WILLA CATHER

WILLA CATHER

STORIES, POEMS,
AND OTHER WRITINGS

THE LIBRARY OF AMERICA

My Mortal Enemy; *Obscure Destinies*; *The Old Beauty and Others*; *April Twilights and Other Poems*; *Not Under Forty*; and "On *Death Comes for the Archbishop*," "On *Shadows on the Rock*," "Escapism," "On *The Professor's House*," "Preface to *The Wagnerian Romances*," "Preface to *Wounds in the Rain*," "Preface to *The Fortunate Mistress*," "My First Novels (There Were Two)," "On the Art of Fiction," and "Light on Adobe Walls," from *Willa Cather on Writing*, published by arrangement with Alfred A. Knopf, Inc.

The paper used in this publication meets the
minimum requirements of the American National Standard for
Information Sciences—Permanence of Paper for Printed
Library Materials, ANSI Z39.48—1984

Distributed to the trade in the United States
and Canada by the Viking Press.

Library of Congress Catalog Number: 91-62294
For cataloging information, see end of Notes.
ISBN 0-940450-71-2

First Printing
The Library of America—57

Manufactured in the United States of America

SHARON O'BRIEN
WROTE THE NOTES AND SELECTED
THE CONTENTS FOR THIS VOLUME

Grateful acknowledgment is made to the National Endowment for the Humanities, the Ford Foundation, and the Andrew W. Mellon Foundation for their generous support of this series.

Contents

UNCOLLECTED STORIES
1892–1929

Contents

Peter

"No, Antone, I have told thee many times, no, thou shalt not sell it until I am gone."

"But I need money; what good is that old fiddle to thee? The very crows laugh at thee when thou art trying to play. Thy hand trembles so thou canst scarce hold the bow. Thou shalt go with me to the Blue to cut wood to-morrow. See to it thou art up early."

"What, on the Sabbath, Antone, when it is so cold? I get so very cold, my son, let us not go to-morrow."

"Yes, to-morrow, thou lazy old man. Do not I cut wood upon the Sabbath? Care I how cold it is? Wood thou shalt cut, and haul it too, and as for the fiddle, I tell thee I will sell it yet." Antone pulled his ragged cap down over his low heavy brow, and went out. The old man drew his stool up nearer the fire, and sat stroking his violin with trembling fingers and muttering, "Not while I live, not while I live."

Five years ago they had come here, Peter Sadelack, and his wife, and oldest son Antone, and countless smaller Sadelacks, here to the dreariest part of south-western Nebraska, and had taken up a homestead. Antone was the acknowledged master of the premises, and people said he was a likely youth, and would do well. That he was mean and untrustworthy every one knew, but that made little difference. His corn was better tended than any in the county, and his wheat always yielded more than other men's.

Of Peter no one knew much, nor had any one a good word to say for him. He drank whenever he could get out of Antone's sight long enough to pawn his hat or coat for whiskey. Indeed there were but two things he would not pawn, his pipe and his violin. He was a lazy, absent minded old fellow, who liked to fiddle better than to plow, though Antone surely got work enough out of them all, for that matter. In the house of which Antone was master there was no one, from the little boy three years old, to the old man of sixty, who did not earn his bread. Still people said that Peter was worthless, and was a great drag on Antone, his son, who never drank,

5

and was a much better man than his father had ever been. Peter did not care what people said. He did not like the country, nor the people, least of all he liked the plowing. He was very homesick for Bohemia. Long ago, only eight years ago by the calendar, but it seemed eight centuries to Peter, he had been a second violinist in the great theatre at Prague. He had gone into the theatre very young, and had been there all his life, until he had a stroke of paralysis, which made his arm so weak that his bowing was uncertain. Then they told him he could go. Those were great days at the theatre. He had plenty to drink then, and wore a dress coat every evening, and there were always parties after the play. He could play in those days, ay, that he could! He could never read the notes well, so he did not play first; but his touch, he had a touch indeed, so Herr Mikilsdoff, who led the orchestra, had said. Sometimes now Peter thought he could plow better if he could only bow as he used to. He had seen all the lovely women in the world there, all the great singers and the great players. He was in the orchestra when Rachel played, and he heard Liszt play when the Countess d'Agoult sat in the stage box and threw the master white lilies. Once, a French woman came and played for weeks, he did not remember her name now. He did not remember her face very well either, for it changed so, it was never twice the same. But the beauty of it, and the great hunger men felt at the sight of it, that he remembered. Most of all he remembered her voice. He did not know French, and could not understand a word she said, but it seemed to him that she must be talking the music of Chopin. And her voice, he thought he should know that in the other world. The last night she played a play in which a man touched her arm, and she stabbed him. As Peter sat among the smoking gas jets down below the footlights with his fiddle on his knee, and looked up at her, he thought he would like to die too, if he could touch her arm once, and have her stab him so. Peter went home to his wife very drunk that night. Even in those days he was a foolish fellow, who cared for nothing but music and pretty faces.

It was all different now. He had nothing to drink and little to eat, and here, there was nothing but sun, and grass, and sky. He had forgotten almost everything, but some things he remembered well enough. He loved his violin and the holy Mary, and above all else he feared the Evil One, and his son Antone.

The fire was low, and it grew cold. Still Peter sat by the fire remembering. He dared not throw more cobs on the fire; Antone would be angry. He did not want to cut wood tomorrow, it would be Sunday, and he wanted to go to mass. Antone might let him do that. He held his violin under his wrinkled chin, his white hair fell over it, and he began to play "Ave Maria." His hand shook more than ever before, and at last refused to work the bow at all. He sat stupefied for a while, then arose, and taking his violin with him, stole out into the old sod stable. He took Antone's shot-gun down from its peg, and loaded it by the moonlight which streamed in through the door. He sat down on the dirt floor, and leaned back against the dirt wall. He heard the wolves howling in the distance, and the night wind screaming as it swept over the snow. Near him he heard the regular breathing of the horses in the dark. He put his crucifix above his heart, and folding his hands said brokenly all the Latin he had ever known, *"Pater noster, qui in cœlum est."* Then he raised his head and sighed, "Not one kreutzer will Antone pay them to pray for my soul, not one kreutzer, he is so careful of his money, is Antone, he does not waste it in drink, he is a better man than I, but hard sometimes. He works the girls too hard, women were not made to work so. But he shall not sell thee, my fiddle, I can play thee no more, but they shall not part us. We have seen it all together, and we will forget it together, the French woman and all." He held his fiddle under his chin a moment, where it had lain so often, then put it across his knee and broke it through the middle. He pulled off his old boot, held the gun between his knees with the muzzle against his forehead, and pressed the trigger with his toe.

In the morning Antone found him stiff, frozen fast in a pool of blood. They could not straighten him out enough to fit a coffin, so they buried him in a pine box. Before the funeral Antone carried to town the fiddle-bow which Peter had forgotten to break. Antone was very thrifty, and a better man than his father had been.

The Mahogany Tree, May 21, 1892

On the Divide

NEAR RATTLESNAKE CREEK, on the side of a little draw stood Canute's shanty. North, east, south, stretched the level Nebraska plain of long rust-red grass that undulated constantly in the wind. To the west the ground was broken and rough, and a narrow strip of timber wound along the turbid, muddy little stream that had scarcely ambition enough to crawl over its black bottom. If it had not been for the few stunted cottonwoods and elms that grew along its banks, Canute would have shot himself years ago. The Norwegians are a timber-loving people, and if there is even a turtle pond with a few plum bushes around it they seem irresistibly drawn toward it.

As to the shanty itself, Canute had built it without aid of any kind, for when he first squatted along the banks of Rattlesnake Creek there was not a human being within twenty miles. It was built of logs split in halves, the chinks stopped with mud and plaster. The roof was covered with earth and was supported by one gigantic beam curved in the shape of a round arch. It was almost impossible that any tree had ever grown in that shape. The Norwegians used to say that Canute had taken the log across his knee and bent it into the shape he wished. There were two rooms, or rather there was one room with a partition made of ash saplings interwoven and bound together like big straw basket work. In one corner there was a cook stove, rusted and broken. In the other a bed made of unplaned planks and poles. It was fully eight feet long, and upon it was a heap of dark bed clothing. There was a chair and a bench of colossal proportions. There was an ordinary kitchen cupboard with a few cracked dirty dishes in it, and beside it on a tall box a tin wash-basin. Under the bed was a pile of pint flasks, some broken, some whole, all empty. On the wood box lay a pair of shoes of almost incredible dimensions. On the wall hung a saddle, a gun, and some ragged clothing, conspicuous among which was a suit of dark cloth, apparently new, with a paper collar carefully wrapped in a red silk handkerchief and pinned to the sleeve. Over the door hung a wolf and a badger skin, and on the door itself a brace of thirty or forty snake skins whose noisy tails rattled ominously every time it opened. The strangest things in the shanty were the wide window-sills. At first glance they looked as though they had been ruthlessly hacked and mutilated with a hatchet, but on closer inspection all the notches and holes in the wood took form and shape. There seemed to be a series of pictures. They were, in a rough way, artistic, but the figures were heavy and labored, as though they had been cut very slowly and with very awkward instruments. There were men plowing with little horned imps sitting on their shoulders and on their horses' heads. There were men praying with a skull hanging over their heads and little demons behind them mocking their attitudes. There were men fighting with big serpents, and skeletons dancing together. All about these pictures were blooming vines and foliage such as never grew in this world, and coiled among the branches of the vines there was always the scaly body of a serpent, and behind every flower there was a serpent's head. It was a veritable Dance of Death by one who had felt its sting. In the wood box lay some boards, and every inch of them was cut up in the same manner. Sometimes the work was very rude and careless, and looked as though the hand of the workman had trembled. It would sometimes have been hard to distinguish the men from their evil geniuses but for one fact, the men were always grave and were either toiling or praying, while the devils were always smiling and dancing. Several of these boards had been split for kindling and it was evident that the artist did not value his work highly.

It was the first day of winter on the Divide. Canute stumbled into his shanty carrying a basket of cobs, and after filling the stove, sat down on a stool and crouched his seven foot frame over the fire, staring drearily out of the window at the wide gray sky. He knew by heart every individual clump of bunch grass in the miles of red shaggy prairie that stretched before his cabin. He knew it in all the deceitful loveliness of its early summer, in all the bitter barrenness of its autumn. He had seen it smitten by all the plagues of Egypt. He had seen it parched by drought, and sogged by rain, beaten by hail, and swept by fire, and in the grasshopper years he had seen it eaten as bare and clean as bones that the vultures have left. After the great fires he had seen it stretch for miles and miles, black and smoking as the floor of hell.

He rose slowly and crossed the room, dragging his big feet heavily as though they were burdens to him. He looked out of the window into the hog corral and saw the pigs burying themselves in the straw before the shed. The leaden gray clouds were beginning to spill themselves, and the snow-flakes were settling down over the white leprous patches of frozen earth where the hogs had gnawed even the sod away. He shuddered and began to walk, tramping heavily with his ungainly feet. He was the wreck of ten winters on the Divide and he knew what they meant. Men fear the winters of the Divide as a child fears night or as men in the North Seas fear the still dark cold of the polar twilight.

His eyes fell upon his gun, and he took it down from the wall and looked it over. He sat down on the edge of his bed and held the barrel towards his face, letting his forehead rest upon it, and laid his finger on the trigger. He was perfectly calm, there was neither passion nor despair in his face, but the thoughtful look of a man who is considering. Presently he laid down the gun, and reaching into the cupboard, drew out a pint bottle of raw white alcohol. Lifting it to his lips, he drank greedily. He washed his face in the tin basin and combed his rough hair and shaggy blond beard. Then he stood in uncertainty before the suit of dark clothes that hung on the wall. For the fiftieth time he took them in his hands and tried to summon courage to put them on. He took the paper collar that was pinned to the sleeve of the coat and cautiously slipped it under his rough beard, looking with timid expectancy into the cracked, splashed glass that hung over the bench. With a short laugh he threw it down on the bed, and pulling on his old black hat, he went out, striking off across the level.

It was a physical necessity for him to get away from his cabin once in a while. He had been there for ten years, dig-ging and plowing and sowing, and reaping what little the hail and the hot winds and the frosts left him to reap. Insanity and suicide are very common things on the Divide. They come on like an epidemic in the hot wind season. Those scorching dusty winds that blow up over the bluffs from Kansas seem to dry up the blood in men's veins as they do the sap in the corn leaves. Whenever the yellow scorch creeps down over the tender inside leaves about the ear, then the coroners prepare for active duty; for the oil of the country is burned out and it does not take long for the flame to eat up the wick. It causes no great sensation there when a Dane is found swinging to his own windmill tower, and most of the Poles after they have become too careless and discouraged to shave themselves keep their razors to cut their throats with.

It may be that the next generation on the Divide will be very happy, but the present one came too late in life. It is useless for men that have cut hemlocks among the mountains of Sweden for forty years to try to be happy in a country as flat and gray and as naked as the sea. It is not easy for men that have spent their youths fishing in the Northern seas to be content with following a plow, and men that have served in the Austrian army hate hard work and coarse clothing and the loneliness of the plains, and long for marches and excitement and tavern company and pretty barmaids. After a man has passed his fortieth birthday it is not easy for him to change the habits and conditions of his life. Most men bring with them to the Divide only the dregs of the lives that they have squandered in other lands and among other peoples.

Canute Canuteson was as mad as any of them, but his madness did not take the form of suicide or religion but of alcohol. He had always taken liquor when he wanted it, as all Norwegians do, but after his first year of solitary life he settled down to it steadily. He exhausted whisky after a while, and went to alcohol, because its effects were speedier and surer. He was a big man with a terrible amount of resistant force, and it took a great deal of alcohol even to move him. After nine years of drinking, the quantities he could take would seem fabulous to an ordinary drinking man. He never let it interfere with his work, he generally drank at night and on Sundays. Every night, as soon as his chores were done, he began to drink. While he was able to sit up he would play on his mouth harp or hack away at his window sills with his jack knife. When the liquor went to his head he would lie down on his bed and stare out of the window until he went to sleep. He drank alone and in solitude not for pleasure or good cheer, but to forget the awful loneliness and level of the Divide. Milton made a sad blunder when he put mountains in hell. Mountains postulate faith and aspiration. All mountain peoples are religious. It was the cities of the plains that, because of their utter lack of spirituality and the mad caprice of their vice, were cursed of God.

Alcohol is perfectly consistent in its effects upon man. Drunkenness is merely an exaggeration. A foolish man drunk becomes maudlin; a bloody man, vicious; a coarse man, vulgar. Canute was none of these, but he was morose and gloomy, and liquor took him through all the hells of Dante. As he lay on his giant's bed all the horrors of this world and every other were laid bare to his chilled senses. He was a man who knew no joy, a man who toiled in silence and bitterness. The skull and the serpent were always before him, the symbols of eternal futileness and of eternal hate.

When the first Norwegians near enough to be called neighbors came, Canute rejoiced, and planned to escape from his bosom vice. But he was not a social man by nature and had not the power of drawing out the social side of other people. His new neighbors rather feared him because of his great strength and size, his silence and his lowering brows. Perhaps, too, they knew that he was mad, mad from the eternal treachery of the plains, which every spring stretch green and rustle with the promises of Eden, showing long grassy lagoons full of clear water and cattle whose hoofs are stained with wild roses. Before autumn the lagoons are dried up, and the ground is burnt dry and hard until it blisters and cracks open.

So instead of becoming a friend and neighbor to the men that settled about him, Canute became a mystery and a terror. They told awful stories of his size and strength and of the alcohol he drank. They said that one night, when he went out to see to his horses just before he went to bed, his steps were unsteady and the rotten planks of the floor gave way and threw him behind the feet of a fiery young stallion. His foot was caught fast in the floor, and the nervous horse began kicking frantically. When Canute felt the blood trickling down in his eyes from a scalp wound in his head, he roused himself from his kingly indifference, and with the quiet stoical courage of a drunken man leaned forward and wound his arms about the horse's hind legs and held them against his breast with crushing embrace. All through the darkness and cold of the night he lay there, matching strength against strength. When little Jim Peterson went over the next morning at four o'clock to go with him to the Blue to cut wood, he found him so, and the horse was on its fore knees, trembling and whinnying with fear. This is the story the Norwegians tell of him, and if it is true it is no wonder that they feared and hated this Holder of the Heels of Horses.

One spring there moved to the next "eighty" a family that made a great change in Canute's life. Ole Yensen was too drunk most of the time to be afraid of any one, and his wife Mary was too garrulous to be afraid of any one who listened to her talk, and Lena, their pretty daughter, was not afraid of man nor devil. So it came about that Canute went over to take his alcohol with Ole oftener than he took it alone. After a while the report spread that he was going to marry Yensen's daughter, and the Norwegian girls began to tease Lena about the great bear she was going to keep house for. No one could quite see how the affair had come about, for Canute's tactics of courtship were somewhat peculiar. He apparently never spoke to her at all: he would sit for hours with Mary chattering on one side of him and Ole drinking on the other and watch Lena at her work. She teased him, and threw flour in his face and put vinegar in his coffee, but he took her rough jokes with silent wonder, never even smiling. He took her to church occasionally, but the most watchful and curious people never saw him speak to her. He would sit staring at her while she giggled and flirted with the other men.

Next spring Mary Lee went to town to work in a steam laundry. She came home every Sunday, and always ran across to Yensens to startle Lena with stories of ten cent theaters, firemen's dances, and all the other esthetic delights of metropolitan life. In a few weeks Lena's head was completely turned, and she gave her father no rest until he let her go to town to seek her fortune at the ironing board. From the time she came home on her first visit she began to treat Canute with contempt. She had bought a plush cloak and kid gloves, had her clothes made by the dress-maker, and assumed airs and graces that made the other women of the neighborhood cordially detest her. She generally brought with her a young man from town who waxed his mustache and wore a red necktie, and she did not even introduce him to Canute.

The neighbors teased Canute a good deal until he knocked one of them down. He gave no sign of suffering from her neglect except that he drank more and avoided the other Norwegians more carefully than ever. He lay around in his den and no one knew what he felt or thought, but little Jim Peterson, who had seen him glowering at Lena in church one Sunday when she was there with the town man, said that he would not give an acre of his wheat for Lena's life or the town chap's either; and Jim's wheat was so wondrously worthless that the statement was an exceedingly strong one.

Canute had bought a new suit of clothes that looked as nearly like the town man's as possible. They had cost him half a millet crop; for tailors are not accustomed to fitting giants and they charge for it. He had hung those clothes in his shanty two months ago and had never put them on, partly from fear of ridicule, partly from discouragement, and partly because there was something in his own soul that revolted at the littleness of the device.

Lena was at home just at this time. Work was slack in the laundry and Mary had not been well, so Lena stayed at home, glad enough to get an opportunity to torment Canute once more.

She was washing in the side kitchen, singing loudly as she worked. Mary was on her knees, blacking the stove and scolding violently about the young man who was coming out from town that night. The young man had committed the fatal error of laughing at Mary's ceaseless babble and had never been forgiven.

"He is no good, and you will come to a bad end by running with him! I do not see why a daughter of mine should act so. I do not see why the Lord should visit such a punishment upon me as to give me such a daughter. There are plenty of good men you can marry."

Lena tossed her head and answered curtly, "I don't happen to want to marry any man right away, and so long as Dick dresses nice and has plenty of money to spend, there is no harm in my going with him."

"Money to spend? Yes, and that is all he does with it I'll be bound. You think it very fine now, but you will change your tune when you have been married five years and see your children running naked and your cupboard empty. Did Anne Hermanson come to any good end by marrying a town man?"

"I don't know anything about Anne Hermanson, but I know any of the laundry girls would have Dick quick enough if they could get him."

"Yes, and a nice lot of store clothes huzzies you are too. Now there is Canuteson who has an 'eighty' proved up and fifty head of cattle and——"

"And hair that ain't been cut since he was a baby, and a big dirty beard, and he wears overalls on Sundays, and drinks like a pig. Besides he will keep. I can have all the fun I want, and when I am old and ugly like you he can have me and take care of me. The Lord knows there ain't nobody else going to marry him."

Canute drew his hand back from the latch as though it were red hot. He was not the kind of a man to make a good eavesdropper, and he wished he had knocked sooner. He pulled himself together and struck the door like a battering ram. Mary jumped and opened it with a screech.

"God! Canute, how you scared us! I thought it was crazy Lou,—he has been tearing around the neighborhood trying to convert folks. I am afraid as death of him. He ought to be sent off, I think. He is just as liable as not to kill us all, or burn the barn, or poison the dogs. He has been worrying even the poor minister to death, and he laid up with the rheumatism, too! Did you notice that he was too sick to preach last Sunday? But don't stand there in the cold,—come in. Yensen isn't here, but he just went over to Sorenson's for the mail; he won't be gone long. Walk right in the other room and sit down."

Canute followed her, looking steadily in front of him and not noticing Lena as he passed her. But Lena's vanity would not allow him to pass unmolested. She took the wet sheet she was wringing out and cracked him across the face with it, and ran giggling to the other side of the room. The blow stung his cheeks and the soapy water flew in his eyes, and he involuntarily began rubbing them with his hands. Lena giggled with delight at his discomfiture, and the wrath in Canute's face grew blacker than ever. A big man humiliated is vastly more undignified than a little one. He forgot the sting of his face in the bitter consciousness that he had made a fool of himself. He stumbled blindly into the living room, knocking his head against the door jamb because he forgot to stoop. He dropped into a chair behind the stove, thrusting his big feet back helplessly on either side of him.

Ole was a long time in coming, and Canute sat there, still and silent, with his hands clenched on his knees, and the skin of his face seemed to have shriveled up into little wrinkles that trembled when he lowered his brows. His life had been one long lethargy of solitude and alcohol, but now he was awakening, and it was as when the dumb stagnant heat of summer breaks out into thunder.

When Ole came staggering in, heavy with liquor, Canute rose at once.

"Yensen," he said quietly, "I have come to see if you will let me marry your daughter today."

"Today!" gasped Ole.

"Yes, I will not wait until tomorrow. I am tired of living alone."

Ole braced his staggering knees against the bedstead, and stammered eloquently: "Do you think I will marry my daughter to a drunkard? a man who drinks raw alcohol? a man who sleeps with rattle snakes? Get out of my house or I will kick you out for your impudence." And Ole began looking anxiously for his feet.

Canute answered not a word, but he put on his hat and went out into the kitchen. He went up to Lena and said without looking at her, "Get your things on and come with me!"

The tones of his voice startled her, and she said angrily, dropping the soap, "Are you drunk?"

"If you do not come with me, I will take you,—you had better come," said Canute quietly.

She lifted a sheet to strike him, but he caught her arm roughly and wrenched the sheet from her. He turned to the wall and took down a hood and shawl that hung there, and began wrapping her up. Lena scratched and fought like a wild thing. Ole stood in the door, cursing, and Mary howled and screeched at the top of her voice. As for Canute, he lifted the girl in his arms and went out of the house. She kicked and struggled, but the helpless wailing of Mary and Ole soon died away in the distance, and her face was held down tightly on Canute's shoulder so that she could not see whither he was taking her. She was conscious only of the north wind whistling in her ears, and of rapid steady motion and of a great breast that heaved beneath her in quick, irregular breaths. The harder she struggled the tighter those iron arms that had held the heels of horses crushed about her, until she felt as if they would crush the breath from her, and lay still with fear. Canute was striding across the level fields at a pace at which man never went before, drawing the stinging north wind into his lungs in great gulps. He walked with his eyes half closed and looking straight in front of him, only lowering them when he bent his head to blow away the snow flakes that settled on her hair. So it was that Canute took her to his home, even as his bearded barbarian ancestors took the fair frivolous women of the South in their hairy arms and bore them down to their war ships. For ever and anon the soul becomes weary of the conventions that are not of it, and with a single stroke shatters the civilized lies with which it is unable to cope, and the strong arm reaches out and takes by force what it cannot win by cunning.

When Canute reached his shanty he placed the girl upon a chair, where she sat sobbing. He stayed only a few minutes. He filled the stove with wood and lit the lamp, drank a huge swallow of alcohol and put the bottle in his pocket. He paused a moment, staring heavily at the weeping girl, then he went off and locked the door and disappeared in the gathering gloom of the night.

Wrapped in flannels and soaked with turpentine, the little Norwegian preacher sat reading his Bible, when he heard a thundering knock at his door, and Canute entered, covered with snow and with his beard frozen fast to his coat.

"Come in, Canute, you must be frozen," said the little man, shoving a chair towards his visitor.

Canute remained standing with his hat on and said quietly, "I want you to come over to my house tonight to marry me to Lena Yensen."

"Have you got a license, Canute?"

"No, I don't want a license. I want to be married."

"But I can't marry you without a license, man. It would not be legal."

A dangerous light came in the big Norwegian's eye. "I want you to come over to my house to marry me to Lena Yensen."

"No, I can't, it would kill an ox to go out in a storm like this, and my rheumatism is bad tonight."

"Then if you will not go I must take you," said Canute with a sigh.

He took down the preacher's bearskin coat and bade him put it on while he hitched up his buggy. He went out and closed the door softly after him. Presently he returned and found the frightened minister crouching before the fire with his coat lying beside him. Canute helped him put it on and gently wrapped his head in his big muffler. Then he picked him up and carried him out and placed him in his buggy. As he tucked the buffalo robes around him he said: "Your horse is old, he might flounder or lose his way in this storm. I will lead him."

The minister took the reins feebly in his hands and sat shivering with the cold. Sometimes when there was a lull in the wind, he could see the horse struggling through the snow with the man plodding steadily beside him. Again the blowing snow would hide them from him altogether. He had no idea where they were or what direction they were going. He felt as though he were being whirled away in the heart of the storm, and he said all the prayers he knew. But at last the long four miles were over, and Canute set him down in the snow while he unlocked the door. He saw the bride sitting by the fire with her eyes red and swollen as though she had been weeping. Canute placed a huge chair for him, and said roughly,—

"Warm yourself."

Lena began to cry and moan afresh, begging the minister to take her home. He looked helplessly at Canute. Canute said simply,—

"If you are warm now, you can marry us."

"My daughter, do you take this step of your own free will?" asked the minister in a trembling voice.

"No sir, I don't, and it is disgraceful he should force me into it! I won't marry him."

"Then, Canute, I cannot marry you," said the minister, standing as straight as his rheumatic limbs would let him.

"Are you ready to marry us now, sir?" said Canute, laying one iron hand on his stooped shoulder. The little preacher was a good man, but like most men of weak body he was a coward and had a horror of physical suffering, although he had known so much of it. So with many qualms of conscience he began to repeat the marriage service. Lena sat sullenly in her chair, staring at the fire. Canute stood beside her, listening with his head bent reverently and his hands folded on his breast. When the little man had prayed and said amen, Canute began bundling him up again.

"I will take you home, now," he said as he carried him out and placed him in his buggy, and started off with him through the fury of the storm, floundering among the snow drifts that brought even the giant himself to his knees.

After she was left alone, Lena soon ceased weeping. She was not of a particularly sensitive temperament, and had little pride beyond that of vanity. After the first bitter anger wore itself out, she felt nothing more than a healthy sense of humiliation and defeat. She had no inclination to run away, for she was married now, and in her eyes that was final and all rebellion was useless. She knew nothing about a license, but she knew that a preacher married folks. She consoled herself by thinking that she had always intended to marry Canute some day, any way.

She grew tired of crying and looking into the fire, so she got up and began to look about her. She had heard queer tales about the inside of Canute's shanty, and her curiosity soon got the better of her rage. One of the first things she noticed was the new black suit of clothes hanging on the wall. She was dull, but it did not take a vain woman long to interpret anything so decidedly flattering, and she was pleased in spite of herself. As she looked through the cupboard, the general air of neglect and discomfort made her pity the man who lived there.

"Poor fellow, no wonder he wants to get married to get somebody to wash up his dishes. Batchin's pretty hard on a man."

It is easy to pity when once one's vanity has been tickled. She looked at the window sill and gave a little shudder and wondered if the man were crazy. Then she sat down again and sat a long time wondering what her Dick and Ole would do.

"It is queer Dick didn't come right over after me. He surely came, for he would have left town before the storm began and he might just as well come right on as go back. If he'd hurried he would have gotten here before the preacher came. I suppose he was afraid to come, for he knew Canuteson could pound him to jelly, the coward!" Her eyes flashed angrily.

The weary hours wore on and Lena began to grow horribly lonesome. It was an uncanny night and this was an uncanny place to be in. She could hear the coyotes howling hungrily a little way from the cabin, and more terrible still were all the unknown noises of the storm. She remembered the tales they told of the big log overhead and she was afraid of those snaky things on the window sills. She remembered the man who had been killed in the draw, and she wondered what she would do if she saw crazy Lou's white face glaring into the window. The rattling of the door became unbearable, she thought the latch must be loose and took the lamp to look at it. Then for the first time she saw the ugly brown snake skins whose death rattle sounded every time the wind jarred the door.

"Canute, Canute!" she screamed in terror.

Outside the door she heard a heavy sound as of a big dog getting up and shaking himself. The door opened and Canute stood before her, white as a snow drift.

"What is it?" he asked kindly.

"I am cold," she faltered.

He went out and got an armful of wood and a basket of cobs and filled the stove. Then he went out and lay in the snow before the door. Presently he heard her calling again.

"What is it?" he said, sitting up.

"I'm so lonesome, I'm afraid to stay in here all alone."

"I will go over and get your mother." And he got up.

"She won't come."

"I'll bring her," said Canute grimly.

"No, no. I don't want her, she will scold all the time."

"Well, I will bring your father."

She spoke again and it seemed as though her mouth was close up to the key-hole. She spoke lower than he had ever heard her speak before, so low that he had to put his ear up to the lock to hear her.

"I don't want him either, Canute, — I'd rather have you."

For a moment she heard no noise at all, then something like a groan. With a cry of fear she opened the door, and saw Canute stretched in the snow at her feet, his face in his hands, sobbing on the door step.

Overland Monthly, January 1896

Eric Hermannson's Soul

I.

IT WAS a great night at the Lone Star schoolhouse—a night when the Spirit was present with power and when God was very near to man. So it seemed to Asa Skinner, servant of God and Free Gospeller. The schoolhouse was crowded with the saved and sanctified, robust men and women, trembling and quailing before the power of some mysterious psychic force. Here and there among this cowering, sweating multitude crouched some poor wretch who had felt the pangs of an awakened conscience, but had not yet experienced that complete divestment of reason, that frenzy born of a convulsion of the mind, which, in the parlance of the Free Gospellers, is termed "the Light." On the floor, before the mourners' bench, lay the unconscious figure of a man in whom outraged nature had sought her last resort. This "trance" state is the highest evidence of grace among the Free Gospellers, and indicates a close walking with God.

Before the desk stood Asa Skinner, shouting of the mercy and vengeance of God, and in his eyes shone a terrible earnestness, an almost prophetic flame. Asa was a converted train gambler who used to run between Omaha and Denver. He was a man made for the extremes of life; from the most debauched of men he had become the most ascetic. His was a bestial face, a face that bore the stamp of Nature's eternal injustice. The forehead was low, projecting over the eyes, and the sandy hair was plastered down over it and then brushed back at an abrupt right angle. The chin was heavy, the nostrils were low and wide, and the lower lip hung loosely except in his moments of spasmodic earnestness, when it shut like a steel trap. Yet about those coarse features there were deep, rugged furrows, the scars of many a hand-to-hand struggle with the weakness of the flesh, and about that drooping lip were sharp, strenuous lines that had conquered it and taught it to pray. Over those seamed cheeks there was a certain pallor, a grayness caught from many a vigil. It was as though, after Nature had done her worst with that face, some fine chisel had gone over it, chastening and almost transfiguring it. To-night, as his muscles twitched with emotion, and the perspiration dropped from his hair and chin, there was a certain convincing power in the man. For Asa Skinner was a man possessed of a belief, of that sentiment of the sublime before which all inequalities are leveled, that transport of conviction which seems superior to all laws of condition, under which debauchees have become martyrs; which made a tinker an artist and a camel-driver the founder of an empire. This was with Asa Skinner to-night, as he stood proclaiming the vengeance of God.

It might have occurred to an impartial observer that Asa Skinner's God was indeed a vengeful God if he could reserve vengeance for those of his creatures who were packed into the Lone Star schoolhouse that night. Poor exiles of all nations; men from the south and the north, peasants from almost every country of Europe, most of them from the mountainous, night-bound coast of Norway. Honest men for the most part, but men with whom the world had dealt hardly; the failures of all countries, men sobered by toil and saddened by exile, who had been driven to fight for the dominion of an untoward soil, to sow where others should gather, the advance-guard of a mighty civilization to be.

Never had Asa Skinner spoken more earnestly than now. He felt that the Lord had this night a special work for him to do. To-night Eric Hermannson, the wildest lad on all the Divide, sat in his audience with a fiddle on his knee, just as he had dropped in on his way to play for some dance. The violin is an object of particular abhorrence to the Free Gospellers. Their antagonism to the church organ is bitter enough, but the fiddle they regard as a very incarnation of evil desires, singing forever of worldly pleasures and inseparably associated with all forbidden things.

Eric Hermannson had long been the object of the prayers of the revivalists. His mother had felt the power of the Spirit weeks ago, and special prayer-meetings had been held at her house for her son. But Eric had only gone his ways laughing, the ways of youth, which are short enough at best, and none too flowery on the Divide. He slipped away from the prayer-meetings to meet the Campbell boys in Genereau's saloon, or hug the plump little French girls at Chevalier's dances, and sometimes, of a summer night, he even went across the dewy cornfields and through the wild-plum thicket to play the fiddle for Lena Hanson, whose name was a reproach through all the Divide country, where the women are usually too plain and too busy and too tired to depart from the ways of virtue. On such occasions Lena, attired in a pink wrapper and silk stockings and tiny pink slippers, would sing to him, accompanying herself on a battered guitar. It gave him a delicious sense of freedom and experience to be with a woman who, no matter how, had lived in big cities and knew the ways of town-folk, who had never worked in the fields and had kept her hands white and soft, her throat fair and tender, who had heard great singers in Denver and Salt Lake, and who knew the strange language of flattery and idleness and mirth.

Yet, careless as he seemed, the frantic prayers of his mother were not altogether without their effect upon Eric. For days he had been fleeing before them as a criminal from his pursuers, and over his pleasures had fallen the shadow of something dark and terrible that dogged his steps. The harder he danced, the louder he sang, the more was he conscious that this phantom was gaining upon him, that in time it would track him down. One Sunday afternoon, late in the fall, when he had been drinking beer with Lena Hanson and listening to a song which made his cheeks burn, a rattlesnake had crawled out of the side of the sod house and thrust its ugly head in under the screen door. He was not afraid of snakes, but he knew enough of Gospellism to feel the significance of the reptile lying coiled there upon her doorstep. His lips were cold when he kissed Lena good-by, and he went there no more.

The final barrier between Eric and his mother's faith was his violin, and to that he clung as a man sometimes will cling to his dearest sin, to the weakness more precious to him than all his strength. In the great world beauty comes to men in many guises, and art in a hundred forms, but for Eric there was only his violin. It stood, to him, for all the manifestations of art; it was his only bridge into the kingdom of the soul.

It was to Eric Hermannson that the evangelist directed his impassioned pleading that night.

"*Saul, Saul, why persecutest thou me?* Is there a Saul here to-night who has stopped his ears to that gentle pleading, who has thrust a spear into that bleeding side? Think of it, my brother; you are offered this wonderful love and you prefer the worm that dieth not and the fire which will not be quenched. What right have you to lose one of God's precious souls? *Saul, Saul, why persecutest thou me?*"

A great joy dawned in Asa Skinner's pale face, for he saw that Eric Hermannson was swaying to and fro in his seat. The minister fell upon his knees and threw his long arms up over his head.

"O my brothers! I feel it coming, the blessing we have prayed for. I tell you the Spirit is coming! Just a little more prayer, brothers, a little more zeal, and he will be here. I can feel his cooling wing upon my brow. Glory be to God forever and ever, amen!"

The whole congregation groaned under the pressure of this spiritual panic. Shouts and hallelujahs went up from every lip. Another figure fell prostrate upon the floor. From the mourners' bench rose a chant of terror and rapture:

> "Eating honey and drinking wine,
> *Glory to the bleeding Lamb!*
> I am my Lord's and he is mine,
> *Glory to the bleeding Lamb!*"

The hymn was sung in a dozen dialects and voiced all the vague yearning of these hungry lives, of these people who had starved all the passions so long, only to fall victims to the basest of them all, fear.

A groan of ultimate anguish rose from Eric Hermannson's bowed head, and the sound was like the groan of a great tree when it falls in the forest.

The minister rose suddenly to his feet and threw back his head, crying in a loud voice:

"*Lazarus, come forth!* Eric Hermannson, you are lost, going down at sea. In the name of God, and Jesus Christ his Son, I throw you the life-line. Take hold! Almighty God, my soul for his!" The minister threw his arms out and lifted his quivering face.

Eric Hermannson rose to his feet; his lips were set and the

lightning was in his eyes. He took his violin by the neck and crushed it to splinters across his knee, and to Asa Skinner the sound was like the shackles of sin broken audibly asunder.

II.

For more than two years Eric Hermannson kept the austere faith to which he had sworn himself, kept it until a girl from the East came to spend a week on the Nebraska Divide. She was a girl of other manners and conditions, and there were greater distances between her life and Eric's than all the miles which separated Rattlesnake Creek from New York city. Indeed, she had no business to be in the West at all; but ah! across what leagues of land and sea, by what improbable chances, do the unrelenting gods bring to us our fate!

It was in a year of financial depression that Wyllis Elliot came to Nebraska to buy cheap land and revisit the country where he had spent a year of his youth. When he had graduated from Harvard it was still customary for moneyed gentlemen to send their scapegrace sons to rough it on ranches in the wilds of Nebraska or Dakota, or to consign them to a living death in the sage-brush of the Black Hills. These young men did not always return to the ways of civilized life. But Wyllis Elliot had not married a half-breed, nor been shot in a cow-punchers' brawl, nor wrecked by bad whisky, nor appropriated by a smirched adventuress. He had been saved from these things by a girl, his sister, who had been very near to his life ever since the days when they read fairy tales together and dreamed the dreams that never come true. On this, his first visit to his father's ranch since he left it six years before, he brought her with him. She had been laid up half the winter from a sprain received while skating, and had had too much time for reflection during those months. She was restless and filled with a desire to see something of the wild country of which her brother had told her so much. She was to be married the next winter, and Wyllis understood her when she begged him to take her with him on this long, aimless jaunt across the continent, to taste the last of their freedom together. It comes to all women of her type—that desire to taste the unknown which allures and terrifies, to run one's whole soul's length out to the wind—just once.

It had been an eventful journey. Wyllis somehow understood that strain of gypsy blood in his sister, and he knew where to take her. They had slept in sod houses on the Platte River, made the acquaintance of the personnel of a third-rate opera company on the train to Deadwood, dined in a camp of railroad constructors at the world's end beyond New Castle, gone through the Black Hills on horseback, fished for trout in Dome Lake, watched a dance at Cripple Creek, where the lost souls who hide in the hills gathered for their besotted revelry. And now, last of all, before the return to thraldom, there was this little shack, anchored on the windy crest of the Divide, a little black dot against the flaming sunsets, a scented sea of cornland bathed in opalescent air and blinding sunlight.

Margaret Elliot was one of those women of whom there are so many in this day, when old order, passing, giveth place to new; beautiful, talented, critical, unsatisfied, tired of the world at twenty-four. For the moment the life and people of the Divide interested her. She was there but a week; perhaps had she stayed longer, that inexorable ennui which travels faster even than the Vestibule Limited would have overtaken her. The week she tarried there was the week that Eric Hermannson was helping Jerry Lockhart thresh; a week earlier or a week later, and there would have been no story to write.

It was on Thursday and they were to leave on Saturday. Wyllis and his sister were sitting on the wide piazza of the ranchhouse, staring out into the afternoon sunlight and protesting against the gusts of hot wind that blew up from the sandy river-bottom twenty miles to the southward.

The young man pulled his cap lower over his eyes and remarked:

"This wind is the real thing; you don't strike it anywhere else. You remember we had a touch of it in Algiers and I told you it came from Kansas. It's the key-note of this country."

Wyllis touched her hand that lay on the hammock and continued gently:

"I hope it's paid you, Sis. Roughing it's dangerous business; it takes the taste out of things."

She shut her fingers firmly over the brown hand that was so like her own.

"Paid? Why, Wyllis, I haven't been so happy since we were children and were going to discover the ruins of Troy together some day. Do you know, I believe I could just stay on here forever and let the world go on its own gait. It seems as though the tension and strain we used to talk of last winter were gone for good, as though one could never give one's strength out to such petty things any more."

Wyllis brushed the ashes of his pipe away from the silk handkerchief that was knotted about his neck and stared moodily off at the sky-line.

"No, you're mistaken. This would bore you after a while. You can't shake the fever of the other life. I've tried it. There was a time when the gay fellows of Rome could trot down into the Thebaid and burrow into the sandhills and get rid of it. But it's all too complex now. You see we've made our dissipations so dainty and respectable that they've gone further in than the flesh, and taken hold of the ego proper. You couldn't rest, even here. The war-cry would follow you."

"You don't waste words, Wyllis, but you never miss fire. I talk more than you do, without saying half so much. You must have learned the art of silence from these taciturn Norwegians. I think I like silent men."

"Naturally," said Wyllis, "since you have decided to marry the most brilliant talker you know."

Both were silent for a time, listening to the sighing of the hot wind through the parched morning-glory vines. Margaret spoke first.

"Tell me, Wyllis, were many of the Norwegians you used to know as interesting as Eric Hermannson?"

"Who, Siegfried? Well, no. He used to be the flower of the Norwegian youth in my day, and he's rather an exception, even now. He has retrograded, though. The bonds of the soil have tightened on him, I fancy."

"Siegfried? Come, that's rather good, Wyllis. He looks like a dragon-slayer. What is it that makes him so different from the others? I can talk to him; he seems quite like a human being."

"Well," said Wyllis, meditatively, "I don't read Bourget as

much as my cultured sister, and I'm not so well up in analysis, but I fancy it's because one keeps cherishing a perfectly unwarranted suspicion that under that big, hulking anatomy of his, he may conceal a soul somewhere. Nicht wahr?"

"Something like that," said Margaret, thoughtfully, "except that it's more than a suspicion, and it isn't groundless. He has one, and he makes it known, somehow, without speaking."

"I always have my doubts about loquacious souls," Wyllis remarked, with the unbelieving smile that had grown habitual with him.

Margaret went on, not heeding the interruption. "I knew it from the first, when he told me about the suicide of his cousin, the Bernstein boy. That kind of blunt pathos can't be summoned at will in anybody. The earlier novelists rose to it, sometimes, unconsciously. But last night when I sang for him I was doubly sure. Oh, I haven't told you about that yet! Better light your pipe again. You see, he stumbled in on me in the dark when I was pumping away at that old parlor organ to please Mrs. Lockhart. It's her household fetish and I've forgotten how many pounds of butter she made and sold to buy it. Well, Eric stumbled in, and in some inarticulate manner made me understand that he wanted me to sing for him. I sang just the old things, of course. It's queer to sing familiar things here at the world's end. It makes one think how the hearts of men have carried them around the world, into the wastes of Iceland and the jungles of Africa and the islands of the Pacific. I think if one lived here long enough one would quite forget how to be trivial, and would read only the great books that we never get time to read in the world, and would remember only the great music, and the things that are really worth while would stand out clearly against that horizon over there. And of course I played the intermezzo from 'Cavalleria Rusticana' for him; it goes rather better on an organ than most things do. He shuffled his feet and twisted his big hands up into knots and blurted out that he didn't know there was any music like that in the world. Why, there were tears in his voice, Wyllis! Yes, like Rossetti, I *heard* his tears. Then it dawned upon me that it was probably the first good music he had ever heard in all his life. Think of it, to care for music as he does and never to hear it, never to know that it exists on earth! To long for it as we long for other perfect experiences that never come. I can't tell you what music means to that man. I never saw any one so susceptible to it. It gave him speech, he became alive. When I had finished the inter-mezzo, he began telling me about a little crippled brother who died and whom he loved and used to carry everywhere in his arms. He did not wait for encouragement. He took up the story and told it slowly, as if to himself, just sort of rose up and told his own woe to answer Mascagni's. It over-came me."

"Poor devil," said Wyllis, looking at her with mysterious eyes, "and so you've given him a new woe. Now he'll go on wanting Grieg and Schubert the rest of his days and never getting them. That's a girl's philanthropy for you!"

Jerry Lockhart came out of the house screwing his chin over the unusual luxury of a stiff white collar, which his wife insisted upon as a necessary article of toilet while Miss Elliot was at the house. Jerry sat down on the step and smiled his broad, red smile at Margaret.

"Well, I've got the music for your dance, Miss Elliot. Olaf Oleson will bring his accordion and Mollie will play the or-gan, when she isn't lookin' after the grub, and a little chap from Frenchtown will bring his fiddle—though the French don't mix with the Norwegians much."

"Delightful! Mr. Lockhart, that dance will be the feature of our trip, and it's so nice of you to get it up for us. We'll see the Norwegians in character at last," cried Margaret, cordially.

"See here, Lockhart, I'll settle with you for backing her in this scheme," said Wyllis, sitting up and knocking the ashes out of his pipe. "She's done crazy things enough on this trip, but to talk of dancing all night with a gang of half-mad Nor-wegians and taking the carriage at four to catch the six o'clock train out of Riverton—well, it's tommy-rot, that's what it is!"

"Wyllis, I leave it to your sovereign power of reason to decide whether it isn't easier to stay up all night than to get up at three in the morning. To get up at three, think what that means! No, sir, I prefer to keep my vigil and then get into a sleeper."

"But what do you want with the Norwegians? I thought you were tired of dancing."

"So I am, with some people. But I want to see a Norwegian dance, and I intend to. Come, Wyllis, you know how seldom it is that one really wants to do anything nowadays. I wonder when I have really wanted to go to a party before. It will be something to remember next month at Newport, when we have to and don't want to. Remember your own theory that contrast is about the only thing that makes life endurable. This is my party and Mr. Lockhart's; your whole duty to-morrow night will consist in being nice to the Norwegian girls. I'll warrant you were adept enough at it once. And you'd better be very nice indeed, for if there are many such young valkyrs as Eric's sister among them, they would simply tie you up in a knot if they suspected you were guying them."

Wyllis groaned and sank back into the hammock to consider his fate, while his sister went on.

"And the guests, Mr. Lockhart, did they accept?"

Lockhart took out his knife and began sharpening it on the sole of his plowshoe.

"Well, I guess we'll have a couple dozen. You see it's pretty hard to get a crowd together here any more. Most of 'em have gone over to the Free Gospellers, and they'd rather put their feet in the fire than shake 'em to a fiddle."

Margaret made a gesture of impatience.

"Those Free Gospellers have just cast an evil spell over this country, haven't they?"

"Well," said Lockhart, cautiously, "I don't just like to pass judgment on any Christian sect, but if you're to know the chosen by their works, the Gospellers can't make a very proud showin', an' that's a fact. They're responsible for a few suicides, and they've sent a good-sized delegation to the state insane asylum, an' I don't see as they've made the rest of us much better than we were before. I had a little herdboy last spring, as square a little Dane as I want to work for me, but after the Gospellers got hold of him and sanctified him, the little beggar used to get down on his knees out on the prairie and pray by the hour and let the cattle get into the corn, an' I had to fire him. That's about the way it goes. Now there's

Eric; that chap used to be a hustler and the spryest dancer in all this section — called all the dances. Now he's got no ambition and he's glum as a preacher. I don't suppose we can even get him to come in to-morrow night."

"Eric? Why, he must dance, we can't let him off," said Margaret, quickly. "Why, I intend to dance with him myself!"

"I'm afraid he won't dance. I asked him this morning if he'd help us out and he said, 'I don't dance now, any more,'" said Lockhart, imitating the labored English of the Norwegian.

"'The Miller of Hoffbau, the Miller of Hoffbau, O my Princess!'" chirped Wyllis, cheerfully, from his hammock.

The red on his sister's cheek deepened a little, and she laughed mischievously. "We'll see about that, sir. I'll not admit that I am beaten until I have asked him myself."

Every night Eric rode over to St. Anne, a little village in the heart of the French settlement, for the mail. As the road lay through the most attractive part of the Divide country, on several occasions Margaret Elliot and her brother had accompanied him. To-night Wyllis had business with Lockhart, and Margaret rode with Eric, mounted on a frisky little mustang that Mrs. Lockhart had broken to the side-saddle. Margaret regarded her escort very much as she did the servant who always accompanied her on long rides at home, and the ride to the village was a silent one. She was occupied with thoughts of another world, and Eric was wrestling with more thoughts than had ever been crowded into his head before. He rode with his eyes riveted on that slight figure before him, as though he wished to absorb it through the optic nerves and hold it in his brain forever. He understood the situation perfectly. His brain worked slowly, but he had a keen sense of the values of things. This girl represented an entirely new species of humanity to him, but he knew where to place her. The prophets of old, when an angel first appeared unto them, never doubted its high origin.

Eric was patient under the adverse conditions of his life, but he was not servile. The Norse blood in him had not entirely lost its self-reliance. He came of a proud fisher line, men who were not afraid of anything but the ice and the devil, and he had prospects before him when his father went down off the North Cape in the long Arctic night, and his mother, seized by a violent horror of seafaring life, had followed her brother to America. Eric was eighteen then, handsome as young Siegfried, a giant in stature, with a skin singularly pure and delicate, like a Swede's; hair as yellow as the locks of Tennyson's amorous Prince, and eyes of a fierce, burning blue, whose flash was most dangerous to women. He had in those days a certain pride of bearing, a certain confidence of approach, that usually accompanies physical perfection. It was even said of him then that he was in love with life, and inclined to levity, a vice most unusual on the Divide. But the sad history of those Norwegian exiles, transplanted in an arid soil and under a scorching sun, had repeated itself in his case. Toil and isolation had sobered him, and he grew more and more like the clods among which he labored. It was as though some red-hot instrument had touched for a moment those delicate fibers of the brain which respond to acute pain or pleasure, in which lies the power of exquisite sensation, and had seared them quite away. It is a painful thing to watch the light die out of the eyes of those Norsemen, leaving an expression of impenetrable sadness, quite passive, quite hopeless, a shadow that is never lifted. With some this change comes almost at once, in the first bitterness of homesickness, with others it comes more slowly, according to the time it takes each man's heart to die.

Oh, those poor Northmen of the Divide! They are dead many a year before they are put to rest in the little graveyard on the windy hill where exiles of all nations grow akin.

The peculiar species of hypochondria to which the exiles of his people sooner or later succumb had not developed in Eric until that night at the Lone Star schoolhouse, when he had broken his violin across his knee. After that, the gloom of his people settled down upon him, and the gospel of maceration began its work. *"If thine eye offend thee, pluck it out,"* et cetera. The pagan smile that once hovered about his lips was gone, and he was one with sorrow. Religion heals a hundred hearts for one that it embitters, but when it destroys, its work is quick and deadly, and where the agony of the cross has been, joy will not come again. This man understood things literally:

one must live without pleasure to die without fear; to save the soul it was necessary to starve the soul.

The sun hung low above the cornfields when Margaret and her cavalier left St. Anne. South of the town there is a stretch of road that runs for some three miles through the French settlement, where the prairie is as level as the surface of a lake. There the fields of flax and wheat and rye are bordered by precise rows of slender, tapering Lombard poplars. It was a yellow world that Margaret Elliot saw under the wide light of the setting sun.

The girl gathered up her reins and called back to Eric, "It will be safe to run the horses here, won't it?"

"Yes, I think so, now," he answered, touching his spur to his pony's flank. They were off like the wind. It is an old saying in the West that new-comers always ride a horse or two to death before they get broken in to the country. They are tempted by the great open spaces and try to outride the horizon, to get to the end of something. Margaret galloped over the level road, and Eric, from behind, saw her long veil fluttering in the wind. It had fluttered just so in his dreams last night and the night before. With a sudden inspiration of courage he overtook her and rode beside her, looking intently at her half-averted face. Before, he had only stolen occasional glances at it, seen it in blinding flashes, always with more or less embarrassment, but now he determined to let every line of it sink into his memory. Men of the world would have said that it was an unusual face, nervous, finely cut, with clear, elegant lines that betokened ancestry. Men of letters would have called it a historic face, and would have conjectured at what old passions, long asleep, what old sorrows forgotten time out of mind, doing battle together in ages gone, had curved those delicate nostrils, left their unconscious memory in those eyes. But Eric read no meaning in these details. To him this beauty was something more than color and line; it was as a flash of white light, in which one cannot distinguish color because all colors are there. To him it was a complete revelation, an embodiment of those dreams of impossible loveliness that linger by a young man's pillow on midsummer nights; yet, because it held something more than the attraction of health and youth and shapeliness, it troubled him, and in its presence he felt as the Goths before the white marbles in the Roman Capitol, not knowing whether they were men or gods. At times he felt like uncovering his head before it, again the fury seized him to break and despoil, to find the clay in this spirit-thing and stamp upon it. Away from her, he longed to strike out with his arms, and take and hold; it maddened him that this woman whom he could break in his hands should be so much stronger than he. But near her, he never questioned this strength; he admitted its potentiality as he admitted the miracles of the Bible; it enervated and conquered him. To-night, when he rode so close to her that he could have touched her, he knew that he might as well reach out his hand to take a star.

Margaret stirred uneasily under his gaze and turned questioningly in her saddle.

"This wind puts me a little out of breath when we ride fast," she said.

Eric turned his eyes away.

"I want to ask you if I go to New York to work, if I maybe hear music like you sang last night? I been a purty good hand to work," he asked, timidly.

Margaret looked at him with surprise, and then, as she studied the outline of his face, pityingly.

"Well, you might—but you'd lose a good deal else. I shouldn't like you to go to New York—and be poor, you'd be out of atmosphere, some way," she said, slowly. Inwardly she was thinking: "There he would be altogether sordid, impossible—a machine who would carry one's trunks upstairs, perhaps. Here he is every inch a man, rather picturesque; why is it?" "No," she added aloud, "I shouldn't like that."

"Then I not go," said Eric, decidedly.

Margaret turned her face to hide a smile. She was a trifle amused and a trifle annoyed. Suddenly she spoke again.

"But I'll tell you what I do want you to do, Eric. I want you to dance with us to-morrow night and teach me some of the Norwegian dances; they say you know them all. Won't you?"

Eric straightened himself in his saddle and his eyes flashed as they had done in the Lone Star schoolhouse when he broke his violin across his knee.

"Yes, I will," he said, quietly, and he believed that he delivered his soul to hell as he said it.

They had reached the rougher country now, where the road wound through a narrow cut in one of the bluffs along the creek, when a beat of hoofs ahead and the sharp neighing of horses made the ponies start and Eric rose in his stirrups. Then down the gulch in front of them and over the steep clay banks thundered a herd of wild ponies, nimble as monkeys and wild as rabbits, such as horse-traders drive east from the plains of Montana to sell in the farming country. Margaret's pony made a shrill sound, a neigh that was almost a scream, and started up the clay bank to meet them, all the wild blood of the range breaking out in an instant. Margaret called to Eric just as he threw himself out of the saddle and caught her pony's bit. But the wiry little animal had gone mad and was kicking and biting like a devil. Her wild brothers of the range were all about her, neighing, and pawing the earth, and striking her with their fore feet and snapping at her flanks. It was the old liberty of the range that the little beast fought for.

"Drop the reins and hold tight, tight!" Eric called, throwing all his weight upon the bit, struggling under those frantic fore feet that now beat at his breast, and now kicked at the wild mustangs that surged and tossed about him. He succeeded in wrenching the pony's head toward him and crowding her withers against the clay bank, so that she could not roll.

"Hold tight, tight!" he shouted again, launching a kick at a snorting animal that reared back against Margaret's saddle. If she should lose her courage and fall now, under those hoofs—— He struck out again and again, kicking right and left with all his might. Already the negligent drivers had galloped into the cut, and their long quirts were whistling over the heads of the herd. As suddenly as it had come, the struggling, frantic wave of wild life swept up out of the gulch and on across the open prairie, and with a long despairing whinny of farewell the pony dropped her head and stood trembling in her sweat, shaking the foam and blood from her bit.

Eric stepped close to Margaret's side and laid his hand on

her saddle. "You are not hurt?" he asked, hoarsely. As he
raised his face in the soft starlight she saw that it was white
and drawn and that his lips were working nervously.

"No, no, not at all. But you, you are suffering; they struck
you!" she cried in sharp alarm.

He stepped back and drew his hand across his brow.

"No, it is not that," he spoke rapidly now, with his hands
clenched at his side. "But if they had hurt you, I would beat
their brains out with my hands, I would kill them all. I was
never afraid before. You are the only beautiful thing that has
ever come close to me. You came like an angel out of the sky.
You are like the music you sing, you are like the stars and the
snow on the mountains where I played when I was a little
boy. You are like all that I wanted once and never had, you
are all that they have killed in me. I die for you to-night,
to-morrow, for all eternity. I am not a coward; I was afraid
because I love you more than Christ who died for me, more
than I am afraid of hell, or hope for heaven. I was never afraid
before. If you had fallen—oh, my God!" he threw his arms
out blindly and dropped his head upon the pony's mane,
leaning limply against the animal like a man struck by some
sickness. His shoulders rose and fell perceptibly with his
labored breathing. The horse stood cowed with exhaustion
and fear. Presently Margaret laid her hand on Eric's head and
said gently:

"You are better now, shall we go on? Can you get your
horse?"

"No, he has gone with the herd. I will lead yours, she is not
safe. I will not frighten you again." His voice was still husky,
but it was steady now. He took hold of the bit and tramped
home in silence.

When they reached the house, Eric stood stolidly by the
pony's head until Wyllis came to lift his sister from the saddle.

"The horses were badly frightened, Wyllis. I think I was
pretty thoroughly scared myself," she said as she took her
brother's arm and went slowly up the hill toward the house.
"No, I'm not hurt, thanks to Eric. You must thank him for
taking such good care of me. He's a mighty fine fellow. I'll
tell you all about it in the morning, dear. I was pretty well
shaken up and I'm going right to bed now. Good-night."

When she reached the low room in which she slept, she sank upon the bed in her riding-dress face downward.

"Oh, I pity him! I pity him!" she murmured, with a long sigh of exhaustion. She must have slept a little. When she rose again, she took from her dress a letter that had been waiting for her at the village post-office. It was closely written in a long, angular hand, covering a dozen pages of foreign note-paper, and began: —

"My Dearest Margaret: If I should attempt to say *how like a winter hath thine absence been*, I should incur the risk of being tedious. Really, it takes the sparkle out of everything. Having nothing better to do, and not caring to go anywhere in particular without you, I remained in the city until Jack Courtwell noted my general despondency and brought me down here to his place on the sound to manage some open-air theatricals he is getting up. 'As You Like It' is of course the piece selected. Miss Harrison plays Rosalind. I wish you had been here to take the part. Miss Harrison reads her lines well, but she is either a maiden-all-forlorn or a tomboy; in-sists on reading into the part all sorts of deeper meanings and highly colored suggestions wholly out of harmony with the pastoral setting. Like most of the professionals, she exagger-ates the emotional element and quite fails to do justice to Rosalind's facile wit and really brilliant mental qualities. Gerard will do Orlando, but rumor says he is épris of your sometime friend, Miss Meredith, and his memory is treach-erous and his interest fitful.

"My new pictures arrived last week on the 'Gascogne.' The Puvis de Chavannes is even more beautiful than I thought it in Paris. A pale dream-maiden sits by a pale dream-cow, and a stream of anemic water flows at her feet. The Constant, you will remember, I got because you admired it. It is here in all its florid splendor, the whole dominated by a glowing sensu-osity. The drapery of the female figure is as wonderful as you said; the fabric all barbaric pearl and gold, painted with an easy, effortless voluptuousness, and that white, gleaming line of African coast in the background recalls memories of you very precious to me. But it is useless to deny that Constant irritates me. Though I cannot prove the charge against him, his brilliancy always makes me suspect him of cheapness."

Here Margaret stopped and glanced at the remaining pages of this strange love-letter. They seemed to be filled chiefly with discussions of pictures and books, and with a slow smile she laid them by.

She rose and began undressing. Before she lay down she went to open the window. With her hand on the sill, she hesitated, feeling suddenly as though some danger were lurking outside, some inordinate desire waiting to spring upon her in the darkness. She stood there for a long time, gazing at the infinite sweep of the sky.

"Oh, it is all so little, so little there," she murmured. "When everything else is so dwarfed, why should one expect love to be great? Why should one try to read highly colored suggestions into a life like that? If only I could find one thing in it all that mattered greatly, one thing that would warm me when I am alone! Will life never give me that one great moment?"

As she raised the window, she heard a sound in the plum-bushes outside. It was only the house-dog roused from his sleep, but Margaret started violently and trembled so that she caught the foot of the bed for support. Again she felt herself pursued by some overwhelming longing, some desperate necessity for herself, like the outstretching of helpless, unseen arms in the darkness, and the air seemed heavy with sighs of yearning. She fled to her bed with the words, "I love you more than Christ, who died for me!" ringing in her ears.

III.

About midnight the dance at Lockhart's was at its height. Even the old men who had come to "look on" caught the spirit of revelry and stamped the floor with the vigor of old Silenus. Eric took the violin from the Frenchman, and Minna Oleson sat at the organ, and the music grew more and more characteristic—rude, half-mournful music, made up of the folk-songs of the North, that the villagers sing through the long night in hamlets by the sea, when they are thinking of the sun, and the spring, and the fishermen so long away. To Margaret some of it sounded like Grieg's Peer Gynt music. She found something irresistibly infectious in the mirth of these people who were so seldom merry, and she felt almost one of them. Something seemed struggling for freedom in them to-night, something of the joyous childhood of the nations which exile had not killed. The girls were all boisterous with delight. Pleasure came to them but rarely, and when it came, they caught at it wildly and crushed its fluttering wings in their strong brown fingers. They had a hard life enough, most of them. Torrid summers and freezing winters, labor and drudgery and ignorance, were the portion of their girlhood; a short wooing, a hasty, loveless marriage, unlimited maternity, thankless sons, premature age and ugliness, were the dower of their womanhood. But what matter? To-night there was hot liquor in the glass and hot blood in the heart; to-night they danced.

To-night Eric Hermannson had renewed his youth. He was no longer the big, silent Norwegian who had sat at Margaret's feet and looked hopelessly into her eyes. To-night he was a man, with a man's rights and a man's power. To-night he was Siegfried indeed. His hair was yellow as the heavy wheat in the ripe of summer, and his eyes flashed like the blue water between the ice-packs in the North Seas. He was not afraid of Margaret to-night, and when he danced with her he held her firmly. She was tired and dragged on his arm a little, but the strength of the man was like an all-pervading fluid, stealing through her veins, awakening under her heart some nameless, unsuspected existence that had slumbered there all these years and that went out through her throbbing finger-tips to his that answered. She wondered if the hoydenish blood of some lawless ancestor, long asleep, were calling out in her to-night, some drop of a hotter fluid that the centuries had failed to cool, and why, if this curse were in her, it had not spoken before. But was it a curse, this awakening, this wealth before undiscovered, this music set free? For the first time in her life her heart held something stronger than herself, was not this worth while? Then she ceased to wonder. She lost sight of the lights and the faces, and the music was drowned by the beating of her own arteries. She saw only the blue eyes that flashed above her, felt only the warmth of that throbbing hand which held hers and which the blood of his heart fed. Dimly, as in a dream, she saw the drooping shoulders, high white forehead and tight, cynical mouth of the man she was to marry in December. For an hour she had been crowding back the memory of that face with all her strength.

"Let us stop, this is enough," she whispered. His only answer was to tighten the arm behind her. She sighed and let that masterful strength bear her where it would. She forgot that this man was little more than a savage, that they would part at dawn. The blood has no memories, no reflections, no regrets for the past, no consideration of the future.

"Let us go out where it is cooler," she said when the music stopped; thinking, "I am growing faint here, I shall be all right in the open air." They stepped out into the cool, blue air of the night.

Since the older folk had begun dancing, the young Norwegians had been slipping out in couples to climb the windmill tower into the cooler atmosphere, as is their custom.

"You like to go up?" asked Eric, close to her ear.

She turned and looked at him with suppressed amusement. "How high is it?"

"Forty feet, about. I not let you fall." There was a note of irresistible pleading in his voice, and she felt that he tremendously wished her to go. Well, why not? This was a night of the unusual, when she was not herself at all, but was living an unreality. To-morrow, yes, in a few hours, there would be the Vestibule Limited and the world.

"Well, if you'll take good care of me. I used to be able to climb, when I was a little girl."

Once at the top and seated on the platform, they were silent. Margaret wondered if she would not hunger for that scene all her life, through all the routine of the days to come. Above them stretched the great Western sky, serenely blue, even in the night, with its big, burning stars, never so cold and dead and far away as in denser atmospheres. The moon would not be up for twenty minutes yet, and all about the horizon, that wide horizon, which seemed to reach around the world, lingered a pale, white light, as of a universal dawn. The weary wind brought up to them the heavy odors of the cornfields. The music of the dance sounded faintly from below. Eric leaned on his elbow beside her, his legs swinging down on the ladder. His great shoulders looked more than ever like those of the stone Doryphorus, who stands in his perfect, reposeful strength in the Louvre, and had often made her wonder if such men died forever with the youth of Greece.

"How sweet the corn smells at night," said Margaret nervously.

"Yes, like the flowers that grow in paradise, I think."

She was somewhat startled by this reply, and more startled when this taciturn man spoke again.

"You go away to-morrow?"

"Yes, we have stayed longer than we thought to now."

"You not come back any more?"

"No, I expect not. You see, it is a long trip; half-way across the continent."

"You soon forget about this country, I guess." It seemed to him now a little thing to lose his soul for this woman, but that she should utterly forget this night into which he threw all his life and all his eternity, that was a bitter thought.

"No, Eric, I will not forget. You have all been too kind to me for that. And you won't be sorry you danced this one night, will you?"

"I never be sorry. I have not been so happy before. I not be so happy again, ever. You will be happy many nights yet, I only this one. I will dream sometimes, maybe."

The mighty resignation of his tone alarmed and touched her. It was as when some great animal composes itself for death, as when a great ship goes down at sea.

She sighed, but did not answer him. He drew a little closer and looked into her eyes.

"You are not always happy, too?" he asked.

"No, not always, Eric; not very often, I think."

"You have a trouble?"

"Yes, but I cannot put it into words. Perhaps if I could do that, I could cure it."

He clasped his hands together over his heart, as children do when they pray, and said falteringly, "If I own all the world, I give him you."

Margaret felt a sudden moisture in her eyes, and laid her hand on his.

"Thank you, Eric; I believe you would. But perhaps even

then I should not be happy. Perhaps I have too much of it already."

She did not take her hand away from him; she did not dare. She sat still and waited for the traditions in which she had always believed to speak and save her. But they were dumb. She belonged to an ultra-refined civilization which tries to cheat nature with elegant sophistries. Cheat nature? Bah! One generation may do it, perhaps two, but the third—— Can we ever rise above nature or sink below her? Did she not turn on Jerusalem as upon Sodom, upon St. Anthony in his desert as upon Nero in his seraglio? Does she not always cry in brutal triumph: "I am here still, at the bottom of things, warming the roots of life; you cannot starve me nor tame me nor thwart me; I made the world, I rule it, and I am its destiny."

This woman, on a windmill tower at the world's end with a giant barbarian, heard that cry to-night, and she was afraid! Ah! the terror and the delight of that moment when first we fear ourselves! Until then we have not lived.

"Come, Eric, let us go down; the moon is up and the music has begun again," she said.

He rose silently and stepped down upon the ladder, putting his arm about her to help her. That arm could have thrown Thor's hammer out in the cornfields yonder, yet it scarcely touched her, and his hand trembled as it had done in the dance. His face was level with hers now and the moonlight fell sharply upon it. All her life she had searched the faces of men for the look that lay in his eyes. She knew that that look had never shone for her before, would never shine for her on earth again, that such love comes to one only in dreams or in impossible places like this, unattainable always. This was Love's self, in a moment it would die. Stung by the agonized appeal that emanated from the man's whole being, she leaned forward and laid her lips on his. Once, twice and again she heard the deep respirations rattle in his throat while she held them there, and the riotous force under her heart became an engulfing weakness. He drew her up to him until he felt all the resistance go out of her body, until every nerve relaxed and yielded. When she drew her face back from his, it was white with fear.

"Let us go down, oh, my God! let us go down!" she muttered. And the drunken stars up yonder seemed reeling to some appointed doom as she clung to the rounds of the ladder. All that she was to know of love she had left upon his lips.

"The devil is loose again," whispered Olaf Oleson, as he saw Eric dancing a moment later, his eyes blazing.

But Eric was thinking with an almost savage exultation of the time when he should pay for this. Ah, there would be no quailing then! If ever a soul went fearlessly, proudly down to the gates infernal, his should go. For a moment he fancied he was there already, treading down the tempest of flame, hugging the fiery hurricane to his breast. He wondered whether in ages gone, all the countless years of sinning in which men had sold and lost and flung their souls away, any man had ever so cheated Satan, had ever bartered his soul for so great a price.

It seemed but a little while till dawn.

The carriage was brought to the door and Wyllis Elliot and his sister said good-by. She could not meet Eric's eyes as she gave him her hand, but as he stood by the horse's head, just as the carriage moved off, she gave him one swift glance that said, "I will not forget." In a moment the carriage was gone.

Eric changed his coat and plunged his head into the water-tank and went to the barn to hook up his team. As he led his horses to the door, a shadow fell across his path, and he saw Skinner rising in his stirrups. His rugged face was pale and worn with looking after his wayward flock, with dragging men into the way of salvation.

"Good-morning, Eric. There was a dance here last night?" he asked, sternly.

"A dance? Oh, yes, a dance," replied Eric, cheerfully.

"Certainly you did not dance, Eric?"

"Yes, I danced. I danced all the time."

The minister's shoulders drooped, and an expression of profound discouragement settled over his haggard face. There was almost anguish in the yearning he felt for this soul.

"Eric, I didn't look for this from you. I thought God had set his mark on you if he ever had on any man. And it is for things like this that you set your soul back a thousand years from God. O foolish and perverse generation!"

Eric drew himself up to his full height and looked off to where the new day was gilding the corn-tassels and flooding the uplands with light. As his nostrils drew in the breath of the dew and the morning, something from the only poetry he had ever read flashed across his mind, and he murmured, half to himself, with dreamy exultation:

" 'And a day shall be as a thousand years, and a thousand years as a day.' "

Cosmopolitan, April 1900

The Sentimentality of William Tavener

It takes a strong woman to make any sort of success of living in the West, and Hester undoubtedly was that. When people spoke of William Tavener as the most prosperous farmer in McPherson County, they usually added that his wife was a "good manager." She was an executive woman, quick of tongue and something of an imperatrix. The only reason her husband did not consult her about his business was that she did not wait to be consulted.

It would have been quite impossible for one man, within the limited sphere of human action, to follow all Hester's advice, but in the end William usually acted upon some of her suggestions. When she incessantly denounced the "shiftlessness" of letting a new threshing machine stand unprotected in the open, he eventually built a shed for it. When she sniffed contemptuously at his notion of fencing a hog corral with sod walls, he made a spiritless beginning on the structure—merely to "show his temper," as she put it—but in the end he went off quietly to town and bought enough barbed wire to complete the fence. When the first heavy rains came on, and the pigs rooted down the sod wall and made little paths all over it to facilitate their ascent, he heard his wife relate with relish the story of the little pig that built a mud house, to the minister at the dinner table, and William's gravity never relaxed for an instant. Silence, indeed, was William's refuge and his strength.

William set his boys a wholesome example to respect their mother. People who knew him very well suspected that he even admired her. He was a hard man towards his neighbors, and even towards his sons; grasping, determined and ambitious.

There was an occasional blue day about the house when William went over the store bills, but he never objected to items relating to his wife's gowns or bonnets. So it came about that many of the foolish, unnecessary little things that Hester bought for boys, she had charged to her personal account.

One spring night Hester sat in a rocking chair by the sitting room window, darning socks. She rocked violently and sent her long needle vigorously back and forth over her gourd, and it took only a very casual glance to see that she was wrought up over something. William sat on the other side of the table reading his farm paper. If he had noticed his wife's agitation, his calm, clean-shaven face betrayed no sign of concern. He must have noticed the sarcastic turn of her remarks at the supper table, and he must have noticed the moody silence of the older boys as they ate. When supper was but half over little Billy, the youngest, had suddenly pushed back his plate and slipped away from the table, manfully trying to swallow a sob. But William Tavener never heeded ominous forecasts in the domestic horizon, and he never looked for a storm until it broke.

After supper the boys had gone to the pond under the willows in the big cattle corral, to get rid of the dust of plowing. Hester could hear an occasional splash and a laugh ringing clear through the stillness of the night, as she sat by the open window. She sat silent for almost an hour reviewing in her mind many plans of attack. But she was too vigorous a woman to be much of a strategist, and she usually came to her point with directness. At last she cut her thread and suddenly put her darning down, saying emphatically:

"William, I don't think it would hurt you to let the boys go to that circus in town to-morrow."

William continued to read his farm paper, but it was not Hester's custom to wait for an answer. She usually divined his arguments and assailed them one by one before he uttered them.

"You've been short of hands all summer, and you've worked the boys hard, and a man ought use his own flesh and blood as well as he does his hired hands. We're plenty able to afford it, and it's little enough our boys ever spend. I don't see how you can expect 'em to be steady and hard workin', unless you encourage 'em a little. I never could see much harm in circuses, and our boys have never been to one. Oh, I know Jim Howley's boys get drunk an' carry on when they go, but our boys ain't that sort, an' you know it, William. The animals are real instructive, an' our boys don't get to see much out here on the prairie. It was different where we were raised, but the boys have got no advantages here, an' if you don't take care, they'll grow up to be greenhorns."

Hester paused a moment, and William folded up his paper, but vouchsafed no remark. His sisters in Virginia had often said that only a quiet man like William could ever have lived with Hester Perkins. Secretly, William was rather proud of his wife's "gift of speech," and of the fact that she could talk in prayer meeting as fluently as a man. He confined his own efforts in that line to a brief prayer at Covenant meetings.

Hester shook out another sock and went on.

"Nobody was ever hurt by goin' to a circus. Why, law me! I remember I went to one myself once, when I was little. I had most forgot about it. It was over at Pewtown, an' I remember how I had set my heart on going. I don't think I'd ever forgiven my father if he hadn't taken me, though that red clay road was in a frightful way after the rain. I mind they had an elephant and six poll parrots, an' a Rocky Mountain lion, an' a cage of monkeys, an' two camels. My! but they were a sight to me then!"

Hester dropped the black sock and shook her head and smiled at the recollection. She was not expecting anything from William yet, and she was fairly startled when he said gravely, in much the same tone in which he announced the hymns in prayer meeting:

"No, there was only one camel. The other was a dromedary."

She peered around the lamp and looked at him keenly.

"Why, William, how come you to know?"

William folded his paper and answered with some hesitation, "I was there, too."

Hester's interest flashed up.—"Well, I never, William! To think of my finding it out after all these years! Why, you couldn't have been much bigger'n our Billy then. It seems queer I never saw you when you was little, to remember about you. But then you Back Creek folks never have anything to do with us Gap people. But how come you to go? Your father was stricter with you than you are with your boys."

"I reckon I shouldn't 'a gone," he said slowly, "but boys

will do foolish things. I had done a good deal of fox hunting the winter before, and father let me keep the bounty money. I hired Tom Smith's Tap to weed the corn for me, an' I slipped off unbeknownst to father an' went to the show."

Hester spoke up warmly: "Nonsense, William! It didn't do you no harm, I guess. You was always worked hard enough. It must have been a big sight for a little fellow. That clown must have just tickled you to death."

William crossed his knees and leaned back in his chair.

"I reckon I could tell all that fool's jokes now. Sometimes I can't help thinkin' about 'em in meetin' when the sermon's long. I mind I had on a pair of new boots that hurt me like the mischief, but I forgot all about 'em when that fellow rode the donkey. I recall I had to take them boots off as soon as I got out of sight o' town, and walked home in the mud barefoot"

"O poor little fellow!" Hester ejaculated, drawing her chair nearer and leaning her elbows on the table. "What cruel shoes they did use to make for children. I remember I went up to Back Creek to see the circus wagons go by. They came down from Romney, you know. The circus men stopped at the creek to water the animals, an' the elephant got stubborn an' broke a big limb off the yellow willow tree that grew there by the toll house porch, an' the Scribners were 'fraid as death he'd pull the house down. But this much I saw him do; he waded in the creek an' filled his trunk with water, and squirted it in at the window and nearly ruined Ellen Scribner's pink lawn dress that she had just ironed an' laid out on the bed ready to wear to the circus."

"I reckon that must have been a trial to Ellen," chuckled William, "for she was mighty prim in them days."

Hester drew her chair still nearer William's. Since the children had begun growing up, her conversation with her husband had been almost wholly confined to questions of economy and expense. Their relationship had become purely a business one, like that between landlord and tenant. In her desire to indulge her boys she had unconsciously assumed a defensive and almost hostile attitude towards her husband. No debtor ever haggled with his usurer more doggedly than did Hester with her husband in behalf of her sons. The stra-

tegic contest had gone on so long that it had almost crowded
out the memory of a closer relationship. This exchange of
confidences to-night, when common recollections took them
unawares and opened their hearts, had all the miracle of ro-
mance. They talked on and on; of old neighbors, of old famil-
iar faces in the valley where they had grown up, of long
forgotten incidents of their youth—weddings, picnics, sleigh-
ing parties and baptizings. For years they had talked of noth-
ing else but butter and eggs and the prices of things, and now
they had as much to say to each other as people who meet
after a long separation.

When the clock struck ten, William rose and went over to
his walnut secretary and unlocked it. From his red leather
wallet he took out a ten dollar bill and laid it on the table
beside Hester.

"Tell the boys not to stay late, an' not to drive the horses
hard," he said quietly, and went off to bed.

Hester blew out the lamp and sat still in the dark a long
time. She left the bill lying on the table where William had
placed it. She had a painful sense of having missed something,
or lost something; she felt that somehow the years had
cheated her.

The little locust trees that grew by the fence were white
with blossoms. Their heavy odor floated in to her on the
night wind and recalled a night long ago, when the first whip-
poor-Will of the Spring was heard, and the rough, buxom
girls of Hawkins Gap had held her laughing and struggling
under the locust trees, and searched in her bosom for a lock
of her sweetheart's hair, which is supposed to be on every
girl's breast when the first whip-poor-Will sings. Two of
those same girls had been her bridesmaids. Hester had been a
very happy bride. She rose and went softly into the room
where William lay. He was sleeping heavily, but occasionally
moved his hand before his face to ward off the flies. Hester
went into the parlor and took the piece of mosquito net from
the basket of wax apples and pears that her sister had made
before she died. One of the boys had brought it all the way
from Virginia, packed in a tin pail, since Hester would not
risk shipping so precious an ornament by freight. She went
back to the bed room and spread the net over William's head.

Then she sat down by the bed and listened to his deep, regular breathing until she heard the boys returning. She went out to meet them and warn them not to waken their father.

"I'll be up early to get your breakfast, boys. Your father says you can go to the show." As she handed the money to the eldest, she felt a sudden throb of allegiance to her husband and said sharply, "And you be careful of that, an' don't waste it. Your father works hard for his money."

The boys looked at each other in astonishment and felt that they had lost a powerful ally.

Library, May 12, 1900

The Namesake

S EVEN OF US, students, sat one evening in Hartwell's
studio on the Boulevard St. Michel. We were all fellow-
countrymen; one from New Hampshire, one from Colorado,
another from Nevada, several from the farm lands of the
Middle West, and I myself from California. Lyon Hartwell,
though born abroad, was simply, as every one knew, "from
America." He seemed, almost more than any other one living
man, to mean all of it—from ocean to ocean. When he was in
Paris, his studio was always open to the seven of us who were
there that evening, and we intruded upon his leisure as often
as we thought permissible.

Although we were within the terms of the easiest of all
intimacies, and although the great sculptor, even when he was
more than usually silent, was at all times the most gravely
cordial of hosts, yet, on that long remembered evening, as the
sunlight died on the burnished brown of the horse-chestnuts
below the windows, a perceptible dullness yawned through
our conversation.

We were, indeed, somewhat low in spirit, for one of our
number, Charley Bentley, was leaving us indefinitely, in re-
sponse to an imperative summons from home. To-morrow his
studio, just across the hall from Hartwell's, was to pass into
other hands, and Bentley's luggage was even now piled in
discouraged resignation before his door. The various bales
and boxes seemed literally to weigh upon us as we sat in his
neighbor's hospitable rooms, drearily putting in the time un-
til he should leave us to catch the ten o'clock express for
Dieppe.

The day we had got through very comfortably, for Bentley
made it the occasion of a somewhat pretentious luncheon at
Maxim's. There had been twelve of us at table, and the two
young Poles were thirsty, the Gascon so fabulously entertain-
ing, that it was near upon five o'clock when we put down our
liqueur glasses for the last time, and the red, perspiring
waiter, having pocketed the reward of his arduous and pro-
tracted services, bowed us affably to the door, flourishing his

napkin and brushing back the streaks of wet, black hair from
his rosy forehead. Our guests having betaken themselves be-
lated to their respective engagements, the rest of us returned
with Bentley—only to be confronted by the depressing array
before his door. A glance about his denuded rooms had suf-
ficed to chill the glow of the afternoon, and we fled across the
hall in a body and begged Lyon Hartwell to take us in.

Bentley had said very little about it, but we all knew what it
meant to him to be called home. Each of us knew what it
would mean to himself, and each had felt something of that
quickened sense of opportunity which comes at seeing an-
other man in any way counted out of the race. Never had the
game seemed so enchanting, the chance to play it such a piece
of unmerited, unbelievable good fortune.

It must have been, I think, about the middle of October,
for I remember that the sycamores were almost bare in the
Luxembourg Gardens that morning, and the terrace about the
queens of France were strewn with crackling brown leaves.
The fat red roses, out the summer long on the stand of the
old flower woman at the corner, had given place to dahlias
and purple asters. First glimpses of autumn toilettes flashed
from the carriages; wonderful little bonnets nodded at one
along the Champs-Elysées; and in the Quarter an occasional
feather boa, red or black or white, brushed one's coat sleeve
in the gay twilight of the early evening. The crisp, sunny au-
tumn air was all day full of the stir of people and carriages and
of the cheer of salutations; greetings of the students, returned
brown and bearded from their holiday, gossip of people come
back from Trouville, from St. Valery, from Dieppe, from all
over Brittany and the Norman coast. Everywhere was the joy-
ousness of return, the taking up again of life and work and
play.

I had felt ever since early morning that this was the saddest
of all possible seasons for saying good-by to that old, old city
of youth, and to that little corner of it on the south shore
which since the Dark Ages themselves—yes, and before—has
been so peculiarly the land of the young.

I can recall our very postures as we lounged about Hart-
well's rooms that evening, with Bentley making occasional
hurried trips to his desolated workrooms across the hall—as

if haunted by a feeling of having forgotten something—or
stopping to poke nervously at his *perroquets*, which he had
bequeathed to Hartwell, gilt cage and all. Our host himself
sat on the couch, his big, bronze-like shoulders backed up
against the window, his shaggy head, beaked nose, and long
chin cut clean against the gray light.

Our drowsing interest, in so far as it could be said to be
fixed upon anything, was centered upon Hartwell's new fig-
ure, which stood on the block ready to be cast in bronze,
intended as a monument for some American battlefield. He
called it "The Color Sergeant." It was the figure of a young
soldier running, clutching the folds of a flag, the staff of
which had been shot away. We had known it in all the stages
of its growth, and the splendid action and feeling of the thing
had come to have a kind of special significance for the half
dozen of us who often gathered at Hartwell's rooms—
though, in truth, there was as much to dishearten one as to
inflame, in the case of a man who had done so much in a field
so amazingly difficult; who had thrown up in bronze all the
restless, teeming force of that adventurous wave still climbing
westward in our own land across the waters. We recalled his
"Scout," his "Pioneer," his "Gold Seekers," and those monu-
ments in which he had invested one and another of the heroes
of the Civil War with such convincing dignity and power.

"Where in the world does he get the heat to make an idea
like that carry?" Bentley remarked morosely, scowling at the
clay figure. "Hang me, Hartwell, if I don't think it's just be-
cause you're not really an American at all, that you can look at
it like that."

The big man shifted uneasily against the window. "Yes," he
replied smiling, "perhaps there is something in that. My citi-
zenship was somewhat belated and emotional in its flowering.
I've half a mind to tell you about it, Bentley." He rose uncer-
tainly, and, after hesitating a moment, went back into his
workroom, where he began fumbling among the litter in the
corners.

At the prospect of any sort of personal expression from
Hartwell, we glanced questioningly at one another; for al-
though he made us feel that he liked to have us about, we
were always held at a distance by a certain diffidence of his.

There were rare occasions—when he was in the heat of work or of ideas—when he forgot to be shy, but they were so exceptional that no flattery was quite so seductive as being taken for a moment into Hartwell's confidence. Even in the matter of opinions—the commonest of currency in our circle—he was niggardly and prone to qualify. No man ever guarded his mystery more effectually. There was a singular, intense spell, therefore, about those few evenings when he had broken through this excessive modesty, or shyness, or melancholy, and had, as it were, committed himself.

When Hartwell returned from the back room, he brought with him an unframed canvas which he put on an easel near his clay figure. We drew close about it, for the darkness was rapidly coming on. Despite the dullness of the light, we instantly recognized the boy of Hartwell's "Color Sergeant." It was the portrait of a very handsome lad in uniform, standing beside a charger impossibly rearing. Not only in his radiant countenance and flashing eyes, but in every line of his young body there was an energy, a gallantry, a joy of life, that arrested and challenged one.

"Yes, that's where I got the notion," Hartwell remarked, wandering back to his seat in the window. "I've wanted to do it for years, but I've never felt quite sure of myself. I was afraid of missing it. He was an uncle of mine, my father's half-brother, and I was named for him. He was killed in one of the big battles of Sixty-four, when I was a child. I never saw him—never knew him until he had been dead for twenty years. And then, one night, I came to know him as we sometimes do living persons—intimately, in a single moment."

He paused to knock the ashes out of his short pipe, refilled it, and puffed at it thoughtfully for a few moments with his hands on his knees. Then, settling back heavily among the cushions and looking absently out of the window, he began his story. As he proceeded further and further into the experience which he was trying to convey to us, his voice sank so low and was sometimes so charged with feeling, that I almost thought he had forgotten our presence and was remembering aloud. Even Bentley forgot his nervousness in astonishment and sat breathless under the spell of the man's thus breathing his memories out into the dusk.

"It was just fifteen years ago this last spring that I first went home, and Bentley's having to cut away like this brings it all back to me.

"I was born, you know, in Italy. My father was a sculptor, though I dare say you've not heard of him. He was one of those first fellows who went over after Story and Powers,— went to Italy for 'Art,' quite simply; to lift from its native bough the willing, iridescent bird. Their story is told, informingly enough, by some of those ingenuous marble things at the Metropolitan. My father came over some time before the outbreak of the Civil War, and was regarded as a renegade by his family because he did not go home to enter the army. His half-brother, the only child of my grandfather's second marriage, enlisted at fifteen and was killed the next year. I was ten years old when the news of his death reached us. My mother died the following winter, and I was sent away to a Jesuit school, while my father, already ill himself, stayed on at Rome, chipping away at his Indian maidens and marble goddesses, still gloomily seeking the thing for which he had made himself the most unhappy of exiles.

"He died when I was fourteen, but even before that I had been put to work under an Italian sculptor. He had an almost morbid desire that I should carry on his work, under, as he often pointed out to me, conditions so much more auspicious. He left me in the charge of his one intimate friend, an American gentleman in the consulate at Rome, and his instructions were that I was to be educated there and to live there until I was twenty-one. After I was of age, I came to Paris and studied under one master after another until I was nearly thirty. Then, almost for the first time, I was confronted by a duty which was not my pleasure.

"My grandfather's death, at an advanced age, left an invalid maiden sister of my father's quite alone in the world. She had suffered for years from a cerebral disease, a slow decay of the faculties which rendered her almost helpless. I decided to go to America and, if possible, bring her back to Paris, where I seemed on my way toward what my poor father had wished for me.

"On my arrival at my father's birthplace, however, I found that this was not to be thought of. To tear this timid, feeble, shrinking creature, doubly aged by years and illness, from the spot where she had been rooted for a lifetime, would have been little short of brutality. To leave her to the care of strangers seemed equally heartless. There was clearly nothing for me to do but to remain and wait for that slow and painless malady to run its course. I was there something over two years.

"My grandfather's home, his father's homestead before him, lay on the high banks of a river in Western Pennsylvania. The little town twelve miles down the stream, whither my great-grandfather used to drive his ox-wagon on market days, had become, in two generations, one of the largest manufacturing cities in the world. For hundreds of miles about us the gentle hill slopes were honeycombed with gas wells and coal shafts; oil derricks creaked in every valley and meadow; the brooks were sluggish and discolored with crude petroleum, and the air was impregnated by its searching odor. The great glass and iron manufactories had come up and up the river almost to our very door; their smoky exhalations brooded over us, and their crashing was always in our ears. I was plunged into the very incandescence of human energy. But, though my nerves tingled with the feverish, passionate endeavor which snapped in the very air about me, none of these great arteries seemed to feed me; this tumultuous life did not warm me. On every side were the great muddy rivers, the ragged mountains from which the timber was being ruthlessly torn away, the vast tracts of wild country, and the gulches that were like wounds in the earth; everywhere the glare of that relentless energy which followed me like a searchlight and seemed to scorch and consume me. I could only hide myself in the tangled garden, where the dropping of a leaf or the whistle of a bird was the only incident.

"The Hartwell homestead had been sold away little by little, until all that remained of it was garden and orchard. The house, a square brick structure, stood in the midst of a great garden which sloped toward the river, ending in a grassy bank which fell some forty feet to the water's edge. The garden was now little more than a tangle of neglected shrubbery; damp, rank, and of that intense blue-green peculiar to vegetation in smoky places where the sun shines but rarely, and the mists form early in the evening and hang late in the morning.

"I shall never forget it as I saw it first, when I arrived there in the chill of a backward June. The long, rank grass, thick and soft and falling in billows, was always wet until midday. The gravel walks were bordered with great lilac-bushes, mock-orange, and bridal-wreath. Back of the house was a neglected rose garden, surrounded by a low stone wall over which the long suckers trailed and matted. They had wound their pink, thorny tentacles, layer upon layer, about the lock and the hinges of the rusty iron gate. Even the porches of the house, and the very windows, were damp and heavy with growth: wistaria, clematis, honeysuckle, and trumpet vine. The garden was grown up with trees, especially that part of it which lay above the river. The bark of the old locusts was blackened by the smoke that crept continually up the valley, and their feathery foliage, so merry in its movement and so yellow and joyous in its color, seemed peculiarly precious under that somber sky. There were sycamores and copper beeches; gnarled apple-trees, too old to bear; and fall pear-trees, hung with a sharp, hard fruit in October; all with a leafage singularly rich and luxuriant, and peculiarly vivid in color. The oaks about the house had been old trees when my great-grandfather built his cabin there, more than a century before, and this garden was almost the only spot for miles along the river where any of the original forest growth still survived. The smoke from the mills was fatal to trees of the larger sort, and even these had the look of doomed things— bent a little toward the town and seemed to wait with head inclined before that on-coming, shrieking force.

"About the river, too, there was a strange hush, a tragic submission—it was so leaden and sullen in its color, and it flowed so soundlessly forever past our door.

"I sat there every evening, on the high veranda overlooking it, watching the dim outlines of the steep hills on the other shore, the flicker of the lights on the island, where there was a boat-house, and listening to the call of the boatmen through the mist. The mist came as certainly as night, whitened by moonshine or starshine. The tin water-pipes went splash, splash, with it all evening, and the wind, when it rose at all, was little more than a sighing of the old boughs and a troubled breath in the heavy grasses.

"At first it was to think of my distant friends and my old life that I used to sit there; but after awhile it was simply to watch the days and weeks go by, like the river which seemed to carry them away.

"Within the house I was never at home. Month followed month, and yet I could feel no sense of kinship with anything there. Under the roof where my father and grandfather were born, I remained utterly detached. The somber rooms never spoke to me, the old furniture never seemed tinctured with race. This portrait of my boy uncle was the only thing to which I could draw near, the only link with anything I had ever known before.

"There is a good deal of my father in the face, but it is my father transformed and glorified; his hesitating discontent drowned in a kind of triumph. From my first day in that house, I continually turned to this handsome kinsman of mine, wondering in what terms he had lived and had his hope; what he had found there to look like that, to bound at one, after all those years, so joyously out of the canvas.

"From the timid, clouded old woman over whose life I had come to watch, I learned that in the backyard, near the old rose garden, there was a locust-tree which my uncle had planted. After his death, while it was still a slender sapling, his mother had a seat built round it, and she used to sit there on summer evenings. His grave was under the apple-trees in the old orchard.

"My aunt could tell me little more than this. There were days when she seemed not to remember him at all.

"It was from an old soldier in the village that I learned the boy's story. Lyon was, the old man told me, but fourteen when the first enlistment occurred, but was even then eager to go. He was in the court-house square every evening to watch the recruits at their drill, and when the home company was ordered off he rode into the city on his pony to see the men board the train and to wave them good-by. The next year he spent at home with a tutor, but when he was fifteen he held his parents to their promise and went into the army. He was color sergeant of his regiment and fell in a charge upon the breastworks of a fort about a year after his enlistment.

"The veteran showed me an account of this charge which had been written for the village paper by one of my uncle's comrades who had seen his part in the engagement. It seems that as his company were running at full speed across the bottom lands toward the fortified hill, a shell burst over them. This comrade, running beside my uncle, saw the colors waver and sink as if falling, and looked to see that the boy's hand and forearm had been torn away by the exploding shrapnel. The boy, he thought, did not realize the extent of his injury, for he laughed, shouted something which his comrade did not catch, caught the flag in his left hand, and ran on up the hill. They went splendidly up over the breastworks, but just as my uncle, his colors flying, reached the top of the embankment, a second shell carried away his left arm at the arm-pit, and he fell over the wall with the flag settling about him.

"It was because this story was ever present with me, because I was unable to shake it off, that I began to read such books as my grandfather had collected upon the Civil War. I found that this war was fought largely by boys, that more men enlisted at eighteen than at any other age. When I thought of those battlefields—and I thought of them much in those days—there was always that glory of youth above them, that impetuous, generous passion stirring the long lines on the march, the blue battalions in the plain. The bugle, whenever I have heard it since, has always seemed to me the very golden throat of that boyhood which spent itself so gaily, so incredibly.

"I used often to wonder how it was that this uncle of mine, who seemed to have possessed all the charm and brilliancy allotted to his family and to have lived up its vitality in one splendid hour, had left so little trace in the house where he was born and where he had awaited his destiny. Look as I would, I could find no letters from him, no clothing or books that might have been his. He had been dead but twenty years, and yet nothing seemed to have survived except the tree he had planted. It seemed incredible and cruel that no physical memory of him should linger to be cherished among his kindred,—nothing but the dull image in the brain of that aged sister. I used to pace the garden walks in the evening, wondering that no breath of his, no echo of his laugh, of his call to his pony or his whistle to his dogs, should linger about those shaded paths where the pale roses exhaled their dewy, country smell. Sometimes, in the dim starlight, I have thought that I heard on the grasses beside me the stir of a footfall lighter than my own, and under the black arch of the lilacs I have fancied that he bore me company.

"There was, I found, one day in the year for which my old aunt waited, and which stood out from the months that were all of a sameness to her. On the thirtieth of May she insisted that I should bring down the big flag from the attic and run it up upon the tall flagstaff beside Lyon's tree in the garden. Later in the morning she went with me to carry some of the garden flowers to the grave in the orchard,—a grave scarcely larger than a child's.

"I had noticed, when I was hunting for the flag in the attic, a leather trunk with my own name stamped upon it, but was unable to find the key. My aunt was all day less apathetic than usual; she seemed to realize more clearly who I was, and to wish me to be with her. I did not have an opportunity to return to the attic until after dinner that evening, when I carried a lamp up-stairs and easily forced the lock of the trunk. I found all the things that I had looked for; put away, doubtless, by his mother, and still smelling faintly of lavender and rose leaves; his clothes, his exercise books, his letters from the army, his first boots, his riding-whip, some of his toys, even. I took them out and replaced them gently. As I was about to shut the lid, I picked up a copy of the Æneid, on the fly-leaf of which was written in a slanting, boyish hand,

Lyon Hartwell, January, 1862.

He had gone to the wars in Sixty-three, I remembered.

"My uncle, I gathered, was none too apt at his Latin, for the pages were dog-eared and rubbed and interlined, the margins mottled with pencil sketches—bugles, stacked bayonets, and artillery carriages. In the act of putting the book down, I happened to run over the pages to the end, and on the fly-leaf at the back I saw his name again, and a drawing—with his initials and a date—of the Federal flag; above it, written in a kind of arch and in the same unformed hand:

'Oh, say, can you see by the dawn's early light
What so proudly we hailed at the twilight's last gleaming?'

It was a stiff, wooden sketch, not unlike a detail from some Egyptian inscription, but, the moment I saw it, wind and color seemed to touch it. I caught up the book, blew out the lamp, and rushed down into the garden.

"I seemed, somehow, at last to have known him; to have been with him in that careless, unconscious moment and to have known him as he was then.

"As I sat there in the rush of this realization, the wind began to rise, stirring the light foliage of the locust over my head and bringing, fresher than before, the woody odor of the pale roses that overran the little neglected garden. Then, as it grew stronger, it brought the sound of something sighing and stirring over my head in the perfumed darkness.

"I thought of that sad one of the Destinies who, as the Greeks believed, watched from birth over those marked for a violent or untimely death. Oh, I could see him, there in the shine of the morning, his book idly on his knee, his flashing eyes looking straight before him, and at his side that grave figure, hidden in her draperies, her eyes following his, but seeing so much farther—seeing what he never saw, that great moment at the end, when he swayed above his comrades on the earthen wall.

"All the while, the bunting I had run up in the morning flapped fold against fold, heaving and tossing softly in the dark—against a sky so black with rain clouds that I could see above me only the blur of something in soft, troubled motion.

"The experience of that night, coming so overwhelmingly to a man so dead, almost rent me in pieces. It was the same feeling that artists know when we, rarely, achieve truth in our work; the feeling of union with some great force, of purpose and security, of being glad that we have lived. For the first time I felt the pull of race and blood and kindred, and felt beating within me things that had not begun with me. It was as if the earth under my feet had grasped and rooted me, and were pouring its essence into me. I sat there until the dawn of morning, and all night long my life seemed to be pouring out of me and running into the ground."

Hartwell drew a long breath that lifted his heavy shoulders, and then let them fall again. He shifted a little and faced more squarely the scattered, silent company before him. The darkness had made us almost invisible to each other, and, except for the occasional red circuit of a cigarette end traveling upward from the arm of a chair, he might have supposed us all asleep.

"And so," Hartwell added thoughtfully, "I naturally feel an interest in fellows who are going home. It's always an experience."

No one said anything, and in a moment there was a loud rap at the door,—the concierge, come to take down Bentley's luggage and to announce that the cab was below. Bentley got his hat and coat, enjoined Hartwell to take good care of his *perroquets*, gave each of us a grip of the hand, and went briskly down the long flights of stairs. We followed him into the street, calling our good wishes, and saw him start on his drive across the lighted city to the Gare St. Lazare.

McClure's, March 1907

The Enchanted Bluff

W<small>E HAD</small> our swim before sundown, and while we were cooking our supper the oblique rays of light made a dazzling glare on the white sand about us. The translucent red ball itself sank behind the brown stretches of corn field as we sat down to eat, and the warm layer of air that had rested over the water and our clean sand-bar grew fresher and smelled of the rank ironweed and sunflowers growing on the flatter shore. The river was brown and sluggish, like any other of the half-dozen streams that water the Nebraska corn lands. On one shore was an irregular line of bald clay bluffs where a few scrub-oaks with thick trunks and flat, twisted tops threw light shadows on the long grass. The western shore was low and level, with corn fields that stretched to the sky-line, and all along the water's edge were little sandy coves and beaches where slim cottonwoods and willow saplings flickered.

The turbulence of the river in spring-time discouraged milling, and, beyond keeping the old red bridge in repair, the busy farmers did not concern themselves with the stream; so the Sandtown boys were left in undisputed possession. In the autumn we hunted quail through the miles of stubble and fodder land along the flat shore, and, after the winter skating season was over and the ice had gone out, the spring freshets and flooded bottoms gave us our great excitement of the year. The channel was never the same for two successive seasons. Every spring the swollen stream undermined a bluff to the east, or bit out a few acres of corn field to the west and whirled the soil away to deposit it in spumy mud banks somewhere else. When the water fell low in midsummer, new sand-bars were thus exposed to dry and whiten in the August sun. Sometimes these were banked so firmly that the fury of the next freshet failed to unseat them; the little willow seedlings emerged triumphantly from the yellow froth, broke into spring leaf, shot up into summer growth, and with their mesh of roots bound together the moist sand beneath them against the batterings of another April. Here and there a cottonwood soon glittered among them, quivering in the low current of air that, even on breathless days when the dust hung like smoke above the wagon road, trembled along the face of the water.

It was on such an island, in the third summer of its yellow green, that we built our watch-fire; not in the thicket of dancing willow wands, but on the level terrace of fine sand which had been added that spring; a little new bit of world, beautifully ridged with ripple marks, and strewn with the tiny skeletons of turtles and fish, all as white and dry as if they had been expertly cured. We had been careful not to mar the freshness of the place, although we often swam out to it on summer evenings and lay on the sand to rest.

This was our last watch-fire of the year, and there were reasons why I should remember it better than any of the others. Next week the other boys were to file back to their old places in the Sandtown High School, but I was to go up to the Divide to teach my first country school in the Norwegian district. I was already homesick at the thought of quitting the boys with whom I had always played; of leaving the river, and going up into a windy plain that was all windmills and corn fields and big pastures; where there was nothing wilful or unmanageable in the landscape, no new islands, and no chance of unfamiliar birds—such as often followed the watercourses.

Other boys came and went and used the river for fishing or skating, but we six were sworn to the spirit of the stream, and we were friends mainly because of the river. There were the two Hassler boys, Fritz and Otto, sons of the little German tailor. They were the youngest of us; ragged boys of ten and twelve, with sunburned hair, weather-stained faces, and pale blue eyes. Otto, the elder, was the best mathematician in school, and clever at his books, but he always dropped out in the spring term as if the river could not get on without him. He and Fritz caught the fat, horned catfish and sold them about the town, and they lived so much in the water that they were as brown and sandy as the river itself.

There was Percy Pound, a fat, freckled boy with chubby cheeks, who took half a dozen boys' story-papers and was always being kept in for reading detective stories behind his desk. There was Tip Smith, destined by his freckles and red hair to be the buffoon in all our games, though he walked like a timid little old man and had a funny, cracked laugh. Tip worked hard in his father's grocery store every afternoon, and swept it out before school in the morning. Even his recreations were laborious. He collected cigarette cards and tin tobacco-tags indefatigably, and would sit for hours humped up over a snarling little scroll-saw which he kept in his attic. His dearest possessions were some little pill-bottles that purported to contain grains of wheat from the Holy Land, water from the Jordan and the Dead Sea, and earth from the Mount of Olives. His father had bought these dull things from a Baptist missionary who peddled them, and Tip seemed to derive great satisfaction from their remote origin.

The tall boy was Arthur Adams. He had fine hazel eyes that were almost too reflective and sympathetic for a boy, and such a pleasant voice that we all loved to hear him read aloud. Even when he had to read poetry aloud at school, no one ever thought of laughing. To be sure, he was not at school very much of the time. He was seventeen and should have finished the High School the year before, but he was always off somewhere with his gun. Arthur's mother was dead, and his father, who was feverishly absorbed in promoting schemes, wanted to send the boy away to school and get him off his hands; but Arthur always begged off for another year and promised to study. I remember him as a tall, brown boy with an intelligent face, always lounging among a lot of us little fellows, laughing at us oftener than with us, but such a soft, satisfied laugh that we felt rather flattered when we provoked it. In after-years people said that Arthur had been given to evil ways even as a lad, and it is true that we often saw him with the gambler's sons and with old Spanish Fanny's boy, but if he learned anything ugly in their company he never betrayed it to us. We would have followed Arthur anywhere, and I am bound to say that he led us into no worse places than the cattail marshes and the stubble fields. These, then, were the boys who camped with me that summer night upon the sand-bar.

After we finished our supper we beat the willow thicket for driftwood. By the time we had collected enough, night had fallen, and the pungent, weedy smell from the shore increased with the coolness. We threw ourselves down about the fire and made another futile effort to show Percy Pound the Little Dipper. We had tried it often before, but he could never be got past the big one.

"You see those three big stars just below the handle, with the bright one in the middle?" said Otto Hassler; "that's Orion's belt, and the bright one is the clasp." I crawled behind Otto's shoulder and sighted up his arm to the star that seemed perched upon the tip of his steady forefinger. The Hassler boys did seine-fishing at night, and they knew a good many stars.

Percy gave up the Little Dipper and lay back on the sand, his hands clasped under his head. "I can see the North Star," he announced, contentedly, pointing toward it with his big toe. "Any one might get lost and need to know that."

We all looked up at it.

"How do you suppose Columbus felt when his compass didn't point north any more?" Tip asked.

Otto shook his head. "My father says that there was another North Star once, and that maybe this one won't last always. I wonder what would happen to us down here if anything went wrong with it?"

Arthur chuckled. "I wouldn't worry, Ott. Nothing's apt to happen to it in your time. Look at the Milky Way! There must be lots of good dead Indians."

We lay back and looked, meditating, at the dark cover of the world. The gurgle of the water had become heavier. We had often noticed a mutinous, complaining note in it at night, quite different from its cheerful daytime chuckle, and seeming like the voice of a much deeper and more powerful stream. Our water had always these two moods: the one of sunny complaisance, the other of inconsolable, passionate regret.

"Queer how the stars are all in sort of diagrams," remarked Otto. "You could do most any proposition in geometry with 'em. They always look as if they meant something. Some folks say everybody's fortune is all written out in the stars, don't they?"

"They believe so in the old country," Fritz affirmed.

But Arthur only laughed at him. "You're thinking of Napoleon, Fritzey. He had a star that went out when he began to lose battles. I guess the stars don't keep any close tally on Sandtown folks."

We were speculating on how many times we could count a hundred before the evening star went down behind the corn fields, when some one cried, "There comes the moon, and it's as big as a cart wheel!"

We all jumped up to greet it as it swam over the bluffs behind us. It came up like a galleon in full sail; an enormous, barbaric thing, red as an angry heathen god.

"When the moon came up red like that, the Aztecs used to sacrifice their prisoners on the temple top," Percy announced.

"Go on, Perce. You got that out of *Golden Days*. Do you believe that, Arthur?" I appealed.

Arthur answered, quite seriously: "Like as not. The moon was one of their gods. When my father was in Mexico City he saw the stone where they used to sacrifice their prisoners."

As we dropped down by the fire again some one asked whether the Mound-Builders were older than the Aztecs. When we once got upon the Mound-Builders we never willingly got away from them, and we were still conjecturing when we heard a loud splash in the water.

"Must have been a big cat jumping," said Fritz. "They do sometimes. They must see bugs in the dark. Look what a track the moon makes!"

There was a long, silvery streak on the water, and where the current fretted over a big log it boiled up like gold pieces.

"Suppose there ever *was* any gold hid away in this old river?" Fritz asked. He lay like a little brown Indian, close to the fire, his chin on his hand and his bare feet in the air. His brother laughed at him, but Arthur took his suggestion seriously.

"Some of the Spaniards thought there was gold up here somewhere. Seven cities chuck full of gold, they had it, and Coronado and his men came up to hunt it. The Spaniards were all over this country once."

Percy looked interested. "Was that before the Mormons went through?"

We all laughed at this.

"Long enough before. Before the Pilgrim Fathers, Perce.

Maybe they came along this very river. They always followed the watercourses."

"I wonder where this river really does begin?" Tip mused. That was an old and a favorite mystery which the map did not clearly explain. On the map the little black line stopped somewhere in western Kansas; but since rivers generally rose in mountains, it was only reasonable to suppose that ours came from the Rockies. Its destination, we knew, was the Missouri, and the Hassler boys always maintained that we could embark at Sandtown in flood-time, follow our noses, and eventually arrive at New Orleans. Now they took up their old argument. "If us boys had grit enough to try it, it wouldn't take no time to get to Kansas City and St. Joe."

We began to talk about the places we wanted to go to. The Hassler boys wanted to see the stock-yards in Kansas City, and Percy wanted to see a big store in Chicago. Arthur was interlocutor and did not betray himself.

"Now it's your turn, Tip."

Tip rolled over on his elbow and poked the fire, and his eyes looked shyly out of his queer, tight little face. "My place is awful far away. My uncle Bill told me about it."

Tip's Uncle Bill was a wanderer, bitten with mining fever, who had drifted into Sandtown with a broken arm, and when it was well had drifted out again.

"Where is it?"

"Aw, it's down in New Mexico somewheres. There aren't no railroads or anything. You have to go on mules, and you run out of water before you get there and have to drink canned tomatoes."

"Well, go on, kid. What's it like when you do get there?"

Tip sat up and excitedly began his story.

"There's a big red rock there that goes right up out of the sand for about nine hundred feet. The country's flat all around it, and this here rock goes up all by itself, like a monument. They call it the Enchanted Bluff down there, because no white man has ever been on top of it. The sides are smooth rock, and straight up, like a wall. The Indians say that hundreds of years ago, before the Spaniards came, there was a village away up there in the air. The tribe that lived there had some sort of steps, made out of wood and bark, hung down over the face of the bluff, and the braves went down to hunt and carried water up in big jars swung on their backs. They kept a big supply of water and dried meat up there, and never went down except to hunt. They were a peaceful tribe that made cloth and pottery, and they went up there to get out of the wars. You see, they could pick off any war party that tried to get up their little steps. The Indians say they were a handsome people, and they had some sort of a queer religion. Uncle Bill thinks they were Cliff-Dwellers who had got into trouble and left home. They weren't fighters, anyhow.

"One time the braves were down hunting and an awful storm came up—a kind of waterspout—and when they got back to their rock they found their little staircase had been all broken to pieces, and only a few steps were left hanging away up in the air. While they were camped at the foot of the rock, wondering what to do, a war party from the north came along and massacred 'em to a man, with all the old folks and women looking on from the rock. Then the war party went on south and left the village to get down the best way they could. Of course they never got down. They starved to death up there, and when the war party came back on their way north, they could hear the children crying from the edge of the bluff where they had crawled out, but they didn't see a sign of a grown Indian, and nobody has ever been up there since."

We exclaimed at this dolorous legend and sat up.

"There couldn't have been many people up there," Percy demurred. "How big is the top, Tip?"

"Oh, pretty big. Big enough so that the rock doesn't look nearly as tall as it is. The top's bigger than the base. The bluff is sort of worn away for several hundred feet up. That's one reason it's so hard to climb."

I asked how the Indians got up, in the first place.

"Nobody knows how they got up or when. A hunting party came along once and saw that there was a town up there, and that was all."

Otto rubbed his chin and looked thoughtful. "Of course there must be some way to get up there. Couldn't people get a rope over someway and pull a ladder up?"

Tip's little eyes were shining with excitement. "I know a

way. Me and Uncle Bill talked it all over. There's a kind of
rocket that would take a rope over—life-savers use 'em—and
then you could hoist a rope-ladder and peg it down at the
bottom and make it tight with guy-ropes on the other side.
I'm going to climb that there bluff, and I've got it all planned
out."

Fritz asked what he expected to find when he got up there.

"Bones, maybe, or the ruins of their town, or pottery, or
some of their idols. There might be 'most anything up there.
Anyhow, I want to see."

"Sure nobody else has been up there, Tip?" Arthur asked.

"Dead sure. Hardly anybody ever goes down there. Some
hunters tried to cut steps in the rock once, but they didn't get
higher than a man can reach. The Bluff's all red granite, and
Uncle Bill thinks it's a boulder the glaciers left. It's a queer
place, anyhow. Nothing but cactus and desert for hundreds of
miles, and yet right under the bluff there's good water and
plenty of grass. That's why the bison used to go down there."

Suddenly we heard a scream above our fire, and jumped up
to see a dark, slim bird floating southward far above us—a
whooping-crane, we knew by her cry and her long neck. We
ran to the edge of the island, hoping we might see her alight,
but she wavered southward along the rivercourse until we lost
her. The Hassler boys declared that by the look of the heavens
it must be after midnight, so we threw more wood on our
fire, put on our jackets, and curled down in the warm sand.
Several of us pretended to doze, but I fancy we were really
thinking about Tip's Bluff and the extinct people. Over in the
wood the ring-doves were calling mournfully to one another,
and once we heard a dog bark, far away. "Somebody getting
into old Tommy's melon patch," Fritz murmured, sleepily,
but nobody answered him. By and by Percy spoke out of the
shadow.

"Say, Tip, when you go down there will you take me with
you?"

"Maybe."

"Suppose one of us beats you down there, Tip?"

"Whoever gets to the Bluff first has got to promise to tell
the rest of us exactly what he finds," remarked one of the
Hassler boys, and to this we all readily assented.

Somewhat reassured, I dropped off to sleep. I must have dreamed about a race for the Bluff, for I awoke in a kind of fear that other people were getting ahead of me and that I was losing my chance. I sat up in my damp clothes and looked at the other boys, who lay tumbled in uneasy attitudes about the dead fire. It was still dark, but the sky was blue with the last wonderful azure of night. The stars glistened like crystal globes, and trembled as if they shone through a depth of clear water. Even as I watched, they began to pale and the sky brightened. Day came suddenly, almost instantaneously. I turned for another look at the blue night, and it was gone. Everywhere the birds began to call, and all manner of little insects began to chirp and hop about in the willows. A breeze sprang up from the west and brought the heavy smell of ripened corn. The boys rolled over and shook themselves. We stripped and plunged into the river just as the sun came up over the windy bluffs.

When I came home to Sandtown at Christmas time, we skated out to our island and talked over the whole project of the Enchanted Bluff, renewing our resolution to find it.

Although that was twenty years ago, none of us have ever climbed the Enchanted Bluff. Percy Pound is a stockbroker in Kansas City and will go nowhere that his red touring-car cannot carry him. Otto Hassler went on the railroad and lost his foot braking; after which he and Fritz succeeded their father as the town tailors.

Arthur sat about the sleepy little town all his life—he died before he was twenty-five. The last time I saw him, when I was home on one of my college vacations, he was sitting in a steamer-chair under a cottonwood tree in the little yard behind one of the two Sandtown saloons. He was very untidy and his hand was not steady, but when he rose, unabashed, to greet me, his eyes were as clear and warm as ever. When I had talked with him for an hour and heard him laugh again, I wondered how it was that when Nature had taken such pains with a man, from his hands to the arch of his long foot, she had ever lost him in Sandtown. He joked about Tip Smith's Bluff, and declared he was going down there just as soon as the weather got cooler; he thought the Grand Cañon might be worth while, too.

I was perfectly sure when I left him that he would never get beyond the high plank fence and the comfortable shade of the cottonwood. And, indeed, it was under that very tree that he died one summer morning.

Tip Smith still talks about going to New Mexico. He married a slatternly, unthrifty country girl, has been much tied to a perambulator, and has grown stooped and gray from irregular meals and broken sleep. But the worst of his difficulties are now over, and he has, as he says, come into easy water. When I was last in Sandtown I walked home with him late one moonlight night, after he had balanced his cash and shut up his store. We took the long way around and sat down on the schoolhouse steps, and between us we quite revived the romance of the lone red rock and the extinct people. Tip insists that he still means to go down there, but he thinks now he will wait until his boy, Bert, is old enough to go with him. Bert has been let into the story, and thinks of nothing but the Enchanted Bluff.

Harper's, April 1909

The Joy of Nelly Deane

NELL AND I were almost ready to go on for the last act of "Queen Esther," and we had for the moment got rid of our three patient dressers, Mrs. Dow, Mrs. Freeze, and Mrs. Spinny. Nell was peering over my shoulder into the little cracked looking-glass that Mrs. Dow had taken from its nail on her kitchen wall and brought down to the church under her shawl that morning. When she realized that we were alone, Nell whispered to me in the quick, fierce way she had:

"Say, Peggy, won't you go up and stay with me to-night? Scott Spinny's asked to take me home, and I don't want to walk up with him alone."

"I guess so, if you'll ask my mother."

"Oh, I'll fix her!" Nell laughed, with a toss of her head which meant that she usually got what she wanted, even from people much less tractable than my mother.

In a moment our tiring-women were back again. The three old ladies — at least they seemed old to us — fluttered about us, more agitated than we were ourselves. It seemed as though they would never leave off patting Nell and touching her up. They kept trying things this way and that, never able in the end to decide which way was best. They wouldn't hear to her using rouge, and as they powdered her neck and arms, Mrs. Freeze murmured that she hoped we wouldn't get into the habit of using such things. Mrs. Spinny divided her time between pulling up and tucking down the "illusion" that filled in the square neck of Nelly's dress. She didn't like things much low, she said; but after she had pulled it up, she stood back and looked at Nell thoughtfully through her glasses. While the excited girl was reaching for this and that, buttoning a slipper, pinning down a curl, Mrs. Spinny's smile softened more and more until, just before *Esther* made her entrance, the old lady tiptoed up to her and softly tucked the illusion down as far as it would go.

"She's so pink; it seems a pity not," she whispered apologetically to Mrs. Dow.

Every one admitted that Nelly was the prettiest girl in

Riverbend, and the gayest—oh, the gayest! When she was not singing, she was laughing. When she was not laid up with a broken arm, the outcome of a foolhardy coasting feat, or suspended from school because she ran away at recess to go buggy-riding with Guy Franklin, she was sure to be up to mischief of some sort. Twice she broke through the ice and got soused in the river because she never looked where she skated or cared what happened so long as she went fast enough. After the second of these duckings our three dressers declared that she was trying to be a Baptist despite herself.

Mrs. Spinny and Mrs. Freeze and Mrs. Dow, who were always hovering about Nelly, often whispered to me their hope that she would eventually come into our church and not "go with the Methodists"; her family were Wesleyans. But to me these artless plans of theirs never wholly explained their watchful affection. They had good daughters themselves,— except Mrs. Spinny, who had only the sullen Scott,—and they loved their plain girls and thanked God for them. But they loved Nelly differently. They were proud of her pretty figure and yellow-brown eyes, which dilated so easily and sparkled with a kind of golden effervescence. They were always making pretty things for her, always coaxing her to come to the sewing-circle, where she knotted her thread, and put in the wrong sleeve, and laughed and chattered and said a great many things that she should not have said, and somehow always warmed their hearts. I think they loved her for her unquenchable joy.

All the Baptist ladies liked Nell, even those who criticized her most severely, but the three who were first in fighting the battles of our little church, who held it together by their prayers and the labor of their hands, watched over her as they did over Mrs. Dow's century-plant before it blossomed. They looked for her on Sunday morning and smiled at her as she hurried, always a little late, up to the choir. When she rose and stood behind the organ and sang "There Is a Green Hill," one could see Mrs. Dow and Mrs. Freeze settle back in their accustomed seats and look up at her as if she had just come from that hill and had brought them glad tidings.

It was because I sang contralto, or, as we said, alto, in the Baptist choir that Nell and I became friends. She was so gay and grown up, so busy with parties and dances and picnics, that I would scarcely have seen much of her had we not sung together. She liked me better than she did any of the older girls, who tried clumsily to be like her, and I felt almost as solicitous and admiring as did Mrs. Dow and Mrs. Spinny. I think even then I must have loved to see her bloom and glow, and I loved to hear her sing, in "The Ninety and Nine,"

But one was out on the hills away

in her sweet, strong voice. Nell had never had a singing lesson, but she had sung from the time she could talk, and Mrs. Dow used fondly to say that it was singing so much that made her figure so pretty.

After I went into the choir it was found to be easier to get Nelly to choir practice. If I stopped outside her gate on my way to church and coaxed her, she usually laughed, ran in for her hat and jacket, and went along with me. The three old ladies fostered our friendship, and because I was "quiet," they esteemed me a good influence for Nelly. This view was propounded in a sewing-circle discussion and, leaking down to us through our mothers, greatly amused us. Dear old ladies! It was so manifestly for what Nell was that they loved her, and yet they were always looking for "influences" to change her.

The "Queen Esther" performance had cost us three months of hard practice, and it was not easy to keep Nell up to attending the tedious rehearsals. Some of the boys we knew were in the chorus of Assyrian youths, but the solo cast was made up of older people, and Nell found them very poky. We gave the cantata in the Baptist church on Christmas eve, "to a crowded house," as the Riverbend "Messenger" truly chronicled. The country folk for miles about had come in through a deep snow, and their teams and wagons stood in a long row at the hitch-bars on each side of the church door. It was certainly Nelly's night, for however much the tenor—he was her schoolmaster, and naturally thought poorly of her— might try to eclipse her in his dolorous solos about the rivers of Babylon, there could be no doubt as to whom the people had come to hear—and to see.

After the performance was over, our fathers and mothers

came back to the dressing-rooms—the little rooms behind the baptistry where the candidates for baptism were robed —to congratulate us, and Nell persuaded my mother to let me go home with her. This arrangement may not have been wholly agreeable to Scott Spinny, who stood glumly waiting at the baptistry door; though I used to think he dogged Nell's steps not so much for any pleasure he got from being with her as for the pleasure of keeping other people away. Dear little Mrs. Spinny was perpetually in a state of humiliation on account of his bad manners, and she tried by a very special tenderness to make up to Nelly for the remissness of her ungracious son.

Scott was a spare, muscular fellow, good-looking, but with a face so set and dark that I used to think it very like the castings he sold. He was taciturn and domineering, and Nell rather liked to provoke him. Her father was so easy with her that she seemed to enjoy being ordered about now and then. That night, when every one was praising her and telling her how well she sang and how pretty she looked, Scott only said, as we came out of the dressing-room:

"Have you got your high shoes on?"

"No; but I've got rubbers on over my low ones. Mother doesn't care."

"Well, you just go back and put 'em on as fast as you can."

Nell made a face at him and ran back, laughing. Her mother, fat, comfortable Mrs. Deane, was immensely amused at this.

"That's right, Scott," she chuckled. "You can do enough more with her than I can. She walks right over me an' Jud."

Scott grinned. If he was proud of Nelly, the last thing he wished to do was to show it. When she came back he began to nag again. "What are you going to do with all those flowers? They'll freeze stiff as pokers."

"Well, there won't none of *your* flowers freeze, Scott Spinny, so there!" Nell snapped. She had the best of him that time, and the Assyrian youths rejoiced. They were most of them high-school boys, and the poorest of them had "chipped in" and sent all the way to Denver for *Queen Esther's* flowers. There were bouquets from half a dozen townspeople, too, but none from Scott. Scott was a prosperous hardware merchant and notoriously penurious, though he saved his face, as the boys said, by giving liberally to the church.

"There's no use freezing the fool things, anyhow. You get me some newspapers, and I'll wrap 'em up." Scott took from his pocket a folded copy of the Riverbend "Messenger" and began laboriously to wrap up one of the bouquets. When we left the church door he bore three large newspaper bundles, carrying them as carefully as if they had been so many newly frosted wedding-cakes, and left Nell and me to shift for ourselves as we floundered along the snow-burdened sidewalk.

Although it was after midnight, lights were shining from many of the little wooden houses, and the roofs and shrubbery were so deep in snow that Riverbend looked as if it had been tucked down into a warm bed. The companies of people, all coming from church, tramping this way and that toward their homes and calling "Good night" and "Merry Christmas" as they parted company, all seemed to us very unusual and exciting.

When we got home, Mrs. Deane had a cold supper ready, and Jud Deane had already taken off his shoes and fallen to on his fried chicken and pie. He was so proud of his pretty daughter that he must give her her Christmas presents then and there, and he went into the sleeping-chamber behind the dining-room and from the depths of his wife's closet brought out a short sealskin jacket and a round cap and made Nelly put them on.

Mrs. Deane, who sat busy between a plate of spice cake and a tray piled with her famous whipped-cream tarts, laughed inordinately at his behavior.

"Ain't he worse than any kid you ever see? He's been running to that closet like a cat shut away from her kittens. I wonder Nell ain't caught on before this. I did think he'd make out now to keep 'em till Christmas morning; but he's never made out to keep anything yet."

That was true enough, and fortunately Jud's inability to keep anything seemed always to present a highly humorous aspect to his wife. Mrs. Deane put her heart into her cooking, and said that so long as a man was a good provider she had no cause to complain. Other people were not so charitable toward Jud's failing. I remember how many strictures were passed upon that little sealskin and how he was censured for his extravagance. But what a public-spirited thing, after all, it was for him to do! How, the winter through, we all enjoyed seeing Nell skating on the river or running about the town with the brown collar turned up about her bright cheeks and her hair blowing out from under the round cap! "No seal," Mrs. Dow said, "would have begrudged it to her. Why should we?" This was at the sewing-circle, when the new coat was under grave discussion.

At last Nelly and I got up-stairs and undressed, and the pad of Jud's slippered feet about the kitchen premises—where he was carrying up from the cellar things that might freeze—ceased. He called "Good night, daughter," from the foot of the stairs, and the house grew quiet. But one is not a prima donna the first time for nothing, and it seemed as if we could not go to bed. Our light must have burned long after every other in Riverbend was out. The muslin curtains of Nell's bed were drawn back; Mrs. Deane had turned down the white counterpane and taken off the shams and smoothed the pillows for us. But their fair plumpness offered no temptation to two such hot young heads. We could not let go of life even for a little while. We sat and talked in Nell's cozy room, where there was a tiny, white fur rug—the only one in Riverbend—before the bed; and there were white sash curtains, and the prettiest little desk and dressing-table I had ever seen. It was a warm, gay little room, flooded all day long with sunlight from east and south windows that had climbing-roses all about them in summer. About the dresser were photographs of adoring high-school boys; and one of Guy Franklin, much groomed and barbered, in a dress-coat and a boutonnière. I never liked to see that photograph there. The home boys looked properly modest and bashful on the dresser, but he seemed to be staring impudently all the time.

I knew nothing definite against Guy, but in Riverbend all "traveling-men" were considered worldly and wicked. He traveled for a Chicago dry-goods firm, and our fathers did n't like him because he put extravagant ideas into our mothers' heads. He had very smooth and flattering ways, and he introduced into our simple community a great variety of perfumes and scented soaps, and he always reminded me of the merchants in Cæsar, who brought into Gaul "those things which effeminate the mind," as we translated that delightfully easy passage.

Nell was sitting before the dressing-table in her nightgown, holding the new fur coat and rubbing her cheek against it, when I saw a sudden gleam of tears in her eyes. "You know, Peggy," she said in her quick, impetuous way, "this makes me feel bad. I 've got a secret from my daddy."

I can see her now, so pink and eager, her brown hair in two springy braids down her back, and her eyes shining with tears and with something even softer and more tremulous.

"I 'm engaged, Peggy," she whispered, "really and truly."

She leaned forward, unbuttoning her nightgown, and there on her breast, hung by a little gold chain about her neck, was a diamond ring—Guy Franklin's solitaire; every one in Riverbend knew it well.

"I 'm going to live in Chicago, and take singing lessons, and go to operas, and do all those nice things—oh, everything! I know you don't like him, Peggy, but you know you *are* a kid. You 'll see how it is yourself when you grow up. He 's so *different* from our boys, and he 's just terribly in love with me. And then, Peggy,"—flushing all down over her soft shoulders,—"I 'm awfully fond of him, too. Awfully."

"Are you, Nell, truly?" I whispered. She seemed so changed to me by the warm light in her eyes and that delicate suffusion of color. I felt as I did when I got up early on picnic mornings in summer, and saw the dawn come up in the breathless sky above the river meadows and make all the cornfields golden.

"Sure I do, Peggy; don't look so solemn. It 's nothing to look that way about, kid. It 's nice." She threw her arms about me suddenly and hugged me.

"I hate to think about your going so far away from us all, Nell."

"Oh, you 'll love to come and visit me. Just you wait."

She began breathlessly to go over things Guy Franklin had told her about Chicago, until I seemed to see it all looming up out there under the stars that kept watch over our little sleeping town. We had neither of us ever been to a city, but we knew what it would be like. We heard it throbbing like great engines, and calling to us, that far-away world. Even after we had opened the windows and scurried into bed, we seemed to feel a pulsation across all the miles of snow. The winter silence trembled with it, and the air was full of something new that seemed to break over us in soft waves. In that snug, warm little bed I had a sense of imminent change and danger. I was somehow afraid for Nelly when I heard her breathing so quickly beside me, and I put my arm about her protectingly as we drifted toward sleep.

In the following spring we were both graduated from the Riverbend high school, and I went away to college. My family moved to Denver, and during the next four years I heard very little of Nelly Deane. My life was crowded with new people and new experiences, and I am afraid I held her little in mind. I heard indirectly that Jud Deane had lost what little property he owned in a luckless venture in Cripple Creek, and that he had been able to keep his house in Riverbend only through the clemency of his creditors. Guy Franklin had his route changed and did not go to Riverbend any more. He married the daughter of a rich cattle-man out near Long Pine, and ran a dry-goods store of his own. Mrs. Dow wrote me a long letter about once a year, and in one of these she told me that Nelly was teaching in the sixth grade in the Riverbend school.

"Dear Nelly does not like teaching very well. The children try her, and she is so pretty it seems a pity for her to be tied down to uncongenial employment. Scott is still very attentive, and I have noticed him look up at the window of Nelly's room in a very determined way as he goes home to dinner. Scott continues prosperous; he has made money during these hard times and now owns both our hardware stores. He is close, but a very honorable fellow. Nelly seems to hold off, but I think Mrs. Spinny has hopes. Nothing would please her more. If Scott were more careful about his appearance, it would help. He of course gets black about his business, and Nelly, you know, is very dainty. People do say his mother does his courting for him, she is so eager. If only Scott does not turn out hard and penurious like his father! We must all have our schooling in this life, but I don't want Nelly's to be too severe. She is a dear girl, and keeps her color."

Mrs. Dow's own schooling had been none too easy. Her husband had long been crippled with rheumatism, and was bitter and faultfinding. Her daughters had married poorly, and one of her sons had fallen into evil ways. But her letters were always cheerful, and in one of them she gently remonstrated with me because I "seemed inclined to take a sad view of life."

In the winter vacation of my senior year I stopped on my way home to visit Mrs. Dow. The first thing she told me when I got into her old buckboard at the station was that "Scott had at last prevailed," and that Nelly was to marry him in the spring. As a preliminary step, Nelly was about to join the Baptist church. "Just think, you will be here for her baptizing! How that will please Nelly! She is to be immersed to-morrow night."

I met Scott Spinny in the post-office that morning, and he gave me a hard grip with one black hand. There was something grim and saturnine about his powerful body and bearded face and his strong, cold hands. I wondered what perverse fate had driven him for eight years to dog the footsteps of a girl whose charm was due to qualities naturally distasteful to him. It still seems strange to me that in easy-going Riverbend, where there were so many boys who could have lived contentedly enough with my little grasshopper, it was the pushing ant who must have her and all her careless ways.

By a kind of unformulated etiquette one did not call upon candidates for baptism on the day of the ceremony, so I had my first glimpse of Nelly that evening. The baptistry was a cemented pit directly under the pulpit rostrum, over which we had our stage when we sang "Queen Esther." I sat through the sermon somewhat nervously. After the minister, in his long, black gown, had gone down into the water and the choir had finished singing, the door from the dressing-room opened, and, led by one of the deacons, Nelly came down the steps into the pool. Oh, she looked so little and meek and chastened! Her white cashmere robe clung about her, and her brown hair was brushed straight back and hung in two soft braids from a little head bent humbly. As she stepped down into the water I shivered with the cold of it, and I remembered sharply how much I had loved her. She went down until the water was well above her waist, and stood white and small, with her hands crossed on her breast, while the minister said the words about being buried with Christ in baptism. Then, lying in his arm, she disappeared under the dark water. "It will be like that when she dies," I thought, and a quick pain caught my heart. The choir began to sing "Washed in the Blood of the Lamb" as she rose again, the door behind the baptistry opened, revealing those three dear guardians, Mrs. Dow, Mrs. Freeze, and Mrs. Spinny, and she went up into their arms.

I went to see Nell next day, up in the little room of many memories. Such a sad, sad visit! She seemed changed—a little embarrassed and quietly despairing. We talked of many of the old Riverbend girls and boys, but she did not mention Guy Franklin or Scott Spinny, except to say that her father had got work in Scott's hardware store. She begged me, putting her hands on my shoulders with something of her old impulsiveness, to come and stay a few days with her. But I was afraid—afraid of what she might tell me and of what I might say. When I sat in that room with all her trinkets, the foolish harvest of her girlhood, lying about, and the white curtains and the little white rug, I thought of Scott Spinny with positive terror and could feel his hard grip on my hand again. I made the best excuse I could about having to hurry on to Denver; but she gave me one quick look, and her eyes ceased to plead. I saw that she understood me perfectly. We had known each other so well. Just once, when I got up to go and had trouble with my veil, she laughed her old merry laugh and told me there were some things I would never learn, for all my schooling.

The next day, when Mrs. Dow drove me down to the station to catch the morning train for Denver, I saw Nelly hurrying to school with several books under her arm. She had been working up her lessons at home, I thought. She was never quick at her books, dear Nell.

It was ten years before I again visited Riverbend. I had been in Rome for a long time, and had fallen into bitter homesickness. One morning, sitting among the dahlias and asters that bloom so bravely upon those gigantic heaps of earth-red ruins that were once the palaces of the Cæsars, I broke the seal of one of Mrs. Dow's long yearly letters. It brought so much sad news that I resolved then and there to go home to Riverbend, the only place that had ever really been home to me. Mrs. Dow wrote me that her husband, after years of illness, had died in the cold spell last March. "So good and patient toward the last," she wrote, "and so afraid of giving extra trouble." There was another thing she saved until the last. She wrote on and on, dear woman, about new babies and village improvements, as if she could not bear to tell me; and then it came:

"You will be sad to hear that two months ago our dear Nelly left us. It was a terrible blow to us all. I cannot write about it yet, I fear. I wake up every morning feeling that I ought to go to her. She went three days after her little boy was born. The baby is a fine child and will live, I think, in spite of everything. He and her little girl, now eight years old, whom she named Margaret, after you, have gone to Mrs. Spinny's. She loves them more than if they were her own. It seems as if already they had made her quite young again. I wish you could see Nelly's children."

Ah, that was what I wanted, to see Nelly's children! The wish came aching from my heart along with the bitter homesick tears; along with a quick, torturing recollection that flashed upon me, as I looked about and tried to collect myself, of how we two had sat in our sunny seat in the corner of the old bare school-room one September afternoon and learned the names of the seven hills together. In that place, at that moment, after so many years, how it all came back to me— the warm sun on my back, the chattering girl beside me, the curly hair, the laughing yellow eyes, the stubby little finger on the page! I felt as if even then, when we sat in the sun with our heads together, it was all arranged, written out like a story, that at this moment I should be sitting among the crumbling bricks and drying grass, and she should be lying in the place I knew so well, on that green hill far away.

Mrs. Dow sat with her Christmas sewing in the familiar

sitting-room, where the carpet and the wall-paper and the table-cover had all faded into soft, dull colors, and even the chromo of Hagar and Ishmael had been toned to the sobriety of age. In the bay-window the tall wire flower-stand still bore its little terraces of potted plants, and the big fuchsia and the Martha Washington geranium had blossomed for Christmas-tide. Mrs. Dow herself did not look greatly changed to me. Her hair, thin ever since I could remember it, was now quite white, but her spare, wiry little person had all its old activity, and her eyes gleamed with the old friendliness behind her silver-bowed glasses. Her gray house-dress seemed just like those she used to wear when I ran in after school to take her angel-food cake down to the church supper.

The house sat on a hill, and from behind the geraniums I could see pretty much all of Riverbend, tucked down in the soft snow, and the air above was full of big, loose flakes, falling from a gray sky which betokened settled weather. Indoors the hard-coal burner made a tropical temperature, and glowed a warm orange from its isinglass sides. We sat and visited, the two of us, with a great sense of comfort and completeness. I had reached Riverbend only that morning, and Mrs. Dow, who had been haunted by thoughts of shipwreck and suffering upon wintry seas, kept urging me to draw nearer to the fire and suggesting incidental refreshment. We had chattered all through the winter morning and most of the afternoon, taking up one after another of the Riverbend girls and boys, and agreeing that we had reason to be well satisfied with most of them. Finally, after a long pause in which I had listened to the contented ticking of the clock and the crackle of the coal, I put the question I had until then held back:

"And now, Mrs. Dow, tell me about the one we loved best of all. Since I got your letter I've thought of her every day. Tell me all about Scott and Nelly."

The tears flashed behind her glasses, and she smoothed the little pink bag on her knee.

"Well, dear, I'm afraid Scott proved to be a hard man, like his father. But we must remember that Nelly always had Mrs. Spinny. I never saw anything like the love there was between those two. After Nelly lost her own father and mother, she looked to Mrs. Spinny for everything. When Scott was too unreasonable, his mother could 'most always prevail upon him. She never lifted a hand to fight her own battles with Scott's father, but she was never afraid to speak up for Nelly. And then Nelly took great comfort of her little girl. Such a lovely child!"

"Had she been very ill before the little baby came?"

"No, Margaret; I'm afraid 't was all because they had the wrong doctor. I feel confident that either Doctor Tom or Doctor Jones could have brought her through. But, you see, Scott had offended them both, and they'd stopped trading at his store, so he would have young Doctor Fox, a boy just out of college and a stranger. He got scared and didn't know what to do. Mrs. Spinny felt he wasn't doing right, so she sent for Mrs. Freeze and me. It seemed like Nelly had got discouraged. Scott would move into their big new house before the plastering was dry, and though 't was summer, she had taken a terrible cold that seemed to have drained her, and she took no interest in fixing the place up. Mrs. Spinny had been down with her back again and wasn't able to help, and things was just anyway. We won't talk about that, Margaret; I think 't would hurt Mrs. Spinny to have you know. She nearly died of mortification when she sent for us, and blamed her poor back. We did get Nelly fixed up nicely before she died. I prevailed upon Doctor Tom to come in at the last, and it 'most broke his heart. 'Why, Mis' Dow,' he said, 'if you'd only have come and told me how 't was, I'd have come and carried her right off in my arms.'"

"Oh, Mrs. Dow," I cried, "then it needn't have been?"

Mrs. Dow dropped her needle and clasped her hands quickly. "We mustn't look at it that way, dear," she said tremulously and a little sternly; "we mustn't let ourselves. We must just feel that our Lord wanted her *then*, and took her to Himself. When it was all over, she did look so like a child of God, young and trusting, like she did on her baptizing night, you remember?"

I felt that Mrs. Dow did not want to talk any more about Nelly then, and, indeed, I had little heart to listen; so I told her I would go for a walk, and suggested that I might stop at Mrs. Spinny's to see the children.

Mrs. Dow looked up thoughtfully at the clock. "I doubt if

you'll find little Margaret there now. It's half-past four, and she'll have been out of school an hour and more. She'll be most likely coasting on Lupton's Hill. She usually makes for it with her sled the minute she is out of the school-house door. You know, it's the old hill where you all used to slide. If you stop in at the church about six o'clock, you'll likely find Mrs. Spinny there with the baby. I promised to go down and help Mrs. Freeze finish up the tree, and Mrs. Spinny said she'd run in with the baby, if 't was n't too bitter. She won't leave him alone with the Swede girl. She's like a young woman with her first."

Lupton's Hill was at the other end of town, and when I got there the dusk was thickening, drawing blue shadows over the snowy fields. There were perhaps twenty children creeping up the hill or whizzing down the packed sled-track. When I had been watching them for some minutes, I heard a lusty shout, and a little red sled shot past me into the deep snow-drift beyond. The child was quite buried for a moment, then she struggled out and stood dusting the snow from her short coat and red woolen comforter. She wore a brown fur cap, which was too big for her and of an old-fashioned shape, such as girls wore long ago, but I would have known her without the cap. Mrs. Dow had said a beautiful child, and there would not be two like this in Riverbend. She was off before I had time to speak to her, going up the hill at a trot, her sturdy little legs plowing through the trampled snow. When she reached the top she never paused to take breath, but threw herself upon her sled and came down with a whoop that was quenched only by the deep drift at the end.

"Are you Margaret Spinny?" I asked as she struggled out in a cloud of snow.

"Yes, 'm." She approached me with frank curiosity, pulling her little sled behind her. "Are you the strange lady staying at Mrs. Dow's?" I nodded, and she began to look my clothes over with respectful interest.

"Your grandmother is to be at the church at six o'clock, is n't she?"

"Yes, 'm."

"Well, suppose we walk up there now. It's nearly six, and all the other children are going home." She hesitated, and looked up at the faintly gleaming track on the hill-slope. "Do you want another slide? Is that it?" I asked.

"Do you mind?" she asked shyly.

"No. I'll wait for you. Take your time; don't run."

Two little boys were still hanging about the slide, and they cheered her as she came down, her comforter streaming in the wind.

"Now," she announced, getting up out of the drift, "I'll show you where the church is."

"Shall I tie your comforter again?"

"No, 'm, thanks. I'm plenty warm." She put her mittened hand confidingly in mine and trudged along beside me.

Mrs. Dow must have heard us tramping up the snowy steps of the church, for she met us at the door. Every one had gone except the old ladies. A kerosene lamp flickered over the Sunday-school chart, with the lesson-picture of the Wise Men, and the little barrel-stove threw out a deep glow over the three white heads that bent above the baby. There the three friends sat, patting him, and smoothing his dress, and playing with his hands, which made theirs look so brown.

"You ain't seen nothing finer in all your travels," said Mrs. Spinny, and they all laughed.

They showed me his full chest and how strong his back was; had me feel the golden fuzz on his head, and made him look at me with his round, bright eyes. He laughed and reared himself in my arms as I took him up and held him close to me. He was so warm and tingling with life, and he had the flush of new beginnings, of the new morning and the new rose. He seemed to have come so lately from his mother's heart! It was as if I held her youth and all her young joy. As I put my cheek down against his, he spied a pink flower in my hat, and making a gleeful sound, he lunged at it with both fists.

"Don't let him spoil it," murmured Mrs. Spinny. "He loves color so—like Nelly."

Century, October 1911

The Bohemian Girl

THE TRANS-CONTINENTAL EXPRESS swung along the
windings of the Sand River Valley, and in the rear seat of
the observation car a young man sat greatly at his ease, not in
the least discomfited by the fierce sunlight which beat in upon
his brown face and neck and strong back. There was a look of
relaxation and of great passivity about his broad shoulders,
which seemed almost too heavy until he stood up and squared
them. He wore a pale flannel shirt and a blue silk necktie with
loose ends. His trousers were wide and belted at the waist,
and his short sack-coat hung open. His heavy shoes had seen
good service. His reddish-brown hair, like his clothes, had a
foreign cut. He had deep-set, dark blue eyes under heavy red-
dish eyebrows. His face was kept clean only by close shaving,
and even the sharpest razor left a glint of yellow in the
smooth brown of his skin. His teeth and the palms of his
hands were very white. His head, which looked hard and
stubborn, lay indolently in the green cushion of the wicker
chair, and as he looked out at the ripe summer country a
teasing, not unkindly smile played over his lips. Once, as he
basked thus comfortably, a quick light flashed in his eyes,
curiously dilating the pupils, and his mouth became a hard,
straight line, gradually relaxing into its former smile of rather
kindly mockery. He told himself, apparently, that there was
no point in getting excited; and he seemed a master hand at
taking his ease when he could. Neither the sharp whistle of
the locomotive nor the brakeman's call disturbed him. It was
not until after the train had stopped that he rose, put on a
Panama hat, took from the rack a small valise and a flute-case,
and stepped deliberately to the station platform. The baggage
was already unloaded, and the stranger presented a check for
a battered sole-leather steamer-trunk.

"Can you keep it here for a day or two?" he asked the
agent. "I may send for it, and I may not."

"Depends on whether you like the country, I suppose?" de-
manded the agent in a challenging tone.

"Just so."

The agent shrugged his shoulders, looked scornfully at the small trunk, which was marked "N. E.," and handed out a claim check without further comment. The stranger watched him as he caught one end of the trunk and dragged it into the express room. The agent's manner seemed to remind him of something amusing. "Doesn't seem to be a very big place," he remarked, looking about.

"It's big enough for us," snapped the agent, as he banged the trunk into a corner.

That remark, apparently, was what Nils Ericson had wanted. He chuckled quietly as he took a leather strap from his pocket and swung his valise around his shoulder. Then he settled his Panama securely on his head, turned up his trousers, tucked the flute-case under his arm, and started off across the fields. He gave the town, as he would have said, a wide berth, and cut through a great fenced pasture, emerging, when he rolled under the barbed wire at the farther corner, upon a white dusty road which ran straight up from the river valley to the high prairies, where the ripe wheat stood yellow and the tin roofs and weather-cocks were twinkling in the fierce sunlight. By the time Nils had done three miles, the sun was sinking and the farm-wagons on their way home from town came rattling by, covering him with dust and making him sneeze. When one of the farmers pulled up and offered to give him a lift, he clambered in willingly. The driver was a thin, grizzled old man with a long lean neck and a foolish sort of beard, like a goat's. "How fur ye goin'?" he asked, as he clucked to his horses and started off.

"Do you go by the Ericson place?"

"Which Ericson?" The old man drew in his reins as if he expected to stop again.

"Preacher Ericson's."

"Oh, the Old Lady Ericson's!" He turned and looked at Nils. "La, me! If you're goin' out there you might 'a' rid out in the automobile. That's a pity, now. The Old Lady Ericson was in town with her auto. You might 'a' heard it snortin' anywhere about the post-office er the butcher-shop."

"Has she a motor?" asked the stranger absently.

" 'Deed an' she has! She runs into town every night about this time for her mail and meat for supper. Some folks say she's afraid her auto won't get exercise enough, but I say that's jealousy."

"Aren't there any other motors about here?"

"Oh, yes! we have fourteen in all. But nobody else gets around like the Old Lady Ericson. She's out, rain er shine, over the whole county, chargin' into town and out amongst her farms, an' up to her sons' places. Sure you ain't goin' to the wrong place?" He craned his neck and looked at Nils' flute-case with eager curiosity. "The old woman ain't got any piany that I knows on. Olaf, he has a grand. His wife's musical; took lessons in Chicago."

"I'm going up there to-morrow," said Nils imperturbably. He saw that the driver took him for a piano-tuner.

"Oh, I see!" The old man screwed up his eyes mysteriously. He was a little dashed by the stranger's non-communicativeness, but he soon broke out again.

"I'm one o' Mis' Ericson's tenants. Look after one of her places. I did own the place myself oncet, but I lost it a while back, in the bad years just after the World's Fair. Just as well, too, I say. Lets you out o' payin' taxes. The Ericsons do own most of the county now. I remember the old preacher's fav'rite text used to be, 'To them that hath shall be given.' They've spread something wonderful—run over this here country like bindweed. But I ain't one that begretches it to 'em. Folks is entitled to what they kin git; and they're hustlers. Olaf, he's in the Legislature now, and a likely man fur Congress. Listen, if that ain't the old woman comin' now. Want I should stop her?"

Nils shook his head. He heard the deep chug-chug of a motor vibrating steadily in the clear twilight behind them. The pale lights of the car swam over the hill, and the old man slapped his reins and turned clear out of the road, ducking his head at the first of three angry snorts from behind. The motor was running at a hot, even speed, and passed without turning an inch from its course. The driver was a stalwart woman who sat at ease in the front seat and drove her car bareheaded. She left a cloud of dust and a trail of gasoline behind her. Her tenant threw back his head and sneezed.

"Whew! I sometimes say I'd as lief be *before* Mrs. Ericson as behind her. She does beat all! Nearly seventy, and never lets another soul touch that car. Puts it into commission herself every morning, and keeps it tuned up by the hitch-bar all day. I never stop work for a drink o' water that I don't hear her a-churnin' up the road. I reckon her darter-in-laws never sets down easy nowadays. Never know when she'll pop in. Mis' Otto, she says to me: 'We're so afraid that thing'll blow up and do Ma some injury yet, she's so turrible venturesome.' Says I: 'I wouldn't stew, Mis' Otto; the old lady'll drive that car to the funeral of every darter-in-law she's got.' That was after the old woman had jumped a turrible bad culvert."

The stranger heard vaguely what the old man was saying. Just now he was experiencing something very much like homesickness, and he was wondering what had brought it about. The mention of a name or two, perhaps; the rattle of a wagon along a dusty road; the rank, resinous smell of sun-flowers and ironweed, which the night damp brought up from the draws and low places; perhaps, more than all, the dancing lights of the motor that had plunged by. He squared his shoulders with a comfortable sense of strength.

The wagon, as it jolted westward, climbed a pretty steady upgrade. The country, receding from the rough river valley, swelled more and more gently, as if it had been smoothed out by the wind. On one of the last of the rugged ridges, at the end of a branch road, stood a grim square house with a tin roof and double porches. Behind the house stretched a row of broken, wind-racked poplars, and down the hill-slope to the left straggled the sheds and stables. The old man stopped his horses where the Ericsons' road branched across a dry sand creek that wound about the foot of the hill.

"That's the old lady's place. Want I should drive in?"

"No, thank you. I'll roll out here. Much obliged to you. Good night."

His passenger stepped down over the front wheel, and the old man drove on reluctantly, looking back as if he would like to see how the stranger would be received.

As Nils was crossing the dry creek he heard the restive tramp of a horse coming toward him down the hill. Instantly he flashed out of the road and stood behind a thicket of wild plum bushes that grew in the sandy bed. Peering through the dusk, he saw a light horse, under tight rein, descending the hill at a sharp walk. The rider was a slender woman—barely visible against the dark hillside—wearing an old-fashioned derby hat and a long riding-skirt. She sat lightly in the saddle, with her chin high, and seemed to be looking into the distance. As she passed the plum thicket her horse snuffed the air and shied. She struck him, pulling him in sharply, with an angry exclamation, *"Blázne!"* in Bohemian. Once in the main road, she let him out into a lope, and they soon emerged upon the crest of high land, where they moved along the skyline, silhouetted against the band of faint color that lingered in the west. This horse and rider, with their free, rhythmical gallop, were the only moving things to be seen on the face of the flat country. They seemed, in the last sad light of evening, not to be there accidentally, but as an inevitable detail of the landscape.

Nils watched them until they had shrunk to a mere moving speck against the sky, then he crossed the sand creek and climbed the hill. When he reached the gate the front of the house was dark, but a light was shining from the side windows. The pigs were squealing in the hog corral, and Nils could see a tall boy, who carried two big wooden buckets, moving about among them. Half way between the barn and the house, the windmill wheezed lazily. Following the path that ran around to the back porch, Nils stopped to look through the screen door into the lamp-lit kitchen. The kitchen was the largest room in the house; Nils remembered that his older brothers used to give dances there when he was a boy. Beside the stove stood a little girl with two light yellow braids and a broad, flushed face, peering anxiously into a frying-pan. In the dining-room beyond, a large, broad-shouldered woman was moving about the table. She walked with an active, springy step. Her face was heavy and florid, almost without wrinkles, and her hair was black at seventy. Nils felt proud of her as he watched her deliberate activity; never a momentary hesitation, or a movement that did not tell. He waited until she came out into the kitchen and, brushing the child aside, took her place at the stove. Then he tapped on the screen door and entered.

"It's nobody but Nils, Mother. I expect you weren't looking for me."

Mrs. Ericson turned away from the stove and stood staring at him. "Bring the lamp, Hilda, and let me look."

Nils laughed and unslung his valise. "What's the matter, Mother? Don't you know me?"

Mrs. Ericson put down the lamp. "You must be Nils. You don't look very different, anyway."

"Nor you, Mother. You hold your own. Don't you wear glasses yet?"

"Only to read by. Where's your trunk, Nils?"

"Oh, I left that in town. I thought it might not be convenient for you to have company so near threshing-time."

"Don't be foolish, Nils." Mrs. Ericson turned back to the stove. "I don't thresh now. I hitched the wheat land onto the next farm and have a tenant. Hilda, take some hot water up to the company room, and go call little Eric."

The tow-haired child, who had been standing in mute amazement, took up the tea-kettle and withdrew, giving Nils a long, admiring look from the door of the kitchen stairs.

"Who's the youngster?" Nils asked, dropping down on the bench behind the kitchen stove.

"One of your Cousin Henrik's."

"How long has Cousin Henrik been dead?"

"Six years. There are two boys. One stays with Peter and one with Anders. Olaf is their guardeen."

There was a clatter of pails on the porch, and a tall, lanky boy peered wonderingly in through the screen door. He had a fair, gentle face and big gray eyes, and wisps of soft yellow hair hung down under his cap. Nils sprang up and pulled him into the kitchen, hugging him and slapping him on the shoulders. "Well, if it isn't my kid! Look at the size of him! Don't you know me, Eric?"

The boy reddened under his sunburn and freckles, and hung his head. "I guess it's Nils," he said shyly.

"You're a good guesser," laughed Nils, giving the lad's hand a swing. To himself he was thinking: "That's why the little girl looked so friendly. He's taught her to like me. He was only six when I went away, and he's remembered for twelve years."

Eric stood fumbling with his cap and smiling. "You look just like I thought you would," he ventured.

"Go wash your hands, Eric," called Mrs. Ericson. "I've got cob corn for supper, Nils. You used to like it. I guess you don't get much of that in the old country. Here's Hilda; she'll take you up to your room. You'll want to get the dust off you before you eat."

Mrs. Ericson went into the dining-room to lay another plate, and the little girl came up and nodded to Nils as if to let him know that his room was ready. He put out his hand and she took it, with a startled glance up at his face. Little Eric dropped his towel, threw an arm about Nils and one about Hilda, gave them a clumsy squeeze, and then stumbled out to the porch.

During supper Nils heard exactly how much land each of his eight grown brothers farmed, how their crops were coming on, and how much live stock they were feeding. His mother watched him narrowly as she talked. "You've got better looking, Nils," she remarked abruptly, whereupon he grinned and the children giggled. Eric, although he was eighteen and as tall as Nils, was always accounted a child, being the last of so many sons. His face seemed childlike, too, Nils thought, and he had the open, wandering eyes of a little boy. All the others had been men at his age.

After supper Nils went out to the front porch and sat down on the step to smoke a pipe. Mrs. Ericson drew a rocking-chair up near him and began to knit busily. It was one of the few old-world customs she had kept up, for she could not bear to sit with idle hands.

"Where's little Eric, Mother?"

"He's helping Hilda with the dishes. He does it of his own will; I don't like a boy to be too handy about the house."

"He seems like a nice kid."

"He's very obedient."

Nils smiled a little in the dark. It was just as well to shift the line of conversation. "What are you knitting there, Mother?"

"Baby stockings. The boys keep me busy." Mrs. Ericson chuckled and clicked her needles.

"How many grandchildren have you?"

"Only thirty-one now. Olaf lost his three. They were sickly, like their mother."

"I supposed he had a second crop by this time!"

"His second wife has no children. She's too proud. She tears about on horseback all the time. But she'll get caught up with, yet. She sets herself very high, though nobody knows what for. They were low enough Bohemians she came of. I never thought much of Bohemians; always drinking."

Nils puffed away at his pipe in silence, and Mrs. Ericson knitted on. In a few moments she added grimly: "She was down here to-night, just before you came. She'd like to quarrel with me and come between me and Olaf, but I don't give her the chance. I suppose you'll be bringing a wife home some day."

"I don't know. I've never thought much about it."

"Well, perhaps it's best as it is," suggested Mrs. Ericson hopefully. "You'd never be contented tied down to the land. There was roving blood in your father's family, and it's come out in you. I expect your own way of life suits you best." Mrs. Ericson had dropped into a blandly agreeable tone which Nils well remembered. It seemed to amuse him a good deal and his white teeth flashed behind his pipe. His mother's strategies had always diverted him, even when he was a boy—they were so flimsy and patent, so illy proportioned to her vigor and force. "They've been waiting to see which way I'd jump," he reflected. He felt that Mrs. Ericson was pondering his case deeply as she sat clicking her needles.

"I don't suppose you've ever got used to steady work," she went on presently. "Men ain't apt to if they roam around too long. It's a pity you didn't come back the year after the World's Fair. Your father picked up a good bit of land cheap then, in the hard times, and I expect maybe he'd have give you a farm. It's too bad you put off comin' back so long, for I always thought he meant to do something by you."

Nils laughed and shook the ashes out of his pipe. "I'd have missed a lot if I had come back then. But I'm sorry I didn't get back to see father."

"Well, I suppose we have to miss things at one end or the other. Perhaps you are as well satisfied with your own doings, now, as you'd have been with a farm," said Mrs. Ericson reassuringly.

"Land's a good thing to have," Nils commented, as he lit another match and sheltered it with his hand.

His mother looked sharply at his face until the match burned out. "Only when you stay on it!" she hastened to say.

Eric came round the house by the path just then, and Nils rose, with a yawn. "Mother, if you don't mind, Eric and I will take a little tramp before bed-time. It will make me sleep."

"Very well; only don't stay long. I'll sit up and wait for you. I like to lock up myself."

Nils put his hand on Eric's shoulder, and the two tramped down the hill and across the sand creek into the dusty high-road beyond. Neither spoke. They swung along at an even gait, Nils puffing at his pipe. There was no moon, and the white road and the wide fields lay faint in the starlight. Over everything was darkness and thick silence, and the smell of dust and sunflowers. The brothers followed the road for a mile or more without finding a place to sit down. Finally Nils perched on a stile over the wire fence, and Eric sat on the lower step.

"I began to think you never would come back, Nils," said the boy softly.

"Didn't I promise you I would?"

"Yes; but people don't bother about promises they make to babies. Did you really know you were going away for good when you went to Chicago with the cattle that time?"

"I thought it very likely, if I could make my way."

"I don't see how you did it, Nils. Not many fellows could." Eric rubbed his shoulder against his brother's knee.

"The hard thing was leaving home—you and father. It was easy enough, once I got beyond Chicago. Of course I got awful homesick; used to cry myself to sleep. But I'd burned my bridges."

"You had always wanted to go, hadn't you?"

"Always. Do you still sleep in our little room? Is that cottonwood still by the window?"

Eric nodded eagerly and smiled up at his brother in the gray darkness.

"You remember how we always said the leaves were whispering when they rustled at night? Well, they always whispered to me about the sea. Sometimes they said names out of the geography books. In a high wind they had a desperate sound, like something trying to tear loose."

"How funny, Nils," said Eric dreamily, resting his chin on his hand. "That tree still talks like that, and 'most always it talks to me about you."

They sat a while longer, watching the stars. At last Eric whispered anxiously: "Hadn't we better go back now? Mother will get tired waiting for us." They rose and took a short cut home, through the pasture.

II

The next morning Nils woke with the first flood of light that came with dawn. The white-plastered walls of his room reflected the glare that shone through the thin window-shades, and he found it impossible to sleep. He dressed hurriedly and slipped down the hall and up the back stairs to the half-story room which he used to share with his little brother. Eric, in a skimpy night-shirt, was sitting on the edge of the bed, rubbing his eyes, his pale yellow hair standing up in tufts all over his head. When he saw Nils, he murmured something confusedly and hustled his long legs into his trousers. "I didn't expect you'd be up so early, Nils," he said, as his head emerged from his blue shirt.

"Oh, you thought I was a dude, did you?" Nils gave him a playful tap which bent the tall boy up like a clasp-knife. "See here; I must teach you to box." Nils thrust his hands into his pockets and walked about. "You haven't changed things much up here. Got most of my old traps, haven't you?"

He took down a bent, withered piece of sapling that hung over the dresser. "If this isn't the stick Lou Sandberg killed himself with!"

The boy looked up from his shoe-lacing.

"Yes; you never used to let me play with that. Just how did he do it, Nils? You were with father when he found Lou, weren't you?"

"Yes. Father was going off to preach somewhere, and, as we drove along, Lou's place looked sort of forlorn, and we thought we'd stop and cheer him up. When we found him father said he'd been dead a couple days. He'd tied a piece of binding twine round his neck, made a noose in each end, fixed the nooses over the ends of a bent stick, and let the stick spring straight; strangled himself."

"What made him kill himself such a silly way?"

The simplicity of the boy's question set Nils laughing. He clapped little Eric on the shoulder. "What made him such a silly as to kill himself at all, I should say!"

"Oh, well! But his hogs had the cholera, and all up and died on him, didn't they?"

"Sure they did; but he didn't have cholera; and there were plenty of hogs left in the world, weren't there?"

"Well, but, if they weren't his, how could they do him any good?" Eric asked, in astonishment.

"Oh, scat! He could have had lots of fun with other people's hogs. He was a chump, Lou Sandberg. To kill yourself for a pig—think of that, now!" Nils laughed all the way downstairs, and quite embarrassed little Eric, who fell to scrubbing his face and hands at the tin basin. While he was parting his wet hair at the kitchen looking-glass, a heavy tread sounded on the stairs. The boy dropped his comb. "Gracious, there's Mother. We must have talked too long." He hurried out to the shed, slipped on his overalls, and disappeared with the milking-pails.

Mrs. Ericson came in, wearing a clean white apron, her black hair shining from the application of a wet brush.

"Good morning, Mother. Can't I make the fire for you?"

"No, thank you, Nils. It's no trouble to make a cob fire, and I like to manage the kitchen stove myself." Mrs. Ericson paused with a shovel full of ashes in her hand. "I expect you will be wanting to see your brothers as soon as possible. I'll take you up to Anders' place this morning. He's threshing, and most of our boys are over there."

"Will Olaf be there?"

Mrs. Ericson went on taking out the ashes, and spoke between shovels. "No; Olaf's wheat is all in, put away in his new barn. He got six thousand bushel this year. He's going to town to-day to get men to finish roofing his barn."

"So Olaf is building a new barn?" Nils asked absently.

"Biggest one in the county, and almost done. You'll likely be here for the barn-raising. He's going to have a supper and a dance as soon as everybody's done threshing. Says it keeps the voters in a good humor. I tell him that's all nonsense; but Olaf has a long head for politics."

"Does Olaf farm all Cousin Henrik's land?"

Mrs. Ericson frowned as she blew into the faint smoke curling up about the cobs. "Yes; he holds it in trust for the children, Hilda and her brothers. He keeps strict account of everything he raises on it, and puts the proceeds out at compound interest for them."

Nils smiled as he watched the little flames shoot up. The door of the back stairs opened, and Hilda emerged, her arms behind her, buttoning up her long gingham apron as she came. He nodded to her gaily, and she twinkled at him out of her little blue eyes, set far apart over her wide cheek-bones.

"There, Hilda, you grind the coffee—and just put in an extra handful; I expect your Cousin Nils likes his strong," said Mrs. Ericson, as she went out to the shed.

Nils turned to look at the little girl, who gripped the coffee-grinder between her knees and ground so hard that her two braids bobbed and her face flushed under its broad spattering of freckles. He noticed on her middle finger something that had not been there last night, and that had evidently been put on for company: a tiny gold ring with a clumsily set garnet stone. As her hand went round and round he touched the ring with the tip of his finger, smiling.

Hilda glanced toward the shed door through which Mrs. Ericson had disappeared. "My Cousin Clara gave me that," she whispered bashfully. "She's Cousin Olaf's wife."

III

Mrs. Olaf Ericson—Clara Vavrika, as many people still called her—was moving restlessly about her big bare house that morning. Her husband had left for the county town before his wife was out of bed—her lateness in rising was one of the many things the Ericson family had against her. Clara seldom came downstairs before eight o'clock, and this morning she was even later, for she had dressed with unusual care. She put on, however, only a tight-fitting black dress, which people thereabouts thought very plain. She was a tall, dark woman of thirty, with a rather sallow complexion and a touch of dull salmon red in her cheeks, where the blood seemed to burn under her brown skin. Her hair, parted evenly above her low forehead, was so black that there were distinctly blue lights in it. Her black eyebrows were delicate half-moons and her lashes were long and heavy. Her eyes slanted a little, as if she had a strain of Tartar or gypsy blood, and were sometimes full of fiery determination and sometimes dull and opaque. Her expression was never altogether amiable; was often, indeed, distinctly sullen, or, when she was animated, sarcastic. She was most attractive in profile, for then one saw to advantage her small, well-shaped head and delicate ears, and felt at once that here was a very positive, if not an altogether pleasing, personality.

The entire management of Mrs. Olaf's household devolved upon her aunt, Johanna Vavrika, a superstitious, doting woman of fifty. When Clara was a little girl her mother died, and Johanna's life had been spent in ungrudging service to her niece. Clara, like many self-willed and discontented persons, was really very apt, without knowing it, to do as other people told her, and to let her destiny be decided for her by intelligences much below her own. It was her Aunt Johanna who had humored and spoiled her in her girlhood, who had got her off to Chicago to study piano, and who had finally persuaded her to marry Olaf Ericson as the best match she would be likely to make in that part of the country. Johanna Vavrika had been deeply scarred by smallpox in the old country. She was short and fat, homely and jolly and sentimental. She was so broad, and took such short steps when she walked, that her brother, Joe Vavrika, always called her his duck. She adored her niece because of her talent, because of her good looks and masterful ways, but most of all because of her selfishness.

Clara's marriage with Olaf Ericson was Johanna's particular triumph. She was inordinately proud of Olaf's position, and she found a sufficiently exciting career in managing Clara's house, in keeping it above the criticism of the Ericsons, in pampering Olaf to keep him from finding fault with his wife, and in concealing from every one Clara's domestic infelicities. While Clara slept of a morning, Johanna Vavrika was bustling about, seeing that Olaf and the men had their breakfast, and that the cleaning or the butter-making or the washing was properly begun by the two girls in the kitchen. Then, at about eight o'clock, she would take Clara's coffee up to her, and chat with her while she drank it, telling her what was going on in the house. Old Mrs. Ericson frequently said that her daughter-in-law would not know what day of the week it was if Johanna did not tell her every morning. Mrs. Ericson despised and pitied Johanna, but did not wholly dislike her. The one thing she hated in her daughter-in-law above everything else was the way in which Clara could come it over people. It enraged her that the affairs of her son's big, barnlike house went on as well as they did, and she used to feel that in this world we have to wait over-long to see the guilty punished. "Suppose Johanna Vavrika died or got sick?" the old lady used to say to Olaf. "Your wife wouldn't know where to look for her own dish-cloth." Olaf only shrugged his shoulders. The fact remained that Johanna did not die, and, although Mrs. Ericson often told her she was looking poorly, she was never ill. She seldom left the house, and she slept in a little room off the kitchen. No Ericson, by night or day, could come prying about there to find fault without her knowing it. Her one weakness was that she was an incurable talker, and she sometimes made trouble without meaning to.

This morning Clara was tying a wine-colored ribbon about her throat when Johanna appeared with her coffee. After putting the tray on a sewing-table, she began to make Clara's bed, chattering the while in Bohemian.

"Well, Olaf got off early, and the girls are baking. I'm going down presently to make some poppy-seed bread for Olaf. He asked for prune preserves at breakfast, and I told him I was out of them, and to bring some prunes and honey and cloves from town."

Clara poured her coffee. "Ugh! I don't see how men can eat so much sweet stuff. In the morning, too!"

Her aunt chuckled knowingly. "Bait a bear with honey, as we say in the old country."

"Was he cross?" her niece asked indifferently.

"Olaf? Oh, no! He was in fine spirits. He's never cross if you know how to take him. I never knew a man to make so little fuss about bills. I gave him a list of things to get a yard long, and he didn't say a word; just folded it up and put it in his pocket."

"I can well believe he didn't say a word," Clara remarked with a shrug. "Some day he'll forget how to talk."

"Oh, but they say he's a grand speaker in the Legislature. He knows when to keep quiet. That's why he's got such influence in politics. The people have confidence in him." Johanna beat up a pillow and held it under her fat chin while she slipped on the case. Her niece laughed.

"Maybe we could make people believe we were wise, Aunty, if we held our tongues. Why did you tell Mrs. Ericson that Norman threw me again last Saturday and turned my foot? She's been talking to Olaf."

Johanna fell into great confusion. "Oh, but, my precious, the old lady asked for you, and she's always so angry if I can't give an excuse. Anyhow, she needn't talk; she's always tearing up something with that motor of hers."

When her aunt clattered down to the kitchen, Clara went to dust the parlor. Since there was not much there to dust, this did not take very long. Olaf had built the house new for her before their marriage, but her interest in furnishing it had been short-lived. It went, indeed, little beyond a bath-tub and her piano. They had disagreed about almost every other article of furniture, and Clara had said she would rather have her house empty than full of things she didn't want. The house was set in a hillside, and the west windows of the parlor looked out above the kitchen yard thirty feet below. The east windows opened directly into the front yard. At one of the latter, Clara, while she was dusting, heard a low whistle. She did not turn at once, but listened intently as she drew her cloth slowly along the round of a chair. Yes, there it was:

"I dreamt that I dwelt in ma-a-arble halls,"

She turned and saw Nils Ericson laughing in the sunlight, his hat in his hand, just outside the window. As she crossed the room he leaned against the wire screen. "Aren't you at all surprised to see me, Clara Vavrika?"

"No; I was expecting to see you. Mother Ericson telephoned Olaf last night that you were here."

Nils squinted and gave a long whistle. "Telephoned? That

must have been while Eric and I were out walking. Isn't she enterprising? Lift this screen, won't you?"

Clara lifted the screen, and Nils swung his leg across the window-sill. As he stepped into the room she said: "You didn't think you were going to get ahead of your mother, did you?"

He threw his hat on the piano. "Oh, I do sometimes. You see, I'm ahead of her now. I'm supposed to be in Anders' wheat-field. But, as we were leaving, Mother ran her car into a soft place beside the road and sank up to the hubs. While they were going for horses to pull her out, I cut away behind the stacks and escaped." Nils chuckled. Clara's dull eyes lit up as she looked at him admiringly.

"You've got them guessing already. I don't know what your mother said to Olaf over the telephone, but he came back looking as if he'd seen a ghost, and he didn't go to bed until a dreadful hour—ten o'clock, I should think. He sat out on the porch in the dark like a graven image. It had been one of his talkative days, too." They both laughed, easily and lightly, like people who have laughed a great deal together; but they remained standing.

"Anders and Otto and Peter looked as if they had seen ghosts, too, over in the threshing-field. What's the matter with them all?"

Clara gave him a quick, searching look. "Well, for one thing, they've always been afraid you have the other will."

Nils looked interested. "The other will?"

"Yes. A later one. They knew your father made another, but they never knew what he did with it. They almost tore the old house to pieces looking for it. They always suspected that he carried on a clandestine correspondence with you, for the one thing he would do was to get his own mail himself. So they thought he might have sent the new will to you for safekeeping. The old one, leaving everything to your mother, was made long before you went away, and it's understood among them that it cuts you out—that she will leave all the property to the others. Your father made the second will to prevent that. I've been hoping you had it. It would be such fun to spring it on them." Clara laughed mirthfully, a thing she did not often do now.

Nils shook his head reprovingly. "Come, now, you're malicious."

"No, I'm not. But I'd like something to happen to stir them all up, just for once. There never was such a family for having nothing ever happen to them but dinner and threshing. I'd almost be willing to die, just to have a funeral. *You* wouldn't stand it for three weeks."

Nils bent over the piano and began pecking at the keys with the finger of one hand. "I wouldn't? My dear young lady, how do you know what I can stand? *You* wouldn't wait to find out."

Clara flushed darkly and frowned. "I didn't believe you would ever come back—" she said defiantly.

"Eric believed I would, and he was only a baby when I went away. However, all's well that ends well, and I haven't come back to be a skeleton at the feast. We mustn't quarrel. Mother will be here with a search-warrant pretty soon." He swung round and faced her, thrusting his hands into his coat pockets. "Come, you ought to be glad to see me, if you want something to happen. I'm something, even without a will. We can have a little fun, can't we? I think we can!"

She echoed him, "I think we can!" They both laughed and their eyes sparkled. Clara Vavrika looked ten years younger than when she had put the velvet ribbon about her throat that morning.

"You know, I'm so tickled to see mother," Nils went on. "I didn't know I was so proud of her. A regular pile-driver. How about little pigtails, down at the house? Is Olaf doing the square thing by those children?"

Clara frowned pensively. "Olaf has to do something that looks like the square thing, now that he's a public man!" She glanced drolly at Nils. "But he makes a good commission out of it. On Sundays they all get together here and figure. He lets Peter and Anders put in big bills for the keep of the two boys, and he pays them out of the estate. They are always having what they call accountings. Olaf gets something out of it, too. I don't know just how they do it, but it's entirely a family matter, as they say. And when the Ericsons say that—" Clara lifted her eyebrows.

Just then the angry *honk-honk* of an approaching motor

sounded from down the road. Their eyes met and they began to laugh. They laughed as children do when they can not contain themselves, and can not explain the cause of their mirth to grown people, but share it perfectly together. When Clara Vavrika sat down at the piano after he was gone, she felt that she had laughed away a dozen years. She practised as if the house were burning over her head.

When Nils greeted his mother and climbed into the front seat of the motor beside her, Mrs. Ericson looked grim, but she made no comment upon his truancy until she had turned her car and was retracing her revolutions along the road that ran by Olaf's big pasture. Then she remarked dryly:

"If I were you I wouldn't see too much of Olaf's wife while you are here. She's the kind of woman who can't see much of men without getting herself talked about. She was a good deal talked about before he married her."

"Hasn't Olaf tamed her?" Nils asked indifferently.

Mrs. Ericson shrugged her massive shoulders. "Olaf don't seem to have much luck, when it comes to wives. The first one was meek enough, but she was always ailing. And this one has her own way. He says if he quarreled with her she'd go back to her father, and then he'd lose the Bohemian vote. There are a great many Bohunks in this district. But when you find a man under his wife's thumb you can always be sure there's a soft spot in him somewhere."

Nils thought of his own father, and smiled. "She brought him a good deal of money, didn't she, besides the Bohemian vote?"

Mrs. Ericson sniffed. "Well, she has a fair half section in her own name, but I can't see as that does Olaf much good. She will have a good deal of property some day, if old Vavrika don't marry again. But I don't consider a saloonkeeper's money as good as other people's money."

Nils laughed outright. "Come, Mother, don't let your prejudices carry you that far. Money's money. Old Vavrika's a mighty decent sort of saloonkeeper. Nothing rowdy about him."

Mrs. Ericson spoke up angrily: "Oh, I know you always stood up for them! But hanging around there when you were a boy never did you any good, Nils, nor any of the other boys who went there. There weren't so many after her when she married Olaf, let me tell you. She knew enough to grab her chance."

Nils settled back in his seat. "Of course I liked to go there, Mother, and you were always cross about it. You never took the trouble to find out that it was the one jolly house in this country for a boy to go to. All the rest of you were working yourselves to death, and the houses were mostly a mess, full of babies and washing and flies. Oh, it was all right—I understand that; but you are young only once, and I happened to be young then. Now, Vavrika's was always jolly. He played the violin, and I used to take my flute, and Clara played the piano, and Johanna used to sing Bohemian songs. She always had a big supper for us—herrings and pickles and poppy-seed bread, and lots of cake and preserves. Old Joe had been in the army in the old country, and he could tell lots of good stories. I can see him cutting bread, at the head of the table, now. I don't know what I'd have done when I was a kid if it hadn't been for the Vavrikas, really."

"And all the time he was taking money that other people had worked hard in the fields for," Mrs. Ericson observed.

"So do the circuses, Mother, and they're a good thing. People ought to get fun for some of their money. Even father liked old Joe."

"Your father," Mrs. Ericson said grimly, "liked everybody."

As they crossed the sand creek and turned into her own place, Mrs. Ericson observed, "There's Olaf's buggy. He's stopped on his way from town." Nils shook himself and prepared to greet his brother, who was waiting on the porch.

Olaf was a big, heavy Norwegian, slow of speech and movement. His head was large and square, like a block of wood. When Nils, at a distance, tried to remember what his brother looked like, he could recall only his heavy head, high forehead, large nostrils, and pale-blue eyes, set far apart. Olaf's features were rudimentary: the thing one noticed was the face itself, wide and flat and pale, devoid of any expression, betraying his fifty years as little as it betrayed anything else, and powerful by reason of its very stolidity. When Olaf shook hands with Nils he looked at him from under his light eyebrows, but Nils felt that no one could ever say what that pale look might mean. The one thing he had always felt in Olaf was a heavy stubbornness, like the unyielding stickiness of wet loam against the plow. He had always found Olaf the most difficult of his brothers.

"How do you do, Nils? Expect to stay with us long?"

"Oh, I may stay forever," Nils answered gaily. "I like this country better than I used to."

"There's been some work put into it since you left," Olaf remarked.

"Exactly. I think it's about ready to live in now—and I'm about ready to settle down." Nils saw his brother lower his big head. ("Exactly like a bull," he thought.) "Mother's been persuading me to slow down now, and go in for farming," he went on lightly.

Olaf made a deep sound in his throat. "Farming ain't learned in a day," he brought out, still looking at the ground.

"Oh, I know! But I pick things up quickly." Nils had not meant to antagonize his brother, and he did not know now why he was doing it. "Of course," he went on, "I shouldn't expect to make a big success, as you fellows have done. But then, I'm not ambitious. I won't want much. A little land, and some cattle, maybe."

Olaf still stared at the ground, his head down. He wanted to ask Nils what he had been doing all these years, that he didn't have a business somewhere he couldn't afford to leave; why he hadn't more pride than to come back with only a little sole-leather trunk to show for himself, and to present himself as the only failure in the family. He did not ask one of these questions, but he made them all felt distinctly.

"Humph!" Nils thought. "No wonder the man never talks, when he can butt his ideas into you like that without ever saying a word. I suppose he uses that kind of smokeless powder on his wife all the time. But I guess she has her innings." He chuckled, and Olaf looked up. "Never mind me, Olaf. I laugh without knowing why, like little Eric. He's another cheerful dog."

"Eric," said Olaf slowly, "is a spoiled kid. He's just let his mother's best cow go dry because he don't milk her right. I was hoping you'd take him away somewhere and put him into business. If he don't do any good among strangers, he never will." This was a long speech for Olaf, and as he finished it he climbed into his buggy.

Nils shrugged his shoulders. "Same old tricks," he thought. "Hits from behind you every time. What a whale of a man!" He turned and went round to the kitchen, where his mother was scolding little Eric for letting the gasoline get low.

IV

Joe Vavrika's saloon was not in the county-seat, where Olaf and Mrs. Ericson did their trading, but in a cheerfuller place, a little Bohemian settlement which lay at the other end of the county, ten level miles north of Olaf's farm. Clara rode up to see her father almost every day. Vavrika's house was, so to speak, in the back yard of his saloon. The garden between the two buildings was inclosed by a high board fence as tight as a partition, and in summer Joe kept beer-tables and wooden benches among the gooseberry bushes under his little cherry tree. At one of these tables Nils Ericson was seated in the late afternoon, three days after his return home. Joe had gone in to serve a customer, and Nils was lounging on his elbows, looking rather mournfully into his half-emptied pitcher, when he heard a laugh across the little garden. Clara, in her riding-habit, was standing at the back door of the house, under the grapevine trellis that old Joe had grown there long ago. Nils rose.

"Come out and keep your father and me company. We've been gossiping all afternoon. Nobody to bother us but the flies."

She shook her head. "No, I never come out here any more. Olaf doesn't like it. I must live up to my position, you know."

"You mean to tell me you never come out and chat with the boys, as you used to? He *has* tamed you! Who keeps up these flower-beds?"

"I come out on Sundays, when father is alone, and read the Bohemian papers to him. But I am never here when the bar is open. What have you two been doing?"

"Talking, as I told you. I've been telling him about my travels. I find I can't talk much at home, not even to Eric."

Clara reached up and poked with her riding-whip at a white moth that was fluttering in the sunlight among the vine leaves. "I suppose you will never tell me about all those things."

"Where can I tell them? Not in Olaf's house, certainly. What's the matter with our talking here?" He pointed persuasively with his hat to the bushes and the green table, where the flies were singing lazily above the empty beer-glasses.

Clara shook her head weakly. "No, it wouldn't do. Besides, I am going now."

"I'm on Eric's mare. Would you be angry if I overtook you?"

Clara looked back and laughed. "You might try and see. I can leave you if I don't want you. Eric's mare can't keep up with Norman."

Nils went into the bar and attempted to pay his score. Big Joe, six feet four, with curly yellow hair and mustache, clapped him on the shoulder. "Not a God-damn a your money go in my drawer, you hear? Only next time you bring your flute, te-te-te-te-te-ty." Joe wagged his fingers in imitation of the flute-player's position. "My Clara, she come all-a-time Sundays an' play for me. She not like to play at Ericson's place." He shook his yellow curls and laughed. "Not a God-damn a fun at Ericson's. You come a Sunday. You like-a fun. No forget de flute." Joe talked very rapidly and always tumbled over his English. He seldom spoke it to his customers, and had never learned much.

Nils swung himself into the saddle and trotted to the west end of the village, where the houses and gardens scattered into prairie-land and the road turned south. Far ahead of him, in the declining light, he saw Clara Vavrika's slender figure, loitering on horseback. He touched his mare with the whip, and shot along the white, level road, under the reddening sky. When he overtook Olaf's wife he saw that she had been crying. "What's the matter, Clara Vavrika?" he asked kindly.

"Oh, I get blue sometimes. It was awfully jolly living there with father. I wonder why I ever went away."

Nils spoke in a low, kind tone that he sometimes used with women: "That's what I've been wondering these many years.

You were the last girl in the country I'd have picked for a wife for Olaf. What made you do it, Clara?"

"I suppose I really did it to oblige the neighbors"—Clara tossed her head. "People were beginning to wonder."

"To wonder?"

"Yes—why I didn't get married. I suppose I didn't like to keep them in suspense. I've discovered that most girls marry out of consideration for the neighborhood."

Nils bent his head toward her and his white teeth flashed. "I'd have gambled that one girl I knew would say, 'Let the neighborhood be damned.'"

Clara shook her head mournfully. "You see, they have it on you, Nils; that is, if you're a woman. They say you're beginning to go off. That's what makes us get married: we can't stand the laugh."

Nils looked sidewise at her. He had never seen her head droop before. Resignation was the last thing he would have expected of her. "In your case, there wasn't something else?"

"Something else?"

"I mean, you didn't do it to spite somebody? Somebody who didn't come back?"

Clara drew herself up. "Oh, I never thought you'd come back. Not after I stopped writing to you, at least. *That* was all over, long before I married Olaf."

"It never occurred to you, then, that the meanest thing you could do to me was to marry Olaf?"

Clara laughed. "No; I didn't know you were so fond of Olaf."

Nils smoothed his horse's mane with his glove. "You know, Clara Vavrika, you are never going to stick it out. You'll cut away some day, and I've been thinking you might as well cut away with me."

Clara threw up her chin. "Oh, you don't know me as well as you think. I won't cut away. Sometimes, when I'm with father, I feel like it. But I can hold out as long as the Ericsons can. They've never got the best of me yet, and one can live, so long as one isn't beaten. If I go back to father, it's all up with Olaf in politics. He knows that, and he never goes much beyond sulking. I've as much wit as the Ericsons. I'll never leave them unless I can show them a thing or two."

"You mean unless you can come it over them?"

"Yes—unless I go away with a man who is cleverer than they are, and who has more money."

Nils whistled. "Dear me, you are demanding a good deal. The Ericsons, take the lot of them, are a bunch to beat. But I should think the excitement of tormenting them would have worn off by this time."

"It has, I'm afraid," Clara admitted mournfully.

"Then why don't you cut away? There are more amusing games than this in the world. When I came home I thought it might amuse me to bully a few quarter sections out of the Ericsons; but I've almost decided I can get more fun for my money somewhere else."

Clara took in her breath sharply. "Ah, you have got the other will! That was why you came home!"

"No, it wasn't. I came home to see how you were getting on with Olaf."

Clara struck her horse with the whip, and in a bound she was far ahead of him. Nils dropped one word, "Damn!" and whipped after her; but she leaned forward in her saddle and fairly cut the wind. Her long riding-skirt rippled in the still air behind her. The sun was just sinking behind the stubble in a vast, clear sky, and the shadows drew across the fields so rapidly that Nils could scarcely keep in sight the dark figure on the road. When he overtook her he caught her horse by the bridle. Norman reared, and Nils was frightened for her; but Clara kept her seat.

"Let me go, Nils Ericson!" she cried. "I hate you more than any of them. You were created to torture me, the whole tribe of you—to make me suffer in every possible way."

She struck her horse again and galloped away from him. Nils set his teeth and looked thoughtful. He rode slowly home along the deserted road, watching the stars come out in the clear violet sky. They flashed softly into the limpid heavens, like jewels let fall into clear water. They were a reproach, he felt, to a sordid world. As he turned across the sand creek, he looked up at the North Star and smiled, as if there were an understanding between them. His mother scolded him for being late for supper.

v

On Sunday afternoon Joe Vavrika, in his shirt-sleeves
and carpet-slippers, was sitting in his garden, smoking a long-
tasseled porcelain pipe with a hunting scene painted on
the bowl. Clara sat under the cherry tree, reading aloud to
him from the weekly Bohemian papers. She had worn a
white muslin dress under her riding-habit, and the leaves of
the cherry tree threw a pattern of sharp shadows over her
skirt. The black cat was dozing in the sunlight at her feet, and
Joe's dachshund was scratching a hole under the scarlet gera-
niums and dreaming of badgers. Joe was filling his pipe for
the third time since dinner, when he heard a knocking on the
fence. He broke into a loud guffaw and unlatched the little
door that led into the street. He did not call Nils by name,
but caught him by the hand and dragged him in. Clara stiff-
ened and the color deepened under her dark skin. Nils, too,
felt a little awkward. He had not seen her since the night
when she rode away from him and left him alone on the level
road between the fields. Joe dragged him to the wooden
bench beside the green table.

"You bring de flute," he cried, tapping the leather case un-
der Nils' arm. "Ah, das-a good! Now we have some liddle fun
like old times. I got somet'ing good for you." Joe shook his
finger at Nils and winked his blue eyes, a bright clear eye, full
of fire, though the tiny blood-vessels on the ball were always a
little distended. "I got somet'ing for you from"—he paused
and waved his hand—"Hongarie. You know Hongarie? You
wait!" He pushed Nils down on the bench, and went through
the back door of his saloon.

Nils looked at Clara, who sat frigidly with her white
skirts drawn tight about her. "He didn't tell you he had asked
me to come, did he? He wanted a party and proceeded to
arrange it. Isn't he fun? Don't be cross; let's give him a good
time."

Clara smiled and shook out her skirt. "Isn't that like father?
And he has sat here so meekly all day. Well, I won't pout. I'm
glad you came. He doesn't have very many good times now

any more. There are so few of his kind left. The second gen-
eration are a tame lot."

Joe came back with a flask in one hand and three wine-
glasses caught by the stems between the fingers of the other.
These he placed on the table with an air of ceremony, and,
going behind Nils, held the flask between him and the sun,
squinting into it admiringly. "You know dis, Tokai? A great
friend of mine, he bring dis to me, a present out of Hongarie.
You know how much it cost, dis wine? Chust so much what it
weigh in gold. Nobody but de nobles drink him in Bohemie.
Many, many years I save him up, dis Tokai." Joe whipped out
his official cork-screw and delicately removed the cork. "De
old man die what bring him to me, an' dis wine he lay on his
belly in my cellar an' sleep. An' now," carefully pouring out
the heavy yellow wine, "an' now he wake up; and maybe he
wake us up, too!" He carried one of the glasses to his daugh-
ter and presented it with great gallantry.

Clara shook her head, but, seeing her father's disappoint-
ment, relented. "You taste it first. I don't want so much."

Joe sampled it with a beatific expression, and turned to
Nils. "You drink him slow, dis wine. He very soft, but he go
down hot. You see!"

After a second glass Nils declared that he couldn't take any
more without getting sleepy. "Now get your fiddle, Vavrika,"
he said as he opened his flute-case.

But Joe settled back in his wooden rocker and wagged his
big carpet-slipper. "No-no-no-no-no-no-no! No play fiddle
now any more: too much ache in de finger," waving them,
"all-a-time rheumatiz. You play de flute, te-tety-te-tety-te. Bo-
hemie songs."

"I've forgotten all the Bohemian songs I used to play with
you and Johanna. But here's one that will make Clara pout.
You remember how her eyes used to snap when we called her
the Bohemian Girl?" Nils lifted his flute and began "When
Other Lips and Other Hearts," and Joe hummed the air in a
husky baritone, waving his carpet-slipper. "Oh-h-h, das-a fine
music," he cried, clapping his hands as Nils finished. "Now
'Marble Halls, Marble Halls'! Clara, you sing him."

Clara smiled and leaned back in her chair, beginning softly:

> *"I dreamt that I dwelt in ma-a-arble halls,*
> *With vassals and serfs at my knee,"*

and Joe hummed like a big bumble-bee.

"There's one more you always played," Clara said quietly; "I remember that best." She locked her hands over her knee and began "The Heart Bowed Down," and sang it through without groping for the words. She was singing with a good deal of warmth when she came to the end of the old song:

> *"For memory is the only friend*
> *That grief can call its own."*

Joe flashed out his red silk handkerchief and blew his nose, shaking his head. "No-no-no-no-no-no-no! Too sad, too sad! I not like-a dat. Play quick somet'ing gay now."

Nils put his lips to the instrument, and Joe lay back in his chair, laughing and singing, "Oh, Evelina, Sweet Evelina!" Clara laughed, too. Long ago, when she and Nils went to high school, the model student of their class was a very homely girl in thick spectacles. Her name was Evelina Oleson; she had a long, swinging walk which somehow suggested the measure of that song, and they used mercilessly to sing it at her.

"Dat ugly Oleson girl, she teach in de school," Joe gasped, "an' she still walk chust like dat, yup-a, yup-a, yup-a, chust like a camel she go! Now, Nils, we have some more li'l drink. Oh, yes-yes-ycs-ycs-yes-yes-*yes!* Dis time you haf to drink, and Clara she haf to, so she show she not jealous. So, we all drink to your girl. You not tell her name, eh? No-no-no, I no make you tell. She pretty, eh? She make good sweetheart? I bet!" Joe winked and lifted his glass. "How soon you get married?"

Nils screwed up his eyes. "That I don't know. When she says."

Joe threw out his chest. "Das-a way boys talks. No way for mans. Mans say, 'You come to de church, an' get a hurry on you.' Das-a way mans talks."

"Maybe Nils hasn't got enough to keep a wife," put in Clara ironically. "How about that, Nils?" she asked him frankly, as if she wanted to know.

Nils looked at her coolly, raising one eyebrow. "Oh, I can keep her, all right."

"The way she wants to be kept?"

"With my wife, I'll decide that," replied Nils calmly. "I'll give her what's good for her."

Clara made a wry face. "You'll give her the strap, I expect, like old Peter Oleson gave his wife."

"When she needs it," said Nils lazily, locking his hands behind his head and squinting up through the leaves of the cherry tree. "Do you remember the time I squeezed the cherries all over your clean dress, and Aunt Johanna boxed my ears for me? My gracious, weren't you mad! You had both hands full of cherries, and I squeezed 'em and made the juice fly all over you. I liked to have fun with you; you'd get so mad."

"We *did* have fun, didn't we? None of the other kids ever had so much fun. We knew how to play."

Nils dropped his elbows on the table and looked steadily across at her. "I've played with lots of girls since, but I haven't found one who was such good fun."

Clara laughed. The late afternoon sun was shining full in her face, and deep in the back of her eyes there shone something fiery, like the yellow drops of Tokai in the brown glass bottle. "Can you still play, or are you only pretending?"

"I can play better than I used to, and harder."

"Don't you ever work, then?" She had not intended to say it. It slipped out because she was confused enough to say just the wrong thing.

"I work between times." Nils' steady gaze still beat upon her. "Don't you worry about my working, Mrs. Ericson. You're getting like all the rest of them." He reached his brown, warm hand across the table and dropped it on Clara's, which was cold as an icicle. "Last call for play, Mrs. Ericson!" Clara shivered, and suddenly her hands and cheeks grew warm. Her fingers lingered in his a moment, and they looked at each other earnestly. Joe Vavrika had put the mouth of the bottle to his lips and was swallowing the last drops of the Tokai, standing. The sun, just about to sink behind his shop, glistened on the bright glass, on his flushed face and curly yellow hair. "Look," Clara whispered; "that's the way I want to grow old."

VI

On the day of Olaf Ericson's barn-raising, his wife, for once in a way, rose early. Johanna Vavrika had been baking cakes and frying and boiling and spicing meats for a week beforehand, but it was not until the day before the party was to take place that Clara showed any interest in it. Then she was seized with one of her fitful spasms of energy, and took the wagon and little Eric and spent the day on Plum Creek, gathering vines and swamp goldenrod to decorate the barn.

By four o'clock in the afternoon buggies and wagons began to arrive at the big unpainted building in front of Olaf's house. When Nils and his mother came at five, there were more than fifty people in the barn, and a great drove of children. On the ground floor stood six long tables, set with the crockery of seven flourishing Ericson families, lent for the occasion. In the middle of each table was a big yellow pumpkin, hollowed out and filled with woodbine. In one corner of the barn, behind a pile of green-and-white-striped watermelons, was a circle of chairs for the old people; the younger guests sat on bushel measures or barbed-wire spools, and the children tumbled about in the haymow. The box-stalls Clara had converted into booths. The framework was hidden by goldenrod and sheaves of wheat, and the partitions were covered with wild grapevines full of fruit. At one of these Johanna Vavrika watched over her cooked meats, enough to provision an army; and at the next her kitchen girls had ranged the ice-cream freezers, and Clara was already cutting pies and cakes against the hour of serving. At the third stall, little Hilda, in a bright pink lawn dress, dispensed lemonade throughout the afternoon. Olaf, as a public man, had thought it inadvisable to serve beer in his barn; but Joe Vavrika had come over with two demijohns concealed in his buggy, and after his arrival the wagon-shed was much frequented by the men.

"Hasn't Cousin Clara fixed things lovely?" little Hilda whispered, when Nils went up to her stall and asked for lemonade.

Nils leaned against the booth, talking to the excited little girl and watching the people. The barn faced the west, and the sun, pouring in at the big doors, filled the whole interior with a golden light, through which filtered fine particles of dust from the haymow, where the children were romping. There was a great chattering from the stall where Johanna Vavrika exhibited to the admiring women her platters heaped with fried chicken, her roasts of beef, boiled tongues, and baked hams with cloves stuck in the crisp brown fat and garnished with tansy and parsley. The older women, having assured themselves that there were twenty kinds of cake, not counting cookies, and three dozen fat pies, repaired to the corner behind the pile of watermelons, put on their white aprons, and fell to their knitting and fancy-work. They were a fine company of old women, and a Dutch painter would have loved to find them there together, where the sun made bright patches on the floor and sent long, quivering shafts of gold through the dusky shade up among the rafters. There were fat, rosy old women who looked hot in their best black dresses; spare, alert old women with brown, dark-veined hands; and several of almost heroic frame, not less massive than old Mrs. Ericson herself. Few of them wore glasses, and old Mrs. Svendsen, a Danish woman, who was quite bald, wore the only cap among them. Mrs. Oleson, who had twelve big grandchildren, could still show two braids of yellow hair as thick as her own wrists. Among all these grandmothers there were more brown heads than white. They all had a pleased, prosperous air, as if they were more than satisfied with themselves and with life. Nils, leaning against Hilda's lemonade-stand, watched them as they sat chattering in four languages, their fingers never lagging behind their tongues.

"Look at them over there," he whispered, detaining Clara as she passed him. "Aren't they the Old Guard? I've just counted thirty hands. I guess they've wrung many a chicken's neck and warmed many a boy's jacket for him in their time."

In reality he fell into amazement when he thought of the Herculean labors those fifteen pairs of hands had performed: of the cows they had milked, the butter they had made, the gardens they had planted, the children and grandchildren they had tended, the brooms they had worn out, the mountains of food they had cooked. It made him dizzy. Clara Vavrika smiled a hard, enigmatical smile at him and walked rapidly away. Nils' eyes followed her white figure as she went toward the house. He watched her walking alone in the sunlight, looked at her slender, defiant shoulders and her little hard-set head with its coils of blue-black hair. "No," he reflected; "she'd never be like them, not if she lived here a hundred years. She'd only grow more bitter. You can't tame a wild thing; you can only chain it. People aren't all alike. I mustn't lose my nerve." He gave Hilda's pigtail a parting tweak and set out after Clara. "Where to?" he asked, as he came upon her in the kitchen.

"I'm going to the cellar for preserves."

"Let me go with you. I never get a moment alone with you. Why do you keep out of my way?"

Clara laughed. "I don't usually get in anybody's way."

Nils followed her down the stairs and to the far corner of the cellar, where a basement window let in a stream of light. From a swinging shelf Clara selected several glass jars, each labeled in Johanna's careful hand. Nils took up a brown flask. "What's this? It looks good."

"It is. It's some French brandy father gave me when I was married. Would you like some? Have you a corkscrew? I'll get glasses."

When she brought them, Nils took them from her and put them down on the window-sill. "Clara Vavrika, do you remember how crazy I used to be about you?"

Clara shrugged her shoulders. "Boys are always crazy about somebody or other. I dare say some silly has been crazy about Evelina Oleson. You got over it in a hurry."

"Because I didn't come back, you mean? I had to get on, you know, and it was hard sledding at first. Then I heard you'd married Olaf."

"And then you stayed away from a broken heart," Clara laughed.

"And then I began to think about you more than I had since I first went away. I began to wonder if you were really as you had seemed to me when I was a boy. I thought I'd like to see. I've had lots of girls, but no one ever pulled me the same way. The more I thought about you, the more I remembered how it used to be—like hearing a wild tune you can't resist, calling you out at night. It had been a long while since anything had pulled me out of my boots, and I wondered whether anything ever could again." Nils thrust his hands into his coat pockets and squared his shoulders, as his mother sometimes squared hers, as Olaf, in a clumsier manner, squared his. "So I thought I'd come back and see. Of course the family have tried to do me, and I rather thought I'd bring out father's will and make a fuss. But they can have their old land; they've put enough sweat into it." He took the flask and filled the two glasses carefully to the brim. "I've found out what I want from the Ericsons. Drink *skoal*, Clara." He lifted his glass, and Clara took hers with downcast eyes. "Look at me, Clara Vavrika. *Skoal!*"

She raised her burning eyes and answered fiercely: "*Skoal!*"

The barn supper began at six o'clock and lasted for two hilarious hours. Yense Nelson had made a wager that he could eat two whole fried chickens, and he did. Eli Swanson stowed away two whole custard pies, and Nick Hermanson ate a chocolate layer cake to the last crumb. There was even a cooky contest among the children, and one thin, slablike Bohemian boy consumed sixteen and won the prize, a gingerbread pig which Johanna Vavrika had carefully decorated with red candies and burnt sugar. Fritz Sweiheart, the German carpenter, won in the pickle contest, but he disappeared soon after supper and was not seen for the rest of the evening. Joe Vavrika said that Fritz could have managed the pickles all right, but he had sampled the demijohn in his buggy too often before sitting down to the table.

While the supper was being cleared away the two fiddlers began to tune up for the dance. Clara was to accompany them on her old upright piano, which had been brought down from her father's. By this time Nils had renewed old acquaintances. Since his interview with Clara in the cellar, he had been busy telling all the old women how young they looked, and all the young ones how pretty they were, and assuring the men that they had here the best farm-land in the world. He had made himself so agreeable that old Mrs. Ericson's friends began to come up to her and tell how lucky she was to get her smart son back again, and please to get him to play his flute.

Joe Vavrika, who could still play very well when he forgot that he had rheumatism, caught up a fiddle from Johnny Oleson and played a crazy Bohemian dance tune that set the wheels going. When he dropped the bow every one was ready to dance.

Olaf, in a frock-coat and a solemn made-up necktie, led the grand march with his mother. Clara had kept well out of *that* by sticking to the piano. She played the march with a pompous solemnity which greatly amused the prodigal son, who went over and stood behind her.

"Oh, aren't you rubbing it into them, Clara Vavrika? And aren't you lucky to have me here, or all your wit would be thrown away."

"I'm used to being witty for myself. It saves my life."

The fiddles struck up a polka, and Nils convulsed Joe Vavrika by leading out Evelina Oleson, the homely schoolteacher. His next partner was a very fat Swedish girl, who, although she was an heiress, had not been asked for the first dance, but had stood against the wall in her tight, high-heeled shoes, nervously fingering a lace handkerchief. She was soon out of breath, so Nils led her, pleased and panting, to her seat, and went over to the piano, from which Clara had been watching his gallantry. "Ask Olena Yenson," she whispered. "She waltzes beautifully."

Olena, too, was rather inconveniently plump, handsome in a smooth, heavy way, with a fine color and good-natured, sleepy eyes. She was redolent of violet sachet powder, and had warm, soft, white hands, but she danced divinely, moving as smoothly as the tide coming in. "There, that's something like," Nils said as he released her. "You'll give me the next waltz, won't you? Now I must go and dance with my little cousin."

Hilda was greatly excited when Nils went up to her stall and held out his arm. Her little eyes sparkled, but she declared that she could not leave her lemonade. Old Mrs. Ericson, who happened along at this moment, said she would attend to that, and Hilda came out, as pink as her pink dress. The dance was a schottische, and in a moment her yellow braids were fairly standing on end. "Bravo!" Nils cried encouragingly. "Where did you learn to dance so nicely?"

"My Cousin Clara taught me," the little girl panted.

Nils found Eric sitting with a group of boys who were too awkward or too shy to dance, and told him that he must dance the next waltz with Hilda.

The boy screwed up his shoulders. "Aw, Nils, I can't dance. My feet are too big; I look silly."

"Don't be thinking about yourself. It doesn't matter how boys look."

Nils had never spoken to him so sharply before, and Eric made haste to scramble out of his corner and brush the straw from his coat.

Clara nodded approvingly. "Good for you, Nils. I've been trying to get hold of him. They dance very nicely together; I sometimes play for them."

"I'm obliged to you for teaching him. There's no reason why he should grow up to be a lout."

"He'll never be that. He's more like you than any of them. Only he hasn't your courage." From her slanting eyes Clara shot forth one of those keen glances, admiring and at the same time challenging, which she seldom bestowed on any one, and which seemed to say, "Yes, I admire you, but I am your equal."

Clara was proving a much better host than Olaf, who, once the supper was over, seemed to feel no interest in anything but the lanterns. He had brought a locomotive headlight from town to light the revels, and he kept skulking about it as if he feared the mere light from it might set his new barn on fire. His wife, on the contrary, was cordial to every one, was animated and even gay. The deep salmon color in her cheeks burned vividly, and her eyes were full of life. She gave the piano over to the fat Swedish heiress, pulled her father away from the corner where he sat gossiping with his cronies, and made him dance a Bohemian dance with her. In his youth Joe had been a famous dancer, and his daughter got him so limbered up that every one sat round and applauded them. The old ladies were particularly delighted, and made them go through the dance again. From their corner where they watched and commented, the old women kept time with their feet and hands, and whenever the fiddles struck up a new air old Mrs. Svendsen's white cap would begin to bob.

Clara was waltzing with little Eric when Nils came up to them, brushed his brother aside, and swung her out among the dancers. "Remember how we used to waltz on rollers at the old skating-rink in town? I suppose people don't do that any more. We used to keep it up for hours. You know, we never did moon around as other boys and girls did. It was dead serious with us from the beginning. When we were most in love with each other, we used to fight. You were always pinching people; your fingers were like little nippers. A regular snapping-turtle, you were. Lord, how you'd like Stockholm! Sit out in the streets in front of cafés and talk all night in summer. Just like a reception—officers and ladies and funny English people. Jolliest people in the world, the Swedes, once you get them going. Always drinking things— champagne and stout mixed, half-and-half; serve it out of big pitchers, and serve plenty. Slow pulse, you know; they can stand a lot. Once they light up, they're glow-worms, I can tell you."

"All the same, you don't really like gay people."

"*I* don't?"

"No; I could see that when you were looking at the old women there this afternoon. They're the kind you really admire, after all; women like your mother. And that's the kind you'll marry."

"Is it, Miss Wisdom? You'll see who I'll marry, and she won't have a domestic virtue to bless herself with. She'll be a snapping-turtle, and she'll be a match for me. All the same, they're a fine bunch of old dames over there. You admire them yourself."

"No, I don't; I detest them."

"You won't, when you look back on them from Stockholm or Budapest. Freedom settles all that. Oh, but you're the real Bohemian Girl, Clara Vavrika!" Nils laughed down at her sullen frown and began mockingly to sing:

> *"Oh, how could a poor gypsy maiden like me*
> *Expect the proud bride of a baron to be?"*

Clara clutched his shoulder. "Hush, Nils; every one is looking at you."

"I don't care. They can't gossip. It's all in the family, as the Ericsons say when they divide up little Hilda's patrimony amongst them. Besides, we'll give them something to talk about when we hit the trail. Lord, it will be a godsend to them! They haven't had anything so interesting to chatter about since the grasshopper year. It'll give them a new lease of life. And Olaf won't lose the Bohemian vote, either. They'll have the laugh on him so that they'll vote two apiece. They'll send him to Congress. They'll never forget his barn party, or us. They'll always remember us as we're dancing together now. We're making a legend. Where's my waltz, boys?" he called as they whirled past the fiddlers.

The musicians grinned, looked at each other, hesitated, and began a new air; and Nils sang with them, as the couples fell from a quick waltz to a long, slow glide:

> *"When other lips and other hearts*
> *Their tale of love shall tell,*
> *In language whose excess imparts*
> *The power they feel so well,"*

The old women applauded vigorously. "What a gay one he is, that Nils!" And old Mrs. Svendsen's cap lurched dreamily from side to side to the flowing measure of the dance.

> *"Of days that have as ha-a-p-py been,*
> *And you'll remember me."*

VII

The moonlight flooded that great, silent land. The reaped fields lay yellow in it. The straw stacks and poplar windbreaks threw sharp black shadows. The roads were white rivers of dust. The sky was a deep, crystalline blue, and the stars were few and faint. Everything seemed to have succumbed, to have sunk to sleep, under the great, golden, tender, midsummer moon. The splendor of it seemed to transcend human life and human fate. The senses were too feeble to take it in, and every time one looked up at the sky one felt unequal to it, as if one were sitting deaf under the waves of a great river of melody.

Near the road, Nils Ericson was lying against a straw stack in Olaf's wheat-field. His own life seemed strange and unfamiliar to him, as if it were something he had read about, or dreamed, and forgotten. He lay very still, watching the white road that ran in front of him, lost itself among the fields, and then, at a distance, reappeared over a little hill. At last, against this white band he saw something moving rapidly, and he got up and walked to the edge of the field. "She is passing the row of poplars now," he thought. He heard the padded beat of hoofs along the dusty road, and as she came into sight he stepped out and waved his arms. Then, for fear of frightening the horse, he drew back and waited. Clara had seen him, and she came up at a walk. Nils took the horse by the bit and stroked his neck.

"What are you doing out so late, Clara Vavrika? I went to the house, but Johanna told me you had gone to your father's."

"Who can stay in the house on a night like this? Aren't you out yourself?"

"Ah, but that's another matter."

Nils turned the horse into the field.

"What are you doing? Where are you taking Norman?"

"Not far, but I want to talk to you to-night; I have something to say to you. I can't talk to you at the house, with Olaf sitting there on the porch, weighing a thousand tons."

Clara laughed. "He won't be sitting there now. He's in bed by this time, and asleep—weighing a thousand tons."

Nils plodded on across the stubble. "Are you really going to spend the rest of your life like this, night after night, summer after summer? Haven't you anything better to do on a night like this than to wear yourself and Norman out tearing across the country to your father's and back? Besides, your father won't live forever, you know. His little place will be shut up or sold, and then you'll have nobody but the Ericsons. You'll have to fasten down the hatches for the winter then."

Clara moved her head restlessly. "Don't talk about that. I try never to think of it. If I lost father I'd lose everything, even my hold over the Ericsons."

"Bah! You'd lose a good deal more than that. You'd lose your race, everything that makes you yourself. You've lost a good deal of it now."

"Of what?"

"Of your love of life, your capacity for delight."

Clara put her hands up to her face. "I haven't, Nils Ericson, I haven't! Say anything to me but that. I won't have it!" she declared vehemently.

Nils led the horse up to a straw stack, and turned to Clara, looking at her intently, as he had looked at her that Sunday afternoon at Vavrika's. "But why do you fight for that so? What good is the power to enjoy, if you never enjoy? Your hands are cold again; what are you afraid of all the time? Ah, you're afraid of losing it; that's what's the matter with you! And you will, Clara Vavrika, you will! When I used to know you—listen; you've caught a wild bird in your hand, haven't you, and felt its heart beat so hard that you were afraid it would shatter its little body to pieces? Well, you used to be just like that, a slender, eager thing with a wild delight inside you. That is how I remembered you. And I come back and find you—a bitter woman. This is a perfect ferret fight here; you live by biting and being bitten. Can't you remember what life used to be? Can't you remember that old delight? I've never forgotten it, or known its like, on land or sea."

He drew the horse under the shadow of the straw stack. Clara felt him take her foot out of the stirrup, and she slid softly down into his arms. He kissed her slowly. He was a deliberate man, but his nerves were steel when he wanted anything. Something flashed out from him like a knife out of a sheath. Clara felt everything slipping away from her; she was flooded by the summer night. He thrust his hand into his pocket, and then held it out at arm's length. "Look," he said. The shadow of the straw stack fell sharp across his wrist, and in the palm of his hand she saw a silver dollar shining. "That's my pile," he muttered; "will you go with me?"

Clara nodded, and dropped her forehead on his shoulder.

Nils took a deep breath. "Will you go with me to-night?"

"Where?" she whispered softly.

"To town, to catch the midnight flyer."

Clara lifted her head and pulled herself together. "Are you crazy, Nils? We couldn't go away like that."

"That's the only way we ever will go. You can't sit on the bank and think about it. You have to plunge. That's the way I've always done, and it's the right way for people like you and me. There's nothing so dangerous as sitting still. You've only got one life, one youth, and you can let it slip through your fingers if you want to; nothing easier. Most people do that. You'd be better off tramping the roads with me than you are here." Nils held back her head and looked into her eyes. "But I'm not that kind of a tramp, Clara. You won't have to take in sewing. I'm with a Norwegian shipping line; came over on business with the New York offices, but now I'm going straight back to Bergen. I expect I've got as much money as the Ericsons. Father sent me a little to get started. They never knew about that. There, I hadn't meant to tell you; I wanted you to come on your own nerve."

Clara looked off across the fields. "It isn't that, Nils, but something seems to hold me. I'm afraid to pull against it. It comes out of the ground, I think."

"I know all about that. One has to tear loose. You're not needed here. Your father will understand; he's made like us. As for Olaf, Johanna will take better care of him than ever you could. It's now or never, Clara Vavrika. My bag's at the station; I smuggled it there yesterday."

Clara clung to him and hid her face against his shoulder. "Not to-night," she whispered. "Sit here and talk to me to-night. I don't want to go anywhere to-night. I may never love you like this again."

Nils laughed through his teeth. "You can't come that on me. That's not my way, Clara Vavrika. Eric's mare is over there behind the stacks, and I'm off on the midnight. It's good-by, or off across the world with me. My carriage won't wait. I've written a letter to Olaf; I'll mail it in town. When he reads it he won't bother us—not if I know him. He'd rather have the land. Besides, I could demand an investigation of his administration of Cousin Henrik's estate, and that would be bad for a public man. You've no clothes, I know; but you can sit up to-night, and we can get everything on the way. Where's your old dash, Clara Vavrika? What's become of your Bohemian blood? I used to think you had courage enough for anything. Where's your nerve—what are you waiting for?"

Clara drew back her head, and he saw the slumberous fire in her eyes. "For you to say one thing, Nils Ericson."

"I never say that thing to any woman, Clara Vavrika." He leaned back, lifted her gently from the ground, and whispered through his teeth: "But I'll never, never let you go, not to any man on earth but me! Do you understand me? Now, wait here."

Clara sank down on a sheaf of wheat and covered her face with her hands. She did not know what she was going to do—whether she would go or stay. The great, silent country seemed to lay a spell upon her. The ground seemed to hold her as if by roots. Her knees were soft under her. She felt as if she could not bear separation from her old sorrows, from her old discontent. They were dear to her, they had kept her alive, they were a part of her. There would be nothing left of her if she were wrenched away from them. Never could she pass beyond that sky-line against which her restlessness had beat so many times. She felt as if her soul had built itself a nest there on that horizon at which she looked every morning and every evening, and it was dear to her, inexpressibly dear. She pressed her fingers against her eyeballs to shut it out. Beside her she heard the tramping of horses in the soft earth. Nils said nothing to her. He put his hands under her arms and lifted her lightly to her saddle. Then he swung himself into his own.

"We shall have to ride fast to catch the midnight train. A last gallop, Clara Vavrika. Forward!"

There was a start, a thud of hoofs along the moonlit road, two dark shadows going over the hill; and then the great, still land stretched untroubled under the azure night. Two shadows had passed.

VIII

A year after the flight of Olaf Ericson's wife, the night train was steaming across the plains of Iowa. The conductor was hurrying through one of the day-coaches, his lantern on his arm, when a lank, fair-haired boy sat up in one of the plush seats and tweaked him by the coat.

"What is the next stop, please, sir?"

"Red Oak, Iowa. But you go through to Chicago, don't you?" He looked down, and noticed that the boy's eyes were red and his face was drawn, as if he were in trouble.

"Yes. But I was wondering whether I could get off at the next place and get a train back to Omaha."

"Well, I suppose you could. Live in Omaha?"

"No. In the western part of the State. How soon do we get to Red Oak?"

"Forty minutes. You'd better make up your mind, so I can tell the baggageman to put your trunk off."

"Oh, never mind about that! I mean, I haven't got any," the boy added, blushing.

"Run away," the conductor thought, as he slammed the coach door behind him.

Eric Ericson crumpled down in his seat and put his brown hand to his forehead. He had been crying, and he had had no supper, and his head was aching violently. "Oh, what shall I do?" he thought, as he looked dully down at his big shoes. "Nils will be ashamed of me; I haven't got any spunk."

Ever since Nils had run away with his brother's wife, life at home had been hard for little Eric. His mother and Olaf both suspected him of complicity. Mrs. Ericson was harsh and fault-finding, constantly wounding the boy's pride; and Olaf was always getting her against him.

Joe Vavrika heard often from his daughter. Clara had always been fond of her father, and happiness made her kinder. She wrote him long accounts of the voyage to Bergen, and of the trip she and Nils took through Bohemia to the little town where her father had grown up and where she herself was born. She visited all her kinsmen there, and sent her father news of his brother, who was a priest; of his sister, who had married a horse-breeder—of their big farm and their many children. These letters Joe always managed to read to little Eric. They contained messages for Eric and Hilda. Clara sent presents, too, which Eric never dared to take home and which poor little Hilda never even saw, though she loved to hear Eric tell about them when they were out getting the eggs together. But Olaf once saw Eric coming out of Vavrika's house,—the old man had never asked the boy to come into his saloon,—and Olaf went straight to his mother and told her. That night Mrs. Ericson came to Eric's room after he was in bed and made a terrible scene. She could be very terrifying when she was really angry. She forbade him ever to speak to Vavrika again, and after that night she would not allow him to go to town alone. So it was a long while before Eric got any more news of his brother. But old Joe suspected what was going on, and he carried Clara's letters about in his pocket. One Sunday he drove out to see a German friend of his, and chanced to catch sight of Eric, sitting by the cattle-pond in the big pasture. They went together into Fritz Oberlies' barn, and read the letters and talked things over. Eric admitted that things were getting hard for him at home. That very night old Joe sat down and laboriously penned a statement of the case to his daughter.

Things got no better for Eric. His mother and Olaf felt that, however closely he was watched, he still, as they said, "heard." Mrs. Ericson could not admit neutrality. She had sent Johanna Vavrika packing back to her brother's, though Olaf would much rather have kept her than Anders' eldest daughter, whom Mrs. Ericson installed in her place. He was not so high-handed as his mother, and he once sulkily told her that she might better have taught her granddaughter to cook before she sent Johanna away. Olaf could have borne a good deal for the sake of prunes spiced in honey, the secret of which Johanna had taken away with her.

At last two letters came to Joe Vavrika: one from Nils, inclosing a postal order for money to pay Eric's passage to Bergen, and one from Clara, saying that Nils had a place for Eric in the offices of his company, that he was to live with them, and that they were only waiting for him to come. He was to leave New York on one of the boats of Nils' own line; the captain was one of their friends, and Eric was to make himself known at once.

Nils' directions were so explicit that a baby could have followed them, Eric felt. And here he was, nearing Red Oak, Iowa, and rocking backward and forward in despair. Never had he loved his brother so much, and never had the big world called to him so hard. But there was a lump in his throat which would not go down. Ever since nightfall he had been tormented by the thought of his mother, alone in that big house that had sent forth so many men. Her unkindness now seemed so little, and her loneliness so great. He remembered everything she had ever done for him: how frightened she had been when he tore his hand in the corn-sheller, and how she wouldn't let Olaf scold him. When Nils went away he didn't leave his mother all alone, or he would never have gone. Eric felt sure of that.

The train whistled. The conductor came in, smiling not unkindly. "Well, young man, what are you going to do? We stop at Red Oak in three minutes."

"Yes, thank you. I'll let you know." The conductor went out, and the boy doubled up with misery. He couldn't let his one chance go like this. He felt for his breast pocket and crackled Nils' kind letter to give him courage. He didn't want Nils to be ashamed of him. The train stopped. Suddenly he remembered his brother's kind, twinkling eyes, that always looked at you as if from far away. The lump in his throat softened. "Ah, but Nils, Nils would *understand*!" he thought. "That's just it about Nils; he always understands."

A lank, pale boy with a canvas telescope stumbled off the train to the Red Oak siding, just as the conductor called, "All aboard!"

The next night Mrs. Ericson was sitting alone in her wooden rocking-chair on the front porch. Little Hilda had been sent to bed and had cried herself to sleep. The old woman's knitting was in her lap, but her hands lay motionless on top of it. For more than an hour she had not moved a muscle. She simply sat, as only the Ericsons and the mountains can sit. The house was dark, and there was no sound but the croaking of the frogs down in the pond of the little pasture.

Eric did not come home by the road, but across the fields, where no one could see him. He set his telescope down softly in the kitchen shed, and slipped noiselessly along the path to the front porch. He sat down on the step without saying anything. Mrs. Ericson made no sign, and the frogs croaked on. At last the boy spoke timidly.

"I've come back, Mother."

"Very well," said Mrs. Ericson.

Eric leaned over and picked up a little stick out of the grass. "How about the milking?" he faltered.

"That's been done, hours ago."

"Who did you get?"

"Get? I did it myself. I can milk as good as any of you."

Eric slid along the step nearer to her. "Oh, Mother, why did you?" he asked sorrowfully. "Why didn't you get one of Otto's boys?"

"I didn't want anybody to know I was in need of a boy," said Mrs. Ericson bitterly. She looked straight in front of her and her mouth tightened. "I always meant to give you the home farm," she added.

The boy started and slid closer. "Oh, Mother," he faltered, "I don't care about the farm. I came back because I thought you might be needing me, maybe." He hung his head and got no further.

"Very well," said Mrs. Ericson. Her hand went out from her suddenly and rested on his head. Her fingers twined themselves in his soft, pale hair. His tears splashed down on the boards; happiness filled his heart.

McClure's, August 1912

Consequences

HENRY EASTMAN, a lawyer, aged forty, was standing beside the Flatiron building in a driving November rainstorm, signaling frantically for a taxi. It was six-thirty, and everything on wheels was engaged. The streets were in confusion about him, the sky was in turmoil above him, and the Flatiron building, which seemed about to blow down, threw water like a mill-shoot. Suddenly, out of the brutal struggle of men and cars and machines and people tilting at each other with umbrellas, a quiet, well-mannered limousine paused before him, at the curb, and an agreeable, ruddy countenance confronted him through the open window of the car.

"Don't you want me to pick you up, Mr. Eastman? I'm running directly home now."

Eastman recognized Kier Cavenaugh, a young man of pleasure, who lived in the house on Central Park South, where he himself had an apartment.

"Don't I?" he exclaimed, bolting into the car. "I'll risk getting your cushions wet without compunction. I came up in a taxi, but I didn't hold it. Bad economy. I thought I saw your car down on Fourteenth Street about half an hour ago."

The owner of the car smiled. He had a pleasant, round face and round eyes, and a fringe of smooth, yellow hair showed under the rim of his soft felt hat. "With a lot of little broilers fluttering into it? You did. I know some girls who work in the cheap shops down there. I happened to be down-town and I stopped and took a load of them home. I do sometimes. Saves their poor little clothes, you know. Their shoes are never any good."

Eastman looked at his rescuer. "Aren't they notoriously afraid of cars and smooth young men?" he inquired.

Cavenaugh shook his head. "They know which cars are safe and which are chancy. They put each other wise. You have to take a bunch at a time, of course. The Italian girls can never come along; their men shoot. The girls understand, all right; but their fathers don't. One gets to see queer places, sometimes, taking them home."

Eastman laughed drily. "Every time I touch the circle of your acquaintance, Cavenaugh, it's a little wider. You must know New York pretty well by this time."

"Yes, but I'm on my good behavior below Twenty-third Street," the young man replied with simplicity. "My little friends down there would give me a good character. They're wise little girls. They have grand ways with each other, a romantic code of loyalty. You can find a good many of the lost virtues among them."

The car was standing still in a traffic block at Fortieth Street, when Cavenaugh suddenly drew his face away from the window and touched Eastman's arm. "Look, please. You see that hansom with the bony gray horse—driver has a broken hat and red flannel around his throat. Can you see who is inside?"

Eastman peered out. The hansom was just cutting across the line, and the driver was making a great fuss about it, bobbing his head and waving his whip. He jerked his dripping old horse into Fortieth Street and clattered off past the Public Library grounds toward Sixth Avenue. "No, I couldn't see the passenger. Someone you know?"

"Could you see whether there was a passenger?" Cavenaugh asked.

"Why, yes. A man, I think. I saw his elbow on the apron. No driver ever behaves like that unless he has a passenger."

"Yes, I may have been mistaken," Cavenaugh murmured absent-mindedly. Ten minutes or so later, after Cavenaugh's car had turned off Fifth Avenue into Fifty-eighth Street, Eastman exclaimed, "There's your same cabby, and his cart's empty. He's headed for a drink now, I suppose." The driver in the broken hat and the red flannel neck cloth was still brandishing the whip over his old gray. He was coming from the west now, and turned down Sixth Avenue, under the elevated.

Cavenaugh's car stopped at the bachelor apartment house between Sixth and Seventh Avenues where he and Eastman lived, and they went up in the elevator together. They were still talking when the lift stopped at Cavenaugh's floor, and Eastman stepped out with him and walked down the hall, finishing his sentence while Cavenaugh found his latch-key. When he opened the door, a wave of fresh cigarette smoke greeted them. Cavenaugh stopped short and stared into his hallway. "Now how in the devil—!" he exclaimed angrily.

"Someone waiting for you? Oh, no, thanks. I wasn't coming in. I have to work to-night. Thank you, but I couldn't." Eastman nodded and went up the two flights to his own rooms.

Though Eastman did not customarily keep a servant he had this winter a man who had been lent to him by a friend who was abroad. Rollins met him at the door and took his coat and hat.

"Put out my dinner clothes, Rollins, and then get out of here until ten o'clock. I've promised to go to a supper to-night. I shan't be dining. I've had a late tea and I'm going to work until ten. You may put out some kumiss and biscuit for me."

Rollins took himself off, and Eastman settled down at the big table in his sitting-room. He had to read a lot of letters submitted as evidence in a breach of contract case, and before he got very far he found that long paragraphs in some of the letters were written in German. He had a German dictionary at his office, but none here. Rollins had gone, and anyhow, the bookstores would be closed. He remembered having seen a row of dictionaries on the lower shelf of one of Cavenaugh's bookcases. Cavenaugh had a lot of books, though he never read anything but new stuff. Eastman prudently turned down his student's lamp very low—the thing had an evil habit of smoking—and went down two flights to Cavenaugh's door.

The young man himself answered Eastman's ring. He was freshly dressed for the evening, except for a brown smoking jacket, and his yellow hair had been brushed until it shone. He hesitated as he confronted his caller, still holding the door knob, and his round eyes and smooth forehead made their best imitation of a frown. When Eastman began to apologize, Cavenaugh's manner suddenly changed. He caught his arm and jerked him into the narrow hall. "Come in, come in. Right along!" he said excitedly. "Right along," he repeated as he pushed Eastman before him into his sitting-room. "Well I'll—" he stopped short at the door and looked about his own room with an air of complete mystification. The back window was wide open and a strong wind was blowing in.

Cavenaugh walked over to the window and stuck out his head, looking up and down the fire escape. When he pulled his head in, he drew down the sash.

"I had a visitor I wanted you to see," he explained with a nervous smile. "At least I thought I had. He must have gone out that way," nodding toward the window.

"Call him back. I only came to borrow a German dictionary, if you have one. Can't stay. Call him back."

Cavenaugh shook his head despondently. "No use. He's beat it. Nowhere in sight."

"He must be active. Has he left something?" Eastman pointed to a very dirty white glove that lay on the floor under the window.

"Yes, that's his." Cavenaugh reached for his tongs, picked up the glove, and tossed it into the grate, where it quickly shriveled on the coals. Eastman felt that he had happened in upon something disagreeable, possibly something shady, and he wanted to get away at once. Cavenaugh stood staring at the fire and seemed stupid and dazed; so he repeated his request rather sternly, "I think I've seen a German dictionary down there among your books. May I have it?"

Cavenaugh blinked at him. "A German dictionary? Oh, possibly! Those were my father's. I scarcely know what there is." He put down the tongs and began to wipe his hands nervously with his handkerchief.

Eastman went over to the bookcase behind the Chesterfield, opened the door, swooped upon the book he wanted and stuck it under his arm. He felt perfectly certain now that something shady had been going on in Cavenaugh's rooms, and he saw no reason why he should come in for any hangover. "Thanks. I'll send it back to-morrow," he said curtly as he made for the door.

Cavenaugh followed him. "Wait a moment. I wanted you to see him. You did see his glove," glancing at the grate.

Eastman laughed disagreeably. "I saw a glove. That's not evidence. Do your friends often use that means of exit? Somewhat inconvenient."

Cavenaugh gave him a startled glance. "Wouldn't you think so? For an old man, a very rickety old party? The ladders are steep, you know, and rusty." He approached the window again and put it up softly. In a moment he drew his head back with a jerk. He caught Eastman's arm and shoved him toward the window. "Hurry, please. Look! Down there." He pointed to the little patch of paved court four flights down.

The square of pavement was so small and the walls about it were so high, that it was a good deal like looking down a well. Four tall buildings backed upon the same court and made a kind of shaft, with flagstones at the bottom, and at the top a square of dark blue with some stars in it. At the bottom of the shaft Eastman saw a black figure, a man in a caped coat and a tall hat stealing cautiously around, not across the square of pavement, keeping close to the dark wall and avoiding the streak of light that fell on the flagstones from a window in the opposite house. Seen from that height he was of course fore-shortened and probably looked more shambling and decrepit than he was. He picked his way along with exaggerated care and looked like a silly old cat crossing a wet street. When he reached the gate that led into an alley way between two buildings, he felt about for the latch, opened the door a mere crack, and then shot out under the feeble lamp that burned in the brick arch over the gateway. The door closed after him.

"He'll get run in," Eastman remarked curtly, turning away from the window. "That door shouldn't be left unlocked. Any crook could come in. I'll speak to the janitor about it, if you don't mind," he added sarcastically.

"Wish you would." Cavenaugh stood brushing down the front of his jacket, first with his right hand and then with his left. "You saw him, didn't you?"

"Enough of him. Seems eccentric. I have to see a lot of buggy people. They don't take me in any more. But I'm keeping you and I'm in a hurry myself. Good night."

Cavenaugh put out his hand detainingly and started to say something; but Eastman rudely turned his back and went down the hall and out of the door. He had never felt anything shady about Cavenaugh before, and he was sorry he had gone down for the dictionary. In five minutes he was deep in his papers; but in the half hour when he was loafing before he dressed to go out, the young man's curious behavior came into his mind again.

Eastman had merely a neighborly acquaintance with Cave-
naugh. He had been to a supper at the young man's rooms
once, but he didn't particularly like Cavenaugh's friends; so
the next time he was asked, he had another engagement. He
liked Cavenaugh himself, if for nothing else than because he
was so cheerful and trim and ruddy. A good complexion is
always at a premium in New York, especially when it shines
reassuringly on a man who does everything in the world to
lose it. It encourages fellow mortals as to the inherent vigor
of the human organism and the amount of bad treatment it
will stand for. "Footprints that perhaps another," etc.

Cavenaugh, he knew, had plenty of money. He was the son
of a Pennsylvania preacher, who died soon after he discovered
that his ancestral acres were full of petroleum, and Kier had
come to New York to burn some of the oil. He was thirty-two
and was still at it; spent his life, literally, among the breakers.
His motor hit the Park every morning as if it were the first
time ever. He took people out to supper every night. He
went from restaurant to restaurant, sometimes to half-a-dozen
in an evening. The head waiters were his hosts and their cor-
diality made him happy. They made a life-line for him up
Broadway and down Fifth Avenue. Cavenaugh was still fresh
and smooth, round and plump, with a lustre to his hair and
white teeth and a clear look in his round eyes. He seemed
absolutely unwearied and unimpaired; never bored and never
carried away.

Eastman always smiled when he met Cavenaugh in the
entrance hall, serenely going forth to or returning from glad-
iatorial combats with joy, or when he saw him rolling
smoothly up to the door in his car in the morning after a
restful night in one of the remarkable new roadhouses he was
always finding. Eastman had seen a good many young men
disappear on Cavenaugh's route, and he admired this young
man's endurance.

To-night, for the first time, he had got a whiff of something
unwholesome about the fellow—bad nerves, bad company,
something on hand that he was ashamed of, a visitor old and
vicious, who must have had a key to Cavenaugh's apartment,
for he was evidently there when Cavenaugh returned at seven
o'clock. Probably it was the same man Cavenaugh had seen in

the hansom. He must have been able to let himself in, for Cavenaugh kept no man but his chauffeur; or perhaps the janitor had been instructed to let him in. In either case, and whoever he was, it was clear enough that Cavenaugh was ashamed of him and was mixing up in questionable business of some kind.

Eastman sent Cavenaugh's book back by Rollins, and for the next few weeks he had no word with him beyond a casual greeting when they happened to meet in the hall or the elevator. One Sunday morning Cavenaugh telephoned up to him to ask if he could motor out to a roadhouse in Connecticut that afternoon and have supper; but when Eastman found there were to be other guests he declined.

On New Year's eve Eastman dined at the University Club at six o'clock and hurried home before the usual manifestations of insanity had begun in the streets. When Rollins brought his smoking coat, he asked him whether he wouldn't like to get off early.

"Yes, sir. But won't you be dressing, Mr. Eastman?" he inquired.

"Not to-night." Eastman handed him a bill. "Bring some change in the morning. There'll be fees."

Rollins lost no time in putting everything to rights for the night, and Eastman couldn't help wishing that he were in such a hurry to be off somewhere himself. When he heard the hall door close softly, he wondered if there were any place, after all, that he wanted to go. From his window he looked down at the long lines of motors and taxis waiting for a signal to cross Broadway. He thought of some of their probable destinations and decided that none of those places pulled him very hard. The night was warm and wet, the air was drizzly. Vapor hung in clouds about the *Times* Building, half hid the top of it, and made a luminous haze along Broadway. While he was looking down at the army of wet, black carriage-tops and their reflected headlights and tail-lights, Eastman heard a ring at his door. He deliberated. If it were a caller, the hall porter would have telephoned up. It must be the janitor. When he opened the door, there stood a rosy young man in a tuxedo, without a coat or hat.

"Pardon. Should I have telephoned? I half thought you wouldn't be in."

Eastman laughed. "Come in, Cavenaugh. You weren't sure whether you wanted company or not, eh, and you were trying to let chance decide it? That was exactly my state of mind. Let's accept the verdict." When they emerged from the narrow hall into his sitting-room, he pointed out a seat by the fire to his guest. He brought a tray of decanters and soda bottles and placed it on his writing table.

Cavenaugh hesitated, standing by the fire. "Sure you weren't starting for somewhere?"

"Do I look it? No, I was just making up my mind to stick it out alone when you rang. Have one?" he picked up a tall tumbler.

"Yes, thank you. I always do."

Eastman chuckled. "Lucky boy! So will I. I had a very early dinner. New York is the most arid place on holidays," he continued as he rattled the ice in the glasses. "When one gets too old to hit the rapids down there, and tired of gobbling food to heathenish dance music, there is absolutely no place where you can get a chop and some milk toast in peace, unless you have strong ties of blood brotherhood on upper Fifth Avenue. But you, why aren't you starting for somewhere?"

The young man sipped his soda and shook his head as he replied:

"Oh, I couldn't get a chop, either. I know only flashy people, of course." He looked up at his host with such a grave and candid expression that Eastman decided there couldn't be anything very crooked about the fellow. His smooth cheeks were positively cherubic.

"Well, what's the matter with them? Aren't they flashing to-night?"

"Only the very new ones seem to flash on New Year's eve. The older ones fade away. Maybe they are hunting a chop, too."

"Well"—Eastman sat down—"holidays do dash one. I was just about to write a letter to a pair of maiden aunts in my old home town, up-state; old coasting hill, snow-covered pines, lights in the church windows. That's what you've saved me from."

Cavenaugh shook himself. "Oh, I'm sure that wouldn't have been good for you. Pardon me," he rose and took a photograph from the bookcase, a handsome man in shooting clothes. "Dudley, isn't it? Did you know him well?"

"Yes. An old friend. Terrible thing, wasn't it? I haven't got over the jolt yet."

"His suicide? Yes, terrible! Did you know his wife?"

"Slightly. Well enough to admire her very much. She must be terribly broken up. I wonder Dudley didn't think of that."

Cavenaugh replaced the photograph carefully, lit a cigarette, and standing before the fire began to smoke. "Would you mind telling me about him? I never met him, but of course I'd read a lot about him, and I can't help feeling interested. It was a queer thing."

Eastman took out his cigar case and leaned back in his deep chair. "In the days when I knew him best he hadn't any story, like the happy nations. Everything was properly arranged for him before he was born. He came into the world happy, healthy, clever, straight, with the right sort of connections and the right kind of fortune, neither too large nor too small. He helped to make the world an agreeable place to live in until he was twenty-six. Then he married as he should have married. His wife was a Californian, educated abroad. Beautiful. You have seen her picture?"

Cavenaugh nodded. "Oh, many of them."

"She was interesting, too. Though she was distinctly a person of the world, she had retained something, just enough of the large Western manner. She had the habit of authority, of calling out a special train if she needed it, of using all our ingenious mechanical contrivances lightly and easily, without over-rating them. She and Dudley knew how to live better than most people. Their house was the most charming one I have ever known in New York. You felt freedom there, and a zest of life, and safety—absolute sanctuary—from everything sordid or petty. A whole society like that would justify the creation of man and would make our planet shine with a soft, peculiar radiance among the constellations. You think I'm putting it on thick?"

The young man sighed gently. "Oh, no! One has always felt there must be people like that. I've never known any."

"They had two children, beautiful ones. After they had been married for eight years, Rosina met this Spaniard. He must have amounted to something. She wasn't a flighty woman. She came home and told Dudley how matters stood. He persuaded her to stay at home for six months and try to pull up. They were both fair-minded people, and I'm as sure as if I were the Almighty, that she did try. But at the end of the time, Rosina went quietly off to Spain, and Dudley went to hunt in the Canadian Rockies. I met his party out there. I didn't know his wife had left him and talked about her a good deal. I noticed that he never drank anything, and his light used to shine through the log chinks of his room until all hours, even after a hard day's hunting. When I got back to New York, rumors were creeping about. Dudley did not come back. He bought a ranch in Wyoming, built a big log house and kept splendid dogs and horses. One of his sisters went out to keep house for him, and the children were there when they were not in school. He had a great many visitors, and everyone who came back talked about how well Dudley kept things going.

"He put in two years out there. Then, last month, he had to come back on business. A trust fund had to be settled up, and he was administrator. I saw him at the club; same light, quick step, same gracious handshake. He was getting gray, and there was something softer in his manner; but he had a fine red tan on his face and said he found it delightful to be here in the season when everything is going hard. The Madison Avenue house had been closed since Rosina left it. He went there to get some things his sister wanted. That, of course, was the mistake. He went alone, in the afternoon, and didn't go out for dinner—found some sherry and tins of biscuit in the sideboard. He shot himself sometime that night. There were pistols in his smoking-room. They found burnt out candles beside him in the morning. The gas and electricity were shut off. I suppose there, in his own house, among his own things, it was too much for him. He left no letters."

Cavenaugh blinked and brushed the lapel of his coat. "I suppose," he said slowly, "that every suicide is logical and reasonable, if one knew all the facts."

Eastman roused himself. "No, I don't think so. I've known

too many fellows who went off like that—more than I deserve, I think—and some of them were absolutely inexplicable. I can understand Dudley; but I can't see why healthy bachelors, with money enough, like ourselves, need such a device. It reminds me of what Dr. Johnson said, that the most discouraging thing about life is the number of fads and hobbies and fake religions it takes to put people through a few years of it."

"Dr. Johnson? The specialist? Oh, the old fellow!" said Cavenaugh imperturbably. "Yes, that's interesting. Still, I fancy if one knew the facts— Did you know about Wyatt?"

"I don't think so."

"You wouldn't, probably. He was just a fellow about town who spent money. He wasn't one of the *forestieri*, though. Had connections here and owned a fine old place over on Staten Island. He went in for botany, and had been all over, hunting things; rusts, I believe. He had a yacht and used to take a gay crowd down about the South Seas, botanizing. He really did botanize, I believe. I never knew such a spender— only not flashy. He helped a lot of fellows and he was awfully good to girls, the kind who come down here to get a little fun, who don't like to work and still aren't really tough, the kind you see talking hard for their dinner. Nobody knows what becomes of them, or what they get out of it, and there are hundreds of new ones every year. He helped dozens of 'em; it was he who got me curious about the little shop girls. Well, one afternoon when his tea was brought, he took prussic acid instead. He didn't leave any letters, either; people of any taste don't. They wouldn't leave any material reminder if they could help it. His lawyers found that he had just $314.72 above his debts when he died. He had planned to spend all his money, and then take his tea; he had worked it out carefully."

Eastman reached for his pipe and pushed his chair away from the fire. "That looks like a considered case, but I don't think philosophical suicides like that are common. I think they usually come from stress of feeling and are really, as the newspapers call them, desperate acts; done without a motive. You remember when Anna Karenina was under the wheels, she kept saying, 'Why am I here?' "

Cavenaugh rubbed his upper lip with his pink finger and made an effort to wrinkle his brows. "May I, please?" reaching for the whiskey. "But have you," he asked, blinking as the soda flew at him, "have you ever known, yourself, cases that were really inexplicable?"

"A few too many. I was in Washington just before Captain Jack Purden was married and I saw a good deal of him. Popular army man, fine record in the Philippines, married a charming girl with lots of money; mutual devotion. It was the gayest wedding of the winter, and they started for Japan. They stopped in San Francisco for a week and missed their boat because, as the bride wrote back to Washington, they were too happy to move. They took the next boat, were both good sailors, had exceptional weather. After they had been out for two weeks, Jack got up from his deck chair one afternoon, yawned, put down his book, and stood before his wife. 'Stop reading for a moment and look at me.' She laughed and asked him why. 'Because you happen to be good to look at.' He nodded to her, went back to the stern and was never seen again. Must have gone down to the lower deck and slipped overboard, behind the machinery. It was the luncheon hour, not many people about; steamer cutting through a soft green sea. That's one of the most baffling cases I know. His friends raked up his past, and it was as trim as a cottage garden. If he'd so much as dropped an ink spot on his fatigue uniform, they'd have found it. He wasn't emotional or moody; wasn't, indeed, very interesting; simply a good soldier, fond of all the pompous little formalities that make up a military man's life. What do you make of that, my boy?"

Cavenaugh stroked his chin. "It's very puzzling, I admit. Still, if one knew everything——"

"But we do know everything. His friends wanted to find something to help them out, to help the girl out, to help the case of the human creature."

"Oh, I don't mean things that people could unearth," said Cavenaugh uneasily. "But possibly there were things that couldn't be found out."

Eastman shrugged his shoulders. "It's my experience that when there are 'things' as you call them, they're very apt to be found. There is no such thing as a secret. To make any move at all one has to employ human agencies, employ at least one human agent. Even when the pirates killed the men who buried their gold for them, the bones told the story."

Cavenaugh rubbed his hands together and smiled his sunny smile.

"I like that idea. It's reassuring. If we can have no secrets, it means that we can't, after all, go so far afield as we might," he hesitated, "yes, as we might."

Eastman looked at him sourly. "Cavenaugh, when you've practised law in New York for twelve years, you find that people can't go far in any direction, except—" He thrust his forefinger sharply at the floor. "Even in that direction, few people can do anything out of the ordinary. Our range is limited. Skip a few baths, and we become personally objectionable. The slightest carelessness can rot a man's integrity or give him ptomaine poisoning. We keep up only by incessant cleansing operations, of mind and body. What we call character, is held together by all sorts of tacks and strings and glue."

Cavenaugh looked startled. "Come now, it's not so bad as that, is it? I've always thought that a serious man, like you, must know a lot of Launcelots." When Eastman only laughed, the younger man squirmed about in his chair. He spoke again hastily, as if he were embarrassed. "Your military friend may have had personal experiences, however, that his friends couldn't possibly get a line on. He may accidentally have come to a place where he saw himself in too unpleasant a light. I believe people can be chilled by a draft from outside, somewhere."

"Outside?" Eastman echoed. "Ah, you mean the far outside! Ghosts, delusions, eh?"

Cavenaugh winced. "That's putting it strong. Why not say tips from the outside? Delusions belong to a diseased mind, don't they? There are some of us who have no minds to speak of, who yet have had experiences. I've had a little something in that line myself and I don't look it, do I?"

Eastman looked at the bland countenance turned toward him. "Not exactly. What's your delusion?"

"It's not a delusion. It's a haunt."

The lawyer chuckled. "Soul of a lost Casino girl?"

"No; an old gentleman. A most unattractive old gentleman, who follows me about."

"Does he want money?"

Cavenaugh sat up straight. "No. I wish to God he wanted anything—but the pleasure of my society! I'd let him clean me out to be rid of him. He's a real article. You saw him yourself that night when you came to my rooms to borrow a dictionary, and he went down the fire-escape. You saw him down in the court."

"Well, I saw somebody down in the court, but I'm too cautious to take it for granted that I saw what you saw. Why, anyhow, should I see your haunt? If it was your friend I saw, he impressed me disagreeably. How did you pick him up?"

Cavenaugh looked gloomy. "That was queer, too. Charley Burke and I had motored out to Long Beach, about a year ago, sometime in October, I think. We had supper and stayed until late. When we were coming home, my car broke down. We had a lot of girls along who had to get back for morning rehearsals and things; so I sent them all into town in Charley's car, and he was to send a man back to tow me home. I was driving myself, and didn't want to leave my machine. We had not taken a direct road back; so I was stuck in a lonesome, woody place, no houses about. I got chilly and made a fire, and was putting in the time comfortably enough, when this old party steps up. He was in shabby evening clothes and a top hat, and had on his usual white gloves. How he got there, at three o'clock in the morning, miles from any town or railway, I'll leave it to you to figure out. *He* surely had no car. When I saw him coming up to the fire, I disliked him. He had a silly, apologetic walk. His teeth were chattering, and I asked him to sit down. He got down like a clothes-horse folding up. I offered him a cigarette, and when he took off his gloves I couldn't help noticing how knotted and spotty his hands were. He was asthmatic, and took his breath with a wheeze. 'Haven't you got anything—refreshing in there?' he asked, nodding at the car. When I told him I hadn't, he sighed. 'Ah, you young fellows are greedy. You drink it all up. You drink it all up, all up—up!' he kept chewing it over."

Cavenaugh paused and looked embarrassed again. "The thing that was most unpleasant is difficult to explain. The old man sat there by the fire and leered at me with a silly sort of admiration that was—well, more than humiliating. 'Gay boy, gay dog!' he would mutter, and when he grinned he showed his teeth, worn and yellow—shells. I remembered that it was better to talk casually to insane people; so I remarked carelessly that I had been out with a party and got stuck.

" 'Oh yes, I remember,' he said, 'Flora and Lottie and Maybelle and Marcelline, and poor Kate.'

"He had named them correctly; so I began to think I had been hitting the bright waters too hard.

"Things I drank never had seemed to make me woody; but you can never tell when trouble is going to hit you. I pulled my hat down and tried to look as uncommunicative as possible; but he kept croaking on from time to time, like this: 'Poor Kate! Splendid arms, but dope got her. She took up with Eastern religions after she had her hair dyed. Got to going to a Swami's joint, and smoking opium. Temple of the Lotus, it was called, and the police raided it.'

"This was nonsense, of course; the young woman was in the pink of condition. I let him rave, but I decided that if something didn't come out for me pretty soon, I'd foot it across Long Island. There wasn't room enough for the two of us. I got up and took another try at my car. He hopped right after me.

" 'Good car,' he wheezed, 'better than the little Ford.'

"I'd had a Ford before, but so has everybody; that was a safe guess.

" 'Still,' he went on, 'that run in from Huntington Bay in the rain wasn't bad. Arrested for speeding, he-he.'

"It was true I had made such a run, under rather unusual circumstances, and had been arrested. When at last I heard my life-boat snorting up the road, my visitor got up, sighed, and stepped back into the shadow of the trees. I didn't wait to see what became of him, you may believe. That was visitation number one. What do you think of it?"

Cavenaugh looked at his host defiantly. Eastman smiled.

"I think you'd better change your mode of life, Cavenaugh. Had many returns?" he inquired.

"Too many, by far." The young man took a turn about the room and came back to the fire. Standing by the mantel he lit another cigarette before going on with his story:

"The second visitation happened in the street, early in the evening, about eight o'clock. I was held up in a traffic block before the Plaza. My chauffeur was driving. Old Nibbs steps up out of the crowd, opens the door of my car, gets in and sits down beside me. He had on wilted evening clothes, same as before, and there was some sort of heavy scent about him. Such an unpleasant old party! A thorough-going rotter; you knew it at once. This time he wasn't talkative, as he had been when I first saw him. He leaned back in the car as if he owned it, crossed his hands on his stick and looked out at the crowd—sort of hungrily.

"I own I really felt a loathing compassion for him. We got down the avenue slowly. I kept looking out at the mounted police. But what could I do? Have him pulled? I was afraid to. I was awfully afraid of getting him into the papers.

" 'I'm going to the New Astor,' I said at last. 'Can I take you anywhere?'

" 'No, thank you,' says he. 'I get out when you do. I'm due on West 44th. I'm dining to-night with Marcelline—all that is left of her!'

"He put his hand to his hat brim with a grewsome salute. Such a scandalous, foolish old face as he had! When we pulled up at the Astor, I stuck my hand in my pocket and asked him if he'd like a little loan.

" 'No, thank you, but'—he leaned over and whispered, ugh!—'but save a little, save a little. Forty years from now —a little—comes in handy. Save a little.'

"His eyes fairly glittered as he made his remark. I jumped out. I'd have jumped into the North River. When he tripped off, I asked my chauffeur if he'd noticed the man who got into the car with me. He said he knew someone was with me, but he hadn't noticed just when he got in. Want to hear any more?"

Cavenaugh dropped into his chair again. His plump cheeks

were a trifle more flushed than usual, but he was perfectly calm. Eastman felt that the young man believed what he was telling him.

"Of course I do. It's very interesting. I don't see quite where you are coming out though."

Cavenaugh sniffed. "No more do I. I really feel that I've been put upon. I haven't deserved it any more than any other fellow of my kind. Doesn't it impress you disagreeably?"

"Well, rather so. Has anyone else seen your friend?"

"You saw him."

"We won't count that. As I said, there's no certainty that you and I saw the same person in the court that night. Has anyone else had a look in?"

"People sense him rather than see him. He usually crops up when I'm alone or in a crowd on the street. He never approaches me when I'm with people I know, though I've seen him hanging about the doors of theatres when I come out with a party; loafing around the stage exit, under a wall; or across the street, in a doorway. To be frank, I'm not anxious to introduce him. The third time, it was I who came upon him. In November my driver, Harry, had a sudden attack of appendicitis. I took him to the Presbyterian Hospital in the car, early in the evening. When I came home, I found the old villain in my rooms. I offered him a drink, and he sat down. It was the first time I had seen him in a steady light, with his hat off.

"His face is lined like a railway map, and as to color— Lord, what a liver! His scalp grows tight to his skull, and his hair is dyed until it's perfectly dead, like a piece of black cloth."

Cavenaugh ran his fingers through his own neatly trimmed thatch, and seemed to forget where he was for a moment.

"I had a twin brother, Brian, who died when we were sixteen. I have a photograph of him on my wall, an enlargement from a kodak of him, doing a high jump, rather good thing, full of action. It seemed to annoy the old gentleman. He kept looking at it and lifting his eyebrows, and finally he got up, tip-toed across the room, and turned the picture to the wall.

" 'Poor Brian! Fine fellow, but died young,' says he.

"Next morning, there was the picture, still reversed."

"Did he stay long?" Eastman asked interestedly.

"Half an hour, by the clock."

"Did he talk?"

"Well, he rambled."

"What about?"

Cavenaugh rubbed his pale eyebrows before answering.

"About things that an old man ought to want to forget. His conversation is highly objectionable. Of course he knows me like a book; everything I've ever done or thought. But when he recalls them, he throws a bad light on them, somehow. Things that weren't much off color, look rotten. He doesn't leave one a shred of self-respect, he really doesn't. That's the amount of it." The young man whipped out his handkerchief and wiped his face.

"You mean he really talks about things that none of your friends know?"

"Oh, dear, yes! Recalls things that happened in school. Anything disagreeable. Funny thing, he always turns Brian's picture to the wall."

"Does he come often?"

"Yes, oftener, now. Of course I don't know how he gets in down-stairs. The hall boys never see him. But he has a key to my door. I don't know how he got it, but I can hear him turn it in the lock."

"Why don't you keep your driver with you, or telephone for me to come down?"

"He'd only grin and go down the fire escape as he did before. He's often done it when Harry's come in suddenly. Everybody has to be alone sometimes, you know. Besides, I don't want anybody to see him. He has me there."

"But why not? Why do you feel responsible for him?"

Cavenaugh smiled wearily. "That's rather the point, isn't it? Why do I? But I absolutely do. That identifies him, more than his knowing all about my life and my affairs."

Eastman looked at Cavenaugh thoughtfully. "Well, I should advise you to go in for something altogether different and new, and go in for it hard; business, engineering, metallurgy, something this old fellow wouldn't be interested in. See if you can make him remember logarithms."

Cavenaugh sighed. "No, he has me there, too. People never really change; they go on being themselves. But I would never make much trouble. Why can't they let me alone, damn it! I'd never hurt anybody, except, perhaps——"

"Except your old gentleman, eh?" Eastman laughed. "Seriously, Cavenaugh, if you want to shake him, I think a year on a ranch would do it. He would never be coaxed far from his favorite haunts. He would dread Montana."

Cavenaugh pursed up his lips. "So do I!"

"Oh, you think you do. Try it, and you'll find out. A gun and a horse beats all this sort of thing. Besides losing your haunt, you'd be putting ten years in the bank for yourself. I know a good ranch where they take people, if you want to try it."

"Thank you. I'll consider. Do you think I'm batty?"

"No, but I think you've been doing one sort of thing too long. You need big horizons. Get out of this."

Cavenaugh smiled meekly. He rose lazily and yawned behind his hand. "It's late, and I've taken your whole evening." He strolled over to the window and looked out. "Queer place, New York; rough on the little fellows. Don't you feel sorry for them, the girls especially? I do. What a fight they put up for a little fun! Why, even that old goat is sorry for them, the only decent thing he kept."

Eastman followed him to the door and stood in the hall, while Cavenaugh waited for the elevator. When the car came up Cavenaugh extended his pink, warm hand. "Good night."

The cage sank and his rosy countenance disappeared, his round-eyed smile being the last thing to go.

Weeks passed before Eastman saw Cavenaugh again. One morning, just as he was starting for Washington to argue a case before the Supreme Court, Cavenaugh telephoned him at his office to ask him about the Montana ranch he had recommended; said he meant to take his advice and go out there for the spring and summer.

When Eastman got back from Washington, he saw dusty trunks, just up from the trunk room, before Cavenaugh's door. Next morning, when he stopped to see what the young man was about, he found Cavenaugh in his shirt sleeves, packing.

"I'm really going; off to-morrow night. You didn't think it of me, did you?" he asked gaily.

"Oh, I've always had hopes of you!" Eastman declared. "But you are in a hurry, it seems to me."

"Yes, I am in a hurry." Cavenaugh shot a pair of leggings into one of the open trunks. "I telegraphed your ranch people, used your name, and they said it would be all right. By the way, some of my crowd are giving a little dinner for me at Rector's to-night. Couldn't you be persuaded, as it's a farewell occasion?" Cavenaugh looked at him hopefully.

Eastman laughed and shook his head. "Sorry, Cavenaugh, but that's too gay a world for me. I've got too much work lined up before me. I wish I had time to stop and look at your guns, though. You seem to know something about guns. You've more than you'll need, but nobody can have too many good ones." He put down one of the revolvers regretfully. "I'll drop in to see you in the morning, if you're up."

"I shall be up, all right. I've warned my crowd that I'll cut away before midnight."

"You won't, though," Eastman called back over his shoulder as he hurried down-stairs.

The next morning, while Eastman was dressing, Rollins came in greatly excited.

"I'm a little late, sir. I was stopped by Harry, Mr. Cavenaugh's driver. Mr. Cavenaugh shot himself last night, sir."

Eastman dropped his vest and sat down on his shoe-box. "You're drunk, Rollins," he shouted. "He's going away to-day!"

"Yes, sir. Harry found him this morning. Ah, he's quite dead, sir. Harry's telephoned for the coroner. Harry don't know what to do with the ticket."

Eastman pulled on his coat and ran down the stairway. Cavenaugh's trunks were strapped and piled before the door. Harry was walking up and down the hall with a long green railroad ticket in his hand and a look of complete stupidity on his face.

"What shall I do about this ticket, Mr. Eastman?" he whispered. "And what about his trunks? He had me tell the transfer people to come early. They may be here any minute. Yes, sir. I brought him home in the car last night, before twelve, as cheerful as could be."

"Be quiet, Harry. Where is he?"

"In his bed, sir."

Eastman went into Cavenaugh's sleeping-room. When he came back to the sitting-room, he looked over the writing table; railway folders, time-tables, receipted bills, nothing else. He looked up for the photograph of Cavenaugh's twin brother. There it was, turned to the wall. Eastman took it down and looked at it; a boy in track clothes, half lying in the air, going over the string shoulders first, above the heads of a crowd of lads who were running and cheering. The face was somewhat blurred by the motion and the bright sunlight. Eastman put the picture back, as he found it. Had Cavenaugh entertained his visitor last night, and had the old man been more convincing than usual? "Well, at any rate, he's seen to it that the old man can't establish identity. What a soft lot they are, fellows like poor Cavenaugh!" Eastman thought of his office as a delightful place.

McClure's, November 1915

The Bookkeeper's Wife

NOBODY but the janitor was stirring about the offices of the Remsen Paper Company, and still Percy Bixby sat at his desk, crouched on his high stool and staring out at the tops of the tall buildings flushed with the winter sunset, at the hundreds of windows, so many rectangles of white electric light, flashing against the broad waves of violet that ebbed across the sky. His ledgers were all in their places, his desk was in order, his office coat on its peg, and yet Percy's smooth, thin face wore the look of anxiety and strain which usually meant that he was behind in his work. He was trying to persuade himself to accept a loan from the company without the company's knowledge. As a matter of fact, he had already accepted it. His books were fixed, the money, in a black-leather bill-book, was already inside his waistcoat pocket.

He had still time to change his mind, to rectify the false figures in his ledger, and to tell Stella Brown that they couldn't possibly get married next month. There he always halted in his reasoning, and went back to the beginning.

The Remsen Paper Company was a very wealthy concern, with easy, old-fashioned working methods. They did a long-time credit business with safe customers, who never thought of paying up very close on their large indebtedness. From the payments on these large accounts Percy had taken a hundred dollars here and two hundred there until he had made up the thousand he needed. So long as he stayed by the books himself and attended to the mail-orders he couldn't possibly be found out. He could move these little shortages about from account to account indefinitely. He could have all the time he needed to pay back the deficit, and more time than he needed.

Although he was so far along in one course of action, his mind still clung resolutely to the other. He did not believe he was going to do it. He was the least of a sharper in the world. Being scrupulously honest even in the most trifling matters was a pleasure to him. He was the sort of young man that Socialists hate more than they hate capitalists. He loved his

154

desk, he loved his books, which had no handwriting in them but his own. He never thought of resenting the fact that he had written away in those books the good red years between twenty-one and twenty-seven. He would have hated to let any one else put so much as a pen-scratch in them. He liked all the boys about the office; his desk, worn smooth by the sleeves of his alpaca coat; his rulers and inks and pens and calendars. He had a great pride in working economics, and he always got so far ahead when supplies were distributed that he had drawers full of pencils and pens and rubber bands against a rainy day.

Percy liked regularity: to get his work done on time, to have his half-day off every Saturday, to go to the theater Saturday night, to buy a new necktie twice a month, to appear in a new straw hat on the right day in May, and to know what was going on in New York. He read the morning and evening papers coming and going on the elevated, and preferred journals of approximate reliability. He got excited about ball-games and elections and business failures, was not above an interest in murders and divorce scandals, and he checked the news off as neatly as he checked his mail-orders. In short, Percy Bixby was like the model pupil who is satisfied with his lessons and his teachers and his holidays, and who would gladly go to school all his life. He had never wanted anything outside his routine until he wanted Stella Brown to marry him, and that had upset everything.

It was n't, he told himself for the hundredth time, that she was extravagant. Not a bit of it. She was like all girls. Moreover, she made good money, and why should she marry unless she could better herself? The trouble was that he had lied to her about his salary. There were a lot of fellows rushing Mrs. Brown's five daughters, and they all seemed to have fixed on Stella as first choice and this or that one of the sisters as second. Mrs. Brown thought it proper to drop an occasional hint in the presence of these young men to the effect that she expected Stella to "do well." It went without saying that hair and complexion like Stella's could scarcely be expected to do poorly. Most of the boys who went to the house and took the girls out in a bunch to dances and movies seemed to realize this. They merely wanted a whirl with Stella before they settled down to one of her sisters. It was tacitly understood that she came too high for them. Percy had sensed all this through those slumbering instincts which awake in us all to befriend us in love or in danger.

But there was one of his rivals, he knew, who was a man to be reckoned with. Charley Greengay was a young salesman who wore tailor-made clothes and spotted waistcoats, and had a necktie for every day in the month. His air was that of a young man who is out for things that come high and who is going to get them. Mrs. Brown was ever and again dropping a word before Percy about how the girl that took Charley would have her flat furnished by the best furniture people, and her china-closet stocked with the best ware, and would have nothing to worry about but nicks and scratches. It was because he felt himself pitted against this pulling power of Greengay's that Percy had brazenly lied to Mrs. Brown, and told her that his salary had been raised to fifty a week, and that now he wanted to get married.

When he threw out this challenge to Mother Brown, Percy was getting thirty-five dollars a week, and he knew well enough that there were several hundred thousand young men in New York who would do his work as well as he did for thirty.

These were the factors in Percy's present situation. He went over them again and again as he sat stooping on his tall stool. He had quite lost track of time when he heard the janitor call good night to the watchman. Without thinking what he was doing, he slid into his overcoat, caught his hat, and rushed out to the elevator, which was waiting for the janitor. The moment the car dropped, it occurred to him that the thing was decided without his having made up his mind at all. The familiar floors passed him, ten, nine, eight, seven. By the time he reached the fifth, there was no possibility of going back; the click of the drop-lever seemed to settle that. The money was in his pocket. Now, he told himself as he hurried out into the exciting clamor of the street, he was not going to worry about it any more.

When Percy reached the Browns' flat on 123d Street that evening he felt just the slightest chill in Stella's greeting. He could make that all right, he told himself, as he kissed her lightly in the dark three-by-four entrance-hall. Percy's court-ing had been prosecuted mainly in the Bronx or in winged pursuit of a Broadway car. When he entered the crowded sitting-room he greeted Mrs. Brown respectfully and the four girls playfully. They were all piled on one couch, reading the continued story in the evening paper, and they did n't think it necessary to assume more formal attitudes for Percy. They looked up over the smeary pink sheets of paper, and handed him, as Percy said, the same old jolly:

"Hullo, Perc'! Come to see me, ain't you? So flattered!"

"Any sweet goods on you, Perc'? Anything doing in the bong-bong line to-night?"

"Look at his new neckwear! Say, Perc', remember me. That tie would go lovely with my new tailored waist."

"Quit your kiddin', girls!" called Mrs. Brown, who was drying shirt-waists on the dining-room radiator. "And, Percy, mind the rugs when you 're steppin' round among them gum-drops."

Percy fired his last shot at the recumbent figures, and followed Stella into the dining-room, where the table and two large easy-chairs formed, in Mrs. Brown's estimation, a proper background for a serious suitor.

"I say, Stell'," he began as he walked about the table with his hands in his pockets, "seems to me we ought to begin buying our stuff." She brightened perceptibly. "Ah," Percy thought, "so that *was* the trouble!" "To-morrow's Saturday; why can't we make an afternoon of it?" he went on cheerfully. "Shop till we 're tired, then go to Houtin's for dinner, and end up at the theater."

As they bent over the lists she had made of things needed, Percy glanced at her face. She was very much out of her sis-ters' class and out of his, and he kept congratulating himself on his nerve. He was going in for something much too hand-some and expensive and distinguished for him, he felt, and it took courage to be a plunger. To begin with, Stella was the sort of girl who had to be well dressed. She had pale primrose hair, with bluish tones in it, very soft and fine, so that it lay smooth however she dressed it, and pale-blue eyes, with blond eyebrows and long, dark lashes. She would have been a

little too remote and languid even for the fastidious Percy had
it not been for her hard, practical mouth, with lips that always
kept their pink even when the rest of her face was pale. Her
employers, who at first might be struck by her indifference,
understood that anybody with that sort of mouth would get
through the work.

After the shopping-lists had been gone over, Percy took up
the question of the honeymoon. Stella said she had been
thinking of Atlantic City. Percy met her with firmness. What-
ever happened, he couldn't leave his books now.

"I want to do my traveling right here on Forty-second
Street, with a high-price show every night," he declared. He
made out an itinerary, punctuated by theaters and restaurants,
which Stella consented to accept as a substitute for Atlantic
City.

"They give your fellows a week off when they're married,
don't they?" she asked.

"Yes, but I'll want to drop into the office every morning to
look after my mail. That's only businesslike."

"I'd like to have you treated as well as the others, though."
Stella turned the rings about on her pale hand and looked at
her polished finger-tips.

"I'll look out for that. What do you say to a little walk,
Stell'?" Percy put the question coaxingly. When Stella was
pleased with him she went to walk with him, since that was
the only way in which Percy could ever see her alone. When
she was displeased, she said she was too tired to go out. To-
night she smiled at him incredulously, and went to put on her
hat and gray fur piece.

Once they were outside, Percy turned into a shadowy side
street that was only partly built up, a dreary waste of derricks
and foundation holes, but comparatively solitary. Stella liked
Percy's steady, sympathetic silences; she was not a chatterbox
herself. She often wondered why she was going to marry
Bixby instead of Charley Greengay. She knew that Charley
would go further in the world. Indeed, she had often coolly
told herself that Percy would never go very far. But, as she
admitted with a shrug, she was "weak to Percy." In the capa-
ble New York stenographer, who estimated values coldly and
got the most for the least outlay, there was something left

that belonged to another kind of woman—something that liked the very things in Percy that were not good business assets. However much she dwelt upon the effectiveness of Greengay's dash and color and assurance, her mind always came back to Percy's neat little head, his clean-cut face, and warm, clear, gray eyes, and she liked them better than Charley's fullness and blurred floridness. Having reckoned up their respective chances with no doubtful result, she opposed a mild obstinacy to her own good sense. "I guess I'll take Percy, *anyway*," she said simply, and that was all the good her clever business brain did her.

Percy spent a night of torment, lying tense on his bed in the dark, and figuring out how long it would take him to pay back the money he was advancing to himself. Any fool could do it in five years, he reasoned, but he was going to do it in three. The trouble was that his expensive courtship had taken every penny of his salary. With competitors like Charley Greengay, you had to spend money or drop out. Certain birds, he reflected ruefully, are supplied with more attractive plumage when they are courting, but nature hadn't been so thoughtful for men. When Percy reached the office in the morning he climbed on his tall stool and leaned his arms on his ledger. He was so glad to feel it there that he was faint and weak-kneed.

Oliver Remsen, Junior, had brought new blood into the Remsen Paper Company. He married shortly after Percy Bixby did, and in the five succeeding years he had considerably enlarged the company's business and profits. He had been particularly successful in encouraging efficiency and loyalty in the employees. From the time he came into the office he had stood for shorter hours, longer holidays, and a generous consideration of men's necessities. He came out of college on the wave of economic reform, and he continued to read and think a good deal about how the machinery of labor is operated. He knew more about the men who worked for him than their mere office records.

Young Remsen was troubled about Percy Bixby because he took no summer vacations—always asked for the two weeks'

extra pay instead. Other men in the office had skipped a vaca-
tion now and then, but Percy had stuck to his desk for five
years, had tottered to his stool through attacks of grippe and
tonsilitis. He seemed to have grown fast to his ledger, and it
was to this that Oliver objected. He liked his men to stay
men, to look like men and live like men. He remembered how
alert and wide-awake Bixby had seemed to him when he him-
self first came into the office. He had picked Bixby out as the
most intelligent and interested of his father's employees, and
since then had often wondered why he never seemed to see
chances to forge ahead. Promotions, of course, went to the
men who went after them. When Percy's baby died, he went
to the funeral, and asked Percy to call on him if he needed
money. Once when he chanced to sit down by Bixby on the
elevated and found him reading Bryce's "American Common-
wealth," he asked him to make use of his own large office
library. Percy thanked him, but he never came for any books.
Oliver wondered whether his bookkeeper really tried to avoid
him.

One evening Oliver met the Bixbys in the lobby of a the-
ater. He introduced Mrs. Remsen to them, and held them for
some moments in conversation. When they got into their mo-
tor, Mrs. Remsen said:

"Is that little man afraid of you, Oliver? He looked like a
scared rabbit."

Oliver snapped the door, and said with a shade of irri-
tation:

"I don't know what's the matter with him. He's the fellow
I've told you about who never takes a vacation. I half believe
it's his wife. She looks pitiless enough for anything."

"She's very pretty of her kind," mused Mrs. Remsen, "but
rather chilling. One can see that she has ideas about ele-
gance."

"Rather unfortunate ones for a bookkeeper's wife. I sur-
mise that Percy felt she was overdressed, and that made him
awkward with me. I've always suspected that fellow of good
taste."

After that, when Remsen passed the counting-room and
saw Percy screwed up over his ledger, he often remembered
Mrs. Bixby, with her cold, pale eyes and long lashes, and her

expression that was something between indifference and discontent. She rose behind Percy's bent shoulders like an apparition.

One spring afternoon Remsen was closeted in his private office with his lawyer until a late hour. As he came down the long hall in the dusk he glanced through the glass partition into the counting-room, and saw Percy Bixby huddled up on his tall stool, though it was too dark to work. Indeed, Bixby's ledger was closed, and he sat with his two arms resting on the brown cover. He did not move a muscle when young Remsen entered.

"You are late, Bixby, and so am I," Oliver began genially as he crossed to the front of the room and looked out at the lighted windows of other tall buildings. "The fact is, I've been doing something that men have a foolish way of putting off. I've been making my will."

"Yes, sir." Percy brought it out with a deep breath.

"Glad to be through with it," Oliver went on. "Mr. Melton will bring the paper back to-morrow, and I'd like to ask you to be one of the witnesses."

"I'd be very proud, Mr. Remsen."

"Thank you, Bixby. Good night." Remsen took up his hat just as Percy slid down from his stool.

"Mr. Remsen, I'm told you're going to have the books gone over."

"Why, yes, Bixby. Don't let that trouble you. I'm taking in a new partner, you know, an old college friend. Just because he is a friend, I insist upon all the usual formalities. But it is a formality, and I'll guarantee the expert won't make a scratch on your books. Good night. You'd better be coming, too." Remsen had reached the door when he heard "Mr. Remsen!" in a desperate voice behind him. He turned, and saw Bixby standing uncertainly at one end of the desk, his hand still on his ledger, his uneven shoulders drooping forward and his head hanging as if he were seasick. Remsen came back and stood at the other end of the long desk. It was too dark to see Bixby's face clearly.

"What is it, Bixby?"

"Mr. Remsen, five years ago, just before I was married, I falsified the books a thousand dollars, and I used the money."

Percy leaned forward against his desk, which took him just across the chest.

"What's that, Bixby?" Young Remsen spoke in a tone of polite surprise. He felt painfully embarrassed.

"Yes, sir. I thought I'd get it all paid back before this. I've put back three hundred, but the books are still seven hundred out of true. I've played the shortages about from account to account these five years, but an expert would find 'em in twenty-four hours."

"I don't just understand how—" Oliver stopped and shook his head.

"I held it out of the Western remittances, Mr. Remsen. They were coming in heavy just then. I was up against it. I hadn't saved anything to marry on, and my wife thought I was getting more money than I was. Since we've been married, I've never had the nerve to tell her. I could have paid it all back if it hadn't been for the unforeseen expenses."

Remsen sighed.

"Being married is largely unforeseen expenses, Percy. There's only one way to fix this up: I'll give you seven hundred dollars in cash to-morrow, and you can give me your personal note, with the understanding that I hold ten dollars a week out of your pay-check until it is paid. I think you ought to tell your wife exactly how you are fixed, though. You can't expect her to help you much when she doesn't know."

That night Mrs. Bixby was sitting in their flat, waiting for her husband. She was dressed for a bridge party, and often looked with impatience from her paper to the Mission clock, as big as a coffin and with nothing but two weights dangling in its hollow framework. Percy had been loath to buy the clock when they got their furniture, and he had hated it ever since. Stella had changed very little since she came into the flat a bride. Then she wore her hair in a Floradora pompadour; now she wore it hooded close about her head like a scarf, in a rather smeary manner, like an Impressionist's brush-work. She heard her husband come in and close the door softly. While he was taking off his hat in the narrow tunnel of a hall, she called to him:

"I hope you've had something to eat down-town. You'll

have to dress right away." Percy came in and sat down. She looked up from the evening paper she was reading. "You've no time to sit down. We must start in fifteen minutes."

He shaded his eyes from the glaring overhead light.

"I'm afraid I can't go anywhere to-night. I'm all in."

Mrs. Bixby rattled her paper, and turned from the theatrical page to the fashions.

"You'll feel better after you dress. We won't stay late."

Her even persistence usually conquered her husband. She never forgot anything she had once decided to do. Her manner of following it up grew more chilly, but never weaker. To-night there was no spring in Percy. He closed his eyes and replied without moving:

"I can't go. You had better telephone the Burks we aren't coming. I have to tell you something disagreeable."

Stella rose.

"I certainly am not going to disappoint the Burks and stay at home to talk about anything disagreeable."

"You're not very sympathetic, Stella."

She turned away.

"If I were, you'd soon settle down into a pretty dull proposition. We'd have no social life now if I didn't keep at you."

Percy roused himself a little.

"Social life? Well, we'll have to trim that pretty close for a while. I'm in debt to the company. We've been living beyond our means ever since we were married."

"We can't live on less than we do," Stella said quietly. "No use in taking that up again."

Percy sat up, clutching the arms of his chair.

"We'll have to take it up. I'm seven hundred dollars short, and the books are to be audited to-morrow. I told young Remsen and he's going to take my note and hold the money out of my pay-checks. He could send me to jail, of course."

Stella turned and looked down at him with a gleam of interest.

"Oh, you've been playing solitaire with the books, have you? And he's found you out! I hope I'll never see that man again. Sugar face!" She said this with intense acrimony. Her forehead flushed delicately, and her eyes were full of hate. Young Remsen was not her idea of a "business man."

Stella went into the other room. When she came back she wore her evening coat and carried long gloves and a black scarf. This she began to arrange over her hair before the mirror above the false fireplace. Percy lay inert in the Morris chair and watched her. Yes, he understood; it was very difficult for a woman with hair like that to be shabby and to go without things. Her hair made her conspicuous, and it had to be lived up to. It had been the deciding factor in his fate.

Stella caught the lace over one ear with a large gold hairpin. She repeated this until she got a good effect. Then turning to Percy, she began to draw on her gloves.

"I'm not worrying any, because I'm going back into business," she said firmly. "I meant to, anyway, if you didn't get a raise the first of the year. I have the offer of a good position, and we can live in an apartment hotel."

Percy was on his feet in an instant.

"I won't have you grinding in any office. That's flat."

Stella's lower lip quivered in a commiserating smile. "Oh, I won't lose my health. Charley Greengay's a partner in his concern now, and he wants a private secretary."

Percy drew back.

"You can't work for Greengay. He's got too bad a reputation. You've more pride than that, Stella."

The thin sweep of color he knew so well went over Stella's face.

"His business reputation seems to be all right," she commented, working the kid on with her left hand.

"What if it is?" Percy broke out. "He's the cheapest kind of a skate. He gets into scrapes with the girls in his own office. The last one got into the newspapers, and he had to pay the girl a wad."

"He don't get into scrapes with his books, anyway, and he seems to be able to stand getting into the papers. I excuse Charley. His wife's a pill."

"I suppose you think he'd have been all right if he'd married you," said Percy, bitterly.

"Yes, I do." Stella buttoned her glove with an air of finishing something, and then looked at Percy without animosity. "Charley and I both have sporty tastes, and we like excitement. You might as well live in Newark if you're going to sit at home in the evening. You ought n't to have married a business woman; you need somebody domestic. There's nothing in this sort of life for either of us."

"That means, I suppose, that you're going around with Greengay and his crowd?"

"Yes, that's my sort of crowd, and you never did fit into it. You're too intellectual. I've always been proud of you, Percy. You're better style than Charley, but that gets tiresome. You will never burn much red fire in New York, now, will you?"

Percy did not reply. He sat looking at the minute-hand of the eviscerated Mission clock. His wife almost never took the trouble to argue with him.

"You're old style, Percy," she went on. "Of course everybody marries and wishes they had n't, but nowadays people get over it. Some women go ahead on the quiet, but I'm giving it to you straight. I'm going to work for Greengay. I like his line of business, and I meet people well. Now I'm going to the Burks'."

Percy dropped his hands limply between his knees.

"I suppose," he brought out, "the real trouble is that you've decided my earning power is not very great."

"That's part of it, and part of it is you're old-fashioned." Stella paused at the door and looked back. "What made you rush me, anyway, Percy?" she asked indulgently. "What did you go and pretend to be a spender and get tied up with me for?"

"I guess everybody wants to be a spender when he's in love," Percy replied.

Stella shook her head mournfully.

"No, you're a spender or you're not. Greengay has been broke three times, fired, down and out, black-listed. But he's always come back, and he always will. You will never be fired, but you'll always be poor." She turned and looked back again before she went out.

Six months later Bixby came to young Oliver Remsen one afternoon and said he would like to have twenty dollars a week held out of his pay until his debt was cleared off.

Oliver looked up at his sallow employee and asked him how he could spare as much as that.

"My expenses are lighter," Bixby replied. "My wife has gone into business with a ready-to-wear firm. She is not living with me any more."

Oliver looked annoyed, and asked him if nothing could be done to readjust his domestic affairs. Bixby said no; they would probably remain as they were.

"But where are you living, Bixby? How have you arranged things?" the young man asked impatiently.

"I'm very comfortable. I live in a boarding-house and have my own furniture. There are several fellows there who are fixed the same way. Their wives went back into business, and they drifted apart."

With a baffled expression Remsen stared at the uneven shoulders under the skin-fitting alpaca desk coat as his book-keeper went out. He had meant to do something for Percy, but somehow, he reflected, one never did do anything for a fellow who had been stung as hard as that.

Century, May 1916

Ardessa

THE GRAND-MANNERED old man who sat at a desk in the reception-room of "The Outcry" offices to receive visitors and incidentally to keep the time-book of the employees, looked up as Miss Devine entered at ten minutes past ten and condescendingly wished him good morning. He bowed profoundly as she minced past his desk, and with an indifferent air took her course down the corridor that led to the editorial offices. Mechanically he opened the flat, black book at his elbow and placed his finger on D, running his eye along the line of figures after the name Devine. "It's banker's hours she keeps, indeed," he muttered. What was the use of entering so capricious a record? Nevertheless, with his usual preliminary flourish he wrote 10:10 under this, the fourth day of May.

The employee who kept banker's hours rustled on down the corridor to her private room, hung up her lavender jacket and her trim spring hat, and readjusted her side combs by the mirror inside her closet door. Glancing at her desk, she rang for an office boy, and reproved him because he had not dusted more carefully and because there were lumps in her paste. When he disappeared with the paste-jar, she sat down to decide which of her employer's letters he should see and which he should not.

Ardessa was not young and she was certainly not handsome. The coquettish angle at which she carried her head was a mannerism surviving from a time when it was more becoming. She shuddered at the cold candor of the new business woman, and was insinuatingly feminine.

Ardessa's employer, like young Lochinvar, had come out of the West, and he had done a great many contradictory things before he became proprietor and editor of "The Outcry." Before he decided to go to New York and make the East take notice of him, O'Mally had acquired a punctual, reliable silver-mine in South Dakota. This silent friend in the background made his journalistic success comparatively easy. He had figured out, when he was a rich nobody in Nevada, that the quickest way to cut into the known world was through the printing-press. He arrived in New York, bought a highly respectable publication, and turned it into a red-hot magazine of protest, which he called "The Outcry." He knew what the West wanted, and it proved to be what everybody secretly wanted. In six years he had done the thing that had hitherto seemed impossible: built up a national weekly, out on the news-stands the same day in New York and San Francisco; a magazine the people howled for, a moving-picture film of their real tastes and interests.

O'Mally bought "The Outcry" to make a stir, not to make a career, but he had got built into the thing more than he ever intended. It had made him a public man and put him into politics. He found the publicity game diverting, and it held him longer than any other game had ever done. He had built up about him an organization of which he was somewhat afraid and with which he was vastly bored. On his staff there were five famous men, and he had made every one of them. At first it amused him to manufacture celebrities. He found he could take an average reporter from the daily press, give him a "line" to follow, a trust to fight, a vice to expose,—this was all in that good time when people were eager to read about their own wickedness,—and in two years the reporter would be recognized as an authority. Other people—Napoleon, Disraeli, Sarah Bernhardt—had discovered that advertising would go a long way; but Marcus O'Mally discovered that in America it would go all the way—as far as you wished to pay its passage. Any human countenance, plastered in three-sheet posters from sea to sea, would be revered by the American people. The strangest thing was that the owners of these grave countenances, staring at their own faces on news-stands and billboards, fell to venerating themselves; and even he, O'Mally, was more or less constrained by these reputations that he had created out of cheap paper and cheap ink.

Constraint was the last thing O'Mally liked. The most engaging and unusual thing about the man was that he couldn't be fooled by the success of his own methods, and no amount of "recognition" could make a stuffed shirt of him. No matter how much he was advertised as a great medicine-man in the councils of the nation, he knew that he was a born gambler and a soldier of fortune. He left his dignified office to take care of itself for a good many months of the year while he played about on the outskirts of social order. He liked being a great man from the East in rough-and-tumble Western cities where he had once been merely an unconsidered spender.

O'Mally's long absences constituted one of the supreme advantages of Ardessa Devine's position. When he was at his post her duties were not heavy, but when he was giving balls in Goldfield, Nevada, she lived an ideal life. She came to the office every day, indeed, to forward such of O'Mally's letters as she thought best, to attend to his club notices and tradesmen's bills, and to taste the sense of her high connections. The great men of the staff were all about her, as contemplative as Buddhas in their private offices, each meditating upon the particular trust or form of vice confided to his care. Thus surrounded, Ardessa had a pleasant sense of being at the heart of things. It was like a mental massage, exercise without exertion. She read and she embroidered. Her room was pleasant, and she liked to be seen at ladylike tasks and to feel herself a graceful contrast to the crude girls in the advertising and circulation departments across the hall. The younger stenographers, who had to get through with the enormous office correspondence, and who rushed about from one editor to another with wire baskets full of letters, made faces as they passed Ardessa's door and saw her cool and cloistered, daintily plying her needle. But no matter how hard the other stenographers were driven, no one, not even one of the five oracles of the staff, dared dictate so much as a letter to Ardessa. Like a sultan's bride, she was inviolate in her lord's absence; she had to be kept for him.

Naturally the other young women employed in "The Outcry" offices disliked Miss Devine. They were all competent girls, trained in the exacting methods of modern business, and they had to make good every day in the week, had to get through with a great deal of work or lose their position. O'Mally's private secretary was a mystery to them. Her exemptions and privileges, her patronizing remarks, formed an exhaustless subject of conversation at the lunch-hour. Ardessa had, indeed, as they knew she must have, a kind of "purchase" on her employer.

When O'Mally first came to New York to break into pub-

licity, he engaged Miss Devine upon the recommendation of
the editor whose ailing publication he bought and rechris-
tened. That editor was a conservative, scholarly gentleman of
the old school, who was retiring because he felt out of place
in the world of brighter, breezier magazines that had been
flowering since the new century came in. He believed that in
this vehement world young O'Mally would make himself
heard and that Miss Devine's training in an editorial office
would be of use to him.

When O'Mally first sat down at a desk to be an editor, all
the cards that were brought in looked pretty much alike to
him. Ardessa was at his elbow. She had long been steeped in
literary distinctions and in the social distinctions which used
to count for much more than they do now. She knew all the
great men, all the nephews and clients of great men. She
knew which must be seen, which must be made welcome, and
which could safely be sent away. She could give O'Mally on
the instant the former rating in magazine offices of nearly
every name that was brought in to him. She could give him
an idea of the man's connections, of the price his work com-
manded, and insinuate whether he ought to be met with the
old punctiliousness or with the new joviality. She was useful
in explaining to her employer the significance of various invi-
tations, and the standing of clubs and associations. At first she
was virtually the social mentor of the bullet-headed young
Westerner who wanted to break into everything, the solitary
person about the office of the humming new magazine who
knew anything about the editorial traditions of the eighties
and nineties which, antiquated as they now were, gave an
editor, as O'Mally said, a background.

Despite her indolence, Ardessa was useful to O'Mally as a
social reminder. She was the card catalogue of his ever-
changing personal relations. O'Mally went in for everything
and got tired of everything; that was why he made a good
editor. After he was through with people, Ardessa was very
skilful in covering his retreat. She read and answered the let-
ters of admirers who had begun to bore him. When great
authors, who had been dined and fêted the month before,
were suddenly left to cool their heels in the reception-room,
thrown upon the suave hospitality of the grand old man at

the desk, it was Ardessa who went out and made soothing
and plausible explanations as to why the editor could not see
them. She was the brake that checked the too-eager neophyte,
the emollient that eased the severing of relationships, the gen-
tle extinguisher of the lights that failed. When there were no
longer messages of hope and cheer to be sent to ardent young
writers and reformers, Ardessa delivered, as sweetly as possi-
ble, whatever messages were left.

In handling these people with whom O'Mally was quite
through, Ardessa had gradually developed an industry which
was immensely gratifying to her own vanity. Not only did she
not crush them; she even fostered them a little. She continued
to advise them in the reception-room and "personally" re-
ceived their manuscripts long after O'Mally had declared that
he would never read another line they wrote. She let them
outline their plans for stories and articles to her, promising to
bring these suggestions to the editor's attention. She denied
herself to nobody, was gracious even to the Shakspere-Bacon
man, the perpetual-motion man, the travel-article man, the
ghosts which haunt every magazine office. The writers who
had had their happy hour of O'Mally's favor kept feeling that
Ardessa might reinstate them. She answered their letters of
inquiry in her most polished and elegant style, and even gave
them hints as to the subjects in which the restless editor was
or was not interested at the moment: she feared it would be
useless to send him an article on "How to Trap Lions," be-
cause he had just bought an article on "Elephant-Shooting in
Majuba Land," etc.

So when O'Mally plunged into his office at 11:30 on this,
the fourth day of May, having just got back from three-days'
fishing, he found Ardessa in the reception-room, surrounded
by a little court of discards. This was annoying, for he always
wanted his stenographer at once. Telling the office boy to give
her a hint that she was needed, he threw off his hat and top-
coat and began to race through the pile of letters Ardessa had
put on his desk. When she entered, he did not wait for her
polite inquiries about his trip, but broke in at once.

"What is that fellow who writes about phossy jaw still
hanging round here for? I don't want any articles on phossy
jaw, and if I did, I wouldn't want his."

"He has just sold an article on the match industry to 'The New Age,' Mr. O'Mally," Ardessa replied as she took her seat at the editor's right.

"Why does he have to come and tell us about it? We've nothing to do with 'The New Age.' And that prison-reform guy, what's he loafing about for?"

Ardessa bridled.

"You remember, Mr. O'Mally, he brought letters of introduction from Governor Harper, the reform Governor of Mississippi."

O'Mally jumped up, kicking over his waste-basket in his impatience.

"That was months ago. I went through his letters and went through him, too. He has n't got anything we want. I've been through with Governor Harper a long while. We're asleep at the switch in here. And let me tell you, if I catch sight of that causes-of-blindness-in-babies woman around here again, I'll do something violent. Clear them out, Miss Devine! Clear them out! We need a traffic policeman in this office. Have you got that article on 'Stealing Our National Water Power' ready for me?"

"Mr. Gerrard took it back to make modifications. He gave it to me at noon on Saturday, just before the office closed. I will have it ready for you to-morrow morning, Mr. O'Mally, if you have not too many letters for me this afternoon," Ardessa replied pointedly.

"Holy Mike!" muttered O'Mally, "we need a traffic policeman for the staff, too. Gerrard's modified that thing half a dozen times already. Why don't they get accurate information in the first place?"

He began to dictate his morning mail, walking briskly up and down the floor by way of giving his stenographer an energetic example. Her indolence and her ladylike deportment weighed on him. He wanted to take her by the elbows and run her around the block. He did n't mind that she loafed when he was away, but it was becoming harder and harder to speed her up when he was on the spot. He knew his correspondence was not enough to keep her busy, so when he was in town he made her type his own breezy editorials and various articles by members of his staff.

Transcribing editorial copy is always laborious, and the only way to make it easy is to farm it out. This Ardessa was usually clever enough to do. When she returned to her own room after O'Mally had gone out to lunch, Ardessa rang for an office boy and said languidly, "James, call Becky, please."

In a moment a thin, tense-faced Hebrew girl of eighteen or nineteen came rushing in, carrying a wire basket full of typewritten sheets. She was as gaunt as a plucked spring chicken, and her cheap, gaudy clothes might have been thrown on her. She looked as if she were running to catch a train and in mortal dread of missing it. While Miss Devine examined the pages in the basket, Becky stood with her shoulders drawn up and her elbows drawn in, apparently trying to hide herself in her insufficient open-work waist. Her wild, black eyes followed Miss Devine's hands desperately. Ardessa sighed.

"This seems to be very smeary copy again, Becky. You don't keep your mind on your work, and so you have to erase continually."

Becky spoke up in wailing self-vindication.

"It ain't that, Miss Devine. It's so many hard words he uses that I have to be at the dictionary all the time. Look! Look!" She produced a bunch of manuscript faintly scrawled in pencil, and thrust it under Ardessa's eyes. "He don't write out the words at all. He just begins a word, and then makes waves for you to guess."

"I see you have n't always guessed correctly, Becky," said Ardessa, with a weary smile. "There are a great many words here that would surprise Mr. Gerrard, I am afraid."

"And the inserts," Becky persisted. "How is anybody to tell where they go, Miss Devine? It's mostly inserts; see, all over the top and sides and back."

Ardessa turned her head away.

"Don't claw the pages like that, Becky. You make me nervous. Mr. Gerrard has not time to dot his i's and cross his t's. That is what we keep copyists for. I will correct these sheets for you,—it would be terrible if Mr. O'Mally saw them,— and then you can copy them over again. It must be done by to-morrow morning, so you may have to work late. See that your hands are clean and dry, and then you will not smear it."

"Yes, ma'am. Thank you, Miss Devine. Will you tell the

janitor, please, it's all right if I have to stay? He was cross because I was here Saturday afternoon doing this. He said it was a holiday, and when everybody else was gone I ought to—"

"That will do, Becky. Yes, I will speak to the janitor for you. You may go to lunch now."

Becky turned on one heel and then swung back.

"Miss Devine," she said anxiously, "will it be all right if I get white shoes for now?"

Ardessa gave her kind consideration.

"For office wear, you mean? No, Becky. With only one pair, you could not keep them properly clean; and black shoes are much less conspicuous. Tan, if you prefer."

Becky looked down at her feet. They were too large, and her skirt was as much too short as her legs were too long.

"Nearly all the girls I know wear white shoes to business," she pleaded.

"They are probably little girls who work in factories or department stores, and that is quite another matter. Since you raise the question, Becky, I ought to speak to you about your new waist. Don't wear it to the office again, please. Those cheap open-work waists are not appropriate in an office like this. They are all very well for little chorus girls."

"But Miss Kalski wears expensive waists to business more open than this, and jewelry—"

Ardessa interrupted. Her face grew hard.

"Miss Kalski," she said coldly, "works for the business department. You are employed in the editorial offices. There is a great difference. You see, Becky, I might have to call you in here at any time when a scientist or a great writer or the president of a university is here talking over editorial matters, and such clothes as you have on to-day would make a bad impression. Nearly all our connections are with important people of that kind, and we ought to be well, but quietly, dressed."

"Yes, Miss Devine. Thank you," Becky gasped and disappeared. Heaven knew she had no need to be further impressed with the greatness of "The Outcry" office. During the year and a half she had been there she had never ceased to tremble. She knew the prices all the authors got as well as

Miss Devine did, and everything seemed to her to be done on a magnificent scale. She hadn't a good memory for long technical words, but she never forgot dates or prices or initials or telephone numbers.

Becky felt that her job depended on Miss Devine, and she was so glad to have it that she scarcely realized she was being bullied. Besides, she was grateful for all that she had learned from Ardessa; Ardessa had taught her to do most of the things that she was supposed to do herself. Becky wanted to learn, she had to learn; that was the train she was always running for. Her father, Isaac Tietelbaum, the tailor, who pressed Miss Devine's skirts and kept her ladylike suits in order, had come to his client two years ago and told her he had a bright girl just out of a commercial high school. He implored Ardessa to find some office position for his daughter. Ardessa told an appealing story to O'Mally, and brought Becky into the office, at a salary of six dollars a week, to help with the copying and to learn business routine. When Becky first came she was as ignorant as a young savage. She was rapid at her shorthand and typing, but a Kafir girl would have known as much about the English language. Nobody ever wanted to learn more than Becky. She fairly wore the dictionary out. She dug up her old school grammar and worked over it at night. She faithfully mastered Miss Devine's fussy system of punctuation.

There were eight children at home, younger than Becky, and they were all eager to learn. They wanted to get their mother out of the three dark rooms behind the tailor shop and to move into a flat up-stairs, where they could, as Becky said, "live private." The young Tietelbaums doubted their father's ability to bring this change about, for the more things he declared himself ready to do in his window placards, the fewer were brought to him to be done. "Dyeing, Cleaning, Ladies' Furs Remodeled"—it did no good.

Rebecca was out to "improve herself," as her father had told her she must. Ardessa had easy way with her. It was one of those rare relationships from which both persons profit. The more Becky could learn from Ardessa, the happier she was; and the more Ardessa could unload on Becky, the greater was her contentment. She easily broke Becky of the gum-chewing habit, taught her to walk quietly, to efface herself at the proper moment, and to hold her tongue. Becky had been raised to eight dollars a week; but she did n't care half so much about that as she did about her own increasing efficiency. The more work Miss Devine handed over to her the happier she was, and the faster she was able to eat it up. She tested and tried herself in every possible way. She now had full confidence that she would surely one day be a high-priced stenographer, a real "business woman."

Becky would have corrupted a really industrious person, but a bilious temperament like Ardessa's could n't make even a feeble stand against such willingness. Ardessa had grown soft and had lost the knack of turning out work. Sometimes, in her importance and serenity, she shivered. What if O'Mally should die, and she were thrust out into the world to work in competition with the brazen, competent young women she saw about her everywhere? She believed herself indispensable, but she knew that in such a mischanceful world as this the very powers of darkness might rise to separate her from this pearl among jobs.

When Becky came in from lunch she went down the long hall to the wash-room, where all the little girls who worked in the advertising and circulation departments kept their hats and jackets. There were shelves and shelves of bright spring hats, piled on top of one another, all as stiff as sheet-iron and trimmed with gay flowers. At the marble wash-stand stood Rena Kalski, the right bower of the business manager, polishing her diamond rings with a nail-brush.

"Hullo, kid," she called over her shoulder to Becky. "I've got a ticket for you for Thursday afternoon."

Becky's black eyes glowed, but the strained look on her face drew tighter than ever.

"I'll never ask her, Miss Kalski," she said rapidly. "I don't dare. I have to stay late to-night again; and I know she'd be hard to please after, if I was to try to get off on a week-day. I thank you, Miss Kalski, but I'd better not."

Miss Kalski laughed. She was a slender young Hebrew, handsome in an impudent, Tenderloin sort of way, with a small head, reddish-brown almond eyes, a trifle tilted, a rapacious mouth, and a beautiful chin.

"Ain't you under that woman's thumb, though! Call her

bluff. She is n't half the prima donna she thinks she is. On my side of the hall we know who 's who about this place."

The business and editorial departments of "The Outcry" were separated by a long corridor and a great contempt. Miss Kalski dried her rings with tissue-paper and studied them with an appraising eye.

"Well, since you 're such a 'fraidy-calf,' " she went on, "maybe I can get a rise out of her myself. Now I 've got you a ticket out of that shirt-front, I want you to go. I 'll drop in on Devine this afternoon."

When Miss Kalski went back to her desk in the business manager's private office, she turned to him familiarly, but not impertinently.

"Mr. Henderson, I want to send a kid over in the editorial stenographers' to the Palace Thursday afternoon. She 's a nice kid, only she 's scared out of her skin all the time. Miss Devine 's her boss, and she 'll be just mean enough not to let the young one off. Would you say a word to her?"

The business manager lit a cigar.

"I 'm not saying words to any of the high-brows over there. Try it out with Devine yourself. You 're not bashful."

Miss Kalski shrugged her shoulders and smiled.

"Oh, very well." She serpentined out of the room and crossed the Rubicon into the editorial offices. She found Ardessa typing O'Mally's letters and wearing a pained expression.

"Good afternoon, Miss Devine," she said carelessly. "Can we borrow Becky over there for Thursday afternoon? We 're short."

Miss Devine looked piqued and tilted her head.

"I don't think it 's customary, Miss Kalski, for the business department to use our people. We never have girls enough here to do the work. Of course if Mr. Henderson feels justified—"

"Thanks awfully, Miss Devine,"—Miss Kalski interrupted her with the perfectly smooth, good-natured tone which never betrayed a hint of the scorn every line of her sinuous figure expressed,—"I will tell Mr. Henderson. Perhaps we can do something for you some day." Whether this was a threat, a kind wish, or an insinuation, no mortal could have told. Miss Kalski's face was always suggesting insolence without being quite insolent. As she returned to her own domain she met the cashier's head clerk in the hall. "That Devine woman's a crime," she murmured. The head clerk laughed tolerantly.

That afternoon as Miss Kalski was leaving the office at 5:15, on her way down the corridor she heard a typewriter clicking away in the empty, echoing editorial offices. She looked in, and found Becky bending forward over the machine as if she were about to swallow it.

"Hello, kid. Do you sleep with that?" she called. She walked up to Becky and glanced at her copy. "What do you let 'em keep you up nights over that stuff for?" she asked contemptuously. "The world wouldn't suffer if that stuff never got printed."

Rebecca looked up wildly. Not even Miss Kalski's French pansy hat or her ear-rings and landscape veil could loosen Becky's tenacious mind from Mr. Gerrard's article on water power. She scarcely knew what Miss Kalski had said to her, certainly not what she meant.

"But I must make progress already, Miss Kalski," she panted.

Miss Kalski gave her low, siren laugh.

"I should say you must!" she ejaculated.

Ardessa decided to take her vacation in June, and she arranged that Miss Milligan should do O'Mally's work while she was away. Miss Milligan was blunt and noisy, rapid and inaccurate. It would be just as well for O'Mally to work with a coarse instrument for a time; he would be more appreciative, perhaps, of certain qualities to which he had seemed insensible of late. Ardessa was to leave for East Hampton on Sunday, and she spent Saturday morning instructing her substitute as to the state of the correspondence. At noon O'Mally burst into her room. All the morning he had been closeted with a new writer of mystery-stories just over from England.

"Can you stay and take my letters this afternoon, Miss Devine? You're not leaving until to-morrow."

Ardessa pouted, and tilted her head at the angle he was tired of.

"I'm sorry, Mr. O'Mally, but I've left all my shopping for this afternoon. I think Becky Tietelbaum could do them for you. I will tell her to be careful."

"Oh, all right." O'Mally bounced out with a reflection of Ardessa's disdainful expression on his face. Saturday afternoon was always a half-holiday, to be sure, but since she had weeks of freedom when he was away— However—

At two o'clock Becky Tietelbaum appeared at his door, clad in the sober office suit which Miss Devine insisted she should wear, her note-book in her hand, and so frightened that her fingers were cold and her lips were pale. She had never taken dictation from the editor before. It was a great and terrifying occasion.

"Sit down," he said encouragingly. He began dictating while he shook from his bag the manuscripts he had snatched away from the amazed English author that morning. Presently he looked up.

"Do I go too fast?"

"No, sir," Becky found strength to say.

At the end of an hour he told her to go and type as many of the letters as she could while he went over the bunch of stuff he had torn from the Englishman. He was with the Hindu detective in an opium den in Shanghai when Becky returned and placed a pile of papers on his desk.

"How many?" he asked, without looking up.

"All you gave me, sir."

"All, so soon? Wait a minute and let me see how many mistakes." He went over the letters rapidly, signing them as he read. "They seem to be all right. I thought you were the girl that made so many mistakes."

Rebecca was never too frightened to vindicate herself.

"Mr. O'Mally, sir, I don't make mistakes with letters. It's only copying the articles that have so many long words, and when the writing isn't plain, like Mr. Gerrard's. I never make many mistakes with Mr. Johnson's articles, or with yours I don't."

O'Mally wheeled round in his chair, looked with curiosity at her long, tense face, her black eyes, and straight brows.

"Oh, so you sometimes copy articles, do you? How does that happen?"

"Yes, sir. Always Miss Devine gives me the articles to do. It's good practice for me."

"I see." O'Mally shrugged his shoulders. He was thinking that he could get a rise out of the whole American public any day easier than he could get a rise out of Ardessa. "What editorials of mine have you copied lately, for instance?"

Rebecca blazed out at him, reciting rapidly:

"Oh, 'A Word about the Rosenbaums,' 'Useless Navy-Yards,' 'Who Killed Cock Robin'—"

"Wait a minute." O'Mally checked her flow. "What was that one about—Cock Robin?"

"It was all about why the secretary of the interior dismissed—"

"All right, all right. Copy those letters, and put them down the chute as you go out. Come in here for a minute on Monday morning."

Becky hurried home to tell her father that she had taken the editor's letters and had made no mistakes. On Monday she learned that she was to do O'Mally's work for a few days. He disliked Miss Milligan, and he was annoyed with Ardessa for trying to put her over on him when there was better material at hand. With Rebecca he got on very well; she was impersonal, unreproachful, and she fairly panted for work. Everything was done almost before he told her what he wanted. She raced ahead with him; it was like riding a good modern bicycle after pumping along on an old hard tire.

On the day before Miss Devine's return O'Mally strolled over for a chat with the business office.

"Henderson, your people are taking vacations now, I suppose? Could you use an extra girl?"

"If it's that thin black one, I can."

O'Mally gave him a wise smile.

"It isn't. To be honest, I want to put one over on you. I want you to take Miss Devine over here for a while and speed her up. I can't do anything. She's got the upper hand of me. I don't want to fire her, you understand, but she makes my life too difficult. It's my fault, of course. I've pampered her. Give her a chance over here; maybe she'll come back. You can be firm with 'em, can't you?"

Henderson glanced toward the desk where Miss Kalski's

lightning eye was skimming over the printing-house bills that he was supposed to verify himself.

"Well, if I can't, I know who can," he replied, with a chuckle.

"Exactly," O'Mally agreed. "I'm counting on the force of Miss Kalski's example. Miss Devine's all right, Miss Kalski, but she needs regular exercise. She owes it to her complexion. I can't discipline people."

Miss Kalski's only reply was a low, indulgent laugh.

O'Mally braced himself on the morning of Ardessa's return. He told the waiter at his club to bring him a second pot of coffee and to bring it hot. He was really afraid of her. When she presented herself at his office at 10:30 he complimented her upon her tan and asked about her vacation. Then he broke the news to her.

"We want to make a few temporary changes about here, Miss Devine, for the summer months. The business department is short of help. Henderson is going to put Miss Kalski on the books for a while to figure out some economies for him, and he is going to take you over. Meantime I'll get Becky broken in so that she could take your work if you were sick or anything."

Ardessa drew herself up.

"I've not been accustomed to commercial work, Mr. O'Mally. I've no interest in it, and I don't care to brush up in it."

"Brushing up is just what we need, Miss Devine." O'Mally began tramping about his room expansively. "I'm going to brush everybody up. I'm going to brush a few people out; but I want you to stay with us, of course. You belong here. Don't be hasty now. Go to your room and think it over."

Ardessa was beginning to cry, and O'Mally was afraid he would lose his nerve. He looked out of the window at a new sky-scraper that was building, while she retired without a word.

At her own desk Ardessa sat down breathless and trembling. The one thing she had never doubted was her unique value to O'Mally. She had, as she told herself, taught him everything. She would say a few things to Becky Tietelbaum, and to that pigeon-breasted tailor, her father, too! The worst of it was that Ardessa had herself brought it all about; she could see that clearly now. She had carefully trained and qualified her successor. Why had she ever civilized Becky? Why had she taught her manners and deportment, broken her of the gum-chewing habit, and made her presentable? In her original state O'Mally would never have put up with her, no matter what her ability.

Ardessa told herself that O'Mally was notoriously fickle; Becky amused him, but he would soon find out her limitations. The wise thing, she knew, was to humor him; but it seemed to her that she could not swallow her pride. Ardessa grew yellower within the hour. Over and over in her mind she bade O'Mally a cold adieu and minced out past the grand old man at the desk for the last time. But each exit she rehearsed made her feel sorrier for herself. She thought over all the offices she knew, but she realized that she could never meet their inexorable standards of efficiency.

While she was bitterly deliberating, O'Mally himself wandered in, rattling his keys nervously in his pocket. He shut the door behind him.

"Now, you're going to come through with this all right, aren't you, Miss Devine? I want Henderson to get over the notion that my people over here are stuck up and think the business department are old shoes. That's where we get our money from, as he often reminds me. You'll be the best-paid girl over there; no reduction, of course. You don't want to go wandering off to some new office where personality doesn't count for anything." He sat down confidentially on the edge of her desk. "Do you, now, Miss Devine?"

Ardessa simpered tearfully as she replied.

"Mr. O'Mally," she brought out, "you'll soon find that Becky is not the sort of girl to meet people for you when you are away. I don't see how you can think of letting her."

"That's one thing I want to change, Miss Devine. You're too soft-handed with the has-beens and the never-was-ers. You're too much of a lady for this rough game. Nearly everybody who comes in here wants to sell us a gold-brick, and you treat them as if they were bringing in wedding presents. Becky is as rough as sandpaper, and she'll clear out a lot of dead wood." O'Mally rose, and tapped Ardessa's shrinking shoulder. "Now, be a sport and go through with it, Miss Devine. I'll see that you don't lose. Henderson thinks you'll refuse to do his work, so I want you to get moved in there before he comes back from lunch. I've had a desk put in his office for you. Miss Kalski is in the bookkeeper's room half the time now."

Rena Kalski was amazed that afternoon when a line of office boys entered, carrying Miss Devine's effects, and when Ardessa herself coldly followed them. After Ardessa had arranged her desk, Miss Kalski went over to her and told her about some matters of routine very good-naturedly. Ardessa looked pretty badly shaken up, and Rena bore no grudges.

"When you want the dope on the correspondence with the paper men, don't bother to look it up. I've got it all in my head, and I can save time for you. If he wants you to go over the printing bills every week, you'd better let me help you with that for a while. I can stay almost any afternoon. It's quite a trick to figure out the plates and over-time charges till you get used to it. I've worked out a quick method that saves trouble."

When Henderson came in at three he found Ardessa, chilly, but civil, awaiting his instructions. He knew she disapproved of his tastes and his manners, but he didn't mind. What interested and amused him was that Rena Kalski, whom he had always thought as cold-blooded as an adding-machine, seemed to be making a hair-mattress of herself to break Ardessa's fall.

At five o'clock, when Ardessa rose to go, the business manager said breezily:

"See you at nine in the morning, Miss Devine. We begin on the stroke."

Ardessa faded out of the door, and Miss Kalski's slender back squirmed with amusement.

"I never thought to hear such words spoken," she admitted; "but I guess she'll limber up all right. The atmosphere is bad over there. They get moldy."

After the next monthly luncheon of the heads of departments, O'Mally said to Henderson, as he feed the coat-boy:

"By the way, how are you making it with the bartered bride?"

Henderson smashed on his Panama as he said:

"Any time you want her back, don't be delicate."

But O'Mally shook his red head and laughed.

"Oh, I'm no Indian giver!"

Century, May 1918

Her Boss

Paul Wanning opened the front door of his house in Orange, closed it softly behind him, and stood looking about the hall as he drew off his gloves.

Nothing was changed there since last night, and yet he stood gazing about him with an interest which a long-married man does not often feel in his own reception hall. The rugs, the two pillars, the Spanish tapestry chairs, were all the same. The Venus di Medici stood on her column as usual and there, at the end of the hall (opposite the front door), was the full-length portrait of Mrs. Wanning, maturely blooming forth in an evening gown, signed with the name of a French painter who seemed purposely to have made his signature indistinct. Though the signature was largely what one paid for, one couldn't ask him to do it over.

In the dining room the colored man was moving about the table set for dinner, under the electric cluster. The candles had not yet been lighted. Wanning watched him with a homesick feeling in his heart. They had had Sam a long while, twelve years, now. His warm hall, the lighted dining-room, the drawing room where only the flicker of the wood fire played upon the shining surfaces of many objects— they seemed to Wanning like a haven of refuge. It had never occurred to him that his house was too full of things. He often said, and he believed, that the women of his household had "perfect taste." He had paid for these objects, sometimes with difficulty, but always with pride. He carried a heavy life-insurance and permitted himself to spend most of the income from a good law practise. He wished, during his life-time, to enjoy the benefits of his wife's discriminating extravagance.

Yesterday Wanning's doctor had sent him to a specialist. Today the specialist, after various laboratory tests, had told him most disconcerting things about the state of very necessary, but hitherto wholly uninteresting, organs of his body.

The information pointed to something incredible; insinuated that his residence in this house was only temporary; that he, whose time was so full, might have to leave not only his house and his office and his club, but a world with which he was extremely well satisfied—the only world he knew anything about.

Wanning unbuttoned his overcoat, but did not take it off. He stood folding his muffler slowly and carefully. What he did not understand was, how he could go while other people stayed. Sam would be moving about the table like this, Mrs. Wanning and her daughters would be dressing upstairs, when he would not be coming home to dinner any more; when he would not, indeed, be dining anywhere.

Sam, coming to turn on the parlor lights, saw Wanning and stepped behind him to take his coat.

"Good evening, Mr. Wanning, sah, excuse me. You entahed so quietly, sah, I didn't heah you."

The master of the house slipped out of his coat and went languidly upstairs.

He tapped at the door of his wife's room, which stood ajar.

"Come in, Paul," she called from her dressing table.

She was seated, in a violet dressing gown, giving the last touches to her coiffure, both arms lifted. They were firm and white, like her neck and shoulders. She was a handsome woman of fifty-five,—still a woman, not an old person, Wanning told himself, as he kissed her cheek. She was heavy in figure, to be sure, but she had kept, on the whole, presentable outlines. Her complexion was good, and she wore less false hair than either of her daughters.

Wanning himself was five years older, but his sandy hair did not show the gray in it, and since his mustache had begun to grow white he kept it clipped so short that it was unobtrusive. His fresh skin made him look younger than he was. Not long ago he had overheard the stenographers in his law office discussing the ages of their employers. They had put him down at fifty, agreeing that his two partners must be considerably older than he—which was not the case. Wanning had an especially kindly feeling for the little new girl, a copyist, who had exclaimed that "Mr. Wanning couldn't be fifty; he seemed so boyish!"

Wanning lingered behind his wife, looking at her in the mirror.

"Well, did you tell the girls, Julia?" he asked, trying to speak casually.

Mrs. Wanning looked up and met his eyes in the glass. "The girls?"

She noticed a strange expression come over his face.

"About your health, you mean? Yes, dear, but I tried not to alarm them. They feel dreadfully. I'm going to have a talk with Dr. Seares myself. These specialists are all alarmists, and I've often heard of his frightening people."

She rose and took her husband's arm, drawing him toward the fireplace.

"You are not going to let this upset you, Paul? If you take care of yourself, everything will come out all right. You have always been so strong. One has only to look at you."

"Did you," Wanning asked, "say anything to Harold?"

"Yes, of course. I saw him in town today, and he agrees with me that Seares draws the worst conclusions possible. He says even the young men are always being told the most terrifying things. Usually they laugh at the doctors and do as they please. You certainly don't look like a sick man, and you don't feel like one, do you?"

She patted his shoulder, smiled at him encouragingly, and rang for the maid to come and hook her dress.

When the maid appeared at the door, Wanning went out through the bathroom to his own sleeping chamber. He was too much dispirited to put on a dinner coat, though such remissness was always noticed. He sat down and waited for the sound of the gong, leaving his door open, on the chance that perhaps one of his daughters would come in.

When Wanning went down to dinner he found his wife already at her chair, and the table laid for four.

"Harold," she explained, "is not coming home. He has to attend a first night in town."

A moment later their two daughters entered, obviously "dressed." They both wore earrings and masses of hair. The daughters' names were Roma and Florence,—Roma, Firenze, one of the young men who came to the house often, but not often enough, had called them. Tonight they were going to a rehearsal of "The Dances of the Nations,"—a benefit performance in which Miss Roma was to lead the Spanish dances, her sister the Grecian.

The elder daughter had often been told that her name suited her admirably. She looked, indeed, as we are apt to think the unrestrained beauties of later Rome must have looked,—but as their portrait busts emphatically declare they did not. Her head was massive, her lips full and crimson, her eyes large and heavy-lidded, her forehead low. At costume balls and in living pictures she was always Semiramis, or Poppea, or Theodora. Barbaric accessories brought out something cruel and even rather brutal in her handsome face. The men who were attracted to her were somehow afraid of her.

Florence was slender, with a long, graceful neck, a restless head, and a flexible mouth—discontent lurked about the corners of it. Her shoulders were pretty, but her neck and arms were too thin. Roma was always struggling to keep within a certain weight—her chin and upper arms grew persistently more solid—and Florence was always striving to attain a certain weight. Wanning used sometimes to wonder why these disconcerting fluctuations could not go the other way; why Roma could not melt away as easily as did her sister, who had to be sent to Palm Beach to save the precious pounds.

"I don't see why you ever put Rickie Allen in charge of the English country dances," Florence said to her sister, as they sat down. "He knows the figures, of course, but he has no real style."

Roma looked annoyed. Rickie Allen was one of the men who came to the house almost often enough.

"He is absolutely to be depended upon, that's why," she said firmly.

"I think he is just right for it, Florence," put in Mrs. Wanning. "It's remarkable he should feel that he can give up the time; such a busy man. He must be very much interested in the movement."

Florence's lip curled drolly under her soup spoon. She shot an amused glance at her mother's dignity.

"Nothing doing," her keen eyes seemed to say.

Though Florence was nearly thirty and her sister a little beyond, there was, seriously, nothing doing. With so many charms and so much preparation, they never, as Florence vulgarly said, quite pulled it off. They had been rushed, time and again, and Mrs. Wanning had repeatedly steeled herself to bear the blow. But the young men went to follow a career in Mexico or the Philippines, or moved to Yonkers, and escaped without a mortal wound.

Roma turned graciously to her father.

"I met Mr. Lane at the Holland House today, where I was lunching with the Burtons, father. He asked about you, and when I told him you were not so well as usual, he said he would call you up. He wants to tell you about some doctor he discovered in Iowa, who cures everything with massage and hot water. It sounds freakish, but Mr. Lane is a very clever man, isn't he?"

"Very," assented Wanning.

"I should think he must be!" sighed Mrs. Wanning. "How in the world did he make all that money, Paul? He didn't seem especially promising years ago, when we used to see so much of them."

"Corporation business. He's attorney for the P. L. and G.," murmured her husband.

"What a pile he must have!" Florence watched the old negro's slow movements with restless eyes. "Here is Jenny, a Contessa, with a glorious palace in Genoa that her father must have bought her. Surely Aldrini had nothing. Have you seen the baby count's pictures, Roma? They're very cunning. I should think you'd go to Genoa and visit Jenny."

"We must arrange that, Roma. It's such an opportunity." Though Mrs. Wanning addressed her daughter, she looked at her husband. "You would get on so well among their friends. When Count Aldrini was here you spoke Italian much better than poor Jenny. I remember when we entertained him, he could scarcely say anything to her at all."

Florence tried to call up an answering flicker of amusement upon her sister's calm, well-bred face. She thought her mother was rather outdoing herself tonight,—since Aldrini had at least managed to say the one important thing to Jenny, somehow, somewhere. Jenny Lane had been Roma's friend and schoolmate, and the Count was an ephemeral hope in Orange. Mrs. Wanning was one of the first matrons to declare that she had no prejudices against foreigners, and at the dinners that were given for the Count, Roma was always put next him to act as interpreter.

Roma again turned to her father.

"If I were you, dear, I would let Mr. Lane tell me about his doctor. New discoveries are often made by queer people."

Roma's voice was low and sympathetic; she never lost her dignity.

Florence asked if she might have her coffee in her room, while she dashed off a note, and she ran upstairs humming "Bright Lights" and wondering how she was going to stand her family until the summer scattering. Why could Roma never throw off her elegant reserve and call things by their names? She sometimes thought she might like her sister, if she would only come out in the open and howl about her disappointments.

Roma, drinking her coffee deliberately, asked her father if they might have the car early, as they wanted to pick up Mr. Allen and Mr. Rydberg on their way to rehearsal.

Wanning said certainly. Heaven knew he was not stingy about his car, though he could never quite forget that in his day it was the young men who used to call for the girls when they went to rehearsals.

"You are going with us, Mother?" Roma asked as they rose.

"I think so dear. Your father will want to go to bed early, and I shall sleep better if I go out. I am going to town tomorrow to pour tea for Harold. We must get him some new silver, Paul. I am quite ashamed of his spoons."

Harold, the only son, was a playwright—as yet "unproduced"—and he had a studio in Washington Square.

A half-hour later, Wanning was alone in his library. He would not permit himself to feel aggrieved. What was more commendable than a mother's interest in her children's pleasures? Moreover, it was his wife's way of following things up, of never letting the grass grow under her feet, that had helped to push him along in the world. She was more ambitious than he,—that had been good for him. He was naturally indolent, and Julia's childlike desire to possess material objects, to buy what other people were buying, had been the spur that made him go after business. It had, moreover, made his house the attractive place he believed it to be.

"Suppose," his wife sometimes said to him when the bills came in from Céleste or Mme. Blanche, "suppose you had homely daughters; how would you like that?"

He wouldn't have liked it. When he went anywhere with his three ladies, Wanning always felt very well done by. He had no complaint to make about them, or about anything. That was why it seemed so unreasonable— He felt along his back incredulously with his hand. Harold, of course, was a trial; but among all his business friends, he knew scarcely one who had a promising boy.

The house was so still that Wanning could hear a faint, metallic tinkle from the butler's pantry. Old Sam was washing up the silver, which he put away himself every night.

Wanning rose and walked aimlessly down the hall and out through the dining-room.

"Any Apollinaris on ice, Sam? I'm not feeling very well to-night."

The old colored man dried his hands.

"Yessah, Mistah Wanning. Have a little rye with it, sah?"

"No, thank you, Sam. That's one of the things I can't do any more. I've been to see a big doctor in the city, and he tells me there's something seriously wrong with me. My kidneys have sort of gone back on me."

It was a satisfaction to Wanning to name the organ that had betrayed him, while all the rest of him was so sound.

Sam was immediately interested. He shook his grizzled head and looked full of wisdom.

"Don't seem like a gen'leman of such a temperate life ought to have anything wrong thar, sah."

"No, it doesn't, does it?"

Wanning leaned against the china closet and talked to Sam for nearly half an hour. The specialist who condemned him hadn't seemed half so much interested. There was not a detail about the examination and the laboratory tests in which Sam did not show the deepest concern. He kept asking Wanning if he could remember "straining himself" when he was a young man.

"I've knowed a strain like that to sleep in a man for yeahs and yeahs, and then come back on him, 'deed I have," he said, mysteriously. "An' again, it might be you got a floatin' kidney, sah. Aftah dey once teah loose, dey sometimes don't make no trouble for quite a while."

When Wanning went to his room he did not go to bed. He sat up until he heard the voices of his wife and daughters in the hall below. His own bed somehow frightened him. In all the years he had lived in this house he had never before looked about his room, at that bed, with the thought that he might one day be trapped there, and might not get out again. He had been ill, of course, but his room had seemed a particularly pleasant place for a sick man; sunlight, flowers,—agreeable, well-dressed women coming in and out.

Now there was something sinister about the bed itself, about its position, and its relation to the rest of the furniture.

II

The next morning, on his way downtown, Wanning got off the subway train at Astor Place and walked over to Washington Square. He climbed three flights of stairs and knocked at his son's studio. Harold, dressed, with his stick and gloves in his hand, opened the door. He was just going over to the Brevoort for breakfast. He greeted his father with the cordial familiarity practised by all the "boys" of his set, clapped him on the shoulder and said in his light, tonsilitis voice:

"Come in, Governor, how delightful! I haven't had a call from you in a long time."

He threw his hat and gloves on the writing table. He was a perfect gentleman, even with his father.

Florence said the matter with Harold was that he had heard people say he looked like Byron, and stood for it.

What Harold would stand for in such matters was, indeed, the best definition of him. When he read his play "The Street Walker" in drawing rooms and one lady told him it had the poetic symbolism of Tchekhov, and another said that it sug-

gested the biting realism of Brieux, he never, in his most se-
cret thoughts, questioned the acumen of either lady. Harold's
speech, even if you heard it in the next room and could not
see him, told you that he had no sense of the absurd,—a
throaty staccato, with never a downward inflection, trustfully
striving to please.

"Just going out?" his father asked. "I won't keep you. Your
mother told you I had a discouraging session with Seares?"

"So awfully sorry you've had this bother, Governor; just as
sorry as I can be. No question about it's coming out all right,
but it's a downright nuisance, your having to diet and that
sort of thing. And I suppose you ought to follow directions,
just to make us all feel comfortable, oughtn't you?" Harold
spoke with fluent sympathy.

Wanning sat down on the arm of a chair and shook his
head. "Yes, they do recommend a diet, but they don't promise
much from it."

Harold laughed precipitately. "Delicious! All doctors are,
aren't they? So profound and oracular! The medicine-man;
it's quite the same idea, you see; with tom-toms."

Wanning knew that Harold meant something subtle,—one
of the subtleties which he said were only spoiled by being
explained—so he came bluntly to one of the issues he had in
mind.

"I would like to see you settled before I quit the harness,
Harold."

Harold was absolutely tolerant.

He took out his cigarette case and burnished it with his
handkerchief.

"I perfectly understand your point of view, dear Governor,
but perhaps you don't altogether get mine. Isn't it so? I am
settled. What you mean by being settled, would unsettle me,
completely. I'm cut out for just such an existence as this; to
live four floors up in an attic, get my own breakfast, and have
a charwoman to do for me. I should be awfully bored with an
establishment. I'm quite content with a little diggings like
this."

Wanning's eyes fell. Somebody had to pay the rent of even
such modest quarters as contented Harold, but to say so
would be rude, and Harold himself was never rude. Wanning

did not, this morning, feel equal to hearing a statement of his son's uncommercial ideals.

"I know," he said hastily. "But now we're up against hard facts, my boy. I did not want to alarm your mother, but I've had a time limit put on me, and it's not a very long one."

Harold threw away the cigarette he had just lighted in a burst of indignation.

"That's the sort of thing I consider criminal, Father, absolutely criminal! What doctor has a right to suggest such a thing? Seares himself may be knocked out tomorrow. What have laboratory tests got to do with a man's will to live? The force of that depends upon his entire personality, not on any organ or pair of organs."

Harold thrust his hands in his pockets and walked up and down, very much stirred. "Really, I have a very poor opinion of scientists. They ought to be made serve an apprenticeship in art, to get some conception of the power of human motives. Such brutality!"

Harold's plays dealt with the grimmest and most depressing matters, but he himself was always agreeable, and he insisted upon high cheerfulness as the correct tone of human intercourse.

Wanning rose and turned to go. There was, in Harold, simply no reality, to which one could break through. The young man took up his hat and gloves.

"Must you go? Let me step along with you to the sub. The walk will do me good."

Harold talked agreeably all the way to Astor Place. His father heard little of what he said, but he rather liked his company and his wish to be pleasant.

Wanning went to his club for luncheon, meaning to spend the afternoon with some of his friends who had retired from business and who read the papers there in the empty hours between two and seven. He got no satisfaction, however. When he tried to tell these men of his present predicament, they began to describe ills of their own in which he could not feel interested. Each one of them had a treacherous organ of which he spoke with animation, almost with pride, as if it were a crafty business competitor whom he was constantly outwitting. Each had a doctor, too, for whom he was ardently soliciting business. They wanted either to telephone their doctor and make an appointment for Wanning, or to take him then and there to the consulting room. When he did not accept these invitations, they lost interest in him and remembered engagements. He called a taxi and returned to the offices of McQuiston, Wade, and Wanning.

Settled at his desk, Wanning decided that he would not go home to dinner, but would stay at the office and dictate a long letter to an old college friend who lived in Wyoming. He could tell Douglas Brown things that he had not succeeded in getting to any one else. Brown, out in the Wind River mountains, couldn't defend himself, couldn't slap Wanning on the back and tell him to gather up the sunbeams.

He called up his house in Orange to say that he would not be home until late. Roma answered the telephone. He spoke mournfully, but she was not disturbed by it.

"Very well, Father. Don't get too tired," she said in her well modulated voice.

When Wanning was ready to dictate his letter, he looked out from his private office into the reception room and saw that his stenographer in her hat and gloves, and furs of the newest cut, was just leaving.

"Goodnight, Mr. Wanning," she said, drawing down her dotted veil.

Had there been important business letters to be got off on the night mail, he would have felt that he could detain her, but not for anything personal. Miss Doane was an expert legal stenographer, and she knew her value. The slightest delay in dispatching office business annoyed her. Letters that were not signed until the next morning awoke her deepest contempt. She was scrupulous in professional etiquette, and Wanning felt that their relations, though pleasant, were scarcely cordial.

As Miss Doane's trim figure disappeared through the outer door, little Annie Wooley, the copyist, came in from the stenographers' room. Her hat was pinned over one ear, and she was scrambling into her coat as she came, holding her gloves in her teeth and her battered handbag in the fist that was already through a sleeve.

"Annie, I wanted to dictate a letter. You were just leaving, weren't you?"

"Oh, I don't mind!" she answered cheerfully, and pulling off her old coat, threw it on a chair. "I'll get my book."

She followed him into his room and sat down by a table,— though she wrote with her book on her knee.

Wanning had several times kept her after office hours to take his private letters for him, and she had always been good-natured about it. On each occasion, when he gave her a dollar to get her dinner, she protested, laughing, and saying that she could never eat so much as that.

She seemed a happy sort of little creature, didn't pout when she was scolded, and giggled about her own mistakes in spelling. She was plump and undersized, always dodging under the elbows of taller people and clattering about on high heels, much run over. She had bright black eyes and fuzzy black hair in which, despite Miss Doane's reprimands, she often stuck her pencil. She was the girl who couldn't believe that Wanning was fifty, and he had liked her ever since he overheard that conversation.

Tilting back his chair—he never assumed this position when he dictated to Miss Doane—Wanning began: "To Mr. D. E. Brown, South Forks, Wyoming."

He shaded his eyes with his hand and talked off a long letter to this man who would be sorry that his mortal frame was breaking up. He recalled to him certain fine months they had spent together on the Wind River when they were young men, and said he sometimes wished that like D. E. Brown, he had claimed his freedom in a big country where the wheels did not grind a man as hard as they did in New York. He had spent all these years hustling about and getting ready to live the way he wanted to live, and now he had a puncture the doctors couldn't mend. What was the use of it?

Wanning's thoughts were fixed on the trout streams and the great silver-firs in the canyons of the Wind River Mountains, when he was disturbed by a soft, repeated sniffling. He looked out between his fingers. Little Annie, carried away by his eloquence, was fairly panting to make dots and dashes fast enough, and she was sopping her eyes with an unpresentable, end-of-the-day handkerchief.

Wanning rambled on in his dictation. Why was she crying? What did it matter to her? He was a man who said good-morning to her, who sometimes took an hour of the precious few she had left at the end of the day and then complained about her bad spelling. When the letter was finished, he handed her a new two dollar bill.

"I haven't got any change tonight; and anyhow, I'd like you to eat a whole lot. I'm on a diet, and I want to see every-body else eat."

Annie tucked her notebook under her arm and stood look-ing at the bill which she had not taken up from the table.

"I don't like to be paid for taking letters to your friends, Mr. Wanning," she said impulsively. "I can run personal let-ters off between times. It ain't as if I needed the money," she added carelessly.

"Get along with you! Anybody who is eighteen years old and has a sweet tooth needs money, all they can get."

Annie giggled and darted out with the bill in her hand.

Wanning strolled aimlessly after her into the reception room.

"Let me have that letter before lunch tomorrow, please, and be sure that nobody sees it." He stopped and frowned. "I don't look very sick, do I?"

"I should say you don't!" Annie got her coat on after con-siderable tugging. "Why don't you call in a specialist? My mother called a specialist for my father before he died."

"Oh, is your father dead?"

"I should say he is! He was a painter by trade, and he fell off a seventy-foot stack into the East River. Mother couldn't get anything out of the company, because he wasn't buckled. He lingered for four months, so I know all about taking care of sick people. I was attending business college then, and sick as he was, he used to give me dictation for practise. He made us all go into professions; the girls, too. He didn't like us to just run."

Wanning would have liked to keep Annie and hear more about her family, but it was nearly seven o'clock, and he knew he ought, in mercy, to let her go. She was the only person to

whom he had talked about his illness who had been frank and
honest with him, who had looked at him with eyes that con-
cealed nothing. When he broke the news of his condition to
his partners that morning, they shut him off as if he were
uttering indecent ravings. All day they had met him with a
hurried, abstracted manner. McQuiston and Wade went out
to lunch together, and he knew what they were thinking, per-
haps talking, about. Wanning had brought into the firm valu-
able business, but he was less enterprising than either of his
partners.

III

In the early summer Wanning's family scattered. Roma
swallowed her pride and sailed for Genoa to visit the Con-
tessa Jenny. Harold went to Cornish to be in an artistic at-
mosphere. Mrs. Wanning and Florence took a cottage at York
Harbor where Wanning was supposed to join them whenever
he could get away from town. He did not often get away. He
felt most at ease among his accustomed surroundings. He
kept his car in the city and went back and forth from his office
to the club where he was living. Old Sam, his butler, came in
from Orange every night to put his clothes in order and make
him comfortable.

Wanning began to feel that he would not tire of his office in
a hundred years. Although he did very little work, it was
pleasant to go down town every morning when the streets
were crowded, the sky clear, and the sunshine bright. From
the windows of his private office he could see the harbor and
watch the ocean liners come down the North River and go
out to sea.

While he read his mail, he often looked out and wondered
why he had been so long indifferent to that extraordinary
scene of human activity and hopefulness. How had a short-
lived race of beings the energy and courage valiantly to begin
enterprises which they could follow for only a few years; to
throw up towers and build sea-monsters and found great
businesses, when the frailest of the materials with which they
worked, the paper upon which they wrote, the ink upon their
pens, had more permanence in this world than they? All this

material rubbish lasted. The linen clothing and cosmetics of the Egyptians had lasted. It was only the human flame that certainly, certainly went out. Other things had a fighting chance; they might meet with mishap and be destroyed, they might not. But the human creature who gathered and shaped and hoarded and foolishly loved these things, he had no chance—absolutely none. Wanning's cane, his hat, his top-coat, might go from beggar to beggar and knock about in this world for another fifty years or so; but not he.

In the late afternoon he never hurried to leave his office now. Wonderful sunsets burned over the North River, wonderful stars trembled up among the towers; more wonderful than anything he could hurry away to. One of his windows looked directly down upon the spire of Old Trinity, with the green churchyard and the pale sycamores far below. Wanning often dropped into the church when he was going out to lunch; not because he was trying to make his peace with Heaven, but because the church was old and restful and familiar, because it and its gravestones had sat in the same place for a long while. He bought flowers from the street boys and kept them on his desk, which his partners thought strange behavior, and which Miss Doane considered a sign that he was failing.

But there were graver things than bouquets for Miss Doane and the senior partner to ponder over.

The senior partner, McQuiston, in spite of his silvery hair and mustache and his important church connections, had rich natural taste for scandal.—After Mr. Wade went away for his vacation, in May, Wanning took Annie Wooley out of the copying room, put her at a desk in his private office, and raised her pay to eighteen dollars a week, explaining to McQuiston that for the summer months he would need a secretary. This explanation satisfied neither McQuiston nor Miss Doane.

Annie was also paid for overtime, and although Wanning attended to very little of the office business now, there was a great deal of overtime. Miss Doane was, of course, 'above' questioning a chit like Annie; but what was he doing with his time and his new secretary, she wanted to know?

If anyone had told her that Wanning was writing a book,

she would have said bitterly that it was just like him. In his youth Wanning had hankered for the pen. When he studied law, he had intended to combine that profession with some tempting form of authorship. Had he remained a bachelor, he would have been an unenterprising literary lawyer to the end of his days. It was his wife's restlessness and her practical turn of mind that had made him a money-getter. His illness seemed to bring back to him the illusions with which he left college.

As soon as his family were out of the way and he shut up the Orange house, he began to dictate his autobiography to Annie Wooley. It was not only the story of his life, but an expression of all his theories and opinions, and a commentary on the fifty years of events which he could remember.

Fortunately, he was able to take great interest in this undertaking. He had the happiest convictions about the clear-cut style he was developing and his increasing felicity in phrasing. He meant to publish the work handsomely, at his own expense and under his own name. He rather enjoyed the thought of how greatly disturbed Harold would be. He and Harold differed in their estimates of books. All the solid works which made up Wanning's library, Harold considered beneath contempt. Anybody, he said, could do that sort of thing.

When Wanning could not sleep at night, he turned on the light beside his bed and made notes on the chapter he meant to dictate the next day.

When he returned to the office after lunch, he gave instructions that he was not to be interrupted by telephone calls, and shut himself up with his secretary.

After he had opened all the windows and taken off his coat, he fell to dictating. He found it a delightful occupation, the solace of each day. Often he had sudden fits of tiredness; then he would lie down on the leather sofa and drop asleep, while Annie read "The Leopard's Spots" until he awoke.

Like many another business man Wanning had relied so long on stenographers that the operation of writing with a pen had become laborious to him. When he undertook it, he wanted to cut everything short. But walking up and down his private office, with the strong afternoon sun pouring in at his windows, a fresh air stirring, all the people and boats moving restlessly down there, he could say things he wanted to say. It was like living his life over again.

He did not miss his wife or his daughters. He had become again the mild, contemplative youth he was in college, before he had a profession and a family to grind for, before the two needs which shape our destiny had made of him pretty much what they make of every man.

At five o'clock Wanning sometimes went out for a cup of tea and took Annie along. He felt dull and discouraged as soon as he was alone. So long as Annie was with him, he could keep a grip on his own thoughts. They talked about what he had just been dictating to her. She found that he liked to be questioned, and she tried to be greatly interested in it all.

After tea, they went back to the office. Occasionally Wanning lost track of time and kept Annie until it grew dark. He knew he had old McQuiston guessing, but he didn't care. One day the senior partner came to him with a reproving air.

"I am afraid Miss Doane is leaving us, Paul. She feels that Miss Wooley's promotion is irregular."

"How is that any business of hers, I'd like to know? She has all my legal work. She is always disagreeable enough about doing anything else."

McQuiston's puffy red face went a shade darker.

"Miss Doane has a certain professional pride; a strong feeling for office organization. She doesn't care to fill an equivocal position. I don't know that I blame her. She feels that there is something not quite regular about the confidence you seem to place in this inexperienced young woman."

Wanning pushed back his chair.

"I don't care a hang about Miss Doane's sense of propriety. I need a stenographer who will carry out my instructions. I've carried out Miss Doane's long enough. I've let that schoolma'am hector me for years. She can go when she pleases."

That night McQuiston wrote to his partner that things were in a bad way, and they would have to keep an eye on Wanning. He had been seen at the theatre with his new stenographer.

That was true. Wanning had several times taken Annie to

the Palace on Saturday afternoon. When all his acquaintances were off motoring or playing golf, when the down-town offices and even the streets were deserted, it amused him to watch a foolish show with a delighted, cheerful little person beside him.

Beyond her generosity, Annie had no shining merits of character, but she had the gift of thinking well of everything, and wishing well. When she was there Wanning felt as if there were someone who cared whether this was a good or a bad day with him. Old Sam, too, was like that. While the old black man put him to bed and made him comfortable, Wanning could talk to him as he talked to little Annie. Even if he dwelt upon his illness, in plain terms, in detail, he did not feel as if he were imposing on them.

People like Sam and Annie admitted misfortune,—admitted it almost cheerfully. Annie and her family did not consider illness or any of its hard facts vulgar or indecent. It had its place in their scheme of life, as it had not in that of Wanning's friends.

Annie came out of a typical poor family of New York. Of eight children, only four lived to grow up. In such families the stream of life is broad enough, but runs shallow. In the children, vitality is exhausted early. The roots do not go down into anything very strong. Illness and deaths and funerals, in her own family and in those of her friends, had come at frequent intervals in Annie's life. Since they had to be, she and her sisters made the best of them. There was something to be got out of funerals, even, if they were managed right. They kept people in touch with old friends who had moved uptown, and revived kindly feelings.

Annie had often given up things she wanted because there was sickness at home, and now she was patient with her boss. What he paid her for overtime work by no means made up to her what she lost.

Annie was not in the least thrifty, nor were any of her sisters. She had to make a living, but she was not interested in getting all she could for her time, or in laying up for the future. Girls like Annie know that the future is a very uncertain thing, and they feel no responsibility about it. The present is what they have—and it is all they have. If Annie missed a chance to go sailing with the plumber's son on Saturday afternoon, why, she missed it. As for the two dollars her boss gave her, she handed them over to her mother. Now that Annie was getting more money, one of her sisters quit a job she didn't like and was staying at home for a rest. That was all promotion meant to Annie.

The first time Annie's boss asked her to work on Saturday afternoon, she could not hide her disappointment. He suggested that they might knock off early and go to a show, or take a run in his car, but she grew tearful and said it would be hard to make her family understand. Wanning thought perhaps he could explain to her mother. He called his motor and took Annie home.

When his car stopped in front of the tenement house on Eighth Avenue, heads came popping out of the windows for six storys up, and all the neighbor women, in dressing sacks and wrappers, gazed down at the machine and at the couple alighting from it. A motor meant a wedding or the hospital.

The plumber's son, Willy Steen, came over from the corner saloon to see what was going on, and Annie introduced him at the doorstep.

Mrs. Wooley asked Wanning to come into the parlor and invited him to have a chair of ceremony between the folding bed and the piano.

Annie, nervous and tearful, escaped to the dining-room— the cheerful spot where the daughters visited with each other and with their friends. The parlor was a masked sleeping chamber and store room.

The plumber's son sat down on the sofa beside Mrs. Wooley, as if he were accustomed to share in the family councils. Mrs. Wooley waited expectant and kindly. She looked the sensible, hard-working woman that she was, and one could see she hadn't lived all her life on Eighth Avenue without learning a great deal.

Wanning explained to her that he was writing a book which he wanted to finish during the summer months when business was not so heavy. He was ill and could not work regularly. His secretary would have to take his dictation when he felt able to give it; must, in short, be a sort of companion to him. He would like to feel that she could go out in his car with him, or even to the theater, when he felt like it. It might have been better if he had engaged a young man for this work, but since he had begun it with Annie, he would like to keep her if her mother was willing.

Mrs. Wooley watched him with friendly, searching eyes. She glanced at Willy Steen, who, wise in such distinctions, had decided that there was nothing shady about Annie's boss. He nodded his sanction.

"I don't want my girl to conduct herself in any such way as will prejudice her, Mr. Wanning," she said thoughtfully. "If you've got daughters, you know how that is. You've been liberal with Annie, and it's a good position for her. It's right she should go to business every day, and I want her to do her work right, but I like to have her home after working hours. I always think a young girl's time is her own after business hours, and I try not to burden them when they come home. I'm willing she should do your work as suits you, if it's her wish; but I don't like to press her. The good times she misses now, it's not you nor me, sir, that can make them up to her. These young things has their feelings."

"Oh, I don't want to press her, either," Wanning said hastily. "I simply want to know that you understand the situation. I've made her a little present in my will as a recognition that she is doing more for me than she is paid for."

"That's something above me, sir. We'll hope there won't be no question of wills for many years yet," Mrs. Wooley spoke heartily. "I'm glad if my girl can be of any use to you, just so she don't prejudice herself."

The plumber's son rose as if the interview were over.

"It's all right, Mama Wooley, don't you worry," he said.

He picked up his canvas cap and turned to Wanning. "You see, Annie ain't the sort of girl that would want to be spotted circulating around with a monied party her folks didn't know all about. She'd lose friends by it."

After this conversation Annie felt a great deal happier. She was still shy and a trifle awkward with poor Wanning when they were outside the office building, and she missed the old freedom of her Saturday afternoons. But she did the best she could, and Willy Steen tried to make it up to her.

In Annie's absence he often came in of an afternoon to have

a cup of tea and a sugar-bun with Mrs. Wooley and the daughter who was "resting." As they sat at the dining-room table, they discussed Annie's employer, his peculiarities, his health, and what he had told Mrs. Wooley about his will.

Mrs. Wooley said she sometimes felt afraid he might disinherit his children, as rich people often did, and make talk; but she hoped for the best. Whatever came to Annie, she prayed it might not be in the form of taxable property.

IV

Late in September Wanning grew suddenly worse. His family hurried home, and he was put to bed in his house in Orange. He kept asking the doctors when he could get back to the office, but he lived only eight days.

The morning after his father's funeral, Harold went to the office to consult Wanning's partners and to read the will. Everything in the will was as it should be. There were no surprises except a codicil in the form of a letter to Mrs. Wanning, dated July 8th, requesting that out of the estate she should pay the sum of one thousand dollars to his stenographer, Annie Wooley, "in recognition of her faithful services."

"I thought Miss Doane was my father's stenographer," Harold exclaimed.

Alec McQuiston looked embarrassed and spoke in a low, guarded tone.

"She was, for years. But this spring,—" he hesitated.

McQuiston loved a scandal. He leaned across his desk toward Harold.

"This spring your father put this little girl, Miss Wooley, a copyist, utterly inexperienced, in Miss Doane's place. Miss Doane was indignant and left us. The change made comment here in the office. It was slightly— No, I will be frank with you, Harold, it was very irregular."

Harold also looked grave. "What could my father have meant by such a request as this to my mother?"

The silver haired senior partner flushed and spoke as if he were trying to break something gently.

"I don't understand it, my boy. But I think, indeed I prefer to think, that your father was not quite himself all this summer. A man like your father does not, in his right senses, find pleasure in the society of an ignorant, common little girl. He does not make a practise of keeping her at the office after hours, often until eight o'clock, or take her to restaurants and to the theater with him; not, at least, in a slanderous city like New York."

Harold flinched before McQuiston's meaning gaze and turned aside in pained silence. He knew, as a dramatist, that there are dark chapters in all men's lives, and this but too clearly explained why his father had stayed in town all summer instead of joining his family.

McQuiston asked if he should ring for Annie Wooley.

Harold drew himself up. "No. Why should I see her? I prefer not to. But with your permission, Mr. McQuiston, I will take charge of this request to my mother. It could only give her pain, and might awaken doubts in her mind."

"We hardly know," murmured the senior partner, "where an investigation would lead us. Technically, of course, I cannot agree with you. But if, as one of the executors of the will, you wish to assume personal responsibility for this bequest, under the circumstances—irregularities beget irregularities."

"My first duty to my father," said Harold, "is to protect my mother."

That afternoon McQuiston called Annie Wooley into his private office and told her that her services would not be needed any longer, and that in lieu of notice the clerk would give her two weeks' salary.

"Can I call up here for references?" Annie asked.

"Certainly. But you had better ask for me, personally. You must know there has been some criticism of you here in the office, Miss Wooley."

"What about?" Annie asked boldly.

"Well, a young girl like you cannot render so much personal service to her employer as you did to Mr. Wanning without causing unfavorable comment. To be blunt with you, for your own good, my dear young lady, your services to your employer should terminate in the office, and at the close of office hours. Mr. Wanning was a very sick man and his judgment was at fault, but you should have known what a girl in your station can do and what she cannot do."

The vague discomfort of months flashed up in little Annie. She had no mind to stand by and be lectured without having a word to say for herself.

"Of course he was sick, poor man!" she burst out. "Not as anybody seemed much upset about it. I wouldn't have given up my half-holidays for anybody if they hadn't been sick, no matter what they paid me. There wasn't anything in it for me."

McQuiston raised his hand warningly.

"That will do, young lady. But when you get another place, remember this: it is never your duty to entertain or to provide amusement for your employer."

He gave Annie a look which she did not clearly understand, although she pronounced him a nasty old man as she hustled on her hat and jacket.

When Annie reached home she found Willy Steen sitting with her mother and sister at the dining-room table. This was the first day that Annie had gone to the office since Wanning's death, and her family awaited her return with suspense.

"Hello yourself," Annie called as she came in and threw her handbag into an empty armchair.

"You're off early, Annie," said her mother gravely. "Has the will been read?"

"I guess so. Yes, I know it has. Miss Wilson got it out of the safe for them. The son came in. He's a pill."

"Was nothing said to you, daughter?"

"Yes, a lot. Please give me some tea, mother." Annie felt that her swagger was failing.

"Don't tantalize us, Ann," her sister broke in. "Didn't you get anything?"

"I got the mit, all right. And some back talk from the old man that I'm awful sore about."

Annie dashed away the tears and gulped her tea.

Gradually her mother and Willy drew the story from her. Willy offered at once to go to the office building and take his stand outside the door and never leave it until he had punched old Mr. McQuiston's face. He rose as if to attend to it at once, but Mrs. Wooley drew him to his chair again and patted his arm.

"It would only start talk and get the girl in trouble, Willy.

When it's lawyers, folks in our station is helpless. I certainly believed that man when he sat here; you heard him yourself. Such a gentleman as he looked."

Willy thumped his great fist, still in punching position, down on his knee.

"Never you be fooled again, Mama Wooley. You'll never get anything out of a rich guy that he ain't signed up in the courts for. Rich is tight. There's no exceptions."

Annie shook her head.

"I didn't want anything out of him. He was a nice, kind man, and he had his troubles, I guess. He wasn't tight."

"Still," said Mrs. Wooley sadly, "Mr. Wanning had no call to hold out promises. I hate to be disappointed in a gentleman. You've had confining work for some time, daughter; a rest will do you good."

Smart Set, October 1919

Uncle Valentine

(Adagio non troppo)

ONE MORNING not long ago I heard Louise Ireland give a singing lesson to a young countrywoman of mine, in her studio in Paris. Ireland must be quite sixty now, but there is not a break in the proud profile; she is still beautiful, still the joy of men, young and old. To hear her give a lesson is to hear a fine performance. The pupil was a girl of exceptional talent, handsome and intelligent, but she had the character-istic deficiency of her generation—she found nothing re-markable. She realized that she was fortunate to get in a few lessons with Ireland, but good fortune was what she expected, and she probably thought Ireland didn't every day find such good material to work with.

When the vocal lesson was over the girl said, "May I try that song you told me to look at?"

"If you wish. Have you done anything with it?"

"I've worked on it a little." The young woman unstrapped a roll of music. "I've tried over most of the songs in his book. I'm crazy about them. I never heard of Valentine Ramsay before."

"Sad for him," murmured the teacher.

"Was he English?"

"No, American, like you," sarcastically.

"I went back to the shop for more of his things, but they had only this one collection. Didn't he do any others?"

"A few. But these are the best."

"But I don't understand. If he could do things like these, why didn't he keep it up? What prevented him?"

"Oh, the things that always prevent one: marriage, money, friends, the general social order. Finally a motor truck pre-vented him, one of the first in Paris. He was struck and killed one night, just out of the window there, as he was going on to the Pont Royal. He was barely thirty."

The girl said "Oh!" in a subdued voice, and actually crossed the room to look out of the window.

"If you wish to know anything further about him, this

American lady can tell you. She knew him in his own country. Now I'll see what you've done with that." Ireland shook her loose sleeves back from her white arms and began to play the song:

I know a wall where red roses grow

I

Yes, I had known Valentine Ramsay. I knew him in a lovely place, at a lovely time, in a bygone period of American life; just at the incoming of this century which has made all the world so different.

I was a girl of sixteen, living with my aunt and uncle at Fox Hill, in Greenacre. My mother and father had died young, leaving me and my little sister, Betty Jane, with scant provision for our future. Aunt Charlotte and Uncle Harry Waterford took us to live with them, and brought us up with their own four little daughters. Harriet, their oldest girl, was two years younger than I, and Elizabeth, the youngest, was just the age of Betty Jane. When cousins agree at all, they agree better than sisters, and we were all extraordinarily happy. The Ramsays were our nearest neighbors; their place, Bonnie Brae, sat on the same hilltop as ours—a houseful of lonely men (and such strange ones!) tyrannized over by a Swedish woman who was housekeeper.

Greenacre was a little railway station where every evening dogcarts and carriages drew up and waited for the express that brought the business men down from the City, and then rolled them along smooth roads to their dwellings, scattered about on the fine line of hills, clad with forest, that rose above a historic American river.

The City up the river it is scarcely necessary to name; a big inland American manufacturing city, older and richer and gloomier than most, also more powerful and important. Greenacre was not a suburb in the modern sense. It was as old as the City, and there were no small holdings. The people who lived there had been born there, and inherited their land from fathers and grandfathers. Every householder had his own stables and pasture land, and hay meadows and orchard. There were plenty of servants in those days.

My Aunt Charlotte lived in the house where she was born, and ever since her marriage she had been playing with it and enlarging it, as if she had foreseen that she was one day to have a large family on her hands. She loved that house and she loved to work on it, making it always more and more just as she wanted it to be, and yet keeping it what it always had been—a big, rambling, hospitable old country house. As one drove up the hill from the station, Fox Hill, under its tall oaks and sycamores, looked like several old farmhouses pieced together; uneven roofs with odd gables and dormer windows sticking out, porches on different levels connected by sagging steps. It was all in the dull tone of scaling brown paint and old brown wood—though often, as we came up the hill in the late afternoon, the sunset flamed wonderfully on the diamond-paned windows that were so gray and inconspicuous by day.

The house kept its rusty outer shell, like an old turtle's, all the while that it was growing richer in color and deeper in comfort within. These changes were made very cautiously, very delicately. Though my aunt was constantly making changes, she was terribly afraid of them. When she brought things back from Spain or Italy for her house, they used to stay in the barn, in their packing cases, for months before she would even try them. Then some day, when we children were all at school and she was alone, they would be smuggled in one at a time—sometimes to vanish forever after a day or two. There was something she wanted to get, in this corner or that, but there was something she was even more afraid of losing. The boldest enterprise she ever undertook was the construction of the new music-room, on the north side of the house, toward the Ramsays'. Even that was done very quietly, by the village workmen. The piano was moved out into the big square hall, and the door between the hall and the scene of the carpenters' activities was closed up. When, after a month or so, it was opened again, there was the new music-room, a proper room for chamber music, such as the petty kings and grand dukes of old Germany had in their castles;

finished and empty, as it was to remain; nothing to be seen but a long room of satisfying proportions, with many wax candles flickering in the polish of the dark wooden walls and floor.

It was into this music-room that Aunt Charlotte called Harriet and me one November afternoon to tell us that Valentine Ramsay was coming home. She was sitting at the piano with a book of Debussy's piano pieces open before her. His music was little known in America then, but when she was alone she played it a great deal. She took a letter from between the leaves of the book. There was a flutter of excitement in her voice and in her features as she told us: "He says he will take the next fast steamer after his letter. He must be on the water now."

"Oh, aren't you happy, Aunt Charlotte!" I cried, knowing well how fond she was of him.

"Very, Marjorie. And a little troubled too. I'm not quite sure that people will be nice to him. The Oglethorpes are very influential, and now that Janet is living here—"

"But she's married again."

"Nevertheless, people feel that Valentine behaved very badly. He'll be here for Christmas, and I've been thinking what we can do for him. We must work very hard on our part songs. Good singing pleases him more than anything. I've been hoping he may fall into the way of composing again while he's with us. His life has been so distracted for the last few years that he's almost given up writing songs. Go to the playroom, Harriet, and tell the little girls to get their school work done early. We'll have a long rehearsal to-night. I suppose they scarcely remember him."

Three years before Valentine Ramsay had been at home for several weeks before his brother Horace died. Even at that sad time his being there was like a holiday for us children, and all the Greenacre people seemed glad to have him back again. But much had happened since then. Valentine had deserted his wife for a singer, notorious for her beauty and misconduct; had, as my friends at school often told me, utterly disgraced himself. His wife, Janet Oglethorpe, was now living in her house in the City. I had seen her twice at Saturday matinées, and I didn't wonder that Valentine had run away with a beautiful woman. The second time I saw her very well—it was a charity performance, and she was sitting in a box with her new husband, a young man who was the perfection of good tailoring, who was reputed handsome, who appeared so, indeed, until you looked closely into his vain, apprehensive face. He was immensely conceited, but not sure of himself, and kept arranging his features as he talked to the women in the box. As for Janet, I thought her an unattractive, red-faced woman, very ordinary, as we said. Aunt Charlotte murmured in my ear that she had once been better looking, but that after her marriage with Valentine she had grown stouter and "coarsened"—my aunt hurried over the word.

Aunt Charlotte had never, I knew, approved of the marriage. When he was a little boy Valentine had been her squire and had loved her devotedly. After his mother died, leaving him in a houseful of grown men, she had looked out for him and tried to direct his studies. She was ten years older than Valentine, and, in the years when Uncle Harry came a-courting, the spoiled neighbor boy was always hanging about and demanding attention. He had a pretty talent for the piano, and for composition; but he wouldn't work regularly at anything, and there was no one to make him. He drifted along until he was a young fellow of twenty, and then he met Janet Oglethorpe.

Valentine had a habit of running up to the City to dawdle about the Steinerts' music store and practice on their pianos. The two young Steinert lads were musical and were great friends of his. It was there, when she went in to buy tickets for a concert, that Janet Oglethorpe first saw Valentine and heard him play. He was a strikingly handsome boy, and picturesque—certainly very different from the canny Oglethorpe men and their friends. Janet took to him at once, began inviting him to the house and asking musicians there to meet him. The Ramsays were greatly pleased; the Oglethorpes were the richest family in a whole cityful of rich people. They owned mines and mills and oil wells and gas works and farms and banks. Unlike some of our great Scotch families, they didn't become idlers and coupon-clippers in the third generation. They held their edge—kept their keenness for money as if they were just beginning, must sink or swim, and hadn't millions behind them. Janet was one of the third generation, and it was well known that she was as shrewd in business as old Duncan himself, the founder of the Oglethorpe fortune, who was still living, having buried three wives, and spry enough to attend directors' meetings and make plenty of trouble for the young men.

Janet was older than Valentine in years, and much older in experience and judgment. Even after she had announced her engagement to him, Aunt Charlotte prevailed upon him to go abroad to study for a little. He was happily settled in Paris, under Saint-Saens, but before the year was out Janet followed him up and married him. They lived abroad. Aunt Charlotte had visited them in Rome, but she never said much about them.

Later, when the scandal came, and everyone in the City, and in Greenacre as well, fell upon Valentine for a worthless scamp, Uncle Harry and Aunt Charlotte always stood up for him, and said that when Janet married a flighty student she took the chance with her eyes open. Some of our friends insisted that he had shattered himself with drink, like so many of the Ramsay men; others hinted that he must 'take something,' meaning drugs. No one could believe that a man entirely in his right mind would run away from so much money—toss it overboard, mills and mines, stocks and bonds; and that when he had none himself, and Bonnie Brae was plastered with mortgages, and old Uncle Jonathan had already two helpless men to take care of.

II

For ten days after his letter came we waited and waited for Valentine. Everyone was restless—except Uncle Jonathan, who often told us that he enjoyed anticipation as much as realization. Uncle Morton, Valentine's much older brother, used to stumble in of an evening, when we were all gathered in the big hall after dinner, to announce the same news about boats that he had given us the evening before, wave his long thin hands a little, and boast in a husky voice about his gifted brother. Aunt Charlotte put her impatience to some account by rehearsing us industriously in the part songs we were working up for Valentine. She called us her sextette, and she trained us very well. Several of us were said to have good voices. My aunt used to declare that she liked us better when we were singing than at any other time, and that drilling us was the chief pleasure she got out of having such a large family.

Aunt Charlotte was the person who felt all that went on about her—and all that did not go on—and understood it. I find that I did not know her very well then. It was not until years afterward, not until after her death, indeed, that I began really to know her. Recalling her quickly, I see a dark, full-figured woman, dressed in dark, rich materials; I remember certain velvet dresses, brown, claret-colored, deep violet, which especially became her, and certain fur hats and capes and coats. Though she was a little overweight, she seemed often to be withdrawing into her clothes, not shrinking, but retiring behind the folds of her heavy cloaks and gowns and soft barricades of fur. She had to do with people constantly, and her house was often overflowing with guests, but she was by nature very shy. I now believe that she suffered all her life from a really painful timidity, and had to keep taking herself in hand. I have said that she was dark; her skin and hair and eyes were all brown. Even when she was out in the garden her face seemed always in shadow.

As a child I understood that my aunt had what we call a strong nature; still, deep and, on the whole, happy. Whatever it is that enables us to make our peace with life, she had found it. She cared more for music than for anything else in the world, and after that for her family and her house and her friends. She was very intelligent, but she had entirely too much respect for the opinions of others. Even in music she was often dominated by people who were much less discerning than she, but more aggressive. If her preference was disputed or challenged, she easily gave up. She knew what she liked, but she was apt to be apologetic about it. When she mentioned a composition or an artist she admired, or spoke the name of a person or place she loved, I remember a dark, rich color used to come into her voice, and sometimes she uttered the name with a curious little intake of the breath.

Aunt Charlotte's real life went on very deep within her, I

suspect, though she seemed so open and cordial, and not especially profound. No one ever thought of her as intellectual, though people often spoke of her wonderful taste; of how, without effort, she was able to make her garden and house exactly right. Our old friends considered taste as something quite apart from intelligence, instead of the flower of it. She read little, it is true; what other people learned from books she learned from music,—all she needed to give her a rich enjoyment of art and life. She played the piano extremely well; it was not an accomplishment with her, but a way of living. The rearing of six little girls did not seem to strain her patience much. She allowed us a great deal of liberty and demanded her own in return. We were permitted to have our own thoughts and feelings, and even Elizabeth and Betty Jane understood that it is a great happiness to be permitted to be glad or sorry in one's own way.

III

On the night of Valentine's return, our household went in a body over to Bonnie Brae to make a short call. It was delightful to see the old house looking so festive, with lights streaming from all the windows. We found the family in the long, pale parlor; the men of the house, and half a dozen Ramsay cousins with their wives and children.

Valentine was standing near the fireplace when we entered, beside his father's armchair. The little girls at once tripped down the long room toward him, Uncle Harry following. But Aunt Charlotte stopped short in the doorway and stood there in the shadow of the curtains, watching Valentine across the heads of the company, as if she wished to remain an outsider. Through the buzz and flutter of greetings, his eyes found her there. He left the others, crossed the room in a flash, and, giving her a quick, sidewise look, put down his head to be kissed, like a little boy. As he stood there for a moment, so close to us, he struck me at once as altogether too young to have had so much history, as very hardy and high-colored and unsubdued. His thick, seal-brown hair grew on his head exactly like fur, there was no part in it anywhere. His short mustache and eyebrows had the same furry look. His red lips and white teeth gave him a striking freshness—there was something very roguish and wayward, very individual about his mouth. He seldom looked at one when he talked to one—he had a habit of frowning at the floor or looking fixedly at some object when he was speaking, but one felt his eyes through the lowered lids—felt his pleasure or his annoyance, his affection or impatience.

Since gay Uncle Horace died the Ramsay men did not often give parties, and that night they roamed about somewhat uneasily, all but Uncle Jonathan, who was always superbly at his ease. He kept his armchair, with a cape about his shoulders to protect him from drafts. The old man's hair and beard were just the color of dirty white snow, and he was averse to having them trimmed. He was a gracious host, having the air of one to whom many congratulations are due. Roland had put on a frock coat and was doing his duty, making himself quietly agreeable to everyone. His handsome silver-gray head and fine physique would have added to the distinction of any company. Uncle Morton was wandering about from group to group, jerking his hands this way and that—a curiously individual gesture from the wrist, as if he were making signals from a world too remote for speech. He fastened himself upon me, as he was very likely to do (finding me out in the little corner sofa to which I had retreated), sat down beside me and began talking about his brother in disconnected sentences, trying to focus his almost insensible eyes upon me.

"My brother is very devoted to your aunt. She must help me with his studio. We are going to make a studio for him off in the wing, for the quiet. Something very nice. I think I shall have the walls upholstered, like cushions, to keep the noise out. It will be handsome, you understand. We can give parties there—receptions. My brother is a fine musician. Could play anything when he was eleven—classical music—the most difficult compositions." In the same expansive spirit Uncle Morton had once planned a sunken garden for my aunt, and a ballroom for Harriet and me.

Molla Carlsen brought in cake and port and sherry. She had been at the door to admit us, and had since been intermittently in the background, disappearing and reappearing as if she were much occupied. She had always this air of moving quietly and efficiently in her own province. Molla was very correct in her deportment, was there and not too much there. She was fair, and good looking, very. The only fault Aunt Charlotte had to find with her appearance was the way she wore her hair. It was yellow enough to be showy in any case, and she made it more so by parting it very low on one side, just over her left ear, indeed, so that it lay across her head in a long curly wave, making her low forehead lower still and giving her an air that, as some of our neighbors declared, was little short of "tough."

After we had sipped our wine the cousins began to gather up their babies for departure, and we younger ones had all to go up to Uncle Jonathan and kiss him good night. It was a rite we shrank from, he was always so strong of tobacco and snuff, but he liked to kiss us, and there was no escape.

When we left, Uncle Valentine put his arm through Aunt Charlotte's and walked with us as far as the summerhouse, looking about him and up overhead through the trees. I heard him say suddenly, as if it had just struck him:

"Isn't it funny, Charlotte; no matter how much things or people ought to be different, what we love them for is for being just the same!"

IV

The next afternoon when Harriet and I got home from Miss Demming's school, we heard two pianos going, and knew that Uncle Valentine was there. The door between the big hall and the music-room was open, and Aunt Charlotte called to us:

"Harriet and Marjorie? Run up-stairs and make yourselves neat. You may have tea with us presently."

When we came down, the music had ceased, and the hall was empty. Black John, coming through with a plate of toast, told us he had taken tea into the study.

My uncle's study was my favorite spot in that house full of lovely places. It was a little room just off the library, very quiet, like a little pond off the main currents of the house. There was but one door, and no one ever passed through it on the way to another room. As it had formerly been a conservatory for winter flowers, it was all glass on two sides, with heavy curtains one could draw at night to shut out the chill. There was always a little coal fire in the grate, Uncle Harry's favorite books on the shelves, and the new ones he was reading arranged on the table, along with his pipes and tobacco jars. Sitting beside the red coals one could look out into the great forking sycamore limbs, with their mottled bark of white and olive green, and off across the bare tops of the winter trees that grew down the hill slopes—until finally one looked into nothingness, into the great stretch of open sky above the river, where the early sunsets burned or brooded over our valley. It was with delight I heard we were to have our tea there.

We found my aunt and Valentine before the grate, the steaming samovar between them, the glass room full of gray light, a little warmed by the glowing coals.

"Aren't you surprised to find us here?" There was just a shade of embarrassment in my aunt's voice. "This was Uncle Valentine's choice." Curious; though she always looked so at ease, so calm in her matronly figure, a little thing like having tea in an unusual room could make her a trifle self-conscious and apologetic.

Valentine, in brown corduroys with a soft shirt and a Chinese-red necktie, was sitting in Uncle Harry's big chair, one foot tucked under him. He told us he had been all over the hills that morning, clear up to Flint Ridge. "I came home by the near side of Blinker's Hill, past the Wakeley place. I wish Belle wouldn't stay abroad so long; it's a shame to keep that jolly old house shut up." He said he liked having tea in the study because the outlook was the same as from his up-stairs room at home. "I was always supposed to be doing lessons there as evening came on. I'm sure I don't know what I was doing—writing serenades for you, probably, Charlotte."

Aunt Charlotte was nursing the samovar along—it never worked very well. "I've been hoping," she murmured, "that you would bring me home some new serenades—or songs of some kind."

"Songs? Oh, hell, Charlotte!" He jerked his foot from under him and sat up straight. "Sorry I swore, but you evidently

don't know what I've been up against these last four years.
You'll have to know, and so will your maidens fair. Anyhow,
if you're to have a rake next door to a houseful of daughters,
you'd better look into it."

Aunt Charlotte caught her breath painfully, glanced at Har-
riet and me and then at the door. Valentine sprang up, went
to the door and closed it. "Oh, don't look so frightened!" he
exclaimed irritably, "and don't send the girls away. Do you
suppose they've heard nothing? What do you think girls
whisper about at school, anyway? You'd better let me explain
a little."

"I think it unnecessary," she murmured entreatingly.

"It isn't unnecessary!" he stamped his foot down upon the
rug. "You mean they'll think what you tell them to—stay
where you put them, like china shepherdesses. Well, they
won't!"

We were almost as much frightened as Aunt Charlotte. He
was standing before us, his brow wrinkled in a heavy frown,
his shoulders lowered, his red lips thrust out petulantly. I am
sure I was hoping that he wouldn't quite explain away the
legend of his awful wickedness. As he addressed us he looked
not at us but at the floor.

"You've heard, haven't you, Harriet and Marjorie, that I
deserted a noble wife and ran away with a wicked woman?
Well, she wasn't a wicked woman. She is kind and generous,
and she ran away with me out of charity, to get me out of the
awful mess I in. The mess, you understand, was just be-
ing married to this noble wife. Janey is all right for her own
kind, for Oglethorpes in general, but she was all wrong for
me."

Here he stopped and made a wry face, as if his pedagogical
tone put a bad taste in his mouth. He glanced at my aunt for
help, but she was looking steadfastly at the samovar.

"Hang it, Charlotte," he broke out, "these girls are not in
the nursery! They must hear what they hear and think what
they think. It's got to come out. You know well enough what
dear Janey is; you've known ever since you stayed with us in
Rome. She's a common, energetic, close-fisted little trades-
woman, who ought to be keeping a shop and doing people
out of their eyeteeth. She thinks, day and night, about

common, trivial, worthless things. And what's worse, she talks about them day and night. She bargains in her sleep. It's what she can get out of this dressmaker or that porter; it's getting the royal suite in a hotel for the price of some other suite. We left you in Rome and dashed off to Venice that fall because she could get a palazzo at a bargain. Some English people had to go home on account of a grandmother dying and had to sub-let in a hurry. That was her only reason for going to Venice. And when we got there she did nothing but beat the house servants down to lower wages, and get herself burned red as a lobster staying out in boats all day to get her money's worth. I was dragged about the world for five years in an atmosphere of commonness and meanness and coarseness. I tell you I was paralyzed by the flood of trivial, vulgar nagging that poured over me and never stopped. Even Dickie—I might have had some fun with the little chap, but she never let me. She never let me have any but the most painful relations with him. With two nurses sitting idle, she'd make me chase off in a cab to demand his linen from special laundresses, or scurry around a whole day to find some silly kind of milk—all utter nonsense. The child was never sick and could take any decent milk. But she likes to make a fuss; calls it 'managing.'

"Sometimes I used to try to get off by myself long enough to return to consciousness, to find whether I had any consciousness left to return to—but she always came pelting after. I got off for Bayreuth one time. Thought I'd covered my tracks so well. She arrived in the middle of the Ring. My God, the agony of having to sit through music with that woman!" Valentine sat down and wiped his forehead. It glistened with perspiration; the roots of his furry hair were quite wet.

After a moment he said doggedly, "I give you my word, Charlotte, there was nothing for it but to make a scandal; to hurt her pride so openly that she'd have to take action. I don't know that she'd have done it then, if Seymour Towne hadn't turned up to sympathize with her. You can't hurt anybody as beefy as that without being a butcher!" He shuddered.

"Louise Ireland offered to be the sacrifice. She hadn't much to lose in the way of—well, of the proprieties, of course. But she's a glorious creature. I couldn't have done it with a horrid woman. Don't think anything nasty of her, any of you, I won't have it. Everything she does is lovely, somehow or other, just as every song she sings is more beautiful than it ever was before. She's been more or less irregular in behavior—as you've doubtless heard with augmentation. She had certainly run away with desperate men before. But behavior, I find, is more or less accidental, Charlotte. Oh, don't look so scared! Your dovelets will have to face facts some day. Æsthetics come back to predestination, if theology doesn't. A woman's behavior may be irreproachable and she herself may be gross—just gross. She may do her duty, and defile everything she touches. And another woman may be erratic, imprudent, self-indulgent if you like, and all the while be—what is it the Bible says? Pure in heart. People are as they are, and that's all there is to life. And now—" Valentine got up and went toward the door to open it.

Aunt Charlotte came out of her lethargy and held up her finger. "Valentine," she said with a deep breath, "I wasn't afraid of letting the girls hear what you had to say—not exactly afraid. But I thought it unnecessary. I understood everything as soon as I looked at you last night. One hasn't watched people from their childhood for nothing."

He wheeled round to her. "Of course *you* would know! But these girls aren't you, my dear! I doubt if they ever will be, even with luck!" The tone in which he said this, the proud, sidelong glance he flashed upon her, made this a rich and beautiful compliment—so violent a one that it seemed almost to hurt that timid woman. Slowly, slowly, the red burned up in her dark cheeks, and it was a long while dying down.

"Now we've finished with this—what a relief!" Valentine knelt down on the window seat between Harriet and me and put an arm lightly around each of us. "There's a fine sunset coming on, come and look at it, Charlotte."

We huddled together, looking out over the descending knolls of bare tree tops into the open space over the river, where the smoky gray atmosphere was taking on a purple tinge, like some thick liquid changing color. The sun, which had all day been a shallow white ring, emerged and swelled into an orange-red globe. It hung there without changing, as if the density of the atmosphere supported it and would not let it sink. We sat hushed and still, living in some strong wave of feeling or memory that came up in our visitor. Valentine had that power of throwing a mood over people. There was nothing imaginary about it; it was as real as any form of pain or pleasure. One had only to look at Aunt Charlotte's face, which had become beautiful, to know that.

It was Uncle Harry who brought us back into the present again. He had caught an early train down from the City, hoping to come upon us just like this, he said. He was almost pathetically eager for anything of this sort he could get, and was glad to come in for cold toast and tea.

"Awfully happy I got here before Valentine got away," he said, as he turned on the light. "And, Charlotte, how rosy you are! It takes you to do that to her, Val." She still had the dusky color which had been her unwilling response to Valentine's compliment.

v

Within a few days Uncle Valentine ran over to beg my aunt to go shopping with him. Something had reminded him that Christmas was very near.

"It's awfully embarrassing," he said. "Nobody in Paris was saying anything about Christmas before I sailed. Here I've come home with empty trunks, and Paris full of things that everybody wants."

Aunt Charlotte laughed at him and said she thought they would find plenty of things from Paris up in the City.

The next morning Valentine appeared before we left for school. He was in a very businesslike mood, and his check book was sticking out from the breast pocket of his fur coat. They were to catch the eight-thirty train. The day was dark and gray, I remember, though our valley was white, for there had been a snowfall the day before. Standing on the porch with my school satchel, I watched them get into the carriage and go down the hill as the train whistled for the station below ours—they would just have time to catch it. Aunt

Charlotte looked so happy. She didn't often have Valentine to herself for a whole day. Well, she deserved it.

I could follow them in my mind: Valentine with his brilliant necktie and foreign-cut clothes, hurrying about the shops, so lightning-quick, when all the men they passed in the street were so slow and ponderous or, when they weren't ponderous, stiff—stiff because they were wooden, or because they weren't wooden and were in constant dread of betraying it. Everybody would be trying not to look at bright-colored, foreign-living, disgracefully divorced Valentine Ramsay; some in contempt—some in secret envy, because everything about him told how free he was. And up there, nobody was free. They were imprisoned in their harsh Calvinism, or in their merciless business grind, or in mere apathy—a mortal dullness.

Oh, I could see those two, walking about the narrow streets of the grim, raw, dark gray old city, cold with its river damp, and severe by reason of the brooding frown of huge stone churches that loomed up even in the most congested part of the shopping district. There were old graveyards round those churches, with gravestones sunken and tilted and blackened—covered this morning with dirty snow—and jangling car lines all about them. The street lamps would be burning all day, on account of the fog, full of black smoke from the furnace chimneys. Hidden away in the grime and damp and noise were the half dozen special shops which imported splendors for the owners of those mills that made the city so dark and so powerful.

Their shopping over, Valentine was going to take Aunt Charlotte to lunch at a hotel where they could get a very fine French wine she loved. What a day they would have! There was only one thing to be feared. They might easily chance to meet one of the Oglethorpe men, there were so many of them, or Janet herself, face to face, or her new husband, Seymour Towne, who had been the idle son of an industrious family, and by idling abroad had stepped into such a good thing that now his hard-working brothers found life bitter in their mouths.

But they didn't meet with anything disagreeable. They came home on the four-thirty train, before the rush, bringing their spoils with them (no motor truck deliveries down the valley in those days), and their faces shone like the righteous in his Heavenly Father's house. Aunt Charlotte admitted that she was tired and went up-stairs to lie down directly after tea. Valentine took me down into the music-room to show me where to put the blossoming mimosa tree he had found for Aunt Charlotte, when it came down on the express to-morrow. The little girls followed us, and when he told them to be still they crept into the corners.

Valentine sat down at the piano and began to play very softly; something dark and rich and shadowy, but not somber, with a silvery air flowing through its mysteriousness. It might, I thought, be something of Debussy's that I had never heard . . . but no, I was sure it was not.

Presently he rose abruptly to go without taking leave, but one of the little girls ran up to him—Helen, probably, she was the most musical—and asked him what he had been playing, please.

"Oh, some old thing, I guess. I wasn't thinking," he muttered vaguely, and escaped through the glass doors that led directly into the garden between our house and his. I felt very sure that it was nothing old, but something new—just beginning, indeed. That would be a pleasant thing to tell Aunt Charlotte. I ran up-stairs; the door of her room was ajar, but all was dark within. I entered on tiptoe and listened; she was sound asleep. What a day she had had!

VI

Aunt Charlotte planned a musical party for Christmas eve and invited a dozen or more of her old friends. They were coming home with her after the evening church service; we were to sing carols, and Uncle Valentine was to play. She telephoned the invitations, and made it very clear that Valentine Ramsay was going to be there. Whoever didn't want to meet him could decline. Nobody declined; some even said it would be a pleasure to hear him play again.

On Christmas eve, after dinner, Uncle Harry and I were left alone in the house. All the children went to the church with Aunt Charlotte; she left me to help Black John arrange the table for a late supper after the music. After I had seen to everything, I had an hour or so alone up-stairs in my own room.

I well remember how beautiful our valley looked from my window that winter night. Through the creaking, shaggy limbs of the great sycamores I could look off at the white, white landscape; the deep folds of the snow-covered hills, the high drifts over the bushes, the gleaming ice on the broken road, and the thin, gauzy clouds driving across the crystal-clear, star-spangled sky.

Across the garden was Bonnie Brae, with so many windows lighted; the parlor, the library, Uncle Jonathan's room, Morton's room, a yellow patch on the snow from Roland's window, which I could not see; off there, at the end of the long, dark, sagging wing, Valentine's study, lit up like a lantern. I often looked over at our neighbors' house and thought about how much life had gone on in it, and about the muted, mysterious lives that still went on there. In the garret were chests full of old letters; all the highly descriptive letters that Uncle Jonathan had written his wife when he was traveling abroad; family letters, love letters, every letter the boys had written home when they were away at school. And in all these letters were tender references to the garden, the old trees, the house itself. And now so many of those who had loved the old place and danced in the long parlor were dead. I wondered, as young people often do, how my elders had managed to bear life at all, either its killing happiness or its despair.

I heard wheels on the drive, and laughter. Looking out I saw guests alighting on one side of the house, and on the other side Uncle Valentine running across the garden, bare-headed in the snow. I started down-stairs with a little faint-ness at heart—I knew how much my aunt had counted on bringing Valentine again into the circle of her friends, under her own roof. I found him in the big hall, surrounded by the ladies—they hadn't yet taken off their wraps—and I surveyed them from the second landing where the stairway turned. They were doing their best, I thought. Some of the younger women kept timidly at the outer edge of the group, but all the ones who counted most were emphatic in their cordi-ality. Deaf old Mrs. Hungerford, who rather directed public opinion in Greenacre, patted him on the back, shouted that now the naughty boy had come home to be good, and thrust out her ear trumpet at him. Julia Knewstubb, who for some reason, I never discovered why, was an important person, stood beside him in a brassy, patronizing way, and Ida Milholland, the intellectual light of the valley, began speaking slow, crusty French at him. In short, all was well.

Salutations over, Aunt Charlotte led the way to the music-room and signaled to her six girls. We sang one carol after another, and a fragment of John Bennett's we had especially practiced for Uncle Valentine—a song about a bluebird flying over a gray landscape and making it all blue; a pretty thing for high voices. But when we finished this and looked about to see whether it had pleased him, Valentine was nowhere to be found. Aunt Charlotte drew me aside while the others went out to supper and told me I must search all through the house, go to Bonnie Brae if necessary, and fetch him. It would never do for him to behave thus, when they had unbent so far as to come and greet him.

I looked out of the window and saw a light in his study at the end of the wing. The rooms between his study and the main house were unused, filled with old furniture. He avoided that chain of dusty, echoing chambers and came and went by a back door that opened into the old apple orchard. I dashed across the garden and ran in upon him without knocking.

There he was, lounging before the fire in his slippers and wine-colored velvet jacket, a pipe in his mouth and a yellow French book on his knee. I gasped and explained to him that he must come at once; the company was waiting for him.

He shrugged and waved his pipe. "I'm not going back at all. Pouf, what's the use? I'd only behave badly if I did. I don't want to lose my temper on Christmas eve."

"But you promised Aunt Charlotte, and she's told them you'd play," I pleaded.

He flung down his book wrathfully. "Oh, I can't stand them! I didn't know who Charlotte was going to ask . . . seems to me she's got together all the most objectionable old birds in the valley. There's Julia Knewstubb, with her nippers hanging on her nose, looking more like a horse than ever.

Old Mrs. Hungerford, poking her ear trumpet at me and stroking me on the back—I can't talk into an ear trumpet—can't think of anything important enough to say! And that bump of intellect, Ida Milholland, creaking at every joint and practicing her French grammar on me. Charlotte knows I hate ugly women—what did she get such a bunch together for? Not much, I'm not going back. Sit down and I'll read you something. I've got a new collection of all the legends about Tristan and Iseult. You can understand French?"

I said I would be dreadfully scolded if I did such a thing. "And you will hurt Aunt Charlotte's feelings, terribly!"

He laughed and poked out his red lower lip at me. "Shall I? Oh, but I can mend them again! Listen, I've got a new song for her, a good one. You sit down, and we'll work a spell on her; we'll wish and wish, and she'll come running over. While we wait I'll play it for you."

He put his pipe on the mantel, went to the piano, and commenced to play the Ballad of the Young Knight, which begins:

> "From the Ancient Kingdoms,
>   Through the wood of dreaming, . . ."

It was the same thing I had heard him trying out the afternoon he and Aunt Charlotte got home from the City.

"Now, you try it over with me, Margie. It's meant for high voice, you see. By the time she comes, we can give her a good performance."

"But she won't come, Uncle Valentine! She can't leave her guests."

"Oh, they'll soon be gone! Old tabbies always get sleepy after supper—you said they were at supper. She'll come."

I was so excited, so distressed and delighted, that I made a poor showing at reading the manuscript, and was well scolded. Valentine always wrote the words of his songs, as well as the music, like the old troubadours, and the words of this one were beautiful. "And what wood do you suppose it is?" He played the dark music with his left hand.

I said it made me think of the wood on the other side of Blinker's hill.

"I guess so," he muttered. "But of course it will be different woods to different people. Don't tell Charlotte, but I'm doing a lot of songs. I think of a new one almost every morning, when I waken up. Our woods are full of them, but they're terribly, terribly coy. You can't trap them, they're too wild. . . . No, you can't catch them . . . sometimes one comes and lights on your shoulder; I always wonder why."

It did not seem very long until Aunt Charlotte entered, bareheaded, her long black cape over her shoulders, a look of distress and anxiety on her face. Valentine sprang up and caught her hand.

"Not a word, Charlotte, don't scold, look before you leap! I kept Margie because I knew you'd come to hunt her, and I didn't just know any other way of getting you here. Now don't be angry, because when you get angry your face puffs up just a little, and I have reason to hate women whose faces swell. Sit down by the fire. We've had a rehearsal, and now we'll sing my new song for you. Don't glare at the child, or she can't sing. Why haven't you taught her to follow manuscript better?"

Aunt Charlotte didn't have a chance to speak until we had gone through with the song. But though my eyes were glued to the page, I knew her face was going through many changes.

"Now," he said exultantly as we finished, "with a song like that under my shirt, did I have to sit over there and let old Ida wise-bump practice her French on me—period of Bossuet, I guess!"

Aunt Charlotte laughed softly and asked us to sing it again. The second time we did better; Valentine hadn't much voice, but of course he knew how. As we finished we heard a queer sound, something like a snore and something like a groan, in the wall behind us. Valentine held up his finger sharply, tiptoed to the door behind the fireplace that led into the old wing, put down his head and listened for a moment. Then he wrenched open the door.

There stood Roland, holding himself steady by an old chest of drawers, his eyes looking blind, tears shining on his white face. He did not say a word; put his hands to his forehead as if to collect himself, and went away through the dark rooms, swaying slightly and groping along the floor with his feet.

"Poor old chap, perfectly soaked! I thought it was Molla Carlsen, spooking round." Valentine threw himself into a chair. "Do you suppose that's the way I'll be keeping Christmas ten years from now, Charlotte? What else is there for us to do, I ask you? Sons of an easy-going, self-satisfied American family, never taught anything until we are too old to learn. What could Roland do when he came home from Germany fifteen years ago? . . . Lord, it's more than that now . . . it's nineteen! Nineteen years!" Valentine dropped his head into his hands and rumpled his hair as if he were washing it, which was a sign with him that a situation was too hopeless for discussion. "Well, what could he have done, Charlotte? What could he do now? Teach piano, take the bread out of somebody's mouth? My son Dickie, he'll be an Oglethorpe! He'll get on, and won't carry this damned business any farther."

On Christmas morning Molla Carlsen came over and reported with evident satisfaction that Roland and Valentine had made a night of it, and were both keeping their rooms in consequence. Aunt Charlotte was sad and downcast all day long.

VII

Molla Carlsen loved to give my aunt the worst possible account of the men she kept house for, though in talking to outsiders I think she was discreet and loyal. She was a strange woman, then about forty years old, and she had been in the Ramsay household for more than twelve years. She managed everything over there, and was paid very high wages. She was grasping, but as honest as she was heartless. The house was well conducted, though it was managed, as Valentine said, somewhat like an institution. No matter how many thousand roses were blooming in the garden, it never occurred to Molla to cut any and put them in the bare, faded parlor. The men who lived there got no coddling; they were terribly afraid of her. When a wave of red went over Molla's white skin, poor Uncle Morton's shaky hands trembled more than ever, and his far-away eyes shrank to mere pin-points. He was the one who most often angered her, because he dropped things. Once when Aunt Charlotte remonstrated with her about her severity, she replied that a woman who managed a houseful of alcoholics must be a tyrant, or the place would be a sty.

This made us all indignant. Morton, we thought, was the only one who could justly be thus defined. He was the oldest of Uncle Jonathan's sons; tall, narrow, utterly spare, with a long, thin face, a shriveled scalp with a little dry hair on it, parted in the middle, eyes that never looked at you because the pupils were always shrunk so small. Morton was awfully proud of the fact that he was a business man; he alone of that household went up on the business men's train in the morning. He went to an office in the City, climbed upon a high stool, and fastened his distant eyes upon a ledger. (It was a coal business, in which his father owned a good deal of stock, and every night an accountant went over Morton's books and corrected his mistakes.) On his way to the office, he stopped at the bar of a most respectable hotel. He stopped there again before lunch at noon, and on his way to the station in the late afternoon. He often told Uncle Harry that he never took anything during business hours. Nobody ever saw Morton thoroughly intoxicated, but nobody ever saw him quite himself. He had good manners, a kind voice, though husky, and he was usually very quiet.

Uncle Jonathan, to be sure, took a good deal of whisky during the day — but then he ate almost nothing. Whisky and tobacco were his nourishment. He was frail, but he had been so even as a young man, and he outlived all his sons except Morton — lived on until the six little girls at Fox Hill were all grown women. No, I don't think it was alcohol that preserved him; I think it was his fortunate nature, his happy form of self-esteem. He was perfectly satisfied with himself and his family — with whatever they had done and whatever they had not done. He was glad that Roland had declined the nervous strain of an artistic career, and that Morton was in business; in each generation some of the Ramsays had been business men. Uncle Jonathan had loved his wife dearly and he must have missed her, but he was pleased with the verses he had written about her since her death, verses in the manner of Tom Moore, whom he considered an absolutely satisfactory poet. He had, of course, been proud of Valentine's brilliant marriage. The divorce he certainly regretted. But whatever pill life handed out to him he managed to swallow with equanimity.

Uncle Jonathan spent his days in the library, across the hall from the parlor, where he was writing a romance of the French and Indian wars. The room was lined with his father's old brown theological books, and everything one touched there felt dusty. There was always a scattering of tobacco crumbs over the hearth, the floor, the desk, and over Uncle Jonathan's waistcoat and whiskers. It wasn't in Molla Carlsen's contract to keep the tobacco dust off her master.

Roland Ramsay was Uncle Jonathan's much younger brother. When he was a boy of twelve and fourteen, he had been a musical prodigy, had played to large and astonished audiences in New York and Boston and Philadelphia. Later he was sent to Germany to study under Liszt and D'Albert. At twenty-eight he returned to Bonnie Brae—and he had been there ever since. He was a big, handsome man, never ill, but something had happened to his nervous system. He could not play in public, not even in his own city. Ever since Valentine was a little boy, Uncle Roland and his piano had lived upstairs at Bonnie Brae. There were several stories: that he had been broken by a love affair with a German singer; that Wagner had hurt his feelings so cruelly he could never get over it; that at his début in Paris he had forgotten in the middle of his sonata in what key the next movement was written, and had labored through the rest of his program like a man stupefied by drugs.

At any rate, Roland had broken nerves, just as some people have a weak heart, and he lived in solitude and silence. Occasionally when some fine orchestra or a new artist played in the City up the river, Roland's waxy, frozen face was to be seen in the audience; but not often. Five or six times a year he went on a long spree. Then he would shut himself up in his room and play the piano—it couldn't be called practicing—for eight or ten hours a day. Sometimes in the evening Aunt Charlotte would put on a cloak and go out into the garden to listen to him. "Harry," she said once when she came back into the house, "I was walking under Roland's window. Really, he is playing like a god to-night."

Inert and inactive as he was, Roland kept his good physique. He used to sit all afternoon beside his window with a book; as we came up the hill we could see his fine head and shoulders there, motionless as if in a frame. I never liked to look at his face, for his strong, well-cut features never moved. His eyes were large and uncomfortable-looking, under heavy lids with deep hollows beneath—curiously like the eyes of the tired American business men whose pictures appear in the papers when they are getting a divorce.

I had heard it whispered at school that Uncle Jonathan was "in Molla Carlsen's power," because Horace, the wild son, had made vehement advances to her long ago when she first came into the house, and that his bad behavior had hastened his mother's end. However it came about, in her power the lonely men at Bonnie Brae certainly were. When Molla was dressed to go up to the City, she walked down the front steps and got into the carriage with the air of mistress of the place. And her furs, we knew, had cost more than Aunt Charlotte's.

VIII

All that winter Valentine was tremendously busy. He was not only writing ever so many new songs, but was hunting up beautiful old ones for our sextette, and he trained us so industriously that the little girls fell behind in their lessons, and Aunt Charlotte had to limit rehearsals to three nights a week. I remember he made us an arrangement for voices of the minuet in the third movement of Brahms' second symphony, and wrote words to it.

We were not allowed to sing any of Valentine's songs in company, not even for Aunt Charlotte's old friends. He was rather proud and sulky with most of the neighbors, and wouldn't have it. When we tried out his new songs for the home circle, as he said, Uncle Morton was allowed to come over, and Uncle Jonathan in his black cape. Roland came too, and sat off in a corner by himself. Uncle Jonathan thought very well of his own judgment in music. He liked all Valentine's songs, but warned him against writing things without a sufficient "climax," mildly bidding him beware of a too modern manner.

I remember he used to repeat for his son's guidance two lines from one of his favorite poets, accenting the measure with the stogie he held in his fingers—a particularly noxious kind of cigar which he not only smoked but, on occasion, ate!

"Avoid eccentricity, Val," he would say, beaming softly at his son. "Remember this admirable rule for poets and composers:

> Be not the first by whom the new is tried,
> Nor yet the last to lay the old aside."

That year the spring began early. I remember March and April as a succession of long walks and climbs with Valentine. Sometimes Aunt Charlotte went with us, but she was not a nimble walker, and Valentine liked climb and dash and short-cut. We would plunge into the wooded course of Blue Run or Powhatan Creek, and get to the top of Flint Ridge by a quicker route than any path. That long, windy ridge lay behind Blinker's Hill and Fox Hill; the top was a bare expanse, except for a few bleached boulders and twisted oaks. From there we could look off over all the great wrinkles of hills, catch glimpses of the river, and see the black pillar of cloud to the north where the City lay. This dark cloud, as evening came on, took deep rich colors from the sunset; and after the sun was gone it sent out all night an orange glow from the furnace fires that burned there. But that smoke did not come down to us; our evenings were pure and silvery—soft blue skies seen through the budding trees above us, or over the folds and folds of lavender forest below us.

One Saturday afternoon we took Aunt Charlotte along and got to the top of Flint Ridge by the winding roadway. As we were walking upon the crest, curtains of mist began to rise from the river and from between the lines of hills. Soon the darkening sky was full of fleecy clouds, and the countryside below us disappeared into nothingness.

Suddenly, in the low cut between the hills across the river, we saw a luminousness, throbbing and phosphorescent, a ghostly brightness with mists streaming about it and enfolding it, struggling to quench it. We knew it was the moon, but we could see no form, no solid image; it was a flowing, surging, liquid gleaming; now stronger, now softer.

"The Rhinegold!" murmured Valentine and Aunt Charlotte in one breath. The little girls were silent; Betty Jane felt for my hand. They were awed, not so much by the light, as by something in the two voices that had spoken together. Presently we dropped into the dark winding road along Blue Run and got home late for dinner.

While we were at dessert, Uncle Valentine went into the music-room and began to play the Rhine music. He played on as if he would never stop; Siegmund's love song and the Valhalla music and back to the Rhine journey and the Rhine maidens. The cycle was like a plaything in his hands. Presently a shadow fell in the patch of moonlight on the floor, and looking out I saw Roland, without a hat, standing just outside the open window. He often appeared at the window or the doorway when we were singing with Valentine, but if we noticed him, or addressed him, he faded quickly away.

As Valentine stopped for a moment, his uncle tapped on the window glass.

"Going over now, Valentine? It's getting late."

"Yes, I suppose it is. I say, Charlotte, do you remember how we used to play the Ring to each other hours on end, long ago, when Damrosch first brought the German opera over? Why can't people stay young forever?"

"Maybe you will, Val," said Aunt Charlotte, musing. "What a difference Wagner made in the world, after all!"

"It's not a good thing to play Wagner at night," said the gray voice outside the window. "It brings on sleeplessness."

"I'll come along presently, Roland," the nephew called. "I'm warm now; I'll take cold if I go out."

The large figure went slowly away.

"Poor old Roland, isn't he just a coffin of a man!" Valentine got up and lit the fagots in the fireplace. "I feel shivery. I've had him on my hands a good deal this winter. He'll come drifting in through the wing and settle himself in my study and sit there half the night without opening his head."

"Doesn't he talk to you, even?" I asked.

"Hardly, though I get fidgety and talk to him. Sometimes

he plays. He's always interesting at the piano. It's remarkable that he plays as well as he does, when he's so irregular."

"Does he really read? We so often see him sitting by his upstairs window with a book."

"He reads too much, German philosophy and things that aren't good for him. Did you know, Charlotte, that he keeps a diary. At least he writes often in a big ledger Morton brought him from town. Sometimes he's at it for hours. Lord, I'd like to know what he puts down in it!" Valentine plunged his head in his hands and began rumpling his hair. "Can you remember him much before he went abroad, Charlotte?"

"When I was little I was taken to hear him play in Steinway hall, just before he went to Germany. From what I can remember, it was very brilliant. He had splendid hands, and a wonderful memory. When he came back he was much more musical, but he couldn't play in public."

"Queer! How he supports the years as they come and go. . . . Of course, he loves the place, just as I do; that's something. By the way, when I was home three years ago I was let into a family secret; it was Roland who was Molla Carlsen's suitor and made all the row, not poor Horace at all! Oh, shouldn't I have said that before the sextette? They'll forget it. They forget most things. What haunts me about Roland is the feeling of kinship. So often it flashes into my mind: 'Yes, I might be struck dumb some day, just like that.' Oh, don't laugh! It *was* like that, for months and months, while I was trying to live with Janet. My skin would get yellow, and I'd feel a perfect loathing of speech. My jaws would set together so that I couldn't open them. I'd walk along the quais in Paris and go without a newspaper because I couldn't bring myself to say good-morning to the old woman and buy one. I'd wander about awfully hungry because I couldn't bear the sound of talk in a restaurant. I dodged everybody I knew, or cut them."

There was something funny about his self-commiseration, and I wanted to hear more; but just at this point we were told that we must go instantly to bed.

"And I?" Valentine asked, "must I go too?"

"No. You may stay a little longer."

Aunt Charlotte must have thought he needed a serious talking-to, for she almost never saw him alone. Her life was hedged about by very subtle but sure conventionalities, and that was only one of many things she did not permit herself.

IX

Fox Hill was soon besieged on all sides by spring. The first attack came by way of the old apple orchard that ran irregularly behind our carriage house and Uncle Valentine's studio. The foaming, flowery trees were a beautiful sight from his doorstep. Aunt Charlotte and Morton were carrying on a hot rivalry in tulips. Uncle Jonathan now came out to sun himself on the front porch, in a broad-rimmed felt hat and a green plaid shawl which his father used to wear on horseback trips over the hills.

Though spring first attacked us through the orchard, the great assault, for which we children waited, came on the side of the hill next the river; it was violent, blood-red, long drawn-out, and when it was over, our hill belonged to summer. The vivid event of our year was the blooming of the wall.

Along the front of Fox Hill, where the lawn ended in a steep descent, Uncle Harry had put in a stone retaining wall to keep the ground from washing out. This wall, he said, he intended to manage himself, and when he first announced that he was going to cover it with red rambler roses, his wife laughed at him and told him he would spoil the whole hill. But in the event she was converted. Nowhere in the valley did ramblers thrive so well and bloom so gorgeously. From the railway station our home-coming business men could see that crimson wall, running along high on the green hillside.

One Sunday morning when the ramblers were at their height, we all went with Uncle Harry and Valentine down the driveway to admire them. Aunt Charlotte admitted that they were very showy, very decorative, but she added under her breath that she couldn't feel much enthusiasm for scentless roses.

"But they are quite another sort of thing," Uncle Harry expostulated. "They go right about their business and bloom.

I like their being without an odor; it gives them a kind of frankness and innocence."

In the bright sunlight I could see her dark skin flush a little. "Innocence?" she murmured, "I shouldn't call it just that."

I was wondering what she would call it, when our stable-man Bill came up from the post office with his leather bag and emptied the contents on the grass. He always brought the Ramsays' mail with ours, and we often teased Uncle Valentine about certain bright purple letters from Paris, addressed to him in a woman's hand. Because of the curious ways of mail steamers they sometimes came in pairs, and that morning there were actually five of these purple punctuations in the pile of white letters. The children laughed immoderately. Betty Jane and Elizabeth shouted for joy as they fished them out. "Poor Uncle Val! When will you ever get time to answer them all?"

"Ah, that's it!" he said as he began stuffing them away in his pockets.

The next afternoon Aunt Charlotte and I were sewing, seated in the little covered balcony out of her room, with honeysuckle vines all about us. We saw Valentine, hatless, in his striped blazer, come around the corner of the house and seat himself at the tea-table under one of the big sycamores, just below us. We were about to call to him, when he took out those five purple envelopes and spread them on the table before him as if he were going to play a game with them. My aunt looked at me with a sparkle in her eye and put her finger to her lips to keep me quiet. Elizabeth came running across from the summerhouse with her kitten. He called to her.

"Just a moment, Elizabeth. I want you to choose one of these."

"But how? What for?" she asked, much astonished.

"Oh, just choose one, any one," he said carelessly. "Put your finger down." He took out a lead pencil. "Now, we'll mark that 1. Choose again; very well, that's number 2; another, another. Thank you. Now the one that's left will necessarily be 5, won't it?"

"But, Uncle Val, aren't these the ones that came yesterday? And you haven't read them yet?"

"Hush, not so loud, dear." He took up his half-burned cigarette. "You see, when so many come at once, it's not easy to know which should be read first. But you've settled that difficulty for me." He swept them lightly into the two side pockets of his blazer and sprang up. "Where are the others? Can't we go off for a tramp somewhere? Up Blue Run, to see the wild azaleas?"

Elizabeth came into the house calling for us, and Aunt Charlotte and I went down to him.

"We're going up Blue Run to see the azaleas, Charlotte, won't you come?"

She looked wistful. "It's very hot. I'm afraid I ought not to climb, and you'll want to go the steep way."

She waited, hoping to be urged, but he said no more about it. He was sometimes quite heartless.

That evening we came home tired, and the little girls were sent to bed soon after dinner. It was the most glorious of summer nights; I couldn't think of giving it up and going to sleep. Our valley was still, breathlessly still, and full of white moonlight. The garden gave off a heavy perfume, the lawn and house were mottled with intense black and intense white, a mosaic so perplexing that I could hardly find my way along the familiar paths. There was a languorous spirit of beauty abroad—warm, sensuous, oppressive, like the pressure of a warm, clinging body. I felt vaguely afraid to be alone.

I looked for Aunt Charlotte, and found her in the little balcony off her bedroom, where we had been sitting that morning. She spoke to me impatiently, in a way that quite hurt my feelings.

"You must go to bed, Marjorie. I have a headache and I can't be with anyone to-night."

I could feel that she did not want me near her, that my intrusion was most unwelcome. I went downstairs. Uncle Harry was in his study, doing accounts.

"Fine night, isn't it?" he said cheerfully. "I'm going out to see a little of it presently. Almost done my figures." His accounts must have troubled him sometimes; his household cost a great deal of money.

I retreated to the apple orchard. Seeing that the door of

Valentine's study was open, I approached cautiously and looked in. He was on his divan, which he had pulled up into the moonlight, lying on his back with his arms under his head.

"Run away, Margie, I'm busy," he muttered, not looking at me but staring past me.

I walked alone about the garden, smelling the stocks until I could smell them no more. I noticed how many moonflowers had come out on the Japanese summerhouse that stood on the line between our ground and the Ramsays'. As I drew near it I heard a groan, not loud, but long, long, as if the unhappiness of a whole lifetime were coming out in one despairing breath. I looked in through the vines. There sat Roland, his head in his hands, the moonlight on his silver hair. I stole softly away through the grass. It seemed that to-night every-one wanted to be alone with his ghost.

Going home through the garden I heard a low call: "Wait, wait a minute!" Uncle Morton came out of the darkness of the vine-covered side porch and beckoned me to follow him. He led me to the plot where his finest roses were in bloom and stopped before a bush that had a great many buds on it, but only one open flower—a great white rose, almost as big as a moonflower, its petals beautifully curled.

"Wait a minute," he whispered again. He took out his pocket knife, and with great care and considerable difficulty managed to cut the rose with a long stem. He held it out to me in his shaking hand. "There," he said proudly. "That's my best one, the Queen of Savoy. I've been waiting for someone to give it to!"

This was a bold adventure for Morton. I saw that he meant it as a high compliment, and that he was greatly pleased with himself as he wavered back along the white path and disappeared into the darkness under the honeysuckle vines.

X

The next morning Valentine went up to town with Morton on the early train, and at six o'clock that evening Morton came back without him. Aunt Charlotte, who was watching in the garden, went quickly across the Ramsays' lawn.

"Morton, where is Valentine?"

Morton stood holding his straw hat before him in both hands, telling her vaguely that Valentine was going to spend the night in town, at a hotel. "He has to be near the cable office—been sending messages all day—something very important."

Valentine remained in the City for several days. We did not see him again until he joined us one afternoon when we were having tea in the garden. He looked fresh and happy, in new white flannels and one of his gayest neckties.

"Oh, it's delightful to be back, Charlotte!" he exclaimed as he sank into a chair near her.

"We've missed you, Valentine." She, too, looked radiantly happy.

"I should hope so! Because you're probably going to have a great deal of me. Likely I'm here forever, like Roland and the oak trees. I've been staying up in the City, on neutral ground for a few days, to find out what I really want. Do you know, Betty Jane and Elizabeth, that's a sure test; the place you wish for the first moment you're awake in the morning, is the place where you most want to be. I often want to do two things at once, be in two places at once, but this time I don't think I had a moment's indecision." He did not say about what, but presently he drew off a seal ring he wore on his little finger and began playing with it. I knew it was Louise Ireland's ring, he had told me so once. It was an intaglio, a three-masted ship under full sail, and over it, in old English letters, *Telle est la Vie*.

He sat playing with the ring, tossing it up into the sunlight and catching it in his palm, while he addressed my aunt.

"Ireland's leaving Paris. Off for a long tour in South Africa and Australia. She's like a sea gull or a swallow, that woman, forever crossing water. I'm sorry I can't be with her. She's the best friend I've ever had—except you, Charlotte." He did not look at my aunt, but the drop in his voice was a look. "I do seem to be tied to you."

"It's the valley you're tied to. The place is necessary to you, Valentine."

"Yes, it's the place, and it's you and the children—it's even Morton and Roland, God knows why!"

Aunt Charlotte was right. It was the place. The people were secondary. Indeed, I have often wondered, had he been left to his own will, how long he would have been content there. A man under thirty does not settle down to live with old men and children. But the place was vocal to him. During the year that he was with us he wrote all of the thirty-odd songs by which he lives. Some artists profit by exile. He was one of those who do not. And his country was not a continent, but a few wooded hills in a river valley, a few old houses and gardens that were home.

XI

The summer passed joyously. Valentine went on making new songs for us and we went on singing them. I expected life to be like that forever. The golden year, Aunt Charlotte called it, when I visited her at Fox Hill years afterward. September came and went, and then a cold wind blew down upon us.

Uncle Harry and Morton came home one night with disturbing news. It was said in the City that the old Wakeley estate had been sold. Miss Belle Wakeley, the sole heir, had lived in Italy for several years; her big house on the unwooded side of Blinker's Hill had been shut up, her many acres rented out or lying idle.

Very soon after Uncle Harry startled us with this news, Valentine came over to ask whether such a thing were possible. No large tract of land had changed hands in Greenacre for many years.

"I rather think it's true," said Uncle Harry. "I'm going to the agent to-morrow to find out any particulars I can. It seems to be a very guarded transaction. I suppose this means that Belle has decided to live abroad for good. I'm sorry."

"It's very wrong of her," said Aunt Charlotte, "and I think she'll regret it. If she hasn't any feeling for her property now, she will have some day. Why, her grandfather was born there!"

"Yes, I'm disappointed. I thought Belle had a great deal of sentiment underneath." Uncle Harry had always been Miss Wakeley's champion, liked her independent ways, and was amused by her brusque manners.

Valentine was standing by the fireplace, abstracted and deeply concerned.

"Just how much does the Wakeley property take in, Harry? I've never known exactly."

"A great deal. It covers the courses of both creeks, Blue Run and Powhatan creek, and runs clear back to the top of Flint Ridge. It's our biggest estate, by long odds."

Valentine began pacing the floor. "Did you know she wanted to sell? Couldn't the neighbors have clubbed together and bought it, rather than let strangers in?"

Uncle Harry laughed and shook his head. "I'm afraid we're not rich enough, Val. It's worth a tremendous lot of money. Most of us have all the land we can take care of."

"I suppose so," he muttered. "Father's pretty well mortgaged up, isn't he?"

"Pretty well," Uncle Harry admitted. "Don't worry. I'll see what I can find out to-morrow. I can't think Belle would sell to a speculator, and let her estate be parceled out. She'd have too much consideration for the rest of us. She was the finest kind of neighbor. I wish we had her back."

"It never occurred to me, Harry, that the actual countryside could be sold; the creeks and woods and hills. That shouldn't be permitted. They ought to be kept just as they are, since they give the place its character."

Uncle Harry said he was afraid the only way of keeping a place the same, in this country, was to own it.

"But there are some things one doesn't think of in terms of money," Valentine persisted. "If I'd had bushels of money when I came home last winter, it would never have occurred to me to try to buy Blinker's Hill, any more than the sky over it. I didn't know that the Wakeleys or anybody else owned the creeks, and the forest up toward the Ridge."

Aunt Charlotte rose and went up to Uncle Harry's chair. "Is it really too late to do anything? Too late to cable Belle and ask her to give her neighbors a chance to buy it in first?"

"My dear, you never do realize much about the cost of things. But remember, Belle is a shrewd business woman. She knows well enough that no dozen of her neighbors could raise so much ready money. I understand it's a cash transaction."

Aunt Charlotte looked hurt. "Well, I can only say it was

faithless of her. People have some responsibility toward the place where they were born, and toward their old friends."

Dinner was announced, and Valentine was urged to stay, but he refused.

"I don't want any dinner, I'm too nervous. I'm awfully fussed by this affair, Charlotte." He stood beside my aunt at the door for a moment, hanging his head despondently, and went away.

That evening my aunt and uncle could talk of nothing but the sale of the Wakeley property. Uncle Harry said sadly that he had never before so wished that he were a rich man. "Though even if I were, I don't know that I'd have thought of making Belle an offer. I'm as impractical as Valentine. But if I'd had money, I do believe Belle would have given me the first chance. We're her nearest neighbors, and whoever buys Blinker's Hill has to be a part of our landscape, and to come into our life more or less."

"Have you any suspicion who it may be?" She spoke very low.

Uncle Harry was standing beside her, his back to the hall fire, smoking his church-warden pipe. "The purchaser? Not the slightest. Have you?"

"Yes." She spoke lower still. "A suspicion that tortures me. It flashed into my mind the moment you told us. I don't know why."

"Then keep it to yourself, my dear," he said resolutely, as if he had all he cared to shoulder. I heard a snap, and saw that he had broken the long stem of his pipe. "There," he said, throwing it into the fire, "you and Valentine have got me worked up with your fussing. I'm as shaky as poor Morton to-night."

XII

The next day Uncle Harry telephoned my aunt from his office in town; Miss Wakeley's agent was not at liberty to disclose the purchaser's name, but assured him that the estate was not sold to a speculator, but an old resident of the City who would preserve the property very much as it was and would respect the feelings of the community.

I was sent over to Bonnie Brae with the good tidings. We all felt so much encouraged that we decided to spend the afternoon in the woods that had been restored to us. It was a yellow October day, and our country had never looked more beautiful. We had tea beside Powhatan creek, where it curved wide and shallow through green bottom land. A plantation of sycamores grew there, their old white roots bursting out of the low banks and forking into the stream itself. The bark of those sycamores was always peculiarly white, and the sunlight played on the silvery interlacing of the great boughs. Dry ledges of slate rock stood out of the cold green water here and there, and on the up-stream side of each ledge lay a little trembling island of yellow leaves, unable to pass the barrier. The meadow in which we lingered was smooth turf, of that intense green of autumn grass that has been already a little touched by frost.

As we sat on the warm slate rocks, we looked up at the wooded side of Blinker's Hill—like a mellow old tapestry. The fiercest autumn colors had burned themselves out; the gold on the smoke-colored beeches was thin and pale, so that through their horizontal branches one could see the colored carpet of leaves on the ground. Only the young oaks held all their ruby leaves, the deepest tone in the whole scale of reds—and they would still be there, a little duller, when the snow was flying.

I remember my aunt's voice, a tone not quite natural, when she said suddenly, "Valentine, how beautiful the Tuilleries gardens are on an afternoon like this—down about the second fountain. The color lasts in the sky so long after dusk comes on,—behind the Eiffel tower."

He was lying on his back. He sat up and looked at her sharply. "Oh, yes!"

"Aren't you beginning to be a little homesick for it?" she asked bashfully.

"A little. But it's rather nice to sit safe and lazy on Fox Hill and be a trifle homesick for far-away places. Even Roland gets homesick for Bavaria in the spring, he tells me. He takes a drink or two and recovers. Are you trying to shove me off somewhere?"

She sighed. "Oh, no! No, indeed, I'm not."

But she had, in some way, broken the magical contentment of the afternoon. The little girls began to seem restless, so we gathered them up and started home.

We followed the road round the foot of Blinker's Hill, to the cleared side on which stood the old Wakeley house. There we saw a man and woman coming down the driveway from the house itself. The man stopped and hesitated, but the woman quickened her pace and came toward us. Aunt Charlotte became very pale. She had recognized them at a distance, and so had I; Janet Oglethorpe and her second husband. I remember exactly how she looked. She was wearing a black and white check out-of-door coat and a hard black turban. Her face, always high-colored, was red and shiny from exercise. She waved to us cordially as she came up, but did not offer to shake hands. Her husband took off his hat and smiled scornfully. He stood well behind her, looking very ill at ease, with his elbows out and his chin high, and as the conversation went on his haughty smile became a nervous grin.

"How do you do, Mrs. Waterford, and how do you do, Valentine," Mrs. Towne began effusively. She spoke very fast, and her lips seemed not to keep up with her enunciation; they were heavy and soft, and made her speech slushy. Her mouth was her bad feature—her teeth were too far apart, there was something crude and inelegant about them. "We are going to be neighbors, Mrs. Waterford. I don't want it noised abroad yet, but I've just bought the Wakeley place. I'm going to do the house over and live down here. I hope you won't mind our coming."

Aunt Charlotte made some reply. Valentine did not utter a sound. He took off his hat, replaced it, and stood with his hands in his jacket pockets, looking at the ground.

"I've always had my eye on this property," Mrs. Towne went on, "but it took Belle a long while to make up her mind. It's too fine a place to be left going to waste. It will be nice for Valentine's boy to grow up here where he did, and to be near his Grandfather Ramsay. I want him to know his Ramsay kin."

Valentine behaved very badly. He addressed her without lifting his eyes from the ground or taking his hands out of his pockets; merely kicked a dead leaf out of the road and said:

"He's not my boy, and the less he sees of the Ramsays, the
better. You've got him, it's your affair to make an Oglethorpe
of him and see that he stays one. What do you want to make
the kid miserable for?"

Mrs. Towne grew as much redder as it was possible to be,
but she spoke indulgently. "Now, Valentine, why can't you be
sensible? Certainly, on Mrs. Waterford's account—"

"Oh, yes!" he muttered. "That's the Oglethorpe notion of
good manners, before people!"

"I'm sorry, Mrs. Waterford. I had no idea he would be so
naughty, or I wouldn't have stopped you. But I did want you
to be the first person to know." Mrs. Towne turned to my
aunt with great self-command and a ready flow of speech.
Her alarmingly high color and a slight swelling of the face,
a puffing-up about her eyes and nose, betrayed her state of
feeling.

The women talked politely for a few moments, while the
two men stood sulking, each in his own way. When the con-
ference was over, Mrs. Towne crossed the road resolutely and
took the path to the station. Towne again took off his hat,
looking nowhere, and followed her. Valentine did not return
the salute.

As our meek band went on around the foot of the hill, he
merely pulled his hat lower over his eyes and said, "She's
Scotch; she couldn't let anything get away—not even me. All
damned bunk about wanting to get Dickie down here. Every-
thing about her's bunk, except her damned money. That's a
fact, and it's got me—it's got me."

Aunt Charlotte's breathing was so irregular that she could
scarcely speak. "Valentine, I've had a presentiment of that,
from the beginning. I scarcely slept at all last night. I can't
have it so. Harry must find some way out."

"No way out, Charlotte," he went along swinging his
shoulders and speaking in a dull sing-song voice. "That was
her creek we were playing along this afternoon; Blue Run,
Powhatan Creek, the big woods, Flint Ridge, Blinker's Hill. I
can't get in or out. What does it say on the rat-bane bottle;
put the poison along all his runways. That's the right idea!"

He did not stop with us, but cut back through the orchard
to his study. After dinner we waited for him, sitting solemnly

about the fire. At last Aunt Charlotte started up as if she could bear it no longer.

"Come on, Harry," she said firmly. "We must see about Valentine."

He looked up at her pathetically. "Take Marjorie, won't you? I really don't want to see the poor chap to-night, Charlotte."

We hurried across the garden. The studio was dark, the fire had gone out. He was lying on the couch, but he did not answer us. I found a box of matches and lit a candle.

One of Uncle Jonathan's rye bottles stood half empty on the mantelpiece. He had had no dinner, had drunk off nearly a pint of whisky and dropped on the couch. He was deathly white, and his eyes were rolled up in his head.

Aunt Charlotte knelt down beside him and covered him with her cloak. "Run for your Uncle Harry, as fast as you can," she said.

XIII

The end? That was the end for us. Within the week workmen were pulling down the wing of the Wakeley house, in order to get as much work as possible done before the cold weather came on. The sound of the stone masons' tools rang out clear across the cut between the two hills; even in Valentine's study one could not escape it. We wished that Morton had carried out his happy idea of making a padded cell of it!

Valentine lingered on at Bonnie Brae for a month, though he never went off his father's place again. He did not sail until the end of November, stayed out his year with us, but he had become a different man. All of us, except Aunt Charlotte, were eager to have him go. He had tonsillitis, I remember, and lay on the couch in his study ill and feverish for two weeks. He seemed not to be working, yet he must have been, for when he went away he left between the leaves of one of my aunt's music books the manuscript of the most beautiful and heart-breaking of all his songs:

I know a wall where red roses grow . . .

He deferred his departure from date to date, changed his passage several times. The night before he went we were sitting by the hall fire, and he said he wished that all the trains and all the boats in the world would stop moving, stop forever.

When his trunks had gone, and his bags were piled up ready to be put into the carriage, he took a latchkey from his pocket and gave it to Aunt Charlotte.

"That's the key to my study. Keep it for me. I don't know that I'll ever need it again, but I'd like to think that you have it."

Less than two years afterward, Valentine was accidentally killed, struck by a motor-truck one night at the Pont Royal, just as he was leaving Louise Ireland's apartment on the Quai.

Aunt Charlotte survived him by eleven years, but after her death we found his latchkey in her jewel box. I have it still. There is now no door for it to open. Bonnie Brae was pulled down during the war. The wave of industrial expansion swept down that valley, and roaring mills belch their black smoke up to the heights where those lovely houses used to stand. Fox Hill is gone, and our wall is gone. *I know a wall where red roses grow*; youngsters sing it still. The roses of song and the roses of memory, they are the only ones that last.

Woman's Home Companion, February–March 1925

Double Birthday

EVEN IN American cities, which seem so much alike, where people seem all to be living the same lives, striving for the same things, thinking the same thoughts, there are still individuals a little out of tune with the times—there are still survivals of a past more loosely woven, there are disconcerting beginnings of a future yet unforeseen.

Coming out of the gray stone Court House in Pittsburgh on a dark November afternoon, Judge Hammersley encountered one of these men whom one does not readily place, whom one is, indeed, a little embarrassed to meet, because they have not got on as they should. The Judge saw him mounting the steps outside, leaning against the wind, holding his soft felt hat on with his hand, his head thrust forward—hurrying with a light, quick step, and so intent upon his own purposes that the Judge could have gone out by a side door and avoided the meeting. But that was against his principles.

"Good day, Albert," he muttered, seeming to feel, himself, all the embarrassment of the encounter, for the other snatched off his hat with a smile of very evident pleasure, and something like pride. His gesture bared an attractive head—small, well-set, definite and smooth, one of those heads that look as if they had been turned out of some hard, rich wood by a workman deft with the lathe. His smooth-shaven face was dark—a warm coffee color—and his hazel eyes were warm and lively. He was not young, but his features had a kind of quick-silver mobility. His manner toward the stiff, frowning Judge was respectful and admiring—not in the least self-conscious.

The Judge inquired after his health and that of his uncle.

"Uncle Albert is splendidly preserved for his age. Frail, and can't stand any strain, but perfectly all right if he keeps to his routine. He's going to have a birthday soon. He will be eighty on the first day of December, and I shall be fifty-five on the same day. I was named after him because I was born on his twenty-fifth birthday."

"Umph." The Judge glanced from left to right as if this

announcement were in bad taste, but he put a good face on it and said with a kind of testy heartiness, "That will be an—occasion. I'd like to remember it in some way. Is there anything your uncle would like, any—recognition?" He stammered and coughed.

Young Albert Engelhardt, as he was called, laughed apologetically, but with confidence. "I think there is, Judge Hammersley. Indeed, I'd thought of coming to you to ask a favor. I am going to have a little supper for him, and you know he likes good wine. In these dirty bootlegging times, it's hard to get."

"Certainly, certainly." The Judge spoke up quickly and for the first time looked Albert squarely in the eye. "Don't give him any of that bootleg stuff. I can find something in my cellar. Come out to-morrow night after eight, with a gripsack of some sort. Very glad to help you out, Albert. Glad the old fellow holds up so well. Thank'ee, Albert," as Engelhardt swung the heavy door open and held it for him to pass.

Judge Hammersley's car was waiting for him, and on the ride home to Squirrel Hill he thought with vexation about the Engelhardts. He was really a sympathetic man, and though so stern of manner, he had deep affections; was fiercely loyal to old friends, old families, and old ideals. He didn't think highly of what is called success in the world to-day, but such as it was he wanted his friends to have it, and was vexed with them when they missed it. He was vexed with Albert for unblushingly, almost proudly, declaring that he was fifty-five years old, when he had nothing whatever to show for it. He was the last of the Engelhardt boys, and they had none of them had anything to show. They all died much worse off in the world than they began. They began with a flourishing glass factory up the river, a comfortable fortune, a fine old house on the park in Allegheny, a good standing in the community; and it was all gone, melted away.

Old August Engelhardt was a thrifty, energetic man, though pig-headed—Judge Hammersley's friend and one of his first clients. August's five sons had sold the factory and wasted the money in fantastic individual enterprises, lost the big house, and now they were all dead except Albert. They ought all to be alive, with estates and factories and families.

To be sure, they had that queer German streak in them; but so had old August, and it hadn't prevented his amounting to something. Their bringing-up was wrong; August had too free a hand, he was too proud of his five handsome boys, and too conceited. Too much tennis, Rhine wine punch, music, and silliness. They were always running over to New York, like this Albert. Somebody, when asked what in the world young Albert had ever done with his inheritance, had laughingly replied that he had spent it on the Pennsylvania Railroad.

Judge Hammersley didn't see how Albert could hold his head up. He had some small job in the County Clerk's office, was dependent upon it, had nothing else but the poor little house on the South Side where he lived with his old uncle. The county took care of him for the sake of his father, who had been a gallant officer in the Civil War, and afterward a public-spirited citizen and a generous employer of labor. But, as Judge Hammersley had bitterly remarked to Judge Merriman when Albert's name happened to come up, "If it weren't for his father's old friends seeing that he got something, that fellow wouldn't be able to make a living." Next to a charge of dishonesty, this was the worst that could be said of any man.

Judge Hammersley's house out on Squirrel Hill sat under a grove of very old oak trees. He lived alone, with his daughter, Margaret Parmenter, who was a widow. She had a great many engagements, but she usually managed to dine at home with her father, and that was about as much society as he cared for. His house was comfortable in an old-fashioned way, well appointed—especially the library, the room in which he lived when he was not in bed or at the Court House. To-night, when he came down to dinner, Mrs. Parmenter was already at the table, dressed for an evening party. She was tall, handsome, with a fine, easy carriage, and her face was both hard and sympathetic, like her father's. She had not, however, his stiffness of manner, that contraction of the muscles which was his unconscious protest at any irregularity in the machinery of life. She accepted blunders and accidents smoothly if not indifferently.

As the old colored man pulled back the Judge's chair for him, he glanced at his daughter from under his eyebrows.

"I saw that son of old Gus Engelhardt's this afternoon," he said in an angry, challenging tone.

As a young girl his daughter had used to take up the challenge and hotly defend the person who had displeased or disappointed her father. But as she grew older she was conscious of that same feeling in herself when people fell short of what she expected; and she understood now that when her father spoke as if he were savagely attacking someone, it merely meant that he was disappointed or sorry for them; he never spoke thus of persons for whom he had no feeling. So she said calmly:

"Oh, did you really? I haven't seen him for years, not since the war. How was he looking? Shabby?"

"Not so shabby as he ought to. That fellow's likely to be in want one of these days."

"I'm afraid so," Mrs. Parmenter sighed. "But I believe he would be rather plucky about it."

The Judge shrugged. "He's coming out here to-morrow night, on some business for his uncle."

"Then I'll have a chance to see for myself. He must look much older. I can't imagine his ever looking really old and settled, though."

"See that you don't ask him to stay. I don't want the fellow hanging around. He'll transact his business and get it over. He had the face to admit to me that he'll be fifty-five years old on the first of December. He's giving some sort of birthday party for old Albert, a-hem." The Judge coughed formally but was unable to check a smile; his lips sarcastic, but his eyes full of sly humor.

"Can he be as old as that? Yes, I suppose so. When we were both at Mrs. Sterrett's, in Rome, I was fifteen, and he must have been about thirty."

Her father coughed. "He'd better have been in Homestead!"

Mrs. Parmenter looked up; that was rather commonplace, for her father. "Oh, I don't know. Albert would never have been much use in Homestead, and he was very useful to Mrs. Sterrett in Rome."

"What did she want the fellow hanging round for? All the men of her family amounted to something."

"To too much! There must be some butterflies if one is going to give house parties, and the Sterretts and Dents were all heavyweights. He was in Rome a long while; three years, I think. He had a gorgeous time. Anyway, he learned to speak Italian very well, and that helps him out now, doesn't it? You still send for him at the Court House when you need an interpreter?"

"That's not often. He picks up a few dollars. Nice business for his father's son."

After dinner the Judge retired to his library, where the gas fire was lit, and his book at hand, with a paper-knife inserted to mark the place where he had left off reading last night at exactly ten-thirty. On his way he went to the front door, opened it, turned on the porch light, and looked at the thermometer, making an entry in a little notebook. In a few moments his daughter, in an evening cloak, stopped at the library door to wish him good night and went down the hall. He listened for the closing of the front door; it was a reassuring sound to him. He liked the feeling of an orderly house, empty for himself and his books all evening. He was deeply read in divinity, philosophy, and in the early history of North America.

II

While Judge Hammersley was settling down to his book, Albert Engelhardt was sitting at home in a garnet velvet smoking-jacket, at an upright piano, playing Schumann's *Kreisleriana* for his old uncle. They lived, certainly, in a queer part of the city, on one of the dingy streets that run uphill off noisy Carson Street, in a little two-story brick house, a workingman's house, that Albert's father had taken over long ago in satisfaction of a bad debt. When his father had acquired this building, it was a mere nothing—the Engelhardts were then living in their big, many-gabled, so-German house on the Park, in Allegheny; and they owned many other buildings, besides the glass factory up the river. After the father's death, when the sons converted houses and lands into cash, this forgotten little house on the South Side had somehow never been sold or mortgaged. A day came when Albert, the last surviving son, found this piece of property the only thing he owned in the world besides his personal effects. His uncle, having had a crushing disappointment, wanted at that time to retire from the practice of medicine, so Albert settled in the South Side house and took his uncle with him.

He had not gone there in any mood of despair. His impoverishment had come about gradually, and before he took possession of these quarters he had been living in a boarding house; the change seemed going up instead of going down in the world. He was delighted to have a home again, to unpack his own furniture and his books and pictures—the most valuable in the world to him, because they were full of his own history and that of his family, were like part of his own personality. All the years and the youth which had slipped away from him still clung to these things.

At his piano, under his Degas drawing in black and red—three ballet girls at the bar—or seated at his beautiful inlaid writing table, he was still the elegant young man who sat there long ago. His rugs were fine ones, his collection of books was large and very personal. It was full of works which, though so recent, were already immensely far away and diminished. The glad, rebellious excitement they had once caused in the world he could recapture only in memory. Their power to seduce and stimulate the young, the living, was utterly gone. There was a complete file of the *Yellow Book*, for instance; who could extract sweet poison from those volumes now? A portfolio of the drawings of Aubrey Beardsley—decadent, had they been called? A slender, padded volume—the complete works of a great new poet, Ernest Dowson. Oscar Wilde, whose wickedness was now so outdone that he looked like the poor old hat of some Victorian belle, wired and feathered and garlanded and faded.

Albert and his uncle occupied only the upper floor of their house. The ground floor was let to an old German glass engraver who had once been a workman in August Engelhardt's factory. His wife was a good cook, and every night sent their dinner up hot on the dumb-waiter. The house opened directly upon the street, and to reach Albert's apartment one went down a narrow paved alley at the side of the building and mounted an outside flight of wooden stairs at the back. They had only four rooms—two bedrooms, a snug sitting room in which they dined, and a small kitchen where Albert got breakfast every morning. After he had gone to work, Mrs. Rudder came up from downstairs to wash the dishes and do the cleaning, and to cheer up old Doctor Engelhardt.

At dinner this evening Albert had told his uncle about meeting Judge Hammersley, and of his particular inquiries after his health. The old man was very proud and received this intelligence as his due, but could not conceal a certain gratification.

"The daughter, she still lives with him? A damned fine-looking woman!" he muttered between his teeth. Uncle Albert, a bachelor, had been a professed connoisseur of ladies in his day.

Immediately after dinner, unless he were going somewhere, Albert always played for his uncle for an hour. He played extremely well. Doctor Albert sat by the fire smoking his cigar. While he listened, the look of wisdom and professional authority faded, and many changes went over his face, as if he were playing a little drama to himself; moods of scorn and contempt, of rakish vanity, sentimental melancholy . . . and something remote and lonely. The Doctor had always flattered himself that he resembled a satyr, because the tops of his ears were slightly pointed; and he used to hint to his nephews that his large pendulous nose was the index of an excessively amorous disposition. His mouth was full of long, yellowish teeth, all crowded irregularly, which he snapped and ground together when he uttered denunciations of modern art or the Eighteenth Amendment. He wore his mustache short and twisted up at the corners. His thick gray hair was cut close and upright, in the bristling French fashion. His hands were small and fastidious, high-knuckled, quite elegant in shape.

Across the Doctor's throat ran a long, jagged scar. He used to mutter to his young nephews that it had been justly inflicted by an outraged husband—a pistol shot in the dark. But his brother August always said that he had been cut by glass, when, wandering about in the garden one night after drinking too much punch, he had fallen into the cold-frames.

After playing Schumann for some time, Albert, without stopping, went into Stravinsky.

Doctor Engelhardt by the gas fire stirred uneasily, turned his important head toward his nephew, and snapped his teeth. "Br-r-r, that stuff! Poverty of imagination, poverty of musical invention; *fin-de-siècle!*"

Albert laughed. "I thought you were asleep. Why will you use that phrase? It shows your vintage. Like this any better?" He began the second act of *Pélleas et Mélisande*.

The Doctor nodded. "Yes, that is better, though I'm not fooled by it." He wrinkled his nose as if he were smelling out something, and squinted with superior discernment. "To this *canaille* that is all very new; but to me it goes back to Bach."

"Yes, if you like."

Albert, like Judge Hammersley, was jealous of his solitude—liked a few hours with his books. It was time for Uncle Doctor to be turning in. He ended the music by playing half a dozen old German songs which the old fellow always wanted but never asked for. The Doctor's chin sank into his shirt front. His face took on a look of deep, resigned sadness; his features, losing their conscious importance, seemed to shrink a good deal. His nephew knew that this was the mood in which he would most patiently turn to rest and darkness. Doctor Engelhardt had had a heavy loss late in life. Indeed, he had suffered the same loss twice.

As Albert left the piano, the Doctor rose and walked a little stiffly across the room. At the door of his chamber he paused, brought his hand up in a kind of military salute and gravely bowed, so low that one saw only the square upstanding gray brush on the top of his head and the long pear-shaped nose. After this he closed the door behind him. Albert sat down to his book. Very soon he heard the bath water running. Having taken his bath, the Doctor would get into bed immediately to avoid catching cold. Luckily, he usually slept well. Perhaps he dreamed of that unfortunate young singer whom he sometimes called, to his nephew and himself, "the lost Lenore."

III

Long years ago, when the Engelhardt boys were still living in the old house in Allegheny with their mother, after their father's death, Doctor Engelhardt was practising medicine, and had an office on the Park, five minutes' walk from his sister-in-law. He usually lunched with the family, after his morning office hours were over. They always had a good cook, and the Allegheny market was one of the best in the world. Mrs. Engelhardt went to market every morning of her life; such vegetables and poultry, such cheeses and sausages and smoked and pickled fish as one could buy there! Soon after she had made her rounds, boys in white aprons would come running across the Park with her purchases. Everyone knew the Engelhardt house, built of many-colored bricks, with gables and turrets, and on the west a large stained-glass window representing a scene on the Grand Canal in Venice, the Church of Santa Maria della Salute in the background, in the foreground a gondola with a slender gondolier. People said August and Mrs. Engelhardt should be solidly seated in the prow to make the picture complete.

Doctor Engelhardt's especial interest was the throat, preferably the singing throat. He had studied every scrap of manuscript that Manuel Garcia had left behind him, every reported conversation with him. He had doctored many singers, and imagined he had saved many voices. Pittsburgh air is not good for the throat, and traveling artists often had need of medical assistance. Conductors of orchestras and singing societies recommended Doctor Engelhardt because he was very lax about collecting fees from professionals, especially if they sent him a photograph floridly inscribed. He had been a medical student in New York while Patti was still singing; his biography fell into chapters of great voices as a turfman's falls into chapters of fast horses. This passion for the voice had given him the feeling of distinction, of being unique in his profession, which had made him all his life a well-satisfied and happy man, and had left him a poor one.

One morning when the Doctor was taking his customary walk about the Park before office hours, he stopped in front of the Allegheny High School building because he heard singing—a chorus of young voices. It was June, and the chapel windows were open. The Doctor listened for a few moments, then tilted his head on one side and laid his forefinger on his pear-shaped nose with an anxious, inquiring squint. Among the voices he certainly heard one Voice. The final bang of the piano was followed by laughter and buzzing. A boy ran down the steps. The Doctor stopped him and learned that this was a rehearsal for Class Day exercises. Just then the piano began again, and in a moment he heard the same voice, alone:

"Still wie die Nacht, tief wie das Meer."

No, he was not mistaken; a full, rich soprano voice, so easy, so sure; a golden warmth, even in the high notes. Before the second verse was over he went softly into the building, into the chapel, and for the first time laid eyes on Marguerite Thiesinger. He saw a sturdy, blooming German girl standing beside the piano; good-natured one knew at a glance, glowing with health. She looked like a big peony just burst into bloom and full of sunshine—sunshine in her auburn hair, in her rather small hazel eyes. When she finished the song, she began waltzing on the platform with one of the boys.

Doctor Albert waited by the door, and accosted her as she came out carrying her coat and schoolbooks. He introduced himself and asked her if she would go over to Mrs. Engelhardt's for lunch and sing for him.

Oh, yes! She knew one of the Engelhardt boys, and she'd always wanted to see that beautiful window from the inside.

She went over at noon and sang for them before lunch, and the family took stock of her. She spoke a very ordinary German and her English was still worse; her people were very ordinary. Her flat, slangy speech was somehow not vulgar because it was so naïve—she knew no other way. The boys were delighted with her because she was jolly and interested in everything. She told them about the glorious good times she had going to dances in suburban Turner halls, and to picnics in the damp, smoke-smeared woods up the Allegheny. The boys roared with laughter at the unpromising places she mentioned. But she had the warm bubble in her blood that makes everything fair; even being a junior in the Allegheny High School was "glorious," she told them!

She came to lunch with them again and again, because she liked the boys, and she thought the house magnificent. The Doctor observed her narrowly all the while. Clearly she had no ambition, no purpose; she sang to be agreeable. She was not very intelligent, but she had a kind of personal warmth that, to his way of thinking, was much better than brains. He took her over to his office and poked and pounded her. When he had finished his examination, he stood before the foolish, happy young thing and inclined his head in his peculiar fashion.

"Miss Thiesinger, I have the honor to announce to you that you are on the threshold of a brilliant, possibly a great career."

She laughed her fresh, ringing laugh. "Aren't you nice, though, to take so much trouble about me!"

The Doctor lifted a forefinger. "But for that you must turn your back on this childishness, these sniveling sapheads you play marbles with. You must uproot this triviality." He made a gesture as if he were wringing a chicken's neck, and Marguerite was thankful she was able to keep back a giggle.

Doctor Engelhardt wanted her to go to New York with him at once, and begin her studies. He was quite ready to finance her. He had made up his mind to stake everything upon this voice.

But not at all. She thought it was lovely of him, but she was very fond of her classmates, and she wanted to graduate with her class next year. Moreover, she had just been given a choir position in one of the biggest churches in Pittsburgh, though she was still a schoolgirl; she was going to have money and pretty clothes for the first time in her life and wouldn't miss it all for anything.

All through the next school year Doctor Albert went regularly to the church where she sang, watched and cherished her, expostulated and lectured, trying to awaken fierce ambition in his big peony flower. She was very much interested in other things just then, but she was patient with him; accepted his devotion with good nature, respected his wisdom, and bore with his "stagey" manners as she called them. She graduated in June, and immediately after Commencement, when she was not quite nineteen, she eloped with an insurance agent and went to Chicago to live. She wrote Doctor Albert: "I do appreciate all your kindness to me, but I guess I will let my voice rest for the present."

He took it hard. He burned her photographs and the foolish little scrawls she had written to thank him for presents. His life would have been dull and empty if he hadn't had so many reproaches to heap upon her in his solitude. How often and how bitterly he arraigned her for the betrayal of so beautiful a gift. Where did she keep it hidden now, that jewel, in the sordid life she had chosen?

Three years after her elopement, suddenly, without warning, Marguerite Thiesinger walked into his office on Arch street one morning and told him she had come back to study! Her husband's "affairs were involved"; he was now quite willing that she should make as much as possible of her voice—and out of it.

"My voice is better than it was," she said, looking at him out of her rather small eyes—greenish yellow, with a glint of gold in them. He believed her. He suddenly realized how uncommonly truthful she had always been. Rather stupid, unimaginative, but carried joyously along on a flood of warm vitality, and truthful to a degree he had hardly known in any woman or in any man. And now she was a woman.

He took her over to his sister-in-law's. Albert, who chanced to be at home, was sent to the piano. She was not mistaken. The Doctor kept averting his head to conceal his delight, to conceal, once or twice, a tear—the moisture that excitement and pleasure brought to his eyes. The voice, after all, he told himself, is a physical thing. She had been growing and ripening like fruit in the sun, and the voice with the body. Doctor Engelhardt stepped softly out of the music room into the conservatory and addressed a potted palm, his lips curling back from his teeth: "So we get that out of you, *Monsieur le commis voyageur*, and now we throw you away like a squeezed lemon."

When he returned to his singer, she addressed him very earnestly from under her spring hat covered with lilacs. "Before my marriage, Doctor Engelhardt, you offered to take me to New York to a teacher, and lend me money to start on. If you still feel like doing it, I'm sure I could repay you before very long. I'll follow your instructions. What was it you used to tell me I must have—application and ambition?"

He glared at her; "Take note, Gretchen, that I change the prescription. There is something vulgar about ambition. Now

we will play for higher stakes; for ambition read aspiration!"
His index finger shot upward.

In New York he had no trouble in awakening the interest of
his friends and acquaintances. Within a week he had got his
protégée to a very fine artist, just then retiring from the Op-
era, a woman who had been a pupil of Pauline Garcia Viar-
dot. In short, Doctor Engelhardt had realized the dream of a
lifetime: he had discovered a glorious voice, backed by a rich
vitality. Within a year Marguerite had one of the best church
positions in New York; she insisted upon repaying her bene-
factor before she went abroad to complete her studies. Doctor
Engelhardt went often to New York to counsel and advise, to
gloat over his treasure. He often shivered as he crossed the
Jersey ferry; he was afraid of Fate. He would tell over her
assets on his fingers to reassure himself. You might have seen
a small, self-important man of about fifty, standing by the rail
of the ferry boat, his head impressively inclined as if he were
addressing an amphitheatre full of students, gravely counting
upon his fingers.

But Fate struck, and from the quarter least under suspi-
cion—through that blooming, rounded, generously molded
young body, from that abundant, glowing health which the
Doctor proudly called peasant vigor. Marguerite's success had
brought to his office many mothers of singing daughters. He
was not insensible to the compliment, but he usually dis-
missed them by dusting his fingers delicately in the air and
growling: "Yes, she can sing a little, she has a voice; *aber
kleine, kleine!*" He exulted in the opulence of his cabbage rose.
To his nephews he used to match her possibilities with the
singers of that period. Emma Eames he called *die Puritan*,
Geraldine Farrar *la voix blanche*, another was *trop raffinée*.

Marguerite had been in New York two years, her path one
of uninterrupted progress, when she wrote the Doctor about
a swelling of some sort; the surgeons wanted to operate.
Doctor Albert took the next train for New York. An oper-
ation revealed that things were very bad indeed; a malignant
growth, so far advanced that the knife could not check it. Her
mother and grandmother had died of the same disease.

Poor Marguerite lived a year in a hospital for incurables.

Every week-end when Doctor Albert went over to see her he found great changes—it was rapid and terrible. That winter and spring he lived like a man lost in a dark morass, the Slave in the Dismal Swamp. He suffered more than his Gretchen, for she was singularly calm and hopeful to the very end, never doubting that she would get well.

The last time he saw her she had given up. But she was noble and sweet in mood, and so piteously apologetic for disappointing him—like a child who has broken something precious and is sorry. She was wasted, indeed, until she was scarcely larger than a child, her beautiful hair cut short, her hands like shadows, but still a stain of color in her cheeks.

"I'm so sorry I didn't do as you wanted instead of running off with Phil," she said. "I see now how little he cared about me—and you've just done everything. If I had my twenty-six years to live over, I'd live them very differently."

Doctor Albert dropped her hand and walked to the window, the tears running down his face. *"Pourquoi, pourquoi?"* he muttered, staring blindly at that brutal square of glass. When he could control himself and came back to the chair at her bedside, she put her poor little sheared head out on his knee and lay smiling and breathing softly.

"I expect you don't believe in the hereafter," she murmured. "Scientific people hardly ever do. But if there is one, I'll not forget you. I'll love to remember you."

When the nurse came to give her her hypodermic, Doctor Albert went out into Central Park and wandered about without knowing where or why, until he smelled something sweet which suddenly stopped his breath, and he sat down under a flowering linden tree. He dropped his face in his hands and cried like a woman. Youth, art, love, dreams, true-heartedness—why must they go out of the summer world into darkness? *Warum, warum?* He thought he had already suffered all that man could, but never had it come down on him like this. He sat on that bench like a drunken man or like a dying man, muttering Heine's words, "God is a grimmer humorist than I. Nobody but God could have perpetrated anything so cruel." She was ashamed, he remembered it afresh and struck his bony head with his clenched fist—ashamed at having been used like this; she was apologetic for the power, whatever it was, that had tricked her. "Yes, by God, she apologized for God!"

The tortured man looked up through the linden branches at the blue arch that never answers. As he looked, his face relaxed, his breathing grew regular. His eyes were caught by puffy white clouds like the cherub-heads in Raphael's pictures, and something within him seemed to rise and travel with those clouds. The moment had come when he could bear no more. . . . When he went back to the hospital that evening, he learned that she had died very quietly between eleven and twelve, the hour when he was sitting on the bench in the park.

Uncle Doctor now sometimes spoke to Albert out of a long silence: "Anyway, I died for her; that was given to me. She never knew a death-struggle—she went to sleep. That struggle took place in my body. Her dissolution occurred within me."

IV

Old Doctor Engelhardt walked abroad very little now. Sometimes on a fine Sunday, his nephew would put him aboard a street car that climbs the hills beyond Mount Oliver and take him to visit an old German graveyard and a monastery. Every afternoon, in good weather, he walked along the pavement which ran past the front door, as far as the first corner, where he bought his paper and cigarettes. If Elsa, the pretty little granddaughter of his housekeeper, ran out to join him and see him over the crossings, he would go a little farther. In the morning, while Mrs. Rudder did the sweeping and dusting, the Doctor took the air on an upstairs back porch, overhanging the court.

The court was bricked, and had an old-fashioned cistern and hydrant, and three ailanthus trees—the last growing things left to the Engelhardts, whose flowering shrubs and greenhouses had once been so well known in Allegheny. In these trees, which he called *les Chinoises*, the Doctor took a great interest. The clothes line ran about their trunks in a triangle, and on Mondays he looked down upon the washing.

He was too near-sighted to be distressed by the sooty flakes descending from neighboring chimneys upon the white sheets. He enjoyed the dull green leaves of his *Chinoises* in summer, scarcely moving on breathless, sticky nights, when the moon came up red over roofs and smokestacks. In autumn he watched the yellow fronds drop down upon the brick pavement like great ferns. Now, when his birthday was approaching, the trees were bare; and he thought he liked them best so, especially when all the knotty, curly twigs were outlined by a scurf of snow.

As he sat there, wrapped up in rugs, a stiff felt hat on his head—he would never hear to a cap—and woolen gloves on his hands, Elsa, the granddaughter, would bring her cross-stitch and chatter to him. Of late she had been sewing on her trousseau, and that amused the Doctor highly—though it meant she would soon go to live in lower Allegheny, and he would lose her. Her young man, Carl Abberbock, had now a half-interest in a butcher stall in the Allegheny market, and was in a hurry to marry.

When Mrs. Rudder had quite finished her work and made the place neat, she would come and lift the rug from his knees and say, "Time to go in, Herr Doctor."

V

The next evening after dinner Albert left the house with a suitcase, the bag that used to make so many trips to New York in the opera season. He stopped downstairs to ask Elsa to carry her sewing up and sit with his uncle for a while, then he took the street car across the Twenty-second Street Bridge by the blazing steel mills. As he waited on Soho Hill to catch a Fifth Avenue car, the heavy, frosty air suddenly began to descend in snow flakes. He wished he had worn his old over-coat; didn't like to get this one wet. He had to consider such things now. He was hesitating about a taxi when his car came, bound for the East End.

He got off at the foot of one of the streets running up Squirrel Hill, and slowly mounted. Everything was white with the softly-falling snow. Albert knew all the places; old school friends lived in many of them. Big, turreted stone houses, set in ample grounds with fine trees and shrubbery and driveways. He stepped aside now and then to avoid a car, rolling from the gravel drives on to the stone-block pavement. If the occupants had recognized Albert, they would have felt sorry for him. But he did not feel sorry for himself. He looked up at the lighted windows, the red gleam on the snowy rhododendron bushes, and shrugged. His old school-fellows went to New York now as often as he had done in his youth; but they went to consult doctors, to put children in school, or to pay the bills of incorrigible sons.

He thought he had had the best of it; he had gone a-Maying while it was May. This solid comfort, this iron-bound security, didn't appeal to him much. These massive houses, after all, held nothing but the heavy domestic routine; all the frictions and jealousies and discontents of family life. Albert felt light and free, going up the hill in his thin over-coat. He believed he had had a more interesting life than most of his friends who owned real estate. He could still amuse himself, and he had lived to the full all the revolutions in art and music that his period covered. He wouldn't at this moment exchange his life and his memories—his memories of his teacher, Rafael Joseffy, for instance—for any one of these massive houses and the life of the man who paid the upkeep. If Mephistopheles were to emerge from the rho-dodendrons and stand behind his shoulder with such an offer, he wouldn't hesitate. Money? Oh, yes, he would like to have some, but not what went with it.

He turned in under Judge Hammersley's fine oak trees. A car was waiting in the driveway, near the steps by which he mounted to the door. The colored man admitted him, and just as he entered the hall Mrs. Parmenter came down the stairs.

"Ah, it's you, Albert! Father said you were coming in this evening, and I've kept the car waiting, to have a glimpse of you."

Albert had dropped his hat and bag, and stood holding her hand with the special grace and appreciation she remembered in him.

"What a pleasure to see you!" he exclaimed, and she knew from his eyes it was. "It doesn't happen often, but it's always such a surprise and pleasure." He held her hand as if he wanted to keep her there. "It's a long while since the Villa Scipione, isn't it?"

They stood for a moment in the shrouded hall light. Mrs. Parmenter was looking very handsome, and Albert was thinking that she had all her father's authority, with much more sweep and freedom. She was impulsive and careless, where he was strong and shrinking—a powerful man terribly afraid of little annoyances. His daughter, Albert believed, was not afraid of anything. She had proved more than once that if you aren't afraid of gossip, it is harmless. She did as she pleased. People took it. Even Parmenter had taken it, and he was rather a stiff sort.

Mrs. Parmenter laughed at his allusion to their summer at Mrs. Sterrett's, in Rome, and gave him her coat to hold.

"You remember, Albert, how you and I used to get up early on fête days, and go down to the garden gate to see the young king come riding in from the country at the head of the horse guards? How the sun flashed on his helmet! Heavens, I saw him last summer! So grizzled and battered."

"And we were always going to run away to Russia together, and now there is no Russia. Everything has changed but you, Mrs. Parmenter."

"Wish I could think so. But you don't know any Mrs. Parmenter. I'm Marjorie, please. How often I think of those gay afternoons I had with you and your brothers in the garden behind your old Allegheny house. There's such a lot I want to talk to you about. And this birthday—when is it? May I send your uncle some flowers? I always remember his goodness to poor Marguerite Thiesinger. He never got over that, did he? But I'm late, and father is waiting. Good-night, you'll have a message from me."

Albert bent and kissed her hand in the old-fashioned way, keeping it a moment and breathing in softly the fragrance of her clothes, her furs, her person, the fragrance of that other world to which he had once belonged and out of which he had slipped so gradually that he scarcely realized it, unless suddenly brought face to face with something in it that was charming. Releasing her, he caught up his hat and opened the door to follow her, but she pushed him back with her arm and smiled over her shoulder. "No, no, father is waiting for you in the library. Good-night."

Judge Hammersley stood in the doorway, fingering a bunch of keys and blinking with impatience to render his service and have done with it. The library opened directly into the hall; he couldn't help overhearing his daughter, and he disliked her free and unreproachful tone with this man who was young when he should be old, single when he should be married, and penniless when he should be well-fixed.

Later, as Albert came down the hill with two bottles of the Judge's best champagne in his bag, he was thinking that the greatest disadvantage of being poor and dropping out of the world was that he didn't meet attractive women any more. The men he could do without, Heaven knew! But the women, the ones like Marjorie Hammersley, were always grouped where the big fires burned—money and success and big houses and fast boats and French cars; it was natural.

Mrs. Parmenter, as she drove off, resolved that she would see more of Albert and his uncle—wondered why she had let an old friendship lapse for so long. When she was a little girl, she used often to spend a week with her aunt in Allegheny. She was fond of the aunt, but not of her cousins, and she used to escape whenever she could to the Engelhardts' garden only a few doors away. No grass in that garden—in Allegheny grass was always dirty—but glittering gravel, and lilac hedges beautiful in spring, and barberry hedges red in the fall, and flowers and bird cages and striped awnings, boys lying about in tennis clothes, making mint juleps before lunch, having coffee under the sycamore trees after dinner. The Engelhardt boys were different, like people in a book or a play. All the young men in her set were scornful of girls until they wanted one; then they grabbed her rather brutally, and it was over. She had felt that the Engelhardt boys admired her without in the least wanting to grab her, that they enjoyed her æsthetically, so to speak, and it pleased her to be liked in that way.

VI

On the afternoon of the first of December, Albert left his desk in the County Clerk's office at four o'clock, feeling very much as he used to when school was dismissed in the middle of the afternoon just before the Christmas holidays. It was his uncle's birthday that was in his mind; his own, of course, gave him no particular pleasure. If one stopped to think of that, there was a shiver waiting round the corner. He walked over the Smithfield Street Bridge. A thick brown fog made everything dark, and there was a feeling of snow in the air. The lights along the sheer cliffs of Mount Washington, high above the river, were already lighted. When Albert was a boy, those cliffs, with the row of lights far up against the sky, always made him think of some far-away, cloud-set city in Asia; the forbidden city, he used to call it. Well, that was a long time ago; a lot of water had run under this bridge since then, and kingdoms and empires had fallen. Meanwhile, Uncle Doctor was still hanging on, and things were not so bad with them as they might be. Better not reflect too much. He hopped on board a street car, and old women with market baskets shifted to make room for him.

When he reached home, the table was already set in the living room. Beautiful table linen had been one of his mother's extravagances (he had boxes of it, meant to give some to Elsa on her marriage), and Mrs. Rudder laundered it with pious care. She had put out the best silver. He had forgotten to order flowers, but the old woman had brought up one of her blooming geraniums for a centerpiece. Uncle Albert was dozing by the fire in his old smoking jacket, a volume of Schiller on his knee.

"I'll put the studs in your shirt for you. Time to dress, Uncle Doctor."

The old man blinked and smiled drolly. "So? *Die* claw-hammer?"

"Of course *die* claw-hammer! Elsa is going to a masquerade with Carl, and they are coming up to see us before they go. I promised her you would dress."

"Albert," the Doctor called him back, beckoned with a mysterious smile; "where did you get that wine now?"

"Oh, you found it when she put it on ice, did you? That's Judge Hammersley's, the best he had. He insisted on sending it to you, with his compliments and good wishes."

Uncle Albert rose and drew up his shoulders somewhat

pompously. "From my own kind I still command recognition." Then dropping into homely vulgarity he added, with a sidelong squint at his nephew, "By God, some of that will feel good, running down the gullet."

"You'll have all you want for once. It's a great occasion. Did you shave carefully? I'll take my bath, and then you must be ready for me."

In half an hour Albert came out in his dress clothes and found his uncle still reading his favorite poet. "The trousers are too big," the Doctor complained. "Why not *die* clawhammer and my old trousers? Elsa wouldn't notice."

"Oh yes, she would! She's seen these every day for five years. Quick change!"

Doctor Engelhardt submitted, and when he was dressed, surveyed himself in his mirror with satisfaction, though he slyly slipped a cotton handkerchief into his pocket instead of the linen one Albert had laid out. When they came back to the sitting room, Mrs. Rudder had been up again and had put on the wine glasses. There was still half an hour before dinner, and Albert sat down to play for his uncle. He was beginning to feel that it was all much ado about nothing, after all.

A gentle tap at the door, and Elsa came in with her young man. She was dressed as a Polish maiden, and Carl Abberbock was in a Highlander's kilt.

"Congratulations on your birthday, Herr Doctor, and I've brought you some flowers." She went to his chair and bent down to be kissed, putting a bunch of violets in his hand.

The Doctor rose and stood looking down at the violets. "Hey, you take me for a Bonapartist? What is Mussolini's flower, Albert? Advise your friends in Rome that a Supreme Dictator should always have a flower." He turned the young girl around in the light and teased her about her thin arms—such an old joke, but she laughed for him.

"But that's the style now, Herr Doctor. Everybody wants to be as thin as possible."

"Bah, there are no styles in such things! A man will always want something to take hold of, till Hell freezes over! Is dat so, Carl?"

Carl, a very broad-faced, smiling young man with outstanding ears, was suddenly frightened into silence by the entrance of a fine lady, and made for the door to get his knotty knees into the shadow. Elsa, too, caught her breath and shrank away.

Without knocking, Mrs. Parmenter, her arms full of roses, appeared in the doorway, and just behind her was her chauffeur, carrying a package. "Put it down there and wait for me," she said to him, then swept into the room and lightly embraced Doctor Engelhardt without waiting to drop the flowers or take off her furs. "I wanted to congratulate you in person. They told me below that you were receiving. Please take these flowers, Albert. I want a moment's chat with Doctor Engelhardt."

The Doctor stood with singular gravity, like someone in a play, the violets still in his hand. "To what," he muttered with his best bow, "to what am I indebted for such distinguished consideration?"

"To your own distinction, my dear sir—always one of the most distinguished men I ever knew."

The Doctor, to whom flattery was thrice dearer than to ordinary men, flushed deeply. But he was not so exalted that he did not notice his little friend of many lonely hours slipping out of the entry-way—the bare-kneed Highland chief had already got down the wooden stairs. "Elsa," he called commandingly, "come here and kiss me good-night." He pulled her forward. "This is Elsa Rudder, Mrs. Parmenter, and my very particular friend. You should have seen her beautiful hair before she cut it off." Elsa reddened and glanced up to see whether the lady understood. Uncle Doctor kissed her on the forehead and ran his hand over her shingled head. "Nineteen years," he said softly. "If the next nineteen are as happy, we won't bother about the rest. *Behüt' dich, Gott!*"

"Thank you, Uncle Doctor. Good-night."

After she fluttered out, he turned to Mrs. Parmenter. "That little girl," he said impressively, "is the rose in winter. She is my heir. Everything I have, I leave to her."

"Everything but my birthday present, please! You must drink that. I've brought you a bottle of champagne."

Both Alberts began to laugh. "But your father has already given us two!"

Mrs. Parmenter looked from one to the other. "My father?

Well, that is a compliment! It's unheard of. Of course he and I have different lockers. We could never agree when to open them. I don't think he's opened his since the Chief Justice dined with him. Now I must leave you. Be as jolly as the night is long; with three bottles you ought to do very well! The good woman downstairs said your dinner would be served in half an hour."

Both men started toward her. "Don't go. Please, please, stay and dine with us! It's the one thing we needed." Albert began to entreat her in Italian, a language his uncle did not understand. He confessed that he had been freezing up for the last hour, couldn't go on with it alone. "One can't do such things without a woman—a beautiful woman."

"Thank you, Albert. But I've a dinner engagement; I ought to be at the far end of Ellsworth Avenue this minute."

"But this is once in a lifetime—for him! Still, if your friends are waiting for you, you can't. Certainly not." He took up her coat and held it for her. But how the light had gone out of his face; he looked so different, so worn, as he stood holding her coat at just the right height. She slipped her arms into it, then pulled them out. "I can't, but I just will! Let me write a note, please. I'll send Henry on with it and tell them I'll drop in after dinner." Albert pressed her hand gratefully and took her to his desk. "Oh, Albert, your Italian writing table, and all the lovely things on it, just as it stood in your room at the Villa Scipione! You used to let me write letters at it. You had the nicest way with young girls. If I had a daughter, I'd want you to do it all over again."

She scratched a note, and Albert put a third place at the table. He noticed Uncle Doctor slip away, and come back with his necktie set straight, attended by a wave of *eau de cologne*. While he was lighting the candles and bringing in the wine cooler, Mrs. Parmenter sat down beside the Doctor, accepted one of his cigarettes, and began to talk to him simply and naturally about Marguerite Thiesinger. Nothing could have been more tactful, Albert knew; nothing could give the old man more pleasure on his birthday. Albert himself couldn't do it any more; he had worn out his power of going over that sad story. He tried to make up for it by playing the songs she had sung.

"Albert," said Mrs. Parmenter when they sat down to dinner, "this is the only spot I know in the world that is before-the-war. You've got a period shut up in here; the last ten years of one century, and the first ten of another. Sitting here, I don't believe in aëroplanes, or jazz, or Cubists. My father is nearly as old as Doctor Engelhardt, and we never buy anything new; yet we haven't kept it out. How do you manage?"

Albert smiled a little ruefully. "I suppose it's because we never have any young people about. They bring it in."

"Elsa," murmured the Doctor. "But I see; she is only a child."

"I'm sorry for the young people now," Mrs. Parmenter went on. "They seem to me coarse and bitter. There's nothing wonderful left for them, poor things; the war destroyed it all. Where could any girl find such a place to escape to as your mother's house, full of chests of linen like this? All houses now are like hotels; nothing left to cherish. Your house was wonderful! And what music we used to have. Do you remember the time you took me to hear Joseffy play the second Brahms, with Gericke? It was the last time I ever heard him. What did happen to him, Albert? Went to pieces in some way, didn't he?"

Albert sighed and shook his head; wine was apt to plunge him into pleasant, poetic melancholy. "I don't know if anyone knows. I stayed in Rome too long to know, myself. Before I went abroad, I'd been taking lessons with him right along—I saw no change in him, though he gave fewer and fewer concerts. When I got back, I wrote him the day I landed in New York—he was living up the Hudson then. I got a reply from his housekeeper, saying that he was not giving lessons, was ill and was seeing nobody. I went out to his place at once. I wasn't asked to come into the house. I was told to wait in the garden. I waited a long while. At last he came out, wearing white clothes, as he often did, a panama hat, carrying a little cane. He shook hands with me, asked me about Mrs. Sterrett—but he was another man, that's all. He was gone; he wasn't there. I was talking to his picture."

"Drugs!" muttered the Doctor out of one corner of his mouth.

"Nonsense!" Albert shrugged in derision. "Or if he did, that was secondary; a result, not a cause. He'd seen the other side of things; he'd let go. Something had happened in his brain that was not paresis."

Mrs. Parmenter leaned forward. "Did he *look* the same? Surely, he had the handsomest head in the world. Remember his forehead? Was he gray? His hair was a reddish chestnut, as I remember."

"A little gray; not much. There was no change in his face, except his eyes. The bright spark had gone out, and his body had a sort of trailing languor when he moved."

"Would he give you a lesson?"

"No. Said he wasn't giving any. Said he was sorry, but he wasn't seeing people at all any more. I remember he sat making patterns in the gravel with his cane. He frowned and said he simply couldn't see people; said the human face had become hateful to him—and the human voice! 'I am sorry,' he said, 'but that is the truth.' I looked at his left hand, lying on his knee. I wonder, Marjorie, that I had the strength to get up and go away. I felt as if everything had been drawn out of me. He got up and took my hand. I understood that I must leave. In desperation I asked him whether music didn't mean anything to him still. 'Music,' he said slowly, with just a ghost of his old smile, 'yes—some music.' He went back into the house. Those were the last words I ever heard him speak."

"Oh dear! And he had everything that is beautiful—and the name of an angel! But we're making the Doctor melancholy. Open another bottle, Albert—father did very well by you. We've not drunk a single toast. Many returns, we take for granted. Why not each drink a toast of our own, to something we care for." She glanced at Doctor Engelhardt, who lifted the bunch of violets by his plate and smelled them absently. "Now, Doctor Engelhardt, a toast!"

The Doctor put down his flowers, delicately took up his glass and held it directly in front of him; everything he did with his hands was deft and sure. A beautiful, a wonderful look came over his face as she watched him.

"I drink," he said slowly, "to a memory; to the lost Lenore."

"And I," said young Albert softly, "to my youth, to my beautiful youth!"

Tears flashed into Mrs. Parmenter's eyes. "Ah," she thought, "that's what liking people amounts to; it's liking their silliness and absurdities. That's what it really is."

"And I," she said aloud, "will drink to the future; to our renewed friendship, and many dinners together. I like you two better than anyone I know."

When Albert came back from seeing Mrs. Parmenter down to her car, he found his uncle standing by the fire, his elbow on the mantle, thoughtfully rolling a cigarette. "Albert," he said in a deeply confidential tone, "good wine, good music, beautiful women; that is all there is worth turning over the hand for."

Albert began to laugh. The old man wasn't often banal. "Why Uncle, you and Martin Luther—"

The Doctor lifted a hand imperiously to stop him, and flushed darkly. He evidently hadn't been aware that he was quoting—it came from the heart. "Martin Luther," he snapped, "was a vulgarian of the first water; cabbage soup!" He paused a moment to light his cigarette. "But don't fool yourself; one like her always knows when a man has had success with women!"

Albert poured a last glass from the bottle and sipped it critically. "Well, you had success to-night, certainly. I could see that Marjorie was impressed. She's coming to take you for a ride to-morrow, after your nap, so you must be ready."

The Doctor passed his flexible, nervous hand lightly over the thick bristles of his French hair-cut. *"Even in our ashes,"* he muttered haughtily.

Forum, February 1929

ALEXANDER'S BRIDGE

Chapter I

LATE ONE brilliant April afternoon Professor Lucius Wilson stood at the head of Chestnut Street, looking about him with the pleased air of a man of taste who does not very often get to Boston. He had lived there as a student, but for twenty years and more, since he had been Professor of Philosophy in a Western university, he had seldom come East except to take a steamer for some foreign port. Wilson was standing quite still, contemplating with a whimsical smile the slanting street, with its worn paving, its irregular, gravely colored houses, and the row of naked trees on which the thin sunlight was still shining. The gleam of the river at the foot of the hill made him blink a little, not so much because it was too bright as because he found it so pleasant. The few passers-by glanced at him unconcernedly, and even the children who hurried along with their school-bags under their arms seemed to find it perfectly natural that a tall brown gentleman should be standing there, looking up through his glasses at the gray housetops.

The sun sank rapidly; the silvery light had faded from the bare boughs and the watery twilight was setting in when Wilson at last walked down the hill, descending into cooler and cooler depths of grayish shadow. His nostril, long unused to it, was quick to detect the smell of wood smoke in the air, blended with the odor of moist spring earth and the saltiness that came up the river with the tide. He crossed Charles Street between jangling street cars and shelving lumber drays, and after a moment of uncertainty wound into Brimmer Street. The street was quiet, deserted, and hung with a thin bluish haze. He had already fixed his sharp eye upon the house which he reasoned should be his objective point, when he noticed a woman approaching rapidly from the opposite direction. Always an interested observer of women, Wilson would have slackened his pace anywhere to follow this one with his impersonal, appreciative glance. She was a person of distinction he saw at once, and, moreover, very handsome. She was tall, carried her beautiful head proudly, and moved with ease and certainty. One immediately took for granted the costly privileges and fine spaces that must lie in the background from which such a figure could emerge with this rapid and elegant gait. Wilson noted her dress, too,—for, in his way, he had an eye for such things,—particularly her brown furs and her hat. He got a blurred impression of her fine color, the violets she wore, her white gloves, and, curiously enough, of her veil, as she turned up a flight of steps in front of him and disappeared.

Wilson was able to enjoy lovely things that passed him on the wing as completely and deliberately as if they had been dug-up marvels, long anticipated, and definitely fixed at the end of a railway journey. For a few pleasurable seconds he quite forgot where he was going, and only after the door had closed behind her did he realize that the young woman had entered the house to which he had directed his trunk from the South Station that morning. He hesitated a moment before mounting the steps. "Can that," he murmured in amazement, —"can that possibly have been Mrs. Alexander?"

When the servant admitted him, Mrs. Alexander was still standing in the hallway. She heard him give his name, and came forward holding out her hand.

"Is it you, indeed, Professor Wilson? I was afraid that you might get here before I did. I was detained at a concert, and Bartley telephoned that he would be late. Thomas will show you your room. Had you rather have your tea brought to you there, or will you have it down here with me, while we wait for Bartley?"

Wilson was pleased to find that he had been the cause of her rapid walk, and with her he was even more vastly pleased than before. He followed her through the drawing-room into the library, where the wide back windows looked out upon the garden and the sunset and a fine stretch of silver-colored river. A harp-shaped elm stood stripped against the pale-colored evening sky, with ragged last year's birds' nests in its forks, and through the bare branches the evening star quivered in the misty air. The long brown room breathed the peace of a rich and amply guarded quiet. Tea was brought in immediately and placed in front of the wood fire. Mrs. Alexander sat down in a high-backed chair and began to pour it, while Wilson sank into a low seat opposite her and took his cup with a great sense of ease and harmony and comfort.

"You have had a long journey, haven't you?" Mrs. Alexander asked, after showing gracious concern about his tea. "And I am so sorry Bartley is late. He's often tired when he's late. He flatters himself that it is a little on his account that you have come to this Congress of Psychologists."

"It is," Wilson assented, selecting his muffin carefully; "and I hope he won't be tired to-night. But, on my own account, I'm glad to have a few moments alone with you, before Bartley comes. I was somehow afraid that my knowing him so well would not put me in the way of getting to know you."

"That's very nice of you." She nodded at him above her cup and smiled, but there was a little formal tightness in her tone which had not been there when she greeted him in the hall.

Wilson leaned forward. "Have I said something awkward? I live very far out of the world, you know. But I didn't mean that you would exactly fade dim, even if Bartley *were* here."

Mrs. Alexander laughed relentingly. "Oh, I'm not so vain! How terribly discerning you are."

She looked straight at Wilson, and he felt that this quick, frank glance brought about an understanding between them.

He liked everything about her, he told himself, but he particularly liked her eyes; when she looked at one directly for a moment they were like a glimpse of fine windy sky that may bring all sorts of weather.

"Since you noticed something," Mrs. Alexander went on, "it must have been a flash of the distrust I have come to feel whenever I meet any of the people who knew Bartley when he was a boy. It is always as if they were talking of some one I had never met. Really, Professor Wilson, it would seem that he grew up among the strangest people. They usually say that he has turned out very well, or remark that he always was a fine fellow. I never know what reply to make."

Wilson chuckled and leaned back in his chair, shaking his left foot gently. "I expect the fact is that we none of us knew him very well, Mrs. Alexander. Though I will say for myself that I was always confident he'd do something extraordinary."

Mrs. Alexander's shoulders gave a slight movement, suggestive of impatience. "Oh, I should think that might have been a safe prediction. Another cup, please?"

"Yes, thank you. But predicting, in the case of boys, is not so easy as you might imagine, Mrs. Alexander. Some get a bad hurt early and lose their courage; and some never get a fair wind. Bartley"—he dropped his chin on the back of his long hand and looked at her admiringly—"Bartley caught the wind early, and it has sung in his sails ever since."

Mrs. Alexander sat looking into the fire with intent pre-occupation, and Wilson studied her half-averted face. He liked the suggestion of stormy possibilities in the proud curve of her lip and nostril. Without that, he reflected, she would be too cold.

"I should like to know what he was really like when he was a boy. I don't believe he remembers," she said suddenly. "Won't you smoke, Mr. Wilson?"

Wilson lit a cigarette. "No, I don't suppose he does. He was never introspective. He was simply the most tremendous response to stimuli I have ever known. We did n't know exactly what to do with him."

A servant came in and noiselessly removed the tea-tray. Mrs. Alexander screened her face from the firelight, which was beginning to throw wavering bright spots on her dress and hair as the dusk deepened.

"Of course," she said, "I now and again hear stories about things that happened when he was in college."

"But that is n't what you want." Wilson wrinkled his brows and looked at her with the smiling familiarity that had come about so quickly. "What you want is a picture of him, standing back there at the other end of twenty years. You want to look down through my memory."

She dropped her hands in her lap. "Yes, yes; that's exactly what I want."

At this moment they heard the front door shut with a jar, and Wilson laughed as Mrs. Alexander rose quickly. "There he is. Away with perspective! No past, no future for Bartley; just the fiery moment. The only moment that ever was or will be in the world!"

The door from the hall opened, a voice called "Winifred?" hurriedly, and a big man came through the drawing-room with a quick, heavy tread, bringing with him a smell of cigar smoke and chill out-of-doors air. When Alexander reached the library door, he switched on the lights and stood six feet and more in the archway, glowing with strength and cordiality and rugged, blond good looks. There were other bridge-builders in the world, certainly, but it was always Alexander's picture that the Sunday Supplement men wanted, because he looked as a tamer of rivers ought to look. Under his tumbled sandy hair his head seemed as hard and powerful as a catapult, and his shoulders looked strong enough in themselves to support a span of any one of his ten great bridges that cut the air above as many rivers.

After dinner Alexander took Wilson up to his study. It was a large room over the library, and looked out upon the black river and the row of white lights along the Cambridge Embankment. The room was not at all what one might expect of an engineer's study. Wilson felt at once the harmony of beautiful things that have lived long together without obtrusions of ugliness or change. It was none of Alexander's doing, of course; those warm consonances of color had been blending and mellowing before he was born. But the wonder was that he was not out of place there,—that it all seemed to glow like the inevitable background for his vigor and vehemence. He sat before the fire, his shoulders deep in the cushions of his chair, his powerful head upright, his hair rumpled above his broad forehead. He sat heavily, a cigar in his large, smooth hand, a flush of after-dinner color in his face, which wind and sun and exposure to all sorts of weather had left fair and clear-skinned.

"You are off for England on Saturday, Bartley, Mrs. Alexander tells me."

"Yes, for a few weeks only. There's a meeting of British engineers, and I'm doing another bridge in Canada, you know."

"Oh, every one knows about that. And it was in Canada that you met your wife, wasn't it?"

"Yes, at Allway. She was visiting her great-aunt there. A most remarkable old lady. I was working with MacKeller then, an old Scotch engineer who had picked me up in London

and taken me back to Quebec with him. He had the con-
tract for the Allway Bridge, but before he began work on it
he found out that he was going to die, and he advised the
committee to turn the job over to me. Otherwise I'd never
have got anything good so early. MacKeller was an old friend
of Mrs. Pemberton, Winifred's aunt. He had mentioned me to
her, so when I went to Allway she asked me to come to see
her. She was a wonderful old lady."

"Like her niece?" Wilson queried.

Bartley laughed. "She had been very handsome, but not in
Winifred's way. When I knew her she was little and fragile,
very pink and white, with a splendid head and a face like fine
old lace, somehow,—but perhaps I always think of that be-
cause she wore a lace scarf on her hair. She had such a flavor
of life about her. She had known Gordon and Livingstone
and Beaconsfield when she was young,—every one. She was
the first woman of that sort I'd ever known. You know how it
is in the West,—old people are poked out of the way. Aunt
Eleanor fascinated me as few young women have ever done. I
used to go up from the works to have tea with her, and sit
talking to her for hours. It was very stimulating, for she
couldn't tolerate stupidity."

"It must have been then that your luck began, Bartley,"
said Wilson, flicking his cigar ash with his long finger. "It's
curious, watching boys," he went on reflectively. "I'm sure I
did you justice in the matter of ability. Yet I always used to
feel that there was a weak spot where some day strain would
tell. Even after you began to climb, I stood down in the
crowd and watched you with—well, not with confidence.
The more dazzling the front you presented, the higher your
façade rose, the more I expected to see a big crack zigzagging
from top to bottom,"—he indicated its course in the air with
his forefinger,—"then a crash and clouds of dust. It was cu-
rious. I had such a clear picture of it. And another curious
thing, Bartley," Wilson spoke with deliberateness and settled
deeper into his chair, "is that I don't feel it any longer. I am
sure of you."

Alexander laughed. "Nonsense! It's not I you feel sure of;
it's Winifred. People often make that mistake."

"No, I'm serious, Alexander. You've changed. You have

decided to leave some birds in the bushes. You used to want them all."

Alexander's chair creaked. "I still want a good many," he said rather gloomily. "After all, life does n't offer a man much. You work like the devil and think you're getting on, and suddenly you discover that you've only been getting yourself tied up. A million details drink you dry. Your life keeps going for things you don't want, and all the while you are being built alive into a social structure you don't care a rap about. I sometimes wonder what sort of chap I'd have been if I had n't been this sort; I want to go and live out his potentialities, too. I have n't forgotten that there are birds in the bushes."

Bartley stopped and sat frowning into the fire, his shoulders thrust forward as if he were about to spring at something. Wilson watched him, wondering. His old pupil always stimulated him at first, and then vastly wearied him. The machinery was always pounding away in this man, and Wilson preferred companions of a more reflective habit of mind. He could not help feeling that there were unreasoning and unreasonable activities going on in Alexander all the while; that even after dinner, when most men achieve a decent impersonality, Bartley had merely closed the door of the engine-room and come up for an airing. The machinery itself was still pounding on.

Bartley's abstraction and Wilson's reflections were cut short by a rustle at the door, and almost before they could rise Mrs. Alexander was standing by the hearth. Alexander brought a chair for her, but she shook her head.

"No, dear, thank you. I only came in to see whether you and Professor Wilson were quite comfortable. I am going down to the music-room."

"Why not practice here? Wilson and I are growing very dull. We are tired of talk."

"Yes, I beg you, Mrs. Alexander," Wilson began, but he got no further.

"Why, certainly, if you won't find me too noisy. I am working on the Schumann 'Carnival,' and, though I don't practice a great many hours, I am very methodical," Mrs. Alexander explained, as she crossed to an upright piano that stood at the back of the room, near the windows.

Wilson followed, and, having seen her seated, dropped into a chair behind her. She played brilliantly and with great musical feeling. Wilson could not imagine her permitting herself to do anything badly, but he was surprised at the cleanness of her execution. He wondered how a woman with so many duties had managed to keep herself up to a standard really professional. It must take a great deal of time, certainly, and Bartley must take a great deal of time. Wilson reflected that he had never before known a woman who had been able, for any considerable while, to support both a personal and an intellectual passion. Sitting behind her, he watched her with perplexed admiration, shading his eyes with his hand. In her dinner dress she looked even younger than in street clothes, and, for all her composure and self-sufficiency, she seemed to him strangely alert and vibrating, as if in her, too, there were something never altogether at rest. He felt that he knew pretty much what she demanded in people and what she demanded from life, and he wondered how she squared Bartley. After ten years she must know him; and however one took him, however much one admired him, one had to admit that he simply would n't square. He was a natural force, certainly, but beyond that, Wilson felt, he was not anything very really or for very long at a time.

Wilson glanced toward the fire, where Bartley's profile was still wreathed in cigar smoke that curled up more and more slowly. His shoulders were sunk deep in the cushions and one hand hung large and passive over the arm of his chair. He had slipped on a purple velvet smoking-coat. His wife, Wilson surmised, had chosen it. She was clearly very proud of his good looks and his fine color. But, with the glow of an immediate interest gone out of it, the engineer's face looked tired, even a little haggard. The three lines in his forehead, directly above the nose, deepened as he sat thinking, and his powerful head drooped forward heavily. Although Alexander was only forty-three, Wilson thought that beneath his vigorous color he detected the dulling weariness of on-coming middle age.

The next afternoon, at the hour when the river was beginning to redden under the declining sun, Wilson again found himself facing Mrs. Alexander at the tea-table in the library.

"Well," he remarked, when he was bidden to give an account of himself, "there was a long morning with the psychologists, luncheon with Bartley at his club, more psychologists, and here I am. I've looked forward to this hour all day."

Mrs. Alexander smiled at him across the vapor from the kettle. "And do you remember where we stopped yesterday?"

"Perfectly. I was going to show you a picture. But I doubt whether I have color enough in me. Bartley makes me feel a faded monochrome. You can't get at the young Bartley except by means of color." Wilson paused and deliberated. Suddenly he broke out: "He wasn't a remarkable student, you know, though he was always strong in higher mathematics. His work in my own department was quite ordinary. It was as a powerfully equipped nature that I found him interesting. That is the most interesting thing a teacher can find. It has the fascination of a scientific discovery. We come across other pleasing and endearing qualities so much oftener than we find force."

"And, after all," said Mrs. Alexander, "that is the thing we all live upon. It is the thing that takes us forward."

Wilson thought she spoke a little wistfully. "Exactly," he assented warmly. "It builds the bridges into the future, over which the feet of every one of us will go."

"How interested I am to hear you put it in that way. The bridges into the future—I often say that to myself. Bartley's bridges always seem to me like that. Have you ever seen his first suspension bridge in Canada, the one he was doing when I first knew him? I hope you will see it sometime. We were married as soon as it was finished, and you will laugh when I tell you that it always has a rather bridal look to me. It is over the wildest river, with mists and clouds always battling about it, and it is as delicate as a cobweb hanging in the sky. It really was a bridge into the future. You have only to look at it to feel that it meant the beginning of a great career. But I have a photograph of it here." She drew a portfolio from behind a bookcase. "And there, you see, on the hill, is my aunt's house."

Wilson took up the photograph. "Bartley was telling me something about your aunt last night. She must have been a delightful person."

Winifred laughed. "The bridge, you see, was just at the foot of the hill, and the noise of the engines annoyed her very much at first. But after she met Bartley she pretended to like it, and said it was a good thing to be reminded that there were things going on in the world. She loved life, and Bartley brought a great deal of it in to her when he came to the house. Aunt Eleanor was very worldly in a frank, Early-Victorian manner. She liked men of action, and disliked young men who were careful of themselves and who, as she put it, were always trimming their wick as if they were afraid of their oil's giving out. MacKeller, Bartley's first chief, was an old friend of my aunt, and he told her that Bartley was a wild, ill-governed youth, which really pleased her very much. I remember we were sitting alone in the dusk after Bartley had been there for the first time. I knew that Aunt Eleanor had found him much to her taste, but she hadn't said anything. Presently she came out, with a chuckle: 'MacKeller found him sowing wild oats in London, I believe. I hope he didn't stop him too soon. Life coquets with dashing fellows. The coming men are always like that. We must have him to dinner, my dear.' And we did. She grew much fonder of Bartley than she was of me. I had been studying in Vienna, and she thought that absurd. She was interested in the army and in politics, and she had a great contempt for music and art and philosophy. She used to declare that the Prince Consort had brought all that stuff over out of Germany. She always sniffed when Bartley asked me to play for him. She considered that a newfangled way of making a match of it."

When Alexander came in a few moments later, he found Wilson and his wife still confronting the photograph. "Oh, let us get that out of the way," he said, laughing. "Winifred, Thomas can bring my trunk down. I've decided to go over to New York to-morrow night and take a fast boat. I shall save two days."

Chapter II

O<small>N THE NIGHT</small> of his arrival in London, Alexander went
immediately to the hotel on the Embankment at which
he always stopped, and in the lobby he was accosted by an old
acquaintance, Maurice Mainhall, who fell upon him with ef-
fusive cordiality and indicated a willingness to dine with him.
Bartley never dined alone if he could help it, and Mainhall
was a good gossip who always knew what had been going on
in town; especially, he knew everything that was not printed
in the newspapers. The nephew of one of the standard Victo-
rian novelists, Mainhall bobbed about among the various
literary cliques of London and its outlying suburbs, careful to
lose touch with none of them. He had written a number of
books himself; among them a "History of Dancing," a "His-
tory of Costume," a "Key to Shakespeare's Sonnets," a study
of "The Poetry of Ernest Dowson," etc. Although Mainhall's
enthusiasm was often tiresome, and although he was often
unable to distinguish between facts and vivid figments of his
imagination, his imperturbable good nature overcame even
the people whom he bored most, so that they ended by be-
coming, in a reluctant manner, his friends. In appearance,
Mainhall was astonishingly like the conventional stage-
Englishman of American drama: tall and thin, with high,
hitching shoulders and a small head glistening with closely
brushed yellow hair. He spoke with an extreme Oxford ac-
cent, and when he was talking well, his face sometimes wore
the rapt expression of a very emotional man listening to mu-
sic. Mainhall liked Alexander because he was an engineer. He
had preconceived ideas about everything, and his idea about
Americans was that they should be engineers or mechanics.
He hated them when they presumed to be anything else.

While they sat at dinner Mainhall acquainted Bartley with
the fortunes of his old friends in London, and as they left the
table he proposed that they should go to see Hugh Mac-
Connell's new comedy, "Bog Lights."

"It's really quite the best thing MacConnell's done," he ex-
plained as they got into a hansom. "It's tremendously well

289

put on, too. Florence Merrill and Cyril Henderson. But Hilda Burgoyne's the hit of the piece. Hugh's written a delightful part for her, and she's quite inexpressible. It's been on only two weeks, and I've been half a dozen times already. I happen to have MacConnell's box for to-night or there'd be no chance of our getting places. There's everything in seeing Hilda while she's fresh in a part. She's apt to grow a bit stale after a time. The ones who have any imagination do."

"Hilda Burgoyne!" Alexander exclaimed mildly. "Why, I haven't heard of her for—years."

Mainhall laughed. "Then you can't have heard much at all, my dear Alexander. It's only lately, since MacConnell and his set have got hold of her, that she's come up. Myself, I always knew she had it in her. If we had one real critic in London —but what can one expect? Do you know, Alexander,"— Mainhall looked with perplexity up into the top of the hansom and rubbed his pink cheek with his gloved finger,—"do you know, I sometimes think of taking to criticism seriously myself. In a way, it would be a sacrifice; but, dear me, we do need some one."

Just then they drove up to the Duke of York's, so Alexander did not commit himself, but followed Mainhall into the theatre. When they entered the stage-box on the left the first act was well under way, the scene being the interior of a cabin in the south of Ireland. As they sat down, a burst of applause drew Alexander's attention to the stage. Miss Burgoyne and her donkey were thrusting their heads in at the half door. "After all," he reflected, "there's small probability of her recognizing me. She doubtless hasn't thought of me for years." He felt the enthusiasm of the house at once, and in a few moments he was caught up by the current of MacConnell's irresistible comedy. The audience had come forewarned, evidently, and whenever the ragged slip of a donkey-girl ran upon the stage there was a deep murmur of approbation, every one smiled and glowed, and Mainhall hitched his heavy chair a little nearer the brass railing.

"You see," he murmured in Alexander's ear, as the curtain fell on the first act, "one almost never sees a part like that done without smartness or mawkishness. Of course, Hilda is Irish,—the Burgoynes have been stage people for generations,

—and she has the Irish voice. It's delightful to hear it in a London theatre. That laugh, now, when she doubles over at the hips—who ever heard it out of Galway? She saves her hand, too. She's at her best in the second act. She's really MacConnell's poetic motif, you see; makes the whole thing a fairy tale."

The second act opened before Philly Doyle's underground still, with Peggy and her battered donkey come in to smuggle a load of potheen across the bog, and to bring Philly word of what was doing in the world without, and of what was happening along the roadsides and ditches with the first gleam of fine weather. Alexander, annoyed by Mainhall's sighs and exclamations, watched her with keen, half-skeptical interest. As Mainhall had said, she was the second act; the plot and feeling alike depended upon her lightness of foot, her lightness of touch, upon the shrewdness and deft fancifulness that played alternately, and sometimes together, in her mirthful brown eyes. When she began to dance, by way of showing the gossoons what she had seen in the fairy rings at night, the house broke into a prolonged uproar. After her dance she withdrew from the dialogue and retreated to the ditch wall back of Philly's burrow, where she sat singing "The Rising of the Moon" and making a wreath of primroses for her donkey.

When the act was over Alexander and Mainhall strolled out into the corridor. They met a good many acquaintances; Mainhall, indeed, knew almost every one, and he babbled on incontinently, screwing his small head about over his high collar. Presently he hailed a tall, bearded man, grim-browed and rather battered-looking, who had his opera cloak on his arm and his hat in his hand, and who seemed to be on the point of leaving the theatre.

"MacConnell, let me introduce Mr. Bartley Alexander. I say! It's going famously to-night, Mac. And what an audience! You'll never do anything like this again, mark me. A man writes to the top of his bent only once."

The playwright gave Mainhall a curious look out of his deep-set faded eyes and made a wry face. "And have I done anything so fool as that, now?" he asked.

"That's what I was saying," Mainhall lounged a little nearer and dropped into a tone even more conspicuously confidential. "And you'll never bring Hilda out like this again. Dear me, Mac, the girl couldn't possibly be better, you know."

MacConnell grunted. "She'll do well enough if she keeps her pace and doesn't go off on us in the middle of the season, as she's more than like to do."

He nodded curtly and made for the door, dodging acquaintances as he went.

"Poor old Hugh," Mainhall murmured. "He's hit terribly hard. He's been wanting to marry Hilda these three years and more. She doesn't take up with anybody, you know. Irene Burgoyne, one of her family, told me in confidence that there was a romance somewhere back in the beginning. One of your countrymen, Alexander, by the way; an American student whom she met in Paris, I believe. I dare say it's quite true that there's never been any one else." Mainhall vouched for her constancy with a loftiness that made Alexander smile, even while a kind of rapid excitement was tingling through him. Blinking up at the lights, Mainhall added in his luxurious, worldly way: "She's an elegant little person, and quite capable of an extravagant bit of sentiment like that. Here comes Sir Harry Towne. He's another who's awfully keen about her. Let me introduce you. Sir Harry Towne, Mr. Bartley Alexander, the American engineer."

Sir Harry Towne bowed and said that he had met Mr. Alexander and his wife in Tokyo.

Mainhall cut in impatiently.

"I say, Sir Harry, the little girl's going famously to-night, isn't she?"

Sir Harry wrinkled his brows judiciously. "Do you know, I thought the dance a bit conscious to-night, for the first time. The fact is, she's feeling rather seedy, poor child. Westmere and I were back after the first act, and we thought she seemed quite uncertain of herself. A little attack of nerves, possibly."

He bowed as the warning bell rang, and Mainhall whispered: "You know Lord Westmere, of course,—the stooped man with the long gray mustache, talking to Lady Dowle. Lady Westmere is very fond of Hilda."

When they reached their box the house was darkened and the orchestra was playing "The Cloak of Old Gaul." In a moment Peggy was on the stage again, and Alexander applauded vigorously with the rest. He even leaned forward over the rail a little. For some reason he felt pleased and flattered by the enthusiasm of the audience. In the half-light he looked about at the stalls and boxes and smiled a little consciously, recalling with amusement Sir Harry's judicial frown. He was beginning to feel a keen interest in the slender, barefoot donkey-girl who slipped in and out of the play, singing, like some one winding through a hilly field. He leaned forward and beamed felicitations as warmly as Mainhall himself when, at the end of the play, she came again and again before the curtain, panting a little and flushed, her eyes dancing and her eager, nervous little mouth tremulous with excitement.

When Alexander returned to his hotel—he shook Mainhall at the door of the theatre—he had some supper brought up to his room, and it was late before he went to bed. He had not thought of Hilda Burgoyne for years; indeed, he had almost forgotten her. He had last written to her from Canada, after he first met Winifred, telling her that everything was changed with him—that he had met a woman whom he would marry if he could; if he could not, then all the more was everything changed for him. Hilda had never replied to his letter. He felt guilty and unhappy about her for a time, but after Winifred promised to marry him he really forgot Hilda altogether. When he wrote her that everything was changed for him, he was telling the truth. After he met Winifred Pemberton he seemed to himself like a different man. One night when he and Winifred were sitting together on the bridge, he told her that things had happened while he was studying abroad that he was sorry for,—one thing in particular,—and he asked her whether she thought she ought to know about them. She considered a moment and then said: "No, I think not, though I am glad you ask me. You see, one can't be jealous about things in general; but about particular, definite, personal things,"—here she had thrown her hands up to his shoulders with a quick, impulsive gesture—"oh, about those I should be very jealous. I should torture my-self—I could n't help it." After that it was easy to forget, actually to forget. He wondered to-night, as he poured his wine, how many times he had thought of Hilda in the last ten years. He had been in London more or less, but he had never happened to hear of her. "All the same," he lifted his glass, "here's to you, little Hilda. You've made things come your way, and I never thought you'd do it.

"Of course," he reflected, "she always had that combination of something homely and sensible, and something utterly wild and daft. But I never thought she'd do anything. She had n't much ambition then, and she was too fond of trifles. She must care about the theatre a great deal more than she used to. Perhaps she has me to thank for something, after all. Sometimes a little jolt like that does one good. She was a daft, generous little thing. I'm glad she's held her own since. After all, we were awfully young. It was youth and poverty and proximity, and everything was young and kindly. I should n't wonder if she could laugh about it with me now. I should n't wonder— But they've probably spoiled her, so that she'd be tiresome if one met her again."

Bartley smiled and yawned and went to bed.

Chapter III

THE NEXT EVENING Alexander dined alone at a club, and at about nine o'clock he dropped in at the Duke of York's. The house was sold out and he stood through the second act. When he returned to his hotel he examined the new directory, and found Miss Burgoyne's address still given as off Bedford Square, though at a new number. He remembered that, in so far as she had been brought up at all, she had been brought up in Bloomsbury. Her father and mother played in the provinces most of the year, and she was left a great deal in the care of an old aunt who was crippled by rheumatism and who had had to leave the stage altogether. In the days when Alexander knew her, Hilda always managed to have a lodging of some sort about Bedford Square, because she clung tenaciously to such scraps and shreds of memories as were connected with it. The mummy room of the British Museum had been one of the chief delights of her childhood. That forbidding pile was the goal of her truant fancy, and she was sometimes taken there for a treat, as other children are taken to the theatre. It was long since Alexander had thought of any of these things, but now they came back to him quite fresh, and had a significance they did not have when they were first told him in his restless twenties. So she was still in the old neighborhood, near Bedford Square. The new number probably meant increased prosperity. He hoped so. He would like to know that she was snugly settled. He looked at his watch. It was a quarter past ten; she would not be home for a good two hours yet, and he might as well walk over and have a look at the place. He remembered the shortest way.

It was a warm, smoky evening, and there was a grimy moon. He went through Covent Garden to Oxford Street, and as he turned into Museum Street he walked more slowly, smiling at his own nervousness as he approached the sullen gray mass at the end. He had not been inside the Museum, actually, since he and Hilda used to meet there; sometimes to set out for gay adventures at Twickenham or Richmond, sometimes to linger about the place for a while and to ponder by Lord Elgin's marbles upon the lastingness of some things, or, in the mummy room, upon the awful brevity of others. Since then Bartley had always thought of the British Museum as the ultimate repository of mortality, where all the dead things in the world were assembled to make one's hour of youth the more precious. One trembled lest before he got out it might somehow escape him, lest he might drop the glass from over-eagerness and see it shivered on the stone floor at his feet. How one hid his youth under his coat and hugged it! And how good it was to turn one's back upon all that vaulted cold, to take Hilda's arm and hurry out of the great door and down the steps into the sunlight among the pigeons—to know that the warm and vital thing within him was still there and had not been snatched away to flush Cæsar's lean cheek or to feed the veins of some bearded Assyrian king. They in their day had carried the flaming liquor, but to-day was his! So the song used to run in his head those summer mornings a dozen years ago. Alexander walked by the place very quietly, as if he were afraid of waking some one.

He crossed Bedford Square and found the number he was looking for. The house, a comfortable, well-kept place enough, was dark except for the four front windows on the second floor, where a low, even light was burning behind the white muslin sash curtains. Outside there were window boxes, painted white and full of flowers. Bartley was making a third round of the Square when he heard the far-flung hoof-beats of a hansom-cab horse, driven rapidly. He looked at his watch, and was astonished to find that it was a few minutes after twelve. He turned and walked back along the iron railing as the cab came up to Hilda's number and stopped. The hansom must have been one that she employed regularly, for she did not stop to pay the driver. She stepped out quickly and lightly. He heard her cheerful "Good-night, cabby," as she ran up the steps and opened the door with a latchkey. In a few moments the lights flared up brightly behind the white curtains, and as he walked away he heard a window raised. But he had gone too far to look up without turning round. He went back to his hotel, feeling that he had had a good evening, and he slept well.

For the next few days Alexander was very busy. He took a

desk in the office of a Scotch engineering firm on Henrietta Street, and was at work almost constantly. He avoided the clubs and usually dined alone at his hotel. One afternoon, after he had tea, he started for a walk down the Embankment toward Westminster, intending to end his stroll at Bedford Square and to ask whether Miss Burgoyne would let him take her to the theatre. But he did not go so far. When he reached the Abbey, he turned back and crossed Westminster Bridge and sat down to watch the trails of smoke behind the Houses of Parliament catch fire with the sunset. The slender towers were washed by a rain of golden light and licked by little flickering flames; Somerset House and the bleached gray pinnacles about Whitehall were floated in a luminous haze. The yellow light poured through the trees and the leaves seemed to burn with soft fires. There was a smell of acacias in the air everywhere, and the laburnums were dripping gold over the walls of the gardens. It was a sweet, lonely kind of summer evening. Remembering Hilda as she used to be, was doubtless more satisfactory than seeing her as she must be now—and, after all, Alexander asked himself, what was it but his own young years that he was remembering?

He crossed back to Westminster, went up to the Temple, and sat down to smoke in the Middle Temple gardens, listening to the thin voice of the fountain and smelling the spice of the sycamores that came out heavily in the damp evening air. He thought, as he sat there, about a great many things: about his own youth and Hilda's; above all, he thought of how glorious it had been, and how quickly it had passed; and, when it had passed, how little worth while anything was. None of the things he had gained in the least compensated. In the last six years his reputation had become, as the saying is, popular. Four years ago he had been called to Japan to deliver, at the Emperor's request, a course of lectures at the Imperial University, and had instituted reforms throughout the islands, not only in the practice of bridge-building but in drainage and road-making. On his return he had undertaken the bridge at Moorlock, in Canada, the most important piece of bridge-building going on in the world,—a test, indeed, of how far the latest practice in bridge structure could be carried. It was a spectacular undertaking by reason of its very size, and Bartley realized that, whatever else he might do, he would probably always be known as the engineer who designed the great Moorlock Bridge, the longest cantilever in existence. Yet it was to him the least satisfactory thing he had ever done. He was cramped in every way by a niggardly commission, and was using lighter structural material than he thought proper. He had vexations enough, too, with his work at home. He had several bridges under way in the United States, and they were always being held up by strikes and delays resulting from a general industrial unrest.

Though Alexander often told himself he had never put more into his work than he had done in the last few years, he had to admit that he had never got so little out of it. He was paying for success, too, in the demands made on his time by boards of civic enterprise and committees of public welfare. The obligations imposed by his wife's fortune and position were sometimes distracting to a man who followed his profession, and he was expected to be interested in a great many worthy endeavors on her account as well as on his own. His existence was becoming a network of great and little details. He had expected that success would bring him freedom and power; but it had brought only power that was in itself another kind of restraint. He had always meant to keep his personal liberty at all costs, as old MacKeller, his first chief, had done, and not, like so many American engineers, to become a part of a professional movement, a cautious board member, a Nestor *de pontibus*. He happened to be engaged in work of public utility, but he was not willing to become what is called a public man. He found himself living exactly the kind of life he had determined to escape. What, he asked himself, did he want with these genial honors and substantial comforts? Hardships and difficulties he had carried lightly; overwork had not exhausted him; but this dead calm of middle life which confronted him,—of that he was afraid. He was not ready for it. It was like being buried alive. In his youth he would not have believed such a thing possible. The one thing he had really wanted all his life was to be free; and there was still something unconquered in him, something besides the strong work-horse that his profession had made of him. He felt rich to-night in the possession of that unstultified survival; in the light of his experience, it was more precious than honors or achievement. In all those busy, successful years there had been nothing so good as this hour of wild light-heartedness. This feeling was the only happiness that was real to him, and such hours were the only ones in which he could feel his own continuous identity—feel the boy he had been in the rough days of the old West, feel the youth who had worked his way across the ocean on a cattle-ship and gone to study in Paris without a dollar in his pocket. The man who sat in his offices in Boston was only a powerful machine. Under the activities of that machine the person who, at such moments as this, he felt to be himself, was fading and dying. He remembered how, when he was a little boy and his father called him in the morning, he used to leap from his bed into the full consciousness of himself. That consciousness was Life itself. Whatever took its place, action, reflection, the power of concentrated thought, were only functions of a mechanism useful to society; things that could be bought in the market. There was only one thing that had an absolute value for each individual, and it was just that original impulse, that internal heat, that feeling of one's self in one's own breast.

When Alexander walked back to his hotel, the red and green lights were blinking along the docks on the farther shore, and the soft white stars were shining in the wide sky above the river.

The next night, and the next, Alexander repeated this same foolish performance. It was always Miss Burgoyne whom he started out to find, and he got no farther than the Temple gardens and the Embankment. It was a pleasant kind of loneliness. To a man who was so little given to reflection, whose dreams always took the form of definite ideas, reaching into the future, there was a seductive excitement in renewing old experiences in imagination. He started out upon these walks half guiltily, with a curious longing and expectancy which were wholly gratified by solitude. Solitude, but not solitariness; for he walked shoulder to shoulder with a shadowy companion—not little Hilda Burgoyne, by any means, but some one vastly dearer to him than she had ever been—his own young self, the youth who had waited for him upon the steps of the British Museum that night, and who, though he had tried to pass so quietly, had known him and come down and linked an arm in his.

It was not until long afterward that Alexander learned that for him this youth was the most dangerous of companions.

One Sunday evening, at Lady Walford's, Alexander did at last meet Hilda Burgoyne. Mainhall had told him that she would probably be there. He looked about for her rather nervously, and finally found her at the farther end of the large drawing-room, the centre of a circle of men, young and old. She was apparently telling them a story. They were all laughing and bending toward her. When she saw Alexander, she rose quickly and put out her hand. The other men drew back a little to let him approach.

"Mr. Alexander! I am delighted. Have you been in London long?"

Bartley bowed, somewhat laboriously, over her hand. "Long enough to have seen you more than once. How fine it all is!"

She laughed as if she were pleased. "I'm glad you think so. I like it. Won't you join us here?"

"Miss Burgoyne was just telling us about a donkey-boy she had in Galway last summer," Sir Harry Towne explained as the circle closed up again. Lord Westmere stroked his long white mustache with his bloodless hand and looked at Alexander blankly. Hilda was a good story-teller. She was sitting on the edge of her chair, as if she had alighted there for a moment only. Her primrose satin gown seemed like a soft sheath for her slender, supple figure, and its delicate color suited her white Irish skin and brown hair. Whatever she wore, people felt the charm of her active, girlish body with its slender hips and quick, eager shoulders. Alexander heard little of the story, but he watched Hilda intently. She must certainly, he reflected, be thirty, and he was honestly delighted to see that the years had treated her so indulgently. If her face had changed at all, it was in a slight hardening of the mouth—still eager enough to be very disconcerting at times, he felt—and in an added air of self-possession and self-reliance. She carried her head, too, a little more resolutely.

When the story was finished, Miss Burgoyne turned point-edly to Alexander, and the other men drifted away.

"I thought I saw you in MacConnell's box with Mainhall one evening, but I supposed you had left town before this."

She looked at him frankly and cordially, as if he were in-deed merely an old friend whom she was glad to meet again.

"No, I've been mooning about here."

Hilda laughed gayly. "Mooning! I see you mooning! You must be the busiest man in the world. Time and success have done well by you, you know. You're handsomer than ever and you've gained a grand manner."

Alexander blushed and bowed. "Time and success have been good friends to both of us. Aren't you tremendously pleased with yourself?"

She laughed again and shrugged her shoulders. "Oh, so-so. But I want to hear about you. Several years ago I read such a lot in the papers about the wonderful things you did in Japan, and how the Emperor decorated you. What was it, Com-mander of the Order of the Rising Sun? That sounds like 'The Mikado.' And what about your new bridge—in Canada, isn't it, and it's to be the longest one in the world and has some queer name I can't remember."

Bartley shook his head and smiled drolly. "Since when have you been interested in bridges? Or have you learned to be interested in everything? And is that a part of success?"

"Why, how absurd! As if I were not always interested!" Hilda exclaimed.

"Well, I think we won't talk about bridges here, at any rate." Bartley looked down at the toe of her yellow slipper which was tapping the rug impatiently under the hem of her gown. "But I wonder whether you'd think me impertinent if I asked you to let me come to see you sometime and tell you about them?"

"Why should I? Ever so many people come on Sunday afternoons."

"I know. Mainhall offered to take me. But you must know that I've been in London several times within the last few years, and you might very well think that just now is a rather inopportune time—"

She cut him short. "Nonsense. One of the pleasantest

things about success is that it makes people want to look one up, if that's what you mean. I'm like every one else—more agreeable to meet when things are going well with me. Don't you suppose it gives me any pleasure to do something that people like?"

"Does it? Oh, how fine it all is, your coming on like this! But I didn't want you to think it was because of that I wanted to see you." He spoke very seriously and looked down at the floor.

Hilda studied him in wide-eyed astonishment for a moment, and then broke into a low, amused laugh. "My dear Mr. Alexander, you have strange delicacies. If you please, that is exactly why you wish to see me. We understand that, do we not?"

Bartley looked ruffled and turned the seal ring on his little finger about awkwardly.

Hilda leaned back in her chair, watching him indulgently out of her shrewd eyes. "Come, don't be angry, but don't try to pose for me, or to be anything but what you are. If you care to come, it's yourself I'll be glad to see, and you thinking well of yourself. Don't try to wear a cloak of humility; it doesn't become you. Stalk in as you are and don't make excuses. I'm not accustomed to inquiring into the motives of my guests. That would hardly be safe, even for Lady Walford, in a great house like this."

"Sunday afternoon, then," said Alexander, as she rose to join her hostess. "How early may I come?"

"I'm at home after four, and I'll be glad to see you, Bartley."

She gave him her hand and flushed and laughed. He bent over it a little stiffly. She went away on Lady Walford's arm, and as he stood watching her yellow train glide down the long floor he looked rather sullen. He felt that he had not come out of it very brilliantly.

Chapter IV

O N Sunday afternoon Alexander remembered Miss Burgoyne's invitation and called at her apartment. He found it a delightful little place and he met charming people there. Hilda lived alone, attended by a very pretty and competent French servant who answered the door and brought in the tea. Alexander arrived early, and some twenty-odd people dropped in during the course of the afternoon. Hugh MacConnell came with his sister, and stood about, managing his tea-cup awkwardly and watching every one out of his deep-set, faded eyes. He seemed to have made a resolute effort at tidiness of attire, and his sister, a robust, florid woman with a splendid joviality about her, kept eyeing his freshly creased clothes apprehensively. It was not very long, indeed, before his coat hung with a discouraged sag from his gaunt shoulders and his hair and beard were rumpled as if he had been out in a gale. His dry humor went under a cloud of absent-minded kindliness which, Mainhall explained, always overtook him here. He was never so witty or so sharp here as elsewhere, and Alexander thought he behaved as if he were an elderly relative come in to a young girl's party.

The editor of a monthly review came with his wife, and Lady Kildare, the Irish philanthropist, brought her young nephew, Robert Owen, who had come up from Oxford, and who was visibly excited and gratified by his first introduction to Miss Burgoyne. Hilda was very nice to him, and he sat on the edge of his chair, flushed with his conversational efforts and moving his chin about nervously over his high collar. Sarah Frost, the novelist, came with her husband, a very genial and placid old scholar who had become slightly deranged upon the subject of the fourth dimension. On other matters he was perfectly rational and he was easy and pleasing in conversation. He looked very much like Agassiz, and his wife, in her old-fashioned black silk dress, overskirted and tight-sleeved, reminded Alexander of the early pictures of Mrs. Browning. Hilda seemed particularly fond of this quaint couple, and Bartley himself was so pleased with their mild and thoughtful converse that he took his leave when they did, and walked with them over to Oxford Street, where they waited for their 'bus. They asked him to come to see them in Chelsea, and they spoke very tenderly of Hilda. "She's a dear, unworldly little thing," said the philosopher absently; "more like the stage people of my young days—folk of simple manners. There are n't many such left. American tours have spoiled them, I'm afraid. They have all grown very smart. Lamb would n't care a great deal about many of them, I fancy."

Alexander went back to Bedford Square a second Sunday afternoon. He had a long talk with MacConnell, but he got no word with Hilda alone, and he left in a discontented state of mind. For the rest of the week he was nervous and unsettled, and kept rushing his work as if he were preparing for immediate departure. On Thursday afternoon he cut short a committee meeting, jumped into a hansom, and drove to Bedford Square. He sent up his card, but it came back to him with a message scribbled across the front.

> *So sorry I can't see you. Will you come and dine with me Sunday evening at half-past seven?*
>
> H. B.

When Bartley arrived at Bedford Square on Sunday evening, Marie, the pretty little French girl, met him at the door and conducted him upstairs. Hilda was writing in her living-room, under the light of a tall desk lamp. Bartley recognized the primrose satin gown she had worn that first evening at Lady Walford's.

"I'm so pleased that you think me worth that yellow dress, you know," he said, taking her hand and looking her over admiringly from the toes of her canary slippers to her smoothly parted brown hair. "Yes, it's very, very pretty. Every one at Lady Walford's was looking at it."

Hilda curtsied. "Is that why you think it pretty? I've no need for fine clothes in Mac's play this time, so I can afford a few duddies for myself. It's owing to that same chance, by the way, that I am able to ask you to dinner. I don't need Marie to dress me this season, so she keeps house for me, and my little Galway girl has gone home for a visit. I should never have asked you if Molly had been here, for I remember you don't like English cookery."

Alexander walked about the room, looking at everything.

"I haven't had a chance yet to tell you what a jolly little place I think this is. Where did you get those etchings? They're quite unusual, aren't they?"

"Lady Westmere sent them to me from Rome last Christmas. She is very much interested in the American artist who did them. They are all sketches made about the Villa d'Este, you see. He painted that group of cypresses for the Salon, and it was bought for the Luxembourg."

Alexander walked over to the bookcases. "It's the air of the whole place here that I like. You haven't got anything that doesn't belong. Seems to me it looks particularly well tonight. And you have so many flowers. I like these little yellow irises."

"Rooms always look better by lamplight—in London, at least. Though Marie is clean—really clean, as the French are. Why do you look at the flowers so critically? Marie got them all fresh in Covent Garden market yesterday morning."

"I'm glad," said Alexander simply. "I can't tell you how glad I am to have you so pretty and comfortable here, and to hear every one saying such nice things about you. You've got awfully nice friends," he added humbly, picking up a little jade elephant from her desk. "Those fellows are all very loyal, even Mainhall. They don't talk of any one else as they do of you."

Hilda sat down on the couch and said seriously: "I've a neat little sum in the bank, too, now, and I own a mite of a hut in Galway. It's not worth much, but I love it. I've managed to save something every year, and that with helping my three sisters now and then, and tiding poor Cousin Mike over bad seasons. He's that gifted, you know, but he will drink and loses more good engagements than other fellows ever get. And I've traveled a bit, too."

Marie opened the door and smilingly announced that dinner was served.

"My dining-room," Hilda explained, as she led the way, "is the tiniest place you have ever seen."

It was a tiny room, hung all round with French prints,

above which ran a shelf full of china. Hilda saw Alexander look up at it.

"It's not particularly rare," she said, "but some of it was my mother's. Heaven knows how she managed to keep it whole, through all our wanderings, or in what baskets and bundles and theatre trunks it hasn't been stowed away. We always had our tea out of those blue cups when I was a little girl, sometimes in the queerest lodgings, and sometimes on a trunk at the theatre—queer theatres, for that matter."

It was a wonderful little dinner. There was watercress soup, and sole, and a delightful omelette stuffed with mushrooms and truffles, and two small rare ducklings, and artichokes, and a dry yellow Rhone wine of which Bartley had always been very fond. He drank it appreciatively and remarked that there was still no other he liked so well.

"I have some champagne for you, too. I don't drink it myself, but I like to see it behave when it's poured. There is nothing else that looks so jolly."

"Thank you. But I don't like it so well as this." Bartley held the yellow wine against the light and squinted into it as he turned the glass slowly about. "You have traveled, you say. Have you been in Paris much these late years?"

Hilda lowered one of the candle-shades carefully. "Oh, yes, I go over to Paris often. There are few changes in the old Quarter. Dear old Madame Anger is dead—but perhaps you don't remember her?"

"Don't I, though! I'm so sorry to hear it. How did her son turn out? I remember how she saved and scraped for him, and how he always lay abed till ten o'clock. He was the laziest fellow at the Beaux Arts; and that's saying a good deal."

"Well, he is still clever and lazy. They say he is a good architect when he will work. He's a big, handsome creature, and he hates Americans as much as ever. But Angel—do you remember Angel?"

"Perfectly. Did she ever get back to Brittany and her *bains de mer*?"

"Ah, no. Poor Angel! She got tired of cooking and scouring the coppers in Madame Anger's little kitchen, so she ran away with a soldier, and then with another soldier. Too bad! She still lives about the Quarter, and, though there is always a *soldat*, she has become a *blanchisseuse de fin*. She did my blouses beautifully the last time I was there, and was so delighted to see me again. I gave her all my old clothes, even my old hats, though she always wears her Breton headdress. Her hair is still like flax, and her blue eyes are just like a baby's, and she has the same three freckles on her little nose, and talks about going back to her *bains de mer*."

Bartley looked at Hilda across the yellow light of the candles and broke into a low, happy laugh. "How jolly it was being young, Hilda! Do you remember that first walk we took together in Paris? We walked down to the Place Saint-Michel to buy some lilacs. Do you remember how sweet they smelled?"

"Indeed I do. Come, we'll have our coffee in the other room, and you can smoke."

Hilda rose quickly, as if she wished to change the drift of their talk, but Bartley found it pleasant to continue it.

"What a warm, soft spring evening that was," he went on, as they sat down in the study with the coffee on a little table between them; "and the sky, over the bridges, was just the color of the lilacs. We walked on down by the river, didn't we?"

Hilda laughed and looked at him questioningly. He saw a gleam in her eyes that he remembered even better than the episode he was recalling.

"I think we did," she answered demurely. "It was on the Quai we met that woman who was crying so bitterly. I gave her a spray of lilac, I remember, and you gave her a franc. I was frightened at your prodigality."

"I expect it was the last franc I had. What a strong brown face she had, and very tragic. She looked at us with such despair and longing, out from under her black shawl. What she wanted from us was neither our flowers nor our francs, but just our youth. I remember it touched me so. I would have given her some of mine off my back, if I could. I had enough and to spare then," Bartley mused, and looked thoughtfully at his cigar.

They were both remembering what the woman had said when she took the money: "God give you a happy love!" It was not in the ingratiating tone of the habitual beggar: it had come out of the depths of the poor creature's sorrow, vibrating with pity for their youth and despair at the terribleness of human life; it had the anguish of a voice of prophecy. Until she spoke, Bartley had not realized that he was in love. The strange woman, and her passionate sentence that rang out so sharply, had frightened them both. They went home sadly with the lilacs, back to the Rue Saint-Jacques, walking very slowly, arm in arm. When they reached the house where Hilda lodged, Bartley went across the court with her, and up the dark old stairs to the third landing; and there he had kissed her for the first time. He had shut his eyes to give him the courage, he remembered, and she had trembled so—

Bartley started when Hilda rang the little bell beside her. "Dear me, why did you do that? I had quite forgotten—I was back there. It was very jolly," he murmured lazily, as Marie came in to take away the coffee.

Hilda laughed and went over to the piano. "Well, we are neither of us twenty now, you know. Have I told you about my new play? Mac is writing one; really for me this time. You see, I'm coming on."

"I've seen nothing else. What kind of a part is it? Shall you wear yellow gowns? I hope so."

He was looking at her round, slender figure, as she stood by the piano, turning over a pile of music, and he felt the energy in every line of it.

"No, it isn't a dress-up part. He doesn't seem to fancy me in fine feathers. He says I ought to be minding the pigs at home, and I suppose I ought. But he's given me some good Irish songs. Listen."

She sat down at the piano and sang. When she finished, Alexander shook himself out of a reverie.

"Sing 'The Harp that Once,' Hilda. You used to sing it so well."

"Nonsense. Of course I can't really sing, except the way my mother and grandmother did before me. Most actresses nowadays learn to sing properly, so I tried a master; but he confused me, just!"

Alexander laughed. "All the same, sing it, Hilda."

Hilda started up from the stool and moved restlessly toward

the window. "It's really too warm in this room to sing. Don't you feel it?"

Alexander went over and opened the window for her. "Are n't you afraid to let the wind blow like that on your neck? Can't I get a scarf or something?"

"Ask a theatre lydy if she's afraid of drafts!" Hilda laughed. "But perhaps, as I'm so warm—give me your handkerchief. There, just in front." He slipped the corners carefully under her shoulder-straps. "There, that will do. It looks like a bib." She pushed his hand away quickly and stood looking out into the deserted square. "Is n't London a tomb on Sunday night?"

Alexander caught the agitation in her voice. He stood a little behind her, and tried to steady himself as he said: "It's soft and misty. See how white the stars are."

For a long time neither Hilda nor Bartley spoke. They stood close together, looking out into the wan, watery sky, breathing always more quickly and lightly, and it seemed as if all the clocks in the world had stopped. Suddenly he moved the clenched hand he held behind him and dropped it violently at his side. He felt a tremor run through the slender yellow figure in front of him.

She caught his handkerchief from her throat and thrust it at him without turning round. "Here, take it. You must go now, Bartley. Good-night."

Bartley leaned over her shoulder, without touching her, and whispered in her ear: "You are giving me a chance?"

"Yes. Take it and go. This is n't fair, you know. Good-night."

Alexander unclenched the two hands at his sides. With one he threw down the window and with the other—still standing behind her—he drew her back against him.

She uttered a little cry, threw her arms over her head, and drew his face down to hers. "Are you going to let me love you a little, Bartley?" she whispered.

Chapter V

IT WAS the afternoon of the day before Christmas. Mrs. Alexander had been driving about all the morning, leaving presents at the houses of her friends. She lunched alone, and as she rose from the table she spoke to the butler: "Thomas, I am going down to the kitchen now to see Norah. In half an hour you are to bring the greens up from the cellar and put them in the library. Mr. Alexander will be home at three to hang them himself. Don't forget the stepladder, and plenty of tacks and string. You may bring the azaleas upstairs. Take the white one to Mr. Alexander's study. Put the two pink ones in this room, and the red one in the drawing-room."

A little before three o'clock Mrs. Alexander went into the library to see that everything was ready. She pulled the window shades high, for the weather was dark and stormy, and there was little light, even in the streets. A foot of snow had fallen during the morning, and the wide space over the river was thick with flying flakes that fell and wreathed the masses of floating ice. Winifred was standing by the window when she heard the front door open. She hurried to the hall as Alexander came stamping in, covered with snow. He kissed her joyfully and brushed away the snow that fell on her hair.

"I wish I had asked you to meet me at the office and walk home with me, Winifred. The Common is beautiful. The boys have swept the snow off the pond and are skating furiously. Did the cyclamens come?"

"An hour ago. What splendid ones! But are n't you frightfully extravagant?"

"Not for Christmas-time. I'll go upstairs and change my coat. I shall be down in a moment. Tell Thomas to get everything ready."

When Alexander reappeared, he took his wife's arm and went with her into the library. "When did the azaleas get here? Thomas has got the white one in my room."

"I told him to put it there."

"But, I say, it's much the finest of the lot!"

310

"That's why I had it put there. There is too much color in that room for a red one, you know."

Bartley began to sort the greens. "It looks very splendid there, but I feel piggish to have it. However, we really spend more time there than anywhere else in the house. Will you hand me the holly?"

He climbed up the stepladder, which creaked under his weight, and began to twist the tough stems of the holly into the framework of the chandelier.

"I forgot to tell you that I had a letter from Wilson, this morning, explaining his telegram. He is coming on because an old uncle up in Vermont has conveniently died and left Wilson a little money—something like ten thousand. He's coming on to settle up the estate. Won't it be jolly to have him?"

"And how fine that he's come into a little money. I can see him posting down State Street to the steamship offices. He will get a good many trips out of that ten thousand. What can have detained him? I expected him here for luncheon."

"Those trains from Albany are always late. He'll be along sometime this afternoon. And now, don't you want to go up-stairs and lie down for an hour? You've had a busy morning and I don't want you to be tired to-night."

After his wife went upstairs Alexander worked energetically at the greens for a few moments. Then, as he was cutting off a length of string, he sighed suddenly and sat down, staring out of the window at the snow. The animation died out of his face, but in his eyes there was a restless light, a look of apprehension and suspense. He kept clasping and unclasping his big hands as if he were trying to realize something. The clock ticked through the minutes of a half-hour and the afternoon outside began to thicken and darken turbidly. Alexander, since he first sat down, had not changed his position. He leaned forward, his hands between his knees, scarcely breathing, as if he were holding himself away from his surroundings, from the room, and from the very chair in which he sat, from everything except the wild eddies of snow above the river on which his eyes were fixed with feverish intentness, as if he were trying to project himself thither. When at last Lucius Wilson was announced, Alexander sprang eagerly to his feet and hurried to meet his old instructor.

"Hello, Wilson. What luck! Come into the library. We are to have a lot of people to dinner to-night, and Winifred's lying down. You will excuse her, won't you? And now what about yourself? Sit down and tell me everything."

"I think I'd rather move about, if you don't mind. I've been sitting in the train for a week, it seems to me." Wilson stood before the fire with his hands behind him and looked about the room. "You *have* been busy. Bartley, if I'd had my choice of all possible places in which to spend Christmas, your house would certainly be the place I'd have chosen. Happy people do a great deal for their friends. A house like this throws its warmth out. I felt it distinctly as I was coming through the Berkshires. I could scarcely believe that I was to see Mrs. Bartley again so soon."

"Thank you, Wilson. She'll be as glad to see you. Shall we have tea now? I'll ring for Thomas to clear away this litter. Winifred says I always wreck the house when I try to do anything. Do you know, I am quite tired. Looks as if I were not used to work, does n't it?" Alexander laughed and dropped into a chair. "You know, I'm sailing the day after New Year's."

"Again? Why, you've been over twice since I was here in the spring, have n't you?"

"Oh, I was in London about ten days in the summer. Went to escape the hot weather more than anything else. I shan't be gone more than a month this time. Winifred and I have been up in Canada for most of the autumn. That Moorlock Bridge is on my back all the time. I never had so much trouble with a job before." Alexander moved about restlessly and fell to poking the fire.

"Have n't I seen in the papers that there is some trouble about a tidewater bridge of yours in New Jersey?"

"Oh, that does n't amount to anything. It's held up by a steel strike. A bother, of course, but the sort of thing one is always having to put up with. But the Moorlock Bridge is a continual anxiety. You see, the truth is, we are having to build pretty well to the strain limit up there. They've crowded me too much on the cost. It's all very well if everything goes well, but these estimates have never been used for anything of such length before. However, there's nothing to be done. They hold me to the scale I've used in shorter bridges. The last thing a bridge commission cares about is the kind of bridge you build."

When Bartley had finished dressing for dinner he went into his study, where he found his wife arranging flowers on his writing-table.

"These pink roses just came from Mrs. Hastings," she said, smiling, "and I am sure she meant them for you."

Bartley looked about with an air of satisfaction at the greens and the wreaths in the windows. "Have you a moment, Winifred? I have just now been thinking that this is our twelfth Christmas. Can you realize it?" He went up to the table and took her hands away from the flowers, drying them with his pocket handkerchief. "They've been awfully happy ones, all of them, have n't they?" He took her in his arms and bent back, lifting her a little and giving her a long kiss. "You are happy, are n't you, Winifred? More than anything else in the world, I want you to be happy. Sometimes, of late, I've thought you looked as if you were troubled."

"No; it's only when you are troubled and harassed that I feel worried, Bartley. I wish you always seemed as you do to-night. But you don't, always." She looked earnestly and inquiringly into his eyes.

Alexander took her two hands from his shoulders and swung them back and forth in his own, laughing his big blond laugh.

"I'm growing older, my dear; that's what you feel. Now, may I show you something? I meant to save them until to-morrow, but I want you to wear them to-night." He took a little leather box out of his pocket and opened it. On the white velvet lay two long pendants of curiously worked gold, set with pearls. Winifred looked from the box to Bartley and exclaimed: —

"Where did you ever find such gold work, Bartley?"

"It's old Flemish. Is n't it fine?"

"They are the most beautiful things, dear. But, you know, I never wear earrings."

"Yes, yes, I know. But I want you to wear them. I have always wanted you to. So few women can. There must be a good ear, to begin with, and a nose"—he waved his hand—"above reproach. Most women look silly in them. They go only with faces like yours—very, very proud, and just a little hard."

Winifred laughed as she went over to the mirror and fitted the delicate springs to the lobes of her ears. "Oh, Bartley, that old foolishness about my being hard. It really hurts my feelings. But I must go down now. People are beginning to come."

Bartley drew her arm about his neck and went to the door with her. "Not hard to me, Winifred," he whispered. "Never, never hard to me."

Left alone, he paced up and down his study. He was at home again, among all the dear familiar things that spoke to him of so many happy years. His house to-night would be full of charming people, who liked and admired him. Yet all the time, underneath his pleasure and hopefulness and satisfaction, he was conscious of the vibration of an unnatural excitement. Amid this light and warmth and friendliness, he sometimes started and shuddered, as if some one had stepped on his grave. Something had broken loose in him of which he knew nothing except that it was sullen and powerful, and that it wrung and tortured him. Sometimes it came upon him softly, in enervating reveries. Sometimes it battered him like the cannon rolling in the hold of the vessel. Always, now, it brought with it a sense of quickened life, of stimulating danger. To-night it came upon him suddenly, as he was walking the floor, after his wife left him. It seemed impossible; he could not believe it. He glanced entreatingly at the door, as if to call her back. He heard voices in the hall below, and knew that he must go down. Going over to the window, he looked out at the lights across the river. How could this happen here, in his own house, among the things he loved? What was it that reached in out of the darkness and thrilled him? As he stood there he had a feeling that he would never escape. He shut his eyes and pressed his forehead against the cold window glass, breathing in the chill that came through it. "That this," he groaned, "that this should have happened to *me!*"

On New Year's day a thaw set in, and during the night torrents of rain fell. In the morning, the morning of Alexander's departure for England, the river was streaked with fog and the rain drove hard against the windows of the breakfast-room. Alexander had finished his coffee and was pacing up and down. His wife sat at the table, watching him. She was pale and unnaturally calm. When Thomas brought the letters, Bartley sank into his chair and ran them over rapidly.

"Here's a note from old Wilson. He's safe back at his grind, and says he had a bully time. 'The memory of Mrs. Bartley will make my whole winter fragrant.' Just like him. He will go on getting measureless satisfaction out of you by his study fire. What a man he is for looking on at life!" Bartley sighed, pushed the letters back impatiently, and went over to the window. "This is a nasty sort of day to sail. I've a notion to call it off. Next week would be time enough."

"That would only mean starting twice. It wouldn't really help you out at all," Mrs. Alexander spoke soothingly. "And you'd come back late for all your engagements."

Bartley began jingling some loose coins in his pocket. "I wish things would let me rest. I'm tired of work, tired of people, tired of trailing about." He looked out at the storm-beaten river.

Winifred came up behind him and put a hand on his shoulder. "That's what you always say, poor Bartley! At bottom you really like all these things. Can't you remember that?"

He put his arm about her. "All the same, life runs smoothly enough with some people, and with me it's always a messy sort of patchwork. It's like the song; peace is where I am not. How can you face it all with so much fortitude?"

She looked at him with that clear gaze which Wilson had so much admired, which he had felt implied such high confidence and fearless pride. "Oh, I faced that long ago, when you were on your first bridge, up at old Allway. I knew then that your paths were not to be paths of peace, but I decided that I wanted to follow them."

Bartley and his wife stood silent for a long time; the fire crackled in the grate, the rain beat insistently upon the windows, and the sleepy Angora looked up at them curiously.

Presently Thomas made a discreet sound at the door. "Shall Edward bring down your trunks, sir?"

"Yes; they are ready. Tell him not to forget the big portfolio on the study table."

Thomas withdrew, closing the door softly. Bartley turned away from his wife, still holding her hand. "It never gets any easier, Winifred."

They both started at the sound of the carriage on the pavement outside. Alexander sat down and leaned his head on his hand. His wife bent over him. "Courage," she said gayly. Bartley rose and rang the bell. Thomas brought him his hat and stick and ulster. At the sight of these, the supercilious Angora moved restlessly, quitted her red cushion by the fire, and came up, waving her tail in vexation at these ominous indications of change. Alexander stooped to stroke her, and then plunged into his coat and drew on his gloves. His wife held his stick, smiling. Bartley smiled too, and his eyes cleared. "I'll work like the devil, Winifred, and be home again before you realize I've gone." He kissed her quickly several times, hurried out of the front door into the rain, and waved to her from the carriage window as the driver was starting his melancholy, dripping black horses. Alexander sat with his hands clenched on his knees. As the carriage turned up the hill, he lifted one hand and brought it down violently. "This time" —he spoke aloud and through his set teeth—"this time I'm going to end it!"

On the afternoon of the third day out, Alexander was sitting well to the stern, on the windward side where the chairs were few, his rugs over him and the collar of his fur-lined coat turned up about his ears. The weather had so far been dark and raw. For two hours he had been watching the low, dirty sky and the beating of the heavy rain upon the iron-colored sea. There was a long, oily swell that made exercise laborious. The decks smelled of damp woolens, and the air was so humid that drops of moisture kept gathering upon his hair and mustache. He seldom moved except to brush them away. The great open spaces made him passive and the restlessness of the water quieted him. He intended during the voyage to decide upon a course of action, but he held all this away from him for the present and lay in a blessed gray oblivion. Deep down in him somewhere his resolution was weakening and strengthening, ebbing and flowing. The thing that perturbed him went on as steadily as his pulse, but he was almost unconscious of it. He was submerged in the vast impersonal grayness about him, and at intervals the sidelong roll of the boat measured off time like the ticking of a clock. He felt released from everything that troubled and perplexed him. It was as if he had tricked and outwitted torturing memories, had actually managed to get on board without them. He thought of nothing at all. If his mind now and again picked a face out of the grayness, it was Lucius Wilson's, or the face of an old schoolmate, forgotten for years; or it was the slim outline of a favorite greyhound he used to hunt jack-rabbits with when he was a boy.

Toward six o'clock the wind rose and tugged at the tarpaulin and brought the swell higher. After dinner Alexander came back to the wet deck, piled his damp rugs over him again, and sat smoking, losing himself in the obliterating blackness and drowsing in the rush of the gale. Before he went below a few bright stars were pricked off between heavily moving masses of cloud.

The next morning was bright and mild, with a fresh breeze. Alexander felt the need of exercise even before he came out of his cabin. When he went on deck the sky was blue and blinding, with heavy whiffs of white cloud, smoke-colored at the edges, moving rapidly across it. The water was roughish, a cold, clear indigo breaking into whitecaps. Bartley walked for two hours, and then stretched himself in the sun until lunchtime.

In the afternoon he wrote a long letter to Winifred. Later, as he walked the deck through a splendid golden sunset, his spirits rose continually. It was agreeable to come to himself again after several days of numbness and torpor. He stayed out until the last tinge of violet had faded from the water.

There was literally a taste of life on his lips as he sat down to dinner and ordered a bottle of champagne. He was late in finishing his dinner, and drank rather more wine than he had meant to. When he went above, the wind had risen and the deck was almost deserted. As he stepped out of the door a gale lifted his heavy fur coat about his shoulders. He fought his way up the deck with keen exhilaration. The moment he stepped, almost out of breath, behind the shelter of the stern, the wind was cut off, and he felt, like a rush of warm air, a sense of close and intimate companionship. He started back and tore his coat open as if something warm were actually clinging to him beneath it. He hurried up the deck and went into the saloon parlor, full of women who had retreated thither from the sharp wind. He threw himself upon them. He talked delightfully to the older ones and played accompaniments for the younger ones until the last sleepy girl had followed her mother below. Then he went into the smoking-room. He played bridge until two o'clock in the morning, and managed to lose a considerable sum of money without really noticing that he was doing so.

After the break of one fine day the weather was pretty consistently dull. When the low sky thinned a trifle, the pale white spot of a sun did no more than throw a bluish lustre on the water, giving it the dark brightness of newly cut lead. Through one after another of those gray days Alexander drowsed and mused, drinking in the grateful moisture. But the complete peace of the first part of the voyage was over. Sometimes he rose suddenly from his chair as if driven out, and paced the deck for hours. People noticed his propensity for walking in rough weather, and watched him curiously as he did his rounds. From his abstraction and the determined set of his jaw, they fancied he must be thinking about his bridge. Every one had heard of the new cantilever bridge in Canada.

But Alexander was not thinking about his work. After the fourth night out, when his will suddenly softened under his hands, he had been continually hammering away at himself. More and more often, when he first wakened in the morning or when he stepped into a warm place after being chilled on the deck, he felt a sudden painful delight at being nearer another shore. Sometimes when he was most despondent, when he thought himself worn out with this struggle, in a flash he was free of it and leaped into an overwhelming consciousness of himself. On the instant he felt that marvelous return of the impetuousness, the intense excitement, the increasing expectancy of youth.

Chapter VI

THE LAST TWO DAYS of the voyage Bartley found almost intolerable. The stop at Queenstown, the tedious passage up the Mersey, were things that he noted dimly through his growing impatience. He had planned to stop in Liverpool; but, instead, he took the boat train for London.

Emerging at Euston at half-past three o'clock in the afternoon, Alexander had his luggage sent to the Savoy and drove at once to Bedford Square. When Marie met him at the door, even her strong sense of the proprieties could not restrain her surprise and delight. She blushed and smiled and fumbled his card in her confusion before she ran upstairs. Alexander paced up and down the hallway, buttoning and unbuttoning his overcoat, until she returned and took him up to Hilda's living-room. The room was empty when he entered. A coal fire was crackling in the grate and the lamps were lit, for it was already beginning to grow dark outside. Alexander did not sit down. He stood his ground over by the windows until Hilda came in. She called his name on the threshold, but in her swift flight across the room she felt a change in him and caught herself up so deftly that he could not tell just when she did it. She merely brushed his cheek with her lips and put a hand lightly and joyously on either shoulder.

"Oh, what a grand thing to happen on a raw day! I felt it in my bones when I woke this morning that something splendid was going to turn up. I thought it might be Sister Kate or Cousin Mike would be happening along. I never dreamed it would be you, Bartley. But why do you let me chatter on like this? Come over to the fire; you're chilled through."

She pushed him toward the big chair by the fire, and sat down on a stool at the opposite side of the hearth, her knees drawn up to her chin, laughing like a happy little girl.

"When did you come, Bartley, and how did it happen? You have n't spoken a word."

"I got in about ten minutes ago. I landed at Liverpool this morning and came down on the boat train."

Alexander leaned forward and warmed his hands before the blaze. Hilda watched him with perplexity.

"There's something troubling you, Bartley. What is it?"

Bartley bent lower over the fire. "It's the whole thing that troubles me, Hilda. You and I."

Hilda took a quick, soft breath. She looked at his heavy shoulders and big, determined head, thrust forward like a catapult in leash.

"What about us, Bartley?" she asked in a thin voice.

He locked and unlocked his hands over the grate and spread his fingers close to the bluish flame, while the coals crackled and the clock ticked and a street vendor began to call under the window. At last Alexander brought out one word: —

"Everything!"

Hilda was pale by this time, and her eyes were wide with fright. She looked about desperately from Bartley to the door, then to the windows, and back again to Bartley. She rose uncertainly, touched his hair with her hand, then sank back upon her stool.

"I'll do anything you wish me to, Bartley," she said tremulously. "I can't stand seeing you miserable."

"I can't live with myself any longer," he answered roughly.

He rose and pushed the chair behind him and began to walk miserably about the room, seeming to find it too small for him. He pulled up a window as if the air were heavy.

Hilda watched him from her corner, trembling and scarcely breathing, dark shadows growing about her eyes.

"It . . . it hasn't always made you miserable, has it?" Her eyelids fell and her lips quivered.

"Always. But it's worse now. It's unbearable. It tortures me every minute."

"But why *now*?" she asked piteously, wringing her hands.

He ignored her question. "I am not a man who can live two lives," he went on feverishly. "Each life spoils the other. I get nothing but misery out of either. The world is all there, just as it used to be, but I can't get at it any more. There is this deception between me and everything."

At that word "deception," spoken with such self-contempt, the color flashed back into Hilda's face as suddenly as if she had been struck by a whiplash. She bit her lip and looked down at her hands, which were clasped tightly in front of her.

"Could you—could you sit down and talk about it quietly, Bartley, as if I were a friend, and not some one who had to be defied?"

He dropped back heavily into his chair by the fire. "It was myself I was defying, Hilda. I have thought about it until I am worn out."

He looked at her and his haggard face softened. He put out his hand toward her as he looked away again into the fire.

She crept across to him, drawing her stool after her. "When did you first begin to feel like this, Bartley?"

"After the very first. The first was—sort of in play, was n't it?"

Hilda's face quivered, but she whispered: "Yes, I think it must have been. But why did n't you tell me when you were here in the summer?"

Alexander groaned. "I meant to, but somehow I could n't. We had only a few days, and your new play was just on, and you were so happy."

"Yes, I was happy, was n't I?" She pressed his hand gently in gratitude. "Were n't you happy then, at all?"

She closed her eyes and took a deep breath, as if to draw in again the fragrance of those days. Something of their troubling sweetness came back to Alexander, too. He moved uneasily and his chair creaked.

"Yes, I was then. You know. But afterward . . ."

"Yes, yes," she hurried, pulling her hand gently away from him. Presently it stole back to his coat sleeve. "Please tell me one thing, Bartley. At least, tell me that you believe I thought I was making you happy."

His hand shut down quickly over the questioning fingers on his sleeves. "Yes, Hilda; I know that," he said simply.

She leaned her head against his arm and spoke softly:—

"You see, my mistake was in wanting you to have everything. I wanted you to eat all the cakes and have them, too. I somehow believed that I could take all the bad consequences for you. I wanted you always to be happy and handsome and successful—to have all the things that a great man ought to have, and, once in a way, the careless holidays that great men are not permitted."

Bartley gave a bitter little laugh, and Hilda looked up and read in the deepening lines of his face that youth and Bartley would not much longer struggle together.

"I understand, Bartley. I was wrong. But I didn't know. You've only to tell me now. What must I do that I've not done, or what must I not do?" She listened intently, but she heard nothing but the creaking of his chair. "You want me to say it?" she whispered. "You want to tell me that you can only see me like this, as old friends do, or out in the world among people? I can do that."

"I can't," he said heavily.

Hilda shivered and sat still. Bartley leaned his head in his hands and spoke through his teeth. "It's got to be a clean break, Hilda. I can't see you at all, anywhere. What I mean is that I want you to promise never to see me again, no matter how often I come, no matter how hard I beg."

Hilda sprang up like a flame. She stood over him with her hands clenched at her side, her body rigid.

"No!" she gasped. "It's too late to ask that. Do you hear me, Bartley? It's too late. I won't promise. It's abominable of you to ask me. Keep away if you wish; when have I ever followed you? But, if you come to me, I'll do as I see fit. The shamefulness of your asking me to do that! If you come to me, I'll do as I see fit. Do you understand? Bartley, you're cowardly!"

Alexander rose and shook himself angrily. "Yes, I know I'm cowardly. I'm afraid of myself. I don't trust myself any more. I carried it all lightly enough at first, but now I don't dare trifle with it. It's getting the better of me. It's different now. I'm growing older, and you've got my young self here with you. It's through him that I've come to wish for you all and all the time." He took her roughly in his arms. "Do you know what I mean?"

Hilda held her face back from him and began to cry bitterly. "Oh, Bartley, what am I to do? Why didn't you let me be angry with you? You ask me to stay away from you because you want me! And I've got nobody but you. I will do anything you say—but that! I will ask the least imaginable, but I must have *something*!"

Bartley turned away and sank down in his chair again. Hilda sat on the arm of it and put her hands lightly on his shoulders.

"Just something, Bartley. I must have you to think of through the months and months of loneliness. I must see you. I must know about you. The sight of you, Bartley, to see you living and happy and successful—can I never make you understand what that means to me?" She pressed his shoulders gently. "You see, loving some one as I love you makes the whole world different. If I'd met you later, if I hadn't loved you so well—but that's all over, long ago. Then came all those years without you, lonely and hurt and discouraged; those decent young fellows and poor Mac, and me never heeding—hard as a steel spring. And then you came back, not caring very much, but it made no difference."

She slid to the floor beside him, as if she were too tired to sit up any longer. Bartley bent over and took her in his arms, kissing her mouth and her wet, tired eyes.

"Don't cry, don't cry," he whispered. "We've tortured each other enough for to-night. Forget everything except that I am here."

"I think I have forgotten everything but that already," she murmured. "Ah, your dear arms!"

Chapter VII

During the fortnight that Alexander was in London he drove himself hard. He got through a great deal of personal business and saw a great many men who were doing interesting things in his own profession. He disliked to think of his visits to London as holidays, and when he was there he worked even harder than he did at home.

The day before his departure for Liverpool was a singularly fine one. The thick air had cleared overnight in a strong wind which brought in a golden dawn and then fell off to a fresh breeze. When Bartley looked out of his windows from the Savoy, the river was flashing silver and the gray stone along the Embankment was bathed in bright, clear sunshine. London had wakened to life after three weeks of cold and sodden rain. Bartley breakfasted hurriedly and went over his mail while the hotel valet packed his trunks. Then he paid his account and walked rapidly down the Strand past Charing Cross Station. His spirits rose with every step, and when he reached Trafalgar Square, blazing in the sun, with its fountains playing and its column reaching up into the bright air, he signaled to a hansom, and, before he knew what he was about, told the driver to go to Bedford Square by way of the British Museum.

When he reached Hilda's apartment she met him, fresh as the morning itself. Her rooms were flooded with sunshine and full of the flowers he had been sending her. She would never let him give her anything else.

"Are you busy this morning, Hilda?" he asked as he sat down, his hat and gloves in his hand.

"Very. I've been up and about three hours, working at my part. We open in February, you know."

"Well, then you've worked enough. And so have I. I've seen all my men, my packing is done, and I go up to Liverpool this evening. But this morning we are going to have a holiday. What do you say to a drive out to Kew and Richmond? You may not get another day like this all winter. It's like a fine April day at home. May I use your telephone? I want to order the carriage."

"Oh, how jolly! There, sit down at the desk. And while you are telephoning I'll change my dress. I shan't be long. All the morning papers are on the table."

Hilda was back in a few moments wearing a long gray squirrel coat and a broad fur hat.

Bartley rose and inspected her. "Why don't you wear some of those pink roses?" he asked.

"But they came only this morning, and they have not even begun to open. I was saving them. I am so unconsciously thrifty!" She laughed as she looked about the room. "You've been sending me far too many flowers, Bartley. New ones every day. That's too often; though I do love to open the boxes, and I take good care of them."

"Why won't you let me send you any of those jade or ivory things you are so fond of? Or pictures? I know a good deal about pictures."

Hilda shook her large hat as she drew the roses out of the tall glass. "No, there are some things you can't do. There's the carriage. Will you button my gloves for me?"

Bartley took her wrist and began to button the long gray suede glove. "How gay your eyes are this morning, Hilda."

"That's because I've been studying. It always stirs me up a little."

He pushed the top of the glove up slowly. "When did you learn to take hold of your parts like that?"

"When I had nothing else to think of. Come, the carriage is waiting. What a shocking while you take."

"I'm in no hurry. We've plenty of time."

They found all London abroad. Piccadilly was a stream of rapidly moving carriages, from which flashed furs and flowers and bright winter costumes. The metal trappings of the harnesses shone dazzlingly, and the wheels were revolving disks that threw off rays of light. The parks were full of children and nursemaids and joyful dogs that leaped and yelped and scratched up the brown earth with their paws.

"I'm not going until to-morrow, you know," Bartley announced suddenly. "I'll cut off a day in Liverpool. I have n't felt so jolly this long while."

Hilda looked up with a smile which she tried not to make too glad. "I think people were meant to be happy, a little," she said.

They had lunch at Richmond and then walked to Twickenham, where they had sent the carriage. They drove back, with a glorious sunset behind them, toward the distant gold-washed city. It was one of those rare afternoons when all the thickness and shadow of London are changed to a kind of shining, pulsing, special atmosphere; when the smoky vapors become fluttering golden clouds, nacreous veils of pink and amber; when all that bleakness of gray stone and dullness of dirty brick trembles in aureate light, and all the roofs and spires, and one great dome, are floated in golden haze. On such rare afternoons the ugliest of cities becomes the most beautiful, the most prosaic becomes the most poetic, and months of sodden days are offset by a moment of miracle.

"It's like that with us Londoners, too," Hilda was saying. "Everything is awfully grim and cheerless, our weather and our houses and our ways of amusing ourselves. But we can be happier than anybody. We can go mad with joy, as the people do out in the fields on a fine Whitsunday. We make the most of our moment."

She thrust her little chin out defiantly over her gray fur collar, and Bartley looked down at her and laughed.

"You are a plucky one, you." He patted her glove with his hand. "Yes, you are a plucky one."

Hilda sighed. "No, I'm not. Not about some things, at any rate. It doesn't take pluck to fight for one's moment, but it takes pluck to go without—a lot. More than I have. I can't help it," she added fiercely.

After miles of outlying streets and little gloomy houses, they reached London itself, red and roaring and murky, with a thick dampness coming up from the river, that betokened fog again to-morrow. The streets were full of people who had worked indoors all through the priceless day and had now come hungrily out to drink the muddy lees of it. They stood in long black lines, waiting before the pit entrances of the theatres—short-coated boys, and girls in sailor hats, all shivering and chatting gayly. There was a blurred rhythm in all the dull city noises—in the clatter of the cab horses and the rumbling of the busses, in the street calls, and in the undulating tramp, tramp of the crowd. It was like the deep vibration of some vast underground machinery, and like the muffled pulsations of millions of human hearts.

"Seems good to get back, does n't it?" Bartley whispered, as they drove from Bayswater Road into Oxford Street. "London always makes me want to live more than any other city in the world. You remember our priestess mummy over in the mummy-room, and how we used to long to go and bring her out on nights like this? Three thousand years! Ugh!"

"All the same, I believe she used to feel it when we stood there and watched her and wished her well. I believe she used to remember," Hilda said thoughtfully.

"I hope so. Now let's go to some awfully jolly place for dinner before we go home. I could eat all the dinners there are in London to-night. Where shall I tell the driver? The Piccadilly Restaurant? The music's good there."

"There are too many people there whom one knows. Why not that little French place in Soho, where we went so often when you were here in the summer? I love it, and I've never been there with any one but you. Sometimes I go by myself, when I am particularly lonely."

"Very well, the sole's good there. How many street pianos there are about to-night! The fine weather must have thawed them out. We've had five miles of 'Il Trovatore' now. They always make me feel jaunty. Are you comfy, and not too tired?"

"I'm not tired at all. I was just wondering how people can ever die. Why did you remind me of the mummy? Life seems the strongest and most indestructible thing in the world. Do you really believe that all those people rushing about down there, going to good dinners and clubs and theatres, will be dead some day, and not care about anything? I don't believe it, and I know I shan't die, ever! You see, I feel too—too powerful!"

The carriage stopped. Bartley sprang out and swung her quickly to the pavement. As he lifted her in his two hands he whispered: "You are—powerful!"

Chapter VIII

T HE LAST REHEARSAL was over, a tedious dress rehearsal which had lasted all day and exhausted the patience of every one who had to do with it. When Hilda had dressed for the street and came out of her dressing-room, she found Hugh MacConnell waiting for her in the corridor.

"The fog's thicker than ever, Hilda. There have been a great many accidents to-day. It's positively unsafe for you to be out alone. Will you let me take you home?"

"How good of you, Mac. If you are going with me, I think I'd rather walk. I've had no exercise to-day, and all this has made me nervous."

"I shouldn't wonder," said MacConnell dryly. Hilda pulled down her veil and they stepped out into the thick brown wash that submerged St. Martin's Lane. MacConnell took her hand and tucked it snugly under his arm. "I'm sorry I was such a savage. I hope you didn't think I made an ass of myself."

"Not a bit of it. I don't wonder you were peppery. Those things are awfully trying. How do you think it's going?"

"Magnificently. That's why I got so stirred up. We are going to hear from this, both of us. And that reminds me; I've got news for you. They are going to begin repairs on the theatre about the middle of March, and we are to run over to New York for six weeks. Bennett told me yesterday that it was decided."

Hilda looked up delightedly at the tall gray figure beside her. He was the only thing she could see, for they were moving through a dense opaqueness, as if they were walking at the bottom of the ocean.

"Oh, Mac, how glad I am! And they love your things over there, don't they?"

"Shall you be glad for—any other reason, Hilda?"

MacConnell put his hand in front of her to ward off some dark object. It proved to be only a lamp-post, and they beat in farther from the edge of the pavement.

"What do you mean, Mac?" Hilda asked nervously.

"I was just thinking there might be people over there you'd be glad to see," he brought out awkwardly. Hilda said nothing, and as they walked on MacConnell spoke again, apologetically: "I hope you don't mind my knowing about it, Hilda. Don't stiffen up like that. No one else knows, and I didn't try to find out anything. I felt it, even before I knew who he was. I knew there was somebody, and that it wasn't I."

They crossed Oxford Street in silence, feeling their way. The busses had stopped running and the cab-drivers were leading their horses. When they reached the other side, Mac-Connell said suddenly, "I hope you are happy."

"Terribly, dangerously happy, Mac,"—Hilda spoke quietly, pressing the rough sleeve of his greatcoat with her gloved hand.

"You've always thought me too old for you, Hilda,—oh, of course you've never said just that,—and here this fellow is not more than eight years younger than I. I've always felt that if I could get out of my old case I might win you yet. It's a fine, brave youth I carry inside me, only he'll never be seen."

"Nonsense, Mac. That has nothing to do with it. It's because you seem too close to me, too much my own kind. It would be like marrying Cousin Mike, almost. I really tried to care as you wanted me to, away back in the beginning."

"Well, here we are, turning out of the Square. You are not angry with me, Hilda? Thank you for this walk, my dear. Go in and get dry things on at once. You'll be having a great night to-morrow."

She put out her hand. "Thank you, Mac, for everything. Good-night."

MacConnell trudged off through the fog, and she went slowly upstairs. Her slippers and dressing gown were waiting for her before the fire. "I shall certainly see him in New York. He will see by the papers that we are coming. Perhaps he knows it already," Hilda kept thinking as she undressed. "Perhaps he will be at the dock. No, scarcely that; but I may meet him in the street even before he comes to see me." Marie placed the tea-table by the fire and brought Hilda her letters. She looked them over, and started as she came to one in a handwriting that she did not often see; Alexander had written to her only twice before, and he did not allow her to write to him at all. "Thank you, Marie. You may go now."

Hilda sat down by the table with the letter in her hand, still unopened. She looked at it intently, turned it over, and felt its thickness with her fingers. She believed that she sometimes had a kind of second-sight about letters, and could tell before she read them whether they brought good or evil tidings. She put this one down on the table in front of her while she poured her tea. At last, with a little shiver of expectancy, she tore open the envelope and read: —

BOSTON, February ——

MY DEAR HILDA: —

It is after twelve o'clock. Every one else is in bed and I am sitting alone in my study. I have been happier in this room than anywhere else in the world. Happiness like that makes one insolent. I used to think these four walls could stand against anything. And now I scarcely know myself here. Now I know that no one can build his security upon the nobleness of another person. Two people, when they love each other, grow alike in their tastes and habits and pride, but their moral natures (whatever we may mean by that canting expression) are never welded. The base one goes on being base, and the noble one noble, to the end.

The last week has been a bad one; I have been realizing how things used to be with me. Sometimes I get used to being dead inside, but lately it has been as if a window beside me had suddenly opened, and as if all the smells of spring blew in to me. There is a garden out there, with stars overhead, where I used to walk at night when I had a single purpose and a single heart. I can remember how I used to feel there, how beautiful everything about me was, and what life and power and freedom I felt in myself. When the window opens I know exactly how it would feel to be out there. But that garden is closed to me. How is it, I ask myself, that everything can be so different with me when nothing here has changed? I am in my own house, in my own study, in the midst of all these quiet streets where my friends live. They are all safe and at peace with themselves. But I am never at peace. I feel always on the edge of danger and change.

I keep remembering locoed horses I used to see on the range when I was a boy. They changed like that. We used to catch them and put them up in the corral, and they developed great cunning. They would pretend to eat their oats like the other horses, but we knew they were always scheming to get back at the loco.

It seems that a man is meant to live only one life in this world. When he tries to live a second, he develops another nature. I feel as if a second man had been grafted into me. At first he seemed only a pleasure-loving simpleton, of whose company I was rather ashamed, and whom I used to hide under my coat when I walked the Embankment, in London. But now he is strong and sullen, and he is fighting for his life at the cost of mine. That is his one activity: to grow strong. No creature ever wanted so much to live. Eventually, I suppose, he will absorb me altogether. Believe me, you will hate me then.

And what have you to do, Hilda, with this ugly story? Nothing at all. The little boy drank of the prettiest brook in the forest and he became a stag. I write all this because I can never tell it to you, and because it seems as if I could not keep silent any longer. And because I suffer, Hilda. If any one I loved suffered like this, I'd want to know it. Help me, Hilda!

B. A.

Chapter IX

On the last Saturday in April, the New York "Times" published an account of the strike complications which were delaying Alexander's New Jersey bridge, and stated that the engineer himself was in town and at his office on West Tenth Street.

On Sunday, the day after this notice appeared, Alexander worked all day at his Tenth Street rooms. His business often called him to New York, and he had kept an apartment there for years, subletting it when he went abroad for any length of time. Besides his sleeping-room and bath, there was a large room, formerly a painter's studio, which he used as a study and office. It was furnished with the cast-off possessions of his bachelor days and with odd things which he sheltered for friends of his who followed itinerant and more or less artistic callings. Over the fireplace there was a large old-fashioned gilt mirror. Alexander's big work-table stood in front of one of the three windows, and above the couch hung the one picture in the room, a big canvas of charming color and spirit, a study of the Luxembourg Gardens in early spring, painted in his youth by a man who had since become a portrait-painter of international renown. He had done it for Alexander when they were students together in Paris.

Sunday was a cold, raw day and a fine rain fell continuously. When Alexander came back from dinner he put more wood on his fire, made himself comfortable, and settled down at his desk, where he began checking over estimate sheets. It was after nine o'clock and he was lighting a second pipe, when he thought he heard a sound at his door. He started and listened, holding the burning match in his hand; again he heard the same sound, like a firm, light tap. He rose and crossed the room quickly. When he threw open the door he recognized the figure that shrank back into the bare, dimly lit hallway. He stood for a moment in awkward constraint, his pipe in his hand.

"Come in," he said to Hilda at last, and closed the door

333

behind her. He pointed to a chair by the fire and went back to his work-table. "Won't you sit down?"

He was standing behind the table, turning over a pile of blueprints nervously. The yellow light from the student's lamp fell on his hands and the purple sleeves of his velvet smoking-jacket, but his flushed face and big, hard head were in the shadow. There was something about him that made Hilda wish herself at her hotel again, in the street below, anywhere but where she was.

"Of course I know, Bartley," she said at last, "that after this you won't owe me the least consideration. But we sail on Tuesday. I saw that interview in the paper yesterday, telling where you were, and I thought I had to see you. That's all. Good-night; I'm going now." She turned and her hand closed on the door-knob.

Alexander hurried toward her and took her gently by the arm. "Sit down, Hilda; you're wet through. Let me take off your coat—and your boots; they're oozing water." He knelt down and began to unlace her shoes, while Hilda shrank into the chair. "Here, put your feet on this stool. You don't mean to say you walked down—and without overshoes!"

Hilda hid her face in her hands. "I was afraid to take a cab. Can't you see, Bartley, that I'm terribly frightened? I've been through this a hundred times to-day. Don't be any more angry than you can help. I was all right until I knew you were in town. If you'd sent me a note, or telephoned me, or anything! But you won't let me write to you, and I had to see you after that letter, that terrible letter you wrote me when you got home."

Alexander faced her, resting his arm on the mantel behind him, and began to brush the sleeve of his jacket. "Is this the way you mean to answer it, Hilda?" he asked unsteadily.

She was afraid to look up at him. "Didn't—didn't you mean even to say good-by to me, Bartley? Did you mean just to—quit me?" she asked. "I came to tell you that I'm willing to do as you asked me. But it's no use talking about that now. Give me my things, please." She put her hand out toward the fender.

Alexander sat down on the arm of her chair. "Did you think I had forgotten you were in town, Hilda? Do you think

I kept away by accident? Did you suppose I did n't know you were sailing on Tuesday? There is a letter for you there, in my desk drawer. It was to have reached you on the steamer. I was all the morning writing it. I told myself that if I were really thinking of you, and not of myself, a letter would be better than nothing. Marks on paper mean something to you." He paused. "They never did to me."

Hilda smiled up at him beautifully and put her hand on his sleeve. "Oh, Bartley! Did you write to me? Why did n't you telephone me to let me know that you had? Then I would n't have come."

Alexander slipped his arm about her. "I did n't know it before, Hilda, on my honor I did n't, but I believe it was because, deep down in me somewhere, I was hoping I might drive you to do just this. I've watched that door all day. I've jumped up if the fire crackled. I think I have felt that you were coming." He bent his face over her hair.

"And I," she whispered, — "I felt that you were feeling that. But when I came, I thought I had been mistaken."

Alexander started up and began to walk up and down the room.

"No, you were n't mistaken. I've been up in Canada with my bridge, and I arranged not to come to New York until after you had gone. Then, when your manager added two more weeks, I was already committed." He dropped upon the stool in front of her and sat with his hands hanging between his knees. "What am I to do, Hilda?"

"That 's what I wanted to see you about, Bartley. I'm going to do what you asked me to do, when you were in London. Only I'll do it more completely. I'm going to marry."

"Who?"

"Oh, it does n't matter much! One of them. Only not Mac. I'm too fond of him."

Alexander moved restlessly. "Are you joking, Hilda?"

"Indeed I'm not."

"Then you don't know what you're talking about."

"Yes, I know very well. I've thought about it a great deal, and I've quite decided. I never used to understand how women did things like that, but I know now. It 's because they can't be at the mercy of the man they love any longer."

Alexander flushed angrily. "So it's better to be at the mercy of a man you don't love?"

"Under such circumstances, infinitely!"

There was a flash in her eyes that made Alexander's fall. He got up and went over to the window, threw it open, and leaned out. He heard Hilda moving about behind him. When he looked over his shoulder she was lacing her boots. He went back and stood over her.

"Hilda, you'd better think a while longer before you do that. I don't know what I ought to say, but I don't believe you'd be happy; truly I don't. Are n't you trying to frighten me?"

She tied the knot of the last lacing and put her boot-heel down firmly. "No; I'm telling you what I've made up my mind to do. I suppose I would better do it without telling you. But afterward I shan't have an opportunity to explain, for I shan't be seeing you again."

Alexander started to speak, but caught himself. When Hilda rose he sat down on the arm of her chair and drew her back into it.

"I would n't be so much alarmed if I did n't know how utterly reckless you *can* be. Don't do anything like that rashly." His face grew troubled. "You would n't be happy. You are not that kind of woman. I'd never have another hour's peace if I helped to make you do a thing like that." He took her face between his hands and looked down into it. "You see, you are different, Hilda. Don't you know you are?" His voice grew softer, his touch more and more tender. "Some women can do that sort of thing, but you—you can love as queens did, in the old time."

Hilda had heard that soft, deep tone in his voice only once before. She closed her eyes; her lips and eyelids trembled. "Only one, Bartley. Only one. And he threw it back at me a second time."

She felt the strength leap in the arms that held her so lightly.

"Try him again, Hilda. Try him once again."

She looked up into his eyes, and hid her face in her hands.

Chapter X

ON TUESDAY AFTERNOON a Boston lawyer, who had been trying a case in Vermont, was standing on the siding at White River Junction when the Canadian Express pulled by on its northward journey. As the day-coaches at the rear end of the long train swept by him, the lawyer noticed at one of the windows a man's head, with thick rumpled hair. "Curious," he thought; "that looked like Alexander, but what would he be doing back there in the day-coaches?"

It was, indeed, Alexander.

That morning a telegram from Moorlock had reached him, telling him that there was serious trouble with the bridge and that he was needed there at once, so he had caught the first train out of New York. He had taken a seat in a day-coach to avoid the risk of meeting any one he knew, and because he did not wish to be comfortable. When the telegram arrived, Alexander was at his rooms on Tenth Street, packing his bag to go to Boston. On Monday night he had written a long letter to his wife, but when morning came he was afraid to send it, and the letter was still in his pocket. Winifred was not a woman who could bear disappointment. She demanded a great deal of herself and of the people she loved; and she never failed herself. If he told her now, he knew, it would be irretrievable. There would be no going back. He would lose the thing he valued most in the world; he would be destroying himself and his own happiness. There would be nothing for him afterward. He seemed to see himself dragging out a restless existence on the Continent—Cannes, Hyères, Algiers, Cairo—among smartly dressed, disabled men of every nationality; forever going on journeys that led nowhere; hurrying to catch trains that he might just as well miss; getting up in the morning with a great bustle and splashing of water, to begin a day that had no purpose and no meaning; dining late to shorten the night, sleeping late to shorten the day.

And for what? For a mere folly, a masquerade, a little thing that he could not let go. *And he could even let it go,* he told himself. But he had promised to be in London at midsummer, and he knew that he would go. . . . It was impossible to live like this any longer.

And this, then, was to be the disaster that his old professor had foreseen for him: the crack in the wall, the crash, the cloud of dust. And he could not understand how it had come about. He felt that he himself was unchanged, that he was still there, the same man he had been five years ago, and that he was sitting stupidly by and letting some resolute offshoot of himself spoil his life for him. This new force was not he, it was but a part of him. He would not even admit that it was stronger than he; but it was more active. It was by its energy that this new feeling got the better of him. His wife was the woman who had made his life, gratified his pride, given direction to his tastes and habits. The life they led together seemed to him beautiful. Winifred still was, as she had always been, Romance for him, and whenever he was deeply stirred he turned to her. When the grandeur and beauty of the world challenged him—as it challenges even the most self-absorbed people—he always answered with her name. That was his reply to the question put by the mountains and the stars; to all the spiritual aspects of life. In his feeling for his wife there was all the tenderness, all the pride, all the devotion of which he was capable. There was everything but energy; the energy of youth which must register itself and cut its name before it passes. This new feeling was so fresh, so unsatisfied and light of foot. It ran and was not wearied, anticipated him everywhere. It put a girdle round the earth while he was going from New York to Moorlock. At this moment, it was tingling through him, exultant, and live as quicksilver, whispering, "In July you will be in England."

Already he dreaded the long, empty days at sea, the monotonous Irish coast, the sluggish passage up the Mersey, the flash of the boat train through the summer country. He closed his eyes and gave himself up to the feeling of rapid motion and to swift, terrifying thoughts. He was sitting so, his face shaded by his hand, when the Boston lawyer saw him from the siding at White River Junction.

When at last Alexander roused himself, the afternoon had waned to sunset. The train was passing through a gray country and the sky overhead was flushed with a wide flood of clear color. There was a rose-colored light over the gray rocks and hills and meadows. Off to the left, under the approach of a weather-stained wooden bridge, a group of boys were sitting around a little fire. The smell of the wood smoke blew in at the window. Except for an old farmer, jogging along the highroad in his box-wagon, there was not another living creature to be seen. Alexander looked back wistfully at the boys, camped on the edge of a little marsh, crouching under their shelter and looking gravely at their fire. They took his mind back a long way, to a campfire on a sandbar in a Western river, and he wished he could go back and sit down with them. He could remember exactly how the world had looked then.

It was quite dark and Alexander was still thinking of the boys, when it occurred to him that the train must be nearing Allway. In going to his new bridge at Moorlock he had always to pass through Allway. The train stopped at Allway Mills, then wound two miles up the river, and then the hollow sound under his feet told Bartley that he was on his first bridge again. The bridge seemed longer than it had ever seemed before, and he was glad when he felt the beat of the wheels on the solid roadbed again. He did not like coming and going across that bridge, or remembering the man who built it. And was he, indeed, the same man who used to walk that bridge at night, promising such things to himself and to the stars? And yet, he could remember it all so well: the quiet hills sleeping in the moonlight, the slender skeleton of the bridge reaching out into the river, and up yonder, alone on the hill, the big white house; upstairs, in Winifred's window, the light that told him she was still awake and still thinking of him. And after the light went out he walked alone, taking the heavens into his confidence, unable to tear himself away from the white magic of the night, unwilling to sleep because longing was so sweet to him, and because, for the first time since first the hills were hung with moonlight, there was a lover in the world. And always there was the sound of the rushing water underneath, the sound which, more than anything else, meant death; the wearing away of things under the impact of physical forces which men could direct but never circumvent or diminish. Then, in the exaltation of love, more than ever it seemed to him to mean death, the only other thing as strong as love. Under the moon, under the cold, splendid stars, there were only those two things awake and sleepless; death and love, the rushing river and his burning heart.

Alexander sat up and looked about him. The train was tearing on through the darkness. All his companions in the day-coach were either dozing or sleeping heavily, and the murky lamps were turned low. How came he here among all these dirty people? Why was he going to London? What did it mean—what was the answer? How could this happen to a man who had lived through that magical spring and summer, and who had felt that the stars themselves were but flaming particles in the far-away infinitudes of his love?

What had he done to lose it? How could he endure the baseness of life without it? And with every revolution of the wheels beneath him, the unquiet quicksilver in his breast told him that at midsummer he would be in London. He remembered his last night there: the red foggy darkness, the hungry crowds before the theatres, the hand-organs, the feverish rhythm of the blurred, crowded streets, and the feeling of letting himself go with the crowd. He shuddered and looked about him at the poor unconscious companions of his journey, unkempt and travel-stained, now doubled in unlovely attitudes, who had come to stand to him for the ugliness he had brought into the world.

And those boys back there, beginning it all just as he had begun it; he wished he could promise them better luck. Ah, if one could promise any one better luck, if one could assure a single human being of happiness! He had thought he could do so, once; and it was thinking of that that he at last fell asleep. In his sleep, as if it had nothing fresher to work upon, his mind went back and tortured itself with something years and years away, an old, long-forgotten sorrow of his childhood.

When Alexander awoke in the morning, the sun was just rising through pale golden ripples of cloud, and the fresh yellow light was vibrating through the pine woods. The white birches, with their little unfolding leaves, gleamed in the lowlands, and the marsh meadows were already coming to life with their first green, a thin, bright color which had run over them like fire. As the train rushed along the trestles, thousands of wild birds rose screaming into the light. The sky was already a pale blue and of the clearness of crystal. Bartley caught up his bag and hurried through the Pullman coaches until he found the conductor. There was a stateroom unoccupied, and he took it and set about changing his clothes. Last night he would not have believed that anything could be so pleasant as the cold water he dashed over his head and shoulders and the freshness of clean linen on his body.

After he had dressed, Alexander sat down at the window and drew into his lungs deep breaths of the pine-scented air. He had awakened with all his old sense of power. He could not believe that things were as bad with him as they had seemed last night, that there was no way to set them entirely right. Even if he went to London at midsummer, what would that mean except that he was a fool? And he had been a fool before. That was not the reality of his life. Yet he knew that he would go to London.

Half an hour later the train stopped at Moorlock. Alexander sprang to the platform and hurried up the siding, waving to Philip Horton, one of his assistants, who was anxiously looking up at the windows of the coaches. Bartley took his arm and they went together into the station buffet.

"I'll have my coffee first, Philip. Have you had yours? And now, what seems to be the matter up here?"

The young man, in a hurried, nervous way, began his explanation.

But Alexander cut him short. "When did you stop work?" he asked sharply.

The young engineer looked confused. "I haven't stopped work yet, Mr. Alexander. I didn't feel that I could go so far without definite authorization from you."

"Then why didn't you say in your telegram exactly what you thought, and ask for your authorization? You'd have got it quick enough."

"Well, really, Mr. Alexander, I couldn't be absolutely sure, you know, and I didn't like to take the responsibility of making it public."

Alexander pushed back his chair and rose. "Anything I do can be made public, Phil. You say that you believe the lower chords are showing strain, and that even the workmen have been talking about it, and yet you've gone on adding weight."

"I'm sorry, Mr. Alexander, but I had counted on your getting here yesterday. My first telegram missed you somehow. I sent one Sunday evening, to the same address, but it was returned to me."

"Have you a carriage out there? I must stop to send a wire."

Alexander went up to the telegraph-desk and penciled the following message to his wife:—

I may have to be here for some time. Can you come up at once? Urgent.

BARTLEY.

The Moorlock Bridge lay three miles above the town. When they were seated in the carriage, Alexander began to question his assistant further. If it were true that the compression members showed strain, with the bridge only two thirds done, then there was nothing to do but pull the whole structure down and begin over again. Horton kept repeating that he was sure there could be nothing wrong with the estimates.

Alexander grew impatient. "That's all true, Phil, but we never were justified in assuming that a scale that was perfectly safe for an ordinary bridge would work with anything of such length. It's all very well on paper, but it remains to be seen whether it can be done in practice. I should have thrown up the job when they crowded me. It's all nonsense to try to do what other engineers are doing when you know they're not sound."

"But just now, when there is such competition," the younger man demurred. "And certainly that's the new line of development."

Alexander shrugged his shoulders and made no reply.

When they reached the bridge works, Alexander began his examination immediately. An hour later he sent for the superintendent. "I think you had better stop work out there at once, Dan. I should say that the lower chord here might buckle at any moment. I told the Commission that we were using higher unit stresses than any practice has established, and we've put the dead load at a low estimate. Theoretically it worked out well enough, but it had never actually been tried." Alexander put on his overcoat and took the superintendent by the arm. "Don't look so chopfallen, Dan. It's a jolt, but we've got to face it. It is n't the end of the world, you know. Now we'll go out and call the men off quietly. They're already nervous, Horton tells me, and there's no use alarming them. I'll go with you, and we'll send the end riveters in first."

Alexander and the superintendent picked their way out slowly over the long span. They went deliberately, stopping to see what each gang was doing, as if they were on an ordinary round of inspection. When they reached the end of the river span, Alexander nodded to the superintendent, who quietly gave an order to the foreman. The men in the end gang picked up their tools and, glancing curiously at each other, started back across the bridge toward the river-bank. Alexander himself remained standing where they had been working, looking about him. It was hard to believe, as he looked back over it, that the whole great span was incurably disabled, was already as good as condemned, because something was out of line in the lower chord of the cantilever arm.

The end riveters had reached the bank and were dispersing among the tool-houses, and the second gang had picked up their tools and were starting toward the shore. Alexander, still standing at the end of the river span, saw the lower chord of the cantilever arm give a little, like an elbow bending. He shouted and ran after the second gang, but by this time every one knew that the big river span was slowly settling. There was a burst of shouting that was immediately drowned by the scream and cracking of tearing iron, as all the tension work began to pull asunder. Once the chords began to buckle, there were thousands of tons of iron-work, all riveted together and lying in midair without support. It tore itself to pieces with roaring and grinding and noises that were like the shrieks of a steam whistle. There was no shock of any kind; the bridge had no impetus except from its own weight. It lurched neither to right nor left, but sank almost in a vertical line, snapping and breaking and tearing as it went, because no integral part could bear for an instant the enormous strain

loosed upon it. Some of the men jumped and some ran, try-
ing to make the shore.

At the first shriek of the tearing iron, Alexander jumped
from the downstream side of the bridge. He struck the water
without injury and disappeared. He was under the river a
long time and had great difficulty in holding his breath.
When it seemed impossible, and his chest was about to heave,
he thought he heard his wife telling him that he could hold
out a little longer. An instant later his face cleared the water.
For a moment, in the depths of the river, he had realized
what it would mean to die a hypocrite, and to lie dead under
the last abandonment of her tenderness. But once in the light
and air, he knew he should live to tell her and to recover all
he had lost. Now, at last, he felt sure of himself. He was not
startled. It seemed to him that he had been through some-
thing of this sort before. There was nothing horrible about it.
This, too, was life, and life was activity, just as it was in Bos-
ton or in London. He was himself, and there was something
to be done; everything seemed perfectly natural. Alexander
was a strong swimmer, but he had gone scarcely a dozen
strokes when the bridge itself, which had been settling faster
and faster, crashed into the water behind him. Immediately
the river was full of drowning men. A gang of French Cana-
dians fell almost on top of him. He thought he had cleared
them, when they began coming up all around him, clutching
at him and at each other. Some of them could swim, but they
were either hurt or crazed with fright. Alexander tried to beat
them off, but there were too many of them. One caught him
about the neck, another gripped him about the middle, and
they went down together. When he sank, his wife seemed to
be there in the water beside him, telling him to keep his head,
that if he could hold out the men would drown and release
him. There was something he wanted to tell his wife, but he
could not think clearly for the roaring in his ears. Suddenly he
remembered what it was. He caught his breath, and then she
let him go.

The work of recovering the dead went on all day and all
the following night. By the next morning forty-eight bodies
had been taken out of the river, but there were still twenty

missing. Many of the men had fallen with the bridge and were held down under the débris. Early on the morning of the second day a closed carriage was driven slowly along the river-bank and stopped a little below the works, where the river boiled and churned about the great iron carcass which lay in a straight line two thirds across it. The carriage stood there hour after hour, and word soon spread among the crowds on the shore that its occupant was the wife of the Chief Engineer; his body had not yet been found. The widows of the lost workmen, moving up and down the bank with shawls over their heads, some of them carrying babies, looked at the rusty hired hack many times that morning. They drew near it and walked about it, but none of them ventured to peer within. Even half-indifferent sight-seers dropped their voices as they told a newcomer: "You see that carriage over there? That's Mrs. Alexander. They haven't found him yet. She got off the train this morning. Horton met her. She heard it in Boston yesterday—heard the newsboys crying it in the street."

At noon Philip Horton made his way through the crowd with a tray and a tin coffee-pot from the camp kitchen. When he reached the carriage he found Mrs. Alexander just as he had left her in the early morning, leaning forward a little, with her hand on the lowered window, looking at the river. Hour after hour she had been watching the water, the lonely, useless stone towers, and the convulsed mass of iron wreckage over which the angry river continually spat up its yellow foam.

"Those poor women out there, do they blame him very much?" she asked, as she handed the coffee-cup back to Horton.

"Nobody blames him, Mrs. Alexander. If any one is to blame, I'm afraid it's I. I should have stopped work before he came. He said so as soon as I met him. I tried to get him here a day earlier, but my telegram missed him, somehow. He didn't have time really to explain to me. If he'd got here Monday, he'd have had all the men off at once. But, you see, Mrs. Alexander, such a thing never happened before. According to all human calculations, it simply couldn't happen."

Horton leaned wearily against the front wheel of the cab.

He had not had his clothes off for thirty hours, and the stimulus of violent excitement was beginning to wear off.

"Don't be afraid to tell me the worst, Mr. Horton. Don't leave me to the dread of finding out things that people may be saying. If he is blamed, if he needs any one to speak for him,"—for the first time her voice broke and a flush of life, tearful, painful, and confused, swept over her rigid pallor,— "if he needs any one, tell me, show me what to do." She began to sob, and Horton hurried away.

When he came back at four o'clock in the afternoon he was carrying his hat in his hand, and Winifred knew as soon as she saw him that they had found Bartley. She opened the carriage door before he reached her and stepped to the ground.

Horton put out his hand as if to hold her back and spoke pleadingly: "Won't you drive up to my house, Mrs. Alexander? They will take him up there."

"Take me to him now, please. I shall not make any trouble."

The group of men down under the river-bank fell back when they saw a woman coming, and one of them threw a tarpaulin over the stretcher. They took off their hats and caps as Winifred approached, and although she had pulled her veil down over her face they did not look up at her. She was taller than Horton, and some of the men thought she was the tallest woman they had ever seen. "As tall as himself," some one whispered. Horton motioned to the men, and six of them lifted the stretcher and began to carry it up the embankment. Winifred followed them the half-mile to Horton's house. She walked quietly, without once breaking or stumbling. When the bearers put the stretcher down in Horton's spare bedroom, she thanked them and gave her hand to each in turn. The men went out of the house and through the yard with their caps in their hands. They were too much confused to say anything as they went down the hill.

Horton himself was almost as deeply perplexed. "Mamie," he said to his wife, when he came out of the spare room half an hour later, "will you take Mrs. Alexander the things she needs? She is going to do everything herself. Just stay about where you can hear her and go in if she wants you."

Everything happened as Alexander had foreseen in that moment of prescience under the river. With her own hands she washed him clean of every mark of disaster. All night he was alone with her in the still house, his great head lying deep in the pillow. In the pocket of his coat Winifred found the letter that he had written her the night before he left New York, water-soaked and illegible, but because of its length, she knew it had been meant for her.

For Alexander death was an easy creditor. Fortune, which had smiled upon him consistently all his life, did not desert him in the end. His harshest critics did not doubt that, had he lived, he would have retrieved himself. Even Lucius Wilson did not see in this accident the disaster he had once foretold.

When a great man dies in his prime there is no surgeon who can say whether he did well; whether or not the future was his, as it seemed to be. The mind that society had come to regard as a powerful and reliable machine, dedicated to its service, may for a long time have been sick within itself and bent upon its own destruction.

Epilogue

PROFESSOR WILSON had been living in London for six years and he was just back from a visit to America. One afternoon, soon after his return, he put on his frock-coat and drove in a hansom to pay a call upon Hilda Burgoyne, who still lived at her old number, off Bedford Square. He and Miss Burgoyne had been fast friends for a long time. He had first noticed her about the corridors of the British Museum, where he read constantly. Her being there so often had made him feel that he would like to know her, and as she was not an inaccessible person, an introduction was not difficult. The preliminaries once over, they came to depend a great deal upon each other, and Wilson, after his day's reading, often went round to Bedford Square for his tea. They had much more in common than their memories of a common friend. Indeed, they seldom spoke of him. They saved that for the deep moments which do not come often, and then their talk of him was mostly silence. Wilson knew that Hilda had loved him; more than this he had not tried to know.

It was late when Wilson reached Hilda's apartment on this particular December afternoon, and he found her alone. She sent for fresh tea and made him comfortable, as she had such a knack of making people comfortable.

"How good you were to come back before Christmas! I quite dreaded the Holidays without you. You've helped me over a good many Christmases." She smiled at him gayly.

"As if you needed me for that! But, at any rate, I needed *you*. How well you are looking, my dear, and how rested."

He peered up at her from his low chair, balancing the tips of his long fingers together in a judicial manner which had grown on him with years.

Hilda laughed as she carefully poured his cream. "That means that I was looking very seedy at the end of the season, doesn't it? Well, we must show wear at last, you know."

Wilson took the cup gratefully. "Ah, no need to remind a man of seventy, who has just been home to find that he has survived all his contemporaries. I was most gently treated—as

348

a sort of precious relic. But, do you know, it made me feel awkward to be hanging about still."

"Seventy? Never mention it to me." Hilda looked appreciatively at the Professor's alert face, with so many kindly lines about the mouth and so many quizzical ones about the eyes. "You've got to hang about for me, you know. I can't even let you go home again. You must stay put, now that I have you back. You're the realest thing I have."

Wilson chuckled. "Dear me, am I? Out of so many conquests and the spoils of conquered cities! You've really missed me? Well, then, I shall hang. Even if you have at last to put *me* in the mummy-room with the others. You'll visit me often, won't you?"

"Every day in the calendar. Here, your cigarettes are in this drawer, where you left them." She struck a match and lit one for him. "But you did, after all, enjoy being at home again?"

"Oh, yes. I found the long railway journeys trying. People live a thousand miles apart. But I did it thoroughly; I was all over the place. It was in Boston I lingered longest."

"Ah, you saw Mrs. Alexander?"

"Often. I dined with her, and had tea there a dozen different times, I should think. Indeed, it was to see her that I lingered on and on. I found that I still loved to go to the house. It always seemed as if Bartley were there, somehow, and that at any moment one might hear his heavy tramp on the stairs. Do you know, I kept feeling that he must be up in his study." The Professor looked reflectively into the grate. "I should really have liked to go up there. That was where I had my last long talk with him. But Mrs. Alexander never suggested it."

"Why?"

Wilson was a little startled by her tone, and he turned his head so quickly that his cuff-link caught the string of his nose-glasses and pulled them awry. "Why? Why, dear me, I don't know. She probably never thought of it."

Hilda bit her lip. "I don't know what made me say that. I didn't mean to interrupt. Go on, please, and tell me how it was."

"Well, it was like that. Almost as if he were there. In a way, he really is there. She never lets him go. It's the most beautiful and dignified sorrow I've ever known. It's so beautiful that it has its compensations, I should think. Its very completeness is a compensation. It gives her a fixed star to steer by. She does n't drift. We sat there evening after evening in the quiet of that magically haunted room, and watched the sunset burn on the river, and felt him. Felt him with a difference, of course."

Hilda leaned forward, her elbow on her knee, her chin on her hand. "With a difference? Because of her, you mean?"

Wilson's brow wrinkled. "Something like that, yes. Of course, as time goes on, to her he becomes more and more their simple personal relation."

Hilda studied the droop of the Professor's head intently. "You did n't altogether like that? You felt it was n't wholly fair to him?"

Wilson shook himself and readjusted his glasses. "Oh, fair enough. More than fair. Of course, I always felt that my image of him was just a little different from hers. No relation is so complete that it can hold absolutely all of a person. And I liked him just as he was; his deviations, too; the places where he did n't square."

Hilda considered vaguely. "Has she grown much older?" she asked at last.

"Yes, and no. In a tragic way she is even handsomer. But colder. Cold for everything but him. 'Forget thyself to marble'; I kept thinking of that. Her happiness was a happiness *à deux*, not apart from the world, but actually against it. And now her grief is like that. She saves herself for it and does n't even go through the form of seeing people much. I'm sorry. It would be better for her, and might be so good for them, if she could let other people in."

"Perhaps she's afraid of letting him out a little, of sharing him with somebody."

Wilson put down his cup and looked up with vague alarm. "Dear me, it takes a woman to think of that, now! I don't, you know, think we ought to be hard on her. More, even, than the rest of us she did n't choose her destiny. She underwent it. And it has left her chilled. As to her not wishing to take the world into her confidence—well, it is a pretty brutal and stupid world, after all, you know."

Hilda leaned forward. "Yes, I know, I know. Only I can't help being glad that there was something for him even in stupid and vulgar people. My little Marie worshiped him. When she is dusting I always know when she has come to his picture."

Wilson nodded. "Oh, yes! He left an echo. The ripples go on in all of us. He belonged to the people who make the play, and most of us are only onlookers at the best. We shouldn't wonder too much at Mrs. Alexander. She must feel how useless it would be to stir about, that she may as well sit still; that nothing can happen to her after Bartley."

"Yes," said Hilda softly, "nothing can happen to one after Bartley."

They both sat looking into the fire.

THE END

YOUTH
AND THE BRIGHT MEDUSA

"We must not look at Goblin men,
We must not buy their fruits;
Who knows upon what soil they fed
Their hungry, thirsty roots?"
                    Goblin Market

Contents

Coming, Aphrodite!

I

DON HEDGER had lived for four years on the top floor of an old house on the south side of Washington Square, and nobody had ever disturbed him. He occupied one big room with no outside exposure except on the north, where he had built in a many-paned studio window that looked upon a court and upon the roofs and walls of other buildings. His room was very cheerless, since he never got a ray of direct sunlight; the south corners were always in shadow. In one of the corners was a clothes closet, built against the partition, in another a wide divan, serving as a seat by day and a bed by night. In the front corner, the one farther from the window, was a sink, and a table with two gas burners where he sometimes cooked his food. There, too, in the perpetual dusk, was the dog's bed, and often a bone or two for his comfort.

The dog was a Boston bull terrier, and Hedger explained his surly disposition by the fact that he had been bred to the point where it told on his nerves. His name was Caesar III, and he had taken prizes at very exclusive dog shows. When he and his master went out to prowl about University Place or to promenade along West Street, Caesar III was invariably fresh and shining. His pink skin showed through his mottled coat, which glistened as if it had just been rubbed with olive oil, and he wore a brass-studded collar, bought at the smartest saddler's. Hedger, as often as not, was hunched up in an old striped blanket coat, with a shapeless felt hat pulled over his bushy hair, wearing black shoes that had become grey, or brown ones that had become black, and he never put on gloves unless the day was biting cold.

Early in May, Hedger learned that he was to have a new neighbour in the rear apartment—two rooms, one large and one small, that faced the west. His studio was shut off from the larger of these rooms by double doors, which, though they were fairly tight, left him a good deal at the mercy of the occupant. The rooms had been leased, long before he came there, by a trained nurse who considered herself knowing in old furniture. She went to auction sales and bought up mahogany and dirty brass and stored it away here, where she meant to live when she retired from nursing. Meanwhile, she sub-let her rooms, with their precious furniture, to young people who came to New York to "write" or to "paint"— who proposed to live by the sweat of the brow rather than of the hand, and who desired artistic surroundings. When Hedger first moved in, these rooms were occupied by a young man who tried to write plays,—and who kept on trying until a week ago, when the nurse had put him out for unpaid rent.

A few days after the playwright left, Hedger heard an ominous murmur of voices through the bolted double doors: the lady-like intonation of the nurse—doubtless exhibiting her treasures—and another voice, also a woman's, but very different; young, fresh, unguarded, confident. All the same, it would be very annoying to have a woman in there. The only bath-room on the floor was at the top of the stairs in the front hall, and he would always be running into her as he came or went from his bath. He would have to be more careful to see that Caesar didn't leave bones about the hall, too; and she might object when he cooked steak and onions on his gas burner.

As soon as the talking ceased and the women left, he forgot them. He was absorbed in a study of paradise fish at the Aquarium, staring out at people through the glass and green water of their tank. It was a highly gratifying idea; the incommunicability of one stratum of animal life with another, —though Hedger pretended it was only an experiment in unusual lighting. When he heard trunks knocking against the sides of the narrow hall, then he realized that she was moving in at once. Toward noon, groans and deep gasps and the creaking of ropes, made him aware that a piano was arriving. After the tramp of the movers died away down the stairs, somebody touched off a few scales and chords on the instrument, and then there was peace. Presently he heard her lock her door and go down the hall humming something; going out to lunch, probably. He stuck his brushes in a can of turpentine and put on his hat, not stopping to wash his hands. Caesar was smelling along the crack under the bolted doors;

his bony tail stuck out hard as a hickory withe, and the hair was standing up about his elegant collar.

Hedger encouraged him. "Come along, Caesar. You'll soon get used to a new smell."

In the hall stood an enormous trunk, behind the ladder that led to the roof, just opposite Hedger's door. The dog flew at it with a growl of hurt amazement. They went down three flights of stairs and out into the brilliant May afternoon.

Behind the Square, Hedger and his dog descended into a basement oyster house where there were no tablecloths on the tables and no handles on the coffee cups, and the floor was covered with sawdust, and Caesar was always welcome,—not that he needed any such precautionary flooring. All the carpets of Persia would have been safe for him. Hedger ordered steak and onions absentmindedly, not realizing why he had an apprehension that this dish might be less readily at hand hereafter. While he ate, Caesar sat beside his chair, gravely disturbing the sawdust with his tail.

After lunch Hedger strolled about the Square for the dog's health and watched the stages pull out;—that was almost the very last summer of the old horse stages on Fifth Avenue. The fountain had but lately begun operations for the season and was throwing up a mist of rainbow water which now and then blew south and sprayed a bunch of Italian babies that were being supported on the outer rim by older, very little older, brothers and sisters. Plump robins were hopping about on the soil; the grass was newly cut and blindly green. Looking up the Avenue through the Arch, one could see the young poplars with their bright, sticky leaves, and the Brevoort glistening in its spring coat of paint, and shining horses and carriages,—occasionally an automobile, mis-shapen and sullen, like an ugly threat in a stream of things that were bright and beautiful and alive.

While Caesar and his master were standing by the fountain, a girl approached them, crossing the Square. Hedger noticed her because she wore a lavender cloth suit and carried in her arms a big bunch of fresh lilacs. He saw that she was young and handsome,—beautiful, in fact, with a splendid figure and good action. She, too, paused by the fountain and looked back through the Arch up the Avenue. She smiled rather patronizingly as she looked, and at the same time seemed delighted. Her slowly curving upper lip and half-closed eyes seemed to say: "You're gay, you're exciting, you are quite the right sort of thing; but you're none too fine for me!"

In the moment she tarried, Caesar stealthily approached her and sniffed at the hem of her lavender skirt, then, when she went south like an arrow, he ran back to his master and lifted a face full of emotion and alarm, his lower lip twitching under his sharp white teeth and his hazel eyes pointed with a very definite discovery. He stood thus, motionless, while Hedger watched the lavender girl go up the steps and through the door of the house in which he lived.

"You're right, my boy, it's she! She might be worse looking, you know."

When they mounted to the studio, the new lodger's door, at the back of the hall, was a little ajar, and Hedger caught the warm perfume of lilacs just brought in out of the sun. He was used to the musty smell of the old hall carpet. (The nurse-lessee had once knocked at his studio door and complained that Caesar must be somewhat responsible for the particular flavour of that mustiness, and Hedger had never spoken to her since.) He was used to the old smell, and he preferred it to that of the lilacs, and so did his companion, whose nose was so much more discriminating. Hedger shut his door vehemently, and fell to work.

Most young men who dwell in obscure studios in New York have had a beginning, come out of something, have somewhere a home town, a family, a paternal roof. But Don Hedger had no such background. He was a foundling, and had grown up in a school for homeless boys, where book-learning was a negligible part of the curriculum. When he was sixteen, a Catholic priest took him to Greensburg, Pennsylvania, to keep house for him. The priest did something to fill in the large gaps in the boy's education,—taught him to like "Don Quixote" and "The Golden Legend," and encouraged him to mess with paints and crayons in his room up under the slope of the mansard. When Don wanted to go to New York to study at the Art League, the priest got him a night job as packer in one of the big department stores. Since then, Hedger had taken care of himself; that was his only responsibility. He was singularly unencumbered; had no family duties, no social ties, no obligations toward any one but his landlord. Since he travelled light, he had travelled rather far. He had got over a good deal of the earth's surface, in spite of the fact that he never in his life had more than three hundred dollars ahead at any one time, and he had already outlived a succession of convictions and revelations about his art.

Though he was now but twenty-six years old, he had twice been on the verge of becoming a marketable product; once through some studies of New York streets he did for a magazine, and once through a collection of pastels he brought home from New Mexico, which Remington, then at the height of his popularity, happened to see, and generously tried to push. But on both occasions Hedger decided that this was something he didn't wish to carry further,—simply the old thing over again and got nowhere,—so he took enquiring dealers experiments in a "later manner," that made them put him out of the shop. When he ran short of money, he could always get any amount of commercial work; he was an expert draughtsman and worked with lightning speed. The rest of his time he spent in groping his way from one kind of painting into another, or travelling about without luggage, like a tramp, and he was chiefly occupied with getting rid of ideas he had once thought very fine.

Hedger's circumstances, since he had moved to Washington Square, were affluent compared to anything he had ever known before. He was now able to pay advance rent and turn the key on his studio when he went away for four months at a stretch. It didn't occur to him to wish to be richer than this. To be sure, he did without a great many things other people think necessary, but he didn't miss them, because he had never had them. He belonged to no clubs, visited no houses, had no studio friends, and he ate his dinner alone in some decent little restaurant, even on Christmas and New Year's. For days together he talked to nobody but his dog and the janitress and the lame oysterman.

After he shut the door and settled down to his paradise fish on that first Tuesday in May, Hedger forgot all about his new neighbour. When the light failed, he took Caesar out for a walk. On the way home he did his marketing on West

Houston Street, with a one-eyed Italian woman who always cheated him. After he had cooked his beans and scallopini, and drunk half a bottle of Chianti, he put his dishes in the sink and went up on the roof to smoke. He was the only person in the house who ever went to the roof, and he had a secret understanding with the janitress about it. He was to have "the privilege of the roof," as she said, if he opened the heavy trapdoor on sunny days to air out the upper hall, and was watchful to close it when rain threatened. Mrs. Foley was fat and dirty and hated to climb stairs,—besides, the roof was reached by a perpendicular iron ladder, definitely inaccessible to a woman of her bulk, and the iron door at the top of it was too heavy for any but Hedger's strong arm to lift. Hedger was not above medium height, but he practised with weights and dumb-bells, and in the shoulders he was as strong as a gorilla.

So Hedger had the roof to himself. He and Caesar often slept up there on hot nights, rolled in blankets he had brought home from Arizona. He mounted with Caesar under his left arm. The dog had never learned to climb a perpendicular ladder, and never did he feel so much his master's greatness and his own dependence upon him, as when he crept under his arm for this perilous ascent. Up there was even gravel to scratch in, and a dog could do whatever he liked, so long as he did not bark. It was a kind of Heaven, which no one was strong enough to reach but his great, paint-smelling master.

On this blue May night there was a slender, girlish looking young moon in the west, playing with a whole company of silver stars. Now and then one of them darted away from the group and shot off into the gauzy blue with a soft little trail of light, like laughter. Hedger and his dog were delighted when a star did this. They were quite lost in watching the glittering game, when they were suddenly diverted by a sound,—not from the stars, though it was music. It was not the Prologue to Pagliacci, which rose ever and anon on hot evenings from an Italian tenement on Thompson Street, with the gasps of the corpulent baritone who got behind it; nor was it the hurdy-gurdy man, who often played at the corner in the balmy twilight. No, this was a woman's voice, singing the tempestuous, over-lapping phrases of Signor Puccini, then comparatively new in the world, but already so popular that even Hedger recognized his unmistakable gusts of breath. He looked about over the roofs; all was blue and still, with the well-built chimneys that were never used now standing up dark and mournful. He moved softly toward the yellow quadrangle where the gas from the hall shone up through the half-lifted trapdoor. Oh yes! It came up through the hole like a strong draught, a big, beautiful voice, and it sounded rather like a professional's. A piano had arrived in the morning, Hedger remembered. This might be a very great nuisance. It would be pleasant enough to listen to, if you could turn it on and off as you wished; but you couldn't. Caesar, with the gas light shining on his collar and his ugly but sensitive face, panted and looked up for information. Hedger put down a reassuring hand.

"I don't know. We can't tell yet. It may not be so bad."

He stayed on the roof until all was still below, and finally descended, with quite a new feeling about his neighbour. Her voice, like her figure, inspired respect, — if one did not choose to call it admiration. Her door was shut, the transom was dark; nothing remained of her but the obtrusive trunk, unrightfully taking up room in the narrow hall.

II

For two days Hedger didn't see her. He was painting eight hours a day just then, and only went out to hunt for food. He noticed that she practised scales and exercises for about an hour in the morning; then she locked her door, went humming down the hall, and left him in peace. He heard her getting her coffee ready at about the same time he got his. Earlier still, she passed his room on her way to her bath. In the evening she sometimes sang, but on the whole she didn't bother him. When he was working well he did not notice anything much. The morning paper lay before his door until he reached out for his milk bottle, then he kicked the sheet inside and it lay on the floor until evening. Sometimes he read it and sometimes he did not. He forgot there was anything of importance going on in the world outside of his third floor studio. Nobody had ever taught him that he ought to be interested in other people; in the Pittsburgh steel strike, in the Fresh Air Fund, in the scandal about the Babies' Hospital. A grey wolf, living in a Wyoming canyon, would hardly have been less concerned about these things than was Don Hedger.

One morning he was coming out of the bathroom at the front end of the hall, having just given Caesar his bath and rubbed him into a glow with a heavy towel. Before the door, lying in wait for him, as it were, stood a tall figure in a flowing blue silk dressing gown that fell away from her marble arms. In her hands she carried various accessories of the bath.

"I wish," she said distinctly, standing in his way, "I wish you wouldn't wash your dog in the tub. I never heard of such a thing! I've found his hair in the tub, and I've smelled a doggy smell, and now I've caught you at it. It's an outrage!"

Hedger was badly frightened. She was so tall and positive, and was fairly blazing with beauty and anger. He stood blinking, holding on to his sponge and dog-soap, feeling that he ought to bow very low to her. But what he actually said was:

"Nobody has ever objected before. I always wash the tub, —and, anyhow, he's cleaner than most people."

"Cleaner than me?" her eyebrows went up, her white arms and neck and her fragrant person seemed to scream at him like a band of outraged nymphs. Something flashed through his mind about a man who was turned into a dog, or was pursued by dogs, because he unwittingly intruded upon the bath of beauty.

"No, I didn't mean that," he muttered, turning scarlet under the bluish stubble of his muscular jaws. "But I know he's cleaner than I am."

"That I don't doubt!" Her voice sounded like a soft shivering of crystal, and with a smile of pity she drew the folds of her voluminous blue robe close about her and allowed the wretched man to pass. Even Caesar was frightened; he darted like a streak down the hall, through the door and to his own bed in the corner among the bones.

Hedger stood still in the doorway, listening to indignant sniffs and coughs and a great swishing of water about the sides of the tub. He had washed it; but as he had washed it with Caesar's sponge, it was quite possible that a few bristles remained; the dog was shedding now. The playwright had never objected, nor had the jovial illustrator who occupied the front apartment,—but he, as he admitted, "was usually pye-eyed, when he wasn't in Buffalo." He went home to Buffalo sometimes to rest his nerves.

It had never occurred to Hedger that any one would mind using the tub after Caesar;—but then, he had never seen a beautiful girl caparisoned for the bath before. As soon as he beheld her standing there, he realized the unfitness of it. For that matter, she ought not to step into a tub that any other mortal had bathed in; the illustrator was sloppy and left cigarette ends on the moulding.

All morning as he worked he was gnawed by a spiteful desire to get back at her. It rankled that he had been so vanquished by her disdain. When he heard her locking her door to go out for lunch, he stepped quickly into the hall in his messy painting coat, and addressed her.

"I don't wish to be exigent, Miss,"—he had certain grand words that he used upon occasion—"but if this is your trunk, it's rather in the way here."

"Oh, very well!" she exclaimed carelessly, dropping her keys into her handbag. "I'll have it moved when I can get a man to do it," and she went down the hall with her free, roving stride.

Her name, Hedger discovered from her letters, which the postman left on the table in the lower hall, was Eden Bower.

III

In the closet that was built against the partition separating his room from Miss Bower's, Hedger kept all his wearing apparel, some of it on hooks and hangers, some of it on the floor. When he opened his closet door now-a-days, little dust-coloured insects flew out on downy wing, and he suspected that a brood of moths were hatching in his winter overcoat. Mrs. Foley, the janitress, told him to bring down all his heavy clothes and she would give them a beating and hang them in the court. The closet was in such disorder that he shunned the encounter, but one hot afternoon he set himself to the task.

First he threw out a pile of forgotten laundry and tied it up in a sheet. The bundle stood as high as his middle when he had knotted the corners. Then he got his shoes and overshoes together. When he took his overcoat from its place against the partition, a long ray of yellow light shot across the dark enclosure,—a knot hole, evidently, in the high wainscoting of the west room. He had never noticed it before, and without realizing what he was doing, he stooped and squinted through it.

Yonder, in a pool of sunlight, stood his new neighbour, wholly unclad, doing exercises of some sort before a long gilt mirror. Hedger did not happen to think how unpardonable it was of him to watch her. Nudity was not improper to any one who had worked so much from the figure, and he continued to look, simply because he had never seen a woman's body so beautiful as this one,—positively glorious in action. As she swung her arms and changed from one pivot of motion to another, muscular energy seemed to flow through her from her toes to her finger-tips. The soft flush of exercise and the gold of afternoon sun played over her flesh together, enveloped her in a luminous mist which, as she turned and twisted, made now an arm, now a shoulder, now a thigh, dissolve in pure light and instantly recover its outline with the next gesture. Hedger's fingers curved as if he were holding a crayon; mentally he was doing the whole figure in a single running line, and the charcoal seemed to explode in his hand at the point where the energy of each gesture was discharged into the whirling disc of light, from a foot or shoulder, from the up-thrust chin or the lifted breasts.

He could not have told whether he watched her for six minutes or sixteen. When her gymnastics were over, she paused to catch up a lock of hair that had come down, and examined with solicitude a little reddish mole that grew under her left arm-pit. Then, with her hand on her hip, she walked unconcernedly across the room and disappeared through the door into her bedchamber.

Disappeared—Don Hedger was crouching on his knees, staring at the golden shower which poured in through the west windows, at the lake of gold sleeping on the faded Turkish carpet. The spot was enchanted; a vision out of

Alexandria, out of the remote pagan past, had bathed itself there in Helianthine fire.

When he crawled out of his closet, he stood blinking at the grey sheet stuffed with laundry, not knowing what had happened to him. He felt a little sick as he contemplated the bundle. Everything here was different; he hated the disorder of the place, the grey prison light, his old shoes and himself and all his slovenly habits. The black calico curtains that ran on wires over his big window were white with dust. There were three greasy frying pans in the sink, and the sink itself— He felt desperate. He couldn't stand this another minute. He took up an armful of winter clothes and ran down four flights into the basement.

"Mrs. Foley," he began, "I want my room cleaned this afternoon, thoroughly cleaned. Can you get a woman for me right away?"

"Is it company you're having?" the fat, dirty janitress enquired. Mrs. Foley was the widow of a useful Tammany man, and she owned real estate in Flatbush. She was huge and soft as a feather bed. Her face and arms were permanently coated with dust, grained like wood where the sweat had trickled.

"Yes, company. That's it."

"Well, this is a queer time of the day to be asking for a cleaning woman. It's likely I can get you old Lizzie, if she's not drunk. I'll send Willy round to see."

Willy, the son of fourteen, roused from the stupor and stain of his fifth box of cigarettes by the gleam of a quarter, went out. In five minutes he returned with old Lizzie,—she smelling strong of spirits and wearing several jackets which she had put on one over the other, and a number of skirts, long and short, which made her resemble an animated dish-clout. She had, of course, to borrow her equipment from Mrs. Foley, and toiled up the long flights, dragging mop and pail and broom. She told Hedger to be of good cheer, for he had got the right woman for the job, and showed him a great leather strap she wore about her wrist to prevent dislocation of tendons. She swished about the place, scattering dust and splashing soapsuds, while he watched her in nervous despair. He stood over Lizzie and made her scour the sink, directing her roughly, then paid her and got rid of her. Shutting the door on his failure, he hurried off with his dog to lose himself among the stevedores and dock labourers on West Street.

A strange chapter began for Don Hedger. Day after day, at that hour in the afternoon, the hour before his neighbour dressed for dinner, he crouched down in his closet to watch her go through her mysterious exercises. It did not occur to him that his conduct was detestable; there was nothing shy or retreating about this unclad girl,—a bold body, studying itself quite coolly and evidently well pleased with itself, doing all this for a purpose. Hedger scarcely regarded his action as conduct at all; it was something that had happened to him. More than once he went out and tried to stay away for the whole afternoon, but at about five o'clock he was sure to find himself among his old shoes in the dark. The pull of that aperture was stronger than his will,—and he had always considered his will the strongest thing about him. When she threw herself upon the divan and lay resting, he still stared, holding his breath. His nerves were so on edge that a sudden noise made him start and brought out the sweat on his forehead. The dog would come and tug at his sleeve, knowing that something was wrong with his master. If he attempted a mournful whine, those strong hands closed about his throat.

When Hedger came slinking out of his closet, he sat down on the edge of the couch, sat for hours without moving. He was not painting at all now. This thing, whatever it was, drank him up as ideas had sometimes done, and he sank into a stupor of idleness as deep and dark as the stupor of work. He could not understand it; he was no boy, he had worked from models for years, and a woman's body was no mystery to him. Yet now he did nothing but sit and think about one. He slept very little, and with the first light of morning he awoke as completely possessed by this woman as if he had been with her all the night before. The unconscious operations of life went on in him only to perpetuate this excitement. His brain held but one image now—vibrated, burned with it. It was a heathenish feeling; without friendliness, almost without tenderness.

Women had come and gone in Hedger's life. Not having had a mother to begin with, his relations with them, whether amorous or friendly, had been casual. He got on well with janitresses and wash-women, with Indians and with the peasant women of foreign countries. He had friends among the silk-skirt factory girls who came to eat their lunch in Washington Square, and he sometimes took a model for a day in the country. He felt an unreasoning antipathy toward the well-dressed women he saw coming out of big shops, or driving in the Park. If, on his way to the Art Museum, he noticed a pretty girl standing on the steps of one of the houses on upper Fifth Avenue, he frowned at her and went by with his shoulders hunched up as if he were cold. He had never known such girls, or heard them talk, or seen the inside of the houses in which they lived; but he believed them all to be artificial and, in an aesthetic sense, perverted. He saw them enslaved by desire of merchandise and manufactured articles, effective only in making life complicated and insincere and in embroidering it with ugly and meaningless trivialities. They were enough, he thought, to make one almost forget woman as she existed in art, in thought, and in the universe.

He had no desire to know the woman who had, for the time at least, so broken up his life,—no curiosity about her every-day personality. He shunned any revelation of it, and he listened for Miss Bower's coming and going, not to encounter, but to avoid her. He wished that the girl who wore shirt-waists and got letters from Chicago would keep out of his way, that she did not exist. With her he had naught to make. But in a room full of sun, before an old mirror, on a little enchanted rug of sleeping colours, he had seen a woman who emerged naked through a door, and disappeared naked. He thought of that body as never having been clad, or as having worn the stuffs and dyes of all the centuries but his own. And for him she had no geographical associations; unless with Crete, or Alexandria, or Veronese's Venice. She was the immortal conception, the perennial theme.

The first break in Hedger's lethargy occurred one afternoon when two young men came to take Eden Bower out to dine. They went into her music room, laughed and talked for a few minutes, and then took her away with them. They were gone a long while, but he did not go out for food himself; he waited for them to come back. At last he heard them coming down the hall, gayer and more talkative than when they left. One of them sat down at the piano, and they all began to sing. This Hedger found absolutely unendurable. He snatched up his hat and went running down the stairs. Caesar leaped beside him, hoping that old times were coming back. They had supper in the oysterman's basement and then sat down in front of their own doorway. The moon stood full over the Square, a thing of regal glory; but Hedger did not see the moon; he was looking, murderously, for men. Presently two, wearing straw hats and white trousers and carrying canes, came down the steps from his house. He rose and dogged them across the Square. They were laughing and seemed very much elated about something. As one stopped to light a cigarette, Hedger caught from the other:

"Don't you think she has a beautiful talent?"

His companion threw away his match. "She has a beautiful figure." They both ran to catch the stage.

Hedger went back to his studio. The light was shining from her transom. For the first time he violated her privacy at night, and peered through that fatal aperture. She was sitting, fully dressed, in the window, smoking a cigarette and looking out over the housetops. He watched her until she rose, looked about her with a disdainful, crafty smile, and turned out the light.

The next morning, when Miss Bower went out, Hedger followed her. Her white skirt gleamed ahead of him as she sauntered about the Square. She sat down behind the Garibaldi statue and opened a music book she carried. She turned the leaves carelessly, and several times glanced in his direction. He was on the point of going over to her, when she rose quickly and looked up at the sky. A flock of pigeons had risen from somewhere in the crowded Italian quarter to the south, and were wheeling rapidly up through the morning air, soaring and dropping, scattering and coming together, now grey, now white as silver, as they caught or intercepted the sunlight. She put up her hand to shade her eyes and followed them with a kind of defiant delight in her face.

Hedger came and stood beside her. "You've surely seen them before?"

"Oh, yes," she replied, still looking up. "I see them every

day from my windows. They always come home about five o'clock. Where do they live?"

"I don't know. Probably some Italian raises them for the market. They were here long before I came, and I've been here four years."

"In that same gloomy room? Why didn't you take mine when it was vacant?"

"It isn't gloomy. That's the best light for painting."

"Oh, is it? I don't know anything about painting. I'd like to see your pictures sometime. You have such a lot in there. Don't they get dusty, piled up against the wall like that?"

"Not very. I'd be glad to show them to you. Is your name really Eden Bower? I've seen your letters on the table."

"Well, it's the name I'm going to sing under. My father's name is Bowers, but my friend Mr. Jones, a Chicago newspaper man who writes about music, told me to drop the 's.' He's crazy about my voice."

Miss Bower didn't usually tell the whole story,—about anything. Her first name, when she lived in Huntington, Illinois, was Edna, but Mr. Jones had persuaded her to change it to one which he felt would be worthy of her future. She was quick to take suggestions, though she told him she "didn't see what was the matter with 'Edna.' "

She explained to Hedger that she was going to Paris to study. She was waiting in New York for Chicago friends who were to take her over, but who had been detained. "Did you study in Paris?" she asked.

"No, I've never been in Paris. But I was in the south of France all last summer, studying with C——. He's the biggest man among the moderns,—at least I think so."

Miss Bower sat down and made room for him on the bench. "Do tell me about it. I expected to be there by this time, and I can't wait to find out what it's like."

Hedger began to relate how he had seen some of this Frenchman's work in an exhibition, and deciding at once that this was the man for him, he had taken a boat for Marseilles the next week, going over steerage. He proceeded at once to the little town on the coast where his painter lived, and presented himself. The man never took pupils, but because Hedger had come so far, he let him stay. Hedger lived at the master's house and every day they went out together to paint, sometimes on the blazing rocks down by the sea. They wrapped themselves in light woollen blankets and didn't feel the heat. Being there and working with C—— was being in Paradise, Hedger concluded; he learned more in three months than in all his life before.

Eden Bower laughed. "You're a funny fellow. Didn't you do anything but work? Are the women very beautiful? Did you have awfully good things to eat and drink?"

Hedger said some of the women were fine looking, especially one girl who went about selling fish and lobsters. About the food there was nothing remarkable,—except the ripe figs, he liked those. They drank sour wine, and used goat-butter, which was strong and full of hair, as it was churned in a goat skin.

"But don't they have parties or banquets? Aren't there any fine hotels down there?"

"Yes, but they are all closed in summer, and the country people are poor. It's a beautiful country, though."

"How, beautiful?" she persisted.

"If you want to go in, I'll show you some sketches, and you'll see."

Miss Bower rose. "All right. I won't go to my fencing lesson this morning. Do you fence? Here comes your dog. You can't move but he's after you. He always makes a face at me when I meet him in the hall, and shows his nasty little teeth as if he wanted to bite me."

In the studio Hedger got out his sketches, but to Miss Bower, whose favourite pictures were Christ Before Pilate and a redhaired Magdalen of Henner, these landscapes were not at all beautiful, and they gave her no idea of any country whatsoever. She was careful not to commit herself, however. Her vocal teacher had already convinced her that she had a great deal to learn about many things.

"Why don't we go out to lunch somewhere?" Hedger asked, and began to dust his fingers with a handkerchief— which he got out of sight as swiftly as possible.

"All right, the Brevoort," she said carelessly. "I think that's a good place, and they have good wine. I don't care for cocktails."

Hedger felt his chin uneasily. "I'm afraid I haven't shaved this morning. If you could wait for me in the Square? It won't take me ten minutes."

Left alone, he found a clean collar and handkerchief, brushed his coat and blacked his shoes, and last of all dug up ten dollars from the bottom of an old copper kettle he had brought from Spain. His winter hat was of such a complexion that the Brevoort hall boy winked at the porter as he took it and placed it on the rack in a row of fresh straw ones.

IV

That afternoon Eden Bower was lying on the couch in her music room, her face turned to the window, watching the pigeons. Reclining thus she could see none of the neighbouring roofs, only the sky itself and the birds that crossed and recrossed her field of vision, white as scraps of paper blowing in the wind. She was thinking that she was young and handsome and had had a good lunch, that a very easy-going, light-hearted city lay in the streets below her; and she was wondering why she found this queer painter chap, with his lean, bluish cheeks and heavy black eyebrows, more interesting than the smart young men she met at her teacher's studio.

Eden Bower was, at twenty, very much the same person that we all know her to be at forty, except that she knew a great deal less. But one thing she knew: that she was to be Eden Bower. She was like some one standing before a great show window full of beautiful and costly things, deciding which she will order. She understands that they will not all be delivered immediately, but one by one they will arrive at her door. She already knew some of the many things that were to happen to her; for instance, that the Chicago millionaire who was going to take her abroad with his sister as chaperone, would eventually press his claim in quite another manner. He was the most circumspect of bachelors, afraid of everything obvious, even of women who were too flagrantly handsome. He was a nervous collector of pictures and furniture, a nervous patron of music, and a nervous host; very cautious about his health, and about any course of conduct that might make him ridiculous. But she knew that he would at last throw all his precautions to the winds.

People like Eden Bower are inexplicable. Her father sold farming machinery in Huntington, Illinois, and she had grown up with no acquaintances or experiences outside of that prairie town. Yet from her earliest childhood she had not one conviction or opinion in common with the people about her,—the only people she knew. Before she was out of short dresses she had made up her mind that she was going to be an actress, that she would live far away in great cities, that she would be much admired by men and would have everything she wanted. When she was thirteen, and was already singing and reciting for church entertainments, she read in some illustrated magazine a long article about the late Czar of Russia, then just come to the throne or about to come to it. After that, lying in the hammock on the front porch on summer evenings, or sitting through a long sermon in the family pew, she amused herself by trying to make up her mind whether she would or would not be the Czar's mistress when she played in his Capital. Now Edna had met this fascinating word only in the novels of Ouida,— her hard-worked little mother kept a long row of them in the upstairs storeroom, behind the linen chest. In Huntington, women who bore that relation to men were called by a very different name, and their lot was not an enviable one; of all the shabby and poor, they were the shabbiest. But then, Edna had never lived in Huntington, not even before she began to find books like "Sapho" and "Mademoiselle de Maupin," secretly sold in paper covers throughout Illinois. It was as if she had come into Huntington, into the Bowers family, on one of the trains that puffed over the marshes behind their back fence all day long, and was waiting for another train to take her out.

As she grew older and handsomer, she had many beaux, but these small-town boys didn't interest her. If a lad kissed her when he brought her home from a dance, she was indulgent and she rather liked it. But if he pressed her further, she slipped away from him, laughing. After she began to sing in Chicago, she was consistently discreet. She stayed as a guest in rich people's houses, and she knew that she was being watched like a rabbit in a laboratory. Covered up in bed, with the lights out, she thought her own thoughts, and laughed.

This summer in New York was her first taste of freedom. The Chicago capitalist, after all his arrangements were made for sailing, had been compelled to go to Mexico to look after oil interests. His sister knew an excellent singing master in New York. Why should not a discreet, well-balanced girl like Miss Bower spend the summer there, studying quietly? The capitalist suggested that his sister might enjoy a summer on Long Island; he would rent the Griffiths' place for her, with all the servants, and Eden could stay there. But his sister met this proposal with a cold stare. So it fell out, that between selfishness and greed, Eden got a summer all her own,— which really did a great deal toward making her an artist and whatever else she was afterward to become. She had time to look about, to watch without being watched; to select diamonds in one window and furs in another, to select shoulders and moustaches in the big hotels where she went to lunch. She had the easy freedom of obscurity and the consciousness of power. She enjoyed both. She was in no hurry.

While Eden Bower watched the pigeons, Don Hedger sat on the other side of the bolted doors, looking into a pool of dark turpentine, at his idle brushes, wondering why a woman could do this to him. He, too, was sure of his future and knew that he was a chosen man. He could not know, of course, that he was merely the first to fall under a fascination which was to be disastrous to a few men and pleasantly stimulating to many thousands. Each of these two young people sensed the future, but not completely. Don Hedger knew that nothing much would ever happen to him. Eden Bower understood that to her a great deal would happen. But she did not guess that her neighbour would have more tempestuous adventures sitting in his dark studio than she would find in all the capitals of Europe, or in all the latitude of conduct she was prepared to permit herself.

v

One Sunday morning Eden was crossing the Square with a spruce young man in a white flannel suit and a panama hat.

They had been breakfasting at the Brevoort and he was coaxing her to let him come up to her rooms and sing for an hour.

"No, I've got to write letters. You must run along now. I see a friend of mine over there, and I want to ask him about something before I go up."

"That fellow with the dog? Where did you pick him up?" the young man glanced toward the seat under a sycamore where Hedger was reading the morning paper.

"Oh, he's an old friend from the West," said Eden easily. "I won't introduce you, because he doesn't like people. He's a recluse. Good-bye. I can't be sure about Tuesday. I'll go with you if I have time after my lesson." She nodded, left him, and went over to the seat littered with newspapers. The young man went up the Avenue without looking back.

"Well, what are you going to do today? Shampoo this animal all morning?" Eden enquired teasingly.

Hedger made room for her on the seat. "No, at twelve o'clock I'm going out to Coney Island. One of my models is going up in a balloon this afternoon. I've often promised to go and see her, and now I'm going."

Eden asked if models usually did such stunts. No, Hedger told her, but Molly Welch added to her earnings in that way. "I believe," he added, "she likes the excitement of it. She's got a good deal of spirit. That's why I like to paint her. So many models have flaccid bodies."

"And she hasn't, eh? Is she the one who comes to see you? I can't help hearing her, she talks so loud."

"Yes, she has a rough voice, but she's a fine girl. I don't suppose you'd be interested in going?"

"I don't know," Eden sat tracing patterns on the asphalt with the end of her parasol. "Is it any fun? I got up feeling I'd like to do something different today. It's the first Sunday I've not had to sing in church. I had that engagement for breakfast at the Brevoort, but it wasn't very exciting. That chap can't talk about anything but himself."

Hedger warmed a little. "If you've never been to Coney Island, you ought to go. It's nice to see all the people; tailors and bar-tenders and prize-fighters with their best girls, and all sorts of folks taking a holiday."

Eden looked sidewise at him. So one ought to be interested

in people of that kind, ought one? He was certainly a funny fellow. Yet he was never, somehow, tiresome. She had seen a good deal of him lately, but she kept wanting to know him better, to find out what made him different from men like the one she had just left—whether he really was as different as he seemed. "I'll go with you," she said at last, "if you'll leave that at home." She pointed to Caesar's flickering ears with her sunshade.

"But he's half the fun. You'd like to hear him bark at the waves when they come in."

"No, I wouldn't. He's jealous and disagreeable if he sees you talking to any one else. Look at him now."

"Of course, if you make a face at him. He knows what that means, and he makes a worse face. He likes Molly Welch, and she'll be disappointed if I don't bring him."

Eden said decidedly that he couldn't take both of them. So at twelve o'clock when she and Hedger got on the boat at Desbrosses street, Caesar was lying on his pallet, with a bone.

Eden enjoyed the boat-ride. It was the first time she had been on the water, and she felt as if she were embarking for France. The light warm breeze and the plunge of the waves made her very wide awake, and she liked crowds of any kind. They went to the balcony of a big, noisy restaurant and had a shore dinner, with tall steins of beer. Hedger had got a big advance from his advertising firm since he first lunched with Miss Bower ten days ago, and he was ready for anything.

After dinner they went to the tent behind the bathing beach, where the tops of two balloons bulged out over the canvas. A red-faced man in a linen suit stood in front of the tent, shouting in a hoarse voice and telling the people that if the crowd was good for five dollars more, a beautiful young woman would risk her life for their entertainment. Four little boys in dirty red uniforms ran about taking contributions in their pill-box hats. One of the balloons was bobbing up and down in its tether and people were shoving forward to get nearer the tent.

"Is it dangerous, as he pretends?" Eden asked.

"Molly says it's simple enough if nothing goes wrong with the balloon. Then it would be all over, I suppose."

"Wouldn't you like to go up with her?"

"I? Of course not. I'm not fond of taking foolish risks."

Eden sniffed. "I shouldn't think sensible risks would be very much fun."

Hedger did not answer, for just then every one began to shove the other way and shout, "Look out. There she goes!" and a band of six pieces commenced playing furiously.

As the balloon rose from its tent enclosure, they saw a girl in green tights standing in the basket, holding carelessly to one of the ropes with one hand and with the other waving to the spectators. A long rope trailed behind to keep the balloon from blowing out to sea.

As it soared, the figure in green tights in the basket diminished to a mere spot, and the balloon itself, in the brilliant light, looked like a big silver-grey bat, with its wings folded. When it began to sink, the girl stepped through the hole in the basket to a trapeze that hung below, and gracefully descended through the air, holding to the rod with both hands, keeping her body taut and her feet close together. The crowd, which had grown very large by this time, cheered vociferously. The men took off their hats and waved, little boys shouted, and fat old women, shining with the heat and a beer lunch, murmured admiring comments upon the balloonist's figure. "Beautiful legs, she has!"

"That's so," Hedger whispered. "Not many girls would look well in that position." Then, for some reason, he blushed a slow, dark, painful crimson.

The balloon descended slowly, a little way from the tent, and the red-faced man in the linen suit caught Molly Welch before her feet touched the ground, and pulled her to one side. The band struck up "Blue Bell" by way of welcome, and one of the sweaty pages ran forward and presented the balloonist with a large bouquet of artificial flowers. She smiled and thanked him, and ran back across the sand to the tent.

"Can't we go inside and see her?" Eden asked. "You can explain to the door man. I want to meet her." Edging forward, she herself addressed the man in the linen suit and slipped something from her purse into his hand.

They found Molly seated before a trunk that had a mirror in the lid and a "make-up" outfit spread upon the tray. She was wiping the cold cream and powder from her neck with a discarded chemise.

"Hello, Don," she said cordially. "Brought a friend?"

Eden liked her. She had an easy, friendly manner, and there was something boyish and devil-may-care about her.

"Yes, it's fun. I'm mad about it," she said in reply to Eden's questions. "I always want to let go, when I come down on the bar. You don't feel your weight at all, as you would on a stationary trapeze."

The big drum boomed outside, and the publicity man began shouting to newly arrived boatloads. Miss Welch took a last pull at her cigarette. "Now you'll have to get out, Don. I change for the next act. This time I go up in a black evening dress, and lose the skirt in the basket before I start down."

"Yes, go along," said Eden. "Wait for me outside the door. I'll stay and help her dress."

Hedger waited and waited, while women of every build bumped into him and begged his pardon, and the red pages ran about holding out their caps for coins, and the people ate and perspired and shifted parasols against the sun. When the band began to play a two-step, all the bathers ran up out of the surf to watch the ascent. The second balloon bumped and rose, and the crowd began shouting to the girl in a black evening dress who stood leaning against the ropes and smiling. "It's a new girl," they called. "It ain't the Countess this time. You're a peach, girlie!"

The balloonist acknowledged these compliments, bowing and looking down over the sea of upturned faces,—but Hedger was determined she should not see him, and he darted behind the tent-fly. He was suddenly dripping with cold sweat, his mouth was full of the bitter taste of anger and his tongue felt stiff behind his teeth. Molly Welch, in a shirt-waist and a white tam-o'-shanter cap, slipped out from the tent under his arm and laughed up in his face. "She's a crazy one you brought along. She'll get what she wants!"

"Oh, I'll settle with you, all right!" Hedger brought out with difficulty.

"It's not my fault, Donnie. I couldn't do anything with her. She bought me off. What's the matter with you? Are you soft on her? She's safe enough. It's as easy as rolling off a log, if you keep cool." Molly Welch was rather excited herself, and she was chewing gum at a high speed as she stood beside him, looking up at the floating silver cone. "Now watch," she exclaimed suddenly. "She's coming down on the bar. I advised her to cut that out, but you see she does it first-rate. And she got rid of the skirt, too. Those black tights show off her legs very well. She keeps her feet together like I told her, and makes a good line along the back. See the light on those silver slippers,—that was a good idea I had. Come along to meet her. Don't be a grouch; she's done it fine!"

Molly tweaked his elbow, and then left him standing like a stump, while she ran down the beach with the crowd.

Though Hedger was sulking, his eye could not help seeing the low blue welter of the sea, the arrested bathers, standing in the surf, their arms and legs stained red by the dropping sun, all shading their eyes and gazing upward at the slowly falling silver star.

Molly Welch and the manager caught Eden under the arms and lifted her aside, a red page dashed up with a bouquet, and the band struck up "Blue Bell." Eden laughed and bowed, took Molly's arm, and ran up the sand in her black tights and silver slippers, dodging the friendly old women, and the gallant sports who wanted to offer their homage on the spot.

When she emerged from the tent, dressed in her own clothes, that part of the beach was almost deserted. She stepped to her companion's side and said carelessly: "Hadn't we better try to catch this boat? I hope you're not sore at me. Really, it was lots of fun."

Hedger looked at his watch. "Yes, we have fifteen minutes to get to the boat," he said politely.

As they walked toward the pier, one of the pages ran up panting. "Lady, you're carrying off the bouquet," he said, aggrievedly.

Eden stopped and looked at the bunch of spotty cotton roses in her hand. "Of course. I want them for a souvenir. You gave them to me yourself."

"I give 'em to you for looks, but you can't take 'em away. They belong to the show."

"Oh, you always use the same bunch?"

"Sure we do. There ain't too much money in this business."

She laughed and tossed them back to him. "Why are you angry?" she asked Hedger. "I wouldn't have done it if I'd been with some fellows, but I thought you were the sort who wouldn't mind. Molly didn't for a minute think you would."

"What possessed you to do such a fool thing?" he asked roughly.

"I don't know. When I saw her coming down, I wanted to try it. It looked exciting. Didn't I hold myself as well as she did?"

Hedger shrugged his shoulders, but in his heart he forgave her.

The return boat was not crowded, though the boats that passed them, going out, were packed to the rails. The sun was setting. Boys and girls sat on the long benches with their arms about each other, singing. Eden felt a strong wish to propitiate her companion, to be alone with him. She had been curiously wrought up by her balloon trip; it was a lark, but not very satisfying unless one came back to something after the flight. She wanted to be admired and adored. Though Eden said nothing, and sat with her arms limp on the rail in front of her, looking languidly at the rising silhouette of the city and the bright path of the sun, Hedger felt a strange drawing near to her. If he but brushed her white skirt with his knee, there was an instant communication between them, such as there had never been before. They did not talk at all, but when they went over the gang-plank she took his arm and kept her shoulder close to his. He felt as if they were enveloped in a highly charged atmosphere, an invisible network of subtle, almost painful sensibility. They had somehow taken hold of each other.

An hour later, they were dining in the back garden of a little French hotel on Ninth Street, long since passed away. It was cool and leafy there, and the mosquitoes were not very numerous. A party of South Americans at another table were drinking champagne, and Eden murmured that she thought she would like some, if it were not too expensive. "Perhaps it will make me think I am in the balloon again. That was a very nice feeling. You've forgiven me, haven't you?"

Hedger gave her a quick straight look from under his black

eyebrows, and something went over her that was like a chill, except that it was warm and feathery. She drank most of the wine; her companion was indifferent to it. He was talking more to her tonight than he had ever done before. She asked him about a new picture she had seen in his room; a queer thing full of stiff, supplicating female figures. "It's Indian, isn't it?"

"Yes. I call it Rain Spirits, or maybe, Indian Rain. In the Southwest, where I've been a good deal, the Indian traditions make women have to do with the rain-fall. They were supposed to control it, somehow, and to be able to find springs, and make moisture come out of the earth. You see I'm trying to learn to paint what people think and feel; to get away from all that photographic stuff. When I look at you, I don't see what a camera would see, do I?"

"How can I tell?"

"Well, if I should paint you, I could make you understand what I see." For the second time that day Hedger crimsoned unexpectedly, and his eyes fell and steadily contemplated a dish of little radishes. "That particular picture I got from a story a Mexican priest told me; he said he found it in an old manuscript book in a monastery down there, written by some Spanish Missionary, who got his stories from the Aztecs. This one he called 'The Forty Lovers of the Queen,' and it was more or less about rain-making."

"Aren't you going to tell it to me?" Eden asked.

Hedger fumbled among the radishes. "I don't know if it's the proper kind of story to tell a girl."

She smiled; "Oh, forget about that! I've been balloon riding today. I like to hear you talk."

Her low voice was flattering. She had seemed like clay in his hands ever since they got on the boat to come home. He leaned back in his chair, forgot his food, and, looking at her intently, began to tell his story, the theme of which he somehow felt was dangerous tonight.

The tale began, he said, somewhere in Ancient Mexico, and concerned the daughter of a king. The birth of this Princess was preceded by unusual portents. Three times her mother dreamed that she was delivered of serpents, which betokened that the child she carried would have power with the rain gods. The serpent was the symbol of water. The Princess grew up dedicated to the gods, and wise men taught her the rain-making mysteries. She was with difficulty restrained from men and was guarded at all times, for it was the law of the Thunder that she be maiden until her marriage. In the years of her adolescence, rain was abundant with her people. The oldest man could not remember such fertility. When the Princess had counted eighteen summers, her father went to drive out a war party that harried his borders on the north and troubled his prosperity. The King destroyed the invaders and brought home many prisoners. Among the prisoners was a young chief, taller than any of his captors, of such strength and ferocity that the King's people came a day's journey to look at him. When the Princess beheld his great stature, and saw that his arms and breast were covered with the figures of wild animals, bitten into the skin and coloured, she begged his life from her father. She desired that he should practise his art upon her, and prick upon her skin the signs of Rain and Lightning and Thunder, and stain the wounds with herb-juices, as they were upon his own body. For many days, upon the roof of the King's house, the Princess submitted herself to the bone needle, and the women with her marvelled at her fortitude. But the Princess was without shame before the Captive, and it came about that he threw from him his needles and his stains, and fell upon the Princess to violate her honour; and her women ran down from the roof screaming, to call the guard which stood at the gateway of the King's house, and none stayed to protect their mistress. When the guard came, the Captive was thrown into bonds, and he was gelded, and his tongue was torn out, and he was given for a slave to the Rain Princess.

The country of the Aztecs to the east was tormented by thirst, and their king, hearing much of the rain-making arts of the Princess, sent an embassy to her father, with presents and an offer of marriage. So the Princess went from her father to be the Queen of the Aztecs, and she took with her the Captive, who served her in everything with entire fidelity and slept upon a mat before her door.

The King gave his bride a fortress on the outskirts of the city, whither she retired to entreat the rain gods. This fortress was called the Queen's House, and on the night of the new moon the Queen came to it from the palace. But when the moon waxed and grew toward the round, because the god of Thunder had had his will of her, then the Queen returned to the King. Drouth abated in the country and rain fell abundantly by reason of the Queen's power with the stars.

When the Queen went to her own house she took with her no servant but the Captive, and he slept outside her door and brought her food after she had fasted. The Queen had a jewel of great value, a turquoise that had fallen from the sun, and had the image of the sun upon it. And when she desired a young man whom she had seen in the army or among the slaves, she sent the Captive to him with the jewel, for a sign that he should come to her secretly at the Queen's House upon business concerning the welfare of all. And some, after she had talked with them, she sent away with rewards; and some she took into her chamber and kept them by her for one night or two. Afterward she called the Captive and bade him conduct the youth by the secret way he had come, underneath the chambers of the fortress. But for the going away of the Queen's lovers the Captive took out the bar that was beneath a stone in the floor of the passage, and put in its stead a rush-reed, and the youth stepped upon it and fell through into a cavern that was the bed of an underground river, and whatever was thrown into it was not seen again. In this service nor in any other did the Captive fail the Queen.

But when the Queen sent for the Captain of the Archers, she detained him four days in her chamber, calling often for food and wine, and was greatly content with him. On the fourth day she went to the Captive outside her door and said: "Tomorrow take this man up by the sure way, by which the King comes, and let him live."

In the Queen's door were arrows, purple and white. When she desired the King to come to her publicly, with his guard, she sent him a white arrow; but when she sent the purple, he came secretly, and covered himself with his mantle to be hidden from the stone gods at the gate. On the fifth night that the Queen was with her lover, the Captive took a purple arrow to the King, and the King came secretly and found them together. He killed the Captain with his own hand, but the

Queen he brought to public trial. The Captive, when he was put to the question, told on his fingers forty men that he had let through the underground passage into the river. The Captive and the Queen were put to death by fire, both on the same day, and afterward there was scarcity of rain.

Eden Bower sat shivering a little as she listened. Hedger was not trying to please her, she thought, but to antagonize and frighten her by his brutal story. She had often told herself that his lean, big-boned lower jaw was like his bull-dog's, but tonight his face made Caesar's most savage and determined expression seem an affectation. Now she was looking at the man he really was. Nobody's eyes had ever defied her like this. They were searching her and seeing everything; all she had concealed from Livingston, and from the millionaire and his friends, and from the newspaper man. He was testing her, trying her out, and she was more ill at ease than she wished to show.

"That's quite a thrilling story," she said at last, rising and winding her scarf about her throat. "It must be getting late. Almost every one has gone."

They walked down the Avenue like people who have quarrelled, or who wish to get rid of each other. Hedger did not take her arm at the street crossings, and they did not linger in the Square. At her door he tried none of the old devices of the Livingston boys. He stood like a post, having forgotten to take off his hat, gave her a harsh, threatening glance, muttered "goodnight," and shut his own door noisily.

There was no question of sleep for Eden Bower. Her brain was working like a machine that would never stop. After she undressed, she tried to calm her nerves by smoking a cigarette, lying on the divan by the open window. But she grew wider and wider awake, combating the challenge that had flamed all evening in Hedger's eyes. The balloon had been one kind of excitement, the wine another; but the thing that had roused her, as a blow rouses a proud man, was the doubt, the contempt, the sneering hostility with which the painter had looked at her when he told his savage story. Crowds and balloons were all very well, she reflected, but woman's chief adventure is man. With a mind over active and a sense of life over strong, she wanted to walk across the roofs in the star-light, to sail over the sea and face at once a world of which she had never been afraid.

Hedger must be asleep; his dog had stopped sniffing under the double doors. Eden put on her wrapper and slippers and stole softly down the hall over the old carpet; one loose board creaked just as she reached the ladder. The trapdoor was open, as always on hot nights. When she stepped out on the roof she drew a long breath and walked across it, looking up at the sky. Her foot touched something soft; she heard a low growl, and on the instant Caesar's sharp little teeth caught her ankle and waited. His breath was like steam on her leg. Nobody had ever intruded upon his roof before, and he panted for the movement or the word that would let him spring his jaw. Instead, Hedger's hand seized his throat.

"Wait a minute. I'll settle with him," he said grimly. He dragged the dog toward the manhole and disappeared. When he came back, he found Eden standing over by the dark chimney, looking away in an offended attitude.

"I caned him unmercifully," he panted. "Of course you didn't hear anything; he never whines when I beat him. He didn't nip you, did he?"

"I don't know whether he broke the skin or not," she answered aggrievedly, still looking off into the west.

"If I were one of your friends in white pants, I'd strike a match to find whether you were hurt, though I know you are not, and then I'd see your ankle, wouldn't I?"

"I suppose so."

He shook his head and stood with his hands in the pockets of his old painting jacket. "I'm not up to such boy-tricks. If you want the place to yourself, I'll clear out. There are plenty of places where I can spend the night, what's left of it. But if you stay here and I stay here—" He shrugged his shoulders.

Eden did not stir, and she made no reply. Her head drooped slightly, as if she were considering. But the moment he put his arms about her they began to talk, both at once, as people do in an opera. The instant avowal brought out a flood of trivial admissions. Hedger confessed his crime, was reproached and forgiven, and now Eden knew what it was in his look that she had found so disturbing of late.

Standing against the black chimney, with the sky behind and blue shadows before, they looked like one of Hedger's own paintings of that period; two figures, one white and one dark, and nothing whatever distinguishable about them but that they were male and female. The faces were lost, the contours blurred in shadow, but the figures were a man and a woman, and that was their whole concern and their mysterious beauty,—it was the rhythm in which they moved, at last, along the roof and down into the dark hole; he first, drawing her gently after him. She came down very slowly. The excitement and bravado and uncertainty of that long day and night seemed all at once to tell upon her. When his feet were on the carpet and he reached up to lift her down, she twined her arms about his neck as after a long separation, and turned her face to him, and her lips, with their perfume of youth and passion.

One Saturday afternoon Hedger was sitting in the window of Eden's music room. They had been watching the pigeons come wheeling over the roofs from their unknown feeding grounds.

"Why," said Eden suddenly, "don't we fix those big doors into your studio so they will open? Then, if I want you, I won't have to go through the hall. That illustrator is loafing about a good deal of late."

"I'll open them, if you wish. The bolt is on your side."

"Isn't there one on yours, too?"

"No. I believe a man lived there for years before I came in, and the nurse used to have these rooms herself. Naturally, the lock was on the lady's side."

Eden laughed and began to examine the bolt. "It's all stuck up with paint." Looking about, her eye lighted upon a bronze Buddha which was one of the nurse's treasures. Taking him by his head, she struck the bolt a blow with his squatting posteriors. The two doors creaked, sagged, and swung weakly inward a little way, as if they were too old for such escapades. Eden tossed the heavy idol into a stuffed chair. "That's better," she exclaimed exultantly. "So the bolts are always on the lady's side? What a lot society takes for granted!"

Hedger laughed, sprang up and caught her arms roughly. "Whoever takes you for granted— Did anybody, ever?"

"Everybody does. That's why I'm here. You are the only one who knows anything about me. Now I'll have to dress if we're going out for dinner."

He lingered, keeping his hold on her. "But I won't always be the only one, Eden Bower. I won't be the last."

"No, I suppose not," she said carelessly. "But what does that matter? You are the first."

As a long, despairing whine broke in the warm stillness, they drew apart. Caesar, lying on his bed in the dark corner, had lifted his head at this invasion of sunlight, and realized that the side of his room was broken open, and his whole world shattered by change. There stood his master and this woman, laughing at him! The woman was pulling the long black hair of this mightiest of men, who bowed his head and permitted it.

VI

In time they quarrelled, of course, and about an abstraction, —as young people often do, as mature people almost never do. Eden came in late one afternoon. She had been with some of her musical friends to lunch at Burton Ives' studio, and she began telling Hedger about its splendours. He listened a moment and then threw down his brushes. "I know exactly what it's like," he said impatiently. "A very good department-store conception of a studio. It's one of the show places."

"Well, it's gorgeous, and he said I could bring you to see him. The boys tell me he's awfully kind about giving people a lift, and you might get something out of it."

Hedger started up and pushed his canvas out of the way. "What could I possibly get from Burton Ives? He's almost the worst painter in the world; the stupidest, I mean."

Eden was annoyed. Burton Ives had been very nice to her and had begged her to sit for him. "You must admit that he's a very successful one," she said coldly.

"Of course he is! Anybody can be successful who will do

that sort of thing. I wouldn't paint his pictures for all the money in New York."

"Well, I saw a lot of them, and I think they are beautiful."

Hedger bowed stiffly.

"What's the use of being a great painter if nobody knows about you?" Eden went on persuasively. "Why don't you paint the kind of pictures people can understand, and then, after you're successful, do whatever you like?"

"As I look at it," said Hedger brusquely, "I am successful."

Eden glanced about. "Well, I don't see any evidences of it," she said, biting her lip. "He has a Japanese servant and a wine cellar, and keeps a riding horse."

Hedger melted a little. "My dear, I have the most expensive luxury in the world, and I am much more extravagant than Burton Ives, for I work to please nobody but myself."

"You mean you could make money and don't? That you don't try to get a public?"

"Exactly. A public only wants what has been done over and over. I'm painting for painters,—who haven't been born."

"What would you do if I brought Mr. Ives down here to see your things?"

"Well, for God's sake, don't! Before he left I'd probably tell him what I thought of him."

Eden rose. "I give you up. You know very well there's only one kind of success that's real."

"Yes, but it's not the kind you mean. So you've been thinking me a scrub painter, who needs a helping hand from some fashionable studio man? What the devil have you had anything to do with me for, then?"

"There's no use talking to you," said Eden walking slowly toward the door. "I've been trying to pull wires for you all afternoon, and this is what it comes to." She had expected that the tidings of a prospective call from the great man would be received very differently, and had been thinking as she came home in the stage how, as with a magic wand, she might gild Hedger's future, float him out of his dark hole on a tide of prosperity, see his name in the papers and his pictures in the windows on Fifth Avenue.

Hedger mechanically snapped the midsummer leash on Caesar's collar and they ran downstairs and hurried through

Sullivan Street off toward the river. He wanted to be among rough, honest people, to get down where the big drays bumped over stone paving blocks and the men wore corduroy trowsers and kept their shirts open at the neck. He stopped for a drink in one of the sagging bar-rooms on the water front. He had never in his life been so deeply wounded; he did not know he could be so hurt. He had told this girl all his secrets. On the roof, in these warm, heavy summer nights, with her hands locked in his, he had been able to explain all his misty ideas about an unborn art the world was waiting for; had been able to explain them better than he had ever done to himself. And she had looked away to the chattels of this uptown studio and coveted them for him! To her he was only an unsuccessful Burton Ives.

Then why, as he had put it to her, did she take up with him? Young, beautiful, talented as she was, why had she wasted herself on a scrub? Pity? Hardly; she wasn't sentimental. There was no explaining her. But in this passion that had seemed so fearless and so fated to be, his own position now looked to him ridiculous; a poor dauber without money or fame,—it was her caprice to load him with favours. Hedger ground his teeth so loud that his dog, trotting beside him, heard him and looked up.

While they were having supper at the oysterman's, he planned his escape. Whenever he saw her again, everything he had told her, that he should never have told any one, would come back to him; ideas he had never whispered even to the painter whom he worshipped and had gone all the way to France to see. To her they must seem his apology for not having horses and a valet, or merely the puerile boastfulness of a weak man. Yet if she slipped the bolt tonight and came through the doors and said, "Oh, weak man, I belong to you!" what could he do? That was the danger. He would catch the train out to Long Beach tonight, and tomorrow he would go on to the north end of Long Island, where an old friend of his had a summer studio among the sand dunes. He would stay until things came right in his mind. And she could find a smart painter, or take her punishment.

When he went home, Eden's room was dark; she was dining out somewhere. He threw his things into a hold-all he

had carried about the world with him, strapped up some
colours and canvases, and ran downstairs.

VII

Five days later Hedger was a restless passenger on a dirty,
crowded Sunday train, coming back to town. Of course he
saw now how unreasonable he had been in expecting a Hun-
tington girl to know anything about pictures; here was a
whole continent full of people who knew nothing about pic-
tures and he didn't hold it against them. What had such
things to do with him and Eden Bower? When he lay out on
the dunes, watching the moon come up out of the sea, it had
seemed to him that there was no wonder in the world like the
wonder of Eden Bower. He was going back to her because
she was older than art, because she was the most overwhelm-
ing thing that had ever come into his life.

He had written her yesterday, begging her to be at home
this evening, telling her that he was contrite, and wretched
enough.

Now that he was on his way to her, his stronger feeling
unaccountably changed to a mood that was playful and ten-
der. He wanted to share everything with her, even the most
trivial things. He wanted to tell her about the people on the
train, coming back tired from their holiday with bunches of
wilted flowers and dirty daisies; to tell her that the fish-man,
to whom she had often sent him for lobsters, was among the
passengers, disguised in a silk shirt and a spotted tie, and how
his wife looked exactly like a fish, even to her eyes, on which
cataracts were forming. He could tell her, too, that he hadn't
as much as unstrapped his canvases,—that ought to convince
her.

In those days passengers from Long Island came into New
York by ferry. Hedger had to be quick about getting his dog
out of the express car in order to catch the first boat. The East
River, and the bridges, and the city to the west, were burning
in the conflagration of the sunset; there was that great home-
coming reach of evening in the air.

The car changes from Thirty-fourth Street were too many
and too perplexing; for the first time in his life Hedger took a

hansom cab for Washington Square. Caesar sat bolt upright on the worn leather cushion beside him, and they jogged off, looking down on the rest of the world.

It was twilight when they drove down lower Fifth Avenue into the Square, and through the Arch behind them were the two long rows of pale violet lights that used to bloom so beautifully against the grey stone and asphalt. Here and yonder about the Square hung globes that shed a radiance not unlike the blue mists of evening, emerging softly when daylight died, as the stars emerged in the thin blue sky. Under them the sharp shadows of the trees fell on the cracked pavement and the sleeping grass. The first stars and the first lights were growing silver against the gradual darkening, when Hedger paid his driver and went into the house,—which, thank God, was still there! On the hall table lay his letter of yesterday, unopened.

He went upstairs with every sort of fear and every sort of hope clutching at his heart; it was as if tigers were tearing him. Why was there no gas burning in the top hall? He found matches and the gas bracket. He knocked, but got no answer; nobody was there. Before his own door were exactly five bottles of milk, standing in a row. The milk-boy had taken spiteful pleasure in thus reminding him that he forgot to stop his order.

Hedger went down to the basement; it, too, was dark. The janitress was taking her evening airing on the basement steps. She sat waving a palm-leaf fan majestically, her dirty calico dress open at the neck. She told him at once that there had been "changes." Miss Bower's room was to let again, and the piano would go tomorrow. Yes, she left yesterday, she sailed for Europe with friends from Chicago. They arrived on Friday, heralded by many telegrams. Very rich people they were said to be, though the man had refused to pay the nurse a month's rent in lieu of notice,—which would have been only right, as the young lady had agreed to take the rooms until October. Mrs. Foley had observed, too, that he didn't overpay her or Willy for their trouble, and a great deal of trouble they had been put to, certainly. Yes, the young lady was very pleasant, but the nurse said there were rings on the mahogany table where she had put tumblers and wine glasses. It was just as well she was gone. The Chicago man was uppish in his ways, but not much to look at. She supposed he had poor health, for there was nothing to him inside his clothes.

Hedger went slowly up the stairs—never had they seemed so long, or his legs so heavy. The upper floor was emptiness and silence. He unlocked his room, lit the gas, and opened the windows. When he went to put his coat in the closet, he found, hanging among his clothes, a pale, flesh-tinted dressing gown he had liked to see her wear, with a perfume—oh, a perfume that was still Eden Bower! He shut the door behind him and there, in the dark, for a moment he lost his manliness. It was when he held this garment to him that he found a letter in the pocket.

The note was written with a lead pencil, in haste: She was sorry that he was angry, but she still didn't know just what she had done. She had thought Mr. Ives would be useful to him; she guessed he was too proud. She wanted awfully to see him again, but Fate came knocking at her door after he had left her. She believed in Fate. She would never forget him, and she knew he would become the greatest painter in the world. Now she must pack. She hoped he wouldn't mind her leaving the dressing gown; somehow, she could never wear it again.

After Hedger read this, standing under the gas, he went back into the closet and knelt down before the wall; the knot hole had been plugged up with a ball of wet paper,—the same blue note-paper on which her letter was written.

He was hard hit. Tonight he had to bear the loneliness of a whole lifetime. Knowing himself so well, he could hardly believe that such a thing had ever happened to him, that such a woman had lain happy and contented in his arms. And now it was over. He turned out the light and sat down on his painter's stool before the big window. Caesar, on the floor beside him, rested his head on his master's knee. We must leave Hedger thus, sitting in his tank with his dog, looking up at the stars.

COMING, APHRODITE! This legend, in electric lights over the Lexington Opera House, had long announced the return of Eden Bower to New York after years of spectacular success in Paris. She came at last, under the management of an American Opera Company, but bringing her own *chef d'orchestre*.

One bright December afternoon Eden Bower was going down Fifth Avenue in her car, on the way to her broker, in Williams Street. Her thoughts were entirely upon stocks,—Cerro de Pasco, and how much she should buy of it,—when she suddenly looked up and realized that she was skirting Washington Square. She had not seen the place since she rolled out of it in an old-fashioned four-wheeler to seek her fortune, eighteen years ago.

"Arrêtez, Alphonse. Attendez moi," she called, and opened the door before he could reach it. The children who were streaking over the asphalt on roller skates saw a lady in a long fur coat, and short, high-heeled shoes, alight from a French car and pace slowly about the Square, holding her muff to her chin. This spot, at least, had changed very little, she reflected; the same trees, the same fountain, the white arch, and over yonder, Garibaldi, drawing the sword for freedom. There, just opposite her, was the old red brick house.

"Yes, that is the place," she was thinking. "I can smell the carpets now, and the dog,—what was his name? That grubby bathroom at the end of the hall, and that dreadful Hedger —still, there was something about him, you know—" She glanced up and blinked against the sun. From somewhere in the crowded quarter south of the Square a flock of pigeons rose, wheeling quickly upward into the brilliant blue sky. She threw back her head, pressed her muff closer to her chin, and watched them with a smile of amazement and delight. So they still rose, out of all that dirt and noise and squalor, fleet and silvery, just as they used to rise that summer when she was twenty and went up in a balloon on Coney Island!

Alphonse opened the door and tucked her robes about her. All the way down town her mind wandered from Cerro de Pasco, and she kept smiling and looking up at the sky.

When she had finished her business with the broker, she asked him to look in the telephone book for the address of M. Gaston Jules, the picture dealer, and slipped the paper on which he wrote it into her glove. It was five o'clock when she reached the French Galleries, as they were called. On entering she gave the attendant her card, asking him to take it to M. Jules. The dealer appeared very promptly and begged her to come into his private office, where he pushed a great chair toward his desk for her and signalled his secretary to leave the room.

"How good your lighting is in here," she observed, glancing about. "I met you at Simon's studio, didn't I? Oh, no! I never forget anybody who interests me." She threw her muff on his writing table and sank into the deep chair. "I have come to you for some information that's not in my line. Do you know anything about an American painter named Hedger?"

He took the seat opposite her. "Don Hedger? But, certainly! There are some very interesting things of his in an exhibition at V——'s. If you would care to—"

She held up her hand. "No, no. I've no time to go to exhibitions. Is he a man of any importance?"

"Certainly. He is one of the first men among the moderns. That is to say, among the very moderns. He is always coming up with something different. He often exhibits in Paris, you must have seen—"

"No, I tell you I don't go to exhibitions. Has he had great success? That is what I want to know."

M. Jules pulled at his short grey moustache. "But, Madame, there are many kinds of success," he began cautiously.

Madame gave a dry laugh. "Yes, so he used to say. We once quarrelled on that issue. And how would you define his particular kind?"

M. Jules grew thoughtful. "He is a great name with all the young men, and he is decidedly an influence in art. But one can't definitely place a man who is original, erratic, and who is changing all the time."

She cut him short. "Is he much talked about at home? In Paris, I mean? Thanks. That's all I want to know." She rose and began buttoning her coat. "One doesn't like to have been an utter fool, even at twenty."

"*Mais, non!*" M. Jules handed her her muff with a quick, sympathetic glance. He followed her out through the carpeted show-room, now closed to the public and draped in cheesecloth, and put her into her car with words appreciative of the honour she had done him in calling.

Leaning back in the cushions, Eden Bower closed her eyes, and her face, as the street lamps flashed their ugly orange light upon it, became hard and settled, like a plaster cast; so a sail, that has been filled by a strong breeze, behaves when the wind suddenly dies. Tomorrow night the wind would blow again, and this mask would be the golden face of Aphrodite. But a "big" career takes its toll, even with the best of luck.

The Diamond Mine

I

I FIRST became aware that Cressida Garnet was on board when I saw young men with cameras going up to the boat deck. In that exposed spot she was good-naturedly posing for them—amid fluttering lavender scarfs—wearing a most unseaworthy hat, her broad, vigorous face wreathed in smiles. She was too much an American not to believe in publicity. All advertising was good. If it was good for breakfast foods, it was good for prime donne,—especially for a prima donna who would never be any younger and who had just announced her intention of marrying a fourth time.

Only a few days before, when I was lunching with some friends at Sherry's, I had seen Jerome Brown come in with several younger men, looking so pleased and prosperous that I exclaimed upon it.

"His affairs," some one explained, "are looking up. He's going to marry Cressida Garnet. Nobody believed it at first, but since she confirms it he's getting all sorts of credit. That woman's a diamond mine."

If there was ever a man who needed a diamond mine at hand, immediately convenient, it was Jerome Brown. But as an old friend of Cressida Garnet, I was sorry to hear that mining operations were to be begun again.

I had been away from New York and had not seen Cressida for a year; now I paused on the gangplank to note how very like herself she still was, and with what undiminished zeal she went about even the most trifling things that pertained to her profession. From that distance I could recognize her "carrying" smile, and even what, in Columbus, we used to call "the Garnet look."

At the foot of the stairway leading up to the boat deck stood two of the factors in Cressida's destiny. One of them was her sister, Miss Julia; a woman of fifty with a relaxed, mournful face, an ageing skin that browned slowly, like meerschaum, and the unmistakable "look" by which one knew a Garnet. Beside her, pointedly ignoring her, smoking a ciga-

397

rette while he ran over the passenger list with supercilious almond eyes, stood a youth in a pink shirt and a green plush hat, holding a French bull-dog on the leash. This was "Horace," Cressida's only son. He, at any rate, had not the Garnet look. He was rich and ruddy, indolent and insolent, with soft oval cheeks and the blooming complexion of twenty-two. There was the beginning of a silky shadow on his upper lip. He seemed like a ripe fruit grown out of a rich soil; "oriental," his mother called his peculiar lusciousness. His aunt's restless and aggrieved glance kept flecking him from the side, but the two were as motionless as the *bouledogue*, standing there on his bench legs and surveying his travelling basket with loathing. They were waiting, in constrained immobility, for Cressida to descend and reanimate them,—will them to do or to be something. Forward, by the rail, I saw the stooped, eager back for which I was unconsciously looking: Miletus Poppas, the Greek Jew, Cressida's accompanist and shadow. We were all there, I thought with a smile, except Jerome Brown.

The first member of Cressida's party with whom I had speech was Mr. Poppas. When we were two hours out I came upon him in the act of dropping overboard a steamer cushion made of American flags. Cressida never sailed, I think, that one of these vivid comforts of travel did not reach her at the dock. Poppas recognized me just as the striped object left his hand. He was standing with his arm still extended over the rail, his fingers contemptuously sprung back. "Lest we forgedt!" he said with a shrug. "Does Madame Cressida know we are to have the pleasure of your company for this voyage?" He spoke deliberate, grammatical English—he despised the American rendering of the language—but there was an indescribably foreign quality in his voice,—a something muted; and though he aspirated his "th's" with such conscientious thoroughness, there was always the thud of a "d" in them. Poppas stood before me in a short, tightly buttoned grey coat and cap, exactly the colour of his greyish skin and hair and waxed moustache; a monocle on a very wide black ribbon dangled over his chest. As to his age, I could not offer a conjecture. In the twelve years I had known his thin lupine face behind Cressida's shoulder, it had not changed. I was used to his cold, supercilious manner, to his alarming, deep-set eyes,—very close together, in colour a yellowish green, and always gleaming with something like defeated fury, as if he were actually on the point of having it out with you, or with the world, at last.

I asked him if Cressida had engagements in London.

"Quite so; the Manchester Festival, some concerts at Queen's Hall, and the Opera at Covent Garden; a rather special production of the operas of Mozart. That she can still do quite well,—which is not at all, of course, what we might have expected, and only goes to show that our Madame Cressida is now, as always, a charming exception to rules." Poppas' tone about his client was consistently patronizing, and he was always trying to draw one into a conspiracy of two, based on a mutual understanding of her shortcomings.

I approached him on the one subject I could think of which was more personal than his usefulness to Cressida, and asked him whether he still suffered from facial neuralgia as much as he had done in former years, and whether he was therefore dreading London, where the climate used to be so bad for him.

"And is still," he caught me up, "And is still! For me to go to London is martyrdom, *chère Madame*. In New York it is bad enough, but in London it is the *auto de fé*, nothing less. My nervous system is exotic in any country washed by the Atlantic ocean, and it shivers like a little hairless dog from Mexico. It never relaxes. I think I have told you about my favourite city in the middle of Asia, *la sainte Asie*, where the rainfall is absolutely nil, and you are protected on every side by hundreds of metres of warm, dry sand. I was there when I was a child once, and it is still my intention to retire there when I have finished with all this. I would be there now, n-ow-ow," his voice rose querulously, "if Madame Cressida did not imagine that she needs me,—and her fancies, you know," he flourished his hands, "one gives in to them. In humouring her caprices you and I have already played some together."

We were approaching Cressida's deck chairs, ranged under the open windows of her stateroom. She was already recumbent, swathed in lavender scarfs and wearing purple orchids—doubtless from Jerome Brown. At her left, Horace had settled down to a French novel, and Julia Garnet, at her right, was complainingly regarding the grey horizon. On seeing me, Cressida struggled under her fur-lined robes and got to her feet,—which was more than Horace or Miss Julia managed to do. Miss Julia, as I could have foretold, was not pleased. All the Garnets had an awkward manner with me. Whether it was that I reminded them of things they wished to forget, or whether they thought I esteemed Cressida too highly and the rest of them too lightly, I do not know; but my appearance upon their scene always put them greatly on their dignity. After Horace had offered me his chair and Miss Julia had said doubtfully that she thought I was looking rather better than when she last saw me, Cressida took my arm and walked me off toward the stern.

"Do you know, Carrie, I half wondered whether I shouldn't find you here, or in London, because you always turn up at critical moments in my life." She pressed my arm confidentially, and I felt that she was once more wrought up to a new purpose. I told her that I had heard some rumour of her engagement.

"It's quite true, and it's all that it should be," she reassured me. "I'll tell you about it later, and you'll see that it's a real solution. They are against me, of course,—all except Horace. He has been such a comfort."

Horace's support, such as it was, could always be had in exchange for his mother's signature, I suspected. The pale May day had turned bleak and chilly, and we sat down by an open hatchway which emitted warm air from somewhere below. At this close range I studied Cressida's face, and felt reassured of her unabated vitality; the old force of will was still there, and with it her characteristic optimism, the old hope of a "solution."

"You have been in Columbus lately?" she was saying. "No, you needn't tell me about it," with a sigh. "Why is it, Caroline, that there is so little of my life I would be willing to live over again? So little that I can even think of without depression. Yet I've really not such a bad conscience. It may mean that I still belong to the future more than to the past, do you think?"

My assent was not warm enough to fix her attention, and she went on thoughtfully: "Of course, it was a bleak country and a bleak period. But I've sometimes wondered whether the bleakness may not have been in me, too; for it has certainly followed me. There, that is no way to talk!" she drew herself up from a momentary attitude of dejection. "Sea air always lets me down at first. That's why it's so good for me in the end."

"I think Julia always lets you down, too," I said bluntly. "But perhaps that depression works out in the same way."

Cressida laughed. "Julia is rather more depressing than Georgie, isn't she? But it was Julia's turn. I can't come alone, and they've grown to expect it. They haven't, either of them, much else to expect."

At this point the deck steward approached us with a blue envelope. "A wireless for you, Madame Garnet."

Cressida put out her hand with impatience, thanked him graciously, and with every indication of pleasure tore open the blue envelope. "It's from Jerome Brown," she said with some confusion, as she folded the paper small and tucked it between the buttons of her close-fitting gown, "Something he forgot to tell me. How long shall you be in London? Good; I want you to meet him. We shall probably be married there as soon as my engagements are over." She rose. "Now I must write some letters. Keep two places at your table, so that I can slip away from my party and dine with you sometimes."

I walked with her toward her chair, in which Mr. Poppas was now reclining. He indicated his readiness to rise, but she shook her head and entered the door of her deck suite. As she passed him, his eye went over her with assurance until it rested upon the folded bit of blue paper in her corsage. He must have seen the original rectangle in the steward's hand; having found it again, he dropped back between Horace and Miss Julia, whom I think he disliked no more than he did the rest of the world. He liked Julia quite as well as he liked me, and he liked me quite as well as he liked any of the women to whom he would be fitfully agreeable upon the voyage. Once or twice, during each crossing, he did his best and made himself very charming indeed, to keep his hand in,—for the same reason that he kept a dummy keyboard in his stateroom, somewhere down in the bowels of the boat. He practised all the small economies; paid the minimum rate, and never took a deck chair, because, as Horace was usually in the cardroom, he could sit in Horace's.

The three of them lay staring at the swell which was steadily growing heavier. Both men had covered themselves with rugs, after dutifully bundling up Miss Julia. As I walked back and forth on the deck, I was struck by their various degrees of in-expressiveness. Opaque brown eyes, almond-shaped and only half open; wolfish green eyes, close-set and always doing something, with a crooked gleam boring in this direction or in that; watery grey eyes, like the thick edges of broken skylight glass: I would have given a great deal to know what was going on behind each pair of them.

These three were sitting there in a row because they were all woven into the pattern of one large and rather splendid life. Each had a bond, and each had a grievance. If they could have their will, what would they do with the generous, credulous creature who nourished them, I wondered? How deep a humiliation would each egotism exact? They would scarcely have harmed her in fortune or in person (though I think Miss Julia looked forward to the day when Cressida would "break" and could be mourned over),—but the fire at which she warmed herself, the little secret hope,—the illusion, ridiculous or sublime, which kept her going,—that they would have stamped out on the instant, with the whole Garnet pack behind them to make extinction sure. All, except, perhaps, Miletus Poppas. He was a vulture of the vulture race, and he had the beak of one. But I always felt that if ever he had her thus at his mercy,—if ever he came upon the softness that was hidden under so much hardness, the warm credulity under a life so dated and scheduled and "reported" and generally exposed,—he would hold his hand and spare.

The weather grew steadily rougher. Miss Julia at last plucked Poppas by the sleeve and indicated that she wished to be released from her wrappings. When she disappeared, there seemed to be every reason to hope that she might be off the scene for awhile. As Cressida said, if she had not brought Julia, she would have had to bring Georgie, or some other

Garnet. Cressida's family was like that of the unpopular Prince of Wales, of whom, when he died, some wag wrote:

> If it had been his brother,
> Better him than another.
> If it had been his sister,
> No one would have missed her.

Miss Julia was dampening enough, but Miss Georgie was aggressive and intrusive. She was out to prove to the world, and more especially to Ohio, that all the Garnets were as like Cressida as two peas. Both sisters were club-women, social service workers, and directors in musical societies, and they were continually travelling up and down the Middle West to preside at meetings or to deliver addresses. They reminded one of two sombre, bumping electrics, rolling about with no visible means of locomotion, always running out of power and lying beached in some inconvenient spot until they received a check or a suggestion from Cressy. I was only too well acquainted with the strained, anxious expression that the sight of their handwriting brought to Cressida's face when she ran over her morning mail at breakfast. She usually put their letters by to read "when she was feeling up to it" and hastened to open others which might possibly contain something gracious or pleasant. Sometimes these family unburdenings lay about unread for several days. Any other letters would have got themselves lost, but these bulky epistles, never properly fitted to their envelopes, seemed immune to mischance and unfailingly disgorged to Cressida long explanations as to why her sisters had to do and to have certain things precisely upon her account and because she was so much a public personage.

The truth was that all the Garnets, and particularly her two sisters, were consumed by an habitual, bilious, unenterprising envy of Cressy. They never forgot that, no matter what she did for them or how far she dragged them about the world with her, she would never take one of them to live with her in her Tenth Street house in New York. They thought that was the thing they most wanted. But what they wanted, in the last analysis, was to *be* Cressida. For twenty years she had been plunged in struggle; fighting for her life at first, then for a beginning, for growth, and at last for eminence and perfection; fighting in the dark, and afterward in the light,—which, with her bad preparation, and with her uninspired youth already behind her, took even more courage. During those twenty years the Garnets had been comfortable and indolent and vastly self-satisfied; and now they expected Cressida to make them equal sharers in the finer rewards of her struggle. When her brother Buchanan told me he thought Cressida ought "to make herself one of them," he stated the converse of what he meant. They coveted the qualities which had made her success, as well as the benefits which came from it. More than her furs or her fame or her fortune, they wanted her personal effectiveness, her brighter glow and stronger will to live.

"Sometimes," I have heard Cressida say, looking up from a bunch of those sloppily written letters, "sometimes I get discouraged."

For several days the rough weather kept Miss Julia cloistered in Cressida's deck suite with the maid, Luisa, who confided to me that the Signorina Garnet was *"dificile."* After dinner I usually found Cressida unincumbered, as Horace was always in the cardroom and Mr. Poppas either nursed his neuralgia or went through the exercise of making himself interesting to some one of the young women on board. One evening, the third night out, when the sea was comparatively quiet and the sky was full of broken black clouds, silvered by the moon at their ragged edges, Cressida talked to me about Jerome Brown.

I had known each of her former husbands. The first one, Charley Wilton, Horace's father, was my cousin. He was organist in a church in Columbus, and Cressida married him when she was nineteen. He died of tuberculosis two years after Horace was born. Cressida nursed him through a long illness and made the living besides. Her courage during the three years of her first marriage was fine enough to foreshadow her future to any discerning eye, and it had made me feel that she deserved any number of chances at marital happiness. There had, of course, been a particular reason for each subsequent experiment, and a sufficiently alluring promise of success. Her motives, in the case of Jerome Brown, seemed to me more vague and less convincing than those which she had explained to me on former occasions.

"It's nothing hasty," she assured me. "It's been coming on for several years. He has never pushed me, but he was always there—some one to count on. Even when I used to meet him at the Whitings, while I was still singing at the Metropolitan, I always felt that he was different from the others; that if I were in straits of any kind, I could call on him. You can't know what that feeling means to me, Carrie. If you look back, you'll see it's something I've never had."

I admitted that, in so far as I knew, she had never been much addicted to leaning on people.

"I've never had any one to lean on," she said with a short laugh. Then she went on, quite seriously: "Somehow, my relations with people always become business relations in the end. I suppose it's because,—except for a sort of professional personality, which I've had to get, just as I've had to get so many other things,—I've not very much that's personal to give people. I've had to give too much else. I've had to try too hard for people who wouldn't try at all."

"Which," I put in firmly, "has done them no good, and has robbed the people who really cared about you."

"By making me grubby, you mean?"

"By making you anxious and distracted so much of the time; empty."

She nodded mournfully. "Yes, I know. You used to warn me. Well, there's not one of my brothers and sisters who does not feel that I carried off the family success, just as I might have carried off the family silver,—if there'd been any! They take the view that there were just so many prizes in the bag; I reached in and took them, so there were none left for the others. At my age, that's a dismal truth to waken up to." Cressida reached for my hand and held it a moment, as if she needed courage to face the facts in her case. "When one remembers one's first success; how one hoped to go home like a Christmas tree full of presents— How much one learns in a life-time! That year when Horace was a baby and Charley was dying, and I was touring the West with the Williams band, it was my feeling about my own people that made me go at all.

Why I didn't drop myself into one of those muddy rivers, or turn on the gas in one of those dirty hotel rooms, I don't know to this day. At twenty-two you must hope for something more than to be able to bury your husband decently, and what I hoped for was to make my family happy. It was the same afterward in Germany. A young woman must live for human people. Horace wasn't enough. I might have had lovers, of course. I suppose you will say it would have been better if I had."

Though there seemed no need for me to say anything, I murmured that I thought there were more likely to be limits to the rapacity of a lover than to that of a discontented and envious family.

"Well," Cressida gathered herself up, "once I got out from under it all, didn't I? And perhaps, in a milder way, such a release can come again. You were the first person I told when I ran away with Charley, and for a long while you were the only one who knew about Blasius Bouchalka. That time, at least, I shook the Garnets. I wasn't distracted or empty. That time I was all there!"

"Yes," I echoed her, "that time you were all there. It's the greatest possible satisfaction to remember it."

"But even that," she sighed, "was nothing but lawyers and accounts in the end—and a hurt. A hurt that has lasted. I wonder what is the matter with me?"

The matter with Cressida was, that more than any woman I have ever known, she appealed to the acquisitive instinct in men; but this was not easily said, even in the brutal frankness of a long friendship.

We would probably have gone further into the Bouchalka chapter of her life, had not Horace appeared and nervously asked us if we did not wish to take a turn before we went inside. I pleaded indolence, but Cressida rose and disappeared with him. Later I came upon them, standing at the stern above the huddled steerage deck, which was by this time bathed in moonlight, under an almost clear sky. Down there on the silvery floor, little hillocks were scattered about under quilts and shawls; family units, presumably,—male, female, and young. Here and there a black shawl sat alone, nodding. They crouched submissively under the moonlight as if it were a spell. In one of those hillocks a baby was crying, but the sound was faint and thin, a slender protest which aroused no response. Everything was so still that I could hear snatches of the low talk between my friends. Cressida's voice was deep and entreating. She was remonstrating with Horace about his losses at bridge, begging him to keep away from the card-room.

"But what else is there to do on a trip like this, my Lady?" He expostulated, tossing his spark of a cigarette-end over-board. "What is there, now, to do?"

"Oh, Horace!" she murmured, "how can you be so? If I were twenty-two, and a boy, with some one to back me—"

Horace drew his shoulders together and buttoned his top-coat. "Oh, I've not your energy, Mother dear. We make no secret of that. I am as I am. I didn't ask to be born into this charming world."

To this gallant speech Cressida made no answer. She stood with her hand on the rail and her head bent forward, as if she had lost herself in thought. The ends of her scarf, lifted by the breeze, fluttered upward, almost transparent in the argent light. Presently she turned away,—as if she had been alone and were leaving only the night sea behind her,—and walked slowly forward; a strong, solitary figure on the white deck, the smoke-like scarf twisting and climbing and falling back upon itself in the light over her head. She reached the door of her stateroom and disappeared. Yes, she was a Garnet, but she was also Cressida; and she had done what she had done.

II

My first recollections of Cressida Garnet have to do with the Columbus Public Schools; a little girl with sunny brown hair and eager bright eyes, looking anxiously at the teacher and reciting the names and dates of the Presidents: "James Buchanan, 1857–1861; Abraham Lincoln, 1861–1865"; etc. Her family came from North Carolina, and they had that to feel superior about before they had Cressy. The Garnet "look," indeed, though based upon a strong family resemblance, was nothing more than the restless, preoccupied expression of an inflamed sense of importance. The father was a Democrat, in the sense that other men were doctors or lawyers. He scratched up some sort of poor living for his family behind office windows inscribed with the words "Real Estate. Insurance. Investments." But it was his political faith that, in a Republican community, gave him his feeling of eminence and originality. The Garnet children were all in school then, scattered along from the first grade to the ninth. In almost any room of our school building you might chance to enter, you saw the self-conscious little face of one or another of them. They were restrained, uncomfortable children, not frankly boastful, but insinuating, and somehow forever demanding special consideration and holding grudges against teachers and classmates who did not show it them; all but Cressida, who was naturally as sunny and open as a May morning.

It was no wonder that Cressy ran away with young Charley Wilton, who hadn't a shabby thing about him except his health. He was her first music teacher, the choir-master of the church in which she sang. Charley was very handsome; the "romantic" son of an old, impoverished family. He had refused to go into a good business with his uncles and had gone abroad to study music when that was an extravagant and picturesque thing for an Ohio boy to do. His letters home were handed round among the members of his own family and of other families equally conservative. Indeed, Charley and what his mother called "his music" were the romantic expression of a considerable group of people; young cousins and old aunts and quiet-dwelling neighbours, allied by the amity of several generations. Nobody was properly married in our part of Columbus unless Charley Wilton, and no other, played the wedding march. The old ladies of the First Church used to say that he "hovered over the keys like a spirit." At nineteen Cressida was beautiful enough to turn a much harder head than the pale, ethereal one Charley Wilton bent above the organ.

That the chapter which began so gracefully ran on into such a stretch of grim, hard prose, was simply Cressida's relentless bad luck. In her undertakings, in whatever she could lay hold of with her two hands, she was successful; but whatever happened to her was almost sure to be bad. Her family, her husbands, her son, would have crushed any other woman I have ever known. Cressida lived, more than most of us, "for others"; and what she seemed to promote among her beneficiaries was indolence and envy and discord—even dishonesty and turpitude.

Her sisters were fond of saying—at club luncheons—that Cressida had remained "untouched by the breath of scandal," which was not strictly true. There were captious people who objected to her long and close association with Miletus Poppas. Her second husband, Ransome McChord, the foreign representative of the great McChord Harvester Company, whom she married in Germany, had so persistently objected to Poppas that she was eventually forced to choose between them. Any one who knew her well could easily understand why she chose Poppas.

While her actual self was the least changed, the least modified by experience that it would be possible to imagine, there had been, professionally, two Cressida Garnets; the big handsome girl, already a "popular favourite" of the concert stage, who took with her to Germany the raw material of a great voice;—and the accomplished artist who came back. The singer that returned was largely the work of Miletus Poppas. Cressida had at least known what she needed, hunted for it, found it, and held fast to it. After experimenting with a score of teachers and accompanists, she settled down to work her problem out with Poppas. Other coaches came and went—she was always trying new ones—but Poppas survived them all. Cressida was not musically intelligent; she never became so. Who does not remember the countless rehearsals which were necessary before she first sang *Isolde* in Berlin; the disgust of the conductor, the sullenness of the tenor, the rages of the blonde *teufelin*, boiling with the impatience of youth and genius, who sang her *Brangaena*? Everything but her driving power Cressida had to get from the outside.

Poppas was, in his way, quite as incomplete as his pupil. He possessed a great many valuable things for which there is no market; intuitions, discrimination, imagination, a whole twilight world of intentions and shadowy beginnings which were dark to Cressida. I remember that when "Trilby" was published she fell into a fright and said such books ought to be prohibited by law; which gave me an intimation of what their relationship had actually become.

Poppas was indispensable to her. He was like a book in which she had written down more about herself than she could possibly remember—and it was information that she might need at any moment. He was the one person who knew her absolutely and who saw into the bottom of her grief. An artist's saddest secrets are those that have to do with his artistry. Poppas knew all the simple things that were so desperately hard for Cressida, all the difficult things in which she could count on herself; her stupidities and inconsistencies, the chiaroscuro of the voice itself and what could be expected from the mind somewhat mismated with it. He knew where she was sound and where she was mended. With him she could share the depressing knowledge of what a wretchedly faulty thing any productive faculty is.

But if Poppas was necessary to her career, she was his career. By the time Cressida left the Metropolitan Opera Company, Poppas was a rich man. He had always received a retaining fee and a percentage of her salary,—and he was a man of simple habits. Her liberality with Poppas was one of the weapons that Horace and the Garnets used against Cressida, and it was a point in the argument by which they justified to themselves their rapacity. Whatever they didn't get, they told themselves, Poppas would. What they got, therefore, they were only saving from Poppas. The Greek ached a good deal at the general pillage, and Cressida's conciliatory methods with her family made him sarcastic and spiteful. But he had to make terms, somehow, with the Garnets and Horace, and with the husband, if there happened to be one. He sometimes reminded them, when they fell to wrangling, that they must not, after all, overturn the boat under them, and that it would be better to stop just before they drove her wild than just after. As he was the only one among them who understood the sources of her fortune,—and they knew it,—he was able, when it came to a general set-to, to proclaim sanctuary for the goose that laid the golden eggs.

That Poppas had caused the break between Cressida and McChord was another stick her sisters held over her. They pretended to understand perfectly, and were always explaining what they termed her "separation"; but they let Cressida know that it cast a shadow over her family and took a good deal of living down.

A beautiful soundness of body, a seemingly exhaustless vitality, and a certain "squareness" of character as well as of mind, gave Cressida Garnet earning powers that were exceptional even in her lavishly rewarded profession. Managers chose her over the heads of singers much more gifted, because she was so sane, so conscientious, and above all, because she was so sure. Her efficiency was like a beacon to lightly anchored men, and in the intervals between her marriages she had as many suitors as Penelope. Whatever else they saw in her at first, her competency so impressed and delighted them that they gradually lost sight of everything else. Her sterling character was the subject of her story. Once, as she said, she very nearly escaped her destiny. With Blasius Bouchalka she became almost another woman, but not quite. Her "principles," or his lack of them, drove those two apart in the end. It was of Bouchalka that we talked upon that last voyage I ever made with Cressida Garnet, and not of Jerome Brown. She remembered the Bohemian kindly, and since it was the passage in her life to which she most often reverted, it is the one I shall relate here.

III

Late one afternoon in the winter of 189–, Cressida and I were walking in Central Park after the first heavy storm of the year. The snow had been falling thickly all the night before, and all day, until about four o'clock. Then the air grew much warmer and the sky cleared. Overhead it was a soft, rainy blue, and to the west a smoky gold. All around the horizon everything became misty and silvery; even the big, brutal buildings looked like pale violet water-colours on a silver ground. Under the elm trees along the Mall the air was purple as wisterias. The sheep-field, toward Broadway, was smooth and white, with a thin gold wash over it. At five o'clock the carriage came for us, but Cressida sent the driver home to the Tenth Street house with the message that she would dine uptown, and that Horace and Mr. Poppas were not to wait for her. As the horses trotted away we turned up the Mall.

"I won't go indoors this evening for any one," Cressida declared. "Not while the sky is like that. Now we will go back to the laurel wood. They are so black, over the snow, that I could cry for joy. I don't know when I've felt so care-free as I feel tonight. Country winter, country stars—they always make me think of Charley Wilton."

She was singing twice a week, sometimes oftener, at the Metropolitan that season, quite at the flood-tide of her powers, and so enmeshed in operatic routine that to be walking in the park at an unaccustomed hour, unattended by one of the men of her entourage, seemed adventurous. As we strolled along the little paths among the snow banks and the bronze laurel bushes, she kept going back to my poor young cousin, dead so long. "Things happen out of season. That's the worst of living. It was untimely for both of us, and yet," she sighed softly, "since he had to die, I'm not sorry. There was one beautifully happy year, though we were so poor, and it gave him—something! It would have been too hard if he'd had to miss everything." (I remember her simplicity, which never changed any more than winter or Ohio change.) "Yes," she went on, "I always feel very tenderly about Charley. I believe I'd do the same thing right over again, even knowing all that had to come after. If I were nineteen tonight, I'd rather go sleigh-riding with Charley Wilton than anything else I've ever done."

We walked until the procession of carriages on the drive-way, getting people home to dinner, grew thin, and then we went slowly toward the Seventh Avenue gate, still talking of Charley Wilton. We decided to dine at a place not far away, where the only access from the street was a narrow door, like a hole in the wall, between a tobacconist's and a flower shop. Cressida deluded herself into believing that her incognito was more successful in such non-descript places. She was wearing a long sable coat, and a deep fur hat, hung with red cherries, which she had brought from Russia. Her walk had given her a fine colour, and she looked so much a personage that no disguise could have been wholly effective.

The dining-rooms, frescoed with conventional Italian

scenes, were built round a court. The orchestra was playing as we entered and selected our table. It was not a bad orchestra, and we were no sooner seated than the first violin began to speak, to assert itself, as if it were suddenly done with mediocrity.

"We have been recognized," Cressida said complacently. "What a good tone he has, quite unusual. What does he look like?" She sat with her back to the musicians.

The violinist was standing, directing his men with his head and with the beak of his violin. He was a tall, gaunt young man, big-boned and rugged, in skin-tight clothes. His high forehead had a kind of luminous pallour, and his hair was jet black and somewhat stringy. His manner was excited and dramatic. At the end of the number he acknowledged the applause, and Cressida looked at him graciously over her shoulder. He swept her with a brilliant glance and bowed again. Then I noticed his red lips and thick black eyebrows.

"He looks as if he were poor or in trouble," Cressida said. "See how short his sleeves are, and how he mops his face as if the least thing upset him. This is a hard winter for musicians."

The violinist rummaged among some music piled on a chair, turning over the sheets with flurried rapidity, as if he were searching for a lost article of which he was in desperate need. Presently he placed some sheets upon the piano and began vehemently to explain something to the pianist. The pianist stared at the music doubtfully—he was a plump old man with a rosy, bald crown, and his shiny linen and neat tie made him look as if he were on his way to a party. The violinist bent over him, suggesting rhythms with his shoulders and running his bony finger up and down the pages. When he stepped back to his place, I noticed that the other players sat at ease, without raising their instruments.

"He is going to try something unusual," I commented. "It looks as if it might be manuscript."

It was something, at all events, that neither of us had heard before, though it was very much in the manner of the later Russian composers who were just beginning to be heard in New York. The young man made a brilliant dash of it, despite a lagging, scrambling accompaniment by the conservative pianist. This time we both applauded him vigorously and again, as he bowed, he swept us with his eye.

The usual repertory of restaurant music followed, varied by a charming bit from Massenet's "Manon," then little known in this country. After we paid our check, Cressida took out one of her visiting cards and wrote across the top of it: *"We thank you for the unusual music and the pleasure your playing has given us."* She folded the card in the middle, and asked the waiter to give it to the director of the orchestra. Pausing at the door, while the porter dashed out to call a cab, we saw, in the wall mirror, a pair of wild black eyes following us quite despairingly from behind the palms at the other end of the room. Cressida observed as we went out that the young man was probably having a hard struggle. "He never got those clothes here, surely. They were probably made by a country tailor in some little town in Austria. He seemed wild enough to grab at anything, and was trying to make himself heard above the dishes, poor fellow. There are so many like him. I wish I could help them all! I didn't quite have the courage to send him money. His smile, when he bowed to us, was not that of one who would take it, do you think?"

"No," I admitted, "it wasn't. He seemed to be pleading for recognition. I don't think it was money he wanted."

A week later I came upon some curious-looking manuscript songs on the piano in Cressida's music room. The text was in some Slavic tongue with a French translation written underneath. Both the handwriting and the musical script were done in a manner experienced, even distinguished. I was looking at them when Cressida came in.

"Oh, yes!" she exclaimed. "I meant to ask you to try them over. Poppas thinks they are very interesting. They are from that young violinist, you remember,—the one we noticed in the restaurant that evening. He sent them with such a nice letter. His name is Blasius Bouchalka (Boú-kal-ka), a Bohemian."

I sat down at the piano and busied myself with the manuscript, while Cressida dashed off necessary notes and wrote checks in a large square checkbook, six to a page. I supposed her immersed in sumptuary preoccupations when she suddenly looked over her shoulder and said, "Yes, that legend,

Sarka, is the most interesting. Run it through a few times and I'll try it over with you."

There was another, *"Dans les ombres des forêts tristes,"* which I thought quite as beautiful. They were fine songs; very individual, and each had that spontaneity which makes a song seem inevitable and, once for all, "done." The accompaniments were difficult, but not unnecessarily so; they were free from fatuous ingenuity and fine writing.

"I wish he'd indicated his tempi a little more clearly," I remarked as I finished *Sarka* for the third time. "It matters, because he really has something to say. An orchestral accompaniment would be better, I should think."

"Yes, he sent the orchestral arrangement. Poppas has it. It works out beautifully,—so much colour in the instrumentation. The English horn comes in so effectively there," she rose and indicated the passage, "just right with the voice. I've asked him to come next Sunday, so please be here if you can. I want to know what you think of him."

Cressida was always at home to her friends on Sunday afternoon unless she was billed for the evening concert at the Opera House, in which case we were sufficiently advised by the daily press. Bouchalka must have been told to come early, for when I arrived on Sunday, at four, he and Cressida had the music-room quite to themselves and were standing by the piano in earnest conversation. In a few moments they were separated by other early comers, and I led Bouchalka across the hall to the drawing-room. The guests, as they came in, glanced at him curiously. He wore a dark blue suit, soft and rather baggy, with a short coat, and a high double-breasted vest with two rows of buttons coming up to the loops of his black tie. This costume was even more foreign-looking than his skin-tight dress clothes, but it was more becoming. He spoke hurried, elliptical English, and very good French. All his sympathies were French rather than German—the Czecks lean to the one culture or to the other. I found him a fierce, a transfixing talker. His brilliant eyes, his gaunt hands, his white, deeply-lined forehead, all entered into his speech.

I asked him whether he had not recognized Madame Garnet at once when we entered the restaurant that evening more than a week ago.

"*Mais, certainement!* I hear her twice when she sings in the afternoon, and sometimes at night for the last act. I have a friend who buys a ticket for the first part, and he comes out and gives to me his pass-back check, and I return for the last act. That is convenient if I am broke." He explained the trick with amusement but without embarrassment, as if it were a shift that we might any of us be put to.

I told him that I admired his skill with the violin, but his songs much more.

He threw out his red under-lip and frowned. "Oh, I have no instrument! The violin I play from necessity; the flute, the piano, as it happens. For three years now I write all the time, and it spoils the hand for violin."

When the maid brought him his tea, he took both muffins and cakes and told me that he was very hungry. He had to lunch and dine at the place where he played, and he got very tired of the food. "But since," his black eyebrows nearly met in an acute angle, "but since, before, I eat at a bakery, with the slender brown roach on the pie, I guess I better let alone well enough." He paused to drink his tea; as he tasted one of the cakes his face lit with sudden animation and he gazed across the hall after the maid with the tray—she was now holding it before the aged and ossified 'cellist of the Hempfstangle Quartette. "*Des gâteaux,*" he murmured feelingly, "*ou est-ce qu'elle peut trouver de tels gâteaux ici à* New York?"

I explained to him that Madame Garnet had an accomplished cook who made them,—an Austrian, I thought.

He shook his head. "*Austrichienne? Je ne pense pas.*"

Cressida was approaching with the new Spanish soprano, Mme. Bartolas, who was all black velvet and long black feathers, with a lace veil over her rich pallour and even a little black patch on her chin. I beckoned them. "Tell me, Cressida, isn't Ruzenka an Austrian?"

She looked surprised. "No, a Bohemian, though I got her in Vienna." Bouchalka's expression, and the remnant of a cake in his long fingers, gave her the connection. She laughed. "You like them? Of course, they are of your own country. You shall have more of them." She nodded and went away to greet a guest who had just come in.

A few moments later, Horace, then a beautiful lad in Eton

clothes, brought another cup of tea and a plate of cakes for Bouchalka. We sat down in a corner, and talked about his songs. He was neither boastful nor deprecatory. He knew exactly in what respects they were excellent. I decided as I watched his face, that he must be under thirty. The deep lines in his forehead probably came there from his habit of frowning densely when he struggled to express himself, and suddenly elevating his coal-black eyebrows when his ideas cleared. His teeth were white, very irregular and interesting. The corrective methods of modern dentistry would have taken away half his good looks. His mouth would have been much less attractive for any re-arranging of those long, narrow, over-crowded teeth. Along with his frown and his way of thrusting out his lip, they contributed, somehow, to the engaging impetuousness of his conversation. As we talked about his songs, his manner changed. Before that he had seemed responsive and easily pleased. Now he grew abstracted, as if I had taken away his pleasant afternoon and wakened him to his miseries. He moved restlessly in his clothes. When I mentioned Puccini, he held his head in his hands. "Why is it they like that always and always? A little, oh yes, very nice. But so much, always the same thing! Why?" He pierced me with the despairing glance which had followed us out of the restaurant.

I asked him whether he had sent any of his songs to the publishers and named one whom I knew to be discriminating. He shrugged his shoulders. "They not want Bohemian songs. They not want my music. Even the street cars will not stop for me here, like for other people. Every time, I wait on the corner until somebody else make a signal to the car, and then it stop, — but not for me."

Most people cannot become utterly poor; whatever happens, they can right themselves a little. But one felt that Bouchalka was the sort of person who might actually starve or blow his brains out. Something very important had been left out either of his make-up or of his education; something that we are not accustomed to miss in people.

Gradually the parlour was filled with little groups of friends, and I took Bouchalka back to the music-room where Cressida was surrounded by her guests; feathered women, with large sleeves and hats, young men of no importance, in frock coats, with shining hair, and the smile which is intended to say so many flattering things but which really expresses little more than a desire to get on. The older men were standing about waiting for a word *à deux* with the hostess. To these people Bouchalka had nothing to say. He stood stiffly at the outer edge of the circle, watching Cressida with intent, impatient eyes, until, under the pretext of showing him a score, she drew him into the alcove at the back end of the long room, where she kept her musical library. The bookcases ran from the floor to the ceiling. There was a table and a reading-lamp, and a window seat looking upon the little walled garden. Two persons could be quite withdrawn there, and yet be a part of the general friendly scene. Cressida took a score from the shelf, and sat down with Bouchalka upon the window seat, the book open between them, though neither of them looked at it again. They fell to talking with great earnestness. At last the Bohemian pulled out a large, yellowing silver watch, held it up before him, and stared at it a moment as if it were an object of horror. He sprang up, bent over Cressida's hand and murmured something, dashed into the hall and out of the front door without waiting for the maid to open it. He had worn no overcoat, apparently. It was then seven o'clock; he would surely be late at his post in the uptown restaurant. I hoped he would have wit enough to take the elevated.

After supper Cressida told me his story. His parents, both poor musicians,—the mother a singer—died while he was yet a baby, and he was left to the care of an arbitrary uncle who resolved to make a priest of him. He was put into a monastery school and kept there. The organist and choirdirector, fortunately for Blasius, was an excellent musician, a man who had begun his career brilliantly, but who had met with crushing sorrows and disappointments in the world. He devoted himself to his talented pupil, and was the only teacher the young man ever had. At twenty-one, when he was ready for the novitiate, Blasius felt that the call of life was too strong for him, and he ran away out into a world of which he knew nothing. He tramped southward to Vienna, begging and playing his fiddle from town to town. In Vienna he fell in with a gipsy band which was being recruited for a Paris restaurant and went with them to Paris. He played in cafés and in cheap theatres, did transcribing for a music publisher, tried to get pupils. For four years he was the mouse, and hunger was the cat. She kept him on the jump. When he got work he did not understand why; when he lost a job he did not understand why. During the time when most of us acquire a practical sense, get a half-unconscious knowledge of hard facts and market values, he had been shut away from the world, fed like the pigeons in the bell-tower of his monastery. Bouchalka had now been in New York a year, and for all he knew about it, Cressida said, he might have landed the day before yesterday.

Several weeks went by, and as Bouchalka did not reappear on Tenth Street, Cressida and I went once more to the place where he had played, only to find another violinist leading the orchestra. We summoned the proprietor, a Swiss-Italian, polite and solicitous. He told us the gentleman was not playing there any more,—was playing somewhere else, but he had forgotten where. We insisted upon talking to the old pianist, who at last reluctantly admitted that the Bohemian had been dismissed. He had arrived very late one Sunday night three weeks ago, and had hot words with the proprietor. He had been late before, and had been warned. He was a very talented fellow, but wild and not to be depended upon. The old man gave us the address of a French boarding-house on Seventh Avenue where Bouchalka used to room. We drove there at once, but the woman who kept the place said that he had gone away two weeks before, leaving no address, as he never got letters. Another Bohemian, who did engraving on glass, had a room with her, and when he came home perhaps he could tell where Bouchalka was, for they were friends.

It took us several days to run Bouchalka down, but when we did find him Cressida promptly busied herself in his behalf. She sang his *"Sarka"* with the Metropolitan Opera orchestra at a Sunday night concert, she got him a position with the Symphony Orchestra, and persuaded the conservative Hempfstangle Quartette to play one of his chamber compositions from manuscript. She aroused the interest of a publisher in his work, and introduced him to people who were helpful to him.

By the new year Bouchalka was fairly on his feet. He had proper clothes now, and Cressida's friends found him attractive. He was usually at her house on Sunday afternoons; so usually, indeed, that Poppas began pointedly to absent himself. When other guests arrived, the Bohemian and his patroness were always found at the critical point of discussion,—at the piano, by the fire, in the alcove at the end of the room—both of them interested and animated. He was invariably respectful and admiring, deferring to her in every tone and gesture, and she was perceptibly pleased and flattered,—as if all this were new to her and she were tasting the sweetness of a first success.

One wild day in March Cressida burst tempestuously into my apartment and threw herself down, declaring that she had just come from the most trying rehearsal she had ever lived through. When I tried to question her about it, she replied absently and continued to shiver and crouch by the fire. Suddenly she rose, walked to the window, and stood looking out over the Square, glittering with ice and rain and strewn with the wrecks of umbrellas. When she turned again, she approached me with determination.

"I shall have to ask you to go with me," she said firmly. "That crazy Bouchalka has gone and got a pleurisy or something. It may be pneumonia; there is an epidemic of it just now. I've sent Dr. Brooks to him, but I can never tell anything from what a doctor says. I've got to see Bouchalka and his nurse, and what sort of place he's in. I've been rehearsing all day and I'm singing tomorrow night; I can't have so much on my mind. Can you come with me? It will save time in the end."

I put on my furs, and we went down to Cressida's carriage, waiting below. She gave the driver a number on Seventh Avenue, and then began feeling her throat with the alarmed expression which meant that she was not going to talk. We drove in silence to the address, and by this time it was growing dark. The French landlady was a cordial, comfortable person who took Cressida in at a glance and seemed much impressed. Cressida's incognito was never successful. Her black gown was inconspicuous enough, but over it she wore a dark purple velvet carriage coat, lined with fur and furred at the cuffs and collar. The Frenchwoman's eye ran over it delightedly and scrutinized the veil which only half-concealed the well-known face behind it. She insisted upon conducting us up to the fourth floor herself, running ahead of us and turning up the gas jets in the dark, musty-smelling halls. I suspect that she tarried outside the door after we sent the nurse for her walk.

We found the sick man in a great walnut bed, a relic of the better days which this lodging house must have seen. The grimy red plush carpet, the red velvet chairs with broken springs, the double gilt-framed mirror above the mantel, had all been respectable, substantial contributions to comfort in their time. The fireplace was now empty and grateless, and an ill-smelling gas stove burned in its sooty recess under the cracked marble. The huge arched windows were hung with heavy red curtains, pinned together and lightly stirred by the wind which rattled the loose frames.

I was examining these things while Cressida bent over Bouchalka. Her carriage cloak she threw over the foot of his bed, either from a protective impulse, or because there was no place else to put it. After she had greeted him and seated herself, the sick man reached down and drew the cloak up over him, looking at it with weak, childish pleasure and stroking the velvet with his long fingers. *"Couleur de gloire, couleur des reines!"* I heard him murmur. He thrust the sleeve under his chin and closed his eyes. His loud, rapid breathing was the only sound in the room. If Cressida brushed back his hair or touched his hand, he looked up long enough to give her a smile of utter adoration, naïve and uninquiring, as if he were smiling at a dream or a miracle.

The nurse was gone for an hour, and we sat quietly, Cressida with her eyes fixed on Bouchalka, and I absorbed in the strange atmosphere of the house, which seemed to seep in under the door and through the walls. Occasionally we heard a call for *"de l'eau chaude!"* and the heavy trot of a serving woman on the stairs. On the floor below somebody was struggling with Schubert's Marche Militaire on a coarse-toned upright piano. Sometimes, when a door was opened, one could hear a parrot screaming, *"Voilà, voilà, tonnerre!"* The house was built before 1870, as one could tell from windows and mouldings, and the walls were thick. The sounds were not disturbing and Bouchalka was probably used to them.

When the nurse returned and we rose to go, Bouchalka still lay with his cheek on her cloak, and Cressida left it. "It seems to please him," she murmured as we went down the stairs. "I can go home without a wrap. It's not far." I had, of course, to give her my furs, as I was not singing *Donna Anna* tomorrow evening and she was.

After this I was not surprised by any devout attitude in which I happened to find the Bohemian when I entered Cressida's music-room unannounced, or by any radiance on her face when she rose from the window-seat in the alcove and came down the room to greet me.

Bouchalka was, of course, very often at the Opera now. On almost any night when Cressida sang, one could see his narrow black head—high above the temples and rather constrained behind the ears—peering from some part of the house. I used to wonder what he thought of Cressida as an artist, but probably he did not think seriously at all. A great voice, a handsome woman, a great prestige, all added together made a "great artist," the common synonym for success. Her success, and the material evidences of it, quite blinded him. I could never draw from him anything adequate about Anna Straka, Cressida's Slavic rival, and this perhaps meant that he considered comparison disloyal. All the while that Cressida was singing reliably, and satisfying the management, Straka was singing uncertainly and making history. Her voice was primarily defective, and her immediate vocal method was bad. Cressida was always living up to her contract, delivering the whole order in good condition; while the Slav was sometimes almost voiceless, sometimes inspired. She put you off with a hope, a promise, time after time. But she was quite as likely to put you off with a revelation,—with an interpretation that was inimitable, unrepeatable.

Bouchalka was not a reflective person. He had his own idea of what a great prima donna should be like, and he took it for granted that Mme. Garnet corresponded to his conception.

The curious thing was that he managed to impress his idea upon Cressida herself. She began to see herself as he saw her, to try to be like the notion of her that he carried somewhere in that pointed head of his. She was exalted quite beyond herself. Things that had been chilled under the grind came to life in her that winter, with the breath of Bouchalka's adoration. Then, if ever in her life, she heard the bird sing on the branch outside her window; and she wished she were younger, lovelier, freer. She wished there were no Poppas, no Horace, no Garnets. She longed to be only the bewitching creature Bouchalka imagined her.

One April day when we were driving in the Park, Cressida, superb in a green-and-primrose costume hurried over from Paris, turned to me smiling and said: "Do you know, this is the first spring I haven't dreaded. It's the first one I've ever really had. Perhaps people never have more than one, whether it comes early or late." She told me that she was overwhelmingly in love.

Our visit to Bouchalka when he was ill had, of course, been reported, and the men about the Opera House had made of it the only story they have the wit to invent. They could no more change the pattern of that story than the spider could change the design of its web. But being, as she said, "in love" suggested to Cressida only one plan of action; to have the Tenth Street house done over, to put more money into her brothers' business, send Horace to school, raise Poppas' percentage, and then with a clear conscience be married in the Church of the Ascension. She went through this program with her usual thoroughness. She was married in June and sailed immediately with her husband. Poppas was to join them in Vienna in August, when she would begin to work again. From her letters I gathered that all was going well, even beyond her hopes.

When they returned in October, both Cressida and Blasius seemed changed for the better. She was perceptibly freshened and renewed. She attacked her work at once with more vigour and more ease; did not drive herself so relentlessly. A little carelessness became her wonderfully. Bouchalka was less gaunt, and much less flighty and perverse. His frank pleasure in the comfort and order of his wife's establishment was ingratiating, even if it was a little amusing. Cressida had the sewing-room at the top of the house made over into a study for him. When I went up there to see him, I usually found him sitting before the fire or walking about with his hands in his coat pockets, admiring his new possessions. He explained the ingenious arrangement of his study to me a dozen times.

With Cressida's friends and guests, Bouchalka assumed nothing for himself. His deportment amounted to a quiet, unobtrusive appreciation of her and of his good fortune. He was proud to owe his wife so much. Cressida's Sunday afternoons were more popular than ever, since she herself had so much more heart for them. Bouchalka's picturesque presence stimulated her graciousness and charm. One still found them conversing together as eagerly as in the days when they saw each other but seldom. Consequently their guests were never bored. We felt as if the Tenth Street house had a pleasant climate quite its own. In the spring, when the Metropolitan company went on tour, Cressida's husband accompanied her, and afterward they again sailed for Genoa.

During the second winter people began to say that Bouchalka was becoming too thoroughly domesticated, and that since he was growing heavier in body he was less attractive. I noticed his increasing reluctance to stir abroad. Nobody could say that he was "wild" now. He seemed to dread leaving the house, even for an evening. Why should he go out, he said, when he had everything he wanted at home? He published very little. One was given to understand that he was writing an opera. He lived in the Tenth Street house like a tropical plant under glass. Nowhere in New York could he get such cookery as Ruzenka's. Ruzenka ("little Rose") had, like her mistress, bloomed afresh, now that she had a man and a compatriot to cook for. Her invention was tireless, and she took things with a high hand in the kitchen, confident of a perfect appreciation. She was a plump, fair, blue-eyed girl, giggly and easily flattered, with teeth like cream. She was passionately domestic, and her mind was full of homely stories and proverbs and superstitions which she somehow worked into her cookery. She and Bouchalka had between them a whole literature of traditions about sauces and fish and pastry. The cellar was full of the wines he liked, and Ruzenka always knew what wines to serve with the dinner. Blasius' monastery had been famous for good living.

That winter was a very cold one, and I think the even temperature of the house enslaved Bouchalka. "Imagine it," he once said to me when I dropped in during a blinding snowstorm and found him reading before the fire. "To be warm all the time, every day! It is like Aladdin. In Paris I have had weeks together when I was not warm once, when I did not have a bath once, like the cats in the street. The nights were a misery. People have terrible dreams when they are so cold. Here I waken up in the night so warm I do not know what it means. Her door is open, and I turn on my light. I cannot believe in myself until I see that she is there."

I began to think that Bouchalka's wildness had been the desperation which the tamest animals exhibit when they are tortured or terrorized. Naturally luxurious, he had suffered more than most men under the pinch of penury. Those first beautiful compositions, full of the folk-music of his own country, had been wrung out of him by home-sickness and heart-ache. I wondered whether he could compose only under the spur of hunger and loneliness, and whether his talent might not subside with his despair. Some such apprehension must have troubled Cressida, though his gratitude would have been propitiatory to a more exacting task-master. She had always liked to make people happy, and he was the first one who had accepted her bounty without sourness. When he did not accompany her upon her spring tour, Cressida said it was because travelling interfered with composition; but I felt that she was deeply disappointed. Blasius, or Blažej, as his wife had with difficulty learned to call him, was not showy or extravagant. He hated hotels, even the best of them. Cressida had always fought for the hearthstone and the fireside, and the humour of Destiny is sometimes to give us too much of what we desire. I believe she would have preferred even enthusiasm about other women to his utter *oisiveté*. It was his old fire, not his docility, that had won her.

During the third season after her marriage Cressida had only twenty-five performances at the Metropolitan, and she was singing out of town a great deal. Her husband did not bestir himself to accompany her, but he attended, very faithfully, to her correspondence and to her business at home. He had no ambitious schemes to increase her fortune, and he carried out her directions exactly. Nevertheless, Cressida faced her concert tours somewhat grimly, and she seldom talked now about their plans for the future.

The crisis in this growing estrangement came about by accident,—one of those chance occurrences that affect our lives more than years of ordered effort,—and it came in an inverted form of a situation old to comedy. Cressida had been on the road for several weeks; singing in Minneapolis, Cleveland, St. Paul, then up into Canada and back to Boston. From Boston she was to go directly to Chicago, coming down on the five o'clock train and taking the eleven, over the Lake Shore, for the West. By her schedule she would have time to change cars comfortably at the Grand Central station.

On the journey down from Boston she was seized with a great desire to see Blasius. She decided, against her custom, one might say against her principles, to risk a performance with the Chicago orchestra without rehearsal, to stay the night in New York and go west by the afternoon train the next day. She telegraphed Chicago, but she did not telegraph Blasius, because she wished—the old fallacy of affection!—to "surprise" him. She could take it for granted that, at eleven on a cold winter night, he would be in the Tenth Street house and nowhere else in New York. She sent Poppas—paler than usual with accusing scorn—and her trunks on to Chicago, and with only her travelling bag and a sense of being very audacious in her behaviour and still very much in love, she took a cab for Tenth Street.

Since it was her intention to disturb Blasius as little as possible and to delight him as much as possible, she let herself in with her latch-key and went directly to his room. She did not find him there. Indeed, she found him where he should not have been at all. There must have been a trying scene.

Ruzenka was sent away in the morning, and the other two maids as well. By eight o'clock Cressida and Bouchalka had the house to themselves. Nobody had any breakfast. Cressida took the afternoon train to keep her engagement with Theodore Thomas, and to think over the situation. Blasius was left in the Tenth Street house with only the furnace man's wife to look after him. His explanation of his conduct was that he had been drinking too much. His digression, he swore, was casual. It had never occurred before, and he could only appeal to his wife's magnanimity. But it was, on the whole, easier for Cressida to be firm than to be yielding, and she knew herself too well to attempt a readjustment. She had never made shabby compromises, and it was too late for her to begin. When she returned to New York she went to a hotel, and she never saw Bouchalka alone again. Since he admitted her charge, the legal formalities were conducted so quietly that the granting of her divorce was announced in the morning papers before her friends knew that there was the least likelihood of one. Cressida's concert tours had interrupted the hospitalities of the house.

While the lawyers were arranging matters, Bouchalka came to see me. He was remorseful and miserable enough, and I think his perplexity was quite sincere. If there had been an intrigue with a woman of her own class, an infatuation, an affair, he said, he could understand. But anything so venial and accidental— He shook his head slowly back and forth. He assured me that he was not at all himself on that fateful evening, and that when he recovered himself he would have sent Ruzenka away, making proper provision for her, of course. It was an ugly thing, but ugly things sometimes happened in one's life, and one had to put them away and forget them. He could have overlooked any accident that might have occurred when his wife was on the road, with Poppas, for example. I cut him short, and he bent his head to my reproof.

"I know," he said, "such things are different with her. But when have I said that I am noble as she is? Never. But I have appreciated and I have adored. About me, say what you like. But if you say that in this there was any *méprise* to my wife, that is not true. I have lost all my place here. I came in from the streets; but I understand her, and all the fine things in her, better than any of you here. If that accident had not been, she would have lived happy with me for years. As for me, I have never believed in this happiness. I was not born under a good star. How did it come? By accident. It goes by accident. She tried to give good fortune to an unfortunate man, *un misé-rable*; that was her mistake. It cannot be done in this world. The lucky should marry the lucky." Bouchalka stopped and lit a cigarette. He sat sunk in my chair as if he never meant to get up again. His large hands, now so much plumper than when I first knew him, hung limp. When he had consumed his cigarette he turned to me again.

"I, too, have tried. Have I so much as written one note to a lady since she first put out her hand to help me? Some of the artists who sing my compositions have been quite willing to plague my wife a little if I make the least sign. With the Española, for instance, I have had to be very stern, *farouche*; she is so very playful. I have never given my wife the slightest annoyance of this kind. Since I married her, I have not kissed the cheek of one lady! Then one night I am bored and drink too much champagne and I become a fool. What does it matter? Did my wife marry the fool of me? No, she married me, with my mind and my feelings all here, as I am today. But she is getting a divorce from the fool of me, which she would never see *anyhow*! The stupidity which, excuse me, is the thing she will not overlook. Even in her memory of me she will be harsh."

His view of his conduct and its consequences was fatalistic: he was meant to have just so much misery every day of his life; for three years it had been withheld, had been piling up somewhere, underground, overhead; now the accumulation burst over him. He had come to pay his respects to me, he said, to declare his undying gratitude to Madame Garnet, and to bid me farewell. He took up his hat and cane and kissed my hand. I have never seen him since. Cressida made a settlement upon him, but even Poppas, tortured by envy and curiosity, never discovered how much it was. It was very little, she told me. *"Pour des gâteaux,"* she added with a smile that was not unforgiving. She could not bear to think of his being in want when so little could make him comfortable.

He went back to his own village in Bohemia. He wrote her that the old monk, his teacher, was still alive, and that from the windows of his room in the town he could see the pigeons flying forth from and back to the monastery bell-tower all day long. He sent her a song, with his own words, about those pigeons,—quite a lovely thing. He was the bell tower, and *les colombes* were his memories of her.

IV

Jerome Brown proved, on the whole, the worst of Cressida's husbands, and, with the possible exception of her eldest brother, Buchanan Garnet, he was the most rapacious of the men with whom she had had to do. It was one thing to gratify every wish of a cake-loving fellow like Bouchalka, but quite another to stand behind a financier. And Brown would be a financier or nothing. After her marriage with him, Cressida grew rapidly older. For the first time in her life she wanted to go abroad and live—to get Jerome Brown away from the scene of his unsuccessful but undiscouraged activities. But Brown was not a man who could be amused and kept out of mischief in Continental hotels. He had to be a figure, if only a "mark," in Wall street. Nothing else would gratify his peculiar vanity. The deeper he went in, the more affectionately he told Cressida that now all her cares and anxieties were over. To try to get related facts out of his optimism was like trying to find framework in a feather bed. All Cressida knew was that she was perpetually "investing" to save investments. When she told me she had put a mortgage on the Tenth Street house, her eyes filled with tears. "Why is it? I have never cared about money, except to make people happy with it, and it has been the curse of my life. It has spoiled all my relations with people. Fortunately," she added irrelevantly, drying her eyes, "Jerome and Poppas get along well." Jerome could have got along with anybody; that is a promoter's business. His warm hand, his flushed face, his bright eye, and his newest funny story,—Poppas had no weapons that could do execution with a man like that.

Though Brown's ventures never came home, there was nothing openly disastrous until the outbreak of the revolution in Mexico jeopardized his interests there. Then Cressida went to England—where she could always raise money from a faithful public—for a winter concert tour. When she sailed, her friends knew that her husband's affairs were in a bad way; but we did not know how bad until after Cressida's death.

Cressida Garnet, as all the world knows, was lost on the *Titanic*. Poppas and Horace, who had been travelling with her, were sent on a week earlier and came as safely to port as if they had never stepped out of their London hotel. But Cressida had waited for the first trip of the sea monster—she still believed that all advertising was good—and she went down on the road between the old world and the new. She had been ill, and when the collision occurred she was in her stateroom, a modest one somewhere down in the boat, for she was travelling economically. Apparently she never left her cabin. She was not seen on the decks, and none of the survivors brought any word of her.

On Monday, when the wireless messages were coming from the *Carpathia* with the names of the passengers who had been saved, I went, with so many hundred others, down to the White Star offices. There I saw Cressida's motor, her redoubtable initials on the door, with four men sitting in the limousine. Jerome Brown, stripped of the promoter's joviality and looking flabby and old, sat behind with Buchanan Garnet, who had come on from Ohio. I had not seen him for years. He was now an old man, but he was still conscious of being in the public eye, and sat turning a cigar about in his face with that foolish look of importance which Cressida's achievement had stamped upon all the Garnets. Poppas was in front, with Horace. He was gnawing the finger of his chamois glove as it rested on the top of his cane. His head was sunk, his shoulders drawn together; he looked as old as Jewry. I watched them, wondering whether Cressida would come back to them if she could. After the last names were posted, the four men settled back into the powerful car—one of the best made—and the chauffeur backed off. I saw him dash away the tears from his face with the back of his driving glove. He was an Irish boy, and had been devoted to Cressida.

When the will was read, Henry Gilbert, the lawyer, an old friend of her early youth, and I, were named executors. A nice job we had of it. Most of her large fortune had been converted into stocks that were almost worthless. The marketable property realized only a hundred and fifty thousand dollars.

To defeat the bequest of fifty thousand dollars to Poppas,
Jerome Brown and her family contested the will. They brought
Cressida's letters into court to prove that the will did not rep-
resent her intentions, often expressed in writing through
many years, to "provide well" for them.

Such letters they were! The writing of a tired, overdriven
woman; promising money, sending money herewith, asking
for an acknowledgment of the draft sent last month, etc. In
the letters to Jerome Brown she begged for information about
his affairs and entreated him to go with her to some foreign
city where they could live quietly and where she could rest; if
they were careful, there would "be enough for all." Neither
Brown nor her brothers and sisters had any sense of shame
about these letters. It seemed never to occur to them that this
golden stream, whether it rushed or whether it trickled, came
out of the industry, out of the mortal body of a woman. They
regarded her as a natural source of wealth; a copper vein, a
diamond mine.

Henry Gilbert is a good lawyer himself, and he employed
an able man to defend the will. We determined that in this
crisis we would stand by Poppas, believing it would be Cres-
sida's wish. Out of the lot of them, he was the only one who
had helped her to make one penny of the money that had
brought her so much misery. He was at least more deserving
than the others. We saw to it that Poppas got his fifty thou-
sand, and he actually departed, at last, for his city in *la sainte
Asie*, where it never rains and where he will never again have
to hold a hot water bottle to his face.

The rest of the property was fought for to a finish. Poppas
out of the way, Horace and Brown and the Garnets quar-
relled over her personal effects. They went from floor to floor
of the Tenth Street house. The will provided that Cressida's
jewels and furs and gowns were to go to her sisters. Georgie
and Julia wrangled over them down to the last moleskin. They
were deeply disappointed that some of the muffs and stoles
which they remembered as very large, proved, when exhumed
from storage and exhibited beside furs of a modern cut, to be
ridiculously scant. A year ago the sisters were still reasoning
with each other about pearls and opals and emeralds.

I wrote Poppas some account of these horrors, as during

the court proceedings we had become rather better friends than of old. His reply arrived only a few days ago; a photograph of himself upon a camel, under which is written:

> *Traulich und Treu*
> *ist's nur in der Tiefe:*
> *falsch und feig*
> *ist was dort oben sich freut!*

His reply, and the memories it awakens—memories which have followed Poppas into the middle of Asia, seemingly,—prompted this informal narration.

A Gold Slipper

MARSHALL McKANN followed his wife and her friend Mrs. Post down the aisle and up the steps to the stage of the Carnegie Music Hall with an ill-concealed feeling of grievance. Heaven knew he never went to concerts, and to be mounted upon the stage in this fashion, as if he were a "high-brow" from Sewickley, or some unfortunate with a musical wife, was ludicrous. A man went to concerts when he was courting, while he was a junior partner. When he became a person of substance he stopped that sort of nonsense. His wife, too, was a sensible person, the daughter of an old Pittsburgh family as solid and well-rooted as the McKanns. She would never have bothered him about this concert had not the meddlesome Mrs. Post arrived to pay her a visit. Mrs. Post was an old school friend of Mrs. McKann, and because she lived in Cincinnati she was always keeping up with the world and talking about things in which no one else was interested, music among them. She was an aggressive lady, with weighty opinions, and a deep voice like a jovial bassoon. She had arrived only last night, and at dinner she brought it out that she could on no account miss Kitty Ayrshire's recital; it was, she said, the sort of thing no one could afford to miss.

When McKann went into town in the morning he found that every seat in the music-hall was sold. He telephoned his wife to that effect, and, thinking he had settled the matter, made his reservation on the 11.25 train for New York. He was unable to get a drawing-room because this same Kitty Ayrshire had taken the last one. He had not intended going to New York until the following week, but he preferred to be absent during Mrs. Post's incumbency.

In the middle of the morning, when he was deep in his correspondence, his wife called him up to say the enterprising Mrs. Post had telephoned some musical friends in Sewickley and had found that two hundred folding-chairs were to be placed on the stage of the concert-hall, behind the piano, and that they would be on sale at noon. Would he please get seats in the front row? McKann asked if they would not excuse

433

him, since he was going over to New York on the late train, would be tired, and would not have time to dress, etc. No, not at all. It would be foolish for two women to trail up to the stage unattended. Mrs. Post's husband always accompanied her to concerts, and she expected that much attention from her host. He needn't dress, and he could take a taxi from the concert-hall to the East Liberty station.

The outcome of it all was that, though his bag was at the station, here was McKann, in the worst possible humour, facing the large audience to which he was well known, and sitting among a lot of music students and excitable old maids. Only the desperately zealous or the morbidly curious would endure two hours in those wooden chairs, and he sat in the front row of this hectic body, somehow made a party to a transaction for which he had the utmost contempt.

When McKann had been in Paris, Kitty Ayrshire was singing at the Comique, and he wouldn't go to hear her—even there, where one found so little that was better to do. She was too much talked about, too much advertised; always being thrust in an American's face as if she were something to be proud of. Perfumes and petticoats and cutlets were named for her. Some one had pointed Kitty out to him one afternoon when she was driving in the Bois with a French composer— old enough, he judged, to be her father—who was said to be infatuated, carried away by her. McKann was told that this was one of the historic passions of old age. He had looked at her on that occasion, but she was so befrilled and befeathered that he caught nothing but a graceful outline and a small, dark head above a white ostrich boa. He had noted with disgust, however, the stooped shoulders and white imperial of the silk-hatted man beside her, and the senescent line of his back. McKann described to his wife this unpleasing picture only last night, while he was undressing, when he was making every possible effort to avert this concert party. But Bessie only looked superior and said she wished to hear Kitty Ayrshire sing, and that her "private life" was something in which she had no interest.

Well, here he was; hot and uncomfortable, in a chair much too small for him, with a row of blinding footlights glaring in his eyes. Suddenly the door at his right elbow opened. Their seats were at one end of the front row; he had thought they would be less conspicuous there than in the centre, and he had not foreseen that the singer would walk over him every time she came upon the stage. Her velvet train brushed against his trousers as she passed him. The applause which greeted her was neither overwhelming nor prolonged. Her conservative audience did not know exactly how to accept her toilette. They were accustomed to dignified concert gowns, like those which Pittsburgh matrons (in those days!) wore at their daughters' coming-out teas.

Kitty's gown that evening was really quite outrageous—the repartée of a conscienceless Parisian designer who took her hint that she wished something that would be entirely novel in the States. Today, after we have all of us, even in the uttermost provinces, been educated by Bakst and the various Ballets Russes, we would accept such a gown without distrust; but then it was a little disconcerting, even to the well-disposed. It was constructed of a yard or two of green velvet—a reviling, shrieking green which would have made a fright of any woman who had not inextinguishable beauty—and it was made without armholes, a device to which we were then so unaccustomed that it was nothing less than alarming. The velvet skirt split back from a transparent gold-lace petticoat, gold stockings, gold slippers. The narrow train was, apparently, looped to both ankles, and it kept curling about her feet like a serpent's tail, turning up its gold lining as if it were squirming over on its back. It was not, we felt, a costume in which to sing Mozart and Handel and Beethoven.

Kitty sensed the chill in the air, and it amused her. She liked to be thought a brilliant artist by other artists, but by the world at large she liked to be thought a daring creature. She had every reason to believe, from experience and from example, that to shock the great crowd was the surest way to get its money and to make her name a household word. Nobody ever became a household word of being an artist, surely; and you were not a thoroughly paying proposition until your name meant something on the sidewalk and in the barber-shop. Kitty studied her audience with an appraising eye. She liked the stimulus of this disapproval. As she faced this hard-shelled public she felt keen and interested; she knew that she would give such a recital as cannot often be heard for money. She nodded gaily to the young man at the piano, fell into an attitude of seriousness, and began the group of Beethoven and Mozart songs.

Though McKann would not have admitted it, there were really a great many people in the concert-hall who knew what the prodigal daughter of their country was singing, and how well she was doing it. They thawed gradually under the beauty of her voice and the subtlety of her interpretation. She had sung seldom in concert then, and they had supposed her very dependent upon the accessories of the opera. Clean singing, finished artistry, were not what they expected from her. They began to feel, even, the wayward charm of her personality.

McKann, who stared coldly up at the balconies during her first song, during the second glanced cautiously at the green apparition before him. He was vexed with her for having retained a débutante figure. He comfortably classed all singers—especially operatic singers—as "fat Dutchwomen" or "shifty Sadies," and Kitty would not fit into his clever generalization. She displayed, under his nose, the only kind of figure he considered worth looking at—that of a very young girl, supple and sinuous and quick-silverish; thin, eager shoulders, polished white arms that were nowhere too fat and nowhere too thin. McKann found it agreeable to look at Kitty, but when he saw that the authoritative Mrs. Post, red as a turkey-cock with opinions she was bursting to impart, was studying and appraising the singer through her lorgnette, he gazed indifferently out into the house again. He felt for his watch, but his wife touched him warningly with her elbow—which, he noticed, was not at all like Kitty's.

When Miss Ayrshire finished her first group of songs, her audience expressed its approval positively, but guardedly. She smiled bewitchingly upon the people in front, glanced up at the balconies, and then turned to the company huddled on the stage behind her. After her gay and careless bows, she retreated toward the stage door. As she passed McKann, she again brushed lightly against him, and this time she paused long enough to glance down at him and murmur, "Pardon!"

In the moment her bright, curious eyes rested upon him, McKann seemed to see himself as if she were holding a mirror up before him. He beheld himself a heavy, solid figure, unsuitably clad for the time and place, with a florid, square face, well-visored with good living and sane opinions—an inexpressive countenance. Not a rock face, exactly, but a kind of pressed-brick-and-cement face, a "business" face upon which years and feelings had made no mark—in which cocktails might eventually blast out a few hollows. He had never seen himself so distinctly in his shaving-glass as he did in that instant when Kitty Ayrshire's liquid eye held him, when her bright, inquiring glance roamed over his person. After her prehensile train curled over his boot and she was gone, his wife turned to him and said in the tone of approbation one uses when an infant manifests its groping intelligence, "Very gracious of her, I'm sure!" Mrs. Post nodded oracularly. McKann grunted.

Kitty began her second number, a group of romantic German songs which were altogether more her affair than her first number. When she turned once to acknowledge the applause behind her, she caught McKann in the act of yawning behind his hand—he of course wore no gloves—and he thought she frowned a little. This did not embarrass him; it somehow made him feel important. When she retired after the second part of the program, she again looked him over curiously as she passed, and she took marked precaution that her dress did not touch him. Mrs. Post and his wife again commented upon her consideration.

The final number was made up of modern French songs which Kitty sang enchantingly, and at last her frigid public was thoroughly aroused. While she was coming back again and again to smile and curtsy, McKann whispered to his wife that if there were to be encores he had better make a dash for his train.

"Not at all," put in Mrs. Post. "Kitty is going on the same train. She sings in *Faust* at the opera tomorrow night, so she'll take no chances."

McKann once more told himself how sorry he felt for Post. At last Miss Ayrshire returned, escorted by her accompanist, and gave the people what she of course knew they wanted:

the most popular aria from the French opera of which the title-rôle had become synonymous with her name—an opera written for her and to her and round about her, by the veteran French composer who adored her,—the last and not the palest flash of his creative fire. This brought her audience all the way. They clamoured for more of it, but she was not to be coerced. She had been unyielding through storms to which this was a summer breeze. She came on once more, shrugged her shoulders, blew them a kiss, and was gone. Her last smile was for that uncomfortable part of her audience seated behind her, and she looked with recognition at McKann and his ladies as she nodded good night to the wooden chairs.

McKann hurried his charges into the foyer by the nearest exit and put them into his motor. Then he went over to the Schenley to have a glass of beer and a rarebit before traintime. He had not, he admitted to himself, been so much bored as he pretended. The minx herself was well enough, but it was absurd in his fellow-townsmen to look owlish and uplifted about her. He had no rooted dislike for pretty women; he even didn't deny that gay girls had their place in the world, but they ought to be kept in their place. He was born a Presbyterian, just as he was born a McKann. He sat in his pew in the First Church every Sunday, and he never missed a presbytery meeting when he was in town. His religion was not very spiritual, certainly, but it was substantial and concrete, made up of good, hard convictions and opinions. It had something to do with citizenship, with whom one ought to marry, with the coal business (in which his own name was powerful), with the Republican party, and with all majorities and established precedents. He was hostile to fads, to enthusiasms, to individualism, to all changes except in mining machinery and in methods of transportation.

His equanimity restored by his lunch at the Schenley, McKann lit a big cigar, got into his taxi, and bowled off through the sleet.

There was not a sound to be heard or a light to be seen. The ice glittered on the pavement and on the naked trees. No restless feet were abroad. At eleven o'clock the rows of small, comfortable houses looked as empty of the troublesome bubble of life as the Allegheny cemetery itself. Suddenly the cab stopped, and McKann thrust his head out of the window. A woman was standing in the middle of the street addressing his driver in a tone of excitement. Over against the curb a lone electric stood despondent in the storm. The young woman, her cloak blowing about her, turned from the driver to Mc-Kann himself, speaking rapidly and somewhat incoherently.

"Could you not be so kind as to help us? It is Mees Ayrshire, the singer. The juice is gone out and we cannot move. We must get to the station. Mademoiselle cannot miss the train; she sings tomorrow night in New York. It is very important. Could you not take us to the station at East Liberty?"

McKann opened the door. "That's all right, but you'll have to hurry. It's eleven-ten now. You've only got fifteen minutes to make the train. Tell her to come along."

The maid drew back and looked up at him in amazement. "But, the hand-luggage to carry, and Mademoiselle to walk! The street is like glass!"

McKann threw away his cigar and followed her. He stood silent by the door of the derelict, while the maid explained that she had found help. The driver had gone off somewhere to telephone for a car. Miss Ayrshire seemed not at all apprehensive; she had not doubted that a rescuer would be forthcoming. She moved deliberately; out of a whirl of skirts she thrust one fur-topped shoe—McKann saw the flash of the gold stocking above it—and alighted.

"So kind of you! So fortunate for us!" she murmured. One hand she placed upon his sleeve, and in the other she carried an armful of roses that had been sent up to the concert stage. The petals showered upon the sooty, sleety pavement as she picked her way along. They would be lying there tomorrow morning, and the children in those houses would wonder if there had been a funeral. The maid followed with two leather bags. As soon as he had lifted Kitty into his cab she exclaimed:

"My jewel-case! I have forgotten it. It is on the back seat, please. I am so careless!"

He dashed back, ran his hand along the cushions, and discovered a small leather bag. When he returned he found the maid and the luggage bestowed on the front seat, and a place left for him on the back seat beside Kitty and her flowers.

"Shall we be taking you far out of your way?" she asked sweetly. "I haven't an idea where the station is. I'm not even sure about the name. Céline thinks it is East Liberty, but I think it is West Liberty. An odd name, anyway. It is a Bohemian quarter, perhaps? A district where the law relaxes a trifle?"

McKann replied grimly that he didn't think the name referred to that kind of liberty.

"So much the better," sighed Kitty. "I am a Californian; that's the only part of America I know very well, and out there, when we called a place Liberty Hill or Liberty Hollow—well, we meant it. You will excuse me if I'm uncommunicative, won't you? I must not talk in this raw air. My throat is sensitive after a long program." She lay back in her corner and closed her eyes.

When the cab rolled down the incline at East Liberty station, the New York express was whistling in. A porter opened the door. McKann sprang out, gave him a claim check and his Pullman ticket, and told him to get his bag at the check-stand and rush it on that train.

Miss Ayrshire, having gathered up her flowers, put out her hand to take his arm. "Why, it's you!" she exclaimed, as she saw his face in the light. "What a coincidence!" She made no further move to alight, but sat smiling as if she had just seated herself in a drawing-room and were ready for talk and a cup of tea.

McKann caught her arm. "You must hurry, Miss Ayrshire, if you mean to catch that train. It stops here only a moment. Can you run?"

"Can I run!" she laughed. "Try me!"

As they raced through the tunnel and up the inside stairway, McKann admitted that he had never before made a dash with feet so quick and sure stepping out beside him. The white-furred boots chased each other like lambs at play, the gold stockings flashed like the spokes of a bicycle wheel in the sun. They reached the door of Miss Ayrshire's state-room just as the train began to pull out. McKann was ashamed of the way he was panting, for Kitty's breathing was as soft and regular as when she was reclining on the back seat of his taxi. It had somehow run in his head that all these stage women were a poor lot physically—unsound, overfed creatures, like canaries that are kept in a cage and stuffed with song-restorer. He retreated to escape her thanks. "Good night! Pleasant journey! Pleasant dreams!" With a friendly nod in Kitty's direction he closed the door behind him.

He was somewhat surprised to find his own bag, his Pullman ticket in the strap, on the seat just outside Kitty's door. But there was nothing strange about it. He had got the last section left on the train, No. 13, next the drawing-room. Every other berth in the car was made up. He was just starting to look for the porter when the door of the state-room opened and Kitty Ayrshire came out. She seated herself carelessly in the front seat beside his bag.

"Please talk to me a little," she said coaxingly. "I'm always wakeful after I sing, and I have to hunt some one to talk to. Céline and I get so tired of each other. We can speak very low, and we shall not disturb any one." She crossed her feet and rested her elbow on his Gladstone. Though she still wore her gold slippers and stockings, she did not, he thanked Heaven, have on her concert gown, but a very demure black velvet with some sort of pearl trimming about the neck. "Wasn't it funny," she proceeded, "that it happened to be you who picked me up? I wanted a word with you, anyway."

McKann smiled in a way that meant he wasn't being taken in. "Did you? We are not very old acquaintances."

"No, perhaps not. But you disapproved tonight, and I thought I was singing very well. You are very critical in such matters?"

He had been standing, but now he sat down. "My dear young lady, I am not critical at all. I know nothing about 'such matters.'"

"And care less?" she said for him. "Well, then we know where we are, in so far as that is concerned. What did displease you? My gown, perhaps? It may seem a little *outré* here, but it's the sort of thing all the imaginative designers abroad are doing. You like the English sort of concert gown better?"

"About gowns," said McKann, "I know even less than about music. If I looked uncomfortable, it was probably because I was uncomfortable. The seats were bad and the lights were annoying."

Kitty looked up with solicitude. "I was sorry they sold those seats. I don't like to make people uncomfortable in any way. Did the lights give you a headache? They are very trying. They burn one's eyes out in the end, I believe." She paused and waved the porter away with a smile as he came toward them. Half-clad Pittsburghers were tramping up and down the aisle, casting sidelong glances at McKann and his companion. "How much better they look with all their clothes on," she murmured. Then, turning directly to McKann again: "I saw you were not well seated, but I felt something quite hostile and personal. You were displeased with me. Doubtless many people are, but I seldom get an opportunity to question them. It would be nice if you took the trouble to tell me why you were displeased."

She spoke frankly, pleasantly, without a shadow of challenge or hauteur. She did not seem to be angling for compliments. McKann settled himself in his seat. He thought he would try her out. She had come for it, and he would let her have it. He found, however, that it was harder to formulate the grounds of his disapproval than he would have supposed. Now that he sat face to face with her, now that she was leaning against his bag, he had no wish to hurt her.

"I'm a hard-headed business man," he said evasively, "and I don't much believe in any of you fluffy-ruffles people. I have a sort of natural distrust of them all, the men more than the women."

She looked thoughtful. "Artists, you mean?" drawing her words slowly. "What is your business?"

"Coal."

"I don't feel any natural distrust of business men, and I know ever so many. I don't know any coal-men, but I think I could become very much interested in coal. Am I larger-minded than you?"

McKann laughed. "I don't think you know when you are interested or when you are not. I don't believe you know what it feels like to be really interested. There is so much fake about your profession. It's an affectation on both sides. I know a great many of the people who went to hear you tonight, and I know that most of them neither know nor care anything about music. They imagine they do, because it's supposed to be the proper thing."

Kitty sat upright and looked interested. She was certainly a lovely creature—the only one of her tribe he had ever seen that he would cross the street to see again. Those were remarkable eyes she had—curious, penetrating, restless, somewhat impudent, but not at all dulled by self-conceit.

"But isn't that so in everything?" she cried. "How many of your clerks are honest because of a fine, individual sense of honour? They are honest because it is the accepted rule of good conduct in business. Do you know"—she looked at him squarely—"I thought you would have something quite definite to say to me; but this is funny-paper stuff, the sort of objection I'd expect from your office-boy."

"Then you don't think it silly for a lot of people to get together and pretend to enjoy something they know nothing about?"

"Of course I think it silly, but that's the way God made audiences. Don't people go to church in exactly the same way? If there were a spiritual-pressure test-machine at the door, I suspect not many of you would get to your pews."

"How do you know I go to church?"

She shrugged her shoulders. "Oh, people with these old, ready-made opinions usually go to church. But you can't evade me like that." She tapped the edge of his seat with the toe of her gold slipper. "You sat there all evening, glaring at me as if you could eat me alive. Now I give you a chance to state your objections, and you merely criticize my audience. What is it? Is it merely that you happen to dislike my personality? In that case, of course, I won't press you."

"No," McKann frowned, "I perhaps dislike your professional personality. As I told you, I have a natural distrust of your variety."

"Natural, I wonder?" Kitty murmured. "I don't see why you should naturally dislike singers any more than I naturally dislike coal-men. I don't classify people by their occupations. Doubtless I should find some coal-men repulsive, and you may find some singers so. But I have reason to believe that, at least, I'm one of the less repellent."

"I don't doubt it," McKann laughed, "and you're a shrewd woman to boot. But you are, all of you, according to my standards, light people. You're brilliant, some of you, but you've no depth."

Kitty seemed to assent, with a dive of her girlish head. "Well, it's a merit in some things to be heavy, and in others to be light. Some things are meant to go deep, and others to go high. Do you want all the women in the world to be profound?"

"You are all," he went on steadily, watching her with indulgence, "fed on hectic emotions. You are pampered. You don't help to carry the burdens of the world. You are self-indulgent and appetent."

"Yes, I am," she assented, with a candour which he did not expect. "Not all artists are, but I am. Why not? If I could once get a convincing statement as to why I should not be self-indulgent, I might change my ways. As for the burdens of the world—" Kitty rested her chin on her clasped hands and looked thoughtful. "One should give pleasure to others. My dear sir, granting that the great majority of people can't enjoy anything very keenly, you'll admit that I give pleasure to many more people than you do. One should help others who are less fortunate; at present I am supporting just eight people, besides those I hire. There was never another family in California that had so many cripples and hard-luckers as that into which I had the honour to be born. The only ones who could take care of themselves were ruined by the San Francisco earthquake some time ago. One should make personal sacrifices. I do; I give money and time and effort to talented students. Oh, I give something much more than that! something that you probably have never given to any one. I give, to the really gifted ones, my *wish*, my desire, my light, if I have any; and that, Mr. Worldly Wiseman, is like giving one's blood! It's the kind of thing you prudent people never give. That is what was in the box of precious ointment." Kitty threw off her fervour with a slight gesture, as if it were a scarf, and leaned back, tucking her slipper up on the edge of his seat. "If you saw the houses I keep up," she sighed, "and the people I employ, and the motor-cars I run— And, after all, I've only this to do it with." She indicated her slender person, which Marshall could almost have broken in two with his bare hands.

She was, he thought, very much like any other charming woman, except that she was more so. Her familiarity was natural and simple. She was at ease because she was not afraid of him or of herself, or of certain half-clad acquaintances of his who had been wandering up and down the car oftener than was necessary. Well, he was not afraid, either.

Kitty put her arms over her head and sighed again, feeling the smooth part in her black hair. Her head was small—capable of great agitation, like a bird's; or of great resignation, like a nun's. "I can't see why I shouldn't be self-indulgent, when I indulge others. I can't understand your equivocal scheme of ethics. Now I can understand Count Tolstoy's, perfectly. I had a long talk with him once, about his book 'What is Art?' As nearly as I could get it, he believes that we are a race who can exist only by gratifying appetites; the appetites are evil, and the existence they carry on is evil. We were always sad, he says, without knowing why; even in the Stone Age. In some miraculous way a divine ideal was disclosed to us, directly at variance with our appetites. It gave us a new craving, which we could only satisfy by starving all the other hungers in us. Happiness lies in ceasing to be and to cause being, because the thing revealed to us is dearer than any existence our appetites can ever get for us. I can understand that. It's something one often feels in art. It is even the subject of the greatest of all operas, which, because I can never hope to sing it, I love more than all the others." Kitty pulled herself up. "Perhaps you agree with Tolstoy?" she added languidly.

"No; I think he's a crank," said McKann, cheerfully.

"What do you mean by a crank?"

"I mean an extremist."

Kitty laughed. "Weighty word! You'll always have a world full of people who keep to the golden mean. Why bother yourself about me and Tolstoy?"

"I don't, except when you bother me."

"Poor man! It's true this isn't your fault. Still, you did provoke it by glaring at me. Why did you go to the concert?"

"I was dragged."

"I might have known!" she chuckled, and shook her head.

"No, you don't give me any good reasons. Your morality seems to me the compromise of cowardice, apologetic and sneaking. When righteousness becomes alive and burning, you hate it as much as you do beauty. You want a little of each in your life, perhaps—adulterated, sterilized, with the sting taken out. It's true enough they are both fearsome things when they get loose in the world; they don't, often."

McKann hated tall talk. "My views on women," he said slowly, "are simple."

"Doubtless," Kitty responded dryly, "but are they consistent? Do you apply them to your stenographers as well as to me? I take it for granted you have unmarried stenographers. Their position, economically, is the same as mine."

McKann studied the toe of her shoe. "With a woman, everything comes back to one thing." His manner was judicial.

She laughed indulgently. "So we are getting down to brass tacks, eh? I have beaten you in argument, and now you are leading trumps." She put her hands behind her head and her lips parted in a half-yawn. "Does everything come back to one thing? I wish I knew! It's more than likely that, under the same conditions, I should have been very like your stenographers—if they are good ones. Whatever I was, I would have been a good one. I think people are very much alike. You are more different than any one I have met for some time, but I know that there are a great many more at home like you. And even you—I believe there is a real creature down under these custom-made prejudices that save you the trouble of thinking. If you and I were shipwrecked on a desert island, I have no doubt that we would come to a simple and natural understanding. I'm neither a coward nor a shirk. You would find, if you had to undertake any enterprise of danger or difficulty with a woman, that there are several qualifications quite as important as the one to which you doubtless refer."

McKann felt nervously for his watch-chain. "Of course," he brought out, "I am not laying down any generalizations—" His brows wrinkled.

"Oh, aren't you?" murmured Kitty. "Then I totally misunderstood. But remember"—holding up a finger—"it is you, not I, who are afraid to pursue this subject further. Now, I'll tell you something." She leaned forward and clasped her slim, white hands about her velvet knee. "I am as much a victim of these ineradicable prejudices as you. Your stenographer seems to you a better sort. Well, she does to me. Just because her life is, presumably, greyer than mine, she seems better. My mind tells me that dulness, and a mediocre order of ability, and poverty, are not in themselves admirable things. Yet in my heart I always feel that the sales-women in shops and the working girls in factories are more meritorious than I. Many of them, with my opportunities, would be more selfish than I am. Some of them, with their own opportunities, are more selfish. Yet I make this sentimental genuflection before the nun and the charwoman. Tell me, haven't you any weakness? Isn't there any foolish natural thing that unbends you a trifle and makes you feel gay?"

"I like to go fishing."

"To see how many fish you can catch?"

"No, I like the woods and the weather. I like to play a fish and work hard for him. I like the pussy-willows and the cold; and the sky, whether it's blue or grey—night coming on, every thing about it."

He spoke devoutly, and Kitty watched him through half-closed eyes. "And you like to feel that there are light-minded girls like me, who only care about the inside of shops and theatres and hotels, eh? You amuse me, you and your fish! But I mustn't keep you any longer. Haven't I given you every opportunity to state your case against me? I thought you would have more to say for yourself. Do you know, I believe it's not a case you have at all, but a grudge. I believe you are envious; that you'd like to be a tenor, and a perfect lady-killer!" She rose, smiling, and paused with her hand on the door of her state-room. "Anyhow, thank you for a pleasant evening. And, by the way, dream of me tonight, and not of either of those ladies who sat beside you. It does not matter much whom we live with in this world, but it matters a great deal whom we dream of." She noticed his bricky flush. "You are very naïf, after all, but, oh, so cautious! You are naturally afraid of everything new, just as I naturally want to try every-thing: new people, new religions—new miseries, even. If only there were more new things— If only you were really new! I might learn something. I'm like the Queen of Sheba—

I'm not above learning. But you, my friend, would be afraid to try a new shaving soap. It isn't gravitation that holds the world in place; it's the lazy, obese cowardice of the people on it. All the same"—taking his hand and smiling encouragingly—"I'm going to haunt you a little. *Adios!*"

When Kitty entered her state-room, Céline, in her dressing-gown, was nodding by the window.

"Mademoiselle found the fat gentleman interesting?" she asked. "It is nearly one."

"Negatively interesting. His kind always say the same thing. If I could find one really intelligent man who held his views, I should adopt them."

"Monsieur did not look like an original," murmured Céline, as she began to take down her lady's hair.

McKann slept heavily, as usual, and the porter had to shake him in the morning. He sat up in his berth, and, after composing his hair with his fingers, began to hunt about for his clothes. As he put up the window-blind some bright object in the little hammock over his bed caught the sunlight and glittered. He stared and picked up a delicately turned gold slipper.

"Minx! hussy!" he ejaculated. "All that tall talk—! Probably got it from some man who hangs about; learned it off like a parrot. Did she poke this in here herself last night, or did she send that sneak-faced Frenchwoman? I like her nerve!" He wondered whether he might have been breathing audibly when the intruder thrust her head between his curtains. He was conscious that he did not look a Prince Charming in his sleep. He dressed as fast as he could, and, when he was ready to go to the wash-room, glared at the slipper. If the porter should start to make up his berth in his absence— He caught the slipper, wrapped it in his pajama jacket, and thrust it into his bag. He escaped from the train without seeing his tormentor again.

Later McKann threw the slipper into the wastebasket in his room at the Knickerbocker, but the chambermaid, seeing that it was new and mateless, thought there must be a mistake, and placed it in his clothes-closet. He found it there when he returned from the theatre that evening. Considerably mellowed by food and drink and cheerful company, he took the slipper in his hand and decided to keep it as a reminder that absurd things could happen to people of the most clock-like deportment. When he got back to Pittsburgh, he stuck it in a lock-box in his vault, safe from prying clerks.

McKann has been ill for five years now, poor fellow! He still goes to the office, because it is the only place that interests him, but his partners do most of the work, and his clerks find him sadly changed—"morbid," they call his state of mind. He has had the pine-trees in his yard cut down because they remind him of cemeteries. On Sundays or holidays, when the office is empty, and he takes his will or his insurance-policies out of his lock-box, he often puts the tarnished gold slipper on his desk and looks at it. Somehow it suggests life to his tired mind, as his pine-trees suggested death—life and youth. When he drops over some day, his executors will be puzzled by the slipper.

As for Kitty Ayrshire, she has played so many jokes, practical and impractical, since then, that she has long ago forgotten the night when she threw away a slipper to be a thorn in the side of a just man.

Scandal

KITTY AYRSHIRE had a cold, a persistent inflammation of the vocal cords which defied the throat specialist. Week after week her name was posted at the Opera, and week after week it was canceled, and the name of one of her rivals was substituted. For nearly two months she had been deprived of everything she liked, even of the people she liked, and had been shut up until she had come to hate the glass windows between her and the world, and the wintry stretch of the Park they looked out upon. She was losing a great deal of money, and, what was worse, she was losing life; days of which she wanted to make the utmost were slipping by, and nights which were to have crowned the days, nights of incalculable possibilities, were being stolen from her by women for whom she had no great affection. At first she had been courageous, but the strain of prolonged uncertainty was telling on her, and her nervous condition did not improve her larynx. Every morning Miles Creedon looked down her throat, only to put her off with evasions, to pronounce improvement that apparently never got her anywhere, to say that tomorrow he might be able to promise something definite.

Her illness, of course, gave rise to rumours—rumours that she had lost her voice, that at some time last summer she must have lost her discretion. Kitty herself was frightened by the way in which this cold hung on. She had had many sharp illnesses in her life, but always, before this, she had rallied quickly. Was she beginning to lose her resiliency? Was she, by any cursed chance, facing a bleak time when she would have to cherish herself? She protested, as she wandered about her sunny, many-windowed rooms on the tenth floor, that if she was going to have to live frugally, she wouldn't live at all. She wouldn't live on any terms but the very generous ones she had always known. She wasn't going to hoard her vitality. It must be there when she wanted it, be ready for any strain she chose to put upon it, let her play fast and loose with it; and then, if necessary, she would be ill for a while and pay the

piper. But be systematically prudent and parsimonious she
would not.

When she attempted to deliver all this to Doctor Creedon,
he merely put his finger on her lips and said they would
discuss these things when she could talk without injuring
her throat. He allowed her to see no one except the Director
of the Opera, who did not shine in conversation and was not
apt to set Kitty going. The Director was a glum fellow, in-
deed, but during this calamitous time he had tried to be
soothing, and he agreed with Creedon that she must not risk
a premature appearance. Kitty was tormented by a suspicion
that he was secretly backing the little Spanish woman who
had sung many of her parts since she had been ill. He fur-
thered the girl's interests because his wife had a very special
consideration for her, and Madame had that consideration
because— But that was too long and too dreary a story to
follow out in one's mind. Kitty felt a tonsilitis disgust for
opera-house politics, which, when she was in health, she
rather enjoyed, being no mean strategist herself. The worst of
being ill was that it made so many things and people look
base.

She was always afraid of being disillusioned. She wished to
believe that everything for sale in Vanity Fair was worth the
advertised price. When she ceased to believe in these delights,
she told herself, her pulling power would decline and she
would go to pieces. In some way the chill of her disillusion-
ment would quiver through the long, black line which
reached from the box-office down to Seventh Avenue on
nights when she sang. They shivered there in the rain and
cold, all those people, because they loved to believe in her
inextinguishable zest. She was no prouder of what she drew
in the boxes than she was of that long, oscillating tail; little
fellows in thin coats, Italians, Frenchmen, South-Americans,
Japanese.

When she had been cloistered like a Trappist for six weeks,
with nothing from the outside world but notes and flowers
and disquieting morning papers, Kitty told Miles Creedon
that she could not endure complete isolation any longer.

"I simply cannot live through the evenings. They have
become horrors to me. Every night is the last night of a

condemned man. I do nothing but cry, and that makes my throat worse."

Miles Creedon, handsomest of his profession, was better looking with some invalids than with others. His athletic figure, his red cheeks, and splendid teeth always had a cheering effect upon this particular patient, who hated anything weak or broken.

"What can I do, my dear? What do you wish? Shall I come and hold your lovely hand from eight to ten? You have only to suggest it."

"Would you do that, even? No, *caro mio*, I take far too much of your time as it is. For an age now you have been the only man in the world to me, and you have been charming! But the world is big, and I am missing it. Let some one come tonight, some one interesting, but not too interesting. Pierce Tevis, for instance. He is just back from Paris. Tell the nurse I may see him for an hour tonight," Kitty finished pleadingly, and put her fingers on the doctor's sleeve. He looked down at them and smiled whimsically.

Like other people, he was weak to Kitty Ayrshire. He would do for her things that he would do for no one else; would break any engagement, desert a dinner-table, leaving an empty place and an offended hostess, to sit all evening in Kitty's dressing-room, spraying her throat and calming her nerves, using every expedient to get her through a performance. He had studied her voice like a singing master; knew all of its idiosyncracies and the emotional and nervous perturbations which affected it. When it was permissible, sometimes when it was not permissible, he indulged her caprices. On this sunny morning her wan, disconsolate face moved him.

"Yes, you may see Tevis this evening if you will assure me that you will not shed one tear for twenty-four hours. I may depend on your word?" He rose, and stood before the deep couch on which his patient reclined. Her arch look seemed to say, "On what could you depend more?" Creedon smiled, and shook his head. "If I find you worse tomorrow—"

He crossed to the writing-table and began to separate a bunch of tiny flame-coloured rosebuds. "May I?" Selecting one, he sat down on the chair from which he had lately risen, and leaned forward while Kitty pinched the thorns from the stem and arranged the flower in his buttonhole.

"Thank you. I like to wear one of yours. Now I must be off to the hospital. I've a nasty little operation to do this morning. I'm glad it's not you. Shall I telephone Tevis about this evening?"

Kitty hesitated. Her eyes ran rapidly about, seeking a likely pretext. Creedon laughed.

"Oh, I see. You've already asked him to come. You were so sure of me! Two hours in bed after lunch, with all the windows open, remember. Read something diverting, but not exciting; some homely British author; nothing *abandonné*. And don't make faces at me. Until tomorrow!"

When her charming doctor had disappeared through the doorway, Kitty fell back on her cushions and closed her eyes. Her mocking-bird, excited by the sunlight, was singing in his big gilt cage, and a white lilac-tree that had come that morning was giving out its faint sweetness in the warm room. But Kitty looked paler and wearier than when the doctor was with her. Even with him she rose to her part just a little; couldn't help it. And he took his share of her vivacity and sparkle, like every one else. He believed that his presence was soothing to her. But he admired; and whoever admired, blew on the flame, however lightly.

The mocking-bird was in great form this morning. He had the best bird-voice she had ever heard, and Kitty wished there were some way to note down his improvisations; but his intervals were not expressible in any scale she knew. Parker White had brought him to her, from Ojo Caliente, in New Mexico, where he had been trained in the pine forests by an old Mexican and an ill-tempered, lame master-bird, half thrush, that taught young birds to sing. This morning, in his song there were flashes of silvery Southern springtime; they opened inviting roads of memory. In half an hour he had sung his disconsolate mistress to sleep.

That evening Kitty sat curled up on the deep couch before the fire, awaiting Pierce Tevis. Her costume was folds upon folds of diaphanous white over equally diaphanous rose, with a line of white fur about her neck. Her beautiful arms were bare. Her tiny Chinese slippers were embroidered so richly that they resembled the painted porcelain of old vases. She looked like a sultan's youngest, newest bride; a beautiful little toy-woman, sitting at one end of the long room which composed about her,—which, in the soft light, seemed happily arranged for her. There were flowers everywhere: rose-trees; camellia-bushes, red and white; the first forced hyacinths of the season; a feathery mimosa-tree, tall enough to stand under.

The long front of Kitty's study was all windows. At one end was the fireplace, before which she sat. At the other end, back in a lighted alcove, hung a big, warm, sympathetic interior by Lucien Simon,—a group of Kitty's friends having tea in the painter's salon in Paris. The room in the picture was flooded with early lamp-light, and one could feel the grey, chill winter twilight in the Paris streets outside. There stood the cavalier-like old composer, who had done much for Kitty, in his most characteristic attitude, before the hearth. Mme. Simon sat at the tea-table. B——, the historian, and H——, the philologist, stood in animated discussion behind the piano, while Mme. H—— was tying on the bonnet of her lovely little daughter. Marcel Durand, the physicist, sat alone in a corner, his startling black-and-white profile lowered broodingly, his cold hands locked over his sharp knee. A genial, red-bearded sculptor stood over him, about to touch him on the shoulder and waken him from his dream.

This painting made, as it were, another room; so that Kitty's study on Central Park West seemed to open into that charming French interior, into one of the most highly harmonized and richly associated rooms in Paris. There her friends sat or stood about, men distinguished, women at once plain and beautiful, with their furs and bonnets, their clothes that were so distinctly not smart—all held together by the warm lamp-light, by an indescribable atmosphere of graceful and gracious human living.

Pierce Tevis, after he had entered noiselessly and greeted Kitty, stood before her fire and looked over her shoulder at this picture.

"It's nice that you have them there together, now that they are scattered, God knows where, fighting to preserve just that. But your own room, too, is charming," he added at last, taking his eyes from the canvas.

Kitty shrugged her shoulders.

"Bah! I can help to feed the lamp, but I can't supply the dear things it shines upon."

"Well, tonight it shines upon you and me, and we aren't so bad." Tevis stepped forward and took her hand affectionately. "You've been over a rough bit of road. I'm so sorry. It's left you looking very lovely, though. Has it been very hard to get on?"

She brushed his hand gratefully against her cheek and nodded.

"Awfully dismal. Everything has been shut out from me but—gossip. That always gets in. Often I don't mind, but this time I have. People do tell such lies about me."

"Of course we do. That's part of our fun, one of the many pleasures you give us. It only shows how hard up we are for interesting public personages; for a royal family, for romantic fiction, if you will. But I never hear any stories that wound me, and I'm very sensitive about you."

"I'm gossiped about rather more than the others, am I not?"

"I believe! Heaven send that the day when you are not gossiped about is far distant! Do you want to bite off your nose to spite your pretty face? You are the sort of person who makes myths. You can't turn around without making one. That's your singular good luck. A whole staff of publicity men, working day and night, couldn't do for you what you do for yourself. There is an affinity between you and the popular imagination."

"I suppose so," said Kitty, and sighed. "All the same, I'm getting almost as tired of the person I'm supposed to be as of the person I really am. I wish you would invent a new Kitty Ayrshire for me, Pierce. Can't I do something revolutionary? Marry, for instance?"

Tevis rose in alarm.

"Whatever you do, don't try to change your legend. You have now the one that gives the greatest satisfaction to the greatest number of people. Don't disappoint your public. The popular imagination, to which you make such a direct appeal, for some reason wished you to have a son, so it has given you one. I've heard a dozen versions of the story, but it is always a son, never by any chance a daughter. Your public gives you what is best for you. Let well enough alone."

Kitty yawned and dropped back on her cushions.

"He still persists, does he, in spite of never being visible?"

"Oh, but he has been seen by ever so many people. Let me think a moment." He sank into an attitude of meditative ease. "The best description I ever had of him was from a friend of my mother, an elderly woman, thoroughly truthful and matter-of-fact. She has seen him often. He is kept in Russia, in St. Petersburg, that was. He is about eight years old and of marvellous beauty. He is always that in every version. My old friend has seen him being driven in his sledge on the Nevskii Prospekt on winter afternoons; black horses with silver bells and a giant in uniform on the seat beside the driver. He is always attended by this giant, who is responsible to the Grand Duke Paul for the boy. This lady can produce no evidence beyond his beauty and his splendid furs and the fact that all the Americans in Petrograd know he is your son."

Kitty laughed mournfully.

"If the Grand Duke Paul had a son, any old rag of a son, the province of Moscow couldn't contain him! He may, for aught I know, actually pretend to have a son. It would be very like him." She looked at her finger-tips and her rings disapprovingly for a moment. "Do you know, I've been thinking that I would rather like to lay hands on that youngster. I believe he'd be interesting. I'm bored with the world."

Tevis looked up and said quickly:

"Would you like him, really?"

"Of course I should," she said indignantly. "But, then, I like other things, too; and one has to choose. When one has only two or three things to choose from, life is hard; when one has many, it is harder still. No, on the whole, I don't mind that story. It's rather pretty, except for the Grand Duke. But not all of them are pretty."

"Well, none of them are very ugly; at least I never heard but one that troubled me, and that was long ago."

She looked interested.

"That is what I want to know; how do the ugly ones get

started? How did that one get going and what was it about?
Is it too dreadful to repeat?"

"No, it's not especially dreadful; merely rather shabby. If
you really wish to know, and won't be vexed, I can tell you
exactly how it got going, for I took the trouble to find out.
But it's a long story, and you really had nothing whatever to
do with it."

"Then who did have to do with it? Tell me; I should like to
know exactly how even one of them originated."

"Will you be comfortable and quiet and not get into a rage,
and let me look at you as much as I please?"

Kitty nodded, and Tevis sat watching her indolently while
he debated how much of his story he ought not to tell her.
Kitty liked being looked at by intelligent persons. She knew
exactly how good looking she was; and she knew, too, that,
pretty as she was, some of those rather sallow women in the
Simon painting had a kind of beauty which she would never
have. This knowledge, Tevis was thinking, this important re-
alization, contributed more to her loveliness than any other
thing about her; more than her smooth, ivory skin or her
changing grey eyes, the delicate forehead above them, or even
the dazzling smile, which was gradually becoming too bright
and too intentional,—out in the world, at least. Here by her
own fire she still had for her friends a smile less electric than
the one she flashed from stages. She could still be, in short,
intime, a quality which few artists keep, which few ever had.

Kitty broke in on her friend's meditations.

"You may smoke. I had rather you did. I hate to deprive
people of things they like."

"No, thanks. May I have those chocolates on the tea-table?
They are quite as bad for me. May you? No, I suppose not."
He settled himself by the fire, with the candy beside him,
and began in the agreeable voice which always soothed his
listener.

"As I said, it was a long while ago, when you first came
back to this country and were singing at the Manhattan. I
dropped in at the Metropolitan one evening to hear some-
thing new they were trying out. It was an off night, no pullers
in the cast, and nobody in the boxes but governesses and
poor relations. At the end of the first act two people entered

one of the boxes in the second tier. The man was Siegmund Stein, the department-store millionaire, and the girl, so the men about me in the omnibus box began to whisper, was Kitty Ayrshire. I didn't know you then, but I was unwilling to believe that you were with Stein. I could not contradict them at that time, however, for the resemblance, if it was merely a resemblance, was absolute, and all the world knew that you were not singing at the Manhattan that night. The girl's hair was dressed just as you then wore yours. Moreover, her head was small and restless like yours, and she had your colouring, your eyes, your chin. She carried herself with the critical indifference one might expect in an artist who had come for a look at a new production that was clearly doomed to failure. She applauded lightly. She made comments to Stein when comments were natural enough. I thought, as I studied her face with the glass, that her nose was a trifle thinner than yours, a prettier nose, my dear Kitty, but stupider and more inflexible. All the same, I was troubled until I saw her laugh,—and then I knew she was a counterfeit. I had never seen you laugh, but I knew that you would not laugh like that. It was not boisterous; indeed, it was consciously refined,—mirthless, meaningless. In short, it was not the laugh of one whom our friends in there"—pointing to the Simon painting—"would honour with their affection and admiration."

Kitty rose on her elbow and burst out indignantly:

"So you would really have been hood-winked except for that! You may be sure that no woman, no intelligent woman, would have been. Why do we ever take the trouble to look like anything for any of you? I could count on my four fingers" —she held them up and shook them at him—"the men I've known who had the least perception of what any woman really looked like, and they were all dressmakers. Even painters" —glancing back in the direction of the Simon picture— "never get more than one type through their thick heads; they try to make all women look like some wife or mistress. You are all the same; you never see our real faces. What you do see, is some cheap conception of prettiness you got from a coloured supplement when you were adolescents. It's too discouraging. I'd rather take vows and veil my face for ever from

such abominable eyes. In the kingdom of the blind any petti-
coat is a queen." Kitty thumped the cushion with her elbow.
"Well, I can't do anything about it. Go on with your story."

"Aren't you furious, Kitty! And I thought I was so shrewd.
I've quite forgotten where I was. Anyhow, I was not the only
man fooled. After the last curtain I met Villard, the press man
of that management, in the lobby, and asked him whether
Kitty Ayrshire was in the house. He said he thought so. Stein
had telephoned for a box, and said he was bringing one of the
artists from the other company. Villard had been too busy
about the new production to go to the box, but he was quite
sure the woman was Ayrshire, whom he had met in Paris.

"Not long after that I met Dan Leland, a classmate of mine,
at the Harvard Club. He's a journalist, and he used to keep
such eccentric hours that I had not run across him for a long
time. We got to talking about modern French music, and
discovered that we both had a very lively interest in Kitty
Ayrshire.

" 'Could you tell me,' Dan asked abruptly, 'why, with
pretty much all the known world to choose her friends from,
this young woman should flit about with Siegmund Stein?
It prejudices people against her. He's a most objectionable
person.'

" 'Have you,' I asked, 'seen her with him, yourself?'

"Yes, he had seen her driving with Stein, and some of the
men on his paper had seen her dining with him at rather
queer places down town. Stein was always hanging about the
Manhattan on nights when Kitty sang. I told Dan that I
suspected a masquerade. That interested him, and he said
he thought he would look into the matter. In short, we both
agreed to look into it. Finally, we got the story, though Dan
could never use it, could never even hint at it, because Stein
carries heavy advertising in his paper.

"To make you see the point, I must give you a little history
of Siegmund Stein. Any one who has seen him never forgets
him. He is one of the most hideous men in New York, but
it's not at all the common sort of ugliness that comes from
overeating and automobiles. He isn't one of the fat horrors.
He has one of those rigid, horselike faces that never tell any-
thing; a long nose, flattened as if it had been tied down; a

scornful chin; long, white teeth; flat cheeks, yellow as a Mongolian's; tiny, black eyes, with puffy lids and no lashes; dingy, dead-looking hair—looks as if it were glued on.

"Stein came here a beggar from somewhere in Austria. He began by working on the machines in old Rosenthal's garment factory. He became a speeder, a foreman, a salesman; worked his way ahead steadily until the hour when he rented an old dwelling-house on Seventh Avenue and began to make misses' and juniors' coats. I believe he was the first manufacturer to specialize in those particular articles. Dozens of garment manufacturers have come along the same road, but Stein is like none of the rest of them. He is, and always was, a personality. While he was still at the machine, a hideous, underfed little whippersnapper, he was already a youth of manycoloured ambitions, deeply concerned about his dress, his associates, his recreations. He haunted the old Astor Library and the Metropolitan Museum, learned something about pictures and porcelains, took singing lessons, though he had a voice like a crow's. When he sat down to his baked apple and doughnut in a basement lunch-room, he would prop a book up before him and address his food with as much leisure and ceremony as if he were dining at his club. He held himself at a distance from his fellow-workmen and somehow always managed to impress them with his superiority. He had inordinate vanity, and there are many stories about his foppishness. After his first promotion in Rosenthal's factory, he bought a new overcoat. A few days later, one of the men at the machines, which Stein had just quitted, appeared in a coat exactly like it. Stein could not discharge him, but he gave his own coat to a newly arrived Russian boy and got another. He was already magnificent.

"After he began to make headway with misses' and juniors' cloaks, he became a collector—etchings, china, old musical instruments. He had a dancing master, and engaged a beautiful Brazilian widow—she was said to be a secret agent for some South American republic—to teach him Spanish. He cultivated the society of the unknown great; poets, actors, musicians. He entertained them sumptuously, and they regarded him as a deep, mysterious Jew who had the secret of gold, which they had not. His business associates thought him a man of taste and culture, a patron of the arts, a credit to the garment trade.

"One of Stein's many ambitions was to be thought a success with women. He got considerable notoriety in the garment world by his attentions to an emotional actress who is now quite forgotten, but who had her little hour of expectation. Then there was a dancer; then, just after Gorky's visit here, a Russian anarchist woman. After that the coat-makers and shirtwaist-makers began to whisper that Stein's great success was with Kitty Ayrshire.

"It is the hardest thing in the world to disprove such a story, as Dan Leland and I discovered. We managed to worry down the girl's address through a taxi-cab driver who got next to Stein's chauffeur. She had an apartment in a decent-enough house on Waverly Place. Nobody ever came to see her but Stein, her sisters, and a little Italian girl from whom we got the story.

"The counterfeit's name was Ruby Mohr. She worked in a shirtwaist factory, and this Italian girl, Margarita, was her chum. Stein came to the factory when he was hunting for living models for his new department store. He looked the girls over, and picked Ruby out from several hundred. He had her call at his office after business hours, tried her out in cloaks and evening gowns, and offered her a position. She never, however, appeared as a model in the Sixth Avenue store. Her likeness to the newly arrived prima donna suggested to Stein another act in the play he was always putting on. He gave two of her sisters positions as saleswomen, but Ruby he established in an apartment on Waverly Place.

"To the outside world Stein became more mysterious in his behaviour than ever. He dropped his Bohemian friends. No more suppers and theatre-parties. Whenever Kitty sang, he was in his box at the Manhattan, usually alone, but not always. Sometimes he took two or three good customers, large buyers from St. Louis or Kansas City. His coat factory is still the biggest earner of his properties. I've seen him there with these buyers, and they carried themselves as if they were being let in on something; took possession of the box with a proprietory air, smiled and applauded and looked wise as if each and every one of them were friends of Kitty Ayrshire. While they buzzed and trained their field-glasses on the prima donna, Stein was impassive and silent. I don't imagine he even told many lies. He is the most insinuating cuss, anyhow. He probably dropped his voice or lifted his eyebrows when he invited them, and let their own eager imaginations do the rest. But what tales they took back to their provincial capitals!

"Sometimes, before they left New York, they were lucky enough to see Kitty dining with their clever garment man at some restaurant, her back to the curious crowd, her face half concealed by a veil or a fur collar. Those people are like children; nothing that is true or probable interests them. They want the old, gaudy lies, told always in the same way. Siegmund Stein and Kitty Ayrshire—a story like that, once launched, is repeated unchallenged for years among New York factory sports. In St. Paul, St. Jo, Sioux City, Council Bluffs, there used to be clothing stores where a photograph of Kitty Ayrshire hung in the fitting-room or over the proprietor's desk.

"This girl impersonated you successfully to the lower manufacturing world of New York for two seasons. I doubt if it could have been put across anywhere else in the world except in this city, which pays you so magnificently and believes of you what it likes. Then you went over to the Metropolitan, stopped living in hotels, took this apartment, and began to know people. Stein discontinued his pantomime at the right moment, withdrew his patronage. Ruby, of course, did not go back to shirtwaists. A business friend of Stein's took her over, and she dropped out of sight. Last winter, one cold, snowy night, I saw her once again. She was going into a saloon hotel with a tough-looking young fellow. She had been drinking, she was shabby, and her blue shoes left stains in the slush. But she still looked amazingly, convincingly like a battered, hardened Kitty Ayrshire. As I saw her going up the brass-edged stairs, I said to myself—"

"Never mind that." Kitty rose quickly, took an impatient step to the hearth, and thrust one shining porcelain slipper out to the fire. "The girl doesn't interest me. There is nothing I can do about her, and of course she never looked like me at all. But what did Stein do without me?"

"Stein? Oh, he chose a new rôle. He married with great

magnificence—married a Miss Mandelbaum, a California heiress. Her people have a line of department stores along the Pacific Coast. The Steins now inhabit a great house on Fifth Avenue that used to belong to people of a very different sort. To old New-Yorkers, it's an historic house."

Kitty laughed, and sat down on the end of her couch nearest her guest; sat upright, without cushions.

"I imagine I know more about that house than you do. Let me tell you how I made the sequel to your story.

"It has to do with Peppo Amoretti. You may remember that I brought Peppo to this country, and brought him in, too, the year the war broke out, when it wasn't easy to get boys who hadn't done military service out of Italy. I had taken him to Munich to have some singing lessons. After the war came on we had to get from Munich to Naples in order to sail at all. We were told that we could take only hand luggage on the railways, but I took nine trunks and Peppo. I dressed Peppo in knickerbockers, made him brush his curls down over his ears like doughnuts, and carry a little violin-case. It took us eleven days to reach Naples. I got my trunks through purely by personal persuasion. Once at Naples, I had a frightful time getting Peppo on the boat. I declared him as hand-luggage; he was so travel-worn and so crushed by his absurd appearance that he did not look like much else. One inspector had a sense of humour, and passed him at that, but the other was inflexible. I had to be very dramatic. Peppo was frightened, and there is no fight in him, anyhow.

" '*Per me tutto e indifferente, Signorina,*' he kept whimpering. 'Why should I go without it? I have lost it.'

" 'Which?' I screamed. '*Not* the hat-trunk?'

" '*No, no; mia voce.* It is gone since Ravenna.'

"He thought he had lost his voice somewhere along the way. At last I told the inspector that I couldn't live without Peppo, and that I would throw myself into the bay. I took him into my confidence. Of course, when I found I had to play on that string, I wished I hadn't made the boy such a spectacle. But ridiculous as he was, I managed to make the inspector believe that I had kidnapped him, and that he was indispensable to my happiness. I found that incorruptible official, like most people, willing to aid one so utterly depraved.

I could never have got that boy out for any proper, reasonable purpose, such as giving him a job or sending him to school. Well, it's a queer world! But I must cut all that and get to the Steins.

"That first winter Peppo had no chance at the Opera. There was an iron ring about him, and my interest in him only made it all the more difficult. We've become a nest of intrigues down there; worse than the Scala. Peppo had to scratch along just any way. One evening he came to me and said he could get an engagement to sing for the grand rich Steins, but the condition was that I should sing with him. They would pay, oh, anything! And the fact that I had sung a private engagement with him would give him other engagements of the same sort. As you know, I never sing private engagements; but to help the boy along, I consented.

"On the night of the party, Peppo and I went to the house together in a taxi. My car was ailing. At the hour when the music was about to begin, the host and hostess appeared at my dressing-room, up-stairs. Isn't he wonderful? Your description was most inadequate. I never encountered such restrained, frozen, sculptured vanity. My hostess struck me as extremely good natured and jolly, though somewhat intimate in her manner. Her reassuring pats and smiles puzzled me at the time, I remember, when I didn't know that she had anything in particular to be large-minded and charitable about. Her husband made known his willingness to conduct me to the music-room, and we ceremoniously descended a staircase blooming like the hanging-gardens of Babylon. From there I had my first glimpse of the company. They *were* strange people. The women glittered like Christmas-trees. When we were half-way down the stairs, the buzz of conversation stopped so suddenly that some foolish remark I happened to be making rang out like oratory. Every face was lifted toward us. My host and I completed our descent and went the length of the drawing-room through a silence which somewhat awed me. I couldn't help wishing that one could ever get that kind of attention in a concert-hall. In the music-room Stein insisted upon arranging things for me. I must say that he was neither awkward nor stupid, not so wooden as most rich men who rent singers. I was properly affable. One has, under such circumstances, to be either gracious or pouty. Either you have to stand and sulk, like an old-fashioned German singer who wants the piano moved about for her like a tea-wagon, and the lights turned up and the lights turned down,—or you have to be a trifle forced, like a débutante trying to make good. The fixed attention of my audience affected me. I was aware of unusual interest, of a thoroughly enlisted public. When, however, my host at last left me, I felt the tension relax to such an extent that I wondered whether by any chance he, and not I, was the object of so much curiosity. But, at any rate, their cordiality pleased me so well that after Peppo and I had finished our numbers I sang an encore or two, and I stayed through Peppo's performance because I felt that they liked to look at me.

"I had asked not to be presented to people, but Mrs. Stein, of course, brought up a few friends. The throng began closing in upon me, glowing faces bore down from every direction, and I realized that, among people of such unscrupulous cordiality, I must look out for myself. I ran through the drawing-room and fled up the stairway, which was thronged with Old Testament characters. As I passed them, they all looked at me with delighted, cherishing eyes, as if I had at last come back to my native hamlet. At the top of the stairway a young man, who looked like a camel with its hair parted on the side, stopped me, seized my hands and said he must present himself, as he was such an old friend of Siegmund's bachelor days. I said, 'Yes, how interesting!' The atmosphere was somehow so thick and personal that I felt uncomfortable.

"When I reached my dressing-room Mrs. Stein followed me to say that I would, of course, come down to supper, as a special table had been prepared for me. I replied that it was not my custom.

"'But here it is different. With us you must feel perfect freedom. Siegmund will never forgive me if you do not stay. After supper our car will take you home.' She was overpowering. She had the manner of an intimate and indulgent friend of long standing. She seemed to have come to make me a visit. I could only get rid of her by telling her that I must see Peppo at once, if she would be good enough to send him to me. She did not come back, and I began to fear that I would actually be dragged down to supper. It was as if I had been kidnapped. I felt like *Gulliver* among the giants. These people were all too—well, too much what they were. No chill of manner could hold them off. I was defenceless. I must get away. I ran to the top of the staircase and looked down. There was that fool Peppo, beleaguered by a bevy of fair women. They were simply looting him, and he was grinning like an idiot. I gathered up my train, ran down, and made a dash at him, yanked him out of that circle of rich contours, and dragged him by a limp cuff up the stairs after me. I told him that I must escape from that house at once. If he could get to the telephone, well and good; but if he couldn't get past so many deep-breathing ladies, then he must break out of the front door and hunt me a cab on foot. I felt as if I were about to be immured within a harem.

"He had scarcely dashed off when the host called my name several times outside the door. Then he knocked and walked in, uninvited. I told him that I would be inflexible about supper. He must make my excuses to his charming friends; any pretext he chose. He did not insist. He took up his stand by the fireplace and began to talk; said rather intelligent things. I did not drive him out; it was his own house, and he made himself agreeable. After a time a deputation of his friends came down the hall, somewhat boisterously, to say that supper could not be served until we came down. Stein was still standing by the mantel, I remember. He scattered them, without moving or speaking to them, by a portentous look. There is something hideously forceful about him. He took a very profound leave of me, and said he would order his car at once. In a moment Peppo arrived, splashed to the ankles, and we made our escape together.

"A week later Peppo came to me in a rage, with a paper called *The American Gentleman*, and showed me a page devoted to three photographs: Mr. and Mrs. Siegmund Stein, lately married in New York City, and Kitty Ayrshire, operatic soprano, who sang at their house-warming. Mrs. Stein and I were grinning our best, looked frantic with delight, and Siegmund frowned inscrutably between us. Poor Peppo wasn't mentioned. Stein has a publicity sense."

Tevis rose.

"And you have enormous publicity value and no discretion. It was just like you to fall for such a plot, Kitty. You'd be sure to."

"What's the use of discretion?" She murmured behind her hand. "If the Steins want to adopt you into their family circle, they'll get you in the end. That's why I don't feel compassionate about your Ruby. She and I are in the same boat. We are both the victims of circumstance, and in New York so many of the circumstances are Steins."

Paul's Case

IT WAS Paul's afternoon to appear before the faculty of the Pittsburgh High School to account for his various misdemeanours. He had been suspended a week ago, and his father had called at the Principal's office and confessed his perplexity about his son. Paul entered the faculty room suave and smiling. His clothes were a trifle out-grown, and the tan velvet on the collar of his open overcoat was frayed and worn; but for all that there was something of the dandy about him, and he wore an opal pin in his neatly knotted black four-in-hand, and a red carnation in his button-hole. This latter adornment the faculty somehow felt was not properly significant of the contrite spirit befitting a boy under the ban of suspension.

Paul was tall for his age and very thin, with high, cramped shoulders and a narrow chest. His eyes were remarkable for a certain hysterical brilliancy, and he continually used them in a conscious, theatrical sort of way, peculiarly offensive in a boy. The pupils were abnormally large, as though he were addicted to belladonna, but there was a glassy glitter about them which that drug does not produce.

When questioned by the Principal as to why he was there, Paul stated, politely enough, that he wanted to come back to school. This was a lie, but Paul was quite accustomed to lying; found it, indeed, indispensable for overcoming friction. His teachers were asked to state their respective charges against him, which they did with such a rancour and aggrievedness as evinced that this was not a usual case. Disorder and impertinence were among the offences named, yet each of his instructors felt that it was scarcely possible to put into words the real cause of the trouble, which lay in a sort of hysterically defiant manner of the boy's; in the contempt which they all knew he felt for them, and which he seemingly made not the least effort to conceal. Once, when he had been making a synopsis of a paragraph at the blackboard, his English teacher had stepped to his side and attempted to guide his hand. Paul had started back with a shudder and thrust his hands violently behind him. The astonished woman could scarcely have been more hurt and embarrassed had he struck at her. The insult was so involuntary and definitely personal as to be unforgettable. In one way and another, he had made all his teachers, men and women alike, conscious of the same feeling of physical aversion. In one class he habitually sat with his hand shading his eyes; in another he always looked out of the window during the recitation; in another he made a running commentary on the lecture, with humorous intent.

His teachers felt this afternoon that his whole attitude was symbolized by his shrug and his flippantly red carnation flower, and they fell upon him without mercy, his English teacher leading the pack. He stood through it smiling, his pale lips parted over his white teeth. (His lips were continually twitching, and he had a habit of raising his eyebrows that was contemptuous and irritating to the last degree.) Older boys than Paul had broken down and shed tears under that ordeal, but his set smile did not once desert him, and his only sign of discomfort was the nervous trembling of the fingers that toyed with the buttons of his overcoat, and an occasional jerking of the other hand which held his hat. Paul was always smiling, always glancing about him, seeming to feel that people might be watching him and trying to detect something. This conscious expression, since it was as far as possible from boyish mirthfulness, was usually attributed to insolence or "smartness."

As the inquisition proceeded, one of his instructors repeated an impertinent remark of the boy's, and the Principal asked him whether he thought that a courteous speech to make to a woman. Paul shrugged his shoulders slightly and his eyebrows twitched.

"I don't know," he replied. "I didn't mean to be polite or impolite, either. I guess it's a sort of way I have, of saying things regardless."

The Principal asked him whether he didn't think that a way it would be well to get rid of. Paul grinned and said he guessed so. When he was told that he could go, he bowed gracefully and went out. His bow was like a repetition of the scandalous red carnation.

His teachers were in despair, and his drawing master voiced the feeling of them all when he declared there was something about the boy which none of them understood. He added: "I don't really believe that smile of his comes altogether from insolence; there's something sort of haunted about it. The boy is not strong, for one thing. There is something wrong about the fellow."

The drawing master had come to realize that, in looking at Paul, one saw only his white teeth and the forced animation of his eyes. One warm afternoon the boy had gone to sleep at his drawing-board, and his master had noted with amazement what a white, blue-veined face it was; drawn and wrinkled like an old man's about the eyes, the lips twitching even in his sleep.

His teachers left the building dissatisfied and unhappy; humiliated to have felt so vindictive toward a mere boy, to have uttered this feeling in cutting terms, and to have set each other on, as it were, in the grewsome game of intemperate reproach. One of them remembered having seen a miserable street cat set at bay by a ring of tormentors.

As for Paul, he ran down the hill whistling the Soldiers' Chorus from *Faust*, looking wildly behind him now and then to see whether some of his teachers were not there to witness his light-heartedness. As it was now late in the afternoon and Paul was on duty that evening as usher at Carnegie Hall, he decided that he would not go home to supper.

When he reached the concert hall the doors were not yet open. It was chilly outside, and he decided to go up into the picture gallery—always deserted at this hour—where there were some of Raffelli's gay studies of Paris streets and an airy blue Venetian scene or two that always exhilarated him. He was delighted to find no one in the gallery but the old guard, who sat in the corner, a newspaper on his knee, a black patch over one eye and the other closed. Paul possessed himself of the place and walked confidently up and down, whistling under his breath. After a while he sat down before a blue Rico and lost himself. When he bethought him to look at his watch, it was after seven o'clock, and he rose with a start and ran downstairs, making a face at Augustus Cæsar, peering out from the cast-room, and an evil gesture at the Venus of Milo as he passed her on the stairway.

When Paul reached the ushers' dressing-room half-a-dozen

boys were there already, and he began excitedly to tumble into his uniform. It was one of the few that at all approached fitting, and Paul thought it very becoming—though he knew the tight, straight coat accentuated his narrow chest, about which he was exceedingly sensitive. He was always excited while he dressed, twanging all over to the tuning of the strings and the preliminary flourishes of the horns in the music-room; but tonight he seemed quite beside himself, and he teased and plagued the boys until, telling him that he was crazy, they put him down on the floor and sat on him.

Somewhat calmed by his suppression, Paul dashed out to the front of the house to seat the early comers. He was a model usher. Gracious and smiling he ran up and down the aisles. Nothing was too much trouble for him; he carried messages and brought programs as though it were his greatest pleasure in life, and all the people in his section thought him a charming boy, feeling that he remembered and admired them. As the house filled, he grew more and more vivacious and animated, and the colour came to his cheeks and lips. It was very much as though this were a great reception and Paul were the host. Just as the musicians came out to take their places, his English teacher arrived with checks for the seats which a prominent manufacturer had taken for the season. She betrayed some embarrassment when she handed Paul the tickets, and a *hauteur* which subsequently made her feel very foolish. Paul was startled for a moment, and had the feeling of wanting to put her out; what business had she here among all these fine people and gay colours? He looked her over and decided that she was not appropriately dressed and must be a fool to sit downstairs in such togs. The tickets had probably been sent her out of kindness, he reflected, as he put down a seat for her, and she had about as much right to sit there as he had.

When the symphony began Paul sank into one of the rear seats with a long sigh of relief, and lost himself as he had done before the Rico. It was not that symphonies, as such, meant anything in particular to Paul, but the first sigh of the instruments seemed to free some hilarious spirit within him; something that struggled there like the Genius in the bottle found by the Arab fisherman. He felt a sudden zest of life; the lights danced before his eyes and the concert hall blazed into unimaginable splendour. When the soprano soloist came on, Paul forgot even the nastiness of his teacher's being there, and gave himself up to the peculiar intoxication such personages always had for him. The soloist chanced to be a German woman, by no means in her first youth, and the mother of many children; but she wore a satin gown and a tiara, and she had that indefinable air of achievement, that world-shine upon her, which always blinded Paul to any possible defects.

After a concert was over, Paul was often irritable and wretched until he got to sleep,—and tonight he was even more than usually restless. He had the feeling of not being able to let down; of its being impossible to give up this delicious excitement which was the only thing that could be called living at all. During the last number he withdrew and, after hastily changing his clothes in the dressing-room, slipped out to the side door where the singer's carriage stood. Here he began pacing rapidly up and down the walk, waiting to see her come out.

Over yonder the Schenley, in its vacant stretch, loomed big and square through the fine rain, the windows of its twelve stories glowing like those of a lighted card-board house under a Christmas tree. All the actors and singers of any importance stayed there when they were in the city, and a number of the big manufacturers of the place lived there in the winter. Paul had often hung about the hotel, watching the people go in and out, longing to enter and leave school-masters and dull care behind him for ever.

At last the singer came out, accompanied by the conductor, who helped her into her carriage and closed the door with a cordial *auf wiedersehen*,—which set Paul to wondering whether she were not an old sweetheart of his. Paul followed the carriage over to the hotel, walking so rapidly as not to be far from the entrance when the singer alighted and disappeared behind the swinging glass doors which were opened by a negro in a tall hat and a long coat. In the moment that the door was ajar, it seemed to Paul that he, too, entered. He seemed to feel himself go after her up the steps, into the warm, lighted building, into an exotic, a tropical world of shiny, glistening surfaces and basking ease. He reflected upon the mysterious dishes that were brought into the dining-room, the green bottles in buckets of ice, as he had seen them in the supper party pictures of the Sunday supplement. A quick gust of wind brought the rain down with sudden vehemence, and Paul was startled to find that he was still outside in the slush of the gravel driveway; that his boots were letting in the water and his scanty overcoat was clinging wet about him; that the lights in front of the concert hall were out, and that the rain was driving in sheets between him and the orange glow of the windows above him. There it was, what he wanted—tangibly before him, like the fairy world of a Christmas pantomime; as the rain beat in his face, Paul wondered whether he were destined always to shiver in the black night outside, looking up at it.

He turned and walked reluctantly toward the car tracks. The end had to come sometime; his father in his night-clothes at the top of the stairs, explanations that did not explain, hastily improvised fictions that were forever tripping him up, his upstairs room and its horrible yellow wall-paper, the creaking bureau with the greasy plush collar-box, and over his painted wooden bed the pictures of George Washington and John Calvin, and the framed motto, "Feed my Lambs," which had been worked in red worsted by his mother, whom Paul could not remember.

Half an hour later, Paul alighted from the Negley Avenue car and went slowly down one of the side streets off the main thoroughfare. It was a highly respectable street, where all the houses were exactly alike, and where business men of moderate means begot and reared large families of children, all of whom went to Sabbath-school and learned the shorter catechism, and were interested in arithmetic; all of whom were as exactly alike as their homes, and of a piece with the monotony in which they lived. Paul never went up Cordelia Street without a shudder of loathing. His home was next the house of the Cumberland minister. He approached it tonight with the nerveless sense of defeat, the hopeless feeling of sinking back forever into ugliness and commonness that he had always had when he came home. The moment he turned into Cordelia Street he felt the waters close above his head. After each of these orgies of living, he experienced all the physical

depression which follows a debauch; the loathing of respect-
able beds, of common food, of a house permeated by kitchen
odours; a shuddering repulsion for the flavourless, colourless
mass of every-day existence; a morbid desire for cool things
and soft lights and fresh flowers.

The nearer he approached the house, the more absolutely
unequal Paul felt to the sight of it all; his ugly sleeping cham-
ber; the cold bath-room with the grimy zinc tub, the cracked
mirror, the dripping spiggots; his father, at the top of the
stairs, his hairy legs sticking out from his nightshirt, his feet
thrust into carpet slippers. He was so much later than usual
that there would certainly be inquiries and reproaches. Paul
stopped short before the door. He felt that he could not be
accosted by his father tonight; that he could not toss again on
that miserable bed. He would not go in. He would tell his
father that he had no car fare, and it was raining so hard he
had gone home with one of the boys and stayed all night.

Meanwhile, he was wet and cold. He went around to the
back of the house and tried one of the basement windows,
found it open, raised it cautiously, and scrambled down the
cellar wall to the floor. There he stood, holding his breath,
terrified by the noise he had made; but the floor above him
was silent, and there was no creak on the stairs. He found a
soap-box, and carried it over to the soft ring of light that
streamed from the furnace door, and sat down. He was hor-
ribly afraid of rats, so he did not try to sleep, but sat looking
distrustfully at the dark, still terrified lest he might have awak-
ened his father. In such reactions, after one of the experiences
which made days and nights out of the dreary blanks of the
calendar, when his senses were deadened, Paul's head was al-
ways singularly clear. Suppose his father had heard him get-
ting in at the window and had come down and shot him for
a burglar? Then, again, suppose his father had come down,
pistol in hand, and he had cried out in time to save him-
self, and his father had been horrified to think how nearly he
had killed him? Then, again, suppose a day should come when
his father would remember that night, and wish there had
been no warning cry to stay his hand? With this last suppo-
sition Paul entertained himself until daybreak.

The following Sunday was fine; the sodden November chill

was broken by the last flash of autumnal summer. In the morning Paul had to go to church and Sabbath-school, as always. On seasonable Sunday afternoons the burghers of Cordelia Street usually sat out on their front "stoops," and talked to their neighbours on the next stoop, or called to those across the street in neighbourly fashion. The men sat placidly on gay cushions placed upon the steps that led down to the sidewalk, while the women, in their Sunday "waists," sat in rockers on the cramped porches, pretending to be greatly at their ease. The children played in the streets; there were so many of them that the place resembled the recreation grounds of a kindergarten. The men on the steps—all in their shirt sleeves, their vests unbuttoned—sat with their legs well apart, their stomachs comfortably protruding, and talked of the prices of things, or told anecdotes of the sagacity of their various chiefs and overlords. They occasionally looked over the multitude of squabbling children, listened affectionately to their high-pitched, nasal voices, smiling to see their own proclivities reproduced in their offspring, and interspersed their legends of the iron kings with remarks about their sons' progress at school, their grades in arithmetic, and the amounts they had saved in their toy banks.

On this last Sunday of November, Paul sat all the afternoon on the lowest step of his "stoop," staring into the street, while his sisters, in their rockers, were talking to the minister's daughters next door about how many shirt-waists they had made in the last week, and how many waffles some one had eaten at the last church supper. When the weather was warm, and his father was in a particularly jovial frame of mind, the girls made lemonade, which was always brought out in a red-glass pitcher, ornamented with forget-me-nots in blue enamel. This the girls thought very fine, and the neighbours joked about the suspicious colour of the pitcher.

Today Paul's father, on the top step, was talking to a young man who shifted a restless baby from knee to knee. He happened to be the young man who was daily held up to Paul as a model, and after whom it was his father's dearest hope that he would pattern. This young man was of a ruddy complexion, with a compressed, red mouth, and faded, near-sighted eyes, over which he wore thick spectacles, with gold bows that curved about his ears. He was clerk to one of the magnates of a great steel corporation, and was looked upon in Cordelia Street as a young man with a future. There was a story that, some five years ago—he was now barely twenty-six—he had been a trifle 'dissipated,' but in order to curb his appetites and save the loss of time and strength that a sowing of wild oats might have entailed, he had taken his chief's advice, oft reiterated to his employés, and at twenty-one had married the first woman whom he could persuade to share his fortunes. She happened to be an angular school-mistress, much older than he, who also wore thick glasses, and who had now borne him four children, all near-sighted, like herself.

The young man was relating how his chief, now cruising in the Mediterranean, kept in touch with all the details of the business, arranging his office hours on his yacht just as though he were at home, and "knocking off work enough to keep two stenographers busy." His father told, in turn, the plan his corporation was considering, of putting in an electric railway plant at Cairo. Paul snapped his teeth; he had an awful apprehension that they might spoil it all before he got there. Yet he rather liked to hear these legends of the iron kings, that were told and retold on Sundays and holidays; these stories of palaces in Venice, yachts on the Mediterranean, and high play at Monte Carlo appealed to his fancy, and he was interested in the triumphs of cash boys who had become famous, though he had no mind for the cash-boy stage.

After supper was over, and he had helped to dry the dishes, Paul nervously asked his father whether he could go to George's to get some help in his geometry, and still more nervously asked for car-fare. This latter request he had to repeat, as his father, on principle, did not like to hear requests for money, whether much or little. He asked Paul whether he could not go to some boy who lived nearer, and told him that he ought not to leave his school work until Sunday; but he gave him the dime. He was not a poor man, but he had a worthy ambition to come up in the world. His only reason for allowing Paul to usher was that he thought a boy ought to be earning a little.

Paul bounded upstairs, scrubbed the greasy odour of the

dish-water from his hands with the ill-smelling soap he hated, and then shook over his fingers a few drops of violet water from the bottle he kept hidden in his drawer. He left the house with his geometry conspicuously under his arm, and the moment he got out of Cordelia Street and boarded a downtown car, he shook off the lethargy of two deadening days, and began to live again.

The leading juvenile of the permanent stock company which played at one of the downtown theatres was an acquaintance of Paul's, and the boy had been invited to drop in at the Sunday-night rehearsals whenever he could. For more than a year Paul had spent every available moment loitering about Charley Edwards's dressing-room. He had won a place among Edwards's following not only because the young actor, who could not afford to employ a dresser, often found him useful, but because he recognized in Paul something akin to what churchmen term "vocation."

It was at the theatre and at Carnegie Hall that Paul really lived; the rest was but a sleep and a forgetting. This was Paul's fairy tale, and it had for him all the allurement of a secret love. The moment he inhaled the gassy, painty, dusty odour behind the scenes, he breathed like a prisoner set free, and felt within him the possibility of doing or saying splendid, brilliant things. The moment the cracked orchestra beat out the overture from *Martha*, or jerked at the serenade from *Rigoletto*, all stupid and ugly things slid from him, and his senses were deliciously, yet delicately fired.

Perhaps it was because, in Paul's world, the natural nearly always wore the guise of ugliness, that a certain element of artificiality seemed to him necessary in beauty. Perhaps it was because his experience of life elsewhere was so full of Sabbath-school picnics, petty economies, wholesome advice as to how to succeed in life, and the unescapable odours of cooking, that he found this existence so alluring, these smartly-clad men and women so attractive, that he was so moved by these starry apple orchards that bloomed perennially under the lime-light.

It would be difficult to put it strongly enough how convincingly the stage entrance of that theatre was for Paul the actual portal of Romance. Certainly none of the company ever suspected it, least of all Charley Edwards. It was very like the old stories that used to float about London of fabulously rich Jews, who had subterranean halls, with palms, and fountains, and soft lamps and richly apparelled women who never saw the disenchanting light of London day. So, in the midst of that smoke-palled city, enamoured of figures and grimy toil, Paul had his secret temple, his wishing-carpet, his bit of blue-and-white Mediterranean shore bathed in perpetual sunshine.

Several of Paul's teachers had a theory that his imagination had been perverted by garish fiction; but the truth was, he scarcely ever read at all. The books at home were not such as would either tempt or corrupt a youthful mind, and as for reading the novels that some of his friends urged upon him— well, he got what he wanted much more quickly from music; any sort of music, from an orchestra to a barrel organ. He needed only the spark, the indescribable thrill that made his imagination master of his senses, and he could make plots and pictures enough of his own. It was equally true that he was not stage-struck—not, at any rate, in the usual acceptation of that expression. He had no desire to become an actor, any more than he had to become a musician. He felt no necessity to do any of these things; what he wanted was to see, to be in the atmosphere, float on the wave of it, to be carried out, blue league after blue league, away from everything.

After a night behind the scenes, Paul found the school-room more than ever repulsive; the bare floors and naked walls; the prosy men who never wore frock coats, or violets in their buttonholes; the women with their dull gowns, shrill voices, and pitiful seriousness about prepositions that govern the dative. He could not bear to have the other pupils think, for a moment, that he took these people seriously; he must convey to them that he considered it all trivial, and was there only by way of a joke, anyway. He had autograph pictures of all the members of the stock company which he showed his classmates, telling them the most incredible stories of his familiarity with these people, of his acquaintance with the soloists who came to Carnegie Hall, his suppers with them and the flowers he sent them. When these stories lost their effect, and his audience grew listless, he would bid all the boys good-bye, announcing that he was going to travel for awhile; going to Naples, to California, to Egypt. Then, next Monday, he would slip back, conscious and nervously smiling; his sister was ill, and he would have to defer his voyage until spring.

Matters went steadily worse with Paul at school. In the itch to let his instructors know how heartily he despised them, and how thoroughly he was appreciated elsewhere, he mentioned once or twice that he had no time to fool with theorems; adding—with a twitch of the eyebrows and a touch of that nervous bravado which so perplexed them—that he was helping the people down at the stock company; they were old friends of his.

The upshot of the matter was, that the Principal went to Paul's father, and Paul was taken out of school and put to work. The manager at Carnegie Hall was told to get another usher in his stead; the doorkeeper at the theatre was warned not to admit him to the house; and Charley Edwards remorsefully promised the boy's father not to see him again.

The members of the stock company were vastly amused when some of Paul's stories reached them—especially the women. They were hard-working women, most of them supporting indolent husbands or brothers, and they laughed rather bitterly at having stirred the boy to such fervid and florid inventions. They agreed with the faculty and with his father, that Paul's was a bad case.

The east-bound train was ploughing through a January snow-storm; the dull dawn was beginning to show grey when the engine whistled a mile out of Newark. Paul started up from the seat where he had lain curled in uneasy slumber, rubbed the breath-misted window glass with his hand, and peered out. The snow was whirling in curling eddies above the white bottom lands, and the drifts lay already deep in the fields and along the fences, while here and there the long dead grass and dried weed stalks protruded black above it. Lights shone from the scattered houses, and a gang of labourers who stood beside the track waved their lanterns.

Paul had slept very little, and he felt grimy and uncomfortable. He had made the all-night journey in a day coach because he was afraid if he took a Pullman he might be seen by some Pittsburgh business man who had noticed him in Denny & Carson's office. When the whistle woke him, he clutched quickly at his breast pocket, glancing about him with an uncertain smile. But the little, clay-bespattered Italians were still sleeping, the slatternly women across the aisle were in open-mouthed oblivion, and even the crumby, crying babies were for the nonce stilled. Paul settled back to struggle with his impatience as best he could.

When he arrived at the Jersey City station, he hurried through his breakfast, manifestly ill at ease and keeping a sharp eye about him. After he reached the Twenty-third Street station, he consulted a cabman, and had himself driven to a men's furnishing establishment which was just opening for the day. He spent upward of two hours there, buying with endless reconsidering and great care. His new street suit he put on in the fitting-room; the frock coat and dress clothes he had bundled into the cab with his new shirts. Then he drove to a hatter's and a shoe house. His next errand was at Tiffany's, where he selected silver mounted brushes and a scarf-pin. He would not wait to have his silver marked, he said. Lastly, he stopped at a trunk shop on Broadway, and had his purchases packed into various travelling bags.

It was a little after one o'clock when he drove up to the Waldorf, and, after settling with the cabman, went into the office. He registered from Washington; said his mother and father had been abroad, and that he had come down to await the arrival of their steamer. He told his story plausibly and had no trouble, since he offered to pay for them in advance, in engaging his rooms; a sleeping-room, sitting-room and bath.

Not once, but a hundred times Paul had planned this entry into New York. He had gone over every detail of it with Charley Edwards, and in his scrap book at home there were pages of description about New York hotels, cut from the Sunday papers.

When he was shown to his sitting-room on the eighth floor, he saw at a glance that everything was as it should be; there was but one detail in his mental picture that the place did not realize, so he rang for the bell boy and sent him down for flowers. He moved about nervously until the boy returned, putting away his new linen and fingering it delightedly as he did so. When the flowers came, he put them hastily into water, and then tumbled into a hot bath. Presently he came out of his white bath-room, resplendent in his new silk underwear, and playing with the tassels of his red robe. The snow was whirling so fiercely outside his windows that he could scarcely see across the street; but within, the air was deliciously soft and fragrant. He put the violets and jonquils on the tabouret beside the couch, and threw himself down with a long sigh, covering himself with a Roman blanket. He was thoroughly tired; he had been in such haste, he had stood up to such a strain, covered so much ground in the last twenty-four hours, that he wanted to think how it had all come about. Lulled by the sound of the wind, the warm air, and the cool fragrance of the flowers, he sank into deep, drowsy retrospection.

It had been wonderfully simple; when they had shut him out of the theatre and concert hall, when they had taken away his bone, the whole thing was virtually determined. The rest was a mere matter of opportunity. The only thing that at all surprised him was his own courage—for he realized well enough that he had always been tormented by fear, a sort of apprehensive dread that, of late years, as the meshes of the lies he had told closed about him, had been pulling the muscles of his body tighter and tighter. Until now, he could not remember a time when he had not been dreading something. Even when he was a little boy, it was always there—behind him, or before, or on either side. There had always been the shadowed corner, the dark place into which he dared not look, but from which something seemed always to be watching him—and Paul had done things that were not pretty to watch, he knew.

But now he had a curious sense of relief, as though he had at last thrown down the gauntlet to the thing in the corner.

Yet it was but a day since he had been sulking in the traces; but yesterday afternoon that he had been sent to the bank with Denny & Carson's deposit, as usual—but this time he was instructed to leave the book to be balanced. There was above two thousand dollars in checks, and nearly a thousand in the bank notes which he had taken from the book and quietly transferred to his pocket. At the bank he had made

out a new deposit slip. His nerves had been steady enough to
permit of his returning to the office, where he had finished his
work and asked for a full day's holiday tomorrow, Saturday,
giving a perfectly reasonable pretext. The bank book, he
knew, would not be returned before Monday or Tuesday, and
his father would be out of town for the next week. From the
time he slipped the bank notes into his pocket until he
boarded the night train for New York, he had not known a
moment's hesitation.

How astonishingly easy it had all been; here he was, the
thing done; and this time there would be no awakening, no
figure at the top of the stairs. He watched the snow flakes
whirling by his window until he fell asleep.

When he awoke, it was four o'clock in the afternoon. He
bounded up with a start; one of his precious days gone al-
ready! He spent nearly an hour in dressing, watching every
stage of his toilet carefully in the mirror. Everything was quite
perfect; he was exactly the kind of boy he had always wanted
to be.

When he went downstairs, Paul took a carriage and drove
up Fifth avenue toward the Park. The snow had somewhat
abated; carriages and tradesmen's wagons were hurrying
soundlessly to and fro in the winter twilight; boys in woollen
mufflers were shovelling off the doorsteps; the avenue stages
made fine spots of colour against the white street. Here and
there on the corners whole flower gardens blooming behind
glass windows, against which the snow flakes stuck and
melted; violets, roses, carnations, lilies of the valley—some-
how vastly more lovely and alluring that they blossomed thus
unnaturally in the snow. The Park itself was a wonderful stage
winter-piece.

When he returned, the pause of the twilight had ceased,
and the tune of the streets had changed. The snow was falling
faster, lights streamed from the hotels that reared their many
stories fearlessly up into the storm, defying the raging Atlan-
tic winds. A long, black stream of carriages poured down the
avenue, intersected here and there by other streams, tending
horizontally. There were a score of cabs about the entrance of
his hotel, and his driver had to wait. Boys in livery were run-
ning in and out of the awning stretched across the sidewalk,

up and down the red velvet carpet laid from the door to the street. Above, about, within it all, was the rumble and roar, the hurry and toss of thousands of human beings as hot for pleasure as himself, and on every side of him towered the glaring affirmation of the omnipotence of wealth.

The boy set his teeth and drew his shoulders together in a spasm of realization; the plot of all dramas, the text of all romances, the nerve-stuff of all sensations was whirling about him like the snow flakes. He burnt like a faggot in a tempest.

When Paul came down to dinner, the music of the orchestra floated up the elevator shaft to greet him. As he stepped into the thronged corridor, he sank back into one of the chairs against the wall to get his breath. The lights, the chatter, the perfumes, the bewildering medley of colour—he had, for a moment, the feeling of not being able to stand it. But only for a moment; these were his own people, he told himself. He went slowly about the corridors, through the writing-rooms, smoking-rooms, reception-rooms, as though he were exploring the chambers of an enchanted palace, built and peopled for him alone.

When he reached the dining-room he sat down at a table near a window. The flowers, the white linen, the many-coloured wine glasses, the gay toilettes of the women, the low popping of corks, the undulating repetitions of the *Blue Danube* from the orchestra, all flooded Paul's dream with bewildering radiance. When the roseate tinge of his champagne was added—that cold, precious, bubbling stuff that creamed and foamed in his glass—Paul wondered that there were honest men in the world at all. This was what all the world was fighting for, he reflected; this was what all the struggle was about. He doubted the reality of his past. Had he ever known a place called Cordelia Street, a place where fagged looking business men boarded the early car? Mere rivets in a machine they seemed to Paul,—sickening men, with combings of children's hair always hanging to their coats, and the smell of cooking in their clothes. Cordelia Street— Ah, that belonged to another time and country! Had he not always been thus, had he not sat here night after night, from as far back as he could remember, looking pensively over just such shimmering textures, and slowly twirling the stem of a glass like this one between his thumb and middle finger? He rather thought he had.

He was not in the least abashed or lonely. He had no especial desire to meet or to know any of these people; all he demanded was the right to look on and conjecture, to watch the pageant. The mere stage properties were all he contended for. Nor was he lonely later in the evening, in his loge at the Opera. He was entirely rid of his nervous misgivings, of his forced aggressiveness, of the imperative desire to show himself different from his surroundings. He felt now that his surroundings explained him. Nobody questioned the purple; he had only to wear it passively. He had only to glance down at his dress coat to reassure himself that here it would be impossible for anyone to humiliate him.

He found it hard to leave his beautiful sitting-room to go to bed that night, and sat long watching the raging storm from his turret window. When he went to sleep, it was with the lights turned on in his bedroom; partly because of his old timidity, and partly so that, if he should wake in the night, there would be no wretched moment of doubt, no horrible suspicion of yellow wall-paper, or of Washington and Calvin above his bed.

On Sunday morning the city was practically snow-bound. Paul breakfasted late, and in the afternoon he fell in with a wild San Francisco boy, a freshman at Yale, who said he had run down for a "little flyer" over Sunday. The young man offered to show Paul the night side of the town, and the two boys went off together after dinner, not returning to the hotel until seven o'clock the next morning. They had started out in the confiding warmth of a champagne friendship, but their parting in the elevator was singularly cool. The freshman pulled himself together to make his train, and Paul went to bed. He awoke at two o'clock in the afternoon, very thirsty and dizzy, and rang for ice-water, coffee, and the Pittsburgh papers.

On the part of the hotel management, Paul excited no suspicion. There was this to be said for him, that he wore his spoils with dignity and in no way made himself conspicuous. His chief greediness lay in his ears and eyes, and his excesses were not offensive ones. His dearest pleasures were the grey winter twilights in his sitting-room; his quiet enjoyment of his flowers, his clothes, his wide divan, his cigarette and his sense of power. He could not remember a time when he had felt so at peace with himself. The mere release from the necessity of petty lying, lying every day and every day, restored his self-respect. He had never lied for pleasure, even at school; but to make himself noticed and admired, to assert his difference from other Cordelia Street boys; and he felt a good deal more manly, more honest, even, now that he had no need for boastful pretensions, now that he could, as his actor friends used to say, "dress the part." It was characteristic that remorse did not occur to him. His golden days went by without a shadow, and he made each as perfect as he could.

On the eighth day after his arrival in New York, he found the whole affair exploited in the Pittsburgh papers, exploited with a wealth of detail which indicated that local news of a sensational nature was at a low ebb. The firm of Denny & Carson announced that the boy's father had refunded the full amount of his theft, and that they had no intention of prosecuting. The Cumberland minister had been interviewed, and expressed his hope of yet reclaiming the motherless lad, and Paul's Sabbath-school teacher declared that she would spare no effort to that end. The rumour had reached Pittsburgh that the boy had been seen in a New York hotel, and his father had gone East to find him and bring him home.

Paul had just come in to dress for dinner; he sank into a chair, weak in the knees, and clasped his head in his hands. It was to be worse than jail, even; the tepid waters of Cordelia Street were to close over him finally and forever. The grey monotony stretched before him in hopeless, unrelieved years; Sabbath-school, Young People's Meeting, the yellow-papered room, the damp dish-towels; it all rushed back upon him with sickening vividness. He had the old feeling that the orchestra had suddenly stopped, the sinking sensation that the play was over. The sweat broke out on his face, and he sprang to his feet, looked about him with his white, conscious smile, and winked at himself in the mirror. With something of the childish belief in miracles with which he had so often gone to class, all his lessons unlearned, Paul dressed and dashed whistling down the corridor to the elevator.

He had no sooner entered the dining-room and caught the measure of the music, than his remembrance was lightened by his old elastic power of claiming the moment, mounting with it, and finding it all sufficient. The glare and glitter about him, the mere scenic accessories had again, and for the last time, their old potency. He would show himself that he was game, he would finish the thing splendidly. He doubted, more than ever, the existence of Cordelia Street, and for the first time he drank his wine recklessly. Was he not, after all, one of these fortunate beings? Was he not still himself, and in his own place? He drummed a nervous accompaniment to the music and looked about him, telling himself over and over that it had paid.

He reflected drowsily, to the swell of the violin and the chill sweetness of his wine, that he might have done it more wisely. He might have caught an outbound steamer and been well out of their clutches before now. But the other side of the world had seemed too far away and too uncertain then; he could not have waited for it; his need had been too sharp. If he had to choose over again, he would do the same thing tomorrow. He looked affectionately about the dining-room, now gilded with a soft mist. Ah, it had paid indeed!

Paul was awakened next morning by a painful throbbing in his head and feet. He had thrown himself across the bed without undressing, and had slept with his shoes on. His limbs and hands were lead heavy, and his tongue and throat were parched. There came upon him one of those fateful attacks of clear-headedness that never occurred except when he was physically exhausted and his nerves hung loose. He lay still and closed his eyes and let the tide of realities wash over him.

His father was in New York; "stopping at some joint or other," he told himself. The memory of successive summers on the front stoop fell upon him like a weight of black water. He had not a hundred dollars left; and he knew now, more than ever, that money was everything, the wall that stood between all he loathed and all he wanted. The thing was winding itself up; he had thought of that on his first glorious day in New York, and had even provided a way to snap the thread. It lay on his dressing-table now; he had got it out last night when he came blindly up from dinner,—but the shiny metal hurt his eyes, and he disliked the look of it, anyway.

He rose and moved about with a painful effort, succumbing now and again to attacks of nausea. It was the old depression exaggerated; all the world had become Cordelia Street. Yet somehow he was not afraid of anything, was absolutely calm; perhaps because he had looked into the dark corner at last, and knew. It was bad enough, what he saw there; but somehow not so bad as his long fear of it had been. He saw everything clearly now. He had a feeling that he had made the best of it, that he had lived the sort of life he was meant to live, and for half an hour he sat staring at the revolver. But he told himself that was not the way, so he went downstairs and took a cab to the ferry.

When Paul arrived at Newark, he got off the train and took another cab, directing the driver to follow the Pennsylvania tracks out of the town. The snow lay heavy on the roadways and had drifted deep in the open fields. Only here and there the dead grass or dried weed stalks projected, singularly black, above it. Once well into the country, Paul dismissed the carriage and walked, floundering along the tracks, his mind a medley of irrelevant things. He seemed to hold in his brain an actual picture of everything he had seen that morning. He remembered every feature of both his drivers, the toothless old woman from whom he had bought the red flowers in his coat, the agent from whom he had got his ticket, and all of his fellow-passengers on the ferry. His mind, unable to cope with vital matters near at hand, worked feverishly and deftly at sorting and grouping these images. They made for him a part of the ugliness of the world, of the ache in his head, and the bitter burning on his tongue. He stooped and put a handful of snow into his mouth as he walked, but that, too, seemed hot. When he reached a little hillside, where the tracks ran through a cut some twenty feet below him, he stopped and sat down.

The carnations in his coat were drooping with the cold, he noticed; all their red glory over. It occurred to him that all the flowers he had seen in the show windows that first night must have gone the same way, long before this. It was only one splendid breath they had, in spite of their brave mockery at the winter outside the glass. It was a losing game in the end, it seemed, this revolt against the homilies by which the world is run. Paul took one of the blossoms carefully from his coat and scooped a little hole in the snow, where he covered it up. Then he dozed a while, from his weak condition, seeming insensible to the cold.

The sound of an approaching train woke him, and he started to his feet, remembering only his resolution, and afraid lest he should be too late. He stood watching the approaching locomotive, his teeth chattering, his lips drawn away from them in a frightened smile; once or twice he glanced nervously sidewise, as though he were being watched. When the right moment came, he jumped. As he fell, the folly of his haste occurred to him with merciless clearness, the vastness of what he had left undone. There flashed through his brain, clearer than ever before, the blue of Adriatic water, the yellow of Algerian sands.

He felt something strike his chest,—his body was being thrown swiftly through the air, on and on, immeasurably far and fast, while his limbs gently relaxed. Then, because the picture making mechanism was crushed, the disturbing visions flashed into black, and Paul dropped back into the immense design of things.

A Wagner Matinée

I RECEIVED one morning a letter, written in pale ink on glassy, blue-lined note-paper, and bearing the postmark of a little Nebraska village. This communication, worn and rubbed, looking as if it had been carried for some days in a coat pocket that was none too clean, was from my uncle Howard, and informed me that his wife had been left a small legacy by a bachelor relative, and that it would be necessary for her to go to Boston to attend to the settling of the estate. He requested me to meet her at the station and render her whatever services might be necessary. On examining the date indicated as that of her arrival, I found it to be no later than tomorrow. He had characteristically delayed writing until, had I been away from home for a day, I must have missed my aunt altogether.

The name of my Aunt Georgiana opened before me a gulf of recollection so wide and deep that, as the letter dropped from my hand, I felt suddenly a stranger to all the present conditions of my existence, wholly ill at ease and out of place amid the familiar surroundings of my study. I became, in short, the gangling farmer-boy my aunt had known, scourged with chilblains and bashfulness, my hands cracked and sore from the corn husking. I sat again before her parlour organ, fumbling the scales with my stiff, red fingers, while she, beside me, made canvas mittens for the huskers.

The next morning, after preparing my landlady for a visitor, I set out for the station. When the train arrived I had some difficulty in finding my aunt. She was the last of the passengers to alight, and it was not until I got her into the carriage that she seemed really to recognize me. She had come all the way in a day coach; her linen duster had become black with soot and her black bonnet grey with dust during the journey. When we arrived at my boarding-house the landlady put her to bed at once and I did not see her again until the next morning.

Whatever shock Mrs. Springer experienced at my aunt's appearance, she considerately concealed. As for myself, I saw my aunt's battered figure with that feeling of awe and respect with which we behold explorers who have left their ears and fingers north of Franz-Joseph-Land, or their health somewhere along the Upper Congo. My Aunt Georgiana had been a music teacher at the Boston Conservatory, somewhere back in the latter sixties. One summer, while visiting in the little village among the Green Mountains where her ancestors had dwelt for generations, she had kindled the callow fancy of my uncle, Howard Carpenter, then an idle, shiftless boy of twenty-one. When she returned to her duties in Boston, Howard followed her, and the upshot of this infatuation was that she eloped with him, eluding the reproaches of her family and the criticism of her friends by going with him to the Nebraska frontier. Carpenter, who, of course, had no money, took up a homestead in Red Willow County, fifty miles from the railroad. There they had measured off their land themselves, driving across the prairie in a wagon, to the wheel of which they had tied a red cotton handkerchief, and counting its revolutions. They built a dug-out in the red hillside, one of those cave dwellings whose inmates so often reverted to primitive conditions. Their water they got from the lagoons where the buffalo drank, and their slender stock of provisions was always at the mercy of bands of roving Indians. For thirty years my aunt had not been farther than fifty miles from the homestead.

I owed to this woman most of the good that ever came my way in my boyhood, and had a reverential affection for her. During the years when I was riding herd for my uncle, my aunt, after cooking the three meals—the first of which was ready at six o'clock in the morning—and putting the six children to bed, would often stand until midnight at her ironing-board, with me at the kitchen table beside her, hearing me recite Latin declensions and conjugations, gently shaking me when my drowsy head sank down over a page of irregular verbs. It was to her, at her ironing or mending, that I read my first Shakspere, and her old text-book on mythology was the first that ever came into my empty hands. She taught me my scales and exercises on the little parlour organ which her husband had bought her after fifteen years during which she had not so much as seen a musical instrument. She would sit beside me by the hour, darning and counting, while I struggled with the "Joyous Farmer." She seldom talked to me about music, and I understood why. Once when I had been doggedly beating out some easy passages from an old score of *Euryanthe* I had found among her music books, she came up to me and, putting her hands over my eyes, gently drew my head back upon her shoulder, saying tremulously, "Don't love it so well, Clark, or it may be taken from you."

When my aunt appeared on the morning after her arrival in Boston, she was still in a semi-somnambulant state. She seemed not to realize that she was in the city where she had spent her youth, the place longed for hungrily half a lifetime. She had been so wretchedly train-sick throughout the journey that she had no recollection of anything but her discomfort, and, to all intents and purposes, there were but a few hours of nightmare between the farm in Red Willow County and my study on Newbury Street. I had planned a little pleasure for her that afternoon, to repay her for some of the glorious moments she had given me when we used to milk together in the straw-thatched cowshed and she, because I was more than usually tired, or because her husband had spoken sharply to me, would tell me of the splendid performance of the *Huguenots* she had seen in Paris, in her youth.

At two o'clock the Symphony Orchestra was to give a Wagner program, and I intended to take my aunt; though, as I conversed with her, I grew doubtful about her enjoyment of it. I suggested our visiting the Conservatory and the Common before lunch, but she seemed altogether too timid to wish to venture out. She questioned me absently about various changes in the city, but she was chiefly concerned that she had forgotten to leave instructions about feeding half-skimmed milk to a certain weakling calf, "old Maggie's calf, you know, Clark," she explained, evidently having forgotten how long I had been away. She was further troubled because she had neglected to tell her daughter about the freshly-opened kit of mackerel in the cellar, which would spoil if it were not used directly.

I asked her whether she had ever heard any of the Wagnerian operas, and found that she had not, though she was perfectly familiar with their respective situations, and had once possessed the piano score of *The Flying Dutchman*. I began to think it would be best to get her back to Red Willow County without waking her, and regretted having suggested the concert.

From the time we entered the concert hall, however, she was a trifle less passive and inert, and for the first time seemed to perceive her surroundings. I had felt some trepidation lest she might become aware of her queer, country clothes, or might experience some painful embarrassment at stepping suddenly into the world to which she had been dead for a quarter of a century. But, again, I found how superficially I had judged her. She sat looking about her with eyes as impersonal, almost as stony, as those with which the granite Rameses in a museum watches the froth and fret that ebbs and flows about his pedestal. I have seen this same aloofness in old miners who drift into the Brown hotel at Denver, their pockets full of bullion, their linen soiled, their haggard faces unshaven; standing in the thronged corridors as solitary as though they were still in a frozen camp on the Yukon.

The matinée audience was made up chiefly of women. One lost the contour of faces and figures, indeed any effect of line whatever, and there was only the colour of bodices past counting, the shimmer of fabrics soft and firm, silky and sheer; red, mauve, pink, blue, lilac, purple, écru, rose, yellow, cream, and white, all the colours that an impressionist finds in a sunlit landscape, with here and there the dead shadow of a frock coat. My Aunt Georgiana regarded them as though they had been so many daubs of tube-paint on a palette.

When the musicians came out and took their places, she gave a little stir of anticipation, and looked with quickening interest down over the rail at that invariable grouping, perhaps the first wholly familiar thing that had greeted her eye since she had left old Maggie and her weakling calf. I could feel how all those details sank into her soul, for I had not forgotten how they had sunk into mine when I came fresh from ploughing forever and forever between green aisles of corn, where, as in a treadmill, one might walk from daybreak to dusk without perceiving a shadow of change. The clean profiles of the musicians, the gloss of their linen, the dull black of their coats, the beloved shapes of the instruments, the patches of yellow light on the smooth, varnished bellies of the 'cellos and the bass viols in the rear, the restless, wind-tossed forest of fiddle necks and bows—I recalled how, in the first orchestra I ever heard, those long bow-strokes seemed to draw the heart out of me, as a conjurer's stick reels out yards of paper ribbon from a hat.

The first number was the *Tannhauser* overture. When the horns drew out the first strain of the Pilgrim's chorus, Aunt Georgiana clutched my coat sleeve. Then it was I first realized that for her this broke a silence of thirty years. With the battle between the two motives, with the frenzy of the Venusberg theme and its ripping of strings, there came to me an over-whelming sense of the waste and wear we are so powerless to combat; and I saw again the tall, naked house on the prairie, black and grim as a wooden fortress; the black pond where I had learned to swim, its margin pitted with sun-dried cattle tracks; the rain gullied clay banks about the naked house, the four dwarf ash seedlings where the dish-cloths were always hung to dry before the kitchen door. The world there was the flat world of the ancients; to the east, a cornfield that stretched to daybreak; to the west, a corral that reached to sunset; between, the conquests of peace, dearer-bought than those of war.

The overture closed, my aunt released my coat sleeve, but she said nothing. She sat staring dully at the orchestra. What, I wondered, did she get from it? She had been a good pianist in her day, I knew, and her musical education had been broader than that of most music teachers of a quarter of a century ago. She had often told me of Mozart's operas and Meyerbeer's, and I could remember hearing her sing, years ago, certain melodies of Verdi. When I had fallen ill with a fever in her house she used to sit by my cot in the evening—when the cool, night wind blew in through the faded mos-quito netting tacked over the window and I lay watching a certain bright star that burned red above the cornfield—and sing "Home to our mountains, O, let us return!" in a way fit to break the heart of a Vermont boy near dead of homesick-ness already.

I watched her closely through the prelude to *Tristan and Isolde*, trying vainly to conjecture what that seething turmoil of strings and winds might mean to her, but she sat mutely staring at the violin bows that drove obliquely downward, like the pelting streaks of rain in a summer shower. Had this music any message for her? Had she enough left to at all comprehend this power which had kindled the world since she had left it? I was in a fever of curiosity, but Aunt Georgiana sat silent upon her peak in Darien. She preserved this utter immobility throughout the number from *The Flying Dutchman*, though her fingers worked mechanically upon her black dress, as if, of themselves, they were recalling the piano score they had once played. Poor hands! They had been stretched and twisted into mere tentacles to hold and lift and knead with; — on one of them a thin, worn band that had once been a wedding ring. As I pressed and gently quieted one of those groping hands, I remembered with quivering eyelids their services for me in other days.

Soon after the tenor began the "Prize Song," I heard a quick drawn breath and turned to my aunt. Her eyes were closed, but the tears were glistening on her cheeks, and I think, in a moment more, they were in my eyes as well. It never really died, then—the soul which can suffer so excruciatingly and so interminably; it withers to the outward eye only; like that strange moss which can lie on a dusty shelf half a century and yet, if placed in water, grows green again. She wept so throughout the development and elaboration of the melody.

During the intermission before the second half, I questioned my aunt and found that the "Prize Song" was not new to her. Some years before there had drifted to the farm in Red Willow County a young German, a tramp cow-puncher, who had sung in the chorus at Bayreuth when he was a boy, along with the other peasant boys and girls. Of a Sunday morning he used to sit on his gingham-sheeted bed in the hands' bedroom which opened off the kitchen, cleaning the leather of his boots and saddle, singing the "Prize Song," while my aunt went about her work in the kitchen. She had hovered over him until she had prevailed upon him to join the country church, though his sole fitness for this step, in so far as I could gather, lay in his boyish face and his possession of this divine melody. Shortly afterward, he had gone to town on the Fourth of July, been drunk for several days, lost his money at a faro table, ridden a saddled Texas steer on a bet, and disappeared with a fractured collar-bone. All this my aunt told me huskily, wanderingly, as though she were talking in the weak lapses of illness.

"Well, we have come to better things than the old *Trovatore* at any rate, Aunt Georgie?" I queried, with a well meant effort at jocularity.

Her lip quivered and she hastily put her handkerchief up to her mouth. From behind it she murmured, "And you have been hearing this ever since you left me, Clark?" Her question was the gentlest and saddest of reproaches.

The second half of the program consisted of four numbers from the *Ring*, and closed with Siegfried's funeral march. My aunt wept quietly, but almost continuously, as a shallow vessel overflows in a rain-storm. From time to time her dim eyes looked up at the lights, burning softly under their dull glass globes.

The deluge of sound poured on and on; I never knew what she found in the shining current of it; I never knew how far it bore her, or past what happy islands. From the trembling of her face I could well believe that before the last number she had been carried out where the myriad graves are, into the grey, nameless burying grounds of the sea; or into some world of death vaster yet, where, from the beginning of the world, hope has lain down with hope and dream with dream and, renouncing, slept.

The concert was over; the people filed out of the hall chattering and laughing, glad to relax and find the living level again, but my kinswoman made no effort to rise. The harpist slipped the green felt cover over his instrument; the flute-players shook the water from their mouthpieces; the men of the orchestra went out one by one, leaving the stage to the chairs and music stands, empty as a winter cornfield.

I spoke to my aunt. She burst into tears and sobbed pleadingly. "I don't want to go, Clark, I don't want to go!"

I understood. For her, just outside the concert hall, lay the black pond with the cattle-tracked bluffs; the tall, unpainted house, with weather-curled boards, naked as a tower; the crook-backed ash seedlings where the dish-cloths hung to dry; the gaunt, moulting turkeys picking up refuse about the kitchen door.

The Sculptor's Funeral

A GROUP of the townspeople stood on the station siding of a little Kansas town, awaiting the coming of the night train, which was already twenty minutes overdue. The snow had fallen thick over everything; in the pale starlight the line of bluffs across the wide, white meadows south of the town made soft, smoke-coloured curves against the clear sky. The men on the siding stood first on one foot and then on the other, their hands thrust deep into their trousers pockets, their overcoats open, their shoulders screwed up with the cold; and they glanced from time to time toward the southeast, where the railroad track wound along the river shore. They conversed in low tones and moved about restlessly, seeming uncertain as to what was expected of them. There was but one of the company who looked as if he knew exactly why he was there, and he kept conspicuously apart; walking to the far end of the platform, returning to the station door, then pacing up the track again, his chin sunk in the high collar of his overcoat, his burly shoulders drooping forward, his gait heavy and dogged. Presently he was approached by a tall, spare, grizzled man clad in a faded Grand Army suit, who shuffled out from the group and advanced with a certain deference, craning his neck forward until his back made the angle of a jack-knife three-quarters open.

"I reckon she's a-goin' to be pretty late agin tonight, Jim," he remarked in a squeaky falsetto. "S'pose it's the snow?"

"I don't know," responded the other man with a shade of annoyance, speaking from out an astonishing cataract of red beard that grew fiercely and thickly in all directions.

The spare man shifted the quill toothpick he was chewing to the other side of his mouth. "It ain't likely that anybody from the East will come with the corpse, I s'pose," he went on reflectively.

"I don't know," responded the other, more curtly than before.

"It's too bad he didn't belong to some lodge or other. I like an order funeral myself. They seem more appropriate for people of some repytation," the spare man continued, with an ingratiating concession in his shrill voice, as he carefully placed his toothpick in his vest pocket. He always carried the flag at the G. A. R. funerals in the town.

The heavy man turned on his heel, without replying, and walked up the siding. The spare man rejoined the uneasy group. "Jim's ez full ez a tick, ez ushel," he commented commiseratingly.

Just then a distant whistle sounded, and there was a shuffling of feet on the platform. A number of lanky boys, of all ages, appeared as suddenly and slimily as eels wakened by the crack of thunder; some came from the waiting-room, where they had been warming themselves by the red stove, or half asleep on the slat benches; others uncoiled themselves from baggage trucks or slid out of express wagons. Two clambered down from the driver's seat of a hearse that stood backed up against the siding. They straightened their stooping shoulders and lifted their heads, and a flash of momentary animation kindled their dull eyes at that cold, vibrant scream, the world-wide call for men. It stirred them like the note of a trumpet; just as it had often stirred the man who was coming home tonight, in his boyhood.

The night express shot, red as a rocket, from out the eastward marsh lands and wound along the river shore under the long lines of shivering poplars that sentinelled the meadows, the escaping steam hanging in grey masses against the pale sky and blotting out the Milky Way. In a moment the red glare from the headlight streamed up the snow-covered track before the siding and glittered on the wet, black rails. The burly man with the dishevelled red beard walked swiftly up the platform toward the approaching train, uncovering his head as he went. The group of men behind him hesitated, glanced questioningly at one another, and awkwardly followed his example. The train stopped, and the crowd shuffled up to the express car just as the door was thrown open, the man in the G. A. R. suit thrusting his head forward with curiosity. The express messenger appeared in the doorway, accompanied by a young man in a long ulster and travelling cap.

"Are Mr. Merrick's friends here?" inquired the young man.

The group on the platform swayed uneasily. Philip Phelps, the banker, responded with dignity: "We have come to take charge of the body. Mr. Merrick's father is very feeble and can't be about."

"Send the agent out here," growled the express messenger, "and tell the operator to lend a hand."

The coffin was got out of its rough-box and down on the snowy platform. The townspeople drew back enough to make room for it and then formed a close semicircle about it, looking curiously at the palm leaf which lay across the black cover. No one said anything. The baggage man stood by his truck, waiting to get at the trunks. The engine panted heavily, and the fireman dodged in and out among the wheels with his yellow torch and long oil-can, snapping the spindle boxes. The young Bostonian, one of the dead sculptor's pupils who had come with the body, looked about him helplessly. He turned to the banker, the only one of that black, uneasy, stoop-shouldered group who seemed enough of an individual to be addressed.

"None of Mr. Merrick's brothers are here?" he asked uncertainly.

The man with the red beard for the first time stepped up and joined the others. "No, they have not come yet; the family is scattered. The body will be taken directly to the house." He stooped and took hold of one of the handles of the coffin.

"Take the long hill road up, Thompson, it will be easier on the horses," called the liveryman as the undertaker snapped the door of the hearse and prepared to mount to the driver's seat.

Laird, the red-bearded lawyer, turned again to the stranger: "We didn't know whether there would be any one with him or not," he explained. "It's a long walk, so you'd better go up in the hack." He pointed to a single battered conveyance, but the young man replied stiffly: "Thank you, but I think I will go up with the hearse. If you don't object," turning to the undertaker, "I'll ride with you."

They clambered up over the wheels and drove off in the starlight up the long, white hill toward the town. The lamps in the still village were shining from under the low, snow-burdened roofs; and beyond, on every side, the plains reached out into emptiness, peaceful and wide as the soft sky itself, and wrapped in a tangible, white silence.

When the hearse backed up to a wooden sidewalk before a naked, weather-beaten frame house, the same composite, ill-defined group that had stood upon the station siding was huddled about the gate. The front yard was an icy swamp, and a couple of warped planks, extending from the sidewalk to the door, made a sort of rickety foot-bridge. The gate hung on one hinge, and was opened wide with difficulty. Steavens, the young stranger, noticed that something black was tied to the knob of the front door.

The grating sound made by the casket, as it was drawn from the hearse, was answered by a scream from the house; the front door was wrenched open, and a tall, corpulent woman rushed out bareheaded into the snow and flung herself upon the coffin, shrieking: "My boy, my boy! And this is how you've come home to me!"

As Steavens turned away and closed his eyes with a shudder of unutterable repulsion, another woman, also tall, but flat and angular, dressed entirely in black, darted out of the house and caught Mrs. Merrick by the shoulders, crying sharply: "Come, come, mother; you mustn't go on like this!" Her tone changed to one of obsequious solemnity as she turned to the banker: "The parlour is ready, Mr. Phelps."

The bearers carried the coffin along the narrow boards, while the undertaker ran ahead with the coffin-rests. They bore it into a large, unheated room that smelled of dampness and disuse and furniture polish, and set it down under a hanging lamp ornamented with jingling glass prisms and before a "Rogers group" of John Alden and Priscilla, wreathed with smilax. Henry Steavens stared about him with the sickening conviction that there had been a mistake, and that he had somehow arrived at the wrong destination. He looked at the clover-green Brussels, the fat plush upholstery, among the hand-painted china placques and panels and vases, for some mark of identification,—for something that might once conceivably have belonged to Harvey Merrick. It was not until he recognized his friend in the crayon portrait of a little boy in kilts and curls, hanging above the piano, that he felt willing to let any of these people approach the coffin.

"Take the lid off, Mr. Thompson; let me see my boy's face," wailed the elder woman between her sobs. This time Steavens looked fearfully, almost beseechingly into her face, red and swollen under its masses of strong, black, shiny hair. He flushed, dropped his eyes, and then, almost incredulously, looked again. There was a kind of power about her face—a kind of brutal handsomeness, even; but it was scarred and furrowed by violence, and so coloured and coarsened by fiercer passions that grief seemed never to have laid a gentle finger there. The long nose was distended and knobbed at the end, and there were deep lines on either side of it; her heavy, black brows almost met across her forehead, her teeth were large and square, and set far apart—teeth that could tear. She filled the room; the men were obliterated, seemed tossed about like twigs in an angry water, and even Steavens felt himself being drawn into the whirlpool.

The daughter—the tall, raw-boned woman in crêpe, with a mourning comb in her hair which curiously lengthened her long face—sat stiffly upon the sofa, her hands, conspicuous for their large knuckles, folded in her lap, her mouth and eyes drawn down, solemnly awaiting the opening of the coffin. Near the door stood a mulatto woman, evidently a servant in the house, with a timid bearing and an emaciated face pitifully sad and gentle. She was weeping silently, the corner of her calico apron lifted to her eyes, occasionally suppressing a long, quivering sob. Steavens walked over and stood beside her.

Feeble steps were heard on the stairs, and an old man, tall and frail, odorous of pipe smoke, with shaggy, unkept grey hair and a dingy beard, tobacco stained about the mouth, entered uncertainly. He went slowly up to the coffin and stood rolling a blue cotton handkerchief between his hands, seeming so pained and embarrassed by his wife's orgy of grief that he had no consciousness of anything else.

"There, there, Annie, dear, don't take on so," he quavered timidly, putting out a shaking hand and awkwardly patting her elbow. She turned and sank upon his shoulder with such violence that he tottered a little. He did not even glance toward the coffin, but continued to look at her with a dull, frightened, appealing expression, as a spaniel looks at the whip. His sunken cheeks slowly reddened and burned with miserable shame. When his wife rushed from the room, her daughter strode after her with set lips. The servant stole up to the coffin, bent over it for a moment, and then slipped away to the kitchen, leaving Steavens, the lawyer, and the father to themselves. The old man stood looking down at his dead son's face. The sculptor's splendid head seemed even more noble in its rigid stillness than in life. The dark hair had crept down upon the wide forehead; the face seemed strangely long, but in it there was not that repose we expect to find in the faces of the dead. The brows were so drawn that there were two deep lines above the beaked nose, and the chin was thrust forward defiantly. It was as though the strain of life had been so sharp and bitter that death could not at once relax the tension and smooth the countenance into perfect peace—as though he were still guarding something precious, which might even yet be wrested from him.

The old man's lips were working under his stained beard. He turned to the lawyer with timid deference: "Phelps and the rest are comin' back to set up with Harve, ain't they?" he asked. "Thank 'ee, Jim, thank 'ee." He brushed the hair back gently from his son's forehead. "He was a good boy, Jim; always a good boy. He was ez gentle ez a child and the kindest of 'em all—only we didn't none of us ever onderstand him." The tears trickled slowly down his beard and dropped upon the sculptor's coat.

"Martin, Martin! Oh, Martin! come here," his wife wailed from the top of the stairs. The old man started timorously: "Yes, Annie, I'm coming." He turned away, hesitated, stood for a moment in miserable indecision; then reached back and patted the dead man's hair softly, and stumbled from the room.

"Poor old man, I didn't think he had any tears left. Seems as if his eyes would have gone dry long ago. At his age nothing cuts very deep," remarked the lawyer.

Something in his tone made Steavens glance up. While the mother had been in the room, the young man had scarcely seen any one else; but now, from the moment he first glanced into Jim Laird's florid face and blood-shot eyes, he knew that he had found what he had been heartsick at not finding before—the feeling, the understanding, that must exist in some one, even here.

The man was red as his beard, with features swollen and blurred by dissipation, and a hot, blazing blue eye. His face was strained—that of a man who is controlling himself with difficulty—and he kept plucking at his beard with a sort of fierce resentment. Steavens, sitting by the window, watched him turn down the glaring lamp, still its jangling pendants with an angry gesture, and then stand with his hands locked behind him, staring down into the master's face. He could not help wondering what link there had been between the porcelain vessel and so sooty a lump of potter's clay.

From the kitchen an uproar was sounding; when the dining-room door opened, the import of it was clear. The mother was abusing the maid for having forgotten to make the dressing for the chicken salad which had been prepared for the watchers. Steavens had never heard anything in the least like it; it was injured, emotional, dramatic abuse, unique and masterly in its excruciating cruelty, as violent and unrestrained as had been her grief of twenty minutes before. With a shudder of disgust the lawyer went into the dining-room and closed the door into the kitchen.

"Poor Roxy's getting it now," he remarked when he came back. "The Merricks took her out of the poor-house years ago; and if her loyalty would let her, I guess the poor old thing could tell tales that would curdle your blood. She's the mulatto woman who was standing in here a while ago, with her apron to her eyes. The old woman is a fury; there never was anybody like her. She made Harvey's life a hell for him when he lived at home; he was so sick ashamed of it. I never could see how he kept himself sweet."

"He was wonderful," said Steavens slowly, "wonderful; but until tonight I have never known how wonderful."

"That is the eternal wonder of it, anyway; that it can come even from such a dung heap as this," the lawyer cried, with a sweeping gesture which seemed to indicate much more than the four walls within which they stood.

"I think I'll see whether I can get a little air. The room is so close I am beginning to feel rather faint," murmured Steavens, struggling with one of the windows. The sash was stuck, however, and would not yield, so he sat down dejectedly and began pulling at his collar. The lawyer came over, loosened the sash with one blow of his red fist and sent the window up a few inches. Steavens thanked him, but the nausea which had been gradually climbing into his throat for the last half hour left him with but one desire—a desperate feeling that he must get away from this place with what was left of Harvey Merrick. Oh, he comprehended well enough now the quiet bitterness of the smile that he had seen so often on his master's lips!

Once when Merrick returned from a visit home, he brought with him a singularly feeling and suggestive bas-relief of a thin, faded old woman, sitting and sewing something pinned to her knee; while a full-lipped, full-blooded little urchin, his trousers held up by a single gallows, stood beside her, impatiently twitching her gown to call her attention to a butterfly he had caught. Steavens, impressed by the tender and delicate modelling of the thin, tired face, had asked him if it were his mother. He remembered the dull flush that had burned up in the sculptor's face.

The lawyer was sitting in a rocking-chair beside the coffin, his head thrown back and his eyes closed. Steavens looked at him earnestly, puzzled at the line of the chin, and wondering why a man should conceal a feature of such distinction under that disfiguring shock of beard. Suddenly, as though he felt the young sculptor's keen glance, Jim Laird opened his eyes.

"Was he always a good deal of an oyster?" he asked abruptly. "He was terribly shy as a boy."

"Yes, he was an oyster, since you put it so," rejoined Steavens. "Although he could be very fond of people, he always gave one the impression of being detached. He disliked violent emotion; he was reflective, and rather distrustful of himself—except, of course, as regarded his work. He was sure enough there. He distrusted men pretty thoroughly and women even more, yet somehow without believing ill of them. He was determined, indeed, to believe the best; but he seemed afraid to investigate."

"A burnt dog dreads the fire," said the lawyer grimly, and closed his eyes.

Steavens went on and on, reconstructing that whole miser-

able boyhood. All this raw, biting ugliness had been the por-
tion of the man whose mind was to become an exhaustless
gallery of beautiful impressions—so sensitive that the mere
shadow of a poplar leaf flickering against a sunny wall would
be etched and held there for ever. Surely, if ever a man had
the magic word in his finger tips, it was Merrick. Whatever he
touched, he revealed its holiest secret; liberated it from
enchantment and restored it to its pristine loveliness. Upon
whatever he had come in contact with, he had left a beautiful
record of the experience—a sort of ethereal signature; a scent,
a sound, a colour that was his own.

Steavens understood now the real tragedy of his master's
life; neither love nor wine, as many had conjectured; but a
blow which had fallen earlier and cut deeper than anything
else could have done—a shame not his, and yet so unes-
capably his, to hide in his heart from his very boyhood.
And without—the frontier warfare; the yearning of a boy,
cast ashore upon a desert of newness and ugliness and sor-
didness, for all that is chastened and old, and noble with
traditions.

At eleven o'clock the tall, flat woman in black announced
that the watchers were arriving, and asked them to "step into
the dining-room." As Steavens rose, the lawyer said dryly:
"You go on—it'll be a good experience for you. I'm not
equal to that crowd tonight; I've had twenty years of them."

As Steavens closed the door after him he glanced back at
the lawyer, sitting by the coffin in the dim light, with his chin
resting on his hand.

The same misty group that had stood before the door of
the express car shuffled into the dining-room. In the light of
the kerosene lamp they separated and became individuals. The
minister, a pale, feeble-looking man with white hair and
blond chin-whiskers, took his seat beside a small side table
and placed his Bible upon it. The Grand Army man sat down
behind the stove and tilted his chair back comfortably against
the wall, fishing his quill toothpick from his waistcoat pocket.
The two bankers, Phelps and Elder, sat off in a corner behind
the dinner-table, where they could finish their discussion of
the new usury law and its effect on chattel security loans. The
real estate agent, an old man with a smiling, hypocritical face,

soon joined them. The coal and lumber dealer and the cattle
shipper sat on opposite sides of the hard coal-burner, their
feet on the nickel-work. Steavens took a book from his pocket
and began to read. The talk around him ranged through var-
ious topics of local interest while the house was quieting
down. When it was clear that the members of the family were
in bed, the Grand Army man hitched his shoulders and, un-
tangling his long legs, caught his heels on the rounds of his
chair.

"S'pose there'll be a will, Phelps?" he queried in his weak
falsetto.

The banker laughed disagreeably, and began trimming his
nails with a pearl-handled pocket-knife.

"There'll scarcely be any need for one, will there?" he que-
ried in his turn.

The restless Grand Army man shifted his position again,
getting his knees still nearer his chin. "Why, the ole man says
Harve's done right well lately," he chirped.

The other banker spoke up. "I reckon he means by that
Harve ain't asked him to mortgage any more farms lately, so
as he could go on with his education."

"Seems like my mind don't reach back to a time when
Harve wasn't bein' edycated," tittered the Grand Army man.

There was a general chuckle. The minister took out his
handkerchief and blew his nose sonorously. Banker Phelps
closed his knife with a snap. "It's too bad the old man's sons
didn't turn out better," he remarked with reflective authority.
"They never hung together. He spent money enough on
Harve to stock a dozen cattle-farms, and he might as well
have poured it into Sand Creek. If Harve had stayed at home
and helped nurse what little they had, and gone into stock on
the old man's bottom farm, they might all have been well
fixed. But the old man had to trust everything to tenants and
was cheated right and left."

"Harve never could have handled stock none," interposed
the cattleman. "He hadn't it in him to be sharp. Do you re-
member when he bought Sander's mules for eight-year olds,
when everybody in town knew that Sander's father-in-law
give 'em to his wife for a wedding present eighteen years be-
fore, an' they was full-grown mules then?"

The company laughed discreetly, and the Grand Army man rubbed his knees with a spasm of childish delight.

"Harve never was much account for anything practical, and he shore was never fond of work," began the coal and lumber dealer. "I mind the last time he was home; the day he left, when the old man was out to the barn helpin' his hand hitch up to take Harve to the train, and Cal Moots was patchin' up the fence; Harve, he come out on the step and sings out, in his ladylike voice: 'Cal Moots, Cal Moots! please come cord my trunk.'"

"That's Harve for you," approved the Grand Army man. "I kin hear him howlin' yet, when he was a big feller in long pants and his mother used to whale him with a rawhide in the barn for lettin' the cows git foundered in the cornfield when he was drivin' 'em home from pasture. He killed a cow of mine that-a-way onct—a pure Jersey and the best milker I had, an' the ole man had to put up for her. Harve, he was watchin' the sun set acrost the marshes when the anamile got away."

"Where the old man made his mistake was in sending the boy East to school," said Phelps, stroking his goatee and speaking in a deliberate, judicial tone. "There was where he got his head full of nonsense. What Harve needed, of all people, was a course in some first-class Kansas City business college."

The letters were swimming before Steavens's eyes. Was it possible that these men did not understand, that the palm on the coffin meant nothing to them? The very name of their town would have remained for ever buried in the postal guide had it not been now and again mentioned in the world in connection with Harvey Merrick's. He remembered what his master had said to him on the day of his death, after the congestion of both lungs had shut off any probability of recovery, and the sculptor had asked his pupil to send his body home. "It's not a pleasant place to be lying while the world is moving and doing and bettering," he had said with a feeble smile, "but it rather seems as though we ought to go back to the place we came from, in the end. The townspeople will come in for a look at me; and after they have had their say, I shan't have much to fear from the judgment of God!"

The cattleman took up the comment. "Forty's young for a Merrick to cash in; they usually hang on pretty well. Probably he helped it along with whisky."

"His mother's people were not long lived, and Harvey never had a robust constitution," said the minister mildly. He would have liked to say more. He had been the boy's Sunday-school teacher, and had been fond of him; but he felt that he was not in a position to speak. His own sons had turned out badly, and it was not a year since one of them had made his last trip home in the express car, shot in a gambling-house in the Black Hills.

"Nevertheless, there is no disputin' that Harve frequently looked upon the wine when it was red, also variegated, and it shore made an oncommon fool of him," moralized the cattle-man.

Just then the door leading into the parlour rattled loudly and every one started involuntarily, looking relieved when only Jim Laird came out. The Grand Army man ducked his head when he saw the spark in his blue, blood-shot eye. They were all afraid of Jim; he was a drunkard, but he could twist the law to suit his client's needs as no other man in all western Kansas could do, and there were many who tried. The lawyer closed the door behind him, leaned back against it and folded his arms, cocking his head a little to one side. When he assumed this attitude in the court-room, ears were always pricked up, as it usually foretold a flood of withering sarcasm.

"I've been with you gentlemen before," he began in a dry, even tone, "when you've sat by the coffins of boys born and raised in this town; and, if I remember rightly, you were never any too well satisfied when you checked them up. What's the matter, anyhow? Why is it that reputable young men are as scarce as millionaires in Sand City? It might almost seem to a stranger that there was some way something the matter with your progressive town. Why did Ruben Sayer, the brightest young lawyer you ever turned out, after he had come home from the university as straight as a die, take to drinking and forge a check and shoot himself? Why did Bill Merrit's son die of the shakes in a saloon in Omaha? Why was Mr. Thomas's son, here, shot in a gambling-house? Why did young Adams burn his mill to beat the insurance companies and go to the pen?"

The lawyer paused and unfolded his arms, laying one clenched fist quietly on the table. "I'll tell you why. Because you drummed nothing but money and knavery into their ears from the time they wore knickerbockers; because you carped away at them as you've been carping here tonight, holding our friends Phelps and Elder up to them for their models, as our grandfathers held up George Washington and John Adams. But the boys were young, and raw at the business you put them to, and how could they match coppers with such artists as Phelps and Elder? You wanted them to be successful rascals; they were only unsuccessful ones—that's all the difference. There was only one boy ever raised in this borderland between ruffianism and civilization who didn't come to grief, and you hated Harvey Merrick more for winning out than you hated all the other boys who got under the wheels. Lord, Lord, how you did hate him! Phelps, here, is fond of saying that he could buy and sell us all out any time he's a mind to; but he knew Harve wouldn't have given a tinker's damn for his bank and all his cattlefarms put together; and a lack of appreciation, that way, goes hard with Phelps.

"Old Nimrod thinks Harve drank too much; and this from such as Nimrod and me!

"Brother Elder says Harve was too free with the old man's money—fell short in filial consideration, maybe. Well, we can all remember the very tone in which brother Elder swore his own father was a liar, in the county court; and we all know that the old man came out of that partnership with his son as bare as a sheared lamb. But maybe I'm getting personal, and I'd better be driving ahead at what I want to say."

The lawyer paused a moment, squared his heavy shoulders, and went on: "Harvey Merrick and I went to school together, back East. We were dead in earnest, and we wanted you all to be proud of us some day. We meant to be great men. Even I, and I haven't lost my sense of humour, gentlemen, I meant to be a great man. I came back here to practise, and I found you didn't in the least want me to be a great man. You wanted me to be a shrewd lawyer—oh, yes! Our veteran here wanted me to get him an increase of pension, because he had dyspepsia;

Phelps wanted a new county survey that would put the widow Wilson's little bottom farm inside his south line; Elder wanted to lend money at 5 per cent. a month, and get it collected; and Stark here wanted to wheedle old women up in Vermont into investing their annuities in real-estate mortgages that are not worth the paper they are written on. Oh, you needed me hard enough, and you'll go on needing me!

"Well, I came back here and became the damned shyster you wanted me to be. You pretend to have some sort of respect for me; and yet you'll stand up and throw mud at Harvey Merrick, whose soul you couldn't dirty and whose hands you couldn't tie. Oh, you're a discriminating lot of Christians! There have been times when the sight of Harvey's name in some Eastern paper has made me hang my head like a whipped dog; and, again, times when I liked to think of him off there in the world, away from all this hog-wallow, climbing the big, clean up-grade he'd set for himself.

"And we? Now that we've fought and lied and sweated and stolen, and hated as only the disappointed strugglers in a bitter, dead little Western town know how to do, what have we got to show for it? Harvey Merrick wouldn't have given one sunset over your marshes for all you've got put together, and you know it. It's not for me to say why, in the inscrutable wisdom of God, a genius should ever have been called from this place of hatred and bitter waters; but I want this Boston man to know that the drivel he's been hearing here tonight is the only tribute any truly great man could have from such a lot of sick, side-tracked, burnt-dog, land-poor sharks as the here-present financiers of Sand City—upon which town may God have mercy!"

The lawyer thrust out his hand to Steavens as he passed him, caught up his overcoat in the hall, and had left the house before the Grand Army man had had time to lift his ducked head and crane his long neck about at his fellows.

Next day Jim Laird was drunk and unable to attend the funeral services. Steavens called twice at his office, but was compelled to start East without seeing him. He had a presentiment that he would hear from him again, and left his address on the lawyer's table; but if Laird found it, he never acknowledged it. The thing in him that Harvey Merrick had loved must have gone under ground with Harvey Merrick's coffin; for it never spoke again, and Jim got the cold he died of driving across the Colorado mountains to defend one of Phelps's sons who had got into trouble out there by cutting government timber.

"A Death in the Desert"

EVERETT HILGARDE was conscious that the man in the seat across the aisle was looking at him intently. He was a large, florid man, wore a conspicuous diamond solitaire upon his third finger, and Everett judged him to be a travelling salesman of some sort. He had the air of an adaptable fellow who had been about the world and who could keep cool and clean under almost any circumstances.

The "High Line Flyer," as this train was derisively called among railroad men, was jerking along through the hot afternoon over the monotonous country between Holdredge and Cheyenne. Besides the blond man and himself the only occupants of the car were two dusty, bedraggled-looking girls who had been to the Exposition at Chicago, and who were earnestly discussing the cost of their first trip out of Colorado. The four uncomfortable passengers were covered with a sediment of fine, yellow dust which clung to their hair and eyebrows like gold powder. It blew up in clouds from the bleak, lifeless country through which they passed, until they were one colour with the sage-brush and sand-hills. The grey and yellow desert was varied only by occasional ruins of deserted towns, and the little red boxes of station-houses, where the spindling trees and sickly vines in the blue-grass yards made little green reserves fenced off in that confusing wilderness of sand.

As the slanting rays of the sun beat in stronger and stronger through the car-windows, the blond gentleman asked the ladies' permission to remove his coat, and sat in his lavender striped shirt-sleeves, with a black silk handkerchief tucked about his collar. He had seemed interested in Everett since they had boarded the train at Holdredge; kept glancing at him curiously and then looking reflectively out of the window, as though he were trying to recall something. But wherever Everett went, some one was almost sure to look at him with that curious interest, and it had ceased to embarrass or annoy him. Presently the stranger, seeming satisfied with his observation, leaned back in his seat, half closed his eyes, and began softly to whistle the Spring Song from *Proserpine*, the cantata that a dozen years before had made its young composer famous in a night. Everett had heard that air on guitars in Old Mexico, on mandolins at college glees, on cottage organs in New England hamlets, and only two weeks ago he had heard it played on sleighbells at a variety theatre in Denver. There was literally no way of escaping his brother's precocity. Adriance could live on the other side of the Atlantic, where his youthful indiscretions were forgotten in his mature achievements, but his brother had never been able to outrun *Proserpine*,—and here he found it again, in the Colorado sand-hills. Not that Everett was exactly ashamed of *Proserpine*; only a man of genius could have written it, but it was the sort of thing that a man of genius outgrows as soon as he can.

Everett unbent a trifle, and smiled at his neighbour across the aisle. Immediately the large man rose and coming over dropped into the seat facing Hilgarde, extending his card.

"Dusty ride, isn't it? I don't mind it myself; I'm used to it. Born and bred in de briar patch, like Br'er Rabbit. I've been trying to place you for a long time; I think I must have met you before."

"Thank you," said Everett, taking the card; "my name is Hilgarde. You've probably met my brother, Adriance; people often mistake me for him."

The travelling-man brought his hand down upon his knee with such vehemence that the solitaire blazed.

"So I was right after all, and if you're not Adriance Hilgarde you're his double. I thought I couldn't be mistaken. Seen him? Well, I guess! I never missed one of his recitals at the Auditorium, and he played the piano score of *Proserpine* through to us once at the Chicago Press Club. I used to be on the *Commercial* there before I began to travel for the publishing department of the concern. So you're Hilgarde's brother, and here I've run into you at the jumping-off place. Sounds like a newspaper yarn, doesn't it?"

The travelling-man laughed and offering Everett a cigar plied him with questions on the only subject that people ever seemed to care to talk to him about. At length the salesman and the two girls alighted at a Colorado way station, and Everett went on to Cheyenne alone.

The train pulled into Cheyenne at nine o'clock, late by a matter of four hours or so; but no one seemed particularly concerned at its tardiness except the station agent, who grumbled at being kept in the office over time on a summer night. When Everett alighted from the train he walked down the platform and stopped at the track crossing, uncertain as to what direction he should take to reach a hotel. A phaeton stood near the crossing and a woman held the reins. She was dressed in white, and her figure was clearly silhouetted against the cushions, though it was too dark to see her face. Everett had scarcely noticed her, when the switch-engine came puffing up from the opposite direction, and the head-light threw a strong glare of light on his face. The woman in the phaeton uttered a low cry and dropped the reins. Everett started forward and caught the horse's head, but the animal only lifted its ears and whisked its tail in impatient surprise. The woman sat perfectly still, her head sunk between her shoulders and her handkerchief pressed to her face. Another woman came out of the depot and hurried toward the phaeton, crying, "Katharine, dear, what is the matter?"

Everett hesitated a moment in painful embarrassment, then lifted his hat and passed on. He was accustomed to sudden recognitions in the most impossible places, especially from women.

While he was breakfasting the next morning, the head waiter leaned over his chair to murmur that there was a gentleman waiting to see him in the parlour. Everett finished his coffee, and went in the direction indicated, where he found his visitor restlessly pacing the floor. His whole manner betrayed a high degree of agitation, though his physique was not that of a man whose nerves lie near the surface. He was something below medium height, square-shouldered and solidly built. His thick, closely cut hair was beginning to show grey about the ears, and his bronzed face was heavily lined. His square brown hands were locked behind him, and he held his shoulders like a man conscious of responsibilities, yet, as he turned to greet Everett, there was an incongruous diffidence in his address.

"Good-morning, Mr. Hilgarde," he said, extending his hand; "I found your name on the hotel register. My name is

Gaylord. I'm afraid my sister startled you at the station last night, and I've come around to explain."

"Ah! the young lady in the phaeton? I'm sure I didn't know whether I had anything to do with her alarm or not. If I did, it is I who owe an apology."

The man coloured a little under the dark brown of his face.

"Oh, it's nothing you could help, sir, I fully understand that. You see, my sister used to be a pupil of your brother's, and it seems you favour him; when the switch-engine threw a light on your face, it startled her."

Everett wheeled about in his chair. "Oh! *Katharine* Gaylord! Is it possible! Why, I used to know her when I was a boy. What on earth—"

"Is she doing here?" Gaylord grimly filled out the pause. "You've got at the heart of the matter. You know my sister had been in bad health for a long time?"

"No. The last I knew of her she was singing in London. My brother and I correspond infrequently, and seldom get beyond family matters. I am deeply sorry to hear this."

The lines in Charley Gaylord's brow relaxed a little.

"What I'm trying to say, Mr. Hilgarde, is that she wants to see you. She's set on it. We live several miles out of town, but my rig's below, and I can take you out any time you can go."

"At once, then. I'll get my hat and be with you in a moment."

When he came downstairs Everett found a cart at the door, and Charley Gaylord drew a long sigh of relief as he gathered up the reins and settled back into his own element.

"I think I'd better tell you something about my sister before you see her, and I don't know just where to begin. She travelled in Europe with your brother and his wife, and sang at a lot of his concerts; but I don't know just how much you know about her."

"Very little, except that my brother always thought her the most gifted of his pupils. When I knew her she was very young and very beautiful, and quite turned my head for a while."

Everett saw that Gaylord's mind was entirely taken up by his grief. "That's the whole thing," he went on, flecking his horses with the whip.

"She was a great woman, as you say, and she didn't come of a great family. She had to fight her own way from the first. She got to Chicago, and then to New York, and then to Europe, and got a taste for it all; and now she's dying here like a rat in a hole, out of her own world, and she can't fall back into ours. We've grown apart, some way—miles and miles apart—and I'm afraid she's fearfully unhappy."

"It's a tragic story you're telling me, Gaylord," said Everett. They were well out into the country now, spinning along over the dusty plains of red grass, with the ragged blue outline of the mountains before them.

"Tragic!" cried Gaylord, starting up in his seat, "my God, nobody will ever know how tragic! It's a tragedy I live with and eat with and sleep with, until I've lost my grip on everything. You see she had made a good bit of money, but she spent it all going to health resorts. It's her lungs. I've got money enough to send her anywhere, but the doctors all say it's no use. She hasn't the ghost of a chance. It's just getting through the days now. I had no notion she was half so bad before she came to me. She just wrote that she was run down. Now that she's here, I think she'd be happier anywhere under the sun, but she won't leave. She says it's easier to let go of life here. There was a time when I was a brakeman with a run out of Bird City, Iowa, and she was a little thing I could carry on my shoulder, when I could get her everything on earth she wanted, and she hadn't a wish my $80 a month didn't cover; and now, when I've got a little property together, I can't buy her a night's sleep!"

Everett saw that, whatever Charley Gaylord's present status in the world might be, he had brought the brakeman's heart up the ladder with him.

The reins slackened in Gaylord's hand as they drew up before a showily painted house with many gables and a round tower. "Here we are," he said, turning to Everett, "and I guess we understand each other."

They were met at the door by a thin, colourless woman, whom Gaylord introduced as "My sister, Maggie." She asked her brother to show Mr. Hilgarde into the music-room, where Katharine would join him.

When Everett entered the music-room he gave a little start

of surprise, feeling that he had stepped from the glaring Wyoming sunlight into some New York studio that he had always known. He looked incredulously out of the window at the grey plain that ended in the great upheaval of the Rockies.

The haunting air of familiarity perplexed him. Suddenly his eye fell upon a large photograph of his brother above the piano. Then it all became clear enough: this was veritably his brother's room. If it were not an exact copy of one of the many studios that Adriance had fitted up in various parts of the world, wearying of them and leaving almost before the renovator's varnish had dried, it was at least in the same tone. In every detail Adriance's taste was so manifest that the room seemed to exhale his personality.

Among the photographs on the wall there was one of Katharine Gaylord, taken in the days when Everett had known her, and when the flash of her eye or the flutter of her skirt was enough to set his boyish heart in a tumult. Even now, he stood before the portrait with a certain degree of embarrassment. It was the face of a woman already old in her first youth, a trifle hard, and it told of what her brother had called her fight. The *camaraderie* of her frank, confident eyes was qualified by the deep lines about her mouth and the curve of the lips, which was both sad and cynical. Certainly she had more good-will than confidence toward the world. The chief charm of the woman, as Everett had known her, lay in her superb figure and in her eyes, which possessed a warm, life-giving quality like the sunlight; eyes which glowed with a perpetual *salutat* to the world.

Everett was still standing before the picture, his hands behind him and his head inclined, when he heard the door open. A tall woman advanced toward him, holding out her hand. As she started to speak she coughed slightly, then, laughing, said, in a low, rich voice, a trifle husky: "You see I make the traditional Camille entrance. How good of you to come, Mr. Hilgarde."

Everett was acutely conscious that while addressing him she was not looking at him at all, and, as he assured her of his pleasure in coming, he was glad to have an opportunity to collect himself. He had not reckoned upon the ravages of a long illness. The long, loose folds of her white gown had been especially designed to conceal the sharp outlines of her body, but the stamp of her disease was there; simple and ugly and obtrusive, a pitiless fact that could not be disguised or evaded. The splendid shoulders were stooped, there was a swaying unevenness in her gait, her arms seemed disproportionately long, and her hands were transparently white, and cold to the touch. The changes in her face were less obvious; the proud carriage of the head, the warm, clear eyes, even the delicate flush of colour in her cheeks, all defiantly remained, though they were all in a lower key—older, sadder, softer.

She sat down upon the divan and began nervously to arrange the pillows. "Of course I'm ill, and I look it, but you must be quite frank and sensible about that and get used to it at once, for we've no time to lose. And if I'm a trifle irritable you won't mind?—for I'm more than usually nervous."

"Don't bother with me this morning, if you are tired," urged Everett. "I can come quite as well tomorrow."

"Gracious, no!" she protested, with a flash of that quick, keen humour that he remembered as a part of her. "It's solitude that I'm tired to death of—solitude and the wrong kind of people. You see, the minister called on me this morning. He happened to be riding by on his bicycle and felt it his duty to stop. The funniest feature of his conversation is that he is always excusing my own profession to me. But how we are losing time! Do tell me about New York; Charley says you're just on from there. How does it look and taste and smell just now? I think a whiff of the Jersey ferry would be as flagons of cod-liver oil to me. Are the trees still green in Madison Square, or have they grown brown and dusty? Does the chaste Diana still keep her vows through all the exasperating changes of weather? Who has your brother's old studio now, and what misguided aspirants practise their scales in the rookeries about Carnegie Hall? What do people go to see at the theatres, and what do they eat and drink in the world nowadays? Oh, let me die in Harlem!" she was interrupted by a violent attack of coughing, and Everett, embarrassed by her discomfort, plunged into gossip about the professional people he had met in town during the summer, and the musical outlook for the winter. He was diagramming with his pencil some new mechanical device to be used at the Metropolitan in the production of the *Rheingold*, when he became conscious that she was looking at him intently, and that he was talking to the four walls.

Katharine was lying back among the pillows, watching him through half-closed eyes, as a painter looks at a picture. He finished his explanation vaguely enough and put the pencil back in his pocket. As he did so, she said, quietly: "How wonderfully like Adriance you are!"

He laughed, looking up at her with a touch of pride in his eyes that made them seem quite boyish. "Yes, isn't it absurd? It's almost as awkward as looking like Napoleon— But, after all, there are some advantages. It has made some of his friends like me, and I hope it will make you."

Katharine gave him a quick, meaning glance from under her lashes. "Oh, it did that long ago. What a haughty, reserved youth you were then, and how you used to stare at people, and then blush and look cross. Do you remember that night you took me home from a rehearsal, and scarcely spoke a word to me?"

"It was the silence of admiration," protested Everett, "very crude and boyish, but certainly sincere. Perhaps you suspected something of the sort?"

"I believe I suspected a pose; the one that boys often affect with singers. But it rather surprised me in you, for you must have seen a good deal of your brother's pupils."

Everett shook his head. "I saw my brother's pupils come and go. Sometimes I was called on to play accompaniments, or to fill out a vacancy at a rehearsal, or to order a carriage for an infuriated soprano who had thrown up her part. But they never spent any time on me, unless it was to notice the resemblance you speak of."

"Yes," observed Katharine, thoughtfully, "I noticed it then, too; but it has grown as you have grown older. That is rather strange, when you have lived such different lives. It's not merely an ordinary family likeness of features, you know, but the suggestion of the other man's personality in your face— like an air transposed to another key. But I'm not attempting to define it; it's beyond me; something altogether unusual and a trifle—well, uncanny," she finished, laughing.

Everett sat looking out under the red window-blind which

was raised just a little. As it swung back and forth in the wind it revealed the glaring panorama of the desert—a blinding stretch of yellow, flat as the sea in dead calm, splotched here and there with deep purple shadows; and, beyond, the ragged blue outline of the mountains and the peaks of snow, white as the white clouds. "I remember, when I was a child I used to be very sensitive about it. I don't think it exactly displeased me, or that I would have had it otherwise, but it seemed like a birthmark, or something not to be lightly spoken of. It came into even my relations with my mother. Ad went abroad to study when he was very young, and mother was all broken up over it. She did her whole duty by each of us, but it was generally understood among us that she'd have made burnt-offerings of us all for him any day. I was a little fellow then, and when she sat alone on the porch on summer evenings, she used sometimes to call me to her and turn my face up in the light that streamed out through the shutters and kiss me, and then I always knew she was thinking of Adriance."

"Poor little chap," said Katharine, in her husky voice. "How fond people have always been of Adriance! Tell me the latest news of him. I haven't heard, except through the press, for a year or more. He was in Algiers then, in the valley of the Chelif, riding horseback, and he had quite made up his mind to adopt the Mahometan faith and become an Arab. How many countries and faiths has he adopted, I wonder?"

"Oh, that's Adriance," chuckled Everett. "He is himself barely long enough to write checks and be measured for his clothes. I didn't hear from him while he was an Arab; I missed that."

"He was writing an Algerian *suite* for the piano then; it must be in the publisher's hands by this time. I have been too ill to answer his letter, and have lost touch with him."

Everett drew an envelope from his pocket. "This came a month ago. Read it at your leisure."

"Thanks. I shall keep it as a hostage. Now I want you to play for me. Whatever you like; but if there is anything new in the world, in mercy let me hear it."

He sat down at the piano, and Katharine sat near him, absorbed in his remarkable physical likeness to his brother, and trying to discover in just what it consisted. He was of a larger build than Adriance, and much heavier. His face was of the same oval mould, but it was grey, and darkened about the mouth by continual shaving. His eyes were of the same inconstant April colour, but they were reflective and rather dull; while Adriance's were always points of high light, and always meaning another thing than the thing they meant yesterday. It was hard to see why this earnest man should so continually suggest that lyric, youthful face, as gay as his was grave. For Adriance, though he was ten years the elder, and though his hair was streaked with silver, had the face of a boy of twenty, so mobile that it told his thoughts before he could put them into words. A contralto, famous for the extravagance of her vocal methods and of her affections, once said that the shepherd-boys who sang in the Vale of Tempe must certainly have looked like young Hilgarde.

Everett sat smoking on the veranda of the Inter-Ocean House that night, the victim of mournful recollections. His infatuation for Katharine Gaylord, visionary as it was, had been the most serious of his boyish love-affairs. The fact that it was all so done and dead and far behind him, and that the woman had lived her life out since then, gave him an oppressive sense of age and loss.

He remembered how bitter and morose he had grown during his stay at his brother's studio when Katharine Gaylord was working there, and how he had wounded Adriance on the night of his last concert in New York. He had sat there in the box—while his brother and Katharine were called back again and again, and the flowers went up over the footlights until they were stacked half as high as the piano—brooding in his sullen boy's heart upon the pride those two felt in each other's work—spurring each other to their best and beautifully contending in song. The footlights had seemed a hard, glittering line drawn sharply between their life and his. He walked back to his hotel alone, and sat in his window staring out on Madison Square until long after midnight, resolved to beat no more at doors that he could never enter.

Everett's week in Cheyenne stretched to three, and he saw no prospect of release except through the thing he dreaded.

The bright, windy days of the Wyoming autumn passed swiftly. Letters and telegrams came urging him to hasten his trip to the coast, but he resolutely postponed his business engagements. The mornings he spent on one of Charley Gaylord's ponies, or fishing in the mountains. In the afternoon he was usually at his post of duty. Destiny, he reflected, seems to have very positive notions about the sort of parts we are fitted to play. The scene changes and the compensation varies, but in the end we usually find that we have played the same class of business from first to last. Everett had been a stop-gap all his life. He remembered going through a looking-glass labyrinth when he was a boy, and trying gallery after gallery, only at every turn to bump his nose against his own face—which, indeed, was not his own, but his brother's. No matter what his mission, east or west, by land or sea, he was sure to find himself employed in his brother's business, one of the tributary lives which helped to swell the shining current of Adriance Hilgarde's. It was not the first time that his duty had been to comfort, as best he could, one of the broken things his brother's imperious speed had cast aside and forgotten. He made no attempt to analyse the situation or to state it in exact terms; but he accepted it as a commission from his brother to help this woman to die. Day by day he felt her need for him grow more acute and positive; and day by day he felt that in his peculiar relation to her, his own individuality played a smaller part. His power to minister to her comfort lay solely in his link with his brother's life. He knew that she sat by him always watching for some trick of gesture, some familiar play of expression, some illusion of light and shadow, in which he should seem wholly Adriance. He knew that she lived upon this, and that in the exhaustion which followed this turmoil of her dying senses, she slept deep and sweet, and dreamed of youth and art and days in a certain old Florentine garden, and not of bitterness and death.

A few days after his first meeting with Katharine Gaylord, he had cabled his brother to write her. He merely said that she was mortally ill; he could depend on Adriance to say the right thing—that was a part of his gift. Adriance always said not only the right thing, but the opportune, graceful, exquisite thing. He caught the lyric essence of the moment, the poetic suggestion of every situation. Moreover, he usually did the right thing,—except, when he did very cruel things— bent upon making people happy when their existence touched his, just as he insisted that his material environment should be beautiful; lavishing upon those near him all the warmth and radiance of his rich nature, all the homage of the poet and troubadour, and, when they were no longer near, forget- ting—for that also was a part of Adriance's gift.

Three weeks after Everett had sent his cable, when he made his daily call at the gaily painted ranch-house, he found Katharine laughing like a girl. "Have you ever thought," she said, as he entered the music-room, "how much these séances of ours are like Heine's 'Florentine Nights,' except that I don't give you an opportunity to monopolize the conver- sation?" She held his hand longer than usual as she greeted him. "You are the kindest man living, the kindest," she added, softly.

Everett's grey face coloured faintly as he drew his hand away, for he felt that this time she was looking at him, and not at a whimsical caricature of his brother.

She drew a letter with a foreign postmark from between the leaves of a book and held it out, smiling. "You got him to write it. Don't say you didn't, for it came direct, you see, and the last address I gave him was a place in Florida. This deed shall be remembered of you when I am with the just in Para- dise. But one thing you did not ask him to do, for you didn't know about it. He has sent me his latest work, the new so- nata, and you are to play it for me directly. But first for the letter; I think you would better read it aloud to me."

Everett sat down in a low chair facing the window-seat in which she reclined with a barricade of pillows behind her. He opened the letter, his lashes half-veiling his kind eyes, and saw to his satisfaction that it was a long one; wonderfully tactful and tender, even for Adriance, who was tender with his valet and his stable-boy, with his old gondolier and the beggar- women who prayed to the saints for him.

The letter was from Granada, written in the Alhambra, as he sat by the fountain of the Patio di Lindaraxa. The air was heavy with the warm fragrance of the South and full of the sound of splashing, running water, as it had been in a certain old garden in Florence, long ago. The sky was one great turquoise, heated until it glowed. The wonderful Moorish arches threw graceful blue shadows all about him. He had sketched an outline of them on the margin of his note-paper. The letter was full of confidences about his work, and delicate allusions to their old happy days of study and comradeship.

As Everett folded it he felt that Adriance had divined the thing needed and had risen to it in his own wonderful way. The letter was consistently egotistical, and seemed to him even a trifle patronizing, yet it was just what she had wanted. A strong realization of his brother's charm and intensity and power came over him; he felt the breath of that whirlwind of flame in which Adriance passed, consuming all in his path, and himself even more resolutely than he consumed others. Then he looked down at this white, burnt-out brand that lay before him.

"Like him, isn't it?" she said, quietly. "I think I can scarcely answer his letter, but when you see him next you can do that for me. I want you to tell him many things for me, yet they can all be summed up in this: I want him to grow wholly into his best and greatest self, even at the cost of what is half his charm to you and me. Do you understand me?"

"I know perfectly well what you mean," answered Everett, thoughtfully. "And yet it's difficult to prescribe for those fellows; so little makes, so little mars."

Katharine raised herself upon her elbow, and her face flushed with feverish earnestness. "Ah, but it is the waste of himself that I mean; his lashing himself out on stupid and uncomprehending people until they take him at their own estimate."

"Come, come," expostulated Everett, now alarmed at her excitement. "Where is the new sonata? Let him speak for himself."

He sat down at the piano and began playing the first movement, which was indeed the voice of Adriance, his proper speech. The sonata was the most ambitious work he had done up to that time, and marked the transition from his early lyric vein to a deeper and nobler style. Everett played intelligently and with that sympathetic comprehension which seems peculiar to a certain lovable class of men who never accomplish anything in particular. When he had finished he turned to Katharine.

"How he has grown!" she cried. "What the three last years have done for him! He used to write only the tragedies of passion; but this is the tragedy of effort and failure, the thing Keats called hell. This is my tragedy, as I lie here, listening to the feet of the runners as they pass me—ah, God! the swift feet of the runners!"

She turned her face away and covered it with her hands. Everett crossed over to her and knelt beside her. In all the days he had known her she had never before, beyond an occasional ironical jest, given voice to the bitterness of her own defeat. Her courage had become a point of pride with him.

"Don't do it," he gasped. "I can't stand it, I really can't, I feel it too much."

When she turned her face back to him there was a ghost of the old, brave, cynical smile on it, more bitter than the tears she could not shed. "No, I won't; I will save that for the night, when I have no better company. Run over that theme at the beginning again, will you? It was running in his head when we were in Venice years ago, and he used to drum it on his glass at the dinner-table. He had just begun to work it out when the late autumn came on, and he decided to go to Florence for the winter. He lost touch with his idea, I suppose, during his illness. Do you remember those frightful days? All the people who have loved him are not strong enough to save him from himself! When I got word from Florence that he had been ill, I was singing at Monte Carlo. His wife was hurrying to him from Paris, but I reached him first. I arrived at dusk, in a terrific storm. They had taken an old palace there for the winter, and I found him in the library—a long, dark room full of old Latin books and heavy furniture and bronzes. He was sitting by a wood fire at one end of the room, looking, oh, so worn and pale!—as he always does when he is ill, you know. Ah, it is so good that you *do* know! Even his red smoking-jacket lent no colour to his face. His first words were not to tell me how ill he had been, but that that morning he had been well enough to put the last strokes to the score of his '*Souvenirs d' Automne*,' and he was as I most like to remember him; calm and happy, and tired with that heavenly tiredness that comes after a good work done at last. Outside, the rain poured down in torrents, and the wind moaned and sobbed in the garden and about the walls of that desolated old palace. How that night comes back to me! There were no lights in the room, only the wood fire. It glowed on the black walls and floor like the reflection of purgatorial flame. Beyond us it scarcely penetrated the gloom at all. Adriance sat staring at the fire with the weariness of all his life in his eyes, and of all the other lives that must aspire and suffer to make up one such life as his. Somehow the wind with all its world-pain had got into the room, and the cold rain was in our eyes, and the wave came up in both of us at once—that awful vague, universal pain, that cold fear of life and death and God and hope—and we were like two clinging together on a spar in mid-ocean after the shipwreck of everything. Then we heard the front door open with a great gust of wind that shook even the walls, and the servants came running with lights, announcing that Madame had returned, '*and in the book we read no more that night.*'"

She gave the old line with a certain bitter humour, and with the hard, bright smile in which of old she had wrapped her weakness as in a glittering garment. That ironical smile, worn through so many years, had gradually changed the lines of her face, and when she looked in the mirror she saw not herself, but the scathing critic, the amused observer and satirist of herself.

Everett dropped his head upon his hand. "How much you have cared!" he said.

"Ah, yes, I cared," she replied, closing her eyes. "You can't imagine what a comfort it is to have you know how I cared, what a relief it is to be able to tell it to some one."

Everett continued to look helplessly at the floor. "I was not sure how much you wanted me to know," he said.

"Oh, I intended you should know from the first time I looked into your face, when you came that day with Charley. You are so like him, that it is almost like telling him himself. At least, I feel now that he will know some day, and then I will be quite sacred from his compassion."

"And has he never known at all?" asked Everett, in a thick voice.

"Oh! never at all in the way that you mean. Of course, he is accustomed to looking into the eyes of women and finding love there; when he doesn't find it there he thinks he must have been guilty of some discourtesy. He has a genuine fondness for every woman who is not stupid or gloomy, or old or preternaturally ugly. I shared with the rest; shared the smiles and the gallantries and the droll little sermons. It was quite like a Sunday-school picnic; we wore our best clothes and a smile and took our turns. It was his kindness that was hardest."

"Don't; you'll make me hate him," groaned Everett.

Katharine laughed and began to play nervously with her fan. "It wasn't in the slightest degree his fault; that is the most grotesque part of it. Why, it had really begun before I ever met him. I fought my way to him, and I drank my doom greedily enough."

Everett rose and stood hesitating. "I think I must go. You ought to be quiet, and I don't think I can hear any more just now."

She put out her hand and took his playfully. "You've put in three weeks at this sort of thing, haven't you? Well, it ought to square accounts for a much worse life than yours will ever be."

He knelt beside her, saying, brokenly: "I stayed because I wanted to be with you, that's all. I have never cared about other women since I knew you in New York when I was a lad. You are a part of my destiny, and I could not leave you if I would."

She put her hands on his shoulders and shook her head. "No, no; don't tell me that. I have seen enough tragedy. It was only a boy's fancy, and your divine pity and my utter pitiableness have recalled it for a moment. One does not love the dying, dear friend. Now go, and you will come again to-morrow, as long as there are tomorrows." She took his hand with a smile that was both courage and despair, and full of infinite loyalty and tenderness, as she said softly:

> *"For ever and for ever, farewell, Cassius;*
> *If we do meet again, why, we shall smile;*
> *If not, why then, this parting was well made."*

The courage in her eyes was like the clear light of a star to him as he went out.

On the night of Adriance Hilgarde's opening concert in Paris, Everett sat by the bed in the ranch-house in Wyoming, watching over the last battle that we have with the flesh before we are done with it and free of it for ever. At times it seemed that the serene soul of her must have left already and found some refuge from the storm, and only the tenacious animal life were left to do battle with death. She laboured under a delusion at once pitiful and merciful, thinking that she was in the Pullman on her way to New York, going back to her life and her work. When she roused from her stupor, it was only to ask the porter to waken her half an hour out of Jersey City, or to remonstrate about the delays and the rough-ness of the road. At midnight Everett and the nurse were left alone with her. Poor Charley Gaylord had lain down on a couch outside the door. Everett sat looking at the sputtering night-lamp until it made his eyes ache. His head dropped forward, and he sank into heavy, distressful slumber. He was dreaming of Adriance's concert in Paris, and of Adriance, the troubadour. He heard the applause and he saw the flowers going up over the footlights until they were stacked half as high as the piano, and the petals fell and scattered, making crimson splotches on the floor. Down this crimson pathway came Adriance with his youthful step, leading his singer by the hand; a dark woman this time, with Spanish eyes.

The nurse touched him on the shoulder, he started and awoke. She screened the lamp with her hand. Everett saw that Katharine was awake and conscious, and struggling a little. He lifted her gently on his arm and began to fan her. She looked into his face with eyes that seemed never to have wept or doubted. "Ah, dear Adriance, dear, dear!" she whispered.

Everett went to call her brother, but when they came back the madness of art was over for Katharine.

Two days later Everett was pacing the station siding, wait-ing for the west-bound train. Charley Gaylord walked beside him, but the two men had nothing to say to each other. Everett's bags were piled on the truck, and his step was hurried and his eyes were full of impatience, as he gazed again and again up the track, watching for the train. Gaylord's impatience was not less than his own; these two, who had grown so close, had now become painful and impossible to each other, and longed for the wrench of farewell.

As the train pulled in, Everett wrung Gaylord's hand among the crowd of alighting passengers. The people of a German opera company, *en route* for the coast, rushed by them in frantic haste to snatch their breakfast during the stop. Everett heard an exclamation, and a stout woman rushed up to him, glowing with joyful surprise and caught his coat-sleeve with her tightly gloved hands.

"*Herr Gott*, Adriance, *lieber Freund*," she cried.

Everett lifted his hat, blushing. "Pardon me, madame, I see that you have mistaken me for Adriance Hilgarde. I am his brother." Turning from the crestfallen singer he hurried into the car.

MY
MORTAL ENEMY

I

I FIRST MET Myra Henshawe when I was fifteen, but I had known about her ever since I could remember anything at all. She and her runaway marriage were the theme of the most interesting, indeed the only interesting, stories that were told in our family, on holidays or at family dinners. My mother and aunts still heard from Myra Driscoll, as they called her, and Aunt Lydia occasionally went to New York to visit her. She had been the brilliant and attractive figure among the friends of their girlhood, and her life had been as exciting and varied as ours was monotonous.

Though she had grown up in our town, Parthia, in southern Illinois, Myra Henshawe never, after her elopement, came back but once. It was in the year when I was finishing High School, and she must then have been a woman of forty-five. She came in the early autumn, with brief notice by telegraph. Her husband, who had a position in the New York offices of an Eastern railroad, was coming West on business, and they were going to stop over for two days in Parthia. He was to stay at the Parthian, as our new hotel was called, and Mrs. Henshawe would stay with Aunt Lydia.

I was a favourite with my Aunt Lydia. She had three big sons, but no daughter, and she thought my mother scarcely appreciated me. She was always, therefore, giving me what she called "advantages," on the side. My mother and sister were asked to dinner at Aunt Lydia's on the night of the Henshawes' arrival, but she had whispered to me: "I want you to come in early, an hour or so before the others, and get acquainted with Myra."

That evening I slipped quietly in at my aunt's front door, and while I was taking off my wraps in the hall I could see, at the far end of the parlour, a short, plump woman in a black velvet dress, seated upon the sofa and softly playing on Cousin Bert's guitar. She must have heard me, and, glancing up, she saw my reflection in a mirror; she put down the guitar, rose, and stood to await my approach. She stood markedly and pointedly still, with her shoulders back and her head lifted, as if to remind me that it was my business to get to her as quickly as possible and present myself as best I could. I was not accustomed to formality of any sort, but by her attitude she succeeded in conveying this idea to me.

I hastened across the room with so much bewilderment and concern in my face that she gave a short, commiserating laugh as she held out to me her plump, charming little hand.

"Certainly this must be Lydia's dear Nellie, of whom I have heard so much! And you must be fifteen now, by my mournful arithmetic—am I right?"

What a beautiful voice, bright and gay and carelessly kind—but she continued to hold her head up haughtily. She always did this on meeting people—partly, I think, because she was beginning to have a double chin and was sensitive about it. Her deep-set, flashing grey eyes seemed to be taking me in altogether—estimating me. For all that she was no taller than I, I felt quite overpowered by her—and stupid, hopelessly clumsy and stupid. Her black hair was done high on her head, *à la* Pompadour, and there were curious, zigzag, curly streaks of glistening white in it, which made it look like the fleece of a Persian goat or some animal that bore silky fur. I could not meet the playful curiosity of her eyes at all, so I fastened my gaze upon a necklace of carved amethysts she wore inside the square-cut neck of her dress. I suppose I stared, for she said suddenly: "Does this necklace annoy you? I'll take it off if it does."

I was utterly speechless. I could feel my cheeks burning. Seeing that she had hurt me, she was sorry, threw her arm impulsively about me, drew me into the corner of the sofa and sat down beside me.

"Oh, we'll get used to each other! You see, I prod you because I'm certain that Lydia and your mother have spoiled you a little. You've been overpraised to me. It's all very well to be clever, my dear, but you mustn't be solemn about it— nothing is more tiresome. Now, let us get acquainted. Tell me about the things you like best; that's the short cut to friendship. What do you like best in Parthia? The old Driscoll place? I knew it!"

By the time her husband came in I had begun to think she was going to like me. I wanted her to, but I felt I didn't have half a chance with her; her charming, fluent voice, her clear light enunciation bewildered me. And I was never sure whether she was making fun of me or of the thing we were talking about. Her sarcasm was so quick, so fine at the point—it was like being touched by a metal so cold that one doesn't know whether one is burned or chilled. I was fascinated, but very ill at ease, and I was glad when Oswald Henshawe arrived from the hotel.

He came into the room without taking off his overcoat and went directly up to his wife, who rose and kissed him. Again I was some time in catching up with the situation; I wondered for a moment whether they might have come down from Chicago on different trains; for she was clearly glad to see him—glad not merely that he was safe and had got round on time, but because his presence gave her lively personal pleasure. I was not accustomed to that kind of feeling in people long married.

Mr. Henshawe was less perplexing than his wife, and he looked more as I had expected him to look. The prominent bones of his face gave him a rather military air; a broad, rugged forehead, high cheek-bones, a high nose, slightly arched. His eyes, however, were dark and soft, curious in shape—exactly like half-moons—and he wore a limp, drooping moustache, like an Englishman. There was something about him that suggested personal bravery, magnanimity, and a fine, generous way of doing things.

"I am late," he explained, "because I had some difficulty in dressing. I couldn't find my things."

His wife looked concerned for a moment, and then began to laugh softly. "Poor Oswald! You were looking for your new dress shirts that bulge in front. Well, you needn't! I gave them to the janitor's son."

"The janitor's son?"

"Yes. To Willy Bunch, at home. He's probably wearing one to an Iroquois ball to-night, and that's the right place for it."

Mr. Henshawe passed his hand quickly over his smooth, iron-grey hair. "You gave away my six new shirts?"

"Be sure I did. You shan't wear shirts that give you a bosom, not if we go to the poorhouse. You know I can't bear you in ill-fitting things."

Oswald looked at her with amusement, incredulity, and bitterness. He turned away from us with a shrug and pulled up a chair. "Well, all I can say is, what a windfall for Willy!"

"That's the way to look at it," said his wife teasingly. "And now try to talk about something that might conceivably interest Lydia's niece. I promised Liddy to make a salad dressing."

I was left alone with Mr. Henshawe. He had a pleasant way of giving his whole attention to a young person. He "drew one out" better than his wife had done, because he did not frighten one so much. I liked to watch his face, with its outstanding bones and languid, friendly eyes—that perplexing combination of something hard and something soft. Soon my mother and uncle and my boy cousins arrived. When the party was complete I could watch and enjoy the visitors without having to think of what I was going to say next. The dinner was much gayer than family parties usually are. Mrs. Henshawe seemed to remember all the old stories and the old jokes that had been asleep for twenty years.

"How good it is," my mother exclaimed, "to hear Myra laugh again!"

Yes, it was good. It was sometimes terrible, too, as I was to find out later. She had an angry laugh, for instance, that I still shiver to remember. Any stupidity made Myra laugh—I was destined to hear that one very often! Untoward circumstances, accidents, even disasters, provoked her mirth. And it was always mirth, not hysteria; there was a spark of zest and wild humour in it.

II

THE BIG stone house, set in its ten-acre park of trees and surrounded by a high, wrought-iron fence, in which Myra Driscoll grew up, was still, in my time, the finest property in Parthia. At John Driscoll's death it went to the Sisters of the Sacred Heart, and I could remember it only as a convent. Myra was an orphan, and had been taken into this house as a very little girl and brought up by her great-uncle.

John Driscoll made his fortune employing contract labour in the Missouri swamps. He retired from business early, returned to the town where he had been a poor boy, and built a fine house in which he took great pride. He lived in what was considered great splendour in those days. He kept fast horses, and bred a trotter that made a national record. He bought silver instruments for the town band, and paid the salary of the bandmaster. When the band went up to serenade him on his birthday and on holidays, he called the boys in and treated them to his best whisky. If Myra gave a ball or a garden-party, the band furnished the music. It was, indeed, John Driscoll's band.

Myra, as my aunt often said, had everything: dresses and jewels, a fine riding horse, a Steinway piano. Her uncle took her back to Ireland with him, one summer, and had her painted by a famous painter. When they were at home, in Parthia, his house was always open to the young people of the town. Myra's good looks and high spirits gratified the old man's pride. Her wit was of the kind that he could understand, native and racy, and none too squeamish. She was very fond of him, and he knew it. He was a coarse old codger, so unlettered that he made a poor showing with a pen. It was always told of him that when he became president of our national bank, he burned a lot of the treasury notes sent up to his house for him to sign, because he had "spoiled the sig-nay-ture." But he knew a great deal about men and their motives. In his own way he was picturesque, and Myra appreciated it—not many girls would have done so. Indeed, she was a good deal like him; the blood tie was very strong.

There was never a serious disagreement between them until it came to young Henshawe.

Oswald Henshawe was the son of a German girl of good family, and an Ulster Protestant whom Driscoll detested; there was an old grudge of some kind between the two men. This Ulsterman was poor and impractical, a wandering schoolmaster, who had charge for a while of the High School in Parthia, and afterwards taught in smaller towns about. Oswald put himself through Harvard with very little help from his parents. He was not taken account of in our town until he came home from college, a handsome and promising young man. He and Myra met as if for the first time, and fell in love with each other. When old Driscoll found that Oswald was calling on his niece, he forbade him the house. They continued to meet at my grandfather's, however, under the protection of my Aunt Lydia. Driscoll so persecuted the boy that he felt there was no chance for him in Parthia. He roused himself and went to New York. He stayed there two years without coming home, sending his letters to Myra through my aunt.

All Myra's friends were drawn into the web of her romance; half a dozen young men understudied for Oswald so assiduously that her uncle might have thought she was going to marry any one of them. Oswald, meanwhile, was pegging away in New York, at a time when salaries were small and advancement was slow. But he managed to get on, and in two years he was in a position to marry. He wrote to John Driscoll, telling him his resources and prospects, and asked him for his niece's hand. It was then that Driscoll had it out with Myra. He did not come at her in a tantrum, as he had done before, but confronted her with a cold, business proposition. If she married young Henshawe, he would cut her off without a penny. He could do so, because he had never adopted her. If she did not, she would inherit two-thirds of his property—the remaining third was to go to the church. "And I advise ye to think well," he told her. "It's better to be a stray dog in this world than a man without money. I've tried both ways, and I know. A poor man stinks, and God hates him."

Some months after this conversation, Myra went out with a sleighing party. They drove her to a neighbouring town where Oswald's father had a school, and where Oswald himself had quietly arrived the day before. There, in the presence of his parents and of Myra's friends, they were married by the civil authority, and they went away on the Chicago express, which came through at two in the morning.

When I was a little girl my Aunt Lydia used to take me for a walk along the broad stone flagging that ran all the way around the old Driscoll grounds. Through the high iron fence we could see the Sisters, out for recreation, pacing two and two under the apple-trees. My aunt would tell me again about that thrilling night (probably the most exciting in her life), when Myra Driscoll came down that path from the house, and out of those big iron gates, for the last time. She had wanted to leave without taking anything but the clothes she wore—and indeed she walked out of the house with nothing but her muff and her *porte-monnaie* in her hands. My prudent aunt, however, had put her toilet articles and some linen into a travelling-bag, and thrown it out of the back window to one of the boys stationed under an apple-tree.

"I'll never forget the sight of her, coming down that walk and leaving a great fortune behind her," said Aunt Lydia. "I had gone out to join the others before she came—she preferred to leave the house alone. We girls were all in the sleighs and the boys stood in the snow holding the horses. We had begun to think she had weakened, or maybe gone to the old man to try to move him. But we saw by the lights behind when the front door opened and shut, and here she came, with her head high, and that quick little bouncing step of hers. Your Uncle Rob lifted her into the sleigh, and off we went. And that hard old man was as good as his word. Her name wasn't mentioned in his will. He left it all to the Catholic Church and to institutions."

"But they've been happy, anyhow?" I sometimes asked her.

"Happy? Oh, yes! As happy as most people."

That answer was disheartening; the very point of their story was that they should be much happier than other people.

When I was older I used to walk around the Driscoll place alone very often, especially on spring days, after school, and watch the nuns pacing so mildly and measuredly among the blossoming trees where Myra used to give garden-parties and have the band to play for her. I thought of the place as being under a spell, like the Sleeping Beauty's palace; it had been in a trance, or lain in its flowers like a beautiful corpse, ever since that winter night when Love went out of the gates and gave the dare to Fate. Since then, chanting and devotions and discipline, and the tinkle of little bells that seemed forever calling the Sisters in to prayers.

I knew that this was not literally true; old John Driscoll had lived on there for many years after the flight of his niece. I myself could remember his funeral—remember it very vividly —though I was not more than six years old when it happened. I sat with my parents in the front of the gallery, at the back of the church that the old man had enlarged and enriched during the latter days of his life. The high altar blazed with hundreds of candles, the choir was entirely filled by the masses of flowers. The bishop was there, and a flock of priests in gorgeous vestments. When the pall-bearers arrived, Driscoll did not come to the church; the church went to him. The bishop and clergy went down the nave and met that great black coffin at the door, preceded by the cross and boys swinging cloudy censers, followed by the choir chanting to the organ. They surrounded, they received, they seemed to assimilate into the body of the church, the body of old John Driscoll. They bore it up to the high altar on a river of colour and incense and organ-tone; they claimed it and enclosed it.

In after years, when I went to other funerals, stark and grim enough, I thought of John Driscoll as having escaped the end of all flesh; it was as if he had been translated, with no dark conclusion to the pageant, no "night of the grave" about which our Protestant preachers talked. From the freshness of roses and lilies, from the glory of the high altar, he had gone straight to the greater glory, through smoking censers and candles and stars.

After I went home from that first glimpse of the real Myra Henshawe, twenty-five years older than I had always imagined her, I could not help feeling a little disappointed. John Driscoll and his niece had suddenly changed places in my mind, and he had got, after all, the more romantic part. Was it not better to get out of the world with such pomp and dramatic splendour than to linger on in it, having to take account of shirts and railway trains, and getting a double chin into the bargain?

The Henshawes were in Parthia three days, and when they left, it was settled that I was to go on to New York with Aunt Lydia for the Christmas holidays. We were to stay at the old Fifth Avenue Hotel, which, as Myra said, was only a stone's throw from their apartment, "if at any time a body was to feel disposed to throw one, Liddy!"

III

M Y AUNT LYDIA and I arrived at the Jersey City station on the day before Christmas—a soft, grey December morning, with a little snow falling. Myra Henshawe was there to meet us; very handsome, I thought, as she came walking rapidly up the platform, her plump figure swathed in furs,—a fur hat on her head, with a single narrow garnet feather sticking out behind, like the pages' caps in old story-books. She was not alone. She was attended by a tall, elegant young man in a blue-grey ulster. He had one arm through hers, and in the other hand he carried a walking-stick.

"This is Ewan Gray," said Mrs. Henshawe, after she had embraced us. "Doubtless you have seen him play in Chicago. He is meeting an early train, too, so we planned to salute the morn together, and left Oswald to breakfast alone."

The young man took our hand-luggage and walked beside me to the ferryboat, asking polite questions about our trip. He was a Scotchman, of an old theatrical family, a handsome fellow, with a broad, fair-skinned face, sand-coloured hair and moustache, and fine grey eyes, deep-set and melancholy, with black lashes. He took us up to the deck of the ferry, and then Mrs. Henshawe told him he had better leave us. "You must be there when Esther's train gets in—and remember, you are to bring her to dine with us to-morrow night. There will be no one else."

"Thank you, Myra." He stood looking down at her with a grateful, almost humble expression, holding his soft hat against his breast, while the snow-flakes fell about his head. "And may I call in for a few moments to-night, to show you something?"

She laughed as if his request pleased her. "Something for her, I expect? Can't you trust your own judgment?"

"You know I never do," he said, as if that were an old story.

She gave him a little push. "Do put your hat on, or you'll greet Esther with a sneeze. Run along."

She watched him anxiously as he walked away, and groaned: "Oh, the deliberation of him! If I could only make

him hurry once. You'll hear all about him later, Nellie. You'll
have to see a good deal of him, but you won't find it a hard-
ship, I trust!"

The boat was pulling out, and I was straining my eyes to
catch, through the fine, reluctant snow, my first glimpse of
the city we were approaching. We passed the *Wilhelm der
Grosse* coming up the river under tug, her sides covered with
ice after a stormy crossing, a flock of sea-gulls in her wake.
The snow blurred everything a little, and the buildings on the
Battery all ran together—looked like an enormous fortress
with a thousand windows. From the mass, the dull gold
dome of the *World* building emerged like a ruddy autumn
moon at twilight.

From the Twenty-third Street station we took the cross-
town car—people were economical in those days—to the
Fifth Avenue Hotel. After we had unpacked and settled our
things, we went across the Square to lunch at Purcell's, and
there Mrs. Henshawe told us about Ewan Gray. He was in
love with one of her dearest friends, Esther Sinclair, whose
company was coming into New York for the holidays.
Though he was so young, he had, she said, "a rather spotty
past," and Miss Sinclair, who was the daughter of an old New
England family and had been properly brought up, couldn't
make up her mind whether he was stable enough to marry. "I
don't dare advise her, though I'm so fond of him. You can
see; he's just the sort of boy that women pick up and run off
into the jungle with. But he's never wanted to marry before;
it might be the making of him. He's distractedly in love—
goes about like a sleep-walker. Still, I couldn't bear it if any-
thing cruel happened to Esther."

Aunt Lydia and Myra were going to do some shopping.
When we went out into Madison Square again, Mrs. Hen-
shawe must have seen my wistful gaze, for she stopped short
and said: "How would Nellie like it if we left her here, and
picked her up as we come back? That's our house, over there,
second floor—so you won't be far from home. To me this is
the real heart of the city; that's why I love living here." She
waved to me and hurried my aunt away.

Madison Square was then at the parting of the ways; had a
double personality, half commercial, half social, with shops to

the south and residences on the north. It seemed to me so neat, after the raggedness of our Western cities; so protected by good manners and courtesy—like an open-air drawing-room. I could well imagine a winter dancing party being given there, or a reception for some distinguished European visitor.

The snow fell lightly all the afternoon, and friendly old men with brooms kept sweeping the paths—very ready to talk to a girl from the country, and to brush off a bench so that she could sit down. The trees and shrubbery seemed well-groomed and sociable, like pleasant people. The snow lay in clinging folds on the bushes, and outlined every twig of every tree—a line of white upon a line of black. Madison Square Garden, new and spacious then, looked to me so light and fanciful, and Saint Gaudens' Diana, of which Mrs. Henshawe had told me, stepped out freely and fearlessly into the grey air. I lingered long by the intermittent fountain. Its rhythmical splash was like the voice of the place. It rose and fell like something taking deep, happy breaths; and the sound was musical, seemed to come from the throat of spring. Not far away, on the corner, was an old man selling English violets, each bunch wrapped in oiled paper to protect them from the snow. Here, I felt, winter brought no desolation; it was tamed, like a polar bear led on a leash by a beautiful lady.

About the Square the pale blue shadows grew denser and drew closer. The street lamps flashed out all along the Avenue, and soft lights began to twinkle in the tall buildings while it was yet day—violet buildings, just a little denser in substance and colour than the violet sky. While I was gazing up at them I heard a laugh close beside me, and Mrs. Henshawe's arm slipped through mine.

"Why, you're fair moon-struck, Nellie! I've seen the messenger boys dodging all about you!" It was true, droves of people were going through the Square now, and boys carrying potted plants and big wreaths. "Don't you like to watch them? But we can't stay. We're going home to Oswald. Oh, hear the penny whistle! They always find me out." She stopped a thin lad with a cap and yarn comforter but no overcoat, who was playing *The Irish Washerwoman* on a little pipe, and rummaged in her bag for a coin.

The Henshawes' apartment was the second floor of an old brownstone house on the north side of the Square. I loved it from the moment I entered it; such solidly built, high-ceiled rooms, with snug fire-places and wide doors and deep windows. The long, heavy velvet curtains and the velvet chairs were a wonderful plum-colour, like ripe purple fruit. The curtains were lined with that rich cream-colour that lies under the blue skin of ripe figs.

Oswald was standing by the fire, drinking a whisky and soda while he waited for us. He put his glass down on the mantel as we opened the door, and forgot all about it. He pushed chairs up to the hearth for my aunt and me, and stood talking to us while his wife went to change her dress and to have a word with the Irish maid before dinner.

"By the way, Myra," he said, as she left us, "I've put a bottle of champagne on ice; it's Christmas eve."

Everything in their little apartment seemed to me absolutely individual and unique, even the dinner service; the thick grey plates and the soup tureen painted with birds and big, bright flowers—I was sure there were no others like them in the world.

As we were finishing dinner the maid announced Mr. Gray. Henshawe went into the parlour to greet him, and we followed a moment later. The young man was in evening clothes, with a few sprays of white hyacinth in his coat. He stood by the fire, his arm on the mantel. His clean, fair skin and melancholy eyes, his very correct clothes, and something about the shape of his hands, made one conscious of a cool, deliberate fastidiousness in him. In spite of his spotty past he looked, that night, as fresh and undamaged as the flowers he wore. Henshawe took on a slightly bantering tone with him, and seemed to be trying to cheer him up. Mr. Gray would not sit down. After an interval of polite conversation he said to his host: "Will you excuse me if I take Myra away for a few moments? She has promised to do something kind for me."

They went into Henshawe's little study, off the parlour, and shut the door. We could hear a low murmur of voices. When they came back to us Mrs. Henshawe stood beside Gray while he put on his caped cloak, talking encouragingly. "The opals are beautiful, but I'm afraid of them, Ewan.

Oswald would laugh at me, but all the same they have a bad history. Love itself draws on a woman nearly all the bad luck in the world; why, for mercy's sake, add opals? He brought two bracelets for me to decide between them, Oswald, both lovely. However did they let you carry off two, Ewan?"

"They know me there. I always pay my bills, Myra. I don't know why, but I do. I suppose it's the Scotch in me."

He wished us all good-night.

"Give a kiss to Esther for me," said Mrs. Henshawe merrily at the door. He made no reply, but bent over her hand and vanished.

"What he really wanted was to show me some verses he's made for her," said Mrs. Henshawe, as she came back to the fire. "And very pretty ones they are, for sweet-heart poetry."

Mr. Henshawe smiled. "Maybe you obliged him with a rhyme or two, my dear? Lydia—" he sat down by my aunt and put his hand on hers— "I'd never feel sure that I did my own courting, if it weren't that I was a long way off at the time. Myra is so fond of helping young men along. We nearly always have a love affair on hand."

She put her hand over his lips. "Hush! I hate old women who egg on courtships."

When Oswald had finished his cigar we were taken out for a walk. This was primarily for the good of her "figger," Myra said, and incidentally we were to look for a green bush to send to Madame Modjeska. "She's spending the holidays in town, and it will be dismal at her hotel."

At the florist's we found, among all the little trees and potted plants, a glistening holly-tree, full of red berries and pointed like a spire, easily the queen of its companions. "That is naturally hers," said Mrs. Myra.

Her husband shrugged. "It's naturally the most extravagant."

Mrs. Myra threw up her head. "Don't be petty, Oswald. It's not a woollen petticoat or warm mittens that Madame is needing." She gave careful instructions to the florist's man, who was to take the tree to the Savoy; he was to carry with it a box of cakes, "of my baking," she said proudly. He was to ask for Mrs. Hewes, the housekeeper, and under her guidance he was to carry the tree up to Madame Modjeska's rooms

himself. The man showed a sympathetic interest, and prom-
ised to follow instructions. Then Mrs. Henshawe gave him a
silver dollar and wished him a Merry Christmas.

As we walked home she slipped her arm through mine, and
we fell a little behind the other two. "See the moon coming
out, Nellie—behind the tower. It wakens the guilt in me. No
playing with love; and I'd sworn a great oath never to meddle
again. You send a handsome fellow like Ewan Gray to a fine
girl like Esther, and it's Christmas eve, and they rise above us
and the white world around us, and there isn't anybody, not a
tramp on the park benches, that wouldn't wish them well—
and very likely hell will come of it!"

IV

THE NEXT MORNING Oswald Henshawe, in a frock-coat and top-hat, called to take Aunt Lydia and me to church. The weather had cleared before we went to bed, and as we stepped out of our hotel that morning, the sun shone blindingly on the snow-covered park, the gold Diana flashed against a green-blue sky. We were going to Grace Church, and the morning was so beautiful that we decided to walk.

"Lydia," said Henshawe, as he took us each by an arm, "I want you to give me a Christmas present."

"Why, Oswald," she stammered.

"Oh, I have it ready! You've only to present it." He took a little flat package from his pocket and slipped it into her muff. He drew both of us closer to him. "Listen, it's nothing. It's some sleeve-buttons, given me by a young woman who means no harm, but doesn't know the ways of the world very well. She's from a breezy Western city, where a rich girl can give a present whenever she wants to and nobody questions it. She sent these to my office yesterday. If I send them back to her it will hurt her feelings; she would think I had misunderstood her. She'll get hard knocks here, of course, but I don't want to give her any. On the other hand—well, you know Myra; nobody better. She would punish herself and everybody else for this young woman's questionable taste. So I want you to give them to me, Lydia."

"Oh, Oswald," cried my aunt, "Myra is so keen! I'm not clever enough to fool Myra. Can't you just put them away in your office?"

"Not very well. Besides," he gave a slightly embarrassed laugh, "I'd like to wear them. They are very pretty."

"Now, Oswald . . ."

"Oh, it's all right, Lydia, I give you my word it is. But you know how a little thing of that sort can upset my wife. I thought you might give them to me when you come over to dine with us to-morrow night. She wouldn't be jealous of you. But if you don't like the idea . . . why, just take them home with you and give them to some nice boy who would appreciate them."

All through the Christmas service I could see that Aunt Lydia was distracted and perplexed. As soon as we got back to the hotel and were safe in our rooms she took the brown leather case from her muff and opened it. The sleeve-buttons were topazes, winy-yellow, lightly set in crinkly gold. I believe she was seduced by their beauty. "I really think he ought to have them, if he wants them. Everything is always for Myra. He never gets anything for himself. And all the admiration is for her; why shouldn't he have a little? He has been devoted to a fault. It isn't good for any woman to be humoured and pampered as he has humoured her. And she's often most unreasonable with him—most unreasonable!"

The next evening, as we were walking across the Square to the Henshawes, we glanced up and saw them standing together in one of their deep front windows, framed by the plum-coloured curtains. They were looking out, but did not see us. I noticed that she was really quite a head shorter than he, and she leaned a little towards him. When she was peaceful, she was like a dove with its wings folded. There was something about them, as they stood in the lighted window, that would have discouraged me from meddling, but it did not shake my aunt.

As soon as we were in the parlour, before we had taken off our coats, she said resolutely: "Myra, I want to give Oswald a Christmas present. Once an old friend left with me some cuff-links he couldn't keep—unpleasant associations, I suppose. I thought of giving them to one of my own boys, but I brought them for Oswald. I'd rather he would have them than anybody."

Aunt Lydia spoke with an ease and conviction which compelled my admiration. She took the buttons out of her muff, without the box, of course, and laid them in Mrs. Henshawe's hand.

Mrs. Henshawe was delighted. "How clever of you to think of it, Liddy, dear! Yes, they're exactly right for him. There's hardly any other stone I would like, but these are exactly right. Look, Oswald, they're the colour of a fine Moselle." It was Oswald himself who seemed disturbed, and not over-pleased. He grew red, was confused in his remarks, and was genuinely reluctant when his wife insisted upon taking the gold buttons out of his cuffs and putting in the new ones. "I can't get over your canniness, Liddy," she said as she fitted them.

"It's not like me, is it, Myra?" retorted my aunt; "not like me at all to choose the right sort of thing. But did it never occur to you that anyone besides yourself might know what is appropriate for Oswald? No, I'm sure it never did!"

Mrs. Myra took the laugh so heartily to herself that I felt it was a shame to deceive her. So, I am sure, did Oswald. During dinner he talked more than usual, but he was ill at ease. Afterwards, at the opera, when the lights were down, I noticed that he was not listening to the music, but was looking listlessly off into the gloom of the house, with something almost sorrowful in his strange, half-moon eyes. During an *entr'acte* a door at the back was opened, and a draught blew in. As he put his arm back to pull up the cloak which had slipped down from his wife's bare shoulders, she laughed and said: "Oh, Oswald, I love to see your jewels flash!"

He dropped his hand quickly and frowned so darkly that I thought he would have liked to put the topazes under his heel and grind them up. I thought him properly served then, but often since I have wondered at his gentle heart.

V

URING THE WEEK between Christmas and New Year's day I was with Mrs. Henshawe a great deal, but we were seldom alone. It was the season of calls and visits, and she said that meeting so many people would certainly improve my manners and my English. She hated my careless, slangy, Western speech. Her friends, I found, were of two kinds: artistic people—actors, musicians, literary men—with whom she was always at her best because she admired them; and another group whom she called her "moneyed" friends (she seemed to like the word), and these she cultivated, she told me, on Oswald's account. "He is the sort of man who does well in business only if he has the incentive of friendships. He doesn't properly belong in business. We never speak of it, but I'm sure he hates it. He went into an office only because we were young and terribly in love, and had to be married."

The business friends seemed to be nearly all Germans. On Sunday we called at half-a-dozen or more big houses. I remember very large rooms, much upholstered and furnished, walls hung with large paintings in massive frames, and many stiff, dumpy little sofas, in which the women sat two-and-two, while the men stood about the refreshment tables, drinking champagne and coffee and smoking fat black cigars. Among these people Mrs. Myra took on her loftiest and most challenging manner. I could see that some of the women were quite afraid of her. They were in great haste to rush refreshments to her, and looked troubled when she refused anything. They addressed her in German and profusely complimented her upon the way she spoke it. We had a carriage that afternoon, and Myra was dressed in her best—making an especial effort on Oswald's account; but the rich and powerful irritated her. Their solemnity was too much for her sense of humour; there was a biting edge to her sarcasm, a curl about the corners of her mouth that was never there when she was with people whose personality charmed her.

I had one long, delightful afternoon alone with Mrs. Henshawe in Central Park. We walked for miles, stopped to watch the skating, and finally had tea at the Casino, where she told me about some of the singers and actors I would meet at her apartment on New Year's eve. Her account of her friends was often more interesting to me than the people themselves. After tea she hailed a hansom and asked the man to drive us about the park a little, as a fine sunset was coming on. We were jogging happily along under the elms, watching the light change on the crusted snow, when a carriage passed from which a handsome woman leaned out and waved to us. Mrs. Henshawe bowed stiffly, with a condescending smile. "There, Nellie," she exclaimed, "that's the last woman I'd care to have splashing past me, and me in a hansom cab!"

I glimpsed what seemed to me insane ambition. My aunt was always thanking God that the Henshawes got along as well as they did, and worrying because she felt sure Oswald wasn't saving anything. And here Mrs. Myra was wishing for a carriage—with stables and a house and servants, and all that went with a carriage! All the way home she kept her scornful expression, holding her head high and sniffing the purple air from side to side as we drove down Fifth Avenue. When we alighted before her door she paid the driver, and gave him such a large fee that he snatched off his hat and said twice: "Thank you, thank you, my lady!" She dismissed him with a smile and a nod. "All the same," she whispered to me as she fitted her latchkey, "it's very nasty, being poor!"

That week Mrs. Henshawe took me to see a dear friend of hers, Anne Aylward, the poet. She was a girl who had come to New York only a few years before, had won the admiration of men of letters, and was now dying of tuberculosis in her early twenties. Mrs. Henshawe had given me a book of her poems to read, saying: "I want you to see her so that you can remember her in after years, and I want her to see you so that we can talk you over."

Miss Aylward lived with her mother in a small flat overlooking the East River, and we found her in a bathchair, lying in the sun and watching the river boats go by. Her study was a delightful place that morning, full of flowers and plants and baskets of fruit that had been sent her for Christmas. But it was Myra Henshawe herself who made that visit so memorably gay. Never had I seen her so brilliant and strangely charming as she was in that sunlit study up under the roofs. Their talk quite took my breath away; they said such exciting, such fantastic things about people, books, music—anything; they seemed to speak together a kind of highly flavoured special language.

As we were walking home she tried to tell me more about Miss Aylward, but tenderness for her friend and bitter rebellion at her fate choked her voice. She suffered physical anguish for that poor girl. My aunt often said that Myra was incorrigibly extravagant; but I saw that her chief extravagance was in caring for so many people, and in caring for them so much. When she but mentioned the name of some one whom she admired, one got an instant impression that the person must be wonderful, her voice invested the name with a sort of grace. When she liked people she always called them by name a great many times in talking to them, and she enunciated the name, no matter how commonplace, in a penetrating way, without hurrying over it or slurring it; and this, accompanied by her singularly direct glance, had a curious effect. When she addressed Aunt Lydia, for instance, she seemed to be speaking to a person deeper down than the blurred, taken-for-granted image of my aunt that I saw every day, and for a moment my aunt became more individual, less matter-of-fact to me. I had noticed this peculiar effect of Myra's look and vocative when I first met her, in Parthia, where her manner of addressing my relatives had made them all seem a little more attractive to me.

One afternoon when we were at a matinée I noticed in a loge a young man who looked very much like the photographs of a story-writer popular at that time. I asked Mrs. Henshawe whether it could be he. She looked in the direction I indicated, then looked quickly away again.

"Yes, it's he. He used to be a friend of mine. That's a sad phrase, isn't it? But there was a time when he could have stood by Oswald in a difficulty—and he didn't. He passed it up. Wasn't there. I've never forgiven him."

I regretted having noticed the man in the loge, for all the rest of the afternoon I could feel the bitterness working in her. I knew that she was suffering. The scene on the stage was obliterated for her; the drama was in her mind. She was going over it all again; arguing, accusing, denouncing.

As we left the theatre she sighed: "Oh, Nellie, I wish you hadn't seen him! It's all very well to tell us to forgive our enemies; our enemies can never hurt us very much. But oh, what about forgiving our friends?"—she beat on her fur collar with her two gloved hands—"that's where the rub comes!"

The Henshawes always gave a party on New Year's eve. That year most of the guests were stage people. Some of them, in order to get there before midnight, came with traces of make-up still on their faces. I remember old Jefferson de Angelais arrived in his last-act wig, carrying his plumed hat— during the supper his painted eyebrows spread and came down over his eyes like a veil. Most of them are dead now, but it was a fine group that stood about the table to drink the New Year in. By far the handsomest and most distinguished of that company was a woman no longer young, but beautiful in age, Helena Modjeska. She looked a woman of another race and another period, no less queenly than when I had seen her in Chicago as Marie Stuart, and as Katharine in *Henry VIII*. I remember how, when Oswald asked her to propose a toast, she put out her long arm, lifted her glass, and looking into the blur of the candlelight with a grave face, said: "To my coun-n-try!"

As she was not playing, she had come early, some time before the others, bringing with her a young Polish woman who was singing at the Opera that winter. I had an opportunity to watch Modjeska as she sat talking to Myra and Esther Sinclair—Miss Sinclair had once played in her company. When the other guests began to arrive, and Myra was called away, she sat by the fire in a high-backed chair, her head resting lightly on her hand, her beautiful face half in shadow. How well I remember those long, beautifully modelled hands, with so much humanity in them. They were worldly, indeed, but fashioned for a nobler worldliness than ours; hands to hold a sceptre, or a chalice—or, by courtesy, a sword.

The party did not last long, but it was a whirl of high spirits. Everybody was hungry and thirsty. There was a great deal of talk about Sarah Bernhardt's *Hamlet*, which had been running all week and had aroused hot controversy; and about Jean de Reszke's return to the Metropolitan that night, after a long illness in London.

By two o'clock every one had gone but the two Polish ladies. Modjeska, after she put on her long cloak, went to the window, drew back the plum-coloured curtains, and looked out. "See, Myra," she said with that Slav accent she never lost, though she read English verse so beautifully, "the Square is quite white with moonlight. And how still all the ci-ty is, how still!" She turned to her friend; "Emelia, I think you must sing something. Something old . . . yes, from *Norma*." She hummed a familiar air under her breath, and looked about for a chair. Oswald brought one. "Thank you. And we might have less light, might we not?" He turned off the lights.

She sat by the window, half draped in her cloak, the moonlight falling across her knees. Her friend went to the piano and commenced the *Casta Diva* aria, which begins so like the quivering of moonbeams on the water. It was the first air on our old music-box at home, but I had never heard it sung—and I have never heard it sung so beautifully since. I remember Oswald, standing like a statue behind Madame Modjeska's chair, and Myra, crouching low beside the singer, her head in both hands, while the song grew and blossomed like a great emotion.

When it stopped, nobody said anything beyond a low good-bye. Modjeska again drew her cloak around her, and Oswald took them down to their carriage. Aunt Lydia and I followed, and as we crossed the Square we saw their cab going up the Avenue. For many years I associated Mrs. Henshawe with that music, thought of that aria as being mysteriously related to something in her nature that one rarely saw, but nearly always felt; a compelling, passionate, overmastering something for which I had no name, but which was audible, visible in the air that night, as she sat crouching in the shadow. When I wanted to recall powerfully that hidden richness in her, I had only to close my eyes and sing to myself: *"Casta diva, casta diva!"*

VI

ON SATURDAY I was to lunch at the Henshawes' and go alone with Oswald to hear Bernhardt and Coquelin. As I opened the door into the entry hall, the first thing that greeted me was Mrs. Henshawe's angry laugh, and a burst of rapid words that stung like cold water from a spray.

"I tell you, I will know the truth about this key, and I will go through any door your keys open. Is that clear?"

Oswald answered with a distinctly malicious chuckle: "My dear, you'd have a hard time getting through that door. The key happens to open a safety deposit box."

Her voice rose an octave in pitch. "How dare you lie to me, Oswald? How dare you? They told me at your bank that this wasn't a bank key, though it looks like one. I stopped and showed it to them—the day you forgot your keys and telephoned me to bring them down to your office."

"The hell you did!"

I coughed and rapped at the door . . . they took no notice of me. I heard Oswald push back a chair. "Then it was you who took my keys out of my pocket? I might have known it! I never forget to change them. And you went to the bank and made me and yourself ridiculous. I can imagine their amusement."

"Well, you needn't! I know how to get information without giving any. Here is Nellie Birdseye, rapping at the gates. Come in, Nellie. You and Oswald are going over to Martin's for lunch. He and I are quarrelling about a key-ring. There will be no luncheon here to-day."

She went away, and I stood bewildered. This delightful room had seemed to me a place where light-heartedness and charming manners lived—housed there just as the purple curtains and the Kiva rugs and the gay water-colours were. And now everything was in ruins. The air was still and cold like the air in a refrigerating-room. What I felt was fear; I was afraid to look or speak or move. Everything about me seemed evil. When kindness has left people, even for a few moments, we become afraid of them, as if their reason had left them. When it has left a place where we have always found it, it is like shipwreck; we drop from security into something malevolent and bottomless.

"It's all right, Nellie." Oswald recovered himself and put a hand on my shoulder. "Myra isn't half so furious with me as she pretends. I'll get my hat and we'll be off." He was in his smoking-jacket, and had been sitting at his desk, writing. His inkwell was uncovered, and on the blotter lay a half-written sheet of note paper.

I was glad to get out into the sunlight with him. The city seemed safe and friendly and smiling. The air in that room had been like poison. Oswald tried to make it up to me. We walked round and round the Square, and at Martin's he made me drink a glass of sherry, and pointed out the interesting people in the dining-room and told me stories about them. But without his hat, his head against the bright window, he looked tired and troubled. I wondered, as on the first time I saw him, in my own town, at the contradiction in his face: the strong bones, and the curiously shaped eyes without any fire in them. I felt that his life had not suited him; that he possessed some kind of courage and force which slept, which in another sort of world might have asserted themselves brilliantly. I thought he ought to have been a soldier or an explorer. I have since seen those half-moon eyes in other people, and they were always inscrutable, like his; fronted the world with courtesy and kindness, but one never got behind them.

We went to the theatre, but I remember very little of the performance except a dull heartache, and a conviction that I should never like Mrs. Myra so well again. That was on Saturday. On Monday Aunt Lydia and I were to start for home. We positively did not see the Henshawes again. Sunday morning the maid came with some flowers and a note from Myra, saying that her friend Anne Aylward was having a bad day and had sent for her.

On Monday we took an early boat across the ferry, in order to breakfast in the Jersey station before our train started. We had got settled in our places in the Pullman, the moment of departure was near, when we heard an amused laugh, and there was Myra Henshawe, coming into the car in her fur hat, followed by a porter who carried her bags.

"I didn't plot anything so neat as this, Liddy," she laughed, a little out of breath, "though I knew we'd be on the same train. But we won't quarrel, will we? I'm only going as far as Pittsburgh. I've some old friends there. Oswald and I have had a disagreement, and I've left him to think it over. If he needs me, he can quite well come after me."

All day Mrs. Myra was jolly and agreeable, though she treated us with light formality, as if we were new acquaintances. We lunched together, and I noticed, sitting opposite her, that when she was in this mood of high scorn, her mouth, which could be so tender—which cherished the names of her friends and spoke them delicately—was entirely different. It seemed to curl and twist about like a little snake. Letting herself think harm of anyone she loved seemed to change her nature, even her features.

It was dark when we got into Pittsburgh. The Pullman porter took Myra's luggage to the end of the car. She bade us good-bye, started to leave us, then turned back with an icy little smile. "Oh, Liddy dear, you needn't have perjured yourself for those yellow cuff-buttons. I was sure to find out, I always do. I don't hold it against you, but it 's disgusting in a man to lie for personal decorations. A woman might do it, now, . . . for pearls!" With a bright nod she turned away and swept out of the car, her head high, the long garnet feather drooping behind.

Aunt Lydia was very angry. "I'm sick of Myra's dramatics," she declared. "I've done with them. A man never *is* justified, but if ever a man was . . ."

PART II

I

Ｔ

EN YEARS after that visit to New York I happened to be in a sprawling overgrown West-coast city which was in the throes of rapid development—it ran about the shore, stumbling all over itself and finally tumbled untidily into the sea. Every hotel and boarding-house was overcrowded, and I was very poor. Things had gone badly with my family and with me. I had come West in the middle of the year to take a position in a college—a college that was as experimental and unsubstantial as everything else in the place. I found lodgings in an apartment-hotel, wretchedly built and already falling to pieces, although it was new. I moved in on a Sunday morning, and while I was unpacking my trunk, I heard, through the thin walls, my neighbour stirring about; a man, and, from the huskiness of his cough and something measured in his movements, not a young man. The caution of his step, the guarded consideration of his activities, let me know that he did not wish to thrust the details of his housekeeping upon other people any more than he could help.

Presently I detected the ugly smell of gasoline in the air, heard a sound of silk being snapped and shaken, and then a voice humming very low an old German air—yes, Schubert's *Frühlingsglaube*; ta ta te−ta | ta−ta ta−ta ta−ta | ta. In a moment I saw the ends of dark neckties fluttering out of the window next mine.

All this made me melancholy—more than the dreariness of my own case. I was young, and it didn't matter so much about me; for youth there is always the hope, the certainty, of better things. But an old man, a gentleman, living in this shabby, comfortless place, cleaning his neckties of a Sunday morning and humming to himself . . . it depressed me unreasonably. I was glad when his outer door shut softly and I heard no more of him.

There was an indifferent restaurant on the ground floor of the hotel. As I was going down to my dinner that evening, I met, at the head of the stairs, a man coming up and carrying a large black tin tray. His head was bent, and his eyes were lowered. As he drew aside to let me pass, in spite of his thin white hair and stopped shoulders, I recognised Oswald Henshawe, whom I had not seen for so many years—not, indeed, since that afternoon when he took me to see Sarah Bernhardt play *Hamlet*.

When I called his name he started, looked at me, and rested the tray on the sill of the blindless window that lighted the naked stairway.

"Nellie! Nellie Birdseye! Can it be?"

His voice was quite uncertain. He seemed deeply shaken, and pulled out a handkerchief to wipe his forehead. "But, Nellie, you have grown up! I would not know you. What good fortune for Myra! She will hardly believe it when I tell her. She is ill, my poor Myra. Oh, very ill! But we must not speak of that, nor seem to know it. What it will mean to her to see you again! Her friends always were so much to her, you remember? Will you stop and see us as you come up? Her room is thirty-two; rap gently, and I'll be waiting for you. Now I must take her dinner. Oh, I hope for her sake you are staying some time. She has no one here."

He took up the tray and went softly along the uncarpeted hall. I felt little zest for the canned vegetables and hard meat the waitress put before me. I had known that the Henshawes had come on evil days, and were wandering about among the cities of the Pacific coast. But Myra had stopped writing to Aunt Lydia, beyond a word of greeting at Christmas and on her birthday. She had ceased to give us any information about their way of life. We knew that several years after my memorable visit in New York, the railroad to whose president Oswald had long been private secretary, was put into the hands of a receiver, and the retiring president went abroad to live. Henshawe had remained with the new management, but very soon the road was taken over by one of the great trunk lines, and the office staff was cut in two. In the reorganization Henshawe was offered a small position, which he indignantly refused—his wife wouldn't let him think of accepting it. He went to San Francisco as manager of a commission house;

the business failed, and what had happened to them since I did not know.

I lingered long over my dismal dinner. I had not the courage to go up-stairs. Henshawe was not more than sixty, but he looked much older. He had the tired, tired face of one who has utterly lost hope.

Oswald had got his wife up out of bed to receive me. When I entered she was sitting in a wheel-chair by an open window, wrapped in a Chinese dressing-gown, with a bright shawl over her feet. She threw out both arms to me, and as she hugged me, flashed into her old gay laugh.

"Now wasn't it clever of you to find us, Nellie? And we so safely hidden—in earth, like a pair of old foxes! But it was in the cards that we should meet again. Now I understand; a wise woman has been coming to read my fortune for me, and the queen of hearts has been coming up out of the pack when she had no business to; a beloved friend coming out of the past. Well, Nellie, dear, I couldn't think of any old friends that weren't better away, for one reason or another, while we are in temporary eclipse. I gain strength faster if I haven't people on my mind. But you, Nellie . . . that's different." She put my two hands to her cheeks, making a frame for her face. "That's different. Somebody young, and clear-eyed, chock-full of opinions, and without a past. But you may have a past, already? The darkest ones come early."

I was delighted. She was . . . she was herself, Myra Henshawe! I hadn't expected anything so good. The electric bulbs in the room were shrouded and muffled with coloured scarfs, and in that light she looked much less changed than Oswald. The corners of her mouth had relaxed a little, but they could still curl very scornfully upon occasion; her nose was the same sniffy little nose, with its restless, arched nostrils, and her double chin, though softer, was no fuller. A strong cable of grey-black hair was wound on the top of her head, which, as she once remarked, "was no head for a woman at all, but would have graced one of the wickedest of the Roman emperors."

Her bed was in the alcove behind her. In the shadowy dimness of the room I recognised some of the rugs from their

New York apartment, some of the old pictures, with frames peeling and glass cracked. Here was Myra's little inlaid tea-table, and the desk at which Oswald had been writing that day when I dropped in upon their quarrel. At the windows were the dear, plum-coloured curtains, their cream lining streaked and faded—but the sight of them rejoiced me more than I could tell the Henshawes.

"And where did you come from, Nellie? What are you doing here, in heaven's name?"

While I explained myself she listened intently, holding my wrist with one of her beautiful little hands, which were so inexplicably mischievous in their outline, and which, I noticed, were still white and well cared for.

"Ah, but teaching, Nellie! I don't like that, not even for a temporary expedient. It's a cul-de-sac. Generous young people use themselves all up at it; they have no sense. Only the stupid and the phlegmatic should teach."

"But won't you allow me, too, a temporary eclipse?"

She laughed and squeezed my hand. "Ah, *we* wouldn't be hiding in the shadow, if we were five-and-twenty! We were throwing off sparks like a pair of shooting stars, weren't we, Oswald? No, I can't bear teaching for you, Nellie. Why not journalism? You could always make your way easily there."

"Because I hate journalism. I know what I want to do, and I'll work my way out yet, if only you'll give me time."

"Very well, dear." She sighed. "But I'm ambitious for you. I've no patience with young people when they drift. I wish I could live their lives for them; I'd know how! But there it is; by the time you've learned the short cuts, your feet puff up so that you can't take the road at all. Now tell me about your mother and my Lydia."

I had hardly begun when she lifted one finger and sniffed the air. "Do you get it? That bitter smell of the sea? It's apt to come in on the night wind. I live on it. Sometimes I can still take a drive along the shore. Go on; you say that Lydia and your mother are at present in disputation about the posses-sion of your late grandfather's portrait. Why don't you cut it in two for them, Nellie? I remember it perfectly, and half of it would be enough for anybody!"

While I told her any amusing gossip I could remember

about my family, she sat crippled but powerful in her brilliant wrappings. She looked strong and broken, generous and tyrannical, a witty and rather wicked old woman, who hated life for its defeats, and loved it for its absurdities. I recalled her angry laugh, and how she had always greeted shock or sorrow with that dry, exultant chuckle which seemed to say: "Ah-ha, I have one more piece of evidence, one more, against the hideous injustice God permits in this world!"

While we were talking, the silence of the strangely balmy February evening was rudely disturbed by the sound of doors slamming and heavy tramping overhead. Mrs. Henshawe winced, a look of apprehension and helplessness, a tortured expression, came over her face. She turned sharply to her husband, who was resting peacefully in one of their old, deep chairs, over by the muffled light. "There they are, those animals!"

He sat up. "They have just come back from church," he said in a troubled voice.

"Why should I have to know when they come back from church? Why should I have the details of their stupid, messy existence thrust upon me all day long, and half the night?" she broke out bitterly. Her features became tense, as from an attack of pain, and I realised how unable she was to bear things.

"We are unfortunate in the people who live over us," Oswald explained. "They annoy us a great deal. These new houses are poorly built, and every sound carries."

"Couldn't you ask them to walk more quietly?" I suggested.

He smiled and shook his head. "We have, but it seems to make them worse. They are that kind of people."

His wife broke in. "The palavery kind of Southerners; all that slushy gush on the surface, and no sensibilities whatever—a race without consonants and without delicacy. They tramp up there all day long like cattle. The stalled ox would have trod softer. Their energy isn't worth anything, so they use it up gabbling and running about, beating my brains into a jelly."

She had scarcely stopped for breath when I heard a telephone ring overhead, then shrieks of laughter, and two people ran across the floor as if they were running a foot-race.

"You hear?" Mrs. Henshawe looked at me triumphantly. "Those two silly old hens race each other to the telephone as if they had a sweetheart at the other end of it. While I could still climb stairs, I hobbled up to that woman and implored her, and she began gushing about 'mah sistah' and 'mah son,' and what 'rahfined' people they were. . . . Oh, that's the cruelty of being poor; it leaves you at the mercy of such pigs! Money is a protection, a cloak; it can buy one quiet, and some sort of dignity." She leaned back, exhausted, and shut her eyes.

"Come, Nellie," said Oswald, softly. He walked down the hall to my door with me. "I'm sorry the disturbance began while you were there. Sometimes they go to the movies, and stay out later," he said mournfully. "I've talked to that woman and to her son, but they are very unfeeling people."

"But wouldn't the management interfere in a case of sickness?"

Again he shook his head. "No, they pay a higher rent than we do—occupy more rooms. And we are somewhat under obligation to the management."

II

I SOON DISCOVERED the facts about the Henshawes' present existence. Oswald had a humble position, poorly paid, with the city traction company. He had to be at his desk at nine o'clock every day except Sunday. He rose at five in the morning, put on an old duck suit (it happened to be a very smart one, with frogs and a military collar, left over from prosperous times), went to his wife's room and gave her her bath, made her bed, arranged her things, and then got their breakfast. He made the coffee on a spirit lamp, the toast on an electric toaster. This was the only meal of the day they could have together, and as they had it long before the ruthless Poindexters overhead began to tramp, it was usually a cheerful occasion.

After breakfast Oswald washed the dishes. Their one luxury was a private bath, with a large cupboard, which he called his kitchen. Everything else done, he went back to his own room, put it in order, and then dressed for the office. He still dressed very neatly, though how he managed to do it with the few clothes he had, I could not see. He was the only man staying in that shabby hotel who looked well-groomed. As a special favour from his company he was allowed to take two hours at noon, on account of his sick wife. He came home, brought her her lunch from below, then hurried back to his office.

Myra made her own tea every afternoon, getting about in her wheel-chair or with the aid of a cane. I found that one of the kindest things I could do for her was to bring her some little sandwiches or cakes from the Swedish bakery to vary her tinned biscuit. She took great pains to get her tea nicely; it made her feel less shabby to use her own silver tea things and the three glossy English cups she had carried about with her in her trunk. I used often to go in and join her, and we spent some of our pleasantest hours at that time of the day, when the people overhead were usually out. When they were in, and active, it was too painful to witness Mrs. Henshawe's suffering. She was acutely sensitive to sound and light, and the Poindexters did tramp like cattle—except that their brutal

thumping hadn't the measured dignity which the step of ani-
mals always has. Mrs. Henshawe got great pleasure from
flowers, too, and during the late winter months my chief ex-
travagance and my chief pleasure was in taking them to her.

One warm Saturday afternoon, early in April, we went for
a drive along the shore. I had hired a low carriage with a
kindly Negro driver. Supported on his arm and mine, Mrs.
Henshawe managed to get downstairs. She looked much
older and more ill in her black broadcloth coat and a black
taffeta hat that had once been smart. We took with us her furs
and an old steamer blanket. It was a beautiful, soft spring
day. The road, unfortunately, kept winding away from the sea.
At last we came out on a bare headland, with only one old
twisted tree upon it, and the sea beneath.

"Why, Nellie!" she exclaimed, "it's like the cliff in *Lear*,
Gloucester's cliff, so it is! Can't we stay here? I believe this
nice darkey man would fix me up under the tree there and
come back for us later."

We wrapped her in the rug, and she declared that the trunk
of the old cedar, bending away from the sea, made a comfort-
able back for her. The Negro drove away, and I went for a
walk up the shore because I knew she wanted to be alone.
From a distance I could see her leaning against her tree and
looking off to sea, as if she were waiting for something. A few
steamers passed below her, and the gulls dipped and darted
about the headland, the soft shine of the sun on their wings.
The afternoon light, at first wide and watery-pale, grew stron-
ger and yellow, and when I went back to Myra it was beating
from the west on her cliff as if thrown by a burning-glass.

She looked up at me with a soft smile—her face could still
be very lovely in a tender moment. "I've had such a beautiful
hour, dear; or has it been longer? Light and silence: they heal
all one's wounds—all but one, and that is healed by dark and
silence. I find I don't miss clever talk, the kind I always used
to have about me, when I can have silence. It's like cold water
poured over fever."

I sat down beside her, and we watched the sun dropping
lower toward his final plunge into the Pacific. "I'd love to see
this place at dawn," Myra said suddenly. "That is always such
a forgiving time. When that first cold, bright streak comes

over the water, it's as if all our sins were pardoned; as if the sky leaned over the earth and kissed it and gave it absolution. You know how the great sinners always came home to die in some religious house, and the abbot or the abbess went out and received them with a kiss?"

When we got home she was, of course, very tired. Oswald was waiting for us, and he and the driver carried her upstairs. While we were getting her into bed, the noise overhead broke out—tramp, tramp, bang! Myra began to cry.

"Oh, I've come back to it, to be tormented again! I've two fatal maladies, but it's those coarse creatures I shall die of. Why didn't you leave me out there, Nellie, in the wind and night? You ought to get me away from this, Oswald. If I were on my feet, and you laid low, I wouldn't let you be despised and trampled upon."

"I'll go up and see those people to-morrow, Mrs. Henshawe," I promised. "I'm sure I can do something."

"Oh, don't, Nellie!" she looked up at me in affright. "She'd turn a deaf ear to you. You know the Bible says the wicked are deaf like the adder. And, Nellie, she has the wrinkled, white throat of an adder, that woman, and the hard eyes of one. Don't go near her!"

(I went to see Mrs. Poindexter the next day, and she had just such a throat and just such eyes. She smiled, and said that the sick woman underneath was an old story, and she ought to have been sent to a sanatorium long ago.)

"Never mind, Myra. I'll get you away from it yet. I'll manage," Oswald promised as he settled the pillows under her.

She smoothed his hair. "No, my poor Oswald, you'll never stagger far under the bulk of me. Oh, if youth but knew!" She closed her eyes and pressed her hands over them. "It's been the ruin of us both. We've destroyed each other. I should have stayed with my uncle. It was money I needed. We've thrown our lives away."

"Come, Myra, don't talk so before Nellie. You don't mean it. Remember the long time we were happy. That was reality, just as much as this."

"We were never really happy. I am a greedy, selfish, worldly woman; I wanted success and a place in the world. Now I'm old and ill and a fright, but among my own kind I'd still have my circle; I'd have courtesy from people of gentle manners, and not have my brains beaten out by hoodlums. Go away, please, both of you, and leave me!" She turned her face to the wall and covered her head.

We stepped into the hall, and the moment we closed the door we heard the bolt slip behind us. She must have sprung up very quickly. Oswald walked with me to my room. "It's apt to be like this, when she has enjoyed something and gone beyond her strength. There are times when she can't have anyone near her. It was worse before you came."

I persuaded him to come into my room and sit down and drink a glass of cordial.

"Sometimes she has locked me out for days together," he said. "It seems strange—a woman of such generous friendships. It's as if she had used up that part of herself. It's a great strain on me when she shuts herself up like that. I'm afraid she'll harm herself in some way."

"But people don't do things like that," I said hopelessly.

He smiled and straightened his shoulders. "Ah, but she isn't people! She's Molly Driscoll, and there was never anybody else like her. She can't endure, but she has enough desperate courage for a regiment."

III

THE NEXT MORNING I saw Henshawe breakfasting in the restaurant, against his custom, so I judged that his wife was still in retreat. I was glad to see that he was not alone, but was talking, with evident pleasure, to a young girl who lived with her mother at this hotel. I had noticed her respectful admiration for Henshawe on other occasions. She worked on a newspaper, was intelligent and, Oswald thought, promising. We enjoyed talking with her at lunch or dinner. She was perhaps eighteen, overgrown and awkward, with short hair and a rather heavy face; but there was something unusual about her clear, honest eyes that made one wonder. She was always on the watch to catch a moment with Oswald, to get him to talk to her about music, or German poetry, or about the actors and writers he had known. He called her his little chum, and her admiration was undoubtedly a help to him. It was very pretty and naïve. Perhaps that was one of the things that kept him up to the mark in his dress and manner. Among people he never looked apologetic or crushed. He still wore his topaz sleeve-buttons.

On Monday, as I came home from school, I saw that the door of Mrs. Henshawe's room was slightly ajar. She knew my step and called to me: "Can you come in, Nellie?"

She was staying in bed that afternoon, but she had on her best dressing-gown, and she was manicuring her neat little hands—a good sign, I thought.

"Could you stop and have tea with me, and talk? I'll be good to-day, I promise you. I wakened up in the night crying, and it did me good. You see, I was crying about things I never feel now; I'd been dreaming I was young, and the sorrows of youth had set me crying!" She took my hand as I sat down beside her. "Do you know that poem of Heine's, about how he found in his eye a tear that was not of the present, an old one, left over from the kind he used to weep? A tear that belonged to a long dead time of his life and was an anachronism. He couldn't account for it, yet there it was, and he addresses it so prettily: 'Thou old, lonesome tear!' Would you read it for me? There's my little Heine, on the shelf over the sofa. You can easily find the verse, *Du alte, einsame Thräne!*"

I ran through the volume, reading a poem here and there where a leaf had been turned down, or where I saw a line I knew well. It was a fat old book, with yellow pages, bound in tooled leather, and on the fly-leaf, in faint violet ink, was an inscription, "To Myra Driscoll from Oswald," dated 1876.

My friend lay still, with her eyes closed, and occasionally one of those anachronistic tears gathered on her lashes and fell on the pillow, making a little grey spot. Often she took the verse out of my mouth and finished it herself.

"Look for a little short one, about the flower that grows on the suicide's grave, *die Armesünderblum'*, the poor-sinner's-flower. Oh, that's the flower for me, Nellie; *die Arme — sünder — blum'!*" She drew the word out until it was a poem in itself.

"Come, dear," she said presently, when I put down the book, "you don't really like this new verse that's going round, ugly lines about ugly people and common feelings — you don't really?"

When I reminded her that she liked Walt Whitman, she chuckled slyly. "Does that save me? Can I get into your new Parnassus on that dirty old man? I suppose I ought to be glad of any sort of ticket at my age! I like naughty rhymes, when they don't try to be pompous. I like the kind bad boys write on fences. My uncle had a rare collection of such rhymes in his head that he'd picked off fences and out-buildings. I wish I'd taken them down; I might become a poet of note! My uncle was a very unusual man. Did they ever tell you much about him at home? Yes, he had violent prejudices; but that's rather good to remember in these days when so few people have any real passions, either of love or hate. He would help a friend, no matter what it cost him, and over and over again he risked ruining himself to crush an enemy. But he never did ruin himself. Men who hate like that usually have the fist-power to back it up, you'll notice. He gave me fair warning, and then he kept his word. I knew he would; we were enough alike for that. He left his money wisely; part of it went to establish a home for aged and destitute women in Chicago, where it was needed."

While we were talking about this institution and some of the refugees it sheltered, Myra said suddenly: "I wonder if you know about a clause concerning me in that foundation? It states that at any time the founder's niece, Myra Driscoll Henshawe, is to be received into the institution, kept without charge, and paid an allowance of ten dollars a week for pocket money until the time of her death. How like the old Satan that was! Be sure when he dictated that provision to his lawyer, he thought to himself: 'She'd roll herself into the river first, the brach!' And then he probably thought better of me, and maybe died with some decent feeling for me in his heart. We were very proud of each other, and if he'd lived till now, I'd go back to him and ask his pardon; because I know what it is to be old and lonely and disappointed. Yes, and because as we grow old we become more and more the stuff our forbears put into us. I can feel his savagery strengthen in me. We think we are so individual and so misunderstood when we are young; but the nature our strain of blood carries is inside there, waiting, like our skeleton."

It had grown quite dusk while we talked. When I rose and turned on one of the shrouded lights, Mrs. Henshawe looked up at me and smiled drolly. "We've had a fine afternoon, and Biddy forgetting her ails. How the great poets do shine on, Nellie! Into all the dark corners of the world. They have no night."

They shone for her, certainly. Miss Stirling, "a nice young person from the library," as Myra called her, ran in occasionally with new books, but Myra's eyes tired quickly, and she used to shut a new book and lie back and repeat the old ones she knew by heart, the long declamations from *Richard II* or *King John*. As I passed her door I would hear her murmuring at the very bottom of her rich Irish voice:

> *Old John of Gaunt, time-honoured Lan-cas-ter* . . .

IV

ONE AFTERNOON when I got home from school I found a note from Mrs. Henshawe under my door, and went to her at once. She greeted me and kissed me with unusual gravity.

"Nellie, dear, will you do a very special favour for me to-morrow? It is the fifteenth of April, the anniversary of Madame Modjeska's death." She gave me a key and asked me to open an old trunk in the corner. "Lift the tray, and in the bottom, at one end, you will find an old pair of long kid gloves, tied up like sacks. Please give them to me."

I burrowed down under old evening wraps and dinner dresses and came upon the gloves, yellow with age and tied at both ends with corset lacings; they contained something heavy that jingled. Myra was watching my face and chuckled. "Is she thinking they are my wedding gloves, piously preserved? No, my dear; I went before a justice of the peace, and married without gloves, so to speak!" Untying the string, she shook out a little rain of ten- and twenty-dollar gold pieces.

"All old Irish women hide away a bit of money." She took up a coin and gave it to me. "Will you go to St. Joseph's Church and inquire for Father Fay; tell him you are from me, and ask him to celebrate a mass to-morrow for the repose of the soul of Helena Modjeska, Countess Bozenta-Chlapowska. He will remember; last year I hobbled there myself. You are surprised, Nellie? Yes, I broke with the Church when I broke with everything else and ran away with a German free-thinker; but I believe in holy words and holy rites all the same. It is a solace to me to know that to-morrow a mass will be said here in heathendom for the spirit of that noble artist, that beautiful and gracious woman."

When I put the gold back into the trunk and started making the tea, she said: "Oswald, of course, doesn't know the extent of my resources. We've often needed a hundred dollars or two so bitter bad; he wouldn't understand. But that is money I keep for unearthly purposes; the needs of this world don't touch it."

As I was leaving she called me back: "Oh, Nellie, can't we go to Gloucester's cliff on Saturday, if it's fine? I do long to!"

We went again, and again. Nothing else seemed to give her so much pleasure. But the third time I stopped for her, she declared she was not equal to it. I found her sitting in her chair, trying to write to an old friend, an Irish actress I had met at her apartment in New York, one of the guests at that New Year's Eve party. Her son, a young actor, had shot himself in Chicago because of some sordid love affair. I had seen an account of it in the morning paper.

"It touches me very nearly," Mrs. Henshawe told me. "Why, I used to keep Billy with me for weeks together when his mother was off on tour. He was the most truthful, noble-hearted little fellow. I had so hoped he would be happy. You remember his mother?"

I remembered her very well—large and jovial and hearty she was. Myra began telling me about her, and the son, whom she had not seen since he was sixteen.

"To throw his youth away like that, and shoot himself at twenty-three! People are always talking about the joys of youth—but, oh, how youth can suffer! I've not forgotten; those hot southern Illinois nights, when Oswald was in New York, and I had no word from him except through Liddy, and I used to lie on the floor all night and listen to the express trains go by. I've not forgotten."

"Then I wonder why you are sometimes so hard on him now," I murmured.

Mrs. Henshawe did not reply to me at once. The corners of her mouth trembled, then drew tight, and she sat with her eyes closed as if she were gathering herself for something.

At last she sighed, and looked at me wistfully. "It's a great pity, isn't it, Nellie, to reach out a grudging hand and try to spoil the past for any one? Yes, it's a great cruelty. But I can't help it. He's a sentimentalist, always was; he can look back on the best of those days when we were young and loved each other, and make himself believe it was all like that. It wasn't. I was always a grasping, worldly woman; I was never satisfied. All the same, in age, when the flowers are so few, it's a great unkindness to destroy any that are left in a man's heart." The tears rolled down her cheeks, she leaned back, looking up at the ceiling. She had stopped speaking because her voice broke. Presently she began again resolutely. "But I'm made so. People can be lovers and enemies at the same time, you know. We were. . . . A man and woman draw apart from that long embrace, and see what they have done to each other. Perhaps I can't forgive him for the harm I did him. Perhaps that's it. When there are children, that feeling goes through natural changes. But when it remains so personal . . . something gives way in one. In age we lose everything; even the power to love."

"He hasn't," I suggested.

"He has asked you to speak for him, my dear? Then we have destroyed each other indeed!"

"Certainly he hasn't, Mrs. Myra! But you are hard on him, you know, and when there are so many hard things, it seems a pity."

"Yes, it's a great pity." She drew herself up in her chair. "And I'd rather you didn't come any more for the time being, Nellie. I've been thinking the tea made me nervous." She was smiling, but her mouth curled like a little snake, as I had seen it do long ago. "Will you be pleased to take your things and go, Mrs. Casey?" She said it with a laugh, but a very meaning one.

As I rose I watched for some sign of relenting, and I said humbly enough: "Forgive me, if I've said anything I shouldn't. You know I love you very dearly."

She mockingly bowed her tyrant's head. "It's owing to me infirmities, dear Mrs. Casey, that I'll not be able to go as far as me door wid ye."

V

FOR DAYS after that episode I did not see Mrs. Henshawe at all. I saw Oswald at dinner in the restaurant every night, and he reported her condition to me as if nothing had happened. The short-haired newspaper girl often came to our table, and the three of us talked together. I could see that he got great refreshment from her. Her questions woke pleasant trains of recollection, and her straightforward affection was dear to him. Once Myra, in telling me that it was a pleasure to him to have me come into their lives again thus, had remarked: "He was always a man to feel women, you know, in every way." It was true. That crude little girl made all the difference in the world to him. He was generous enough to become quite light-hearted in directing her inexperience and her groping hunger for life. He even read her poor little "specials" and showed her what was worst in them and what was good. She took correction well, he told me.

Early in June Mrs. Henshawe began to grow worse. Her doctors told us a malignant growth in her body had taken hold of a vital organ, and that she would hardly live through the month. She suffered intense pain from pressure on the nerves in her back, and they gave her opiates freely. At first we had two nurses, but Myra hated the night nurse so intensely that we dismissed her, and, as my school was closed for the summer, I took turns with Oswald in watching over her at night. She needed little attention except renewed doses of codeine. She slept deeply for a few hours, and the rest of the night lay awake, murmuring to herself long passages from her old poets.

Myra kept beside her now an ebony crucifix with an ivory Christ. It used to hang on the wall, and I had supposed she carried it about because some friend had given it to her. I felt now that she had it by her for a different reason. Once when I picked it up from her bed to straighten her sheet, she put out her hand quickly and said: "Give it to me. It means nothing to people who haven't suffered."

She talked very little after this last stage of her illness began; she no longer complained or lamented, but toward

Oswald her manner became strange and dark. She had certain illusions; the noise overhead she now attributed entirely to her husband. "Ah, there he's beginning it again," she would say. "He'll wear me down in the end. Oh, let me be buried in the king's highway!"

When Oswald lifted her, or did anything for her now, she was careful to thank him in a guarded, sometimes a cringing tone. "It's bitter enough that I should have to take service from you—you whom I have loved so well," I heard her say to him.

When she asked us to use candles for light during our watches, and to have no more of the electric light she hated, she said accusingly, at him rather than to him: "At least let me die by candlelight; that is not too much to ask."

Father Fay came to see her almost daily now. His visits were long, and she looked forward to them. I was, of course, not in her room when he was there, but if he met me in the corridor he stopped to speak to me, and once he walked down the street with me talking of her. He was a young man, with a fresh face and pleasant eyes, and he was deeply interested in Myra. "She's a most unusual woman, Mrs. Henshawe," he said when he was walking down the street beside me. Then he added, smiling quite boyishly: "I wonder whether some of the saints of the early Church weren't a good deal like her. She's not at all modern in her make-up, is she?"

During those days and nights when she talked so little, one felt that Myra's mind was busy all the while—that it was even abnormally active, and occasionally one got a clue to what occupied it. One night when I was giving her her codeine she asked me a question.

"Why is it, do you suppose, Nellie, that candles are in themselves religious? Not when they are covered by shades, of course—I mean the flame of a candle. Is it because the Church began in the catacombs, perhaps?"

At another time, when she had been lying like a marble figure for a long while, she said in a gentle, reasonable voice:

"Ah, Father Fay, that isn't the reason! Religion is different from everything else; *because in religion seeking is finding.*"

She accented the word "seeking" very strongly, very deeply.

She seemed to say that in other searchings it might be the object of the quest that brought satisfaction, or it might be something incidental that one got on the way; but in religion, desire was fulfilment, it was the seeking itself that rewarded.

One of those nights of watching stands out in my memory as embracing them all, as being the burden and telling the tale of them all. Myra had had a very bad day, so both Oswald and I were sitting up with her. After midnight she was quiet. The candles were burning as usual, one in her alcove. From my chair by the open window I could see her bed. She had been motionless for more than an hour, lying on her back, her eyes closed. I thought she was asleep. The city outside was as still as the room in which we sat. The sick woman began to talk to herself, scarcely above a whisper, but with perfect distinctness; a voice that was hardly more than a soft, passionate breath. I seemed to hear a soul talking.

"I could bear to suffer . . . so many have suffered. But why must it be like this? I have not deserved it. I have been true in friendship; I have faithfully nursed others in sickness. . . . Why must I die like this, alone with my mortal enemy?"

Oswald was sitting on the sofa, his face shaded by his hand. I looked at him in affright, but he did not move or shudder. I felt my hands grow cold and my forehead grow moist with dread. I had never heard a human voice utter such a terrible judgment upon all one hopes for. As I sat on through the night, after Oswald had gone to catch a few hours of sleep, I grew calmer; I began to understand a little what she meant, to sense how it was with her. Violent natures like hers sometimes turn against themselves . . . against themselves and all their idolatries.

VI

ON THE FOLLOWING DAY Mrs. Henshawe asked to be given the Sacrament. After she had taken it she seemed easier in mind and body. In the afternoon she told Henshawe to go to his office and begged me to leave her and let her sleep. The nurse we had sent away that day at her urgent request. She wanted to be cared for by one of the nursing Sisters from the convent from now on, and Father Fay was to bring one to-morrow.

I went to my room, meaning to go back to her in an hour, but once on my bed I slept without waking. It was dark when I heard Henshawe knocking on my door and calling to me. As I opened it, he said in a despairing tone: "She's gone, Nellie, she's gone!"

I thought he meant she had died. I hurried after him down the corridor and into her room. It was empty. He pointed to her empty bed. "Don't you see? She has gone, God knows where!"

"But how could she? A woman so ill? She must be somewhere in the building."

"I've been all over the house. You don't know her, Nellie. She can do anything she wills. Look at this."

On the desk lay a sheet of note paper scribbled in lead pencil: *"Dear Oswald: My hour has come. Don't follow me. I wish to be alone. Nellie knows where there is money for masses."* That was all. There was no signature.

We hurried to the police station. The chief sent a messenger out to the men on the beat to warn them to be on the watch for a distraught woman who had wandered out in delirium. Then we went to Father Fay. "The Church has been on her mind for a long while," said Henshawe. "It is one of her delusions that I separated her from the Church. I never meant to."

The young priest knew nothing. He was distressed, and offered to help us in our search, but we thought he had better stay at home on the chance that she might come to him.

When we got back to the hotel it was after eleven o'clock.

Oswald said he could not stay indoors; I must be there within call, but he would go back to help the police.

After he left I began to search Mrs. Henshawe's room. She had worn her heavy coat and her furs, though the night was warm. When I found that the pair of Austrian blankets was missing, I felt I knew where she had gone. Should I try to get Oswald at the police station? I sat down to think it over. It seemed to me that she ought to be allowed to meet the inevitable end in the way she chose. A yearning strong enough to lift that ailing body and drag it out into the world again should have its way.

At five o'clock in the morning Henshawe came back with an officer and a Negro cabman. The driver had come to the station and reported that at six last night a lady, with her arms full of wraps, had signalled him at the side door of the hotel, and told him to drive her to the boat landing. When they were nearing the landing, she said she did not mean to stop there, but wanted to go farther up the shore, giving him clear directions. They reached the cliff she had indicated. He helped her out of the cab, put her rugs under the tree for her, and she gave him a ten-dollar gold piece and dismissed him. He protested that the fare was too much, and that he was afraid of getting into trouble if he left her there. But she told him a friend was going to meet her, and that it would be all right. The lady had, he said, a very kind, coaxing way with her. When he went to the stable to put up his horse, he heard that the police were looking for a woman who was out of her head, and he was frightened. He went home and talked it over with his wife, who sent him to report at head-quarters.

The cabman drove us out to the headland, and the officer insisted upon going along. We found her wrapped in her blankets, leaning against the cedar trunk, facing the sea. Her head had fallen forward; the ebony crucifix was in her hands. She must have died peacefully and painlessly. There was every reason to believe she had lived to see the dawn. While we watched beside her, waiting for the undertaker and Father Fay to come, I told Oswald what she had said to me about longing to behold the morning break over the sea, and it comforted him.

VII

ALTHOUGH SHE had returned so ardently to the faith of her childhood, Myra Henshawe never changed the clause in her will, which requested that her body should be cremated, and her ashes buried "in some lonely and unfrequented place in the mountains, or in the sea."

After it was all over, and her ashes sealed up in a little steel box, Henshawe called me into her room one morning, where he was packing her things, and told me he was going to Alaska.

"Oh, not to seek my fortune," he said, smiling. "That is for young men. But the steamship company have a place for me in their office there. I have always wanted to go, and now there is nothing to hold me. This poor little box goes with me; I shall scatter her ashes somewhere in those vast waters. And this I want you to keep for remembrance." He dropped into my hands the necklace of carved amethysts she had worn on the night I first saw her.

"And, Nellie——" He paused before me with his arms folded, standing exactly as he stood behind Modjeska's chair in the moonlight on that New Year's night; standing like a statue, or a sentinel, I had said then, not knowing what it was I felt in his attitude; but now I knew it meant indestructible constancy . . . almost indestructible youth. "Nellie," he said, "I don't want you to remember her as she was here. Remember her as she was when you were with us on Madison Square, when she was herself, and we were happy. Yes, happier than it falls to the lot of most mortals to be. After she was stricken, her recollection of those things darkened. Life was hard for her, but it was glorious, too; she had such beautiful friendships. Of course, she was absolutely unreasonable when she was jealous. Her suspicions were sometimes— almost fantastic." He smiled and brushed his forehead with the tips of his fingers, as if the memory of her jealousy was pleasant still, and perplexing still. "But that was just Molly Driscoll! I'd rather have been clawed by her, as she used to say, than petted by any other woman I've ever known. These last years it's seemed to me that I was nursing the mother of the girl who ran away with me. Nothing ever took that girl from me. She was a wild, lovely creature, Nellie. I wish you could have seen her then."

Several years after I said good-bye to him, Oswald Henshawe died in Alaska. I have still the string of amethysts, but they are unlucky. If I take them out of their box and wear them, I feel all evening a chill over my heart. Sometimes, when I have watched the bright beginning of a love story, when I have seen a common feeling exalted into beauty by imagination, generosity, and the flaming courage of youth, I have heard again that strange complaint breathed by a dying woman into the stillness of night, like a confession of the soul: "Why must I die like this, alone with my mortal enemy!"

OBSCURE DESTINIES

Contents

Neighbour Rosicky

I

WHEN DOCTOR BURLEIGH told neighbour Rosicky he had a bad heart, Rosicky protested.

"So? No, I guess my heart was always pretty good. I got a little asthma, maybe. Just a awful short breath when I was pitchin' hay last summer, dat's all."

"Well now, Rosicky, if you know more about it than I do, what did you come to me for? It's your heart that makes you short of breath, I tell you. You're sixty-five years old, and you've always worked hard, and your heart's tired. You've got to be careful from now on, and you can't do heavy work any more. You've got five boys at home to do it for you."

The old farmer looked up at the Doctor with a gleam of amusement in his queer triangular-shaped eyes. His eyes were large and lively, but the lids were caught up in the middle in a curious way, so that they formed a triangle. He did not look like a sick man. His brown face was creased but not wrinkled, he had a ruddy colour in his smooth-shaven cheeks and in his lips, under his long brown moustache. His hair was thin and ragged around his ears, but very little grey. His forehead, naturally high and crossed by deep parallel lines, now ran all the way up to his pointed crown. Rosicky's face had the habit of looking interested,—suggested a contented disposition and a reflective quality that was gay rather than grave. This gave him a certain detachment, the easy manner of an onlooker and observer.

"Well, I guess you ain't got no pills fur a bad heart, Doctor Ed. I guess the only thing is fur me to git me a new one."

Doctor Burleigh swung round in his desk-chair and frowned at the old farmer. "I think if I were you I'd take a little care of the old one, Rosicky."

Rosicky shrugged. "Maybe I don't know how. I expect you mean fur me not to drink my coffee no more."

"I wouldn't, in your place. But you'll do as you choose about that. I've never yet been able to separate a Bohemian from his coffee or his pipe. I've quit trying. But the sure thing is you've got to cut out farm work. You can feed the stock and do chores about the barn, but you can't do anything in the fields that makes you short of breath."

"How about shelling corn?"

"Of course not!"

Rosicky considered with puckered brows.

"I can't make my heart go no longer'n it wants to, can I, Doctor Ed?"

"I think it's good for five or six years yet, maybe more, if you'll take the strain off it. Sit around the house and help Mary. If I had a good wife like yours, I'd want to stay around the house."

His patient chuckled. "It ain't no place fur a man. I don't like no old man hanging round the kitchen too much. An' my wife, she's a awful hard worker her own self."

"That's it; you can help her a little. My Lord, Rosicky, you are one of the few men I know who has a family he can get some comfort out of; happy dispositions, never quarrel among themselves, and they treat you right. I want to see you live a few years and enjoy them."

"Oh, they're good kids, all right," Rosicky assented.

The Doctor wrote him a prescription and asked him how his oldest son, Rudolph, who had married in the spring, was getting on. Rudolph had struck out for himself, on rented land. "And how's Polly? I was afraid Mary mightn't like an American daughter-in-law, but it seems to be working out all right."

"Yes, she's a fine girl. Dat widder woman bring her daughters up very nice. Polly got lots of spunk, an' she got some style, too. Da's nice, for young folks to have some style." Rosicky inclined his head gallantly. His voice and his twinkly smile were an affectionate compliment to his daughter-in-law.

"It looks like a storm, and you'd better be getting home before it comes. In town in the car?" Doctor Burleigh rose.

"No, I'm in de wagon. When you got five boys, you ain't got much chance to ride round in de Ford. I ain't much for cars, noway."

"Well, it's a good road out to your place; but I don't want

you bumping around in a wagon much. And never again on a hay-rake, remember!"

Rosicky placed the Doctor's fee delicately behind the desk-telephone, looking the other way, as if this were an absent-minded gesture. He put on his plush cap and his corduroy jacket with a sheepskin collar, and went out.

The Doctor picked up his stethoscope and frowned at it as if he were seriously annoyed with the instrument. He wished it had been telling tales about some other man's heart, some old man who didn't look the Doctor in the eye so knowingly, or hold out such a warm brown hand when he said good-bye. Doctor Burleigh had been a poor boy in the country before he went away to medical school; he had known Rosicky almost ever since he could remember, and he had a deep affection for Mrs. Rosicky.

Only last winter he had had such a good breakfast at Rosicky's, and that when he needed it. He had been out all night on a long, hard confinement case at Tom Marshall's,—a big rich farm where there was plenty of stock and plenty of feed and a great deal of expensive farm machinery of the newest model, and no comfort whatever. The woman had too many children and too much work, and she was no manager. When the baby was born at last, and handed over to the assisting neighbour woman, and the mother was properly attended to, Burleigh refused any breakfast in that slovenly house, and drove his buggy—the snow was too deep for a car—eight miles to Anton Rosicky's place. He didn't know another farm-house where a man could get such a warm welcome, and such good strong coffee with rich cream. No wonder the old chap didn't want to give up his coffee!

He had driven in just when the boys had come back from the barn and were washing up for breakfast. The long table, covered with a bright oilcloth, was set out with dishes waiting for them, and the warm kitchen was full of the smell of coffee and hot biscuit and sausage. Five big handsome boys, running from twenty to twelve, all with what Burleigh called natural good manners,—they hadn't a bit of the painful self-consciousness he himself had to struggle with when he was a lad. One ran to put his horse away, another helped him off with his fur coat and hung it up, and Josephine, the youngest child and the only daughter, quickly set another place under her mother's direction.

With Mary, to feed creatures was the natural expression of affection,—her chickens, the calves, her big hungry boys. It was a rare pleasure to feed a young man whom she seldom saw and of whom she was as proud as if he belonged to her. Some country housekeepers would have stopped to spread a white cloth over the oilcloth, to change the thick cups and plates for their best china, and the wooden-handled knives for plated ones. But not Mary.

"You must take us as you find us, Doctor Ed. I'd be glad to put out my good things for you if you was expected, but I'm glad to get you any way at all."

He knew she was glad,—she threw back her head and spoke out as if she were announcing him to the whole prairie. Rosicky hadn't said anything at all; he merely smiled his twinkling smile, put some more coal on the fire, and went into his own room to pour the Doctor a little drink in a medicine glass. When they were all seated, he watched his wife's face from his end of the table and spoke to her in Czech. Then, with the instinct of politeness which seldom failed him, he turned to the Doctor and said slyly; "I was just tellin' her not to ask you no questions about Mrs. Marshall till you eat some breakfast. My wife, she's terrible fur to ask questions."

The boys laughed, and so did Mary. She watched the Doctor devour her biscuit and sausage, too much excited to eat anything herself. She drank her coffee and sat taking in everything about her visitor. She had known him when he was a poor country boy, and was boastfully proud of his success, always saying: "What do people go to Omaha for, to see a doctor, when we got the best one in the State right here?" If Mary liked people at all, she felt physical pleasure in the sight of them, personal exultation in any good fortune that came to them. Burleigh didn't know many women like that, but he knew she was like that.

When his hunger was satisfied, he did, of course, have to tell them about Mrs. Marshall, and he noticed what a friendly interest the boys took in the matter.

Rudolph, the oldest one (he was still living at home then),

said: "The last time I was over there, she was lifting them big heavy milk-cans, and I knew she oughtn't to be doing it."

"Yes, Rudolph told me about that when he come home, and I said it wasn't right," Mary put in warmly. "It was all right for me to do them things up to the last, for I was terrible strong, but that woman's weakly. And do you think she'll be able to nurse it, Ed?" She sometimes forgot to give him the title she was so proud of. "And to think of your being up all night and then not able to get a decent breakfast! I don't know what's the matter with such people."

"Why, Mother," said one of the boys, "if Doctor Ed had got breakfast there, we wouldn't have him here. So you ought to be glad."

"He knows I'm glad to have him, John, any time. But I'm sorry for that poor woman, how bad she'll feel the Doctor had to go away in the cold without his breakfast."

"I wish I'd been in practice when these were getting born." The doctor looked down the row of close-clipped heads. "I missed some good breakfasts by not being."

The boys began to laugh at their mother because she flushed so red, but she stood her ground and threw up her head. "I don't care, you wouldn't have got away from this house without breakfast. No doctor ever did. I'd have had something ready fixed that Anton could warm up for you."

The boys laughed harder than ever, and exclaimed at her: "I'll bet you would!" "She would, that!"

"Father, did you get breakfast for the doctor when we were born?"

"Yes, and he used to bring me my breakfast, too, mighty nice. I was always awful hungry!" Mary admitted with a guilty laugh.

While the boys were getting the Doctor's horse, he went to the window to examine the house plants. "What do you do to your geraniums to keep them blooming all winter, Mary? I never pass this house that from the road I don't see your windows full of flowers."

She snapped off a dark red one, and a ruffled new green leaf, and put them in his buttonhole. "There, that looks better. You look too solemn for a young man, Ed. Why don't you git married? I'm worried about you. Settin' at breakfast, I looked at you real hard, and I seen you've got some grey hairs already."

"Oh, yes! They're coming. Maybe they'd come faster if I married."

"Don't talk so. You'll ruin your health eating at the hotel. I could send your wife a nice loaf of nut bread, if you only had one. I don't like to see a young man getting grey. I'll tell you something, Ed; you make some strong black tea and keep it handy in a bowl, and every morning just brush it into your hair, an' it'll keep the grey from showin' much. That's the way I do!"

Sometimes the Doctor heard the gossipers in the drugstore wondering why Rosicky didn't get on faster. He was industrious, and so were his boys, but they were rather free and easy, weren't pushers, and they didn't always show good judgment. They were comfortable, they were out of debt, but they didn't get much ahead. Maybe, Doctor Burleigh reflected, people as generous and warm-hearted and affectionate as the Rosickys never got ahead much; maybe you couldn't enjoy your life and put it into the bank, too.

II

When Rosicky left Doctor Burleigh's office he went into the farm-implement store to light his pipe and put on his glasses and read over the list Mary had given him. Then he went into the general merchandise place next door and stood about until the pretty girl with the plucked eyebrows, who always waited on him, was free. Those eyebrows, two thin India-ink strokes, amused him, because he remembered how they used to be. Rosicky always prolonged his shopping by a little joking; the girl knew the old fellow admired her, and she liked to chaff with him.

"Seems to me about every other week you buy ticking, Mr. Rosicky, and always the best quality," she remarked as she measured off the heavy bolt with red stripes.

"You see, my wife is always makin' goose-fedder pillows, an' de thin stuff don't hold in dem little down-fedders."

"You must have lots of pillows at your house."

"Sure. She makes quilts of dem, too. We sleeps easy. Now she's makin' a fedder quilt for my son's wife. You know Polly, that married my Rudolph. How much my bill, Miss Pearl?"

"Eight eighty-five."

"Chust make it nine, and put in some candy fur de women."

"As usual. I never did see a man buy so much candy for his wife. First thing you know, she'll be getting too fat."

"I'd like dat. I ain't much fur all dem slim women like what de style is now."

"That's one for me, I suppose, Mr. Bohunk!" Pearl sniffed and elevated her India-ink strokes.

When Rosicky went out to his wagon, it was beginning to snow,—the first snow of the season, and he was glad to see it. He rattled out of town and along the highway through a wonderfully rich stretch of country, the finest farms in the county. He admired his High Prairie, as it was called, and always liked to drive through it. His own place lay in a rougher territory, where there was some clay in the soil and it was not so productive. When he bought his land, he hadn't the money to buy on High Prairie; so he told his boys, when they grumbled, that if their land hadn't some clay in it, they wouldn't own it at all. All the same, he enjoyed looking at these fine farms, as he enjoyed looking at a prize bull.

After he had gone eight miles, he came to the graveyard, which lay just at the edge of his own hay-land. There he stopped his horses and sat still on his wagon seat, looking about at the snowfall. Over yonder on the hill he could see his own house, crouching low, with the clump of orchard behind and the windmill before, and all down the gentle hill-slope the rows of pale gold cornstalks stood out against the white field. The snow was falling over the cornfield and the pasture and the hay-land, steadily, with very little wind,—a nice dry snow. The graveyard had only a light wire fence about it and was all overgrown with long red grass. The fine snow, settling into this red grass and upon the few little evergreens and the headstones, looked very pretty.

It was a nice graveyard, Rosicky reflected, sort of snug and homelike, not cramped or mournful,—a big sweep all round it. A man could lie down in the long grass and see the complete arch of the sky over him, hear the wagons go by; in summer the mowing-machine rattled right up to the wire fence. And it was so near home. Over there across the cornstalks his own roof and windmill looked so good to him that he promised himself to mind the Doctor and take care of himself. He was awful fond of his place, he admitted. He wasn't anxious to leave it. And it was a comfort to think that he would never have to go farther than the edge of his own hayfield. The snow, falling over his barnyard and the graveyard, seemed to draw things together like. And they were all old neighbours in the graveyard, most of them friends; there was nothing to feel awkward or embarrassed about. Embarrassment was the most disagreeable feeling Rosicky knew. He didn't often have it,—only with certain people whom he didn't understand at all.

Well, it was a nice snowstorm; a fine sight to see the snow falling so quietly and graciously over so much open country. On his cap and shoulders, on the horses' backs and manes, light, delicate, mysterious it fell; and with it a dry cool fragrance was released into the air. It meant rest for vegetation and men and beasts, for the ground itself; a season of long nights for sleep, leisurely breakfasts, peace by the fire. This and much more went through Rosicky's mind, but he merely told himself that winter was coming, clucked to his horses, and drove on.

When he reached home, John, the youngest boy, ran out to put away his team for him, and he met Mary coming up from the outside cellar with her apron full of carrots. They went into the house together. On the table, covered with oilcloth figured with clusters of blue grapes, a place was set, and he smelled hot coffee-cake of some kind. Anton never lunched in town; he thought that extravagant, and anyhow he didn't like the food. So Mary always had something ready for him when he got home.

After he was settled in his chair, stirring his coffee in a big cup, Mary took out of the oven a pan of *kolache* stuffed with apricots, examined them anxiously to see whether they had got too dry, put them beside his plate, and then sat down opposite him.

Rosicky asked her in Czech if she wasn't going to have any coffee.

She replied in English, as being somehow the right language for transacting business: "Now what did Doctor Ed say, Anton? You tell me just what."

"He said I was to tell you some compliments, but I forgot 'em." Rosicky's eyes twinkled.

"About you, I mean. What did he say about your asthma?"

"He says I ain't got no asthma." Rosicky took one of the little rolls in his broad brown fingers. The thickened nail of his right thumb told the story of his past.

"Well, what is the matter? And don't try to put me off."

"He don't say nothing much, only I'm a little older, and my heart ain't so good like it used to be."

Mary started and brushed her hair back from her temples with both hands as if she were a little out of her mind. From the way she glared, she might have been in a rage with him.

"He says there's something the matter with your heart? Doctor Ed says so?"

"Now don't yell at me like I was a hog in de garden, Mary. You know I always did like to hear a woman talk soft. He didn't say anything de matter wid my heart, only it ain't so young like it used to be, an' he tell me not to pitch hay or run de corn-sheller."

Mary wanted to jump up, but she sat still. She admired the way he never under any circumstances raised his voice or spoke roughly. He was city-bred, and she was country-bred; she often said she wanted her boys to have their papa's nice ways.

"You never have no pain there, do you? It's your breathing and your stomach that's been wrong. I wouldn't believe nobody but Doctor Ed about it. I guess I'll go see him myself. Didn't he give you no advice?"

"Chust to take it easy like, an' stay round de house dis winter. I guess you got some carpenter work for me to do. I kin make some new shelves for you, and I want dis long time to build a closet in de boys' room and make dem two little fellers keep dere clo'es hung up."

Rosicky drank his coffee from time to time, while he considered. His moustache was of the soft long variety and came down over his mouth like the teeth of a buggy-rake over a bundle of hay. Each time he put down his cup, he ran his blue handkerchief over his lips. When he took a drink of water, he managed very neatly with the back of his hand.

Mary sat watching him intently, trying to find any change in his face. It is hard to see anyone who has become like your own body to you. Yes, his hair had got thin, and his high forehead had deep lines running from left to right. But his neck, always clean shaved except in the busiest seasons, was not loose or baggy. It was burned a dark reddish brown, and there were deep creases in it, but it looked firm and full of blood. His cheeks had a good colour. On either side of his mouth there was a half-moon down the length of his cheek, not wrinkles, but two lines that had come there from his habitual expression. He was shorter and broader than when she married him; his back had grown broad and curved, a good deal like the shell of an old turtle, and his arms and legs were short.

He was fifteen years older than Mary, but she had hardly ever thought about it before. He was her man, and the kind of man she liked. She was rough, and he was gentle,—city-bred, as she always said. They had been shipmates on a rough voyage and had stood by each other in trying times. Life had gone well with them because, at bottom, they had the same ideas about life. They agreed, without discussion, as to what was most important and what was secondary. They didn't often exchange opinions, even in Czech,—it was as if they had thought the same thought together. A good deal had to be sacrificed and thrown overboard in a hard life like theirs, and they had never disagreed as to the things that could go. It had been a hard life, and a soft life, too. There wasn't anything brutal in the short, broad-backed man with the three-cornered eyes and the forehead that went on to the top of his skull. He was a city man, a gentle man, and though he had married a rough farm girl, he had never touched her without gentleness.

They had been at one accord not to hurry through life, not to be always skimping and saving. They saw their neighbours buy more land and feed more stock than they did, without discontent. Once when the creamery agent came to the Rosickys to persuade them to sell him their cream, he told them how much money the Fasslers, their nearest neighbours, had made on their cream last year.

"Yes," said Mary, "and look at them Fassler children! Pale, pinched little things, they look like skimmed milk. I'd rather put some colour into my children's faces than put money into the bank."

The agent shrugged and turned to Anton.

"I guess we'll do like she says," said Rosicky.

III

Mary very soon got into town to see Doctor Ed, and then she had a talk with her boys and set a guard over Rosicky. Even John, the youngest, had his father on his mind. If Rosicky went to throw hay down from the loft, one of the boys ran up the ladder and took the fork from him. He sometimes complained that though he was getting to be an old man, he wasn't an old woman yet.

That winter he stayed in the house in the afternoons and carpentered, or sat in the chair between the window full of plants and the wooden bench where the two pails of drinking-water stood. This spot was called "Father's corner," though it was not a corner at all. He had a shelf there, where he kept his Bohemian papers and his pipes and tobacco, and his shears and needles and thread and tailor's thimble. Having been a tailor in his youth, he couldn't bear to see a woman patching at his clothes, or at the boys'. He liked tailoring, and always patched all the overalls and jackets and work shirts. Occasionally he made over a pair of pants one of the older boys had outgrown, for the little fellow.

While he sewed, he let his mind run back over his life. He had a good deal to remember, really; life in three countries. The only part of his youth he didn't like to remember was the two years he had spent in London, in Cheapside, working for a German tailor who was wretchedly poor. Those days, when he was nearly always hungry, when his clothes were dropping off him for dirt, and the sound of a strange language kept him

in continual bewilderment, had left a sore spot in his mind
that wouldn't bear touching.

He was twenty when he landed at Castle Garden in New
York, and he had a protector who got him work in a tailor
shop in Vesey Street, down near the Washington Market. He
looked upon that part of his life as very happy. He became a
good workman, he was industrious, and his wages were in-
creased from time to time. He minded his own business and
envied nobody's good fortune. He went to night school and
learned to read English. He often did overtime work and was
well paid for it, but somehow he never saved anything. He
couldn't refuse a loan to a friend, and he was self-indulgent.
He liked a good dinner, and a little went for beer, a little for
tobacco; a good deal went to the girls. He often stood
through an opera on Saturday nights; he could get standing-
room for a dollar. Those were the great days of opera in New
York, and it gave a fellow something to think about for the
rest of the week. Rosicky had a quick ear, and a childish love
of all the stage splendour; the scenery, the costumes, the
ballet. He usually went with a chum, and after the perfor-
mance they had beer and maybe some oysters somewhere. It
was a fine life; for the first five years or so it satisfied him
completely. He was never hungry or cold or dirty, and every-
thing amused him: a fire, a dog fight, a parade, a storm, a
ferry ride. He thought New York the finest, richest, friendliest
city in the world.

Moreover, he had what he called a happy home life. Very
near the tailor shop was a small furniture-factory, where an
old Austrian, Loeffler, employed a few skilled men and made
unusual furniture, most of it to order, for the rich German
housewives up-town. The top floor of Loeffler's five-storey
factory was a loft, where he kept his choice lumber and stored
the odd pieces of furniture left on his hands. One of the
young workmen he employed was a Czech, and he and Ro-
sicky became fast friends. They persuaded Loeffler to let them
have a sleeping-room in one corner of the loft. They bought
good beds and bedding and had their pick of the furniture
kept up there. The loft was low-pitched, but light and airy,
full of windows, and good-smelling by reason of the fine lum-
ber put up there to season. Old Loeffler used to go down to

the docks and buy wood from South America and the East
from the sea captains. The young men were as foolish about
their house as a bridal pair. Zichec, the young cabinet-maker,
devised every sort of convenience, and Rosicky kept their
clothes in order. At night and on Sundays, when the quiver of
machinery underneath was still, it was the quietest place in
the world, and on summer nights all the sea winds blew in.
Zichec often practised on his flute in the evening. They were
both fond of music and went to the opera together. Rosicky
thought he wanted to live like that for ever.

But as the years passed, all alike, he began to get a little
restless. When spring came round, he would begin to feel
fretted, and he got to drinking. He was likely to drink too
much of a Saturday night. On Sunday he was languid and
heavy, getting over his spree. On Monday he plunged into
work again. So he never had time to figure out what ailed
him, though he knew something did. When the grass turned
green in Park Place, and the lilac hedge at the back of Trinity
churchyard put out its blossoms, he was tormented by a long-
ing to run away. That was why he drank too much; to get a
temporary illusion of freedom and wide horizons.

Rosicky, the old Rosicky, could remember as if it were yes-
terday the day when the young Rosicky found out what was
the matter with him. It was on a Fourth of July afternoon,
and he was sitting in Park Place in the sun. The lower part of
New York was empty. Wall Street, Liberty Street, Broadway,
all empty. So much stone and asphalt with nothing going on,
so many empty windows. The emptiness was intense, like the
stillness in a great factory when the machinery stops and the
belts and bands cease running. It was too great a change, it
took all the strength out of one. Those blank buildings, with-
out the stream of life pouring through them, were like empty
jails. It struck young Rosicky that this was the trouble with
big cities; they built you in from the earth itself, cemented
you away from any contact with the ground. You lived in an
unnatural world, like the fish in an aquarium, who were prob-
ably much more comfortable than they ever were in the sea.

On that very day he began to think seriously about the
articles he had read in the Bohemian papers, describing pros-
perous Czech farming communities in the West. He believed

he would like to go out there as a farm hand; it was hardly possible that he could ever have land of his own. His people had always been workmen; his father and grandfather had worked in shops. His mother's parents had lived in the country, but they rented their farm and had a hard time to get along. Nobody in his family had ever owned any land,—that belonged to a different station of life altogether. Anton's mother died when he was little, and he was sent into the country to her parents. He stayed with them until he was twelve, and formed those ties with the earth and the farm animals and growing things which are never made at all unless they are made early. After his grandfather died, he went back to live with his father and stepmother, but she was very hard on him, and his father helped him to get passage to London.

After that Fourth of July day in Park Place, the desire to return to the country never left him. To work on another man's farm would be all he asked; to see the sun rise and set and to plant things and watch them grow. He was a very simple man. He was like a tree that has not many roots, but one tap-root that goes down deep. He subscribed for a Bohemian paper printed in Chicago, then for one printed in Omaha. His mind got farther and farther west. He began to save a little money to buy his liberty. When he was thirty-five, there was a great meeting in New York of Bohemian athletic societies, and Rosicky left the tailor shop and went home with the Omaha delegates to try his fortune in another part of the world.

IV

Perhaps the fact that his own youth was well over before he began to have a family was one reason why Rosicky was so fond of his boys. He had almost a grandfather's indulgence for them. He had never had to worry about any of them— except, just now, a little about Rudolph.

On Saturday night the boys always piled into the Ford, took little Josephine, and went to town to the moving-picture show. One Saturday morning they were talking at the breakfast table about starting early that evening, so that they would have an hour or so to see the Christmas things in the stores before the show began. Rosicky looked down the table.

"I hope you boys ain't disappointed, but I want you to let me have de car tonight. Maybe some of you can go in with de neighbours."

Their faces fell. They worked hard all week, and they were still like children. A new jack-knife or a box of candy pleased the older ones as much as the little fellow.

"If you and Mother are going to town," Frank said, "maybe you could take a couple of us along with you, anyway."

"No, I want to take de car down to Rudolph's, and let him an' Polly go in to de show. She don't git into town enough, an' I'm afraid she's gettin' lonesome, an' he can't afford no car yet."

That settled it. The boys were a good deal dashed. Their father took another piece of apple-cake and went on: "Maybe next Saturday night de two little fellers can go along wid dem."

"Oh, is Rudolph going to have the car every Saturday night?"

Rosicky did not reply at once; then he began to speak seriously: "Listen, boys; Polly ain't lookin' so good. I don't like to see nobody lookin' sad. It comes hard fur a town girl to be a farmer's wife. I don't want no trouble to start in Rudolph's family. When it starts, it ain't so easy to stop. An American girl don't git used to our ways all at once. I like to tell Polly she and Rudolph can have the car every Saturday night till after New Year's, if it's all right with you boys."

"Sure it's all right, Papa," Mary cut in. "And it's good you thought about that. Town girls is used to more than country girls. I lay awake nights, scared she'll make Rudolph discontented with the farm."

The boys put as good a face on it as they could. They surely looked forward to their Saturday nights in town. That evening Rosicky drove the car the half-mile down to Rudolph's new, bare little house.

Polly was in a short-sleeved gingham dress, clearing away the supper dishes. She was a trim, slim little thing, with blue eyes and shingled yellow hair, and her eyebrows were reduced to a mere brush-stroke, like Miss Pearl's.

"Good evening, Mr. Rosicky. Rudolph's at the barn, I guess." She never called him father, or Mary mother. She was sensitive about having married a foreigner. She never in the world would have done it if Rudolph hadn't been such a handsome, persuasive fellow and such a gallant lover. He had graduated in her class in the high school in town, and their friendship began in the ninth grade.

Rosicky went in, though he wasn't exactly asked. "My boys ain't goin' to town tonight, an' I brought de car over fur you two to go in to de picture show."

Polly, carrying dishes to the sink, looked over her shoulder at him. "Thank you. But I'm late with my work tonight, and pretty tired. Maybe Rudolph would like to go in with you."

"Oh, I don't go to de shows! I'm too old-fashioned. You won't feel so tired after you ride in de air a ways. It's a nice clear night, an' it ain't cold. You go an' fix yourself up, Polly, an' I'll wash de dishes an' leave everything nice fur you."

Polly blushed and tossed her bob. "I couldn't let you do that, Mr. Rosicky. I wouldn't think of it."

Rosicky said nothing. He found a bib apron on a nail behind the kitchen door. He slipped it over his head and then took Polly by her two elbows and pushed her gently toward the door of her own room. "I washed up de kitchen many times for my wife, when de babies was sick or somethin'. You go an' make yourself look nice. I like you to look prettier'n any of dem town girls when you go in. De young folks must have some fun, an' I'm goin' to look out fur you, Polly."

That kind, reassuring grip on her elbows, the old man's funny bright eyes, made Polly want to drop her head on his shoulder for a second. She restrained herself, but she lingered in his grasp at the door of her room, murmuring tearfully: "You always lived in the city when you were young, didn't you? Don't you ever get lonesome out here?"

As she turned round to him, her hand fell naturally into his, and he stood holding it and smiling into her face with his peculiar, knowing, indulgent smile without a shadow of reproach in it. "Dem big cities is all right fur de rich, but dey is terrible hard fur de poor."

"I don't know. Sometimes I think I'd like to take a chance. You lived in New York, didn't you?"

"An' London. Da's bigger still. I learned my trade dere. Here's Rudolph comin', you better hurry."

"Will you tell me about London some time?"

"Maybe. Only I ain't no talker, Polly. Run an' dress yourself up."

The bedroom door closed behind her, and Rudolph came in from the outside, looking anxious. He had seen the car and was sorry any of his family should come just then. Supper hadn't been a very pleasant occasion. Halting in the doorway, he saw his father in a kitchen apron, carrying dishes to the sink. He flushed crimson and something flashed in his eye. Rosicky held up a warning finger.

"I brought de car over fur you an' Polly to go to de picture show, an' I made her let me finish here so you won't be late. You go put on a clean shirt, quick!"

"But don't the boys want the car, Father?"

"Not tonight dey don't." Rosicky fumbled under his apron and found his pants pocket. He took out a silver dollar and said in a hurried whisper: "You go an' buy dat girl some ice cream an' candy tonight, like you was courtin'. She's awful good friends wid me."

Rudolph was very short of cash, but he took the money as if it hurt him. There had been a crop failure all over the county. He had more than once been sorry he'd married this year.

In a few minutes the young people came out, looking clean and a little stiff. Rosicky hurried them off, and then he took his own time with the dishes. He scoured the pots and pans and put away the milk and swept the kitchen. He put some coal in the stove and shut off the draughts, so the place would be warm for them when they got home late at night. Then he sat down and had a pipe and listened to the clock tick.

Generally speaking, marrying an American girl was certainly a risk. A Czech should marry a Czech. It was lucky that Polly was the daughter of a poor widow woman; Rudolph was proud, and if she had a prosperous family to throw up at him, they could never make it go. Polly was one of four sisters, and they all worked; one was book-keeper in the bank, one taught music, and Polly and her younger sister had been clerks, like Miss Pearl. All four of them were musical, had pretty voices, and sang in the Methodist choir, which the eldest sister directed.

Polly missed the sociability of a store position. She missed the choir, and the company of her sisters. She didn't dislike housework, but she disliked so much of it. Rosicky was a little anxious about this pair. He was afraid Polly would grow so discontented that Rudy would quit the farm and take a factory job in Omaha. He had worked for a winter up there, two years ago, to get money to marry on. He had done very well, and they would always take him back at the stockyards. But to Rosicky that meant the end of everything for his son. To be a landless man was to be a wage-earner, a slave, all your life; to have nothing, to be nothing.

Rosicky thought he would come over and do a little carpentering for Polly after the New Year. He guessed she needed jollying. Rudolph was a serious sort of chap, serious in love and serious about his work.

Rosicky shook out his pipe and walked home across the fields. Ahead of him the lamplight shone from his kitchen windows. Suppose he were still in a tailor shop on Vesey Street, with a bunch of pale, narrow-chested sons working on machines, all coming home tired and sullen to eat supper in a kitchen that was a parlour also; with another crowded, angry family quarrelling just across the dumb-waiter shaft, and squeaking pulleys at the windows where dirty washings hung on dirty lines above a court full of old brooms and mops and ash-cans. . . .

He stopped by the windmill to look up at the frosty winter stars and draw a long breath before he went inside. That kitchen with the shining windows was dear to him; but the sleeping fields and bright stars and the noble darkness were dearer still.

v

On the day before Christmas the weather set in very cold; no snow, but a bitter, biting wind that whistled and sang over the flat land and lashed one's face like fine wires. There was baking going on in the Rosicky kitchen all day, and Rosicky sat inside, making over a coat that Albert had outgrown into an overcoat for John. Mary had a big red geranium in bloom for Christmas, and a row of Jerusalem cherry trees, full of berries. It was the first year she had ever grown these; Doctor Ed brought her the seeds from Omaha when he went to some medical convention. They reminded Rosicky of plants he had seen in England; and all afternoon, as he stitched, he sat thinking about those two years in London, which his mind usually shrank from even after all this while.

He was a lad of eighteen when he dropped down into London, with no money and no connexions except the address of a cousin who was supposed to be working at a confectioner's. When he went to the pastry shop, however, he found that the cousin had gone to America. Anton tramped the streets for several days, sleeping in doorways and on the Embankment, until he was in utter despair. He knew no English, and the sound of the strange language all about him confused him. By chance he met a poor German tailor who had learned his trade in Vienna, and could speak a little Czech. This tailor, Lifschnitz, kept a repair shop in a Cheapside basement, underneath a cobbler. He didn't much need an apprentice, but he was sorry for the boy and took him in for no wages but his keep and what he could pick up. The pickings were supposed to be coppers given you when you took work home to a customer. But most of the customers called for their clothes themselves, and the coppers that came Anton's way were very few. He had, however, a place to sleep. The tailor's family lived upstairs in three rooms; a kitchen, a bedroom, where Lifschnitz and his wife and five children slept, and a living-room. Two corners of this living-room were curtained off for lodgers; in one Rosicky slept on an old horsehair sofa, with a feather quilt to wrap himself in. The other corner was rented to a wretched, dirty boy, who was studying the violin. He actually practised there. Rosicky was dirty, too. There was no way to be anything else. Mrs. Lifschnitz got the water she cooked and washed with from a pump in a brick court, four flights down. There were bugs in the place, and multitudes of fleas, though the poor woman did the best she could. Rosicky knew she often went empty to give another potato or a spoonful of dripping to the two hungry, sad-eyed boys who lodged with her. He used to think he would never get out of there, never get a clean shirt to his back again. What would he do, he wondered, when his clothes actually dropped to pieces and the worn cloth wouldn't hold patches any longer?

It was still early when the old farmer put aside his sewing and his recollections. The sky had been a dark grey all day, with not a gleam of sun, and the light failed at four o'clock. He went to shave and change his shirt while the turkey was roasting. Rudolph and Polly were coming over for supper.

After supper they sat round in the kitchen, and the younger boys were saying how sorry they were it hadn't snowed. Everybody was sorry. They wanted a deep snow that would lie long and keep the wheat warm, and leave the ground soaked when it melted.

"Yes, sir!" Rudolph broke out fiercely; "if we have another dry year like last year, there's going to be hard times in this country."

Rosicky filled his pipe. "You boys don't know what hard times is. You don't owe nobody, you got plenty to eat an' keep warm, an' plenty water to keep clean. When you got them, you can't have it very hard."

Rudolph frowned, opened and shut his big right hand, and dropped it clenched upon his knee. "I've got to have a good deal more than that, Father, or I'll quit this farming gamble. I can always make good wages railroading, or at the packing house, and be sure of my money."

"Maybe so," his father answered dryly.

Mary, who had just come in from the pantry and was wiping her hands on the roller towel, thought Rudy and his father were getting too serious. She brought her darning-basket and sat down in the middle of the group.

"I ain't much afraid of hard times, Rudy," she said heartily. "We've had a plenty, but we've always come through. Your father wouldn't never take nothing very hard, not even hard times. I got a mind to tell you a story on him. Maybe you boys can't hardly remember the year we had that terrible hot wind, that burned everything up on the Fourth of July? All the corn an' the gardens. An' that was in the days when we didn't have alfalfa yet,—I guess it wasn't invented.

"Well, that very day your father was out cultivatin' corn, and I was here in the kitchen makin' plum preserves. We had bushels of plums that year. I noticed it was terrible hot, but it's always hot in the kitchen when you're preservin', an' I was too busy with my plums to mind. Anton come in from the field about three o'clock, an' I asked him what was the matter.

" 'Nothin',' he says, 'but it's pretty hot, an' I think I won't work no more today.' He stood round for a few minutes, an' then he says: 'Ain't you near through? I want you should git up a nice supper for us tonight. It's Fourth of July.'

"I told him to git along, that I was right in the middle of preservin', but the plums would taste good on hot biscuit. 'I'm goin' to have fried chicken, too,' he says, and he went off an' killed a couple. You three oldest boys was little fellers, playin' round outside, real hot an' sweaty, an' your father took you to the horse tank down by the windmill an' took off your clothes an' put you in. Them two box-elder trees was little then, but they made shade over the tank. Then he took off all his own clothes, an' got in with you. While he was playin' in the water with you, the Methodist preacher drove into our place to say how all the neighbours was goin' to meet at the schoolhouse that night, to pray for rain. He drove right to the windmill, of course, and there was your father and you three with no clothes on. I was in the kitchen door, an' I had to laugh, for the preacher acted like he ain't never seen a naked man before. He surely was embarrassed, an' your father couldn't git to his clothes; they was all hangin' up on the windmill to let the sweat dry out of 'em. So he laid in the tank where he was, an' put one of you boys on top of him to cover him up a little, an' talked to the preacher.

"When you got through playin' in the water, he put clean clothes on you and a clean shirt on himself, an' by that time I'd begun to get supper. He says: 'It's too hot in here to eat comfortable. Let's have a picnic in the orchard. We'll eat our supper behind the mulberry hedge, under them linden trees.'

"So he carried our supper down, an' a bottle of my wild-grape wine, an' everything tasted good, I can tell you. The wind got cooler as the sun was goin' down, and it turned out pleasant, only I noticed how the leaves was curled up on the linden trees. That made me think, an' I asked your father if that hot wind all day hadn't been terrible hard on the gardens an' the corn.

" 'Corn,' he says, 'there ain't no corn.'

" 'What you talkin' about?' I said. 'Ain't we got forty acres?'

" 'We ain't got an ear,' he says, 'nor nobody else ain't got none. All the corn in this country was cooked by three o'clock today, like you'd roasted it in an oven.'

" 'You mean you won't get no crop at all?' I asked him. I couldn't believe it, after he'd worked so hard.

" 'No crop this year,' he says. 'That's why we're havin' a picnic. We might as well enjoy what we got.'

"An' that's how your father behaved, when all the neighbours was so discouraged they couldn't look you in the face. An' we enjoyed ourselves that year, poor as we was, an' our neighbours wasn't a bit better off for bein' miserable. Some of 'em grieved till they got poor digestions and couldn't relish what they did have."

The younger boys said they thought their father had the best of it. But Rudolph was thinking that, all the same, the neighbours had managed to get ahead more, in the fifteen years since that time. There must be something wrong about his father's way of doing things. He wished he knew what was going on in the back of Polly's mind. He knew she liked his father, but he knew, too, that she was afraid of something. When his mother sent over coffee-cake or prune tarts or a loaf of fresh bread, Polly seemed to regard them with a certain suspicion. When she observed to him that his brothers had nice manners, her tone implied that it was remarkable they should have. With his mother she was stiff and on her guard. Mary's hearty frankness and gusts of good humour irritated her. Polly was afraid of being unusual or conspicuous in any way, of being "ordinary," as she said!

When Mary had finished her story, Rosicky laid aside his pipe.

"You boys like me to tell you about some of dem hard times I been through in London?" Warmly encouraged, he sat rubbing his forehead along the deep creases. It was bothersome to tell a long story in English (he nearly always talked to the boys in Czech), but he wanted Polly to hear this one.

"Well, you know about dat tailor shop I worked in in London? I had one Christmas dere I ain't never forgot. Times was awful bad before Christmas; de boss ain't got much work, an' have it awful hard to pay his rent. It ain't so much fun, bein' poor in a big city like London, I'll say! All de windows is full of good t'ings to eat, an' all de pushcarts in de streets is full, an' you smell 'em all de time, an' you ain't got no money,—not a damn bit. I didn't mind de cold so much, though I didn't have no overcoat, chust a short jacket I'd outgrowed so it wouldn't meet on me, an' my hands was chapped raw. But I always had a good appetite, like you all know, an' de sight of dem pork pies in de windows was awful fur me!

"Day before Christmas was terrible foggy dat year, an' dat fog gits into your bones and makes you all damp like. Mrs. Lifschnitz didn't give us nothin' but a little bread an' drippin' for supper, because she was savin' to try for to give us a good dinner on Christmas Day. After supper de boss say I can go an' enjoy myself, so I went into de streets to listen to de Christmas singers. Dey sing old songs an' make very nice music, an' I run round after dem a good ways, till I got awful hungry. I t'ink maybe if I go home, I can sleep till morning an' forgit my belly.

"I went into my corner real quiet, and roll up in my fedder quilt. But I ain't got my head down, till I smell somet'ing good. Seem like it git stronger an' stronger, an' I can't git to sleep noway. I can't understand dat smell. Dere was a gas light in a hall across de court, dat always shine in at my window a little. I got up an' look round. I got a little wooden box in my corner fur a stool, 'cause I ain't got no chair. I picks up dat box, and under it dere is a roast goose on a platter! I can't believe my eyes. I carry it to de window where de light comes in, an' touch it and smell it to find out, an' den I taste it to be sure. I say, I will eat chust one little bite of dat goose, so I can go to sleep, and tomorrow I won't eat none at all. But I tell you, boys, when I stop, one half of dat goose was gone!"

The narrator bowed his head, and the boys shouted. But little Josephine slipped behind his chair and kissed him on the neck beneath his ear.

"Poor little Papa, I don't want him to be hungry!"

"Da's long ago, child. I ain't never been hungry since I had your mudder to cook fur me."

"Go on and tell us the rest, please," said Polly.

"Well, when I come to realize what I done, of course, I felt terrible. I felt better in de stomach, but very bad in de heart. I set on my bed wid dat platter on my knees, an' it all come to me; how hard dat poor woman save to buy dat goose, and how she get some neighbour to cook it dat got more fire, an' how she put it in my corner to keep it away from dem hungry children. Dey was a old carpet hung up to shut my corner off, an' de children wasn't allowed to go in dere. An' I know she put it in my corner because she trust me more'n she did de violin boy. I can't stand it to face her after I spoil de Christmas. So I put on my shoes and go out into de city. I tell myself I better throw myself in de river; but I guess I ain't dat kind of a boy.

"It was after twelve o'clock, an' terrible cold, an' I start out to walk about London all night. I walk along de river awhile, but dey was lots of drunks all along; men, and women too. I chust move along to keep away from de police. I git onto de Strand, an' den over to New Oxford Street, where dere was a big German restaurant on de ground floor, wid big windows all fixed up fine, an' I could see de people havin' parties inside. While I was lookin' in, two men and two ladies come out, laughin' and talkin' and feelin' happy about all dey been eatin' an' drinkin', and dey was speakin' Czech,—not like de Austrians, but like de home folks talk it.

"I guess I went crazy, an' I done what I ain't never done before nor since. I went right up to dem gay people an' begun to beg dem: 'Fellow-countrymen, for God's sake give me money enough to buy a goose!'

"Dey laugh, of course, but de ladies speak awful kind to me, an' dey take me back into de restaurant and give me hot coffee and cakes, an' make me tell all about how I happened to come to London, an' what I was doin' dere. Dey take my name and where I work down on paper, an' both of dem ladies give me ten shillings.

"De big market at Covent Garden ain't very far away, an' by dat time it was open. I go dere an' buy a big goose an' some pork pies, an' potatoes and onions, an' cakes an' oranges fur de children,—all I could carry! When I git home, everybody is still asleep. I pile all I bought on de kitchen table, an' go in an' lay down on my bed, an' I ain't waken up till I hear dat woman scream when she come out into her kitchen. My goodness, but she was surprise! She laugh an' cry at de same time, an' hug me and waken all de children. She ain't stop fur no breakfast; she git de Christmas dinner ready dat morning, and we all sit down an' eat all we can hold. I ain't never seen dat violin boy have all he can hold before.

"Two three days after dat, de two men come to hunt me up, an' dey ask my boss, and he give me a good report an' tell dem I was a steady boy all right. One of dem Bohemians was very smart an' run a Bohemian newspaper in New York, an' de odder was a rich man, in de importing business, an' dey been travelling togedder. Dey told me how t'ings was easier in New York, an' offered to pay my passage when dey was goin' home soon on a boat. My boss say to me: 'You go. You ain't got no chance here, an' I like to see you git ahead, fur you always been a good boy to my woman, and fur dat fine Christmas dinner you give us all.' An' da's how I got to New York."

That night when Rudolph and Polly, arm in arm, were running home across the fields with the bitter wind at their backs, his heart leaped for joy when she said she thought they might have his family come over for supper on New Year's Eve. "Let's get up a nice supper, and not let your mother help at all; make her be company for once."

"That would be lovely of you, Polly," he said humbly. He was a very simple, modest boy, and he, too, felt vaguely that Polly and her sisters were more experienced and worldly than his people.

VI

The winter turned out badly for farmers. It was bitterly cold, and after the first light snows before Christmas there was no snow at all,—and no rain. March was as bitter as February. On those days when the wind fairly punished the country, Rosicky sat by his window. In the fall he and the boys had put in a big wheat planting, and now the seed had frozen in the ground. All that land would have to be ploughed up and planted over again, planted in corn. It had happened before, but he was younger then, and he never worried about what had to be. He was sure of himself and of Mary; he knew they could bear what they had to bear, that they would always pull through somehow. But he was not so sure about the young ones, and he felt troubled because Rudolph and Polly were having such a hard start.

Sitting beside his flowering window while the panes rattled and the wind blew in under the door, Rosicky gave himself to reflection as he had not done since those Sundays in the loft of the furniture-factory in New York, long ago. Then he was trying to find what he wanted in life for himself; now he was trying to find what he wanted for his boys, and why it was he so hungered to feel sure they would be here, working this very land, after he was gone.

They would have to work hard on the farm, and probably they would never do much more than make a living. But if he could think of them as staying here on the land, he wouldn't have to fear any great unkindness for them. Hardships, certainly; it was a hardship to have the wheat freeze in the ground when seed was so high; and to have to sell your stock because you had no feed. But there would be other years when everything came along right, and you caught up. And what you had was your own. You didn't have to choose between bosses and strikers, and go wrong either way. You didn't have to do with dishonest and cruel people. They were the only things in his experience he had found terrifying and horrible; the look in the eyes of a dishonest and crafty man, of a scheming and rapacious woman.

In the country, if you had a mean neighbour, you could keep off his land and make him keep off yours. But in the city, all the foulness and misery and brutality of your neighbours was part of your life. The worst things he had come upon in his journey through the world were human,— depraved and poisonous specimens of man. To this day he could recall certain terrible faces in the London streets. There were mean people everywhere, to be sure, even in their own country town here. But they weren't tempered, hardened, sharpened, like the treacherous people in cities who live by grinding or cheating or poisoning their fellow-men. He had helped to bury two of his fellow-workmen in the tailoring trade, and he was distrustful of the organized industries that see one out of the world in big cities. Here, if you were sick, you had Doctor Ed to look after you; and if you died, fat Mr. Haycock, the kindest man in the world, buried you.

It seemed to Rosicky that for good, honest boys like his, the worst they could do on the farm was better than the best they would be likely to do in the city. If he'd had a mean boy, now, one who was crooked and sharp and tried to put anything over on his brothers, then town would be the place for him. But he had no such boy. As for Rudolph, the discontented one, he would give the shirt off his back to anyone who touched his heart. What Rosicky really hoped for his boys was that they could get through the world without ever knowing much about the cruelty of human beings. "Their mother and me ain't prepared them for that," he sometimes said to himself.

These thoughts brought him back to a grateful consideration of his own case. What an escape he had had, to be sure! He, too, in his time, had had to take money for repair work from the hand of a hungry child who let it go so wistfully; because it was money due his boss. And now, in all these years, he had never had to take a cent from anyone in bitter need,—never had to look at the face of a woman become like a wolf's from struggle and famine. When he thought of these things, Rosicky would put on his cap and jacket and slip down to the barn and give his work-horses a little extra oats, letting them eat it out of his hand in their slobbery fashion. It was his way of expressing what he felt, and made him chuckle with pleasure.

The spring came warm, with blue skies,—but dry, dry as a bone. The boys began ploughing up the wheat-fields to plant them over in corn. Rosicky would stand at the fence corner and watch them, and the earth was so dry it blew up in clouds of brown dust that hid the horses and the sulky plough and the driver. It was a bad outlook.

The big alfalfa-field that lay between the home place and Rudolph's came up green, but Rosicky was worried because during that open windy winter a great many Russian thistle plants had blown in there and lodged. He kept asking the boys to rake them out; he was afraid their seed would root and "take the alfalfa." Rudolph said that was nonsense. The boys were working so hard planting corn, their father felt he couldn't insist about the thistles, but he set great store by that big alfalfa field. It was a feed you could depend on,—and there was some deeper reason, vague, but strong. The peculiar green of that clover woke early memories in old Rosicky, went back to something in his childhood in the old world. When he was a little boy, he had played in fields of that strong blue-green colour.

One morning, when Rudolph had gone to town in the car, leaving a work-team idle in his barn, Rosicky went over to his son's place, put the horses to the buggy-rake, and set about quietly raking up those thistles. He behaved with guilty caution, and rather enjoyed stealing a march on Doctor Ed, who was just then taking his first vacation in seven years of practice and was attending a clinic in Chicago. Rosicky got the thistles raked up, but did not stop to burn them. That would take some time, and his breath was pretty short, so he thought he had better get the horses back to the barn.

He got them into the barn and to their stalls, but the pain had come on so sharp in his chest that he didn't try to take the harness off. He started for the house, bending lower with every step. The cramp in his chest was shutting him up like a jack-knife. When he reached the windmill, he swayed and caught at the ladder. He saw Polly coming down the hill, running with the swiftness of a slim greyhound. In a flash she had her shoulder under his armpit.

"Lean on me, Father, hard! Don't be afraid. We can get to the house all right."

Somehow they did, though Rosicky became blind with pain; he could keep on his legs, but he couldn't steer his course. The next thing he was conscious of was lying on Polly's bed, and Polly bending over him wringing out bath towels in hot water and putting them on his chest. She stopped only to throw coal into the stove, and she kept the tea-kettle and the black pot going. She put these hot applications on him for nearly an hour, she told him afterwards, and all that time he was drawn up stiff and blue, with the sweat pouring off him.

As the pain gradually loosed its grip, the stiffness went out of his jaws, the black circles round his eyes disappeared, and a little of his natural colour came back. When his daughter-in-law buttoned his shirt over his chest at last, he sighed.

"Da's fine, de way I feel now, Polly. It was a awful bad spell, an' I was so sorry it all come on you like it did."

Polly was flushed and excited. "Is the pain really gone? Can I leave you long enough to telephone over to your place?"

Rosicky's eyelids fluttered. "Don't telephone, Polly. It ain't no use to scare my wife. It's nice and quiet here, an' if I ain't too much trouble to you, just let me lay still till I feel like myself. I ain't got no pain now. It's nice here."

Polly bent over him and wiped the moisture from his face. "Oh, I'm so glad it's over!" she broke out impulsively. "It just broke my heart to see you suffer so, Father."

Rosicky motioned her to sit down on the chair where the tea-kettle had been, and looked up at her with that lively affectionate gleam in his eyes. "You was awful good to me, I won't never forget dat. I hate it to be sick on you like dis. Down at de barn I say to myself, dat young girl ain't had much experience in sickness, I don't want to scare her, an' maybe she's got a baby comin' or somet'ing."

Polly took his hand. He was looking at her so intently and affectionately and confidingly; his eyes seemed to caress her face, to regard it with pleasure. She frowned with her funny streaks of eyebrows, and then smiled back at him.

"I guess maybe there is something of that kind going to happen. But I haven't told anyone yet, not my mother or Rudolph. You'll be the first to know."

His hand pressed hers. She noticed that it was warm again. The twinkle in his yellow-brown eyes seemed to come nearer.

"I like mighty well to see dat little child, Polly," was all he said. Then he closed his eyes and lay half-smiling. But Polly sat still, thinking hard. She had a sudden feeling that nobody in the world, not her mother, not Rudolph, or anyone, really loved her as much as old Rosicky did. It perplexed her. She sat frowning and trying to puzzle it out. It was as if Rosicky had a special gift for loving people, something that was like an ear for music or an eye for colour. It was quiet, unobtrusive; it was merely there. You saw it in his eyes,—perhaps that was why they were merry. You felt it in his hands, too. After he dropped off to sleep, she sat holding his warm, broad, flexible brown hand. She had never seen another in the least like it. She wondered if it wasn't a kind of gypsy hand, it was so alive and quick and light in its communications,—very strange in a farmer. Nearly all the farmers she knew had huge lumps of fists, like mauls, or they were knotty and bony and uncomfortable-looking, with stiff fingers. But Rosicky's was like quick-silver, flexible, muscular, about the colour of a pale cigar, with deep, deep creases across the palm. It wasn't nervous, it wasn't a stupid lump; it was a warm brown human hand, with some cleverness in it, a great deal of generosity, and something else which Polly could only call "gypsy-like,"—something nimble and lively and sure, in the way that animals are.

Polly remembered that hour long afterwards; it had been like an awakening to her. It seemed to her that she had never learned so much about life from anything as from old Rosicky's hand. It brought her to herself; it communicated some direct and untranslatable message.

When she heard Rudolph coming in the car, she ran out to meet him.

"Oh, Rudy, your father's been awful sick! He raked up those thistles he's been worrying about, and afterwards he could hardly get to the house. He suffered so I was afraid he was going to die."

Rudolph jumped to the ground. "Where is he now?"

"On the bed. He's asleep. I was terribly scared, because, you know, I'm so fond of your father." She slipped her arm through his and they went into the house. That afternoon they took Rosicky home and put him to bed, though he protested that he was quite well again.

The next morning he got up and dressed and sat down to breakfast with his family. He told Mary that his coffee tasted better than usual to him, and he warned the boys not to bear any tales to Doctor Ed when he got home. After breakfast he

sat down by his window to do some patching and asked Mary
to thread several needles for him before she went to feed her
chickens,—her eyes were better than his, and her hands
steadier. He lit his pipe and took up John's overalls. Mary had
been watching him anxiously all morning, and as she went
out of the door with her bucket of scraps, she saw that he was
smiling. He was thinking, indeed, about Polly, and how he
might never have known what a tender heart she had if he
hadn't got sick over there. Girls nowadays didn't wear their
heart on their sleeve. But now he knew Polly would make a
fine woman after the foolishness wore off. Either a woman
had that sweetness at her heart or she hadn't. You couldn't
always tell by the look of them; but if they had that, every-
thing came out right in the end.

After he had taken a few stitches, the cramp began in his
chest, like yesterday. He put his pipe cautiously down on the
window-sill and bent over to ease the pull. No use,—he had
better try to get to his bed if he could. He rose and groped
his way across the familiar floor, which was rising and falling
like the deck of a ship. At the door he fell. When Mary came
in, she found him lying there, and the moment she touched
him she knew that he was gone.

Doctor Ed was away when Rosicky died, and for the first
few weeks after he got home he was hard driven. Every day
he said to himself that he must get out to see that family that
had lost their father. One soft, warm moonlight night in early
summer he started for the farm. His mind was on other
things, and not until his road ran by the graveyard did he
realize that Rosicky wasn't over there on the hill where the
red lamplight shone, but here, in the moonlight. He stopped
his car, shut off the engine, and sat there for a while.

A sudden hush had fallen on his soul. Everything here
seemed strangely moving and significant, though signifying
what, he did not know. Close by the wire fence stood Ro-
sicky's mowing-machine, where one of the boys had been
cutting hay that afternoon; his own work-horses had been
going up and down there. The new-cut hay perfumed all the
night air. The moonlight silvered the long, billowy grass that
grew over the graves and hid the fence; the few little ever-

greens stood out black in it, like shadows in a pool. The sky was very blue and soft, the stars rather faint because the moon was full.

For the first time it struck Doctor Ed that this was really a beautiful graveyard. He thought of city cemeteries; acres of shrubbery and heavy stone, so arranged and lonely and unlike anything in the living world. Cities of the dead, indeed; cities of the forgotten, of the "put away." But this was open and free, this little square of long grass which the wind for ever stirred. Nothing but the sky overhead, and the many-coloured fields running on until they met that sky. The horses worked here in summer; the neighbours passed on their way to town; and over yonder, in the cornfield, Rosicky's own cattle would be eating fodder as winter came on. Nothing could be more undeathlike than this place; nothing could be more right for a man who had helped to do the work of great cities and had always longed for the open country and had got to it at last. Rosicky's life seemed to him complete and beautiful.

New York, 1928

Old Mrs. Harris

I

Mrs. David Rosen, cross-stitch in hand, sat looking out of the window across her own green lawn to the ragged, sunburned back yard of her neighbours on the right. Occasionally she glanced anxiously over her shoulder toward her shining kitchen, with a black and white linoleum floor in big squares, like a marble pavement.

"Will dat woman never go?" she muttered impatiently, just under her breath. She spoke with a slight accent—it affected only her *th's*, and, occasionally, the letter *v*. But people in Skyline thought this unfortunate, in a woman whose superiority they recognized.

Mrs. Rosen ran out to move the sprinkler to another spot on the lawn, and in doing so she saw what she had been waiting to see. From the house next door a tall, handsome woman emerged, dressed in white broadcloth and a hat with white lilacs; she carried a sunshade and walked with a free, energetic step, as if she were going out on a pleasant errand.

Mrs. Rosen darted quickly back into the house, lest her neighbour should hail her and stop to talk. She herself was in her kitchen housework dress, a crisp blue chambray which fitted smoothly over her tightly corseted figure, and her lustrous black hair was done in two smooth braids, wound flat at the back of her head, like a braided rug. She did not stop for a hat—her dark, ruddy, salmon-tinted skin had little to fear from the sun. She opened the half-closed oven door and took out a symmetrically plaited coffee-cake, beautifully browned, delicately peppered over with poppy seeds, with sugary margins about the twists. On the kitchen table a tray stood ready with cups and saucers. She wrapped the cake in a napkin, snatched up a little French coffee-pot with a black wooden handle, and ran across her green lawn, through the alley-way and the sandy, unkept yard next door, and entered her neighbour's house by the kitchen.

The kitchen was hot and empty, full of the untempered

619

afternoon sun. A door stood open into the next room; a cluttered, hideous room, yet somehow homely. There, beside a goods-box covered with figured oilcloth, stood an old woman in a brown calico dress, washing her hot face and neck at a tin basin. She stood with her feet wide apart, in an attitude of profound weariness. She started guiltily as the visitor entered.

"Don't let me disturb you, Grandma," called Mrs. Rosen. "I always have my coffee at dis hour in the afternoon. I was just about to sit down to it when I thought: 'I will run over and see if Grandma Harris won't take a cup with me.' I hate to drink my coffee alone."

Grandma looked troubled,—at a loss. She folded her towel and concealed it behind a curtain hung across the corner of the room to make a poor sort of closet. The old lady was always composed in manner, but it was clear that she felt embarrassment.

"Thank you, Mrs. Rosen. What a pity Victoria just this minute went down town!"

"But dis time I came to see you yourself, Grandma. Don't let me disturb you. Sit down there in your own rocker, and I will put my tray on this little chair between us, so!"

Mrs. Harris sat down in her black wooden rocking-chair with curved arms and a faded cretonne pillow on the wooden seat. It stood in the corner beside a narrow spindle-frame lounge. She looked on silently while Mrs. Rosen uncovered the cake and delicately broke it with her plump, smooth, dusky-red hands. The old lady did not seem pleased,— seemed uncertain and apprehensive, indeed. But she was not fussy or fidgety. She had the kind of quiet, intensely quiet, dignity that comes from complete resignation to the chances of life. She watched Mrs. Rosen's deft hands out of grave, steady brown eyes.

"Dis is Mr. Rosen's favourite coffee-cake, Grandma, and I want you to try it. You are such a good cook yourself, I would like your opinion of my cake."

"It's very nice, ma'am," said Mrs. Harris politely, but without enthusiasm.

"And you aren't drinking your coffee; do you like more cream in it?"

"No, thank you. I'm letting it cool a little. I generally drink it that way."

"Of course she does," thought Mrs. Rosen, "since she never has her coffee until all the family are done breakfast!"

Mrs. Rosen had brought Grandma Harris coffee-cake time and again, but she knew that Grandma merely tasted it and saved it for her daughter Victoria, who was as fond of sweets as her own children, and jealous about them, moreover,— couldn't bear that special dainties should come into the house for anyone but herself. Mrs. Rosen, vexed at her failures, had determined that just once she would take a cake to "de old lady Harris," and with her own eyes see her eat it. The result was not all she had hoped. Receiving a visitor alone, unsupervised by her daughter, having cake and coffee that should properly be saved for Victoria, was all so irregular that Mrs. Harris could not enjoy it. Mrs. Rosen doubted if she tasted the cake as she swallowed it,—certainly she ate it without relish, as a hollow form. But Mrs. Rosen enjoyed her own cake, at any rate, and she was glad of an opportunity to sit quietly and look at Grandmother, who was more interesting to her than the handsome Victoria.

It was a queer place to be having coffee, when Mrs. Rosen liked order and comeliness so much: a hideous, cluttered room, furnished with a rocking-horse, a sewing-machine, an empty baby-buggy. A walnut table stood against a blind window, piled high with old magazines and tattered books, and children's caps and coats. There was a wash-stand (two wash-stands, if you counted the oilcloth-covered box as one). A corner of the room was curtained off with some black-and-red-striped cotton goods, for a clothes closet. In another corner was the wooden lounge with a thin mattress and a red calico spread which was Grandma's bed. Beside it was her wooden rocking-chair, and the little splint-bottom chair with the legs sawed short on which her darning-basket usually stood, but which Mrs. Rosen was now using for a tea-table.

The old lady was always impressive, Mrs. Rosen was thinking,—one could not say why. Perhaps it was the way she held her head,—so simply, unprotesting and unprotected; or the gravity of her large, deep-set brown eyes, a warm, reddish brown, though their look, always direct, seemed to ask nothing and hope for nothing. They were not cold, but inscrutable, with no kindling gleam of intercourse in them. There was the kind of nobility about her head that there is about an old lion's: an absence of self-consciousness, vanity, pre-occupation—something absolute. Her grey hair was parted in the middle, wound in two little horns over her ears, and done in a little flat knot behind. Her mouth was large and composed,—resigned, the corners drooping. Mrs. Rosen had very seldom heard her laugh (and then it was a gentle, polite laugh which meant only politeness). But she had observed that whenever Mrs. Harris's grandchildren were about, tumbling all over her, asking for cookies, teasing her to read to them, the old lady looked happy.

As she drank her coffee, Mrs. Rosen tried one subject after another to engage Mrs. Harris's attention.

"Do you feel this hot weather, Grandma? I am afraid you are over the stove too much. Let those naughty children have a cold lunch occasionally."

"No'm, I don't mind the heat. It's apt to come on like this for a spell in May. I don't feel the stove. I'm accustomed to it."

"Oh, so am I! But I get very impatient with my cooking in hot weather. Do you miss your old home in Tennessee very much, Grandma?"

"No'm, I can't say I do. Mr. Templeton thought Colorado was a better place to bring up the children."

"But you had things much more comfortable down there, I'm sure. These little wooden houses are too hot in summer."

"Yes'm, we were more comfortable. We had more room."

"And a flower-garden, and beautiful old trees, Mrs. Templeton told me."

"Yes'm, we had a great deal of shade."

Mrs. Rosen felt that she was not getting anywhere. She almost believed that Grandma thought she had come on an equivocal errand, to spy out something in Victoria's absence. Well, perhaps she had! Just for once she would like to get past the others to the real grandmother,—and the real grandmother was on her guard, as always. At this moment she heard a faint miaow. Mrs. Harris rose, lifting herself by the

wooden arms of her chair, said: "Excuse me," went into the
kitchen, and opened the screen door.

In walked a large, handsome, thickly furred Maltese cat,
with long whiskers and yellow eyes and a white star on his
breast. He preceded Grandmother, waited until she sat down.
Then he sprang up into her lap and settled himself comfort-
ably in the folds of her full-gathered calico skirt. He rested his
chin in his deep bluish fur and regarded Mrs. Rosen. It struck
her that he held his head in just the way Grandmother held
hers. And Grandmother now became more alive, as if some
missing part of herself were restored.

"This is Blue Boy," she said, stroking him. "In winter,
when the screen door ain't on, he lets himself in. He stands
up on his hind legs and presses the thumb-latch with his paw,
and just walks in like anybody."

"He's your cat, isn't he, Grandma?" Mrs. Rosen couldn't
help prying just a little; if she could find but a single thing
that was Grandma's own!

"He's our cat," replied Mrs. Harris. "We're all very fond of
him. I expect he's Vickie's more'n anybody's."

"Of course!" groaned Mrs. Rosen to herself. "Dat Vickie is
her mother over again."

Here Mrs. Harris made her first unsolicited remark. "If you
was to be troubled with mice at any time, Mrs. Rosen, ask
one of the boys to bring Blue Boy over to you, and he'll clear
them out. He's a master mouser." She scratched the thick blue
fur at the back of his neck, and he began a deep purring. Mrs.
Harris smiled. "We call that spinning, back with us. Our
children still say: 'Listen to Blue Boy spin,' though none of
'em is ever heard a spinning-wheel—except maybe Vickie
remembers."

"Did you have a spinning-wheel in your own house,
Grandma Harris?"

"Yes'm. Miss Sadie Crummer used to come and spin for us.
She was left with no home of her own, and it was to give her
something to do, as much as anything, that we had her. I
spun a good deal myself, in my young days." Grandmother
stopped and put her hands on the arms of her chair, as if to
rise. "Did you hear a door open? It might be Victoria."

"No, it was the wind shaking the screen door. Mrs. Templeton won't be home yet. She is probably in my husband's store this minute, ordering him about. All the merchants down town will take anything from your daughter. She is very popular wid de gentlemen, Grandma."

Mrs. Harris smiled complacently. "Yes'm. Victoria was always much admired."

At this moment a chorus of laughter broke in upon the warm silence, and a host of children, as it seemed to Mrs. Rosen, ran through the yard. The hand-pump on the back porch, outside the kitchen door, began to scrape and gurgle.

"It's the children, back from school," said Grandma. "They are getting a cool drink."

"But where is the baby, Grandma?"

"Vickie took Hughie in his cart over to Mr. Holliday's yard, where she studies. She's right good about minding him."

Mrs. Rosen was glad to hear that Vickie was good for something.

Three little boys came running in through the kitchen; the twins, aged ten, and Ronald, aged six, who went to kindergarten. They snatched off their caps and threw their jackets and school bags on the table, the sewing-machine, the rocking-horse.

"Howdy do, Mrs. Rosen." They spoke to her nicely. They had nice voices, nice faces, and were always courteous, like their father. "We are going to play in our back yard with some of the boys, Gram'ma," said one of the twins respectfully, and they ran out to join a troop of schoolmates who were already shouting and racing over that poor trampled back yard, strewn with velocipedes and croquet mallets and toy wagons, which was such an eyesore to Mrs. Rosen.

Mrs. Rosen got up and took her tray.

"Can't you stay a little, ma'am? Victoria will be here any minute."

But her tone let Mrs. Rosen know that Grandma really wished her to leave before Victoria returned.

A few moments after Mrs. Rosen had put the tray down in her own kitchen, Victoria Templeton came up the wooden sidewalk, attended by Mr. Rosen, who had quitted his store half an hour earlier than usual for the pleasure of walking home with her. Mrs. Templeton stopped by the picket fence to smile at the children playing in the back yard,—and it was a real smile, she was glad to see them. She called Ronald over to the fence to give him a kiss. He was hot and sticky.

"Was your teacher nice today? Now run in and ask Grandma to wash your face and put a clean waist on you."

II

That night Mrs. Harris got supper with an effort—had to drive herself harder than usual. Mandy, the bound girl they had brought with them from the South, noticed that the old lady was uncertain and short of breath. The hours from two to four, when Mrs. Harris usually rested, had not been at all restful this afternoon. There was an understood rule that Grandmother was not to receive visitors alone. Mrs. Rosen's call, and her cake and coffee, were too much out of the accepted order. Nervousness had prevented the old lady from getting any repose during her visit.

After the rest of the family had left the supper table, she went into the dining-room and took her place, but she ate very little. She put away the food that was left, and then, while Mandy washed the dishes, Grandma sat down in her rocking-chair in the dark and dozed.

The three little boys came in from playing under the electric light (arc lights had been but lately installed in Skyline) and began begging Mrs. Harris to read *Tom Sawyer* to them. Grandmother loved to read, anything at all, the Bible or the continued story in the Chicago weekly paper. She roused herself, lit her brass "safety lamp," and pulled her black rocker out of its corner to the wash-stand (the table was too far away from her corner, and anyhow it was completely covered with coats and school satchels). She put on her old-fashioned silver-rimmed spectacles and began to read. Ronald lay down on Grandmother's lounge bed, and the twins, Albert and Adelbert, called Bert and Del, sat down against the wall, one on a low box covered with felt, and the other on the little sawed-off chair upon which Mrs. Rosen had served coffee.

They looked intently at Mrs. Harris, and she looked intently at the book.

Presently Vickie, the oldest grandchild, came in. She was fifteen. Her mother was entertaining callers in the parlour, callers who didn't interest Vickie, so she was on her way up to her own room by the kitchen stairway.

Mrs. Harris looked up over her glasses. "Vickie, maybe you'd take the book awhile, and I can do my darning."

"All right," said Vickie. Reading aloud was one of the things she would always do toward the general comfort. She sat down by the wash-stand and went on with the story. Grandmother got her darning-basket and began to drive her needle across great knee-holes in the boys' stockings. Sometimes she nodded for a moment, and her hands fell into her lap. After a while the little boy on the lounge went to sleep. But the twins sat upright, their hands on their knees, their round brown eyes fastened upon Vickie, and when there was anything funny, they giggled. They were chubby, dark-skinned little boys, with round jolly faces, white teeth, and yellow-brown eyes that were always bubbling with fun unless they were sad,—even then their eyes never got red or weepy. Their tears sparkled and fell; left no trace but a streak on the cheeks, perhaps.

Presently old Mrs. Harris gave out a long snore of utter defeat. She had been overcome at last. Vickie put down the book. "That's enough for tonight. Grandmother's sleepy, and Ronald's fast asleep. What'll we do with him?"

"Bert and me'll get him undressed," said Adelbert. The twins roused the sleepy little boy and prodded him up the back stairway to the bare room without window blinds, where he was put into his cot beside their double bed. Vickie's room was across the narrow hallway; not much bigger than a closet, but, anyway, it was her own. She had a chair and an old dresser, and beside her bed was a high stool which she used as a lamp-table,—she always read in bed.

After Vickie went upstairs, the house was quiet. Hughie, the baby, was asleep in his mother's room, and Victoria herself, who still treated her husband as if he were her "beau," had persuaded him to take her down town to the ice-cream parlour. Grandmother's room, between the kitchen and the dining-room, was rather like a passage-way; but now that the children were upstairs and Victoria was off enjoying herself somewhere, Mrs. Harris could be sure of enough privacy to undress. She took off the calico cover from her lounge bed and folded it up, put on her nightgown and white nightcap.

Mandy, the bound girl, appeared at the kitchen door.

"Miz' Harris," she said in a guarded tone, ducking her head, "you want me to rub your feet for you?"

For the first time in the long day the old woman's low composure broke a little. "Oh, Mandy, I would take it kindly of you!" she breathed gratefully.

That had to be done in the kitchen; Victoria didn't like anybody slopping about. Mrs. Harris put an old checked shawl round her shoulders and followed Mandy. Beside the kitchen stove Mandy had a little wooden tub full of warm water. She knelt down and untied Mrs. Harris's garter strings and took off her flat cloth slippers and stockings.

"Oh, Miz' Harris, your feet an' legs is swelled turrible to-night!"

"I expect they air, Mandy. They feel like it."

"Pore soul!" murmured Mandy. She put Grandma's feet in the tub and, crouching beside it, slowly, slowly rubbed her swollen legs. Mandy was tired, too. Mrs. Harris sat in her nightcap and shawl, her hands crossed in her lap. She never asked for this greatest solace of the day; it was something that Mandy gave, who had nothing else to give. If there could be a comparison in absolutes, Mandy was the needier of the two,—but she was younger. The kitchen was quiet and full of shadow, with only the light from an old lantern. Neither spoke. Mrs. Harris dozed from comfort, and Mandy herself was half asleep as she performed one of the oldest rites of compassion.

Although Mrs. Harris's lounge had no springs, only a thin cotton mattress between her and the wooden slats, she usually went to sleep as soon as she was in bed. To be off her feet, to lie flat, to say over the psalm beginning: "*The Lord is my shepherd,*" was comfort enough. About four o'clock in the morning, however, she would begin to feel the hard slats under her, and the heaviness of the old home-made quilts, with weight but little warmth, on top of her. Then she would reach under her pillow for her little comforter (she called it that to herself) that Mrs. Rosen had given her. It was a tan sweater of very soft brushed wool, with one sleeve torn and ragged. A young nephew from Chicago had spent a fortnight with Mrs. Rosen last summer and had left this behind him. One morning, when Mrs. Harris went out to the stable at the back of the yard to pat Buttercup, the cow, Mrs. Rosen ran across the alley-way.

"Grandma Harris," she said, coming into the shelter of the stable, "I wonder if you could make any use of this sweater Sammy left? The yarn might be good for your darning."

Mrs. Harris felt of the article gravely. Mrs. Rosen thought her face brightened. "Yes'm, indeed I could use it. I thank you kindly."

She slipped it under her apron, carried it into the house with her, and concealed it under her mattress. There she had kept it ever since. She knew Mrs. Rosen understood how it was; that Victoria couldn't bear to have anything come into the house that was not for her to dispose of.

On winter nights, and even on summer nights after the cocks began to crow, Mrs. Harris often felt cold and lonely about the chest. Sometimes her cat, Blue Boy, would creep in beside her and warm that aching spot. But on spring and summer nights he was likely to be abroad skylarking, and this little sweater had become the dearest of Grandmother's few possessions. It was kinder to her, she used to think, as she wrapped it about her middle, than any of her own children had been. She had married at eighteen and had had eight children; but some died, and some were, as she said, scattered.

After she was warm in that tender spot under the ribs, the old woman could lie patiently on the slats, waiting for day-break; thinking about the comfortable rambling old house in Tennessee, its feather beds and hand-woven rag carpets and splint-bottom chairs, the mahogany sideboard, and the marble-top parlour table; all that she had left behind to follow Victoria's fortunes.

She did not regret her decision; indeed, there had been no decision. Victoria had never once thought it possible that Ma should not go wherever she and the children went, and Mrs.

Harris had never thought it possible. Of course she regretted Tennessee, though she would never admit it to Mrs. Rosen:—the old neighbours, the yard and garden she had worked in all her life, the apple trees she had planted, the lilac arbour, tall enough to walk in, which she had clipped and shaped so many years. Especially she missed her lemon tree, in a tub on the front porch, which bore little lemons almost every summer, and folks would come for miles to see it.

But the road had led westward, and Mrs. Harris didn't believe that women, especially old women, could say when or where they would stop. They were tied to the chariot of young life, and had to go where it went, because they were needed. Mrs. Harris had gathered from Mrs. Rosen's manner, and from comments she occasionally dropped, that the Jewish people had an altogether different attitude toward their old folks; therefore her friendship with this kind neighbour was almost as disturbing as it was pleasant. She didn't want Mrs. Rosen to think that she was "put upon," that there was anything unusual or pitiful in her lot. To be pitied was the deepest hurt anybody could know. And if Victoria once suspected Mrs. Rosen's indignation, it would be all over. She would freeze her neighbour out, and that friendly voice, that quick pleasant chatter with the little foreign twist, would thenceforth be heard only at a distance, in the alley-way or across the fence. Victoria had a good heart, but she was terribly proud and could not bear the least criticism.

As soon as the grey light began to steal into the room, Mrs. Harris would get up softly and wash at the basin on the oilcloth-covered box. She would wet her hair above her forehead, comb it with a little bone comb set in a tin rim, do it up in two smooth little horns over her ears, wipe the comb dry, and put it away in the pocket of her full-gathered calico skirt. She left nothing lying about. As soon as she was dressed, she made her bed, folding her nightgown and nightcap under the pillow, the sweater under the mattress. She smoothed the heavy quilts, and drew the red calico spread neatly over all. Her towel was hung on its special nail behind the curtain. Her soap she kept in a tin tobacco-box; the children's soap was in a crockery saucer. If her soap or towel got mixed up with the children's, Victoria was always sharp about it. The

little rented house was much too small for the family, and
Mrs. Harris and her "things" were almost required to be in-
visible. Two clean calico dresses hung in the curtained corner;
another was on her back, and a fourth was in the wash. Be-
hind the curtain there was always a good supply of aprons;
Victoria bought them at church fairs, and it was a great
satisfaction to Mrs. Harris to put on a clean one when-
ever she liked. Upstairs, in Mandy's attic room over the
kitchen, hung a black cashmere dress and a black bonnet with
a long crêpe veil, for the rare occasions when Mr. Templeton
hired a double buggy and horses and drove his family to a
picnic or to Decoration Day exercises. Mrs. Harris rather
dreaded these drives, for Victoria was usually cross after-
wards.

When Mrs. Harris went out into the kitchen to get break-
fast, Mandy always had the fire started and the water boiling.
They enjoyed a quiet half-hour before the little boys came
running down the stairs, always in a good humour. In winter
the boys had their breakfast in the kitchen, with Vickie. Mrs.
Harris made Mandy eat the cakes and fried ham the children
left, so that she would not fast so long. Mr. and Mrs. Temple-
ton breakfasted rather late, in the dining-room, and they al-
ways had fruit and thick cream,—a small pitcher of the very
thickest was for Mrs. Templeton. The children were never
fussy about their food. As Grandmother often said feelingly
to Mrs. Rosen, they were as little trouble as children could
possibly be. They sometimes tore their clothes, of course, or
got sick. But even when Albert had an abscess in his ear and
was in such pain, he would lie for hours on Grandmother's
lounge with his cheek on a bag of hot salt, if only she or
Vickie would read aloud to him.

"It's true, too, what de old lady says," remarked Mrs.
Rosen to her husband one night at supper, "dey are nice chil-
dren. No one ever taught them anything, but they have good
instincts, even dat Vickie. And think, if you please, of all the
self-sacrificing mothers we know,—Fannie and Esther, to
come near home; how they have planned for those children
from infancy and given them every advantage. And now in-
gratitude and coldness is what dey meet with."

Mr. Rosen smiled his teasing smile. "Evidently your sister

and mine have the wrong method. The way to make your children unselfish is to be comfortably selfish yourself."

"But dat woman takes no more responsibility for her children than a cat takes for her kittens. Nor does poor young Mr. Templeton, for dat matter. How can he expect to get so many children started in life, I ask you? It is not at all fair!"

Mr. Rosen sometimes had to hear altogether too much about the Templetons, but he was patient, because it was a bitter sorrow to Mrs. Rosen that she had no children. There was nothing else in the world she wanted so much.

III

Mrs. Rosen in one of her blue working dresses, the indigo blue that became a dark skin and dusky red cheeks with a tone of salmon colour, was in her shining kitchen, washing her beautiful dishes—her neighbours often wondered why she used her best china and linen every day—when Vickie Templeton came in with a book under her arm.

"Good day, Mrs. Rosen. Can I have the second volume?"

"Certainly. You know where the books are." She spoke coolly, for it always annoyed her that Vickie never suggested wiping the dishes or helping with such household work as happened to be going on when she dropped in. She hated the girl's bringing-up so much that sometimes she almost hated the girl.

Vickie strolled carelessly through the dining-room into the parlour and opened the doors of one of the big bookcases. Mr. Rosen had a large library, and a great many unusual books. There was a complete set of the Waverley Novels in German, for example; thick, dumpy little volumes bound in tooled leather, with very black type and dramatic engravings printed on wrinkled, yellowing pages. There were many French books, and some of the German classics done into English, such as Coleridge's translation of Schiller's *Wallenstein*.

Of course no other house in Skyline was in the least like Mrs. Rosen's; it was the nearest thing to an art gallery and a museum that the Templetons had ever seen. All the rooms were carpeted alike (that was very unusual), with a soft velvet carpet, little blue and rose flowers scattered on a rose-grey ground. The deep chairs were upholstered in dark blue velvet. The walls were hung with engravings in pale gold frames: some of Raphael's "Hours," a large soft engraving of a castle on the Rhine, and another of cypress trees about a Roman ruin, under a full moon. There were a number of water-colour sketches, made in Italy by Mr. Rosen himself when he was a boy. A rich uncle had taken him abroad as his secretary. Mr. Rosen was a reflective, unambitious man, who didn't mind keeping a clothing-store in a little Western town, so long as he had a great deal of time to read philosophy. He was the only unsuccessful member of a large, rich Jewish family.

Last August, when the heat was terrible in Skyline, and the crops were burned up on all the farms to the north, and the wind from the pink and yellow sand-hills to the south blew so hot that it singed the few green lawns in the town, Vickie had taken to dropping in upon Mrs. Rosen at the very hottest part of the afternoon. Mrs. Rosen knew, of course, that it was probably because the girl had no other cool and quiet place to go—her room at home under the roof would be hot enough! Now, Mrs. Rosen liked to undress and take a nap from three to five,—if only to get out of her tight corsets, for she would have an hour-glass figure at any cost. She told Vickie firmly that she was welcome to come if she would read in the par-lour with the blind up only a little way, and would be as still as a mouse. Vickie came, meekly enough, but she seldom read. She would take a sofa pillow and lie down on the soft carpet and look up at the pictures in the dusky room, and feel a happy, pleasant excitement from the heat and glare outside and the deep shadow and quiet within. Curiously enough, Mrs. Rosen's house never made her dissatisfied with her own; she thought that very nice, too.

Mrs. Rosen, leaving her kitchen in a state of such perfec-tion as the Templetons were unable to sense or to admire, came into the parlour and found her visitor sitting cross-legged on the floor before one of the bookcases.

"Well, Vickie, and how did you get along with *Wilhelm Meister*?"

"I like it," said Vickie.

Mrs. Rosen shrugged. The Templetons always said that; quite as if a book or a cake were lucky to win their approbation.

"Well, *what* did you like?"

"I guess I liked all that about the theatre and Shakspere best."

"It's rather celebrated," remarked Mrs. Rosen dryly. "And are you studying every day? Do you think you will be able to win that scholarship?"

"I don't know. I'm going to try awful hard."

Mrs. Rosen wondered whether any Templeton knew how to try very hard. She reached for her work-basket and began to do cross-stitch. It made her nervous to sit with folded hands.

Vickie was looking at a German book in her lap, an illustrated edition of *Faust*. She had stopped at a very German picture of Gretchen entering the church, with Faustus gazing at her from behind a rose tree, Mephisto at his shoulder.

"I wish I could read this," she said, frowning at the black Gothic text. "It's splendid, isn't it?"

Mrs. Rosen rolled her eyes upward and sighed. "Oh, my dear, one of de world's masterpieces!"

That meant little to Vickie. She had not been taught to respect masterpieces, she had no scale of that sort in her mind. She cared about a book only because it took hold of her.

She kept turning over the pages. Between the first and second parts, in this edition, there was inserted the *Dies Iræ* hymn in full. She stopped and puzzled over it for a long while.

"Here is something I can read," she said, showing the page to Mrs. Rosen.

Mrs. Rosen looked up from her cross-stitch. "There you have the advantage of me. I do not read Latin. You might translate it for me."

Vickie began:

> "Day of wrath, upon that day
>   The world to ashes melts away,
>   As David and the Sibyl say.

"But that don't give you the rhyme; every line ought to end in two syllables."

"Never mind if it doesn't give the metre," corrected Mrs. Rosen kindly; "go on, if you can."

Vickie went on stumbling through the Latin verses, and Mrs. Rosen sat watching her. You couldn't tell about Vickie. She wasn't pretty, yet Mrs. Rosen found her attractive. She liked her sturdy build, and the steady vitality that glowed in her rosy skin and dark blue eyes,—even gave a springy quality to her curly reddish-brown hair, which she still wore in a single braid down her back. Mrs. Rosen liked to have Vickie about because she was never listless or dreamy or apathetic. A half-smile nearly always played about her lips and eyes, and it was there because she was pleased with something, not because she wanted to be agreeable. Even a half-smile made her cheeks dimple. She had what her mother called "a happy disposition."

When she finished the verses, Mrs. Rosen nodded approvingly. "Thank you, Vickie. The very next time I go to Chicago, I will try to get an English translation of *Faust* for you."

"But I want to read this one." Vickie's open smile darkened. "What I want is to pick up any of these books and just read them, like you and Mr. Rosen do."

The dusky red of Mrs. Rosen's cheeks grew a trifle deeper. Vickie never paid compliments, absolutely never; but if she really admired anyone, something in her voice betrayed it so convincingly that one felt flattered. When she dropped a remark of this kind, she added another link to the chain of responsibility which Mrs. Rosen unwillingly bore and tried to shake off—the irritating sense of being somehow responsible for Vickie, since, God knew, no one else felt responsible.

Once or twice, when she happened to meet pleasant young Mr. Templeton alone, she had tried to talk to him seriously about his daughter's future. "She has finished de school here, and she should be getting training of some sort; she is growing up," she told him severely.

He laughed and said in his way that was so honest, and so disarmingly sweet and frank: "Oh, don't remind me, Mrs. Rosen! I just pretend to myself she isn't. I want to keep my little daughter as long as I can." And there it ended.

Sometimes Vickie Templeton seemed so dense, so utterly unperceptive, that Mrs. Rosen was ready to wash her hands of her. Then some queer streak of sensibility in the child would make her change her mind. Last winter, when Mrs. Rosen came home from a visit to her sister in Chicago, she brought with her a new cloak of the sleeveless dolman type, black velvet, lined with grey and white squirrel skins, a grey skin next a white. Vickie, so indifferent to clothes, fell in love with that cloak. Her eyes followed it with delight whenever Mrs. Rosen wore it. She found it picturesque, romantic. Mrs. Rosen had been captivated by the same thing in the cloak, and had bought it with a shrug, knowing it would be quite out of place in Skyline; and Mr. Rosen, when she first produced it from her trunk, had laughted and said: "Where did you get that?—out of *Rigoletto?*" It looked like that—but how could Vickie know?

Vickie's whole family puzzled Mrs. Rosen; their feelings were so much finer than their way of living. She bought milk from the Templetons because they kept a cow—which Mandy milked,—and every night one of the twins brought the milk to her in a tin pail. Whichever boy brought it, she always called him Albert—she thought Adelbert a silly, Southern name.

One night when she was fitting the lid on an empty pail, she said severely:

"Now, Albert, I have put some cookies for Grandma in this pail, wrapped in a napkin. And they are for Grandma, remember, not for your mother or Vickie."

"Yes'm."

When she turned to him to give him the pail, she saw two full crystal globes in the little boy's eyes, just ready to break. She watched him go softly down the path and dash those tears away with the back of his hand. She was sorry. She hadn't thought the little boys realized that their household was somehow a queer one.

Queer or not, Mrs. Rosen liked to go there better than to most houses in the town. There was something easy, cordial, and carefree in the parlour that never smelled of being shut up, and the ugly furniture looked hospitable. One felt a pleasantness in the human relationships. These people didn't seem to know there were such things as struggle or exactness or competition in the world. They were always genuinely glad to

see you, had time to see you, and were usually gay in mood—
all but Grandmother, who had the kind of gravity that people
who take thought of human destiny must have. But even she
liked light-heartedness in others; she drudged, indeed, to keep
it going.

There were houses that were better kept, certainly, but
the housekeepers had no charm, no gentleness of manner,
were like hard little machines, most of them; and some were
grasping and narrow. The Templetons were not selfish or
scheming. Anyone could take advantage of them, and many
people did. Victoria might eat all the cookies her neighbour
sent in, but she would give away anything she had. She was
always ready to lend her dresses and hats and bits of jewellery
for the school theatricals, and she never worked people for
favours.

As for Mr. Templeton (people usually called him "young
Mr. Templeton"), he was too delicate to collect his just debts.
His boyish, eager-to-please manner, his fair complexion and
blue eyes and young face, made him seem very soft to some
of the hard old money-grubbers on Main Street, and the
fact that he always said "Yes, sir," and "No, sir," to men
older than himself furnished a good deal of amusement to
by-standers.

Two years ago, when this Templeton family came to Sky-
line and moved into the house next door, Mrs. Rosen was
inconsolable. The new neighbours had a lot of children, who
would always be making a racket. They put a cow and a horse
into the empty barn, which would mean dirt and flies. They
strewed their back yard with packing-cases and did not pick
them up.

She first met Mrs. Templeton at an afternoon card party, in
a house at the extreme north end of the town, fully half a mile
away, and she had to admit that her new neighbour was an
attractive woman, and that there was something warm and
geniune about her. She wasn't in the least willowy or lan-
guishing, as Mrs. Rosen had usually found Southern ladies to
be. She was high-spirited and direct; a trifle imperious, but
with a shade of diffidence, too, as if she were trying to adjust
herself to a new group of people and to do the right thing.

While they were at the party, a blinding snowstorm came on, with a hard wind. Since they lived next door to each other, Mrs. Rosen and Mrs. Templeton struggled homeward together through the blizzard. Mrs. Templeton seemed delighted with the rough weather; she laughed like a big country girl whenever she made a mis-step off the obliterated sidewalk and sank up to her knees in a snow-drift.

"Take care, Mrs. Rosen," she kept calling, "keep to the right! Don't spoil your nice coat. My, ain't this real winter? We never had it like this back with us."

When they reached the Templetons' gate, Victoria wouldn't hear of Mrs. Rosen's going farther. "No, indeed, Mrs. Rosen, you come right in with me and get dry, and Ma'll make you a hot toddy while I take the baby."

By this time Mrs. Rosen had begun to like her neighbour, so she went in. To her surprise, the parlour was neat and comfortable—the children did not strew things about there, apparently. The hard-coal burner threw out a warm red glow. A faded, respectable Brussels carpet covered the floor, an old-fashioned wooden clock ticked on the walnut bookcase. There were a few easy chairs, and no hideous ornaments about. She rather liked the old oil-chromos on the wall: "Hagar and Ishmael in the Wilderness," and "The Light of the World." While Mrs. Rosen dried her feet on the nickel base of the stove, Mrs. Templeton excused herself and withdrew to the next room,—her bedroom,—took off her silk dress and corsets, and put on a white challis négligée. She reappeared with the baby, who was not crying, exactly, but making eager, passionate, gasping entreaties,—faster and faster, tenser and tenser, as he felt his dinner nearer and nearer and yet not his.

Mrs Templeton sat down in a low rocker by the stove and began to nurse him, holding him snugly but carelessly, still talking to Mrs. Rosen about the card party, and laughing about their wade home through the snow. Hughie, the baby, fell to work so fiercely that beads of sweat came out all over his flushed forehead. Mrs. Rosen could not help admiring him and his mother. They were so comfortable and complete. When he was changed to the other side, Hughie resented the interruption a little; but after a time he became soft and bland, as smooth as oil, indeed; began looking about him as he drew in his milk. He finally dropped the nipple from his lips altogether, turned on his mother's arm, and looked inquiringly at Mrs. Rosen.

"What a beautiful baby!" she exclaimed from her heart. And he was. A sort of golden baby. His hair was like sunshine, and his long lashes were gold over such gay blue eyes. There seemed to be a gold glow in his soft pink skin, and he had the smile of the cherub.

"We think he's a pretty boy," said Mrs. Templeton. "He's the prettiest of my babies. Though the twins were mighty cunning little fellows. I hated the idea of twins, but the minute I saw them, I couldn't resist them."

Just then old Mrs. Harris came in, walking widely in her full-gathered skirt and felt-soled shoes, bearing a tray with two smoking goblets upon it.

"This is my mother, Mrs. Harris, Mrs. Rosen," said Mrs. Templeton.

"I'm glad to know you, ma'am," said Mrs. Harris. "Victoria, let me take the baby, while you two ladies have your toddy."

"Oh, don't take him away, Mrs. Harris, please!" cried Mrs. Rosen.

The old lady smiled. "I won't. I'll set right here. He never frets with his grandma."

When Mrs. Rosen had finished her excellent drink, she asked if she might hold the baby, and Mrs. Harris placed him on her lap. He made a few rapid boxing motions with his two fists, then braced himself on his heels and the back of his head, and lifted himself up in an arc. When he dropped back, he looked up at Mrs. Rosen with his most intimate smile. "See what a smart boy I am!"

When Mrs. Rosen walked home, feeling her way through the snow by following the fence, she knew she could never stay away from a house where there was a baby like that one.

IV

Vickie did her studying in a hammock hung between two tall cottonwood trees over in the Roadmaster's green yard. The Roadmaster had the finest yard in Skyline, on the edge of the town, just where the sandy plain and the sage-brush began. His family went back to Ohio every summer, and Bert and Del Templeton were paid to take care of his lawn, to turn the sprinkler on at the right hours and to cut the grass. They were really too little to run the heavy lawn-mower very well, but they were able to manage because they were twins. Each took one end of the handle-bar, and they pushed together like a pair of fat Shetland ponies. They were very proud of being able to keep the lawn so nice, and worked hard on it. They cut Mrs. Rosen's grass once a week, too, and did it so well that she wondered why in the world they never did anything about their own yard. They didn't have city water, to be sure (it was expensive), but she thought they might pick up a few velocipedes and iron hoops, and dig up the messy "flower-bed," that was even uglier than the naked gravel spots. She was particularly offended by a deep ragged ditch, a miniature arroyo, which ran across the back yard, serving no purpose and looking very dreary.

One morning she said craftily to the twins, when she was paying them for cutting her grass:

"And, boys, why don't you just shovel the sand-pile by your fence into dat ditch, and make your back yard smooth?"

"Oh, no, ma'am," said Adelbert with feeling. "We like to have the ditch to build bridges over!"

Ever since vacation began, the twins had been busy getting the Roadmaster's yard ready for the Methodist lawn party. When Mrs. Holliday, the Roadmaster's wife, went away for the summer, she always left a key with the Ladies' Aid Society and invited them to give their ice-cream social at her place.

This year the date set for the party was June fifteenth. The day was a particularly fine one, and as Mr. Holliday himself had been called to Cheyenne on railroad business, the twins felt personally responsible for everything. They got out to the Holliday place early in the morning, and stayed on guard all day. Before noon the drayman brought a wagon-load of card-tables and folding chairs, which the boys placed in chosen spots under the cottonwood trees. In the afternoon the Methodist ladies arrived and opened up the kitchen to receive the freezers of home-made ice-cream, and the cakes which the congregation donated. Indeed, all the good cake-bakers in town were expected to send a cake. Grandma Harris baked a white cake, thickly iced and covered with freshly grated coconut, and Vickie took it over in the afternoon.

Mr. and Mrs. Rosen, because they belonged to no church, contributed to the support of all, and usually went to the church suppers in winter and the socials in summer. On this warm June evening they set out early, in order to take a walk first. They strolled along the hard gravelled road that led out through the sage toward the sand-hills; tonight it led toward the moon, just rising over the sweep of dunes. The sky was almost as blue as at midday, and had that look of being very near and very soft which it has in desert countries. The moon, too, looked very near, soft and bland and innocent. Mrs. Rosen admitted that in the Adirondacks, for which she was always secretly homesick in summer, the moon had a much colder brilliance, seemed farther off and made of a harder metal. This moon gave the sage-brush plain and the drifted sand-hills the softness of velvet. All countries were beautiful to Mr. Rosen. He carried a country of his own in his mind, and was able to unfold it like a tent in any wilderness.

When they at last turned back toward the town, they saw groups of people, women in white dresses, walking toward the dark spot where the paper lanterns made a yellow light underneath the cottonwoods. High above, the rustling tree-tops stirred free in the flood of moonlight.

The lighted yard was surrounded by a low board fence, painted the dark red Burlington colour, and as the Rosens drew near, they noticed four children standing close together in the shadow of some tall elder bushes just outside the fence. They were the poor Maude children; their mother was the washwoman, the Rosens' laundress and the Templetons'. People said that every one of those children had a different father. But good laundresses were few, and even the members of the Ladies' Aid were glad to get Mrs. Maude's services at a dollar a day, though they didn't like their children to play with hers. Just as the Rosens approached, Mrs. Templeton came out from the lighted square, leaned over the fence, and addressed the little Maudes.

"I expect you children forgot your dimes, now didn't you?

Never mind, here's a dime for each of you, so come along and have your ice-cream."

The Maudes put out small hands and said: "Thank you," but not one of them moved.

"Come along, Francie" (the oldest girl was named Frances). "Climb right over the fence." Mrs. Templeton reached over and gave her a hand, and the little boys quickly scrambled after their sister. Mrs. Templeton took them to a table which Vickie and the twins had just selected as being especially private—they liked to do things together.

"Here, Vickie, let the Maudes sit at your table, and take care they get plenty of cake."

The Rosens had followed close behind Mrs. Templeton, and Mr. Rosen now overtook her and said in his most courteous and friendly manner: "Good evening, Mrs. Templeton. Will you have ice-cream with us?" He always used the local idioms, though his voice and enunciation made them sound altogether different from Skyline speech.

"Indeed I will, Mr. Rosen. Mr. Templeton will be late. He went out to his farm yesterday, and I don't know just when to expect him."

Vickie and the twins were disappointed at not having their table to themselves, when they had come early and found a nice one; but they knew it was right to look out for the dreary little Maudes, so they moved close together and made room for them. The Maudes didn't cramp them long. When the three boys had eaten the last crumb of cake and licked their spoons, Francie got up and led them to a green slope by the fence, just outside the lighted circle. "Now set down, and watch and see how folks do," she told them. The boys looked to Francie for commands and support. She was really Amos Maude's child, born before he ran away to the Klondike, and it had been rubbed into them that this made a difference.

The Templeton children made their ice-cream linger out, and sat watching the crowd. They were glad to see their mother go to Mr. Rosen's table, and noticed how nicely he placed a chair for her and insisted upon putting a scarf about her shoulders. Their mother was wearing her new dotted Swiss, with many ruffles, all edged with black ribbon, and wide ruffly sleeves. As the twins watched her over their spoons, they thought how much prettier their mother was than any of the other women, and how becoming her new dress was. The children got as much satisfaction as Mrs. Harris out of Victoria's good looks.

Mr. Rosen was well pleased with Mrs. Templeton and her new dress, and with her kindness to the little Maudes. He thought her manner with them just right,—warm, spontaneous, without anything patronizing. He always admired her way with her own children, though Mrs. Rosen thought it too casual. Being a good mother, he believed, was much more a matter of physical poise and richness than of sentimentalizing and reading doctor-books. Tonight he was more talkative than usual, and in his quiet way made Mrs. Templeton feel his real friendliness and admiration. Unfortunately, he made other people feel it, too.

Mrs. Jackson, a neighbour who didn't like the Templetons, had been keeping an eye on Mr. Rosen's table. She was a stout square woman of imperturbable calm, effective in regulating the affairs of the community because she never lost her temper, and could say the most cutting things in calm, even kindly, tones. Her face was smooth and placid as a mask, rather good-humoured, and the fact that one eye had a cast and looked askance made it the more difficult to see through her intentions. When she had been lingering about the Rosens' table for some time, studying Mr. Rosen's pleasant attentions to Mrs. Templeton, she brought up a trayful of cake.

"You folks are about ready for another helping," she remarked affably.

Mrs. Rosen spoke. "I want some of Grandma Harris's cake. It's a white coconut, Mrs. Jackson."

"How about you, Mrs. Templeton, would you like some of your own cake?"

"Indeed I would," said Mrs. Templeton heartily. "Ma said she had good luck with it. I didn't see it. Vickie brought it over."

Mrs. Jackson deliberately separated the slices on her tray with two forks. "Well," she remarked with a chuckle that really sounded amiable, "I don't know but I'd like my cakes, if I kept somebody in the kitchen to bake them for me."

Mr. Rosen for once spoke quickly. "If I had a cook like Grandma Harris in my kitchen, I'd live in it!" he declared.

Mrs. Jackson smiled. "I don't know as we feel like that, Mrs. Templeton? I tell Mr. Jackson that my idea of coming up in the world would be to forget I had a cook-stove, like Mrs. Templeton. But we can't all be lucky."

Mr. Rosen could not tell how much was malice and how much was stupidity. What he chiefly detected was self-satisfaction; the craftiness of the coarse-fibred country girl putting catch questions to the teacher. Yes, he decided, the woman was merely showing off,—she regarded it as an accomplishment to make people uncomfortable.

Mrs. Templeton didn't at once take it in. Her training was all to the end that you must give a guest everything you have, even if he happens to be your worst enemy, and that to cause anyone embarrassment is a frightful and humiliating blunder. She felt hurt without knowing just why, but all evening it kept growing clearer to her that this was another of those thrusts from the outside which she couldn't understand. The neighbours were sure to take sides against her, apparently, if they came often to see her mother.

Mr. Rosen tried to distract Mrs. Templeton, but he could feel the poison working. On the way home the children knew something had displeased or hurt their mother. When they went into the house, she told them to go upstairs at once, as she had a headache. She was severe and distant. When Mrs. Harris suggested making her some peppermint tea, Victoria threw up her chin.

"I don't want anybody waiting on me. I just want to be let alone." And she withdrew without saying good-night, or "Are you all right, Ma?" as she usually did.

Left alone, Mrs. Harris sighed and began to turn down her bed. She knew, as well as if she had been at the social, what kind of thing had happened. Some of those prying ladies of the Woman's Relief Corps, or the Woman's Christian Temperance Union, had been intimating to Victoria that her mother was "put upon." Nothing ever made Victoria cross but criticism. She was jealous of small attentions paid to Mrs. Harris, because she felt they were paid "behind her back" or "over her head," in a way that implied reproach to her. Victoria had

been a belle in their own town in Tennessee, but here she was
not very popular, no matter how many pretty dresses she
wore, and she couldn't bear it. She felt as if her mother and
Mr. Templeton must be somehow to blame; at least they
ought to protect her from whatever was disagreeable—they
always had!

v

Mrs. Harris wakened at about four o'clock, as usual, before
the house was stirring, and lay thinking about their position
in this new town. She didn't know why the neighbours acted
so; she was as much in the dark as Victoria. At home, back in
Tennessee, her place in the family was not exceptional, but
perfectly regular. Mrs. Harris had replied to Mrs. Rosen,
when that lady asked why in the world she didn't break
Vickie in to help her in the kitchen: "We are only young
once, and trouble comes soon enough." Young girls, in the
South, were supposed to be carefree and foolish; the fault
Grandmother found in Vickie was that she wasn't foolish
enough. When the foolish girl married and began to have
children, everything else must give way to that. She must be
humoured and given the best of everything, because having
children was hard on a woman, and it was the most important
thing in the world. In Tennessee every young married woman
in good circumstances had an older woman in the house, a
mother or mother-in-law or an old aunt, who managed the
household economies and directed the help.

That was the great difference; in Tennessee there had
been plenty of helpers. There was old Miss Sadie Crummer,
who came to the house to spin and sew and mend; old
Mrs. Smith, who always arrived to help at butchering- and
preserving-time; Lizzie, the coloured girl, who did the
washing and who ran in every day to help Mandy. There
were plenty more, who came whenever one of Lizzie's
barefoot boys ran to fetch them. The hills were full of solitary
old women, or women but slightly attached to some house-
hold, who were glad to come to Miz' Harris's for good food
and a warm bed, and the little present that either Mrs. Harris

or Victoria slipped into their carpet-sack when they went away.

To be sure, Mrs. Harris, and the other women of her age who managed their daughter's house, kept in the background; but it was their own background, and they ruled it jealously. They left the front porch and the parlour to the young married couple and their young friends; the old women spent most of their lives in the kitchen and pantries and back dining-room. But there they ordered life to their own taste, entertained their friends, dispensed charity, and heard the troubles of the poor. Moreover, back there it was Grandmother's own house they lived in. Mr. Templeton came of a superior family and had what Grandmother called "blood," but no property. He never so much as mended one of the steps to the front porch without consulting Mrs. Harris. Even "back home," in the aristocracy, there were old women who went on living like young ones, — gave parties and drove out in their carriage and "went North" in the summer. But among the middle-class people and the country-folk, when a woman was a widow and had married daughters, she considered herself an old woman and wore full-gathered black dresses and a black bonnet and became a housekeeper. She accepted this estate unprotestingly, almost gratefully.

The Templetons' troubles began when Mr. Templeton's aunt died and left him a few thousand dollars, and he got the idea of bettering himself. The twins were little then, and he told Mrs. Harris his boys would have a better chance in Colorado—everybody was going West. He went alone first, and got a good position with a mining company in the mountains of southern Colorado. He had been book-keeper in the bank in his home town, had "grown up in the bank," as they said. He was industrious and honourable, and the managers of the mining company liked him, even if they laughed at his polite, soft-spoken manners. He could have held his position indefinitely, and maybe got a promotion. But the altitude of that mountain town was too high for his family. All the children were sick there; Mrs. Templeton was ill most of the time and nearly died when Ronald was born. Hillary Templeton lost his courage and came north to the flat, sunny, semi-arid country between Wray and Cheyenne, to work for an irrigation project. So far, things had not gone well with him. The pinch told on everyone, but most on Grandmother. Here, in Skyline, she had all her accustomed responsibilities, and no helper but Mandy. Mrs. Harris was no longer living in a feudal society, where there were plenty of landless people glad to render service to the more fortunate, but in a snappy little Western democracy, where every man was as good as his neighbour and out to prove it.

Neither Mrs. Harris nor Mrs. Templeton understood just what was the matter; they were hurt and dazed, merely. Victoria knew that here she was censured and criticized, she who had always been so admired and envied! Grandmother knew that these meddlesome "Northerners" said things that made Victoria suspicious and unlike herself; made her unwilling that Mrs. Harris should receive visitors alone, or accept marks of attention that seemed offered in compassion for her state.

These women who belonged to clubs and Relief Corps lived differently, Mrs. Harris knew, but she herself didn't like the way they lived. She believed that somebody ought to be in the parlour, and somebody in the kitchen. She wouldn't for the world have had Victoria go about every morning in a short gingham dress, with bare arms, and a dust-cap on her head to hide the curling-kids, as these brisk housekeepers did. To Mrs. Harris that would have meant real poverty, coming down in the world so far that one could no longer keep up appearances. Her life was hard now, to be sure, since the family went on increasing and Mr. Templeton's means went on decreasing; but she certainly valued respectability above personal comfort, and she could go on a good way yet if they always had a cool pleasant parlour, with Victoria properly dressed to receive visitors. To keep Victoria different from these "ordinary" women meant everything to Mrs. Harris. She realized that Mrs. Rosen managed to be mistress of any situation, either in kitchen or parlour, but that was because she was "foreign." Grandmother perfectly understood that their neighbour had a superior cultivation which made everything she did an exercise of skill. She knew well enough that their own ways of cooking and cleaning were primitive beside Mrs. Rosen's.

If only Mr. Templeton's business affairs would look up,

they could rent a larger house, and everything would be better. They might even get a German girl to come in and help,—but now there was no place to put her. Grandmother's own lot could improve only with the family fortunes—any comfort for herself, aside from that of the family, was inconceivable to her; and on the other hand she could have no real unhappiness while the children were well, and good, and fond of her and their mother. That was why it was worth while to get up early in the morning and make her bed neat and draw the red spread smooth. The little boys loved to lie on her lounge and her pillows when they were tired. When they were sick, Ronald and Hughie wanted to be in her lap. They had no physical shrinking from her because she was old. And Victoria was never jealous of the children's wanting to be with her so much; that was a mercy!

Sometimes, in the morning, if her feet ached more than usual, Mrs. Harris felt a little low. (Nobody did anything about broken arches in those days, and the common endurance test of old age was to keep going after every step cost something.) She would hang up her towel with a sigh and go into the kitchen, feeling that it was hard to make a start. But the moment she heard the children running down the uncarpeted back stairs, she forgot to be low. Indeed, she ceased to be an individual, an old woman with aching feet; she became part of a group, became a relationship. She was drunk up into their freshness when they burst in upon her, telling her about their dreams, explaining their troubles with buttons and shoelaces and underwear shrunk too small. The tired, solitary old woman Grandmother had been at daybreak vanished; suddenly the morning seemed as important to her as it did to the children, and the mornings ahead stretched out sunshiny, important.

VI

The day after the Methodist social, Blue Boy didn't come for his morning milk; he always had it in a clean saucer on the covered back porch, under the long bench where the tin wash-tubs stood ready for Mrs. Maude. After the children had finished breakfast, Mrs. Harris sent Mandy out to look for the cat.

The girl came back in a minute, her eyes big.

"Law me, Miz' Harris, he's awful sick. He's a-layin' in the straw in the barn. He's swallered a bone, or havin' a fit or somethin'."

Grandmother threw an apron over her head and went out to see for herself. The children went with her. Blue Boy was retching and choking, and his yellow eyes were filled up with rhume.

"Oh, Gram'ma, what's the matter?" the boys cried.

"It's the distemper. How could he have got it?" Her voice was so harsh that Ronald began to cry. "Take Ronald back to the house, Del. He might get bit. I wish I'd kept my word and never had a cat again!"

"Why, Gram'ma!" Albert looked at her. "Won't Blue Boy get well?"

"Not from the distemper, he won't."

"But Gram'ma, can't I run for the veter'nary?"

"You gether up an armful of hay. We'll take him into the coal-house, where I can watch him."

Mrs. Harris waited until the spasm was over, then picked up the limp cat and carried him to the coal-shed that opened off the back porch. Albert piled the hay in one corner—the coal was low, since it was summer—and they spread a piece of old carpet on the hay and made a bed for Blue Boy. "Now you run along with Adelbert. There'll be a lot of work to do on Mr. Holliday's yard, cleaning up after the sociable. Mandy an' me'll watch Blue Boy. I expect he'll sleep for a while."

Albert went away regretfully, but the drayman and some of the Methodist ladies were in Mr. Holliday's yard, packing chairs and tables and ice-cream freezers into the wagon, and the twins forgot the sick cat in their excitement. By noon they had picked up the last paper napkin, raked over the gravel walks where the salt from the freezers had left white patches, and hung the hammock in which Vickie did her studying back in its place. Mr. Holliday paid the boys a dollar a week for keeping up the yard, and they gave the money to their mother—it didn't come amiss in a family where actual cash was so short. She let them keep half the sum Mrs. Rosen paid for her milk every Saturday, and that was more spending money than most boys had. They often made a few extra quarters by cutting grass for other people, or by distributing handbills. Even the disagreeable Mrs. Jackson next door had remarked over the fence to Mrs. Harris: "I do believe Bert and Del are going to be industrious. They must have got it from you, Grandma."

The day came on very hot, and when the twins got back from the Roadmaster's yard, they both lay down on Grandmother's lounge and went to sleep. After dinner they had a rare opportunity; the Roadmaster himself appeared at the front door and invited them to go up to the next town with him on his railroad velocipede. That was great fun: the velocipede always whizzed along so fast on the bright rails, the gasoline engine puffing; and grasshoppers jumped up out of the sage-brush and hit you in the face like sling-shot bullets. Sometimes the wheels cut in two a lazy snake who was sunning himself on the track, and the twins always hoped it was a rattler and felt they had done a good work.

The boys got back from their trip with Mr. Holliday late in the afternoon. The house was cool and quiet. Their mother had taken Ronald and Hughie down town with her, and Vickie was off somewhere. Grandmother was not in her room, and the kitchen was empty. The boys went out to the back porch to pump a drink. The coal-shed door was open, and inside, on a low stool, sat Mrs. Harris beside her cat. Bert and Del didn't stop to get a drink; they felt ashamed that they had gone off for a gay ride and forgotten Blue Boy. They sat down on a big lump of coal beside Mrs. Harris. They would never have known that this miserable rumpled animal was their proud tom. Presently he went off into a spasm and began to froth at the mouth.

"Oh, Gram'ma, can't you do anything?" cried Albert, struggling with his tears. "Blue Boy was such a good cat,— why has he got to suffer?"

"Everything that's alive has got to suffer," said Mrs. Harris. Albert put out his hand and caught her skirt, looking up at her beseechingly, as if to make her unsay that saying, which he only half understood. She patted his hand. She had forgot she was speaking to a little boy.

"Where's Vickie?" Adelbert asked aggrievedly. "Why don't she do something? He's part her cat."

Mrs. Harris sighed. "Vickie's got her head full of things lately; that makes people kind of heartless."

The boys resolved they would never put anything into their heads, then!

Blue Boy's fit passed, and the three sat watching their pet that no longer knew them. The twins had not seen much suffering; Grandmother had seen a great deal. Back in Tennessee, in her own neighbourhood, she was accounted a famous nurse. When any of the poor mountain people were in great distress, they always sent for Miz' Harris. Many a time she had gone into a house where five or six children were all down with scarlet fever or diphtheria, and done what she could. Many a child and many a woman she had laid out and got ready for the grave. In her primitive community the undertaker made the coffin, — he did nothing more. She had seen so much misery that she wondered herself why it hurt so to see her tom-cat die. She had taken her leave of him, and she got up from her stool. She didn't want the boys to be too much distressed.

"Now you boys must wash and put on clean shirts. Your mother will be home pretty soon. We'll leave Blue Boy; he'll likely be easier in the morning." She knew the cat would die at sundown.

After supper, when Bert looked into the coal-shed and found the cat dead, all the family were sad. Ronald cried miserably, and Hughie cried because Ronald did. Mrs. Templeton herself went out and looked into the shed, and she was sorry, too. Though she didn't like cats, she had been fond of this one.

"Hillary," she hold her husband, "when you go down town tonight, tell the Mexican to come and get that cat early in the morning, before the children are up."

The Mexican had a cart and two mules, and he hauled away tin cans and refuse to a gully out in the sage-brush.

Mrs. Harris gave Victoria an indignant glance when she heard this, and turned back to the kitchen. All evening she was gloomy and silent. She refused to read aloud, and the twins took Ronald and went mournfully out to play under the electric light. Later, when they had said good-night to their parents in the parlour and were on their way upstairs, Mrs. Harris followed them into the kitchen, shut the door behind her, and said indignantly:

"Air you two boys going to let that Mexican take Blue Boy and throw him onto some trash-pile?"

The sleepy boys were frightened at the anger and bitterness in her tone. They stood still and looked up at her, while she went on:

"You git up early in the morning, and I'll put him in a sack, and one of you take a spade and go to that crooked old willer tree that grows just where the sand creek turns off the road, and you dig a little grave for Blue Boy, an' bury him right."

They had seldom seen such resentment in their grand-mother. Albert's throat choked up, he rubbed the tears away with his fist.

"Yes'm, Gram'ma, we will, we will," he gulped.

VII

Only Mrs. Harris saw the boys go out next morning. She slipped a bread-and-butter sandwich into the hand of each, but she said nothing, and they said nothing.

The boys did not get home until their parents were ready to leave the table. Mrs. Templeton made no fuss, but told them to sit down and eat their breakfast. When they had fin-ished, she said commandingly:

"Now you march into my room." That was where she heard explanations and administered punishment. When she whipped them, she did it thoroughly.

She followed them and shut the door.

"Now, what were you boys doing this morning?"

"We went off to bury Blue Boy."

"Why didn't you tell me you were going?"

They looked down at their toes, but said nothing. Their mother studied their mournful faces, and her overbearing ex-pression softened.

"The next time you get up and go off anywhere, you come and tell me beforehand, do you understand?"

"Yes'm."

She opened the door, motioned them out, and went with them into the parlour. "I'm sorry about your cat, boys," she said. "That's why I don't like to have cats around; they're always getting sick and dying. Now run along and play. Maybe you'd like to have a circus in the back yard this afternoon? And we'll all come."

The twins ran out in a joyful frame of mind. Their grandmother had been mistaken; their mother wasn't indifferent about Blue Boy, she was sorry. Now everything was all right, and they could make a circus ring.

They knew their grandmother got put out about strange things, anyhow. A few months ago it was because their mother hadn't asked one of the visiting preachers who came to the church conference to stay with them. There was no place for the preacher to sleep except on the folding lounge in the parlour, and no place for him to wash—he would have been very uncomfortable, and so would all the household. But Mrs. Harris was terribly upset that there should be a conference in the town, and they not keeping a preacher! She was quite bitter about it.

The twins called in the neighbour boys, and they made a ring in the back yard, around their turning-bar. Their mother came to the show and paid admission, bringing Mrs. Rosen and Grandma Harris. Mrs. Rosen thought if all the children in the neighbourhood were to be howling and running in a circle in the Templetons' back yard, she might as well be there, too, for she would have no peace at home.

After the dog races and the Indian fight were over, Mrs. Templeton took Mrs. Rosen into the house to revive her with cake and lemonade. The parlour was cool and dusky. Mrs. Rosen was glad to get into it after sitting on a wooden bench in the sun. Grandmother stayed in the parlour with them, which was unusual. Mrs. Rosen sat waving a palm-leaf fan, —she felt the heat very much, because she wore her stays so tight—while Victoria went to make the lemonade.

"De circuses are not so good, widout Vickie to manage them, Grandma," she said.

"No'm. The boys complain right smart about losing Vickie from their plays. She's at her books all the time now. I don't know what's got into the child."

"If she wants to go to college, she must prepare herself, Grandma. I am agreeably surprised in her. I didn't think she'd stick to it."

Mrs. Templeton came in with a tray of tumblers and the glass pitcher all frosted over. Mrs. Rosen wistfully admired her neighbour's tall figure and good carriage; she was wearing no corsets at all today under her flowered organdie afternoon dress, Mrs. Rosen had noticed, and yet she could carry herself so smooth and straight,—after having had so many children, too! Mrs. Rosen was envious, but she gave credit where credit was due.

When Mrs. Templeton brought in the cake, Mrs. Rosen was still talking to Grandmother about Vickie's studying. Mrs. Templeton shrugged carelessly.

"There's such a thing as overdoing it, Mrs. Rosen," she observed as she poured the lemonade. "Vickie's very apt to run to extremes."

"But, my dear lady, she can hardly be too extreme in dis matter. If she is to take a competitive examination with girls from much better schools than ours, she will have to do better than the others, or fail; no two ways about it. We must encourage her."

Mrs. Templeton bridled a little. "I'm sure I don't interfere with her studying, Mrs. Rosen. I don't see where she got this notion, but I let her alone."

Mrs. Rosen accepted a second piece of chocolate cake. "And what do you think about it, Grandma?"

Mrs. Harris smiled politely. "None of our people, or Mr. Templeton's either, ever went to college. I expect it is all on account of the young gentleman who was here last summer."

Mrs. Rosen laughed and lifted her eyebrows. "Something very personal in Vickie's admiration for Professor Chalmers we think, Grandma? A very sudden interest in de sciences, I should say!"

Mrs. Templeton shrugged. "You're mistaken, Mrs. Rosen. There ain't a particle of romance in Vickie."

"But there are several kinds of romance, Mrs. Templeton. She may not have your kind."

"Yes'm, that's so," said Mrs. Harris in a low, grateful voice. She thought that a hard word Victoria had said of Vickie.

"I didn't see a thing in that Professor Chalmers, myself,"
Victoria remarked. "He was a gawky kind of fellow, and
never had a thing to say in company. Did you think he
amounted to much?"

"Oh, widout doubt Doctor Chalmers is a very scholarly
man. A great many brilliant scholars are widout de social
graces, you know." When Mrs. Rosen, from a much wider
experience, corrected her neighbour, she did so somewhat
playfully, as if insisting upon something Victoria capriciously
chose to ignore.

At this point old Mrs. Harris put her hands on the arms of
the chair in preparation to rise. "If you ladies will excuse me, I
think I will go and lie down a little before supper." She rose
and went heavily out on her felt soles. She never really lay
down in the afternoon, but she dozed in her own black
rocker. Mrs. Rosen and Victoria sat chatting about Professor
Chalmers and his boys.

Last summer the young professor had come to Skyline
with four of his students from the University of Michigan,
and had stayed three months, digging for fossils out in the
sand-hills. Vickie had spent a great many mornings at their
camp. They lived at the town hotel, and drove out to their
camp every day in a light spring-wagon. Vickie used to wait
for them at the edge of the town, in front of the Roadmas-
ter's house, and when the spring-wagon came rattling along,
the boys would call: "There's our girl!" slow the horses, and
give her a hand up. They said she was their mascot, and were
very jolly with her. They had a splendid summer,—found a
great bed of fossil elephant bones, where a whole herd must
once have perished. Later on they came upon the bones of a
new kind of elephant, scarcely larger than a pig. They were
greatly excited about their finds, and so was Vickie. That was
why they liked her. It was they who told her about a memo-
rial scholarship at Ann Arbor, which was open to any girl
from Colorado.

VIII

In August Vickie went down to Denver to take her exami-
nations. Mr. Holliday, the Roadmaster, got her a pass, and

arranged that she should stay with the family of one of his passenger conductors.

For three days she wrote examination papers along with other contestants, in one of the Denver high schools, proctored by a teacher. Her father had given her five dollars for incidental expenses, and she came home with a box of mineral specimens for the twins, a singing top for Ronald, and a toy burro for Hughie.

Then began days of suspense that stretched into weeks. Vickie went to the post-office every morning, opened her father's combination box, and looked over the letters, long before he got down town,—always hoping there might be a letter from Ann Arbor. The night mail came in at six, and after supper she hurried to the post-office and waited about until the shutter at the general-delivery window was drawn back, a signal that the mail had all been "distributed." While the tedious process of distribution was going on, she usually withdrew from the office, full of joking men and cigar smoke, and walked up and down under the big cottonwood trees that overhung the side street. When the crowd of men began to come out, then she knew the mail-bags were empty, and she went in to get whatever letters were in the Templeton box and take them home.

After two weeks went by, she grew downhearted. Her young professor, she knew, was in England for his vacation. There would be no one at the University of Michigan who was interested in her fate. Perhaps the fortunate contestant had already been notified of her success. She never asked herself, as she walked up and down under the cottonwoods on those summer nights, what she would do if she didn't get the scholarship. There was no alternative. If she didn't get it, then everything was over.

During the weeks when she lived only to go to the post-office, she managed to cut her finger and get ink into the cut. As a result, she had a badly infected hand and had to carry it in a sling. When she walked her nightly beat under the cottonwoods, it was a kind of comfort to feel that finger throb; it was companionship, made her case more complete.

The strange thing was that one morning a letter came, addressed to Miss Victoria Templeton; in a long envelope such as her father called "legal size," with *"University of Michigan"* in the upper left-hand corner. When Vickie took it from the box, such a wave of fright and weakness went through her that she could scarcely get out of the post-office. She hid the letter under her striped blazer and went a weak, uncertain trail down the sidewalk under the big trees. Without seeing anything or knowing what road she took, she got to the Roadmaster's green yard and her hammock, where she always felt not on the earth, yet of it.

Three hours later, when Mrs. Rosen was just tasting one of those clear soups upon which the Templetons thought she wasted so much pains and good meat, Vickie walked in at the kitchen door and said in a low but somewhat unnatural voice:

"Mrs. Rosen, I got the scholarship."

Mrs. Rosen looked up at her sharply, then pushed the soup back to a cooler part of the stove.

"What is dis you say, Vickie? You have heard from de University?"

"Yes'm. I got the letter this morning." She produced it from under her blazer.

Mrs. Rosen had been cutting noodles. She took Vickie's face in two hot, plump hands that were still floury, and looked at her intently. "Is dat true, Vickie? No mistake? I am delighted—and surprised! Yes, surprised. Den you will *be* something, you won't just sit on de front porch." She squeezed the girl's round, good-natured cheeks, as if she could mould them into something definite then and there. "Now you must stay for lunch and tell us all about it. Go in and announce yourself to Mr. Rosen."

Mr. Rosen had come home for lunch and was sitting, a book in his hand, in a corner of the darkened front parlour where a flood of yellow sun streamed in under the dark green blind. He smiled his friendly smile at Vickie and waved her to a seat, making her understand that he wanted to finish his paragraph. The dark engraving of the pointed cypresses and the Roman tomb was on the wall just behind him.

Mrs. Rosen came into the back parlour, which was the dining-room, and began taking things out of the silver-drawer to lay a place for their visitor. She spoke to her husband rapidly in German.

He put down his book, came over, and took Vickie's
hand.

"Is it true, Vickie? Did you really win the scholarship?"

"Yes, sir."

He stood looking down at her through his kind, remote
smile,—a smile in the eyes, that seemed to come up through
layers and layers of something—gentle doubts, kindly reser-
vations.

"Why do you want to go to college, Vickie?" he asked
playfully.

"To learn," she said with surprise.

"But why do you want to learn? What do you want to do
with it?"

"I don't know. Nothing, I guess."

"Then what do you want it for?"

"I don't know. I just want it."

For some reason Vickie's voice broke there. She had been
terribly strung up all morning, lying in the hammock with her
eyes tight shut. She had not been home at all, she had wanted
to take her letter to the Rosens first. And now one of the
gentlest men she knew made her choke by something strange
and presageful in his voice.

"Then if you want it without any purpose at all, you will
not be disappointed." Mr. Rosen wished to distract her and
help her to keep back the tears. "Listen: a great man once
said: *'Le but n'est rien; le chemin, c'est tout.'* That means: The
end is nothing, the road is all. Let me write it down for you
and give you your first French lesson."

He went to the desk with its big silver ink-well, where he
and his wife wrote so many letters in several languages, and
inscribed the sentence on a sheet of purple paper, in his deli-
cately shaded foreign script, signing under it a name: *J.
Michelet*. He brought it back and shook it before Vickie's
eyes. "There, keep it to remember me by. Slip it into the
envelope with your college credentials,—that is a good place
for it." From his deliberate smile and the twitch of one eye-
brow, Vickie knew he meant her to take it along as an anti-
dote, a corrective for whatever colleges might do to her.
But she had always known that Mr. Rosen was wiser than
professors.

Mrs. Rosen was frowning, she thought that sentence a bad precept to give any Templeton. Moreover, she always promptly called her husband back to earth when he soared a little; though it was exactly for this transcendental quality of mind that she reverenced him in her heart, and thought him so much finer than any of his successful brothers.

"Luncheon is served," she said in the crisp tone that put people in their places. "And Miss Vickie, you are to eat your tomatoes with an oil dressing, as we do. If you are going off into the world, it is quite time you learn to like things that are everywhere accepted."

Vickie said: "Yes'm," and slipped into the chair Mr. Rosen had placed for her. Today she didn't care what she ate, though ordinarily she thought a French dressing tasted a good deal like castor oil.

IX

Vickie was to discover that nothing comes easily in this world. Next day she got a letter from one of the jolly students of Professor Chalmers's party, who was watching over her case in his chief's absence. He told her the scholarship meant admission to the freshman class without further examinations, and two hundred dollars toward her expenses; she would have to bring along about three hundred more to put her through the year.

She took this letter to her father's office. Seated in his re-volving desk-chair, Mr. Templeton read it over several times and looked embarrassed.

"I'm sorry, daughter," he said at last, "but really, just now, I couldn't spare that much. Not this year. I expect next year will be better for us."

"But the scholarship is for this year, Father. It wouldn't count next year. I just have to go in September."

"I really ain't got it, daughter." He spoke, oh so kindly! He had lovely manners with his daughter and his wife. "It's just all I can do to keep the store bills paid up. I'm away behind with Mr. Rosen's bill. Couldn't you study here this winter and get along about as fast? It isn't that I wouldn't like to let you have the money if I had it. And with young children, I can't let my life insurance go."

Vickie didn't say anything more. She took her letter and wandered down Main Street with it, leaving young Mr. Templeton to a very bad half-hour.

At dinner Vickie was silent, but everyone could see she had been crying. Mr. Templeton told *Uncle Remus* stories to keep up the family morale and make the giggly twins laugh. Mrs. Templeton glanced covertly at her daughter from time to time. She was sometimes a little afraid of Vickie, who seemed to her to have a hard streak. If it were a love-affair that the girl was crying about, that would be so much more natural— and more hopeful!

At two o'clock Mrs. Templeton went to the Afternoon Euchre Club, the twins were to have another ride with the Roadmaster on his velocipede, the little boys took their nap on their mother's bed. The house was empty and quiet. Vickie felt an aversion for the hammock under the cotton-woods where she had been betrayed into such bright hopes. She lay down on her grandmother's lounge in the cluttered play-room and turned her face to the wall.

When Mrs. Harris came in for her rest and began to wash her face at the tin basin, Vickie got up. She wanted to be alone. Mrs. Harris came over to her while she was still sitting on the edge of the lounge.

"What's the matter, Vickie child?" She put her hand on her grand-daughter's shoulder, but Vickie shrank away. Young misery is like that, sometimes.

"Nothing. Except that I can't go to college after all. Papa can't let me have the money."

Mrs. Harris settled herself on the faded cushions of her rocker. "How much is it? Tell me about it, Vickie. Nobody's around."

Vickie told her what the conditions were, briefly and dryly, as if she were talking to an enemy. Everyone was an enemy; all society was against her. She told her grandmother the facts and then went upstairs, refusing to be comforted.

Mrs. Harris saw her disappear through the kitchen door, and then sat looking at the door, her face grave, her eyes stern and sad. A poor factory-made piece of joiner's work seldom has to bear a look of such intense, accusing sorrow; as if that flimsy pretence of "grained" yellow pine were the door shut against all young aspiration.

X

Mrs. Harris had decided to speak to Mr. Templeton, but opportunities for seeing him alone were not frequent. She watched out of the kitchen window, and when she next saw him go into the barn to fork down hay for his horse, she threw an apron over her head and followed him. She waylaid him as he came down from the hayloft.

"Hillary, I want to see you about Vickie. I was wondering if you could lay hand on any of the money you got for the sale of my house back home."

Mr. Templeton was nervous. He began brushing his trousers with a little whisk-broom he kept there, hanging on a nail.

"Why, no'm, Mrs. Harris. I couldn't just conveniently call in any of it right now. You know we had to use part of it to get moved up here from the mines."

"I know. But I thought if there was any left you could get at, we could let Vickie have it. A body'd like to help the child."

"I'd like to, powerful well, Mrs. Harris. I would, indeedy. But I'm afraid I can't manage it right now. The fellers I've loaned to can't pay up this year. Maybe next year—" He was like a little boy trying to escape a scolding, though he had never had a nagging word from Mrs. Harris.

She looked downcast, but said nothing.

"It's all right, Mrs. Harris," he took on his brisk business tone and hung up the brush. "The money's perfectly safe. It's well invested."

Invested; that was a word men always held over women, Mrs. Harris thought, and it always meant they could have none of their own money. She sighed deeply.

"Well, if that's the way it is—" She turned away and went back to the house on her flat heelless slippers, just in time;

Victoria was at that moment coming out to the kitchen with Hughie.

"Ma," she said, "can the little boy play out here, while I go down town?"

XI

For the next few days Mrs. Harris was very sombre, and she was not well. Several times in the kitchen she was seized with what she called giddy spells, and Mandy had to help her to a chair and give her a little brandy.

"Don't you say nothin', Mandy," she warned the girl. But Mandy knew enough for that.

Mrs. Harris scarcely noticed how her strength was failing, because she had so much on her mind. She was very proud, and she wanted to do something that was hard for her to do. The difficulty was to catch Mrs. Rosen alone.

On the afternoon when Victoria went to her weekly euchre, the old lady beckoned Mandy and told her to run across the alley and fetch Mrs. Rosen for a minute.

Mrs. Rosen was packing her trunk, but she came at once. Grandmother awaited her in her chair in the play-room.

"I take it very kindly of you to come, Mrs. Rosen. I'm afraid it's warm in here. Won't you have a fan?" She extended the palm leaf she was holding.

"Keep it yourself, Grandma. You are not looking very well. Do you feel badly, Grandma Harris?" She took the old lady's hand and looked at her anxiously.

"Oh, no, ma'am! I'm as well as usual. The heat wears on me a little, maybe. Have you seen Vickie lately, Mrs. Rosen?"

"Vickie? No. She hasn't run in for several days. These young people are full of their own affairs, you know."

"I expect she's backward about seeing you, now that she's so discouraged."

"Discouraged? Why, didn't the child get her scholarship after all?"

"Yes'm, she did. But they write her she has to bring more money to help her out; three hundred dollars. Mr. Templeton can't raise it just now. We had so much sickness in that mountain town before we moved up here, he got behind. Pore Vickie's downhearted."

"Oh, that is too bad! I expect you've been fretting over it, and that is why you don't look like yourself. Now what can we do about it?"

Mrs. Harris sighed and shook her head. "Vickie's trying to muster courage to go around to her father's friends and borrow from one and another. But we ain't been here long, —it ain't like we had old friends here. I hate to have the child do it."

Mrs. Rosen looked perplexed. "I'm sure Mr. Rosen would help her. He takes a great interest in Vickie."

"I thought maybe he could see his way to. That's why I sent Mandy to fetch you."

"That was right, Grandma. Now let me think." Mrs. Rosen put up her plump red-brown hand and leaned her chin upon it. "Day after tomorrow I am going to run on to Chicago for my niece's wedding." She saw her old friend's face fall. "Oh, I shan't be gone long; ten days, perhaps. I will speak to Mr. Rosen tonight, and if Vickie goes to him after I am off his hands, I'm sure he will help her."

Mrs. Harris looked up at her with solemn gratitude. "Vickie ain't the kind of girl would forget anything like that, Mrs. Rosen. Nor I wouldn't forget it."

Mrs. Rosen patted her arm. "Grandma Harris," she exclaimed, "I will just ask Mr. Rosen to do it for you! You know I care more about the old folks than the young. If I take this worry off your mind, I shall go away to the wedding with a light heart. Now dismiss it. I am sure Mr. Rosen can arrange this himself for you, and Vickie won't have to go about to these people here, and our gossipy neighbours will never be the wiser." Mrs. Rosen poured this out in her quick, authoritative tone, converting her *th's* into *d's*, as she did when she was excited.

Mrs. Harris's red-brown eyes slowly filled with tears,— Mrs. Rosen had never seen that happen before. But she simply said, with quiet dignity: "Thank you, ma'am. I wouldn't have turned to nobody else."

"That means I am an old friend already, doesn't it, Grandma? And that's what I want to be. I am very jealous where Grandma Harris is concerned!" She lightly kissed the back of the purple-veined hand she had been holding, and ran home to her packing. Grandma sat looking down at her hand. How easy it was for these foreigners to say what they felt!

XII

Mrs. Harris knew she was failing. She was glad to be able to conceal it from Mrs. Rosen when that kind neighbour dashed in to kiss her good-bye on the morning of her departure for Chicago. Mrs. Templeton was, of course, present, and secrets could not be discussed. Mrs. Rosen, in her stiff little brown travelling-hat, her hands tightly gloved in brown kid, could only wink and nod to Grandmother to tell her all was well. Then she went out and climbed into the "hack" bound for the depot, which had stopped for a moment at the Templetons' gate.

Mrs. Harris was thankful that her excitable friend hadn't noticed anything unusual about her looks, and, above all, that she had made no comment. She got through the day, and that evening, thank goodness, Mr. Templeton took his wife to hear a company of strolling players sing *The Chimes of Normandy* at the Opera House. He loved music, and just now he was very eager to distract and amuse Victoria. Grandma sent the twins out to play and went to bed early.

Next morning, when she joined Mandy in the kitchen, Mandy noticed something wrong.

"You set right down, Miz' Harris, an' let me git you some whisky. 'Deed, ma'am, you look awful porely. You ought to tell Miss Victoria an' let her send for the doctor."

"No, Mandy, I don't want no doctor. I've seen more sickness than ever he has. Doctors can't do no more than linger you out, an' I've always prayed I wouldn't last to be a burden. You git me some whisky in hot water, and pour it on a piece of toast. I feel real empty."

That afternoon when Mrs. Harris was taking her rest, for once she lay down upon her lounge. Vickie came in, tense and excited, and stopped for a moment.

"It's all right, Grandma. Mr. Rosen is going to lend me the

money. I won't have to go to anybody else. He won't ask Father to endorse my note, either. He'll just take my name." Vickie rather shouted this news at Mrs. Harris, as if the old lady were deaf, or slow of understanding. She didn't thank her; she didn't know her grandmother was in any way responsible for Mr. Rosen's offer, though at the close of their interview he had said: "We won't speak of our arrangement to anyone but your father. And I want you to mention it to the old lady Harris. I know she has been worrying about you."

Having brusquely announced her news, Vickie hurried away. There was so much to do about getting ready, she didn't know where to begin. She had no trunk and no clothes. Her winter coat, bought two years ago, was so outgrown that she couldn't get into it. All her shoes were run over at the heel and must go to the cobbler. And she had only two weeks in which to do everything! She dashed off.

Mrs. Harris sighed and closed her eyes happily. She thought with modest pride that with people like the Rosens she had always "got along nicely." It was only with the ill-bred and unclassified, like this Mrs. Jackson next door, that she had disagreeable experiences. Such folks, she told herself, had come out of nothing and knew no better. She was afraid this inquisitive woman might find her ailing and come prying round with unwelcome suggestions.

Mrs. Jackson did, indeed, call that very afternoon, with a miserable contribution of veal-loaf as an excuse (all the Templetons hated veal), but Mandy had been forewarned, and she was resourceful. She met Mrs. Jackson at the kitchen door and blocked the way.

"Sh-h-h, ma'am, Miz' Harris is asleep, havin' her nap. No'm, she ain't porely, she's as usual. But Hughie had the colic last night when Miss Victoria was at the show, an' kep' Miz' Harris awake."

Mrs. Jackson was loath to turn back. She had really come to find out why Mrs. Rosen drove away in the depot hack yesterday morning. Except at church socials, Mrs. Jackson did not meet people in Mrs. Rosen's set.

The next day, when Mrs. Harris got up and sat on the edge of her bed, her head began to swim, and she lay down again. Mandy peeped into the play-room as soon as she came downstairs, and found the old lady still in bed. She leaned over her and whispered:

"Ain't you feelin' well, Miz' Harris?"

"No, Mandy, I'm right porely," Mrs. Harris admitted.

"You stay where you air, ma'am. I'll git the breakfast fur the chillun, an' take the other breakfast in fur Miss Victoria an' Mr. Templeton." She hurried back to the kitchen, and Mrs. Harris went to sleep.

Immediately after breakfast Vickie dashed off about her own concerns, and the twins went to cut grass while the dew was still on it. When Mandy was taking the other breakfast into the dining-room, Mrs. Templeton came through the play-room.

"What's the matter, Ma? Are you sick?" she asked in an accusing tone.

"No, Victoria, I ain't sick. I had a little giddy spell, and I thought I'd lay still."

"You ought to be more careful what you eat, Ma. If you're going to have another bilious spell, when everything is so upset anyhow, I don't know what I'll do!" Victoria's voice broke. She hurried back into her bedroom, feeling bitterly that there was no place in that house to cry in, no spot where one could be alone, even with misery; that the house and the people in it were choking her to death.

Mrs. Harris sighed and closed her eyes. Things did seem to be upset, though she didn't know just why. Mandy, however, had her suspicions. While she waited on Mr. and Mrs. Templeton at breakfast, narrowly observing their manner toward each other and Victoria's swollen eyes and desperate expression, her suspicions grew stronger.

Instead of going to his office, Mr. Templeton went to the barn and ran out the buggy. Soon he brought out Cleveland, the black horse, with his harness on. Mandy watched from the back window. After he had hitched the horse to the buggy, he came into the kitchen to wash his hands. While he dried them on the roller towel, he said in his most business-like tone:

"I likely won't be back tonight, Mandy. I have to go out to my farm, and I'll hardly get through my business there in time to come home."

Then Mandy was sure. She had been through these times before, and at such a crisis poor Mr. Templeton was always called away on important business. When he had driven out through the alley and up the street past Mrs. Rosen's, Mandy left her dishes and went in to Mrs. Harris. She bent over and whispered low:

"Miz' Harris, I 'spect Miss Victoria's done found out she's goin' to have another baby! It looks that way. She's gone back to bed."

Mrs. Harris lifted a warning finger. "Sh-h-h!"

"Oh yes'm, I won't say nothin'. I never do."

Mrs. Harris tried to face this possibility, but her mind didn't seem strong enough—she dropped off into another doze.

All that morning Mrs. Templeton lay on her bed alone, the room darkened and a handkerchief soaked in camphor tied round her forehead. The twins had taken Ronald off to watch them cut grass, and Hughie played in the kitchen under Mandy's eye.

Now and then Victoria sat upright on the edge of the bed, beat her hands together softly and looked desperately at the ceiling, then about at those frail, confining walls. If only she could meet the situation with violence, fight it, conquer it! But there was nothing for it but stupid animal patience. She would have to go through all that again, and nobody, not even Hillary, wanted another baby,—poor as they were, and in this overcrowded house. Anyhow, she told herself, she was ashamed to have another baby, when she had a daughter old enough to go to college! She was sick of it all; sick of dragging this chain of life that never let her rest and periodically knotted and overpowered her; made her ill and hideous for months, and then dropped another baby into her arms. She had had babies enough; and there ought to be an end to such apprehensions some time before you were old and ugly.

She wanted to run away, back to Tennessee, and lead a free, gay life, as she had when she was first married. She could do a great deal more with freedom than ever Vickie could. She was still young, and she was still handsome; why must she be for ever shut up in a little cluttered house with children and fresh babies and an old woman and a stupid bound girl and a husband who wasn't very successful? Life hadn't brought her what she expected when she married Hillary Templeton; life hadn't used her right. She had tried to keep up appearances, to dress well with very little to do it on, to keep young for her husband and children. She had tried, she had tried! Mrs. Templeton buried her face in the pillow and smothered the sobs that shook the bed.

Hillary Templeton, on his drive out through the sagebrush, up into the farming country that was irrigated from the North Platte, did not feel altogether cheerful, though he whistled and sang to himself on the way. He was sorry Victoria would have to go through another time. It was awkward just now, too, when he was so short of money. But he was naturally a cheerful man, modest in his demands upon fortune, and easily diverted from unpleasant thoughts. Before Cleveland had travelled half the eighteen miles to the farm, his master was already looking forward to a visit with his tenants, an old German couple who were fond of him because he never pushed them in a hard year—so far, all the years had been hard—and he sometimes brought them bananas and such delicacies from town.

Mrs. Heyse would open her best preserves for him, he knew, and kill a chicken, and tonight he would have a clean bed in her spare room. She always put a vase of flowers in his room when he stayed overnight with them, and that pleased him very much. He felt like a youth out there, and forgot all the bills he had somehow to meet, and the loans he had made and couldn't collect. The Heyses kept bees and raised turkeys, and had honeysuckle vines running over the front porch. He loved all those things. Mr. Templeton touched Cleveland with the whip, and as they sped along into the grass country, sang softly:

> "Old Jesse was a gem'man,
> Way down in Tennessee."

XIII

Mandy had to manage the house herself that day, and she was not at all sorry. There wasn't a great deal of variety in her life, and she felt very important taking Mrs. Harris's place, giving the children their dinner, and carrying a plate of milk toast to Mrs. Templeton. She was worried about Mrs. Harris, however, and remarked to the children at noon that she thought somebody ought to "set" with their grandma. Vickie wasn't home for dinner. She had her father's office to herself for the day and was making the most of it, writing a long letter to Professor Chalmers. Mr. Rosen had invited her to have dinner with him at the hotel (he boarded there when his wife was away), and that was a great honour.

When Mandy said someone ought to be with the old lady, Bert and Del offered to take turns. Adelbert went off to rake up the grass they had been cutting all morning, and Albert sat down in the play-room. It seemed to him his grandmother looked pretty sick. He watched her while Mandy gave her toast-water with whisky in it, and thought he would like to make the room look a little nicer. While Mrs. Harris lay with her eyes closed, he hung up the caps and coats lying about, and moved away the big rocking-chair that stood by the head of Grandma's bed. There ought to be a table there, he believed, but the small tables in the house all had something on them. Upstairs, in the room where he and Adelbert and Ronald slept, there was a nice clean wooden cracker-box, on which they sat in the morning to put on their shoes and stockings. He brought this down and stood it on end at the head of Grandma's lounge, and put a clean napkin over the top of it.

She opened her eyes and smiled at him. "Could you git me a tin of fresh water, honey?"

He went to the back porch and pumped till the water ran cold. He gave it to her in a tin cup as she had asked, but he didn't think that was the right way. After she dropped back on the pillow, he fetched a glass tumbler from the cupboard, filled it, and set it on the table he had just manufactured. When Grandmother drew a red cotton handkerchief from under her pillow and wiped the moisture from her face, he ran upstairs again and got one of his Sunday-school handkerchiefs, linen ones, that Mrs. Rosen had given him and Del for Christmas. Having put this in Grandmother's hand and taken away the crumpled red one, he could think of nothing else to do—except to darken the room a little. The windows had no blinds, but flimsy cretonne curtains tied back,—not really tied, but caught back over nails driven into the sill. He loosened them and let them hang down over the bright afternoon sunlight. Then he sat down on the low sawed-off chair and gazed about, thinking that now it looked quite like a sick-room.

It was hard for a little boy to keep still. "Would you like me to read *Joe's Luck* to you, Gram'ma?" he said presently.

"You might, Bertie."

He got the "boy's book" she had been reading aloud to them, and began where she had left off. Mrs. Harris liked to hear his voice, and she liked to look at him when she opened her eyes from time to time. She did not follow the story. In her mind she was repeating a passage from the second part of *Pilgrim's Progress*, which she had read aloud to the children so many times; the passage where Christiana and her band come to the arbour on the Hill of Difficulty: *"Then said Mercy, how sweet is rest to them that labour."*

At about four o'clock Adelbert came home, hot and sweaty from raking. He said he had got in the grass and taken it to their cow, and if Bert was reading, he guessed he'd like to listen. He dragged the wooden rocking-chair up close to Grandma's bed and curled up in it.

Grandmother was perfectly happy. She and the twins were about the same age; they had in common all the realest and truest things. The years between them and her, it seemed to Mrs. Harris, were full of trouble and unimportant. The twins and Ronald and Hughie were important. She opened her eyes.

"Where is Hughie?" she asked.

"I guess he's asleep. Mother took him into her bed."

"And Ronald?"

"He's upstairs with Mandy. There ain't nobody in the kitchen now."

"Then you might git me a fresh drink, Del."

"Yes'm, Gram'ma." He tiptoed out to the pump in his brown canvas sneakers.

When Vickie came home at five o'clock, she went to her mother's room, but the door was locked—a thing she couldn't remember ever happening before. She went into the play-room,—old Mrs. Harris was asleep, with one of the twins on guard, and he held up a warning finger. She went into the kitchen. Mandy was making biscuits, and Ronald was helping her to cut them out.

"What's the matter, Mandy? Where is everybody?"

"You know your papa's away, Miss Vickie; an' your mama's got a headache, an' Miz' Harris has had a bad spell. Maybe I'll just fix supper for you an' the boys in the kitchen, so you won't all have to be runnin' through her room."

"Oh, very well," said Vickie bitterly, and she went upstairs. Wasn't it just like them all to go and get sick, when she had now only two weeks to get ready for school, and no trunk and no clothes or anything? Nobody but Mr. Rosen seemed to take the least interest, "when my whole life hangs by a thread," she told herself fiercely. What were families for, anyway?

After supper Vickie went to her father's office to read; she told Mandy to leave the kitchen door open, and when she got home she would go to bed without disturbing anybody. The twins ran out to play under the electric light with the neighbour boys for a little while, then slipped softly up the back stairs to their room. Mandy came to Mrs. Harris after the house was still.

"Kin I rub your legs fur you, Miz' Harris?"

"Thank you, Mandy. And you might get me a clean nightcap out of the press."

Mandy returned with it.

"Lawsie me! But your legs is cold, ma'am!"

"I expect it's about time, Mandy," murmured the old lady. Mandy knelt on the floor and set to work with a will. It brought the sweat out on her, and at last she sat up and wiped her face with the back of her hand.

"I can't seem to git no heat into 'em, Miz' Harris. I got a hot flat-iron on the stove; I'll wrap it in a piece of old blanket and put it to your feet. Why didn't you have the boys tell me you was cold, pore soul?"

Mrs. Harris did not answer. She thought it was probably a cold that neither Mandy nor the flat-iron could do much with. She hadn't nursed so many people back in Tennessee without coming to know certain signs.

After Mandy was gone, she fell to thinking of her blessings. Every night for years, when she said her prayers, she had prayed that she might never have a long sickness or be a burden. She dreaded the heart-ache and humiliation of being helpless on the hands of people who would be impatient under such a care. And now she felt certain that she was going to die tonight, without troubling anybody.

She was glad Mrs. Rosen was in Chicago. Had she been at home, she would certainly have come in, would have seen that her old neighbour was very sick, and bustled about. Her quick eye would have found out all Grandmother's little secrets: how hard her bed was, that she had no proper place to wash, and kept her comb in her pocket; that her nightgowns were patched and darned. Mrs. Rosen would have been indignant, and that would have made Victoria cross. She didn't have to see Mrs. Rosen again to know that Mrs. Rosen thought highly of her and admired her—yes, admired her. Those funny little pats and arch pleasantries had meant a great deal to Mrs. Harris.

It was a blessing that Mr. Templeton was away, too. Appearances had to be kept up when there was a man in the house; and he might have taken it into his head to send for the doctor, and stir everybody up. Now everything would be so peaceful. *"The Lord is my shepherd,"* she whispered gratefully. "Yes, Lord, I always spoiled Victoria. She was so much the prettiest. But nobody won't ever be the worse for it: Mr. Templeton will always humour her, and the children love her more than most. They'll always be good to her; she has that way with her."

Grandma fell to remembering the old place at home: what a dashing, high-spirited girl Victoria was, and how proud she had always been of her; how she used to hear her laughing and teasing out in the lilac arbour when Hillary Templeton was courting her. Toward morning all these pleasant reflections faded out. Mrs. Harris felt that she and her bed were softly sinking, through the darkness to a deeper darkness.

Old Mrs. Harris did not really die that night, but she believed she did. Mandy found her unconscious in the morning. Then there was a great stir and bustle; Victoria, and even Vickie, were startled out of their intense self-absorption. Mrs.

Harris was hastily carried out of the play-room and laid in Victoria's bed, put into one of Victoria's best nightgowns. Mr. Templeton was sent for, and the doctor was sent for. The inquisitive Mrs. Jackson from next door got into the house at last,—installed herself as nurse, and no one had the courage to say her nay. But Grandmother was out of it all, never knew that she was the object of so much attention and excitement. She died a little while after Mr. Templeton got home.

Thus Mrs. Harris slipped out of the Templetons' story; but Victoria and Vickie had still to go on, to follow the long road that leads through things unguessed at and unforeseeable. When they are old, they will come closer and closer to Grandma Harris. They will think a great deal about her, and remember things they never noticed; and their lot will be more or less like hers. They will regret that they heeded her so little; but they, too, will look into the eager, unseeing eyes of young people and feel themselves alone. They will say to themselves: "I was heartless, because I was young and strong and wanted things so much. But now I know."

New Brunswick, 1931

Two Friends

I

EVEN IN EARLY YOUTH, when the mind is so eager for the new and untried, while it is still a stranger to faltering and fear, we yet like to think that there are certain unalterable realities, somewhere at the bottom of things. These anchors may be ideas; but more often they are merely pictures, vivid memories, which in some unaccountable and very personal way give us courage. The sea-gulls, that seem so much creatures of the free wind and waves, that are as homeless as the sea (able to rest upon the tides and ride the storm, needing nothing but water and sky), at certain seasons even they go back to something they have known before; to remote islands and lonely ledges that are their breeding-grounds. The restlessness of youth has such retreats, even though it may be ashamed of them.

Long ago, before the invention of the motor-car (which has made more changes in the world than the War, which indeed produced the particular kind of war that happened just a hundred years after Waterloo), in a little wooden town in a shallow Kansas river valley, there lived two friends. They were "business men," the two most prosperous and influential men in our community, the two men whose affairs took them out into the world to big cities, who had "connections" in St. Joseph and Chicago. In my childhood they represented to me success and power.

R. E. Dillon was of Irish extraction, one of the dark Irish, with glistening jet-black hair and moustache, and thick eyebrows. His skin was very white, bluish on his shaven cheeks and chin. Shaving must have been a difficult process for him, because there were no smooth expanses for the razor to glide over. The bony structure of his face was prominent and unusual; high cheek-bones, a bold Roman nose, a chin cut by deep lines, with a hard dimple at the tip, a jutting ridge over his eyes where his curly black eyebrows grew and met. It was a face in many planes, as if the carver had whittled and modelled and indented to see how far he could go. Yet on meeting him what you saw was an imperious head on a rather small, wiry man, a head held conspicuously and proudly erect, with a carriage unmistakably arrogant and consciously superior. Dillon had a musical, vibrating voice, and the changeable grey eye that is peculiarly Irish. His full name, which he never used, was Robert Emmet Dillon, so there must have been a certain feeling somewhere back in his family.

He was the principal banker in our town, and proprietor of the large general store next the bank; he owned farms up in the grass country, and a fine ranch in the green timbered valley of the Caw. He was, according to our standards, a rich man.

His friend, J. H. Trueman, was what we called a big cattle-man. Trueman was from Buffalo; his family were old residents there, and he had come West as a young man because he was restless and unconventional in his tastes. He was fully ten years older than Dillon,—in his early fifties, when I knew him; large, heavy, very slow in his movements, not given to exercise. His countenance was as unmistakably American as Dillon's was not,—but American of that period, not of this. He did not belong to the time of efficiency and advertising and progressive methods. For any form of pushing or boost-ing he had a cold, unqualified contempt. All this was in his face,—heavy, immobile, rather melancholy, not remarkable in any particular. But the moment one looked at him one felt solidity, an entire absence of anything mean or small, easy carelessness, courage, a high sense of honour.

These two men had been friends for ten years before I knew them, and I knew them from the time I was ten until I was thirteen. I saw them as often as I could, because they led more varied lives than the other men in our town; one could look up to them. Dillon, I believe, was the more intelligent. Trueman had, perhaps, a better tradition, more background.

Dillon's bank and general store stood at the corner of Main Street and a cross-street, and on this cross-street, two short blocks away, my family lived. On my way to and from school, and going on the countless errands that I was sent upon day and night, I always passed Dillon's store. Its long, red brick wall, with no windows except high overhead, ran possibly a hundred feet along the sidewalk of the cross-street. The front door and show windows were on Main Street, and the bank was next door. The board sidewalk along that red brick wall was wider than any other piece of walk in town, smoother, better laid, kept in perfect repair; very good to walk on in a community where most things were flimsy. I liked the store and the brick wall and the sidewalk because they were solid and well built, and possibly I admired Dillon and Trueman for much the same reason. They were secure and established. So many of our citizens were nervous little hopper men, trying to get on. Dillon and Trueman had got on; they stood with easy assurance on a deck that was their own.

In the daytime one did not often see them together—each went about his own affairs. But every evening they were both to be found at Dillon's store. The bank, of course, was locked and dark before the sun went down, but the store was always open until ten o'clock; the clerks put in a long day. So did Dillon. He and his store were one. He never acted as salesman, and he kept a cashier in the wire-screened office at the back end of the store; but he was there to be called on. The thrifty Swedes to the north, who were his best customers, usually came to town and did their shopping after dark—they didn't squander daylight hours in farming season. In these evening visits with his customers, and on his drives in his buckboard among the farms, Dillon learned all he needed to know about how much money it was safe to advance a farmer who wanted to feed cattle, or to buy a steam thrasher or build a new barn.

Every evening in winter, when I went to the post-office after supper, I passed through Dillon's store instead of going round it,—for the warmth and cheerfulness, and to catch sight of Mr. Dillon and Mr. Trueman playing checkers in the office behind the wire screening; both seated on high accountant's stools, with the checker-board on the cashier's desk before them. I knew all Dillon's clerks, and if they were not busy, I often lingered about to talk to them; sat on one of the grocery counters and watched the checker-players from a distance. I remember Mr. Dillon's hand used to linger in the air above the board before he made a move; a well-kept hand, white, marked with blue veins and streaks of strong black hair. Trueman's hands rested on his knees under the desk while he considered; he took a checker, set it down, then dropped his hand on his knee again. He seldom made an unnecessary movement with his hands or feet. Each of the men wore a ring on his little finger. Mr. Dillon's was a large diamond solitaire set in a gold claw, Trueman's the head of a Roman soldier cut in onyx and set in pale twisted gold; it had been his father's, I believe.

Exactly at ten o'clock the store closed. Mr. Dillon went home to his wife and family, to his roomy, comfortable house with a garden and orchard and big stables. Mr. Trueman, who had long been a widower, went to his office to begin the day over. He led a double life, and until one or two o'clock in the morning entertained the poker-players of our town. After everything was shut for the night, a queer crowd drifted into Trueman's back office. The company was seldom the same on two successive evenings, but there were three tireless poker-players who always came: the billiard-hall proprietor, with green-gold moustache and eyebrows, and big white teeth; the horse-trader, who smelled of horses; the dandified cashier of the bank that rivalled Dillon's. The gamblers met in Trueman's place because a game that went on there was respectable, was a social game, no matter how much money changed hands. If the horse-trader or the crooked money-lender got over-heated and broke loose a little, a look or a remark from Mr. Trueman would freeze them up. And his remark was always the same:

"Careful of the language around here."

It was never "your" language, but "the" language,— though he certainly intended no pleasantry. Trueman himself was not a lucky poker man; he was never ahead of the game on the whole. He played because he liked it, and he was willing to pay for his amusement. In general he was large and indifferent about money matters,—always carried a few hundred-dollar bills in his inside coat-pocket, and left his coat hanging anywhere,—in his office, in the bank, in the barber shop, in the cattle-sheds behind the freight yard.

Now, R. E. Dillon detested gambling, often dropped a contemptuous word about "poker bugs" before the horse-trader and the billiard-hall man and the cashier of the other bank. But he never made remarks of that sort in Trueman's presence. He was a man who voiced his prejudices fearlessly and cuttingly, but on this and other matters he held his peace before Trueman. His regard for him must have been very strong.

During the winter, usually in March, the two friends always took a trip together, to Kansas City and St. Joseph. When they got ready, they packed their bags and stepped aboard a fast Santa Fé train and went; the Limited was often signalled to stop for them. Their excursions made some of the rest of us feel less shut away and small-townish, just as their fur over-coats and silk shirts did. They were the only men in Singleton who wore silk shirts. The other business men wore white shirts with detachable collars, high and stiff or low and sprawling, which were changed much oftener than the shirts. Neither of my heroes was afraid of laundry bills. They did not wear waistcoats, but went about in their shirt-sleeves in hot weather; their suspenders were chosen with as much care as their neckties and handkerchiefs. Once when a bee stung my hand in the store (a few of them had got into the brown-sugar barrel), Mr. Dillon himself moistened the sting, put baking soda on it, and bound my hand up with his pocket handkerchief. It was of the smoothest linen, and in one corner was a violet square bearing his initials, R. E. D., in white. There were never any handkerchiefs like that in my family. I cherished it until it was laundered, and I returned it with regret.

It was in the spring and summer that one saw Mr. Dillon and Mr. Trueman at their best. Spring began early with us,—often the first week of April was hot. Every evening when he came back to the store after supper, Dillon had one of his clerks bring two arm-chairs out to the wide sidewalk that ran beside the red brick wall,—office chairs of the old-fashioned sort, with a low round back which formed a half-circle to enclose the sitter, and spreading legs, the front ones slightly higher. In those chairs the two friends would spend the evening. Dillon would sit down and light a good cigar. In a few moments Mr. Trueman would come across from Main Street, walking slowly, spaciously, as if he were used to a great deal of room. As he approached, Mr. Dillon would call out to him:

"Good evening, J. H. Fine weather."

J. H. would take his place in the empty chair.

"Spring in the air," he might remark, if it were April. Then he would relight a dead cigar which was always in his hand, —seemed to belong there, like a thumb or finger.

"I drove up north today to see what the Swedes are doing," Mr. Dillon might begin. "They're the boys to get the early worm. They never let the ground go to sleep. Whatever moisture there is, they get the benefit of it."

"The Swedes are good farmers. I don't sympathize with the way they work their women."

"The women like it, J. H. It's the old-country way; they're accustomed to it, and they like it."

"Maybe. I don't like it," Trueman would reply with something like a grunt.

They talked very much like this all evening; or, rather, Mr. Dillon talked, and Mr. Trueman made an occasional observation. No one could tell just how much Mr. Trueman knew about anything, because he was so consistently silent. Not from diffidence, but from superiority; from a contempt for chatter, and a liking for silence, a taste for it. After they had exchanged a few remarks, he and Dillon often sat in an easy quiet for a long time, watching the passers-by, watching the wagons on the road, watching the stars. Sometimes, very rarely, Mr. Trueman told a long story, and it was sure to be an interesting and unusual one.

But on the whole it was Mr. Dillon who did the talking; he had a wide-awake voice with much variety in it. Trueman's was thick and low,—his speech was rather indistinct and never changed in pitch or tempo. Even when he swore wickedly at the hands who were loading his cattle into freight cars, it was a mutter, a low, even growl. There was a curious attitude in men of his class and time, that of being rather above speech, as they were above any kind of fussiness or eagerness. But I knew he liked to hear Mr. Dillon talk,—anyone did. Dillon had such a crisp, clear enunciation, and he could say things so neatly. People would take a reprimand from him they wouldn't have taken from anyone else, because he put it so well. His voice was never warm or soft—it had a cool, sparkling quality; but it could be very humorous, very kind and considerate, very teasing and stimulating. Every sentence he uttered was alive, never languid, perfunctory, slovenly, unaccented. When he made a remark, it not only meant something, but sounded like something,—sounded like the thing he meant.

When Mr. Dillon was closeted with a depositor in his private room in the bank, and you could not hear his words through the closed door, his voice told you exactly the degree of esteem in which he held that customer. It was interested, encouraging, deliberative, humorous, satisfied, admiring, cold, critical, haughty, contemptuous, according to the deserts and pretensions of his listener. And one could tell when the person closeted with him was a woman; a farmer's wife, or a woman who was trying to run a little business, or a country girl hunting a situation. There was a difference; something peculiarly kind and encouraging. But if it were a foolish, extravagant woman, or a girl he didn't approve of, oh, then one knew it well enough! The tone was courteous, but cold; relentless as the multiplication table.

All these possibilities of voice made his evening talk in the spring dusk very interesting; interesting for Trueman and for me. I found many pretexts for lingering near them, and they never seemed to mind my hanging about. I was very quiet. I often sat on the edge of the sidewalk with my feet hanging down and played jacks by the hour when there was moonlight. On dark nights I sometimes perched on top of one of the big goods-boxes—we called them "store boxes,"—there were usually several of these standing empty on the sidewalk against the red brick wall.

I liked to listen to those two because theirs was the only "conversation" one could hear about the streets. The older men talked of nothing but politics and their business, and the very young men's talk was entirely what they called "josh"; very personal, supposed to be funny, and really not funny at all. It was scarcely speech, but noises, snorts, giggles, yawns, sneezes, with a few abbreviated words and slang expressions which stood for a hundred things. The original Indians of the Kansas plains had more to do with articulate speech than had our promising young men.

To be sure my two aristocrats sometimes discussed politics,

and joked each other about the policies and pretentions of their respective parties. Mr. Dillon, of course, was a Democrat,—it was in the very frosty sparkle of his speech,—and Mr. Trueman was a Republican; his rear, as he walked about the town, looked a little like the walking elephant labelled "G. O. P." in *Puck*. But each man seemed to enjoy hearing his party ridiculed, took it as a compliment.

In the spring their talk was usually about weather and planting and pasture and cattle. Mr. Dillon went about the country in his light buckboard a great deal at that season, and he knew what every farmer was doing and what his chances were, just how much he was falling behind or getting ahead.

"I happened to drive by Oscar Ericson's place today, and I saw as nice a lot of calves as you could find anywhere," he would begin, and Ericson's history and his family would be pretty thoroughly discussed before they changed the subject.

Or he might come out with something sharp: "By the way, J. H., I saw an amusing sight today. I turned in at Sandy Bright's place to get water for my horse, and he had a photographer out there taking pictures of his house and barn. It would be more to the point if he had a picture taken of the mortgages he's put on that farm."

Trueman would give a short, mirthless response, more like a cough than a laugh.

Those April nights, when the darkness itself tasted dusty (or, by the special mercy of God, cool and damp), when the smell of burning grass was in the air, and a sudden breeze brought the scent of wild plum blossoms,—those evenings were only a restless preparation for the summer nights,—nights of full liberty and perfect idleness. Then there was no school, and one's family never bothered about where one was. My parents were young and full of life, glad to have the children out of the way. All day long there had been the excitement that intense heat produces in some people,—a mild drunkenness made of sharp contrasts; thirst and cold water, the blazing stretch of Main Street and the cool of the brick stores when one dived into them. By nightfall one was ready to be quiet. My two friends were always in their best form on those moonlit summer nights, and their talk covered a wide range.

I suppose there were moonless nights, and dark ones with but a silver shaving and pale stars in the sky, just as in the spring. But I remember them all as flooded by the rich indolence of a full moon, or a half-moon set in uncertain blue. Then Trueman and Dillon would sit with their coats off and have a supply of fresh handkerchiefs to mop their faces; they were more largely and positively themselves. One could distinguish their features, the stripes on their shirts, the flash of Mr. Dillon's diamond; but their shadows made two dark masses on the white sidewalk. The brick wall behind them, faded almost pink by the burning of successive summers, took on a carnelian hue at night. Across the street, which was merely a dusty road, lay an open space, with a few stunted box-elder trees, where the farmers left their wagons and teams when they came to town. Beyond this space stood a row of frail wooden buildings, due to be pulled down any day; tilted, crazy, with outside stairs going up to rickety second-storey porches that sagged in the middle. They had once been white, but were now grey, with faded blue doors along the wavy upper porches. These abandoned buildings, an eyesore by day, melted together into a curious pile in the moonlight, became an immaterial structure of velvet-white and glossy blackness, with here and there a faint smear of blue door, or a tilted patch of sage-green that had once been a shutter.

The road, just in front of the sidewalk where I sat and played jacks, would be ankle-deep in dust, and seemed to drink up the moonlight like folds of velvet. It drank up sound, too; muffled the wagon-wheels and hoof-beats; lay soft and meek like the last residuum of material things,—the soft bottom resting-place. Nothing in the world, not snow mountains or blue seas, is so beautiful in moonlight as the soft, dry summer roads in a farming country, roads where the white dust falls back from the slow wagon-wheel.

Wonderful things do happen even in the dullest places—in the cornfields and the wheat-fields. Sitting there on the edge of the sidewalk one summer night, my feet hanging in the warm dust, I saw a transit of Venus. Only the three of us were there. It was a hot night, and the clerks had closed the store and gone home. Mr. Dillon and Mr. Trueman waited on a little while to watch. It was a very blue night, breathless and clear, not the smallest cloud from horizon to horizon. Everything up there overhead seemed as usual, it was the familiar face of a summer-night sky. But presently we saw one bright star moving. Mr. Dillon called to me; told me to watch what was going to happen, as I might never chance to see it again in my lifetime.

That big star certainly got nearer and nearer the moon,—very rapidly, too, until there was not the width of your hand between them—now the width of two fingers—then it passed directly into the moon at about the middle of its girth; absolutely disappeared. The star we had been watching was gone. We waited, I do not know how long, but it seemed to me about fifteen minutes. Then we saw a bright wart on the other edge of the moon, but for a second only,—the machinery up there worked fast. While the two men were exclaiming and telling me to look, the planet swung clear of the golden disk, a rift of blue came between them and widened very fast. The planet did not seem to move, but that inky blue space between it and the moon seemed to spread. The thing was over.

My friends stayed on long past their usual time and talked about eclipses and such matters.

"Let me see," Mr. Trueman remarked slowly, "they reckon the moon's about two hundred and fifty thousand miles away from us. I wonder how far that star is."

"I don't know, J. H., and I really don't much care. When we can get the tramps off the railroad, and manage to run this town with one fancy house instead of two, and have a Federal Government that is as honest as a good banking business, then it will be plenty of time to turn our attention to the stars."

Mr. Trueman chuckled and took his cigar from between his teeth. "Maybe the stars will throw some light on all that, if we get the run of them," he said humorously. Then he added: "Mustn't be a reformer, R. E. Nothing in it. That's the only time you ever get off on the wrong foot. Life is what it always has been, always will be. No use to make a fuss." He got up, said: "Good-night, R. E.," said good-night to me, too, because this had been an unusual occasion, and went down the sidewalk with his wide, sailor-like tread, as if he were walking the deck of his own ship.

When Dillon and Trueman went to St. Joseph, or, as we called it, St. Joe, they stopped at the same hotel, but their diversions were very dissimilar. Mr. Dillon was a family man and a good Catholic; he behaved in St. Joe very much as if he were at home. His sister was Mother Superior of a convent there, and he went to see her often. The nuns made much of him, and he enjoyed their admiration and all the ceremony with which they entertained him. When his two daughters were going to the convent school, he used to give theatre parties for them, inviting all their friends.

Mr. Trueman's way of amusing himself must have tried his friend's patience—Dillon liked to regulate other people's affairs if they needed it. Mr. Trueman had a lot of poker-playing friends among the commission men in St. Joe, and he sometimes dropped a good deal of money. He was supposed to have rather questionable women friends there, too. The grasshopper men of our town used to say that Trueman was financial adviser to a woman who ran a celebrated sporting house. Mary Trent, her name was. She must have been a very unusual woman; she had credit with all the banks, and never got into any sort of trouble. She had formerly been head mistress of a girls' finishing school and knew how to manage young women. It was probably a fact that Trueman knew her and found her interesting, as did many another sound business man of that time. Mr. Dillon must have shut his ears to these rumours,—a measure of the great value he put on Trueman's companionship.

Though they did not see much of each other on these trips, they immensely enjoyed taking them together. They often dined together at the end of the day, and afterwards went to the theatre. They both loved the theatre; not this play or that actor, but the theatre,—whether they saw *Hamlet* or *Pinafore*. It was an age of good acting, and the drama held a more dignified position in the world than it holds today.

After Dillon and Trueman had come home from the city, they used sometimes to talk over the plays they had seen, recalling the great scenes and fine effects. Occasionally an item in the Kansas City *Star* would turn their talk to the stage.

"J. H., I see by the paper that Edwin Booth is very sick," Mr. Dillon announced one evening as Trueman came up to take the empty chair.

"Yes, I noticed." Trueman sat down and lit his dead cigar. "He's not a young man any more." A long pause. Dillon always seemed to know when the pause would be followed by a remark, and waited for it. "The first time I saw Edwin Booth was in Buffalo. It was in *Richard the Second*, and it made a great impression on me at the time." Another pause. "I don't know that I'd care to see him in that play again. I like tragedy, but that play's a little too tragic. Something very black about it. I think I prefer *Hamlet*."

They had seen Mary Anderson in St. Louis once, and talked of it for years afterwards. Mr. Dillon was very proud of her because she was a Catholic girl, and called her "our Mary." It was curious that a third person, who had never seen these actors or read the plays, could get so much of the essence of both from the comments of two business men who used none of the language in which such things are usually discussed, who merely reminded each other of moments here and there in the action. But they saw the play over again as they talked of it, and perhaps whatever is seen by the narrator as he speaks is sensed by the listener, quite irrespective of words. This transference of experience went further: in some way the lives of those two men came across to me as they talked, the strong, bracing reality of successful, large-minded men who had made their way in the world when business was still a personal adventure.

II

Mr. Dillon went to Chicago once a year to buy goods for his store. Trueman would usually accompany him as far as St. Joe, but no farther. He dismissed Chicago as "too big." He didn't like to be one of the crowd, didn't feel at home in a city where he wasn't recognized as J. H. Trueman.

It was one of these trips to Chicago that brought about the end—for me and for them; a stupid, senseless, commonplace end.

Being a Democrat, already somewhat "tainted" by the free-silver agitation, one spring Dillon delayed his visit to Chicago in order to be there for the Democratic Convention—it was the Convention that first nominated Bryan.

On the night after his return from Chicago, Mr. Dillon was seated in his chair on the sidewalk, surrounded by a group of men who wanted to hear all about the nomination of a man from a neighbour State. Mr. Trueman came across the street in his leisurely way, greeted Dillon, and asked him how he had found Chicago,—whether he had had a good trip.

Mr. Dillon must have been annoyed because Trueman didn't mention the Convention. He threw back his head rather haughtily. "Well, J. H., since I saw you last, we've found a great leader in this country, and a great orator." There was a frosty sparkle in his voice that presupposed opposition,—like the feint of a boxer getting ready.

"Great windbag!" muttered Trueman. He sat down in his chair, but I noticed that he did not settle himself and cross his legs as usual.

Mr. Dillon gave an artificial laugh. "It's nothing against a man to be a fine orator. All the great leaders have been eloquent. This Convention was a memorable occasion; it gave the Democratic party a rebirth."

"Gave it a black eye, and a blind spot, I'd say!" commented Trueman. He didn't raise his voice, but he spoke with more heat than I had ever heard from him. After a moment he added: "I guess Grover Cleveland must be a sick man; must feel like he'd taken a lot of trouble for nothing."

Mr. Dillon ignored these thrusts and went on telling the group around him about the Convention, but there was a special nimbleness and exactness in his tongue, a chill politeness in his voice that meant anger. Presently he turned again to Mr. Trueman, as if he could now trust himself:

"It was one of the great speeches of history, J. H.; our grandchildren will have to study it in school, as we did Patrick Henry's."

"Glad I haven't got any grandchildren, if they'd be brought up on that sort of tall talk," said Mr. Trueman. "Sounds like a schoolboy had written it. Absolutely nothing back of it but an unsound theory."

Mr. Dillon's laugh made me shiver; it was like a thin glitter of danger. He arched his curly eyebrows provokingly.

"We'll have four years of currency reform, anyhow. By the end of that time, you old dyed-in-the-wool Republicans will be thinking differently. The under dog is going to have a chance."

Mr. Trueman shifted in his chair. "That's no way for a banker to talk." He spoke very low. "The Democrats will have a long time to be sorry they ever turned Pops. No use talking to you while your Irish is up. I'll wait till you cool off." He rose and walked away, less deliberately than usual, and Mr. Dillon, watching his retreating figure, laughed haughtily and disagreeably. He asked the grain-elevator man to take the vacated chair. The group about him grew, and he sat expounding the reforms proposed by the Democratic candidate until a late hour.

For the first time in my life I listened with breathless interest to a political discussion. Whoever Mr. Dillon failed to convince, he convinced me. I grasped it at once: that gold had been responsible for most of the miseries and inequalities of the world; that it had always been the club the rich and cunning held over the poor; and that "the free and unlimited coinage of silver" would remedy all this. Dillon declared that young Mr. Bryan had looked like the patriots of old when he faced and challenged high finance with: "You shall not press this crown of thorns upon the brow of labour; you shall not crucify mankind upon a cross of gold." I thought that magnificent; I thought the cornfields would show them a thing or two, back there!

R. E. Dillon had never taken an aggressive part in politics. But from that night on, the Democratic candidate and the free-silver plank were the subject of his talks with his customers and depositors. He drove about the country convincing the farmers, went to the neighbouring towns to use his influence with the merchants, organized the Bryan Club and the Bryan Ladies' Quartette in our county, contributed largely to the campaign fund. This was all a new line of conduct for Mr. Dillon, and it sat unsteadily on him. Even his voice became unnatural; there was a sting of comeback in it. His new character made him more like other people and took away from his special personal quality. I wonder whether it was not Trueman, more than Bryan, who put such an edge on him.

While all these things were going on, Trueman kept to his own office. He came to Dillon's bank on business, but he did not "come back to the sidewalk," as I put it to myself. He waited and said nothing, but he looked grim. After a month or so, when he saw that this thing was not going to blow over, when he heard how Dillon had been talking to representative men all over the county, and saw the figure he had put down for the campaign fund, then Trueman remarked to some of his friends that a banker had no business to commit himself to a scatter-brained financial policy which would destroy credit.

The next morning Mr. Trueman went to the bank across the street, the rival of Dillon's, and wrote a cheque on Dillon's bank "for the amount of my balance." He wasn't the sort of man who would ever know what his balance was, he merely kept it big enough to cover emergencies. That afternoon the Merchants' National took the check over to Dillon on its collecting rounds, and by night the word was all over town that Trueman had changed his bank. After this there would be no going back, people said. To change your bank was one of the most final things you could do. The little, unsuccessful men were pleased, as they always are at the destruction of anything strong and fine.

All through the summer and the autumn of that campaign Mr. Dillon was away a great deal. When he was at home, he took his evening airing on the sidewalk, and there was always a group of men about him, talking of the coming election; that was the most exciting presidential campaign people could remember. I often passed this group on my way to the post-office, but there was no temptation to linger now. Mr. Dillon seemed like another man, and my zeal to free humanity from the cross of gold had cooled. Mr. Trueman I seldom saw. When he passed me on the street, he nodded kindly.

The election and Bryan's defeat did nothing to soften Dillon. He had been sure of a Democratic victory. I believe he felt almost as if Trueman were responsible for the triumph of Hanna and McKinley. At least he knew that Trueman was exceedingly well satisfied, and that was bitter to him. He seemed to me sarcastic and sharp all the time now.

I don't believe self-interest would ever have made a breach between Dillon and Trueman. Neither would have taken advantage of the other. If a combination of circumstances had made it necessary that one or the other should take a loss in money or prestige, I think Trueman would have pocketed the loss. That was his way. It was his code, moreover. A gentleman pocketed his gains mechanically, in the day's routine; but he pocketed losses punctiliously, with a sharp, if bitter, relish. I believe now, as I believed then, that this was a quarrel of "principle." Trueman looked down on anyone who could take the reasoning of the Populist party seriously. He was a perfectly direct man, and he showed his contempt. That was enough. It lost me my special pleasure of summer nights: the old stories of the early West that sometimes came to the surface; the minute biographies of the farming people; the clear, detailed, illuminating accounts of all that went on in the great crop-growing, cattle-feeding world; and the silence,—the strong, rich, out-flowing silence between two friends, that was as full and satisfying as the moonlight. I was never to know its like again.

After that rupture nothing went well with either of my two great men. Things were out of true, the equilibrium was gone. Formerly, when they used to sit in their old places on the sidewalk, two black figures with patches of shadow below, they seemed like two bodies held steady by some law of balance, an unconscious relation like that between the earth and the moon. It was this mathematical harmony which gave a third person pleasure.

Before the next presidential campaign came round, Mr. Dillon died (a young man still) very suddenly, of pneumonia. We didn't know that he was seriously ill until one of his clerks came running to our house to tell us he was dead. The same clerk, half out of his wits—it looked like the end of the world to him—ran on to tell Mr. Trueman.

Mr. Trueman thanked him. He called his confidential man, and told him to order flowers from Kansas City. Then he went to his house, informed his housekeeper that he was going away on business, and packed his bag. That same night he boarded the Santa Fé Limited and didn't stop until he was in San Francisco. He was gone all spring. His confidential clerk wrote him letters every week about the business and the new calves, and got telegrams in reply. Trueman never wrote letters.

When Mr. Trueman at last came home, he stayed only a few months. He sold out everything he owned to a stranger from Kansas City; his feeding ranch, his barns and sheds, his house and town lots. It was a terrible blow to me; now only the common, everyday people would be left. I used to walk mournfully up and down before his office while all these deeds were being signed,—there were usually lawyers and notaries inside. But once, when he happened to be alone, he called me in, asked me how old I was now, and how far along I had got in school. His face and voice were more than kind, but he seemed absent-minded, as if he were trying to recall something. Presently he took from his watch-chain a red seal I had always admired, reached for my hand, and dropped the piece of carnelian into my palm.

"For a keepsake," he said evasively.

When the transfer of his property was completed, Mr. Trueman left us for good. He spent the rest of his life among the golden hills of San Francisco. He moved into the Saint Francis Hotel when it was first built, and had an office in a high building at the top of what is now Powell Street. There he read his letters in the morning and played poker at night. I've heard a man whose offices were next his tell how Trueman used to sit tilted back in his desk chair, a half-consumed cigar in his mouth, morning after morning, apparently doing nothing, watching the Bay and the ferry-boats, across a line of wind-racked eucalyptus trees. He died at the Saint Francis about nine years after he left our part of the world.

The breaking-up of that friendship between two men who scarcely noticed my existence was a real loss to me, and has ever since been a regret. More than once, in Southern countries where there is a smell of dust and dryness in the air and the nights are intense, I have come upon a stretch of dusty white road drinking up the moonlight beside a blind wall, and have felt a sudden sadness. Perhaps it was not until the next morning that I knew why,—and then only because I had dreamed of Mr. Dillon or Mr. Trueman in my sleep. When that old scar is occasionally touched by chance, it rouses the old uneasiness; the feeling of something broken that could so easily have been mended; of something delightful that was senselessly wasted, of a truth that was accidentally distorted—one of the truths we want to keep.

Pasadena, 1931

THE OLD BEAUTY
AND OTHERS

Contents

The Old Beauty

I

ONE BRILLIANT September morning in 1922 a slender, fair-skinned man with white moustaches, waxed and turned up at the ends, stepped hurriedly out of the Hôtel Splendide at Aix-les-Bains and stood uncertainly at the edge of the driveway. He stood there for some moments, holding, or rather clutching, his gloves in one hand, a light cane in the other. The pavement was wet, glassy with water. The boys were still sprinkling the walk farther down the hill, and the fuchsias and dahlias in the beds sparkled with water drops. The clear air had the freshness of early morning and the smell of autumn foliage.

Two closed litters, carried by porters, came out of a side door and went joggling down the hill toward the baths. The gentleman standing on the kerb followed these eagerly with his eyes, as if about to dash after them; indeed, his mind seemed to accompany them to the turn in the walk where they disappeared, then to come back to him where he stood and at once to dart off in still another direction.

The gentleman was Mr. Henry Seabury, aged fifty-five, American-born, educated in England, and lately returned from a long business career in China. His evident nervousness was due to a shock: an old acquaintance, who had been one of the brilliant figures in the world of the 1890's, had died a few hours ago in this hotel.

As he stood there he was thinking that he ought to send telegrams . . . but to whom? The lady had no immediate family, and the distinguished men of her time who had cherished the slightest attention from her were all dead. No, there was one (perhaps the most variously gifted of that group) who was still living: living in seclusion down on the Riviera, in a great white mansion set in miles of park and garden. A cloud had come over this man in the midst of a triumphant public life. His opponents had ruined his career by a whispering campaign. They had set going a rumour which would have killed any public man in England at that time. Mr.

Seabury began composing his telegram to Lord H—. Lord H— would recognize that this death was more than the death of an individual. To him her name would recall a society whose manners, dress, conventions, loyalties, codes of honour, were different from anything existing in the world today.

And there were certainly old acquaintances like himself, men not of her intimate circle, scattered about over the world; in the States, in China, India. But how to reach them?

Three young men came up the hill to resolve his perplexity; three newspaper correspondents, English, French, American. The American spoke to his companions. "There's the man I've seen about with her so much. He's the one we want."

The three approached Mr. Seabury, and the American addressed him. "Mr. Seabury, I believe? Excuse my stopping you, but we have just learned through the British Consulate that the former Lady Longstreet died in this hotel last night. We are newspaper men, and must send dispatches to our papers." He paused to introduce his companions by their names and the names of their journals. "We thought you might be good enough to tell us something about Lady Longstreet, Madame de Couçy, as she was known here."

"Nothing but what all the world knows." This intrusion had steadied Mr. Seabury, brought his scattered faculties to a focus.

"But we must jog the world's memory a little. A great many things have happened since Lady Longstreet was known everywhere."

"Certainly. You have only to cable your papers that Madame de Couçy, formerly Lady Longstreet, died here last night. They have in their files more than I could tell you if I stood here all morning."

"But the circumstances of her death?"

"You can get that from the management. Her life was interesting, but she died like anyone else—just as you will, some day."

"Her old friends, everywhere, would of course like to learn something about her life here this summer. No one knew her except as Madame de Couçy, so no one observed her very closely. You were with her a great deal, and the simple story of her life here would be—"

"I understand, but it is quite impossible. Good morning, gentlemen." Mr. Seabury went to his room to write his telegram to Lord H——.

II

Two months ago Henry Seabury had come here almost directly from China. His hurried trip across America and his few weeks in London scarcely counted. He was hunting for something, some spot that was still more or less as it used to be. Here, at Aix-les-Bains, he found the place unchanged,—and in the hotels many people very like those who used to come there.

The first night after he had settled himself at the Splendide he became interested in two old English ladies who dined at a table not far from his own. They had been coming here for many years, he felt sure. They had the old manner. They were at ease and reserved. Their dress was conservative. They were neither painted nor plucked, their nails were neither red nor green. One was plump, distinctly plump, indeed, but as she entered the dining-room he had noticed that she was quick in her movements and light on her feet. She was radiantly cheerful and talkative. But it was the other lady who interested him. She had an air of distinction, that unmistakable thing, which told him she had been a personage. She was tall, had a fine figure and carriage, but either she was much older than her friend, or life had used her more harshly. Something about her eyes and brow teased his memory. Had he once known her, or did he merely recall a type of woman he used to know? No, he felt that he must have met her, at least, long ago, when she was not a stern, gaunt-cheeked old woman with a yellowing complexion. The hotel management informed him that the lady was Madame de Couçy. He had never known anyone of that name.

The next afternoon when he was sitting under the plane trees in the *Place*, he saw the two ladies coming down the hill; the tall one moving with a peculiar drifting ease, looking into the distance as if the unlevel walk beneath her would naturally accommodate itself to her footing. She kept a white fur well up about her cheeks, though the day was hot. The short one

tripped along beside her. They crossed the Square, sat down
under the trees, and had tea brought out from the confec-
tioner's. Then the muffled lady let her fur fall back a little
and glanced about her. He was careful not to stare, but
once, when he suddenly lifted his eyes, she was looking directly
at him. He thought he saw a spark of curiosity, perhaps rec-
ognition.

The two ladies had tea in the *Place* every afternoon unless it
rained; when they did not come Seabury felt disappointed.
Sometimes the taller one would pause before she sat down
and suggest going farther, to the Casino. Once he was near
enough to hear the rosy one exclaiming: "Oh, no! It's much
nicer here, really. You are always dissatisfied when we go to
the Casino. There are more of the kind you hate there."

The older one with a shrug and a mournful smile sat down
resignedly in front of the pastry shop. When she had finished
her tea she drew her wrap up about her chin as if about to
leave, but her companion began to coax: "Let us wait for the
newspaper woman. It's almost time for her, and I do like to
get the home papers."

The other reminded her that there would be plenty of
papers at the hotel.

"Yes, yes, I know. But I like to get them from her. I'm sure
she's glad of our pennies."

When they left their table they usually walked about the
Square for a time, keeping to the less frequented end toward
the Park. They bought roses at the flower booths, and cycla-
men from an old country woman who tramped about with a
basketful of them. Then they went slowly up the hill toward
the hotel.

III

Seabury's first enlightenment about these solitary women
came from a most unlikely source.

Going up to the summit of Mont Revard in the little rail-
way train one morning, he made the acquaintance of an
English family (father, mother, and two grown daughters)
whom he liked very much. He spent the day on the mountain
in their company, and after that he saw a great deal of them.

They were from Devonshire, home-staying people, not tourists. (The daughters had never been on the Continent before.) They had come over to visit the son's grave in one of the war cemeteries in the north of France. The father brought them down to Aix to cheer them up a little. (He and his wife had come there on their honeymoon, long ago.) As the Thompsons were stopping at a cramped, rather mean little hotel down in the town, they spent most of the day out of doors. Usually the mother and one of the daughters sat the whole morning in the *Place*, while the other girl went off tramping with the father. The mother knitted, and the girl read aloud to her. Whichever daughter it happened to be kept watchful eye on Mrs. Thompson. If her face grew too pensive, the girl would close the book and say:

"Now, Mother, do let us have some chocolate and croissants. The breakfast at that hotel is horrid, and I'm famished."

Mr. Seabury often joined them in the morning. He found it very pleasant to be near that kind of family feeling. They felt his friendliness, the mother especially, and were pleased to have him join them at their chocolate, or to go with him to afternoon concerts at the Grand-Cercle.

One afternoon when the mother and both daughters were having tea with him near the Roman Arch, the two English ladies from his hotel crossed the Square and sat down at a table not far away. He noticed that Mrs. Thompson glanced often in their direction. Seabury kept his guests a long while at tea,—the afternoon was hot, and he knew their hotel was stuffy. He was telling the girls something about China, when the two unknown English ladies left their table and got into a taxi. Mrs. Thompson turned to Seabury and said in a low, agitated voice:

"Do you know, I believe the tall one of those two was Lady Longstreet."

Mr. Seabury started. "Oh, no! Could it be possible?"

"I am afraid it is. Yes, she is greatly changed. It's very sad. Six years ago she stayed at a country place near us, in Devonshire, and I used often to see her out on her horse. She still rode then. I don't think I can be mistaken."

In a flash everything came back to Seabury. "You're right, I'm sure of it, Mrs. Thompson. The lady lives at my hotel,

and I've been puzzling about her. I knew Lady Longstreet
slightly many years ago. Now that you tell me, I can see it.
But . . . as you say, she is greatly changed. At the hotel she is
known as Madame de Couçy."

"Yes, she married during the war; a Frenchman. But it
must have been after she had lost her beauty. I had never
heard of the marriage until he was killed,—in '17, I think.
Then some of the English papers mentioned that he was the
husband of Gabrielle Longstreet. It's very sad when those
beautiful ones have to grow old, isn't it? We never have too
many of them, at best."

The younger daughter threw her arms about Mrs. Thomp-
son. "Oh, Mother, I wish you hadn't told us! I'm afraid Mr.
Seabury does, too. It's such a shock."

He protested. "Yes, it is a shock, certainly. But I'm grateful
to Mrs. Thompson. I must be very stupid not to have seen it.
I'm glad to know. The two ladies seem very much alone, and
the older one looks ill. I might be of some service, if she
remembers me. It's all very strange: but one might be useful,
perhaps, Mrs. Thompson?"

"That's the way to look at it, Mr. Seabury." Mrs. Thomp-
son spoke gently. "I think she does remember you. When you
were talking to Dorothy, turned away from them, she glanced
at you often. The lady with her is a friend, don't you think,
not a paid companion?"

He said he was sure of it, and she gave him a warm, grate-
ful glance as if he and she could understand how much that
meant, then turned to her daughters: "Why, there is Father,
come to look for us!" She made a little signal to the stout,
flushed man who was tramping across the Square in climbing
boots.

IV

Mr. Seabury did not go back to his hotel for dinner. He
dined at a little place with tables in the garden, and returned
late to the Splendide. He felt rather knocked up by what Mrs.
Thompson had told him,—felt that in this world people have
to pay an extortionate price for any exceptional gift whatever.
Once in his own room, he lay for a long while in a chaise

longue before an open window, watching the stars and the
fireflies, recalling the whole romantic story, — all he had ever
known of Lady Longstreet. And in this hotel, full of people,
she was unknown — she!

Gabrielle Longstreet was a name known all over the
globe, — even in China, when he went there twenty-seven
years ago. Yet she was not an actress or an adventuress. She
had come into the European world in a perfectly regular, if
somewhat unusual, way.

Sir Wilfred Longstreet, a lover of yachting and adventure
on the high seas, had been driven into Martinique by a trop-
ical hurricane. Strolling about the harbour town, he saw a
young girl coming out of a church with her mother; the girl
was nineteen, the mother perhaps forty. They were the two
most beautiful women he had ever seen. The hurricane passed
and was forgotten, but Sir Wilfred Longstreet's yacht still lay
in the harbour of Fort de France. He sought out the girl's
father, an English colonial from Barbados, who was easily
convinced. The mother not so easily: she was a person of
character as well as severe beauty. Longstreet had sworn that
he would never take his yacht out to sea unless he carried
Gabrielle aboard her. The *Sea Nymph* might lie and rot there.

In time the mother was reassured by letters and documents
from England. She wished to do well for her daughter, and
what very brilliant opportunities were there in Martinique?
As for the girl, she wanted to see the world; she had never
been off the island. Longstreet made a settlement upon Ma-
dame the mother, and submitted to the two services, civil and
religious. He took his bride directly back to England. He had
not advised his friends of his marriage; he was a young man
who kept his affairs to himself.

He kept his wife in the country for some months. When he
opened his town house and took her to London, things went
as he could not possibly have foreseen. In six weeks she was
the fashion of the town; the object of admiration among his
friends, and his father's friends. Gabrielle was not socially
ambitious, made no effort to please. She was not witty or
especially clever, — had no accomplishments beyond speaking
French as naturally as English. She said nothing memorable
in either language. She was beautiful, that was all. And she

was fresh. She came into that society of old London like a quiet country dawn.

She showed no great zest for this life so different from anything she had ever known; a quiet wonderment rather, faintly tinged with pleasure. There was no glitter about her, no sparkle. She never dressed in the mode: refused to wear crinoline in a world that billowed and swelled with it. Into drawing-rooms full of ladies enriched by marvels of hairdressing (switches, ringlets, puffs, pompadours, waves starred with gems), she came with her brown hair parted in the middle and coiled in a small knot at the back of her head. Hair-dressers protested, as one client after another adopted the 'mode Gabrielle.' (The knot at the nape of the neck! Char-women had always worn it; it was as old as mops and pails.)

The English liked high colour, but Lady Longstreet had no red roses in her cheeks. Her skin had the soft glow of orient pearls,—the jewel to which she was most often compared. She was not spirited, she was not witty, but no one ever heard her say a stupid thing. She was often called cold. She seemed unawakened, as if she were still an island girl with reserved island good manners. No woman had been so much discussed and argued about for a long stretch of years. It was to the older men that she was (unconsciously, as it seemed) more gracious. She liked them to tell her about events and personages already in the past; things she had come too late to see.

Longstreet, her husband, was none too pleased by the flutter she caused. It was no great credit to him to have dis-covered a rare creature; since everyone else discovered her the moment they had a glimpse of her. Men much his su-periors in rank and importance looked over his head at his wife, passed him with a nod on their way to her. He began to feel annoyance, and waited for this flurry to pass over. But pass it did not. With her second and third seasons in town her circle grew. Statesmen and officers twenty years Longstreet's senior seemed to find in Gabrielle an escape from long bore-dom. He was jealous without having the common pretexts for jealousy. He began to spend more and more time on his yacht in distant waters. He left his wife in his town house with his spinster cousin as chaperone. Gabrielle's mother came on from Martinique for a season, and was almost as much admired as her daughter. Sir Wilfred found that the Martiniquaises had considerably overshadowed him. He was no longer the interesting 'original' he had once been. His unexpected appearances and disappearances were mere incidents in the house and the life which his wife and his cousin had so well organized. He bore this for six years and then, unexpectedly, demanded divorce. He established the statutory grounds, she petitioning for the decree. He made her a generous settlement.

This brought about a great change in Gabrielle Longstreet's life. She remained in London, and bought a small house near St. James's Park. Longstreet's old cousin, to his great annoyance, stayed on with Gabrielle,—the only one of his family who had not treated her like a poor relation. The loyalty of this spinster, a woman of spirit, Scotch on the father's side, did a good deal to ease Gabrielle's fall in the world. For fall it was, of course. She had her circle, but it was smaller and more intimate. Fewer women invited her now, fewer of the women she used to know. She did not go afield for those who affected art and advanced ideas; they would gladly have championed her cause. She replied to their overtures that she no longer went into society. Her men friends never flinched in their loyalty. Those unembarrassed by wives, the bachelors and widowers, were more assiduous than ever. At that dinner table where Gabrielle and "the Honourable MacPhairson," as the old cousin was called, were sometimes the only women, one met promising young men, not yet settled in their careers, and much older men, so solidly and successfully settled that their presence in a company established its propriety.

Nobody could ever say exactly why Gabrielle's house was so attractive. The men who had the entrée there were not skilful at defining such a thing as 'charm' in words: that was not at all their line. And they would have been reluctant to admit that a negligible thing like temperature had anything to do with the pleasant relaxation they enjoyed there. The chill of London houses had been one of the cruellest trials the young Martiniquaise had to bear. When she took a house of her own, she (secretly, as if it were a disgraceful thing to do) had a hot-air furnace put in her cellar, and she kept coal fires burning in the grates at either end of the drawing-room. In colour, however, the rooms were not warm, but rather cool and spring-like. Always flowers, and not too many. There was something more flower-like than the flowers,—something in Gabrielle herself (now more herself than ever she had been as Lady Longstreet); the soft pleasure that came into her face when she put out her hand to greet a hero of perhaps seventy years, the look of admiration in her calm grey eyes. A century earlier her French grandmothers may have greeted the dignitaries of the Church with such a look,—deep feeling, without eagerness of any kind. To a badgered Minister, who came in out of committee meetings and dirty weather, the warm house, the charming companionship which had no request lurking behind it, must have been grateful. The lingering touch of a white hand on his black sleeve can do a great deal for an elderly man who has left a busy and fruitless day behind him and who is worn down by the unreasonable demands of his own party. Nothing said in that room got out into the world. Gabrielle never repeated one man to another,—and as for the Honourable MacPhairson, she never gave anything away, not even a good story!

In time there came about a succession of Great Protectors, and Gabrielle Longstreet was more talked about than in the days of her sensational debut. Whether any of them were ever her lovers, no one could say. They were all men much older than she, and only one of them was known for light behaviour with women. Young men were sometimes asked to her house, but they were made to feel it was by special kindness. Henry Seabury himself had been taken there by young Hardwick, when he was still an undergraduate. Seabury had not known her well, however, until she leased a house in New York and spent two winters there. A jealous woman, and a very clever one, had made things unpleasant for her in London, and Gabrielle had quitted England for a time.

Sitting alone that night, recalling all he had heard of Lady Longstreet, Seabury tried to remember her face just as it was in the days when he used to know her; the beautiful contour of the cheeks, the low, straight brow, the lovely line from the chin to the base of the throat. Perhaps it was her eyes he remembered best; no glint in them, no sparkle, no drive. When she was moved by admiration, they did not glow, but became more soft, more grave; a kind of twilight shadow deepened in them. That look, with her calm white shoulders, her unconsciousness of her body and whatever clothed it, gave her the air of having come from afar off.

And now it was all gone. There was something tense, a little defiant in the shoulders now. The hands that used to lie on her dress forgotten, as a bunch of white violets might lie there . . . Well, it was all gone.

Plain women, he reflected, when they grow old are—simply plain women. Often they improve. But a beautiful woman may become a ruin. The more delicate her beauty, the more it owes to some exquisite harmony in modelling and line, the more completely it is destroyed. Gabrielle Longstreet's face was now unrecognizable. She gave it no assistance, certainly. She was the only woman in the dining-room who used no make-up. She met the winter barefaced. Cheap counterfeits meant nothing to a woman who had had the real thing for so long. She must have been close upon forty when he knew her in New York,—and where was there such a creature in the world today? Certainly in his hurried trip across America and England he had not been gladdened by the sight of one. He had seen only cinema stars, and women curled and plucked and painted to look like them. Perhaps the few very beautiful women he remembered in the past had been illusions, had benefited by a romantic tradition which played upon them like a kindly light . . . and by an attitude in men which no longer existed.

v

When Mr. Seabury awoke the next day it was clear to him that any approach to Madame de Couçy must be made through the amiable-seeming friend, Madame Allison as she was called at the hotel, who always accompanied her. He had noticed that this lady usually went down into the town alone in the morning. After breakfasting he walked down the hill and loitered about the little streets. Presently he saw Madame

Allison come out of the English bank, with several small parcels tucked under her arm. He stepped beside her.

"Pardon me, Madame, but I am stopping at your hotel, and I have noticed that you are a friend of Madame de Couçy, whom I think I used to know as Gabrielle Longstreet. It was many years ago, and naturally she does not recognize me. Would it displease her if I sent up my name, do you think?"

Mrs. Allison answered brightly. "Oh, she did recognize you, if you are Mr. Seabury. Shall we sit down in the shade for a moment? I find it very warm here, even for August."

When they were seated under the plane trees she turned to him with a friendly smile and frank curiosity. "She is here for a complete rest and isn't seeing people, but I think she would be glad to see an old friend. She remembers you very well. At first she was not sure about your name, but I asked the porter. She recalled it at once and said she met you with Hardwick, General Hardwick, who was killed in the war. Yes, I'm sure she would be glad to see an old friend."

He explained that he was scarcely an old friend, merely one of many admirers; but he used to go to her house when she lived in New York.

"She said you did. She thought you did not recognize her. But we have all changed, haven't we?"

"And have you and I met before, Madame Allison?"

"Oh, drop the Madame, please! We both speak English, and I am Mrs. Allison. No, we never met. You may have seen me, if you went to the Alhambra. I was Cherry Beamish in those days."

"Then I last saw you in an Eton jacket, with your hair cropped. I never had the pleasure of seeing you out of your character parts, which accounts for my not recognizing—"

She cut him short with a jolly laugh. "Oh, thirty years and two stone would account, would account perfectly! I always did boy parts, you remember. They wouldn't have me in skirts. So I had to keep my weight down. Such a comfort not to fuss about it now. One has a right to a little of one's life, don't you think?"

He agreed. "But I saw you in America also. You had great success there."

She nodded. "Yes, three seasons, grand engagements. I laid

by a pretty penny. I was married over there, and divorced over there, quite in the American style! He was a Scotch boy, stranded in Philadelphia. We parted with no hard feelings, but he was too expensive to keep." Seeing the hotel bus, Mrs. Allison hailed it. "I *shall* be glad if Gabrielle feels up to seeing you. She is frightfully dull here and not very well."

VI

The following evening, as Seabury went into the dining-room and bowed to Mrs. Allison, she beckoned him to Madame de Couçy's table. That lady put out her jewelled hand and spoke abruptly.

"Chetty tells me we are old acquaintances, Mr. Seabury. Will you come up to us for coffee after dinner? This is the number of our apartment." As she gave him her card he saw that her hand trembled slightly. Her voice was much deeper than it used to be, and cold. It had always been cool, but soft, like a cool fragrance,—like her eyes and her white arms.

When he rang at Madame de Couçy's suite an hour later, her maid admitted him. The two ladies were seated before an open window, the coffee table near them and the percolator bubbling. Mrs. Allison was the first to greet him. In a moment she retired, leaving him alone with Madame de Couçy.

"It is very pleasant to meet you again, after so many years, Seabury. How did you happen to come?"

Because he had liked the place long ago, he told her.

"And I, for the same reason. I live in Paris now. Mrs. Allison tells me you have been out in China all this while. And how are things there?"

"Not so good now, Lady Longstreet, may I still call you? China is rather falling to pieces."

"Just as here, eh? No, call me as I am known in this hotel, please. When we are alone, you may use my first name; that has survived time and change. As to change, we have got used to it. But you, coming back upon it, this Europe, suddenly . . . it must give you rather a shock."

It was she herself who had given him the greatest shock of

all, and in one quick, penetrating glance she seemed to read that fact. She shrugged: there was nothing to be done about it. "Chetty, where are you?" she called.

Mrs. Allison came quickly from another room and poured the coffee. Her presence warmed the atmosphere considerably. She seemed unperturbed by the grimness of her friend's manner; and she herself was a most comfortable little person. Even her too evident plumpness was comfortable, since she didn't seem to mind it. She didn't like living in Paris very well, she said; something rather stiff and chilly about it. But she often ran away and went home to see her nieces and nephews, and they were a jolly lot. Yes, she found it very pleasant here at Aix. And now that an old friend of Gabrielle's had obligingly turned up, they would have someone to talk to, and that would be a blessing.

Madame de Couçy gave a low, mirthless laugh. "She seems to take a good deal for granted, doesn't she?"

"Not where I am concerned, if you mean that. I should be deeply grateful for someone to talk to. Between the three of us we may find a great deal."

"Be sure we shall," said Mrs. Allison. "We have the past, and the present—which is really very interesting, if only you will let yourself think so. Some of the people here are very novel and amusing, and others are quite like people we used to know. Don't you find it so, Mr. Seabury?"

He agreed with her and turned to Madame de Couçy. "May I smoke?"

"What a question to ask in these days! Yes, you and Chetty may smoke. I will take a liqueur."

Mrs. Allison rose. "Gabrielle has a cognac so old and precious that we keep it locked in a cabinet behind the piano." In opening the cabinet she overturned a framed photograph which fell to the floor. "There goes the General again! No, he didn't break, dear. We carry so many photographs about with us, Mr. Seabury."

Madame de Couçy turned to Seabury. "Do you recognize some of my old friends? There are some of yours, too, perhaps. I think I was never sentimental when I was young, but now I travel with my photographs. My friends mean more to me now than when they were alive. I was too ignorant then to realize what remarkable men they were. I supposed the world was always full of great men."

She left her chair and walked with him about the salon and the long entrance hall, stopping before one and another; uniforms, military and naval, caps and gowns; photographs, drawings, engravings. As she spoke of them the character of her voice changed altogether,—became, indeed, the voice Seabury remembered. The hard, dry tone was a form of disguise, he conjectured; a protection behind which she addressed people from whom she expected neither recognition nor consideration.

"What an astonishing lot they are, seeing them together like this," he exclaimed with feeling. "How can a world manage to get on without them?"

"It hasn't managed very well, has it? You may remember that I was a rather ungrateful young woman. I took what came. A great man's time, his consideration, his affection, were mine in the natural course of things, I supposed. But it's not so now. I bow down to them in admiration . . . gratitude. They are dearer to me than when they were my living friends,—because I understand them better."

Seabury remarked that the men whose pictures looked down at them were too wise to expect youth and deep discernment in the same person.

"I'm not speaking of discernment; that I had, in a way. I mean ignorance. I simply didn't know all that lay behind them. I am better informed now. I read everything they wrote, and everything that has been written about them. That is my chief pleasure."

Seabury smiled indulgently and shook his head. "It wasn't for what you knew about them that they loved you."

She put her hand quickly on his arm. "Ah, you said that before you had time to think! You believe, then, that I did mean something to them?" For the first time she fixed on him the low, level, wondering look that he remembered of old: the woman he used to know seemed breathing beside him. When she turned away from him suddenly, he knew it was to hide the tears in her eyes. He had seen her cry once, a long time ago. He had not forgotten.

He took up a photograph and talked, to bridge over a

silence in which she could not trust her voice. "What a fine likeness of X—! He was my hero, among the whole group. Perhaps his contradictions fascinated me. I could never see how one side of him managed to live with the other. Yet I know that both sides were perfectly genuine. He was a mystery. And his end was mysterious. No one will ever know where or how. A secret departure on a critical mission, and never an arrival anywhere. It was like him."

Madame de Couçy turned, with a glow in her eyes such as he had never seen there in her youth. "The evening his disappearance was announced . . . Shall I ever forget it! I was in London. The newsboys were crying it in the street. I did not go to bed that night. I sat up in the drawing-room until daylight; hoping, saying the old prayers I used to say with my mother. It was all one could do. . . . Young Harney was with him, you remember. I have always been glad of that. Whatever fate was in store for his chief, Harney would have chosen to share it."

Seabury stayed much longer with Madame de Couçy than he had intended. The ice once broken, he felt he might never find her so much herself again. They sat talking about people who were no longer in this world. She knew much more about them than he. Knew so much that her talk brought back not only the men, but their period; its security, the solid exterior, the exotic contradictions behind the screen; the deep, claret-coloured closing years of Victoria's reign. Nobody ever recognizes a period until it has gone by, he reflected: until it lies behind one it is merely everyday life.

VII

The next evening the Thompsons, all four of them, were to dine with Mr. Seabury at the Maison des Fleurs. Their holiday was over, and they would be leaving on the following afternoon. They would stop once more at that spot in the north, to place fresh wreaths, before they took the Channel boat.

When Seabury and his guests were seated and the dinner had been ordered, he was aware that the mother was looking at him rather wistfully. He felt he owed her some confidence, since it was she, really, who had enlightened him. He told her that he had called upon Gabrielle Longstreet last evening.

"And how is she, dear Mr. Seabury? Is she less—less forbidding than when we see her in the Square?"

"She was on her guard at first, but that soon passed. I stayed later than I should have done, but I had a delightful evening. I gather that she is a little antagonistic to the present order,—indifferent, at least. But when she talks about her old friends she is quite herself."

Mrs. Thompson listened eagerly. She hesitated and then asked: "Does she find life pleasant at all, do you think?"

Seabury told her how the lady was surrounded by the photographs and memoirs of her old friends; how she never travelled without them. It had struck him that she was living her life over again,—more understandingly than she lived it the first time.

Mrs. Thompson breathed a little sigh. "Then I know that all is well with her. You have done so much to make our stay here pleasant, Mr. Seabury, but your telling us this is the best of all. Even Father will be interested to know that."

The stout man, who wore an ancient tail coat made for him when he was much thinner, came out indignantly. "Even Father! I like that! One of the great beauties of our time, and very popular before the divorce."

His daughter laughed and patted his sleeve. Seabury went on to tell Mrs. Thompson that she had been quite right in surmising the companion to be a friend, not a paid attendant. "And a very charming person, too. She was one of your cleverest music-hall stars. Cherry Beamish."

Here Father dropped his spoon into his soup. "What's that? Cherry Beamish? But we haven't had such another since! Remember her in that coster song, Mother? It went round the world, that did. We were all crazy about her, the boys called her Cherish Beamy. No monkeyshines for her, never got herself mixed up in anything shady."

"Such a womanly woman in private life," Mrs. Thompson murmured. "My Dorothy went to school with two of her nieces. An excellent school, and quite dear. Their Aunt Chetty

does everything for them. And now she is with Lady Long-
street! One wouldn't have supposed they'd ever meet, those
two. But then things *are* strange now."

There was no lull in conversation at that dinner. After the
father had enjoyed several glasses of champagne he delighted
his daughters with an account of how Cherry Beamish used
to do the tipsy schoolboy coming in at four in the morning
and meeting his tutor in the garden.

VIII

Mr. Seabury sat waiting before the hotel in a comfortable
car which he now hired by the week. Gabrielle and Chetty
drove out with him every day. This afternoon they were to go
to Annecy by the wild road along the Echelles. Presently Mrs.
Allison came down alone. Gabrielle was staying in bed, she
said. Last night Seabury had dined with them in their apart-
ment, and Gabrielle had talked too much, she was afraid.
"She didn't sleep afterward, but I think she will make it up
today if she is quite alone."

Seabury handed her into the car. In a few minutes they
were running past the lake of Bourget.

"This gives me an opportunity, Mrs. Allison, to ask you
how it came about that you've become Lady Longstreet's
protector. It's a beautiful friendship."

She laughed. "And an amazing one? But I think you must
call me Chetty, as she does, if we are to be confidential. Yes, I
suppose it must seem to you the queerest partnership that war
and desolation have made. But you see, she was so strangely
left. When I first began to look after her a little, two years
ago, she was ill in an hotel in Paris (we have taken a flat
since), and there was no one, positively no one but the hotel
people, the French doctor, and an English nurse who had
chanced to be within call. It was the nurse, really, who gave
me my cure. I had sent flowers, with no name, of course.
(What would a bygone music-hall name mean to Gabrielle
Longstreet?) And I called often to inquire. One morning I
met Nurse Ames just as she was going out into the Champs-
Élysées for her exercise, and she asked me to accompany her.
She was an experienced woman, not young. She remembered

when Gabrielle Longstreet's name and photographs were known all over the Continent, and when people at home were keen enough upon meeting her. And here she was, dangerously ill in a foreign hotel, and there was no one, simply no one. To be sure, she was registered under the name of her second husband."

Seabury interrupted. "And who was he, this de Couçy? I have heard nothing about him."

"I know very little myself, I never met him. They had been friends a long while, I believe. He was killed in action—less than a year after they were married. His name was a disguise for her, even then. She came from Martinique, you remember, and she had no relatives in England. Longstreet's people had never liked her. So, you see, she was quite alone."

Seabury took her plump little hand. "And that was where you came in, Chetty?"

She gave his fingers a squeeze. "Thank you! That's nice. It was Nurse Ames who did it. The war made a lot of wise nurses. After Gabrielle was well enough to see people, there was no one for her to see! The same thing that had happened to her friends in England had happened over here. The old men had paid the debt of nature, and the young ones were killed or disabled or had lost touch with her. She once had many friends in Paris. Nurse Ames told me that an old French officer, blinded in the war, sometimes came to see her, guided by his little granddaughter. She said her patient had expressed curiosity about the English woman who had sent so many flowers. I wrote a note, asking whether I could be of any service, and signed my professional name. She might recognize it, she might not. We had been on a committee together during the war. She told the nurse to admit me, and that's how it began."

Seabury took her hand again. "Now I want you to be frank with me. Had she then, or has she now, money worries at all?"

Cherry Beamish chuckled. "Not she, you may believe! But I have had a few for her. On the whole, she's behaved very well. She sold her place in Devonshire to advantage, before the war. Her capital is in British bonds. She seems to you harassed?"

"Sometimes."

Mrs. Allison looked grave and was silent for a little. "Yes," with a sigh, "she gets very low at times. She suffers from strange regrets. She broods on the things she might have done for her friends and didn't,—thinks she was cold to them. Was she, in those days, so indifferent as she makes herself believe?"

Seabury reflected. "Not exactly indifferent. She wouldn't have been so attractive if she'd been that. She didn't take things very hard, perhaps. She used to strike me as . . . well, we might call it unawakened."

"But wasn't she the most beautiful creature then! I used to see her at the races, and at charity bazaars, in my early professional days. After the war broke out and everybody was all mixed up, I was put on an entertainment committee with her. She wasn't quite the Lady Longstreet of my youth, but she still had that grand style. It was the illness in Paris that broke her. She's changed very fast ever since. You see she thought, once the war was over, the world would be just as it used to be. Of course it isn't."

By this time the car had reached Annecy, and they stopped for tea. The shore of the lake was crowded with young people taking their last dip for the day; sunbrowned backs and shoulders, naked arms and legs. As Mrs. Allison was having her tea on the terrace, she watched the bathers. Presently she twinkled a sly smile at her host. "Do you know, I'm rather glad we didn't bring Gabrielle! It puts her out terribly to see young people bathing naked. She makes comments that are indecent, really! If only she had a swarm of young nieces and nephews, as I have, she'd see things quite differently, and she'd be much happier. Legs were never wicked to us stage people, and now all the young things know they are not wicked."

IX

When Madame de Couçy went out with Seabury alone, he missed the companionship of Cherry Beamish. With Cherry the old beauty always softened a little; seemed amused by the other's interest in whatever the day produced: the countryside, the weather, the number of cakes she permitted herself for tea. The imagination which made this strange friendship possible was certainly on the side of Cherry Beamish. For her, he could see, there was something in it; to be the anchor, the refuge, indeed, of one so out of her natural orbit,—selected by her long ago as an object of special admiration.

One afternoon when he called, the maid, answering his ring, said that Madame would not go out this afternoon, but hoped he would stay and have tea with her in her salon. He told the lift boy to dismiss the car and went in to Madame de Couçy. She received him with unusual warmth.

"Chetty is out for the afternoon, with some friends from home. Oh, she still has a great many! She is much younger than I, in every sense. Today I particularly wanted to see you alone. It's curious how the world runs away from one, slips by without one's realizing it."

He reminded her that the circumstances had been unusual. "We have lived through a storm to which the French Revolution, which used to be our standard of horrors, was merely a breeze. A rather gentlemanly affair, as one looks back on it. . . . As for me, I am grateful to be alive, sitting here with you in a comfortable hotel (I might be in a prison full of rats), in a France still undestroyed."

The old lady looked into his eyes with the calm, level gaze so rare with her now. "Are you grateful? I am not. I think one should go out with one's time. I particularly wished to see you alone this afternoon. I want to thank you for your tact and gentleness with me one hideous evening long ago; in my house in New York. You were a darling boy to me that night. If you hadn't come along, I don't know how I would have got over it—out of it, even. One can't call the servants."

"But, Gabrielle, why recall a disagreeable incident when you have so many agreeable ones to remember?"

She seemed not to hear him, but went on, speaking deliberately, as if she were reflecting aloud. "It was strange, your coming in just when you did: that night it seemed to me like a miracle. Afterward, I remembered you had been expected at eight. But I had forgotten all that, forgotten everything. Never before or since have I been so frightened. It was something worse than fear."

There was a knock at the door. Madame de Couçy called:

"*Entrez!*" without turning round. While the tea was brought she sat looking out of the window, frowning. When the waiter had gone she turned abruptly to Seabury:

"After that night I never saw you again until you walked into the dining-room of this hotel a few weeks ago. I had gone into the country somewhere, hiding with friends, and when I came back to New York, you were already on your way to China. I never had a chance to explain."

"There was certainly no need for that."

"Not for you, perhaps. But for me. You may have thought such scenes were frequent in my life. Hear me out, please," as he protested. "That man had come to my house at seven o'clock that evening and sent up a message begging me to see him about some business matters. (I had been stupid enough to let him make investments for me.) I finished dressing and hurried down to the drawing-room." Here she stopped and slowly drank a cup of tea. "Do you know, after you came in I did not see you at all, not for some time, I think. I was mired down in something . . . *the power of the dog*, the English Prayer Book calls it. But the moment I heard your voice, I knew that I was safe . . . I felt the leech drop off. I have never forgot the sound of your voice that night; so calm, with all a man's strength behind it,—and you were only a boy. You merely asked if you had come too early. I felt the leech drop off. After that I remember nothing. I didn't see you, with my eyes, until you gave me your handkerchief. You stayed with me and looked after me all evening.

"You see, I had let the beast come to my house, oh, a number of times! I had asked his advice and allowed him to make investments for me. I had done the same thing at home with men who knew about such matters; they were men like yourself and Hardwick. In a strange country one goes astray in one's reckonings. I had met that man again and again at the houses of my friends,—your friends! Of course his personality was repulsive to me. One knew at once that under his smoothness he was a vulgar person. I supposed that was not unusual in great bankers in the States."

"You simply chose the wrong banker, Gabrielle. The man's accent must have told you that he belonged to a country you did not admire."

"But I tell you I met him at the houses of decent people."

Seabury shook his head. "Yes, I am afraid you must blame us for that. Americans, even those whom you call the decent ones, do ask people to their houses who shouldn't be there. They are often asked *because* they are outrageous,—and therefore considered amusing. Besides, that fellow had a very clever way of pushing himself. If a man is generous in his contributions to good causes, and is useful on committees and commissions, he is asked to the houses of the people who have these good causes at heart."

"And perhaps I, too, was asked because I was considered notorious? A divorcée, known to have more friends among men than among women at home? I think I see what you mean. There are not many shades in your society. I left the States soon after you sailed for China. I gave up my New York house at a loss to be rid of it. The instant I recognized you in the dining-room downstairs, that miserable evening came back to me. In so far as our acquaintance was concerned, all that had happened only the night before."

"Then I am reaping a reward I didn't deserve, some thirty years afterward! If I had not happened to call that evening when you were so—so unpleasantly surprised, you would never have remembered me at all! We shouldn't be sitting together at this moment. Now may I ring for some fresh tea, dear? Let us be comfortable. This afternoon has brought us closer together. And this little spot in Savoie is a nice place to renew old friendships, don't you think?"

X

Some hours later, when Mr. Seabury was dressing for dinner, he was thinking of that strange evening in Gabrielle Longstreet's house on Fifty-third Street, New York.

He was then twenty-four years old. She had been very gracious to him all the winter.

On that particular evening he was to take her to dine at Delmonico's. Her cook and butler were excused to attend a wedding. The maid who answered his ring asked him to go up to the drawing-room on the second floor, where Madame was awaiting him. She followed him as far as the turn of the stairway, then, hearing another ring at the door, she excused herself.

He went on alone. As he approached the wide doorway leading into the drawing-room, he was conscious of something unusual; a sound, or perhaps an unnatural stillness. From the doorway he beheld something quite terrible. At the far end of the room Gabrielle Longstreet was seated on a little French sofa—not seated, but silently struggling. Behind the sofa stood a stout, dark man leaning over her. His left arm, about her waist, pinioned her against the flowered silk upholstery. His right hand was thrust deep into the low-cut bodice of her dinner gown. In her struggle she had turned a little on her side; her right arm was in the grip of his left hand, and she was trying to free the other, which was held down by the pressure of his elbow. Neither of those two made a sound. Her face was averted, half hidden against the blue silk back of the sofa. Young Seabury stood still just long enough to see what the situation really was. Then he stepped across the threshold and said with such coolness as he could command: "Am I too early, Madame Longstreet?"

The man behind her started from his crouching position, darted away from the sofa, and disappeared down the stairway. To reach the stairs he passed Seabury, without lifting his eyes, but his face was glistening wet.

The lady lay without stirring, her face now completely hidden. She looked so crushed and helpless, he thought she must be hurt physically. He spoke to her softly: "Madame Longstreet, shall I call—"

"Oh, don't call! Don't call anyone." She began shuddering violently, her face still turned away. "Some brandy, please. Downstairs, in the dining-room."

He ran down the stairs, had to tell the solicitous maid that Madame wished to be alone for the present. When he came back Gabrielle had caught up the shoulder straps of her gown. Her right arm bore red finger marks. She was shivering and sobbing. He slipped his handkerchief into her hand, and she held it over her mouth. She took a little brandy. Then another fit of weeping came on. He begged her to come nearer to the fire. She put her hand on his arm, but seemed unable to rise. He lifted her from that seat of humiliation and took her, wavering between his supporting hands, to a low chair beside the coal grate. She sank into it, and he put a cushion under her feet. He persuaded her to drink the rest of the brandy. She stopped crying and leaned back, her eyes closed, her hands lying nerveless on the arms of the chair. Seabury thought he had never seen her when she was more beautiful . . . probably that was because she was helpless and he was young.

"Perhaps you would like me to go now?" he asked her.

She opened her eyes. "Oh, no! Don't leave me, please. I am so much safer with you here." She put her hand, still cold, on his for a moment, then closed her eyes and went back into that languor of exhaustion.

Perhaps half an hour went by. She did not stir, but he knew she was not asleep: an occasional trembling of the eyelids, tears stealing out from under her black lashes and glistening unregarded on her cheeks; like pearls he thought they were, transparent shimmers on velvet cheeks gone very white.

When suddenly she sat up, she spoke in her natural voice.

"But, my dear boy, you have gone dinnerless all this while! Won't you stay with me and have just a bit of something up here? Do ring for Hopkins, please."

The young man caught at the suggestion. If once he could get her mind on the duties of caring for a guest, that might lead to something. He must try to be very hungry.

The kitchen maid was in and, under Hopkins's direction, got together a creditable supper and brought it up to the drawing-room. Gabrielle took nothing but the hot soup and a little sherry. Young Seabury, once he tasted food, found he had no difficulty in doing away with cold pheasant and salad.

Gabrielle had quite recovered her self-control. She talked very little, but that was not unusual with her. He told her about Hardwick's approaching marriage. For him, the evening went by very pleasantly. He felt with her a closer intimacy than ever before.

When at midnight he rose to take his leave, she detained him beside her chair, holding his hand. "At some other time I shall explain what you saw here tonight. How could such a thing happen in one's own house, in an English-speaking city . . . ?"

"But that was not an English-speaking man who went out from here. He is an immigrant who has made a lot of money. He does not belong."

"Yes, that is true. I wish you weren't going out to China. Not for long, I hope. It's a bad thing to be away from one's own people." Her voice broke, and tears came again. He kissed her hand softly, devotedly, and went downstairs.

He had not seen her again until his arrival at this hotel some weeks ago, when he did not recognize her.

XI

One evening when Mrs. Allison and Madame de Couçy had been dining with Seabury at the Maison des Fleurs, they went into the tea room to have their coffee and watch the dancing. It was now September, and almost everyone would be leaving next week. The floor was full of young people, English, American, French, moving monotonously to monotonous rhythms,—some of them scarcely moving at all. Gabrielle watched them through her lorgnette, with a look of resigned boredom.

Mrs. Allison frowned at her playfully. "Of course it's all very different," she observed, "but then, so is everything." She turned to Seabury: "You know we used to have to put so much drive into a dance act, or it didn't go at all. Lottie Collins was the only lazy dancer who could get anything over. But the truth was, the dear thing couldn't dance at all; got on by swinging her foot! There must be something in all this new manner, if only one could get it. That couple down by the bar now, the girl with the *very* low back: they are doing it beautifully; she dips and rises like a bird in the air . . . a tired bird, though. That's the disconcerting thing. It all seems so tired."

Seabury agreed with her cheerfully that it was charming, though tired. He felt a gathering chill in the lady on his right. Presently she said impatiently: "Haven't you had enough of this, Chetty?"

Mrs. Allison sighed. "You never see anything in it, do you, dear?"

"I see wriggling. They look to me like lizards dancing—or reptiles coupling."

"Oh, no, dear! No! They are such sweet young things. But they are dancing in a dream. I want to go and wake them up. They are missing so much fun. Dancing ought to be open and free, with the lungs full; not mysterious and breathless. I wish I could see a *spirited* waltz again."

Gabrielle shrugged and gave a dry laugh. "I wish I could dance one! I think I should try, if by any chance I should ever hear a waltz played again."

Seabury rose from his chair. "May I take you up on that? Will you?"

She seemed amused and incredulous, but nodded.

"Excuse me for a moment." He strolled toward the orchestra. When the tango was over he spoke to the conductor, handing him something from his vest pocket. The conductor smiled and bowed, then spoke to his men, who smiled in turn. The saxophone put down his instrument and grinned. The strings sat up in their chairs, pulled themselves up, as it were, tuned for a moment, and sat at attention. At the lift of the leader's hand they began the "Blue Danube."

Gabrielle took Mr. Seabury's arm. They passed a dozen couples who were making a sleepy effort and swung into the open square where the line of tables stopped. Seabury had never danced with Gabrielle Longstreet, and he was astonished. She had attack and style, the grand style, slightly military, quite right for her tall, straight figure. He held her hand very high, accordingly. The conductor caught the idea; smartened the tempo slightly, made the accents sharper. One by one the young couples dropped out and sat down to smoke. The two old waltzers were left alone on the floor. There was a stir of curiosity about the room; who were those two, and why were they doing it? Cherry Beamish heard remarks from the adjoining tables.

"She's rather stunning, the old dear!"

"Aren't they funny?"

"It's so quaint and theatrical. Quite effective in its way."

Seabury had not danced for some time. He thought the musicians drew the middle part out interminably; rather suspected they were playing a joke on him. But his partner lost none of her brilliance and verve. He tried to live up to her. He was grateful when those fiddlers snapped out the last phrase. As he took Gabrielle to her seat, a little breeze of applause broke out from the girls about the room.

"Dear young things!" murmured Chetty, who was flushed with pleasure and excitement. A group of older men who had come in from the dining-room were applauding.

"Let us go now, Seabury. I am afraid we have been making rather an exhibition," murmured Madame de Couçy. As they got into the car awaiting them outside, she laughed good-humouredly. "Do you know, Chetty, I quite enjoyed it!"

XII

The next morning Mrs. Allison telephoned Seabury that Gabrielle had slept well after an amusing evening: felt so fit that she thought they might seize upon this glorious morning for a drive to the Grande-Chartreuse. The drive, by the route they preferred, was a long one, and hitherto she had not felt quite equal to it. Accordingly, the three left the hotel at eleven o'clock with Seabury's trusty young Savoyard driver, and were soon in the mountains.

It was one of those high-heavenly days that often come among the mountains of Savoie in autumn. In the valleys the hillsides were pink with autumn crocuses thrusting up out of the short sunburned grass. The beech trees still held their satiny green. As the road wound higher and higher toward the heights, Seabury and his companions grew more and more silent. The lightness and purity of the air gave one a sense of detachment from everything one had left behind "down there, back yonder." Mere breathing was a delicate physical pleasure. One had the feeling that life would go on thus forever in high places, among naked peaks cut sharp against a stainless sky.

Ever afterward Seabury remembered that drive as strangely impersonal. He and the two ladies were each lost in a companionship much closer than any they could share with one another. The clean-cut mountain boy who drove them seemed lost in thoughts of his own. His eyes were on the road: he never spoke. Once, when the gold tones of an alpine horn floated down from some hidden pasture far overhead, he stopped the car of his own accord and shut off the engine. He threw a smiling glance back at Seabury and then sat still, while the simple, melancholy song floated down through the blue air. When it ceased, he waited a little, looking up. As the horn did not sing again, he drove on without comment.

At last, beyond a sharp turn in the road, the monastery came into view; acres of slate roof, of many heights and pitches, turrets and steep slopes. The terrifying white mountain crags overhung it from behind, and the green beech wood lay all about its walls. The sunlight blazing down upon that mothering roof showed ruined patches: the Government could not afford to keep such a wilderness of leading in repair.

The monastery, superb and solitary among the lonely mountains, was after all a destination: brought Seabury's party down into man's world again, though it was the world of the past. They began to chatter foolishly, after hours of silent reflection. Mrs. Allison wished to see the kitchen of the Carthusians, and the chapel, but she thought Gabrielle should stay in the car. Madame de Couçy insisted that she was not tired: she would walk about the stone courtyard while the other two went into the monastery.

Except for a one armed guard in uniform, the great court was empty. Herbs and little creeping plants grew between the cobblestones. The three walked toward the great open well and leaned against the stone wall that encircled it, looking down into its wide mouth. The hewn blocks of the coping were moss-grown, and there was water at the bottom. Madame de Couçy slipped a little mirror from her handbag and threw a sunbeam down into the stone-lined well. That yellow ray seemed to waken the black water at the bottom: little ripples stirred over the surface. She said nothing, but she smiled as she threw the gold plaque over the water and the wet moss of the lower coping. Chetty and Seabury left her there. When he glanced back, just before they disappeared into the labyrinth of buildings, she was still looking down into the well and playing with her little reflector, a faintly contemptuous smile on her lips.

After nearly two hours at the monastery the party started homeward. Seabury told the driver to regulate his speed so that they would see the last light on the mountains before they reached the hotel.

The return trip was ill-starred: they narrowly escaped a serious accident. As they rounded one of those sharp curves, with a steep wall on their right and an open gulf on the left, the chauffeur was confronted by a small car with two women, crossing the road just in front of him. To avoid throwing them over the precipice he ran sharply to the right, grazing the rock wall until he could bring his car to a stop. His passengers were thrown violently forward over the driver's seat. The light car had been on the wrong side of the road, and had attempted to cross on hearing the Savoyard's horn. His nerve and quickness had brought every one off alive, at least.

Immediately the two women from the other car sprang out and ran up to Seabury with shrill protestations; they were very careful drivers, had run this car twelve thousand miles and never had an accident, etc. They were Americans; bobbed, hatless, clad in dirty white knickers and sweaters. They addressed each other as "Marge" and "Jim." Seabury's forehead was bleeding: they repeatedly offered to plaster it up for him.

The Savoyard was in the road, working with his mudguard and his front wheel. Madame de Couçy was lying back in her seat, pale, her eyes closed, something very wrong with her breathing. Mrs. Allison was fanning her with Seabury's hat. The two girls who had caused all the trouble had lit cigarettes and were swaggering about with their hands in their trousers pockets, giving advice to the driver about his wheel. The Savoyard never lifted his eyes. He had not spoken since he ran his car into the wall. The sharp voices, knowingly ordering him to *"regardez, attendez,"* did not pierce his silence or his contempt. Seabury paid no attention to them because he was alarmed about Madame de Couçy, who looked desperately ill. She ought to lie down, he felt sure, but there was no place to put her—the road was cut along the face of a cliff for a long way back. Chetty had aromatic ammonia in her handbag; she persuaded Gabrielle to take it from the bottle, as they had no cup. While Seabury was leaning over her she opened her eyes and said distinctly:

"I think I am not hurt . . . faintness, a little palpitation. If you could get those creatures away . . ."

He sprang off the running-board and drew the two intruders aside. He addressed them; first politely, then forcibly. Their reply was impertinent, but they got into their dirty little car and went. The Savoyard was left in peace; the situation was simplified. Three elderly people had been badly shaken up and bruised, but the brief submersion in frightfulness was over. At last the driver said he could get his car home safely.

During the rest of the drive Madame de Couçy seemed quite restored. Her colour was not good, but her self-control was admirable.

"You must let me give that boy something on my own account, Seabury. Oh, I know you will be generous with him! But I feel a personal interest. He took a risk, and he took the right one. He couldn't run the chance of knocking two women over a precipice. They happened to be worth nobody's consideration, but that doesn't alter the code."

"Such an afternoon to put you through!" Seabury groaned.

"It was natural, wasn't it, after such a morning? After one has been *exaltée*, there usually comes a shock. Oh, I don't mean the bruises we got! I mean the white breeches." Gabrielle laughed, her good laugh, with no malice in it. She put her hand on his shoulder. "How ever did you manage to dispose of them so quickly?"

When the car stopped before the hotel, Madame de Couçy put a tiny card case into the driver's hand with a smile and a word. But when she tried to rise from the seat, she sank back. Seabury and the Savoyard lifted her out, carried her into the hotel and up the lift, into her own chamber. As they placed her on the bed, Seabury said he would call a doctor. Madame de Couçy opened her eyes and spoke firmly:

"That is not necessary. Chetty knows what to do for me. I shall be myself tomorrow. Thank you both, thank you."

Outside the chamber door Seabury asked Mrs. Allison whether he should telephone for Doctor Françon.

"I think not. A new person would only disturb her. I have

all the remedies her own doctor gave me for these attacks. Quiet is the most important thing, really."

The next morning Seabury was awakened very early, something before six o'clock, by the buzz of his telephone. Mrs. Allison spoke, asking in a low voice if he would come to their apartment as soon as possible. He dressed rapidly. The lift was not yet running, so he went up two flights of stairs and rang at their door. Cherry Beamish, in her dressing-gown, admitted him. From her face he knew, at once,—though her smile was almost radiant as she took his hand.

"Yes, it is over for her, poor dear," she said softly. "It must have happened in her sleep. I was with her until after midnight. When I went in again, a little after five, I found her just as I want you to see her now; before her maid comes, before anyone has been informed."

She led him on tiptoe into Gabrielle's chamber. The first shafts of the morning sunlight slanted through the Venetian blinds. A blue dressing-gown hung on a tall chair beside the bed, blue slippers beneath it. Gabrielle lay on her back, her eyes closed. The face that had outfaced so many changes of fortune had no longer need to muffle itself in furs, to shrink away from curious eyes, or harden itself into scorn. It lay on the pillow regal, calm, victorious,—like an open confession.

Seabury stood for a moment looking down at her. Then he went to the window and peered out through the open slats at the sun, come at last over the mountains into a sky that had long been blue: the same mountains they were driving among yesterday.

Presently Cherry Beamish spoke to him. She pointed to the hand that lay on the turned-back sheet. "See how changed her hands are; like those of a young woman. She forgot to take off her rings last night, or she was too tired. Yes, dear, you needed a long rest. And now you are with your own kind."

"I feel that, too, Chetty. She is with them. All is well. Thank you for letting me come." He stooped for a moment over the hand that had been gracious to his youth. They went out into the salon, carefully closing the door behind them.

"Now, my dear, stay here, with her. I will go to the management, and I will arrange all that must be done."

Some hours later, after he had gone through the formalities required by French law, Seabury encountered the three journalists in front of the hotel.

Next morning the great man from the Riviera to whom Seabury had telegraphed came in person, his car laden with flowers from his conservatories. He stood on the platform at the railway station, his white head uncovered, all the while that the box containing Gabrielle Longstreet's coffin was being carried across and put on the express. Then he shook Seabury's hand in farewell, and bent gallantly over Chetty's. Seabury and Chetty were going to Paris on that same express.

After her illness two years ago Gabrielle de Couçy had bought a lot *à perpétuité* in Père-Lachaise. That was rather a fashion then: Adelina Patti, Sarah Bernhardt, and other ladies who had once held a place in the world made the same choice.

The Best Years

I

O<small>N A BRIGHT</small> September morning in the year 1899 Miss
Evangeline Knightly was driving through the beautiful
Nebraska land which lies between the Platte River and the
Kansas line. She drove slowly, for she loved the country, and
she held the reins loosely in her gloved hand. She drove about
a great deal and always wore leather gauntlets. Her hands
were small, well shaped and very white, but they freckled in
hot sunlight.

Miss Knightly was a charming person to meet—and an un-
usual type in a new country: oval face, small head delicately
set (the oval chin tilting inward instead of the square chin
thrust out), hazel eyes, a little blue, a little green, tiny dots of
brown. . . . Somehow these splashes of colour made light—
and warmth. When she laughed, her eyes positively glowed
with humour, and in each oval cheek a roguish dimple came
magically to the surface. Her laugh was delightful because it
was intelligent, discriminating, not the physical spasm which
seizes children when they are tickled, and growing boys
and girls when they are embarrassed. When Miss Knightly
laughed, it was apt to be because of some happy coincidence
or droll mistake. The farmers along the road always felt flat-
tered if they could make Miss Knightly laugh. Her voice had
as many colours as her eyes—nearly always on the bright
side, though it had a beautiful gravity for people who were in
trouble.

It is only fair to say that in the community where she lived
Miss Knightly was considered an intelligent young woman,
but plain—distinctly plain. The standard of female beauty
seems to be the same in all newly settled countries: Australia,
New Zealand, the farming country along the Platte. It is, and
was, the glowing, smiling calendar girl sent out to advertise
agricultural implements. Colour was everything, modelling
was nothing. A nose was a nose—any shape would do; a
forehead was the place where the hair stopped, chin utterly
negligible unless it happened to be more than two inches long.

Miss Knightly's old mare, Molly, took her time along the dusty, sunflower-bordered roads that morning, occasionally pausing long enough to snatch off a juicy, leafy sunflower top in her yellow teeth. This she munched as she ambled along. Although Molly had almost the slowest trot in the world, she really preferred walking. Sometimes she fell into a doze and stumbled. Miss Knightly also, when she was abroad on these long drives, preferred the leisurely pace. She loved the beautiful autumn country; loved to look at it, to breathe it. She was not a "dreamy" person, but she was thoughtful and very observing. She relished the morning; the great blue of the sky, smiling, cloudless,—and the land that lay level as far as the eye could see. The horizon was like a perfect circle, a great embrace, and within it lay the cornfields, still green, and the yellow wheat stubble, miles and miles of it, and the pasture lands where the white-faced cattle led lives of utter content. All their movements were deliberate and dignified. They grazed through all the morning; approached their metal water tank and drank. If the windmill had run too long and the tank had overflowed, the cattle trampled the overflow into deep mud and cooled their feet. Then they drifted off to graze again. Grazing was not merely eating, it was also a pastime, a form of reflection, perhaps meditation.

Miss Knightly was thinking, as Molly jogged along, that the barbed-wire fences, though ugly in themselves, had their advantages. They did not cut the country up into patterns as did the rail fences and stone walls of her native New England. They were, broadly regarded, invisible—did not impose themselves upon the eye. She seemed to be driving through a fineless land. On her left the Hereford cattle apparently wandered at will: the tall sunflowers hid the wire that kept them off the road. Far away, on the horizon line, a troop of colts were galloping, all in the same direction—purely for exercise, one would say. Between her and the horizon the white wheels of windmills told her where the farmhouses sat.

Miss Knightly was abroad this morning with a special purpose—to visit country schools. She was the County Superintendent of Public Instruction. A grim title, that, to put upon a charming young woman. . . . Fortunately it was seldom used except on reports which she signed, and there it was usually printed. She was not even called "the Superintendent." A country schoolteacher said to her pupils: "I think Miss Knightly will come to see us this week. She was at Walnut Creek yesterday."

After she had driven westward through the pasture lands for an hour or so, Miss Knightly turned her mare north and very soon came into a rich farming district, where the fields were too valuable to be used for much grazing. Big red barns, rows of yellow straw stacks, green orchards, trim white farmhouses, fenced gardens.

Looking at her watch, Miss Knightly found that it was already after eleven o'clock. She touched Molly delicately with the whip and roused her to a jog trot. Presently they stopped before a little one-storey schoolhouse. All the windows were open. At the hitch-bar in the yard five horses were tethered— their saddles and bridles piled in an empty buckboard. There was a yard, but no fence—though on one side of the playground was a woven-wire fence covered with the vines of sturdy rambler roses—very pretty in the spring. It enclosed a cemetery—very few graves, very much sun and waving yellow grass, open to the singing from the schoolroom and the shouts of the boys playing ball at noon. The cemetery never depressed the children, and surely the school cast no gloom over the cemetery.

When Miss Knightly stopped before the door, a boy ran out to hand her from the buggy and to take care of Molly. The little teacher stood on the doorstep, her face lost, as it were, in a wide smile of tremulous gladness.

Miss Knightly took her hand, held it for a moment and looked down into the child's face—she was scarcely more— and said in the very gentlest shade of her many-shaded voice, "Everything going well, Lesley?"

The teacher replied in happy little gasps, "Oh yes, Miss Knightly! It's all so much easier than it was last year. I have some such lovely children—and they're all *good*!"

Miss Knightly took her arm, and they went into the schoolroom. The pupils grinned a welcome to the visitor. The teacher asked the conventional question: What recitation would she like to hear?

Whatever came next in the usual order, Miss Knightly said.

The class in geography came next. The children were "bounding" the States. When the North Atlantic States had been disposed of with more or less accuracy, the little teacher said they would now jump to the Middle West, to bring the lesson nearer home.

"Suppose we begin with Illinois. That is your State, Edward, so I will call on you."

A pale boy rose and came front of the class; a little fellow aged ten, maybe, who was plainly a newcomer—wore knee pants and stockings, instead of long trousers or blue overalls like the other boys. His hands were clenched at his sides, and he was evidently much frightened. Looking appealingly at the little teacher, he began in a high treble: "The State of Illinois is bounded on the north by Lake Michigan, on the east by Lake Michigan . . ." He felt he had gone astray, and language utterly failed. A quick shudder ran over him from head to foot, and an accident happened. His dark blue stockings grew darker still, and his knickerbockers very dark. He stood there as if nailed to the floor. The teacher went up to him and took his hand and led him to his desk.

"You're too tired, Edward," she said. "We're all tired, and it's almost noon. So you can all run out and play, while I talk to Miss Knightly and tell her how naughty you all are."

The children laughed (all but poor Edward), laughed heartily, as if they were suddenly relieved from some strain. Still laughing and punching each other they ran out into the sunshine.

Miss Knightly and the teacher (her name, by the way, was Lesley Ferguesson) sat down on a bench in the corner.

"I'm so sorry that happened, Miss Knightly. I oughtn't to have called on him. He's so new here, and he's a nervous little boy. I thought he'd like to speak up for his State. He seems homesick."

"My dear, I'm glad you did call on him, and I'm glad the poor little fellow had an accident,—if he doesn't get too much misery out of it. The way those children behaved astonished me. Not a wink, or grin, or even a look. Not a wink from the Haymaker boy. I watched him. His mother has no such delicacy. They have just the best kind of good manners. How do you do it, Lesley?"

Lesley gave a happy giggle and flushed as red as a poppy. "Oh, I don't do anything! You see they really *are* nice children. You remember last year I did have a little trouble — till they got used to me."

"But they all passed their finals, and one girl, who was older than her teacher, got a school."

"Hush, hush, ma'am! I'm afraid for the walls to hear it! Nobody knows our secret but my mother."

"I'm very well satisfied with the results of our crime, Lesley."

The girl blushed again. She loved to hear Miss Knightly speak her name, because she always sounded the *s* like a *z*, which made it seem gentler and more intimate. Nearly everyone else, even her mother, hissed the *s* as if it were spelled "Lessley." It was embarrassing to have such a queer name, but she respected it because her father had chosen it for her.

"Where are you going to stay all night, Miss Knightly?" she asked rather timidly.

"I think Mrs. Ericson expects me to stay with her."

"Mrs. Hunt, where I stay, would be awful glad to have you, but I know you'll be more comfortable at Mrs. Ericson's. She's a lovely housekeeper." Lesley resigned the faint hope that Miss Knightly would stay where she herself boarded, and broke out eagerly:

"Oh, Miss Knightly, have you seen any of our boys lately? Mother's too busy to write to me often."

"Hector looked in at my office last week. He came to the Court House with a telegram for the sheriff. He seemed well and happy."

"Did he? But Miss Knightly, I wish he hadn't taken that messenger job. I hate so for him to quit school."

"Now, I wouldn't worry about that, my dear. School isn't everything. He'll be getting good experience every day at the depot."

"Do you think so? I haven't seen him since he went to work."

"Why, how long has it been since you were home?"

"It's over a month now. Not since my school started. Father has been working all our horses on the farm. Maybe you can share my lunch with me?"

"I brought a lunch for the two of us, my dear. Call your favourite boy to go to my buggy and get my basket for us. After lunch I would like to hear the advanced arithmetic class."

While the pupils were doing their sums at the blackboard, Miss Knightly herself was doing a little figuring. This was Thursday. Tomorrow she would visit two schools, and she had planned to spend Friday night with a pleasant family on Farmers' Creek. But she could change her schedule and give this homesick child a visit with her family in the county seat. It would inconvenience her very little.

When the class in advanced arithmetic was dismissed, Miss Knightly made a joking little talk to the children and told them about a very bright little girl in Scotland who knew nearly a whole play of Shakespeare's by heart, but who wrote in her diary: "Nine times nine is the Devil"; which proved, she said, that there are two kinds of memory, and God is very good to anyone to whom he gives both kinds. Then she asked if the pupils might have a special recess of half an hour, as a present from her. They gave her a cheer and out they trooped, the boys to the ball ground, and the girls to the cemetery, to sit neatly on the headstones and discuss Miss Knightly.

During their recess the Superintendent disclosed her plan. "I've been wondering, Lesley, whether you wouldn't like to go back to town with me after school tomorrow. We could get into MacAlpin by seven o'clock, and you could have all of Saturday and Sunday at home. Then we would make an early start Monday morning, and I would drop you here at the schoolhouse at nine o'clock."

The little teacher caught her breath—she became quite pale for a moment.

"Oh Miss Knightly, could you? Could you?"

"Of course I can. I'll stop for you here at four o'clock to-morrow afternoon."

II

The dark secret between Lesley and Miss Knightly was that only this September had the girl reached the legal age for teachers, yet she had been teaching all last year when she was still under age!

Last summer, when the applicants for teachers' certificates took written examinations in the County Superintendent's offices at the Court House in MacAlpin, Lesley Ferguesson had appeared with some twenty-six girls and nine boys. She wrote all morning and all afternoon for two days. Miss Knightly found her paper one of the best in the lot. A week later, when all the papers were filed, Miss Knightly told Lesley she could certainly give her a school. The morning after she had thus notified Lesley, she found the girl herself waiting on the sidewalk in front of the house where Miss Knightly boarded.

"Could I walk over to the Court House with you, Miss Knightly? I ought to tell you something," she blurted out at once. "On that paper I didn't put down my real age. I put down sixteen, and I won't be fifteen until this September."

"But I checked you with the high-school records, Lesley."

"I know. I put it down wrong there, too. I didn't want to be the class baby, and I hoped I could get a school soon, to help out at home."

The County Superintendent thought she would long remember that walk to the Court House. She could see that the child had spent a bad night; and she had walked up from her home down by the depot, quite a mile away, probably without breakfast.

"If your age is wrong on both records, why do you tell me about it now?"

"Oh, Miss Knightly, I got to thinking about it last night, how if you did give me a school it might all come out, and mean people would say you knew about it and broke the law."

Miss Knightly was thoughtless enough to chuckle. "But, my dear, don't you see that if I didn't know about it until this moment, I am completely innocent?"

The child who was walking beside her stopped short and burst into sobs. Miss Knightly put her arm around those thin, eager, forward-reaching shoulders.

"Don't cry, dear. I was only joking. There's nothing very dreadful about it. You didn't give your age under oath, you know." The sobs didn't stop. "Listen, let me tell you some-

thing. That big Hatch boy put his age down as nineteen, and
I know he was teaching down in Nemaha County four years
ago. I can't always be sure about the age applicants put down.
I have to use my judgment."

The girl lifted her pale, troubled face and murmured,
"Judgment?"

"Yes. Some girls are older at thirteen than others are at
eighteen. Your paper was one of the best handed in this year,
and I am going to give you a school. Not a big one, but a
nice one, in a nice part of the county. Now let's go into Er-
nie's coffee shop and have some more breakfast. You have a
long walk home."

Of course, fourteen was rather young for a teacher in an
ungraded school, where she was likely to have pupils of six-
teen and eighteen in her classes. But Miss Knightly's "judg-
ment" was justified by the fact that in June the school
directors of the Wild Rose district asked to have "Miss Fer-
guesson" back for the following year.

III

At four o'clock on Friday afternoon Miss Knightly stopped
at the Wild Rose schoolhouse to find the teacher waiting by
the roadside, and the pupils already scattering across the
fields, their tin lunch pails flashing back the sun. Lesley was
standing almost in the road itself, her grey "telescope" bag at
her feet. The moment old Molly stopped, she stowed her bag
in the back of the buggy and climbed in beside Miss
Knightly. Her smile was so eager and happy that her friend
chuckled softly. "You still get a little homesick, don't you,
Lesley?"

She didn't deny it. She gave a guilty laugh and murmured,
"I do miss the boys."

The afternoon sun was behind them, throwing over the
pastures and the harvested, resting fields that wonderful light,
so yellow that it is actually orange. The three hours and the
fourteen miles seemed not overlong. As the buggy neared the
town of MacAlpin, Miss Knightly thought she could feel
Lesley's heart beat. The girl had been silent a long while
when she exclaimed:

"Look, there's the standpipe!"

The object of this emotion was a red sheet-iron tube which thrust its naked ugliness some eighty feet into the air and held the water supply for the town of MacAlpin. As it stood on a hill, it was the first thing one saw on approaching the town from the west. Old Molly, too, seemed to have spied this heartening landmark, for she quickened her trot without encouragement from the whip. From that point on, Lesley said not a word. There were two more low hills (very low), and then Miss Knightly turned off the main road and drove by a short cut through the baseball ground, to the south appendix of the town proper, the "depot settlement" where the Ferguessons lived.

Their house stood on a steep hillside—a storey-and-a-half frame house with a basement on the downhill side, faced with brick up to the first-floor level. When the buggy stopped before the yard gate, two little boys came running out of the front door. Miss Knightly's passenger vanished from her side—she didn't know just when Lesley alighted. Her attention was distracted by the appearance of the mother, with a third boy, still in kilts, trotting behind her.

Mrs. Ferguesson was not a person who could be overlooked. All the merchants in MacAlpin admitted that she was a fine figure of a woman. As she came down the little yard and out of the gate, the evening breeze ruffled her wavy auburn hair. Her quick step and alert, upright carriage gave one the impression that she got things done. Coming up to the buggy, she took Miss Knightly's hand.

"Why, it's Miss Knightly! And she's brought our girl along to visit us. That was mighty clever of you, Miss, and these boys will surely be a happy family. They do miss their sister." She spoke clearly, distinctly, but with a slight Missouri turn of speech.

By this time Lesley and her brothers had become telepathically one. Miss Knightly couldn't tell what the boys said to her, or whether they said anything, but they had her old canvas bag out of the buggy and up on the porch in no time at all. Lesley ran toward the front door, hurried back to thank Miss Knightly, and then disappeared, holding fast to the little chap in skirts. She had forgotten to ask at what time Miss

Knightly would call for her on Monday, but her mother attended to that. When Mrs. Ferguesson followed the children through the hall and the little back parlour into the dining-room, Lesley turned to her and asked breathlessly, almost sharply:

"Where's Hector?"

"He's often late on Friday night, dear. He telephoned me from the depot and said not to wait supper for him—he'd get a sandwich at the lunch counter. Now how *are* you, my girl?" Mrs. Ferguesson put her hands on Lesley's shoulders and looked into her glowing eyes.

"Just fine, Mother. I like my school so much! And the scholars are nicer even than they were last year. I just love some of them."

At this the little boy in kilts (the fashion of the times, though he was four years old) caught his sister's skirt in his two hands and jerked it to get her attention. "No, no!" he said mournfully, "you don't love anybody but us!"

His mother laughed, and Lesley stooped and gave him the tight hug he wanted.

The family supper was over. Mrs. Ferguesson put on her apron. "Sit right down, Lesley, and talk to the children. No, I won't let you help me. You'll help me most by keeping them out of my way. I'll scramble you an egg and fry you some ham, so sit right down in your own place. I have some stewed plums for your dessert, and a beautiful angel cake I bought at the Methodist bake sale. Your father's gone to some political meeting, so we had supper early. You'll be a nice surprise for him when he gets home. He hadn't been gone half an hour when Miss Knightly drove up. Sit still, dear, it only bothers me if anybody tries to help me. I'll let you wash the dishes afterward, like we always do."

Lesley sat down at the half-cleared table; an oval-shaped table which could be extended by the insertion of "leaves" when Mrs. Ferguesson had company. The room was already dusky (twilights are short in a flat country), and one of the boys switched on the light which hung by a cord high above the table. A shallow china shade over the bulb threw a glaring white light down on the sister and the boys who stood about her chair. Lesley wrinkled up her brow, but it didn't occur to her that the light was too strong. She gave herself up to the feeling of being at home. It went all through her, that feeling, like getting into a warm bath when one is tired. She was safe from everything, was where she wanted to be, where she ought to be. A plant that has been washed out by a rain storm feels like that, when a kind gardener puts it gently back into its own earth with its own group.

The two older boys, Homer and Vincent, kept interrupting each other, trying to tell her things, but she didn't really listen to what they said. The little fellow stood close beside her chair, holding on to her skirt, fingering the glass buttons on her jacket. He was named Bryan, for his father's hero, but he didn't fit the name very well. He was a rather wistful and timid child.

Mrs. Ferguesson brought the ham and eggs and the warmed-up coffee. Then she sat down opposite her daughter to watch her enjoy her supper. "Now don't talk to her, boys. Let her eat in peace."

Vincent spoke up. "Can't I just tell her what happened to my lame pigeon?"

Mrs. Ferguesson merely shook her head. She had control in that household, sure enough!

Before Lesley had quite finished her supper she heard the front door open and shut. The boys started up, but the mother raised a warning finger. They understood; a surprise. They were still as mice, and listened: A pause in the hall . . . he was hanging up his cap. Then he came in—the flower of the family.

For a moment he stood speechless in the doorway, the "incandescent" glaring full on his curly yellow hair and his amazed blue eyes. He was surprised indeed!

"Lesley!" he breathed, as if he were talking in his sleep.

She couldn't sit still. Without knowing that she got up and took a step, she had her arms around her brother. "It's me, Hector! Ain't I lucky? Miss Knightly brought me in."

"What time did you get here? You might have telephoned me, Mother."

"Dear, she ain't been here much more than half an hour."

"And Miss Knightly brought you in with old Molly, did

she?" Oh, the lovely voice he had, that Hector!—warm, deliberate . . . it made the most commonplace remark full of meaning. He had to say merely that—and it told his appreciation of Miss Knightly's kindness, even a playful gratitude to Molly, her clumsy, fat, road-pounding old mare. He was tall for his age, was Hector, and he had the fair pink-cheeked complexion which Lesley should have had and didn't.

Mrs. Ferguesson rose. "Now let's all go into the parlour and talk. We'll come back and clear up afterward." With this she opened the folding doors, and they followed her and found comfortable chairs—there was even a home-made hassock for Bryan. There were real books in the sectional bookcases (old Ferg's fault), and there was a real Brussels carpet in soft colours on the floor. That was Lesley's fault. Most of her savings from her first year's teaching had gone into that carpet. She had chosen it herself from the samples which Marshall Field's travelling man brought to MacAlpin. There were comfortable old-fashioned pictures on the walls— "Venice by Moonlight" and such. Lesley and Hector thought it a beautiful room.

Of course the room was pleasant because of the feeling the children had for one another, and because in Mrs. Ferguesson there was authority and organization. Here the family sat and talked until Father came home. He was always treated a little like company. His wife and his children had a deep respect for him and for experimental farming, and profound veneration for William Jennings Bryan. Even little Bryan knew he was named for a great man, and must some day stop being afraid of the dark.

James Grahame Ferguesson was a farmer. He spent most of his time on what he called an "experimental farm." (The neighbours had other names for it—some of them amusing.) He was a loosely built man; had drooping shoulders carried with a forward thrust. He was a ready speaker, and usually made the Fourth of July speech in MacAlpin—spoke from a platform in the Court House grove, and even the farmers who joked about Ferguesson came to hear him. Alf Delaney declared: "I like to see anything done well—even talking. If

old Ferg could shuck corn as fast as he can rustle the dictio-
nary, I'd hire him, even if he is a Pop."

Old Ferg was not at all old—just turned forty—but he was
fussy about the spelling of his name. He wrote it James Fer-
guesson. The merchants, even the local newspaper, simply
would not spell it that way. They left letters out, or they put
letters in. He complained about this repeatedly, and the result
was that he was simply called "Ferg" to his face, and "old
Ferg" to his back. His neighbours, both in town and in the
country where he farmed, liked him because he gave them so
much to talk about. He couldn't keep a hired man long at any
wages. His habits were too unconventional. He rose early,
saw to the chores like any other man, and went into the field
for the morning. His lunch was a cold spread from his wife's
kitchen, reinforced by hot tea. (The hired man was expected
to bring his own lunch—outrageous!) After lunch Mr. Fer-
guesson took off his boots and lay down on the blue gingham
sheets of a wide bed, and remained there until what he called
"the cool of the afternoon." When that refreshing season
arrived, he fed and watered his work horses, put the young
gelding to his buckboard, and drove four miles to MacAlpin
for his wife's hot supper. Mrs. Ferguesson, though not at all a
meek woman or a stupid one, unquestioningly believed him
when he told her that he did his best thinking in the after-
noon. He hinted to her that he was working out in his head
something that would benefit the farmers of the county more
than all the corn and wheat they could raise even in a good
year.

Sometimes Ferguesson did things she regretted—not be-
cause they were wrong, but because other people had mean
tongues. When a fashion came in for giving names to farms
which had hitherto been designated by figures (range, section,
quarter, etc.), and his neighbours came out with "Lone Tree
Farm," "Cold Spring Farm," etc., Ferguesson tacked on a
cottonwood tree by his gate a neatly painted board inscribed:
WIDE AWAKE FARM.

His neighbours, who could never get used to his afternoon
siesta, were not long in converting this prophetic christening
into "Hush-a-bye Farm." Mrs. Ferguesson overheard some of
this joking on a Saturday night (she was marketing late after a

lodge meeting on top of a busy day), and she didn't like it. On Sunday morning when he was dressing for church, she asked her husband why he ever gave the farm such a foolish name. He explained to her that the important crop on that farm was an idea. His farm was like an observatory where one watched the signs of the times and saw the great change that was coming for the benefit of all mankind. He even quoted Tennyson about looking into the future "far as human eye could see." It had been a long time since he had quoted any poetry to her. She sighed and dropped the matter.

On the whole, Ferg did himself a good turn when he put up that piece of nomenclature. People drove out of their way for miles to see it. They felt more kindly toward old Ferg because he wrote himself down such an ass. In a hard-working farming community a good joke is worth something. Ferguesson himself felt a gradual warming toward him among his neighbours. He ascribed it to the power of his oratory. It was really because he had made himself so absurd, but this he never guessed. Idealists are seldom afraid of ridicule—if they recognize it.

The Ferguesson children believed that their father was misunderstood by people of inferior intelligence, and that conviction gave them a "cause" which bound them together. They must do better than other children; better in school, and better on the playground. They must turn in a quarter of a dollar to help their mother out whenever they could. Experimental farming wasn't immediately remunerative.

Fortunately there was never any rent to pay. They owned their house down by the depot. When Mrs. Ferguesson's father died down in Missouri, she bought that place with what he left her. She knew that was the safe thing to do, her husband being a thinker. Her children were bound to her, and to that house, by the deepest, the most solemn loyalty. They never spoke of that covenant to each other, never even formulated it in their own minds—never. It was a consciousness they shared, and it gave them a family complexion.

On this Saturday of Lesley's surprise visit home, Father was with the family for breakfast. That was always a pleasant way to begin the day—especially on Saturday, when no one was in a hurry. He had grave good manners toward his wife and his children. He talked to them as if they were grown-up, reasonable beings—talked a trifle as if from a rostrum, perhaps,—and he never indulged in small-town gossip. He was much more likely to tell them what he had read in the *Omaha World-Herald* yesterday; news of the State capital and the national capital. Sometimes he told them what a grasping, selfish country England was. Very often he explained to them how the gold standard had kept the poor man down. The family seldom bothered him about petty matters—such as that Homer needed new shoes, or that the iceman's bill for the whole summer had come in for the third time. Mother would take care of that.

On this particular Saturday morning Ferguesson gave especial attention to Lesley. He asked her about her school, and had her name her pupils. "I think you are fortunate to have the Wild Rose school, Lesley," he said as he rose from the table. "The farmers up there are open-minded and prosperous. I have sometimes wished that I had settled up there, though there are certain advantages in living at the county seat. The educational opportunities are better. Your friendship with Miss Knightly has been a broadening influence."

He went out to hitch up the buckboard to drive to the farm, while his wife put up the lunch he was to take along with him, and Lesley went upstairs to make the beds.

"Upstairs" was a story in itself, a secret romance. No caller or neighbour had ever been allowed to go up there. All the children loved it—it was their very own world where there were no older people poking about to spoil things. And it was unique—not at all like other people's upstairs chambers. In her stuffy little bedroom out in the country Lesley had more than once cried for it.

Lesley and the boys liked space, not tight cubbyholes. Their upstairs was a long attic which ran the whole length of the house, from the front door downstairs to the kitchen at the back. Its great charm was that it was unlined. No plaster, no beaver-board lining; just the roof shingles, supported by long, unplaned, splintery rafters that sloped from the sharp roof-peak down to the floor of the attic. Bracing these long roof rafters were cross rafters on which one could hang things—a little personal washing, a curtain for tableaux, a rope swing for Bryan.

In this spacious, undivided loft were two brick chimneys, going up in neat little stair-steps from the plank floor to the shingle roof—and out of it to the stars! The chimneys were of red, unglazed brick, with lines of white mortar to hold them together.

Last year, after Lesley first got her school, Mrs. Ferguesson exerted her authority and partitioned off a little room over the kitchen end of the "upstairs" for her daughter. Before that, all the children slept in this delightful attic. The three older boys occupied two wide beds, their sister her little single bed. Bryan, subject to croup, still slumbered downstairs near his mother, but he looked forward to his ascension as to a state of pure beatitude.

There was certainly room enough up there for widely scattered quarters, but the three beds stood in a row, as in a hospital ward. The children liked to be close enough together to share experiences.

Experiences were many. Perhaps the most exciting was when the driving, sleety snowstorms came on winter nights. The roof shingles were old and had curled under hot summer suns. In a driving snowstorm the frozen flakes sifted in through all those little cracks, sprinkled the beds and the children, melted on their faces, in their hair! That was delightful. The rest of you was snug and warm under blankets and comforters, with a hot brick at one's feet. The wind howled outside; sometimes the white light from the snow and the half-strangled moon came in through the single end window. Each child had his own dream-adventure. They did not exchange confidences; every "fellow" had a right to his own. They never told their love.

If they turned in early, they had a good while to enjoy the outside weather; they never went to sleep until after ten o'clock, for then came the sweetest morsel of the night. At that hour Number Seventeen, the westbound passenger, whistled in. The station and the engine house were perhaps an eighth of a mile down the hill, and from far away across the meadows the children could hear that whistle. Then came the heavy pants of the locomotive in the frosty air. Then a hissing—then silence: she was taking water.

On Saturdays the children were allowed to go down to the depot to see Seventeen come in. It was a fine sight on winter nights. Sometimes the great locomotive used to sweep in armoured in ice and snow, breathing fire like a dragon, its great red eye shooting a blinding beam along the white roadbed and shining wet rails. When it stopped, it panted like a great beast. After it was watered by the big hose from the overhead tank, it seemed to draw long deep breaths, ready to charge afresh over the great Western land.

Yes, they were grand old warriors, those towering locomotives of other days. They seemed to mean power, conquest, triumph—Jim Hill's dream. They set children's hearts beating from Chicago to Los Angeles. They were the awakeners of many a dream.

As she made the boys' beds that Saturday morning and put on clean sheets, Lesley was thinking she would give a great deal to sleep out here as she used to. But when she got her school last year, her mother had said she must have a room of her own. So a carpenter brought sheathing and "lined" the end of the long loft—the end over the kitchen; and Mrs. Ferguesson bought a little yellow washstand and a bowl and pitcher, and said with satisfaction: "Now you see, Lesley, if you were sick, we would have some place to take the doctor." To be sure, the doctor would have to be admitted through the kitchen, and then come up a dark winding stairway with two turns. (Mr. Ferguesson termed it "the turnpike." His old Scotch grandmother, he said, had always thus called a winding stairway.) And Lesley's room, when you got there, was very like a snug wooden box. It was possible, of course, to leave her door open into the long loft, where the wood was brown and the chimneys red and the weather always so close to one. Out there things were still wild and rough—it wasn't a bedroom or a chamber—it was a hall, in the old baronial sense, reminded her of the lines in their *Grimm's Fairy Tales* book:

> Return, return, thou youthful bride,
> This is a robbers' hall inside.

IV

When her daughter had put the attic to rights, Mrs. Ferguesson went uptown to do her Saturday marketing. Lesley slipped out through the kitchen door and sat down on the back porch. The front porch was kept neat and fit to receive callers, but the back porch was given over to the boys. It was a messy-looking place, to be sure. From the wooden ceiling hung two trapezes. At one corner four boxing gloves were piled in a broken chair. In the trampled, grassless back yard, two-by-fours, planted upright, supported a length of lead pipe on which Homer practised bar exercises. Lesley sat down on the porch floor, her feet on the ground, and sank into idleness and safety and perfect love.

The boys were much the dearest things in the world to her. To love them so much was just . . . happiness. To think about them was the most perfect form of happiness. Had they been actually present, swinging on the two trapezes, turning on the bar, she would have been too much excited, too actively happy to be perfectly happy. But sitting in the warm sun, with her feet on the good ground, even her mother away, she almost ceased to exist. The feeling of being at home was complete, absolute: it made her sleepy. And that feeling was not so much the sense of being protected by her father and mother as of being with, and being one with, her brothers. It was the clan feeling, which meant life or death for the blood, not for the individual. For some reason, or for no reason, back in the beginning, creatures wanted the blood to continue.

After the noonday dinner Mrs. Ferguesson thoughtfully confided to her daughter while they were washing the dishes:
"Lesley, I'm divided in my mind. I would so appreciate a quiet afternoon with you, but I've a sort of engagement with the P.E.O. A lady from Canada is to be there to talk to us, and I've promised to introduce her. And just when I want to have a quiet time with you."
Lesley gave a sigh of relief and thought how fortunate it is that circumstances do sometimes make up our mind for us. In

that battered canvas bag upstairs there was a roll of arithmetic papers and "essays" which hung over her like a threat. Now she would have a still hour in their beautiful parlour to correct them; the shades drawn down, just enough light to read by, her father's unabridged at hand, and the boys playing bat and pitch in the back yard.

Lesley and her brothers were proud of their mother's good looks, and that she never allowed herself to become a household drudge, as so many of her neighbours did. She "managed," and the boys helped her to manage. For one thing, there were never any dreary tubs full of washing standing about, and there was no ironing day to make a hole in the week. They sent all the washing, even the sheets, to the town steam laundry. Hector, with his weekly wages as messenger boy, and Homer and Vincent with their stable jobs, paid for it. That simple expedient did away with the worst blight of the working man's home.

Mrs. Ferguesson was "public-spirited," and she was the friend of all good causes. The business men of the town agreed that she had a great deal of influence, and that her name added strength to any committee. She was generally spoken of as a very *practical* woman, with an emphasis which implied several things. She was a "joiner," too! She was a Royal Neighbor, and a Neighborly Neighbor, and a P.E.O., and an Eastern Star. She had even joined the Methodist Win-a-Couple, though she warned them that she could not attend their meetings, as she liked to spend some of her evenings at home.

Promptly at six thirty Monday morning Miss Knightly's old mare stopped in front of the Ferguessons' house. The four boys were all on the front porch. James himself carried Lesley's bag down and put it into the buggy. He thanked the Superintendent very courteously for her kindness and kissed his daughter good-bye.

It had been at no trifling sacrifice that Miss Knightly was able to call for Lesley at six thirty. Customarily she started on her long drives at nine o'clock. This morning she had to give an extra half-dollar to the man who came to curry and harness her mare. She herself got no proper breakfast, but a cold sandwich and a cup of coffee at the station lunch counter—the only eating-place open at six o'clock. Most serious of all, she must push Molly a little on the road, to land her passenger at the Wild Rose schoolhouse at nine o'clock. Such small inconveniences do not sum up to an imposing total, but we assume them only for persons we really care for.

V

It was Christmas Eve. The town was busy with Christmas "exercises," and all the churches were lit up. Hector Ferguesson was going slowly up the hill which separated the depot settlement from the town proper. He walked at no messenger-boy pace tonight, crunching under his feet the snow which had fallen three days ago, melted, and then frozen hard. His hands were in the pockets of his new overcoat, which was so long that it almost touched the ground when he toiled up the steepest part of the hill. It was very heavy and not very warm. In those days there was a theory that in topcoats very little wool was necessary if they were woven tight enough and hard enough to "keep out the cold." A barricade was the idea. Hector carried the weight and clumsiness bravely, proudly. His new overcoat was a Christmas present from his sister. She had gone to the big town in the next county to shop for it, and bought it with her own money. He was thinking how kind Lesley was, and how hard she had worked for that money, and how much she had to put up with in the rough farmhouse where she boarded, out in the country. It was usually a poor housekeeper who was willing to keep a teacher, since they paid so little. Probably the amount Lesley spent for that coat would have kept her at a comfortable house all winter. When he grew up, and made lots of money (a brakeman—maybe an engineer), he would certainly be good to his sister.

Hector was a strange boy; a blend of the soft and the hard. In action he was practical, executive, like his mother. But in his mind, in his thoughts and plans, he was extravagant, often absurd. His mother suspected that he was "dreamy." Tonight, as he trailed up the frozen wooden sidewalk toward the town, he kept looking up at the stars, which were unusually bright, as they always seem over a stretch of snow. He was wondering if there were angels up there, watching the world on Christmas Eve. They came before, on the first Christmas Eve, he knew. Perhaps they kept the Anniversary. He thought about a beautiful coloured picture tacked up in Lesley's bedroom; two angels with white robes and long white wings, flying toward a low hill in the early dawn before sunrise, and on that distant hill, against the soft daybreak light, were three tiny crosses. He never doubted angels looked like that. He was credulous and truthful by nature. There was that look in his blue eyes. He would get it knocked out of him, his mother knew. But she believed he would always keep some of it— enough to make him open-handed and open-hearted.

Tonight Hector had his leather satchel full of Christmas telegrams. After he had delivered them all, he would buy his presents for his mother and the children. The stores sold off their special Christmas things at a discount after eleven o'clock on Christmas Eve.

VI

Miss Knightly was in Lincoln, attending a convention of Superintendents of Public Instruction, when the long-to-be-remembered blizzard swept down over the prairie State. Travel and telephone service were discontinued. A Chicago passenger train was stalled for three days in a deep cut west of W—. There she lay, and the dining-car had much ado to feed the passengers.

Miss Knightly was snowbound in Lincoln. She tarried there after the convention was dismissed and her fellow superintendents had gone home to their respective counties. She was caught by the storm because she had stayed over to see Julia Marlowe (then young and so fair!) in *The Love Chase*. She was not inconsolable to be delayed for some days. Why worry? She was staying at a small but very pleasant hotel, where the food was good and the beds were comfortable. She was New England born and bred, too conscientious to stay over in the city from mere self-indulgence, but quite willing to be lost to MacAlpin and X— County by the intervention of fate. She stayed, in fact, a week, greatly enjoying such luxuries as plenty of running water, hot baths, and steam heat. At that date MacAlpin houses, and even her office in the Court House, were heated by hard-coal stoves.

At last she was jogging home on a passenger train which left Lincoln at a convenient hour (it was two hours late, travel was still disorganized), when she was pleased to see Mr. Redman in conductor's uniform come into the car. Two of his boys had been her pupils when she taught in high school, before she was elected to a county office. Mr. Redman also seemed pleased, and after he had been through the train to punch tickets, he came back and sat down in the green plush seat opposite Miss Knightly and began to "tease."

"I hear there was a story going up at the Court House that you'd eloped. I was hoping you hadn't made a mistake."

"No. I thought it over and avoided the mistake. But what about you, Mr. Redman? You belong on the run west out of MacAlpin, don't you?"

"I don't know where I belong, Ma'm, and nobody else does. This is Jack Kelly's run, but he got his leg broke trying to help the train crew shovel the sleeping-car loose in that deep cut out of W——. The passengers were just freezing. This blizzard has upset everything. There's got to be better organization from higher up. This has taught us we just can't handle an emergency. Hard on stock, hard on people. A little neighbour of ours—why, you must know her, she was one of your teachers—Jim Ferguesson's little girl. She got pneumonia out there in the country and died out there."

Miss Knightly went so white that Redman without a word hurried to the end of the car and brought back a glass of water. He kept muttering that he was sorry . . . that he "always put his foot in it."

She did not disappoint him. She came back quickly. "That's all right, Mr. Redman. I'd rather hear it before I get home. Did she get lost in the storm? I don't understand."

Mr. Redman sat down and did the best he could to repair damages.

"No, Ma'm, little Lesley acted very sensible, didn't lose her head. You see, the storm struck us about three o'clock in the afternoon. The whole day it had been mild and soft, like spring. Then it came down instanter, like a thousand tons of snow dumped out of the sky. My wife was out in the back yard taking in some clothes she'd hung to dry. She hadn't even a shawl over her head. The suddenness of it confused her so (she couldn't see three feet before her), she wandered around in our back yard, couldn't find her way back to the house. Pretty soon our old dog—he's part shepherd—came yappin' and whinin'. She dropped the clothes and held onto his hair, and he got her to the back porch. That's how bad it was in MacAlpin."

"And Lesley?" Miss Knightly murmured.

"Yes, Ma'm! I'm coming to that. Her scholars tell about how the schoolroom got a little dark, and they all looked out, and there was no graveyard, and no horses that some of them had rode to school on. The boys jumped up to run out and see after the horses, but Lesley stood with her back against the door and wouldn't let 'em go out. Told 'em it would be over in a few minutes. Well, you see it wasn't. Over four feet of snow fell in less'n an hour. About six o'clock some of the fathers of the children that lived aways off started out on horseback, but the horses waded belly-deep, and a wind come up and it turned cold.

"Ford Robertson is the nearest neighbour, you know,—scarcely more than across the road—eighth of a mile, maybe. As soon as he come in from his corral—the Herefords had all bunched up together, over a hundred of 'em, under the lee of a big haystack, and he knew they wouldn't freeze. As soon as he got in, the missus made him go over to the schoolhouse an' take a rope along an' herd 'em all over to her house, teacher an' all, with the boys leading their horses. That night Mrs. Robertson cooked nearly everything in the house for their supper, and she sent Ford upstairs to help Lesley make shakedown beds on the floor. Mrs. Robertson remembers when the big supper was ready and the children ate like wolves, Lesley didn't eat much—said she had a little head-ache. Next morning she was pretty sick. That day all the fathers came on horseback for the children. Robertson got one of them to go for old Doctor Small, and he came down on his horse. Doctor said it was pneumonia, and there wasn't much he could do. She didn't seem to have strength to rally. She was out of her head when he got there. She was mostly unconscious for three days, and just slipped out. The funeral is tomorrow. The roads are open now. They were to bring her home today."

The train stopped at a station, and Mr. Redman went to attend to his duties. When he next came through the car Miss Knightly spoke to him. She had recovered herself. Her voice was steady, though very low and very soft when she asked him:

"Were any of her family out there with her when she was ill?"

"Why, yes, Mrs. Ferguesson was out there. That boy Hector got his mother through, before the roads were open. He'd stop at a farmhouse and explain the situation and borrow a team and get the farmer or one of his hands to give them a lift to the next farm, and there they'd get a lift a little further. Everybody knew about the school and the teacher by that time, and wanted to help, no matter how bad the roads were. You see, Miss Knightly, everything would have gone better if it hadn't come on so freezing cold, and if the snow hadn't been so darn soft when it first fell. That family are terrible broke up. We all are, down at the depot. She didn't recognize them when they got there, I heard."

VII

Twenty years after that historic blizzard Evangeline Knightly—now Mrs. Ralph Thorndike—alighted from the fast eastbound passenger at the MacAlpin station. No one at the station knew who she was except the station master, and he was not quite sure. She looked older, but she also looked more prosperous, more worldly. When she approached him at his office door and asked, "Isn't this Mr. Beardsley?" he recognized her voice and speech.

"That's who. And it's my guess this is, or used to be, Miss Knightly. I've been here almost forever. No ambition. But you left us a long time ago. You're looking fine, Ma'm, if I may say so."

She thanked him and asked him to recommend a hotel where she could stay for a day or two.

He scratched his head. "Well, the Plummer House ain't no

Waldorf-Astoria, but the travelling men give a good report of
it. The Bishop always stays there when he comes to town.
You like me to telephone for an otto [automobile] to take you
up? Lord, when you left here there wasn't an otto in the
town!"

Mrs. Thorndike smiled. "Not many in the world, I think.
And can you tell me, Mr. Beardsley, where the Ferguessons
live?"

"The depot Ferguessons? Oh, they live uptown now. Ferg
built right west of the Court House, right next to where the
Donaldsons used to live. You'll find lots of changes. Some's
come up, and some's come down. We used to laugh at Ferg
and tell him politics didn't bring in the bacon. But he's got it
on us now. The Democrats are sure grand job-givers. Throw
'em round for value received. I still vote the Republican
ticket. Too old to change. Anyhow, all those new jobs don't
affect the railroads much. They can't put a college professor
on to run trains. Now I'll telephone for an otto for you."

Miss Knightly, after going to Denver, had married a very
successful young architect, from New England, like herself,
and now she was on her way back to Brunswick, Maine, to
revisit the scenes of her childhood. Although she had never
been in MacAlpin since she left it fifteen years ago, she faith-
fully read the MacAlpin *Messenger* and knew the important
changes in the town.

After she had settled her room at the hotel, and unpacked
her toilet articles, she took a cardboard box she had brought
with her in the sleeping-car, and went out on a personal
errand. She came back to the hotel late for lunch—had a tray
sent up to her room, and at four o'clock went to the office in
the Court House which used to be her office. This was the
autumn of the year, and she had a great desire to drive out
among the country schools and see how much fifteen years
had changed the land, the pupils, the teachers.

When she introduced herself to the present incumbent, she
was cordially received. The young Superintendent seemed a
wide-awake, breezy girl, with bobbed blond hair and crimson
lips. Her name was Wanda Bliss.

Mrs. Thorndike explained that her stay would not be long

enough to let her visit all the country schools, but she would like Miss Bliss's advice as to which were the most interesting.

"Oh, I can run you around to nearly all of them in a day, in my car!"

Mrs. Thorndike thanked her warmly. She liked young people who were not in the least afraid of life or luck or responsibility. In her own youth there were very few like that. The teachers, and many of the pupils out in the country schools, were eager—but anxious. She laughed and told Miss Bliss that she meant to hire a buggy, if there was such a thing left in MacAlpin, and drive out into the country alone.

"I get you. You want to put on an old-home act. You might phone around to any farmers you used to know. Some of them still keep horses for haying."

Mrs. Thorndike got a list of the country teachers and the districts in which they taught. A few of them had been pupils in the schools she used to visit. Those she was determined to see.

The following morning she made the call she had stopped off at MacAlpin to make. She rang the doorbell at the house pointed out to her, and through the open window heard a voice call: "Come in, come in, please. I can't answer the bell."

Mrs. Thorndike opened the door into a shining oak hall with a shining oak stairway.

"Come right through, please. I'm in the back parlour. I sprained my ankle and can't walk yet."

The visitor followed the voice and found Mrs. Ferguesson sitting in a spring rocker, her bandaged right foot resting on a low stool.

"Come in, Ma'm. I have a bad sprain, and the little girl who does for me is downtown marketing. Maybe you came to see Mr. Ferguesson, but his office is—" here she broke off and looked up sharply—intently—at her guest. When the guest smiled, she broke out: "Miss Knightly! *Are* you Miss Knightly? Can it be?"

"They call me Mrs. Thorndike now, but I'm Evangeline Knightly just the same." She put out her hand, and Mrs. Ferguesson seized it with both her own.

"It's too good to be true!" she gasped with tears in her

voice, "just too good to be true. The things we dream about that way don't happen." She held fast to Mrs. Thorndike's hand as if she were afraid she might vanish. "When did you come to town, and why didn't they let me know!"

"I came only yesterday, Mrs. Ferguesson, and I wanted to slip in on you just like this, with no one else around."

"Mr. Ferguesson must have known. But his mind is always off on some trail, and he never brings me any news when I'm laid up like this. Dear me! It's a long time." She pressed the visitor's hand again before she released it. "Get yourself a comfortable chair, dear, and sit down by me. I do hate to be helpless like this. It wouldn't have happened but for those slippery front stairs. Mr. Ferguesson just wouldn't put a carpet on them, because he says folks don't carpet hardwood stairs, and I tried to answer the doorbell in a hurry, and this is what come of it. I'm not naturally a clumsy woman on my feet."

Mrs. Thorndike noticed an aggrieved tone in her talk which had never been there in the old days when she had so much to be aggrieved about. She brought a chair and sat down close to Mrs. Ferguesson, facing her. The good woman had not changed much, she thought. There was a little grey in her crinkly auburn hair, and there were lines about her mouth which used not to be there, but her eyes had all the old fire.

"How comfortably you are fixed here, Mrs. Ferguesson! I'm so glad to find you like this."

"Yes, we're comfortable—now that they're all gone! It's mostly his taste. He took great interest." She spoke rather absently, and kept looking out through the polished hall toward the front door, as if she were expecting someone. It seemed a shame that anyone naturally so energetic should be enduring this foolish antiquated method of treating a sprain. The chief change in her, Mrs. Thorndike thought, was that she had grown softer. She reached for the visitor's hand again and held it fast. Tears came to her eyes.

Mrs. Thorndike ventured that she had found the town much changed for the better.

Yes, Mrs. Ferguesson supposed it was.

Then Mrs. Thorndike began in earnest. "How wonderful it is that all your sons have turned out so well! I take the

MacAlpin paper chiefly to keep track of the Ferguesson boys. You and Mr. Ferguesson must be very proud."

"Yes'm, we are. We are thankful."

"Even the Denver papers have long articles about Hector and Homer and their great sheep ranches in Wyoming. And Vincent has become such a celebrated chemist, and is helping to destroy all the irreducible elements that I learned when I went to school. And Bryan is with Marshall Field!"

Mrs. Ferguesson nodded and pressed her hand, but she still kept looking down the hall toward the front door. Suddenly she turned with all herself to Mrs. Thorndike and with a storm of tears cried out from her heart: "Oh, Miss Knightly, talk to me about my Lesley! Seems so many have forgot her, but I know you haven't."

"No, Mrs. Ferguesson, I never forget her. Yesterday morning I took a box of roses that I brought with me from my own garden down to where she sleeps. I was glad to find a little seat there, so that I could stay for a long while and think about her."

"Oh, I wish I could have gone with you, Miss Knightly! (I can't call you anything else.) I wish we could have gone together. I can't help feeling she knows. *Anyhow*, we know! And there's nothing in all my life so precious to me to remember and think about as my Lesley. I'm no soft woman, either. The boys will tell you that. They'll tell you they got on because I always had a firm hand over them. They're all true to Lesley, my boys. Every time they come home they go down there. They feel it like I do, as if it had happened yesterday. Their father feels it, too, when he's not taken up with his abstractions. Anyhow, I don't think men feel things like women and boys. My boys have stayed boys. I do believe they feel as bad as I do about moving up here. We have four nice bedrooms upstairs to make them comfortable, should they all come home at once, and they're polite about us and tell us how well fixed we are. But Miss Knightly, I know at the bottom of their hearts they wish they was back in the old house down by the depot, sleeping in the attic."

Mrs. Thorndike stroked her hand. "I looked for the old house as I was coming up from the station. I made the driver stop."

"Ain't it dreadful, what's been done to it? If I'd foreseen, I'd never have let Mr. Ferguesson sell it. It was in my name. I'd have kept it to go back to and remember sometimes. Folks in middle age make a mistake when they think they can better themselves. They can't, not if they have any heart. And the other kind don't matter—they aren't real people—just poor put-ons, that try to be like the advertisements. Father even took me to California one winter. I was miserable all the time. And there were plenty more like me—miserable underneath. The women lined up in cafeterias, carrying their little trays— like convicts, seemed to me—and running to beauty shops to get their poor old hands manicured. And the old men, Miss Knightly, I pitied them most of all! Old bent-backed farmers, standing round in their shirt-sleeves, in plazas and alleyways, pitching horseshoes like they used to do at home. I tell you, people are happiest where they've had their children and struggled along and been real folks, and not tourists. What do you think about all this running around, Miss Knightly? You're an educated woman, I never had much schooling."

"I don't think schooling gives people any wisdom, Mrs. Ferguesson. I guess only life does that."

"Well, this I know: our best years are when we're working hardest and going right ahead when we can hardly see our way out. Times I was a good deal perplexed. But I always had one comfort. I did own our own house. I never had to worry about the rent. Don't it seem strange to you, though, that all our boys are so practical, and their father such a dreamer?"

Mrs. Thorndike murmured that some people think boys are most likely to take after their mother.

Mrs. Ferguesson smiled absently and shook her head. Presently she came out with: "It's a comfort to me up here, on a still night I can still hear the trains whistle in. Sometimes, when I can't sleep, I lie and listen for them. And I can almost think I am down there, with my children up in the loft. We were very happy." She looked up at her guest and smiled bravely. "I suppose you go away tonight?"

Mrs. Thorndike explained her plan to spend a day in the country.

"You're going out to visit the little schools? Why, God bless you, dear! You're still our Miss Knightly! But you'd better take a car, so you can get up to the Wild Rose school and back in one day. Do go there! The teacher is Mandy Perkins—she was one of her little scholars. You'll like Mandy, an' she loved Lesley. You must get Bud Sullivan to drive you. Engage him right now—the telephone's there in the hall, and the garage is 306. He'll creep along for you, if you tell him. He does for me. I often go out to the Wild Rose school, and over to see dear Mrs. Robertson, who ain't so young as she was then. I can't go with Mr. Ferguesson. He drives so fast it's no satisfaction. And then he's not always mindful. He's had some accidents. When he gets to thinking, he's just as likely to run down a cow as not. He's had to pay for one. You know cows will cross the road right in front of a car. Maybe their grandchildren calves will be more modern-minded."

Mrs. Thorndike did not see her old friend again, but she wrote her a long letter from Wiscasset, Maine, which Mrs. Ferguesson sent to her son Hector, marked, "To be returned, but first pass on to your brothers."

Before Breakfast

HENRY GRENFELL, of Grenfell & Saunders, got resentfully out of bed after a bad night. The first sleepless night he had ever spent in his own cabin, on his own island, where nobody knew that he was senior partner of Grenfell & Saunders, and where the business correspondence was never forwarded to him. He slipped on a blanket dressing-gown over his pyjamas (island mornings in the North Atlantic are chill before dawn), went to the front windows of his bedroom, and ran up the heavy blue shades which shut out the shameless blaze of the sunrise if one wanted to sleep late—and he usually did on the first morning after arriving. (The trip up from Boston was long and hard, by trains made up of the cast-off coaches of liquidated railroads, and then by the two worst boats in the world.) The cabin modestly squatted on a tiny clearing between a tall spruce wood and the sea,— sat about fifty yards back from the edge of the red sandstone cliff which dropped some two hundred feet to a narrow beach—so narrow that it was covered at high tide. The cliffs rose sheer on this side of the island, were undercut in places, and faced the east.

The east was already lightening; a deep red streak burnt over the sky-line water, and the water itself was thick and dark, indigo blue—occasionally a silver streak, where the tide was going out very quietly. While Grenfell stood at his window, a big snowshoe hare ran downhill from the spruce wood, bounded into the grass plot at the front door, and began nervously nibbling the clover. He was puzzled and furtive; his jaws quivered, and his protruding eyes kept watch behind him as well as before. Grenfell was sure it was the hare that used to come every morning two summers ago and had become quite friendly. But now he seemed ill at ease; presently he started, sat still for an instant, then scampered up the grassy hillside and disappeared into the dark spruce wood. Silly thing! Still, it was a kind of greeting.

Grenfell left the window and went to his walnut washstand (no plumbing) and mechanically prepared to take a shower in the shed room behind his sleeping-chamber. He began his morning routine, still thinking about the hare.

First came the eye-drops. Tilting his head back, thus staring into the eastern horizon, he raised the glass dropper, but he didn't press the bulb. He saw something up there. While he was watching the rabbit the sky had changed. Above the red streak on the water line the sky had lightened to faint blue, and across the horizon a drift of fleecy rose cloud was floating. And through it a white-bright, gold-bright planet was shining. The morning star, of course. At this hour, and so near the sun, it would be Venus.

Behind her rose-coloured veils, quite alone in the sky already blue, she seemed to wait. She had come in on her beat, taken her place in the figure. Serene, impersonal splendour. Merciless perfection, ageless sovereignty. The poor hare and his clover, poor Grenfell and his eye-drops!

He braced himself against his washstand and still stared up at her. Something roused his temper so hot that he began to mutter aloud:

"And what's a hundred and thirty-six million years to you, Madam? That Professor needn't blow. You were winking and blinking up there maybe a hundred and thirty-six million times before that date they are so proud of. The rocks can't tell any tales on you. You were doing your stunt up there long before there was anything down here but—God knows what! Let's leave that to the professors, Madam, you and me!"

This childish bitterness toward "millions" and professors was the result of several things. Two of Grenfell's sons were "professors"; Harrison a distinguished physicist at thirty. This morning, however, Harrison had not popped up in his father's mind. Grenfell was still thinking of a pleasant and courtly scientist whom he had met on the boat yesterday—a delightful man who had, temporarily at least, wrecked Grenfell's life with civilities and information.

It was natural, indeed inevitable, that two clean, close-shaven gentlemen in tailored woods clothes, passengers on the worst tub owned by the Canadian Steamships Company and both bound for a little island off the Nova Scotia coast, should get into conversation. It was all the more natural since the scientist was accompanied by a lovely girl—his daughter.

It was a pleasure to look at her, just as it is a pleasure to look at any comely creature who shows breeding, delicate preferences. She had lovely eyes, lovely skin, lovely manners. She listened closely when Grenfell and her father talked, but she didn't bark up with her opinions. When he asked her about their life on the island last summer, he liked everything she said about the place and the people. She answered him lightly, as if her impressions could matter only to herself, but, having an opinion, it was only good manners to admit it. "Sweet, but decided," was his rough estimate.

Since they were both going to an island which wasn't even on the map, supposed to be known only to the motor launches that called after a catch of herring, it was natural that the two gentlemen should talk about that bit of wooded rock in the sea. Grenfell always liked to talk about it to the right person. At first he thought Professor Fairweather was a right person. He had felt alarm when Fairweather mentioned that last summer he had put up a portable house on the shore about two miles from Grenfell's cabin. But he added that it would soon vanish as quietly as it had come. His geological work would be over this autumn, and his portable house would be taken to pieces and shipped to an island in the South Pacific. Having thus reassured him, Fairweather carelessly, in quite the tone of weather-comment small talk, proceeded to wreck one of Grenfell's happiest illusions; the escape-avenue he kept in the back of his mind when he was at his desk at Grenfell & Saunders, Bonds. The Professor certainly meant no harm. He was a man of the world, urbane, not self-important. He merely remarked that the island was interesting geologically because the two ends of the island belonged to different periods, yet the ice seemed to have brought them both down together.

"And about how old would our end be, Professor?" Grenfell meant simply to express polite interest, but he gave himself away, parted with his only defence—indifference.

"We call it a hundred and thirty-six million years," was the answer he got.

"Really? That's getting it down pretty fine, isn't it? I'm just a blank where science is concerned. I went to work when I was thirteen—didn't have any education. Of course some business men read up on science. But I have to struggle with reports and figures a good deal. When I do read I like something human—the old fellows: Scott and Dickens and Fielding. I get a great kick out of them."

The Professor was a perfect gentleman, but he couldn't resist the appeal of ignorance. He had sensed in half an hour that this man loved the island. (His daughter had sensed it a year ago, as soon as she arrived there with her father. Something about his cabin, the little patch of lawn in front, and the hedge of wild roses that fenced it in, told her that.) In their talk Professor Fairweather had come to realize that this man had quite an unusual feeling for the island, therefore he would certainly like to know more about it—all he could tell him!

The sun leaped out of the sea—the planet vanished. Grenfell rejected his eye-drops. Why patch up? What was the use . . . of anything? Why tear a man loose from his little rock and shoot him out into the eternities? All that stuff was inhuman. A man had his little hour, with heat and cold and a time-sense suited to his endurance. If you took that away from him you left him spineless, accidental, unrelated to anything. He himself was, he realized, sitting in his bathrobe by his washstand, limp! No wonder: what a night! What a dreadful night! The speeds which machinists had worked up in the last fifty years were mere baby-talk to what can go through a man's head between dusk and daybreak. In the last ten hours poor Grenfell had travelled over seas and continents, gone through boyhood and youth, founded a business, made a great deal of money, and brought up an expensive family. (There were three sons, to whom he had given every advantage and who had turned out well, two of them brilliantly.) And all this meant nothing to him except negatively—"to avoid worse rape," he quoted Milton to himself.

Last night had been one of those nights of revelation, revaluation, when everything seems to come clear . . . only to fade out again in the morning. In a low cabin on a high red cliff overhanging the sea, everything that was shut up in him, under lock and bolt and pressure, simply broke jail, spread out into the spaciousness of the night, undraped, unashamed.

ಶಿ

When his father died, Henry had got a job as messenger boy with the Western Union. He always remembered those years with a certain pride. His mother took in sewing. There were two little girls, younger than he. When he looked back on that time, there was nothing in it to be ashamed of. Those are the years, he often told the reformers, that make character, make proficiency. A business man should have early training, like a pianist, *at the instrument*. The sense of responsibility makes a little boy a citizen: for him there is no "dangerous age." From his first winter with the telegraph company he knew he could get on if he tried hard, since most lads emphatically did not try hard. He read law at night, and when he was twenty was confidential clerk with one of the most conservative legal firms in Colorado.

Everything went well until he took his first long vacation— bicycling in the mountains above Colorado Springs. One morning he was pedalling hard uphill when another bicycle came round a curve and collided with him; a girl coasting. Both riders were thrown. She got her foot caught in her wheel; sprain and lacerations. Henry ran two miles down to her hotel and her family. New York people; the father's name was a legend in Henry's credulous Western world. And they liked him, Henry, these cultivated, clever, experienced people! The mother was the ruling power—remarkable woman. What she planned, she put through—relentless determination. He ought to know, for he married that only daughter one year after she coasted into him. A warning unheeded, that first meeting. It was his own intoxicated vanity that sealed his fate. He had never been "made much over" before.

It had worked out as well as most marriages, he supposed. Better than many. The intelligent girl had been no discredit to him, certainly. She had given him two remarkable sons, any man would be proud of them. . . .

Here Grenfell had flopped over in bed and suddenly sat up,

muttering aloud. "But God, they're as cold as ice! I can't see through it. They've never lived at all, those two fellows. They've never run after the ball—they're so damned clever they don't *have* to. They just reach out and *take* the ball. Yes, fine hands, like their grandmother's; long . . . white . . . beautiful nails. The way Harrison picked up that book! I'm glad my paws are red and stubby."

For a moment he recalled sharply a little scene. Three days ago he was packing for his escape to this island. Harrison, the eldest son, the physicist, after knocking, had entered to his father's "Come in!" He came to ask who should take care of his personal mail (that which came to the house) if Miss O'Doyle should go on her vacation before he returned. He put the question rather grimly. The family seemed to resent the fact that, though he worked like a steam shovel while he was in town, when he went on a vacation he never told them how long he would be away or where he was going.

"Oh, I meant to tell you, Harrison, before I leave. But it was nice of you to think of it. Miss O'Doyle has decided to put off her vacation until the middle of October, and then she'll take a long one." He was sure he spoke amiably as he stood looking at his son. He was always proud of Harrison's fine presence, his poise and easy reserve. The little travelling bag (made to his order) which on a journey he always carried himself, never trusted to a porter, lay open on his writing table. On top of his pyjamas and razor case lay two little books bound in red leather. Harrison picked up one and glanced at the lettering on the back. *King Henry IV, Part I*.

"Light reading?" he remarked. Grenfell was stung by such impertinence. He resented any intrusion on his private, personal, non-family life.

"Light or heavy," he remarked dryly, "they're good company. And they're mighty human."

"They have that reputation," his son admitted.

A spark flashed into Grenfell's eye. Was the fellow sarcastic, or merely patronizing?

"Reputation, hell!" he broke out. "I don't carry books around with my toothbrushes and razors on account of their reputation."

"No, I wouldn't accuse you of that." The young man spoke

quietly, not warmly, but as if he meant it. He hesitated and left the room.

Sitting up in his bed in the small hours of the morning, Grenfell wondered if he hadn't flared up too soon. Maybe the fellow hadn't meant to be sarcastic. All the same he had no business to touch anything in his father's bag. That bag was like his coat pocket. Grenfell never bothered his family with his personal diversions, and he never intruded upon theirs. Harrison and his mother were a team—a close corporation! Grenfell respected it absolutely. No questions, no explanations demanded by him. The bills came in; Miss O'Doyle wrote the checks and he signed them. He hadn't the curiosity, the vulgarity to look at them.

Of course, he admitted, there were times when he got back at the corporation just a little. That usually occurred when his dyspepsia had kept him on very light food all day and, the dinner at home happening to be "rich," he confined himself to graham crackers and milk. He remembered such a little dinner scene last month. Harrison and his mother came downstairs dressed to go out for the evening. Soon after the soup was served, Harrison wondered whether Koussevitzky would take the slow movement in the Brahms Second as he did last winter. His mother said she still remembered Muck's reading, and preferred it.

The theoretical head of the house spoke up. "I take it that this is Symphony night, and that my family are going. You have ordered the car? Well, I am going to hear John McCormack sing *Kathleen Mavourneen*."

His wife rescued him as she often did (in an innocent, well-bred way) by refusing to recognize his rudeness. "Dear me! I haven't heard McCormack since he first came out in Italy years and years ago. His success was sensational. He was singing Mozart then."

Yes, when he was irritable and the domestic line-up got the better of him, Margaret, by being faultlessly polite, often saved the situation.

When he thought everything over, here in this great quiet, in this great darkness, he admitted that his shipwreck had not been on the family rock. The bitter truth was that his worst enemy was closer even than the wife of his bosom—was his bosom itself!

Grenfell had what he called a hair-trigger stomach. When he was in his New York office he worked like a whirlwind; and to do it he had to live on a diet that would have tried the leanest anchorite. The doctors said he did everything too hard. He knew that—he always had done things hard, from the day he first went to work for the Western Union. Mother and two little sisters, no schooling—the only capital he had was the ginger to care hard and work hard. Apparently it was not the brain that desired and achieved. At least, the expense account came out of a very other part of one. Perhaps he was a throw-back to the Year One, when in the stomach was the only constant, never sleeping, never quite satisfied desire.

The humiliation of being "delicate" was worse than the actual hardship. He had found the one way in which he could make it up to himself, could feel like a whole man, not like a miserable dyspeptic. That way was by living rough, not by living soft. There wasn't a big-game country in North America where he hadn't hunted; mountain sheep in the wild Rockies, moose in darkest Canada, caribou in Newfoundland. Long before he could really afford it, he took four months out of every year to go shooting. His greatest triumph was a white bear in Labrador. His guide and pack-men and canoe men never guessed that he was a frail man. Out there, up there, he wasn't! Out there he was just a "city man" who paid well; eccentric, but a fairly good shot. That was what he had got out of hard work and very good luck. He had got ahead wonderfully . . . but, somehow, ahead on the wrong road.

❧

At this point in his audit Grenfell had felt his knees getting cold, so he got out of bed, opened a clothes closet, and found his eiderdown bathrobe hanging on the hook where he had left it two summers ago. That was a satisfaction. (He liked to be orderly, and it made this cabin seem more his own to find things, year after year, just as he had left them.) Feeling comfortably warm, he ran up the dark window blinds which last night he had pulled down to shut out the disturbing sight of the stars. He bethought him of his eye-drops, tilted back his head, and there was that planet, serene, terrible and splendid, looking in at him . . . immortal beauty . . . yes, but only when somebody *saw* it, he fiercely answered back!

He thought about it until his head went round. He would get out of this room and get out quick. He began to dress —wool stockings, moccasins, flannel shirt, leather coat. He would get out and find his island. After all, it still existed. The Professor hadn't put it in his pocket, he guessed! He scrawled a line for William, his man Friday: "BREAKFAST WHEN I RETURN," and stuck it on a hook in his dining-car kitchen. William was "boarded out" in a fisherman's family. (Grenfell wouldn't stand anyone in the cabin with him. He wanted all this glorious loneliness for himself. He had paid dearly for it.)

He hurried out of the kitchen door and up the grassy hillside to the spruce wood. The spruces stood tall and still as ever in the morning air; the same dazzling spears of sunlight shot through their darkness. The path underneath had the dampness, the magical softness which his feet remembered. On either side of the trail yellow toadstools and white mushrooms lifted the heavy thatch of brown spruce needles and made little damp tents. Everything was still in the wood. There was not a breath of wind; deep shadow and new-born light, yellow as gold, a little unsteady like other new-born things. It was blinking, too, as if its own reflection on the dewdrops was too bright. Or maybe the light had been asleep down under the sea and was just waking up.

"Hello, Grandfather!" Grenfell cried as he turned a curve in the path. The grandfather was a giant spruce tree that had been struck by lightning (must have been about a hundred years ago, the islanders said). It still lay on a slant along a steep hillside, its shallow roots in the air, all its great branches bleached greyish white, like an animal skeleton long exposed to the weather. Grenfell put out his hand to twitch off a twig as he passed, but it snapped back at him like a metal spring. He stopped in astonishment, his hand smarted, actually.

"Well, Grandfather! Lasting pretty well, I should say. Compliments! You get good drainage on this hillside, don't you?"

Ten minutes more on the winding uphill path brought him to the edge of the spruce wood and out on a bald headland that topped a cliff two hundred feet above the sea. He sat down on a rock and grinned. Like Christian of old, he thought, he had left his burden at the bottom of the hill. Now why had he let Doctor Fairweather's perfectly unessential information give him a miserable night? He had always known this island existed long before he discovered it, and that it must once have been a naked rock. The soil-surface was very thin. Almost anywhere on the open downs you could cut with a spade through the dry turf and roll it back from the rock as you roll a rug back from the floor. One knew that the rock itself, since it rested on the bottom of the ocean, must be very ancient.

But that fact had nothing to do with the green surface where men lived and trees lived and blue flags and buttercups and daisies and meadowsweet and steeplebush and goldenrod crowded one another in all the clearings. Grenfell shook himself and hurried along up the cliff trail. He crossed the first brook on stepping-stones. Must have been recent rain, for the water was rushing down the deep-cut channel with sound and fury till it leaped hundreds of feet over the face of the cliff and fell into the sea: a white waterfall that never rested.

The trail led on through a long jungle of black alder . . . then through a lazy, rooty, brown swamp . . . and then out on another breezy, grassy headland which jutted far out into the air in a horseshoe curve. There one could stand beside a bushy rowan tree and see four waterfalls, white as silver, pouring down the perpendicular cliff walls.

Nothing had changed. Everything was the same, and he, Henry Grenfell, was the same: the relationship was unchanged. Not even a tree blown down; the stunted beeches (precious because so few) were still holding out against a climate unkind to them. The old white birches that grew on the edge of the cliff had been so long beaten and tormented by east wind and north wind that they grew more down than up, and hugged the earth that was kinder than the stormy air. Their growth was all one-sided, away from the sea, and their land-side branches actually lay along the ground and crept up the hillside through the underbrush, persistent, nearly naked, like great creeping vines, and at last, when they got into the sunshine, burst into tender leafage.

This knob of grassy headland with the bushy rowan tree had been his vague objective when he left the cabin. From this elbow he could look back on the cliff wall, both north and south, and see the four silver waterfalls in the morning light. A splendid sight, Grenfell was thinking, and all his own. Not even a gull—they had gone screaming down the coast toward the herring weirs when he first left his cabin. Not a living creature—but wait a minute: there was something moving down there, on the shingle by the water's edge. A human figure, in a long white bathrobe—and a rubber cap! Then it must be a woman? Queer. No island woman would go bathing at this hour, not even in the warm inland ponds. Yes, it was a woman! A girl, and he knew *what* girl! In the miseries of the night he had forgotten her. The geologist's daughter.

How had she got down there without breaking her neck? She picked her way along the rough shingle; presently stopped and seemed to be meditating, seemed to be looking out at an old sliver of rock that was almost submerged at high tide. She opened her robe, a grey thing lined with white. Her bathing-suit was pink. If a clam stood upright and graciously opened its shell, it would look like that. After a moment she drew her shell together again—felt the chill of the morning air, probably. People are really themselves only when they believe they are absolutely alone and unobserved, he was thinking. With a quick motion she shed her robe, kicked off her sandals, and took to the water.

At the same moment Grenfell kicked off his moccasins. "Crazy kid! What does she think she's doing? This is the North Atlantic, girl, you can't treat it like that!" As he muttered, he was getting off his fox-lined jacket and loosening his braces. Just how he would get down to the shingle he didn't know, but he guessed he'd have to. He was getting ready while, so far, she was doing nicely. Nothing is more embarrassing than to rescue people who don't want to be rescued. The tide was out, slack—she evidently knew its schedule.

She reached the rock, put up her arms and rested for a moment, then began to weave her way back. The distance wasn't much, but Lord! the cold,—in the early morning! When he saw her come out dripping and get into her shell, he began to shuffle on his fur jacket and his moccasins. He kept on scolding. "Silly creature! Why couldn't she wait till afternoon, when the death-chill is off the water?"

He scolded her ghost all the way home, but he thought he knew just how she felt. Probably she used to take her swim at that hour last summer, and she had forgot how cold the water was. When she first opened her long coat the nip of the air had startled her a little. There was no one watching her, she didn't have to keep face—except to herself. That she had to do and no fuss about it. She hadn't dodged. She had gone out, and she had come back. She would have a happy day. He knew just how she felt. She surely did look like a little pink clam in her white shell!

He was walking fast down the winding trails. Everything since he left the cabin had been reassuring, delightful—everything was the same, and so was he! The air, or the smell of fir trees—something had sharpened his appetite. He was hungry. As he passed the grandfather tree he waved his hand, but didn't stop. Plucky youth is more bracing than enduring age. He crossed the sharp line from the deep shade to the sunny hillside behind his cabin and saw the wood smoke rising from the chimney. The door of the dining-car kitchen stood open, and the smell of coffee drowned the spruce smell and sea smell. William hadn't waited; he was wisely breakfasting.

As he came down the hill Grenfell was chuckling to himself: "Anyhow, when that first amphibious frog-toad found his water-hole dried up behind him, and jumped out to hop along till he could find another—well, he started on a long hop."

APRIL TWILIGHTS

AND OTHER POEMS

To my Father
for a Valentine

Contents

Part I

"Grandmither, think not I forget"

Grandmither, think not I forget, when I come back to town,
An' wander the old ways again an' tread them up an' down.
I never smell the clover bloom, nor see the swallows pass,
Without I mind how good ye were unto a little lass.
I never hear the winter rain a-pelting all night through,
Without I think and mind me of how cold it falls on you.
And if I come not often to your bed beneath the thyme,
Mayhap 't is that I'd change wi' ye, and gie my bed for thine,
  Would like to sleep in thine.

I never hear the summer winds among the roses blow,
Without I wonder why it was ye loved the lassie so.
Ye gave me cakes and lollipops and pretty toys a score,—
I never thought I should come back and ask ye now for more.
Grandmither, gie me your still, white hands, that lie upon
  your breast,
For mine do beat the dark all night and never find me rest;
They grope among the shadows an' they beat the cold black
  air,
They go seekin' in the darkness, an' they never find him there,
  An' they never find him there.

Grandmither, gie me your sightless eyes, that I may never see
His own a-burnin' full o' love that must not shine for me.
Grandmither, gie me your peaceful lips, white as the kirkyard
  snow,
For mine be red wi' burnin' thirst, an' he must never know.
Grandmither, gie me your clay-stopped ears, that I may never
  hear
My lad a-singin' in the night when I am sick wi' fear;
A-singin' when the moonlight over a' the land is white—
Aw God! I'll up an' go to him a-singin' in the night,
  A-callin' in the night.

Grandmither, gie me your clay-cold heart that has forgot to
  ache,

For mine be fire within my breast and yet it cannot break.
It beats an' throbs forever for the things that must not be,—
An' can ye not let me creep in an' rest awhile by ye?
A little lass afeard o' dark slept by ye years agone—
Ah, she has found what night can hold 'twixt sunset an' the
    dawn!
So when I plant the rose an' rue above your grave for ye,
Ye'll know it's under rue an' rose that I would like to be,
    That I would like to be.

Fides, Spes

Joy is come to the little
    Everywhere;
Pink to the peach and pink to the apple,
    White to the pear.
Stars are come to the dogwood,
    Astral, pale;
Mists are pink on the red-bud,
    Veil after veil.
Flutes for the feathery locusts,
    Soft as spray;
Tongues of lovers for chestnuts, poplars,
    Babbling May.
Yellow plumes for the willows'
    Wind-blown hair;
Oak trees and sycamores only
    Comfortless, bare.
Sore from steel and the watching,
    Somber and old,
(Wooing robes for the beeches, larches,
    Splashed with gold,
Breath of love from the lilacs,
    Warm with noon,)
Great hearts cold when the little
    Beat mad so soon.
What is their faith to bear it
    Till it come,
Waiting with rain-cloud and swallow,
    Frozen, dumb?

The Tavern

In the tavern of my heart
  Many a one has sat before,
Drunk red wine and sung a stave,
  And, departing, come no more.
When the night was cold without,
  And the ravens croaked of storm,
They have sat them at my hearth,
  Telling me my house was warm.

As the lute and cup went round,
  They have rhymed me well in lay; —
When the hunt was on at morn,
  Each, departing, went his way.
On the walls, in compliment,
  Some would scrawl a verse or two,
Some have hung a willow branch,
  Or a wreath of corn-flowers blue.

Ah! my friend, when thou dost go,
  Leave no wreath of flowers for me;
Not pale daffodils nor rue,
  Violets nor rosemary.
Spill the wine upon the lamps,
  Tread the fire, and bar the door;
So despoil the wretched place,
  None will come forevermore.

The Hawthorn Tree

Across the shimmering meadows —
Ah, when he came to me!
In the spring-time,
In the night-time,
In the starlight,
Beneath the hawthorn tree.

Up from the misty marsh-land —
Ah, when he climbed to me!
To my white bower,

To my sweet rest,
To my warm breast,
Beneath the hawthorn tree.

Ask of me what the birds sang,
High in the hawthorn tree;
What the breeze tells,
What the rose smells,
What the stars shine—
Not what he said to me!

The Poor Minstrel

Does the darkness cradle thee
Than mine arms more tenderly?
Do the angels God hath put
        There to guard thy lonely sleep—
One at head and one at foot—
        Watch more fond and constant keep?
When the black-bird sings in May,
        And the spring is in the wood,
Would you never trudge the way
        Over hill-tops, if you could?
Was my harp so hard a load
        Even on the sunny morns
When the plumèd huntsmen rode
        To the music of their horns?
Hath the love that lit the stars,
        Fills the sea and moulds the flowers,
Whose completeness nothing mars,
        Made forgot what once was ours?
Christ hath perfect rest to give—
        Stillness and perpetual peace;
You, who found it hard to live,
        Sleep and sleep, without surcease.

Christ hath stars to light thy porch,
        Silence after fevered song;—
I had but a minstrel's torch
        And the way was wet and long.

Sleep. No more on winter nights,
 Harping at some castle gate,
Thou must see the revel lights
 Stream upon our cold estate.
Bitter was the bread of song
 While you tarried in my tent,
And the jeering of the throng
 Hurt you, as it came and went.
When you slept upon my breast
 Grief had wed me long ago:
Christ hath his perpetual rest
 For thy weariness. But oh!
When I sleep beside the road,
 Thanking God thou liest not so,
Brother to the owl and toad,
 Could'st thou, Dear, but let me know,
Does the darkness cradle thee
Than mine arms more tenderly?

Antinous

With attributes of gods they sculptured him,
 Hermes, Osiris, but were never wise
To lift the level, frowning brow of him
 Or dull the mortal misery in his eyes,
The scornful weariness of every limb,
 The dust-begotten doubt that never dies,
Antinous, beneath thy lids, though dim,
The curling smoke of altars rose to thee,
Conjuring thee to comfort and content.
 An emperor sent his galleys wide and far
To seek thy healing for thee. Yea, and spent
 Honour and treasure and red fruits of war
 To lift thy heaviness, lest thou should'st mar
The head that was an empire's glory, bent
A little, as the heavy poppies are.
 Did the perfection of thy beauty pain
Thy limbs to bear it? Did it ache to be,
 As song hath ached in men, or passion vain?

Or lay it like some heavy robe on thee?
   Was thy sick soul drawn from thee like the rain,
Or drunk up as the dead are drunk each hour
To feed the colour of some tulip flower?

London Roses

"Rowses, Rowses! Penny a bunch!" they tell you—
   Slattern girls in Trafalgar, eager to sell you,
Roses, roses, red in the Kensington sun,
Holland Road, High Street, Bayswater, see you and smell
     you—
Roses of London town, red till the summer is done.

Roses, roses, locust and lilac, perfuming
West End, East End, wondrously budding and blooming
Out of the black earth, rubbed in a million hands,
Foot-trod, sweat-sour over and under, entombing
Highways of darkness, deep gutted with iron bands.

"Rowses, rowses! Penny a bunch!" they tell you,
   Ruddy blooms of corruption, see you and smell you,
Born of stale earth, fallowed with squalor and tears—
North shire, south shire, none are like these, I tell you,
Roses of London perfumed with a thousand years.

Winter at Delphi

Cold are the stars of the night,
   Wild is the tempest crying,
Fast through the velvet dark
   Little white flakes are flying.
Still is the House of Song.
   But the fire on the hearth is burning;
And the lamps are trimmed, and the cup
   Is full for his day of returning.
His watchers are fallen asleep,
   They wait but his call to follow,
Ay, to the ends of the earth—
   But Apollo, the god, Apollo?

Sick is the heart in my breast,
    Mine eyes are blinded with weeping;
The god who never comes back,
    The watch that forever is keeping.
Service of gods is hard;
    Deep lies the snow on my pillow.
For him the laurel and song,
    Weeping for me and the willow:
Empty my arms and cold
    As the nest forgot of the swallow;
Birds will come back with the spring,—
    But Apollo, the god, Apollo?

Hope will come back with the spring,
    Joy with the lark's returning;
Love must awake betimes,
    When crocus buds are a-burning.
Hawthorns will follow the snow,
    The robin his tryst be keeping;
Winds will blow in the May,
    Waking the pulses a-sleeping.
Snowdrops will whiten the hills,
    Violets hide in the hollow:
Pan will be drunken and rage—
    But Apollo, the god, Apollo?

Paradox

I knew them both upon Miranda's isle,
    Which is of youth a sea-bound seigniory:
Misshapen Caliban, so seeming vile,
    And Ariel, proud prince of minstrelsy,
Who did forsake the sunset for my tower
    And like a star above my slumber burned.
The night was held in silver chains by power
    Of melody, in which all longings yearned—
Star-grasping youth in one wild strain expressed,
    Tender as dawn, insistent as the tide;

The heart of night and summer stood confessed.
I rose aglow and flung the lattice wide—
Ah, jest of art, what mockery and pang!
Alack, it was poor Caliban who sang.

In Media Vita

Streams of the spring a-singing,
    Winds of the May that blow,
Birds from the Southland winging,
    Buds in the grasses below.
Clouds that speed hurrying over,
    And the climbing rose by the wall,
Singing of bees in the clover,
    And the dead, under all!

Lads and their sweethearts lying
    In the cleft of the windy hill;
Hearts that are hushed of their sighing,
    Lips that are tender and still.
Stars in the purple gloaming,
    Flowers that suffuse and fall,
Twitter of bird-mates homing,
    And the dead, under all!

Herdsman abroad with his collie,
    Girls on their way to the fair,
Young lads a-chasing their folly,
    Parsons a-praying their prayer.
Children their kites a-flying,
    Grandsires that nod by the wall,
Mothers soft lullabies sighing,
    And the dead, under all!

Evening Song

Dear love, what thing of all the things that be
Is ever worth one thought from you or me,
    Save only Love,
    Save only Love?

The days so short, the nights so quick to flee,
The world so wide, so deep and dark the sea,
        So dark the sea;

So far the suns and every listless star,
Beyond their light—Ah! dear, who knows how far,
        Who knows how far?

One thing of all dim things I know is true,
The heart within me knows, and tells it you,
        And tells it you.

So blind is life, so long at last is sleep,
And none but Love to bid us laugh or weep,
        And none but Love,
        And none but Love.

Lament for Marsyas

Marsyas sleeps. Oh, never wait,
Maidens, by the city gate,
Till he come to plunder gold
Of the daffodils you hold,
Or your branches white with may;
He is whiter gone than they.
He will startle you no more
When along the river shore
Damsels beat the linen clean.
Nor when maidens play at ball
Will he catch it where it fall:
Though ye wait for him and call,
He will answer not, I ween.

Happy Earth to hold him so,
Still and satisfied and low,
Giving him his will—ah, more
Than a woman could before!
Still forever holding up
To his parted lips the cup
Which hath eased him, when to bless
All who loved were powerless.

Ah! for that too-lovely head,
Low among the laureled dead,
Many a rose earth oweth yet;
Many a yellow jonquil brim,
Many a hyacinth dewy-dim,
For the singing breath of him—
Sweeter than the violet.

"I Sought the Wood in Winter"

I sought the wood in summer
    When every twig was green;
The rudest boughs were tender,
    And buds were pink between.
Light-fingered aspens trembled
    In fitful sun and shade,
And daffodils were golden
    In every starry glade.
The brook sang like a robin—
    My hand could check him where
The lissome maiden willows
    Shook out their yellow hair.

"How frail a thing is Beauty,"
    I said, "when every breath
She gives the vagrant summer
    But swifter woos her death.
For this the star dust troubles,
    For this have ages rolled:
To deck the wood for bridal
    And slay her with the cold."

I sought the wood in winter
    When every leaf was dead;
Behind the wind-whipped branches
    The winter sun set red.
The coldest star was rising
    To greet that bitter air,
The oaks were writhen giants;
    Nor bud nor bloom was there.

The birches, white and slender,
        In deathless marble stood,
The brook, a white immortal,
        Slept silent in the wood.

"How sure a thing is Beauty,"
        I cried. "No bolt can slay,
No wave nor shock despoil her,
        No ravishers dismay.
Her warriors are the angels
        That cherish from afar,
Her warders people Heaven
        And watch from every star.
The granite hills are slighter,
        The sea more like to fail;
Behind the rose the planet,
        The Law behind the veil."

"Sleep, Minstrel, Sleep"

Sleep, minstrel, sleep; the winter wind's awake,
        And yellow April's buried deep and cold.
The wood is black, and songful things forsake
        The haunted forest when the year is old.
Above the drifted snow the aspens quake,
        The scourging clouds a shrunken moon enfold,
Denying all that nights of summer spake
        And swearing false the summer's globe of gold.

Sleep, minstrel, sleep; in such a bitter night
        Thine azure song would seek the stars in vain;
Thy rose and roundelay the winter's spite
        Would scarcely spare—O never wake again!
These leaden skies do not thy masques invite,
        Thy sunny breath would warm not their disdain;
How should'st thou sing to boughs with winter dight,
        Or gather marigolds in winter rain?

Sleep, minstrel, sleep; we do not grow more kind;
        Your cloak was thin, your wound was wet and deep;
More bitter breath there was than winter wind,

And hotter tears than now thy lovers weep.
Upon the world-old breast of comfort find
How gentle Darkness thee will gently keep.
Thou wert the summer's, and thy joy declined
When winter winds awoke. Sleep, minstrel, sleep.

In Rose-Time

Oh, this is the joy of the rose:
That it blows,
And goes.

Winter lasts a five-month,
Spring-time stays but one;
Yellow blow the rye-fields
When the rose is done.
Pines are clad at Yuletide
When the birch is bare,
And the holly's greenest
In the frosty air.

Sorrow keeps a stone house
Builded grim and gray;
Pleasure hath a straw thatch
Hung with lanterns gay.
On her petty savings
Niggard Prudence thrives,
Passion, ere the moonset,
Bleeds a thousand lives.

Virtue hath a warm hearth—
Folly's dead and drowned;
Friendship hath her own when
Love is underground.
Ah! for me the madness
Of the spendthrift flower,
Burning myriad sunsets
In a single hour.

For this is the joy of the rose:
That it blows,
And goes.

Poppies on Ludlow Castle

Through halls of vanished pleasure,
    And hold of vanished power,
And crypt of faith forgotten,
    I came to Ludlow tower.

A-top of arch and stairway,
    Of crypt, and donjon cell,
Of council hall, and chamber,
    Of wall, and ditch, and well,

High over grated turrets
    Where clinging ivies run,
A thousand scarlet poppies
    Enticed the rising sun,

Upon the topmost turret,
    With death and damp below,—
Three hundred years of spoilage,—
    The crimson poppies grow.

This hall it was that bred him,
    These hills that knew him brave,
The gentlest English singer
    That fills an English grave.

How have they heart to blossom
    So cruel gay and red,
When beauty so hath perished
    And valour so hath sped?

When knights so fair are rotten,
    And captains true asleep,
And singing lips are dust-stopped
    Six English earth-feet deep?

When ages old remind me
    How much hath gone for naught,
What wretched ghost remaineth
    Of all that flesh hath wrought;

Of love and song and warring,
    Of adventure and play,
Of art and comely building,
    Of faith and form and fray—

I'll mind the flowers of pleasure,
    Of short-lived youth and sleep,
That drank the sunny weather
    A-top of Ludlow keep.

Prairie Dawn

A crimson fire that vanquishes the stars;
A pungent odor from the dusty sage;
A sudden stirring of the huddled herds;
A breaking of the distant table-lands
Through purple mists ascending, and the flare
Of water-ditches silver in the light;
A swift, bright lance hurled low across the world;
A sudden sickness for the hills of home.

Aftermath

Canst thou conjure a vanished morn of spring,
    Or bid the ashes of the sunset glow
Again to redness? Are we strong to wring
    From trodden grapes the juice drunk long ago?
Can leafy longings stir in autumn's blood,
    Or can I wear a pearl dissolved in wine,
Or go a-Maying in a winter wood,
    Or paint with youth thy wasted cheek, or mine?
What bloom, then, shall abide, since ours hath sped?
    Thou art more lost to me than they who dwell
In Egypt's sepulchres, long ages fled;
    And would I touch—Ah me! I might as well
Covet the gold of Helen's vanished head,
    Or kiss back Cleopatra from the dead!

Thou Art the Pearl

I read of knights who laid their armour down,
    And left the tourney's prize for other hands,
And clad them in a pilgrim's sober gown,
    To seek a holy cup in desert lands.
For them no more the torch of victory;
    For them lone vigils and the starlight pale,
So they in dreams the Blessed Cup may see—
      Thou art the Grail!

An Eastern king once smelled a rose in sleep,
    And on the morrow laid his scepter down.
His heir his titles and his lands might keep,—
    The rose was sweeter wearing than the crown.
Nor cared he that its life was but an hour,
    A breath that from the crimson summer blows,
Who gladly paid a kingdom for a flower—
      Thou art the Rose!

A merchant man, who knew the worth of things,
    Beheld a pearl more priceless than a star;
And straight returning, all he hath he brings
    And goes upon his way, ah, richer far!
Laughter of merchants in the market-place,
    Nor taunting gibe nor scornful lips that curl,
Can ever cloud the rapture on his face—
      Thou art the Pearl!

Arcadian Winter

Woe is me to tell it thee,
Winter winds in Arcady!
Scattered is thy flock and fled
From the glades where once it fed,
And the snow lies drifted white
In the bower of our delight,
Where the beech threw gracious shade
On the cheek of boy and maid:
And the bitter blasts make roar
Through the fleshless sycamore.

White enchantment holds the spring,
Where thou once wert wont to sing,
And the cold hath cut to death
Reeds melodious of thy breath.
He, the rival of thy lyre,
Nightingale with note of fire,
Sings no more; but far away,
From the windy hill-side gray,
Calls the broken note forlorn
Of an aged shepherd's horn.

Still about the fire they tell
How it long ago befell
That a shepherd maid and lad
Met and trembled and were glad;
When the swift spring waters ran,
And the wind to boy or man
Brought the aching of his sires—
Song and love and all desires.
Ere the starry dogwoods fell.
They were lovers, so they tell.

Woe is me to tell it thee,
Winter winds in Arcady!
Broken pipes and vows forgot,
Scattered flocks returning not,
Frozen brook and drifted hill,
Ashen sun and song-birds still;
Songs of summer and desire
Crooned about the winter fire;
Shepherd lads with silver hair,
Shepherd maids no longer fair.

Provençal Legend

On his little grave and wild,
Faustinus, the martyr child,
  Candytuft and mustards grow.
Ah, how many a June has smiled
  On the turf he lies below.

Ages gone they laid him there,
Quit of sun and wholesome air,
    Broken flesh and tortured limb;
Leaving all his faith the heir
    Of his gentle hope and him.

Yonder, under pagan skies,
Bleached by rains, the circus lies,
    Where they brought him from his play.
Comeliest his of sacrifice,
    Youth and tender April day.

"Art thou not the shepherd's son? —
There the hills thy lambkins run? —
    These the fields thy brethren keep?"
"On a higher hill than yon
    Doth my Father lead His sheep."

"Bring thy ransom, then," they say,
"Gold enough to pave the way
    From the temple to the Rhone."
When he came, upon his day,
    Slender, tremulous, alone,

Mustard flowers like these he pressed,
Golden, flame-like, to his breast,
    Blooms the early weanlings eat.
When his Triumph brought him rest,
    Yellow bloom lay at his feet.

Golden play-days came: the air
Called him, weanlings bleated there,
    Roman boys ran fleet with spring;
Shorn of youth and usage fair,
    Hope nor hill-top days they bring.

But the shepherd children still
Come at Easter, warm or chill,
    Come with violets gathered wild
From his sloping pasture hill,
    Play-fellows who would fulfill
    Play-time to that martyr child.

The Encore

No garlands in the winter-time,
    No trumpets in the night!
The song ye praise was done lang syne,
    And was its own delight.
O' God's name take the wreath away,
    Since now the music's sped;
Ye never cry, "Long live the king!"
    Until the king is dead.

When I came piping through the land,
    One morning in the spring,
With cockle-burrs upon my coat,
    'Twas then I was a king:
A mullein sceptre in my hand,
    My order daisies three,
With song's first freshness on my lips—
    And then ye pitied me!

Song

Troubadour, when you were gay,
You wooed with rose and roundelay,
Singing harp-strings, sweet as May.
From beneath the crown of bay
Fell the wild, abundant hair.
Scent of cherry bloom and pear
With you from the south did fare,
Buds of myrtle for your wear.
Soft as summer stars thine eyes,
Planets pale in violet skies;
Summer wind that sings and dies
Was the music of thy sighs.

Troubadour, one winter's night,
When the pasture-lands were white
And the cruel stars were bright,
Fortune held thee in despite.
Then beneath my tower you bore

Rose nor rondel as of yore,
But a heavy grief and sore
Laid in silence at my door.
April yearneth, April goes;
Not for me her violet blows,
I have done for long with those.
At my breast thy sorrow grows,
Nearer to my heart, God knows,
Than ever roundelay or rose!

L'Envoi

Where are the loves that we have loved before
When once we are alone, and shut the door?
No matter whose the arms that held me fast,
The arms of Darkness hold me at the last.
No matter down what primrose path I tend,
I kiss the lips of Silence in the end.
No matter on what heart I found delight,
I come again unto the breast of Night.
No matter when or how love did befall,
'Tis Loneliness that loves me best of all,
And in the end she claims me, and I know
That she will stay, though all the rest may go.
No matter whose the eyes that I would keep
Near in the dark, 'tis in the eyes of Sleep
That I must look and look forever more,
When once I am alone, and shut the door.

Part II

The Palatine

(In the "Dark Ages")

"Have you been with the King to Rome,
    Brother, big brother?"
"I've been there and I've come home.
    Back to your play, little brother."

"Oh, how high is Caesar's house,
    Brother, big brother?"
"Goats about the doorways browse:
Night hawks nest in the burnt roof-tree,
Home of the wild bird and home of the bee.
A thousand chambers of marble lie
Wide to the sun and the wind and the sky.
Poppies we find amongst our wheat
Grow on Caesar's banquet seat.
Cattle crop and neatherds drowse
On the floors of Caesar's house."

"But what has become of Caesar's gold,
    Brother, big brother?"
"The times are bad and the world is old—
Who knows the where of the Caesars' gold?
Night comes black on the Caesars' hill;
The wells are deep and the tales are ill.
Fire-flies gleam in the damp and mould,—
All that is left of the Caesars' gold.
    Back to your play, little brother."

"What has become of the Caesars' men,
    Brother, big brother?"
"Dogs in the kennel and wolf in the den
Howl for the fate of the Caesars' men.
Slain in Asia, slain in Gaul,
By Dacian border and Persian wall;
Rhineland orchard and Danube fen
Fatten their roots on Caesar's men."

794

"Why is the world so sad and wide,
            Brother, big brother?"
"Saxon boys by their fields that bide
 Need not know if the world is wide.
 Climb no mountain but Shire-end Hill,
 Cross no water but goes to mill;
 Ox in the stable and cow in the byre,
 Smell of the wood smoke and sleep by the fire;
 Sun-up in seed-time—a likely lad
 Hurts not his head that the world is sad.
            Back to your play, little brother."

The Gaul in the Capitol

The murmur of old, old water,
        The yellow of old, old stone,
The fountain that sings through the silence,
        The river-god, dreaming alone;
The Antonine booted and mounted
        In his sun-lit, hill-top place,
The Julians, gigantic in armour,
        The low-browed Claudian race.

The wolf and the twin boys she suckled,
        And the powerful breed they bred;
Caesars of duplicate empires,
        All under one roof-stead.
Fronting these fronts triumphant,
        Conquest on conquest pressed
By these marching, arrogant masters,
        Who could have hoped for the West?

At the feet of his multiple victors,
        Beaten and dazed and dumb,
One, from the wild new races,
        Clay of the kings to come.
Hail, in the halls of the Caesars!
        Hail, from the thrones oversea!
Sheath of the sword-like vigour,
        Sap of the kings to be!

A Likeness

(PORTRAIT BUST OF AN UNKNOWN, CAPITOL, ROME)

In every line a supple beauty—
    The restless head a little bent—
Disgust of pleasure, scorn of duty,
    The unseeing eyes of discontent.
I often come to sit beside him,
    This youth who passed and left no trace
Of good or ill that did betide him,
    Save the disdain upon his face.

The hope of all his House, the brother
    Adored, the golden-hearted son,
Whom Fortune pampered like a mother;
    And then—a shadow on the sun.
Whether he followed Caesar's trumpet,
    Or chanced the riskier game at home
To find how favour played the strumpet
    In fickle politics at Rome;

Whether he dreamed a dream in Asia
    He never could forget by day,
Or gave his youth to some Aspasia,
    Or gamed his heritage away—
Once lost, across the Empire's border
    This man would seek his peace in vain;
His look arraigns a social order
    Somehow entrammelled with his pain.

"The dice of gods are always loaded";
    One gambler, arrogant as they,
Fierce, and by fierce injustice goaded,
    Left both his hazard and the play.
Incapable of compromises,
    Unable to forgive or spare,
The strange awarding of the prizes
    He had no fortitude to bear.

Tricked by the forms of things material,—
　　The solid-seeming arch and stone,
The noise of war, the pomp Imperial,
　　The heights and depths about a throne—
He missed, among the shapes diurnal,
　　The old, deep-travelled road from pain,
The thoughts of men, which are eternal,
　　In which, eternal, men remain.

Ritratto d'ignoto; defying
　　Things unsubstantial as a dream—
An empire, long in ashes lying—
　　His face still set against the stream—
Yes, so he looked, that gifted brother
　　I loved, who passed and left no trace,
Not even—luckier than this other—
　　His sorrow in a marble face.

The Swedish Mother
(NEBRASKA)

"You shall hear the tale again—
　　Hush, my red-haired daughter."
Brightly burned the sunset gold
　　On the black pond water.

Red the pasture ridges gleamed
　　Where the sun was sinking.
Slow the windmill rasped and wheezed
　　Where the herd was drinking.

On the kitchen doorstep low
　　Sat a Swedish mother;
In her arms one baby slept,
　　By her sat another.

"All time, 'way back in old countree,
　Your grandpa, he been good to me.
　Your grandpa, he been young man, too,
　And I been yust li'l' girl, like you.

All time in spring, when evening come,
We go bring sheep an' li'l' lambs home.
We go big field, 'way up on hill,
Ten times high like our windmill.
One time your grandpa leave me wait
While he call sheep down. By de gate
I sit still till night come dark;
Rabbits run an' strange dogs bark,
Old owl hoot, an' your modder cry,
She been so 'fraid big bear come by.
Last, 'way off, she hear de sheep,
Li'l' bells ring and li'l' lambs bleat.
Then all sheep come over de hills,
Big white dust, an' old dog Nils.
Then come grandpa, in his arm
Li'l' sick lamb dat somet'ing harm.
He so young then, big and strong,
Pick li'l' girl up, take her 'long,—
Poor li'l' tired girl, yust like you,—
Lift her up an' take her too.
Hold her tight an' carry her far,—
Ain't no light but yust one star.
Sheep go 'bah-h,' an' road so steep;
Li'l' girl she go fast asleep."

Every night the red-haired child
    Begs to hear the story,
When the pasture ridges burn
    With the sunset glory.

She can never understand,
    Since the tale ends gladly,
Why her mother, telling it,
    Always smiles so sadly.

Wonderingly she looks away
    Where her mother's gazing;
Only sees the drifting herd,
    In the sunset grazing.

Spanish Johnny

The old West, the old time,
    The old wind singing through
The red, red grass a thousand miles,
    And, Spanish Johnny, you!
He'd sit beside the water-ditch
    When all his herd was in,
And never mind a child, but sing
    To his mandolin.

The big stars, the blue night,
    The moon-enchanted plain:
The olive man who never spoke,
    But sang the songs of Spain.
His speech with men was wicked talk—
    To hear it was a sin;
But those were golden things he said
    To his mandolin.

The gold songs, the gold stars,
    The world so golden then:
And the hand so tender to a child
    Had killed so many men.
He died a hard death long ago
    Before the Road came in;
The night before he swung, he sang
    To his mandolin.

Autumn Melody

In the autumn days, the days of parting,
    Days that in a golden silence fall,
When the air is quick with bird-wings starting,
    And the asters darken by the wall;

Strong and sweet the wine of heaven is flowing,
    Bees and sun and sleep and golden dyes;
Long forgot is budding-time and blowing,
    Sunk in honeyed sleep the garden lies.

Spring and storm and summer midnight madness
    Dream within the grape but never wake;
Bees and sun and sweetness,—oh, and sadness!
    Sun and sweet that reach the heart—and break.

Ah, the pain at heart forever starting,
    Ah, the cup untasted that we spilled
In the autumn days, the days of parting!
    Would our shades could drink it, and be stilled.

Prairie Spring

Evening and the flat land,
Rich and somber and always silent;
The miles of fresh-plowed soil,
Heavy and black, full of strength and harshness;
The growing wheat, the growing weeds,
The toiling horses, the tired men;
The long, empty roads,
Sullen fires of sunset, fading,
The eternal, unresponsive sky.
Against all this, Youth,
Flaming like the wild roses,
Singing like the larks over the plowed fields,
Flashing like a star out of the twilight;
Youth with its insupportable sweetness,
Its fierce necessity,
Its sharp desire;
Singing and singing,
Out of the lips of silence,
Out of the earthy dusk.

Macon Prairie

(NEBRASKA)

She held me for a night against her bosom,
The aunt who died when I was yet a baby,
The girl who scarcely lived to be a woman.
Stricken, she left familiar earth behind her,

Mortally ill, she braved the boisterous ocean,
Dying, she crossed irrevocable rivers,
Hailed the blue Lakes, and saw them fade forever,
Hungry for distances;—her heart exulting
That God had made so many seas and countries
To break upon the eye and sweep behind her.
From one whose love was tempered by discretion,
From all the net of caution and convenience
She snatched her high heart for the great adventure,
Broke her bright bubble under far horizons,—
Among the skirmishers that teased the future,
Precursors of the grave slow-moving millions
Already destined to the Westward-faring.

They came, at last, to where the railway ended,
The strange troop captained by a dying woman;
The father, the old man of perfect silence,
The mother, unresisting, broken-hearted,
The gentle brother and his wife, both timid,
Not knowing why they left their native hamlet;
Going as in a dream, but ever going.

In all the glory of an Indian summer,
The lambent transmutations of October,
They started with the great ox-teams from Hastings
And trekked in a southwesterly direction,
Boring directly toward the fiery sunset.
Over the red grass prairies, shaggy-coated,
Without a goal the caravan proceeded;
Across the tablelands and rugged ridges,
Through the coarse grasses which the oxen breasted,
Blue-stem and bunch-grass, red as sea-marsh samphire.
Always the similar, soft undulations
Of the free-breathing earth in golden sunshine,
The hardy wind, and dun hawks flying over
Against the unstained firmament of heaven.

In the front wagon, under the white cover,
Stretched on her feather-bed and propped with pillows,
Never dismayed by the rude oxen's scrambling,
The jolt of the tied wheel or brake or hold-back,

She lay, the leader of the expedition;
And with her burning eyes she took possession
Of the red waste,—for hers, and theirs, forever.

A wagon-top, rocking in seas of grasses,
A camp-fire on a prairie chartless, trackless,
A red spark under the dark tent of heaven.
Surely, they said, by day she saw a vision,
Though her exhausted strength could not impart it,—
Her breathing hoarser than the tired cattle.

When cold, bright stars the sunburnt days succeeded,
She took me in her bed to sleep beside her,—
A sturdy bunch of life, born on the ocean.
Always she had the wagon cover lifted
Before her face. The sleepless hours till daybreak
She read the stars.

"Plenty of time for sleep," she said, "hereafter."

She pointed out the spot on Macon prairie,
Telling my father that she wished to lie there.
"And plant, one day, an apple orchard round me,
In memory of woman's first temptation,
And man's first cowardice."
That night, within her bosom,
I slept.
                    Before the morning
I cried because the breast was cold behind me.

Now, when the sky blazes like blue enamel,
Brilliant and hard over the blond cornfields,
And through the autumn days our wind is blowing
Like the creative breath of God Almighty—
Then I rejoice that offended love demanded
Such wide retreat, and such self-restitution;
Forged an explorer's will in a frail woman,
Asked of her perfect faith and renunciation,
Hardships and perils, prophecy and vision,
The leadership of kin, and happy ending
On the red rolling land of Macon prairie.

Street in Packingtown
(Chicago)

In the gray dust before a frail gray shed,
By a board fence obscenely chalked in red,
A gray creek willow, left from country days,
Flickers pallid in the haze.

Beside the gutter of the unpaved street,
Tin cans and broken glass about his feet,
And a brown whisky bottle, singled out
For play from prosier crockery strewn about,
Twisting a shoestring noose, a Polack's brat
Joylessly torments a cat.

His dress, some sister's cast-off wear,
Is rolled to leave his stomach bare.
His arms and legs with scratches bleed;
He twists the cat and pays no heed.
He mauls her neither less nor more
Because her claws have raked him sore.
His eyes, faint-blue and moody, stare
From under a pale shock of hair.
Neither resentment nor surprise
Lights the desert of those eyes—
To hurt and to be hurt; he knows
All he will know on earth, or need to know.

But there, beneath his willow tree,
His tribal, tutelary tree,
The tortured cat across his knee,
With hate, perhaps, a threat, maybe,
Lithuania looks at me.

A Silver Cup

In Venice,
Under the Rialto bridge, one summer morning,
In a mean shop I bought a silver goblet.
It was a place of poor and sordid barter,
A damp hole filled with rags and rusty kettles,

Fire-tongs and broken grates and mended bellows,
And common crockery, coarse in use and fashion.
Everything spoke the desperate needs of body,
The breaking up and sale of wretched shelters,
The frail continuance even of hunger.
Misery under all—and that so fleeting!
The fight to fill the pots and pans soon over,
And then this wretched litter left from living.

The goblet
Stood in a dusty window full of charcoal,
The only bright, the only gracious object.
Because my heart was full to overflowing,
Because my day to weep had not come near me,
Because the world was full of love, I bought it.
From all the wreckage there I took no warning;—
Those ugly things outlasting hearts and houses,
And all the life that men build into houses.
Out of the jaws of hunger toothed with iron,
Into the sun exultantly I bore it.
Then, in the brightness of the summer sunshine,
I saw the loops and flourishes of letters,
The scattered trace of some outworn inscription,—
Six lines or more, rubbed flat into the silver,
Dashes and strokes, like rain-marks in a snowdrift.
Was it a prize, perhaps, or gift of friendship?
Was its inscription hope, or recognition?
Not heeding still, I bade my oarsman quicken,
And once ashore, across the Square I hastened,
Precipitate through the idlers and the pigeons,
Behind the Clock Tower, to a cunning craftsman,
There to exhort and urge the deft engraver,
And crowd upon my cup another story;
A name and promise in my memory singing.

In Venice,
Under the Rialto bridge, I bought you.
Now you come back to me, such long years after,
Your promise never kept, your hope defeated,
Your legend now a thing for tears and laughter;—

Though both your names are names of living people,
Cut by the steady hand of that engraver
While I stood over him and urged his deftness.
He played the part; nor stopped to smile and tell me
That for such words his art was too enduring.
His living was to cut such stuff in silver!
And now I have you, what to do, I wonder?
The names, another smith can soon efface them,—
But leave, so beautifully cut, the legend.
Not from a poet's book, but from the living
Sad mouth of a young peasant boy, I took it;
Four words, which mean that life is sweet together.

In some dark junk-shop window I shall leave you,
Some place of poor effects from broken houses,
Where desperate women go to sell a saucepan
And frightened men to buy a baby's cradle.
Here, in New York, a city full of exiles,
Short marriages and early deaths and heart-breaks:
In some such window, with the blue glass vases,
The busts of Presidents in plaster, gilded,
Pawned watches, and the rings and chains and bracelets
Given for love and sold for utter anguish,
There I shall leave you, a sole gracious object.

And hope some blind, bright eye will one day spy you—
Some boy with too much love and empty pockets
May read with quickening pulse your brief inscription,
Cut in his mother-language, half forgotten,
Four words which mean that life is sweet together;
Rush in and count his coins upon the table,
(A cup his own as if his heart had made it!)
And bear you off to one who hopes as he does.
So, one day, may the wish, for you, be granted.
They will not know, these two, the names you cover;
Mine and another, razed by violence from you,
Nor his, worn down by time, the first possessor's—
Who had his story, which you never told me.

Recognition

The old volcanic mountains
That slope up from the sea—
They dream and dream a thousand years
And watch what-is-to-be.

What gladness shines upon them
When, white as white sea-foam,
To the old, old ports of Beauty
A new sail comes home!

Going Home
(BURLINGTON ROUTE)

How smoothly the trains run beyond the Missouri;
Even in my sleep I know when I have crossed the river.
The wheels turn as if they were glad to go;
The sharp curves and windings left behind,
The roadway wide open,
(*The crooked straight*
And the rough places plain.)

They run smoothly, they run softly, too.
There is not noise enough to trouble the lightest sleeper.
Nor jolting to wake the weary-hearted.
I open my window and let the air blow in,
The air of morning,
That smells of grass and earth—
Earth, the grain-giver.

How smoothly the trains run beyond the Missouri;
Even in my sleep I know when I have crossed the river.
The wheels turn as if they were glad to go;
They run like running water,
Like Youth, running away . . .
They spin bright along the bright rails,
Singing and humming,
Singing and humming.
They run remembering,
They run rejoicing,
As if they, too, were going home.

Poor Marty

A lament for Martha, the old kitchenmaid, by her fellow servant, the stableman. The servants are not Negroes, but 'poor whites.'
(*Old Virginia*)

I

Who will scour the pots and pans,
Now Marty's gone away?
Who will scald the milking cans
And put the cream away?
Who will wash the goblets tall,
And chiney plates along the wall,
Platters big and platters small,
Never let one crack or fall,
Now Marty's gone away?
Ding-dong-dell, ding-dong-dell, poor Marty's gone away.

Who will clean the kitchen sink,
Ringed with grease as black as ink?
Not the Mistress, strict and cold,
Not the Master, meek and old,
Not our Miss in lawn and lace,
White of hand and fair of face.
Nor her sister, Marty's dear,
Played the harp for her to hear.
(Ever would the poor soul smile,
Rocking on her tired feet
When the harp strings sounded sweet—
Wiping all her goblets clear
To the music of her dear.)
Who will wash the things away,
Wash them three times every day?
Sixty years she never missed
While her hand hung to her wrist,
Never broke a plate or cup.
Who will wash our dishes up,
Now Marty's gone away?
Ding-dong-dell, ding-dong-dell, poor Marty's gone away.

Who will start the kitchen fire,

Now Marty's gone away?
When the house is all but dead,
Maids and mistress fast abed,
Windows rattle, stair steps groan,
Cookstove gray and cold as stone,
And the handle of the door
Froze to make your fingers sore.
Marty she was thin and old,
Little fleshed against the cold.
But she loved the maidies well,
Ever feared abroad to dwell.
All her life she feared to fall
Unto strangers after all,
To abide the poorhouse end.
Love and fear can both befriend.

Who will feed the winter birds,
Now Marty's gone away?
Snowbirds brown and robins red
Used to flutter round her head,
At the window open wide.
'T was our Mistress' fantasy
Neither cat nor dog might bide
For poor Marty's company,
But the birds came through the air
For the crust she had to spare.
Ding-dong-dell, ding-dong-dell, poor Marty's laid away.

II

On a moonlit winter night
Marty made her kitchen bright,
Wiped the pot-black from her hand
For before her Lord to stand,
She knew no other way.
No man earthly saw her go,
But she was gone afar we know
Before the break of day.
Mistress rang her silver bell,
Fixed to scold poor Marty well;

Master drummed his pewter pot
For his shaving water hot;
Miss and Missy waited long
Never thinking aught was wrong.
I must give my beasts their corn
With no bite or sup that morn,
For Marty's gone away.

Little had she here to leave,
Naught to will and none to grieve.
Hire nor wages did she draw
But her keep and bed of straw.
'T was our Mistress' fantasy
Marty might not trusted be
With fire to warm nor light to see,
In her kitchen loft.
But our Mistress could not bar
Light from moon or light from star,
Or from farther off.

'Martha,' said the angel, 'rise;
Come with me to Paradise.
Never heed thy needy shift,
Hers the shame who gave the gift.
Never hide thy choppy hand;
He, who waits, will understand
When He sees thee. Martha, rise;
Come with me to Paradise.'

Would that I prepared might be,
Clean of all this world like she;
Hands that never gathered aught,
But in faithful service wrought.
Naked as a babe new born
Went she forth that winter morn,
And not a stain she bare.
She, I pray, may housèd be
With Kindness, Love, and Charity—
Better off in ease than we,
Now poor Marty's gone.

NOT UNDER FORTY

Prefatory Note

The title of this book is meant to be "arresting" only in the literal sense, like the signs put up for motorists: "ROAD UNDER REPAIR," etc. It means that the book will have little interest for people under forty years of age. The world broke in two in 1922 or thereabouts, and the persons and prejudices recalled in these sketches slid back into yesterday's seven thousand years. Thomas Mann, to be sure, belongs immensely to the forward-goers, and they are concerned only with his forwardness. But he also goes back a long way, and his backwardness is more gratifying to the backward. It is for the backward, and by one of their number, that these sketches were written.

THE AUTHOR

Contents

A Chance Meeting

IT HAPPENED at Aix-les-Bains, one of the pleasantest places in the world. I was staying at the Grand-Hôtel d'Aix, which opens on the sloping little square with the bronze head of Queen Victoria, commemorating her visits to that old watering-place in Savoie. The Casino and the Opera are next door, just across the gardens. The hotel was built for the travellers of forty years ago, who liked large rooms and large baths, and quiet. It is not at all smart, but very comfortable. Long ago I used to hear old Pittsburghers and Philadelphians talk of it. The newer hotels, set on the steep hills above the town, have the fashionable trade; the noise and jazz and dancing.

In the dining-room I often noticed, at a table not far from mine, an old lady, a Frenchwoman, who usually lunched and dined alone. She seemed very old indeed, well over eighty, and somewhat infirm, though not at all withered or shrunken. She was not stout, but her body had that rather shapeless heaviness which for some detestable reason often settles upon people in old age. The thing one especially noticed was her fine head, so well set upon her shoulders and beautiful in shape, recalling some of the portrait busts of Roman ladies. Her forehead was low and straight, her nose made just the right angle with it, and there was something quite lovely about her temples, something one very rarely sees.

As I watched her entering and leaving the dining-room I observed that she was slightly lame, and that she utterly disregarded it—walked with a quick, short step and great impatience, holding her shoulders well back. One saw that she was contemptuously intolerant of the limitations of old age. As she passed my table she often gave me a keen look and a half-smile (her eyes were extremely bright and clear), as if she were about to speak. But I remained blank. I am a poor linguist, and there would be no point in uttering commonplaces to this old lady; one knew that much about her, at a glance. If one spoke to her at all, one must be at ease.

Several times in the early morning I happened to see her leave the hotel in her motor, and each time her chauffeur brought down and placed in the car a camp chair, an easel, and canvases and colour boxes strapped together. Then they drove off toward the mountains. A plucky old lady, certainly, to go sketching in that very hot weather—for this was in the latter part of August 1930, one of the hottest seasons Aix-les-Bains had ever known. Every evening after dinner the old lady disappeared into the lift and went to her own rooms. But often she reappeared later, dressed for the opera, and went out, attended by her maid.

One evening, when there was no opera, I found her smoking a cigarette in the lounge, where I had gone to write letters. It was a very hot night, and all the windows were open; seeing her pull her lace shawl closer about her shoulders, I went to shut one of them. Then she spoke to me in excellent English:—

"I think that draught blows out from the dining-room. If you will ask the boy to close the doors, we shall not feel the air."

I found the boy and had the doors closed. When I returned, the old lady thanked me, motioned to a chair at her side, and asked if I had time for a cigarette.

"You are stopping at Aix for some time, I judge?" she asked as I sat down.

I replied that I was.

"You like it, then? You are taking a cure? You have been here before?"

No, I was not taking a cure. I had been here before, and had come back merely because I liked the place.

"It has changed less than most places, I think," she remarked. "I have been coming here for thirty-five years; I have old associations with Aix-les-Bains. Besides, I enjoy the music here. I live in the South, at Antibes. You attend the Grand-Cercle? You heard the performance of *Tristan and Iseult* last night?"

I had not heard it. I told her I had thought the evening too frightfully hot to sit in a theatre.

"But it was no hotter there than anywhere else. I was not uncomfortable."

There was a reprimand in her tone, and I added the further excuse that I had thought the principals would probably not be very good, and that I liked to hear that opera well sung.

"They were well enough," she declared. "With Wagner I do not so much care about the voices. It is the orchestra I go to hear. The conductor last night was Albert Wolff, one of our best *Kapellmeister*."

I said I was sorry I had missed the opera.

"Are you going to his classical concert tomorrow afternoon? He will give a superb rendering of Ravel's *La Valse*—if you care for modern music."

I hastily said that I meant to go.

"But have you reserved your places? No? Then I would advise you to do so at once. The best way here is to have places for the entire chain of performances. One need not go to all, of course; but it is the best way. There is little else to do here in the evening, unless one plays at the gaming tables. Besides, it is almost September; the days are lowering now, and one needs the theatre." The old lady stopped, frowned, and made an impatient gesture with her very interesting hand. "What should I have said then? Lowering is not the word, but I seldom have opportunity to speak English."

"You might say the days are growing shorter, but I think lowering a very good word."

"*Mais un peu poétique, n'est-ce pas?*"

"Perhaps; but it is the right kind of poetic."

"And by that you mean?"

"That it's not altogether bookish or literary. The country people use it in some parts of England, I think. I have heard old-fashioned farmers use it in America, in the South."

The old lady gave a dry little laugh. "So if the farmers use a word it is quite safe, eh?"

Yes, I told her, that was exactly what I meant; safe.

We talked a little longer on that first occasion. She asked if I had been to Chamonix, and strongly advised me to go to a place near Sallanches, where she had lately been visiting friends, on her way to Aix-les-Bains. In replying to her questions I fell into the stupid way one sometimes adopts when speaking to people of another language; tried to explain something in very simple words. She frowned and checked me with: "Speak idiomatically, please. I knew English quite well at one time. If I speak it badly, it is because now I have no practice."

I said good-night and sat down at a desk to write letters. But on the way to my room I stopped to tell the friend with whom I was travelling that the old French lady we had so often admired spoke very good English, and spoke it easily; that she seemed, indeed, to have a rather special feeling for language.

II

The next day was intensely hot. In the morning the beautiful mountain ridges which surround Aix stood out sharp and clear, but the vineyards looked wilted. Toward noon the hills grew misty, and the sun poured down through a slightly milky atmosphere. I rather dreaded the heat of a concert hall, but at two o'clock I went to Albert Wolff's concert, and heard such a rendition of Ravel's *La Valse* as I do not expect to hear again; a small orchestra, wonderfully trained, and a masterly conductor.

The program was long, with two intermissions. The last group did not seem to be especially interesting, and the concert was quite long enough, and fine enough, without those numbers. I decided that I could miss them. I would go up to the Square and have tea beside the Roman arch. As I left the hall by the garden entrance, I saw the old French lady seated on the veranda with her maid, wearing a white dress and a white lace garden hat, fanning herself vigorously, the beads of moisture on her face making dark streaks in the powder. She beckoned to me and asked whether I had enjoyed the music. I told her that I had, very much indeed; but now my capacity for enjoying, or even listening, was quite spent, and I was going up to the Square for tea.

"Oh, no," said she, "that is not necessary. You can have your tea here at the Maison des Fleurs quite well, and still have time to go back for the last group."

I thanked her and went across the garden, but I did not mean to see the concert through. Seeing things through was evidently a habit with this old lady: witness the way she was

seeing life through, going to concerts and operas in this wilt-
ing heat; being concerned that other people should go, more-
over, and caring about the way in which Ravel was played,
when in the course of nature her interest in new music should
have stopped with César Franck, surely.

I left the Casino gardens through a grotto that gave into
the street, went up to the Square, and had tea with some nice
English people I had met on Mont Revard, a young business
man and his wife come over for their holiday. I felt a little as
if I had escaped from an exacting preceptress. The old lady
took it for granted that one wished to accomplish as much as
possible in a given space of time. I soon found that, to her,
life meant just that—accomplishing things; "doing them al-
ways a little better and better," as she once remarked after I
came to know her.

While I was dressing for dinner I decided to go away for a
few days, up into the high mountains of Haute-Savoie, under
Mont Blanc. That evening, when the old lady stopped me to
discuss the concert, I asked her for some suggestions about
the hotels there, since at our first meeting she had said I must
certainly go to some of the mountain places easily reached
from Sallanches.

She at once recommended a hotel that was very high and
cool, and then told me of all the excursions I must make from
that place, outlining a full program which I knew I should
not follow. I was going away merely to escape the heat and to
regard Mont Blanc from an advantageous point—not to be-
come acquainted with the country.

III

My trip into the mountains was wholly successful. All the
suggestions the old lady had given me proved excellent, and I
felt very grateful to her. I stayed away longer than I had
intended. I returned to Aix-les-Bains late one night, got up
early the next morning, and went to the bank, feeling that Aix
is always a good place to come back to. When I returned to
the hotel for lunch, there was the old lady, sitting in a chair
just outside the door, looking worn and faded. Why, since
she had her car and her driver there, she had not run away

from the heat, I do not know. But she had stayed through it, and gone out sketching every morning. She greeted me very cordially, asked whether I had an engagement for the evening, and suggested that we should meet in the salon after dinner.

I was dining with my friend, and after dinner we both went into the writing-room where the old lady was awaiting us. Our acquaintance seemed to have progressed measurably in my absence, though neither of us as yet knew the other's name. Her name, I thought, would mean very little; she was what she was. No one could fail to recognize her distinction and authority; it was in the carriage of her head, in her fine hands, in her voice, in every word she uttered in any language, in her brilliant, very piercing eyes. I had no curiosity about her name; that would be an accident and could scarcely matter.

We talked very comfortably for a time. The old lady made some comment on the Soviet experiment in Russia. My friend remarked that it was fortunate for the great group of Russian writers that none of them had lived to see the Revolution; Gogol, Tolstoi, Turgeniev.

"Ah, yes," said the old lady with a sigh, "for Turgeniev, especially, all this would have been very terrible. I knew him well at one time."

I looked at her in astonishment. Yes, of course, it was possible. She was very old. I told her I had never met anyone who had known Turgeniev.

She smiled. "No? I saw him very often when I was a young girl. I was much interested in German, in the great works. I was making a translation of *Faust*, for my own pleasure, merely, and Turgeniev used to go over my translation and correct it from time to time. He was a great friend of my uncle. I was brought up in my uncle's house." She was becoming excited as she spoke, her face grew more animated, her voice warmer, something flashed in her eyes, some strong feeling awoke in her. As she went on, her voice shook a little. "My mother died at my birth, and I was brought up in my uncle's house. He was more than father to me. My uncle also was a man of letters, Gustave Flaubert, you may perhaps know . . ." She murmured the last phrase in a curious tone, as if she had said something indiscreet and were evasively dismissing it.

The meaning of her words came through to me slowly; so this must be the "Caro" of the *Lettres à sa Nièce Caroline*. There was nothing to say, certainly. The room was absolutely quiet, but there was nothing to say to this disclosure. It was like being suddenly brought up against a mountain of memories. One could not see round it; one could only stupidly realize that in this mountain which the old lady had conjured up by a phrase and a name or two lay most of one's mental past. Some moments went by. There was no word with which one could greet such a revelation. I took one of her lovely hands and kissed it, in homage to a great period, to the names that made her voice tremble.

She laughed an embarrassed laugh, and spoke hurriedly. "Oh, that is not necessary! That is not at all necessary." But the tone of distrust, the faint challenge in that "you may perhaps know . . ." had disappeared. *"Vous connaissez bien les œuvres de mon oncle?"*

Who did not know them? I asked her.

Again the dry tone, with a shrug. "Oh, I almost never meet anyone who really knows them. The name, of course, its place in our literature, but not the works themselves. I never meet anyone now who cares much about them."

Great names are awkward things in conversation, when one is a chance acquaintance. One cannot be too free with them; they have too much value. The right course, I thought, was to volunteer nothing, above all to ask no questions; to let the old lady say what she would, ask what she would. She wished, it seemed, to talk about *les œuvres de mon oncle*. Her attack was uncertain; she touched here and there. It was a large subject. She told me she had edited the incomplete *Bouvard et Pécuchet* after his death, that *La Tentation de Saint Antoine* had been his own favourite among his works; she supposed I would scarcely agree with his choice?

No, I was sorry, but I could not.

"I suppose you care most for *Madame Bovary*?"

One can hardly discuss that book; it is a fact in history. One knows it too well to know it well.

"And yet," she murmured, "my uncle got only five hundred

francs for it from the publisher. Of course, he did not write for money. Still, he would have been pleased . . . Which one, then, do you prefer?"

I told her that a few years ago I had reread *L'Éducation sentimentale*, and felt that I had never risen to its greatness before.

She shook her head. "Ah, too long, prolix, *trop de conversation*. And Frédéric is very weak."

But there was an eagerness in her face, and I knew by something in her voice that this was like Garibaldi's proclamation to his soldiers on the retreat from Rome, when he told them he could offer them cold and hunger and sickness and misery. He offered something else, too, but the listeners must know that for themselves.

It had seemed to me when I last read *L'Éducation sentimentale* that its very faults were of a noble kind. It is too cold, certainly, to justify the subtitle, *Roman d'un jeune homme*; for youth, even when it has not generous enthusiasm, has at least fierce egotism. But I had wondered whether this cool, dispassionate, almost contemptuous presentation of Frédéric were not a protest against the overly sympathetic manner of Balzac in his stories of young men: Eugène de Rastignac, Lucien de Rubempré, Horace Bianchon, and all the others. Certainly Balzac's habit of playing up his characters, of getting into the ring and struggling and sweating with them, backing them with all his animal heat, must have been very distasteful to Flaubert. It was perhaps this quality of salesmanship in Balzac which made Flaubert say of him in a letter to this same niece Caroline: "He is as ignorant as a pot, and bourgeois to the marrow."

Of course, a story of youth, which altogether lacks that gustatory zest, that exaggerated concern for trivialities, is scarcely successful. In *L'Éducation* the trivialities are there (for life is made up of them), but not the voracious appetite which drives young people through silly and vulgar experiences. The story of Frédéric is a story of youth with the heart of youth left out; and of course it is often dull. But the latter chapters of the book justify one's journey through it. Then all the hero's young life becomes more real than it was as one followed it from year to year, and the story ends on a high plateau. From that great and quiet last scene, seated by the fire with the two middle-aged friends (who were never really friends, but who had been young together), one looks back over Frédéric's life and finds that one has it all, even the dull stretches. It is something one has lived through, not a story one has read; less diverting than a story, perhaps, but more inevitable. One is "left with it," in the same way that one is left with a weak heart after certain illnesses. A shadow has come into one's consciousness that will not go out again.

The old French lady and I talked for some time about *L'Éducation sentimentale*. She spoke with warm affection, with tenderness, of Madame Arnoux.

"Ah yes, Madame Arnoux, she is beautiful!" The moisture in her bright eyes, the flush on her cheeks, and the general softening of her face said much more. That charming and good woman of the middle classes, the wife who holds the story together (as she held Frédéric himself together), passed through the old lady's mind so vividly that it was as if she had entered the room. Madame Arnoux was there with us, in that hotel at Aix, on the evening of September 5, 1930, a physical presence, in the charming costume of her time, as on the night when Frédéric first dined at 24 rue de Choiseul. The niece had a very special feeling for this one of her uncle's characters. She lingered over the memory, recalling her as she first appears, sitting on the bench of a passenger boat on the Seine, in her muslin gown sprigged with green and her wide straw hat with red ribbons. Whenever the old lady mentioned Madame Arnoux it was with some mark of affection; she smiled, or sighed, or shook her head as we do when we speak of something that is quite unaccountably fine: "Ah yes, she is lovely, Madame Arnoux! She is very complete."

The old lady told me that she had at home the corrected manuscript of *L'Éducation sentimentale*. "Of course I have many others. But this he gave me long before his death. You shall see it when you come to my place at Antibes. I call my place the Villa Tanit, *pour la déesse*," she added with a smile.

The name of the goddess took us back to *Salammbô*, which is the book of Flaubert I like best. I like him in those great reconstructions of the remote and cruel past. When I happened to speak of the splendid final sentence of *Hérodias*, where the fall of the syllables is so suggestive of the hurrying footsteps of John's disciples, carrying away with them their prophet's severed head, she repeated that sentence softly: *"Comme elle était très lourde, ils la portaient al-ter-na-tiv-e-ment."*

The hour grew late. The maid had been standing in the corridor a long while, waiting for her mistress. At last the old lady rose and drew her wrap about her.

"Good night, madame. May you have pleasant dreams. As for me, I shall not sleep; you have recalled too much." She went toward the lift with the energetic, unconquered step with which she always crossed the dining-room, carrying with hardihood a body no longer perfectly under her control.

When I reached my room and opened my windows I, too, felt that sleep was far from me. The full moon (like the moon in *Salammbô*) stood over the little square and flooded the gardens and quiet streets and the misty mountains with light. The old lady had brought that great period of French letters very near; a period which has meant so much in the personal life of everyone to whom French literature has meant anything at all.

IV

Probably all those of us who had the good fortune to come upon the French masters accidentally, and not under the chilling guidance of an instructor, went through very much the same experience. We all began, of course, with Balzac. And to young people, for very good reasons, he seems the final word. They read and reread him, and live in his world; to inexperience, that world is neither overpeopled nor overfurnished. When they begin to read Flaubert—usually *Madame Bovary* is the introduction—they resent the change of tone; they miss the glow, the ardour, the temperament. (It is scarcely exaggeration to say that if one is not a little mad about Balzac at twenty, one will never live; and if at forty one can still take Rastignac and Lucien de Rubempré at Balzac's own estimate, one has lived in vain.) We first read *Bovary* with a certain hostility; the wine is too dry for us. We try, perhaps, another work of Flaubert, and with a shrug go back to Balzac. But young people who are at all sensitive to certain qualities in writing will not find the Balzac they left. Something has happened to them which dampens their enjoyment. For a time it looks as if they had lost both Balzac and Flaubert. They recover both, eventually, and read each for what he is, having learned that an artist's limitations are quite as important as his powers; that they are a definite asset, not a deficiency, and that both go to form his flavour, his personality, the thing by which the ear can immediately recognize Flaubert, Stendhal, Mérimée, Thomas Hardy, Conrad, Brahms, César Franck.

The fact remains that Balzac, like Dickens and Scott, has a strong appeal for the great multitudes of humanity who have no feeling for any form of art, and who read him only in poor translations. This is overwhelming evidence of the vital force in him, which no rough handling can diminish. Also it implies the lack in him of certain qualities which matter to only a few people, but matter very much. The time in one's life when one first began to sense the things which Flaubert stood for, to admire (almost against one's will) that peculiar integrity of language and vision, that coldness which, in him, is somehow noble—that is a pleasant chapter of one's life to remember, and Madame Franklin Grout had brought it back within arm's length of me that night.

V

For that was her name. Next morning the *valet de chambre* brought me a visiting card on which was engraved:

Madame Franklin Grout
Antibes

In one corner *Villa Tanit* was written in purple ink.

In the evening we sat in the writing-room again, and Madame Grout's talk touched upon many things. On the Franco-Prussian War, for instance, and its effect upon her uncle. He had seen to it that she herself was comfortably settled in England through most of that troubled time. And during the late war of 1914 she had been in Italy a great deal. She loved Italian best of all the languages she spoke so well.

(She spoke Swedish, even; she had lived for a time in Sweden during the life of her first husband, who had business interests there.)

She talked of Turgeniev, of her uncle's affection for him and great admiration for him as an artist.[1] She liked to recall his pleasant visits to Croisset, which were the reward of long anticipation on the part of the hosts. Turgeniev usually fixed the date by letter, changed it by another letter, then again by telegram—and sometimes he did not come at all. Flaubert's mother prepared for these visits by inspecting all the beds in the house, but she never found one long enough to hold "le Moscove" comfortably.

Madame Grout seemed to remember with especial pleasure the evenings when he used to sit at the table with her, going over her translation of *Faust*: "That noble man, to give his time to my childish efforts!" She well remembered the period during which he was writing *Les Eaux printanières*, and her own excitement when she first read that work. Like Henry James, she seemed to resent Turgeniev's position in the Viardot household; recalling it, even after such a long stretch of time, with vexation. "And when they gave a hunt, he looked after the dogs!" she murmured under her breath. She talked one evening of his sad latter years: of his disappointment in his daughter, of his long and painful illness, of the way in which the death of his friends, going one after another, contracted his life and made it bleak. But these were very personal memories, and if Madame Grout had wished to make them public, she would have written them herself.

Madame Viardot she had known very well, and for many years after Turgeniev's death. "Pauline Viardot was a superb artist, very intelligent and engaging as a woman, with a great

---

[1] Madame Grout's regard for Turgeniev seems to have been warmly returned. In a letter written to her in 1873, immediately after one of Turgeniev's visits to Croisset, Flaubert says: "Mon Moscove m'a quitté ce matin. . . . Tu l'as tout à fait séduit, mon loulou! car à plusieurs reprises il m'a parlé de 'mon adorable nièce,' de 'ma charmante nièce,' 'ravissante femme,' etc., etc. Enfin le Moscove t'adore! ce qui me fait bien plaisir, car c'est un homme exquis. Tu ne t'imagines pas ce qu'il sait! Il m'a répété, par cœur, des morceaux des tragédies de Voltaire, et de Luce de Lancival! Il connaît, je crois, *toutes* les littératures jusque dans leurs bas-fonds! Et si modeste avec tout cela! si bonhomme! si *vache*!"

charm—and, *au fond*, very Spanish!" she said. Of Monsieur
Louis Viardot she did not think highly. I gathered that he
was agreeable, but not much more than that. When I asked
her whether Monsieur Viardot had not translated some of
Turgeniev's books into French, the old lady lifted her brows
and there was a mocking glint in her eyes.

"Turgeniev himself translated them; Viardot may have
looked over his shoulder!"

George Sand she did not like. Yes, she readily admitted, her
men friends were very loyal to her, had a great regard for her;
mon oncle valued her comradeship; but Madame Grout found
the lady's personality distasteful.

I gathered that, for Madame Grout, George Sand did not
really fill any of the great rôles she assigned herself: the de-
voted mistress, the staunch comrade and "good fellow," the
self-sacrificing mother. George Sand's men friends believed
her to be all these things; and certainly she herself believed
that she was. But Madame Grout seemed to feel that in these
various relations Madame Dudevant was self-satisfied rather
than self-forgetful; always self-admiring and a trifle unctuous.
Madame Grout's distaste for this baffling kind of falseness
was immediate and instinctive—it put her teeth on edge.
Turgeniev, that penetrating reader of women, seems never to
have felt this shallowness in his friend. But in Chopin's later
letters one finds that he, to his bitter cost, had become aware
of it—curiously enough, through Madame Dudevant's be-
haviour toward her own children! It is clear that he had come
upon something so subtly false, so excruciatingly aslant, that
when he briefly refers to it his sentences seem to shudder.

Though I tried to let Madame Grout direct our conversa-
tions without suggestion from me, and never to question her,
I did ask her whether she read Marcel Proust with pleasure.

"*Trop dur et trop fatigant,*" she murmured, and dismissed
the greatest French writer of his time with a wave of her
hand.

When I made some reference to Anatole France she said
quickly: "Oh, I like him very much! But I like him most
where he is most indebted to my uncle!"

When she was tired, or deeply moved, Madame Grout
usually spoke French; but when she spoke English it was as

flexible as it was correct. She spoke like an Englishwoman, with no French accent at all.

What astonished me in her was her keen and sympathetic interest in modern music; in Ravel, Scriabin, Albéniz, Stravinsky, De Falla. Only a few days before I quitted Aix I found her at the box office in person, getting exactly the seats she wanted for a performance of *Boris Godounov*. She must change her habitual seat, as she had asked some friends to come over from Sallanches to hear the opera with her. "You will certainly hear it? Albert Wolff is conducting for the last time this season, and he does it very well," she explained.

It was interesting to observe Madame Grout at the opera that night, to watch the changes that went over her face as she listened with an attention that never wandered, looking younger and stronger than she ever did by day, as if the music were some very potent stimulant. Any form of pleasure, I had noticed, made her keener, more direct and positive, more authoritative, revived in her the stamp of a period which had achieved a great style in art. In a letter which Flaubert wrote her when she was a young woman, he said: —

> "C'est une joie profonde pour moi, mon pauvre lou-lou, que de t'avoir donné le goût des occupations intellectuelles. Que d'ennuis et de sottises il vous épargne!"

Certainly those interests had stood her in good stead, and for many more years than the uncle himself lived through. She had still, at eighty-four, a capacity for pleasure such as very few people in this world ever know at all.

VI

The next morning I told Madame Grout that, because of the illness of a friend, I must start at once for Paris.

And when, she asked, could I return and go south to Antibes and the Villa Tanit, to see her Flaubert collection, and the interior of his study, which she had brought down there thirty-five years ago?

I told her I was afraid that visit must be put off until next summer.

She gave a very charming laugh. "At my age, of course, the future is somewhat uncertain!" Then she asked whether, on her return to Antibes, she could send me some souvenir of our meeting; would I like to have something that had belonged to her uncle, or some letter written by him?

I told her that I was not a collector; that manuscripts and autographed letters meant very little to me. The things of her uncle that were valuable to me I already had, and had had for years. It rather hurt me that she should think I wanted any material reminder of her or of Flaubert. It was the Flaubert in her mind and heart that was to give me a beautiful memory.

On the following day, at *déjeuner*, I said good-bye to Madame Grout; I was leaving on the two o'clock train. It was a hurried and mournful parting, but there was real feeling on both sides. She had counted upon my staying longer, she said. But she did not for a moment take on a slightly aggrieved tone, as many privileged old ladies would have done. There was nothing "wayward" or self-indulgent about Madame Grout; the whole discipline of her life had been to the contrary. One had one's objective, and one went toward it; one had one's duty, and one did it as best one could.

The last glimpse I had of her was as she stood in the dining-room, the powder on her face quite destroyed by tears, her features agitated, but her head erect and her eyes flashing. And the last words I heard from her expressed a hope that I would always remember the pleasure we had had together in talking unreservedly about *les œuvres de mon oncle*. Standing there, she seemed holding to that name as to a staff. A great memory and a great devotion were the things she lived upon, certainly; they were her armour against a world concerned with insignificant matters.

VII

When I got back to Paris and began to re-read the *Lettres de Flaubert à sa Nièce Caroline*, I found that the personality of Madame Grout sent a wonderful glow over the pages. I was now almost startled (in those letters written her when she was still a child) by his solicitude about her progress in her English lessons—those lessons by which I was to profit seventy-three years afterward!

The five hundred pages of that book were now peopled for me with familiar figures, like the chronicles of a family I myself had known. It will always be for me one of the most delightful of books; and in none of his letters to other correspondents does Gustave Flaubert himself seem so attractive.

In reading over those letters, covering a stretch of twenty-four years, with the figure of Madame Grout in one's mind, one feels a kind of happiness and contentment about the whole situation—yes, and gratitude to Fate! The great man might have written very charming and tender and warmly confidential letters to a niece who was selfish, vain, intelligent merely in a conventional way—because she was the best he had! One can never be sure about such things; a heartless and stupid woman may be so well educated, after all!

But having known Madame Grout, I know that she had the root of the matter in her; that no one could be more sensitive than she to all that was finest in Flaubert's work, or more quick to admit the qualities he did not have—which is quite as important.

During all his best working years he had in his house beside him, or within convenient distance for correspondence, one of his own blood, younger and more ardent than he, who absolutely understood what he was doing; who could feel the great qualities of his failures, even. Could any situation be happier for a man of letters? How many writers have found one understanding ear among their sons or daughters?

Moreover, Caroline was the daughter of a sister whom Flaubert had devotedly loved. He took her when she was an infant into his house at Croisset, where he lived alone with his old mother. What delight for a solitary man of letters and an old lady to have a baby to take care of, the little daughter of a beloved daughter! They had all the pleasure of her little girlhood—and she must have been an irresistible little girl! Flaubert spent a great deal of time attending to her early education, and when he was seated at his big writing-table, or working in bed, he liked to have her in the room, lying on a rug in the corner with her book. For hours she would not speak, she told me; she was so passionately proud of the fact that he wanted her to be there. When she was just beginning to read, she liked to think, as she lay in her corner, that she was shut in a cage with some powerful wild animal, a tiger or a lion or a bear, who had devoured his keeper and would spring upon anyone else who opened his door, but with whom she was "quite safe and conceited," as she said with a chuckle.

During his short stays in Paris, Flaubert writes to Caroline about her favourite rabbit, and the imaginary characters with whom she had peopled the garden at Croisset. He sends his greetings to Caroline's doll, Madame Robert:—

> "Remercie de ma part Mme. Robert qui a bien voulu se rappeler de moi. Présente-lui mes respects et conseille-lui un régime fortifiant, car elle me paraît un peu pale, et je ne suis pas sans inquiétude sur sa santé."

In a letter from Paris, dated just a year later, when Caroline was eleven, he tells her that he is sending her Thierry's *Récits des temps mérovingiens*, and adds:—

> "Je suis bien aise que les *Récits mérovingiens* t'amusent; relis-les quand tu auras fini; *apprends des dates*, tu as tes programmes, et passe tous les jours quelque temps à regarder une carte de géographie."

One sees from the letters with what satisfaction Flaubert followed every step of Caroline's development. Her facility in languages was a matter of the greatest pride to him, though even after she is married and living abroad he occasionally finds fault with her orthography:—

> "Un peu d'orthographe ne te nuirait pas, mon bibi! car tu écris *aplomb* par deux *p*: 'Moral et physique sont d'applomb,' trois *p* marqueraient encore plus d'énergie! Ça m'a amusé, parce que ça te ressemble."

Yes, it was like her, certainly; like her as she walked across the floor of that hotel dining-room in Aix-les-Bains, so many years afterward.

Though she had been married twice, Madame Grout, in our conversations, did not talk of either of her husbands. Her uncle had always been the great figure in her life, and even a short acquaintance with her made me feel that she possessed every quality for comradeship with him. Besides her devotion to him, her many gifts, her very unusual intelligence and intuition in art, she had moral qualities which he must have loved: poise, great good sense, and a love of fairness and justice. She had the habit of searching out facts and weighing evidence, for her own satisfaction. Her speech, when she was explaining something, had the qualities of good Latin prose: economy, elegance, and exactness. She was not an idealist; she had lived through two wars. She was one of the least visionary and sentimental persons I have ever met. She knew that conditions and circumstances, not their own wishes, dictate the actions of men. In her mind there was a kind of large enlightenment, like that of the many-windowed workroom at Croisset, with the cool, tempered northern light pouring into it. In her, Flaubert had not only a companion, but a "daughter of the house" to cherish and protect. And he had her all his life, until the short seizure which took him off in an hour. And she, all her life, kept the handkerchief with which they had wiped the moisture from his brow a few moments before he died.

VIII

I sailed for Quebec in October. In November, while I was at Jaffrey, New Hampshire, a letter came from Madame Grout; the envelope had been opened and almost destroyed. I have received letters from Borneo and Java that looked much less travel-worn. She had addressed it to me in care of an obscure bookseller, on a small street in Paris, from whom she had got one of my books. (I suppose, in her day, all booksellers were publishers.) The letter had been forwarded through three publishing houses, and a part of its contents had got lost. In her letter Madame Grout writes that she is sending me "ci-joint une lettre de mon oncle Gustave Flaubert adressée à George Sand—elle doit être, je crois, de 1866.

Il me semble qu'elle vous fera plaisir et j'ai plaisir à vous l'envoyer."

This enclosure had been removed. I regretted its loss chiefly because I feared it would distress Madame Grout. But I wrote her, quite truthfully, that her wish that I should have one of her uncle's letters meant a great deal more to me than the actual possession of it could mean. Nevertheless, it was an awkward explanation to make, and I delayed writing it until late in December. I did not hear from her again.

In February my friends in Paris sent me a clipping from the *Journal des Débats* which read: —

MORT DE MME. FRANKLIN-GROUT

Nous apprenons avec tristesse la mort de Mme. Franklin-Grout, qui s'est éteinte à Antibes, à la suite d'une courte maladie.

Nièce de Gustave Flaubert, Mme. Franklin-Grout a joué un rôle important dans la diffusion et le succès des œuvres de son oncle. Exécutrice testamentaire du grand romancier, qui l'avait élevée et instruite, Mme. Franklin-Grout a publié la correspondance de son oncle, si précieuse pour sa psychologie littéraire, et qui nous a révélé les doctrines de Flaubert et sa vie de travail acharné. Mme. Franklin-Grout publia aussi *Bouvard et Pécuchet.* . . . Mme. Franklin-Grout était une personne charmante et distinguée, très attachée à ses amis et qui, jusqu'à la plus extrême vieillesse, avait conservé l'intelligence et la bonté souriante d'une spirituelle femme du monde.

The Novel Démeublé

THE NOVEL, for a long while, has been over-furnished. The property-man has been so busy on its pages, the importance of material objects and their vivid presentation have been so stressed, that we take it for granted whoever can observe, and can write the English language, can write a novel. Often the latter qualification is considered unnecessary.

In any discussion of the novel, one must make it clear whether one is talking about the novel as a form of amusement, or as a form of art; since they serve very different purposes and in very different ways. One does not wish the egg one eats for breakfast, or the morning paper, to be made of the stuff of immortality. The novel manufactured to entertain great multitudes of people must be considered exactly like a cheap soap or a cheap perfume, or cheap furniture. Fine quality is a distinct disadvantage in articles made for great numbers of people who do not want quality but quantity, who do not want a thing that "wears," but who want change,—a succession of new things that are quickly threadbare and can be lightly thrown away. Does anyone pretend that if the Woolworth store windows were piled high with Tanagra figurines at ten cents, they could for a moment compete with Kewpie brides in the popular esteem? Amusement is one thing; enjoyment of art is another.

Every writer who is an artist knows that his "power of observation," and his "power of description," form but a low part of his equipment. He must have both, to be sure; but he knows that the most trivial of writers often have a very good observation. Mérimée said in his remarkable essay on Gogol: "L'art de choisir parmi les innombrable traits que nous offre la nature est, après tout, bien plus difficile que celui de les observer avec attention et de les rendre avec exactitude."

There is a popular superstition that "realism" asserts itself in the cataloguing of a great number of material objects, in explaining mechanical processes, the methods of operating manufactories and trades, and in minutely and unsparingly describing physical sensations. But is not realism, more than it is anything else, an attitude of mind on the part of the writer toward his material, a vague indication of the sympathy and candour with which he accepts, rather than chooses, his theme? Is the story of a banker who is unfaithful to his wife and who ruins himself by speculation in trying to gratify the caprices of his mistresses, at all reinforced by a masterly exposition of banking, our whole system of credits, the methods of the Stock Exchange? Of course, if the story is thin, these things do reinforce it in a sense,—any amount of red meat thrown into the scale to make the beam dip. But are the banking system and the Stock Exchange worth being written about at all? Have such things any proper place in imaginative art?

The automatic reply to this question is the name of Balzac. Yes, certainly, Balzac tried out the value of literalness in the novel, tried it out to the uttermost, as Wagner did the value of scenic literalness in the music drama. He tried it, too, with the passion of discovery, with the inflamed zest of an unexampled curiosity. If the heat of that furnace could not give hardness and sharpness to material accessories, no other brain will ever do it. To reproduce on paper the actual city of Paris; the houses, the upholstery, the food, the wines, the game of pleasure, the game of business, the game of finance: a stupendous ambition—but, after all, unworthy of an artist. In exactly so far as he succeeded in pouring out on his pages that mass of brick and mortar and furniture and proceedings in bankruptcy, in exactly so far he defeated his end. The things by which he still lives, the types of greed and avarice and ambition and vanity and lost innocence of heart which he created—are as vital today as they were then. But their material surroundings, upon which he expended such labour and pains . . . the eye glides over them. We have had too much of the interior decorator and the "romance of business" since his day. The city he built on paper is already crumbling. Stevenson said he wanted to blue-pencil a great deal of Balzac's "presentation"—and he loved him beyond all modern novelists. But where is the man who could cut one sentence from the stories of Mérimée? And who wants any more detail as to how Carmencita and her fellow factory-girls made cigars? Another sort of novel? Truly. Isn't it a better sort?

In this discussion another great name naturally occurs. Tol-
stoi was almost as great a lover of material things as Balzac,
almost as much interested in the way dishes were cooked, and
people were dressed, and houses were furnished. But there is
this determining difference: the clothes, the dishes, the haunt-
ing interiors of those old Moscow houses, are always so much
a part of the emotions of the people that they are perfectly
synthesized; they seem to exist, not so much in the author's
mind, as in the emotional penumbra of the characters them-
selves. When it is fused like this, literalness ceases to be liter-
alness—it is merely part of the experience.

If the novel is a form of imaginative art, it cannot be at the
same time a vivid and brilliant form of journalism. Out of the
teeming, gleaming stream of the present it must select
the eternal material of art. There are hopeful signs that some
of the younger writers are trying to break away from mere
verisimilitude, and, following the development of modern
painting, to interpret imaginatively the material and social
investiture of their characters; to present their scene by sug-
gestion rather than by enumeration. The higher processes of
art are all processes of simplification. The novelist must learn
to write, and then he must unlearn it; just as the modern
painter learns to draw, and then learns when utterly to disre-
gard his accomplishment, when to subordinate it to a higher
and truer effect. In this direction only, it seems to me, can the
novel develop into anything more varied and perfect than all
the many novels that have gone before.

One of the very earliest American romances might well
serve as a suggestion to later writers. In *The Scarlet Letter* how
truly in the spirit of art is the mise-en-scène presented. That
drudge, the theme-writing high-school student, could scarcely
be sent there for information regarding the manners and dress
and interiors of Puritan society. The material investiture of
the story is presented as if unconsciously; by the reserved,
fastidious hand of an artist, not by the gaudy fingers of a
showman or the mechanical industry of a department-store
window-dresser. As I remember it, in the twilight melancholy
of that book, in its consistent mood, one can scarcely ever see
the actual surroundings of the people; one feels them, rather,
in the dusk.

Whatever is felt upon the page without being specifically named there—that, one might say, is created. It is the inexplicable presence of the thing not named, of the overtone divined by the ear but not heard by it, the verbal mood, the emotional aura of the fact or the thing or the deed, that gives high quality to the novel or the drama, as well as to poetry itself.

Literalness, when applied to the presenting of mental reactions and of physical sensations, seems to be no more effective than when it is applied to material things. A novel crowded with physical sensations is no less a catalogue than one crowded with furniture. A book like *The Rainbow* by D. H. Lawrence sharply reminds one how vast a distance lies between emotion and mere sensory reactions. Characters can be almost dehumanized by a laboratory study of the behaviour of their bodily organs under sensory stimuli—can be reduced, indeed, to mere animal pulp. Can one imagine anything more terrible than the story of *Romeo and Juliet* rewritten in prose by D. H. Lawrence?

How wonderful it would be if we could throw all the furniture out of the window; and along with it, all the meaningless reiterations concerning physical sensations, all the tiresome old patterns, and leave the room as bare as the stage of a Greek theatre, or as that house into which the glory of Pentacost descended; leave the scene bare for the play of emotions, great and little—for the nursery tale, no less than the tragedy, is killed by tasteless amplitude. The elder Dumas enunciated a great principle when he said that to make a drama, a man needed one passion, and four walls.

148 Charles Street

LATE IN THE WINTER of 1908 Mrs. Louis Brandeis conducted me along a noisy street in Boston and rang at a door hitherto unknown to me. Sometimes entering a new door can make a great change in one's life. That afternoon I had set out from the Parker House (the old, the real Parker House, before it was "modernized") to make a call on Mrs. Brandeis. When I reached her house in Otis Place she told me that we would go farther: she thought I would enjoy meeting a very charming old lady who was a near neighbour of hers, the widow of James T. Fields, of the publishing firm of Ticknor and Fields. The name of that firm meant something to me. In my father's bookcase there were little volumes of Longfellow and Hawthorne with that imprint. I wondered how the widow of one of the partners could still be living. Mrs. Brandeis explained that when James T. Fields was a man in middle life, a publisher of international reputation and a widower, he married Annie Adams, then a girl of nineteen. She had naturally survived him by many years.

When the door at 148 Charles Street was opened we waited a few moments in a small reception-room just off the hall, then went up a steep, thickly carpeted stairway and entered the "long drawing-room," where Mrs. Fields and Miss Jewett sat at tea. That room ran the depth of the house, its front windows, heavily curtained, on Charles Street, its back windows looking down on a deep garden. Directly above the garden wall lay the Charles River and, beyond, the Cambridge shore. At five o'clock in the afternoon the river was silvery from a half-hidden sun; over the great open space of water the western sky was dove-coloured with little ripples of rose. The air was full of soft moisture and the hint of approaching spring. Against this screen of pale winter light were the two ladies: Mrs. Fields reclining on a green sofa, directly under the youthful portrait of Charles Dickens (now in the Boston Art Museum), Miss Jewett seated, the low tea-table between them.

Mrs. Fields wore the widow's lavender which she never

abandoned except for black velvet, with a scarf of Venetian lace on her hair. She was very slight and fragile in figure, with a great play of animation in her face and a delicate flush of pink on her cheeks. Like her friend Mrs. John Gardner, she had a skin which defied age. As for Miss Jewett—she looked very like the youthful picture of herself in the game of "Authors" I had played as a child, except that she was fuller in figure and a little grey. I do not at all remember what we talked about. Mrs. Brandeis asked that I be shown some of the treasures of the house, but I had no eyes for the treasures, I was too intent upon the ladies.

That winter afternoon began a friendship, impoverished by Miss Jewett's death sixteen months later, but enduring until Mrs. Fields herself died, in February 1915.

In 1922 M. A. DeWolfe Howe, Mrs. Fields' literary executor, published a book of extracts from her diaries under the title *Memories of a Hostess*, a book which delighted all who had known her and many who had not, because of its vivid pictures of the Cambridge and Concord groups in the '60s and '70s, not as "celebrities" but as friends and fellow citizens. When Mr. Howe's book appeared, I wrote for *The Literary Review* an appreciation of it, very sketchy, but done with genuine enthusiasm, which I here incorporate without quotation marks.

In his book made up from the diaries of Mrs. James T. Fields, Mr. DeWolfe Howe presents a record of beautiful memories and, as its subtitle declares, "a chronicle of eminent friendships." For a period of sixty years Mrs. Fields' Boston house, at 148 Charles Street, extended its hospitality to the aristocracy of letters and art. During that long stretch of time there was scarcely an American of distinction in art or public life who was not a guest in that house; scarcely a visiting foreigner of renown who did not pay his tribute there.

It was not only men of letters, Dickens, Thackeray, and Matthew Arnold, who met Mrs. Fields' friends there; Salvini and Modjeska and Edwin Booth and Christine Nilsson and Joseph Jefferson and Ole Bull, Winslow Homer and Sargent, came and went, against the background of closely united friends who were a part of the very Charles Street scene.

Longfellow, Emerson, Whittier, Hawthorne, Lowell, Sumner, Norton, Oliver Wendell Holmes—the list sounds like something in a school-book; but in Mrs. Fields' house one came to believe that they had been very living people—to feel that they had not been long absent from the rooms so full of their thoughts, of their letters, their talk, their remembrances sent at Christmas to the hostess, or brought to her from foreign lands. Even in the garden flourished guelder roses and flowering shrubs which some of these bearers of school-book names had brought in from Cambridge or Concord and set out there. At 148 Charles Street an American of the Apache period and territory could come to inherit a Colonial past.

Although Mrs. Fields was past seventy when I was first conducted into the long drawing-room, she did not seem old to me. Frail, diminished in force, yes; but, emphatically, *not* old. "The personal beauty of her younger years, long retained, and even at the end of such a stretch of life not quite lost," to quote Henry James, may have had something to do with the impression she gave; but I think it was even more because, as he also said of her, "all her implications were gay." I had seldom heard so young, so merry, so musical a laugh; a laugh with countless shades of relish and appreciation and kindness in it. And, on occasion, a short laugh from that same fragile source could positively do police duty! It could put an end to a conversation that had taken an unfortunate turn, absolutely dismiss and silence impertinence or presumption. No woman could have been so great a hostess, could have made so many highly developed personalities happy under her roof, could have blended so many strongly specialized and keenly sensitive people in her drawing-room, without having a great power to control and organize. It was a power so sufficient that one seldom felt it as one lived in the harmonious atmosphere it created—an atmosphere in which one seemed absolutely safe from everything ugly. Nobody can cherish the flower of social intercourse, can give it sun and sustenance and a tempered clime, without also being able very completely to dispose of anything that threatens it—not only the slug, but even the cold draught that ruffles its petals.

Mrs. Fields was in her own person flower-like; the remarkable fineness of her skin and pinkness of her cheeks gave one the comparison—and the natural ruby of her lips she never lost. It always struck one afresh (along with her clear eyes and their quick flashes of humour), that large, generous, mobile mouth, with its rich freshness of colour. "A *woman's* mouth," I used to think as I watched her talking to someone who pleased her; "not an old woman's!" One rejoiced in her little triumphs over colour-destroying age and its infirmities, as at the play one rejoices in the escape of the beautiful and frail from the pursuit of things powerful and evil. It was a drama in which the heroine must be sacrificed in the end: but for how long did she make the outward voyage delightful, with how many a *divertissement* and bright scene did she illumine the respite and the long wait at Aulis!

Sixty years of hospitality, so smooth and unruffled for the recipients, cost the hostess something—cost her a great deal. The Fieldses were never people of liberal means, and the Charles Street house was not a convenient house to entertain in. The basement kitchen was a difficulty. On the first floor were the reception-room and the dining-room, on the second floor was the "long drawing-room," running the depth of the house. Mrs. Fields' own apartments were on the third floor, and the guest-rooms on the fourth. A house so constructed took a great deal of managing. Yet there was never an hour in the day when the order and calm of the drawing-room were not such that one might have sat down to write a sonnet or a sonata. The sweeping and dusting were done very early in the morning, the flowers arranged before the guests were awake.

Besides being distinctly young on the one hand, on the other Mrs. Fields seemed to me to reach back to Waterloo. As Mr. Howe reminds us, she had talked to Leigh Hunt about Shelley and his starlike beauty of face—and it is now more than a century since Shelley was drowned. She had known Severn well, and it was he who gave her a lock of Keats' hair, which, under glass with a drawing of Keats by the same artist, was one of the innumerable treasures of that house. With so much to tell, Mrs. Fields never became a set story-teller. She had no favourite stories—there were too many. Stories were told from time to time, but only as things of today reminded her of things of yesterday. When we came home from the opera, she could tell one what Chorley had said on such and such an occasion. And then if one did not "go at" her, but talked of Chorley just as if he were Philip Hale or W. J. Henderson, one might hear a great deal about him.

When one was staying at that house the past lay in wait for one in all the corners; it exuded from the furniture, from the pictures, the rare editions, and the cabinets of manuscript—the beautiful, clear manuscripts of a typewriterless age, which even the printers had respected and kept clean. The unique charm of Mrs. Fields' house was not that it was a place where one could hear about the past, but that it was a place where the past lived on—where it was protected and cherished, had sanctuary from the noisy push of the present. In casual conversation, at breakfast or tea, you might at any time unconsciously press a spring which liberated recollection, and one of the great shades seemed quietly to enter the room and to take the chair or the corner he had preferred in life.

One afternoon I showed her an interesting picture of Pauline Viardot I had brought from Paris, and my hostess gave me such an account of hearing Viardot sing Gluck's *Orpheus* that I felt I had heard it myself. Then she told me how, when she saw Dickens in London, just after he had returned from giving a reading in Paris, he said: "Oh, yes, the house was sold out. But the important thing is that Viardot came, and sat in a front seat and never took her glorious eyes off me. So, of course," with a flourish of his hand, "nothing else mattered!" A little-known Russian gentleman, Mr. Turgeniev, must have been staying at Madame Viardot's country house at that time. Did he accompany her to the reading, one wonders? If he had, it would probably have meant very little to "Mr. Dickens."

It was at tea-time, I used to think, that the great shades were most likely to appear; sometimes they seemed to come up the deeply carpeted stairs, along with living friends. At that hour the long room was dimly lighted, the fire bright, and through the wide windows the sunset was flaming, or softly brooding, upon the Charles River and the Cambridge shore beyond. The ugliness of the world, all possibility of wrenches and jars and wounding contacts, seemed securely shut out. It was indeed the peace of the past, where the tawdry and cheap have been eliminated and the enduring things have taken their proper, happy places.

Mrs. Fields read aloud beautifully, especially Shakespeare and Milton, for whom she had, even in age, a wonderful depth of voice. I loved to hear her read *Richard II*, or the great, melancholy speeches of *Henry IV* in the Palace at Westminster:

> "And changes fill the cup of altera-ti-on
> With divers liquors."

Many of those lines I can only remember with the colour, the slight unsteadiness, of that fine old voice.

Once I was sitting on the sofa beside her, helping her to hold a very heavy, very old, calf-bound Milton, while she read:

> "In courts and palaces he also reigns,
> And in luxurious cities, where the noise
> Of riot ascends above their loftiest towers,
> And injury and outrage."

When she paused in the solemn evocation for breath, I tried to fill in the interval by saying something about such lines calling up the tumult of Rome and Babylon.

"Or New York," she said slyly, glancing sidewise, and then at once again attacked the mighty page.

Naturally, she was rich in reference and quotation. I recall how she once looked up from a long reverie and said: "You know, my dear, I think we sometimes forget how much we owe to Dryden's prefaces." To my shame, I have not to this day discovered the full extent of my indebtedness. On another occasion Mrs. Fields murmured something about *"A bracelet of bright hair about the bone."* "That's very nice," said I, "but I don't recognize it."

"Surely," she said, "that would be Dr. Donne."

I never pretended to Mrs. Fields—I would have had to pretend too much. "And who," I brazenly asked, "was Dr. Donne?"

I knew before morning. She had a beautiful patience with Bœotian ignorance, but I was strongly encouraged to take two fat volumes of Dr. Donne to bed with me that night.

I love to remember one charming visit in her summer house at Manchester-by-the-Sea, when Sarah Orne Jewett was there. I had just come from Italy bringing word of the places they most loved and about which they had often written me, entreating, nay, commanding me to visit them. Had I gone riding on the Pincian Hill? Mrs. Fields asked. No, I hadn't; I didn't think many people rode there now. Well, said Mrs. Fields, the Brownings' little boy used to ride there, in his velvets. When he complained to her that the Pincio was the same every day, no variety, she suggested that he might ride out into the Campagna. But he sighed and shook his head. "Oh, no! My pony and I have to go there. We are one of the sights of Rome, you know!" As this was the son of a friend, one didn't comment upon the child's speech or the future it suggested.

The second evening after my arrival happened to be a rainy one—no visitors. After dinner Mrs. Fields began to read a little—warmed to her work, and read all of Matthew Arnold's *Scholar Gypsy* and *Tristan and Iseult*. Miss Jewett said she didn't believe the latter poem had been read aloud in that house since Matthew Arnold himself read it there.

At Manchester, when there were no guests, Mrs. Fields had tea on the back veranda, overlooking a wild stretch of woodland. Down in this wood, directly beneath us, were a tea-table and seats built under the trees, where they used to have tea when the hostess was younger—now the climb was too steep for her. It was a little sad, perhaps, to sit and look out over a shrinking kingdom; but if she felt it, she never showed it. Miss Jewett and I went down into the wood, and she told me she hated to go there now, as it reminded her that much was already lost, and what was left was so at the mercy of chance! It seemed as if a strong wind might blow away that beloved friend of many years. We talked in low voices. Who could have believed that Mrs. Fields was to outlive Miss Jewett, so much the younger, by nearly six years, as she outlived Mr. Fields by thirty-four! She had the very genius of survival. She was not, as she once laughingly told me, "to escape anything, not even free verse or the Cubists!" She was not in the least dashed by either. Oh, no, she said, the Cubists weren't any queerer than Manet and the Impressionists were when they first came to Boston, and people used to run in for tea and ask her whether she had ever heard of such a thing as "blue snow," or a man's black hat being purple in the sun!

As in Boston tea was the most happy time for reminiscences, in Manchester it was at the breakfast hour that they were most likely to throng. Breakfasts were long, as country breakfasts have a right to be. We had always been out of doors first and were very hungry.

One morning when the cantaloupes were particularly fine Mrs. Fields began to tell me of Henry James' father,—apropos of the melons, though I forget whether it was that he liked them very much or couldn't abide them. She told me a great deal about him; but I was most interested in what she said regarding his faith in his son. When the young man's first essays and stories began to come back across the Atlantic from Rome and Paris they did not meet with approval in Boston; they were thought self-conscious, artificial, shallow. His father's friends feared the young man had mistaken his calling. Mr. James the elder, however, was altogether pleased. He came down to Manchester one summer to have a talk with the great publisher about Henry, and expressed his satisfaction and confidence. "Believe me," he said, sitting at this very table, "the boy will make his mark in letters, Fields."

The next summer I was visiting Mrs. Fields at Manchester in a season of intense heat. We were daily expecting the arrival of Henry James, Jr., himself. One morning came a spluttery letter from the awaited friend, containing bitter references to the "Great American summer," and saying that he was "lying at Nahant," prostrated by the weather. I was very much disappointed, but Mrs. Fields said wisely: "My dear, it is just as well. Mr. James is always greatly put about by the heat, and at Nahant there is the chance of a breeze."

The house at Manchester was called Thunderbolt Hill. Mr. Howe thinks the name incongruous, but that depends on what associations you choose to give it. When I went a-calling with Mrs. Fields and left her card with Thunderbolt Hill engraved in the corner, I felt that I was paying calls with the lady Juno herself. Why shouldn't such a name befit a hill of high decisions and judgments? Moreover, Mrs. Fields was not at all responsible for that name; it came, as she and Miss

Jewett liked proverbs and place-names to come, from the native folk. Long years before James T. Fields bought the hill to build a summer cottage, some fine trees at the top of it had been destroyed by lightning; the country people thereabouts had ever afterward called it Thunderbolt Hill.

Mrs. Fields' Journal tells us how in her young married days she always moved from Boston to Manchester-by-the-Sea in early summer, just as she still did when I knew her. I remember one characteristic passage in the Journal, written at Manchester and dated July 16, 1870:

It is a perfect summer day, she says. Mr. Fields does not go up to town but stays at home with a bag full of MSS. He and his wife go to a favourite spot in a pasture by the sea, and she reads him a new story which has just come in from Henry James, Jr., then a very young man—*Compagnons de Voyage*, in "execrable" handwriting. They find the quality good. "I do not know," Mrs. Fields wrote in her diary that evening, "why success in work should affect one so powerfully, but I could have wept as I finished reading, not from the sweet, low pathos of the tale, but from the knowledge of the writer's success. It is so difficult to do anything well in this mysterious world."

Yes, one says to oneself, that is Mrs. Fields, at her best. She rose to meet a fine performance, always—to the end. At eighty she could still entertain new people, new ideas, new forms of art. And she brought to her greeting of the new all the richness of her rich past: a long, unbroken chain of splendid contacts, beautiful friendships.

As one follows the diary down through the years, the reader must feel a certain pride in the determined way in which the New England group refused to be patronized by glittering foreign celebrities—by any celebrities! At dinner Dr. Holmes holds himself a little apart from the actor guests, Jefferson and Warren, and addresses them as "you gentlemen of the stage" in a way that quite disturbed Longfellow and, one may judge, the hostess. They all come to dine with Dickens in his long stays with the Fieldses, come repeatedly, but they seem ever a little on their guard. Emerson cannot be got to believe him altogether genuine and sincere. He insists to Mrs. Fields that Dickens has "too much talent for his genius," and that he is "too consummate an artist to have a thread of nature left"! Thackeray made a long visit at 148 Charles Street. (It is said that he finished *Henry Esmond* there.) In the guest-room which he occupied, with an alcove study, hung a little drawing he had made of himself, framed with the note he had written the hostess telling her that, happy as he was here, he must go home to England for Christmas.

When Mrs. Fields was still a young woman, she noted in her diary that Aristotle says: "Virtue is concerned with action; art with production." "The problem in life," she adds, "is to harmonize these two." In a long life she went far toward working out this problem. She knew how to appreciate the noble in behaviour and the noble in art. In the patriot, the philanthropist, the statesman, she could forgive abominable taste. In the artist, the true artist, she could forgive vanity, sensitiveness, selfishness, indecision, and vacillation of will. She was generous and just in her judgment of men and women because she understood Aristotle's axiom. "With a great gift," I once heard her murmur thoughtfully, "we must be willing to bear greatly, because it has already greatly borne."

Today, in 1936, a garage stands on the site of 148 Charles Street. Only in memory exists the long, green-carpeted, softly lighted drawing-room, and the dining-table where Learning and Talent met, enjoying good food and good wit and rare vintages, looking confidently forward to the growth of their country in the finer amenities of life. Perhaps the garage and all it stands for represent the only real development, and have altogether taken the place of things formerly cherished on that spot. If we try to imagine those dinner-parties which Mrs. Fields describes, the scene is certainly not to us what it was to her: the lighting has changed, and the guests seem hundreds of years away from us. Their portraits no longer hang on the walls of our academies, nor are their "works" much discussed there. The English classes, we are told, can be "interested" only in contemporary writers, the newer the better. A letter from a prep-school boy puts it tersely: "D. H. Lawrence is rather rated a back-number here, but Faulkner keeps his end up."

Not the prep-school boys only are blithe to leave the past untroubled: their instructors pretty generally agree with them. And the retired professors who taught these instructors do not see Shelley plain as they once did. The faith of the elders has been shaken.

Just how did this change come about, one wonders. When and where were the Arnolds overthrown and the Brownings devaluated? Was it at the Marne? At Versailles, when a new geography was being made on paper? Certainly the literary world which emerged from the war used a new coinage. In England and America the "masters" of the last century diminished in stature and pertinence, became remote and shadowy.

But Mrs. Fields never entered this strange twilight. She rounded out her period, from Dickens and Thackeray and Tennyson, through Hardy and Meredith to the Great War, with her standards unshaken. For her there was no revaluation. She died with her world (the world of "letters" which mattered most to her) unchallenged. Marcel Proust somewhere said that when he came to die he would take all his great men with him: since his Beethoven and his Wagner could never be at all the same to anyone else, they would go with him like the captives who were slain at the funeral pyres of Eastern potentates. It was thus Mrs. Fields died, in that house of memories, with the material keepsakes of the past about her.

Miss Jewett[1]

I

IN READING OVER a package of letters from Sarah Orne Jewett, I find this observation: *"The thing that teases the mind over and over for years, and at last gets itself put down rightly on paper—whether little or great, it belongs to Literature."* Miss Jewett was very conscious of the fact that when a writer makes anything that belongs to Literature (limiting the term here to imaginative literature, which she of course meant), his material goes through a process very different from that by which he makes merely a good story. No one can define this process exactly; but certainly persistence, survival, recurrence in the writer's mind, are highly characteristic of it. The shapes and scenes that have "teased" the mind for years, when they do at last get themselves rightly put down, make a much higher order of writing, and a much more costly, than the most vivid and vigorous transfer of immediate impressions.

In some of Miss Jewett's earlier books, *Deephaven, Country Byways, Old Friends and New,* one can find first sketches, first impressions, which later crystallized into almost flawless examples of literary art. One can, as it were, watch in process the two kinds of making: the first, which is full of perception and feeling but rather fluid and formless; the second, which is tightly built and significant in design. The design is, indeed, so happy, so right, that it seems inevitable; the design is the story and the story is the design. The "Pointed Fir" sketches are living things caught in the open, with light and freedom and air-spaces about them. They melt into the land and the life of the land until they are not stories at all, but life itself.

A great many stories were being written upon New England themes at the same time that Miss Jewett was writing; stories that to many contemporary readers may have seemed more interesting than hers, because they dealt with more def-

[1]Much of Part I of this sketch was originally written as a preface to a two-volume collection of Miss Jewett's stories published by Houghton Mifflin in 1925.

inite "situations" and were more heavily accented. But they are not very interesting to reread today; they have not the one thing that survives all arresting situations, all good writing and clever story-making—inherent, individual beauty.

Walter Pater said that every truly great drama must, in the end, linger in the reader's mind as a sort of ballad. One might say that every fine story must leave in the mind of the sensitive reader an intangible residuum of pleasure; a cadence, a quality of voice that is exclusively the writer's own, individual, unique. A quality which one can remember without the volume at hand, can experience over and over again in the mind but can never absolutely define, as one can experience in memory a melody, or the summer perfume of a garden. The magnitude of the subject-matter is not of primary importance, seemingly. An idyll of Theocritus, concerned with sheep and goats and shade and pastures, is today as much alive as the most dramatic passages of the *Iliad*—stirs the reader's feeling quite as much, perhaps.

It is a common fallacy that a writer, if he is talented enough, can achieve this poignant quality by improving upon his subject-matter, by using his "imagination" upon it and twisting it to suit his purpose. The truth is that by such a process (which is not imaginative at all!) he can at best produce only a brilliant sham, which, like a badly built and pretentious house, looks poor and shabby after a few years. If he achieves anything noble, anything enduring, it must be by giving himself absolutely to his material. And this gift of sympathy is his great gift; is the fine thing in him that alone can make his work fine.

The artist spends a lifetime in pursuing the things that haunt him, in having his mind "teased" by them, in trying to get these conceptions down on paper exactly as they are to him and not in conventional poses supposed to reveal their character; trying this method and that, as a painter tries different lightings and different attitudes with his subject to catch the one that presents it more suggestively than any other. And at the end of a lifetime he emerges with much that is more or less happy experimenting, and comparatively little that is the very flower of himself and his genius.

The best of Miss Jewett's work, read by a student fifty years from now, will give him the characteristic flavour, the spirit, the cadence, of an American writer of the first order,—and of a New England which will then be a thing of the past.

Even in the stories which fall short of being Miss Jewett's best, one has the pleasure of her society and companionship—if one likes that sort of companionship. I remember she herself had a fondness for "The Hiltons' Holiday,"—the slightest of stories: a hard-worked New England farmer takes his two little girls to town, some seventeen miles away (a long drive by wagon), for a treat. That is all, yet the story is a little miracle. It simply *is the look*—shy, kind, a little wistful—which shines out at one from good country faces on remote farms; it is the look *itself*. To have got it down upon the printed page is like bringing the tenderest of early spring flowers from the deep wood into the hot light of noon without bruising its petals.

To note an artist's limitations is but to define his talent. A reporter can write equally well about everything that is presented to his view, but a creative writer can do his best only with what lies within the range and character of his deepest sympathies. These stories of Miss Jewett's have much to do with fisher-folk and seaside villages; with juniper pastures and lonely farms, neat grey country houses and delightful, well-seasoned old men and women. That, when one thinks of it in a flash, is New England. I remember hearing an English actor say that until he made a motor trip through the New England country he had supposed that the Americans killed their aged in some merciful fashion, for he saw none in the cities where he played.

There are many kinds of people in the State of Maine, and neighbouring States, who are not found in Miss Jewett's books. There may be Othellos and Iagos and Don Juans; but they are not highly characteristic of the country, they do not come up spontaneously in the juniper pastures as the everlasting does. Miss Jewett wrote of everyday people who grew out of the soil, not about exceptional individuals at war with their environment. This was not a creed with her, but an instinctive preference.

Born within the scent of the sea but not within sight of it, in a beautiful old house full of strange and lovely things brought home from all over the globe by seafaring ancestors, she spent much of her childhood driving about the country with her doctor father on his professional rounds among the farms. She early learned to love her country for what it was. What is quite as important, she saw it as it was. She happened to have the right nature, the right temperament, to see it so—and to understand by intuition the deeper meaning of what she saw.

She had not only the eye, she had the ear. From her early years she must have treasured up those pithy bits of local speech, of native idiom, which enrich and enliven her pages. The language her people speak to each other is a native tongue. No writer can invent it. It is made in the hard school of experience, in communities where language has been un-disturbed long enough to take on colour and character from the nature and experiences of the people. The "sayings" of a community, its proverbs, are its characteristic comment upon life; they imply its history, suggest its attitude toward the world and its way of accepting life. Such an idiom makes the finest language any writer can have; and he can never get it with a notebook. He himself must be able to think and feel in that speech—it is a gift from heart to heart.

Much of Miss Jewett's delightful humour comes from her delicate and tactful handling of this native language of the waterside and countryside, never overdone, never pushed a shade too far; from this, and from her own fine attitude to-ward her subject-matter. This attitude in itself, though unspo-ken, is everywhere felt, and constitutes one of the most potent elements of grace and charm in her stories. She had with her own stories and her own characters a very charming relation; spirited, gay, tactful, noble in its essence and a little arch in its expression. In this particular relationship many of our most gifted writers are unfortunate. If a writer's attitude toward his characters and his scene is as vulgar as a showman's, as merce-nary as an auctioneer's, vulgar and meretricious will his prod-uct for ever remain.

II

"The distinguished outward stamp"—it was that one felt immediately upon meeting Miss Jewett: a lady, in the old high sense. It was in her face and figure, in her carriage, her smile, her voice, her way of greeting one. There was an ease, a graciousness, a light touch in conversation, a delicate unobtrusive wit. You quickly recognized that her gift with the pen was one of many charming personal attributes. In the short period when I knew her, 1908 and 1909, she was not writing at all, and found life full enough without it. Some six years before, she had been thrown from a carriage on a country road (sad fate for an enthusiastic horsewoman) and suffered a slight concussion. She recovered, after a long illness, but she did not write again—felt that her best working power was spent.

She had never been one of those who "live to write." She lived for a great many things, and the stories by which we know her were one of many preoccupations. After the carriage accident she was not strong enough to go out into the world a great deal; before that occurred her friendships occupied perhaps the first place in her life. She had friends among the most interesting and gifted people of her time, and scores of friends among the village and country people of her own State—people who knew her as Doctor Jewett's daughter and regarded "Sarah's writing" as a ladylike accomplishment. These country friends, she used to say, were the wisest of all, because they could never be fooled about fundamentals. Even after her long illness she was at home to a few visitors almost every afternoon; friends from England and France were always coming and going. Small dinner-parties and luncheons were part of the regular routine when she was with Mrs. Fields on Charles Street or at Manchester-by-the-Sea. When she was at home, in South Berwick, there were the old friends of her childhood to whom she must be always accessible. At the time I knew her she had, as she said, forgone all customary exercises—except a little gardening in spring and summer. But as a young woman she devoted her mornings to horseback riding in fine weather, and was skilful with a sailboat. Every day, in every season of the year, she enjoyed the beautiful country in which she had the good fortune to be born. Her love of the Maine country and seacoast was the supreme happiness of her life. Her stories were but reflections, quite incidental, of that peculiar and intensely personal pleasure.

Take, for instance, that clear, daybreak paragraph which be-
gins "By the Morning Boat":

> "On the coast of Maine, where many green islands
> and salt inlets fringe the deep-cut shore line; where bal-
> sam firs and bayberry bushes send their fragrance far
> seaward, and song-sparrows sing all day, and the tide
> runs plashing in and out among the weedy ledges;
> where cowbells tinkle on the hills and herons stand in
> the shady coves—on the lonely coast of Maine stood a
> small gray house facing the morning light."

Wherever Miss Jewett might be in the world, in the Alps,
the Pyrenees, the Apennines, she carried the Maine shore-
country with her. She loved it by instinct, and in the light of
wide experience, from near and from afar.

"You must know the world before you can know the vil-
lage," she once said to me. Quoted out of its context this
remark sounds like a wise pronouncement, but Miss Jewett
never made wise pronouncements. Her personal opinions she
voiced lightly, half-humorously; any expression of them was
spontaneous, the outgrowth of the immediate conversation.
This remark was a supplementary comment, apropos of a
story we had both happened to read: a story about a mule,
introduced by the magazine which published it with an edito-
rial note to the effect that (besides being "fresh" and "prom-
ising") it was authentic, as the young man who wrote it was a
mule-driver and had never been anything else. When I asked
Miss Jewett if she had seen it, she gave no affirmative but a
soft laugh, rather characteristic of her, something between
amusement and forbearance, and exclaimed:

"Poor lad! But his mule could have done better! A mule, by
God's grace, is a mule, with the mettle of his kind. Besides,
the mule would be grammatical. It's not in his sure-footed
nature to slight syntax. A horse might tangle himself up in his
sentences or his picket rope, but never a mule."

III

Miss Jewett had read too widely, and had too fine a literary
sense, to overestimate her own performance. Every Sunday

book section of the New York dailies announces half a dozen "great" books, and calls our attention to more great writers than the Elizabethan age and the nineteenth century put together could muster. Miss Jewett applied that adjective very seldom (to Tolstoi, Flaubert, and a few others), certainly never to herself or to anything of her own. She spoke of "the Pointed Fir papers" or "the Pointed Fir sketches"; I never heard her call them stories. She had, as Henry James said of her, "a sort of elegance of humility, or fine flame of modesty." She was content to be slight, if she could be true. The closing sentences of "Marsh Rosemary" might stand as an unconscious piece of self-criticism,—or perhaps as a gentle apology for the art of all new countries, which must grow out of a thin soil and bear its fate:

> "Who can laugh at my Marsh Rosemary, or who can cry, for that matter? The gray primness of the plant is made up from a hundred colors if you look close enough to find them. This Marsh Rosemary stands in her own place, and holds her dry leaves and tiny blossoms steadily toward the same sun that the pink lotus blooms for, and the white rose."

For contemporary writers of much greater range than her own, she had the most reverent and rejoicing admiration. She was one of the first Americans to see the importance of Joseph Conrad. Indeed, she was reading a new volume of Conrad, late in the night, when the slight cerebral hæmorrhage occurred from which she died some months later.

At a time when machine-made historical novels were the literary fashion in the United States, when the magazines were full of dreary dialect stories, and the works of John Fox, Jr., were considered profound merely because they were very dull and heavy as clay, Miss Jewett quietly developed her own medium and confined herself to it. At that time Henry James was the commanding figure in American letters, and his was surely the keenest mind any American ever devoted to the art of fiction. But it was devoted almost exclusively to the study of other and older societies than ours. He was interested in his countrymen chiefly as they appeared in relation to the European scene. As an American writer he seems to claim, and

richly to deserve, a sort of personal exemption. Stephen Crane
came upon the scene, a young man of definite talent, brilliant
and brittle,—dealing altogether with the surfaces of things,
but in a manner all his own. He died young, but he had done
something real. One can read him today. If we glance back
over the many novels which have challenged our attention
since Crane's time, it is like taking a stroll through a World's
Fair grounds some years after the show is over. Palaces with
the stucco peeling off, oriental villages stripped to beaver-
board and cement, broken fountains, lakes gone to mud and
weeds. We realize that whatever it is that makes a book hold
together, most of these hadn't it.

Among those glittering novelties which have now become
old-fashioned Miss Jewett's little volumes made a small show-
ing. A taste for them must always remain a special taste,—but
it will remain. She wrote for a limited audience, and she still
has it, both here and abroad. To enjoy her the reader must
have a sympathetic relation with the subject-matter and a
sensitive ear; especially must he have a sense of "pitch" in
writing. He must recognize when the quality of feeling comes
inevitably out of the theme itself; when the language, the
stresses, the very structure of the sentences are imposed upon
the writer by the special mood of the piece.

It is easy to understand why some of the young students
who have turned back from the present to glance at Miss
Jewett find very little on her pages. Imagine a young man, or
woman, born in New York City, educated at a New York uni-
versity, violently inoculated with Freud, hurried into journal-
ism, knowing no more about New England country people
(or country folk anywhere) than he has caught from motor
trips or observed from summer hotels: what is there for him
in *The Country of the Pointed Firs*?

This hypothetical young man is perhaps of foreign descent:
German, Jewish, Scandinavian. To him English is merely a
means of making himself understood, of communicating his
ideas. He may write and speak American English correctly,
but only as an American may learn to speak French correctly.
It is a surface speech: he clicks the words out as a bank clerk
clicks out silver when you ask for change. For him the lan-

guage has no emotional roots. How could he find the talk of the Maine country people anything but "dialect"? Moreover, the temper of the people which lies behind the language is incomprehensible to him. He can see what these Yankees *have not* (hence an epidemic of "suppressed desire" plays and novels), but what they *have*, their actual preferences and their fixed scale of values, are absolutely dark to him. When he tries to put himself in the Yankee's place, he attempts an impossible substitution.

But the adopted American is not alone in being cut off from an instinctive understanding of "the old moral harmonies." There is the new American, whom Mr. Santayana describes as "the untrained, pushing, cosmopolitan orphan, cocksure in manner but none too sure in his morality, to whom the old Yankee, with his sour integrity, is almost a foreigner."[1]

When we find ourselves on shipboard, among hundreds of strangers, we very soon recognize those who are sympathetic to us. We find our own books in the same way. We like a writer much as we like individuals; for what he is, simply, underneath his accomplishments. Oftener than we realize, it is for some moral quality, some ideal which he himself cherishes, though it may be little discernible in his behaviour in the world. It is the light behind his books and is the living quality in his sentences.

It is this very personal quality of perception, a vivid and intensely personal experience of life, which make a "style"; Mark Twain had it, at his best, and Hawthorne. But among fifty thousand books you will find very few writers who ever achieved a style at all. The distinctive thing about Miss Jewett is that she had an individual voice; "a sense for the finest kind of truthful rendering, the sober, tender note, the temperately touched, whether in the ironic or pathetic," as Henry James said of her. During the twenty-odd clamorous years since her death "masterpieces" have been bumping down upon us like trunks pouring down the baggage chutes from an over-

---

[1]George Santayana: *Character and Opinion in the United States.* New York: Charles Scribner's Sons, 1920.

crowded ocean steamer. But if you can get out from under them and go to a quiet spot and take up a volume of Miss Jewett, you will find the voice still there, with a quality which any ear trained in literature must recognize.

"Joseph and His Brothers"

I

IN THE PROLOGUE of his great work Thomas Mann says of it: "Its theme is the first and last of all our questioning and speaking and all our necessity; the nature of man." But it is not the nature of man as the Behaviourists or the biologists see it. This is a double nature, struggling with itself, and the struggle is not to keep the physical machine running smoothly. These ancient people know very little about their physical structure. Their attention is fixed upon something within themselves which they feel to be their real life, consciousness; where it came from and what becomes of it. In this book men ask themselves the questions they asked æons ago when they found themselves in an unconscious world. From the Old Testament, that greatest record of the orphan soul trying to find its kin somewhere in the universe, and from the cruder superstitions of the neighbouring Semitic peoples, Mann has made something like an orchestral arrangement of all the Semitic religions and philosophies.

There are two ways in which a story-teller can approach a theme set in the distant past. The way most familiar to us is that which Flaubert took in *Salammbô*. The writer stands in present time, his own time, and looks backward. He works and thinks in a long-vanished society. His mind is naturally fixed upon contrasting that world with our own; upon religions, institutions, manners, ways of thinking, all very unlike ours. The reader sees the horrors and splendours of *Salammbô* from a distance; partly because it was a point of ethics with Flaubert to encourage no familiarity at any time, but particularly because in this book he himself was engaged with the feeling of distance, strangeness, difference.

Mann approaches an even more distant past by another route; he gets behind the epoch of his story and looks forward. He begins with a Prologue which is informed by all the discoveries science has lately made about the beginnings of human existence on this globe; the beginnings long before the known beginning, the long ages when men "did battle with the flying newts" and life was little more than a misery which persisted. From the depths without a history he comes up through the ages of orally transmitted legend; every legend, he believes, having a fact behind it, an occurrence of critical importance to the breed of man.

After the tremendous preparation of the Prologue (a marvel of imaginative power), he rises out of the bottomless depths to the period of his story; not much more than three thousand years ago, he says, when men were very much like ourselves, "aside from a measure of dreamy indefiniteness in their habits of thought."

This same dreamy indefiniteness, belonging to a people without any of the relentless mechanical gear which directs every moment of modern life toward accuracy, this indefiniteness is one of the most effective elements of verity in this great work. We are among a shepherd people; the story has almost the movement of grazing sheep. The characters live at that pace. Perhaps no one who has not lived among sheep can realize the rightness of the rhythm. A shepherd people is not driving toward anything. With them, truly, as Michelet said of quite another form of journeying, the end is nothing, the road is all. In fact, the road and the end are literally one.

There is nothing in *Joseph and His Brothers* more admirable than the tempo, the deliberate, sustained pace. (In this age of blinding speed and shattering sound!) Never was there a happier conjunction of writer and subject-matter. Thomas Mann's natural tempo is deliberate; his sentences come out of reflection, not out of an impulse. It is possible for him to write the story of a shepherd people at the right pace and with the right kind of development,—continual circling and digression—which here is not digression since it is his purpose. He can listen to the herdsmen telling their stories over and over, go backward and forward with their "dreamily indefinite" habits of thought. He has all the time there is; Mediterranean time, 1700 B.C.

When I refer to a passage in the book to refresh my memory, I find myself reading on and on, largely from pleasure in this rich deliberateness which is never without intensity and deep vibration. It is not a kind of writing adapted to all subjects, certainly, but here it is in the very nature of the theme; it gives, along with this distinctive rhythm, a warm homeliness, communicates a brooding tenderness which is in the author's mind. For in this book Herr Mann is enamoured of his theme, wholly given to it, and this favouritism, held in check by his native temperateness, is itself a source of pleasure; the strong feeling under the strong hand.

At the end of his Prologue the author declares that he is glad to come up from the bottomless pit of prehistoric struggle, and the undecipherable riddle of the old legends, to something relatively near, rather like a home-coming. We, too, are glad. With a sense of escape we approach something already known to us; not glacier ages or a submerged Atlantis, but the very human Mediterranean shore, on a moonlight night in the season of spring.

We have all been there before, even if we have never crossed salt water. (Perhaps this is not strictly accurate, but even the Agnostic and the Behaviourist would have to admit that his great-grandfather had been there.) The Bible countries along the Mediterranean shore were very familiar to most of us in our childhood. Whether we were born in New Hampshire or Virginia or California, Palestine lay behind us. We took it in unconsciously and unthinkingly perhaps, but we could not escape it. It was all about us, in the pictures on the walls, in the songs we sang in Sunday school, in the "opening exercises" at day school, in the talk of the old people, wherever we lived. And it was in our language—fixedly, indelibly. The effect of the King James translation of the Bible upon English prose has been repeated down through the generations, leaving its mark on the minds of all children who had any but the most sluggish emotional nature.

We emerge from Mann's Prologue to find ourselves not only in a familiar land, but among people we have always known, Joseph and Jacob: and they are talking about their remote ancestors, whom we also know. The Book of Genesis lies like a faded tapestry deep in the consciousness of almost every individual who is more than forty years of age. Moreover, as it is the background of nearly all the art of Western Europe, even today's college Senior must have come upon it, if only by the cheerless road of reference reading. We are familiar with Mann's characters and their history, not only through Moses and the Prophets, but through Milton and Dante and Racine, Bach and Hayden and Handel, through painters and architects and stone-cutters innumerable. We begin the book with the great imaginings and the great imaginators already in our minds—we are dyed through and through with them. That is the take-off of the story.

II

The first volume of the work is the book of Jacob,—of Jacob and his forbears. In a family which held itself so much apart from other tribes and sects, the connection between each man and a long line of grandfathers was very close. There were external features common to all the Semitic religions; hence the shallow and light-minded of the descendants of Abraham were often backsliders, marrying with women of other tribes and troubling themselves very little about the one great idea that had brought Abraham out of Chaldea and isolated him from his own and all other peoples. Whenever that conception of God was very strong in one of Abraham's descendants (was indeed the burning purpose of his inner life, as it was of Jacob's), that man was virtually Abraham's grandson, no matter how many physical generations had gone between, and he was the true and direct inheritor of the "blessing," aside from any accident of primogeniture.

Throughout this first volume one gradually becomes aware that Abraham's seed were not so much the "chosen people" as they were *the people who chose*. They chose to renounce not only sacred images, "idols," but all the spells and incantations and rites to which men resorted for comfort of mind, and to wander forth searching for a God of whom no image could be made by mortal hand. A God who was not a form, but a force, an essence; felt, but not imprisoned in matter. "The God of the ages," Mann puts it, "for whom he [Abraham] sought a name and found none sufficient, wherefore he gave Him the plural, calling Him, provisionally, Elohim, the Godhead."

Herr Mann accounts for Abraham's quest in this wise:

"What had set him in motion was unrest of the spirit, a need of God, and if—as there can be no doubt—dispensations were vouchsafed him, they had reference to the irradiations of his personal experience of God, which was of a new kind altogether; and his whole concern from the beginning had been to win for it sympathy and adherence. He suffered; and when he compared the measure of his inward distress with that of the great majority, he drew the conclusion that it was pregnant with the future. Not in vain, so he heard from the newly beheld God, shall have been thy torment and thine unrest; for it shall fructify many souls and make proselytes in numbers like to the sands of the seas; and it shall give impulse to great expansions of life hidden in it as in a seed; and in one word, thou shalt be a blessing. A blessing? It is unlikely that the word gives the true meaning of that which happened to him in his very sight and which corresponded to his temperament and to his experience of himself. For the word 'blessing' carries with it an idea which but ill describes men of his sort: men, that is, of roving spirit and discomfortable mind, whose novel conception of the deity is destined to make its mark upon the future. The life of men with whom new histories begin can seldom or never be a sheer unclouded blessing; not this it is which their consciousness of self whispers in their ears. 'And thou shalt be a destiny': such is the purer and more precise meaning of the promise, in whatever language it may have been spoken."

The idea was a leap centuries ahead into the dark. Yet it must have been born in the mind of one man: such revelations never come to committees or bureaus of research. Abraham's descendants could not always live up to it, but tradition held them together, and the rite of circumcision set them apart. The rite and the form can be continued even in the sluggish generations when the significance is lost. But Mann's work begins when the quest which drove Abraham

out of a stupefied materialistic world is burning bright again
in Jacob, who, by stratagems outwardly crooked but inwardly
inevitable, "had saved his life, his precious, covenanted life,
for God and the future."

Jacob, apparently, was the first of Abraham's descendants
who had the power of realizing and experiencing God more
and more sharply through all the variations of a life incredibly
eventful and long. He experienced Him in meditation, in the
unforeseeable but strangely logical working-out of events in
his own life—and in dreams. Dreams so full of meaning that
they were to him promises. After Abraham's people had cut
themselves off from the comfortableness and commonplace-
ness of anthropomorphic gods, there still remained the ladder
of dreams, by which the orphan soul could mount and the
ministers of grace descend.

Jacob the constant lover, who served seven years for
Rachel: the trickery of Laban: the rivalry between the sisters:
these are great stories which have lived through the centuries.
But the greatest, the most moving story is what the author
terms "Jacob's labouring upon the Godhead." Jacob is a
many-sided man,—but the painting of his contradictions
must be left to Thomas Mann himself. He has done it as no
one else could. The creation of Jacob, in the flesh and in the
spirit, is the great achievement of his work. The man who
knows that he bears the "blessing" and who sees further into
destiny than any of his tribe or time, must, sometimes by pur-
posed indirection, sometimes by stepping aside and shutting
his eyes, "save his precious, covenanted life for God and the
future." For the aim of the law is worth more than any letter
of it, and a trivial transaction or a question of family govern-
ment must not be allowed to interfere with those fruitful sea-
sons of thought which are well called "labour upon the
Godhead."

For every lapse in conduct and shirking of responsibility
Jacob paid, of course. But the payment, however cruel, seems
always to set him a long way forward in his incommunicable
spiritual quest,—which certainly proves that his way was for
him the right way. With every sorrow he brought upon him-
self for failing in a plain duty, the immortal jewel he carried
within became brighter, and his faith in the way his fathers

had chosen more sure. His shirking in the matter of restraining Leah's sons from their revenge for Dinah cost him Rachel, who died because she was forced to travel by mule-back when she was close upon her confinement. (Another contributing cause comes in here, very characteristic of Jacob, and, one might say, of the author's mind as well.) Rachel died by the roadside, giving birth to Benjamin. It was as Jacob sat beside her under the mulberry tree, aware that she was dying, that there came over him the greatest of his understandings, loftier than all his visions:

> "And then it was that he directed upwards into the silvery light of those worlds above their heads, almost as a confession that he understood, his question: 'Lord, what dost Thou?'
> "To such questions there is no answer. Yet it is the glory of the human spirit that in this silence it does not depart from God, but rather learns to grasp the majesty of the ungraspable and to thrive thereon. Beside him the Chaldæan women and slaves chanted their litanies and invocations, thinking to bind to human wishes the unreasoning powers. But Jacob had never yet so clearly understood as in this hour, why all that was false, and why Abram had left Ur to escape it. The vision vouchsafed him into this immensity was full of horror but also of power; his labour upon the godhead, which always betrayed itself in his care-worn mien, made in this awful night a progress not unconnected with Rachel's agonies."

III

Volume two is the Book of Young Joseph, but it is also still the book of Jacob, though there is a lull in the vicissitudes of his life. The beauty and promise of Rachel's son fill his days,—until there occurs the great shock which arouses him again to the old struggle to comprehend, in some measure, the dealings of God with man; to justify God, as it were, and find some benign purpose behind the brutality of accident and mischance.

The character of the relation between father and son we

have known ever since the long conversation between them
on that spring night beside the well. There all Jacob's anxieties
were at once revealed; his fear that the nature of the boy's
gifts may lead him astray to admire the softer graces of other
peoples,—their arts and sciences, which were irrelevant to a
life for the Godhead, and should not concern the boy to
whom he would undoubtedly give the "blessing." In short,
the lad was already worldly, and with scant opportunity had
managed to learn a great deal about other languages and
other manners than those of his shepherd people. In this pre-
cocity Jacob sensed a danger. But he feared other dangers,—
love can always see many. He is troubled to find the boy
abroad at night, where a wild beast might fall upon him; a
lion has been seen in the neighbourhood. And he is always ill
at ease when the boy is near a well, a hole in the earth. Before
Joseph's birth his grandfather, Laban, had consulted a heathen
seer who foretold of the child Rachel carried that he should
go down into a pit.

As for Joseph's attitude toward his father, it is what the
good son's always will be. He loves Jacob because it is easy for
him to love, respects him for all he has been and is, and pities
him because his mind is shut against whatever is new and
delightfully strange; against interesting languages and reli-
gions, against the clamour of founded cities and the customs
of foreign peoples. He himself already knows a great deal
more than Jacob, although he admits he is not so wise and has
not been through so much.

When the second volume opens, Joseph is seventeen. He
has learned many things since that night when he talked with
Jacob by the well, but he is scarcely more mature. To pick up a
new language easily, to astonish his father by his knowledge
of tradition and the spiritual meaning of natural phenomena,
to be the ornament and, indeed, the intellect, of his family; all
this is quite enough to fill the days pleasantly at seventeen.

Very seldom does the personal charm of a character myste-
riously reach out to one from the printed page. All authors
claim it for their favourite creations, but their failure to make
good their claim is so usual that we seldom stop to say to the
writer: "But this is mere writing, I get no feeling of this

person." For me, at least, Herr Mann wholly succeeds in communicating Joseph's highly individual charm. Mann's own consciousness of it is very strong, with something paternal in it, since he so often feels Joseph through Jacob's senses. When, only a few hours after its birth, Jacob first sees this baby which had seemed so unwilling to be born at all, when he regards the unusual shape and firmness of the head and the "strangely complete little hand," he knows that here is something different from all the other sturdy little animals which have been born to him. From that moment the reader also is able to believe in the special loveliness and equability and fine fibre of this child; here is no shepherd clod, but something that can take a high finish.

The misfortune of young Joseph is that he never meets with anything difficult enough to challenge his very unusual mind. What there is to be learned from his old teacher, and from the routine of a shepherds' camp, is mere child's play. Nothing very interesting ever happens now in Jacob's great family; so Joseph decorates the trivial events: he exaggerates, gossips, talks too much, and is extravagantly given to dreams. These are not the dreams of lassitude, nor are they sensual. They are violent, dizzy,—nightmares of grandeur. The qualities which are to make his great future are in him, potential realities, just as they were in Napoleon at seventeen; and they have nothing to grapple with.

It was this "something," this innate superiority in the boy himself, which the brothers hated even more than they hated the father's favourite: a deeper and more galling kind of jealousy. The story of Joseph and his brothers is not only forever repeated in literature, it forever repeats itself in life. The natural antagonism between the sane and commonplace, and the exceptional and inventive, is never so bitter as when it occurs in a family: and Joseph certainly did nothing to conciliate his stolid brethren. He insisted upon believing (he had to insist, for he was not vain to the point of stupidity) that all his family rejoiced in his good looks and brilliancy and general superiority. Was he not an ornament to them? It did not occur to him that families which lead self-respecting, simple, industrious lives are not pleased with or benefited by ornaments of this kind—which put them in a false position, indeed. The richness of his own fancy and vitality was quite enough for the youth. Upon this limitation in Joseph the author comments as follows:

> "Indifference to the inner life of other human beings, ignorance of their feelings, display an entirely warped attitude toward real life, they give rise to a certain blindness. Since the days of Adam and Eve, since the time when one became two, nobody has been able to live without wanting to put himself in his neighbour's place and explore his situation, even while trying to see it objectively. Imagination, the art of divining the emotional life of others—in other words, sympathy—is not only commendable inasmuch as it breaks down the limitations of the ego; it is always an indispensable means of self-preservation. But of these rules Joseph knew nothing. His blissful self-confidence was like that of a spoilt child; it persuaded him, despite all evidence to the contrary, that everyone loved him, even more than themselves."

Joseph heeded no preliminary warnings; he was awakened from his agreeable self-satisfaction only by a shock so terrible that he barely survived it at all, and this awakening was followed by a long and hazardous servitude among a hostile people. Life put him to the test, to many tests, and proved him; he was one of those whom mischances enlighten and refine. Behind the bright promise in him there was the sound seed which would grow to its full measure under any circumstances and could not be circumvented. The world is always full of brilliant youth which fades into grey and embittered middle age: the first flowering takes everything. The great men are those who have developed slowly, or who have been able to survive the glamour of their early florescence and to go on learning from life. If we could

> *look into the seeds of time,*
> *And say which grain will grow and which will not,*

our hopes for young talent would be disappointed less often. Yet in that very mystery lies much of the fascination which gifted young people have for their elders. Kindly effort to shelter them from struggle with the hard facts of existence is often to take away the bread (or the lack of it) by which they grow, if the power of growth is in them. Perhaps if young Joseph had been sent into Egypt on a pension fund or a travelling scholarship the end might have been very different.

The manner in which he actually sets out for Egypt is a challenge to fate, certainly: disinherited, bruised in body, rocking on the camel of Ishmaelite merchants who have bought him as a slave. Thus he vanishes from the story. We do not know at what point in his adventures we are first to see him again in Mann's third volume, but we know that his father is not to see him again until there has been such a reversal of fortune as seldom happens—even in old legends, with the direct intervention of the gods. Though he is brought so low when he leaves us, his state is not utterly hopeless. The brothers have beaten the conceit and joy out of him; all his sunny youth he has left behind him in the pit, and he has come out into the world naked as when he was born, without father or family or friends, owning not even his own body. But he is going toward a country where, if he really possesses the lively intelligence Jacob and old Eliezer imputed to him, it will find plenty to work upon.

The book ends with Jacob, for however much the story is Joseph's, it is always Jacob's. He is the compass, the north star, the seeking mind behind events; he divines their hidden causes. He knows that even external accidents often have their roots, their true beginnings, in personal feeling. He accepts the evidence of the bloody coat and believes that Joseph was devoured by a boar or a lion, yet his glance at the brothers is always accusing. But for their hatred, the wild beast might not have come down upon Joseph.

Jacob is the understanding witness of the whole play, and we know, when we close the second volume, that he will live to behold the unimaginable conclusion in Egypt. This is one of the advantages of making a new story out of an old one which is a very part of the readers' consciousness. The course of destiny is already known and fixed for us, it is not some story-teller's make-believe (though for strangeness no reckless improviser could surpass this one). What we most love is not bizarre invention, but to have the old story brought home to us closer than ever before, enriched by all that the right man could draw from it and, by sympathetic insight, put into it. Shakespeare knew this fact very well, and the Greek dramatists long before him.

Herr Mann stresses Joseph's charm of person and address with good reason. They are stressed even in the highly condensed account in the Book of Genesis. They are, indeed, the subject of Joseph's story. Had the Ishmaelites not recognized very exceptional values in him, they would have sold him in any slave market. Being sure of special qualities in this piece of merchandise, they held him for a high purchaser and disposed of him to the Captain of Pharaoh's guard. He charmed Potiphar and, to his misfortune, Potiphar's wife. When he was thrown into a dungeon, his jailor gave him the management of the prison. When he was brought before Pharaoh, he was given the management of the kingdom.

He had come into Egypt a slave, born of a half-savage people whom the cultivated Egyptians despised, and he had been trained to an occupation they despised. We are told in Genesis that "every shepherd was an abomination to the Egyptians." (We are not told why: perhaps because the Egyptian cotton market was already an important thing in the world?) It is not easy to find a parallel situation: suppose that a Navajo Indian shepherd boy had been gathered up by the Spanish explorers and sold to one of the world-roving merchant ships from Saint-Malo. Suppose, further, that we find this red Indian boy at the age of thirty become the virtual ruler of France, a Richelieu or a Mazarin.

How much of his remarkable career Herr Mann will accredit to Joseph's aptness in worldly affairs (that quality of which old Jacob was so distrustful), and how much to his direct inheritance from Jacob, that "blessing" (never formally given) which he carried with him into a land of subtleties and highly organized social life, I wait with impatience to learn. I suspect that I shall still find the father mightier than the son, and more remarkable as an imaginative creation.

Jacob is the rod of measure. He saw the beginning, the new-born creature, and believed even then that this was the child of destiny. He knew Joseph before Joseph knew himself. When the "true son" disappeared into darkness at the dawn of his promise, it was Jacob, not Joseph, who bore the full weight of the catastrophe and tasted the bitterness of death. And he lived to see the beautiful conclusion; not the worldly triumph only, but the greatness of heart which could forgive wrongs so shameful and cruel. Had not Jacob been there to recognize and to foresee, to be destroyed by grief and raised up again, the story of Joseph would lose its highest value. Joseph is the brilliant actor in the scene, but Jacob is the mind which created the piece itself. His brooding spirit wraps the legend in a loftiness and grandeur which actual events can never, in themselves, possess. Take Jacob out of the history of Joseph, and it becomes simply the story of young genius; its cruel discipline, its ultimate triumph and worldly success. A story ever new and always gratifying, but one which never wakens the deep vibrations of the soul.

Katherine Mansfield

I

LATE IN THE AUTUMN of 1920, on my way home from Naples, I had a glimpse of Katherine Mansfield through the eyes of a fellow passenger. As I have quite forgotten his real name, I shall call him Mr. J—. He was a New Englander, about sixty-five years of age, I conjectured; long, lean, bronzed, clear blue eyes, not very talkative. His face, however, had a way of talking to itself. When he sat reading, or merely looking at the water, changes went over his thin lips and brown cheeks which betokened silent soliloquy; amusement, doubtful deliberation, very often a good-humoured kind of scorn, accompanied by an audible sniff which was not the result of a cold. His profession was the law, I gathered, though he seemed to know a great deal about mines and mining engineering. Early American history was his personal passion, Francis Parkman and Sir George Otto Trevelyan. Though in both writers he found inconsistencies, he referred to these not superciliously but rather affectionately.

The voyage was very rough (we were delayed three days by bad weather), the cabin passengers were few and the wind and cold kept most of them in their staterooms. I found Mr. J— good company. He wore well. Though I have forgotten his name, I have not forgotten him. He was an original, a queer stick, intelligent but whimsical and crochety, quickly prejudiced for or against people by trifling mannerisms. He dined alone at a small table and always dressed for dinner though no one else did.

He was an agreeable companion chiefly because he was so unexpected. For example: one morning when he was muttering dry witticisms about the boat's having lost so much time, he threw off carelessly that he was trying to get home for his mother's *ninetieth* birthday celebration, "though we are not on good terms, by any means," he chuckled.

I said I had supposed that family differences were outlawed at ninety.

"Not in our family," he brought out with relish.

He was a true chip, and proud of the old block. He was bringing a present home to her—a great bundle of leopard skins, which he showed to me. (He had lately been in Africa.)

He was a bachelor, of course, but when we were filling out declarations for customs, he had a number of expensive toys to declare (besides the leopard skins) and sport clothes for young men. Nephews, I asked? Not altogether, with a twist of the face. Some of his old friends had done him the compliment of naming sons after him. Yes, I thought, a bachelor of this kidney was just the man who would be welcome in other men's homes; he would be a cheerful interruption in the domestic monotony of correct, sound people like himself. Possibly he would have friends among people very unlike himself.

One afternoon as he sat down in his deck chair he picked up a volume of Synge's plays lying on my rug. He looked at it and observed:

"Trevelyan is the one English writer I would really like to meet. The old man."

He glanced through my book for a few moments, then put it back on my knee and asked abruptly: "What do you think of Katherine Mansfield?"

I told him I had read her very little (English friends had sent me over a story of hers from time to time), but I thought her very talented.

"You think so, do you." It was not a question, but a verdict, delivered in his driest manner, with a slight sniff. After a moment he said he had letters to write and went away. Why a specialist in the American Revolution and the French and Indian wars should ask me about a girl then scarcely heard of in America, and why he should be displeased at my answer—

The next morning I saw him doing his usual half-hour on the deck. "Climbing the deck," he called it, because now, in addition to the inconveniences of rough weather, we had a very bad list. Mr. J— explained that it came about because the coal hadn't been properly trimmed and had shifted. Very dangerous with a heavy sea every day . . . disgrace to seamanship . . . couldn't have happened on a British steamer . . . Italians and French in the engine room. After climbing and descending the deck until he had satisfied his conscience, he sat down beside me and flapped his rug over his knees.

"The young lady we were speaking of yesterday: she writes under a *nom de plume*. Her true name is not Mansfield, but Beauchamp."

"That I didn't know. I know nothing about her, really."

He relapsed into one of his long silences, and I went on reading.

"May I send the deck steward to my cabin for some sherry, instead of that logwood he would bring us from the bar?"

The sherry appeared. After we had drunk a few glasses, Mr. J— began: "The young lady we were speaking of; I happen to have seen her several times, though I certainly don't move in literary circles."

I expressed surprise and interest, but he did not go on at once. He sent the steward for more biscuit, and got up to test the lashings of his deck chair and mine. We were on the port side where the wind was milder but the list was worse. At last he made himself comfortable and began to tell me that he had once gone out to Australia and New Zealand on business matters. He was very specific as to dates, geography, boat and railway connections. He elaborated upon these details. I suppose because they were safe and sane, things you could check up on, while the real subject of his communication proved to be very vague. I did not listen attentively; I had only the dimmest conception of those distant British colonies. He was telling me about a boat trip he had made from New Zealand to some Australian port, when gradually his manner changed; he rambled and was more wary. As he became more cautious I became more interested. I wish I could repeat his story exactly as he told it, but his way of talking was peculiar to himself and I can only give the outline:

Among the people who were coming on board his steamer when he left New Zealand, Mr. J— noticed a family party: several children, a man who was evidently their father, and an old lady who seemed of quite a different class than the other passengers. She was quiet, gentle, had the children perfectly under control. She conducted them below as soon as the boat took off. When they reappeared on deck they had changed their shore things for play clothes. Mr. J— remembered very little about the father, "the usual pushing colonial type," but he distinctly remembered the old lady, and a little girl with thin legs and large eyes who wandered away from the family and apparently wished to explore the steamer for herself. Presently she came and sat down next Mr. J—, which pleased him. She was shy, but so happy to be going on a journey that she answered his questions and talked to him as if he were not a stranger. She was delighted with everything; the boat, the water, the weather, the gulls which followed the steamer. "But have you ever seen them *eat*?" she asked. "That is terrible!"

The next morning Mr. J— was up and out very early; found the deck washed down and empty. But up in the bow he saw his little friend of yesterday, doing some sort of gymnastic exercises, "quick as a bird." He joined her and asked if she had breakfasted. No, she was waiting for the others.

"Mustn't exercise too much before breakfast," he told her. "Come and sit down with me." As they walked toward his chair he noticed that she had put on a fresh dress for the morning. Mr. J— said it was "embroidered" (probably cross-stitched) with yellow ducks, all in a row round the hem. He complimented her upon the ducks.

"I thought they would astonish you," she said complacently.

As they sat and talked she kept smoothing her skirt and settling her sleeves, which had a duck on each cuff. Something pleased Mr. J— very much as he recalled the little girl, and her satisfaction with her fresh dress on that fresh morning aboard a little coasting steamer. His eyes twinkled and he chuckled. "She adopted me for the rest of the voyage," he concluded.

No, he couldn't say exactly what the charm of the child was. She struck him as intensely alert, with a deep curiosity altogether different from the flighty, excited curiosity usual in children. She turned things over in her head and asked him questions which surprised him. She was sometimes with her grandmother and the other children, but oftener alone, going about the boat, looking the world over with quiet satisfaction. When she was with him, he did not talk to her a great deal, because he liked better to watch her "taking it all in." It was on her account he had always remembered that short trip, out of many boat trips. She told him her name, and he easily remembered it "because of *Beauchamp's Career*, you see."

"And now do you want chapter two?" Mr. J— asked me. He twisted his face and rubbed his chin.

A few years ago he had been in London on a confidential mission for a client who was also an old friend. The nature of his business took him more or less among people not of his kind and not especially to his liking. (He paused here as if taking counsel with his discretion, and I wondered whether we were to have another version of Henry James' *The Ambassadors*.) In the places frequented by this uncongenial "circle" he heard talk of a girl from New Zealand who "could knock the standard British authors into a cocked hat," though she didn't very easily find a publisher. She scorned conventions, and had got herself talked about. He heard her name spoken. There could be no doubt; from the same part of the world, and the name he had never forgotten. The young lady herself was pointed out to him once in a restaurant, by the young man whose affairs he had come over to manage. She was just back from the Continent, and her friends were giving a dinner for her. As he expected; the same face, the same eyes. She did not fit the gossip he had been hearing; quite the contrary. She looked to him almost demure,—except for something challenging in her eyes, perhaps. And she seemed very frail. He felt a strong inclination to look her up. He decided to write to her, but he thought he had better inform himself a little first. He asked his client whether he had anything Miss Mansfield had written. The young man, doubtless with humorous intent, produced a pamphlet which had been privately printed: *Je ne parle pas français*. After reading it, Mr. J— felt there would be no point in meeting the young writer. He saw her once afterward, at the theatre. When the play was on and the lights were down, she looked, he thought, ill and unhappy. He heartily wished he had never seen or heard of her since that boat trip.

Mr. J— turned to me sharply: "*Je ne parle pas français* —and what do you think of that story, may I ask?"

I had not read it.

"Well, I have. I didn't dismiss it lightly; artificial, and un-
pleasantly hysterical, full of affectations; she had none as a
child." He spoke rather bitterly: his disappointment was
genuine.

II

Every writer and critic of discernment who looked into
Katherine Mansfield's first volume of short stories must have
felt that here was a very individual talent. At this particular
time few writers care much about their medium except as a
means for expressing ideas. But in Katherine Mansfield one
recognized virtuosity, a love for the medium she had chosen.

The qualities of a second-rate writer can easily be defined,
but a first-rate writer can only be experienced. It is just the
thing in him which escapes analysis that makes him first-rate.
One can catalogue all the qualities that he shares with other
writers, but the thing that is his very own, his timbre, this
cannot be defined or explained any more than the quality of a
beautiful speaking voice can be.

It was usually Miss Mansfield's way to approach the major
forces of life through comparatively trivial incidents. She
chose a small reflector to throw a luminous streak out into the
shadowy realm of personal relationships. I feel that personal
relationships, especially the uncatalogued ones, the seemingly
unimportant ones, interested her most. To my thinking, she
never measured herself up so fully as in the two remarkable
stories about an English family in New Zealand, "Prelude"
and "At the Bay."

I doubt whether any contemporary writer has made one
feel more keenly the many kinds of personal relations which
exist in an everyday "happy family" who are merely going on
living their daily lives, with no crises or shocks or bewildering
complications to try them. Yet every individual in that house-
hold (even the children) is clinging passionately to his indi-
vidual soul, is in terror of losing it in the general family
flavour. As in most families, the mere struggle to have any-
thing of one's own, to be one's self at all, creates an element
of strain which keeps everybody almost at the breaking-point.

One realizes that even in harmonious families there is this

double life: the group life, which is the one we can observe in our neighbour's household, and, underneath, another—secret and passionate and intense—which is the real life that stamps the faces and gives character to the voices of our friends. Always in his mind each member of these social units is escaping, running away, trying to break the net which circumstances and his own affections have woven about him. One realizes that human relationships are the tragic necessity of human life; that they can never be wholly satisfactory, that every ego is half the time greedily seeking them, and half the time pulling away from them. In those simple relationships of loving husband and wife, affectionate sisters, children and grandmother, there are innumerable shades of sweetness and anguish which make up the pattern of our lives day by day, though they are not down in the list of subjects from which the conventional novelist works.

Katherine Mansfield's peculiar gift lay in her interpretation of these secret accords and antipathies which lie hidden under our everyday behaviour, and which more than any outward events make our lives happy or unhappy. Had she lived, her development would have gone on in this direction more than in any other. When she touches this New Zealand family and those far-away memories ever so lightly, as in "The Doll's House," there is a magic one does not find in the other stories, fine as some of them are. With this theme the very letters on the page become alive. She communicates vastly more than she actually writes. One goes back and runs through the pages to find the text which made one know certain things about Linda or Burnell or Beryl, and the text is not there—but something was there, all the same—is there, though no typesetter will ever set it. It is this overtone, which is too fine for the printing press and comes through without it, that makes one know that this writer had something of the gift which is one of the rarest things in writing, and quite the most precious. That she had not the happiness of developing her powers to the full, is sad enough. She wrote the truth from Fontainebleau a few weeks before she died: *"The old mechanism isn't mine any longer, and I can't control the new."* She had lived through the first stage, had outgrown her young art, so that it seemed false to her in comparison with the new light that was breaking within. The "new mechanism," big enough to convey the new knowledge, she had not the bodily strength to set in motion.

III

Katherine Mansfield's published *Journal* begins in 1914 and ends in 1922, some months before her death. It is the record of a long struggle with illness, made more cruel by lack of money and by the physical hardships that war conditions brought about in England and France. At the age of twenty-two (when most young people have a secret conviction that they are immortal), she was already ill in a Bavarian *pension*. From the time when she left New Zealand and came back to England to make her own way, there was never an interval in which she did not have to drive herself beyond her strength. She never reached the stage when she could work with a relaxed elbow. In her story "Prelude," when the family are moving, and the storeman lifts the little girl into the dray and tucks her up, he says: "Easy does it." She knew this, long afterward, but she never had a chance to put that method into practice. In all her earlier stories there is something fierce about her attack, as if she took up a new tale in the spirit of overcoming it. "Do or die" is the mood,—indeed, she must have faced that alternative more than once: a girl come back to make her living in London, without health or money or influential friends,—with no assets but talent and pride.

In her volume of stories entitled *Bliss*, published in 1920 (most of them had been written some years before and had appeared in periodicals), she throws down her glove, utters her little challenge in the high language which she knew better than did most of her readers:

> But I tell you, my lord fool, out of this nettle, danger, we pluck this flower, safety.

A fine attitude, youthful and fiery: out of all the difficulties of life and art we will snatch *something*. No one was ever less afraid of the nettle; she was defrauded unfairly of the physical vigour which seems the natural accompaniment of a high and daring spirit.

At thirteen Katherine Mansfield made the long voyage to England with her grandmother, to go to school in London. At eighteen she returned to her own family in Wellington, New Zealand. It was then the struggle against circumstances began. She afterward burned all her early diaries, but it is those I should have liked to read. Exile may be easy to bear for those who have lived their lives. But at eighteen, after four years of London, to be thrown back into a prosperous commercial colony at the end of the world, was starvation. There is no homesickness and no hunger so unbearable. Many a young artist would sell his future, all his chances, simply to get back to the world where other people are doing the only things that, to his inexperience, seem worth doing at all.

Years afterward, when Katherine Mansfield had begun to do her best work but was rapidly sinking in vitality, her homesickness stretched all the other way—backwards, for New Zealand and that same crude Wellington. Unpromising as it was for her purpose, she felt that it was the only territory she could claim, in the deepest sense, as her own. The *Journal* tells us how often she went back to it in her sleep. She recounts these dreams at some length: but the entry which makes one realize that homesickness most keenly is a short one, made in Cornwall in 1918:

> "*June 20th*. The twentieth of June 1918.
>
> C'est de la misère.
>
> Non, pas ça exactement. Il y a quelque chose—une profonde malaise me suive comme un ombre.
>
> Oh, why write bad French? Why write at all? 11,500 miles are so many—too many by 11,499¾ for me."

Eleven thousand five hundred miles is the distance from England to New Zealand.

By this, 1918, she had served her apprenticeship. She had gone through a succession of enthusiasms for this master and that, formed friendships with some of the young writers of her own time. But the person who had freed her from the self-consciousness and affectations of the experimenting young writer, and had brought her to her realest self, was not one of her literary friends but, quite simply, her own brother.

He came over in 1915 to serve as an officer. He was younger than she, and she had not seen him for six years. After a short visit with her in London he went to the front, and a few weeks later was killed in action. But he had brought to his sister the New Zealand of their childhood, and out of those memories her best stories were to grow. For the remaining seven years of her life (she died just under thirty-five) her brother seems to have been almost constantly in her mind. A great change comes over her feelings about art; what it is, and why it is. When she prays to become "humble," it is probably the slightly showy quality in the early stories that she begs to be delivered from—and forgiven for. The *Journal* from 1918 on is a record of a readjustment to life, a changing sense of its deepest realities. One of the entries in 1919 recounts a dream in which her brother, "Chummie," came back to her:

> "I hear his hat and stick thrown on to the hall-table. He runs up the stairs, three at a time. 'Hullo, darling!' But I can't move—I can't move. He puts his arm round me, holding me tightly, and we kiss—a long, firm, family kiss. And the kiss means: We are of the same blood; we have absolute confidence in each other; we love; all is well; nothing can ever come between us."

In the same year she writes:

> "Now it is May 1919. Six o'clock. I am sitting in my own room thinking of Mother: I want to cry. But my thoughts are beautiful and full of gaiety. I think of *our* house, *our* garden, *us* children—the lawn, the gate, and Mother coming in. 'Children! Children!' I really only ask for time to write it all."

But she did not find too late the things she cared for most. She could not have written that group of New Zealand stories when she first came to London. There had to be a long period of writing for writing's sake. The spontaneous untutored outpouring of personal feeling does not go very far in art. It is only the practised hand that can make the natural gesture,—and the practised hand has often to grope its way.

She tells us that she made four false starts on "At the Bay," and when she finished the story it took her nearly a month to recover.

The *Journal*, painful though it is to read, is not the story of utter defeat. She had not, as she said, the physical strength to write what she now knew were, to her, the most important things in life. But she had found them, she possessed them, her mind fed on them. On them, and on the language of her greatest poet. (She read Shakespeare continually, when she was too ill to leave her bed.) The inexhaustible richness of that language seems to have been like a powerful cordial, warmed her when bodily nourishment failed her.

Among the stories she left unfinished there is one of singular beauty, written in the autumn of 1922, a few months before her death, the last piece of work she did. She called it "Six Years After": Linda and Burnell grown old, and the boy six years dead. It has the same powerful slightness which distinguishes the other New Zealand stories, and an even deeper tenderness.

Of the first of the New Zealand stories, "Prelude," Miss Mansfield wrote in answer to the inquiries of an intimate friend:

> "This is about as much as I can say about it. You know, if the truth were known, I have a perfect passion for the island where I was born. Well, in the early morning there I always remember feeling that this little island has dipped back into the dark blue sea during the night only to rise again at gleam of day, all hung with bright spangles and glittering drops. (When you ran over the dewy grass you positively felt that your feet tasted salt.) I tried to catch that moment—with something of its sparkle and its flavour. And just as on those mornings white milky mists rise and uncover some beauty, then smother it again and then again disclose it, I tried to lift that mist from my people and let them be seen and then to hide them again. . . . It's so difficult to describe all this and it sounds perhaps over-ambitious and vain."

An unpretentious but very suggestive statement of how an artist sets to work, and of the hazy sort of thing that almost surely lies behind and directs interesting or beautiful design.

And not with the slighter talents only. Tolstoi himself, one knows from the different Lives and letters, went to work in very much the same way. The long novels, as well as the short tales, grew out of little family dramas, personal intolerances and predilections,—promptings not apparent to the casual reader and incomprehensible to the commercial novel-maker.

SELECTED
REVIEWS AND ESSAYS
1895–1940

Contents

Mark Twain

IF THERE is anything which should make an American sick and disgusted at the literary taste of his country, and almost swerve his allegiance to his flag it is that controversy between Mark Twain and Max O'Rell, in which the Frenchman proves himself a wit and a gentleman and the American shows himself little short of a clown and an all around tough. The squabble arose apropos of Paul Bourget's new book on America, "Outre Mer," a book which deals more fairly and generously with this country than any book yet written in a foreign tongue. Mr. Clemens did not like the book, and like all men of his class, and limited mentality, he cannot criticise without becoming personal and insulting. He cannot be scathing without being a blackguard. He tried to demolish a serious and well considered work by publishing a scurrilous, slangy and loosely written article about it. In this article Mr. Clemens proves very little against Mr. Bourget and a very great deal against himself. He demonstrates clearly that he is neither a scholar, a reader or a man of letters and very little of a gentleman. His ignorance of French literature is something appalling. Why, in these days it is as necessary for a literary man to have a wide knowledge of the French masterpieces as it is for him to have read Shakespeare or the Bible. What man who pretends to be an author can afford to neglect those models of style and composition. George Meredith, Thomas Hardy and Henry James excepted, the great living novelists are Frenchmen.

Mr. Clemens asks what the French sensualists can possibly teach the great American people about novel writing or morality? Well, it would not seriously hurt the art of the classic author of "Puddin' Head Wilson" to study Daudet, De Maupassant, Hugo and George Sand, whatever it might do to his morals. Mark Twain is a humorist of a kind. His humor is always rather broad, so broad that the polite world can justly call it coarse. He is not a reader nor a thinker nor a man who loves art of any kind. He is a clever Yankee who has made a "good thing" out of writing. He has been published in the

North American Review and in the Century, but he is not and never will be a part of literature. The association and companionship of cultured men has given Mark Twain a sort of professional veneer, but it could not give him fine instincts or nice discriminations or elevated tastes. His works are pure and suitable for children, just as the work of most shallow and mediocre fellows. House dogs and donkeys make the most harmless and chaste companions for young innocence in the world. Mark Twain's humor is of the kind that teamsters use in bantering with each other, and his laugh is the gruff "haw-haw" of the backwoodsman. He is still the rough, awkward, good-natured boy who swore at the deck hands on the river steamer and chewed uncured tobacco when he was three years old. Thoroughly likeable as a good fellow, but impossible as a man of letters. It is an unfortunate feature of American literature that a hostler with some natural cleverness and a great deal of assertion receives the same recognition as a standard American author that a man like Lowell does. The French academy is a good thing after all. It at least divides the sheep from the goats and gives a sheep the consolation of knowing that he is a sheep.

It is rather a pity that Paul Bourget should have written "Outre Mer," thoroughly creditable book though it is. Mr. Bourget is a novelist, and he should not content himself with being an essayist, there are far too many of them in the world already. He can develop strong characters, invent strong situations, he can write the truth and he should not drift into penning opinions and platitudes. When God has made a man a creator, it is a great mistake for him to turn critic. It is rather an insult to God and certainly a very great wrong to man.

Nebraska State Journal, May 5, 1895

———————

I got a letter last week from a little boy just half-past seven who had just read "Huckleberry Finn" and "Tom Sawyer." He said: "If there are any more books like them in the world, send them to me quick." I had to humbly confess to him that if there were any others I had not the good fortune to know of them. What a red-letter-day it is to a boy, the day he first opens "Tom Sawyer." I would rather sail on the raft down the Missouri again with "Huck" Finn and Jim than go down the Nile in December or see Venice from a gondola in May. Certainly Mark Twain is much better when he writes of his Missouri boys than when he makes sickley romances about Joan of Arc. And certainly he never did a better piece of work than "Prince and Pauper." One seems to get at the very heart of old England in that dearest of children's books, and in its pages the frail boy king, and his gloomy sister Mary who in her day wrought so much woe for unhappy England, and the dashing Princess Elizabeth who lived to rule so well, seem to live again. A friend of Mr. Clemens' once told me that he said he wrote that book so that when his little daughters grew up they might know that their tired old jester of a father could be serious and gentle sometimes.

The Home Monthly, May 1897

William Dean Howells

C ERTAINLY NOW in his old age Mr. Howells is selecting queer titles for his books. A while ago we had that feeble tale, "The Coast of Bohemia," and now we have "My Literary Passions." "Passions," literary or otherwise, were never Mr. Howells' forte and surely no man could be further from even the coast of Bohemia.

Apropos of "My Literary Passions" which has so long strung out in the Ladies' Home Journal along with those thrilling articles about how Henry Ward Beecher tied his necktie and what kind of coffee Mrs. Hall Cain likes, why did Mr. Howells write it? Doesn't Mr. Howells know that at one time or another every one raves over Don Quixote, imitates Heine, worships Tourgueneff and calls Tolstoi a prophet? Does Mr. Howells think that no one but he ever had youth and enthusiasm and aspirations? Doesn't he know that the only thing that makes the world worth living in at all is that once, when we are young, we all have that great love for books and impersonal things, all reverence and dream? We have all known the time when Porthos, Athos and d'Artagan were vastly more real and important to us than the folks who lived next door. We have all dwelt in that country where Anna Karenina and the Levins were the only people who mattered much. We have all known that intoxicating period when we thought we "understood life," because we had read Daudet, Zola and Guy de Maupassant, and like Mr. Howells we all looked back rather fondly upon the time when we believed that books were the truth and art was all. After a while books grow matter of fact like everything else and we always think enviously of the days when they were new and wonderful and strange. That's a part of existence. We lose our first keen relish for literature just as we lose it for ice-cream and confectionery. The taste grows older, wiser and more subdued. We would all wear out of very enthusiasm if it did not. But why should Mr. Howells tell the world this common experience in detail as though it were his and his alone. He might as well write a detailed account of how he had the measles and the whooping cough. It was all right and proper for Mr. Howells to like Heine and Hugo, but, in the words of the circus clown, "We've all been there."

Nebraska State Journal, July 14, 1895

Edgar Allan Poe

My tantalized spirit
    Here blandly reposes,
Forgetting, or never
    Regretting its roses,
Its old agitations
    Of myrtles and roses.

For now, while so quietly
    Lying, it fancies
A holier odor
    About it, of pansies—
A rosemary odor
    Commingled with pansies.—
With rue and the beautiful
    Puritan pansies.
                    —Edgar Allan Poe.

THE SHAKESPEARE SOCIETY of New York, which is really about the only useful literary organization in this country, is making vigorous efforts to redress an old wrong and atone for a long neglect. Sunday, Sept. 22, it held a meeting at the Poe cottage on Kingsbridge road near Fordham, for the purpose of starting an organized movement to buy back the cottage, restore it to its original condition and preserve it as a memorial of Poe. So it has come at last. After helping build monuments to Shelley, Keats and Carlyle we have at last remembered this man, the greatest of our poets and the most unhappy. I am glad that this movement is in the hands of American actors, for it was among them that Poe found his best friends and warmest admirers. Some way he always seemed to belong to the strolling Thespians who were his mother's people.

Among all the thousands of life's little ironies that make history so diverting, there is none more paradoxical than that Edgar Poe should have been an American. Look at his face. Had we ever another like it? He must have been a strange figure in his youth, among those genial, courtly Virginians, this handsome, pale fellow, violent in his enthusiasm, ardent in his worship, but spiritually cold in his affections. Now playing heavily for the mere excitement of play, now worshipping at the shrine of a woman old enough to be his mother, merely because her voice was beautiful; now swimming six miles up the James river against a heavy current in the glaring sun of a June midday. He must have seemed to them an unreal figure, a sort of stage man who was wandering about the streets with his mask and buskins on, a theatrical figure who had escaped by some strange mischance into the prosaic daylight. His speech and actions were unconsciously and sincerely dramatic, always as though done for effect. He had that nervous, egotistic, self-centered nature common to stage children who seem to have been dazzled by the footlights and maddened by the applause before they are born. It was in his blood. With the exception of two women who loved him, lived for him, died for him, he went through life friendless, misunderstood, with that dense, complete, hopeless misunderstanding which, as Amiel said, is the secret of that sad smile upon the lips of the great. Men tried to befriend him, but in some way or other he hurt and disappointed them. He tried to mingle and share with other men, but he was always shut from them by that shadow, light as gossamer but unyielding as adamant, by which, from the beginning of the world, art has shielded and guarded and protected her own, that God concealing mist in which the heroes of old were hidden, immersed in that gloom and solitude which, if we could but know it here, is but the shadow of God's hand as it falls upon his elect.

We lament our dearth of great prose. With the exception of Henry James and Hawthorne, Poe is our only master of pure prose. We lament our dearth of poets. With the exception of Lowell, Poe is our only great poet. Poe found short story writing a bungling makeshift. He left it a perfect art. He wrote the first perfect short stories in the English language. He first gave the short story purpose, method, and artistic form. In a careless reading one can not realize the wonderful literary art, the cunning devices, the masterly effects that those entrancing tales conceal. They are simple and direct enough to delight us when we are children, subtle and artistic enough to be our marvel when we are old. To this day they are the wonder and admiration of the French, who are the acknowledged masters of craft and form. How in his wandering, laborious life, bound to the hack work of the press and crushed by an ever-growing burden of want and debt, did he ever come upon all this deep and mystical lore, this knowledge of all history, of all languages, of all art, this penetration into the hidden things of the East? As Steadman says, "The self training of genius is always a marvel." The past is spread before us all and most of us spend our lives in learning those things which we do not need to know, but genius reaches out instinctively and takes only the vital detail, by some sort of spiritual gravitation goes directly to the right thing.

Poe belonged to the modern French school of decorative and discriminating prose before it ever existed in France. He rivalled Gautier, Flaubert and de Maupassant before they were born. He clothed his tales in a barbaric splendor and persuasive unreality never before heard of in English. No such profusion of color, oriental splendor of detail, grotesque combinations and mystical effects had ever before been wrought into language. There are tales as grotesque, as monstrous, unearthly as the stone griffens and gargoyles that are cut up among the unvisited niches and towers of Notre Dame, stories as poetic and delicately beautiful as the golden lace work chased upon an Etruscan ring. He fitted his words together as the Byzantine jewelers fitted priceless stones. He found the inner harmony and kinship of words. Where lived another man who could blend the beautiful and the horrible, the gorgeous and the grotesque in such intricate and inexplicable fashion? Who could delight you with his noun and disgust you with his verb, thrill you with his adjective and chill you with his adverb, make you run the whole gamut of human emotions in a single sentence? Sitting in that miserable cottage at Fordham he wrote of the splendor of dream palaces beyond the dreams of art. He hung those grimy walls with dream tapestries, paved those narrow halls with black marble and polished onyx, and into those low-roofed chambers he brought all the treasured imagery of fancy, from the "huge carvings of untutored Egypt" to "mingled and conflicting perfumes, reeking up from strange convolute censers, together with multitudinous, flaring and flickering tongues of purple and violet fire." Hungry and ragged he wrote of Epicurean feasts and luxury that would have beggared the purpled pomp of pagan Rome and put Nero and his Golden House to shame.

And this mighty master of the organ of language, who knew its every stop and pipe, who could awaken at will the thin silver tones of its slenderest reeds or the solemn cadence of its deepest thunder, who could make it sing like a flute or roar like a cataract, he was born into a country without a literature. He was of that ornate school which usually comes last in a national literature, and he came first. American taste had been vitiated by men like Griswold and N. P. Willis until it was at the lowest possible ebb. Willis was considered a genius, that is the worst that could possibly be said. In the North a new race of great philosophers was growing up, but Poe had neither their friendship nor encouragement. He went indeed, sometimes, to the chilly *salon* of Margaret Fuller, but he was always a discord there. He was a mere artist and he had no business with philosophy, he had no theories as to the "higher life" and the "true happiness." He had only his unshapen dreams that battled with him in dark places, the unborn that struggled in his brain for birth. What time has an artist to learn the multiplication table or to talk philosophy? He was not afraid of them. He laughed at Willis, and flung Longfellow's lie in his teeth, the lie the rest of the world was twenty years in finding. He scorned the obtrusive learning of the transcendentalists and he disliked their hard talkative women. He left them and went back to his dream women, his *Berenice*, his *Ligeia*, his *Marchesa Aphrodite*, pale and cold as the mist maidens of the North, sad as the Norns who weep for human woe.

The tragedy of Poe's life was not alcohol, but hunger. He died when he was forty, when his work was just beginning. Thackeray had not touched his great novels at forty, George Eliot was almost unknown at that age. Hugo, Goethe, Hawthorne, Lowell and Dumas all did their great work after they were forty years old. Poe never did his great work. He could not endure the hunger. This year the Drexel Institute has put over sixty thousand dollars into a new edition of Poe's poems and stories. He himself never got six thousand for them alto-gether. If one of the great and learned institutions of the land had invested one tenth of that amount in the living author forty years ago we should have had from him such works as would have made the name of this nation great. But he sold "The Masque of the Red Death" for a few dollars, and now the Drexel Institute pays a publisher thousands to publish it beautifully. It is enough to make Satan laugh until his ribs ache, and all the little devils laugh and heap on fresh coals. I don't wonder they hate humanity. It's so dense, so hopelessly stupid.

Only a few weeks before Poe's death he said he had never had time or opportunity to make a serious effort. All his tales were merely experiments, thrown off when his day's work as a journalist was over, when he should have been asleep. All those voyages into the mystical unknown, into the gleaming, impalpable kingdom of pure romance from which he brought back such splendid trophies, were but experiments. He was only getting his tools into shape getting ready for his great effort, the effort that never came.

Bread seems a little thing to stand in the way of genius, but it can. The simple sordid facts were these, that in the bitterest storms of winter Poe seldom wrote by a fire, that after he was twenty-five years old he never knew what it was to have enough to eat without dreading tomorrow's hunger. Chatterton had only himself to sacrifice, but Poe saw the woman he loved die of want before his very eyes, die smiling and begging him not to give up his work. They saw the depths together in those long winter nights when she lay in that cold room, wrapped in Poe's only coat, he, with one hand holding hers, and with the other dashing off some of the most perfect masterpieces of English prose. And when he would wince and turn white at her coughing, she would always whisper: "Work on, my poet, and when you have finished read it to me. I am happy when I listen." O, the devotion of women and the madness of art! They are the two most awesome things on earth, and surely this man knew both to the full.

I have wondered so often how he did it. How he kept his purpose always clean and his taste always perfect. How it was that hard labor never wearied nor jaded him, never limited his imagination, that the jarring clamor about him never drowned the fine harmonies of his fancy. His discrimination remained always delicate, and from the constant strain of toil his fancy always rose strong and unfettered. Without encouragement or appreciation of any sort, without models or precedents he built up that pure style of his that is without peer in the language, that style of which every sentence is a drawing by Vedder. Elizabeth Barrett and a few great artists over in France knew what he was doing, they knew that in literature he was making possible a new heaven and a new earth. But he never knew that they knew it. He died without the assurance that he was or ever would be understood. And yet through all this, with the whole world of art and letters against him, betrayed by his own people, he managed to keep that lofty ideal of perfect work. What he suffered never touched or marred his work, but it wrecked his character. Poe's character was made by his necessity. He was a liar and an egotist; a man who had to beg for bread at the hands of his publishers and critics could be nothing but a liar, and had he not had the insane egotism and conviction of genius, he would have broken down and written the drivelling trash that his countrymen delighted to read. Poe lied to his publishers sometimes, there is no doubt of that, but there were two to whom he was never false, his wife and his muse. He drank sometimes too, when for very ugly and relentless reasons he could not eat. And then he forgot what he suffered. For Bacchus is the kindest of the gods after all. When Aphrodite has fooled us and left us and Athene has betrayed us in battle, then poor tipsy Bacchus, who covers his head with vine leaves where the curls are getting thin, holds out his cup to us and says, "forget." It's poor consolation, but he means it well.

The Transcendentalists were good conversationalists, that in fact was their principal accomplishment. They used to talk a great deal of genius, that rare and capricious spirit that visits earth so seldom, that is wooed by so many, and won by so few. They had grand theories that all men should be poets, that the visits of that rare spirit should be made as frequent and universal as afternoon calls. O, they had plans to make a whole generation of little geniuses. But she only laughed her scornful laughter, that deathless lady of the immortals, up in her echoing chambers that are floored with dawn and roofed with the spangled stars. And she snatched from them the only man of their nation she had ever deigned to love, whose lips she had touched with music and whose soul with song. In his youth she had shown him the secrets of her beauty and his manhood had been one pursuit of her, blind to all else, like Anchises, who on the night that he knew the love of Venus, was struck sightless, that he might never behold the face of a mortal woman. For Our Lady of Genius has no care for the prayers and groans of mortals, nor for their hecatombs sweet of savor. Many a time of old she has foiled the plans of seers and none may entreat her or take her by force. She favors no one nation or clime. She takes one from the millions, and when she gives herself unto a man it is without his will or that of his fellows, and he pays for it, dear heaven, he pays!

> "The sun comes forth and many reptiles spawn,
> He sets and each ephemeral insect then
> Is gathered unto death without a dawn,
> And the immortal stars awake again."

Yes, "and the immortal stars awake again." None may thwart the unerring justice of the gods, not even the Transcendentalists. What matter that one man's life was miserable, that one man was broken on the wheel? His work lives and his crown is eternal. That the work of his age was undone, that is the pity, that the work of his youth was done, that is the glory. The man is nothing. There are millions of men. The work is everything. There is so little perfection. We lament our dearth of poets when we let Poe starve. We are like the Hebrews who stoned their prophets and then marvelled that the voice of God was silent. We will wait a long time for another. There are Griswold and N. P. Willis, our chosen ones, let us turn to them. Their names are forgotten. God is just. They are,

> "Gathered unto death without a dawn.
> And the immortal stars awake again."

The Courier, October 12, 1895

———————————

You can afford to give a little more care and attention to this imaginative boy of yours than to any of your other children. His nerves are more finely strung and all his life he will need your love more than the others. Be careful to get him the books he likes and see that they are good ones. Get him a volume of Poe's short stories. I know many people are prejudiced against Poe because of the story that he drank himself to death. But that myth has been exploded long ago. Poe drank less than even the average man of his time. No, the most artistic of all American story tellers did not die because he drank too much, but because he ate too little. And yet we, his own countrymen who should be so proud of him, are not content with having starved him and wronged him while he lived, we must even go on slandering him after he has been dead almost fifty years. But get his works for this imaginative boy of yours and he will tell you how great a man the author of "The Gold Bug" and "The Masque of the Red Death" was. Children are impartial critics and sometimes very good ones. They do not reason about a book, they just like it or dislike it intensely, and after all that is the conclusion of the whole matter. I am very sure that "The Fall of the House of Usher," "The Pit and the Pendulum" and "The Black Cat" will give this woolgathering lad of yours more pleasure than a new bicycle could.

The Home Monthly, May 1897

Walt Whitman

SPEAKING OF MONUMENTS reminds one that there is more
talk about a monument to Walt Whitman, "the good,
gray poet." Just why the adjective good is always applied to
Whitman it is difficult to discover, probably because people
who could not understand him at all took it for granted that
he meant well. If ever there was a poet who had no literary
ethics at all beyond those of nature, it was he. He was neither
good nor bad, any more than are the animals he continually
admired and envied. He was a poet without an exclusive sense
of the poetic, a man without the finer discriminations, enjoy-
ing everything with the unreasoning enthusiasm of a boy. He
was the poet of the dung hill as well as of the mountains,
which is admirable in theory but excruciating in verse. In the
same paragraph he informs you that, "The pure contralto
sings in the organ loft," and that "The malformed limbs are
tied to the table, what is removed drop horribly into a pail."
No branch of surgery is poetic, and that hopelessly prosaic
word "pail" would kill a whole volume of sonnets. Whitman's
poems are reckless rhapsodies over creation in general, some
times sublime, some times ridiculous. He declares that the
ocean with its "imperious waves, commanding" is beautiful,
and that the fly-specks on the walls are also beautiful. Such
catholic taste may go in science, but in poetry their results are
sad. The poet's task is usually to select the poetic. Whitman
never bothers to do that, he takes everything in the universe
from fly-specks to the fixed stars. His "Leaves of Grass" is a
sort of dictionary of the English language, and in it is the
name of everything in creation set down with great reverence
but without any particular connection.

But however ridiculous Whitman may be there is a primi-
tive elemental force about him. He is so full of hardiness and
of the joy of life. He looks at all nature in the delighted, ad-
miring way in which the old Greeks and the primitive poets
did. He exults so in the red blood in his body and the
strength in his arms. He has such a passion for the warmth
and dignity of all that is natural. He has no code but to be

natural, a code that this complex world has so long outgrown. He is sensual, not after the manner of Swinbourne and Gautier, who are always seeking for perverted and bizarre effects on the senses, but in the frank fashion of the old barbarians who ate and slept and married and smacked their lips over the mead horn. He is rigidly limited to the physical, things that quicken his pulses, please his eyes or delight his nostrils. There is an element of poetry in all this, but it is by no means the highest. If a joyous elephant should break forth into song, his lay would probably be very much like Whitman's famous "song of myself." It would have just about as much delicacy and deftness and discriminations. He says:

"I think I could turn and live with the animals. They are so placid and self-contained, I stand and look at them long and long. They do not sweat and whine about their condition. They do not lie awake in the dark and weep for their sins. They do not make me sick discussing their duty to God. Not one is dissatisfied nor not one is demented with the mania of many things. Not one kneels to another nor to his kind that lived thousands of years ago. Not one is respectable or unhappy, over the whole earth." And that is not irony on nature, he means just that, life meant no more to him. He accepted the world just as it is and glorified it, the seemly and unseemly, the good and the bad. He had no conception of a difference in people or in things. All men had bodies and were alike to him, one about as good as another. To live was to fulfil all natural laws and impulses. To be comfortable was to be happy. To be happy was the ultimatum. He did not realize the existence of a conscience or a responsibility. He had no more thought of good or evil than the folks in Kipling's Jungle book.

And yet there is an undeniable charm about this optimistic vagabond who is made so happy by the warm sunshine and the smell of spring fields. A sort of good fellowship and whole-heartedness in every line he wrote. His veneration for things physical and material, for all that is in water or air or land, is so real that as you read him you think for the moment that you would rather like to live so if you could. For the time you half believe that a sound body and a strong arm are the greatest things in the world. Perhaps no book shows so much as "Leaves of Grass" that keen senses do not make a poet. When you read it you realize how spirited a thing poetry really is and how great a part spiritual perceptions play in apparently sensuous verse, if only to select the beautiful from the gross.

Nebraska State Journal, January 19, 1896

Henry James

THEIR MANIA for careless and hasty work is not confined
to the lesser men. Howells and Hardy have gone with
the crowd. Now that Stevenson is dead I can think of but one
English speaking author who is really keeping his self-respect
and sticking for perfection. Of course I refer to that mighty
master of language and keen student of human actions and
motives, Henry James. In the last four years he has published,
I believe, just two small volumes, "The Lesson of the Master"
and "Terminations," and in those two little volumes of short
stories he who will may find out something of what it means
to be really an artist. The framework is perfect and the polish
is absolutely without flaw. They are sometimes a little hard,
always calculating and dispassionate, but they are perfect. I
wish James would write about modern society, about "degen-
eracy" and the new woman and all the rest of it. Not that he
would throw any light on it. He seldom does; but he would
say such awfully clever things about it, and turn on so many
side-lights. And then his sentences! If his character novels
were all wrong one could read him forever for the mere
beauty of his sentences. He never lets his phrases run away
with him. They are never dull and never too brilliant. He
subjects them to the general tone of his sentence and has his
whole paragraph partake of the same predominating color.
You are never startled, never surprised, never thrilled or never
enraptured; always delighted by that masterly prose that is as
correct, as classical, as calm and as subtle as the music of
Mozart.

The Courier, November 16, 1895

It is strange that from "Felicia" down, the stage novel has
never been a success. Henry James' "Tragic Muse" is the only
theatrical novel that has a particle of the real spirit of the stage
in it, a glimpse of the enthusiasm, the devotion, the exaltation
and the sordid, the frivolous and the vulgar which are so

strangely and inextricably blended in that life of the green room. For although Henry James cannot write plays he can write passing well of the people who enact them. He has put into one book all those inevitable attendants of the drama, the patronizing theatre goer who loves it above all things and yet feels so far superior to it personally; the old tragedienne, the queen of a dying school whose word is law and whose judgments are to a young actor as the judgments of God; and of course there is the girl, the aspirant, the tragic muse who beats and beats upon those brazen doors that guard the unapproachable until one fine morning she beats them down and comes into her kingdom, the kingdom of unborn beauty that is to live through her. It is a great novel, that book of the master's, so perfect as a novel that one does not realize what a masterly study it is of the life and ends and aims of the people who make plays live.

Nebraska State Journal, March 29, 1896

Harold Frederic

"THE MARKET-PLACE." Harold Frederic. $1.50. New York: F. A. Stokes & Co. Pittsburg: J. R. Weldin & Co.

UNUSUAL INTEREST is attached to the posthumous work of that great man whose career ended so prematurely and so tragically. The story is a study in the ethics and purposes of money-getting, in the romantic element in modern business. In it finance is presented not as being merely the province of shrewdness, or greediness, or petty personal gratification, but of great projects, of great brain-battles, a field for the exercising of talent, daring, imagination, appealing to the strength of a strong man, filling the same place in men's lives that was once filled by the incentives of war, kindling in man the desire for the leadership of men. The hero of the story, "Joel Thorpe," is one of those men, huge of body, keen of brain, with cast iron nerves, as sound a heart as most men, and a magnificent capacity for bluff. He has lived and risked and lost in a dozen countries, been almost within reach of fortune a dozen times, and always missed her until, finally, in London, by promoting a great rubber syndicate he becomes a multi-millionaire. He marries the most beautiful and one of the most impecunious peeresses in England and retires to his country estate. There, as a gentleman of leisure, he loses his motive in life, loses power for lack of opportunity, and grows less commanding even in the eyes of his wife, who misses the uncompromising, barbaric strength which took her by storm and won her. Finally he evolves a gigantic philanthropic scheme of spending his money as laboriously as he made it.

Mr. Frederic says:

"Napoleon was the greatest man of his age—one of the greatest men of all ages—not only in war but in a hundred other ways. He spent the last six years of his life at St. Helena in excellent health, with companions that he talked freely to, and in all the extraordinarily copious reports of his conversations there, we don't get a single sentence worth repeating. The greatness had entirely evaporated from him the moment he was put on an island where he had nothing to do."

It is very fitting that Mr. Frederic's last book should be in praise of action, the thing that makes the world go round; of force, however misspent, which is the sum of life as distinguished from the inertia of death. In the forty-odd years of his life he wrote almost as many pages as Balzac, most of it mere newspaper copy, it is true, read and forgotten, but all of it vigorous and with the stamp of a strong man upon it. And he played just as hard as he worked—alas, it was the play that killed him! The young artist who illustrated the story gave to the pictures of "Joel Thorpe" very much the look of Harold Frederic himself, and they might almost stand for his portraits. I fancy the young man did not select his model carelessly. In this big, burly adventurer who took fortune and women by storm, who bluffed the world by his prowess and fought his way to the front with battle-ax blows, there is a great deal of Harold Frederic, the soldier of fortune, the Utica milk boy who fought his way from the petty slavery of a provincial newspaper to the foremost ranks of the journalists of the world and on into literature, into literature worth the writing. The man won his place in England much as his hero won his, by defiance, by strong shoulder blows, by his self-sufficiency and inexhaustible strength, and when he finished his book he did not know that his end would be so much less glorious than his hero's, that it would be his portion not to fall manfully in the thick of the combat and the press of battle, but to die poisoned in the tent of Chryseis. For who could foresee a tragedy so needless, so blind, so brutal in its lack of dignity, or know that such strength could perish through such insidious weakness, that so great a man could be stung to death by a mania born in little minds?

In point of execution and literary excellence, both "The Market Place" and "Gloria Mundi" are vastly inferior to "The Damnation of Theron Ware," or that exquisite London idyl, "March Hares." The first 200 pages of "Theron Ware" are as good as anything in American fiction, much better than most of it. They are not so much the work of a literary artist as of a vigorous thinker, a man of strong opinions and an intimate and comprehensive knowledge of men. The whole work, despite its irregularities and indifference to form, is full of brain stuff, the kind of active, healthful, masterful intellect that some men put into politics, some into science and a few, a very few, into literature. Both "Gloria Mundi" and "The Market Place" bear unmistakable evidences of the slack rein and the hasty hand. Both of them contain considerable padding, the stamp of the space writer. They are imperfectly developed, and are not packed with ideas like his earlier novels. Their excellence is in flashes; it is not the searching, evenly distributed light which permeates his more careful work. There were, as we know too well, good reasons why Mr. Frederic should work hastily. He needed a large income and he worked heroically, writing many thousands of words a day to obtain it. From the experience of the ages we have learned to expect to find, coupled with great strength, a proportionate weakness, and usually it devours the greater part, as the seven lean kine devoured the seven fat in Pharaoh's vision. Achilles was a god in all his nobler parts, but his feet were of the earth and to the earth they held him down, and he died stung by an arrow in the heel.

Pittsburg Leader, June 10, 1899

Kate Chopin

"THE AWAKENING." Kate Chopin. $1.25. Chicago: H. S. Stone & Co. Pittsburg: J. R. Weldin & Co.

A CREOLE "Bovary" is this little novel of Miss Chopin's. Not that the heroine is a creole exactly, or that Miss Chopin is a Flaubert—save the mark!—but the theme is similar to that which occupied Flaubert. There was, indeed, no need that a second "Madame Bovary" should be written, but an author's choice of themes is frequently as inexplicable as his choice of a wife. It is governed by some innate temperamental bias that cannot be diagrammed. This is particularly so in women who write, and I shall not attempt to say why Miss Chopin has devoted so exquisite and sensitive, well-governed a style to so trite and sordid a theme. She writes much better than it is ever given to most people to write, and hers is a genuinely literary style; of no great elegance or solidity; but light, flexible, subtle and capable of producing telling effects directly and simply. The story she has to tell in the present instance is new neither in matter nor treatment. "Edna Pontellier," a Kentucky girl, who, like "Emma Bovary," had been in love with innumerable dream heroes before she was out of short skirts, married "Leonce Pontellier" as a sort of reaction from a vague and visionary passion for a tragedian whose unresponsive picture she used to kiss. She acquired the habit of liking her husband in time, and even of liking her children. Though we are not justified in presuming that she ever threw articles from her dressing table at them, as the charming "Emma" had a winsome habit of doing, we are told that "she would sometimes gather them passionately to her heart, she would sometimes forget them." At a creole watering place, which is admirably and deftly sketched by Miss Chopin, "Edna" met "Robert Lebrun," son of the landlady, who dreamed of a fortune awaiting him in Mexico while he occupied a petty clerical position in New Orleans. "Robert" made it his business to be agreeable to his mother's boarders, and "Edna," not being a creole, much against his wish and will, took him seriously. "Robert" went to Mexico but found that fortunes were no easier to make there than in New Orleans. He returns and does not even call to pay his respects to her. She encounters him at the home of a friend and takes him home with her. She wheedles him into staying for dinner, and we are told she sent the maid off "in search of some delicacy she had not thought of for herself, and she recommended great care in the dripping of the coffee and having the omelet done to a turn."

Only a few pages back we were informed that the husband, "M. Pontellier," had cold soup and burnt fish for his dinner. Such is life. The lover of course disappointed her, was a coward and ran away from his responsibilities before they began. He was afraid to begin a chapter with so serious and limited a woman. She remembered the sea where she had first met "Robert." Perhaps from the same motive which threw "Anna Keraninna" under the engine wheels, she threw herself into the sea, swam until she was tired and then let go.

> "She looked into the distance, and for a moment the old terror flamed up, then sank again. She heard her father's voice, and her sister Margaret's. She heard the barking of an old dog that was chained to the sycamore tree. The spurs of the cavalry officer clanged as he walked across the porch. There was a hum of bees, and the musky odor of pinks filled the air."

"Edna Pontellier" and "Emma Bovary" are studies in the same feminine type; one a finished and complete portrayal, the other a hasty sketch, but the theme is essentially the same. Both women belong to a class, not large, but forever clamoring in our ears, that demands more romance out of life than God put into it. Mr. G. Barnard Shaw would say that they are the victims of the over-idealization of love. They are the spoil of the poets, the Iphigenias of sentiment. The unfortunate feature of their disease is that it attacks only women of brains, at least of rudimentary brains, but whose development is one-sided; women of strong and fine intuitions, but without the faculty of observation, comparison, reasoning about things. Probably, for emotional people, the most convenient thing about being able to think is that it occasionally gives them a rest from feeling. Now with women of the "Bovary" type, this relaxation and recreation is impossible. They are not critics of life, but, in the most personal sense, partakers of life. They receive impressions through the fancy. With them everything begins with fancy, and passions rise in the brain rather than in the blood, the poor, neglected, limited one-sided brain that might do so much better things than badgering itself into frantic endeavors to love. For these are the people who pay with their blood for the fine ideals of the poets, as Marie Delclasse paid for Dumas' great creation, "Marguerite Gauthier." These people really expect the passion of love to fill and gratify every need of life, whereas nature only intended that it should meet one of many demands. They insist upon making it stand for all the emotional pleasures of life and art, expecting an individual and self-limited passion to yield infinite variety, pleasure and distraction, to contribute to their lives what the arts and the pleasurable exercise of the intellect gives to less limited and less intense idealists. So this passion, when set up against Shakespeare, Balzac, Wagner, Raphael, fails them. They have staked everything on one hand, and they lose. They have driven the blood until it will drive no further, they have played their nerves up to the point where any relaxation short of absolute annihilation is impossible. Every idealist abuses his nerves, and every sentimentalist brutally abuses them. And in the end, the nerves get even. Nobody ever cheats them, really. Then "the awakening" comes. Sometimes it comes in the form of arsenic, as it came to "Emma Bovary," sometimes it is carbolic acid taken covertly in the police station, a goal to which unbalanced idealism not infrequently leads. "Edna Pontellier," fanciful and romantic to the last, chose the sea on a summer night and went down with the sound of her first lover's spurs in her ears, and the scent of pinks about her. And next time I hope that Miss Chopin will devote that flexible, iridescent style of hers to a better cause.

Pittsburg Leader, July 8, 1899

Stephen Crane

"WAR IS KIND." Stephen Crane. $2.50. New York: F. A. Stokes & Co. Pittsburg: J. R. Weldin & Co.

THIS TRULY REMARKABLE BOOK is printed on dirty gray blotting paper, on each page of which is a mere dot of print over a large I of vacancy. There are seldom more than ten lines on a page, and it would be better if most of those lines were not there at all. Either Mr. Crane is insulting the public or insulting himself, or he has developed a case of atavism and is chattering the primeval nonsense of the apes. His "Black Riders," uneven as it was, was a casket of polished masterpieces when compared with "War Is Kind." And it is not kind at all, Mr. Crane; when it provokes such verses as these, it is all that Sherman said it was.

The only production in the volume that is at all coherent is the following, from which the book gets its title:

Do not weep, maiden, for war is kind,
Because your lover threw wild hands toward the sky,
And the affrighted steed ran on alone.
　　　　Do not weep,
　　　　War is kind.

Hoarse booming drums of the regiment,
Little souls who thirst for fight,
　　　These men were born to drill and die.
The unexplained glory flies above them.
Great is the battle-god, great, and his kingdom—
　　　A field where a thousand corpses lie.

Do not weep, babe, for war is kind,
Because your father tumbled in the yellow trenches,
Raged at the breast, gulped and died.
　　　　Do not weep,
　　　　War is kind.

Swift-blazing flag of the regiment,
Eagle with crest of red and gold,

913

These men were born to drill and die.
Point for them the virtue of slaughter,
Make plain to them the excellence of killing,
        And a field where a thousand corpses lie.

Mother whose heart hung humble as a button
On the bright, splendid shroud of your son,
            Do not weep,
            War is kind.

Of course, one may have objections to hearts hanging like humble buttons, or to buttons being humble at all, but one should not stop to quarrel about such trifles with a poet who can perpetrate the following:

Thou art my love,
And thou art the beard
On another man's face—
Woe is me.

Thou art my love,
And thou art a temple,
And in this temple is an altar,
And on this temple is my heart—
Woe is me.

Thou art my love,
And thou art a wretch.
Let these sacred love-lies choke thee.
For I am come to where I know your lies as truth
And your truth as lies—
Woe is me.

Now, if you please, is the object of these verses animal, mineral or vegetable? Is the expression, "Thou art the beard on another man's face," intended as a figure, or was it written by a barber? Certainly, after reading this, "Simple Simon" is a ballade of perfect form, and "Jack and Jill" or "Hickity, Pickity, My Black Hen," are exquisite lyrics. But of the following what shall be said:

Now let me crunch you
With full weight of affrighted love.

I doubted you
—I doubted you—
And in this short doubting
My love grew like a genie
For my further undoing.

Beware of my friends,
Be not in speech too civil,
For in all courtesy
My weak heart sees specters,
Mists of desire
Arising from the lips of my chosen;
Be not civil.

This is somewhat more lucid as evincing the bard's exquisite sensitiveness:

Ah, God, the way your little finger moved
As you thrust a bare arm backward.
And made play with your hair
And a comb, a silly gilt comb
—Ah, God, that I should suffer
Because of the way a little finger moved.

Mr. Crane's verselets are illustrated by some Bradley pictures, which are badly drawn, in bad taste, and come with bad grace. On page 33 of the book there are just two lines which seem to completely sum up the efforts of both poet and artist:

"My good friend," said a learned bystander,
"Your operations are mad."

Yet this fellow Crane has written short stories equal to some of Maupassant's.

Pittsburg Leader, June 3, 1899

After reading such a delightful newspaper story as Mr. Frank Norris' "Blix," it is with assorted sensations of pain and discomfort that one closes the covers of another newspaper novel, "Active Service," by Stephen Crane. If one happens to

have some trifling regard for pure English, he does not come
forth from the reading of this novel unscathed. The hero of
this lurid tale is a newspaper man, and he edits the Sunday
edition of the New York "Eclipse," and delights in publishing
"stories" about deformed and sightless infants. "The office of
the 'Eclipse' was at the top of an immense building on Broad-
way. It was a sheer mountain to the heights of which the
interminable thunder of the streets rose faintly. The Hudson
was a broad path of silver in the distance." This leaves little
doubt as to the fortunate journal which had secured Rufus
Coleman as its Sunday editor. Mr. Coleman's days were spent
in collecting yellow sensations for his paper, and we are told
that he "planned for each edition as for a campaign." The
following elevating passage is one of the realistic paragraphs
by which Mr. Crane makes the routine of Coleman's life
known to us:

> Suddenly there was a flash of light and a cage of
> bronze, gilt and steel dropped magically from above.
> Coleman yelled "Down!" * * * A door flew open. Cole-
> man stepped upon the elevator. "Well, Johnnie," he said
> cheerfully to the lad who operated the machine, "is busi-
> ness good?" "Yes, sir, pretty good," answered the boy,
> grinning. The little cage sank swiftly. Floor after floor
> seemed to be rising with marvelous speed; the whole
> building was winging straight into the sky. There was
> soaring lights, figures and the opalescent glow of
> ground glass doors marked with black inscriptions.
> Other lights were springing heavenward. All the lofty
> corridors rang with cries. "Up!" "Down!" "Down!"
> "Up!!" The boy's hand grasped a lever and his machine
> obeyed his lightest movement with sometimes an unbal-
> ancing swiftness.

Later, when Coleman reached the street, Mr. Crane de-
scribes the cable cars as marching like panoplied elephants,
which is rather far, to say the least. The gentleman's nights
were spent something as follows:

> "In the restaurant he first ordered a large bottle of
> champagne. The last of the wine he finished in somber

mood like an unbroken and defiant man who chews the straw that litters his prison house. During his dinner he was continually sending out messenger boys. He was arranging a poker party. Through a window he watched the beautiful moving life of upper Broadway at night, with its crowds and clanging cable cars and its electric signs, mammoth and glittering like the jewels of a giantess.

"Word was brought to him that poker players were arriving. He arose joyfully, leaving his cheese. In the broad hall, occupied mainly by miscellaneous people and actors, all deep in leather chairs, he found some of his friends waiting. They trooped upstairs to Coleman's rooms, where, as a preliminary, Coleman began to hurl books and papers from the table to the floor. A boy came with drinks. Most of the men, in order to prepare for the game, removed their coats and cuffs and drew up the sleeves of their shirts. The electric globes shed a blinding light upon the table. The sound of clinking chips arose; the elected banker spun the cards, careless and dextrous."

The atmosphere of the entire novel is just that close and enervating. Every page is like the next morning taste of a champagne supper, and is heavy with the smell of stale cigarettes. There is no fresh air in the book and no sunlight, only the "blinding light shed by the electric globes." If the life of New York newspaper men is as unwholesome and sordid as this, Mr. Crane, who has experienced it, ought to be sadly ashamed to tell it. Next morning when Coleman went for breakfast in the grill room of his hotel he ordered eggs on toast and a pint of champagne for breakfast and discoursed affably to the waiter.

"May be you had a pretty lively time last night, Mr. Coleman?"

"Yes, Pat," answered Coleman. "I did. It was all because of an unrequitted affection, Patrick." The man stood near, a napkin over his arm. Coleman went on impressively. "The ways of the modern lover are strange. Now, I, Patrick, am a modern lover, and when, yesterday, the dagger of disappointment was driven deep into my heart, I immediately played poker as hard as I could, and incidentally got loaded. This is the modern point of view. I understand on good authority that in old times lovers used to languish. That is probably a lie, but at any rate we do not, in these times, languish to any great extent. We get drunk. Do you understand Patrick?"

The waiter was used to a harangue at Coleman's breakfast time. He placed his hand over his mouth and giggled. "Yessir."

"Of course," continued Coleman, thoughtfully. "It might be pointed out by uneducated persons that it is difficult to maintain a high standard of drunkenness for the adequate length of time, but in the series of experiments which I am about to make, I am sure I can easily prove them to be in the wrong."

"I am sure, sir," said the waiter, "the young ladies would not like to be hearing you talk this way."

"Yes; no doubt, no doubt. The young ladies have still quite medieval ideas. They don't understand. They still prefer lovers to languish."

"At any rate, sir, I don't see that your heart is sure enough broken. You seem to take it very easy."

"Broken!" cried Coleman. "Easy? Man, my heart is in fragments. Bring me another small bottle."

After this Coleman went to Greece to write up the war for the "Eclipse," and incidentally to rescue his sweetheart from the hands of the Turks and make "copy" of it. Very valid arguments might be advanced that the lady would have fared better with the Turks. On the voyage Coleman spent all his days and nights in the card room and avoided the deck, since fresh air was naturally disagreeable to him. For all that he saw of Greece or that Mr. Crane's readers see of Greece Coleman might as well have stayed in the card room of the steamer, or in the card room of his New York hotel for that matter. Wherever he goes he carries the atmosphere of the card room with him and the "blinding glare of the electrics." In Greece he makes love when he has leisure, but he makes "copy" much more ardently, and on the whole is quite as lurid and sordid and showy as his worst Sunday editions. Some good bits of battle descriptions there are, of the "Red Badge of Courage" order, but one cannot make a novel of clever descriptions of earthworks and poker games. The book concerns itself not with large, universal interests or principles, but with a yellow journalist grinding out yellow copy in such a wooden fashion that the Sunday "Eclipse" must have been even worse than most. In spite of the fact that Mr. Crane has written some of the most artistic short stories in the English language, I begin to wonder whether, blinded by his youth and audacity, two qualities which the American people love, we have not taken him too seriously. It is a grave matter for a man in good health and with a bank account to have written a book so coarse and dull and charmless as "Active Service." Compared with this "War was kind," indeed.

Pittsburg Leader, November 11, 1899

Frank Norris

A NEW and a great book has been written. The name of it is "McTeague, a Story of San Francisco," and the man who wrote it is Mr. Frank Norris. The great presses of the country go on year after year grinding out commonplace books, just as each generation goes on busily reproducing its own mediocrity. When in this enormous output of ink and paper, these thousands of volumes that are yearly rushed upon the shelves of the book stores, one appears which contains both power and promise, the reader may be pardoned some enthusiasm. Excellence always surprises: we are never quite prepared for it. In the case of "McTeague, a Story of San Francisco," it is even more surprising than usual. In the first place the title is not alluring, and not until you have read the book, can you know that there is an admirable consistency in the stiff, uncompromising commonplaceness of that title. In the second place the name of the author is as yet comparatively unfamiliar, and finally the book is dedicated to a member of the Harvard faculty, suggesting that whether it be a story of San Francisco or Dawson City, it must necessarily be vaporous, introspective and chiefly concerned with "literary" impressions. Mr. Norris is, indeed, a "Harvard man," but that he is a good many other kinds of a man is self-evident. His book is, in the language of Mr. Norman Hapgood, the work of "a large human being, with a firm stomach, who knows and loves the people."

In a novel of such high merit as this, the subject matter is the least important consideration. Every newspaper contains the essential material for another "Comedie Humaine." In this case "McTeague," the central figure, happens to be a dentist practicing in a little side street of San Francisco. The novel opens with this description of him:

> "It was Sunday, and, according to his custom on that day, McTeague took his dinner at two in the afternoon at the car conductor's coffee joint on Polk street. He had a thick, gray soup, heavy, underdone meat, very hot, on a cold plate; two kinds of vegetables; and a sort

of suet pudding, full of strong butter and sugar. Once in his office, or, as he called it on his sign-board, 'Dental Parlors,' he took off his coat and shoes, unbuttoned his vest, and, having crammed his little stove with coke, he lay back in his operating chair at the bay window, reading the paper, drinking steam beer, and smoking his huge porcelain pipe while his food digested; crop-full, stupid and warm."

McTeague had grown up in a mining camp in the mountains. He remembered the years he had spent there trundling heavy cars of ore in and out of the tunnel under the direction of his father. For thirteen days out of each fortnight his father was a steady, hard-working shift-boss of the mine. Every other Sunday he became an irresponsible animal, a beast, a brute, crazed with alcohol. His mother cooked for the miners. Her one ambition was that her son should enter a profession. He was apprenticed to a traveling quack dentist and after a fashion, learned the business.

"Then one day at San Francisco had come the news of his mother's death; she had left him some money—not much, but enough to set him up in business; so he had cut loose from the charlatan and had opened his 'Dental Parlors' on Polk street, an 'accommodation street' of small shops in the residence quarter of the town. Here he had slowly collected a clientele of butcher boys, shop girls, drug clerks and car conductors. He made but few acquaintances. Polk street called him the 'doctor' and spoke of his enormous strength. For McTeague was a young giant, carrying his huge shock of blonde hair six feet three inches from the ground; moving his immense limbs, heavy with ropes of muscle, slowly, ponderously. His hands were enormous, red, and covered with a fell of stiff yellow hair; they were as hard as wooden mallets, strong as vices, the hands of the old-time car boy. Often he dispensed with forceps and extracted a refractory tooth with his thumb and finger. His head was square-cut, angular; the jaw salient: like that of the carnivora.

"But for one thing McTeague would have been perfectly contented. Just outside his window was his sign-board—a modest affair—that read: 'Doctor McTeague. Dental Parlors. Gas Given;' but that was all. It was his ambition, his dream, to have projecting from that corner window a huge gilded tooth, a molar with enormous prongs, something gorgeous and attractive. He would have it some day, but as yet it was far beyond his means."

Then Mr. Norris launches into a description of the street in which "McTeague" lives. He presents that street as it is on Sunday, as it is on working days; as it is in the early dawn when the workmen are going out with pickaxes on their shoulders, as it is at ten o'clock when the women are out purchasing from the small shopkeepers, as it is at night when the shop girls are out with the soda-fountain tenders and the motor cars dash by full of theatre-goers, and the Salvationists sing before the saloon on the corner. In four pages he reproduces the life in a by-street of a great city, the little tragedy of the small shopkeeper. There are many ways of handling environment—most of them bad. When a young author has very little to say and no story worth telling, he resorts to environment. It is frequently used to disguise a weakness of structure, as ladies who paint landscapes put their cows knee-deep in water to conceal the defective drawing of the legs. But such description as one meets throughout Mr. Norris' book is in itself convincing proof of power, imagination and literary skill. It is a positive and active force, stimulating the reader's imagination, giving him an actual command, a realizing sense of this world into which he is suddenly transplanted. It gives to the book perspective, atmosphere, effects of time and distance, creates the illusion of life. This power of mature, and accurate and comprehensive description is very unusual among the younger American writers. Most of them observe the world through a temperament, and are more occupied with their medium than the objects they see. And temperament is a glass which distorts most astonishingly. But this young man sees with a clear eye, and reproduces with a touch firm and decisive, strong almost to brutalness. Yet this hand that can depict so powerfully the brute strength and brute passions of a "McTeague," can deal very finely and adroitly with the feminine element of his story. This is his portrait of the little Swiss girl, "Trina," whom the dentist marries:

> "Trina was very small and prettily made. Her face was round and rather pale; her eyes long and narrow and blue, like the half-opened eyes of a baby; her lips and the lobes of her tiny ears were pale, a little suggestive of anaemia. But it was to her hair that one's attention was most attracted. Heaps and heaps of blue-black coils and braids, a royal crown of swarthy bands, a veritable sable tiara, heavy, abundant and odorous. All the vitality that should have given color to her face seemed to have been absorbed by that marvelous hair: It was the coiffure of a queen that shadowed the temples of this little bourgeoise."

The tragedy of the story dates from a chance, a seeming stroke of good fortune, one of those terrible gifts of the Danai. A few weeks before her marriage "Trina" drew $5 000 from a lottery ticket. From that moment her passion for hoarding money becomes the dominant theme of the story, takes command of the book and its characters. After their marriage the dentist is disbarred from practice. They move into a garret where she starves her husband and herself to save that precious hoard. She sells even his office furniture, everything but his concertina and his canary bird, with which he stubbornly refuses to part and which are destined to become very important accessories in the property room of the theatre where this drama is played. This removal from their first home is to this story what Gervaise's removal from her shop is to L'Assommoir; it is the fatal episode of the third act, the sacrifice of self-respect, the beginning of the end. From that time the money stands between "Trina" and her husband. Outraged and humiliated, hating her for her meanness, demoralized by his idleness and despair, he begins to abuse her. The story becomes a careful and painful study of the disintegration of this union, a penetrating and searching analysis of the degeneration of these two souls, the woman's corroded by greed, the man's poisoned by disappointment and hate.

And all the while this same painful theme is placed in a lower key. Maria, the housemaid who took care of "Mc-Teague's" dental parlors in his better days, was a half-crazy girl from somewhere in Central America, she herself did not remember just where. But she had a wonderful story about her people owning a dinner service of pure gold with a punch bowl you could scarcely lift, which rang like a church bell when you struck it. On the strength of this story "Zercow," the Jew junk man, marries her, and believing that she knows where this treasure is hidden, bullies and tortures her to force her to disclose her secret. At last "Maria" is found with her throat cut, and "Zercow" is picked up by the wharf with a sack full of rusty tin cans, which in his dementia he must have thought the fabled dinner service of gold.

From this it is a short step to "McTeague's" crime. He kills his wife to get possession of her money, and escapes to the mountains. While he is on his way south, pushing toward Mexico, he is overtaken by his murdered wife's cousin and former suitor. Both men are half mad with thirst, and there in the desert wastes of Death's Valley, they spring to their last conflict. The cousin falls, but before he dies he slips a hand-cuff over "McTeague's" arm, and so the author leaves his hero in the wastes of Death's Valley, a hundred miles from water, with a dead man chained to his arm. As he stands there the canary bird, the survivor of his happier days, to which he had clung with stubborn affection, begins "chittering feebly in its little gilt prison." It reminds one a little of Stevenson's use of poor "Goddedaal's" canary in "The Wrecker." It is just such sharp, sure strokes that bring out the high lights in a story and separate excellence from the commonplace. They are at once dramatic and revelatory. Lacking them, a novel which may otherwise be a good one, lacks its chief reason for being. The fault with many worthy attempts at fiction lies not in what they are, but in what they are not.

Mr. Norris' model, if he will admit that he has followed one, is clearly no less a person than M. Zola himself. Yet there is no discoverable trace of imitation in his book. He has simply taken a method which has been most successfully applied in the study of French life and applied it in studying American life, as one uses certain algebraic formulae to solve certain problems. It is perhaps the only truthful literary method of dealing with that part of society which environment and heredity hedge about like the walls of a prison. It is true that Mr. Norris now and then allows his "method" to become too prominent, that his restraint savors of constraint, yet he has written a true story of the people, courageous, dramatic, full of matter and warm with life. He has addressed himself seriously to art, and he seems to have no ambition to be clever. His horizon is wide, his invention vigorous and bold, his touch heavy and warm and human. This man is not limited by literary prejudices: he sees the people as they are, he is close to them and not afraid of their unloveliness. He has looked at truth in the depths, among men begrimed by toil and besotted by ignorance, and still found her fair. "McTeague" is an achievement for a young man. It may not win at once the success which it deserves, but Mr. Norris is one of those who can afford to wait.

The Courier, April 8, 1899

If you want to read a story that is all wheat and no chaff, read "Blix." Last winter that brilliant young Californian, Mr. Norris, published a remarkable and gloomy novel, "McTeague," a book deep in insight, rich in promise and splendid in execution, but entirely without charm and as disagreeable as only a great piece of work can be. And now this gentleman, who is not yet thirty, turns around and gives us an idyll that sings through one's brain like a summer wind and makes one feel young enough to commit all manner of indiscretions. It may be that Mr. Norris is desirous of showing us his versatility and that he can follow any suit, or it may have been a process of reaction. I believe it was after M. Zola had completed one of his greatest and darkest novels of Parisian life that he went down to the seaside and wrote "La Reve," a book that every girl should read when she is eighteen, and then again when she is eighty. Powerful and solidly built as

"McTeague" is, one felt that there method was carried almost too far, that Mr. Norris was too consciously influenced by his French masters. But "Blix" belongs to no school whatever, and there is not a shadow of pedantry or pride of craft in it from cover to cover. "Blix" herself is the method, the motives and the aim of the book. The story is an exhalation of youth and spring; it is the work of a man who breaks loose and forgets himself. Mr. Norris was married only last summer, and the march from "Lohengrin" is simply sticking out all over "Blix." It is the story of a San Francisco newspaper man and a girl. The newspaper man "came out" in fiction, so to speak, in the drawing room of Mr. Richard Harding Davis, and has languished under that gentleman's chaperonage until he has come to be regarded as a fellow careful of nothing but his toilet and his dinner. Mr. Davis' reporters all bathed regularly and all ate nice things, but beyond that their tastes were rather colorless. I am glad to see one red-blooded newspaper man, in the person of "Landy Rivers," of San Francisco, break into fiction; a real live reporter with no sentimental loyalty for his "paper," and no Byronic poses about his vices, and no astonishing taste about his clothes, and no money whatever, which is the natural and normal condition of all reporters. "Blix" herself was just a society girl, and "Landy" took her to theatres and parties and tried to make himself believe he was in love with her. But it wouldn't work, for "Landy" couldn't love a society girl, not though she were as beautiful as the morning and terrible as an army with banners, and had "round full arms," and "the skin of her face was white and clean, except where it flushed into a most charming pink upon her smooth, cool cheeks." For while "Landy Rivers" was at college he had been seized with the penchant for writing short stories, and had worshiped at the shrines of Maupassant and Kipling, and when a man is craft mad enough to worship Maupassant truly and know him well, when he has that tingling for technique in his fingers, not Aphrodite herself, new risen from the waves, could tempt him into any world where craft was not lord and king. So it happened that their real love affair never began until one morning when "Landy" had to go down to the wharf to write up a whaleback, and "Blix" went along, and an old sailor told them a story and "Blix" recognized the literary possibilities of it, and they had lunch in a Chinese restaurant, and "Landy" because he was a newspaper man and it was the end of the week, didn't have any change about his clothes, and "Blix" had to pay the bill. And it was in that green old tea house that "Landy" read "Blix" one of his favorite yarns by Kipling, and she in a calm, off-handed way, recognized one of the fine, technical points in it, and "Landy" almost went to pieces for joy of her doing it. That scene in the Chinese restaurant is one of the prettiest bits of color you'll find to rest your eyes upon, and mighty good writing it is. I wonder, though if when Mr. Norris adroitly mentioned the "clack and snarl" of the banjo "Landy" played, he remembered the "silver snarling trumpets" of Keats? After that, things went on as such things will, and "Blix" quit the society racket and went to queer places with "Landy," and got interested in his work, and she broke him of wearing red neckties and playing poker, and she made him work, she did, for she grew to realize how much that meant to him, and she jacked him up when he didn't work, and she suggested an ending for one of his stories that was better than his own; just this big, splendid girl, who had never gone to college to learn how to write novels. And so how, in the name of goodness, could he help loving her? So one morning down by the Pacific, with "Blix" and "The Seven Seas," it all came over "Landy," that "living was better than reading and life was better than literature." And so it is; once, and only once, for each of us; and that is the tune that sings and sings through one's head when one puts the book away.

The Courier, January 13, 1900

AN HEIR APPARENT.

Last winter a young Californian, Mr. Frank Norris, published a novel with the unpretentious title, "McTeague: a Story of San Francisco." It was a book that could not be ignored nor dismissed with a word. There was something very unusual about it, about its solidity and mass, the thorough-

ness and firmness of texture, and it came down like a blow
from a sledge hammer among the slighter and more sprightly
performances of the hour.

The most remarkable thing about the book was its maturity
and compactness. It has none of the ear-marks of those enter-
taining "young writers" whom every season produces as inev-
itably as its debutantes, young men who surprise for an hour
and then settle down to producing industriously for the class
with which their peculiar trick of phrase has found favor. It
was a book addressed to the American people and to the crit-
ics of the world, the work of a young man who had set him-
self to the art of authorship with an almighty seriousness, and
who had no ambition to be clever. "McTeague" was not an
experiment in style nor a pretty piece of romantic folly, it was
a true story of the people—having about it, as M. Zola
would say, "the smell of the people"—courageous, dramatic,
full of matter and warm with life. It was realism of the most
uncompromising kind. The theme was such that the author
could not have expected sudden popularity for his book, such
as sometimes overtakes monstrosities of style in these discour-
aging days when Knighthood is in Flower to the extent of a
quarter of a million copies, nor could he have hoped for
pressing commissions from the fire-side periodicals. The life
story of a quack dentist who sometimes extracted molars with
his fingers, who mistreated and finally murdered his wife, is
not, in itself, attractive. But, after all, the theme counts for
very little. Every newspaper contains the essential subject mat-
ter for another *Comedie Humaine*. The important point is that
a man considerably under thirty could take up a subject so
grim and unattractive, and that, for the mere love of doing
things well, he was able to hold himself down to the task of
developing it completely, that he was able to justify this
quack's existence in literature, to thrust this hairy, blonde
dentist with the "salient jaw of the carnivora," in amongst the
immortals.

It was after M. Zola had completed one of the greatest and
gloomiest of his novels of Parisian life, that he went down by
the sea and wrote "La Reve," that tender, adolescent story of
love and purity and youth. So, almost simultaneously with
"McTeague," Mr. Norris published "Blix," another San Fran-

cisco story, as short as "McTeague" was lengthy, as light as "McTeague" was heavy, as poetic and graceful as "McTeague" was somber and charmless. Here is a man worth waiting on; a man who is both realist and poet, a man who can teach

> "Not only by a comet's rush,
> But by a rose's birth."

Yet unlike as they are, in both books the source of power is the same, and, for that matter, it was even the same in his first book, "Moran of the Lady Letty." Mr. Norris has dispensed with the conventional symbols that have crept into art, with the trite, half-truths and circumlocutions, and got back to the physical basis of things. He has abjured tea-table psychology, and the analysis of figures in the carpet and subtle dissections of intellectual impotencies, and the diverting game of words and the whole literature of the nerves. He is big and warm and sometimes brutal, and the strength of the soil comes up to him with very little loss in the transmission. His art strikes deep down into the roots of life and the foundation of Things as They Are—not as we tell each other they are at the tea-table. But he is realistic art, not artistic realism. He is courageous, but he is without bravado.

He sees things freshly, as though they had not been seen before, and describes them with singular directness and vividness, not with morbid acuteness, with a large, wholesome joy of life. Nowhere is this more evident than in his insistent use of environment. I recall the passage in which he describes the street in which McTeague lives. He represents that street as it is on Sunday, as it is on working days, as it is in the early dawn when the workmen are going out with pickaxes on their shoulders, as it is at ten o'clock when the women are out marketing among the small shopkeepers, as it is at night when the shop girls are out with the soda fountain tenders and the motor cars dash by full of theater-goers, and the Salvationists sing before the saloon on the corner. In four pages he reproduces in detail the life in a by-street of a great city, the little tragedy of the small shopkeeper. There are many ways of handling environment—most of them bad. When a young author has very little to say and no story worth telling, he resorts to environment. It is frequently used to disguise a weakness of structure, as ladies who paint landscapes put their cows knee-deep in water to conceal the defective drawing of the legs. But such description as one meets throughout Mr. Norris' book is in itself convincing proof of power, imagination and literary skill. It is a positive and active force, stimulating the reader's imagination, giving him an actual command, a realizing sense of this world into which he is suddenly transported. It gives to the book perspective, atmosphere, effects of time and distance, creates the illusion of life. This power of mature and comprehensive description is very unusual among the younger American writers. Most of them observe the world through a temperament, and are more occupied with their medium than the objects they watch. And temperament is a glass which distorts most astonishingly. But this young man sees with a clear eye, and reproduces with a touch, firm and decisive, strong almost to brutalness.

Mr. Norris approaches things on their physical side; his characters are personalities of flesh before they are anything else, types before they are individuals. Especially is this true of his women. His Trina is "very small and prettily made. Her face was round and rather pale; her eyes long and narrow and blue, like the half-opened eyes of a baby; her lips and the lobes of her tiny ears were pale, a little suggestive of anaemia. But it was to her hair that one's attention was most attracted. Heaps and heaps of blue-black coils and braids, a royal crown of swarthy bands, a veritable sable tiara, heavy, abundant and odorous. All the vitality that should have given color to her face seems to have been absorbed by that marvelous hair. It was the coiffure of a queen that shadowed the temples of this little bourgeoise." Blix had "round, full arms," and "the skin of her face was white and clean, except where it flushed into a most charming pink upon her smooth, cool cheeks." In this grasp of the element of things, this keen, clean, frank pleasure at color and odor and warmth, this candid admission of the negative of beauty, which is co-existent with and inseparable from it, lie much of his power and promise. Here is a man catholic enough to include the extremes of physical and moral life, strong enough to handle the crudest colors and darkest shadows. Here is a man who has an appetite for the physical universe, who loves the rank smells of crowded alley-ways, or the odors of boudoirs, or the delicate perfume exhaled from a woman's skin; who is not afraid of Pan, be he ever so shaggy, and redolent of the herd.

Structurally, where most young novelists are weak, Mr. Norris is very strong. He has studied the best French masters, and he has adopted their methods quite simply, as one selects an algebraic formula to solve his particular problem. As to his style, that is, as expression always is, just as vigorous as his thought compels it to be, just as vivid as his conception warrants. If God Almighty has given a man ideas, he will get himself a style from one source or another. Mr. Norris, fortunately, is not a conscious stylist. He has too much to say to be exquisitely vain about his medium. He has the kind of brain stuff that would vanquish difficulties in any profession, that might be put to building battleships, or solving problems of finance, or to devising colonial policies. Let us be thankful that he has put it to literature. Let us be thankful, moreover, that he is not introspective and that his intellect does not devour itself, but feeds upon the great race of man, and, above all, let us rejoice that he is not a "temperamental" artist, but something larger, for a great brain and an assertive temperament seldom dwell together.

There are clever men enough in the field of American letters, and the fault of most of them is merely one of magnitude; they are not large enough; they travel in small orbits, they play on muted strings. They sing neither of the combats of Atriedes nor the labors of Cadmus, but of the tea-table and the Odyssey of the Rialto. Flaubert said that a drop of water contained all the elements of the sea, save one—immensity. Mr. Norris is concerned only with serious things, he has only large ambitions. His brush is bold, his color is taken fresh from the kindly earth, his canvas is large enough to hold American life, the real life of the people. He has come into the court of the troubadours singing the song of Elys, the song of warm, full nature. He has struck the true note of the common life. He is what Mr. Norman Hapgood said the great American dramatist must be: "A large human being, with a firm stomach, who knows and loves the people."

The Courier, April 7, 1900

When I Knew Stephen Crane

IT WAS, I think, in the spring of '94 that a slender, narrow-chested fellow in a shabby grey suit, with a soft felt hat pulled low over his eyes, sauntered into the office of the managing editor of the Nebraska State Journal and introduced himself as Stephen Crane. He stated that he was going to Mexico to do some work for the Bacheller Syndicate and get rid of his cough, and that he would be stopping in Lincoln for a few days. Later he explained that he was out of money and would be compelled to wait until he got a check from the East before he went further. I was a Junior at the Nebraska State University at the time, and was doing some work for the State Journal in my leisure time, and I happened to be in the managing editor's room when Mr. Crane introduced himself. I was just off the range; I knew a little Greek and something about cattle and a good horse when I saw one, and beyond horses and cattle I considered nothing of vital importance except good stories and the people who wrote them. This was the first man of letters I had ever met in the flesh, and when the young man announced who he was, I dropped into a chair behind the editor's desk where I could stare at him without being too much in evidence.

Only a very youthful enthusiasm and a large propensity for hero worship could have found anything impressive in the young man who stood before the managing editor's desk. He was thin to emaciation, his face was gaunt and unshaven, a thin dark moustache straggled on his upper lip, his black hair grew low on his forehead and was shaggy and unkempt. His grey clothes were much the worse for wear and fitted him so badly it seemed unlikely he had ever been measured for them. He wore a flannel shirt and a slovenly apology for a necktie, and his shoes were dusty and worn gray about the toes and were badly run over at the heel. I had seen many a tramp printer come up the Journal stairs to hunt a job, but never one who presented such a disreputable appearance as this story-maker man. He wore gloves, which seemed rather a contradiction to the general slovenliness of his attire, but when he took them off to search his pockets for his credentials, I noticed that his hands were singularly fine; long, white, and delicately shaped, with thin, nervous fingers. I have seen pictures of Aubrey Beardsley's hands that recalled Crane's very vividly.

At that time Crane was but twenty-four, and almost an unknown man. Hamlin Garland had seen some of his work and believed in him, and had introduced him to Mr. Howells, who recommended him to the Bacheller Syndicate. "The Red Badge of Courage" had been published in the State Journal that winter along with a lot of other syndicate matter, and the grammatical construction of the story was so faulty that the managing editor had several times called on me to edit the copy. In this way I had read it very carefully, and through the careless sentence-structure I saw the wonder of that remarkable performance. But the grammar certainly was bad. I remember one of the reporters who had corrected the phrase "it don't" for the tenth time remarked savagely, "If I couldn't write better English than this, I'd quit."

Crane spent several days in the town, living from hand to mouth and waiting for his money. I think he borrowed a small amount from the managing editor. He lounged about the office most of the time, and I frequently encountered him going in and out of the cheap restaurants on Tenth Street. When he was at the office he talked a good deal in a wandering, absent-minded fashion, and his conversation was uniformly frivolous. If he could not evade a serious question by a joke, he bolted. I cut my classes to lie in wait for him, confident that in some unwary moment I could trap him into serious conversation, that if one burned incense long enough and ardently enough, the oracle would not be dumb. I was Maupassant mad at the time, a malady particularly unattractive in a Junior, and I made a frantic effort to get an expression of opinion from him on "Le Bonheur." "Oh, you're Moping, are you?" he remarked with a sarcastic grin, and went on reading a little volume of Poe that he carried in his pocket. At another time I cornered him in the Funny Man's room and succeeded in getting a little out of him. We were taught literature by an exceedingly analytical method at the University, and we probably distorted the method, and I was busy trying to find the least common multiple of *Hamlet* and the greatest common divisor of *Macbeth*, and I began asking him whether stories were constructed by cabalistic formulae. At length he sighed wearily and shook his drooping shoulders, remarking:

"Where did you get all that rot? Yarns aren't done by mathematics. You can't do it by rule any more than you can dance by rule. You have to have the itch of the thing in your fingers, and if you haven't,—well, you're damned lucky, and you'll live long and prosper, that's all."—And with that he yawned and went down the hall.

Crane was moody most of the time, his health was bad and he seemed profoundly discouraged. Even his jokes were exceedingly drastic. He went about with the tense, preoccupied, self-centered air of a man who is brooding over some impending disaster, and I conjectured vainly as to what it might be. Though he was seemingly entirely idle during the few days I knew him, his manner indicated that he was in the throes of work that told terribly on his nerves. His eyes I remember as the finest I have ever seen, large and dark and full of lustre and changing lights, but with a profound melancholy always lurking deep in them. They were eyes that seemed to be burning themselves out.

As he sat at the desk with his shoulders drooping forward, his head low, and his long, white fingers drumming on the sheets of copy paper, he was as nervous as a race horse fretting to be on the track. Always, as he came and went about the halls, he seemed like a man preparing for a sudden departure. Now that he is dead it occurs to me that all his life was a preparation for sudden departure. I remember once when he was writing a letter he stopped and asked me about the spelling of a word, saying carelessly, "I haven't time to learn to spell."

Then, glancing down at his attire, he added with an absent-minded smile, "I haven't time to dress either; it takes an awful slice out of a fellow's life."

He said he was poor, and he certainly looked it, but four years later when he was in Cuba, drawing the largest salary ever paid a newspaper correspondent, he clung to this same untidy manner of dress, and his ragged overalls and buttonless shirt were eyesores to the immaculate Mr. Davis, in his spotless linen and neat khaki uniform, with his Gibson chin always freshly shaven. When I first heard of his serious illness, his old throat trouble aggravated into consumption by his reckless exposure in Cuba, I recalled a passage from Maeterlinck's essay, "The Pre-Destined," on those doomed to early death: "As children, life seems nearer to them than to other children. They appear to know nothing, and yet there is in their eyes so profound a certainty that we feel they must know all.—In all haste, but wisely and with minute care do they prepare themselves to live, and this very haste is a sign upon which mothers can scarce bring themselves to look." I remembered, too, the young man's melancholy and his tenseness, his burning eyes, and his way of slurring over the less important things, as one whose time is short.

I have heard other people say how difficult it was to induce Crane to talk seriously about his work, and I suspect that he was particularly averse to discussions with literary men of wider education and better equipment than himself, yet he seemed to feel that this fuller culture was not for him. Perhaps the unreasoning instinct which lies deep in the roots of our lives, and which guides us all, told him that he had not time enough to acquire it.

Men will sometimes reveal themselves to children, or to people whom they think never to see again, more completely than they ever do to their confreres. From the wise we hold back alike our folly and our wisdom, and for the recipients of our deeper confidences we seldom select our equals. The soul has no message for the friends with whom we dine every week. It is silenced by custom and convention, and we play only in the shallows. It selects its listeners willfully, and seemingly delights to waste its best upon the chance wayfarer who meets us in the highway at a fated hour. There are moments too, when the tides run high or very low, when self-revelation is necessary to every man, if it be only to his valet or his gardener. At such a moment, I was with Mr. Crane.

The hoped for revelation came unexpectedly enough. It was on the last night he spent in Lincoln. I had come back from the theatre and was in the Journal office writing a notice of the play. It was eleven o'clock when Crane came in. He had expected his money to arrive on the night mail and it had not done so, and he was out of sorts and deeply despondent. He sat down on the ledge of the open window that faced on the street, and when I had finished my notice I went over and took a chair beside him. Quite without invitation on my part, Crane began to talk, began to curse his trade from the first throb of creative desire in a boy to the finished work of the master. The night was oppressively warm; one of those dry winds that are the curse of that country was blowing up from Kansas. The white, western moonlight threw sharp, blue shadows below us. The streets were silent at that hour, and we could hear the gurgle of the fountain in the Post Office square across the street, and the twang of banjos from the lower verandah of the Hotel Lincoln, where the colored waiters were serenading the guests. The drop lights in the office were dull under their green shades, and the telegraph sounder clicked faintly in the next room. In all his long tirade, Crane never raised his voice; he spoke slowly and monotonously and even calmly, but I have never known so bitter a heart in any man as he revealed to me that night. It was an arraignment of the wages of life, an invocation to the ministers of hate.

Incidentally he told me the sum he had received for "The Red Badge of Courage," which I think was something like ninety dollars, and he repeated some lines from "The Black Riders," which was then in preparation. He gave me to understand that he led a double literary life; writing in the first place the matter that pleased himself, and doing it very slowly; in the second place, any sort of stuff that would sell. And he remarked that his poor was just as bad as it could possibly be. He realized, he said, that his limitations were absolutely impassable. "What I can't do, I can't do at all, and I can't acquire it. I only hold one trump."

He had no settled plans at all. He was going to Mexico wholly uncertain of being able to do any successful work there, and he seemed to feel very insecure about the financial end of his venture. The thing that most interested me was what he said about his slow method of composition. He declared that there was little money in story-writing at best, and practically none in it for him, because of the time it took him to work up his detail. Other men, he said, could sit down and write up an experience while the physical effect of it, so to speak, was still upon them, and yesterday's impressions made to-day's "copy." But when he came in from the streets to write up what he had seen there, his faculties were benumbed, and he sat twirling his pencil and hunting for words like a schoolboy.

I mentioned "The Red Badge of Courage," which was written in nine days, and he replied that, though the writing took very little time, he had been unconsciously working the detail of the story out through most of his boyhood. His ancestors had been soldiers, and he had been imagining war stories ever since he was out of knickerbockers, and in writing his first war story he had simply gone over his imaginary campaigns and selected his favorite imaginary experiences. He declared that his imagination was hide bound; it was there, but it pulled hard. After he got a notion for a story, months passed before he could get any sort of personal contract with it, or feel any potency to handle it. "The detail of a thing has to filter through my blood, and then it comes out like a native product, but it takes forever," he remarked. I distinctly remember the illustration, for it rather took hold of me.

I have often been astonished since to hear Crane spoken of as "the reporter in fiction," for the reportorial faculty of superficial reception and quick transference was what he conspicuously lacked. His first newspaper account of his shipwreck on the filibuster "Commodore" off the Florida coast was as lifeless as the "copy" of a police court reporter. It was many months afterwards that the literary product of his terrible experience appeared in that marvellous sea story "The Open Boat," unsurpassed in its vividness and constructive perfection.

At the close of our long conversation that night, when the copy boy came in to take me home, I suggested to Crane that in ten years he would probably laugh at all his temporary discomfort. Again his body took on that strenuous tension and he clenched his hands, saying, "I can't wait ten years, I haven't time."

The ten years are not up yet, and he has done his work and gathered his reward and gone. Was ever so much experience and achievement crowded into so short a space of time? A great man dead at twenty-nine! That would have puzzled the ancients. Edward Garnett wrote of him in The Academy of

December 17, 1899: "I cannot remember a parallel in the literary history of fiction. Maupassant, Meredith, Henry James, Mr. Howells and Tolstoy, were all learning their expression at an age where Crane had achieved his and achieved it triumphantly." He had the precocity of those doomed to die in youth. I am convinced that when I met him he had a vague premonition of the shortness of his working day, and in the heart of the man there was that which said, "That thou doest, do quickly."

At twenty-one this son of an obscure New Jersey rector, with but a scant reading knowledge of French and no training, had rivaled in technique the foremost craftsmen of the Latin races. In the six years since I met him, a stranded reporter, he stood in the firing line during two wars, knew hairbreadth 'scapes on land and sea, and established himself as the first writer of his time in the picturing of episodic, fragmentary life. His friends have charged him with fickleness, but he was a man who was in the preoccupation of haste. He went from country to country, from man to man, absorbing all that was in them for him. He had no time to look backward. He had no leisure for *camaraderie*. He drank life to the lees, but at the banquet table where other men took their ease and jested over their wine, he stood a dark and silent figure, sombre as Poe himself, not wishing to be understood; and he took his portion in haste, with his loins girded, and his shoes on his feet, and his staff in his hand, like one who must depart quickly.

The Library, June 23, 1900

On the Art of Fiction

ONE IS SOMETIMES asked about the "obstacles" that confront young writers who are trying to do good work. I should say the greatest obstacles that writers today have to get over, are the dazzling journalistic successes of twenty years ago, stories that surprised and delighted by their sharp photographic detail and that were really nothing more than lively pieces of reporting. The whole aim of that school of writing was novelty—never a very important thing in art. They gave us, altogether, poor standards—taught us to multiply our ideas instead of to condense them. They tried to make a story out of every theme that occurred to them and to get returns on every situation that suggested itself. They got returns, of a kind. But their work, when one looks back on it, now that the novelty upon which they counted so much is gone, is journalistic and thin. The especial merit of a good reportorial story is that it shall be intensely interesting and pertinent today and shall have lost its point by tomorrow.

Art, it seems to me, should simplify. That, indeed, is very nearly the whole of the higher artistic process; finding what conventions of form and what detail one can do without and yet preserve the spirit of the whole—so that all that one has suppressed and cut away is there to the reader's consciousness as much as if it were in type on the page. Millet had done hundreds of sketches of peasants sowing grain, some of them very complicated and interesting, but when he came to paint the spirit of them all into one picture, "The Sower," the composition is so simple that it seems inevitable. All the discarded sketches that went before made the picture what it finally became, and the process was all the time one of simplifying, of sacrificing many conceptions good in themselves for one that was better and more universal.

Any first rate novel or story must have in it the strength of a dozen fairly good stories that have been sacrificed to it. A good workman can't be a cheap workman; he can't be stingy about wasting material, and he cannot compromise. Writing ought either to be the manufacture of stories for which there is a market demand—a business as safe and commendable as making soap or breakfast foods—or it should be an art, which is always a search for something for which there is no market demand, something new and untried, where the values are intrinsic and have nothing to do with standardized values. The courage to go on without compromise does not come to a writer all at once—nor, for that matter, does the ability. Both are phases of natural development. In the beginning, the artist, like his public, is wedded to old forms, old ideals, and his vision is blurred by the memory of old delights he would like to recapture.

The Borzoi, 1920

Preface to
"Alexander's Bridge"

IT IS DIFFICULT to comply with the publisher's request that I write a preface for this new edition of an early book. "Alexander's Bridge" was my first novel, and does not deal with the kind of subject-matter in which I now find myself most at home. The people and the places of the story interested me intensely at the time when it was written, because they were new to me and were in themselves attractive. "Alexander's Bridge" was written in 1911, and "O Pioneers!" the following year. The difference in quality in the two books is an illustration of the fact that it is not always easy for the inexperienced writer to distinguish between his own material and that which he would like to make his own. Everything is new to the young writer, and everything seems equally personal. That which is outside his deepest experience, which he observes and studies, often seems more vital than that which he knows well, because he regards it with all the excitement of discovery. The things he knows best he takes for granted, since he is not continually thrilled by new discoveries about them. They lie at the bottom of his consciousness, whether he is aware of it or no, and they continue to feed him, but they do not stimulate him.

There is a time in a writer's development when his "life line" and the line of his personal endeavor meet. This may come early or late, but after it occurs his work is never quite the same. After he has once or twice done a story that formed itself, inevitably, in his mind, he will not often turn back to the building of external stories again. The inner feeling produces for him a deeper excitement than the thrill of novelty or the glitter of the passing show.

The writer, at the beginning of his career, is often more interested in his discoveries about his art than in the homely truths which have been about him from his cradle. He is likely to feel that writing is one of the most important things, if not the most important thing, in the world, and that what he learns about it is his one really precious possession. He understands, of course, that he must know a great deal about life, but he thinks this knowledge is something he can get by going out to look for it, as one goes to a theatre. Perhaps it is just as well for him to believe this until he has acquired a little facility and strength of hand; to work through his youthful vanities and gaudy extravagances before he comes to deal with the material that is truly his own. One of the few really helpful words I ever heard from an older writer, I had from Sarah Orne Jewett when she said to me: "Of course, one day you will write about your own country. In the meantime, get all you can. One must know the world *so well* before one can know the parish."

There have been notable and beautiful exceptions, but I think usually the young writer must have his affair with the external material he covets; must imitate and strive to follow the masters he most admires, until he finds he is starving for reality and cannot make this go any longer. Then he learns that it is not the adventure he sought, but the adventure that sought him, which has made the enduring mark upon him.

When a writer once begins to work with his own material, he realizes that, no matter what his literary excursions may have been, he has been working with it from the beginning—by living it. With this material he is another writer. He has less and less power of choice about the moulding of it. It seems to be there of itself, already moulded. If he tries to meddle with its vague outline, to twist it into some categorical shape, above all if he tries to adapt or modify its mood, he destroys its value. In working with this material he finds that he need have little to do with literary devices; he comes to depend more and more on something else—the thing by which our feet find the road home on a dark night, accounting of themselves for roots and stones which we had never noticed by day. This guide is not always with him, of course. He loses it and wanders. But when it is with him it corresponds to what Mr. Bergson calls the wisdom of intuition as opposed to that of intellect. With this to shape his course, a writer contrives and connives only as regards mechanical details, and questions of effective presentation, always debatable. About the essential matter of his story he cannot argue this way or that; he has seen it, has been enlightened about it in flashes that are as unreasoning, often as unreasonable, as life itself.

WHALE COVE COTTAGE
 GRAND MANAN, N.B.
  September, 1922

Introduction to
Daniel Defoe's
"The Fortunate Mistress"

DEFOE WAS WRITING *Roxanna, or, The Fortunate Mistress* in 1720, twenty years before Richardson produced *Pamela*. He was a writer in much the same sense that he was a hosier, and drove both trades as well as he could. A practical journalist, he wrote on politics, commerce, religion, publishing in pamphlets because there was no periodic press. When he was past fifty, and had been writing all his life, he discovered that there was a much larger public for narratives than for political articles. The success of *Robinson Crusoe* astonished him, and he decided to follow a winning lead. His family expenses were heavy, he was burdened with marriageable daughters, and his hosiery business in London was not flourishing enough to provide portions for them. Stories, he saw, could be made to pay better than either hose or instructive pamphlets.

The material for *Robinson Crusoe* Defoe came upon by chance—by one of those chances which are always happening to the born journalist. He met Alexander Selkirk at the house of a friend in Bristol, and got the story of the shipwrecked man's adventures from his own lips. Selkirk afterward declared that he had handed over his papers to this sympathetic listener. Defoe's literal method never worked out so well again as in *Robinson Crusoe*—at least, not for readers of our time. Robinson, like all his other heroes, lived by his wits, but since he practised his ingenuity upon a desert island and the untamed forces of nature, the details are not so revolting as in the narratives in which the hero uses his wits upon the persons and pocket-books of his fellow mortals. Moreover, since Robinson has the scene to himself, the modern reader does not miss so much the thousand flowers of courtesy and sympathy and fine feeling he has come to expect in the narrative that deals with human intercourse.

Defoe was upwards of sixty when he began *The Fortunate*

Mistress: the story of a daughter of French Protestant parents who fled to England in 1683, married at fifteen to a London brewer, with whom she lives for more than eight years and by whom she has five children. The husband dissipates his own fortune and hers in drinking and hunting, finally deserts her, and goes abroad to enlist in foreign military service. Young and handsome, with five children, no money, and many debts, Roxanna is left to shift for herself—and she demonstrates that she is mightily competent to do so. She embarks almost at once upon a career which it would be absurdly euphuistic to call a career of amatory adventure. A life of adventure it certainly is, though the adventure is always the same. The monetary gains vary somewhat in her various engagements, but they are always large. Defoe undertook to tell the story of a fortunate mistress, one who concerned herself only with men of quality, wealth, and boundless good nature; one who managed her affairs successfully and practised her profession with good sense, shrewdness, and economy until she was well past fifty.

Roxanna's story is told by herself; the entire novel is written in the first person, the fortunate mistress being the narrator. She leaves nothing untold, and there is much to relate. Her story ought to be absorbingly interesting, but it is only inversely so. The most interesting thing about it is that, with such a warehouse of inflammatory material to draw from, it remains so dull.

Here we have the novel (or we may be academic and call it the "romance"), stripped to its bare bones; and what have we? It happens to be much easier to say what we have not. Defoe is a writer of ready invention but no imagination—with none of the personal attributes which, fused together somehow, make imagination. His narrative runs smoothly, evenly, convincingly; the best thing about it is his vigorous, unornamented English. There is a strong weave in the sentences as they follow each other that gives pleasure to the eye, as the feel of good hand-woven linen does to the fingertips. But after a while one demands something more. There is never a change of tempo, never a modulation of voice, or a quickening of sympathy. The episodes of Roxanna's narrative never

emerge from the level text and become "scenes." Fifty years
before Defoe, Bunyan had written much of *The Pilgrim's
Progress* in scenes of the most satisfying kind; where little is
said but much is felt and communicated: one has only to
recall the delightful episodes of Christiana's sojourn at the
House Beautiful, or Mercy's descent into the Valley of
Humiliation. The "scene" in fiction is not a mere matter of
construction, any more than it is in life. When we have a vivid
experience in social intercourse, pleasant or unpleasant, it
records itself in our memory in the form of a scene; and when
it flashes back to us, all sorts of apparently unimportant de-
tails are flashed back with it. When a writer has a strong or
revelatory experience with his characters, he unconsciously
creates a scene; gets a depth of picture, and writes, as it were,
in three dimensions instead of two. The absence of these
warm and satisfying moments in any work of fiction is final
proof of the author's poverty of emotion and lack of imag-
ination.

There are no scenes in Roxanna's narrative, and there is no
atmosphere. Her adventures in France are exactly like those in
England; one is not conscious of the slightest change in her
surroundings or way of living. Defoe had travelled, and so
does his heroine. But all countries and all cities are alike to
Roxanna, just as all well-to-do men are alike to her. When she
is touring with her French Prince, she goes to Venice for her
"lying-in"—but it is all one with Spitalfields. The child died
after two months, and she says that she was on the whole not
sorry, considering the inconvenience of travelling with an in-
fant. About the city itself, or her way of living there, she does
not drop a remark. While one may much prefer this reticence
to the travelogue school of fiction, it certainly adds to the
evidence of a curious insensibility in Roxanna and her author.
The whole book, indeed, is a mass of evidence upon that
point, and that is its chief interest. The reader gets no impres-
sion of Roxanna's physical surroundings at any time; her
houses and retinues in England, France, and Holland are
mere names. The only things in her material investiture which
interest either her or her creator are her clothes. She does
enumerate at some length the gowns and jewels the Prince
bought for her—enumerates them more like a merchant

taking stock than like a pretty woman describing her costumes. We are never told anything so foolish as that the Prince liked her in this or that. One can say this for Roxanna: she is never sentimental.

There are no scenes in this novel, there is no atmosphere, no picturing of rooms or gardens or household gear which for one reason or another were dear to the narrator—as a particular cushion is dear to a cat, or a corner by the fire to a dog. There is no conversation, or almost none. Talk is used chiefly to present arguments. While conversation was slow to develop in the English novel, there is living human intercourse through conversation in *The Pilgrim's Progress*, and many of the theological discussions between Christian and Faithful are more lively and full of feeling than any of Roxanna's dialogues with her lovers.

Roxanna had enough sense of character for her purpose. Of her hard-riding, hard-drinking first husband she paints a good picture; one gets a sense of the man's personality. Her maid, the sprightly and resourceful Amy, the companion and sharer of her adventures, is, after Roxanna herself, the most living person in the book. In discussing her lovers, our heroine is concerned with only one quality, their generosity. When she deigns to be personal, her strokes tell, and one does manage to find out something about these men beyond the ample provision they made for Roxanna. If she and her author had not been so blind to everything but francs and pounds, they might have passed on a good deal to us.

As against so many things that are absent from Defoe's story, one thing is amazingly, powerfully, unflaggingly present: verisimilitude. From the first paragraph one never doubts that this is a woman's actual story, told by a woman. The author never gets outside his character, never insinuates anything through her, has no feelings about her beyond those she has about herself. The reader forgets Daniel Defoe altogether; he is reading a woman's autobiography. And what a woman! One cannot imagine the most starved little girl drudge, in the cruelest age of domestic service, if this book had fallen into her hands, lingering wistfully over its pages and coveting Roxanna's Prince or her diamonds. One cannot believe that the most mush-headed boy would long to take her over from the Prince. The starved and the mush-headed are romantic; they want what goes with the Prince and the diamonds, they believe in their own capacity for pleasure. But Defoe and Roxanna knew well enough that they had none, and no more unromantic pair ever got themselves into print. Their great, their saving quality is that they do not try to be what they are not, and never for one moment pretend to any of the fine feelings they do not possess. This mental integrity makes the narrative, as a piece of writing, almost flawless; as self-sufficient as a column of figures correctly added. Lewd situations are dispatched without lewdness. The book is as safe as sterilized gauze. One is bumped up smartly against the truth, old enough but always new, that in novels, as in poetry, the facts are nothing, the feeling is everything.

Open any volume of M. Fabre's studies of insect life, and one can find passages about the life-struggle of beetles, the love-makings and domestic cares of ants or grasshoppers, passages that are so warm and rich and full of colour, so full of wisdom and humour and the sense of tragedy and beauty, that they make poor Roxanna, with her thirty years of profitable engagements, seem not animal, but mineral. With Fabre, the poetic Provençal was always getting the better of the scientist. When the lights are put out, and the moths he has vainly enticed for weeks at last come flying through the summer night to court the lady under a gauze tent on his study table, it is Fabre, and his breathless children, hidden in the dark, who have the romance and the adventure, not the moths. And they have more in their silent half-hour than Defoe is able to beat up for Roxanna and her dozen lovers in five hundred pages. M. Fabre is much more wonderful than his insects; but Defoe is not at all more remarkable than Roxanna. They are both most remarkable in that, lacking all the most valuable gifts a writer can have except one, they made themselves an immortal place in English, in European, literature.

Defoe seems to have had only one deep interest, and that was in making a living. Read *The Complete British Tradesman* and marvel at how intensely, how acutely, every mean device and petty economy appealed to him; how every stingy trim, every possible twist and sharp practice in shopkeeping and servant-grinding, stirred him and gratified him. All the misers in fiction are sentimental, inexpert, and unresourceful, judged by the standards advocated in this work written for the guidance of Defoe's fellow tradesmen. It is one of the meanest and most sordid books ever written. It makes one ashamed of being human.

Defoe was concerned not only about the matter of making his own living, he was intensely interested in the way other people made theirs; in all the shifts by which we feed and clothe ourselves, and buy a business and get together a property. It must have been much harder to wring a livelihood from a stony world then than it is now: in the profound concern of this small, mean, vigorous spirit, we get some aching sense of the cruel pressure of the times.

In one book Defoe's single theme was quite enough. It happened that the way in which Robinson Crusoe made a living was extremely interesting: nearly everyone would like to try it for a month or two. Except for the moralizing, which few of us read, Defoe's immortal work is an account of how Robinson maintained himself and acquired property on a desert island.

The Fortunate Mistress is an account of how a woman maintained herself and acquired property—and her way of doing it is not interesting. Her profession, of course, is an old theme in art; and of the queens of that profession great artists have left portraits of enduring beauty in sculpture and painting and literature. But such a theme, in the hands of Roxanna and that thrifty hosier, Daniel Defoe——! Shakespeare himself could never have created two such characters; he wouldn't have had the patience. They remind us of what Heine said, that no irony can compete with God's irony.

Some sentimental critics, of the kind that Defoe himself called "high-flying," have tried to make out a case for *The British Tradesman* as a masterpiece of irony. Its author would have said that you might as well call the multiplication table irony. Defoe attempted ironical treatment more than once, in imitation of Swift, but he could never sustain that mood for long. He was as devoid of humour as he was of idealism, of romance, and of geniality. *Robinson Crusoe* and *The Fortunate Mistress* splendidly illustrate to what different ends a writer can put the same talent. The one book has what Stevenson called charm of circumstance, the other emphatically has not; but in both the same nature is effectively asserting itself; mean enough and vital enough—invulnerable because it never affects qualities which it neither comprehends nor admires.

1924

Preface to Gertrude Hall's
"The Wagnerian Romances"

I KNOW of only two books in English on the Wagnerian operas that are at all worthy of their subject; Bernard Shaw's "The Perfect Wagnerite" and "The Wagnerian Romances" by Gertrude Hall. For the most part "guides to the opera" are written by very unintelligent people, who know little about writing and even less about opera. This book of Miss Hall's is beautifully written, and the writer is a discerning critic who has spent her life among musicians of the first rank. The Wagnerian music-dramas, indeed, have been a part of her life, and she has closely followed the work of the best conductors and interpreters of German opera here and abroad. All these facts might be true of a dull writer, of course. This book is good—so good as to be unique among its kind—because the writer has the rare gift of being able to reproduce the emotional effect of the Wagner operas upon the printed page; to suggest the setting, the scenic environment, the dramatic action, the personality of the characters. Moreover, she is able, in a way all her own, to suggest the character of the music itself.

I first came upon this book when I was staying in a thinly peopled part of the Southwest, far enough from the Metropolitan Opera House. I first read the chapter on *Parsifal*, with increasing delight. I was astonished to find how vividly it recalled to me all the best renderings of that opera I had ever heard. Just the right word was said to start the music going in one's memory, as if one had heard the themes given out on a piano. The essay recalled the scenes, the personages of the drama, and the legendary beauty, the truly religious feeling that haunts it from end to end. I next turned to "The Master-Singers of Nuremberg" and it seemed to me that the rich life of that old German city and the joyous comedy of the piece has seldom stood out on any stage as it did on these pages.

What Miss Hall does, it seems to me, is to reproduce the emotional effect of one art through the medium of another

art. This, of course, can scarcely be done in the case of a sym-
phony or a sonata; efforts to do it are usually unsuccessful
and often ludicrous. But opera is a hybrid art,—partly literary
to begin with. It happens that in the Wagnerian music-drama
the literary part of the work is not trivial, as it is so often in
operas, but is truly the mate of the music, done by the same
hand. The music is throughout concerned with words, and
with things that can be presented in language; with human
beings and their passions and sorrows, and with places and
with periods of time, with particular rivers and particular
mountains, even;—with Nuremberg, even. All this feeling for
places and the character of landscape and architecture is, in
the hands of the right person, readily translatable into words.

I have used the word translate; what horrid deeds that
word has been made to cover where the Wagnerian operas are
concerned! What a frightful jargon Tristan and Isolde speak
to each other in the "authorized libretto," what insulting
expletives Siegfried and Brünnhilde shout at each other on
the rock! Miss Hall, in her introduction, says she respects
the libretto-makers for having managed to fit their verse-
rendering to the extremely difficult music in any way whatso-
ever. But in her rendering of the text the right word does not
have to come in for the right beat. She is free to make a noble
passage of the German into noble English. In the dialogue,
when the characters are singing to each other, she translates
Wagner's own text most effectively and sympathetically into
English prose. Miss Hall is an accomplished linguist, and Ger-
man is the language in which she is, musically, most at home.
All the dialogue in these chapters is Wagner's own, exquisitely
done into English,—English that has everywhere the right
shading; the right shading for the god, the right shading for
the gnome. I know of no other English rendering of Wag-
ner's poems that has anything of the character of the origi-
nal,—any character at all, for that matter. And the words are
here not divorced from the action, but vividly accompanied
by the action (in narrative) as Wagner meant them to be. A
mere literal translation of the written scene in which *Walther*
for the first time sings before the Master-singers, for instance,
means very little. And the words of *Walther's* song, literally
translated, without the feeling of the accompanying actions,

mean almost nothing. Miss Hall's rendering of that scene is a brilliant piece of virtuosity. She builds it up, with its influences and counter-influences, themes and counter-themes, very much as the music itself is built up. If you wish to know how difficult it is to transfer the feeling of an operatic scene upon a page of narrative, try it! I had to attempt it once, in the course of a novel, and I paid Miss Hall the highest compliment one writer can pay another; I stole from her.

I have a great many friends who live in distant parts of the country where operas are not given. I believe that after they have read these chapters on the "Ring of the Nibelungs" they will have got a great deal of the beauty of the cycle. Those who are able to spell out parts of the score on the piano will get just so much more. I am deeply interested in the revival of this book by a publisher who will give it a wide audience, because I know it will give great pleasure to many friends of mine, and to great numbers of people who have the intelligence to appreciate the Wagner operas but not the opportunity to hear them. There are innumerable Women's Clubs, for instance, who take a sort of silent course in music, and conscientiously read the dull books that have been written about operas. When they read this book, they will get, not some foolish facts, but an emotional experience of Wagner's Romances, of those noble, mysterious, significant dramas in roughly made verse. And persons who have heard the operas sung, and beautifully sung, many times, but who are now living in remote places, will find this book potent in reviving their recollections; the scenes will float before them, as they did before me in the blue air of New Mexico when I first made the acquaintance of these delicately suggestive pages.

New York
April 1925

Introduction to Stephen Crane's
"Wounds in the Rain"

THE SKETCHES in this volume are most of them low-pressure writing, done during, or soon after, Crane's illness in Cuba. He hadn't the vitality to make stories, to pull things together into a sharp design—though "The Price of the Harness" just misses being a fine war story. In one of them the writing is rather commonplace, the sketch "God Rest Ye, Merry Gentlemen"—the only story of Crane's I know which seems distinctly old-fashioned. It is done in an outworn manner that was considered smart in the days when Richard Harding Davis was young, and the war correspondent and his "kit" was a romantic figure. This sketch indulges in a curiously pompous kind of humour which seemed very swagger then:

"He was hideously youthful and innocent and unaware."

"Walkley departed tearlessly for Jamaica, soon after he had bestowed upon his friends much tinned goods and blankets."

"But they departed joyfully before the sun was up and passed into Siboney."

They always departed in that school of writing, they never went anywhere. This chesty manner, doubtless, came in with Kipling. When one re-reads the young Kipling it seems a little absurd, but it still seems to belong. After it became a general affectation, however, it was surely one of the most foolish of literary fashions. But only this one of Crane's war sketches is much tainted by the war-correspondent idiom of the times. In the others he wrote better than the people of his day, and he wrote like himself. The fact that there is not much design, that these are for the most part collections of impressions which could be arranged as well in one way as another, gives one a chance to examine the sentences, which are part, but only part, of the material out of which stories are made.

When you examine the mere writing in this unorganized material, you see at once that Crane was one of the first post-impressionists; that he began it before the French painters began it, or at least as early as the first of them. He simply knew from the beginning how to handle detail. He estimated it at its true worth—made it serve his purpose and felt no further responsibility about it. I doubt whether he ever spent a laborious half-hour in doing his duty by detail—in enumerating, like an honest, grubby auctioneer. If he saw one thing that engaged him in a room, he mentioned it. If he saw one thing in a landscape that thrilled him, he put it on paper, but he never tried to make a faithful report of everything else within his field of vision, as if he were a conscientious salesman making out his expense-account. "The red sun was pasted in the sky like a wafer," that careless observation which Mr. Hergesheimer admires so much, isn't exceptional with Crane. (He wrote like that when he was writing well.) What about the clouds, and the light on the hills, and the background, and the foreground? Well, Crane left that for his successors to write, and they have been doing it ever since: accounting for everything, as trustees of an estate are supposed to do, thoroughly good business methods applied to art; "doing" landscapes and interiors like house-decorators, putting up the curtains and tacking down the carpets.

Perhaps it was because Stephen Crane had read so little, was so slightly acquainted with the masterpieces of fiction, that he felt no responsibility to be accurate or painstaking in accounting for things and people. He is rather the best of our writers in what is called "description" because he is the least describing. Cuba didn't tempt him to transfer tropical landscapes to paper, any more than New York State had tempted him to do his duty by the countryside.

"The day wore down to the Cuban dusk. . . . The sun threw his last lance through the foliage. The steep mountain-range on the right turned blue and as without detail as a curtain. The tiny ruby of light ahead meant that the ammunition guard were cooking their supper." Enough, certainly. He didn't follow the movement of troops there much more literally than he had in THE RED BADGE OF COURAGE. He knew that the movement of troops was the officers' business, not his. He was in Cuba to write about soldiers and soldiering, and he did; often something like this: "With his heavy roll of blanket and the half of a shelter tent crossing his right

shoulder and under his left arm, each man presented the ap-
pearance of being clasped from behind, wrestler-fashion, by a
pair of thick white arms.

"There was something distinctive in the way they carried
their rifles. There was the grace of the old hunter somewhere
in it, the grace of a man whose rifle has become absolutely a
part of himself. Furthermore, almost every blue shirt-sleeve
was rolled to the elbow, disclosing forearms of almost incred-
ible brawn. The rifles seemed light, almost fragile, in the
hands that were at the end of those arms, never fat but always
rolling with muscles and veins that seemed on the point of
bursting."

That is much more to his purpose than what these men
were about. That is important, all of it—and that sense of the
curious smallness of rifle-butts in the hands of regulars is most
important of all.

The most interesting things in the bundle of impressions
called "War Memories" are the death of Surgeon Gibbs,
Crane's observations about the regulars, "the men," and his
admiration for Admiral Sampson. Sometimes when a man is
writing carelessly, without the restraint he puts upon himself
when he is in good form, one can surprise some of his secrets
and read rather more than he perhaps intended. He admired
Sampson because he wasn't like the time-honoured concep-
tion of a bluff seaman. "It is his distinction not to resemble
the preconceived type of his standing. When I first met him
he seemed immensely bored by the war and with the com-
mand of the North Atlantic Squadron. I perceived a manner,
where I thought I perceived a mood, a point of view."

He admired the Admiral because he wasn't theatrical, de-
tested noise and show. "No bunting, no arches, no fireworks;
nothing but the perfect management of a big fleet. That is a
record for you. No trumpets, no cheers of the populace. Just
plain, pure, unsauced accomplishment. But ultimately he will
reap his reward in—in what? In text-books on sea campaigns.
No more. The people choose their own, and they choose the
kind they like. Who has a better right? Anyhow, he is a great
man. And when you are once started you can continue to be a
great man without the help of bouquets and banquets."

And that point of view caused Mr. Crane's biographer no

little trouble. He himself managed so conspicuously to elude the banquets and bouquets of his own calling that he left a very meagre tradition among "literary people." Had he been more expansive at coffee-houses and luncheon clubs where his art was intelligently discussed, had he even talked about his own tales among a few friends, or written a few papers about his works for reviews, what a convenience for Thomas Beer! But there is every evidence that he was a reticent and unhelpful man, with no warm-hearted love of giving out opinions. His ideal, apparently, was "just plain, pure, unsauced accomplishment."

NEW YORK, N. Y.
January, 1926.

On "Death Comes for the Archbishop"

To the Editor of The Commonweal:—You have asked me to give you a short account of how I happened to write Death Comes for the Archbishop.

When I first went into the Southwest some fifteen years ago, I stayed there for a considerable period of time. It was then much harder to get about than it is today. There were no automobile roads and no hotels off the main lines of railroad. One had to travel by wagon and carry a camp outfit. One traveled slowly, and had plenty of time for reflection. It was then very difficult to find anyone who would tell me anything about the country, or even about the roads. One of the most intelligent and inspiriting persons I found in my travels was a Belgian priest, Father Haltermann, who lived with his sister in the parsonage behind the beautiful old church at Santa Cruz, New Mexico, where he raised fancy poultry and sheep and had a wonderful vegetable and flower garden. He was a florid, full-bearded farmer priest, who drove about among his eighteen Indian missions with a spring wagon and a pair of mules. He knew a great deal about the country and the Indians and their traditions. He went home during the war to serve as a chaplain in the French army, and when I last heard of him he was an invalid.

The longer I stayed in the Southwest, the more I felt that the story of the Catholic Church in that country was the most interesting of all its stories. The old mission churches, even those which were abandoned and in ruins, had a moving reality about them; the hand-carved beams and joists, the utterly unconventional frescoes, the countless fanciful figures of the saints, not two of them alike, seemed a direct expression of some very real and lively human feeling. They were all fresh, individual, first-hand. Almost every one of those many remote little adobe churches in the mountains or the desert had something lovely that was its own. In lonely, sombre villages in the mountains the church decorations were sombre, the martyrdoms bloodier, the grief of the Virgin more agonized, the figure of Death more terrifying. In warm, gentle valleys everything about the churches was milder. I used to wish there were some written account of the old times when those churches were built; but I soon felt that no record of them could be as real as they are themselves. They are their own story, and it is a foolish convention that we must have everything interpreted for us in written language. There are other ways of telling what one feels, and the people who built and decorated those many, many little churches found their way and left their message.

May I say here that within the last few years some of the newer priests down in that country have been taking away from those old churches their old homely images and decorations, which have a definite artistic and historic value, and replacing them by conventional, factory-made church furnishings from New York? It is a great pity. All Catholics will be sorry about it, I think, when it is too late, when all those old paintings and images and carved doors that have so much feeling and individuality are gone—sold to some collector in New York or Chicago, where they mean nothing.

During the twelve years that followed my first year in New Mexico and Arizona I went back as often as I could, and the story of the Church and the Spanish missionaries was always what most interested me; but I hadn't the most remote idea of trying to write about it. I was working on things of a very different nature, and any story of the Church in the Southwest was certainly the business of some Catholic writer, and not mine at all.

Meanwhile Archbishop Lamy, the first Bishop of New Mexico, had become a sort of invisible personal friend. I had heard a great many interesting stories about him from very old Mexicans and traders who still remembered him, and I never passed the life-size bronze of him which stands under a locust tree before the Cathedral in Santa Fé without wishing that I could learn more about a pioneer churchman who looked so well-bred and distinguished. In his pictures one felt the same thing, something fearless and fine and very, very well-bred—something that spoke of race. What I felt curious about was the daily life of such a man in a crude frontier society.

Two years ago, in Santa Fé, that curiosity was gratified. I

came upon a book printed years ago on a country press at
Pueblo, Colorado: The Life of the Right Reverend Joseph P.
Machebeuf, by William Joseph Howlett, a priest who had
worked with Father Machebeuf in Denver. The book is an
admirable piece of work, almost as revelatory about Father
Lamy as about Father Machebeuf, since the two men were so
closely associated from early youth. Father Howlett had gone
to France and got his information about Father Machebeuf's
youth direct from his sister, Philomène. She gave him her
letters from Father Machebeuf, telling all the little details of
his life in New Mexico, and Father Howlett inserted dozens
of them, splendidly translated, into his biography. At last I
found out what I wanted to know about how the country and
the people of New Mexico seemed to those first missionary
priests from France. Without these letters in Father Howlett's
book to guide me, I would certainly never have dared to write
my book. Of course, many of the incidents I used were expe-
riences of my own, but in these letters I learned how experi-
ences very similar to them affected Father Machebeuf and
Father Lamy.

My book was a conjunction of the general and the particu-
lar, like most works of the imagination. I had all my life
wanted to do something in the style of legend, which is abso-
lutely the reverse of dramatic treatment. Since I first saw the
Puvis de Chavannes frescoes of the life of Saint Geneviève in
my student days, I have wished that I could try something a
little like that in prose; something without accent, with none
of the artificial elements of composition. In the Golden Leg-
end the martyrdoms of the saints are no more dwelt upon
than are the trivial incidents of their lives; it is as though all
human experiences, measured against one supreme spiritual
experience, were of about the same importance. The essence
of such writing is not to hold the note, not to use an incident
for all there is in it—but to touch and pass on. I felt that such
writing would be a delightful kind of discipline in these days
when the "situation" is made to count for so much in writing,
when the general tendency is to force things up. In this kind
of writing the mood is the thing—all the little figures and
stories are mere improvisations that come out of it. What I
got from Father Machebeuf's letters was the mood, the spirit

in which they accepted the accidents and hardships of a desert country, the joyful energy that kept them going. To attempt to convey this hardihood of spirit one must use language a little stiff, a little formal, one must not be afraid of the old trite phraseology of the frontier. Some of those time-worn phrases I used as the note from the piano by which the violinist tunes his instrument. Not that there was much difficulty in keeping the pitch. I did not sit down to write the book until the feeling of it had so teased me that I could not get on with other things. The writing of it took only a few months, because the book had all been lived many times before it was written, and the happy mood in which I began it never paled. It was like going back and playing the early composers after a surfeit of modern music.

One friendly reviewer says that to write the book I soaked myself in Catholic lore; perhaps it would have been better if I had. But too much information often makes one pompous, and it's rather deadening. Some things I had to ask about. I had no notion of the manner in which a missionary from the new world would be received by the Pope, so I simply asked an old friend, Father Dennis Fitzgerald, the resident priest in Red Cloud, Nebraska, where my parents live. He was a student in Rome in his youth, so I asked him to tell me something about the procedure of a formal audience with the Pope. There again I had to exercise self-restraint, for he told me such interesting things that I was strongly tempted to make Father Vaillant's audience stand out too much, to particularize it. Knowledge that one hasn't got first-hand is a dangerous thing for a writer, it comes too easily!

Writing this book (the title, by the way, which has caused a good deal of comment, was simply taken from Dürer's Dance of Death) was like a happy vacation from life, a return to childhood, to early memories. As a writer I had the satisfaction of working in a special genre which I had long wished to try. As a human being, I had the pleasure of paying an old debt of gratitude to the valiant men whose life and work have given me so many hours of pleasant reflection in far-away places where certain unavoidable accidents and physical discomforts gave me a feeling of close kinship with them. In the main, I followed the life story of the two Bishops very much as it was, though I used many of my own experiences, and some of my father's. In actual fact, of course, Bishop Lamy died first of the two friends, and it was Bishop Machebeuf who went to his funeral. Often have I heard from the old people of how he broke down when he rose to speak and was unable to go on.

I am amused that so many of the reviews of this book begin with the statement, "This book is hard to classify." Then why bother? Many more assert vehemently that it is not a novel. Myself, I prefer to call it a narrative. In this case I think that term most appropriate. But a novel, it seems to me, is merely a work of the imagination in which a writer tries to present the experiences and emotions of a group of people by the light of his own. That is what he really does, whether his method is "objective" or "subjective."

I hope that I have told you what you wished to know about my book, and I remain,

                    Very sincerely yours,

The Commonweal, November 23, 1927

My First Novels
(There Were Two)

M^{Y FIRST NOVEL}, *Alexander's Bridge*, was very like what painters call a studio picture. It was the result of meeting some interesting people in London. Like most young writers I thought a book should be made out of 'interesting material', and at that time I found the new more exciting than the familiar. The impressions I tried to communicate on paper were genuine, but they were very shallow. I still find people who like that book because it follows the most conventional pattern, and because it is more or less laid in London. London is supposed to be more engaging than, let us say, Gopher Prairie; even if the writer knows Gopher Prairie very well and London very casually. Soon after the book was published I went for six months to Arizona and New Mexico. The longer I stayed in a country I really did care about, and among people who were a part of the country, the more unnecessary and superficial a book like *Alexander's Bridge* seemed to me. I did no writing down there, but I recovered from the conventional editorial point of view.

When I got back to Pittsburgh I began to write a book entirely for myself; a story about some Scandinavians and Bohemians who had been neighbors of ours when I lived on a ranch in Nebraska, when I was eight or nine years old. I found it a much more absorbing occupation than writing *Alexander's Bridge*; a different process altogether. Here there was no arranging or 'inventing'; everything was spontaneous and took its own place, right or wrong. This was like taking a ride through a familiar country on a horse that knew the way, on a fine morning when you felt like riding. The other was like riding in a park, with someone not altogether congenial, to whom you had to be talking all the time. Since I wrote this book for myself, I ignored all the situations and accents that were then generally thought to be necessary. The 'novel of the soil' had not then come into fashion in this country. The drawing-room was considered the proper setting for a novel, and the only characters worth reading about were smart people or clever people. O. Henry had made the short story go into the world of the cheap boarding-house and the shop girl and the truck-driver. But Henry James and Mrs. Wharton were our most interesting novelists, and most of the younger writers followed their manner, without having their qualifications.

O Pioneers! interested me tremendously, because it had to do with a kind of country I loved, because it was about old neighbors, once very dear, whom I had almost forgotten in the hurry and excitement of growing up and finding out what the world was like and trying to get on in it. But I did not in the least expect that other people would see anything in a slow-moving story, without 'action', without 'humor', without a 'hero'; a story concerned entirely with heavy farming people, with cornfields and pasture lands and pig yards—set in Nebraska, of all places! As every one knows, Nebraska is distinctly déclassé as a literary background; its very name throws the delicately attuned critic into a clammy shiver of embarrassment. Kansas is almost as unpromising. Colorado, on the contrary, is considered quite possible. Wyoming really has some class, of its own kind, like well-cut riding breeches. But a New York critic voiced a very general opinion when he said, "I simply don't care a damn what happens in Nebraska, no matter who writes about it."

O Pioneers! was not only about Nebraska farmers, the farmers were Swedes! At that time, 1912, the Swede had never appeared on the printed page in this country except in broadly humorous sketches; and the humor was based on two peculiarities: his physical strength, and his inability to pronounce the letter "j". I had certainly good reasons for supposing that the book I had written for myself would remain faithfully with me, and continue to be exclusively my property. I sent it to Mr. Ferris Greenslet, of Houghton Mifflin, who had published *Alexander's Bridge*, and was truly astonished when he wrote me they would publish it.

I was very much pleased when William Heinemann decided to publish it in England. I had met Mr. Heinemann in London several times, when I was on the editorial staff of *McClure's Magazine*, and I had the highest opinion of his taste and judgment. His personal taste was a thing quite apart from his business, and it was uncompromising. The fact that a second-rate book sold tremendously never made him hedge and insist there must be something good in it after all. Most publishers, like most writers, are ruined by their successes.

When my third book, *The Song of the Lark*, came along, Heinemann turned it down. I had never heard from him directly that he liked *O Pioneers!* but now I had a short handwritten letter from him, telling me that he admired it very much; that he was declining *The Song of the Lark* because he thought in that book I had taken the wrong road, and that the full-blooded method, which told everything about everybody, was not natural to me and was not the one in which I would ever take satisfaction. As for myself, he wrote, he always found "the friendly confidential tone of writing of this sort distressingly familiar, even when the subject matter is very fine."

At that time I did not altogether agree with Mr. Heinemann, nor with Randolph Bourne, in this country, who said in his review almost the same thing. One is always a little on the defensive about one's last book. But when the next book, *My Ántonia*, came along, quite of itself and with no direction from me, it took the road of *O Pioneers!*, not the road of *The Song of the Lark*. Too much detail is apt, like any other form of extravagance, to become slightly vulgar; and it quite destroys in a book a very satisfying element analogous to what painters call 'composition'.

The Colophon, June 1931

On "Shadows on the Rock"

DEAR GOVERNOR CROSS:—
   I want to thank you most heartily for the most understanding review I have seen of my new book. You seem to have seen what a different kind of method I tried to use from that which I used in the "Archbishop." I tried, as you say, to state the mood and the viewpoint in the title. To me the rock of Quebec is not only a stronghold on which many strange figures have for a little time cast a shadow in the sun; it is the curious endurance of a kind of culture, narrow but definite. There another age persists. There, among the country people and the nuns, I caught something new to me; a kind of feeling about life and human fate that I could not accept, wholly, but which I could not but admire. It is hard to state that feeling in language; it was more like an old song, incomplete but uncorrupted, than like a legend. The text was mainly anacoluthon, so to speak, but the meaning was clear. I took the incomplete air and tried to give it what would correspond to a sympathetic musical setting; tried to develop it into a prose composition not too conclusive, not too definite: a series of pictures remembered rather than experienced; a kind of thinking, a mental complexion inherited, left over from the past, lacking in robustness and full of pious resignation.

   Now, it seemed to me that the mood of the misfits among the early settlers (and there were a good many) must have been just that. An orderly little French household that went on trying to live decently, just as ants begin to rebuild when you kick their house down, interests me more than Indian raids or the wild life in the forests. And, as you seem to recognize, once having adopted a tone so definite, once having taken your seat in the close air by the apothecary's fire, you can't explode into military glory, any more than you can pour champagne into a salad dressing. (I don't believe much in rules, but Stevenson laid down a good one when he said: *You can't mix kinds*.) And really, a new society begins with the salad dressing more than with the destruction of Indian villages. Those people brought a kind of French culture there

966

and somehow kept it alive on that rock, sheltered it and tended it and on occasion died for it, as if it really were a sacred fire—and all this temperately and shrewdly, with emotion always tempered by good sense.

It's very hard for an American to catch that rhythm—it's so unlike us. But I made an honest try, and I got a great deal of pleasure out of it, if nobody else does! And surely you'll agree with me that our writers experiment too little, and produce their own special brand too readily.

With deep appreciation of the compliment you pay me in taking the time to review the book, and my friendliest regards always,

Faithfully,

The Saturday Review of Literature, October 17, 1931

Escapism

M<small>Y DEAR</small> M<small>R.</small> W<small>ILLIAMS</small>:
    You were asking me what I thought about a new term in criticism: the Art of "Escape." Isn't the phrase tautological? What has art ever been but escape? To be sure, this definition is for the moment used in a derogatory sense, implying an evasion of duty, something like the behavior of a poltroon. When the world is in a bad way, we are told, it is the business of the composer and the poet to devote himself to propaganda and fan the flames of indignation.

But the world has a habit of being in a bad way from time to time, and art has never contributed anything to help matters—except escape. Hundreds of years ago, before European civilization had touched this continent, the Indian women in the old rock-perched pueblos of the Southwest were painting geometrical patterns on the jars in which they carried water up from the streams. Why did they take the trouble? These people lived under the perpetual threat of drought and famine; they often shaped their graceful cooking pots when they had nothing to cook in them. Anyone who looks over a collection of pre-historic Indian pottery dug up from old burial-mounds knows at once that the potters experimented with form and color to gratify something that had no concern with food and shelter. The major arts (poetry, painting, architecture, sculpture, music) have a pedigree all their own. They did not come into being as a means of increasing the game supply or promoting tribal security. They sprang from an unaccountable predilection of the one unaccountable thing in man.

At the moment, we hear the same cry which went up during the French Revolution: the one really important thing for every individual is his citizenship, his loyalty to a cause—which, of course, always means his loyalty to a party. The composer should be Citizen Beethoven, the painter Citizen Rembrandt, the poet Citizen Shelley, and they should step into line and speed their pen or brush in helping to solve the economic problems which confront society. There have been generous and bold spirits among the artists: Courbet tried to kick down the Vendôme Column and got himself exiled, Citizen Shelley stepped into line and drove his pen — but he was not very useful to the reforms which fired his imagination. He was "useful" if you like that word, only as all true poets are, because they refresh and recharge the spirit of those who can read their language.

"Face the stern realities, you skulking Escapist!" the Radical editor cries. Yes, but usually the poor Escapist has so little cleverness when he struggles with stern realities. Schubert could easily write a dozen songs a day, but he couldn't keep himself in shirts. Suppose the Radical editor, or the head of the Works Project, had to write a dozen songs a day? I can't believe that if Tolstoi and Goethe and Viollet-le-Duc and Descartes and Sir Isaac Newton were brought together and induced to work with a will, their opinions, voiced in their various special languages and formulae, would materially help Mayor La Guardia to better living conditions in New York City. Nearly all the Escapists in the long past have managed their own budget and their social relations so unsuccessfully that I wouldn't want them for my landlords, or my bankers, or my neighbors. They were valuable, like powerful stimulants, only when they were left out of the social and industrial routine which goes on every day all over the world. Industrial life has to work out its own problems.

Give the people a new word, and they think they have a new fact. The pretentious-sounding noun, Escapist, isn't even new. Just now, it is applied to writers with more acrimony than to composers or sculptors. Since poets and novelists do not speak in symbols or a special language, but in the plain speech which all men use and all men may, after some fashion, read, they are told that their first concern should be to cry out against social injustice. This, of course, writers have always done. The Hebrew prophets and the Greek dramatists went much deeper; they considered the greed and selfishness innate in every individual; the valor which leads to power, and the tyranny which power begets. They even cried out against the seeming original injustice that creatures so splendidly aspiring should be inexorably doomed to fail; the unfairness of the contest in which beings whose realest life is in thought or endeavor are kept always under the shackles of their physical body, and are, as Ulysses said, "the slaves of the belly." Since no patriarchal family was without its hatreds and jealousies and treacheries, the old poets could not see how a great number of families brought together into a State could be much better. This seems to be the writer's natural way of looking at the suffering of the world. Seventy-five years ago Dostoievsky was the idol of the Revolutionary party; but who could now consider his novels propaganda? Certainly they are very unlike the product of the young man who goes to spend a year in a factory town and writes a novel on the abuses of factory labor.

Why does the man who wants to reform industrial conditions so seldom follow the method of the pamphleteers? Only by that method can these subjects be seriously and fairly discussed. And the people who are able to do anything toward improving such conditions will read only such a discussion: they will take little account of facts presented in a coating of stock cinema situations.

Why do the propagandists use a vehicle which they consider rickety and obsolete, to convey a message which they believe all-important? When I first lived in New York and was working on the editorial staff of a magazine, I became disillusioned about social workers and reformers. So many of them, when they brought in an article on fire-trap tenements or sweat-shop labor, apologetically explained that they were making these investigations "to collect material for fiction." I couldn't believe that any honest welfare worker, or any honest novelist, went to work in this way. The man who wants to get reforms put through does his investigating in a very different spirit, and the man who has a true vocation for imaginative writing doesn't have to go hunting among the ash cans on Sullivan Street for his material. There were exceptions to these double-purposed, faltering soldiers of good causes— and the exceptions were splendid. The exceptions nearly always are. And their exceptionalness, oftener than not, comes not only from a superior endowment, but from a deeper purpose, and a willingness to pay the cost instead of being paid for it.

But doesn't the new social restlessness spring from a desire to do away with the exceptional? And isn't this desire partly the result of thwarted ambitions? Eighteen or twenty years ago there were graduated from our universities a company of unusually promising men, who were also extravagantly ambitious. The world was changing, and they meant to play a conspicuous part in this change: to make a new kind of thought and a new kind of expression; in language, color, form, sound. They were to bring about a renaissance within a decade or so. Failing in this, they made a career of destroying the past. The only new thing they offered us was contempt for the old. Then began the flood of belittling biography which has poured over us ever since. We were told how shallow had been all the great philosophers, what educated dullards were Goethe, Rousseau, Spinoza, Pascal. Shakespeare and Dante were easily disposed of; the one because he was somebody else, the other because he was a cryptogram and did not at all mean to say what the greatest lines in the Italian language make him say. Able research work was done on the bodily diseases and physical imperfections of Beethoven, Schubert, Hugo Wolff and all the German composers. Not even their teeth were overlooked.

Is this a natural, unprejudiced way to study history? What does it lead to? Nothing very worthy. And what it comes from is less worthy still.

Some of these iconoclasts and tomb-breakers were undoubtedly sincere. They attacked the old popular heroes in a spirit of dreary hopelessness rather than with a disgust bred of the chagrin from disappointed ambitions. The false past must be destroyed, they said, before the new and the true can be born.

Not at all: spare yourselves that disagreeable duty. Give us a new work of genius of any kind, and if it is alive, and fired with some more vital feeling than contempt, you will see how automatically the old and false makes itself air before the new and true.

The revolt against individualism naturally calls artists severely to account, because the artist is of all men the most individual: those who were not have been long forgotten. The condition every art requires is, not so much freedom from restriction, as freedom from adulteration and from the intrusion of foreign matter; considerations and purposes which have nothing to do with spontaneous invention. The great body of Russian literature was produced when the censorship was at its strictest. The art of Italy flowered when the painters were confined almost entirely to religious subjects. In the great age of Gothic architecture sculptors and stone-cutters told the same stories (with infinite variety and fresh invention) over and over, on the faces of all the cathedrals and churches of Europe. How many clumsy experiments in government, futile revolutions and reforms, those buildings have looked down upon without losing a shadow of their dignity and power—of their importance. Religion and art spring from the same root and are close kin. Economics and art are strangers.

The literary radicals tell us there must be a new kind of poetry. There will be, whenever there is a new poet—a genuine one. The thesis that no one can ever write a noble sonnet on a noble theme without repeating Wordsworth, or a mysteriously lovely lyric without repeating Shelley, is an evasion. As well argue that because so many thumb-prints have already been taken, there must be a new method of identification. No fine poet can ever write like another. His poetry is simply his individuality. And the themes of true poetry, of great poetry, will be the same until all the values of human life have changed and all the strongest emotional responses have become different—which can hardly occur until the physical body itself has fundamentally changed.

So far, the effort to make a new kind of poetry, "pure poetry," which eschews (or renounces) the old themes as shop-worn, and confines itself to regarding the grey of a wet oyster shell against the sand of a wet beach through a drizzle of rain, has not produced anything very memorable: not even when the workmanship was good and when a beat in the measure was unexpectedly dropped here and there with what one of the poet's admirers calls a "heart-breaking effect." Certainly the last thing such poetry should attempt is to do any heart breaking.

Now, my dear Mr. Williams, I have already said much too much about a fleeting fashion which perhaps is not to be taken seriously at all. As Mary Colum remarked in the *Yale Review*: "The people who talk about the art of escape simply know nothing about art at all." *At all,* I echo!

Sincerely yours,

The Commonweal, April 17, 1936

On "*The Professor's House*"

L ET ME TRY to answer your question. When I wrote "The Professor's House," I wished to try two experiments in form. The first is the device often used by the early French and Spanish novelists; that of inserting the *Nouvelle* into the *Roman*. "Tom Outland's Story" has been published in French and Polish and Dutch, as a short narrative for school children studying English.

But the experiment which interested me was something a little more vague, and was very much akin to the arrangement followed in sonatas in which the academic sonata form was handled somewhat freely. Just before I began the book I had seen, in Paris, an exhibition of old and modern Dutch paintings. In many of them, the scene presented was a living room warmly furnished, or a kitchen full of food and coppers. But in most of the interiors, whether drawing-room or kitchen, there was a square window, open, through which one saw the masts of ships or a stretch of gray sea. The feeling of the sea that one got through those square windows was remarkable, and gave me a sense of the fleets of Dutch ships that ply quietly on all the waters of the globe — to Java, etc.

In my book I tried to make Professor St. Peter's house rather overcrowded and stuffy with new things; American proprieties, clothes, furs, petty ambitions, quivering jealousies — until one got rather stifled. Then I wanted to open the square window and let in the fresh air that blew off the Blue Mesa, and the fine disregard of trivialities which was in Tom Outland's face and in his behaviour.

The above concerned me as a writer only, but the Blue Mesa (the Mesa Verde) actually was discovered by a young cow-puncher in just this way. The great explorer, Norden-kjold, wrote a scientific book about this discovery, and I myself had the good fortune to hear the story of it from a very old man, brother to Dick Wetherell. Dick Wetherell as a young boy forded Mancos River and rode into the Mesa after lost cattle. I followed the real story very closely in Tom Outland's narrative.

The News Letter of the College
English Association, October 1940

Light on Adobe Walls

EVERY ARTIST knows that there is no such thing as "freedom" in art. The first thing an artist does when he begins a new work is to lay down the barriers and limitations; he decides upon a certain composition, a certain key, a certain relation of creatures of objects to each other. He is never free, and the more splendid his imagination, the more intense his feeling, the farther he goes from general truth and general emotion. Nobody can paint the sun, or sunlight. He can only paint the tricks that shadows play with it, or what it does to forms. He cannot even paint those relations of light and shade—he can only paint some emotion they give him, some man-made arrangement of them that happens to give him personal delight—a conception of clouds over distant mesas (or over the towers of St. Sulpice) that makes one nerve in him thrill and tremble. At bottom all he can give you is the thrill of his own poor little nerve—the projection in paint of a fleeting pleasure in a certain combination of form and colour, as temporary and almost as physical as a taste on the tongue. This oft-repeated pleasure in a painter becomes of course a "style," a way of seeing and feeling things, a favourite mood. What could be more different than Leonardo's treatment of daylight, and Velasquez'? Light is pretty much the same in Italy and Spain—southern light. Each man painted what he got out of light—what it did to him.

No art can do anything at all with great natural forces or great elemental emotions. No poet can write of love, hate, jealousy. He can only touch these things as they affect the people in his drama and his story, and unless he is more interested in his own little story and his foolish little people than in the Preservation of the Indian or Sex or Tuberculosis, then he ought to be working in a laboratory or a bureau.

Art is a concrete and personal and rather childish thing after all—no matter what people do to graft it into science and make it sociological and psychological; it is no good at all unless it is let alone to be itself—a game of make-believe, or re-production, very exciting and delightful to people who have an ear for it or an eye for it. Art is too terribly human to be very "great," perhaps. Some very great artists have outgrown art, the men were bigger than the game. Tolstoi did, and Leonardo did. When I hear the last opuses, I think Beethoven did. Shakespeare died at fifty-three, but there is an awful veiled threat in *The Tempest* that he too felt he had outgrown his toys, was about to put them away and free that spirit of Comedy and Lyrical Poetry and all the rest he held captive—quit play-making and verse-making for ever and turn his attention—to what, he did not hint, but it was probably merely to enjoy with all his senses that Warwickshire country which he loved to weakness—with a warm physical appetite. But he died before he had tried to grow old, never became a bitter old man wrangling with abstractions or creeds. . . .

Alphabetical List of Titles
and Authors Reviewed

Chronology

1873   Born December 7 in Back Creek Valley, near Winchester, Virginia, in the home of maternal grandmother, Rachel Seibert Boak, first child of Charles Fectigue Cather (b. 1848) and Mary Virginia ("Jennie") Boak Cather (b. 1850). Named Wilella for aunt who died of diptheria; called "Willie" by parents. (Cather family had emigrated from Northern Ireland and settled in the Winchester area after the Revolutionary War. Maternal grandfather, William Boak, served in the Virginia House of Delegates, and two of Cather's Boak uncles fought in the Confederate Army.) Father, who had studied law but never practiced, raises sheep for sale in Baltimore and Washington.

1874   Family moves to grandfather William Cather's nearby farm, Willow Shade, accompanied by Rachel Boak. Father manages his father's sheep farm until 1883 (later Cather often will accompany him on his rounds).

1877   Grandparents William and Caroline Cather emigrate with three daughters to Webster County, Nebraska, where their son George and his wife, Frances, are successful farmers. Brother Roscoe born.

1879–82   Strongly affected by reunion of household servant and her daughter, who had escaped from slavery to Canada before the Civil War. Taught to read by Grandmother Boak from the Bible, *Pilgrim's Progress*, and *Peter Parley's Universal History*. Listens to stories told by local women who come to Willow Shade to make quilts, especially Mary Ann Anderson, whose mildly retarded daughter, Marjorie (Margie), works for the Cathers as a housemaid. Brother Douglass born 1880 and sister Jessica in 1881. Begins to call herself "Willa Love Cather," claiming to be named after uncle William Seibert Boak, killed in the Civil War, and the Dr. Love who had attended her birth.

1883   When sheep barn burns down and grandfather refuses to rebuild, Willow Shade is sold. Family, along with Rachel Boak, Marjorie Anderson and her brother, and cousins Bess Seymour and Will Andrews, moves to the Nebraska

Divide (the high plains between the Republican and Little Blue rivers) and lives for a year and a half on grandparents' farm. Mother becomes ill and suffers a miscarriage. Distressed at first by change from sheltered to exposed landscape "as bare as a piece of sheet iron," Cather soon adapts to the prairie. Briefly attends school during winter. Visits homesteads of immigrant settlers from Scandinavia, Russia, Germany, France, and Bohemia and develops friendships with pioneer farm women; listens to stories of their homelands. Ill for part of year (possibly with mild case of polio), but makes full recovery.

1884　　In September father sells livestock and farm equipment and family moves into small frame house in Red Cloud, prairie town sixteen miles southeast. Household includes Rachel Boak, Marjorie Anderson, and Bess Seymour. Father opens a real estate and loan office and Cather attends school. Meets Englishman William Ducker, a storekeeper who teaches her Greek and Latin (they read Virgil, Ovid, Homer, and Anacreon together), and the Wieners, French- and German-speaking neighbors who introduce her to European literature. Discovers romantic adventure fiction and enjoys becoming "Caesar or Napoleon at will."

1885　　Sees plays for the first time at newly opened Red Cloud Opera House. Becomes close friends with the Miner sisters (Mary, Margie, Irene, and Carrie), daughters of a local storekeeper, and participates in amateur theatricals with them (will retain lifelong ties with Irene and Carrie).

1886　　Cather crops her long hair and often wears boys' clothes; sometimes calls herself "William Cather, M.D." (I was determined then to be a surgeon.)

1888　　Brother James is born and mother is ill. Cather's interest in science leads to experiments with dissection and vivisection. Plays Beauty's father in *The Beauty and the Beast*, performed with friends at the Opera House. Begins personal library with Pope's translation of *The Iliad* (soon includes Jacob Abbott's *Histories of Cyrus the Great and Alexander the Great*, George Eliot's *The Spanish Gypsy*,

Thomas Carlyle's *Sartor Resartus*, and Shakespeare's *Antony and Cleopatra*).

1890   June, graduates from Red Cloud High School in class of three and delivers speech "Superstition versus Investigation" in defense of scientific inquiry and experimentation. September, moves to Lincoln and enrolls as a second-year student in the Latin School, two-year preparatory school of the University of Nebraska. Sister Elsie born.

1891   First published essay, "Concerning Thos. Carlyle," appears March 1 in the *Nebraska State Journal* (signed "W.C."), submitted by her English instructor; appears unsigned in the university paper *Hesperian*. Becomes more interested in literature than in science. September, matriculates as freshman at the University of Nebraska, where she studies Greek (for three years, including Pindar, Homer, Herodotus, drama and lyric poetry), Latin (for two years), Anglo-Saxon, Shakespeare and other Elizabethan dramatists, Browning and other 19th-century writers (including Tennyson, Emerson, Hawthorne, and Ruskin), French (reads Daudet, Gautier, Balzac, Racine, and Taine), German (for one year), as well as courses in history, philosophy, rhetoric, journalism, chemistry, and mathematics; is particularly drawn to French literature and to the classics. Friends and fellow students include Louise Pound, Mariel Gere, and Dorothy Canfield. Becomes active in student publications and literary, debating, and theatrical societies, and attends the theater. Changes middle name from "Love" to "Lova." In November essay "Shakespeare and Hamlet" published in the *Nebraska State Journal*.

1892   May, first short story, "Peter," published in Boston literary weekly *The Mahogany Tree* after submission by another teacher. First poem, "Shakespeare: A Freshman Theme," published in the June *Hesperian*. (Will publish short fiction in the *Hesperian* throughout her university career.) Before returning to Red Cloud for the summer, writes Louise Pound expressing her affection. Becomes literary editor of the *Hesperian* in fall and appears in two plays. Brother John Esten (Jack) is born. Begins to let hair grow out.

1893   Grandmother Rachel Boak and old friend and teacher William Ducker die. Louise Pound declines an invitation to Red Cloud for the summer and the friendship cools. Becomes managing editor of the *Hesperian* in the fall and in November begins to contribute regularly to the *Nebraska State Journal*, writing both columns and drama reviews (continues until 1900). Develops reputation for scathing "meat-ax" criticism. Attacks the "primal slime" of Zola's and Hamlin Garland's journalistic naturalism and praises the romantic fiction of Kipling, Stevenson, Dumas, and Anthony Hope.

1894   In the spring publishes lampoon of a "University Graduate" in the *Hesperian*. ("He loves to take rather weak minded persons and browbeat them, argue them down, Latin them into a corner, and botany them into a shapeless mass.") The Pound family identifies the character as Louise's brother Roscoe Pound and breaks with Cather. (Though friendship with Louise cools, she and Cather later resume correspondence.) Becomes literary editor of the school annual, *Sombrero*.

1895   Travels to Chicago in March to attend opera—the beginning of an enduring fascination—and has photograph taken wearing a cape trimmed with Persian lamb and a hat with an ostrich feather. June, reads paper on Poe to joint meeting of the literary societies. ("With the exception of Henry James and Hawthorne, Poe is our only master of pure prose.") Graduates from the university. Remains in Lincoln through the fall as an associate editor for the Lincoln *Courier*, where she comments on women novelists in her column "The Passing Show": "When a woman writes a story of adventure, a stout sea tale, a manly battle yarn, anything without wine, women and love, then I will begin to hope for something great from them."

1896   Returns to Red Cloud. Continues writing for the *Journal* and visits Lincoln frequently to see plays and friends. Publishes "On the Divide," first story in a national magazine, in January *Overland Monthly*. Complains to Mariel Gere of isolation and boredom, datelining her letters "Siberia." Tries to obtain teaching position at the University of Nebraska but is rejected. Leaves for Pittsburgh in June after securing, with help of friends, job as editor of the *Home Monthly*, a women's magazine designed to compete with the *Ladies' Home Journal*. Stays in home of publisher, then moves to a boarding house at 309 South Highland Avenue. Meets Rudyard Kipling, whose "virile" sensibility she admires. Writes Mariel Gere in August, "There is no God but one God and Art is his revealer: that's my creed and I'll follow it to the end, to a hotter place than Pittsburgh if need be." Finds the magazine's editorial policy "namby-pamby" and the work uncongenial but determines to succeed. Publishes several stories and poems, employing a variety of pseudonyms, continues to send drama column "The Passing Show" to Lincoln papers, and writes drama reviews for the *Pittsburg Leader*.

1897   January, begins to contribute a book column to the *Home Monthly* (signed "Helen Delay"). "The Count of the Crow's Nest" published in *Home Monthly* after Cather declines offer of $100 from *Cosmopolitan*. Begins an active social life, enjoying boat excursions and picnics, and enters the city's theatrical and musical circles. Becomes close friends with George and Helen Seibel and reads French literature (Flaubert, Hugo, de Musset, Verlaine, Baudelaire) with them. In the spring sees a week of Wagnerian opera at the Carnegie Music Hall and enjoys a visit from Dorothy Canfield. Visits Red Cloud for the summer. Resigns from *Home Monthly* when it changes ownership (continues to contribute book column until February 1898). Returns to Pittsburgh in September to work on the *Leader*'s telegraph desk, earning $75 a month, and is paid extra for drama criticism. Moves to boarding house at 304 Craig Street. In October begins writing "Books and Magazines" column for the *Leader*. Reads A. E. Housman's *A Shropshire Lad* and decides they are "brothers in exile." Begins friendships with actress Lizzie Hudson Collier and composer Ethelbert Nevin. November, uses "Sibert" as pseudonym for the first time, a name associated with uncle William Seibert Boak, killed fighting for the Confederacy.

1898   Spends week in New York in February where she reviews plays for the New York *Sun*, attends the Metropolitan Opera, and lunches with Polish actress Helena Modjeska. Returns to Pittsburgh in time to write the *Leader*'s headlines on the sinking of the *Maine*. In May spends two weeks in Washington, D.C., with cousin James Howard Gore, professor of geography at Columbian University (later George Washington), and his Norwegian wife, Lillian. In August travels to Red Cloud, the Black Hills, and Wyoming. Becomes ill with the "grippe" after returning to Pittsburgh and spends several days with Dorothy Canfield in Columbus, Ohio, recuperating.

1899   In Lizzie Collier's dressing room, is introduced to Isabelle McClung, 21-year-old daughter of wealthy and prominent Pittsburgh judge Samuel McClung and his wife, Fannie. Drawn together by shared interests in theater, music, and literature, they begin a close friendship that lasts throughout McClung's lifetime. Visits often at McClung household ("chez the goddess"). Under McClung's influence develops greater interest in female dress, favoring satins, velvets, and bright colors. Attacks Gertrude Atherton in *Leader* book column for imitating Henry James in *The Daughter of the Vine* and criticizes Kate Chopin for creating a "self-limited" romantic heroine in *The Awakening*. Moves to boarding house at 341 Sheridan Avenue. August, returns to Red Cloud by way of the Great Lakes, stopping at Mackinac Island in Michigan.

1900   "Eric Hermannson's Soul" published in the April *Cosmopolitan* (signed "Willa Sibert Cather," which remains her professional signature until 1920). Begins contributing stories, poems, and articles to new Pittsburgh literary magazine, *The Library*. Resigns from the *Leader* in the spring. On May 12 last drama column appears in Lincoln *Courier*. Partly fictional reminiscence, "When I Knew Stephen Crane," published in the June *Library* (signed "Henry Nicklemann"), in which she claims to have met Crane during his 1895 visit to Lincoln. Moves to boarding house at 6012 Harvard Street. Goes to Washington, D.C., in the fall, where she translates French materials for Gore in connection with his service as juror at the Paris International Exposition and as government consultant. Contributes columns on the Washington scene to the *Nebraska State Journal* and the *Index of Pittsburgh Life*.

1901   Ethelbert Nevin dies, February 17, at the age of 38; Cather attends funeral in Pittsburgh. Visits Washington home of popular sentimental novelist Mrs. E.D.E.N. Southworth

(1819–99). Impressed by the thousands of letters sent by Southworth's readers, writes in *Journal* column that this devotion far exceeds that elicited by Henry James. "Jack-a-boy" is published in the March *Saturday Evening Post*. Returns to Pittsburgh in the spring to live with Isabelle McClung and her family in their elegant Murray Hill Avenue home, and is given her own study (remains until 1906). Teaches Latin at Central High School at salary of $650 a year. Spends the summer in Lincoln, where she is guest editor of the *Courier* in August. Returns to Pittsburgh in September to teach English at Central.

1902   Publishes four poems in *Harper's Weekly*, *Lippincott's*, and *Youth's Companion*, including "The Namesake," about William Seibert Boak. ("Lies a lad beneath the pine / Who once bore a name like mine.") Makes first trip to Europe in June, accompanied by Isabelle McClung. Visits western England, London, Paris, Marseilles, and Provence and sends travel letters back to the *Journal*. Joined by Dorothy Canfield in London. Visits A. E. Housman at his Highgate lodgings, but is disappointed by his reserve. In Paris visits the tombs of Balzac, Alfred de Musset, the younger Dumas, and Heine. Returns to Pittsburgh in September.

1903   January, " 'A Death in the Desert' " appears in *Scribner's*. *April Twilights*, collection of thirty-seven poems, published in April by Richard G. Badger. Sends several stories to S. S. McClure, who invites her to New York; at initial meeting on May 1, he promises to publish stories in *McClure's Magazine* and in book form. Returns to Nebraska for the summer where she meets Edith Lewis, a Lincoln native and recent graduate of Smith College. Begins teaching English at Pittsburgh's Allegheny High School in September.

1904   "A Wagner Matinée," published in the February *Everybody's Magazine*, criticized in Nebraska for its bleak portrayal of a farm woman's life. Spends the summer working on a collection of short stories and visits Edith Lewis in New York for a week, where Lewis works for the Century Publishing Company.

1905   "The Sculptor's Funeral" published in January *McClure's*. March, *The Troll Garden*, collection of seven short stories, including four new stories ("Flavia and Her Artists," "The Garden Lodge," "The Marriage of Phædra," "Paul's Case") and three most recent magazine works, published by McClure, Phillips & Co. Spends the summer in the West with Isabelle McClung: visits Douglass in Cheyenne, camps with Roscoe in the Black Hills, and stays with parents in Red Cloud for a month. Goes to New York for a week at end of summer, sees S. S. McClure and stays with Edith Lewis. Returns to Pittsburgh at start of school year. Attends birthday dinner for Mark Twain on December 5 at Delmonico's in New York.

1906   Accepts offer from S. S. McClure of job at *McClure's Magazine* when several staff members, including Ida Tarbell and Lincoln Steffens, resign to form a rival publication. Moves to New York in late spring and lives in the same Greenwich Village apartment building as Edith Lewis at 60 Washington Square South. Colleagues at *McClure's* include Viola Roseboro, Witter Bynner, Ellery Sedgwick, Cameron Mackenzie, and eventually Edith Lewis (who later described life at the magazine as "working in a high wind" in which S. S. McClure was the "storm center").

1907   Moves to Boston on assignment for *McClure's*, verifying, researching, and extensively rewriting Georgine Milmine's *The Life of Mary Baker G. Eddy and the History of Christian Science*. Lives in the Parker House hotel, then moves to an apartment on Chestnut Street. Enjoys an active social life, meeting editor Ferris Greenslet, poet Louise Imogen Guiney, novelist Margaret Deland, and attorney Louis Brandeis and his wife, Alice. Publishes four stories in 1907 (three in *McClure's* and one in *Century*) and a poem, "The Star Dial," in which she assumes the persona of Sappho.

1908   In March meets Annie Fields, widow of Boston publisher James T. Fields, and Sarah Orne Jewett at Fields' Beacon Hill home at 148 Charles Street—the "house of memories." Develops close friendships with both women, visiting often in Boston, Thunderbolt Hill (Fields' summer home in Manchester, Massachusetts), and Jewett's home in South Berwick, Maine. Travels to Europe in late spring with Isabelle McClung, spending several weeks in Italy. Returns to New York in fall and moves into an apartment at 82 Washington Place with Edith Lewis. Becomes managing editor of *McClure's*. November, Jewett writes of her "delight" in "On the Gull's Road," which appears in the December *McClure's*. ("It makes me the more sure that you are far on your road toward a fine and long story of very high class.") Cather writes Jewett of her nervous exhaustion and despair that her literary talents are not developing. Jewett reassures Cather of her artistic promise, praising "The Sculptor's Funeral," and urging her to find the "time and quiet to perfect your work."

1909   January, rejects several poems submitted by future playwright Zoë Akins; the two women begin a lifelong correspondence and friendship. Publishes "The Enchanted Bluff," story drawing on her Nebraska past, in the April *Harper's*. May, travels to London to solicit manuscripts and contact authors for *McClure's*. Meets drama critic William Archer, H. G. Wells, and Ford Madox Ford, and attends performances of the Abbey Theatre with Lady Gregory. Sarah Orne Jewett dies, June 24. Cather writes Fields that life is "dark and purposeless" without her. Visits Red Cloud in September and October. Returns to New York and assumes sole responsibility for editing *McClure's* when S. S. McClure leaves for Europe. Gives 1875 as year of birth in her first submission to *Who's Who*.

1910   Meets Elizabeth Sergeant, a young Bryn Mawr graduate who had submitted an article on sweatshop workers to *McClure's*. Sergeant becomes close friend and literary confidante for several years.

1911   February, suffers attack of mastoiditis and spends several weeks in the hospital. Travels to England for *McClure's* after recovery. Visits South Berwick in the spring, where she stays with Sarah Orne Jewett's sister, Mary. Meets Elizabeth Sergeant in Gloucester, Massachusetts, and the two visit Annie Fields in Boston. Returns to Boston in May for a week with Fields and in June again visits South Berwick. Annie Fields' edition of *Letters of Sarah Orne Jewett*, including correspondence with Cather, appears. Over the summer begins *Alexander's Bridge*. "The Joy of Nelly Deane" published in *Century*. Takes leave of absence from *McClure's* in October and spends three months with Isabelle McClung in Cherry Valley, New York; there she rests, revises *Alexander's Bridge*, and writes "The Bohemian Girl" and finishes "Alexandra" (later incorporated into *O Pioneers!*); both stories have Western settings. Returns to New York at the end of the year.

1912　Has small surgical operation in Boston in January. *Alexander's Bridge* published as *Alexander's Masquerade* in *McClure's* in three installments beginning in February. Ferris Greenslet had accepted the novel for Houghton Mifflin, and it appears in April (under original title). Brings "The Bohemian Girl" to Cameron Mackenzie, McClure's son-in-law, now managing editor at *McClure's*, who offers $750 for the story; Cather accepts only $500, the standard payment during her editorship. After attending W. D. Howells' seventy-fifth birthday dinner celebration, leaves in March to visit brother Douglass in Winslow, Arizona, and spends the next few months exploring the Southwest—the beginning of a strong attachment to this region. Visits Indian ruins, explores canyons and cliff dwellings, and attends a Hopi snake dance. Becomes infatuated with young Mexican man living in Winslow and writes to Elizabeth Sergeant describing his beauty and elegance. Spends June in Nebraska where she sees the wheat harvest for the first time in several years. Extends leave from *McClure's*, though agrees to accept a few special editing assignments. Stays with the McClungs in Pittsburgh through the fall, writing "The White Mulberry Tree" (will combine with "Alexandra" to form basis of *O Pioneers!*).

1913　January, returns to New York and moves with Edith Lewis into seven-room apartment at 5 Bank Street. They hire Josephine Bourda, a Frenchwoman, to cook and keep house for them. Returns to *McClure's* on half-time basis. Interviews (for *McClure's*) Wagnerian soprano Olive Fremstad and they become friends. Begins ghost-writing S. S. McClure's autobiography, working from his spoken reminiscences. June, *O Pioneers!*, dedicated to Sarah Orne Jewett, published by Houghton Mifflin Company to enthusiastic critical reception. Travels to childhood home in Virginia with Isabelle McClung in September and spends the fall in Pittsburgh working on *The Song of the Lark*. *My Autobiography*, credited solely to McClure, runs in *McClure's* from October to May 1914 (published as a book by Frederick A. Stokes Co. in September 1914). Returns to New York in November.

1914 Hospitalized in February for blood poisoning resulting from hat-pin scratch. Spends most of the year in Pittsburgh writing *The Song of the Lark*, with summer visits to Olive Fremstad in Maine and to Nebraska and the Southwest.

1915 Saddened by Annie Fields' death in February. Continues working on *The Song of the Lark* and sends most of the manuscript to Ferris Greenslet at Houghton Mifflin in March. Spends summer in the Southwest with Edith Lewis, traveling to Mesa Verde, Taos, and Santa Fe, and returns to Pittsburgh in the fall. Judge McClung dies in October and Cather stays with Isabelle through the winter. *The Song of the Lark* published by Houghton Mifflin in October to good reviews, including H. L. Mencken's announcement that "Miss Cather, indeed, here steps definitely into the small class of American novelists who are seriously to be reckoned with."

1916 Isabelle McClung marries violinist Jan Hambourg in April. Cather is surprised and devastated. "The Bookkeeper's Wife" published in the May *Century* and "The Diamond Mine" in the October *McClure's*. Signs with literary agent Paul Reynolds and resolves to let him handle placement of short fiction and serialization. Accompanied by Edith Lewis, returns to Santa Fe and Taos in the summer and goes alone to visit brother Roscoe in Wyoming, stopping off in Red Cloud on the way east. Returns to Bank Street in fall and works on *My Ántonia*. Commissions artist W. T. Benda to do the illustrations and consults with him frequently. Fights to keep illustrations when Houghton Mifflin balks at their cost.

1917 "A Gold Slipper" appears in the January *Century*. Visits Lincoln in June to accept first honorary degree, a Doctor of Letters from the University of Nebraska (others honored include fellow graduates Roscoe Pound and General

Pershing). Visits Isabelle and Jan Hambourg at the Shattuck Inn in Jaffrey, New Hampshire, and stays through the summer and fall, working on *My Ántonia* in a tent pitched in a meadow.

1918   Ill for several weeks in January and February; progress on *My Ántonia* slows. "Ardessa" appears in the May *Century*. Sends last of *My Ántonia* to Houghton Mifflin in June and spends several weeks in Jaffrey, then travels to Red Cloud. Cooks for family while mother is ill. Reads letters written to her aunt Frances by Frances' son, G. P. Cather, killed in action at Cantigny in May. Begins to plan novel *Claude* (later retitled *One of Ours*) inspired by his life and death. September, *My Ántonia*, dedicated to Irene and Carrie Miner, published by Houghton Mifflin to positive reviews from H. L. Mencken and Randolph Bourne. Slow sales are disappointing (earns $1,300 in first year of publication, $400 in the second). Spends the fall interviewing soldiers and working on *Claude*.

1919   Becomes increasingly dissatisfied with Houghton Mifflin's approach to book design, advertising, sales, and marketing. Works on *Claude* during the spring at Bank Street and the summer and fall in Toronto (during stay with the Hambourgs) and in Jaffrey. Two articles on the war effort—"Roll Call on the Prairies" and "The Education You Have to Fight For"—appear in *Red Cross Magazine*. Ill for several weeks with influenza in the fall. Enjoys a weeklong visit from father in November. Writes "Coming, Aphrodite!" during the Christmas holidays.

1920   Impressed with his list and attention to book design, signs contract with recently established publisher Alfred Knopf for *Youth and the Bright Medusa*, collection of eight stories, four of them revised versions of stories from *The Troll Garden*. Agreement marks beginning of long and important professional relationship (and eventually develops into close friendship with Knopf and his wife, Blanche). Travels to Paris with Edith Lewis in late spring, researching French background for *Claude*. Tours battlefields with Isabelle and Jan Hambourg and visits G. P. Cather's grave. Sees friends in Italy and returns to New York in November. Expurgated version of "Coming, Aphrodite!"

(retitled "Coming, Eden Bower!") appears in the August issue of Mencken's *Smart Set*. September, *Youth and the Bright Medusa* published by Alfred A. Knopf. Name on the title page appears as "Willa Cather"; retains "Sibert" only for signing checks. Spends fall and winter working on *Claude*.

1921 January, tells Ferris Greenslet of her decision to move permanently to Knopf. Reestablishes college friendship with Dorothy Canfield, now a well-known novelist and book reviewer. Stays with the Hambourgs in Toronto from April until August, working on novel, then goes with Lewis to Grand Manan, New Brunswick, an isolated island in the Bay of Fundy. Visits Nebraska in the fall. Tells a Lincoln journalist, "All my stories have been written with the material that was gathered — no, God save us! not gathered but absorbed — before I was fifteen years old." Finishes *Claude* and reluctantly agrees to Knopf's suggestion that it be retitled *One of Ours*.

1922 January, hospitalized for tonsillectomy; spends several weeks recuperating in a sanatorium in Wernersville, Pennsylvania, where she reads proof, writes letters, and complains about the food. "The Novel Démeublé," statement of aesthetic principles, appears in the April 12 *New Republic*. ("If the novel is a form of imaginative art, it cannot be at the same time a vivid and brilliant form of journalism. Out of the teeming, gleaming stream of the present it must select the eternal material of art.") July, teaches for three weeks at the Bread Loaf Writers' Conference in Middlebury, Vermont. Vacations on Grand Manan, and begins work on *A Lost Lady*. September, *One of Ours* published by Alfred A. Knopf. Distressed by negative reviews criticizing her for romanticizing the war, but controversy helps sales. Novel is commercial success, with 40,500 copies in print by November. Visits Red Cloud from Thanksgiving until New Year's for parents' fiftieth wedding anniversary. December 27, confirmed with her parents in the Episcopal Church by Dr. George Beecher, the Bishop of Nebraska, a family friend.

1923 *A Lost Lady* serialized in *Century*, April to June. April, *April Twilights and Other Poems*, dedicated to her father, published by Alfred A. Knopf. Retains twenty-four poems from the 1903 collection and adds twelve (in 1933 will add one more poem). Hires secretary to help with manuscript typing and correspondence. Sails to France for extended visit with the Hambourgs at their new villa at Ville d'Avray outside of Paris. Awarded Pulitzer Prize for Fiction for *One of Ours*. Suffers from neuritis in right arm and shoulder and is unable to write. Portrait, commissioned by the Omaha Public Library, painted by Léon Bakst; finds it unflattering. *A Lost Lady* published by Alfred A. Knopf in September, and by December is in sixth printing (50,000 copies). *One of Ours* has four additional printings (20,400 copies). Earns $19,000 in royalties from Knopf for year.

1924   Knopf sells film rights to *A Lost Lady* to Warner Brothers for $12,000. Cather agrees to edit a two-volume collection of Sarah Orne Jewett's fiction for Houghton Mifflin. Meets D. H. Lawrence, who comes to Bank Street for tea. June, receives honorary degree from the University of Michigan. Summers on Grand Manan and goes to Jaffrey in the fall. Works on the Jewett edition and *The Professor's House*. Introduction to Daniel Defoe's *The Fortunate Mistress* appears in new Knopf edition.

1925   Film version of *A Lost Lady* opens. Dismayed, Cather resolves never to permit another screen adaptation of her work. "Uncle Valentine" serialized, beginning in the February *Woman's Home Companion*. March, attends birthday dinner for Robert Frost in New York and presents him with copy of the recently published *The Best Short Stories of Sarah Orne Jewett*. April, receives letter from F. Scott Fitzgerald informing her that similar passages concerning the heroine's attractiveness in *A Lost Lady* and *The Great Gatsby* suggest a "case of apparent plagiarism," but that he had written his before reading her novel. Cather replies that she finds no cause for suspicion. "Katherine Mansfield" appears in *The Borzoi, 1925*, collection of essays published by Knopf. Works on *My Mortal Enemy*. Writes introductions to Gertrude Hall's *The Wagnerian Romances* and the Knopf edition of Stephen Crane's *Wounds in the Rain*. *The Professor's House* serialized in *Collier's* beginning in June and published by Knopf in September. Buys a

mink coat with *Collier's* money and tells a friend that "her
professor" has made the purchase. Travels with Edith
Lewis to the Southwest for the summer. Stays in Mabel
Dodge Luhan's guest house in Taos for two weeks and
visits D. H. and Frieda Lawrence on their ranch. Reads
Father W. J. Howlett's *Life of the Right Reverend Joseph P.
Machebeuf,* biography of 19th-century French missionary
in the Southwest. Spends fall in Jaffrey working on *Death
Comes for the Archbishop,* drawn in part from Howlett's
book. Has cottage built for her on Grand Manan.

1926   Revises introduction to *My Ántonia* for new edition pub-
          lished by Houghton Mifflin. Returns with Edith Lewis to
          New Mexico for the summer. Visits Acoma and the Mesa
          Encantada and stays in Mary Austin's house in Santa Fe.
          Stops in Red Cloud to visit her sick mother on the way
          home. Works on *Death Comes for the Archbishop* in July
          while in residence at the MacDowell Colony in Peterboro,
          New Hampshire. Spends fall in Jaffrey. *My Mortal Enemy*
          published by Knopf in October. Finishes *Death Comes for
          the Archbishop* and obtains from Knopf one-time increase
          in royalties from 15 to 16 percent.

1927   *Death Comes for the Archbishop* serialized in *The Forum*
          January–June, published by Knopf in September. Summer
          trip through Big Horn Mountains in Wyoming is cut
          short when father suffers severe attack of angina; returns
          to New York after visit to Red Cloud. Moves with Edith
          Lewis to the Grosvenor Hotel, 35 Fifth Avenue, when
          Bank Street apartment house is torn down. (Intends stay
          to be temporary, but lives there for five years.) Spends the
          fall in Jaffrey and returns to Red Cloud for Christmas.

1928   Returns to New York in late February. Father dies of heart
          attack, March 3. Travels to Red Cloud for the funeral
          and stays several weeks, experiencing, along with grief,
          renewed sense of connection to her family and past. Re-
          turns to New York in late April after stopping off at the
          Mayo Clinic for treatment. Writes story "Neighbour
          Rosicky." Becomes ill with influenza. June, receives hon-
          orary degree from Columbia University. Spends summer
          on Grand Manan. Rereads Francis Parkman's histories
          during visit to Quebec City with Edith Lewis and meets

Abbé Henri Arthur Scott, Canadian ecclesiastical historian. Fall, begins *Shadows on the Rock* in New York. Returns to Quebec at Thanksgiving for two weeks of further research on Frontenac era. Marjorie Anderson dies and is buried in the Cather family plot. December, mother has paralytic stroke while staying with family in California.

1929   Spends spring in Long Beach, California, with her mother, who is partially paralyzed and unable to speak. Tries to work on *Shadows on the Rock* but finds concentration difficult due to intense distress over mother's condition. Elected to National Institute of Arts and Letters. June, receives honorary degree from Yale University. Visits Quebec and spends summer on Grand Manan. Goes to Jaffrey in fall, then returns to New York before spending Christmas in Quebec.

1930   Visits mother, now in Pasadena sanatorium, in the spring. "Neighbor Rosicky" serialized in the *Woman's Home Companion* (April–May). Sails for France in May with Edith Lewis. Stays with the Hambourgs in Paris and tours Brittany with them. Introduced by Jan Hambourg to Moshe and Marutha Menuhin and their children Yehudi, Hephzibah, and Yaltah. Meets and talks with Madame Franklin Grout, Flaubert's niece, in hotel dining room in Aix-les-Bains (reminiscence of encounter, "A Chance Meeting," appears in February 1933 *Atlantic Monthly*). Sails to Quebec in September and spends most of fall there and in Jaffrey. November, awarded Howells Medal for Fiction by the American Academy of Arts and Letters for *Death Comes for the Archbishop*. December, finishes *Shadows on the Rock*.

1931   Spends spring in Pasadena with mother; writes "Two Friends." Receives honorary degrees from the University of California at Berkeley and from Princeton University. Spends summer on Grand Manan. Writes "Old Mrs. Harris," featuring characters based on grandmother, mother, and herself. Mother dies August 30. Cather is unable to leave Grand Manan in time to attend funeral; writes Dorothy Canfield: "I feel a good deal like a ghost." *Shadows on the Rock* published in August by Knopf and taken as a Book-of-the-Month Club selection. Reviews are unenthusiastic, but sales reach 160,000 by Christmas. Travels to Red Cloud for family reunion at Christmas (her last visit to Nebraska); continues to send money and food to several local farm families severely affected by the Depression. (Will also contribute regularly to fund for support of now-destitute S. S. McClure, organized by Ida Tarbell.)

1932   "Two Friends" appears in the July *Woman's Home Companion*. Refuses Houghton Mifflin permission to sell film rights to *The Song of the Lark*. "Old Mrs. Harris" (under title "Three Women") serialized in the *Ladies' Home Journal*, September–November. Vacations on Grand Manan in summer, stays at Jaffrey in fall. *Obscure Destinies*, collection comprised of "Neighbour Rosicky," "Old Mrs. Harris," and "Two Friends," published by Knopf in August. Friendship deepens with Menuhin children, who regard her as "Aunt Willa"; reads Shakespeare, walks in Central Park with them. December, moves to new apartment at 570 Park Avenue despite continuing unhappiness with New York (remains in city partially because of Edith Lewis's job as copywriter at J. Walter Thompson advertising agency); encouraged by Josephine Bourda's return as housekeeper and cook (works for Cather until her return to France in 1935).

1933   Wins first Prix Femina Americain, prestigious French literary award, for *Shadows on the Rock*, after being nominated by panel of American women writers and literary figures. Begins work on *Lucy Gayheart*. June, receives honorary degree from Smith College. Spends summer on Grand Manan and fall in Jaffrey. Enjoys visit during island stay from niece Mary Virginia Auld, daughter of sister Jessica. Sprains tendons in left wrist, which becomes chronically inflamed (inflammation later spreads to right hand). Condition, which persists for remainder of her life, often necessitates an immobilizing brace and drastically interferes with writing of fiction, since she finds it impossible to dictate anything except correspondence.

1934   Finishes *Lucy Gayheart* in spring. Spends summer on Grand Manan, and at Jaffrey. Angered by new Warner Brothers film version of *A Lost Lady*, begins to take legal measures to prevent further screen adaptations of her work (eventually writes prohibitory provision into will). Sells serial rights to *Lucy Gayheart* to raise money for friends in Nebraska.

1935   *Lucy Gayheart* serialized in *Woman's Home Companion* March–July, published by Knopf in August. Reviewers accuse Cather of "supine romanticism" and criticize her for ignoring contemporary social problems. March, Isabelle Hambourg arrives in the United States, seriously ill with kidney disease. Cather visits her daily in hospital in New York for three weeks. Goes to Chicago with the Hambourgs in late spring; after six weeks in Italy with Edith Lewis during summer, rejoins Hambourgs after their return to France. Stays with them in Paris for two months. November, returns to New York.

1936   Develops friendship with young British aristocrat and writer Stephen Tennant. Spends summer on Grand Manan entertaining nieces Mary Virginia Auld and Margaret and Elizabeth (Roscoe Cather's twin daughters) and part of fall at Jaffrey. *Not Under Forty*, collection of essays, published by Knopf in November. In introduction expressing alienation from modern American life since the war, writes "the world broke in two in 1922 or thereabouts" and that she belongs to the former half. Writes "The Old Beauty" in autumn.

1937   Helps Houghton Mifflin prepare the "Autograph Edition" of her collected works. *O Pioneers!* becomes volume 1. Extensively cuts *The Song of the Lark*, which appears as volume 2, and places *Alexander's Bridge* and *April Twilights* together as volume 3. (Twelve volumes published by 1938.) When "The Old Beauty" is accepted by *Woman's Home Companion* without enthusiasm, Cather withdraws manuscript and makes no further attempt to arrange magazine publication. Begins work on *Sapphira and the Slave Girl* in spring, drawing heavily upon childhood memories and family stories from Virginia. Vacations on Grand Manan with nieces. Douglass Cather visits on her birthday.

1938–39 In the spring visits Virginia childhood home with Edith Lewis. Injures hand in accident in June. Elected to American Academy of Arts and Letters. Greatly distraught at deaths of brother Douglass in June and Isabelle Hambourg in October. Writes to Zoë Akins: "I think people often write books for just one person, and for me Isabelle was that person." Spends fall 1938 in Jaffrey but has trouble writing and is distressed at damage done to woods by recent hurricane. Works on *Sapphira* in New York into July of 1939, unwilling to interrupt work for a vacation.

1940   Deeply dismayed by surrender of French Army in June. September, finishes *Sapphira and the Slave Girl* while on Grand Manan. Writes Canfield: "I cannot tell you how much pleasure I had in listening to those voices which had been nonexistent for me for so many years, when other sounds silenced them." *Sapphira and the Slave Girl* published by Knopf on birthday. Spends Christmas holidays in the French Hospital in New York for treatment of right hand.

1941   Travels to San Francisco in spring to see brother Roscoe, who is recovering from a heart attack. Visits Victoria, British Columbia, and returns home by the Canadian Pacific Railroad. Begins novel set in Avignon, France. (Works on it intermittently over several years but is unable to make progress due to recurring hand pain and other health problems.) Enters the French Hospital in New York for week of rest in autumn.

1942   Develops friendship with Norwegian novelist Sigrid Undset (that "undaunted exile") after introduction by Alfred and Blanche Knopf. July, has gall bladder and appendix removed at Presbyterian Hospital. Recovers from operation but never regains full health. Fall, spends several weeks at the Williams Inn in Williamstown, Massachusetts, registered as "Miss Carter" to protect privacy. Follows war news closely and is deeply distressed by sense that civilization is crumbling.

1943   Unable to travel to Grand Manan due to war conditions. Spends summer (and the three succeeding) at the Asticou Inn on Mount Desert, an island off Maine. Receives hundreds of letters from servicemen reading her books in special armed forces editions and tries to answer some of them. Sees much of nephew and nieces.

1944   Writes "Before Breakfast." Receives Gold Medal of the National Institute of Arts and Letters. Embraces S. S. Mc-Clure, now 87, during ceremony.

1945   Writes story "The Best Years" during summer in Maine (appears with "The Old Beauty" and "Before Breakfast" in *The Old Beauty and Others*, published by Knopf in 1948). Brother Roscoe dies.

1946   Writes Zoë Akins of her physical and spiritual weakness since Roscoe's death. Has influenza in spring and spends month in Atlantic City convalescing. Informs Houghton Mifflin that she is not interested in Viking's proposal to publish *The Portable Willa Cather*. ("I simply refuse to be a 'portable.' [I]t seems to me the worst form of anthology yet devised.")

1947   Sees Yehudi and Hephzibah Menuhin in March before their departure for England. Dies at home in New York City on the afternoon of April 24 from cerebral hemorrhage. Buried in Jaffrey, New Hampshire, on April 28.

Note on the Texts

This volume contains short fiction, poetry, essays, reviews, and prefaces written by Willa Cather from 1892 to 1946. Included here are two novellas, *Alexander's Bridge* (1912) and *My Mortal Enemy* (1926); three collections of short stories, *Youth and the Bright Medusa* (1920), *Obscure Destinies* (1932), and *The Old Beauty and Others* (published posthumously in 1948); a collection of poetry, *April Twilights and Other Poems* (1933); and a collection of essays, *Not Under Forty* (1936). Almost all of the contents of these volumes first appeared in periodicals and were then revised by Cather for their first book publication. With the exception of the pieces in *The Old Beauty and Others*, they were all included in the "Autograph Edition" of her works published by Houghton Mifflin in 1937–38. Cather generally made few revisions for this edition, which contains extensive changes in punctuation, spelling, and paragraphing that reflect the house style of the Houghton Mifflin editors rather than Cather's own style. She took no part in preparing the English editions of her works, which were produced either by using the American sheets or by resetting from the American texts. The present volume includes an additional fourteen short stories and twenty one reviews and essays selected from writings Cather herself never collected in book form.

The texts of the fourteen uncollected stories included in this volume are taken from their original periodical appearances. "Peter," Cather's first published story, is the only story that appeared in several journals: *The Mahogany Tree*, May 21, 1892; *Hesperian*, November 24, 1892; and *The Library*, July 21, 1900. Cather made revisions in each of these versions, but because it is the first story she published, the text printed here is that of the earliest version in *The Mahogany Tree*. The texts of the other stories are as follows: "On the Divide," from *Overland Monthly*, January 1896; "Eric Hermannson's Soul," from *Cosmopolitan*, April 1900; "The Sentimentality of William Tavener," from *The Library*, May 12, 1900; "The Namesake," from *McClure's Magazine*, March 1907; "The Enchanted Bluff," from *Harper's Magazine*, April 1909; "The Joy of Nelly Deane," from *Century Magazine*, October 1911; "The Bohemian Girl," from *McClure's Magazine*, August 1912; "Consequences," from *McClure's Magazine*, November 1915; "The Bookkeeper's Wife," from *Century Magazine*, May 1916; "Ardessa," from *Century Magazine*, May 1918; "Her Boss," from *Smart Set*, October 1919; "Uncle Valentine," from *Woman's Home Companion*, February 1925; and "Double Birthday," from *Forum*, February 1929. ("Double Birthday" was anthologized in several collections during Cather's lifetime but not revised by her. It was selected for *Best Short Stories of 1929*, edited by E. J. O'Brien, who also included it in his *Modern Short Stories*, published in 1932. The story was also included in *A Modern Galaxy*, published by Houghton Mifflin in 1930.)

Cather completed writing *Alexander's Bridge* in December 1911. It was serialized in *McClure's Magazine* in three installments, February through April 1912, under the title "Alexander's Masquerade." Cather made some verbal revisions in the magazine version before its publication in book form by Houghton Mifflin Company on April 20, 1912. Cather wrote a preface for the second American edition, brought out by Houghton Mifflin in 1922, but made no revisions in the text for that edition. *Alexander's Bridge* was included, together with *April Twilights*, in the third volume of the Houghton Mifflin "Autograph Edition" in December 1937. This edition omits the preface and includes a few minor verbal changes as well as many changes that reflect the house style of the editors. The text printed here is that of the first book edition. (Cather's preface is included in the section of Reviews and Essays in this volume.)

The eight stories in *Youth and the Bright Medusa*, Cather's second collection of short stories, had all appeared previously in periodical publications: "Coming Aphrodite!" (*Smart Set*, August 1920, under the title "Coming, Eden Bower!"; re-written and toned down sexually from Cather's original version), "The Diamond Mine" (*McClure's Magazine*, October 1916), "A Gold Slipper" (*Harper's Magazine*, January 1917), "Scandal" (*Century Magazine*, August 1919), "Paul's Case" (*McClure's Magazine*, May 1905), "A Wagner Matinée" (*Every-*

body's Magazine, February 1904), "The Sculptor's Funeral" (*McClure's Magazine*, January 1905), and "'A Death in the Desert'" (*Scribner's Magazine*, January 1903). In preparing the stories for book publication, Cather revised the periodical versions of the first four stories (in some cases restoring her original wording), and further revised the last four, which had been included in her first collection, *The Troll Garden* (1905), making the most extensive alterations and cuts in "The Sculptor's Funeral" and "A Wagner Matinée." The book was published by Alfred A. Knopf in September 1920. Cather made some revisions to the collection again when she prepared it as volume 6 in the "Autograph Edition" published by Houghton Mifflin in 1937; most significantly, she dropped "'A Death in the Desert'" and made additional cuts in "A Wagner Matinée." Even more changes were made by the editors of the edition in accordance with house style. The text printed here is that of the 1920 Knopf edition.

My Mortal Enemy first appeared in the March 1926 number of *McCall's Magazine* before being published by Alfred A. Knopf in October 1926. There are many differences in punctuation between the magazine and book versions that seem to reflect the style of *McCall's* editors rather than Cather's own usage. Some verbal changes were made in the magazine as well to soften the tone (for example, "hell" was changed to "wretchedness"). Cather made further verbal revisions in the proofs of the book edition. When she prepared the text for inclusion in the "Autograph Edition," she made very few changes, but the editors at Houghton Mifflin again made numerous alterations in Cather's punctuation, paragraphing, and spelling before the work was published in volume 11 (with *Lucy Gayheart*) in March 1938. The text printed here is that of the first book edition, published by Knopf in 1926.

All three of the stories in *Obscure Destinies* were first published in magazines. Two of them appeared in *Woman's Home Companion*: "Neighbour Rosicky" in April and May 1930, and "Two Friends" in July 1932. "Old Mrs. Harris" appeared (under the title "Three Women") in the September, October, and November 1932 numbers of *Ladies' Home Journal*. Cather carefully revised the magazine versions for the book, which was published by Alfred A. Knopf on August 5, 1932. Cather made no further revisions for the "Autograph Edition," but changes were made by the house editors before the work was published in volume 12 with *Literary Encounters* (title changed from *Not Under Forty*) by Houghton Mifflin in 1938. The text printed here is that of the 1932 Knopf edition.

The Old Beauty and Others, published posthumously by Knopf on September 13, 1948, is a collection of three stories— "The Old Beauty" (written 1936), "The Best Years" (written 1945), and "Before Breakfast" (written 1944)—which had not appeared in print during Cather's lifetime. The text of that edition is printed here.

April Twilights, Cather's first book, was published (with a subsidy from Cather) by Richard G. Badger: The Gorham Press, Boston, in spring 1903. Ten of the thirty-seven poems in the volume had appeared earlier in journals and had been revised for book publication, and one had been printed about the same time in another Badger publication. Apparently dissatisfied with the book, Cather bought and destroyed the remainder of the stock in 1908. In 1923 she dropped thirteen of the earlier poems, reordered and revised the remaining twenty-four, and added twelve new poems, six of which had appeared earlier in periodicals, in a second section. *April Twilights and Other Poems* was brought out by Alfred A. Knopf in two editions: a signed limited edition of 450 copies published February 20, 1923, and a trade edition of 1,500 copies published April 1923. An unchanged second printing of the trade edition appeared in January 1924. For the third printing in 1933, Cather added a new poem, "Poor Marty." The work was included in the "Autograph Edition" in 1937 (volume 3, with *Alexander's Bridge*), titled *April Twilights*. Cather dropped two poems from this edition, "In Media Vita" and "Song," and made revisions in a few other poems, but the bulk of the differences were made by the editors at Houghton Mifflin. The text printed here is that of the third, 1933, printing of the trade edition.

Not Under Forty is the only collection of nonfiction prose published by Cather during her lifetime. All six of the essays had appeared previously, some in very different versions. "A

Chance Meeting" (*Atlantic Monthly*, February 1933) was slightly revised for book publication; "The Novel Démeublé" (*The New Republic*, April 12, 1922) was revised verbally in a number of places; "148 Charles Street" ("The House on Charles Street," *New York Evening Post Literary Review*, November 4, 1922) was lengthened and extensively revised; "Miss Jewett" (Preface to *The Best Short Stories of Sarah Orne Jewett*, Boston: Houghton Mifflin, 1925) was extensively revised (two sections were added, and some of the original text was cut); "'Joseph and His Brothers'" ("The Birth of Personality: An Appreciation of Thomas Mann's Trilogy," *Saturday Review of Literature*, June 6, 1936) was revised and lengthened to restore material that was cut by the magazine for reasons of space; "Katherine Mansfield" (*The Borzoi 1925*, Knopf, 1925) was extensively revised, and parts I and III were added. *Not Under Forty* was published by Alfred A. Knopf in November 1936. When the book was included in the "Autograph Edition" (in volume 12, with *Obscure Destinies*, 1938), Cather changed the title to *Literary Encounters* and dropped her prefatory note. She made no revisions in the text and all other differences are due to the editorial staff at Houghton Mifflin. The text printed here is that of the 1936 Knopf edition.

This volume prints twenty-one reviews and essays that were not collected by Cather during her lifetime. The texts presented here are from their original appearances as follows: "Mark Twain," from *Nebraska State Journal*, May 5, 1895, and *The Home Monthly*, May 1897; "William Dean Howells," from *Nebraska State Journal*, July 14, 1895; "Edgar Allan Poe," from *The Courier*, October 12, 1895, and *The Home Monthly*, May 1897; "Walt Whitman," from *Nebraska State Journal*, January 19, 1896; "Henry James," from *The Courier*, November 16, 1895, and *Nebraska State Journal*, March 29, 1896; "Harold Frederic," from *Pittsburg Leader*, June 10, 1899; "Kate Chopin," from *Pittsburg Leader*, July 8, 1899; "Stephen Crane," from *Pittsburg Leader*, June 3, 1899, and November 11, 1899; "Frank Norris," from *The Courier*, April 8, 1899, January 13 and April 7, 1900; "When I Knew Stephen Crane," from *The Library*, June 23, 1900; "On the Art of Fiction," from *The Borzoi 1920*

(Knopf, 1920); "Preface to *Alexander's Bridge*" (Knopf, 1922); "Introduction to Daniel Defoe's *The Fortunate Mistress*" (Knopf, 1924); "Preface to Gertrude Hall's *The Wagnerian Romances*" (Knopf, 1925); "Introduction to Stephen Crane's *Wounds in the Rain and Other Impressions of War*," in *The Work of Stephen Crane*, volume 9 (Knopf, 1926); "On *Death Comes for the Archbishop*," from *Commonweal*, November 23, 1927; "My First Novels (There Were Two)," from *Colophon*, June 1931; "On *Shadows on the Rock*," from *Saturday Review of Literature*, October 17, 1931; "Escapism," from *Commonweal*, April 17, 1936; "On *The Professor's House*," from *The News Letter of the College English Association*, October 1940 (under title "Literary Experimentation"); and "Light on Adobe Walls," from *Willa Cather on Writing* (Knopf, 1949).

This volume presents the texts of the original printings chosen for inclusion here but does not attempt to reproduce features of their typographic design, such as magazine text breaks and the display capitalization of chapter openings. The texts are printed without change, except for the correction of typographical errors. Spelling, punctuation, and capitalization are often expressive features, and they are not altered, even when inconsistent or irregular. The following is a list of typographical errors corrected, cited by page and line number: 15.16, "eighty"; 44.5, lips. "The; 46.3, undoubtly; 47.24, emphatically;; 47.34, its; 47.37, nevre; 48.12, Noboby; 48.18, pol; 49.9, kness; 50.32, sloftly; 51.6, eldset; 62.3–4, "Oh, . . . gleaming?"; 66.16, ready; 106.23, Bokunks; 123.32, Budapesth; 138.15, 0 ; 151.14, you; 169.16, message; 204.10, Manning; 250.7, unforseen; 262.27, growling; 310.2, Mrs; 375.10, Griffith's; 385.15, men; 387.32, Buddah; 397.35–36, meerchaum; 416.40, Eaton; 435.15, Baskt; 504.30, Stevens; 516.35, other.; 519.25–26, pupils. "Everett; 527.12, Katherine; 576.3, there's; 578.24, *Dear*; 590.22, slyly;; 608.20, Rudolf; 637.11, Templeton's; 663.27, Deed; 889.31, author; 890.7, medoicre; 890.34, Huclkeberry; 896.26, Bazantine; 896.36, marbled; 897.1, multitudious; 899.31, gettting thin, out; 899.32, Its; 903.21, irony or; 916.32, street and; 917.10, joyfuly; 917.25, books; 920.15, books; 921.2–3, "Dental Parlors,"; 921.7, porceclain; 921.8–9, warm." McTeague; 921.9, mountains." ¶ He; 921.23, "Dental Parlors";

921.23–24, "accommodation street"; 921.28, "doctor"; 922.3, Given;"; 922.14, shopkeers; 924.18, "McTeague's; 925.38, their; 926.3, himself; 931.13, equisitely; 933.11, of the of the; 966.16–17, anacolouthon.

Notes

In the notes that follow, the reference numbers denote page and line of this volume (the line count includes chapter headings). No note is made for material found in standard desk-reference books such as *Webster's Biographical* and *Webster's Collegiate* dictionaries. Quotations from Shakespeare have been keyed to *The Riverside Shakespeare*, ed. G. Blakemore Evans (Boston: Houghton Mifflin, 1974). Notes at the foot of the page in the text are Cather's own. For more detailed notes and references to other studies, see: William A. Curtin, ed., *The World and the Parish: Willa Cather's Articles and Reviews 1893–1902* (2 vols., Lincoln: University of Nebraska Press, 1970); Joan Crane, *Willa Cather: A Bibliography* (Lincoln: University of Nebraska Press, 1982); Margaret Anne O'Connor, "A Guide to the Letters of Willa Cather," *Resources for American Literary Study*, vol. 4, Autumn 1974, pp. 145–72. Bernice Slote, ed., *The Kingdom of Art: Willa Cather's First Principles and Critical Statements 1893–1896* (Lincoln: University of Nebraska Press, 1966).

UNCOLLECTED STORIES 1892–1929

6.21–31   French woman . . . him.]   Sarah Bernhardt (1845–1923) in Victorien Sardou's *La Tosca* (1887).

7.21   *"Pater . . . est."*]   "Our Father, who art in heaven."

8.1   *Divide*]   High plains in southern Nebraska between the Republican and Little Blue rivers.

12.5–6   Milton . . . hell.]   Cf. *Paradise Lost*, Book II, line 620.

13.14   "eighty"]   An 80-acre section of land. In the Midwest, public lands were surveyed in townships six miles square, each containing 36 sections of 640 acres. Quarter sections (160 acres), half sections (320), and eighties were common subdivisions; the Homestead Act of 1862 offered sections to anyone who would settle and cultivate the land for five years.

15.16   proved up]   Cultivated. To "prove up" meant to fulfill the legal conditions for the right to a government grant of land.

17.39   soaked with turpentine]   A purified form of turpentine was the main ingredient in a stimulating liniment.

24.40   *"Saul . . . me?"*]   Acts 9:4, 22:7, 26:14. The conversion of Saul (later called Paul) began on the road to Damascus, when in a vision he heard Jesus call to him.

25.4—5   worm . . . quenched.]   A reference to damnation in Isaiah 66:24 and Mark 9:44, 46, 48.

25.33   "*Lazarus, come forth!*]   John 11:43.

28.32   Siegfried]   A hero of Germanic legends, including *Der Ring Nibelungenlied* (c. 1200), and Wagner's operas *Siegfried* and *Götterdämmerung* (*Twilight of the Gods*), based on the legends.

29.4   Nicht wahr?]   Not true?

29.32—33   'Cavalleria Rusticana']   *Rustic Chivalry*, a one-act opera (1888) composed by Pietro Mascagni, based on the Giovanni Verga story and play (1880) of the same title.

29.37   Rossetti, . . . tears.]   Dante Gabriel Rossetti, "The Blessed Damozel," last line: "And laid her face between her hands, / And wept. (I heard her tears.)"

32.11—12   " 'The Miller . . . Princess!' "]   "The Indifference of the Miller of Hofbau" (1895) in *The Heart of the Princess Osra*, by Anthony Hope.

33.6—7   hair . . . Prince]   *The Princess* (1847), I, lines 1—3: "A Prince I was, blue-eyed, and fair in face, / Of temper amorous as the first of May, / With lengths of yellow ringlet. . . ."

33.35   "*If . . . out,*"]   Matthew 18:9.

38.9—10   how . . . been]   Cf. Shakespeare's "Sonnet 97," line 1. In the sonnet, "thine absence" reads "my absence."

38.25   épris]   Enamoured; in love with; smitten.

38.31   Constant]   French painter Benjamin Constant (1845—1902), whose paintings of Oriental subjects, inspired by a trip to Spain and Morocco in 1871, established his reputation.

38.35   barbaric pearl and gold]   Cf. Milton's *Paradise Lost*, Book II, lines 3—4: ". . . where the gorgeous East with richest hand / Showers on her kings barbaric pearl and gold."

39.30—31   old Silenus]   Son of a nymph and a god, Silenus is the companion of Dionysius. He is often represented as old, fat, bald, and intoxicated.

42.1   stone Doryphorus]   A Roman copy in marble, one of several still in existence, of the original bronze statue made around 450—440 B.C. by Polyclitus the Elder. Called the "Spear Bearer," it is also known as "The Canon" because it was made to embody the proportions of the ideal male form.

45.9—10   " 'And a day . . . a day.' "]   Cf. 2 Peter 3:8.

53.18   queens of France]   Statues of queens and illustrious women of France that line the terrace.

53.23   Quarter]   The Latin Quarter (*Quartier latin*), the university quarter of Paris on the left bank of the Seine.

54.2   *perroquets*]   Parrots.

62.18   Destinies]   In later Greek mythology, the Destinies or Fates are three goddesses who watch over human lives: Clotho attends the moment of birth, Lachesis spins out the actions and events of individual lives with threads of various lengths, and Atropos finally cuts the thread of life with a pair of scissors.

63.21   Gare]   Railroad Station.

65.17   Divide]   See note 8.1.

67.16–17   Columbus . . . north any more?]   On September 13, 1492, after a week of sailing west from the Canary Islands, Columbus observed that his ships' compasses declined or varied to the northwest in the evening and to the northeast in the morning, as compared to the North Star. This was an effect of two causes: the degree of declination or variation of the magnetic pole from true north, which changed as the ships moved westward, and of the movement of the North Star (relative to the surface of the earth), which in 1492 prescribed a circle of 3 degrees 27 minutes radius around the north celestial pole, significantly more than the circle of 78 minutes it prescribes today. Columbus correctly deduced that the North Star moved as well as the compasses.

67.18–19   another North Star]   Because of the precession of the earth's axis, the polestar changes over the centuries. In 2300 B.C. it was Thuban in the constellation Draco, and by A.D. 12000, Vega, in the constellation Lyra, will be the polestar. The present polestar is Polaris in the constellation Ursa Minor.

67.39–40   Napoleon . . . star]   Napoleon, who believed in signs and omens, thought he was guided to military glory by a star. "In Italy rose Napoleon's 'star,'" writes Ida M. Tarbell in *A Life of Napoleon Bonaparte* (1914), "that mysterious guide which he followed from Lodi [site of an important victory in his first Italian campaign] to Waterloo." Cf. also Byron's "Napoleon," lines 8–9: "Since he, miscalled the Morning Star, / Nor man nor fiend hath fallen so far."

68.12   *Golden Days*.]   *Golden Days for Boys and Girls* (1880–1907), a weekly of serialized fiction, published by James Elverson.

69.32–70.25   "There's a big . . . since."]   Cather retells the same legend in "Tom Outland's Story" in *The Professor's House*. The Enchanted Mesa is a sandstone butte 430 feet high near the pueblo of Acoma, west of Albuquerque, in central New Mexico.

74.3   "Queen Esther,"]   *Esther* (1732), by George Frederick Handel.

75.35—36   "There . . . Hill,"]   "There Is a Green Hill Far Away" (1848), hymn by Cecil Frances Alexander.

76.7   "The Ninety and Nine,"]   Methodist hymn; cf. Matthew 18:13.

80.1—3   merchants . . . mind,"]   *Commentaries on the Gallic War*, Book I, Section 1, line 3.

82.26—27   grasshopper . . . ant]   The grasshopper spends the summer singing while the toiling ant piles up winter stores in the fable "The Grasshopper and the Ant," by Jean de La Fontaine (1621—95).

89.1   *The Bohemian Girl*]   The songs in this story are from *The Bohemian Girl* (1843), an opera by the Irish composer Michael Balfe. Alfred Bunn wrote the libretto. It was one of the most popular English operas of its time, and a number of its songs were adapted and popularized.

91.22   'To them . . . given.']   Cf. Matthew 13:12, 25:29, Mark 4:25, Luke 8:18.

106.29   fair half section]   See note 13.14.

138.11   "Footprints . . . another,"]   Henry Wadsworth Longfellow, "A Psalm of Life" (1839), stanza 8, line 1. (In an earlier version, "Footprints" read "Footsteps.")

162.33—34   Floradora pompadour]   The hairstyle of the six "Florodora Girls" featured in the popular musical comedy *Florodora* (1899) by Leslie Stuart and Owen Hall. First performed in England, it ran for more than 500 performances after opening in New York on November 10, 1900. It was frequently revived.

167.29—30   Lochinvar . . . West]   Cf. Walter Scott, "Lochinvar," stanza 1: "Oh, young Lochinvar came out of the West." The ballad is in *Marmion: A Tale of Flodden Field* (1808), Canto V.

171.18—19   Shakspere-Bacon man]   A believer in the theory, first introduced in the mid-19th century, that Sir Francis Bacon wrote the works attributed to William Shakespeare.

171.19   perpetual-motion man]   A proponent of the theory that a mechanism could be invented that, once set in motion, would continually perform useful work.

171.38   phossy jaw]   Phosphorous necrosis of the jaw, a disease involving localized death of tissue, was an occupational hazard for match girls and match factory laborers.

191.21   Apollinaris]   Apollinaris water, an effervescent mineral water pro-
duced in Apollinarisburg, Germany.

200.35   "The Leopard's Spots"]   By Thomas Dixon (1902). It is subtitled
A Romance of the White Man's Burden.

207.31   got the mit]   "To get the mitten" meant "to be dismissed." It
could also mean "to be jilted."

209.2   *(Adagio non troppo)*]   A musical direction, usually written "Adagio
ma non troppo," meaning "Slowly, but not too much."

221.27–28   Bayreuth . . . Ring.]   A city in Bavaria, Germany, known for
its annual Wagner festival, a tradition that began in 1882. It is held in the
Festspielhaus, the theater Wagner had built for performances of great German
works, including his *Der Ring des Nibelungen* cycle, first performed as a whole
when the theater opened in 1876. (Despite Wagner's intention, only his
operas are performed there.)

222.15   Pure in heart.]   Matthew 5:8.

227.10   John Bennett]   John Bennet (1575?–1614) was an English madrigal
composer.

227.39   nippers]   Slang for eyeglasses, especially pince-nez.

228.9   Tristan and Iseult]   In the many medieval French and English ver-
sions of the legend, Tristan and Iseult, wife of Cornwall's King Mark, are
lovers. Having unknowingly consumed a love potion, they are dominated by
an irresistible passion for each other. In most versions, when the potion loses
its power, they repent and separate. Modern versions include poems by
Matthew Arnold and Swinburne and an opera by Wagner, *Tristan und Isolde*
(1865), in which the reunited lovers die together.

234.11–12   Be not . . . aside."]   Alexander Pope, "Essay on Criticism,"
lines 334–35.

235.11–14   Rhine music . . . maidens.]   The four *Ring* operas, based on
early German and Norse sagas, are: *Das Rheingold* (1869; *The Rhine Gold*), the
story of the theft of gold from the Rhine maidens by Albrecht, King of the
Nibelungs, his forging of the magic ring, and its theft by Wotan; *Die Walküre*
(1870; *The Valkyrie*), the story of the lovers Sieglinde and Siegmond, and
Wotan's putting to sleep of the Valkyrie, Brünnhilde, whom he surrounds
with a ring of fire; *Siegfried* (1876), the story of Sieglinde and Siegmond's son,
who obtains the magic ring, passes through the fire, and wakes Brünnhilde;
and *Götterdämmerung* (1876; *Twilight of the Gods*), in which the Rhine maid-
ens recover the magic ring after the tragic deaths of Siegfried and Brünnhilde.

235.25   Damrosch]   The German conductor and composer Leopold Dam-
rosch (1832–85), a friend of Wagner, came to the United States in 1871. He
organized and conducted the first German opera season at the Metropolitan

Opera in New York, 1884–85, which included the first complete American production of Wagner's *Die Walküre*, and led American premieres of many of Wagner's works.

241.27–28 *Telle est la Vie.*] Such is life.

255.25 *Yellow Book*] Illustrated quarterly of art and literature (1894–97) associated with an art-for-art's-sake philosophy and an emphasis on modern aesthetics that caused a public storm. It was published by John Lane, edited by Henry Harland, and its first art editor was Aubrey Beardsley.

256.29 Eighteenth Amendment] The amendment prohibited the manufacture, sale, or transportation of intoxicating liquors within the United States. Ratified in 1919, it took effect in 1920 and was repealed by the Twenty-first Amendment in 1933.

257.7 *Pélleas et Mélisande.*] Opera (1902) composed by Claude Debussy to Maeterlink's play (1892) of the same name.

257.35 "the lost Lenore."] From "The Raven" (1845) by Edgar Allan Poe.

259.6 *"Still . . . Meer."*] "Still as the night, deep as the sea," from "Still Wie die Nacht," by Carl Bohm (1851–1920).

261.30 *Monsieur . . . voyageur*] Mr. Commercial Traveler.

262.6–7 Pauline Garcia Viardot] Celebrated French opera singer Viardot-Garcia (1821–1910). She developed her own teaching method, and after retiring from the stage in 1863 taught at the Paris Conservatory from 1871 to 1875. She was the sister of Manuel Patricio Garcia, doctor, inventor of the laryngioscope, and singing teacher.

262.27–28 *aber kleine, kleine!*] But small, small!

262.30–31 Emma . . . Farrar] American sopranos and stars of the New York Metropolitan Opera Company. Eames (1865–1952) sang with the Metropolitan from 1891 to 1909, and Farrar (1882–1967) performed with the company more than 500 times from 1906 to 1922.

262.31 *la voix . . . raffinée.*] The white (i.e., pale, without effect) voice . . . too refined.

263.3–4 Slave . . . Swamp] The title of a poem (1842) by Henry Wadsworth Longfellow. The Dismal Swamp along the coast of southeast Virginia and northeast North Carolina frequently appears in literature as a refuge for runaway slaves.

263.18 *"Pourquoi,*] Why?

263.33 *Warum,*] Why?

263.36–38 Heine's . . . cruel."] *Confessions* (1854).

264.36 *les Chinoises*] The Chinese.

266.22   Rafael Joseffy]   A Hungarian pianist, Joseffy came to the United States around 1888 and taught at the National Conservatory of Music.

270.28–29   violets . . . Bonapartist?]   It is said that after his abdication following the fall of Paris in April 1814, Napoleon I vowed to return from exile on the island of Elba in the spring. His followers then began to wear violets, a spring flower, as a badge.

271.31   *Behüt' dich, Gott!*]   God bless you!

274.38–39   lost Lenore."]   See note 257.35.

275.29   *"Even in our ashes,"*]   Thomas Gray, *Elegy Written in a Country Churchyard* (1750), stanza 23: "E'en from the tomb the voice of nature cries, / E'en in our ashes live their wonted fires."

ALEXANDER'S BRIDGE

288.25–26   Prince Consort]   The German prince who married Queen Victoria in 1840, Albert of Saxe-Coburg-Gotha (1819–61), was granted precedence next to the queen and in 1851 received the title Prince Consort of Great Britain. A musician himself and a patron of the arts, he was a prime mover of the Great Exhibition of 1851 and helped to endow the South Kensington (later Victoria and Albert) Museum.

291.9   potheen]   Poteen is illegally distilled Irish whiskey.

291.18–19   gossoons]   From "garçon"; youths or servant boys.

295.36   Twickenham or Richmond]   In the 19th century, these Thames-side villages southwest of London were favorite sites for boating parties and picnickers.

297.22–23   Temple, . . . Middle Temple]   Two of the four Inns of Court (societies for the study of law), located on the south side of Fleet Street.

298.27   *de pontibus.*]   Of bridges.

301.18–19   Commander . . . Sun]   One of the classes of the chivalric order.

301.20   'The Mikado.']   *The Mikado, or The Town of Titipu* (1885), an operetta by W. S. Gilbert and Arthur Sullivan that debunked the Orientalia fashionable at the time.

303.31   fourth dimension]   The dimension beyond length, breadth, and thickness, therefore, something beyond ordinary human perception.

304.9   Lamb . . . care]   In his essay "The New Style of Acting," Charles Lamb (1775–1834) expresses a fondness for simple, unaffected acting.

305.10   Salon]   An annual exhibition in Paris of the works of living artists. The first Salon was held in 1667 in a large room (salon) of the Louvre palace.

306.30   Beaux Arts] École des Beaux-Arts (School of Fine-Arts).

306.35–36   *bains de mer*] Sea bathing.

307.1   *soldat . . . fin.*] Soldier . . . fine laundress (or clear-starcher).

308.32   'The Harp that Once,'] "The Harp that once through Tara's Halls," musical setting of a poem by the Irish poet Thomas Moore (1779–1852).

328.25   'Il Trovatore'] *The Troubadour*, opera (1853) composed by Giuseppe Verdi.

332.15–16   The little boy . . . stag.] In the Greek myth, Actaeon inadvertently wanders into a grove where Artemis and her nymphs are bathing. The enraged goddess splashes him with water, transforming him into a stag, and as he flees his own hounds pursue him and tear him to pieces.

333.20–22   study . . . renown] Perhaps a reference to John Singer Sargent (1856–1925), who began his formal studies at the École des Beaux-Arts in 1874, and whose paintings include *The Luxembourg Gardens at Twilight*.

338.27   It put . . . earth] In Shakespeare's *A Midsummer Night's Dream*, II.i.175–76, Puck says: "I'll put a girdle round about the earth / In forty minutes."

350.25–26   'Forget . . . marble'] Milton, *Il Penseroso*, line 42.

YOUTH AND THE BRIGHT MEDUSA

353.7   *Goblin Market*] By Christina Rossetti (1862). The epigraph was retained from Cather's first book of stories, *The Troll Garden* (1905), in which "Paul's Case," "A Wagner Matinée," "The Sculptor's Funeral," and " 'A Death in the Desert' " appeared.

359.29   Brevoort] Brevoort House was a hotel at the corner of Fifth Avenue and 8th Street.

360.35   "Don . . . Legend,"] *Don Quixote* (1605–15) by Miguel de Cervantes, and *The Golden Legend*, a medieval manual of church lore including lives of saints, sermons for saints' days, and commentary on church services (first printed in English by William Caxton around 1483).

362.36   Pagliacci] *I Pagliacci* (1892), opera by Ruggiero Leoncavallo.

364.26–27   man . . . dogs] See note 332.15–16.

365.27   Eden Bower] From Dante Gabriel Rossetti's poem "Eden Bower" (1870).

367.2   Helianthine fire] Helianthin is an analine dye of orange-yellow color.

374.28   "Sapho . . . Maupin,"] French novels. *Sapho* (1884) by Alphonse Daudet is the story of the courtesan Fanny Legrand and her lovers, including a young artist whom she subjugates completely, bringing about his moral and spiritual disintegration. In Théophile Gautier's *Mademoiselle de Maupin* (1835), a pair of lovers are smitten by Théodore, an exceptionally handsome young squire (Mlle. de Maupin in disguise). De Maupin grants the hero a night of "perfect love," but unable to truly love or commit herself to anyone, she soon leaves for further adventures.

394.6   Cerro de Pasco] Mining town in the gold, silver, and copper-mine district of central Peru.

394.11   *"Arrêtez . . . moi,"*] "Stop, Alphonse. Wait for me."

397.35–36   ageing skin . . . meerschaum] Pipes made of the white meerschaum are prized for the change in color that comes through use.

399.28   *la sainte Asie*] Holy Asia.

403.2–6   Prince . . . *missed her.*] Frederick Louis (1705–51), Prince of Wales, was the eldest son of George II. The verses are a version of those that appear in *Memoires of the Last Ten Years of the Reign of George II* (posthumously published in 1822), by Horace Walpole (1717–97).

409.30–33   Isolde . . . Brangaena] In Wagner's *Tristan und Isolde* (1865). A *teufelin* is a she-devil. (See also note 228.9.)

409.39   "Trilby"] In the novel (1894) by George du Maurier, Trilby is at first repelled by Svengali, but after falling under his spell she becomes a superb singer. They become lovers, and although Svengali exploits her, Trilby wastes away and dies after his death.

415.1   Sarka] Symphonic poem in the cycle *Má Vlast* (composed 1874–79) by Bedřich Smetana. (Sarka is the leader of Bohemian Amazons.)

415.3   *"Dans . . . tristes,"*] "In the shadows of sad forests."

416.24–25   *"Des gâteaux,"* . . . New York?"] "Cakes," . . . "where does she find such cakes here in New York?"

416.28   *"Austrichienne . . . pas."*] "Austrian? I don't think so."

421.26–27   *"Couleur . . . reines!"*] "Color of glory, color of queens!"

421.37   *"de l'eau chaude!"*] "Some hot water!"

422.1   *"Voilà, voilà, tonnerre!"*] "There, there, thunder!"

422.10   *Donna Anna*]   In Mozart's *Don Giovanni* (1787).

425.35   *oisiveté*]   Idleness; indolence.

427.34   *méprise*]   Wrong, offense, scorn.

428.33   *"Pour des gâteaux,"*]   "For some cakes."

429.3   *les colombes*]   The pigeons.

430.4–16   *Titanic. . . . Carpathia*]   The British liner carrying 2,224 persons struck an iceberg on the night of Sunday, April 14, 1912, and sank early Monday morning, April 15, with the loss of 1,513 lives. Its radio distress signal was heard by the smaller British liner *Carpathia*, which arrived 20 minutes after the *Titanic* went down, in time to rescue 711 survivors.

432.4–7   *Traulich . . . freut!*]   "Trusted and true / are down below: / false and cowardly / exalt on high!" from the Rhine maidens' song in the last act of Wagner's *Das Rheingold*.

433.7   Sewickley]   Borough west northwest of Pittsburgh, Pennsylvania.

434.17   Comique]   The Opéra-Comique, established in 1715.

437.36   *Faust*]   Opera (1859) composed by Charles Gounod.

444.27–28   San Francisco earthquake]   The earthquake of April 18, 1906, and the ensuing three-day fire destroyed most of the city.

451.23   Vanity Fair]   A sophisticated review of art, literature, and society (1913–36).

452.11   *caro mio*]   My dear.

461.7   Gorky's visit]   The year after the failed revolution of 1905, the Russian novelist came to the United States to raise funds for the Russian socialist movement abroad.

463.28   *'Per . . . indifferente,*]   "For me, it's all the same."

470.20   *Faust*]   See note 437.36.

470.35   Rico]   Martin Rico (1835–1908), Spanish landscape painter.

471.39–40   Genius . . . fisherman]   "The History of the Fisherman and the Genie" in *The Arabian Nights' Entertainments*.

477.25   *Martha . . . Rigoletto*]   Operas by Friedrich von Flotow (1847) and Giuseppe Verdi (1851).

483.24–25   *Blue Danube*]   Waltz (1867) by Johann Strauss II (1825–99).

491.5   *Euryanthe*]   Opera (1823) by Karl Maria von Weber.

491.22–23   *Huguenots*]   Opera (1836) by Giacomo Meyerbeer.

493.38   "Home . . . return!"] Popular song derived from an aria in
Verdi's *Il Trovatore*.

494.9   silent . . . Darien] In "On First Looking into Chapman's
Homer" (1816), John Keats compares his reaction to that of Cortez, who is
"Silent upon a peak in Darien" when he first sights the Pacific Ocean. (Keats
confused Cortez with Balboa, who crossed the Isthmus of Darien, now Pan-
ama, in 1513.)

494.19   "Prize Song,"] Courtship song that concludes Wagner's comic
opera *Die Meistersinger von Nürnberg* (1867).

494.33   Bayreuth] See note 221.27–28.

495.9   *Trovatore*] See note 328.25.

495.24   happy islands] In Greek mythology and literature, the final rest-
ing place of heroic and noble souls.

497.21   Grand Army] The Grand Army of the Republic (G.A.R.) was an
organization of Union Army veterans.

499.10   palm leaf] Sign of the *Palmes académiques*, a French order of
merit established in 1808 to reward academic excellence.

500.30   Rogers . . . Priscilla] John Rogers (1829–1904), popular Ameri-
can sculptor, used catalogues and mail order to sell thousands of plaster
copies of his small-group sculptures, often based on historical or literary
subjects. John Alden (c. 1599–1687) was a *Mayflower* Pilgrim who held various
colonial positions, and married Priscilla Mullens (or Molines). A legend
about their romance arose in the 19th century and is told in Henry Wads-
worth Longfellow's narrative poem *The Courtship of Miles Standish* (1858).

508.13   wine . . . red] Proverbs 23:31–32: "Look not thou upon the wine
when it is red, when it giveth his colour in the cup, when it moveth itself
aright. At the last it biteth like a serpent, and stingeth like an adder."

512.1   *"A Death in the Desert"*] The title is from a Robert Browning poem
(in *Dramatis Personae*, 1864) concerning the death of John the Apostle in the
desert near Ephesus.

513.19   Br'er Rabbit] A character in the *Uncle Remus* tales and poems of
Joel Chandler Harris (1848–1908).

517.34   Camille] The doomed, consumptive heroine of *Camille* by Alex-
andre Dumas the younger, a play popular in late-19th-century America based
on his novel *La Dame aux Camélias* (1848).

518.30   *Diana*] A statue of the Greek goddess Diana, by Augustus Saint-
Gaudens (1848–1907), stood atop the tower of Madison Square Garden from
1892 to 1925.

519.1   *Rheingold*] See note 235.4.

521.14   Tempe]   Valley in Thessaly.

525.6   Keats . . . hell]   "There is not a fiercer hell than the failure in a great object." Preface to *Endymion* (1818).

526.18−19   *'and the book . . . night.'*]   Francesca da Rimini's description of the beginning of her adulterous affair with Paolo, in Dante's *Inferno*, Canto V, line 138.

527.37−39   *"For ever . . . made."*]   Brutus's farewell to Cassius in Shakespeare's *Julius Caesar* (V.i.119−21), spoken shortly before his suicide and Cassius's death.

529.11   *"Herr Gott . . . Freund,"*]   Lord God . . . dear friend.

MY MORTAL ENEMY

535.37   Iroquois ball]   From the mid-19th century to the early 1900s, men's lodges such as the Loyal Order of Red Men and the New Confederacy of the Five Nations flourished in which white men imitated Indian dress, customs, and rituals and performed community service, such as holding charity balls.

539.16   *porte-monnaie*]   Purse.

540.30   "night of the grave"]   A reference to the belief that the dead will remain in their graves only until they are resurrected on Judgment Day; see, for example, John 5:28, 1 Thessalonians 4:13−16, 1 Corinthians 15:42−55.

544.13−15   Madison . . . Diana]   See note 518.30.

554.12−13   Jefferson de Angelais]   An American comedian, de Angelis (1859−1933) appeared in light operas, vaudeville, and plays, including *Fleur-de-Lis* in 1895, *The Jolly Musketeer* in 1899, and *Fantana* in 1905.

554.21   Marie Stuart]   One of Modjeska's starring roles was in *Maria Stuart* (1800) by Friedrich von Schiller.

555.1−2   Sarah . . . controversy]   Bernhardt's *Hamlet* roused controversy in London, Paris, and New York, because Bernhardt both took the lead role and used a new French prose translation of Shakespeare's play.

555.3   Jean de Reszke's]   De Reszke (1850−1925), a Pole (originally Jean Mieczyslaw), was the leading tenor with the Metropolitan Opera from 1891−1901.

555.12   *Norma*]   Opera (1831) composed by Vincenzo Bellini to Felice Romani's libretto.

555.18   *Casta Diva*]   "Chaste Goddess."

566.16   Gloucester's cliff]   Cf. Shakespeare, *King Lear*, IV.i.73–74, where Gloucester says: "There is a cliff, whose high and bending head / Looks fearfully in the confined deep."

567.19–20   Bible . . . adder.]   Cf. Psalm 58:4.

569.32–33   poem of Heine's]   Poem from "Die Heimkehr" ("The Home-coming") in *Buch der Lieder* (1823–24; "Book of Songs").

570.12–13   little short one . . . grave]   Poem 62 from Heine's *Lyrisches Intermezzo* (*Lyrical Intermezzo*).

571.10   brach!]   Bitch.

571.33   *Old John . . . Lan-cas-ter*]   Cf. *Richard II*, I.i.1.

572.25   Bozenta-Chlapowska]   Modjeska's second husband, with whom she came to the United States in 1876, was Karol Bozenta-Chlapowski.

576.4–5   Oh, . . . highway]   Cf. Shakespeare's *Richard II*, III.iii.155.

OBSCURE DESTINIES

583.1   OBSCURE DESTINIES]   Cf. Thomas Gray, "Elegy Written in a Country Churchyard" (1751), stanza 8: "Let not ambition mock their useful toil, / Their homely joys, and destiny obscure; / Nor grandeur hear with a disdainful smile, / The short and simple annals of the poor."

594.36   *kolache*]   Tea cakes.

598.3   Castle Garden]   Immigrants were processed at Castle Garden on the Battery from 1855 to 1892, before Ellis Island was opened. Originally a fort called Castle Clinton (built 1808), the site was first called Castle Garden when it was made into an opera house and amusement hall in 1823. After World War II it became Castle Clinton National Monument.

600.25–26   Bohemian athletic societies]   First established in Prague in 1862, gymnastic societies, or Sokols, were the most important social organizations for Czech immigrants in the United States, fostering patriotic education through athletic and cultural activities.

625.9   bound girl]   Indentured servant.

631.28   Waverly Novels]   By Walter Scott (1771–1832).

632.38–39   *Wilhelm Meister*]   *Wilhelm Meisters Lehrjahre* (*Apprenticeship*, written 1795–96) and *Wilhelm Meisters Wanderjahre* (*Travels*, written 1821–29) by Johann Wolfgang von Goethe.

633.15   *Faust*]   By Goethe. In *Part One* (1808) Faust, at the instigation of Mephistopheles, seduces Gretchen. (*Part Two* was published in 1832.)

633.26−27   *Dies Iræ*]   Medieval hymn, words attributed to Tomasso di Celano (c. 1185−c.1255). It was part of the Requiem Mass.

633.35−37   "Day . . . say.]   In Latin, the first stanza reads: "*Dies irae, dies illa / Solvet saeclum in favilla / Teste David cum Sibylla.*"

635.13   *Rigoletto*]   See note 477.25.

638.37   Roadmaster]   A railroad employee having charge of railroad bed maintenance in a division.

646.23   curling-kids]   A small device made of wire covered with soft leather used for curling hair.

659.7   *Uncle Remus*]   See note 513.19.

663.20−21   *The Chimes of Normandy*]   *Les Cloches de Cornveille* (1877), a light opera by Robert Planquette. It was also called *The Bells of Cornveille*.

667.32−33   "Old . . . Tennessee."]   "Old Jesse," an African-American ballad sung on plantations before the Civil War that crossed over into white audiences. In an earlier version, the chorus goes: "Ole Jesse was a gemman, / Among de olden times."

669.8   *Joe's Luck*]   Boy's novel (1878) by Horatio Alger, Jr.

669.15   *Pilgrim's Progress*]   *The Pilgrim's Progress, from this World to that which is to come, Part II* (1684), by John Bunyan.

674.6   Robert Emmet Dillon]   Irish revolutionary Robert Emmet (1778−1803) led an unsuccessful insurrection against England in July 1803. He was hanged for treason.

675.9   hopper men]   A term of contempt or reproach for men who live improvidently.

680.6   *Puck*]   Magazine (1877−1918) popular for its cartoons and political, religious, and social satire. Founded by Joseph Keppler and the printer A. Schwarzmann, it was originally an English version of the German-language edition that began in New York in 1876. (In German folklore, Puck is a name for malevolent spirits.)

683.34   *Pinafore*]   *H.M.S. Pinafore, or The Lass that loved a Sailor* (1878), comic opera by W. S. Gilbert and Arthur Sullivan.

685.1−2   free-silver agitation]   In 1862 Congress expanded the money supply by authorizing the treasury to issue paper currency irredeemable in gold ("greenbacks"). Under the specie resumption act of 1875, which took effect on January 1, 1879, the government was again obligated to redeem on demand its paper money with gold coin. The resumption act contributed to a substantial contraction of the money supply and increasing demands, primarily by in-debted farmers and small businesspeople in the South and West, for a new currency expansion, based upon the "free and unlimited coinage of silver." Silver proponents advocated backing the currency with silver as well as gold, with their relative value fixed at a ratio of 16 to 1. Opponents of the measure denounced it as dangerously inflationary, since the market value of silver was well below the proposed 16 to 1 ratio, and harmful to American standing in international finance and trade, which was conducted on a gold basis.

685.3–4   Democratic . . . Bryan.]   William Jennings Bryan (1860–1925), a former congressman from Nebraska (1891–95) and a leading advocate of "free silver," was nominated for president on the fifth ballot on July 11, 1896. Bryan was also the unsuccessful Democratic candidate in the 1900 and 1908 presidential elections.

685.27–28   Grover . . . nothing."]   During his second administration (1893–97) President Grover Cleveland resisted calls for the free coinage of silver and sought to maintain bullion reserves at a level sufficient to keep the currency on a gold basis. His policy caused a bitter split within the Demo-cratic party and was repudiated by the 1896 convention, which adopted a free-silver platform and nominated Bryan, an outspoken critic of the president.

685.35–36   Patrick Henry's]   Probably a reference to Henry's speech to the Virginia Convention on March 23, 1775, which contained the phrase "as for me, give me liberty or give me death!"

686.9   Pops.]   Populists, a common name for supporters of the People's party, which first ran candidates in the 1890 congressional and state elections. In the 1892 presidential election its platform called for an expanded and flex-ible currency system using gold, silver, and paper money backed by the credit of the government, public ownership of railroads and telegraphs, a graduated income tax, an eight-hour working day, direct election of U.S. senators, a single presidential term, and the national adoption of the secret ballot. Its candidate, James B. Weaver (1833–1912), won 22 electoral votes in Colorado, Idaho, Kansas, Nevada, North Dakota, and Oregon. In 1896 it endorsed the free-silver candidacy of Democratic nominee William Jennings Bryan.

686.25–27   "You . . . gold."]   From Bryan's speech delivered on July 9, 1896, in support of "free silver," during the platform debate at the Democratic national convention.

THE OLD BEAUTY AND OTHERS

706.27   Alhambra]   New York theater at Seventh Avenue and 126th Street that opened in 1905 and specialized in respectable vaudeville.

716.19   *the power of the dog,*]   Psalm 22:20: "Deliver my soul from the sword: my darling from the power of the dog."

721.21   "Blue Danube."]   See note 483.24−25.

723.14   leading]   Sheets or strips of lead used to cover a roof.

724.34   *"regardez, attendez,"*]   "Watch out, pay attention."

727.13   *à perpétuité*]   In perpetuity.

727.13   Père-Lachaise.]   Parisian cemetery where, as Cather noted in a 1902 dispatch from her European trip, many famous artists are buried, including de Musset, Fauré, Chopin, Balzac, Racine, Molière. These are "names," she quoted Balzac, "that make one dream."

729.30   fineless]   Infinite, boundless.

740.2   Pop.]   See note 686.9.

740.32−33   section, quarter.]   See note 13.14.

741.8−9   "far as human eye could see."]   "Locksley Hall" (1842), line 119.

743.33   They . . . love.]   Cf. Shakespeare, *Twelfth Night*, II.iv.110: "she never told her love."

744.36−39   *Grimm's* . . . inside.]   In the tale "The Robber's Bridegroom."

745.33   P.E.O.]   P.E.O. was a secretive women's society founded in 1870 at Iowa Wesleyan College. Only the initiated knew the meaning of the letters, although they are believed to stand for "Protect Each Other."

746.25   Eastern Star]   The Order of the Eastern Star is a subsidiary Masonic group limited to Master Masons and their female relatives.

748.31   Julia . . . *Chase.*]   On a tour in 1889−90, Julia Marlowe (1870−1950) starred in a revival of the 1837 comedy by James Sheridan Knowles.

761.34   "to avoid worse rape,"]   *Paradise Lost*, Book I, line 505.

764.28   *Kathleen Mavourneen*]   By Frederich Nichols Crouch (1808−96).

767.4−5   Christian . . . hill.]   In *Pilgrim's Progress*, Christian's burden of sins, which he carries on his back, drops off when he reaches the cross at the top of the hill representing Calvary and disappears into the mouth of the sepulchre below.

APRIL TWILIGHTS AND OTHER POEMS

776.10   *Fides, Spes*]   Faith, Hope.

780.22   *Delphi*]   Site in Pocis, Greece, sacred to Apollo and seat of the most famous oracle of antiquity.

781.26   Miranda's isle]   In Shakespeare's *The Tempest*, Miranda and her father Prospero are on an island inhabited by the semi-human Caliban, son of the witch Sycorax. Ariel is an airy spirit whose name was often later identified with poetic inspiration.

782.5   *In Media Vita*]   "In the midst of life," from the Anglican *Book of Common Prayer*: "In the midst of life we are in death."

783.14   *Marsyas*]   In Greek mythology, a satyr who challenged Apollo to compete with him in musical skill. After Marsyas lost, the god flayed him alive and fastened his skin to a tree. Marsyas was lamented by the fauns, satyrs, and dryads, and by the Muses who judged the contest.

787.1   *Ludlow Castle*]   Norman castle built in the 11th century in Ludlow, Shropshire. Cather visited the castle during her first European trip in 1902, and wrote about it in a letter, dated July 11, for the *Nebraska State Journal* ("Out of the Beaten Track," July 27, 1902). In it, she mentioned the ruins of the great hall, built for the council of the governing heads of Wales, and the banquet halls built for the entertainment of Queen Elizabeth and her peers, when Sir Henry Sidney "renewed and enlarged" the castle in the 16th century.

787.20   English singer]   In her letter, Cather writes about the poet Philip Sidney (1554–86), son of Sir Henry, who "spent the formative part of his boyhood and youth in that country which is surely the country for the making of poets if ever one was."

788.1   Of love . . . warring,]   In her letter, Cather also wrote: "The castle and its lords played an exceedingly prominent part in the war of the roses, as it was the place of residence of Richard Plantagenet, Duke of York, and the two sons of Edward IV, who were afterward murdered in the tower, were reared and educated there. There Prince Arthur, son of Henry VII, died, leaving his wife an inheritance to his brother, Henry VIII." She also tells the story of the Norman knight who built the castle's keep, Joce de Dinan, and his "mortal foe," Walter de Lacy, who while confined in the castle fell in love with Marion de la Bruyere, a maiden reared in de Dinan's household. Marion helped de Lacy to escape, and 11 months later, while de Dinan was away, sent word that it was safe for the knight to visit her. De Lacy returned with 100 armed knights who, while he was with Marion, slew the sleeping garrison and slaughtered everyone in the town below the castle. Discovering this perfidy when she woke the next morning, Marion killed her lover with his own sword and threw herself "from her window down the side of the cliff that is now so white with dog roses and alder bloom."

790.33   Faustinus]   In 1868, the names of Faustinus, his sister Beatrice, and brother Simplicus, were found engraved in a church at the cemetery of Generosa on the road to Porto. According to legend, the brothers were martyred in Rome c. A.D. 304 for refusing to pay homage to idols. (Their sister was put to death because she buried their bodies.)

795.21   twin boys] Romulus and Remus, sons of Mars and the vestal Rhea Silvia, cast into the Tiber to drown but, protected by the gods, washed ashore and were suckled by a she-wolf. Romulus became the founder of Rome.

796.27   "The dice . . . loaded"] A Greek proverb.

797.9   *Ritratto d'ignoto*] Portrait of an unknown person.

800.9   *Prairie Spring*] The poem also appears as the epigraph to *O Pioneers!*

803.24   All . . . know.] Cf. John Keats, "Ode on a Grecian Urn" (1819): " 'Beauty is truth, truth beauty,—that is all ye know on earth, and all ye need to know.' "

803.29   Lithuania . . . me.] Many of the immigrants working in Chicago packing factories in the early 20th century were from Lithuania.

806.11   BURLINGTON] A major 19th-century railway line that ran from Burlington, Iowa, on the Mississippi, crossed the Missouri at Council Bluffs, and then joined the Union Pacific at Kearny, Nebraska.

806.17—18   *(The crooked . . . plain.)*] From Handel's *Messiah* (see Isaiah 40:4).

NOT UNDER FORTY

817.6   Albert Wolff,] Wolff (1884–1970), French conductor and composer, was with the Opéra-Comique in Paris as chorusmaster, conductor, music director (1921–24), and theater director (1945–46). He was with the Metropolitan Opera Company in New York from 1919–21.

817.10   Ravel's *La Valse*] After serving in World War I from 1914 to 1918, Maurice Ravel completed the *La Valse* (1920), which has been described as capturing the "savage flavor" of an era coming to an end.

817.25   *"Mais . . . pas?"*] "But a little poetic, isn't it?"

820.30   *Faust*] Novel in two parts (1808, 1832) by Goethe.

821.18—19   *"Vous . . . oncle?"*] "Do you know well the works of my uncle?"

822.7—8   *trop . . . Frédéric*] "Too much conversation." Frédéric Moreau, hero of *Sentimental Education* (1869), is a young law student in Paris when the novel begins.

822.10—11   Garibaldi's proclamation] In *Garibaldi's Defense of the Roman Republic* (1907) by George Macaulay Trevelyan, he is quoted as saying: "I offer neither pay, nor quarters, nor provisions; I offer hunger, thirst, forced marches, battles, and death. Let him who loves his country in his heart and not with his lips only, follow me." During the Italian *risorgimento*, Giuseppe Garibaldi led an improvised force to Rome in 1849 to fight for Mazzini's short-lived republic against the French aiding Pius IX. Their retreat was through central Italy.

822.17   *Roman d'un jeune homme*]   *Story of a Young Man.*

822.22−23   Eugène . . . Bianchon,]   Characters in *Comédie Humaine*. In *Le Père Goriot* (1834−35), Rastignac is a young law student, and Bianchon a medical student. Rubempré is a young poet in *Illusions perdues* (1837−43).

823.36−37   *pour . . . Salammbô*]   "For the goddess." In Flaubert's novel (1862), the tragic Salammbô is a priestess in the temple of the Carthaginian goddess Tanit.

824.4−5   "*Comme . . . al-ter-na-tiv-e-ment.*"]   When John the Baptist's head is discarded among the remains of Herod's banquet, three of his disciples take it and carry it toward Galilee. "Because it was very heavy, they carried it alternately (by turns)."

825.32−33   Franco-Prussian . . . uncle.]   Although initially distressed by France's declaration of war on July 19, 1870, Flaubert (1821−80) became committed to the defense of his country and eventually joined the national guard. After the Prussians entered Rouen, his estate was commandeered and Flaubert became disillusioned by the eventual French surrender as well as personally humiliated by the occupation of his estate. He later wrote George Sand that the Prussian occupation had been the worst experience of his life.

826.6   Croisset]   His parents' country estate on the Seine near Rouen, where Flaubert and his mother continued to make their home after his father's death in 1846.

826.17   *Les Eaux printanières*]   Novel (1870); English translations of the title include *Spring-Torrents*, *Torrents of Spring*, *Spring Floods*.

826.19−20   Viardot household]   Ivan Sergeivich Turgenev, who had become an admirer of Pauline Viardot-Garcia in 1843, left Russia to be near her. He was living in Paris on the upper floor of a house he shared with her and her husband, Louis Viardot, when Henry James met him in 1875. See also note 262.6−7.

826.34−41   "Mon . . . *vache!*"]   "My Moscovite left me this morning. . . . You have completely bewitched him, my loulou! because he could not stop talking about 'my adorable niece,' of 'my charming niece,' 'delightful woman,' etc., etc. In short, the Moscovite adores you! which pleases me very much, because he is an exquisite man. You can't imagine what he knows! He repeated to me, by heart, bits of the tragedies of Voltaire, and of Luce de

Lancival! He knows, I think, *all* literatures even to their lowest levels! And so modest with all this! such a simple man! so gentlemanly! so *vache!*"

826.35 loulou!] A term of endearment; literally, "lapdog."

826.39 Luce de Lancival] Jean Luce de Lancival (1764–1810) was a poet and dramatist.

826.41 *vache*] Literally, "cow." In his essay "Ivan Turgénieff" (1884), Henry James says Turgenev "repeated to me a figurative epithet which Flaubert (of whom he was extremely fond) applied to him—an epithet intended to characterise a certain expansive softness, a comprehensive indecision, which pervaded his nature, just as it pervades so many of the characters he painted. He enjoyed Flaubert's use of this term, good-naturedly opprobrious, more even than Flaubert himself, and recognized perfectly the element of truth in it."

827.24–27 Chopin's . . . children!] After his nine-year relationship with George Sand ended in 1847, Frédéric Chopin (1810–49) supported her daughter Solange's attempt to repair her bond with Sand, seeing the estrangement as the mother's fault. In a letter to his sister, Ludwika Jedrzejewicz, January 1847, he wrote that Sand "harrows up her daughter's life; with her son too it will end badly . . . she is now in the strangest paroxysm of motherhood, playing the part of a juster and better mother than she really is."

827.33 "*Trop . . . fatigant,*"] "Too long and too tiring."

828.7 *Boris Godounov*] Opera (1874) composed by Modest Mussorgsky to his own libretto, based on Alexander Pushkin's *Boris Godunov* (1831) and Nikolay Karamzin's *History of the Russian Empire* (1829).

828.21–23 "C'est . . . épargne!"] "It is a profound joy for me, my poor loulou, that I have given you a taste for intellectual pursuits. What boredom and nonsense it spares you!"

829.13 *déjeuner*] Lunch.

831.14–17 "Remercie . . . santé."] "Convey my thanks to Mme. Robert who was gracious enough to remember me. Give her my respects, and advise her on a fortifying regimen, because she strikes me as a bit pale, and I'm a little concerned about her health."

831.21–24 "Je suis . . . géographie."] "I am very glad that *Accounts of the Merovingians' Times* amuses you; re-read them when you have finished; *learn the dates*, you have your course of study, and spend some time every day looking at a geography map."

831.30–33 "Un peu . . . ressemble."] "A little spelling won't hurt you, my pet! for you write *aplomb* with two *p*'s: 'Moral and physical are upright [applomb],' three *p*'s would indicate too much energy! That amuses me, because that's like you."

832.36–833.2   "ci-joint . . . l'envoyer."] "Enclosed a letter from my uncle Gustave Flaubert addressed to George Sand—it must be, I think, from 1866. I thought this would please you, and I am glad to send it to you."

833.12–28   MORT . . . monde.]   The clipping reads:
DEATH OF MME. FRANKLIN-GROUT
    We learn with sadness of the death of Mme. Franklin-Grout, who passed away at Antibes, after a short illness.
    Niece of Gustave Flaubert, Mme. Franklin-Grout played an important role in the dissemination and the success of her uncle's work. Testamentary executor for the great novelist, who raised and educated her, Mme. Franklin-Grout published her uncle's correspondence, so valuable for its literary psychology, and which revealed Flaubert's principles and his life of arduous labor. Mme. Franklin-Grout also published *Bouvard et Pécuchet*. . . . Mme. Franklin-Grout was a charming and distinguished person who was very attached to her friends; and she was someone who, until the last years of her life, displayed the intelligence and the good humor of a witty woman of the world.

834.1   *Démeublé*]   Unfurnished, stripped of furniture.

834.21   Tanagra figurines]   Terra-cotta statuettes, now considered valuable art, were made in Tanagra, an ancient city of Boetia, Greece, and shipped for sale to Mediterranean countries. Tanagra figurines dating from around the 4th and 3rd centuries B.C. were first found in tombs near the city.

834.22–23   Kewpie brides]   Kewpies were fat winged babies with topknots of hair, first created by American illustrator and author Rose O'Neill (1874–1944) and popular in the 1920s, when dolls were fashioned after O'Neill's drawings.

834.30–32   "L'art . . . exactitude."]   "The art of choosing among the innumerable traits that nature offers us, is, after all, even more difficult than that of observing them with attention and rendering them with exactitude."

835.34–36   Stevenson . . . novelists.]   Cf. letter to R.A.M. Stevenson, October 1833, in *The Letters of Robert Louis Stevenson to his Family and Friends*, edited by Sidney Calvin (1899).

835.39   Carmencita . . . cigars?]   In the short novel *Carmen* (1847), the title character, a gypsy, is employed in a cigar factory in Seville.

836.29   *The Scarlet Letter*]   By Nathaniel Hawthorne.

837.27–29   elder Dumas . . . walls]   In a February 9, 1896, column in the *Nebraska Journal*, Cather quoted Dumas as saying "in a now forgotten magazine" that " 'I needed only four walls, four boards, two actors and one passion.' " In 1897 she wrote, "Once, when the elder Dumas was asked what were the materials he required to make a play, he replied: 'A stage, four walls, two characters and one passion'" (*Leader*, Nov. 23). In 1901 she wrote: "Old Dumas said that to make a play he needed but four walls, two people and one passion" (*The Courier*, Aug. 10).

838.12   Ticknor and Fields] A 19th-century American publishing house that eventually became Houghton Mifflin, publishers of Cather's first four novels.

839.4   Mrs. John Gardner] The art collector and socialite Isabella Stewart Gardner (1840–1924), who left her home and gallery (now the Isabella Stuart Gardner Museum, on the Fenway) to the city of Boston.

839.36   Salvini] Italian tragedian Tommasso Salvini (1829–1916). From 1873 to 1879 he made five visits to the United States, appearing in successful productions of Shakespeare, including bilingual productions of *Othello* and *Hamlet* in which Edwin Booth also acted.

839.37   Christine Nilsson] Nilsson (1843–1921), a Swedish operatic soprano, made appearances in New York from 1870 to 1874 and 1883 to 1884.

840.16–20   "The personal . . . gay."] In James's essay "Mr. and Mrs. James T. Fields" (1915).

841.13   long wait at Aulis] In Euripides' play *Iphigenia at Aulis*, Iphigenia waits to be sacrificed to the goddess Artemis in order to secure a wind that will carry the ships of her father, King Agammemnon, to Troy.

841.40–842.3   Chorley, . . . Henderson,] An influential music critic, Henry Fothergill Chorley (1808–72) wrote for the English weekly magazine *Athenaeum* from 1831 to 1868, and was also a librettist, novelist, and playwright. Philip Hale (1854–1934), music critic for the Boston newspapers *Post* (1890–91), *Journal* (1891–93), and *Herald* (1903–34), also wrote the Boston Symphony Orchestra program notes from 1901 until his death. In New York, W. J. Henderson (1855–1937) was on the staff of the *Times* (1883–1902) before becoming music critic for the *Sun* (1902–37). His books about music included a study of Wagnerian opera.

842.18–19   Pauline Viardot] See note 262.6–7.

843.8–9   "And changes . . . liquors."] *2 Henry IV*, III.i.52–53.

843.15–18   "In courts . . . outrage."] *Paradise Lost*, Book I, lines 497–500.

843.29–30   *"A bracelet . . . bone."*] "The Relic," stanza 1, by John Donne (1572–1631).

843.37   Bœotian ignorance,] Boeotia, a region of ancient Greece, was proverbial for the stupidity of its inhabitants, who were supposedly rude and illiterate, more concerned with physical strength than with mental excellence.

845.32   Nahant]   A seaside town a few miles north of Boston and about fifteen miles south of Manchester.

846.15   *Compagnons de Voyage*]   "Traveling Companions," published in *The Atlantic Monthly* (Nov.–Dec. 1870).

846.33–36   Dr. Holmes . . . the hostess.]   Mrs. Fields writes in her journal entry for May 22, 1872: "Dr. Holmes had a way at the table of talking of 'you actors,' 'you gentlemen of the stage,' until I saw Longfellow was quite disturbed at the unsympathetic unmannerliness of it, in appearance, and tried to talk more than ever in a different strain."

846.34   Jefferson . . . Warren]   Joseph Jefferson (1829–1905) and William Warren Jr. (1812–88), great American comedians.

848.4   Shelley plain]   Robert Browning, "Memorabilia" (1855), line 1: "Ah, did you once see Shelley plain."

848.8   Marne . . . Versailles]   German advances on Paris were repulsed at both the first (September 1914) and second (July 1918) battles of the Marne. Under the peace treaty signed at Versailles on June 28, 1919, Germany returned Alsace and Lorraine to France, ceded West Prussia and part of Posen province to Poland, and lost its overseas colonies. Plebescites held under the treaty resulted in the further cession of German territory to Belgium, Denmark, and Poland. It also established Danzig as a free city and placed the Saarland under French administration for 15 years.

850.5–6   Walter Pater . . . ballad.]   In his essay "Shakespeare's English Kings" in *Appreciations: with an Essay on Style* (1889).

852.36   ever remain.]   For *Not Under Forty*, Cather made minor revisions and changed the order of some paragraphs in the 1925 preface, but the major change was the addition of parts II and III. The preface ended:

Gilbert Murray has illustrated the two kinds of beauty in writing by a happy similitude. There is a kind of beauty, he says, which comes from rich ornamentation; like the splendor one might admire on a Chinese junk, gorgeously gilded and painted, hung with rich embroideries and tapestries. Then there is the beauty of a modern yacht, where there is no ornamentation at all; our whole sensation of pleasure in watching a yacht under sail comes from the fact that every line of the craft is designed for one purpose, that everything about it furthers that purpose, so that it has an organic, living simplicity and directness. This, he says, is the beauty for which the Greek writers strove; it is certainly that for which Miss Jewett strove.

If I were asked to name three American books which have the possibility of a long, long life, I would say at once, "The Scarlet Letter," "Huckleberry Finn," and "The Country of the Pointed Firs." I can think of no others that confront time and change so serenely. The latter book seems to me fairly to shine with the reflection of its long joyous future.

It is so tightly yet so lightly built, so little encumbered with heavy materialism that deteriorates and grows old-fashioned. I like to think with what pleasure, with what a sense of rich discovery, the young student of American literature in far distant years to come will take up this book and say, "A masterpiece!" as proudly as if he himself had made it. It will be a message to the future, a message in a universal language, like the tuft of meadow flowers in Robert Frost's fine poem, which the mower abroad in the early morning left standing, just skirted by the scythe, for the mower of the afternoon to gaze upon and wonder at—the one message that even the scythe of Time spares.

852.38   "The distinguished outward stamp"]   See note 840.16–20.

855.9   "a sort . . . modesty."]   See note 840.16–20.

857.31–33   "a sense . . . pathetic,"]   See note 840.16–20.

859.22   *Salammbô*]   A novel (1862) set in Carthage during the mercenaries' revolt (240–237 B.C.) after the first Punic War. Flaubert spent years researching ancient Carthage and depicted it in precise historical and archaeological detail.

865.30   Book . . . Joseph,]   *Der Junge Joseph* (1934), translated in 1935.

868.34–35   *look . . . will not,*]   Shakespeare, *Macbeth*, I.iii.58–59.

869.11   third volume,]   *Joseph in Ägypten* (1936), translated *Joseph in Egypt* (1938).

870.34   I wait . . . learn.]   The last volume, *Joseph der Ernährer*, was published in 1943 and the translation, *Joseph the Provider*, in 1944.

876.3   *Beauchamp's Career*]   Novel (1876) by George Meredith.

876.12–13   *The Ambassadors*]   In the novel (1903), James depicts the complex reaction of an American in Europe to manners and customs very different from those in his world in America.

876.32   *Je . . . français.*]   The story (1919) represents a homoerotic male relationship.

878.37   Fontainebleau]   Hoping to regain her health, Mansfield entered Georgei Gurdjieff's Institute for the Harmonious Development of Man near Fontainebleau the year it was founded, 1922. She died there of tuberculosis in January 1923.

879.17   storeman]   A man who keeps a store or shop.

879.30–31   *But I . . . safety.*]   *1 Henry IV*: II.iii.9.

880.27–29   C'est . . . ombre.]   It's a misery. No, not that exactly. There's something else—a profound malaise follows me like a shadow.

SELECTED REVIEWS AND ESSAYS 1895–1940

889.4–5   controversy . . . O'Rell]   Mark Twain's article, "What Paul Bourget Thinks of Us," appeared in the *North American Review*, January 1895. Max O'Rell's response appeared in March. O'Rell was the nom de plume of French author Paul Blouet (1848–1903), whose books include *A Frenchman in America* (1892).

889.9   "Outre Mer"]   Overseas.

889.31   "Puddin' Head Wilson"]   Twain's novel appeared serially in *Century Magazine*, December 1893–June 1894, titled *Pudd'nhead Wilson, A Tale*, and as a book, *Pudd'nhead Wilson*, in 1895.

891.7–8   Joan of Arc.]   *Personal Recollections of Joan of Arc*, first published in *Harper's Magazine* beginning April 1895, and as a book in 1896.

892.20   Porthos, Athos and d'Artagan]   In *The Three Musketeers* (1844), *Twenty Years After* (1845), and *Vicomte de Bragelonne* (1848–50), by Alexandre Dumas *père* (1802–70).

892.22–23   Anna . . . Levins]   In Lev Tolstoi's *Anna Karenina*, written 1873–77.

894.2–15   My tantalized . . . pansies.]   "For Annie" (1849), stanzas 9 and 10.

894.21   Poe . . . Fordham,]   Edgar Allan Poe (1809–49) moved with his wife, Virginia Clemm Poe, and his aunt, Maria Clemm, to the cottage in Fordham in 1846.

894.30–31   Thespians . . . people.]   His mother, Elizabeth Arnold Poe, was the daughter of Elizabeth Smith Arnold, a prominent actress in early American theater. (Both of Poe's parents were actors.)

895.15   two women]   Virginia Clemm Poe, who married Poe in 1836 at the age of 13, and died in 1847, and his foster mother, Frances Allan, who died in 1829.

895.18–19   as Amiel . . . great.]   "To be misunderstood even by those whom one loves is the cross and bitterness of life. It is the secret smile on the lips of the great men which so few understand," in French writer and critic Henri Amiel's *Journal Intime* (1881; *Private Journal*), Volume I, translated by Mrs. Humphry Ward (1885).

896.7–8   As Steadman . . . marvel."]   Introduction to *Works of Edgar Allan Poe* (1894–95), edited by Edmund Clarence Stedman and George Woodberry.

896.38–897.2   "huge carvings . . . fire."]   In "The Assignation" (1834).

897.4–5   Golden House]   Nero called his palace, which was adorned with gold and precious stones, his "golden house." It was built after the great fire that destroyed half of Rome in A.D. 64.

897.30   *Berenice, . . . Aphrodite*]   In the short stories "Berenice" (1835), "Ligeia" (1834), and "The Assignation." Ligeia also appears in the poem "Al Aaraaf."

898.6   "Masque . . . dollars,]   As editor of *Graham's Magazine*, Poe received a salary of $800 plus an additional small sum for pieces he contributed. "The Masque of the Red Death" appeared in the magazine Spring 1842.

898.7   Drexel Institute]   Chartered in 1894 as Drexel Institute for Art, Science and Technology, in Philadelphia.

898.27−32   woman . . . prose]   Virginia Clemm Poe died of tuberculosis January 30, 1847. Unwell since suffering a burst blood vessel in 1842, she had become a semi-invalid by 1846 when Poe, also ill and suffering from severe depression, was writing, among other works, "The Cask of Amontillado" and "The Philosophy of Composition." During that year the family was mentioned as pitiable charity cases in New York and Pennsylvania papers, and Poe wrote that Virginia was ". . . my *greatest* and *only* stimulus now, to battle with this uncongenial, unsatisfactory, and ungrateful life."

900.18−21   "The sun . . . again."]   Percy Bysshe Shelley, "Adonais" (1821), XXIX, lines 1−4.

902.3−4   "the good, gray poet."]   The sobriquet derived from *The Good Gray Poet* (1866), a defense of Whitman written by his friend William Douglas O'Connor after the poet was dismissed from a government post because *Leaves of Grass* was deemed an immoral book.

902.15−17   "The pure . . . pail."]   Cf. the *Leaves of Grass* poem "Song of Myself," section 15, lines 1 and 14−15.

902.22   "imperious . . . commanding"]   Cf. *Leaves of Grass*, "In Cabin'd Ships at Sea," lines 2−3: "The boundless blue on every side expanding, / With whistling winds and music of the waves, the large imperious waves." Line 22 also ends "imperious waves."

903.13−21   "I think . . . earth.]   Cf. *Leaves of Grass*, "Song of Myself," section 32, lines 1−8.

905.30   "Felicia"]   By Fanny N. D. Murfree (1891).

907.5−6   career ended . . . tragically.]   Harold Frederic (1856−1898), a Christian Scientist, died following a stroke for which he refused medical help.

908.9   young artist . . . story]   Harrison Fisher was 21 years old when *Market Place* was published in 1899.

909.15−16   seven . . . vision.]   Genesis 41:1−4.

912.9−10   Marie . . . Gauthier."]   Alexandre Dumas *fils* based the reformed courtesan Marguerite Gautier in *La Dame aux Camélias* (1848) on the

Parisian courtesan Marie Duplessis (1824–47; real name Alphonsine Plessis). "Delclasse" may be a printer's error.

913.14   Sherman . . . was.]   In his September 12, 1864, letter to the mayor and city council of Atlanta, Major General William Tecumseh Sherman wrote: "War is cruelty, and you cannot refine it . . ."

914.13–27   Thou . . . me.]   "Intrigue," stanzas 6–8.

914.31–33   "Simple . . . Hen,"]   "Mother Goose" rhymes.

914.35–915.12   Now . . . civil.]   "Intrigue," stanzas 18–19.

915.15–20   Ah, . . . moved.]   Cf. "Intrigue," stanza 21. In Crane, line 5 of this stanza reads: "Ah God—that I should suffer."

915.21   Bradley]   Will Bradley, artist, author, and designer of several type-faces.

915.25–26   "My good . . . mad."]   The poems are untitled; the poem is identified by the first line: "Forth went the candid man," lines 7–8. In Crane, "friend" reads "fool."

916.10   fortunate journal]   Hearst's *Journal*, for which Crane covered the campaign in Puerto Rico in 1898 after being fired from Joseph Pulitzer's *World*.

918.27   Greece . . . war]   The Greco-Turkish War (1897). Crane had cov-ered this war for the McClure syndicate.

920.18–19   member . . . faculty]   Professor Lewis E. Gates, under whose direction Norris worked on drafts of *McTeague* and *Vandover and the Brute* in 1894. Norris had studied at Berkeley from 1890 to 1894, then entered Harvard for a year to take a writing course and study French. He revised and com-pleted *McTeague* in San Francisco in 1897.

920.29   "Comedie Humaine."]   *The Human Comedy*, novels and tales by Honoré de Balzac (1799–1850) in which more than 2,000 characters appear and reappear at various stages in their lives. Balzac arranged the novels to form a composite whole, and they were published in 17 volumes as a collected edition from 1842 to 1848.

923.19–20   the Danai.]   In Virgil's *Aeneid*, Aenaeus says with reference to the Trojan horse: "Timeo Danaos et dona ferentes." (Book II, line 49—"I fear the Greeks even when they bring gifts.")

923.31–32   Gervaise's . . . L'Assommoir,]   In the novel (1877) by Émile Zola, Gervaise, once abandoned, finds happiness and stability when she re-marries and runs a flourishing laundry business. She loses her shop when her husband begins squandering their money at *l'assommoir* (drinking shop) and she too begins to drink, becoming lazy and greedy. With the loss of her laundry, life becomes hopeless and senseless, and Gervaise dies impoverished within a few months. *L'Assommoir* is the eighth in a cycle of 20 novels, *Les Rougon-Macquart* (1871–93).

926.9   march . . . "Lohengrin"]   The Bridal Chorus, frequently adapted by organists for weddings, and known as the "Wedding March." It occurs in Act II, scene i, of Wagner's opera (1850).

927.13–14   "silver . . . Keats?]   "Eve of Saint Agnes" (1820), stanza 4, line 4.

928.21   Knighthood . . . Flower]   *When Knighthood Was in Flower* (1898), a historical romance, was Indiana author Charles Major's most popular book.

929.5–6   "Not only . . . birth."]   Cf. Robert Browning, *The Ring and the Book* (1868–69), Book VI, "Guiseppe Caponsacchi," lines 2065–66.

931.27   Atriedes]   Atreide or Atride (sons of Atreus) is the patronymic given Agammemnon and Menelaus by Homer.

931.28   Rialto.]   Term, now obsolete, for the New York theater district. It was first used around 1870, and continued into the 20th century.

932.1   *When . . . Crane*]   The article was published under the pseudonym Henry Nicklemann, a name used by Cather for several articles published in the Pittsburgh weekly *Library* in 1900.

934.36   in Cuba]   Crane covered the Cuban campaign for the *World* in 1898. (He was fired after being sent back from the war zone to recover from fever and exhaustion.)

934.39–40   Mr. Davis . . . chin]   Richard Harding Davis, a correspondent with Crane during the 1895–98 Cuban revolution against Spain, was a model for illustrations by Charles Dana Gibson (1867–1944).

935.4   "The Pre-Destined,"]   In *The Treasure of the Humble* (1896) by Maurice Maeterlink.

937.23–24   shipwreck . . . coast]   Crane left to cover the Cuban revolution for McClure's syndicate aboard the *Commodore*, a steamship carrying filibusters (American participants in foreign revolutions), arms, and ammunition, on December 31, 1896. The vessel sank January 2, 1897. His account, "Stephen Crane's Own Story," is dated January 6.

938.8–9   "That . . . do quickly."]   John 13:27.

945.1–2   French . . . 1683]   During the last decades of the 17th century, Louis XIV's intensified persecution of French Protestants (Huguenots) triggered a wave of migration to countries friendlier to their religious beliefs— England, Holland, and Germany.

949.30–31   Heine . . . irony.]   *Confessions* (1854).

951.1–2   *Gertrude . . . Romances*"]   Hall (1863–1961) was a poet, author, and translator of Verlaine and Rostand. *The Wagnerian Romances* was first published in 1907.

952.16   Tristan and Isolde]   See note 228.9.

952.18–19   Siegfried . . . rock!]   On the rock of the Valkyrie, Siegfried, who is under a spell, wrests the ring from Brünnhilde, in *Götterdämmerung*. See note 235.11–14.

953.7–8   novel . . . her.]   *Song of the Lark* (1915).

954.4–5   Crane's . . . Cuba.]   See note 916.10.

955.11–12   "The red . . . wafer,"]   *The Red Badge of Courage* (1895), Chapter 9.

955.30–34   "The day . . . supper."]   "The Price of the Harness," I (1898).

955.39–956.12   "With this . . . bursting."]   "The Price of the Harness," II.

956.18   death . . . Gibbs]   John Blair Gibbs, an army surgeon whose death Crane witnessed and reported.

958.2   Editor . . . Commonweal:]   Michael Williams, who founded the Catholic magazine in 1924 and was its editor until 1937.

959.28   Archbishop Lamy]   The model for Bishop Jean Marie Latour in the novel.

960.4   Father Machebeuf]   The model for Father Joseph Vaillant.

960.28–29   Golden Legend]   See note 360.35.

963.12–13   Gopher Prairie]   The small, stultifying midwestern town where Carol Kennicott lives in Sinclair Lewis's *Main Street*.

966.2   Governor Cross:]   Wilbur Cross, governor of Connecticut from 1931 to 1939 and before that dean of Yale Graduate School.

968.2   Mr. Williams:]   See note 958.2.

969.13   Works Project,]   The Works Progress Administration was a federal agency established by President Franklin D. Roosevelt in 1935 to combat unemployment as part of his New Deal Policy. The WPA administered several cultural programs, including the Federal Art Project, the Federal Writers' Project, and the Federal Theatre Project, as well as a vast program of public road, bridge, and building construction. The agency was abolished in 1943.

973.1   Mary Colum]   Irish-born critic and writer (1887–1957), literary editor of *The Forum* and critic for *The New York Times* and the *Tribune* and author of, among other books, *From These Roots: the ideas that have made modern literature* (1938).

974.2   your question.]   An editorial introduction to the column, head-lined "Literary Experimentation," reads in part: "Members of the CEA will recall the discussion started by Mr. Henry Canby and carried on in these columns over the desirability of English courses exclusively devoted to con-temporary literature. In the course of the argument it was pointed out that much writing of the moment is experimental, and that the author himself is testing devices and techniques which later may be abandoned. Miss Willa Cather . . . graciously permits us to reprint the following paragraphs from a letter to a friend which will serve to illustrate her own experimental attitude in one of her books."

974.5–6   *Nouvelle . . . Roman*]   *Nouvelle* is a short fictitious narrative that differs from the *roman* (novel) in that it deals with only a single situation.

977.6   threat . . . *Tempest*]   Cather, like many other readers, identifies Shakespeare with the magician Prospero, who in the last act renounces his powers of transformation, saying: "I'll break my staff, / Bury it certain fath-oms in the earth, / And deeper than did ever plummet sound / I'll drown my book" (V.i.54–57).

CATALOGING INFORMATION

Cather, Willa, 1873–1947.
    Stories, poems, and other writings / Willa Cather.
    Edited by Sharon O'Brien.

    (The Library of America ; 57)
        Contents: Uncollected stories (1892–1929)—Alexander's bridge—
    Youth and the bright Medusa—My mortal enemy—Obscure destinies
    —The old beauty and others—April twilights and other poems—
    Not under forty—Selected reviews and essays (1895–1940).
        I. Title.   II. Title: Alexander's bridge.   III. Title: Youth and
    the bright Medusa.   IV. Title: My mortal enemy.   V. Title: Obscure
    destinies.   VI. Title: Old beauty and others.   VII. Title: April
    twilights and other poems.   VIII. Title: Not under forty.
    IX. Series.
PS3505.A87A6   1992b   91–62294
813'.52—dc20
ISBN 0–940450–71–2 (alk. paper)

This book is set in 10 point Linotron Galliard,
a face designed for photocomposition by Matthew Carter
and based on the sixteenth-century face Granjon. The paper
is acid-free Ecusta Nyalite and meets the requirements for perma-
nence of the American National Standards Institute. The binding
material is Brillianta, a 100% woven rayon cloth made by
Van Heek-Scholco Textielfabrieken, Holland. The com-
position is by Haddon Craftsmen, Inc., and The
Clarinda Company. Printing and binding
by R. R. Donnelley & Sons Company.
Designed by Bruce Campbell.

THE LIBRARY OF AMERICA SERIES